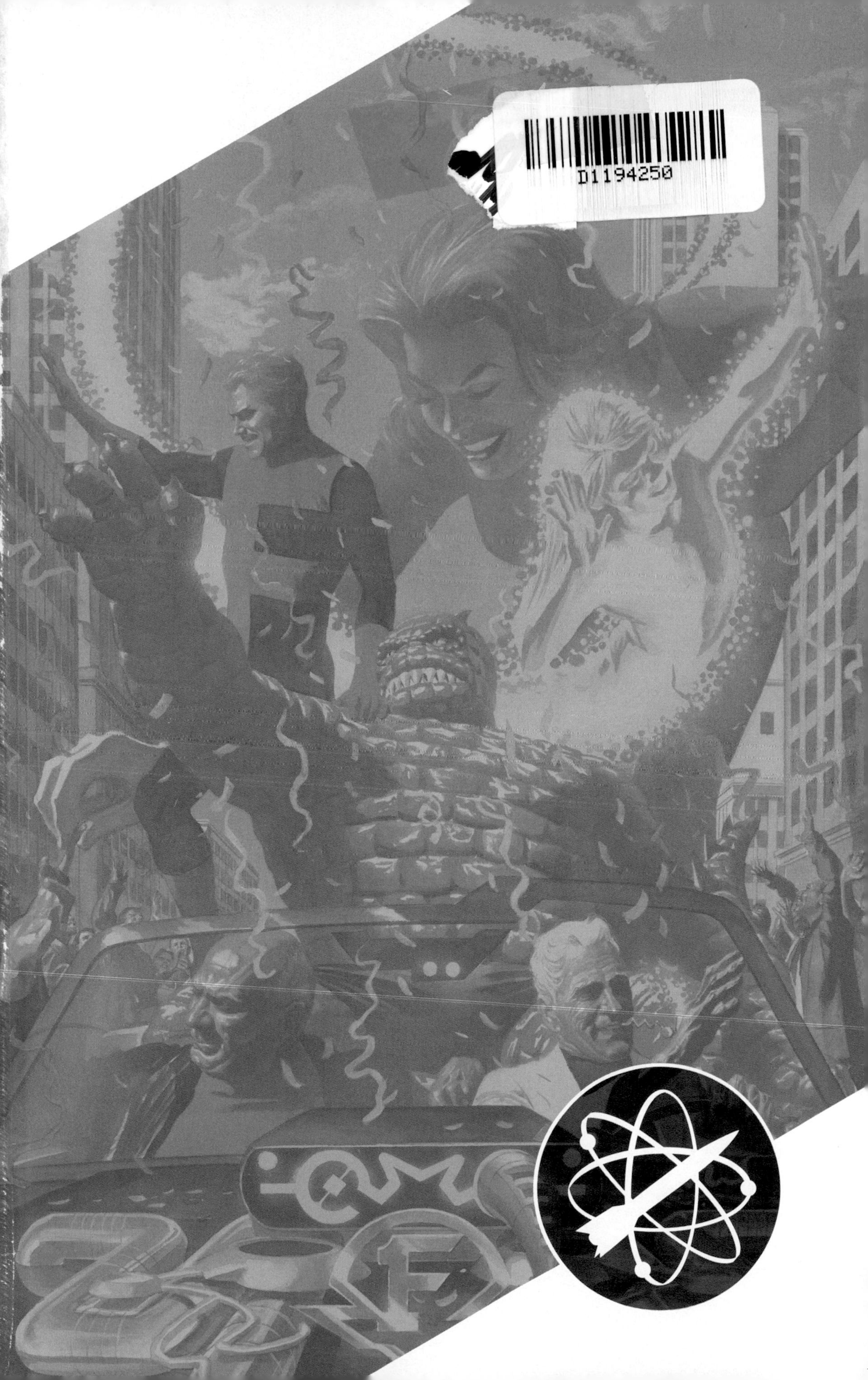

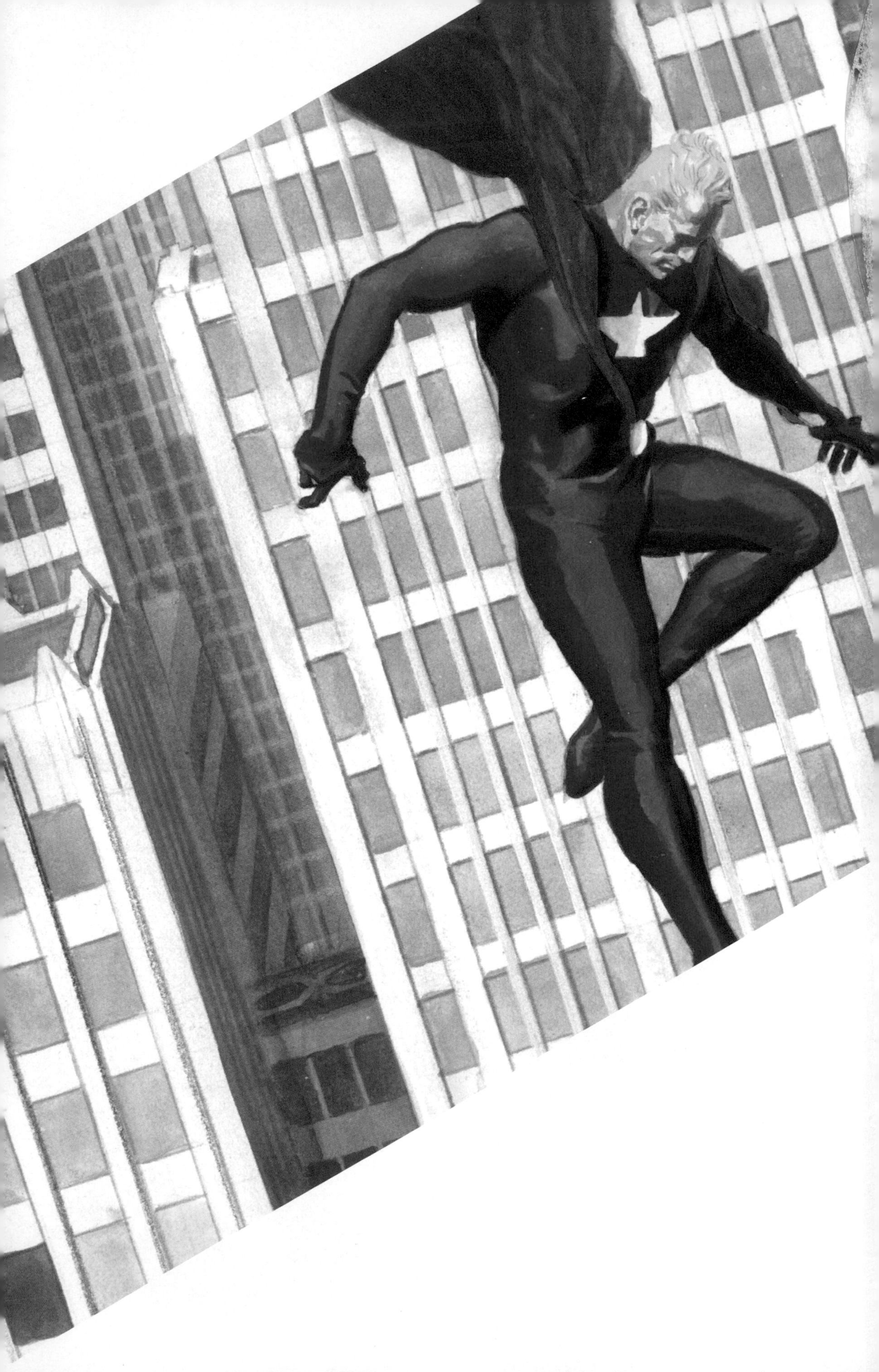

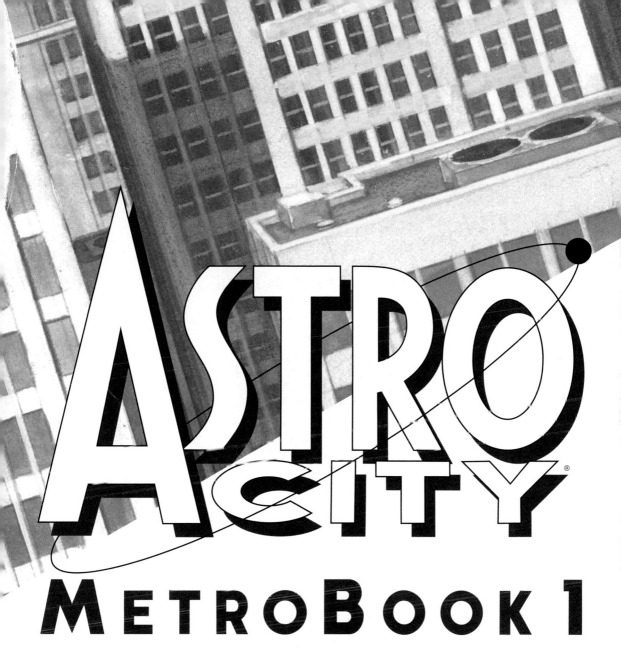

ASTRO CITY®
MetroBook 1

KURT BUSIEK · Writer
BRENT ERIC ANDERSON · Artist
ALEX ROSS · Covers & Character Designs

WILL BLYBERG · Inker, Chapters 7-19
with **GARY MARTIN** · Chapter 18

STEVE BUCCELLATO &
ELECTRIC CRAYON · Colors Chapters 1-6
ALEX SINCLAIR · Colors Chapters 7-19
JOHN ROSHELL of **COMICRAFT** · LETTERING

BUSIEK, ANDERSON & ROSS · Creators

ALEX ROSS
Cover Art

KEL SYMONS
Collection Editor

ANN HUNTINGTON BUSIEK
JONATHAN PETERSON
Original Series Editors

COMICRAFT'S TYLER SMITH
Book Design

RICHARD STARKINGS
Logo Design

Originally Presented in
KURT BUSIEK'S ASTRO CITY #1-6,
KURT BUSIEK'S ASTRO CITY VOL. 2 #1-12
& WIZARD PRESENTS ASTRO CITY #1/2

ASTRO CITY METROBOOK VOL 1. First Printing. March 2022. Published by Image Comics, Inc. Office of publication: PO Box 14457 Portland, OR 97293. Copyright © 1995, 1996, 1997, 2022 Juke Box Productions. All rights reserved. Contains material originally published in single magazine form as KURT BUSIEK'S ASTRO CITY #1-6, KURT BUSIEK'S ASTRO CITY Vol. 2 #1-12 and WIZARD PRESENTS ASTRO CITY #1/2. "Astro City," the Astro City logo(s), and the likenesses of all characters herein are trademarks of Juke Box Productions, unless otherwise expressly noted. "Image" and the Image Comics logos are registered trademarks of Image Comics, Inc. No part of this publication may be reproduced or transmitted, in any form or by any means (except for short excerpts for journalistic or review purposes) without the express written permission of Juke Box Productions or Image Comics, Inc. All names, characters, institutions, events, and places in this publication are entirely fictional. Any resemblance to actual persons (living or dead), institutions, events, or places, without satirical intent, is coincidental. Printed in Canada. For international rights, contact foreignlicensing@imagecomics.com. Representation: Law Offices of Harris M. Miller II, p.c. (rights.inquiries@gmail.com). ISBN: 978-1-5343-2204-2.

CONTENTS

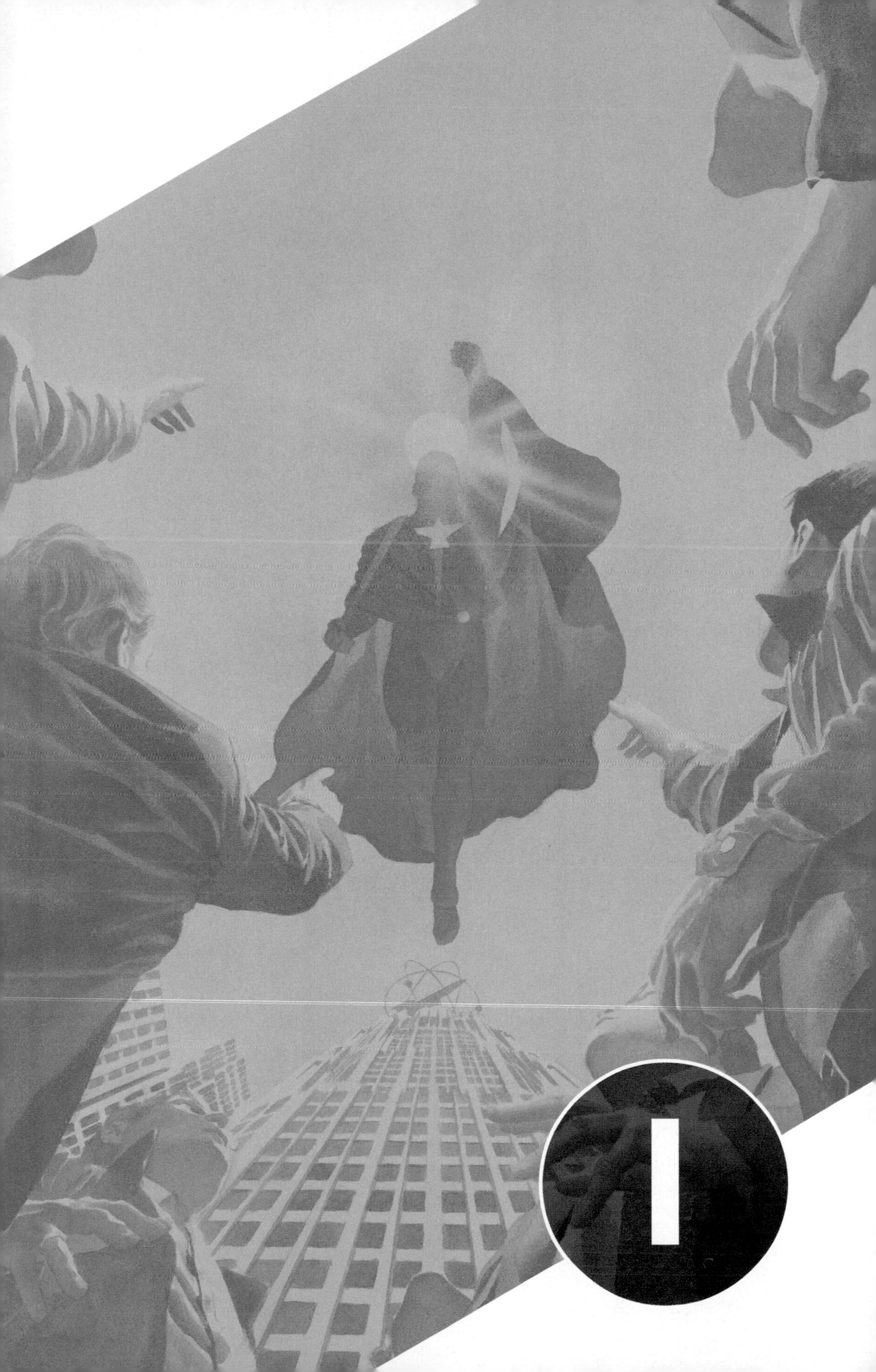

I

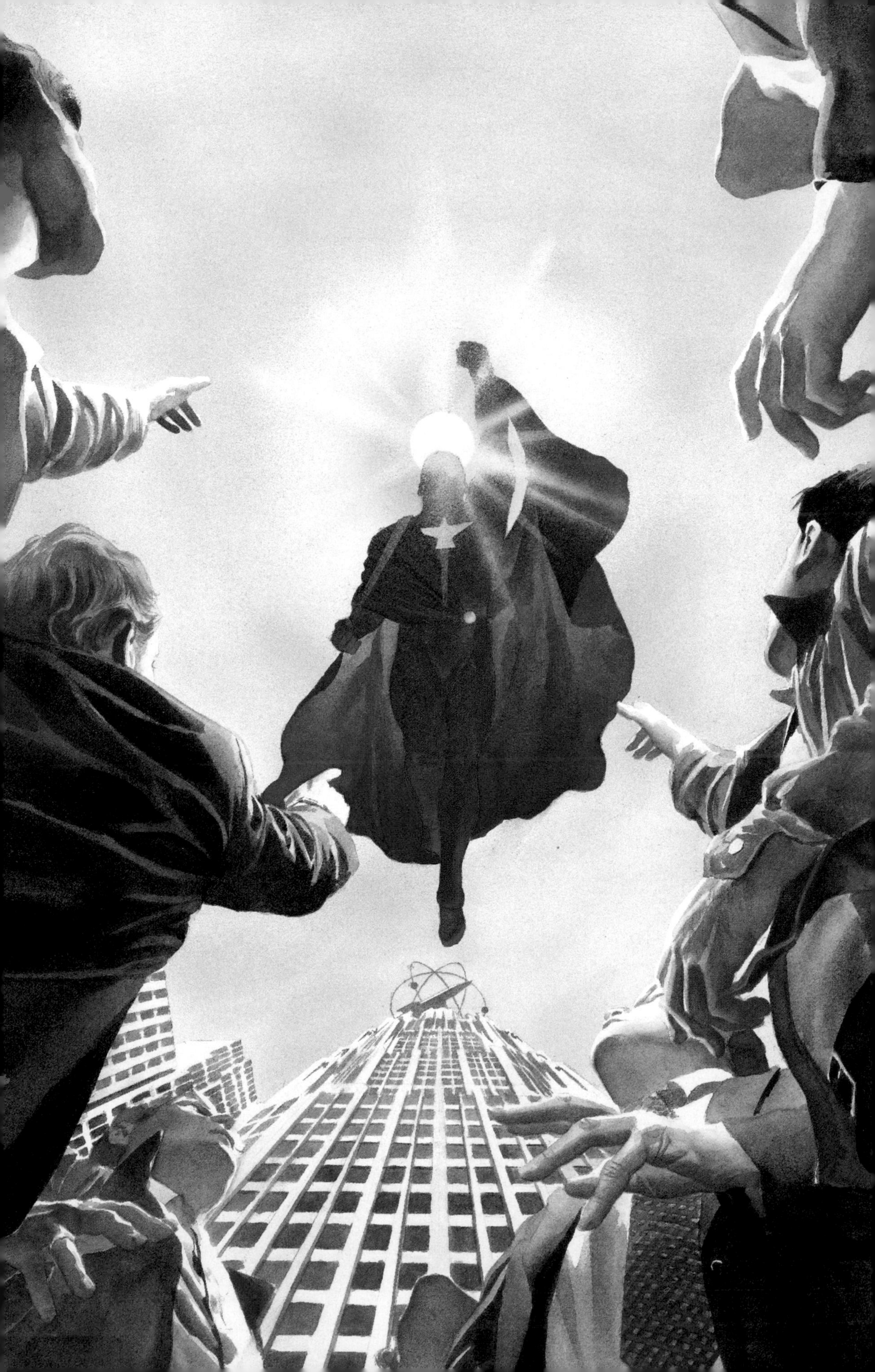

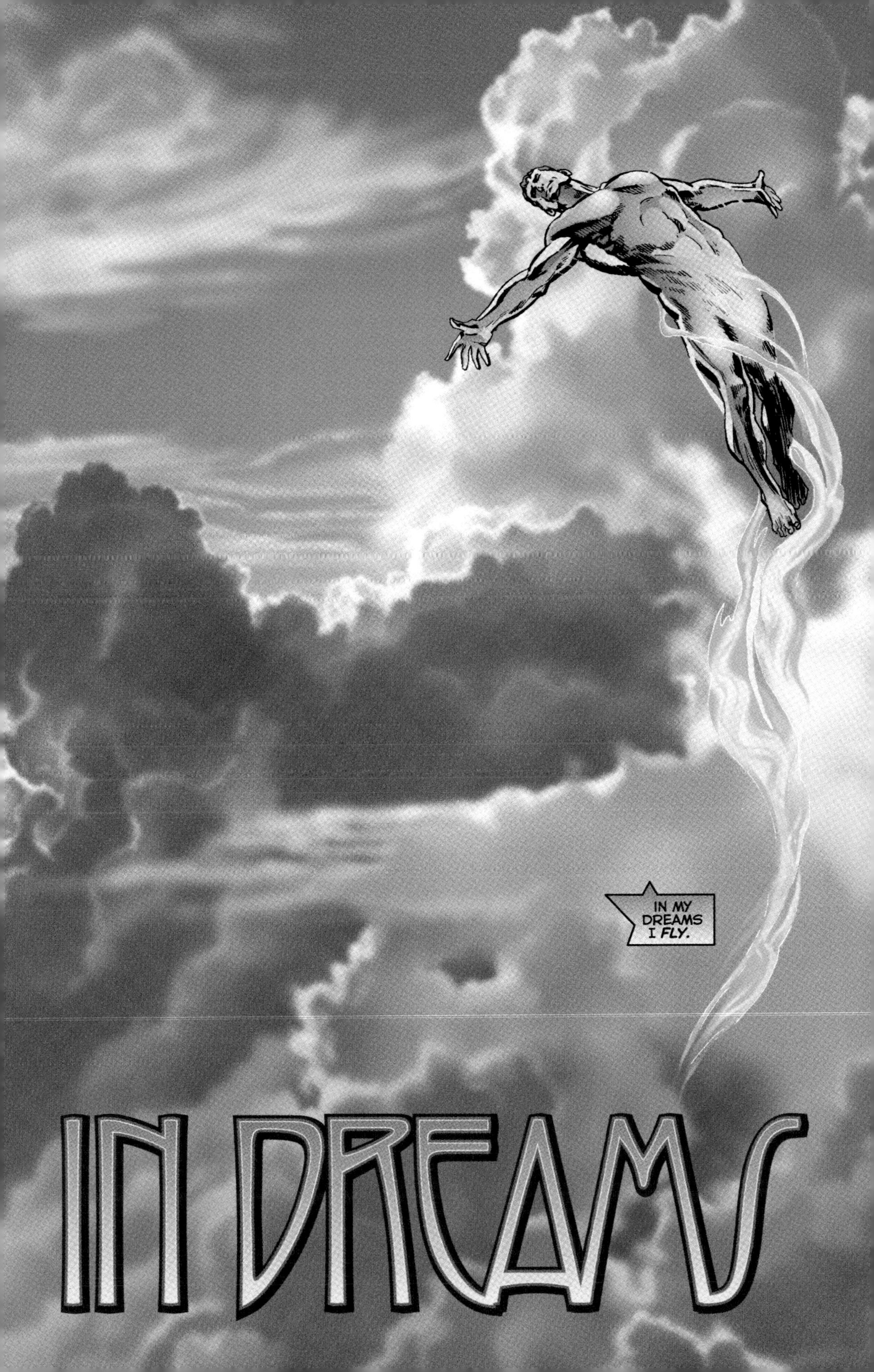
IN MY DREAMS I FLY.
IN DREAMS

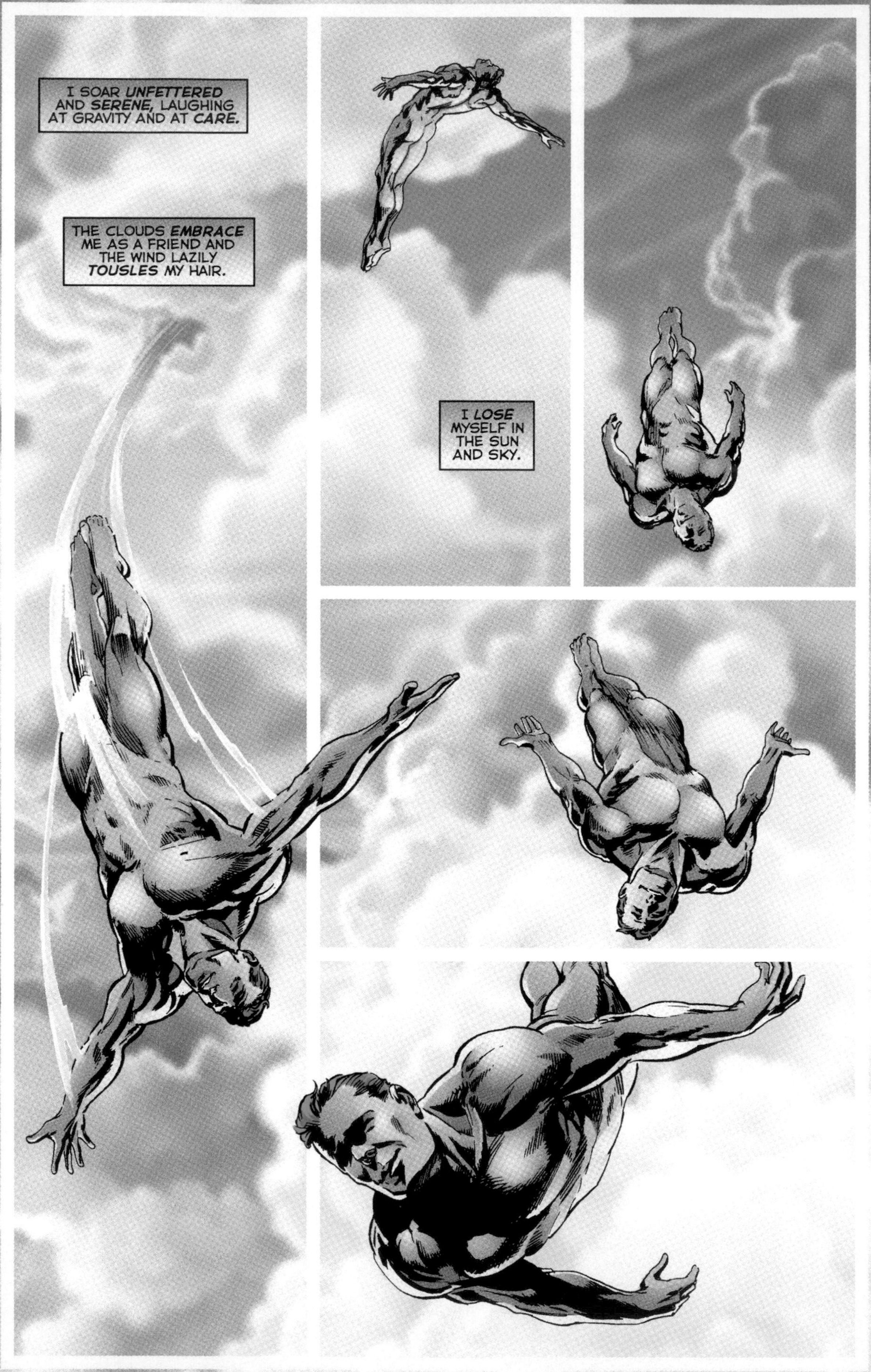
I SOAR UNFETTERED AND SERENE, LAUGHING AT GRAVITY AND AT CARE.
THE CLOUDS EMBRACE ME AS A FRIEND AND THE WIND LAZILY TOUSLES MY HAIR.
I LOSE MYSELF IN THE SUN AND SKY.

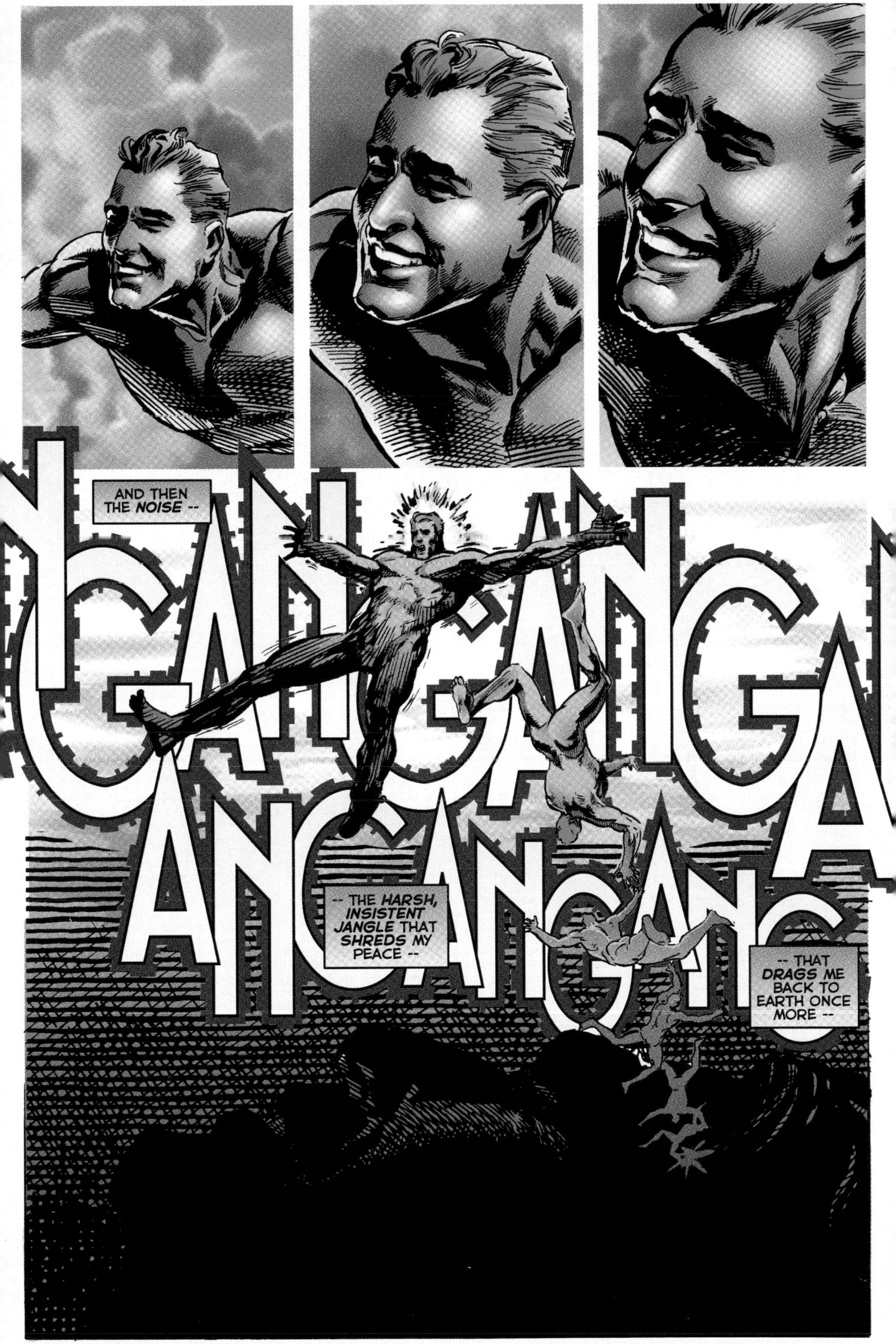
AND THEN THE NOISE --
-- THE HARSH, INSISTENT JANGLE THAT SHREDS MY PEACE --
-- THAT DRAGS ME BACK TO EARTH ONCE MORE --

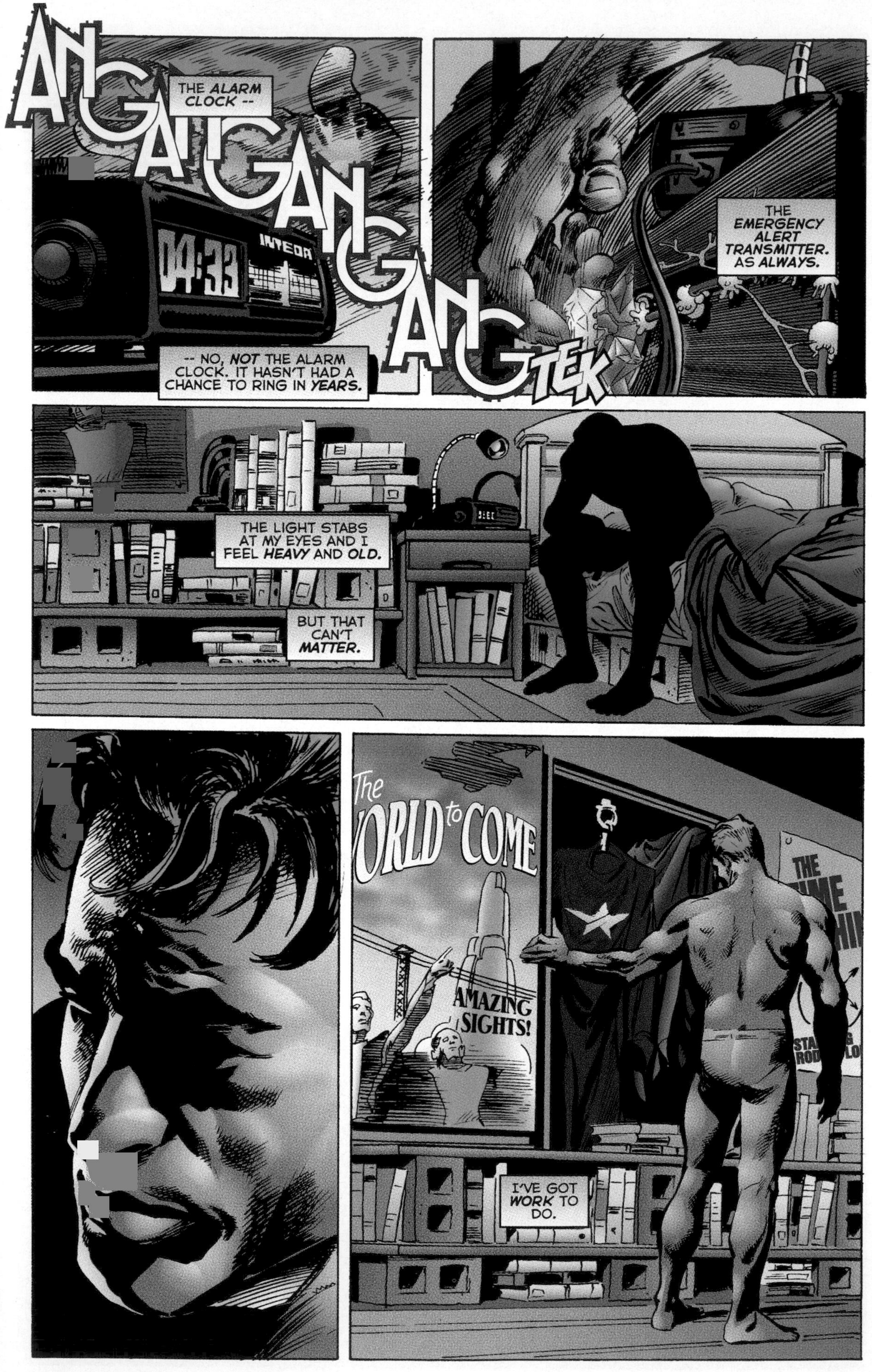
THE ALARM CLOCK --
-- NO, NOT THE ALARM CLOCK. IT HASN'T HAD A CHANCE TO RING IN YEARS.
THE EMERGENCY ALERT TRANSMITTER. AS ALWAYS.
THE LIGHT STABS AT MY EYES AND I FEEL HEAVY AND OLD.
BUT THAT CAN'T MATTER.
The WORLD to COME
AMAZING SIGHTS!
I'VE GOT WORK TO DO.

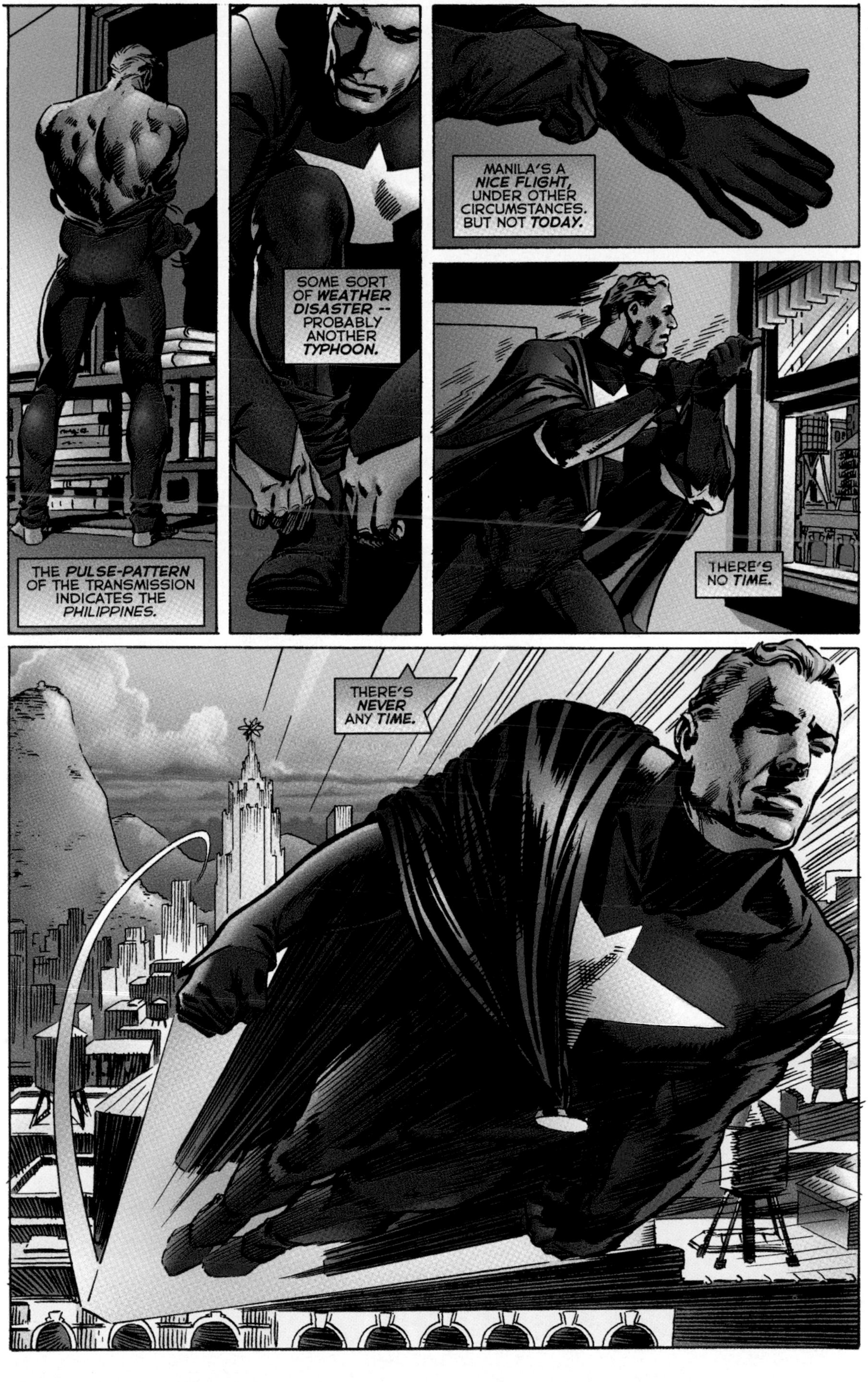
THE PULSE-PATTERN OF THE TRANSMISSION INDICATES THE PHILIPPINES.
SOME SORT OF WEATHER DISASTER -- PROBABLY ANOTHER TYPHOON.
MANILA'S A NICE FLIGHT, UNDER OTHER CIRCUMSTANCES. BUT NOT TODAY.
THERE'S NO TIME.
THERE'S NEVER ANY TIME.

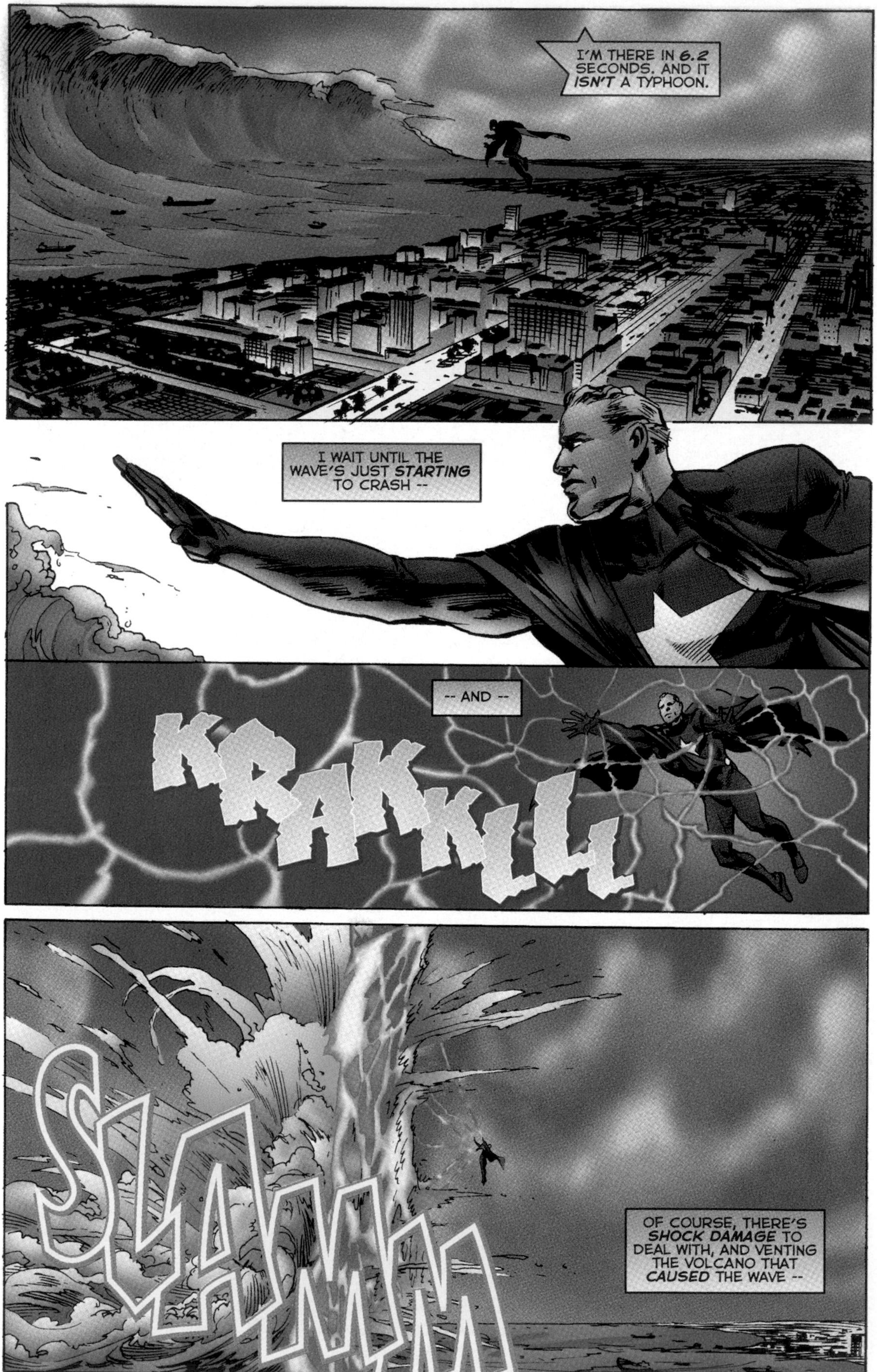
I'M THERE IN 6.2 SECONDS. AND IT ISN'T A TYPHOON.
I WAIT UNTIL THE WAVE'S JUST STARTING TO CRASH --
-- AND --
KRAKKLLL
SLAMMM
OF COURSE, THERE'S SHOCK DAMAGE TO DEAL WITH, AND VENTING THE VOLCANO THAT CAUSED THE WAVE --

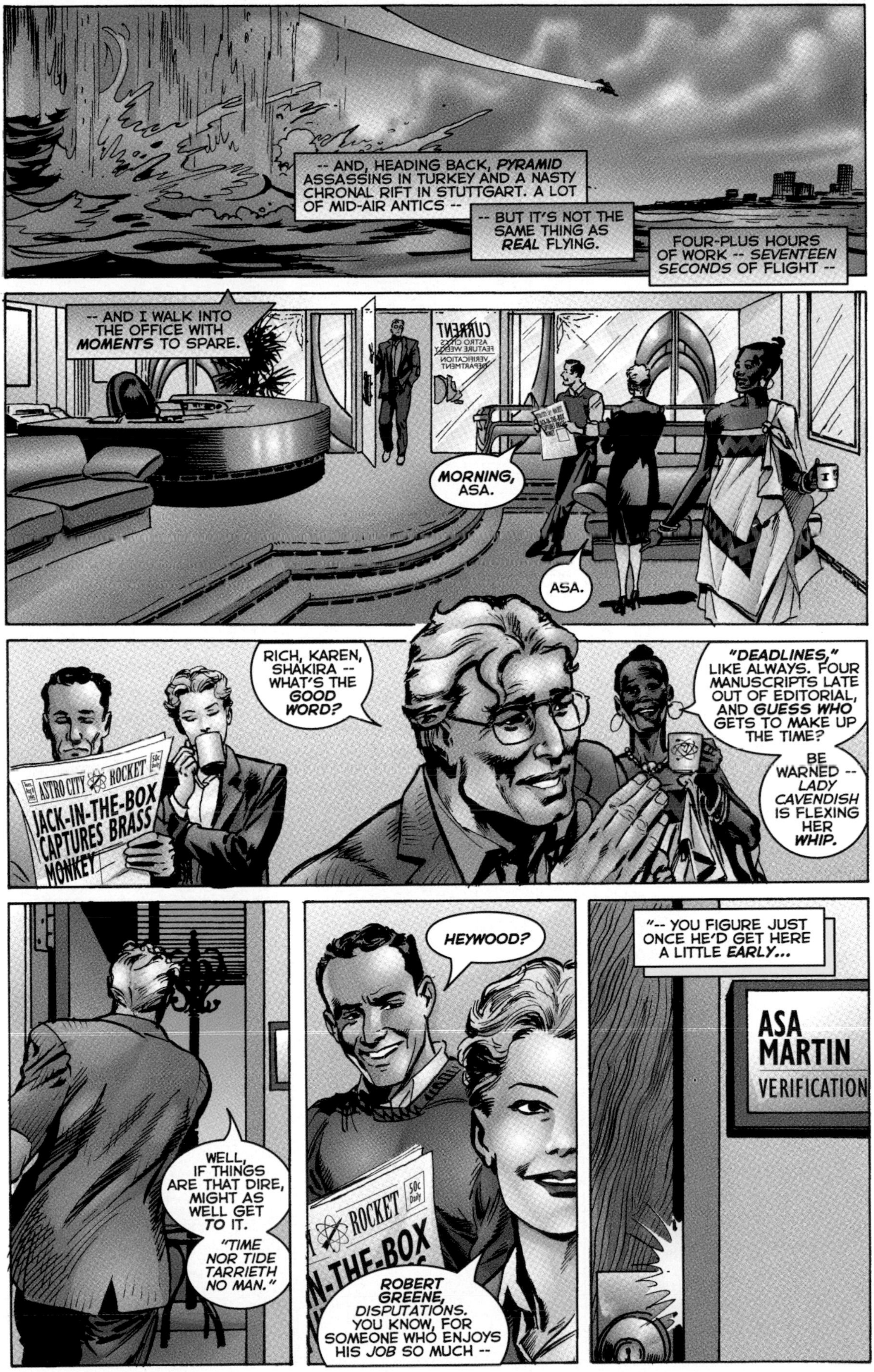
-- AND, HEADING BACK, PYRAMID ASSASSINS IN TURKEY AND A NASTY CHRONAL RIFT IN STUTTGART. A LOT OF MID-AIR ANTICS --
-- BUT IT'S NOT THE SAME THING AS REAL FLYING.
FOUR-PLUS HOURS OF WORK -- SEVENTEEN SECONDS OF FLIGHT --
-- AND I WALK INTO THE OFFICE WITH MOMENTS TO SPARE.
CURRENT
ASTRO CITY'S FEATURE WEEKLY
VERIFICATION DEPARTMENT
MORNING, ASA.
ASA.
RICH, KAREN, SHAKIRA -- WHAT'S THE GOOD WORD?
"DEADLINES," LIKE ALWAYS. FOUR MANUSCRIPTS LATE OUT OF EDITORIAL, AND GUESS WHO GETS TO MAKE UP THE TIME?
BE WARNED -- LADY CAVENDISH IS FLEXING HER WHIP.
ASTRO CITY ROCKET
50¢ Daily
JACK-IN-THE-BOX CAPTURES BRASS MONKEY
WELL, IF THINGS ARE THAT DIRE, MIGHT AS WELL GET TO IT.
"TIME NOR TIDE TARRIETH NO MAN."
HEYWOOD?
ROCKET
50¢ Daily
N-THE-BOX
ROBERT GREENE, DISPUTATIONS. YOU KNOW, FOR SOMEONE WHO ENJOYS HIS JOB SO MUCH --
"-- YOU FIGURE JUST ONCE HE'D GET HERE A LITTLE EARLY...
ASA MARTIN
VERIFICATION

ASIDE FROM YESTERDAY'S STUFF, I GET TWO NEW PIECES TO FACT-CHECK. THE FIRST FAMILY PIECE IS A *TRIPLE RUSH*.

FAMOUS "FIRSTS"
45 Years and Three Generations of Adventure

NOT BAD -- A LITTLE *FLORID*, BUT IT CAPTURES THE SUBJECT WELL.

I POWER THE *ZYXOMETER* UP, AND PROGRAM IT FOR THE MORNING'S WORK -- PHONE CALLS, REFERENCE CITES, REPORT GENERATION.

I ALREADY KNOW WHAT THE *ANSWERS* WILL BE, AND EVEN WHICH ERRORS WILL GO *UNCAUGHT* --

-- BUT THEY NEED THEIR *PROCEDURES* FOLLOWED. AND I NEED THEIR COMPUTER SYSTEM'S *NETWORK CONNECTIONS*.

BIPBIPBIPBIP

LOOKS LIKE IT'S GOING TO BE A *BUSY MORNING*.

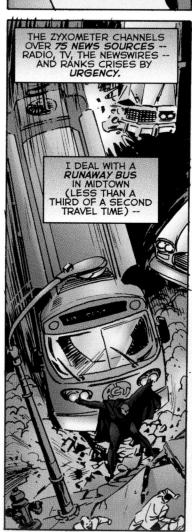

THE ZYXOMETER CHANNELS OVER *75 NEWS SOURCES* -- RADIO, TV, THE NEWSWIRES -- AND RANKS CRISES BY *URGENCY*.

I DEAL WITH A *RUNAWAY BUS* IN MIDTOWN (LESS THAN A THIRD OF A SECOND TRAVEL TIME) --

-- AN ATTACK ON THE *DENVER* CITY HALL BY *DR. SATURDAY* (1.1 SECONDS) --

-- AND A NEAR-DISASTER AT FBU'S *BIO LABS* (HALF A SECOND, BUT ONLY TO AVOID THE AIRPORT).

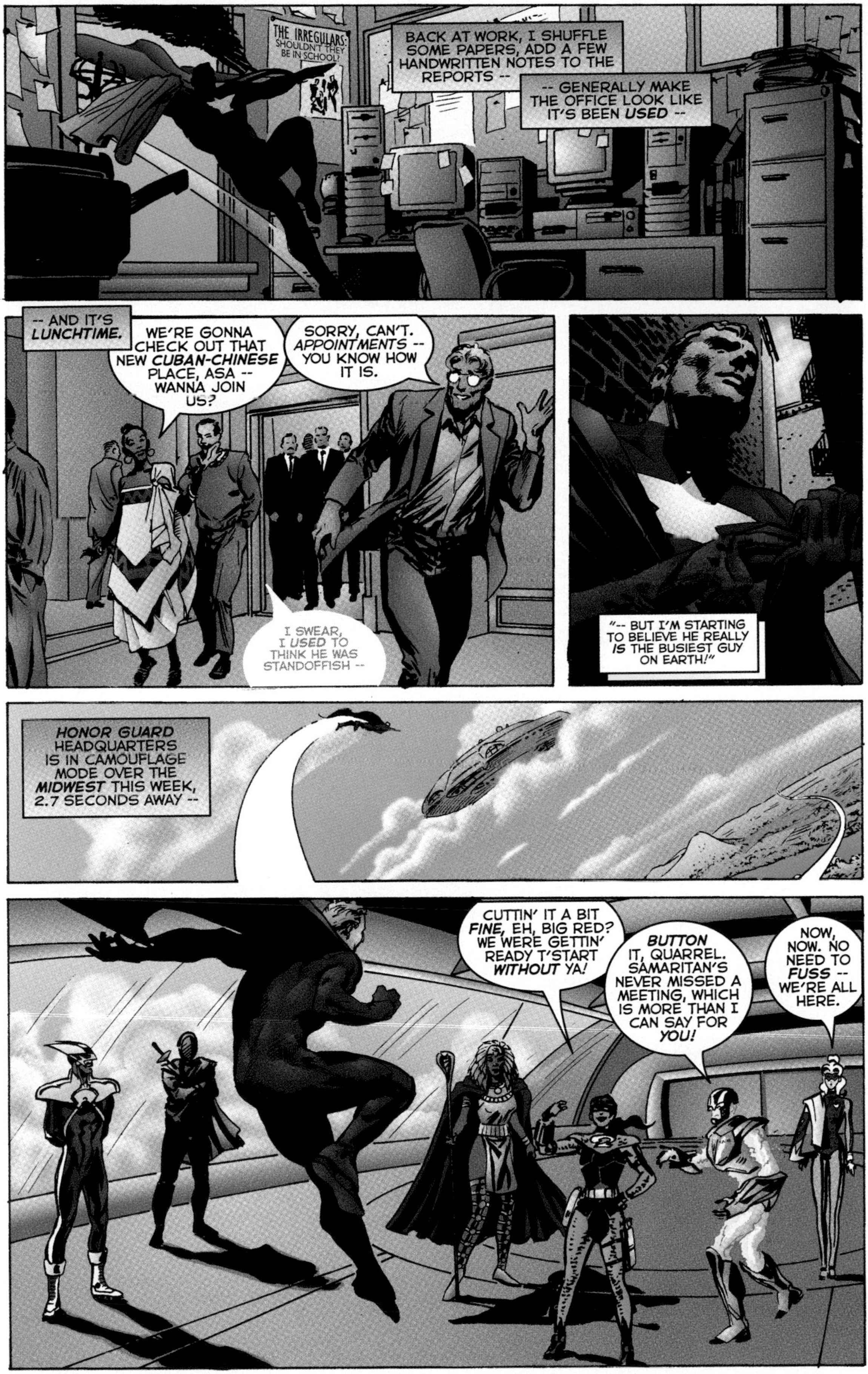
THE IRREGULARS: SHOULDN'T THEY BE IN SCHOOL?
BACK AT WORK, I SHUFFLE SOME PAPERS, ADD A FEW HANDWRITTEN NOTES TO THE REPORTS --
-- GENERALLY MAKE THE OFFICE LOOK LIKE IT'S BEEN *USED* --
-- AND IT'S *LUNCHTIME.*
WE'RE GONNA CHECK OUT THAT NEW *CUBAN-CHINESE* PLACE, ASA -- WANNA JOIN US?
SORRY, CAN'T. *APPOINTMENTS* -- YOU KNOW HOW IT IS.
I SWEAR, I *USED* TO THINK HE WAS STANDOFFISH --
"-- BUT I'M STARTING TO BELIEVE HE REALLY *IS* THE BUSIEST GUY ON EARTH!"
HONOR GUARD HEADQUARTERS IS IN CAMOUFLAGE MODE OVER THE *MIDWEST* THIS WEEK, 2.7 SECONDS AWAY --
CUTTIN' IT A BIT *FINE,* EH, BIG RED? WE WERE GETTIN' READY T'START *WITHOUT* YA!
BUTTON IT, QUARREL. SAMARITAN'S NEVER MISSED A MEETING, WHICH IS MORE THAN I CAN SAY FOR *YOU!*
NOW, NOW. NO NEED TO *FUSS* -- WE'RE ALL HERE.

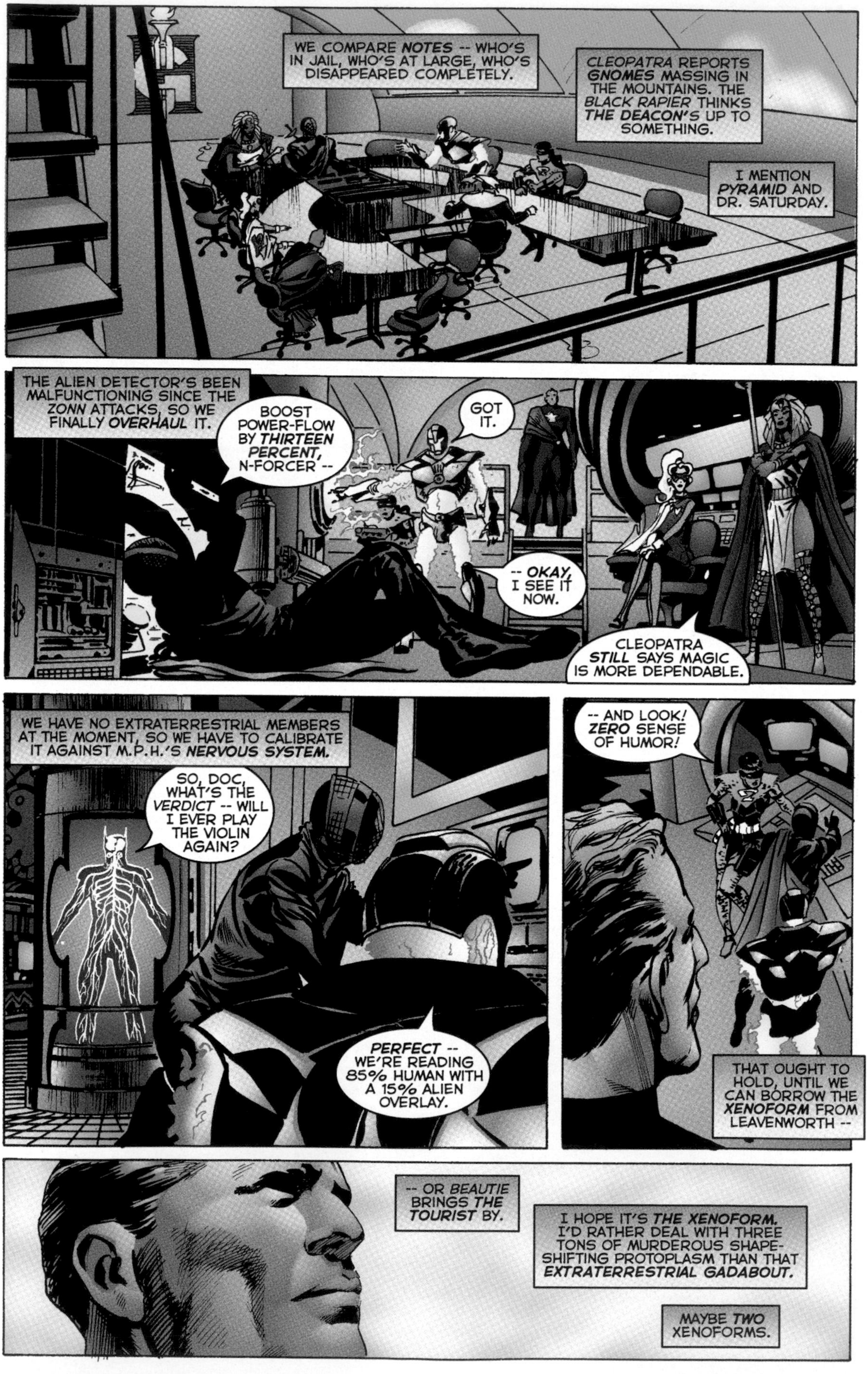
WE COMPARE NOTES -- WHO'S IN JAIL, WHO'S AT LARGE, WHO'S DISAPPEARED COMPLETELY.
CLEOPATRA REPORTS GNOMES MASSING IN THE MOUNTAINS. THE BLACK RAPIER THINKS THE DEACON'S UP TO SOMETHING.
I MENTION PYRAMID AND DR. SATURDAY.
THE ALIEN DETECTOR'S BEEN MALFUNCTIONING SINCE THE ZONN ATTACKS, SO WE FINALLY OVERHAUL IT.
BOOST POWER-FLOW BY THIRTEEN PERCENT, N-FORCER --
GOT IT.
-- OKAY, I SEE IT NOW.
CLEOPATRA STILL SAYS MAGIC IS MORE DEPENDABLE.
WE HAVE NO EXTRATERRESTRIAL MEMBERS AT THE MOMENT, SO WE HAVE TO CALIBRATE IT AGAINST M.P.H.'S NERVOUS SYSTEM.
SO, DOC, WHAT'S THE VERDICT -- WILL I EVER PLAY THE VIOLIN AGAIN?
PERFECT -- WE'RE READING 85% HUMAN WITH A 15% ALIEN OVERLAY.
-- AND LOOK! ZERO SENSE OF HUMOR!
THAT OUGHT TO HOLD, UNTIL WE CAN BORROW THE XENOFORM FROM LEAVENWORTH --
-- OR BEAUTIE BRINGS THE TOURIST BY.
I HOPE IT'S THE XENOFORM. I'D RATHER DEAL WITH THREE TONS OF MURDEROUS SHAPE-SHIFTING PROTOPLASM THAN THAT EXTRATERRESTRIAL GADABOUT.
MAYBE TWO XENOFORMS.

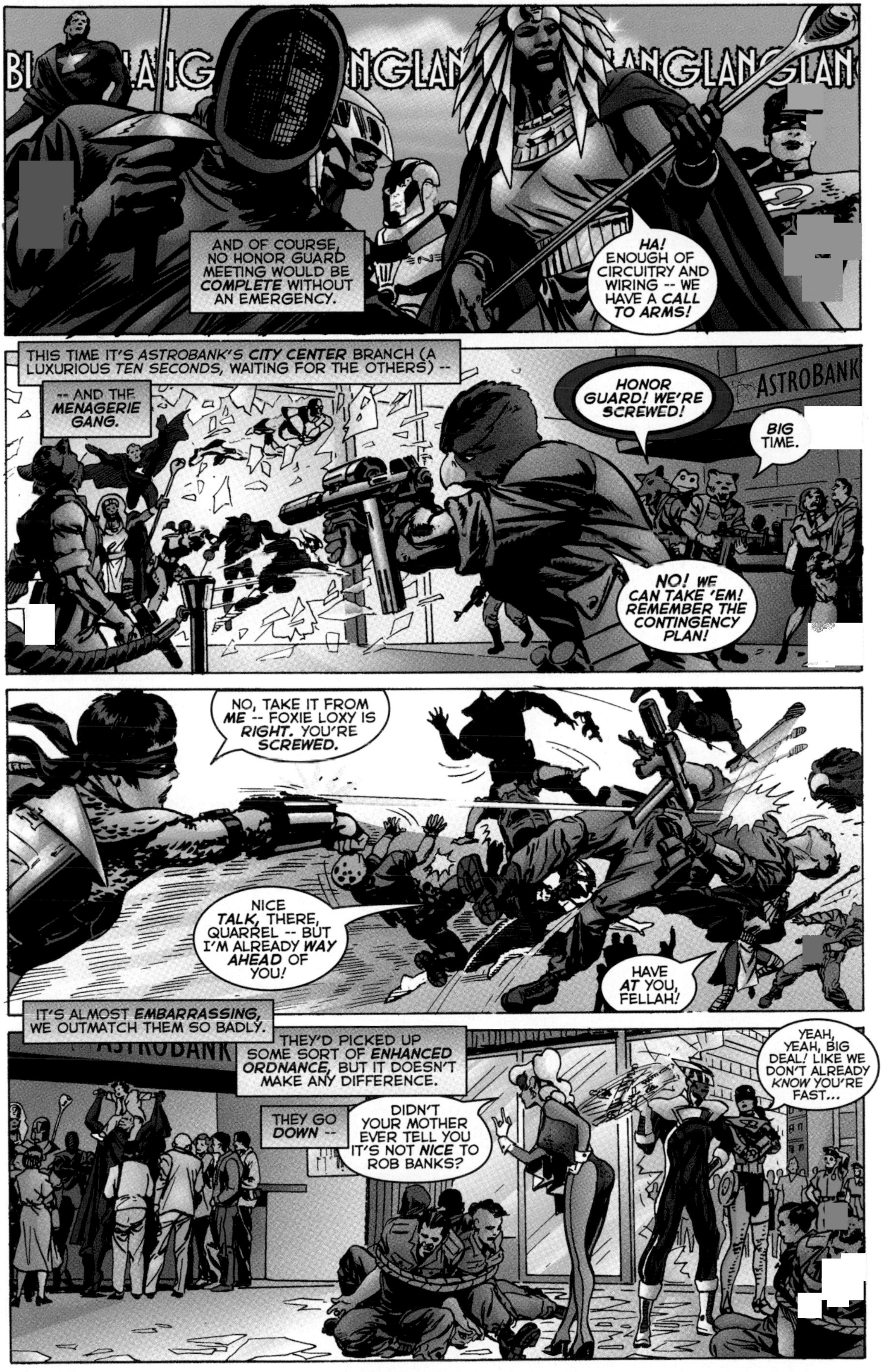
AND OF COURSE, NO HONOR GUARD MEETING WOULD BE COMPLETE WITHOUT AN EMERGENCY.
HA! ENOUGH OF CIRCUITRY AND WIRING -- WE HAVE A CALL TO ARMS!
THIS TIME IT'S ASTROBANK'S CITY CENTER BRANCH (A LUXURIOUS TEN SECONDS, WAITING FOR THE OTHERS) --
-- AND THE MENAGERIE GANG.
ASTROBANK
HONOR GUARD! WE'RE SCREWED!
BIG TIME.
NO! WE CAN TAKE 'EM! REMEMBER THE CONTINGENCY PLAN!
NO, TAKE IT FROM ME -- FOXIE LOXY IS RIGHT. YOU'RE SCREWED.
NICE TALK, THERE, QUARREL -- BUT I'M ALREADY WAY AHEAD OF YOU!
HAVE AT YOU, FELLAH!
IT'S ALMOST EMBARRASSING, WE OUTMATCH THEM SO BADLY.
THEY'D PICKED UP SOME SORT OF ENHANCED ORDNANCE, BUT IT DOESN'T MAKE ANY DIFFERENCE.
YEAH, YEAH, BIG DEAL! LIKE WE DON'T ALREADY KNOW YOU'RE FAST...
THEY GO DOWN --
DIDN'T YOUR MOTHER EVER TELL YOU IT'S NOT NICE TO ROB BANKS?

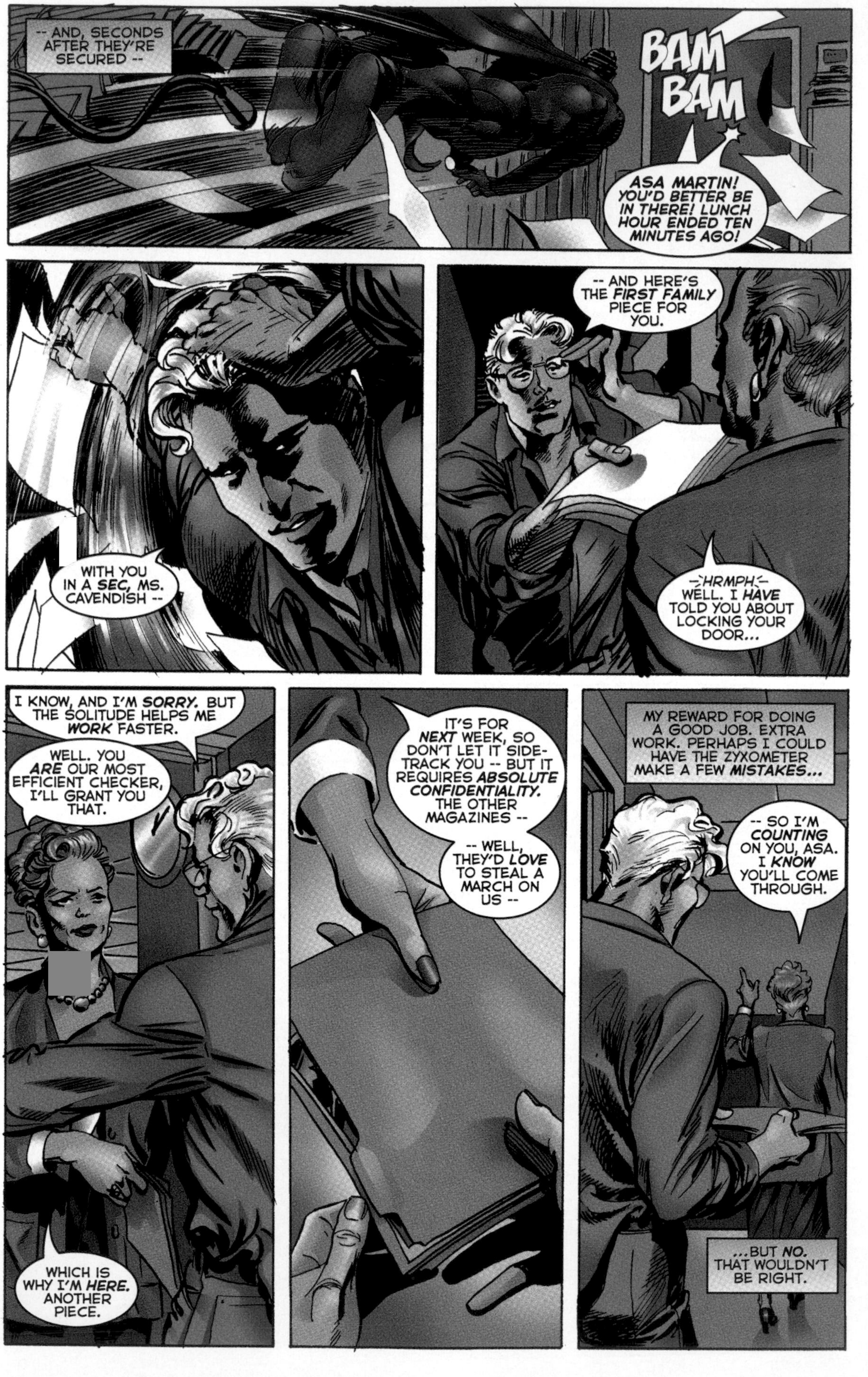
-- AND, SECONDS AFTER THEY'RE SECURED --
BAM BAM
ASA MARTIN! YOU'D BETTER BE IN THERE! LUNCH HOUR ENDED TEN MINUTES AGO!
WITH YOU IN A SEC, MS. CAVENDISH --
-- AND HERE'S THE FIRST FAMILY PIECE FOR YOU.
-HRMPH.- WELL. I HAVE TOLD YOU ABOUT LOCKING YOUR DOOR...
I KNOW, AND I'M SORRY. BUT THE SOLITUDE HELPS ME WORK FASTER.
WELL. YOU ARE OUR MOST EFFICIENT CHECKER, I'LL GRANT YOU THAT.
WHICH IS WHY I'M HERE. ANOTHER PIECE.
IT'S FOR NEXT WEEK, SO DON'T LET IT SIDE-TRACK YOU -- BUT IT REQUIRES ABSOLUTE CONFIDENTIALITY. THE OTHER MAGAZINES --
-- WELL, THEY'D LOVE TO STEAL A MARCH ON US --
MY REWARD FOR DOING A GOOD JOB. EXTRA WORK. PERHAPS I COULD HAVE THE ZYXOMETER MAKE A FEW MISTAKES...
-- SO I'M COUNTING ON YOU, ASA. I KNOW YOU'LL COME THROUGH.
...BUT NO. THAT WOULDN'T BE RIGHT.

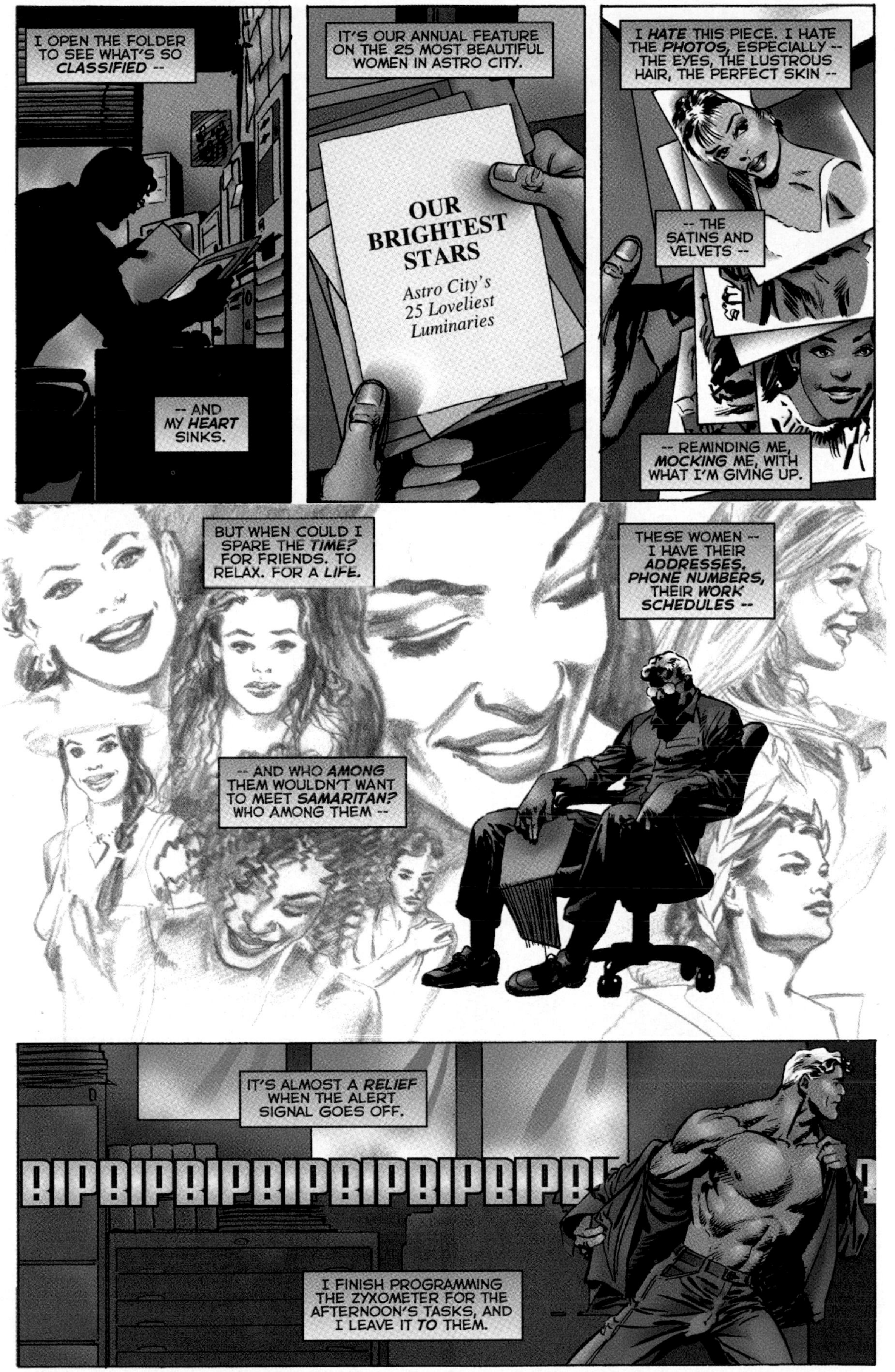
I OPEN THE FOLDER TO SEE WHAT'S SO *CLASSIFIED* --
-- AND MY *HEART* SINKS.
IT'S OUR ANNUAL FEATURE ON THE 25 MOST BEAUTIFUL WOMEN IN ASTRO CITY.
OUR BRIGHTEST STARS
Astro City's 25 Loveliest Luminaries
I *HATE* THIS PIECE. I HATE THE *PHOTOS,* ESPECIALLY -- THE EYES, THE LUSTROUS HAIR, THE PERFECT SKIN --
-- THE SATINS AND VELVETS --
-- REMINDING ME, *MOCKING* ME, WITH WHAT I'M GIVING UP.
BUT WHEN COULD I SPARE THE *TIME?* FOR FRIENDS. TO RELAX. FOR A *LIFE.*
THESE WOMEN -- I HAVE THEIR *ADDRESSES. PHONE NUMBERS,* THEIR *WORK SCHEDULES* --
-- AND WHO *AMONG* THEM WOULDN'T WANT TO MEET *SAMARITAN?* WHO AMONG THEM --
IT'S ALMOST A *RELIEF* WHEN THE ALERT SIGNAL GOES OFF.
BIPBIPBIPBIPBIPBIPBIPBIP
I FINISH PROGRAMMING THE ZYXOMETER FOR THE AFTERNOON'S TASKS, AND I LEAVE IT *TO* THEM.

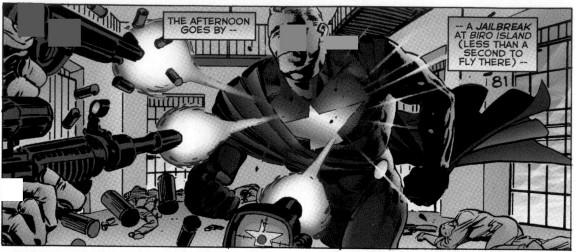

THE AFTERNOON GOES BY --

-- A *JAILBREAK* AT *BIRO ISLAND* (LESS THAN A SECOND TO FLY THERE) --

-- HELPING THE MARITIME MUSEUM RAISE THE *SEA BLAZE,* SUNK IN 1665 OFF THE FLORIDA COAST (THREE SECONDS) --

-- AND A *FRIGHTENED* LITTLE BALL OF *ORANGE AND WHITE* ON CICERO STREET.

I SLOW DOWN (TWO SECONDS) TO LET THE LITTLE GIRL *SEE* ME CLEARLY AND REASSURE HER THAT IT'S ALL RIGHT --

-- AND IT ALMOST COSTS A MAN IN BOSTON HIS *LIFE.*

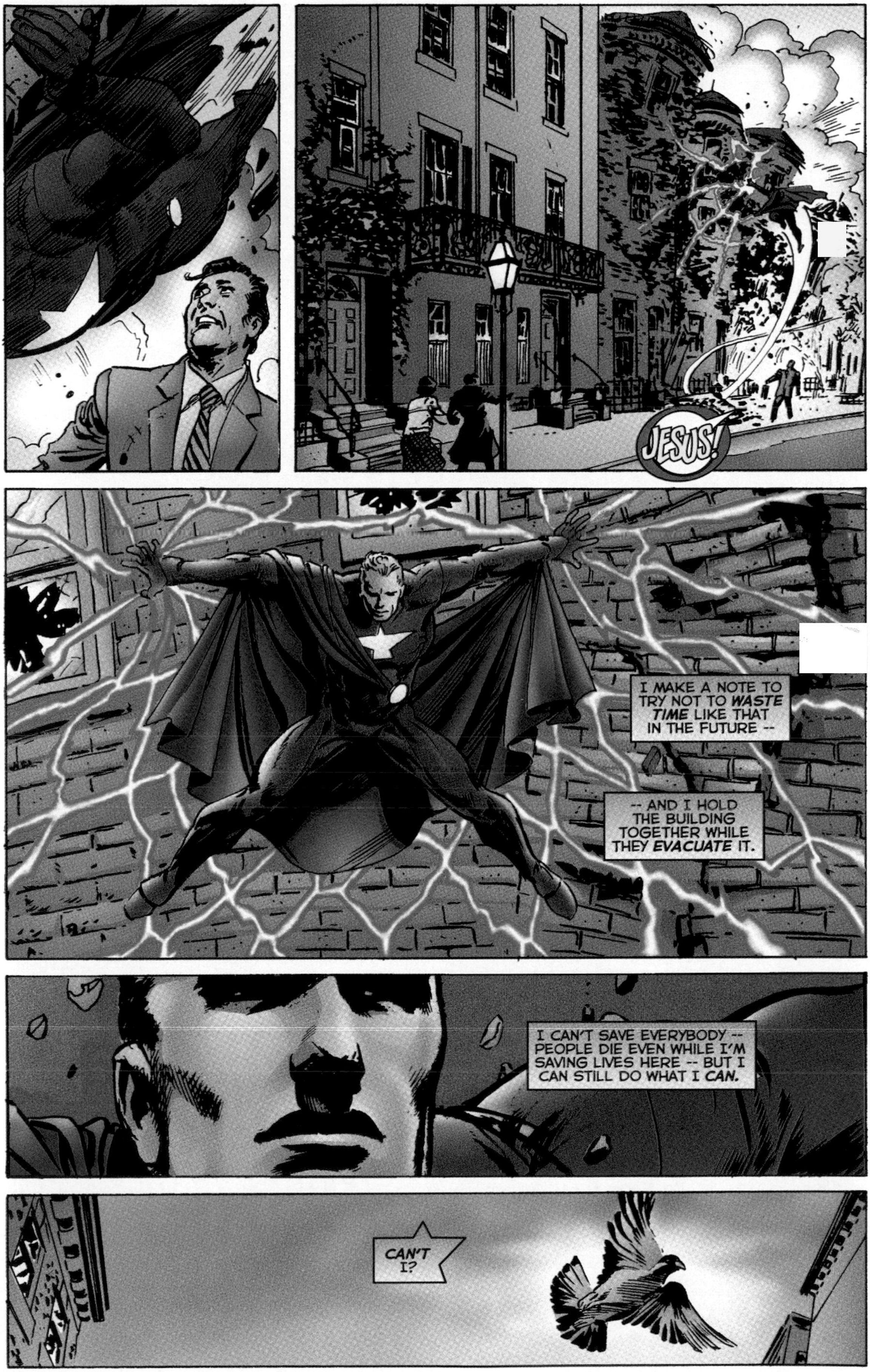
JESUS!
I MAKE A NOTE TO TRY NOT TO WASTE TIME LIKE THAT IN THE FUTURE --
-- AND I HOLD THE BUILDING TOGETHER WHILE THEY EVACUATE IT.
I CAN'T SAVE EVERYBODY -- PEOPLE DIE EVEN WHILE I'M SAVING LIVES HERE -- BUT I CAN STILL DO WHAT I CAN.
CAN'T I?

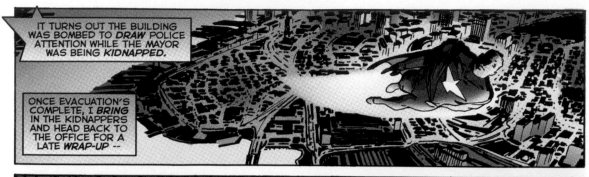

IT TURNS OUT THE BUILDING WAS BOMBED TO *DRAW* POLICE ATTENTION WHILE THE MAYOR WAS BEING *KIDNAPPED*.

ONCE EVACUATION'S COMPLETE, I *BRING* IN THE KIDNAPPERS AND HEAD BACK TO THE OFFICE FOR A LATE *WRAP-UP* --

-- AND IN TIME TO GET READY FOR *DINNER*.

TONIGHT, IT'S THE *FIREFIGHTERS ASSOCIATION.*

-- WITH THE *GREATEST HONOR*, AND *DEEPEST* SENSE OF *GRATITUDE*, THAT I *PRESENT* THIS TOKEN OF OUR ESTEEM TO THE MAN WHO --

ACFA
PRESENTED BY THE
ASTRO CITY
FIREFIGHTERS ASSOCIATION
WITH GRATITUDE AND RESPECT, TO
SAMARITAN
AUGUST 5, 1995

I TRIED ONCE TO SIMPLY *IGNORE* THESE EVENTS, BUT IT OFFENDED PEOPLE --

-- GREAT HONOR. I *THANK* YOU, AND WILL CONTINUE TO DO MY BEST, FOR THE PEOPLE OF *ASTRO CITY* AND THE ENTIRE --

-- AS IF I WAS SAYING I WAS *TOO GOOD* FOR THEM.

ACFA

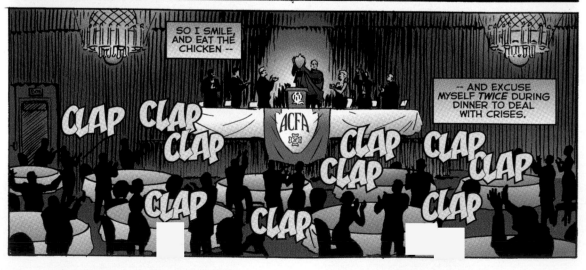

SO I SMILE AND EAT THE CHICKEN --

-- AND EXCUSE MYSELF *TWICE* DURING DINNER TO DEAL WITH CRISES.

CLAP CLAP CLAP CLAP CLAP CLAP CLAP CLAP CLAP CLAP CLAP

ACFA

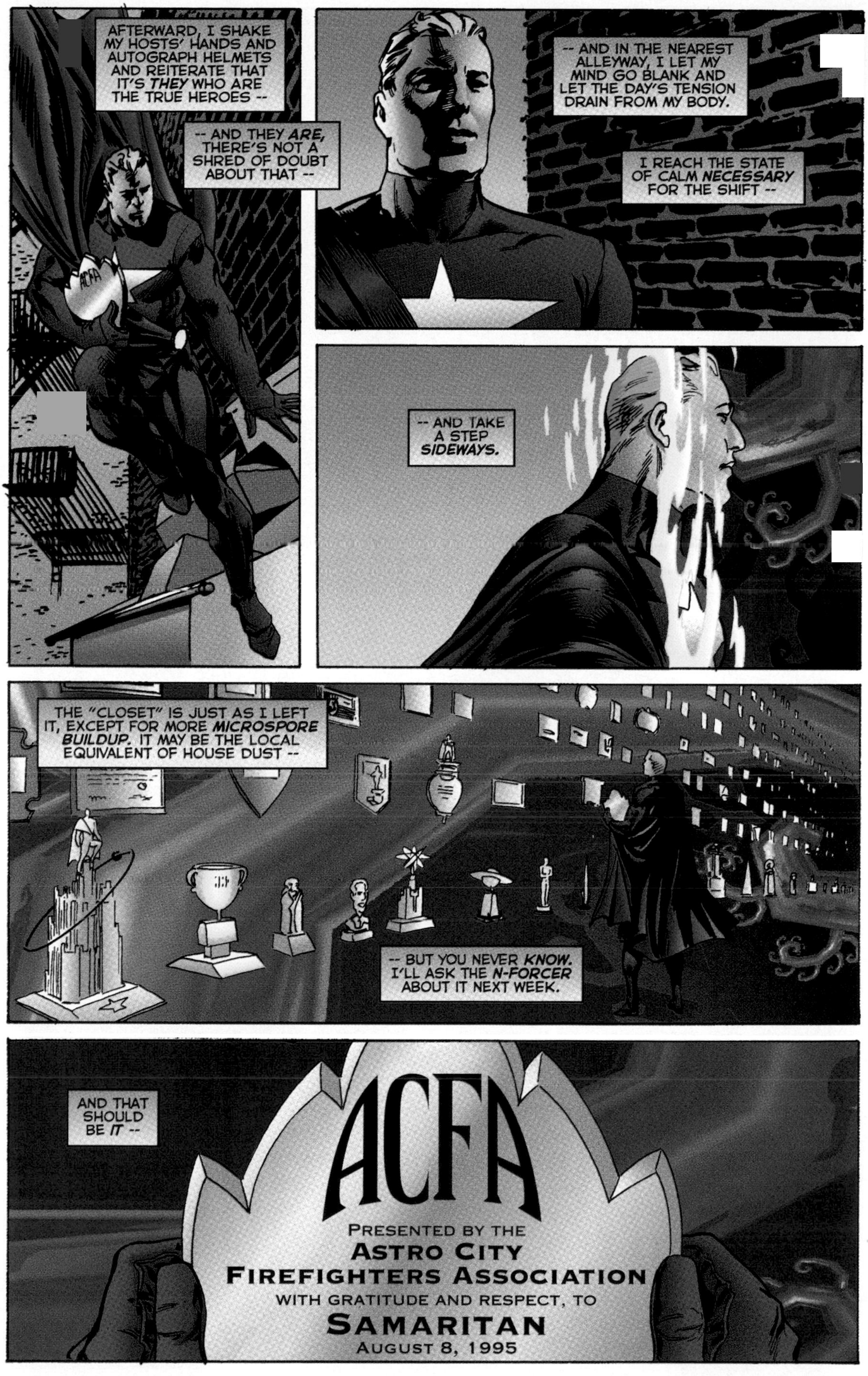
AFTERWARD, I SHAKE MY HOSTS' HANDS AND AUTOGRAPH HELMETS AND REITERATE THAT IT'S *THEY* WHO ARE THE TRUE HEROES --
-- AND THEY *ARE,* THERE'S NOT A SHRED OF DOUBT ABOUT THAT --
ACFA
-- AND IN THE NEAREST ALLEYWAY, I LET MY MIND GO BLANK AND LET THE DAY'S TENSION DRAIN FROM MY BODY.
I REACH THE STATE OF CALM *NECESSARY* FOR THE SHIFT --
-- AND TAKE A STEP *SIDEWAYS.*
THE "CLOSET" IS JUST AS I LEFT IT, EXCEPT FOR MORE *MICROSPORE BUILDUP.* IT MAY BE THE LOCAL EQUIVALENT OF HOUSE DUST --
-- BUT YOU NEVER *KNOW.* I'LL ASK THE *N-FORCER* ABOUT IT NEXT WEEK.
AND THAT SHOULD BE *IT* --
ACFA
PRESENTED BY THE
ASTRO CITY
FIREFIGHTERS ASSOCIATION
WITH GRATITUDE AND RESPECT, TO
SAMARITAN
AUGUST 8, 1995

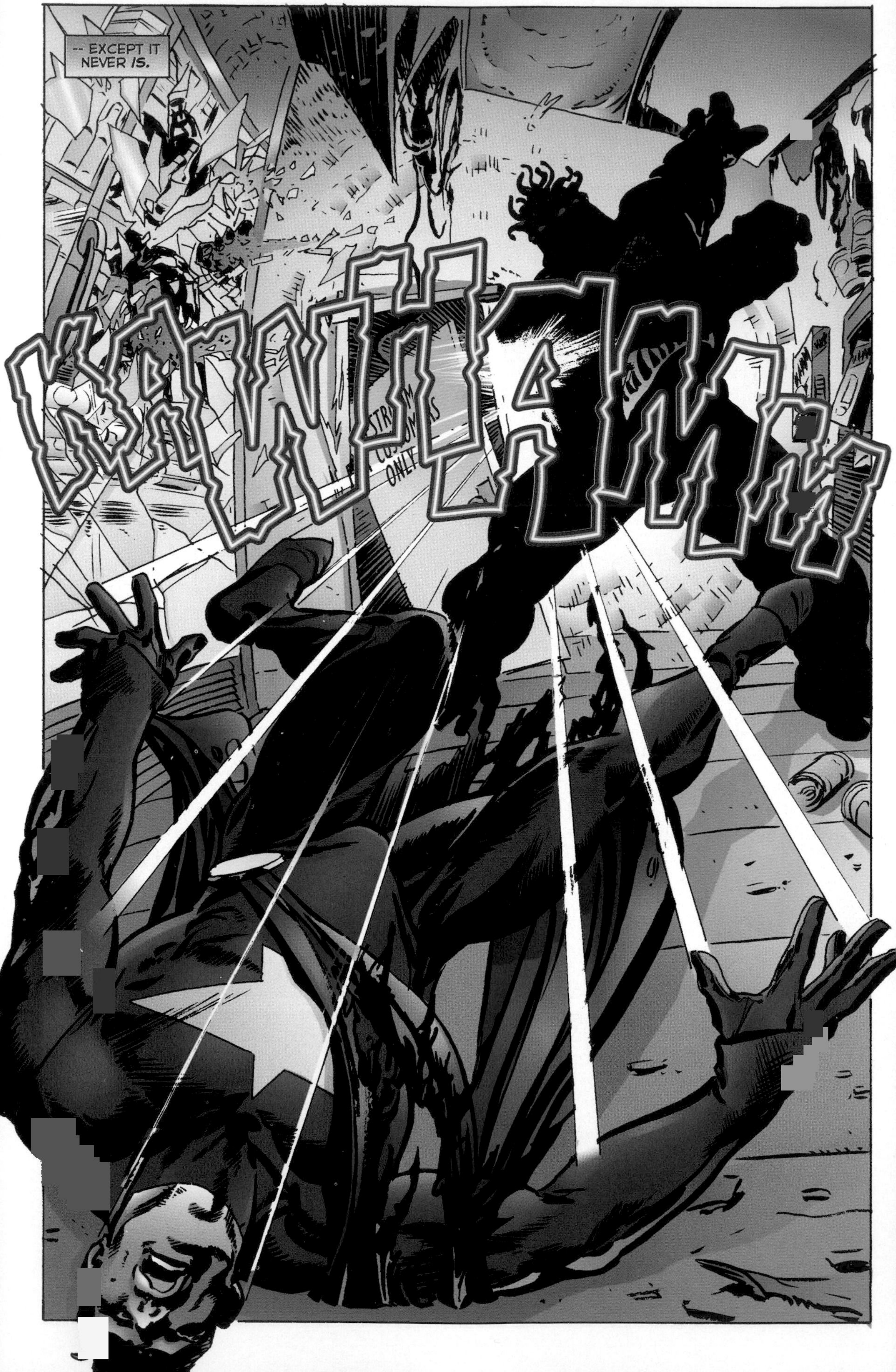
-- EXCEPT IT NEVER IS.

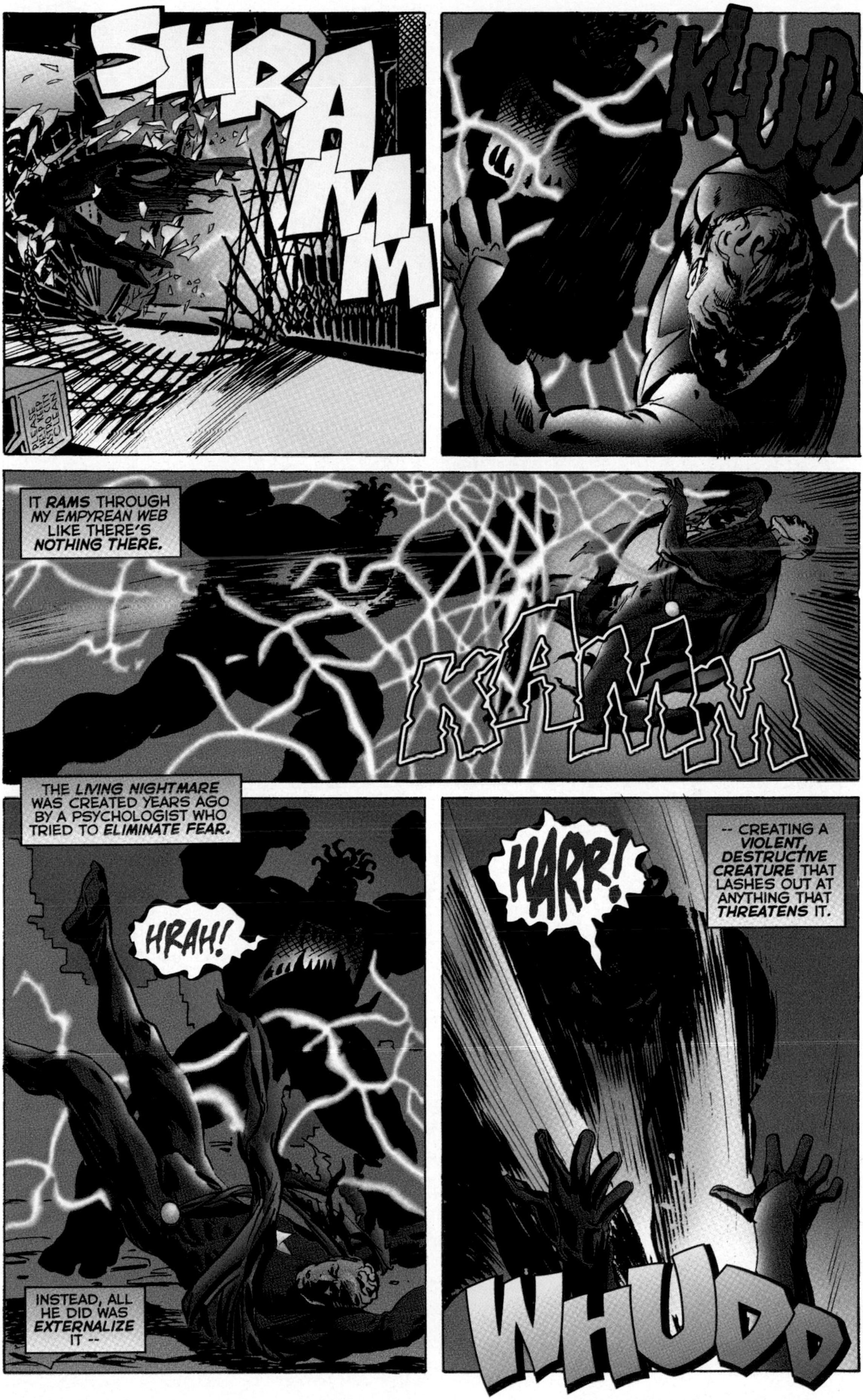
SHRAMM
KLUDD
IT RAMS THROUGH MY EMPYREAN WEB LIKE THERE'S NOTHING THERE.
KRAMM
THE LIVING NIGHTMARE WAS CREATED YEARS AGO BY A PSYCHOLOGIST WHO TRIED TO ELIMINATE FEAR.
HRAH!
INSTEAD, ALL HE DID WAS EXTERNALIZE IT --
HARR!
-- CREATING A VIOLENT, DESTRUCTIVE CREATURE THAT LASHES OUT AT ANYTHING THAT THREATENS IT.
WHUDD

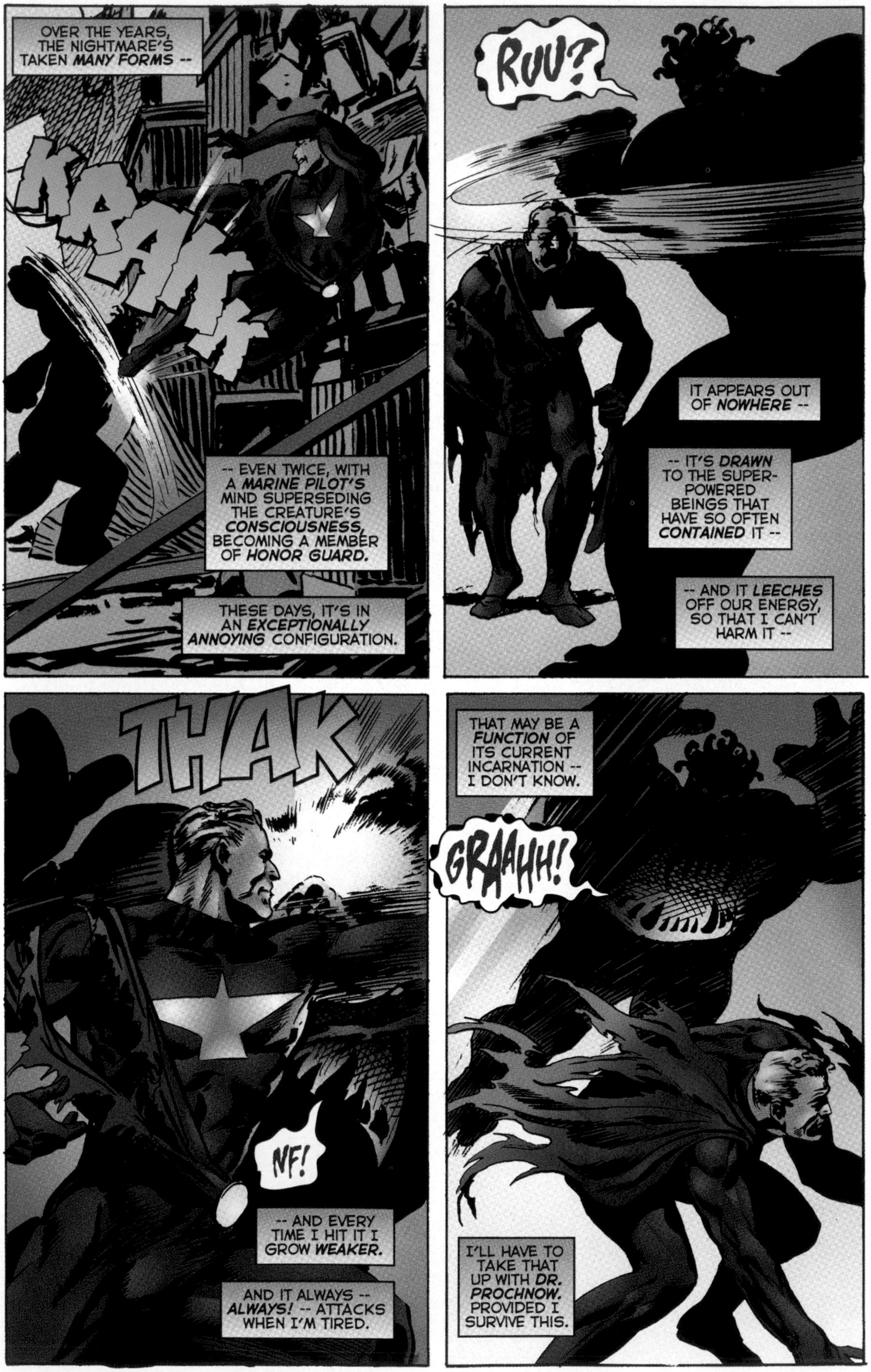
OVER THE YEARS, THE NIGHTMARE'S TAKEN MANY FORMS --
KRAKK
-- EVEN TWICE, WITH A MARINE PILOT'S MIND SUPERSEDING THE CREATURE'S CONSCIOUSNESS, BECOMING A MEMBER OF HONOR GUARD.
THESE DAYS, IT'S IN AN EXCEPTIONALLY ANNOYING CONFIGURATION.
RUU?
IT APPEARS OUT OF NOWHERE --
-- IT'S DRAWN TO THE SUPER-POWERED BEINGS THAT HAVE SO OFTEN CONTAINED IT --
-- AND IT LEECHES OFF OUR ENERGY, SO THAT I CAN'T HARM IT --
THAK
NF!
-- AND EVERY TIME I HIT IT I GROW WEAKER.
AND IT ALWAYS -- ALWAYS! -- ATTACKS WHEN I'M TIRED.
THAT MAY BE A FUNCTION OF ITS CURRENT INCARNATION -- I DON'T KNOW.
GRAAHH!
I'LL HAVE TO TAKE THAT UP WITH DR. PROCHNOW. PROVIDED I SURVIVE THIS.

ONE THING I'LL SAY FOR THE NIGHTMARE, THOUGH --

GARRARRAR!

-- IT'S DEPENDABLY STUPID. I FINALLY MANEUVER IT DIRECTLY ON TOP OF ME --

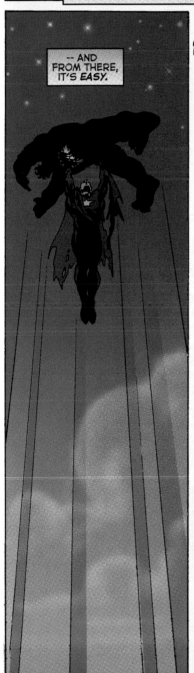

-- AND FROM THERE, IT'S EASY.

BRARGH!

THE TRIP INTO ORBIT DOESN'T LAST LONG ENOUGH FOR IT TO DRAIN ME TOO BADLY --

-- AND THERE'S NOTHING IT CAN HURT BETWEEN HERE AND THE SUN.

BUT SURE ENOUGH, IT BLINKS OUT OF EXISTENCE AS SOON AS IT'S FAR ENOUGH AWAY FROM THE EMOTIONS THAT POWER IT.

IN SOME WAYS, THAT'S THE MOST FRUSTRATING PART OF THE ENTIRE BATTLE.

I'D LIKE TO TAKE MY *TIME* HEADING BACK. I'M BRUISED, EXHAUSTED, AND EARTH IS SO *LOVELY* BY STARLIGHT.

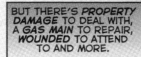

BUT THERE'S *PROPERTY DAMAGE* TO DEAL WITH, A *GAS MAIN* TO REPAIR, *WOUNDED* TO ATTEND TO AND MORE.

IT'S PAST *ONE A.M.* BY THE TIME I GET BACK TO MY APARTMENT.

I TALLY UP THE DAY.

FIFTY-SIX SECONDS. BEST DAY SINCE *MARCH.*

I'M *SLIPPING AWAY* BEFORE MY HEAD HITS THE PILLOW.

AND I SLEEP --

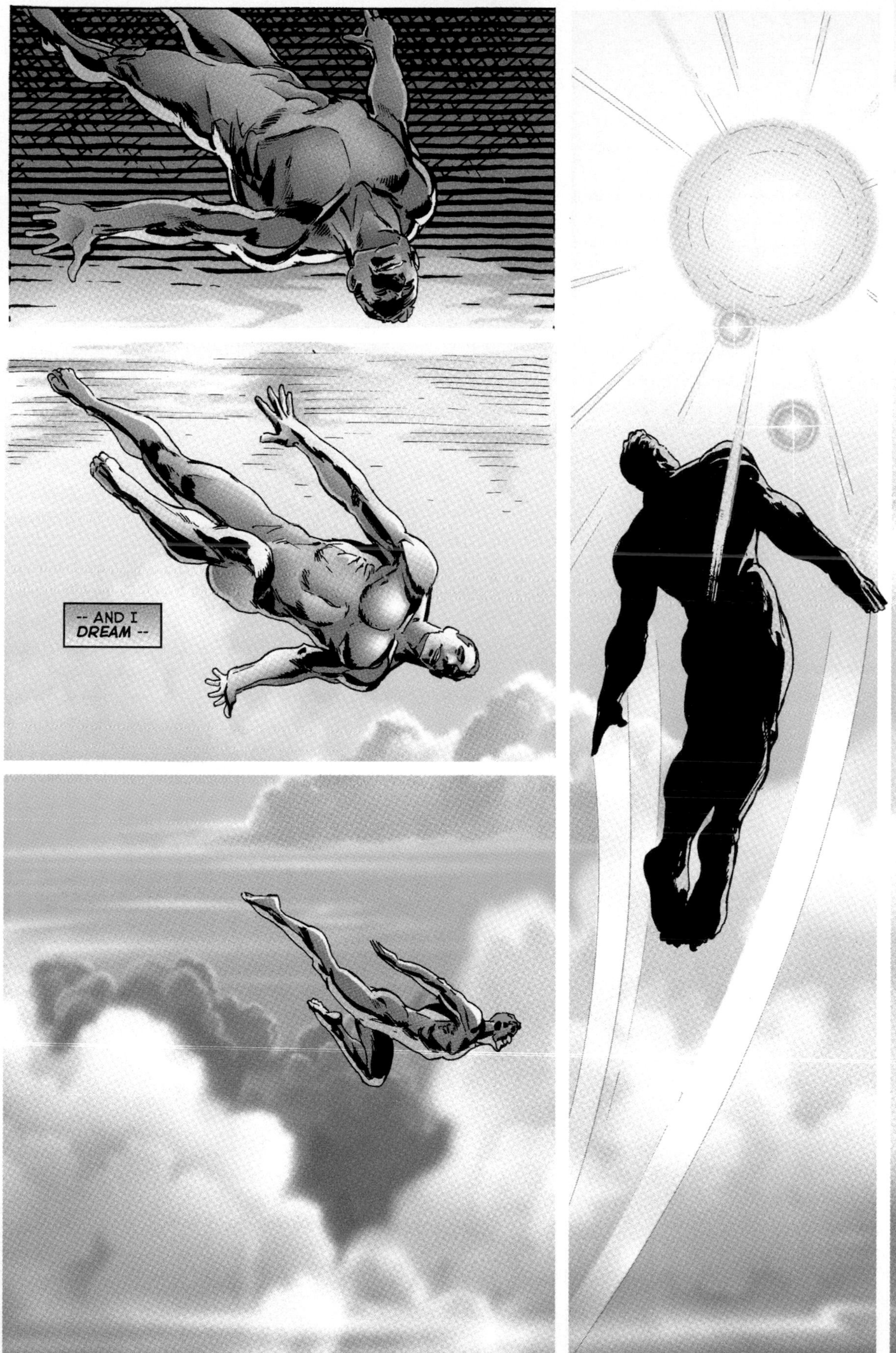
-- AND I DREAM --

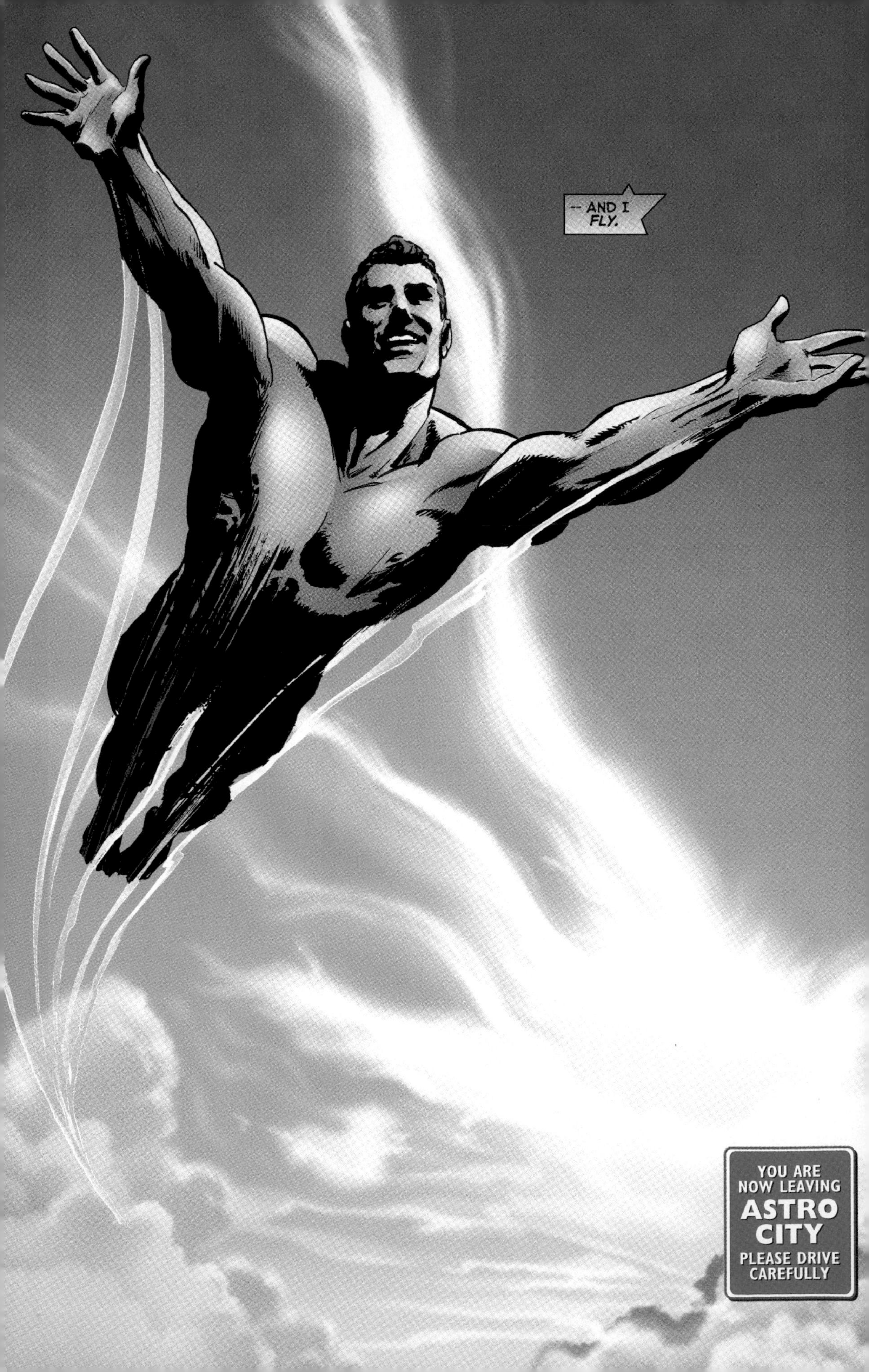
-- AND I FLY.
YOU ARE NOW LEAVING ASTRO CITY PLEASE DRIVE CAREFULLY

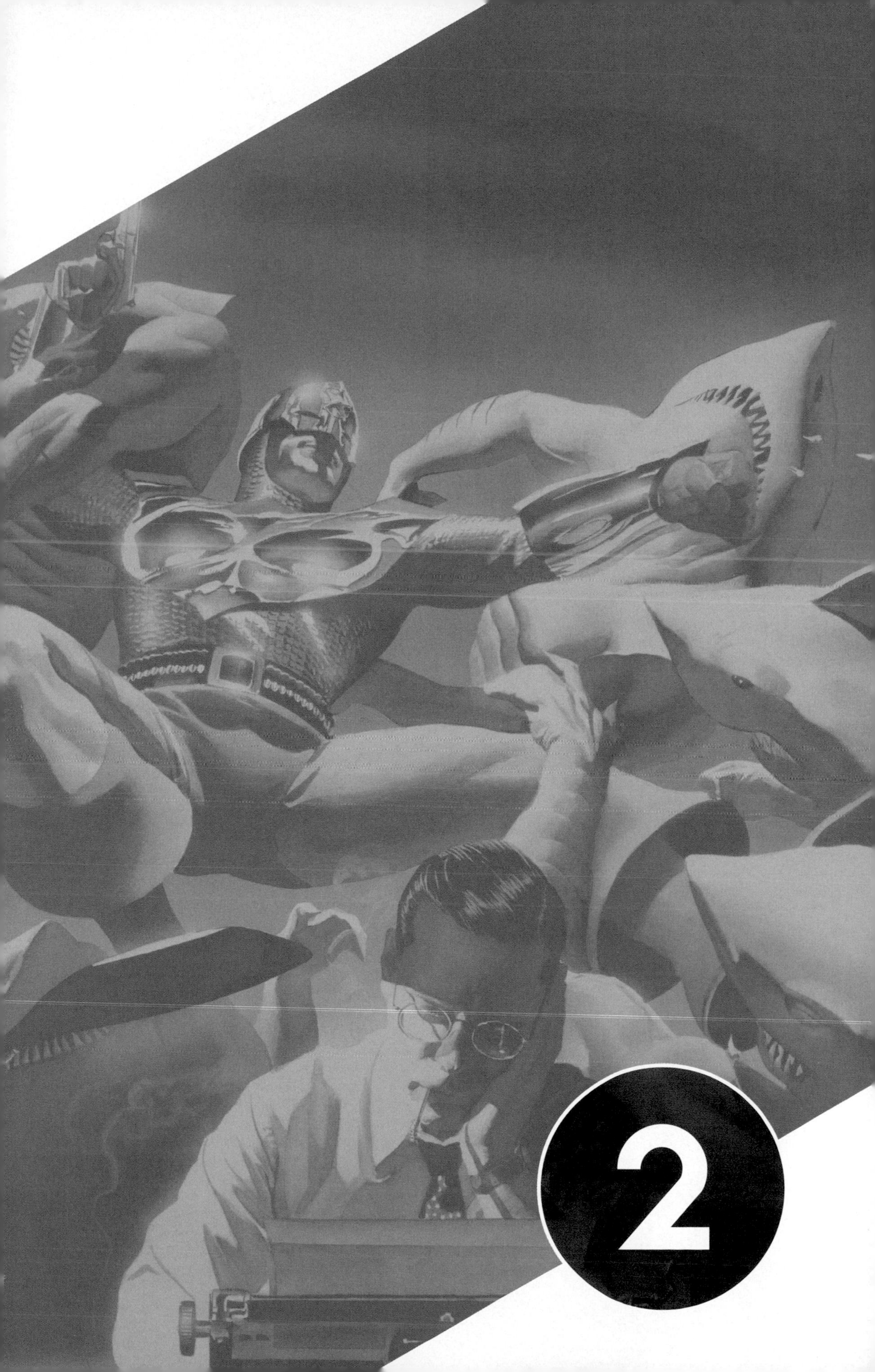

2

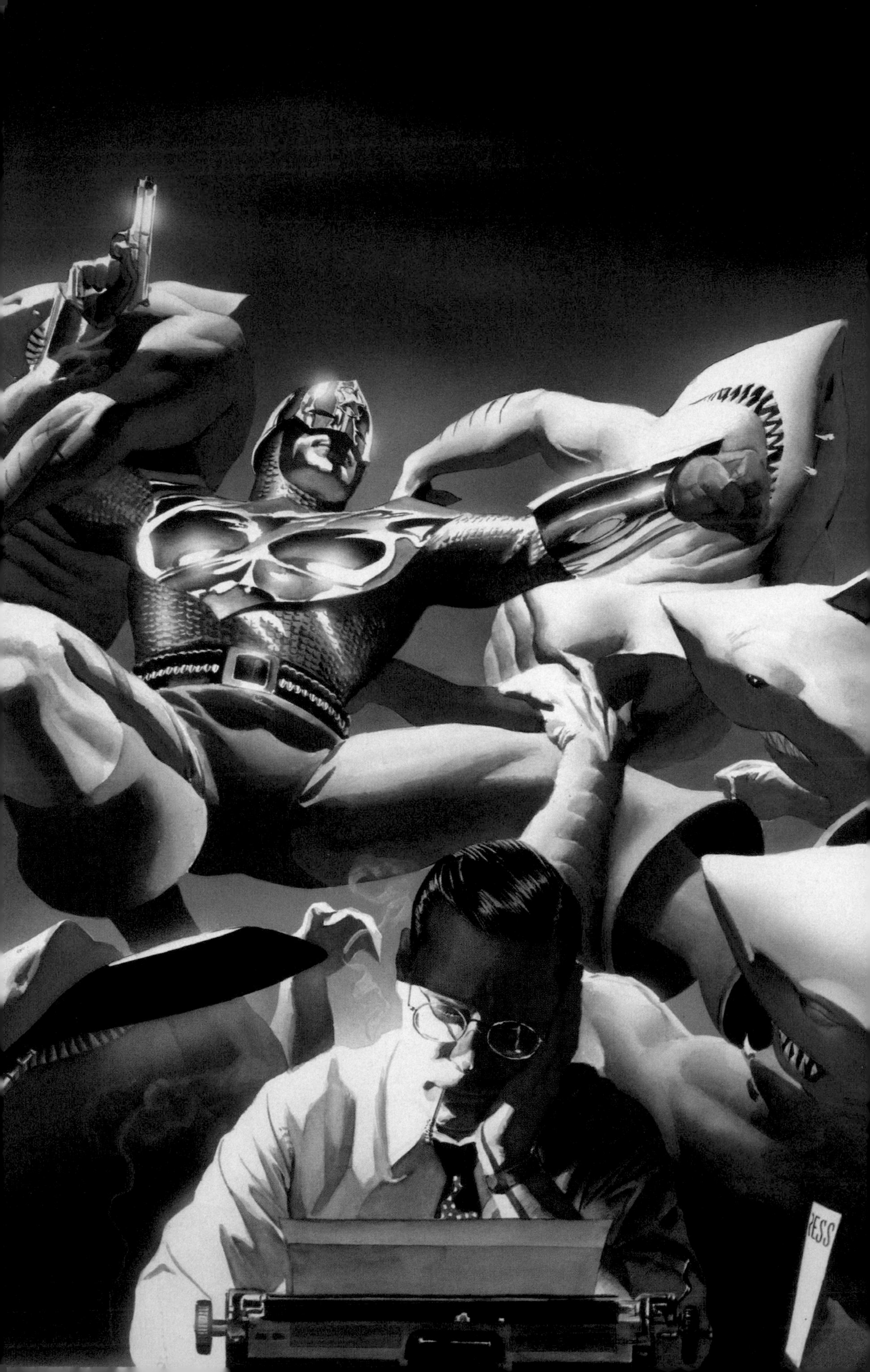

"THE SALARY'S *ACCEPTABLE*, THEN?"

ROCKET!

GETCHER MORNING *ROCKET!*

ASTRO CITY ROCKET
SAMARITAN CHECKS NIGHTMARE RAMPAGE
Damage Contained, No Deaths

ASTRO CITY ROCKET
SAMARITAN CHECKS NIGHTMARE RAMPAGE
Damage Contained, No Deaths

UH, YES -- YES, IT'S *FINE.*

GOOD. THEN WELCOME TO THE *ASTRO CITY ROCKET*, SON. I EXPECT *GREAT THINGS* FROM YOU.

I'LL TRY TO *LIVE UP* TO THAT, MISTER MILLS.

PLEASE, IT'S *ELLIOT.* I'M ONLY "MISTER MILLS" WHEN YOU'VE DONE SOMETHING WRONG.

UH, YES SIR, MISTER-- I MEAN, *ELLIOT.*

DON'T *WORRY,* KID. I'M NOT GOING TO *BITE* YOU.

I HAD SALLY MAKE US LUNCH RESERVATIONS AT THE PRESS CLUB. I'LL INTRODUCE YOU TO SOME OF THE GUYS YOU'LL BE WORKING WITH.

THAT ALL RIGHT WITH *YOU?*

THE *PRESS CLUB?* THAT...THAT'LL BE FINE!

GOOD. WE'VE GOT A FEW MINUTES BEFORE IT'S TIME TO HEAD DOWN, THEN.

RELAX. LOOSEN YOUR *TIE,* MAYBE -- YOU LOOK LIKE YOU'RE *CHOKING.*

THANK YOU, SIR.

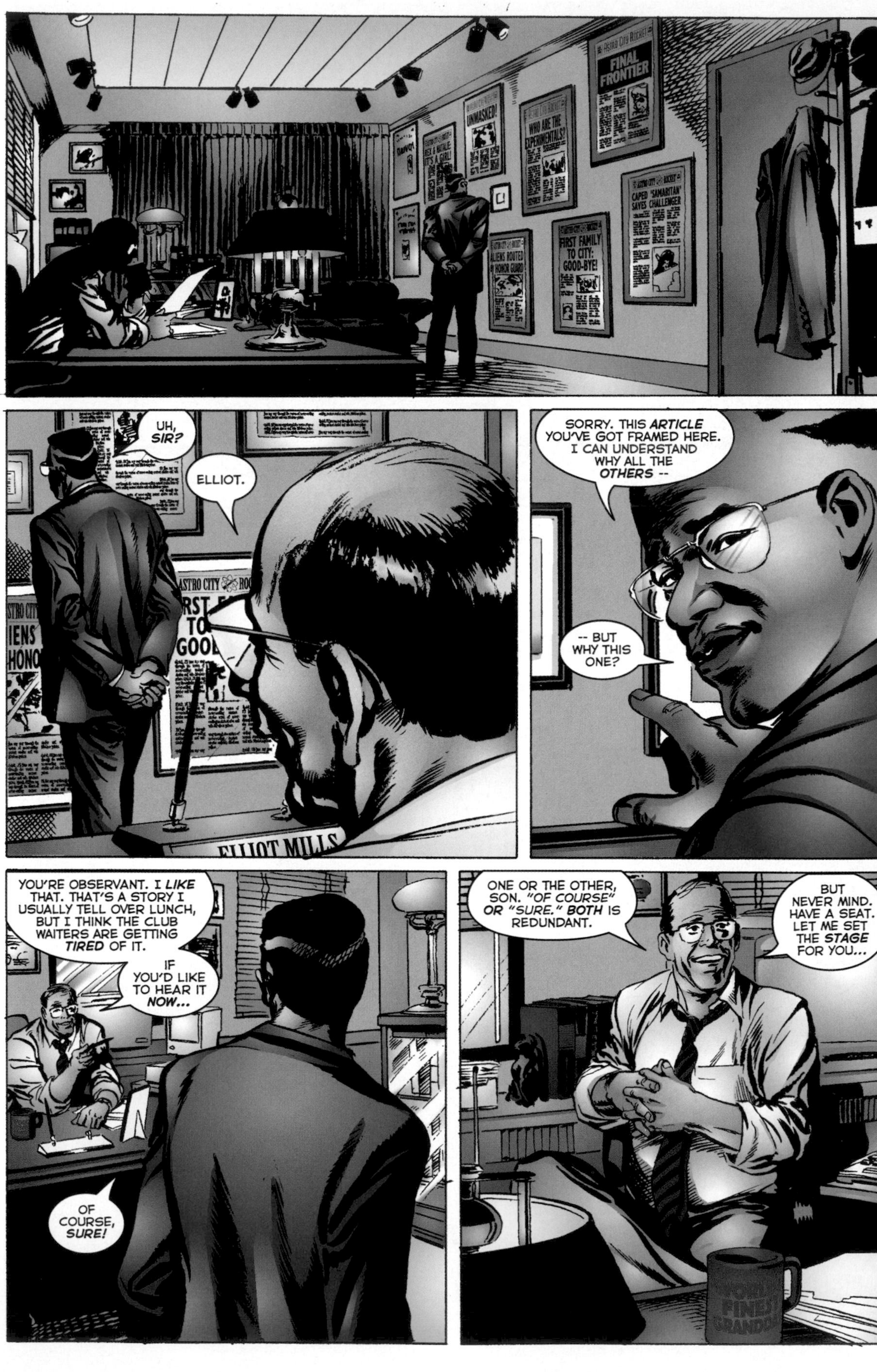
ASTRO CITY ROCKET
FINAL FRONTIER
UNMASKED!
REX & NATALIE: IT'S A GIRL!
WHO ARE THE EXPERIMENTALS?
CAPED 'SAMARITAN' SAVES CHALLENGER
FIRST FAMILY TO CITY: GOOD-BYE!
ALIENS ROUTED BY HONOR GUARD
UH, SIR?
ELLIOT.
ELLIOT MILLS
SORRY. THIS ARTICLE YOU'VE GOT FRAMED HERE. I CAN UNDERSTAND WHY ALL THE OTHERS --
-- BUT WHY THIS ONE?
YOU'RE OBSERVANT. I LIKE THAT. THAT'S A STORY I USUALLY TELL OVER LUNCH, BUT I THINK THE CLUB WAITERS ARE GETTING TIRED OF IT.
IF YOU'D LIKE TO HEAR IT NOW...
OF COURSE, SURE!
ONE OR THE OTHER, SON. "OF COURSE" OR "SURE." BOTH IS REDUNDANT.
BUT NEVER MIND. HAVE A SEAT. LET ME SET THE STAGE FOR YOU...

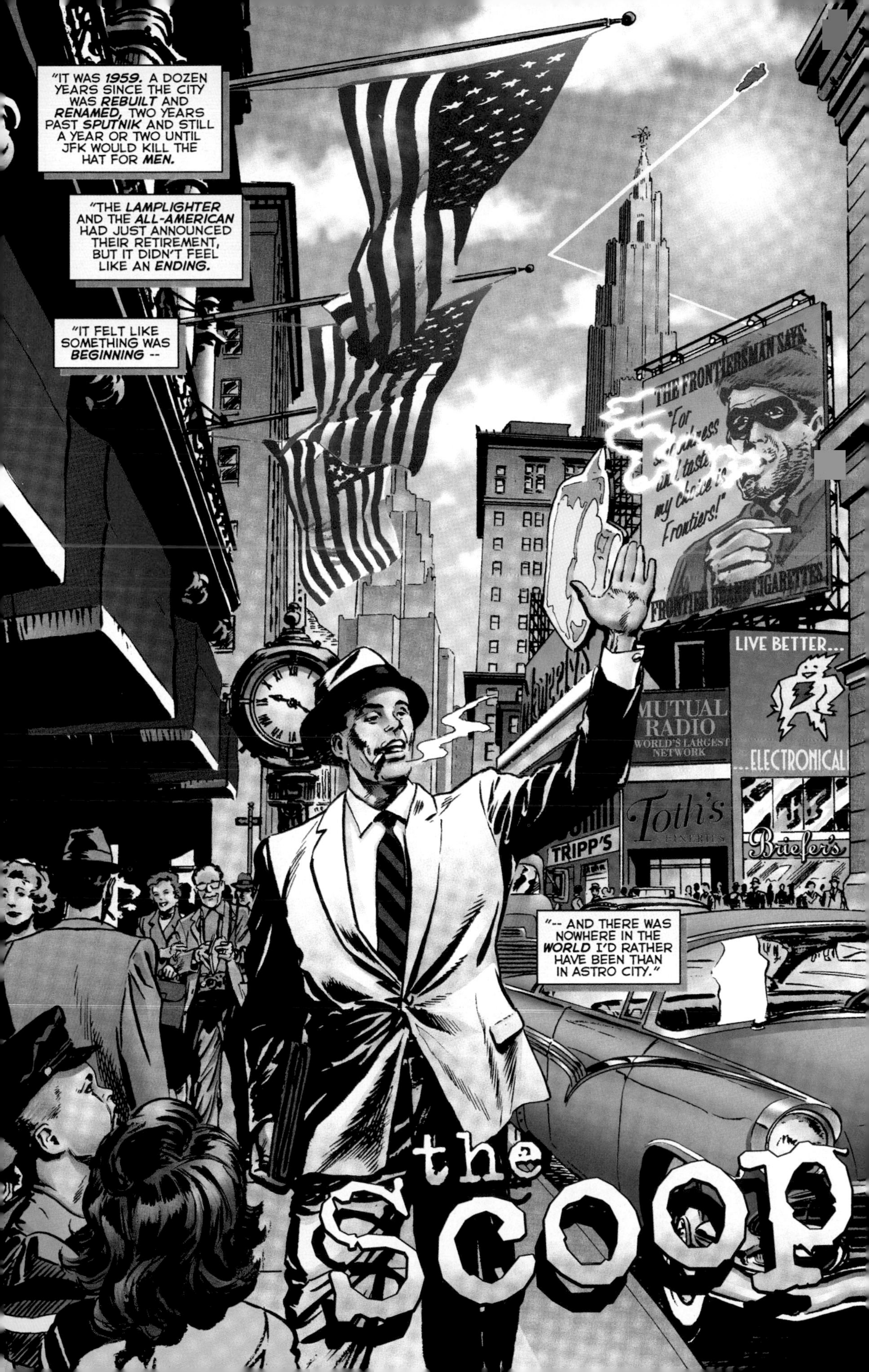
"IT WAS 1959. A DOZEN YEARS SINCE THE CITY WAS REBUILT AND RENAMED, TWO YEARS PAST SPUTNIK AND STILL A YEAR OR TWO UNTIL JFK WOULD KILL THE HAT FOR MEN.
"THE LAMPLIGHTER AND THE ALL-AMERICAN HAD JUST ANNOUNCED THEIR RETIREMENT, BUT IT DIDN'T FEEL LIKE AN ENDING.
"IT FELT LIKE SOMETHING WAS BEGINNING --
THE FRONTIERSMAN SAYS:
FRONTIER BRAND CIGARETTES
LIVE BETTER...
...ELECTRONICALI
MUTUAL RADIO
WORLD'S LARGEST NETWORK
Toth's
TRIPP'S
Briefer's
"-- AND THERE WAS NOWHERE IN THE WORLD I'D RATHER HAVE BEEN THAN IN ASTRO CITY."
the SCOOP

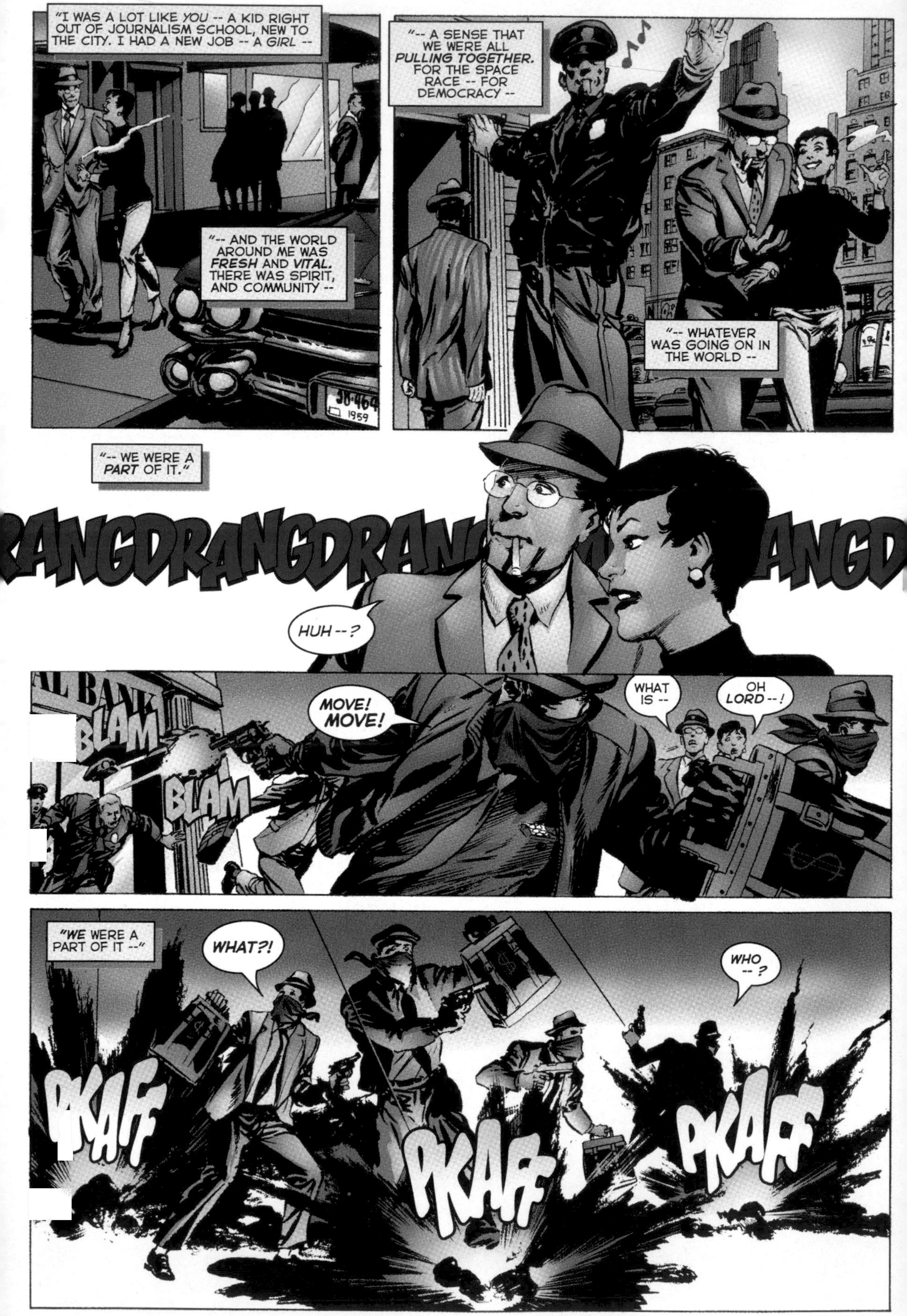
"I WAS A LOT LIKE YOU -- A KID RIGHT OUT OF JOURNALISM SCHOOL, NEW TO THE CITY. I HAD A NEW JOB -- A GIRL --
"-- AND THE WORLD AROUND ME WAS FRESH AND VITAL. THERE WAS SPIRIT, AND COMMUNITY --
JU-464 1959
"-- A SENSE THAT WE WERE ALL PULLING TOGETHER. FOR THE SPACE RACE -- FOR DEMOCRACY --
"-- WHATEVER WAS GOING ON IN THE WORLD --
"-- WE WERE A PART OF IT."
RANGDRANGDRANG
ANGD
HUH --?
BLAM
BLAM
MOVE! MOVE!
WHAT IS --
OH LORD --!
"WE WERE A PART OF IT --"
WHAT?!
WHO -- ?
PKAFF
PKAFF
PKAFF

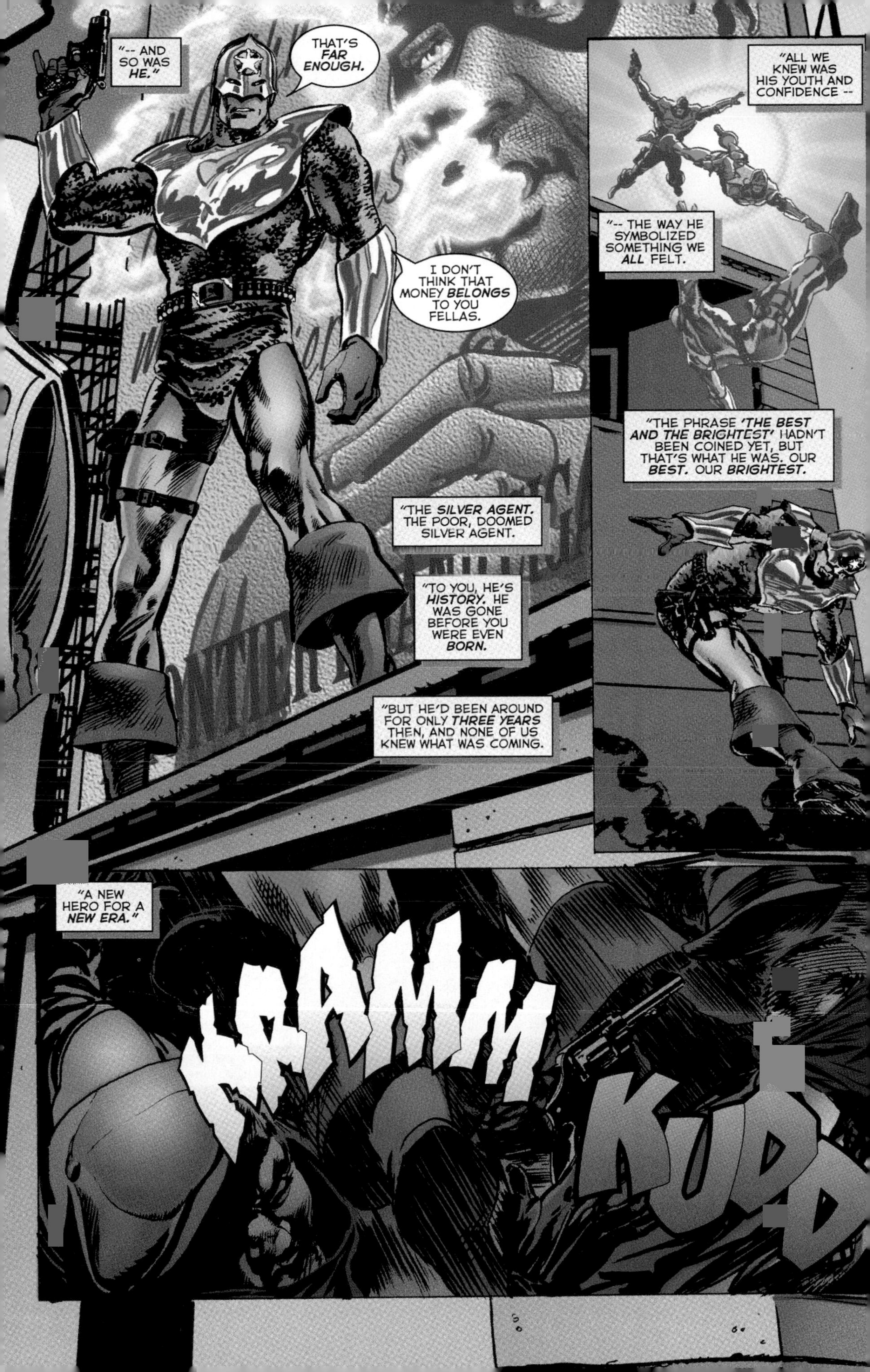
"-- AND SO WAS HE."
THAT'S FAR ENOUGH.
I DON'T THINK THAT MONEY BELONGS TO YOU FELLAS.
"THE SILVER AGENT. THE POOR, DOOMED SILVER AGENT.
"TO YOU, HE'S HISTORY. HE WAS GONE BEFORE YOU WERE EVEN BORN.
"BUT HE'D BEEN AROUND FOR ONLY THREE YEARS THEN, AND NONE OF US KNEW WHAT WAS COMING.
"ALL WE KNEW WAS HIS YOUTH AND CONFIDENCE --
"-- THE WAY HE SYMBOLIZED SOMETHING WE ALL FELT.
"THE PHRASE 'THE BEST AND THE BRIGHTEST' HADN'T BEEN COINED YET, BUT THAT'S WHAT HE WAS. OUR BEST. OUR BRIGHTEST.
"A NEW HERO FOR A NEW ERA."
KRAMM
KUDD

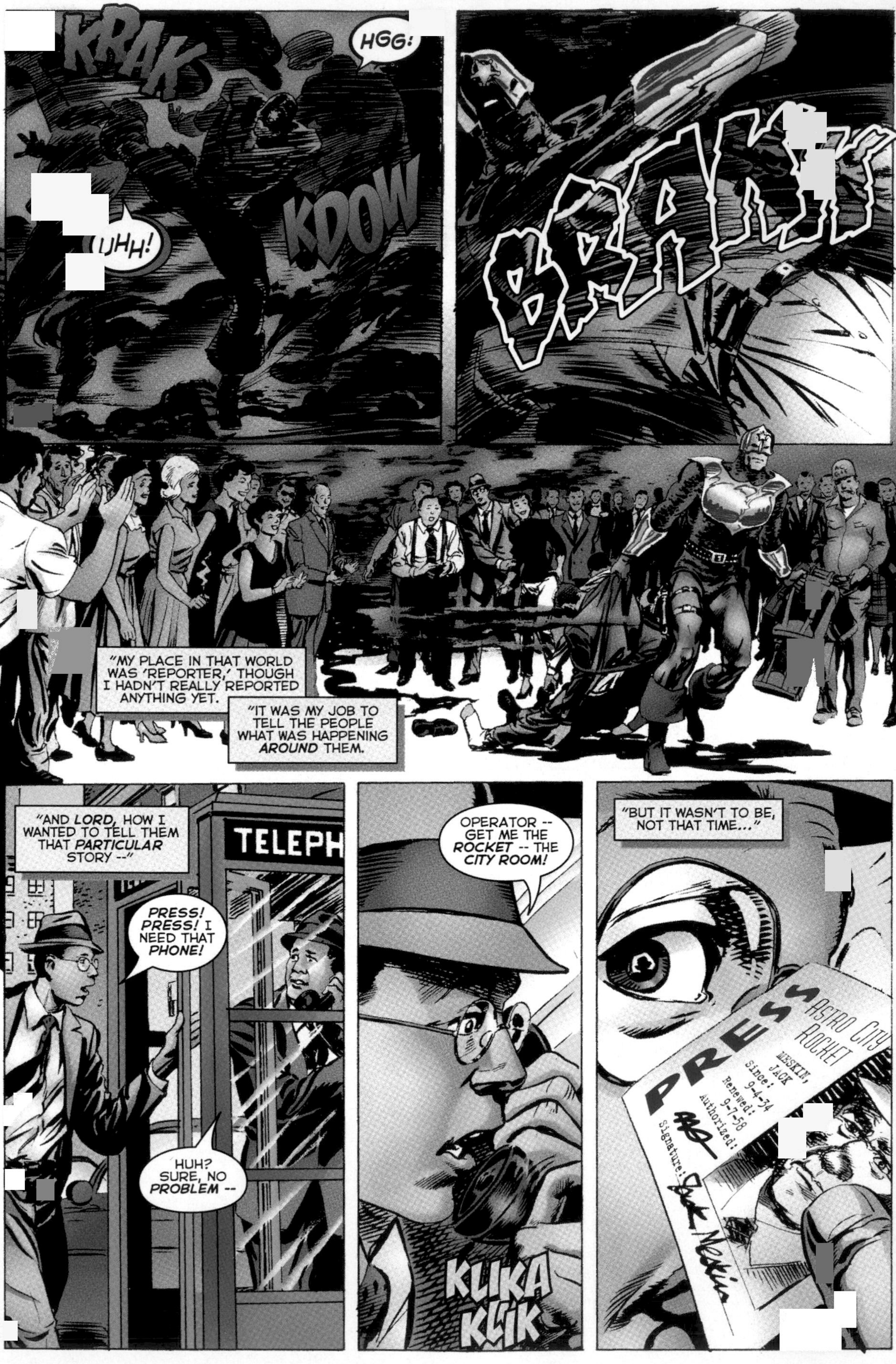
KRAK
HGG!
UHH!
KDOW
BRAK
"MY PLACE IN THAT WORLD WAS 'REPORTER,' THOUGH I HADN'T REALLY REPORTED ANYTHING YET.
"IT WAS MY JOB TO TELL THE PEOPLE WHAT WAS HAPPENING AROUND THEM.
"AND LORD, HOW I WANTED TO TELL THEM THAT PARTICULAR STORY --"
TELEPH
PRESS! PRESS! I NEED THAT PHONE!
HUH? SURE, NO PROBLEM --
OPERATOR -- GET ME THE ROCKET -- THE CITY ROOM!
KLIKA KLIK
"BUT IT WASN'T TO BE, NOT THAT TIME..."
PRESS
Astro City Rocket
MESKIN, JACK
Since: 9-4-34
Renewed: 9-7-58
Authorized:
Signature:

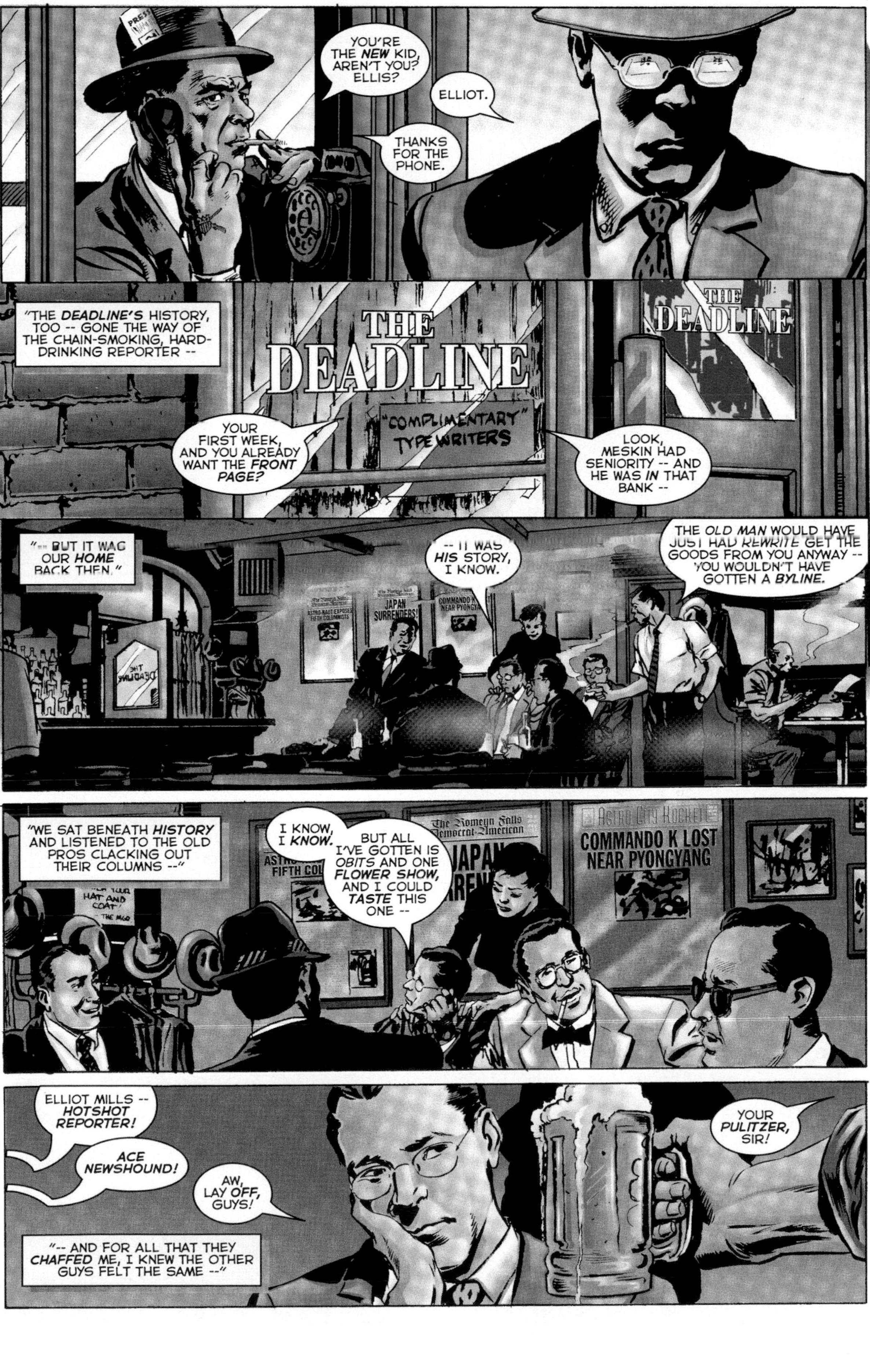
YOU'RE THE NEW KID, AREN'T YOU? ELLIS?
ELLIOT.
THANKS FOR THE PHONE.
"THE DEADLINE'S HISTORY, TOO -- GONE THE WAY OF THE CHAIN-SMOKING, HARD-DRINKING REPORTER --
THE DEADLINE
"COMPLIMENTARY" TYPEWRITERS
THE DEADLINE
YOUR FIRST WEEK, AND YOU ALREADY WANT THE FRONT PAGE?
LOOK, MESKIN HAD SENIORITY -- AND HE WAS IN THAT BANK --
"-- BUT IT WAS OUR HOME BACK THEN."
-- IT WAS HIS STORY, I KNOW.
THE OLD MAN WOULD HAVE JUST HAD REWRITE GET THE GOODS FROM YOU ANYWAY -- YOU WOULDN'T HAVE GOTTEN A BYLINE.
JAPAN SURRENDERS!
"WE SAT BENEATH HISTORY AND LISTENED TO THE OLD PROS CLACKING OUT THEIR COLUMNS --"
I KNOW, I KNOW.
BUT ALL I'VE GOTTEN IS OBITS AND ONE FLOWER SHOW, AND I COULD TASTE THIS ONE --
The Romeyn Falls Democrat-American
ASTRO CITY ROCKET
COMMANDO K LOST NEAR PYONGYANG
ELLIOT MILLS -- HOTSHOT REPORTER!
ACE NEWSHOUND!
AW, LAY OFF, GUYS!
YOUR PULITZER, SIR!
"-- AND FOR ALL THAT THEY CHAFFED ME, I KNEW THE OTHER GUYS FELT THE SAME --"

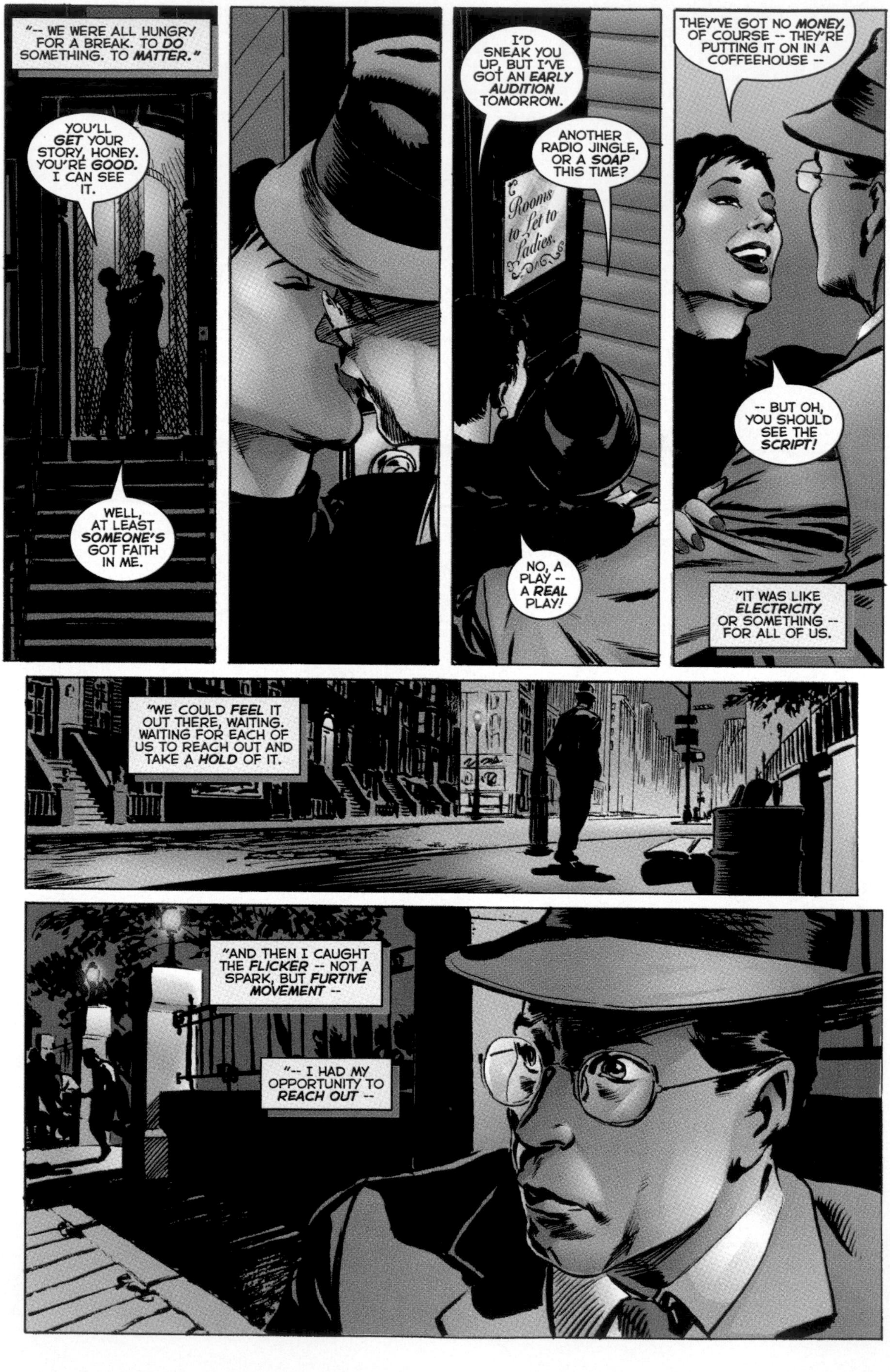
"-- WE WERE ALL HUNGRY FOR A BREAK. TO DO SOMETHING. TO MATTER."
YOU'LL GET YOUR STORY, HONEY. YOU'RE GOOD. I CAN SEE IT.
WELL, AT LEAST SOMEONE'S GOT FAITH IN ME.
I'D SNEAK YOU UP, BUT I'VE GOT AN EARLY AUDITION TOMORROW.
ANOTHER RADIO JINGLE, OR A SOAP THIS TIME?
Rooms to Let to Ladies.
NO, A PLAY -- A REAL PLAY!
THEY'VE GOT NO MONEY, OF COURSE -- THEY'RE PUTTING IT ON IN A COFFEEHOUSE --
-- BUT OH, YOU SHOULD SEE THE SCRIPT!
"IT WAS LIKE ELECTRICITY OR SOMETHING -- FOR ALL OF US.
"WE COULD FEEL IT OUT THERE, WAITING. WAITING FOR EACH OF US TO REACH OUT AND TAKE A HOLD OF IT.
"AND THEN I CAUGHT THE FLICKER -- NOT A SPARK, BUT FURTIVE MOVEMENT --
"-- I HAD MY OPPORTUNITY TO REACH OUT --

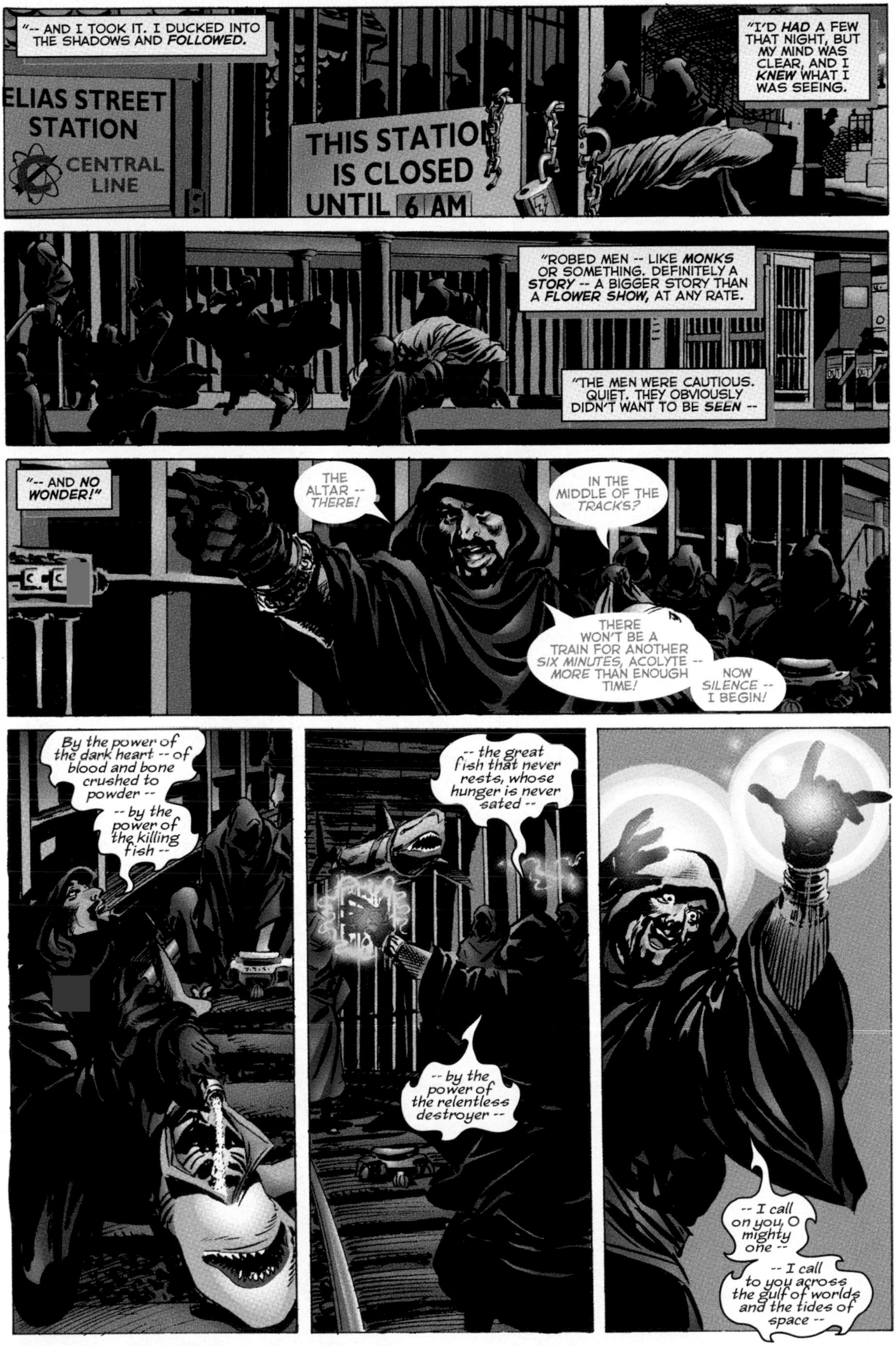
"-- AND I TOOK IT. I DUCKED INTO THE SHADOWS AND FOLLOWED.
ELIAS STREET STATION
CENTRAL LINE
THIS STATIO IS CLOSED UNTIL 6 AM
"I'D HAD A FEW THAT NIGHT, BUT MY MIND WAS CLEAR, AND I KNEW WHAT I WAS SEEING.
"ROBED MEN -- LIKE MONKS OR SOMETHING. DEFINITELY A STORY -- A BIGGER STORY THAN A FLOWER SHOW, AT ANY RATE.
"THE MEN WERE CAUTIOUS. QUIET. THEY OBVIOUSLY DIDN'T WANT TO BE SEEN --
"-- AND NO WONDER!"
THE ALTAR -- THERE!
IN THE MIDDLE OF THE TRACKS?
THERE WON'T BE A TRAIN FOR ANOTHER SIX MINUTES, ACOLYTE -- MORE THAN ENOUGH TIME!
NOW SILENCE -- I BEGIN!
By the power of the dark heart -- of blood and bone crushed to powder --
-- by the power of the killing fish --
-- the great fish that never rests, whose hunger is never sated --
-- by the power of the relentless destroyer --
-- I call on you, O mighty one --
-- I call to you across the gulf of worlds and the tides of space --

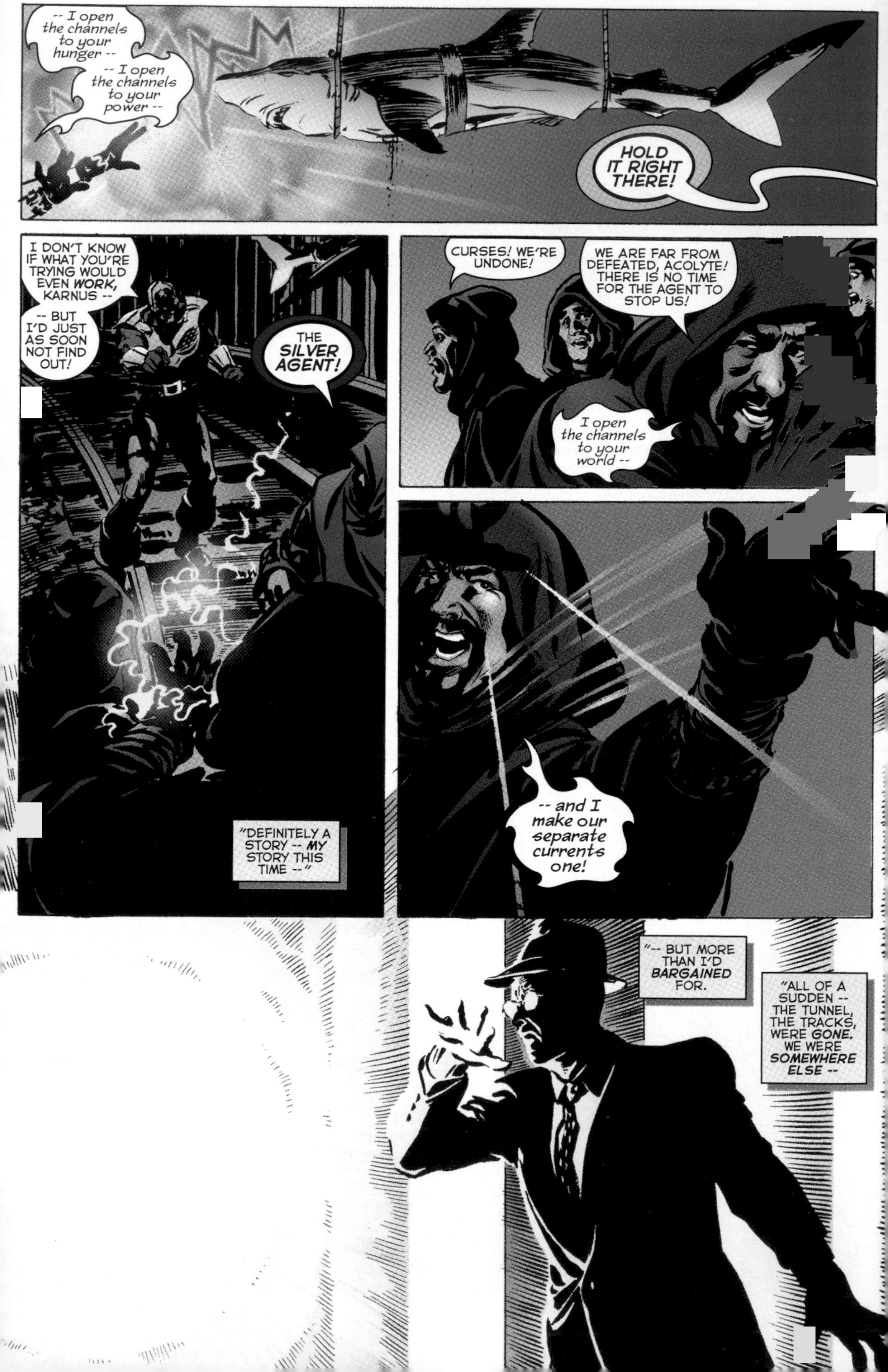
-- I open the channels to your hunger --
-- I open the channels to your power --
HOLD IT RIGHT THERE!
I DON'T KNOW IF WHAT YOU'RE TRYING WOULD EVEN WORK, KARNUS --
-- BUT I'D JUST AS SOON NOT FIND OUT!
THE SILVER AGENT!
"DEFINITELY A STORY -- MY STORY THIS TIME --"
CURSES! WE'RE UNDONE!
WE ARE FAR FROM DEFEATED, ACOLYTE! THERE IS NO TIME FOR THE AGENT TO STOP US!
I open the channels to your world --
-- and I make our separate currents one!
"-- BUT MORE THAN I'D BARGAINED FOR.
"ALL OF A SUDDEN -- THE TUNNEL, THE TRACKS, WERE GONE. WE WERE SOMEWHERE ELSE --

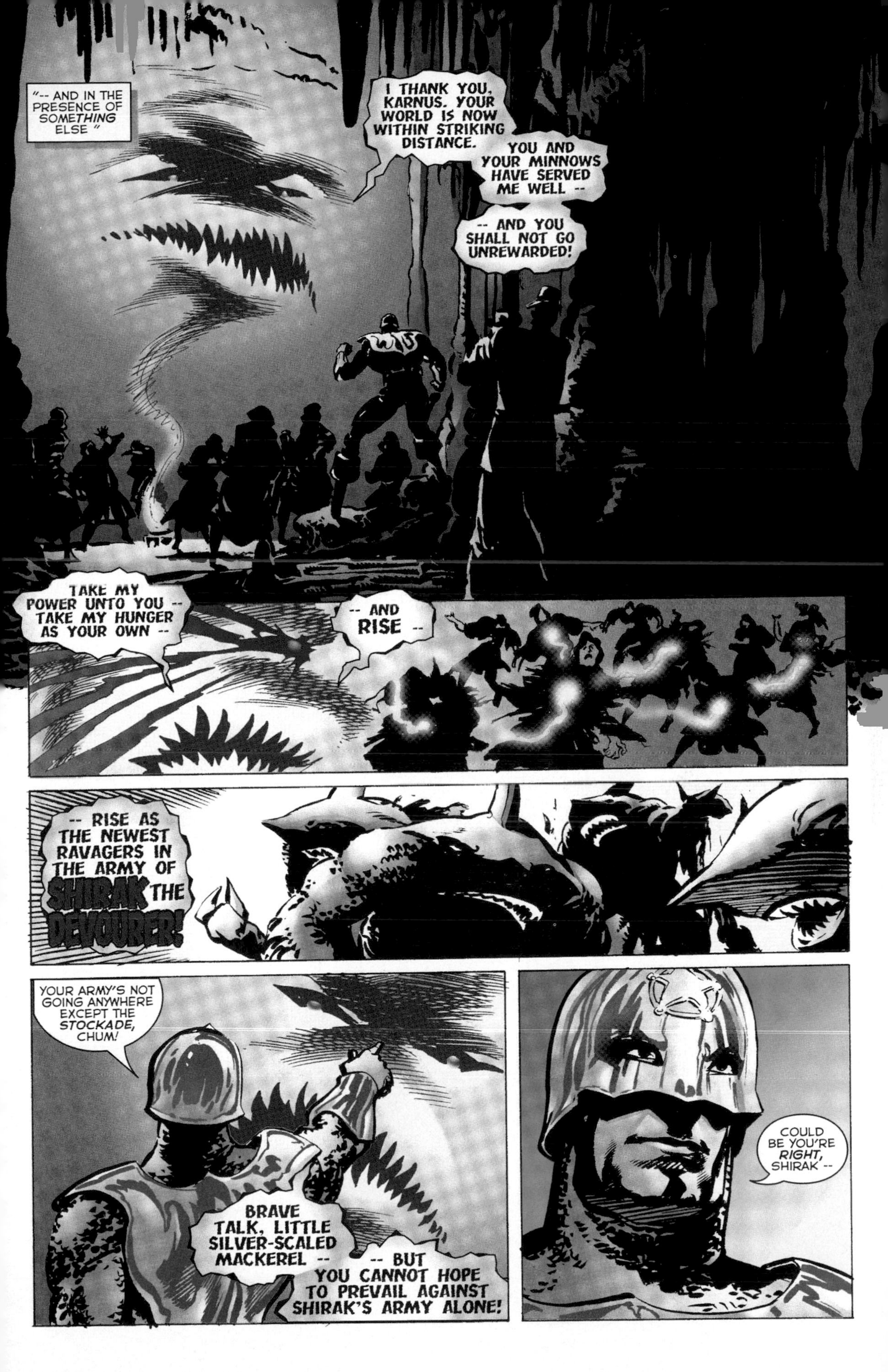
"-- AND IN THE PRESENCE OF SOMETHING ELSE"
I THANK YOU, KARNUS. YOUR WORLD IS NOW WITHIN STRIKING DISTANCE.
YOU AND YOUR MINNOWS HAVE SERVED ME WELL --
-- AND YOU SHALL NOT GO UNREWARDED!
TAKE MY POWER UNTO YOU -- TAKE MY HUNGER AS YOUR OWN --
-- AND RISE --
-- RISE AS THE NEWEST RAVAGERS IN THE ARMY OF SHIRAK THE DEVOURER!
YOUR ARMY'S NOT GOING ANYWHERE EXCEPT THE STOCKADE, CHUM!
BRAVE TALK, LITTLE SILVER-SCALED MACKEREL --
-- BUT YOU CANNOT HOPE TO PREVAIL AGAINST SHIRAK'S ARMY ALONE!
COULD BE YOU'RE RIGHT, SHIRAK --

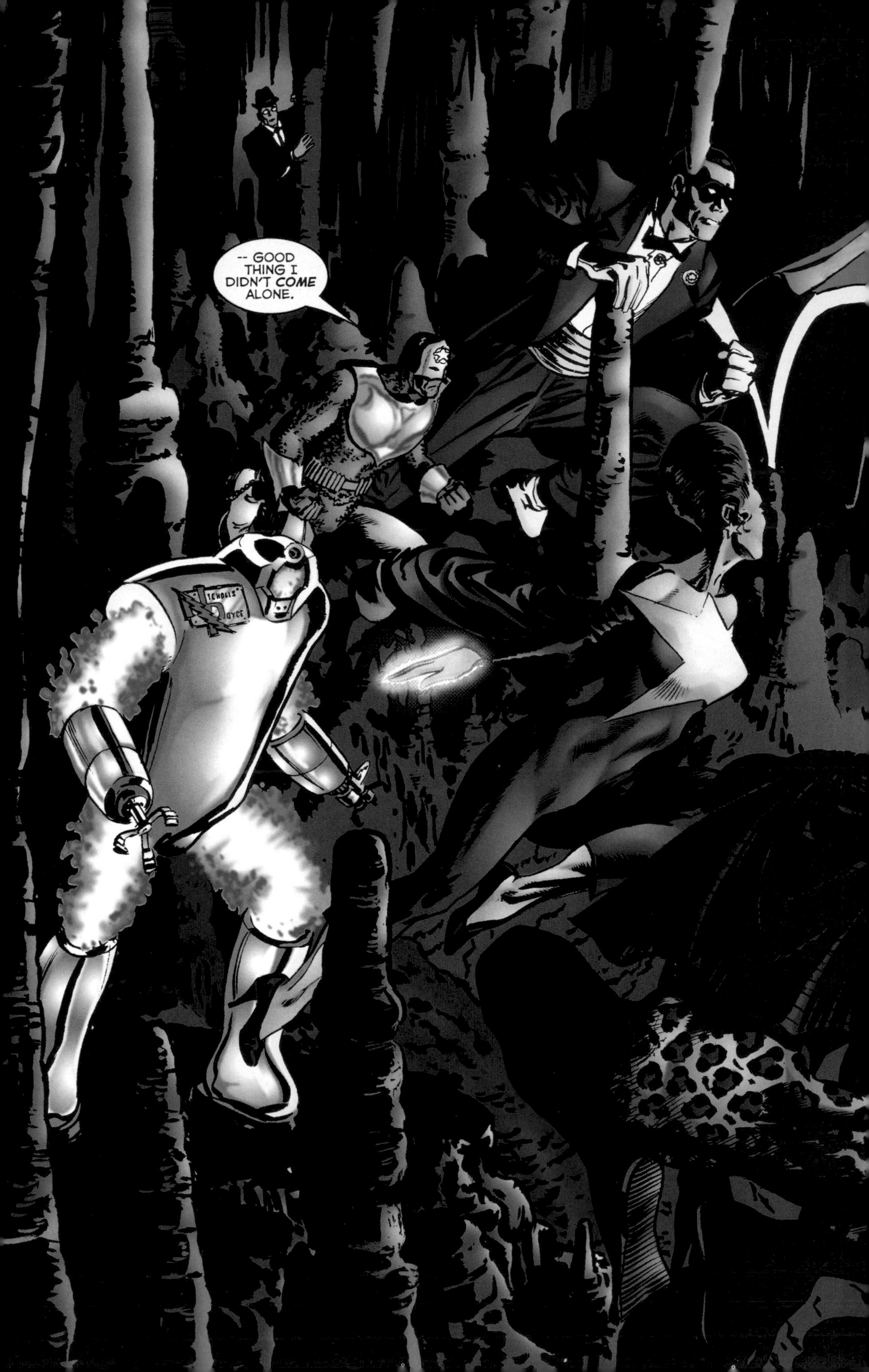
-- GOOD THING I DIDN'T COME ALONE.

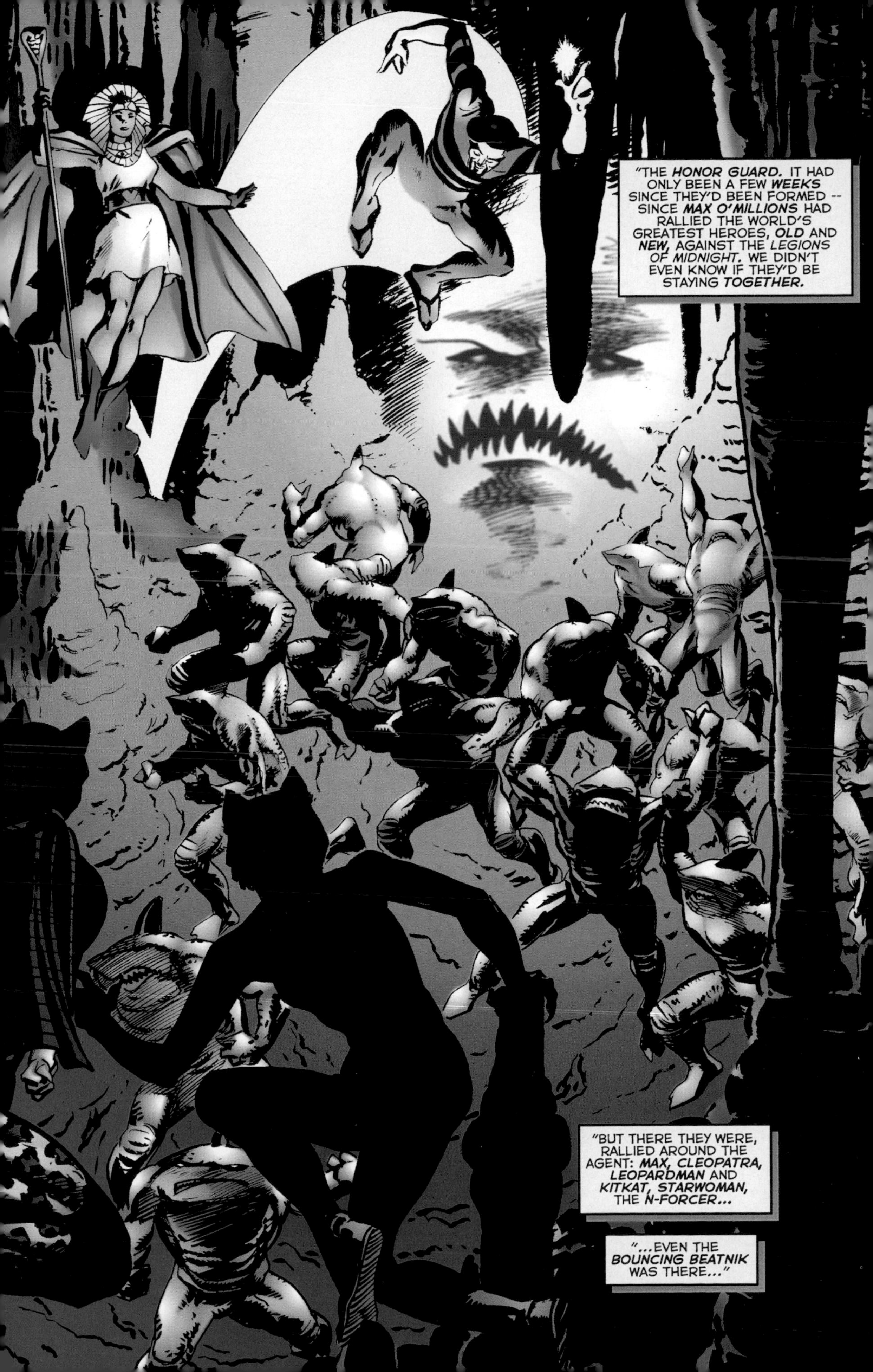
"THE HONOR GUARD. IT HAD ONLY BEEN A FEW WEEKS SINCE THEY'D BEEN FORMED -- SINCE MAX O'MILLIONS HAD RALLIED THE WORLD'S GREATEST HEROES, OLD AND NEW, AGAINST THE LEGIONS OF MIDNIGHT. WE DIDN'T EVEN KNOW IF THEY'D BE STAYING TOGETHER.
"BUT THERE THEY WERE, RALLIED AROUND THE AGENT: MAX, CLEOPATRA, LEOPARDMAN AND KITKAT, STARWOMAN, THE N-FORCER...
"...EVEN THE BOUNCING BEATNIK WAS THERE..."

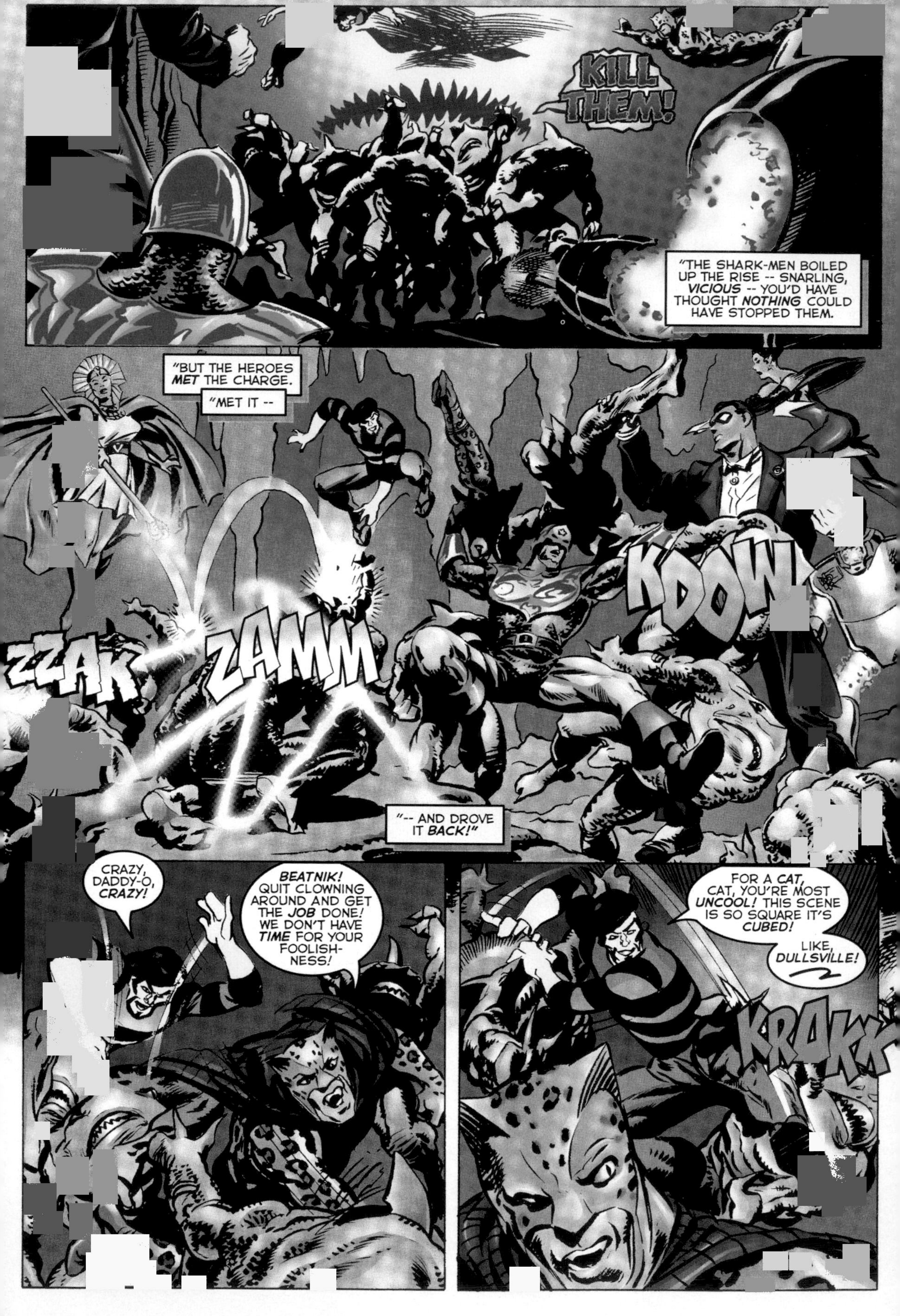
KILL THEM!
"THE SHARK-MEN BOILED UP THE RISE -- SNARLING, VICIOUS -- YOU'D HAVE THOUGHT NOTHING COULD HAVE STOPPED THEM.
"BUT THE HEROES MET THE CHARGE.
"MET IT --
ZZAK
ZAMM
KDOW
"-- AND DROVE IT BACK!"
CRAZY, DADDY-O, CRAZY!
BEATNIK! QUIT CLOWNING AROUND AND GET THE JOB DONE! WE DON'T HAVE TIME FOR YOUR FOOLISHNESS!
FOR A CAT, CAT, YOU'RE MOST UNCOOL! THIS SCENE IS SO SQUARE IT'S CUBED!
LIKE, DULLSVILLE!
KRAKK

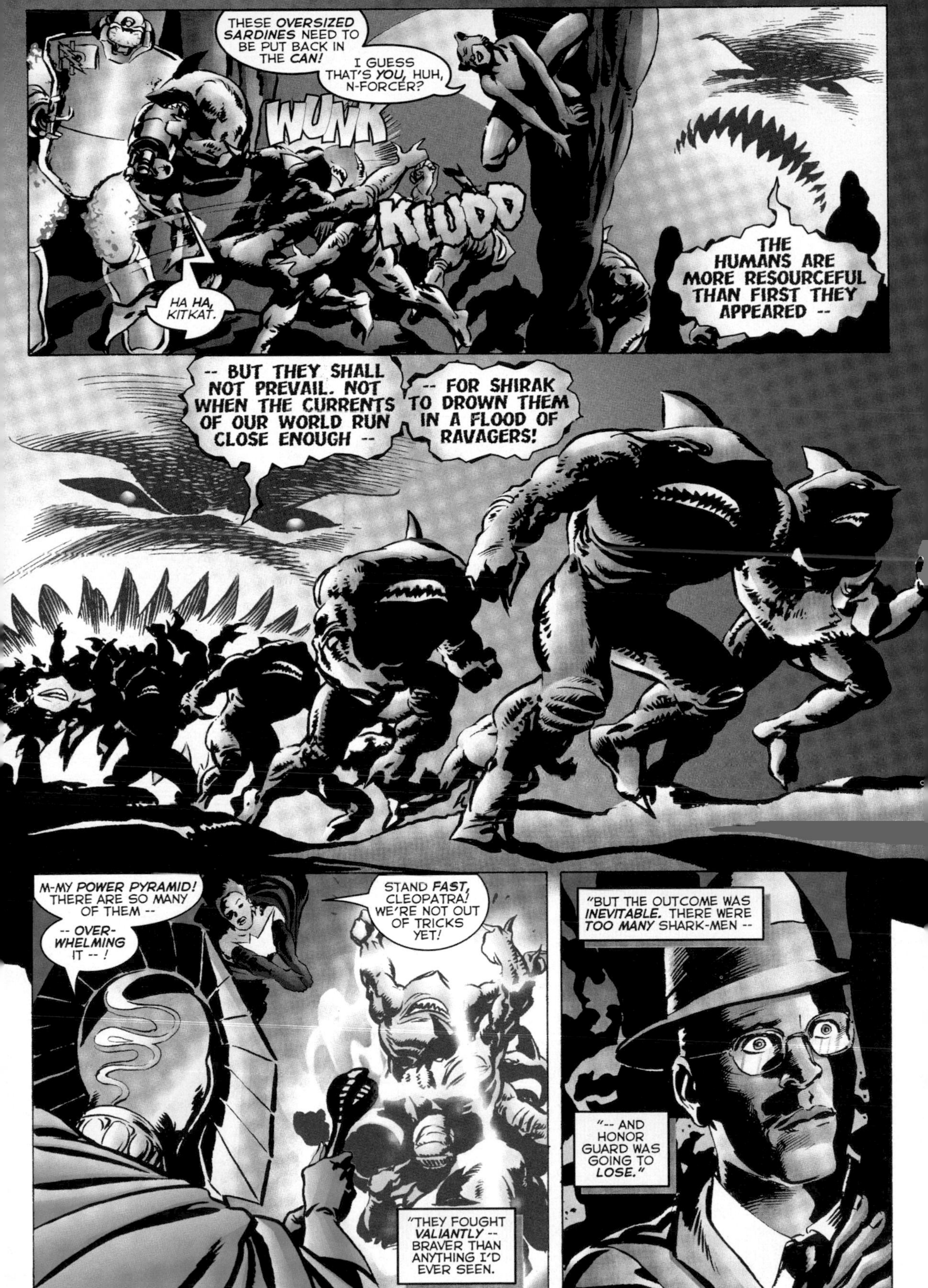
THESE OVERSIZED SARDINES NEED TO BE PUT BACK IN THE CAN!
I GUESS THAT'S YOU, HUH, N-FORCER?
WUNK
KLUDD
HA HA, KITKAT.
THE HUMANS ARE MORE RESOURCEFUL THAN FIRST THEY APPEARED --
-- BUT THEY SHALL NOT PREVAIL. NOT WHEN THE CURRENTS OF OUR WORLD RUN CLOSE ENOUGH --
-- FOR SHIRAK TO DROWN THEM IN A FLOOD OF RAVAGERS!
M-MY POWER PYRAMID! THERE ARE SO MANY OF THEM --
-- OVER-WHELMING IT -- !
STAND FAST, CLEOPATRA! WE'RE NOT OUT OF TRICKS YET!
"THEY FOUGHT VALIANTLY -- BRAVER THAN ANYTHING I'D EVER SEEN.
"BUT THE OUTCOME WAS INEVITABLE. THERE WERE TOO MANY SHARK-MEN --
"-- AND HONOR GUARD WAS GOING TO LOSE."

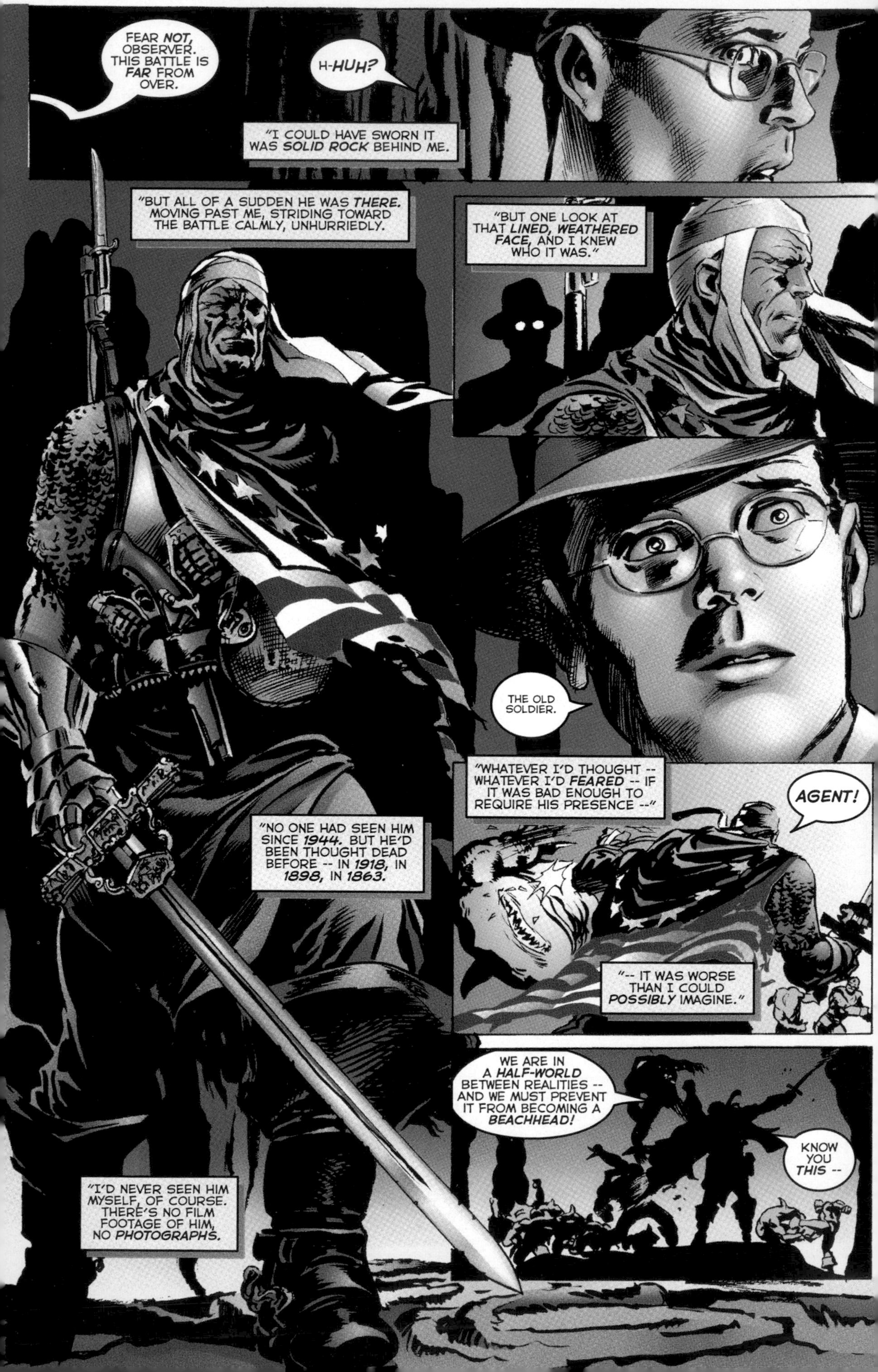
FEAR NOT, OBSERVER. THIS BATTLE IS FAR FROM OVER.
H-HUH?
"I COULD HAVE SWORN IT WAS SOLID ROCK BEHIND ME.
"BUT ALL OF A SUDDEN HE WAS THERE. MOVING PAST ME, STRIDING TOWARD THE BATTLE CALMLY, UNHURRIEDLY.
"BUT ONE LOOK AT THAT LINED, WEATHERED FACE, AND I KNEW WHO IT WAS."
THE OLD SOLDIER.
"NO ONE HAD SEEN HIM SINCE 1944. BUT HE'D BEEN THOUGHT DEAD BEFORE -- IN 1918, IN 1898, IN 1863.
"WHATEVER I'D THOUGHT -- WHATEVER I'D FEARED -- IF IT WAS BAD ENOUGH TO REQUIRE HIS PRESENCE --"
AGENT!
"-- IT WAS WORSE THAN I COULD POSSIBLY IMAGINE."
"I'D NEVER SEEN HIM MYSELF, OF COURSE. THERE'S NO FILM FOOTAGE OF HIM, NO PHOTOGRAPHS.
WE ARE IN A HALF-WORLD BETWEEN REALITIES -- AND WE MUST PREVENT IT FROM BECOMING A BEACHHEAD!
KNOW YOU THIS --

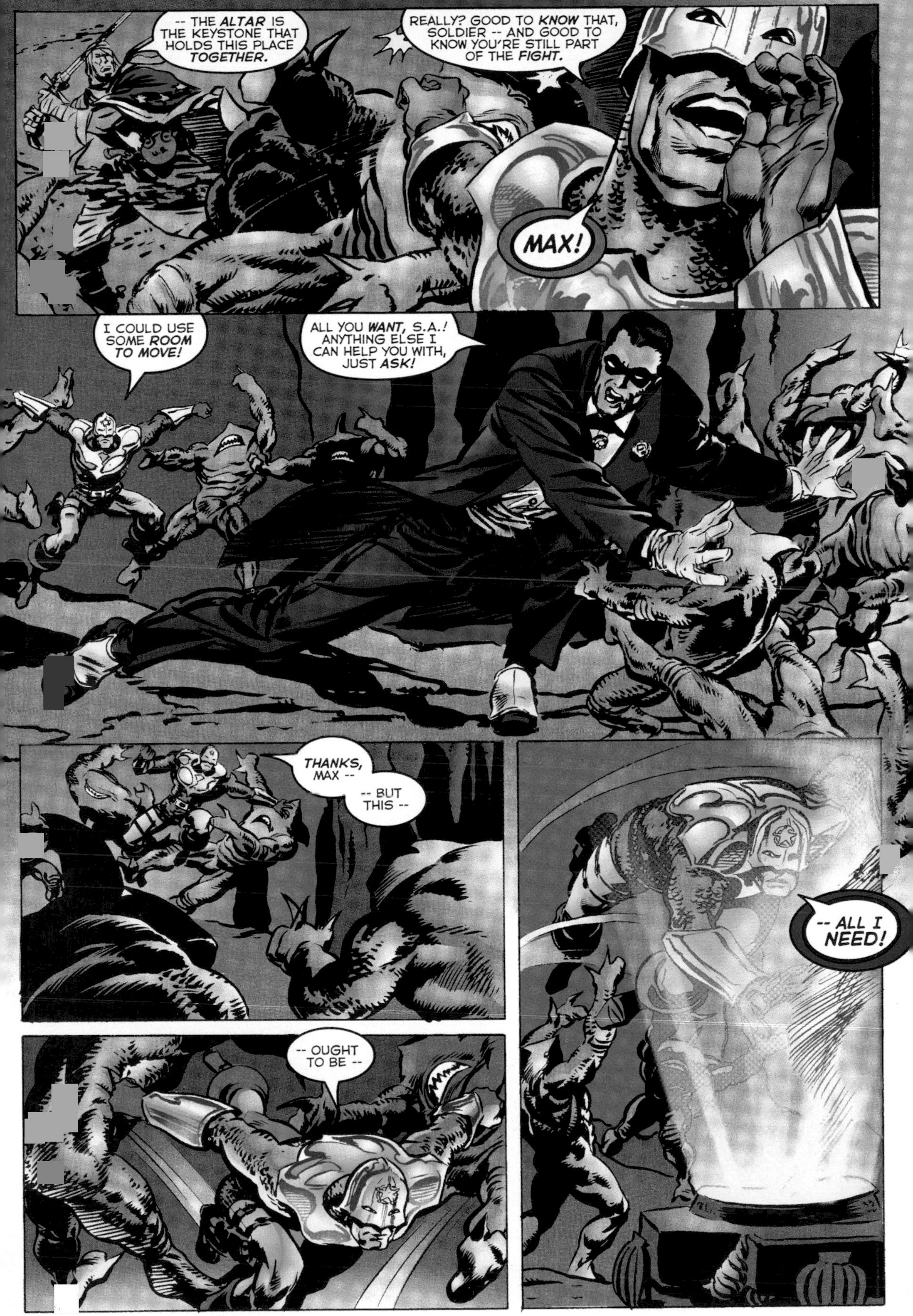
-- THE ALTAR IS THE KEYSTONE THAT HOLDS THIS PLACE TOGETHER.
REALLY? GOOD TO KNOW THAT, SOLDIER -- AND GOOD TO KNOW YOU'RE STILL PART OF THE FIGHT.
MAX!
I COULD USE SOME ROOM TO MOVE!
ALL YOU WANT, S.A.! ANYTHING ELSE I CAN HELP YOU WITH, JUST ASK!
THANKS, MAX --
-- BUT THIS --
-- OUGHT TO BE --
-- ALL I NEED!

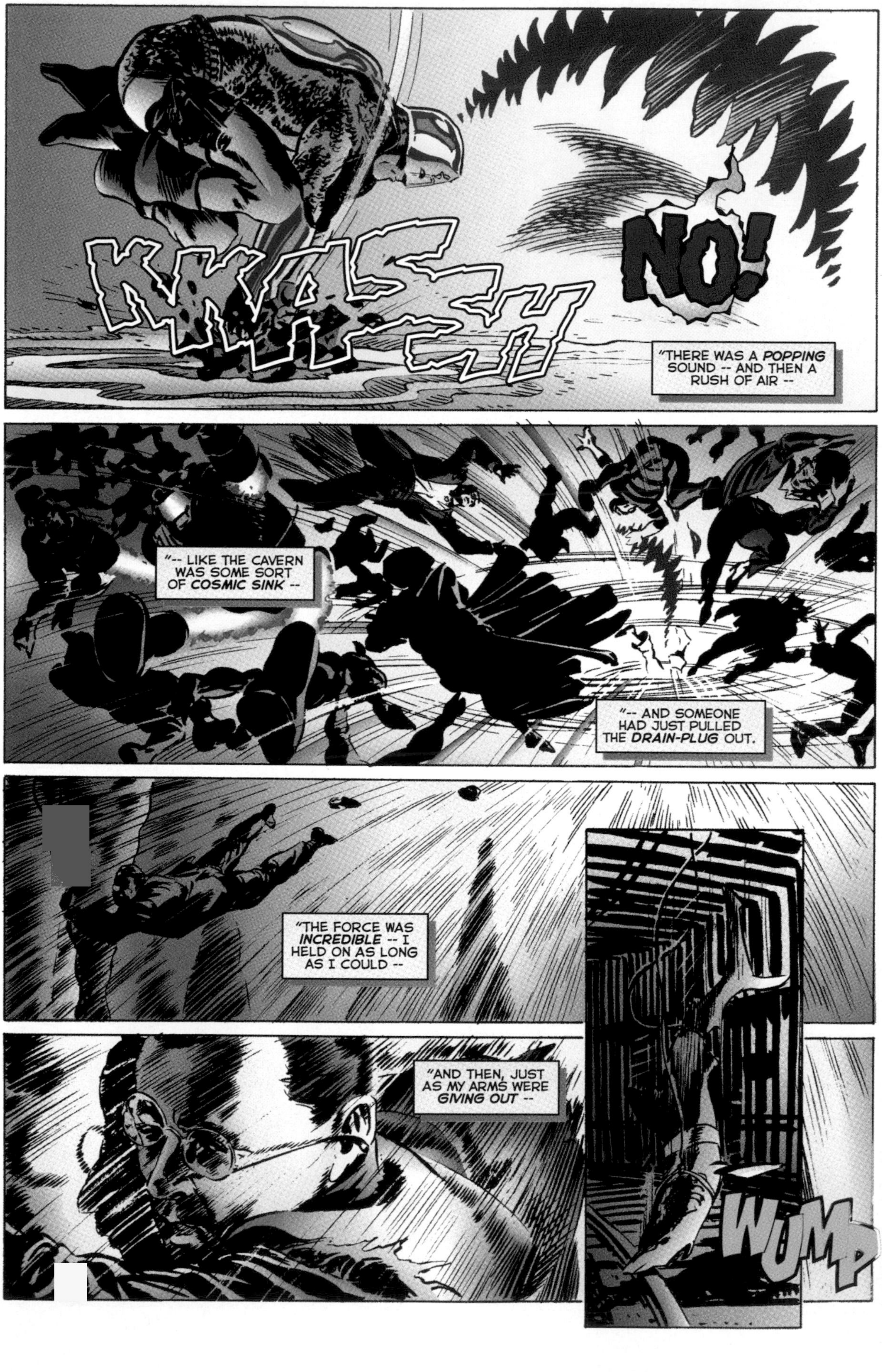
KKKASSHH
NO!
"THERE WAS A POPPING SOUND -- AND THEN A RUSH OF AIR --
"-- LIKE THE CAVERN WAS SOME SORT OF COSMIC SINK --
"-- AND SOMEONE HAD JUST PULLED THE DRAIN-PLUG OUT.
"THE FORCE WAS INCREDIBLE -- I HELD ON AS LONG AS I COULD --
"AND THEN, JUST AS MY ARMS WERE GIVING OUT --
WUMP

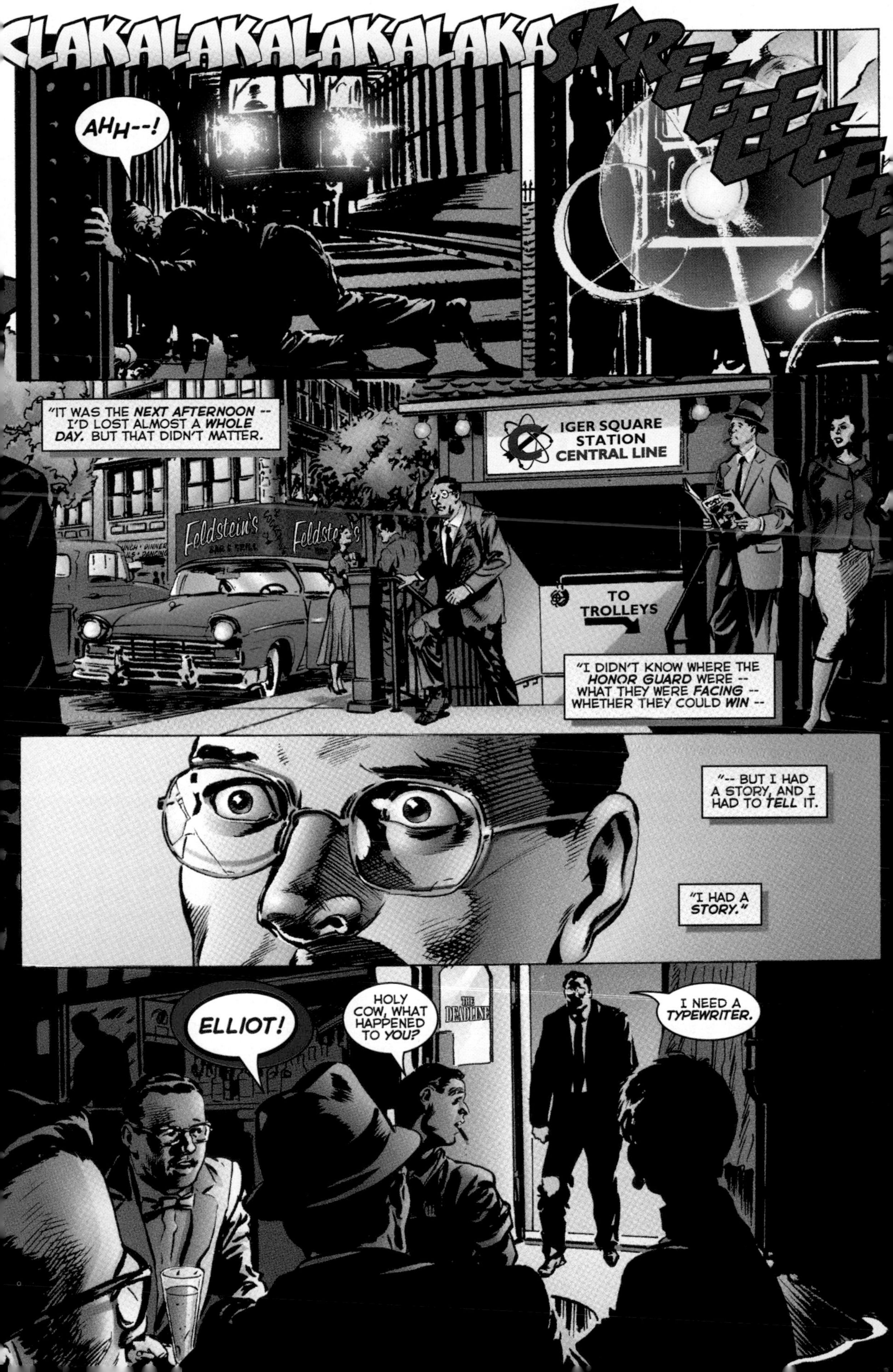

CLAKALAKALAKALAKA
AHH--!
SKREEEEEEEEE
"IT WAS THE NEXT AFTERNOON -- I'D LOST ALMOST A WHOLE DAY. BUT THAT DIDN'T MATTER.
IGER SQUARE STATION CENTRAL LINE
Feldstein's
TO TROLLEYS
"I DIDN'T KNOW WHERE THE HONOR GUARD WERE -- WHAT THEY WERE FACING -- WHETHER THEY COULD WIN --
"-- BUT I HAD A STORY, AND I HAD TO TELL IT.
"I HAD A STORY."
ELLIOT!
HOLY COW, WHAT HAPPENED TO YOU?
THE DEADLINE
I NEED A TYPEWRITER.

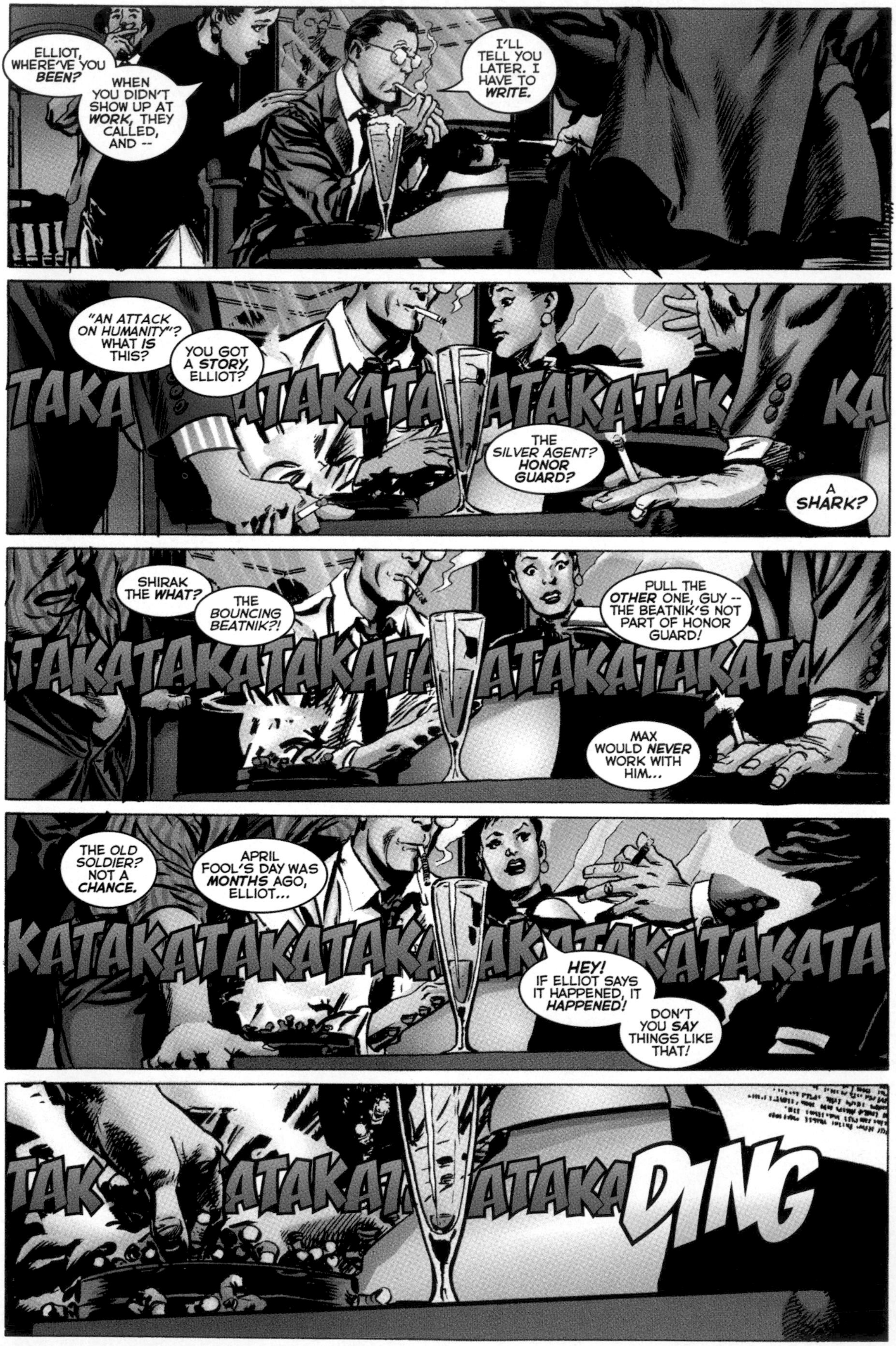
ELLIOT, WHERE'VE YOU BEEN?
WHEN YOU DIDN'T SHOW UP AT WORK, THEY CALLED, AND --
I'LL TELL YOU LATER. I HAVE TO WRITE.
"AN ATTACK ON HUMANITY"? WHAT IS THIS?
YOU GOT A STORY, ELLIOT?
TAKA ATAKATA ATAKATAK KA
THE SILVER AGENT? HONOR GUARD?
A SHARK?
SHIRAK THE WHAT?
THE BOUNCING BEATNIK?!
PULL THE OTHER ONE, GUY -- THE BEATNIK'S NOT PART OF HONOR GUARD!
TAKATAKATAKATA ATAKATAKATA
MAX WOULD NEVER WORK WITH HIM...
THE OLD SOLDIER? NOT A CHANCE.
APRIL FOOL'S DAY WAS MONTHS AGO, ELLIOT...
KATAKATAKATAKA AKATAKATAKATA
HEY! IF ELLIOT SAYS IT HAPPENED, IT HAPPENED!
DON'T YOU SAY THINGS LIKE THAT!
TAK ATAKAT ATAKADING

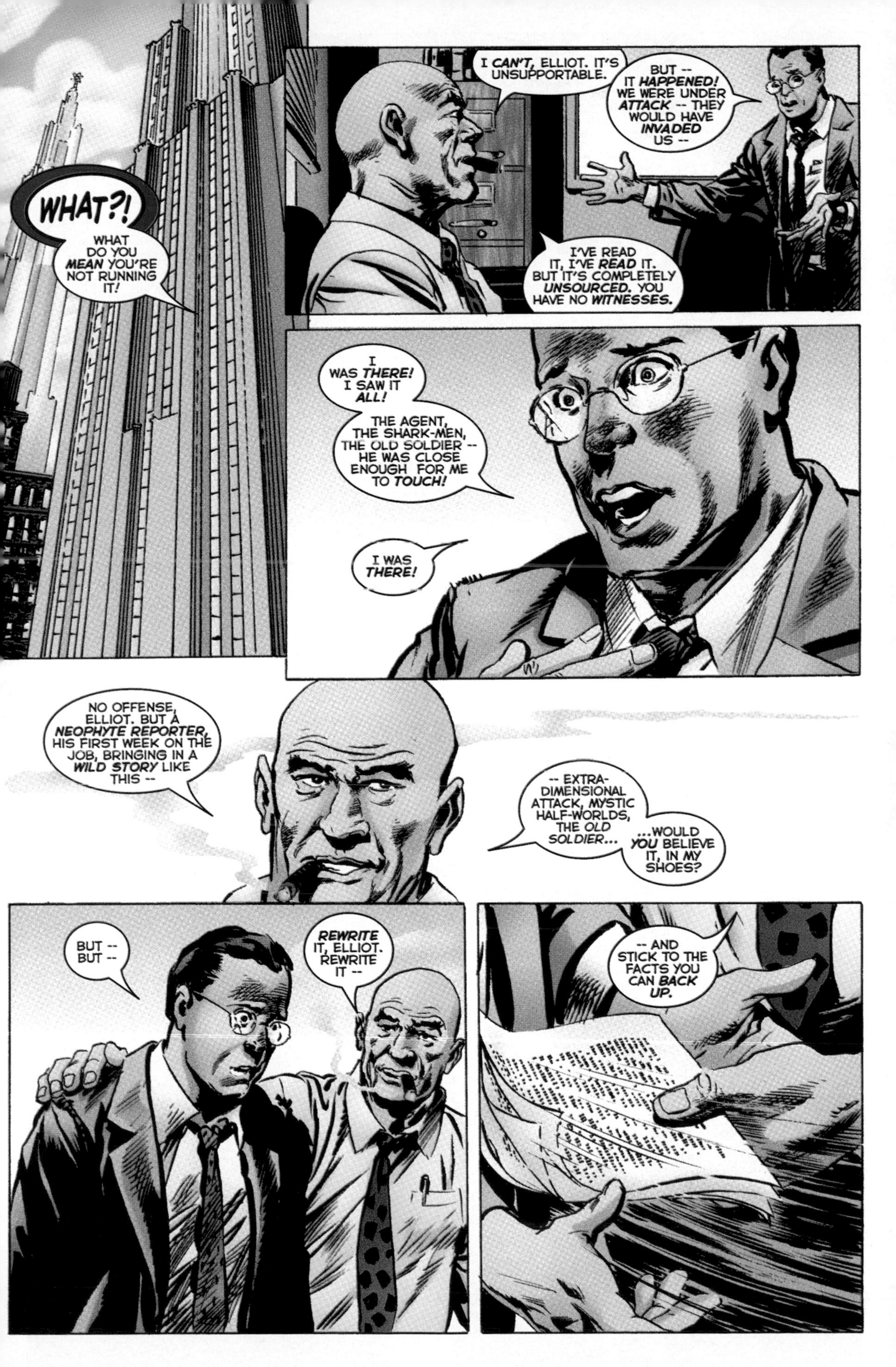
WHAT?!
WHAT DO YOU MEAN YOU'RE NOT RUNNING IT!
I CAN'T, ELLIOT. IT'S UNSUPPORTABLE.
BUT -- IT HAPPENED! WE WERE UNDER ATTACK -- THEY WOULD HAVE INVADED US --
I'VE READ IT, I'VE READ IT. BUT IT'S COMPLETELY UNSOURCED. YOU HAVE NO WITNESSES.
I WAS THERE! I SAW IT ALL!
THE AGENT, THE SHARK-MEN, THE OLD SOLDIER -- HE WAS CLOSE ENOUGH FOR ME TO TOUCH!
I WAS THERE!
NO OFFENSE, ELLIOT. BUT A NEOPHYTE REPORTER, HIS FIRST WEEK ON THE JOB, BRINGING IN A WILD STORY LIKE THIS --
-- EXTRA-DIMENSIONAL ATTACK, MYSTIC HALF-WORLDS, THE OLD SOLDIER...
...WOULD YOU BELIEVE IT, IN MY SHOES?
BUT -- BUT --
REWRITE IT, ELLIOT. REWRITE IT --
-- AND STICK TO THE FACTS YOU CAN BACK UP.

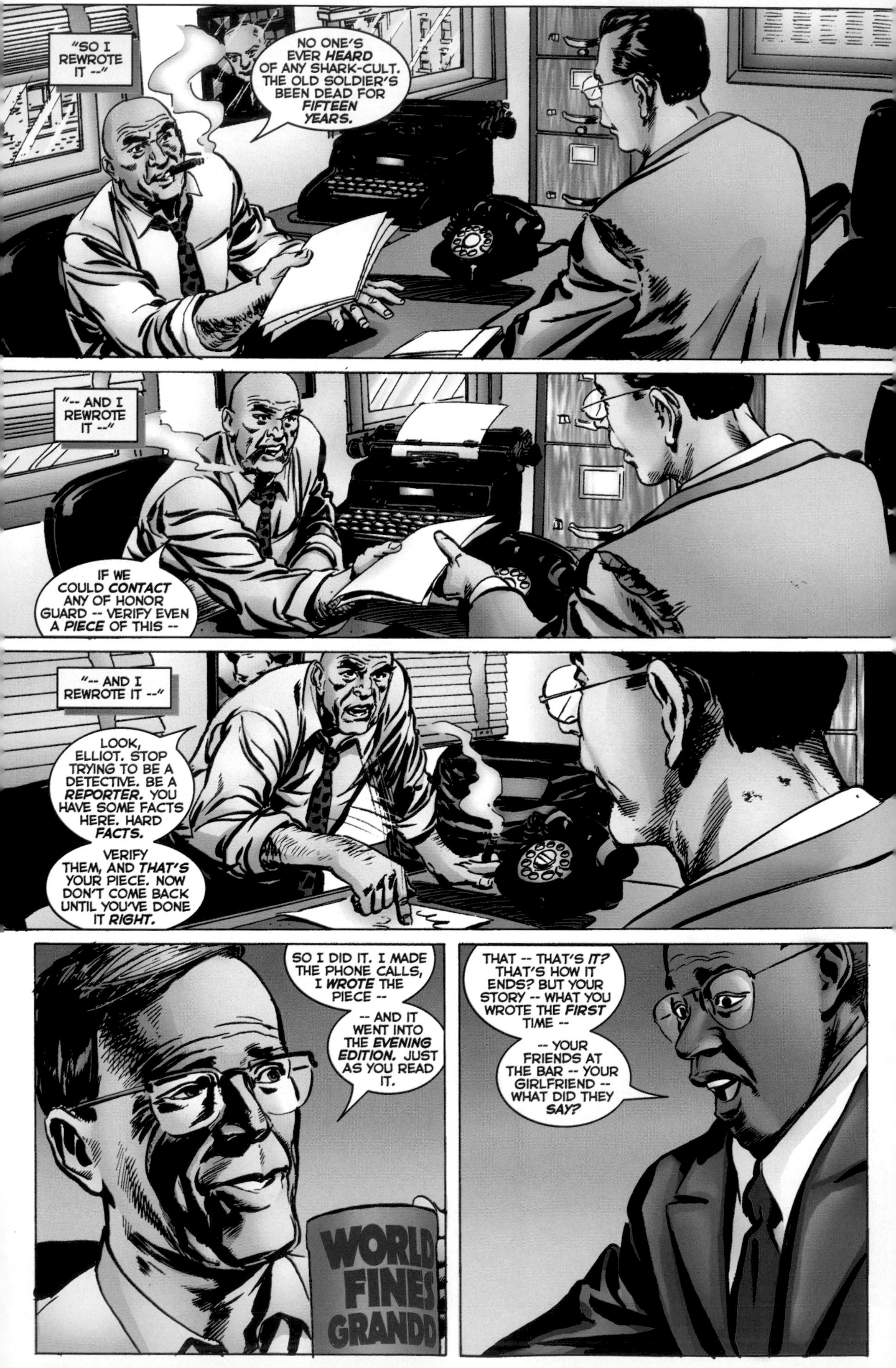
"SO I REWROTE IT --"
NO ONE'S EVER *HEARD* OF ANY SHARK-CULT. THE OLD SOLDIER'S BEEN DEAD FOR *FIFTEEN YEARS.*
"-- AND I REWROTE IT --"
IF WE COULD *CONTACT* ANY OF HONOR GUARD -- VERIFY EVEN A *PIECE* OF THIS --
"-- AND I REWROTE IT --"
LOOK, ELLIOT. STOP TRYING TO BE A DETECTIVE. BE A *REPORTER.* YOU HAVE SOME FACTS HERE. HARD *FACTS.*
VERIFY THEM, AND *THAT'S* YOUR PIECE. NOW DON'T COME BACK UNTIL YOU'VE DONE IT *RIGHT.*
SO I DID IT. I MADE THE PHONE CALLS, I *WROTE* THE PIECE --
-- AND IT WENT INTO THE *EVENING EDITION.* JUST AS YOU READ IT.
WORLD FINES GRANDD
THAT -- THAT'S *IT?* THAT'S HOW IT ENDS? BUT YOUR STORY -- WHAT YOU WROTE THE *FIRST* TIME --
-- YOUR FRIENDS AT THE BAR -- YOUR GIRLFRIEND -- WHAT DID THEY *SAY?*

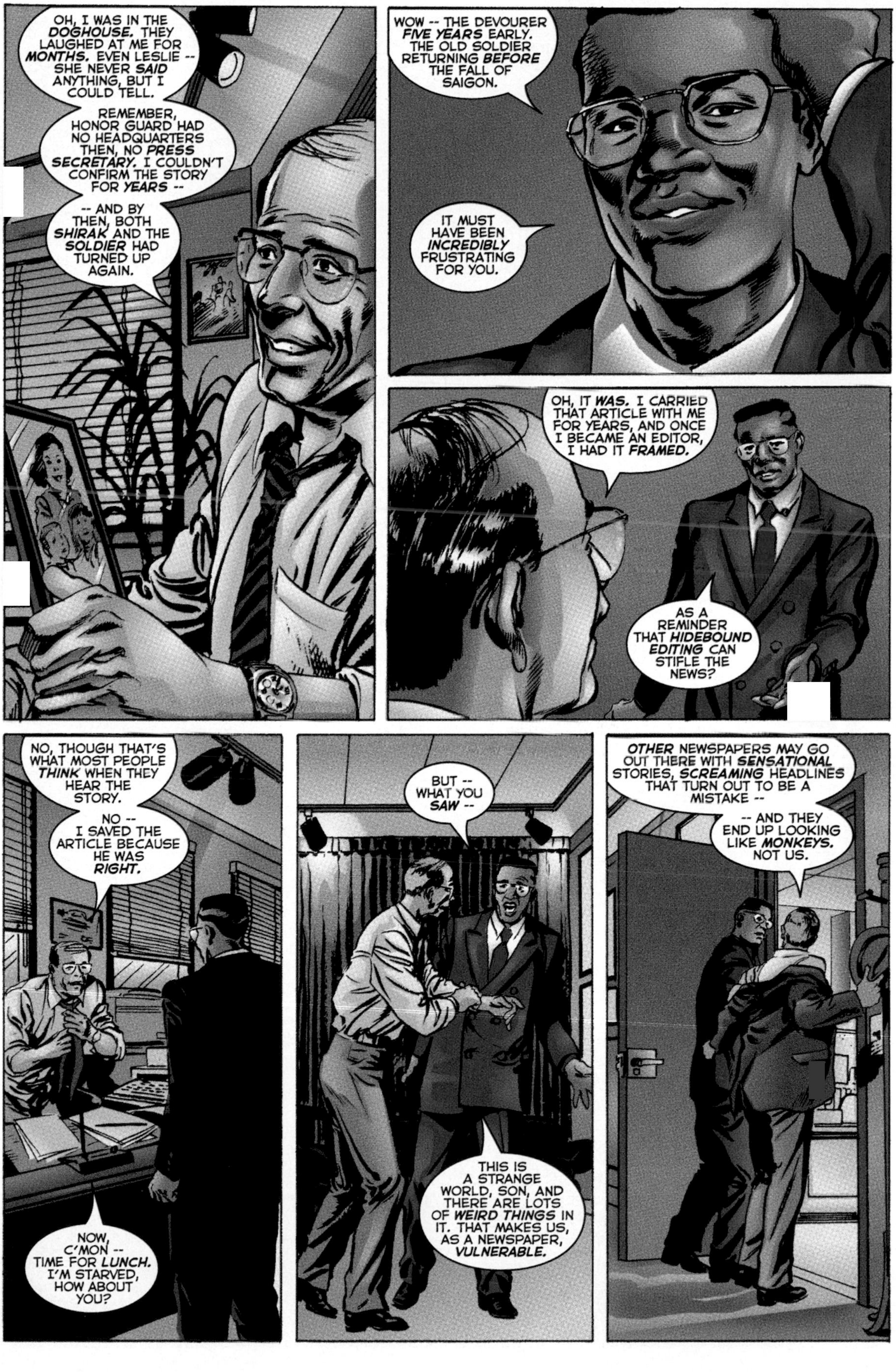
OH, I WAS IN THE DOGHOUSE. THEY LAUGHED AT ME FOR MONTHS. EVEN LESLIE -- SHE NEVER SAID ANYTHING, BUT I COULD TELL.
REMEMBER, HONOR GUARD HAD NO HEADQUARTERS THEN, NO PRESS SECRETARY. I COULDN'T CONFIRM THE STORY FOR YEARS --
-- AND BY THEN, BOTH SHIRAK AND THE SOLDIER HAD TURNED UP AGAIN.
WOW -- THE DEVOURER FIVE YEARS EARLY. THE OLD SOLDIER RETURNING BEFORE THE FALL OF SAIGON.
IT MUST HAVE BEEN INCREDIBLY FRUSTRATING FOR YOU.
OH, IT WAS. I CARRIED THAT ARTICLE WITH ME FOR YEARS, AND ONCE I BECAME AN EDITOR, I HAD IT FRAMED.
AS A REMINDER THAT HIDEBOUND EDITING CAN STIFLE THE NEWS?
NO, THOUGH THAT'S WHAT MOST PEOPLE THINK WHEN THEY HEAR THE STORY.
NO -- I SAVED THE ARTICLE BECAUSE HE WAS RIGHT.
NOW, C'MON -- TIME FOR LUNCH. I'M STARVED, HOW ABOUT YOU?
BUT -- WHAT YOU SAW --
THIS IS A STRANGE WORLD, SON, AND THERE ARE LOTS OF WEIRD THINGS IN IT. THAT MAKES US, AS A NEWSPAPER, VULNERABLE.
OTHER NEWSPAPERS MAY GO OUT THERE WITH SENSATIONAL STORIES, SCREAMING HEADLINES THAT TURN OUT TO BE A MISTAKE --
-- AND THEY END UP LOOKING LIKE MONKEYS. NOT US.

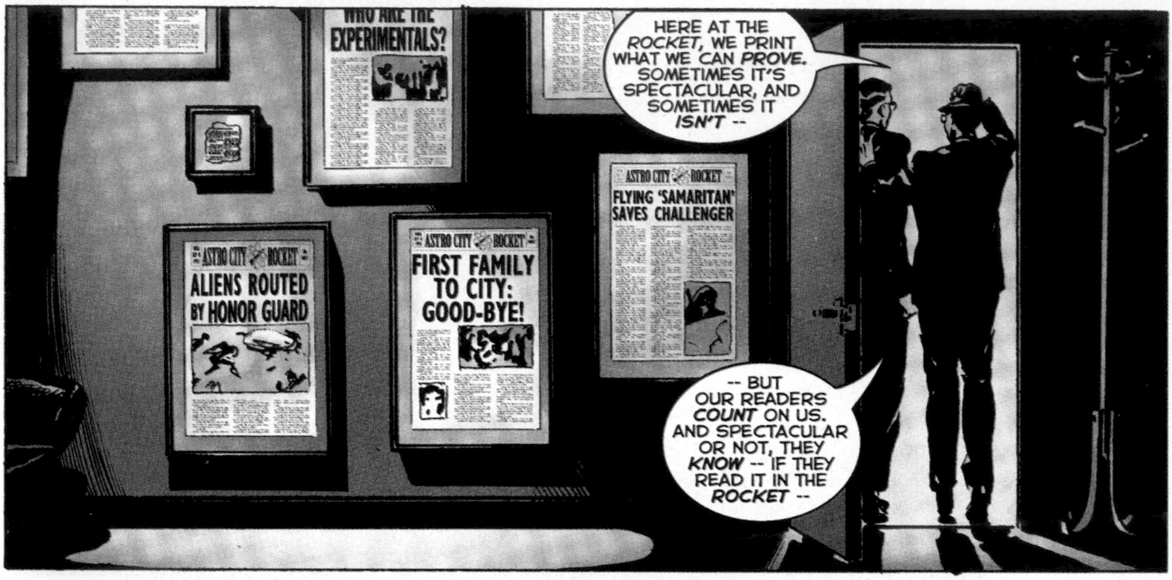
WHO ARE THE EXPERIMENTALS?
ASTRO CITY ROCKET
FLYING 'SAMARITAN' SAVES CHALLENGER
ASTRO CITY ROCKET
ALIENS ROUTED BY HONOR GUARD
ASTRO CITY ROCKET
FIRST FAMILY TO CITY: GOOD-BYE!
HERE AT THE *ROCKET*, WE PRINT WHAT WE CAN *PROVE*. SOMETIMES IT'S SPECTACULAR, AND SOMETIMES IT *ISN'T* --
-- BUT OUR READERS *COUNT* ON US. AND SPECTACULAR OR NOT, THEY *KNOW* -- IF THEY READ IT IN THE *ROCKET* --

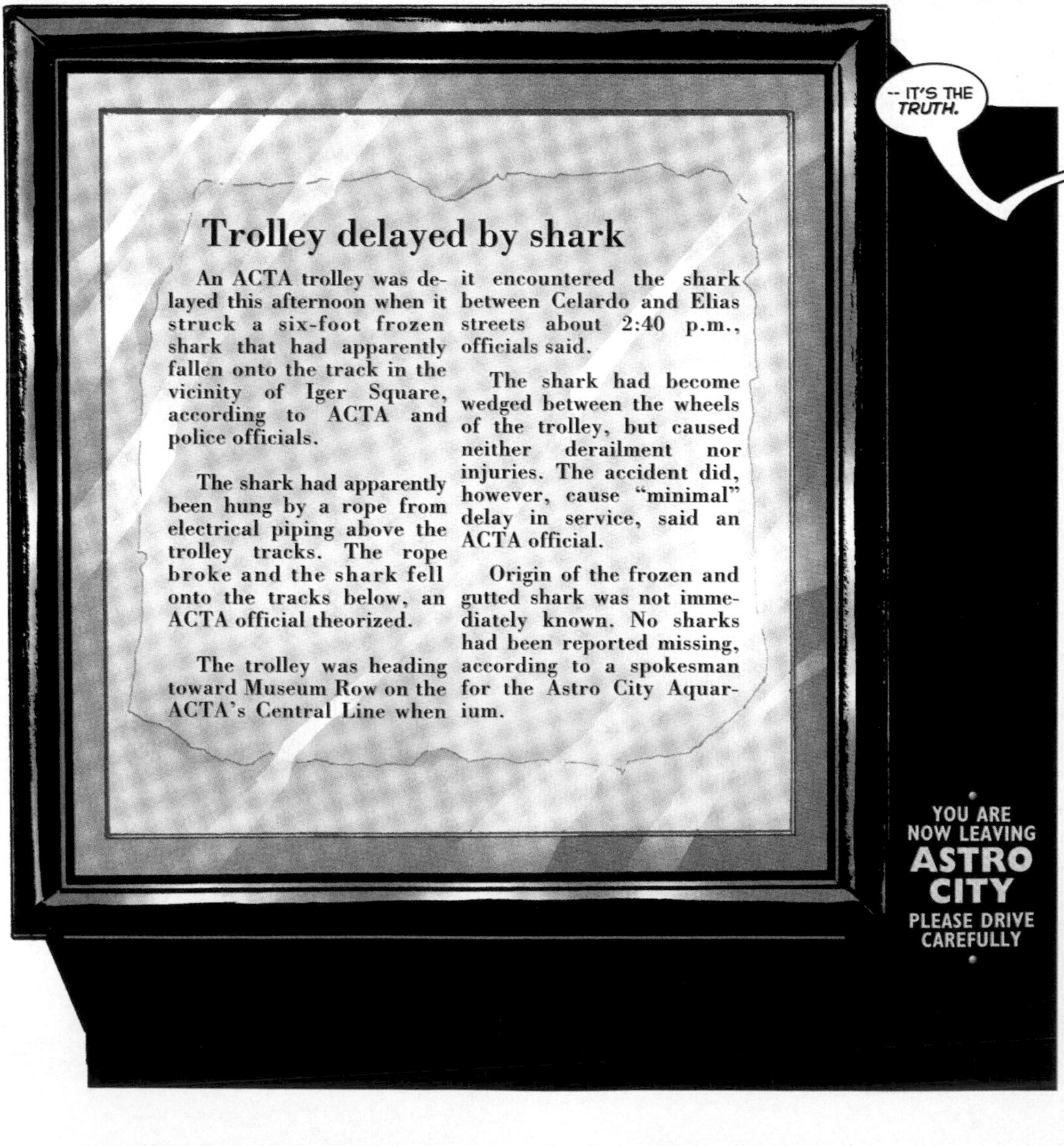

Trolley delayed by shark

An ACTA trolley was delayed this afternoon when it struck a six-foot frozen shark that had apparently fallen onto the track in the vicinity of Iger Square, according to ACTA and police officials.

The shark had apparently been hung by a rope from electrical piping above the trolley tracks. The rope broke and the shark fell onto the tracks below, an ACTA official theorized.

The trolley was heading toward Museum Row on the ACTA's Central Line when it encountered the shark between Celardo and Elias streets about 2:40 p.m., officials said.

The shark had become wedged between the wheels of the trolley, but caused neither derailment nor injuries. The accident did, however, cause "minimal" delay in service, said an ACTA official.

Origin of the frozen and gutted shark was not immediately known. No sharks had been reported missing, according to a spokesman for the Astro City Aquarium.

-- IT'S THE *TRUTH.*
YOU ARE NOW LEAVING ASTRO CITY
PLEASE DRIVE CAREFULLY

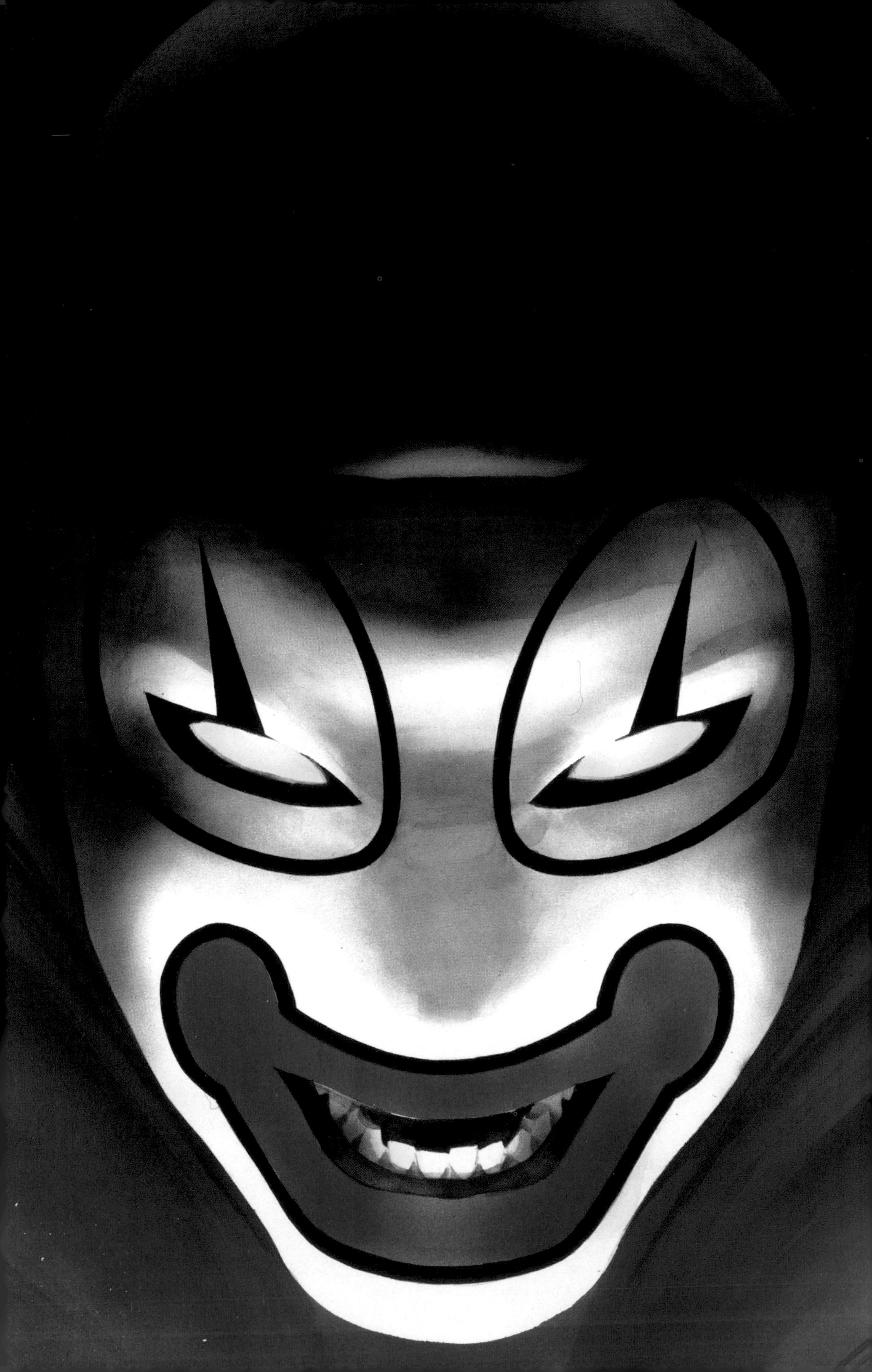

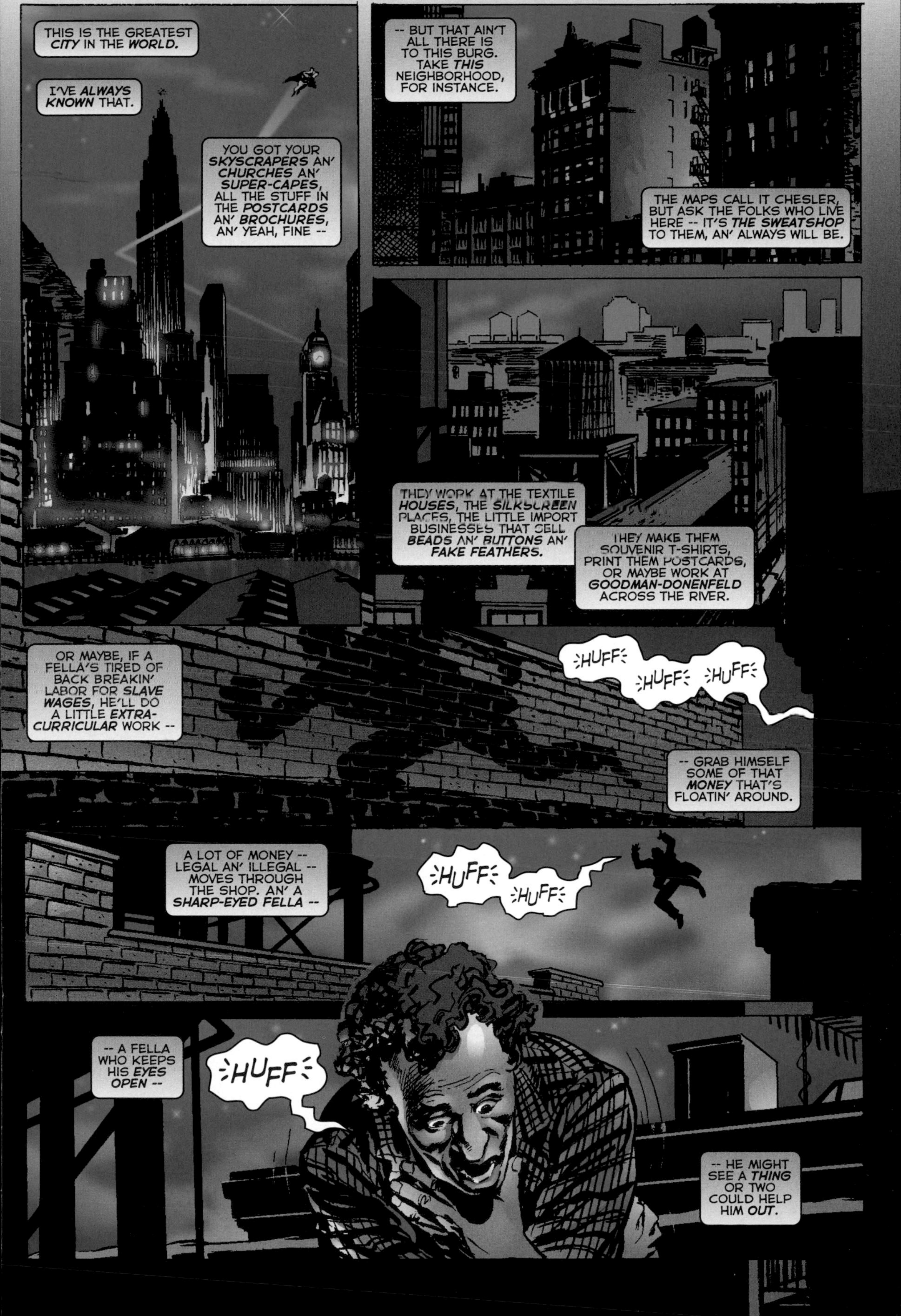
THIS IS THE GREATEST CITY IN THE WORLD.
I'VE ALWAYS KNOWN THAT.
YOU GOT YOUR SKYSCRAPERS AN' CHURCHES AN' SUPER-CAPES, ALL THE STUFF IN THE POSTCARDS AN' BROCHURES, AN' YEAH, FINE --
-- BUT THAT AIN'T ALL THERE IS TO THIS BURG. TAKE THIS NEIGHBORHOOD, FOR INSTANCE.
THE MAPS CALL IT CHESLER, BUT ASK THE FOLKS WHO LIVE HERE -- IT'S THE SWEATSHOP TO THEM, AN' ALWAYS WILL BE.
THEY WORK AT THE TEXTILE HOUSES, THE SILKSCREEN PLACES, THE LITTLE IMPORT BUSINESSES THAT SELL BEADS AN' BUTTONS AN' FAKE FEATHERS.
THEY MAKE THEM SOUVENIR T-SHIRTS, PRINT THEM POSTCARDS, OR MAYBE WORK AT GOODMAN-DONENFELD ACROSS THE RIVER.
OR MAYBE, IF A FELLA'S TIRED OF BACK BREAKIN' LABOR FOR SLAVE WAGES, HE'LL DO A LITTLE EXTRA-CURRICULAR WORK --
HUFF
HUFF
HUFF
-- GRAB HIMSELF SOME OF THAT MONEY THAT'S FLOATIN' AROUND.
A LOT OF MONEY -- LEGAL AN' ILLEGAL -- MOVES THROUGH THE SHOP. AN' A SHARP-EYED FELLA --
HUFF
HUFF
-- A FELLA WHO KEEPS HIS EYES OPEN --
HUFF
-- HE MIGHT SEE A THING OR TWO COULD HELP HIM OUT.

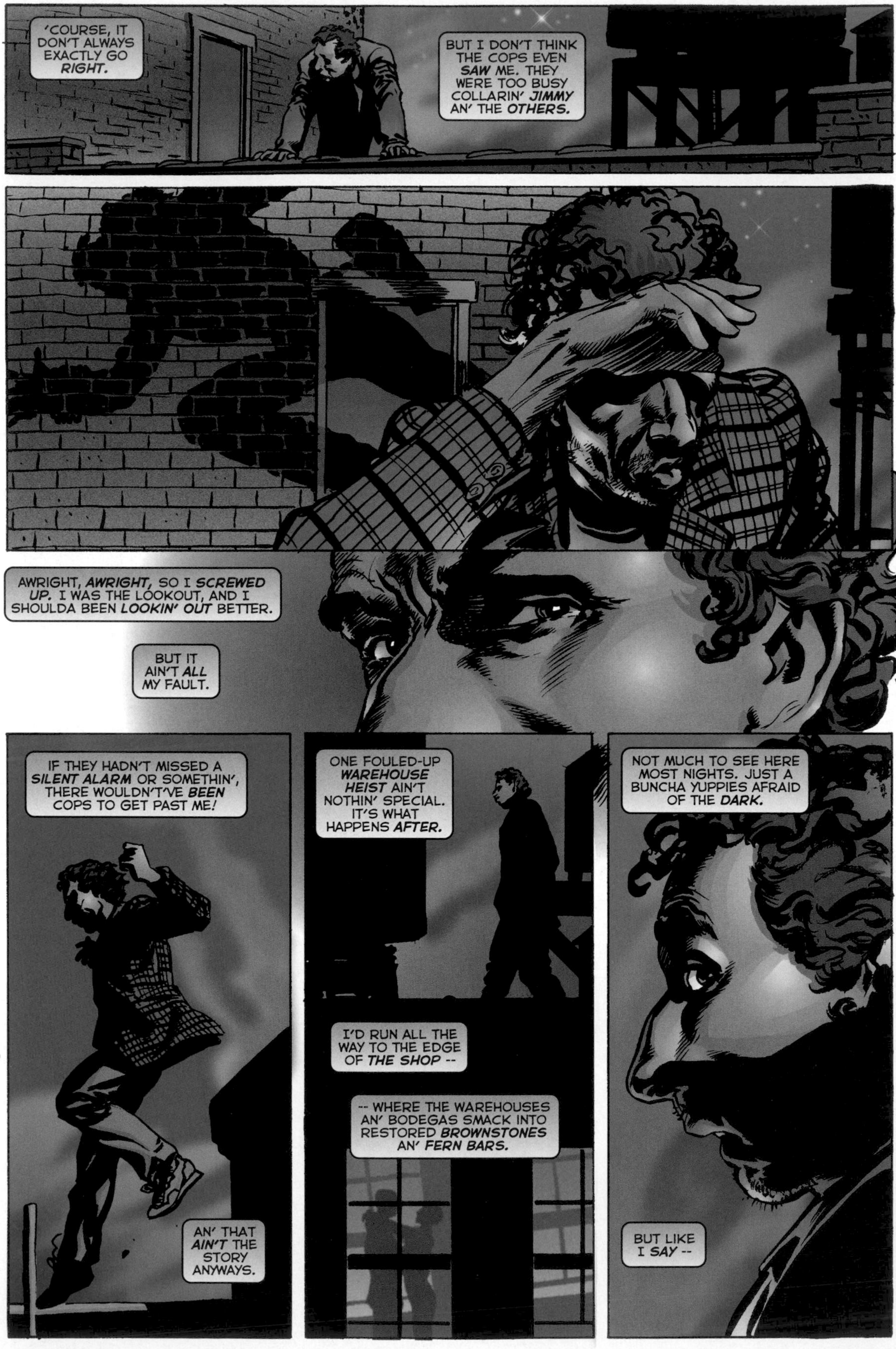
'COURSE, IT DON'T ALWAYS EXACTLY GO RIGHT.
BUT I DON'T THINK THE COPS EVEN SAW ME. THEY WERE TOO BUSY COLLARIN' JIMMY AN' THE OTHERS.
AWRIGHT, AWRIGHT, SO I SCREWED UP. I WAS THE LOOKOUT, AND I SHOULDA BEEN LOOKIN' OUT BETTER.
BUT IT AIN'T ALL MY FAULT.
IF THEY HADN'T MISSED A SILENT ALARM OR SOMETHIN', THERE WOULDN'T'VE BEEN COPS TO GET PAST ME!
AN' THAT AIN'T THE STORY ANYWAYS.
ONE FOULED-UP WAREHOUSE HEIST AIN'T NOTHIN' SPECIAL. IT'S WHAT HAPPENS AFTER.
I'D RUN ALL THE WAY TO THE EDGE OF THE SHOP --
-- WHERE THE WAREHOUSES AN' BODEGAS SMACK INTO RESTORED BROWNSTONES AN' FERN BARS.
NOT MUCH TO SEE HERE MOST NIGHTS. JUST A BUNCHA YUPPIES AFRAID OF THE DARK.
BUT LIKE I SAY --

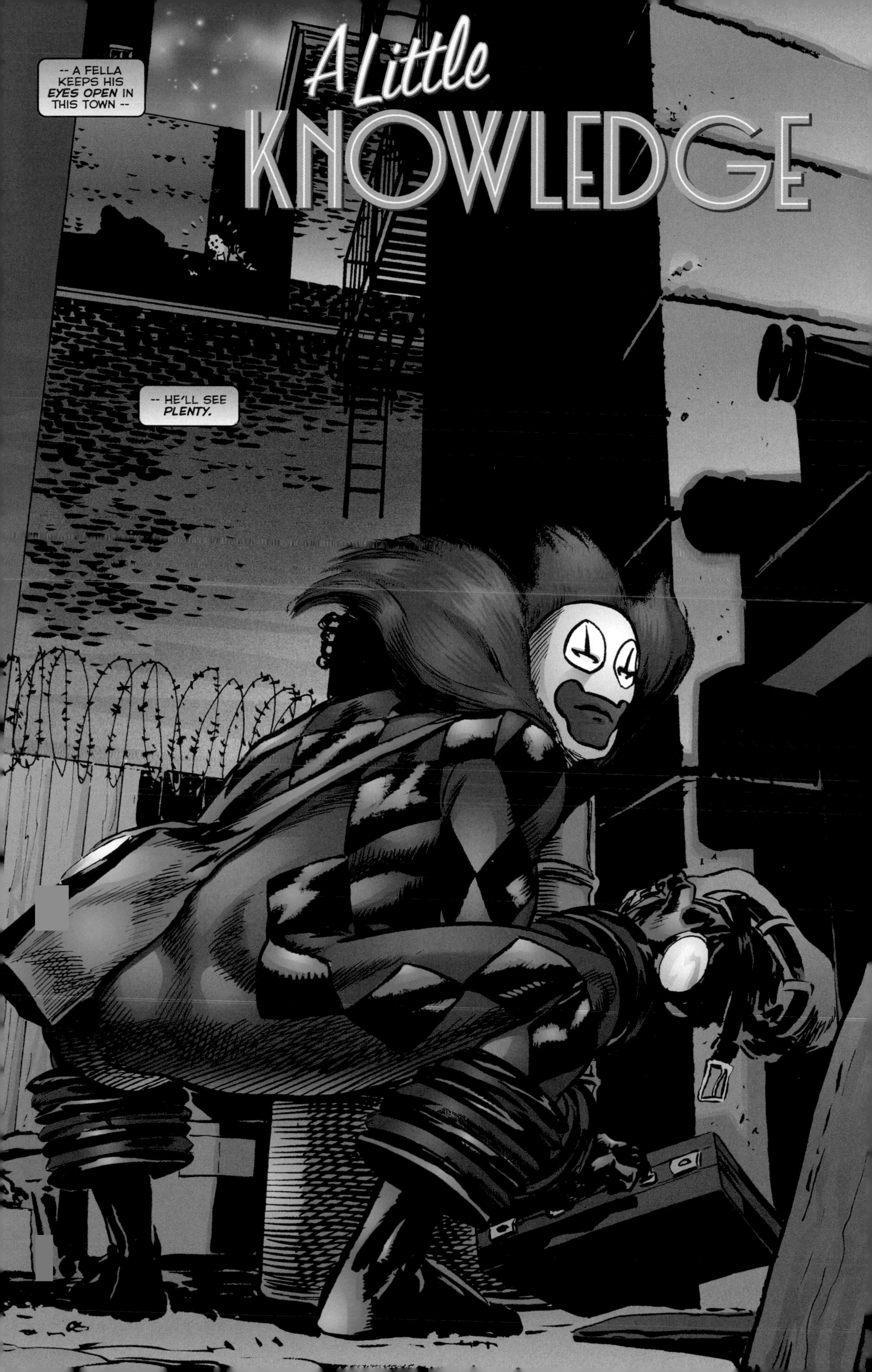

A Little
KNOWLEDGE
-- A FELLA KEEPS HIS EYES OPEN IN THIS TOWN --
-- HE'LL SEE PLENTY.

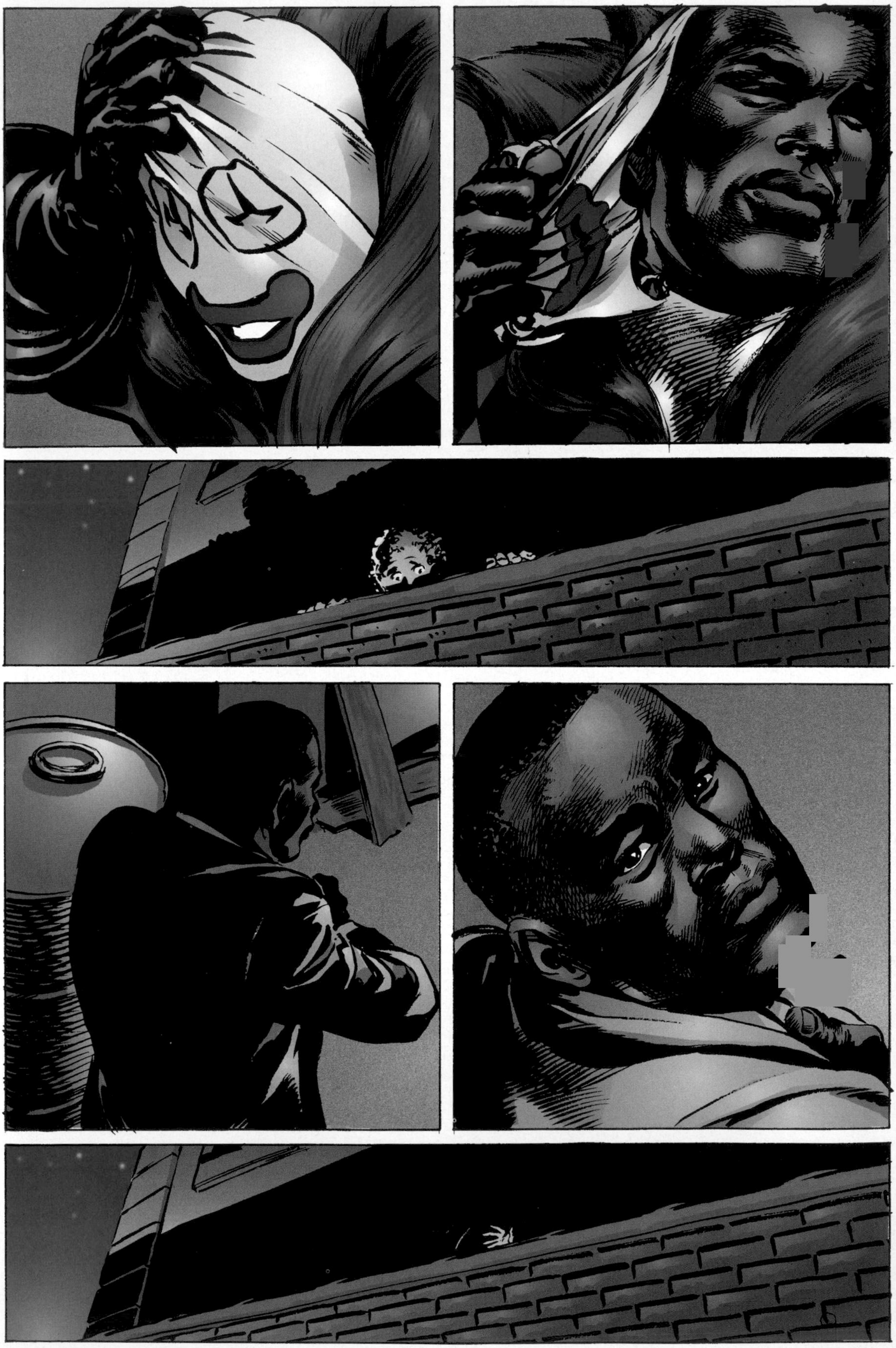

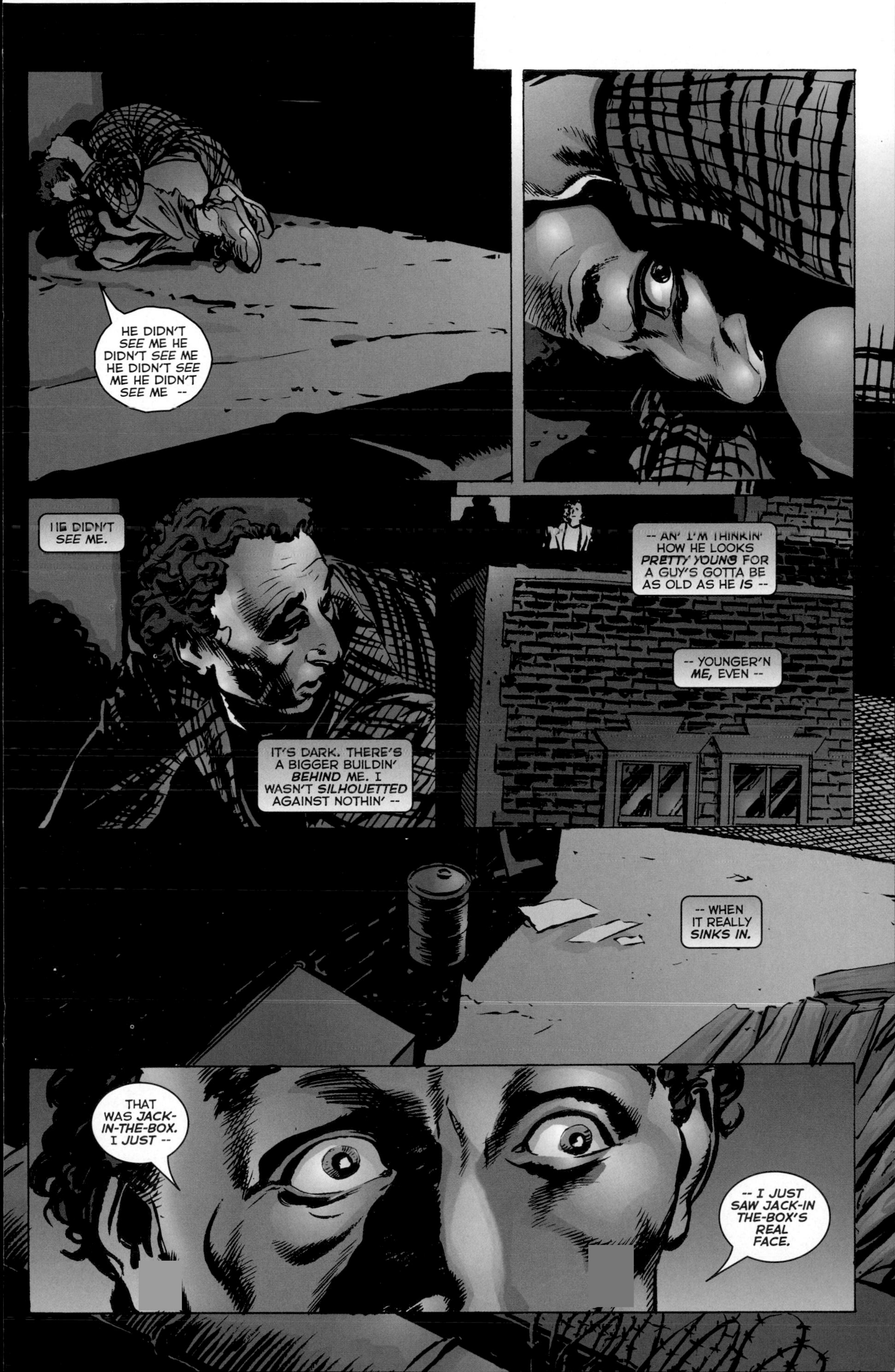
HE DIDN'T SEE ME HE DIDN'T SEE ME HE DIDN'T SEE ME HE DIDN'T SEE ME --
HE DIDN'T SEE ME.
IT'S DARK. THERE'S A BIGGER BUILDIN' BEHIND ME. I WASN'T SILHOUETTED AGAINST NOTHIN' --
-- AN' I'M THINKIN' HOW HE LOOKS PRETTY YOUNG FOR A GUY'S GOTTA BE AS OLD AS HE IS --
-- YOUNGER'N ME, EVEN --
-- WHEN IT REALLY SINKS IN.
THAT WAS JACK-IN-THE-BOX. I JUST --
-- I JUST SAW JACK-IN THE-BOX'S REAL FACE.

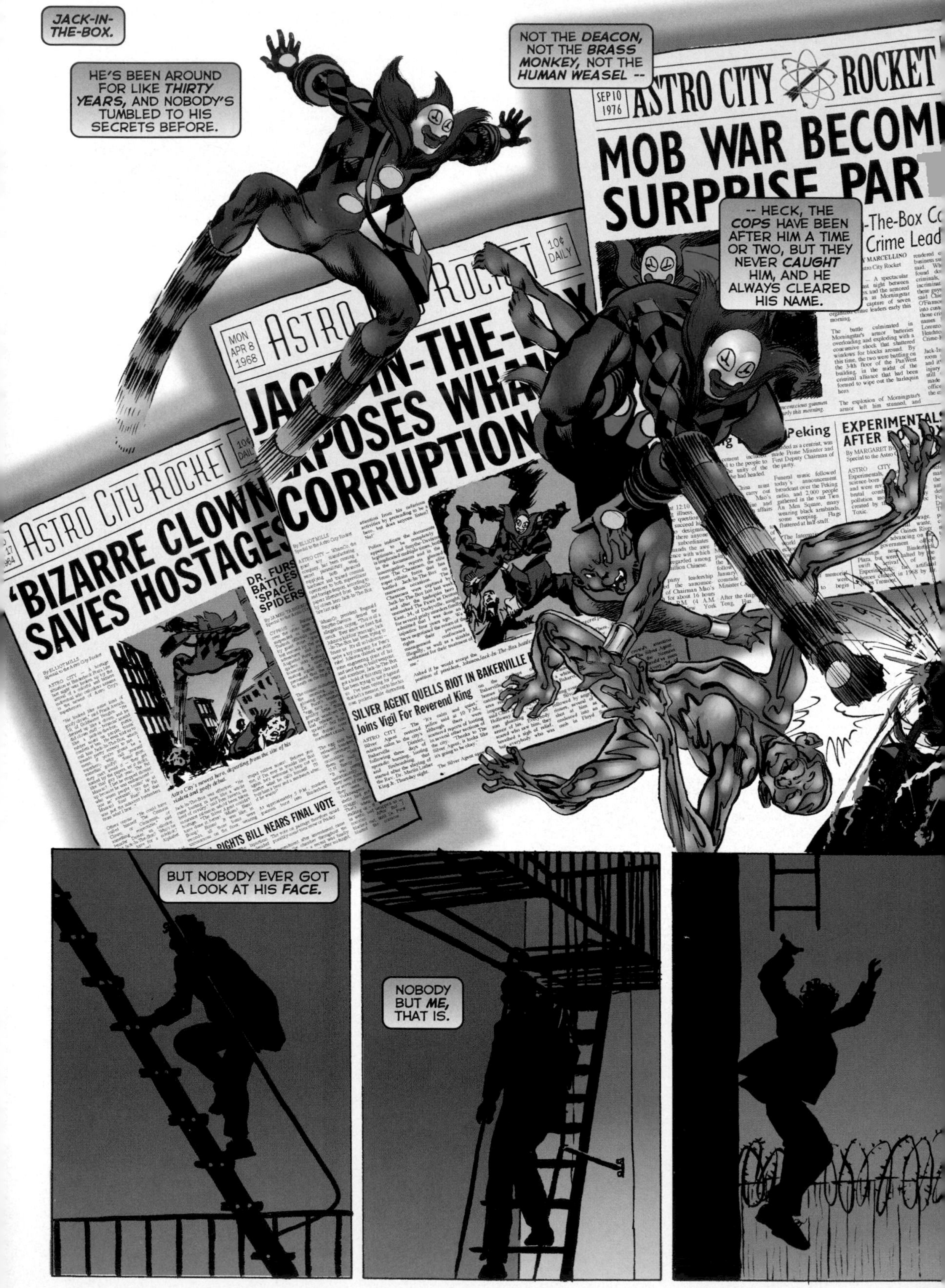
JACK-IN-THE-BOX.
HE'S BEEN AROUND FOR LIKE *THIRTY YEARS,* AND NOBODY'S TUMBLED TO HIS SECRETS BEFORE.
NOT THE *DEACON,* NOT THE *BRASS MONKEY,* NOT THE *HUMAN WEASEL* --
-- HECK, THE *COPS* HAVE BEEN AFTER HIM A TIME OR TWO, BUT THEY NEVER *CAUGHT* HIM, AND HE ALWAYS CLEARED HIS NAME.
ASTRO CITY ROCKET
SEP 10 1976
MOB WAR BECOM
SURPRISE PAR
ASTRO CITY ROCKET
MON. APR 8 1968
10¢ DAILY
EXPOSES WHA
CORRUPTION
SILVER AGENT QUELLS RIOT IN BAKERVILLE
Joins Vigil For Reverend King
ASTRO CITY ROCKET
'BIZARRE CLOWN
SAVES HOSTAGES
BUT NOBODY EVER GOT A LOOK AT HIS *FACE.*
NOBODY BUT *ME,* THAT IS.

FRI OCT 14 1983

ASTRO CITY ⚛ ROCKET

JACK-IN-THE-BOX TRAPPED IN FIERY EXPLOSION

Is Harlequin Hero Dead?

By BRETT SONNENSCHEIN
Special to the Astro City Rocket

REAGAN

FRI MAY 5 1989

ASTRO CITY ⚛ ROCKET

JACK'S BACK

MIA HERO RETURNS — VEIDT ST. SHOOT

By EDWARD NG
Special to the Astro City Rocket

Blue Knight Implicated In Slayings

By MARGARET BOCANNON
Special to the Astro City Rocket

Venus Probe Launched

HALF THE GUYS ON BIRO ISLAND GOT JUGGED BY JACK-IN-THE-BOX ONE TIME OR ANOTHER. AN' HALF THE GUYS WALKIN' LOOSE --

-- THEY KNOW WHAT IT'S LIKE TO GET *CONFETTIED* -- OR TO BE ZAPPED STUPID BY ONE A' THOSE FREAKY *RUBBER NOSES* A' HIS.

THAT'S THE *TRICK,* AIN'T IT? YOU GOTTA KEEP YOUR *EYES* OPEN --

-- YOU GOTTA LOOK FOR YOUR *OPPORTUNITIES* --

-- BUT *STILL* --

-- THIS IS A *GREAT TOWN.*

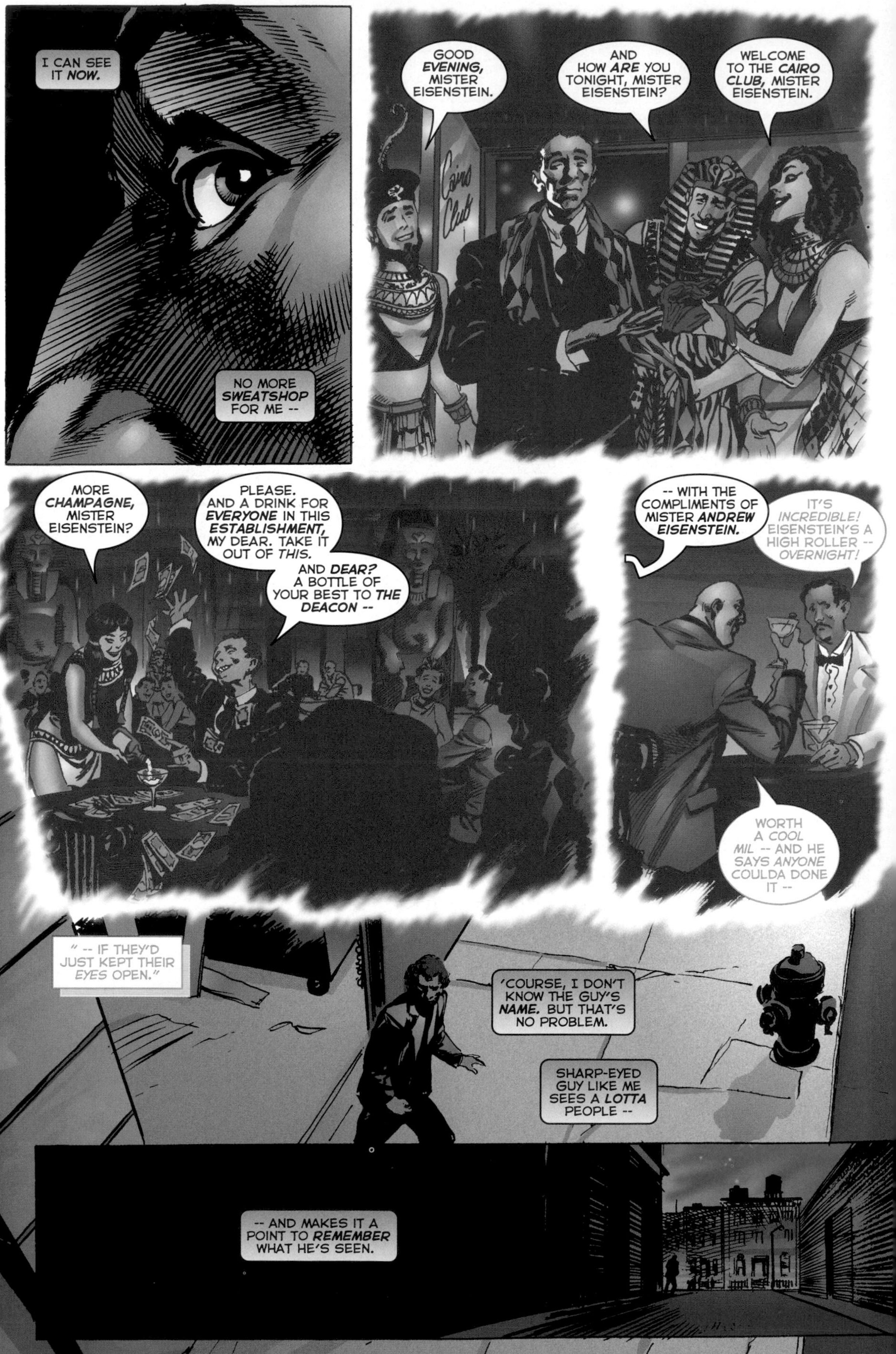
I CAN SEE IT NOW.
NO MORE SWEATSHOP FOR ME --
GOOD EVENING, MISTER EISENSTEIN.
AND HOW ARE YOU TONIGHT, MISTER EISENSTEIN?
WELCOME TO THE CAIRO CLUB, MISTER EISENSTEIN.
Cairo Club
MORE CHAMPAGNE, MISTER EISENSTEIN?
PLEASE. AND A DRINK FOR EVERYONE IN THIS ESTABLISHMENT, MY DEAR. TAKE IT OUT OF THIS.
AND DEAR? A BOTTLE OF YOUR BEST TO THE DEACON --
-- WITH THE COMPLIMENTS OF MISTER ANDREW EISENSTEIN.
IT'S INCREDIBLE! EISENSTEIN'S A HIGH ROLLER -- OVERNIGHT!
WORTH A COOL MIL -- AND HE SAYS ANYONE COULDA DONE IT --
" -- IF THEY'D JUST KEPT THEIR EYES OPEN."
'COURSE, I DON'T KNOW THE GUY'S NAME. BUT THAT'S NO PROBLEM.
SHARP-EYED GUY LIKE ME SEES A LOTTA PEOPLE --
-- AND MAKES IT A POINT TO REMEMBER WHAT HE'S SEEN.

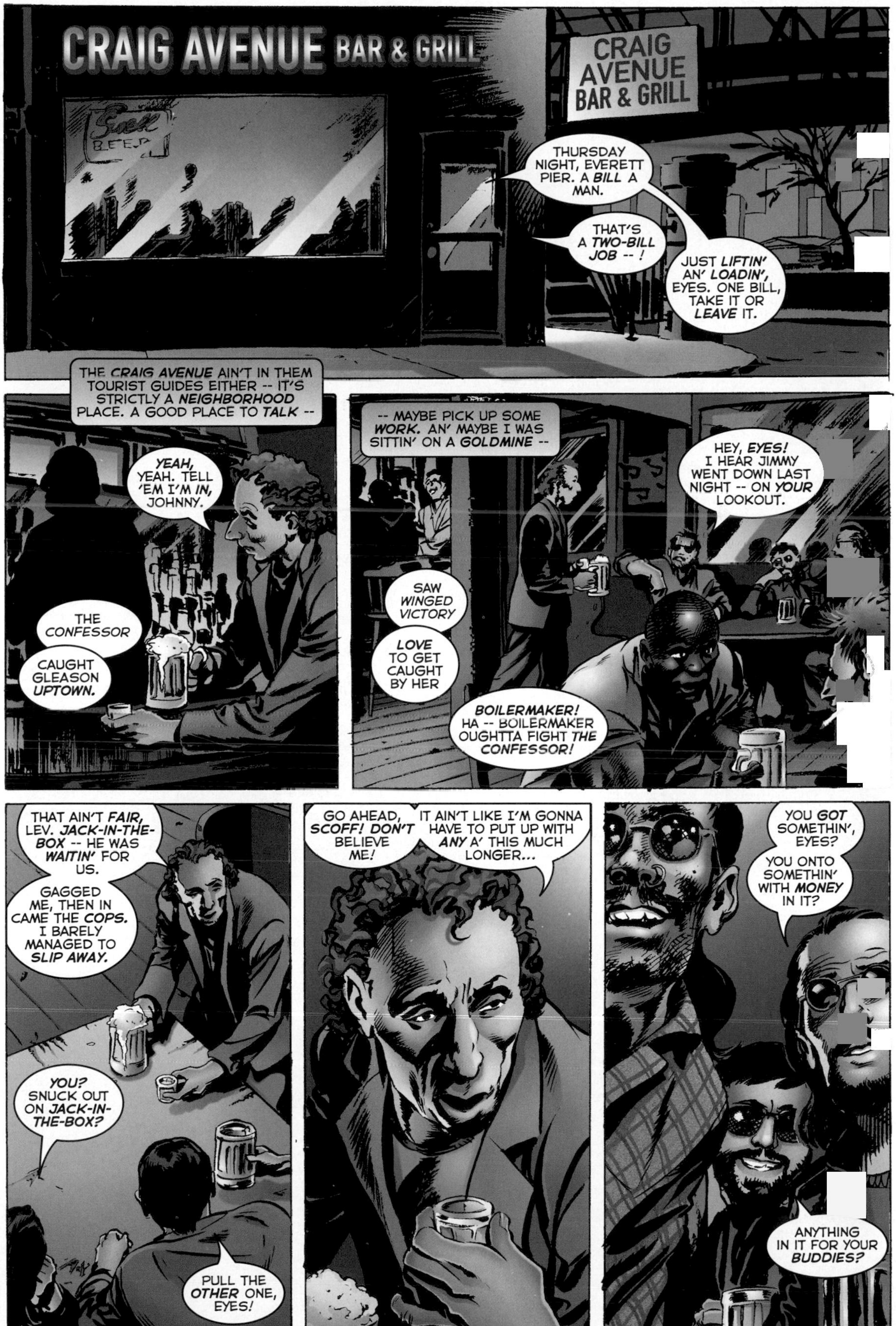
CRAIG AVENUE BAR & GRILL
CRAIG AVENUE BAR & GRILL
THURSDAY NIGHT, EVERETT PIER. A BILL A MAN.
THAT'S A TWO-BILL JOB -- !
JUST LIFTIN' AN' LOADIN', EYES. ONE BILL, TAKE IT OR LEAVE IT.
THE CRAIG AVENUE AIN'T IN THEM TOURIST GUIDES EITHER -- IT'S STRICTLY A NEIGHBORHOOD PLACE. A GOOD PLACE TO TALK --
YEAH, YEAH. TELL 'EM I'M IN, JOHNNY.
THE CONFESSOR
CAUGHT GLEASON UPTOWN.
-- MAYBE PICK UP SOME WORK. AN' MAYBE I WAS SITTIN' ON A GOLDMINE --
HEY, EYES! I HEAR JIMMY WENT DOWN LAST NIGHT -- ON YOUR LOOKOUT.
SAW WINGED VICTORY
LOVE TO GET CAUGHT BY HER
BOILERMAKER! HA -- BOILERMAKER OUGHTTA FIGHT THE CONFESSOR!
THAT AIN'T FAIR, LEV. JACK-IN-THE-BOX -- HE WAS WAITIN' FOR US.
GAGGED ME, THEN IN CAME THE COPS. I BARELY MANAGED TO SLIP AWAY.
YOU? SNUCK OUT ON JACK-IN-THE-BOX?
PULL THE OTHER ONE, EYES!
GO AHEAD, SCOFF! DON'T BELIEVE ME!
IT AIN'T LIKE I'M GONNA HAVE TO PUT UP WITH ANY A' THIS MUCH LONGER...
YOU GOT SOMETHIN', EYES?
YOU ONTO SOMETHIN' WITH MONEY IN IT?
ANYTHING IN IT FOR YOUR BUDDIES?

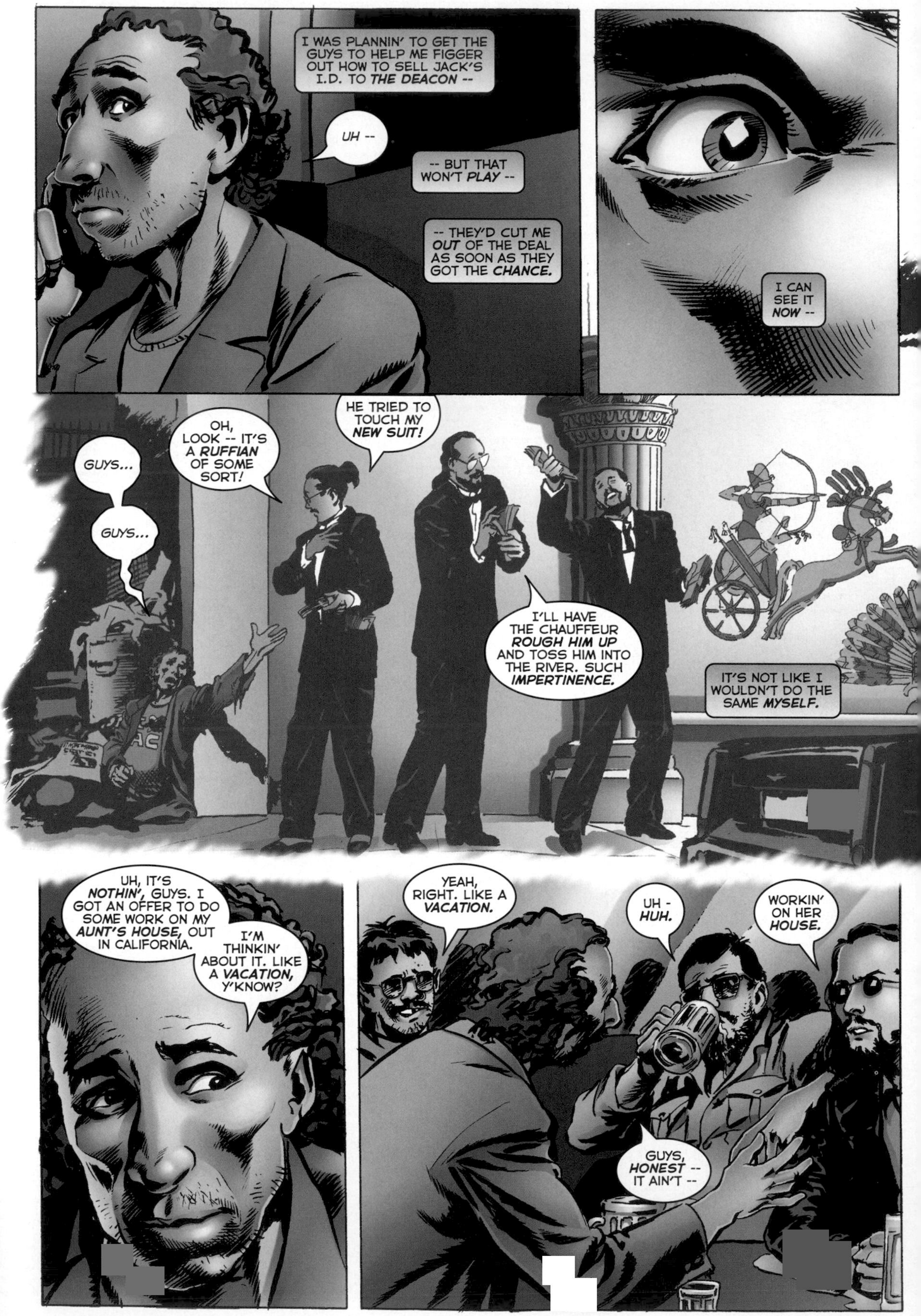
I WAS PLANNIN' TO GET THE GUYS TO HELP ME FIGGER OUT HOW TO SELL JACK'S I.D. TO THE DEACON --
UH --
-- BUT THAT WON'T PLAY --
-- THEY'D CUT ME OUT OF THE DEAL AS SOON AS THEY GOT THE CHANCE.
I CAN SEE IT NOW --
GUYS...
GUYS...
OH, LOOK -- IT'S A RUFFIAN OF SOME SORT!
HE TRIED TO TOUCH MY NEW SUIT!
I'LL HAVE THE CHAUFFEUR ROUGH HIM UP AND TOSS HIM INTO THE RIVER. SUCH IMPERTINENCE.
IT'S NOT LIKE I WOULDN'T DO THE SAME MYSELF.
UH, IT'S NOTHIN', GUYS. I GOT AN OFFER TO DO SOME WORK ON MY AUNT'S HOUSE, OUT IN CALIFORNIA.
I'M THINKIN' ABOUT IT. LIKE A VACATION, Y'KNOW?
YEAH, RIGHT. LIKE A VACATION.
UH - HUH.
WORKIN' ON HER HOUSE.
GUYS, HONEST -- IT AIN'T --

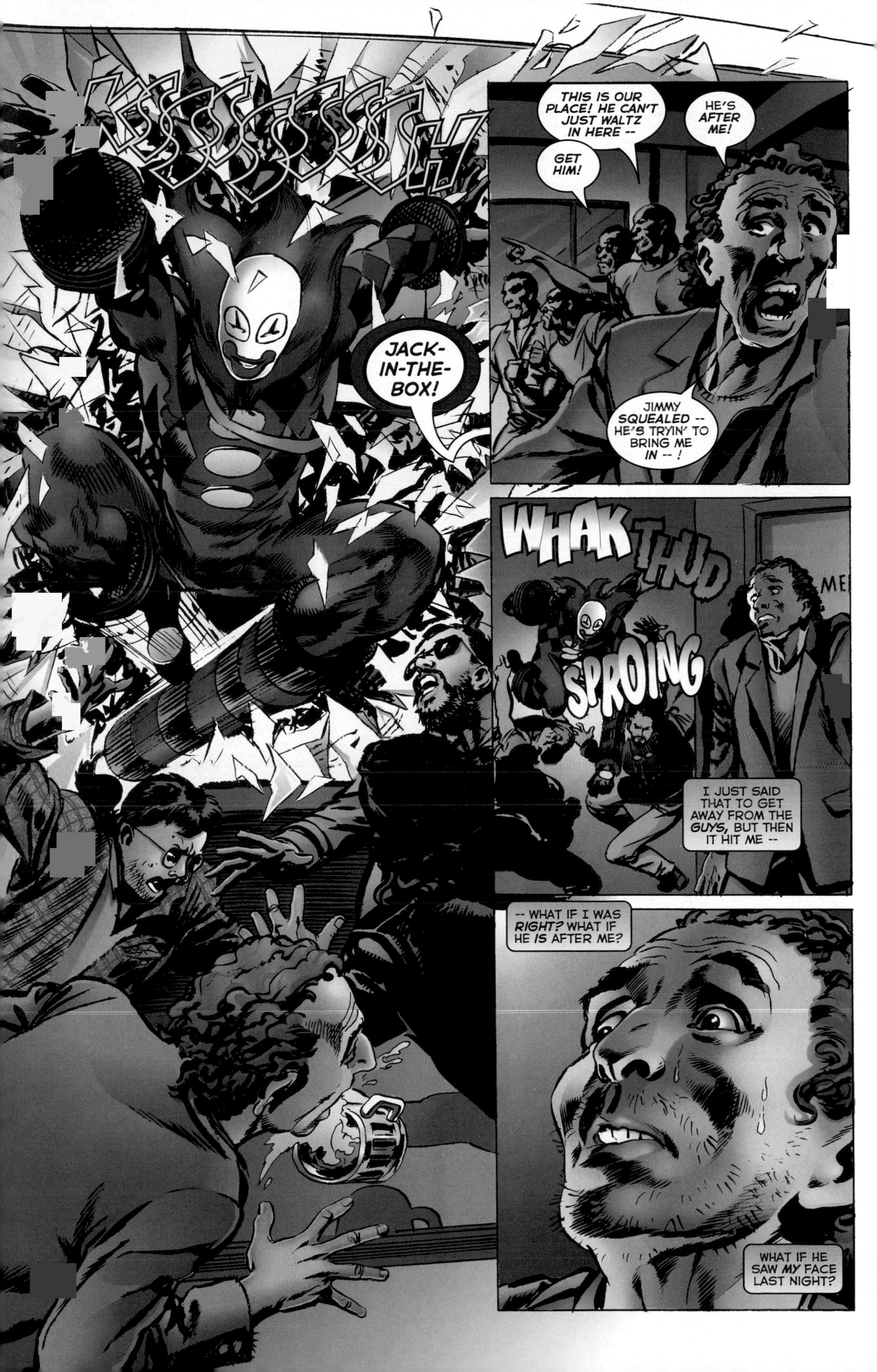
KSSSSSSSSH
JACK-IN-THE-BOX!
THIS IS OUR PLACE! HE CAN'T JUST WALTZ IN HERE --
GET HIM!
HE'S AFTER ME!
JIMMY SQUEALED -- HE'S TRYIN' TO BRING ME IN -- !
WHAK
THUD
SPROING
I JUST SAID THAT TO GET AWAY FROM THE GUYS, BUT THEN IT HIT ME --
-- WHAT IF I WAS RIGHT? WHAT IF HE IS AFTER ME?
WHAT IF HE SAW MY FACE LAST NIGHT?

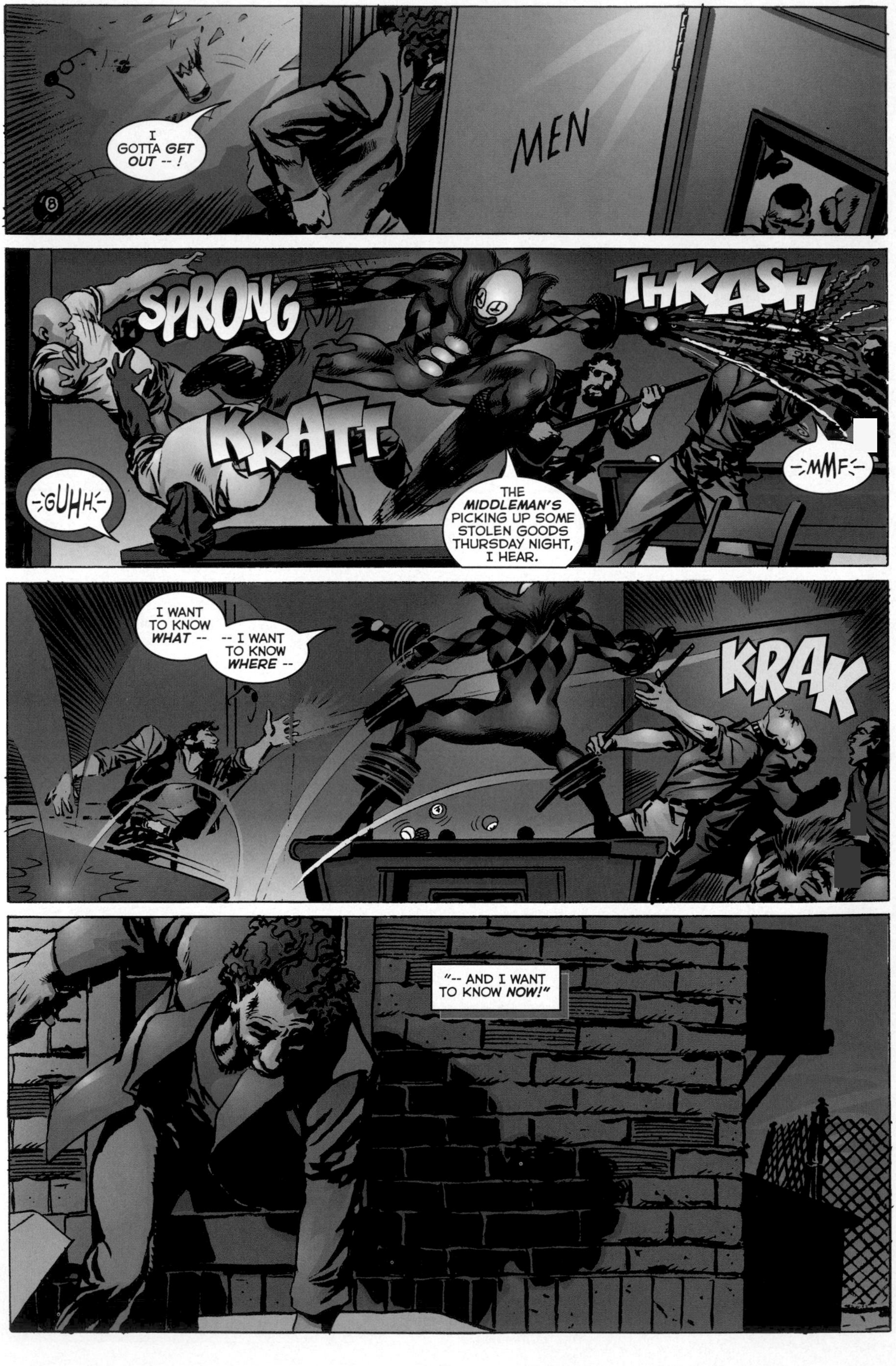
I GOTTA GET OUT -- !
MEN
SPRONG
THKASH
KRATT
-GUHH-
THE MIDDLEMAN'S PICKING UP SOME STOLEN GOODS THURSDAY NIGHT, I HEAR.
-MMF-
I WANT TO KNOW WHAT --
-- I WANT TO KNOW WHERE --
KRAK
"-- AND I WANT TO KNOW NOW!"

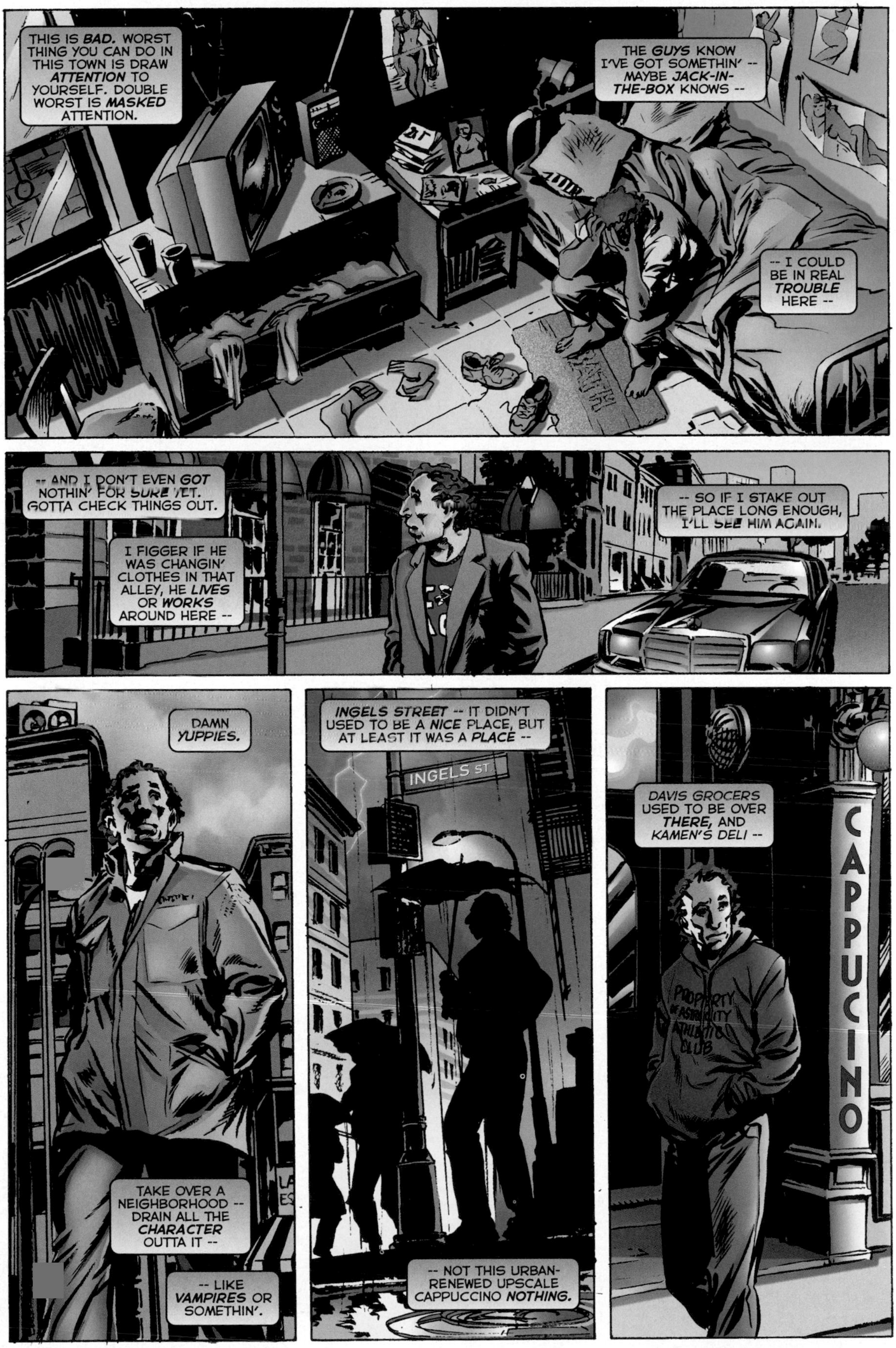
THIS IS *BAD.* WORST THING YOU CAN DO IN THIS TOWN IS DRAW *ATTENTION* TO YOURSELF. DOUBLE WORST IS *MASKED* ATTENTION.
THE *GUYS* KNOW I'VE GOT SOMETHIN' -- MAYBE *JACK-IN-THE-BOX* KNOWS --
-- I COULD BE IN REAL *TROUBLE* HERE --
-- AND I DON'T EVEN *GOT* NOTHIN' FOR *SURE YET.* GOTTA CHECK THINGS OUT.
I FIGGER IF HE WAS CHANGIN' CLOTHES IN THAT ALLEY, HE *LIVES* OR *WORKS* AROUND HERE --
-- SO IF I STAKE OUT THE PLACE LONG ENOUGH, I'LL *SEE* HIM AGAIN.
DAMN *YUPPIES.*
TAKE OVER A NEIGHBORHOOD -- DRAIN ALL THE *CHARACTER* OUTTA IT --
-- LIKE *VAMPIRES* OR SOMETHIN'.
INGELS STREET -- IT DIDN'T USED TO BE A *NICE* PLACE, BUT AT LEAST IT WAS A *PLACE* --
INGELS ST
-- NOT THIS URBAN-RENEWED UPSCALE CAPPUCCINO *NOTHING.*
DAVIS GROCERS USED TO BE OVER *THERE,* AND *KAMEN'S DELI* --
CAPPUCINO

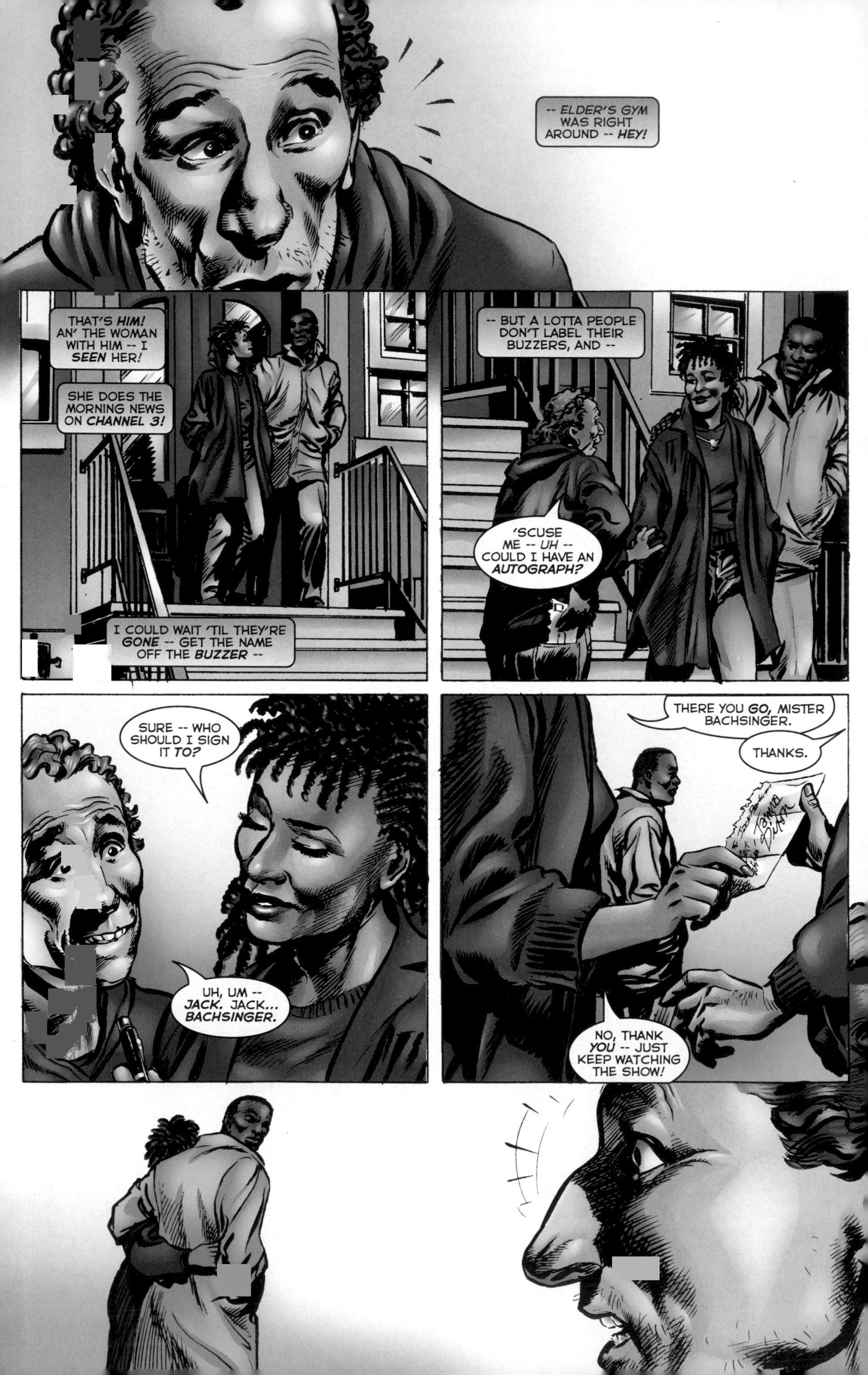
-- ELDER'S GYM WAS RIGHT AROUND -- HEY!
THAT'S HIM! AN' THE WOMAN WITH HIM -- I SEEN HER!
SHE DOES THE MORNING NEWS ON CHANNEL 3!
I COULD WAIT 'TIL THEY'RE GONE -- GET THE NAME OFF THE BUZZER --
-- BUT A LOTTA PEOPLE DON'T LABEL THEIR BUZZERS, AND --
'SCUSE ME -- UH -- COULD I HAVE AN AUTOGRAPH?
SURE -- WHO SHOULD I SIGN IT TO?
UH, UM -- JACK. JACK... BACHSINGER.
THERE YOU GO, MISTER BACHSINGER.
THANKS.
NO, THANK YOU -- JUST KEEP WATCHING THE SHOW!

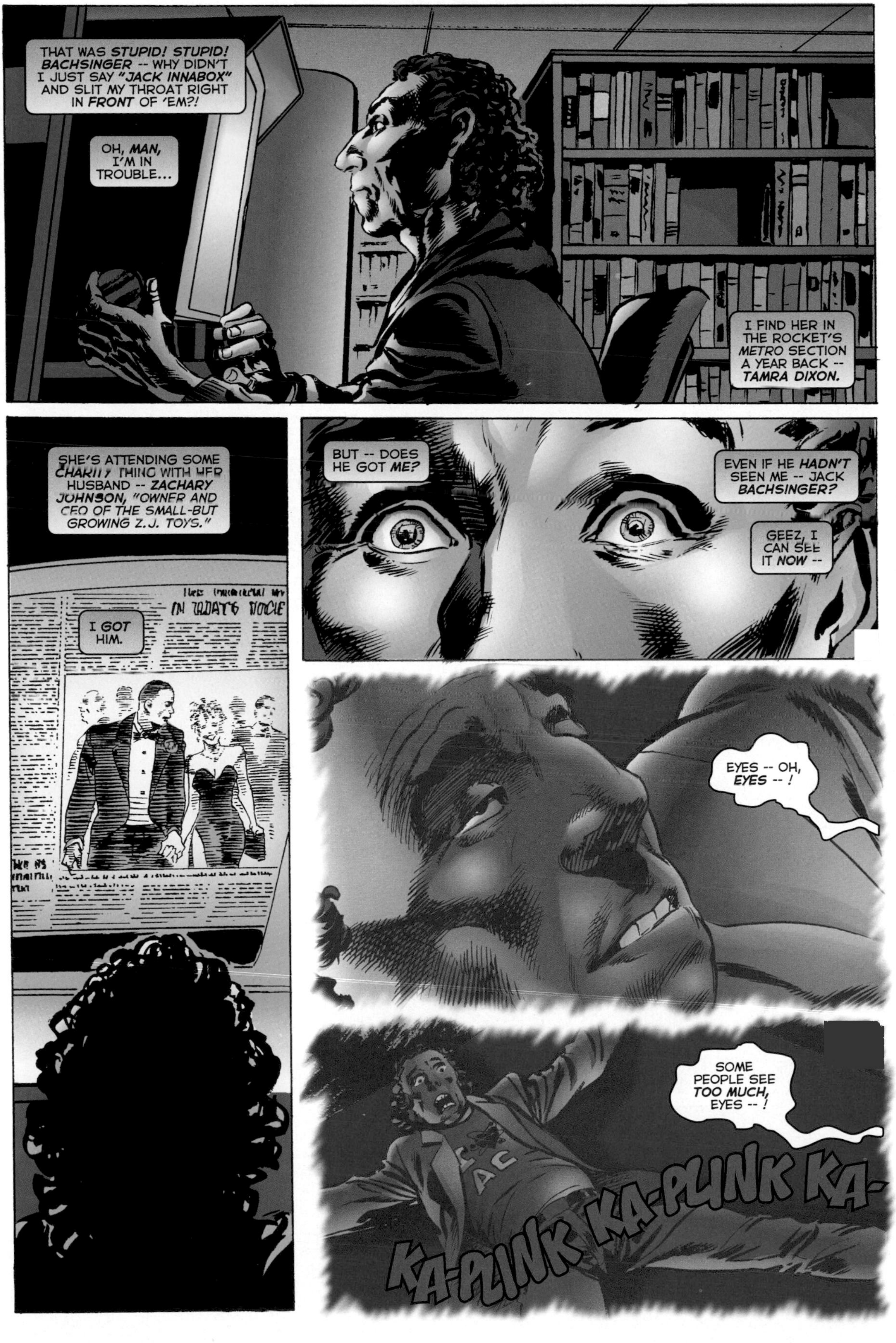

THAT WAS STUPID! STUPID! BACHSINGER -- WHY DIDN'T I JUST SAY "JACK INNABOX" AND SLIT MY THROAT RIGHT IN FRONT OF 'EM?!
OH, MAN, I'M IN TROUBLE...
I FIND HER IN THE ROCKET'S METRO SECTION A YEAR BACK -- TAMRA DIXON.
SHE'S ATTENDING SOME CHARITY THING WITH HER HUSBAND -- ZACHARY JOHNSON, "OWNER AND CEO OF THE SMALL-BUT GROWING Z.J. TOYS."
I GOT HIM.
BUT -- DOES HE GOT ME?
EVEN IF HE HADN'T SEEN ME -- JACK BACHSINGER?
GEEZ, I CAN SEE IT NOW --
EYES -- OH, EYES -- !
SOME PEOPLE SEE TOO MUCH, EYES -- !
KA-PLINK KA-PLINK KA-

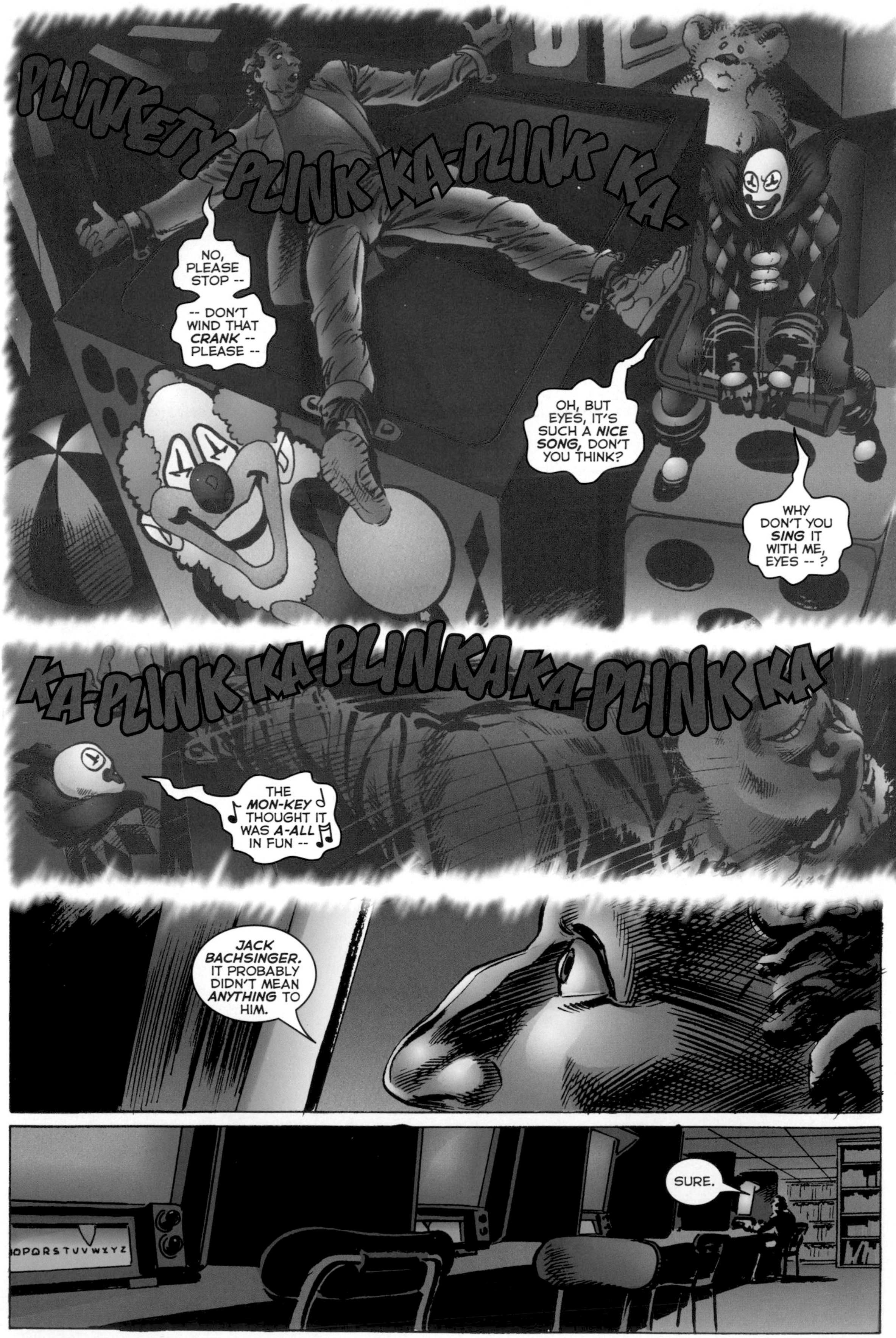
PLINKETTY PLINK KA-PLINK KA-
NO, PLEASE STOP --
-- DON'T WIND THAT CRANK -- PLEASE --
OH, BUT EYES, IT'S SUCH A NICE SONG, DON'T YOU THINK?
WHY DON'T YOU SING IT WITH ME, EYES -- ?
KA-PLINK KA-PLINKA KA-PLINK KA-
THE MON-KEY THOUGHT IT WAS A-ALL IN FUN --
JACK BACHSINGER. IT PROBABLY DIDN'T MEAN ANYTHING TO HIM.
SURE.

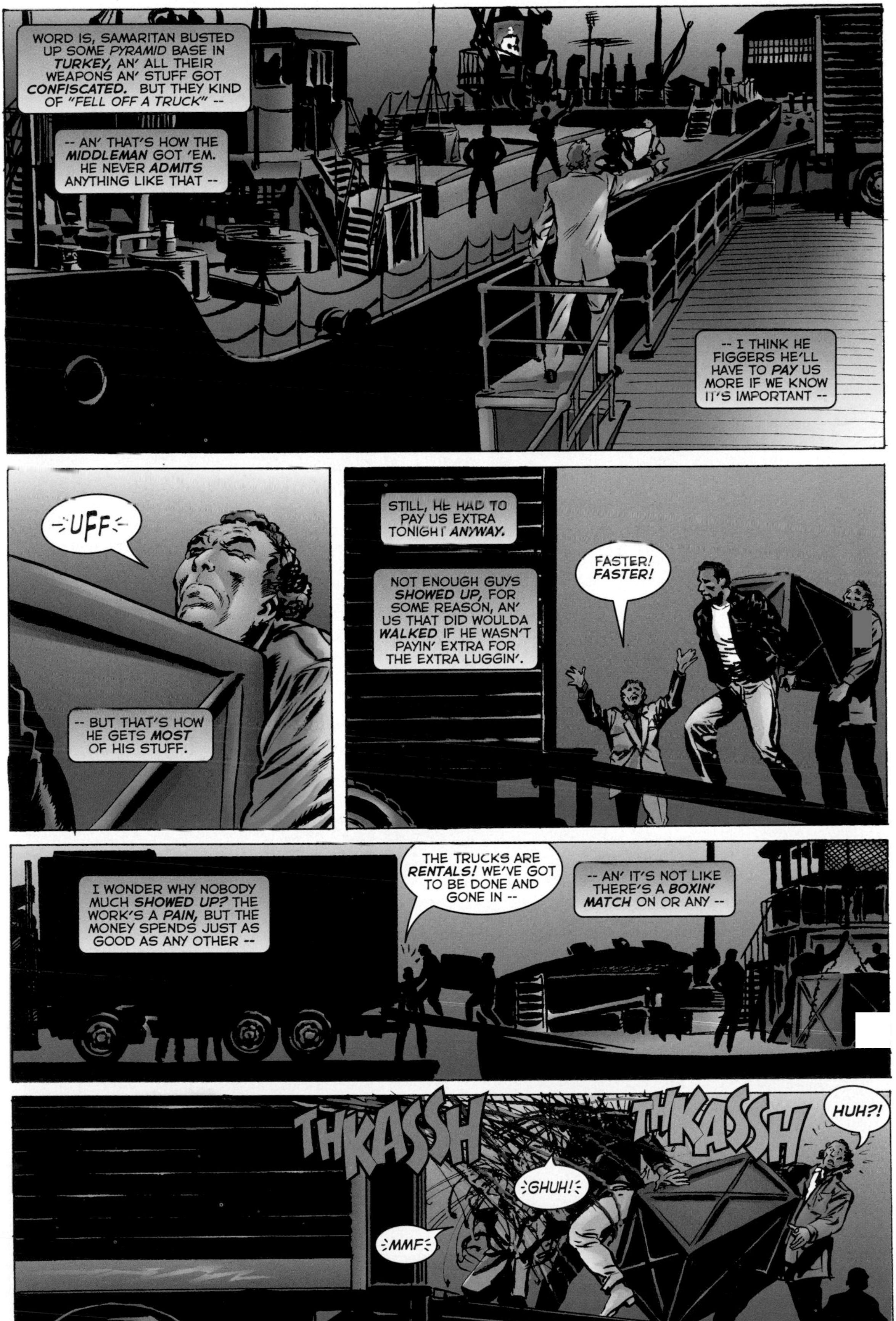
WORD IS, SAMARITAN BUSTED UP SOME *PYRAMID* BASE IN *TURKEY,* AN' ALL THEIR WEAPONS AN' STUFF GOT *CONFISCATED.* BUT THEY KIND OF *"FELL OFF A TRUCK"* --
-- AN' THAT'S HOW THE *MIDDLEMAN* GOT 'EM. HE NEVER *ADMITS* ANYTHING LIKE THAT --
-- I THINK HE FIGGERS HE'LL HAVE TO *PAY* US MORE IF WE KNOW IT'S IMPORTANT --
UFF
-- BUT THAT'S HOW HE GETS *MOST* OF HIS STUFF.
STILL, HE HAD TO PAY US EXTRA TONIGHT *ANYWAY.*
NOT ENOUGH GUYS *SHOWED UP,* FOR SOME REASON, AN' US THAT DID WOULDA *WALKED* IF HE WASN'T PAYIN' EXTRA FOR THE EXTRA LUGGIN'.
FASTER! *FASTER!*
I WONDER WHY NOBODY MUCH *SHOWED UP?* THE WORK'S A *PAIN,* BUT THE MONEY SPENDS JUST AS GOOD AS ANY OTHER --
THE TRUCKS ARE *RENTALS!* WE'VE GOT TO BE DONE AND GONE IN --
-- AN' IT'S NOT LIKE THERE'S A *BOXIN' MATCH* ON OR ANY --
THKASSH
THKASSH
HUH?!
GHUH!
MMF

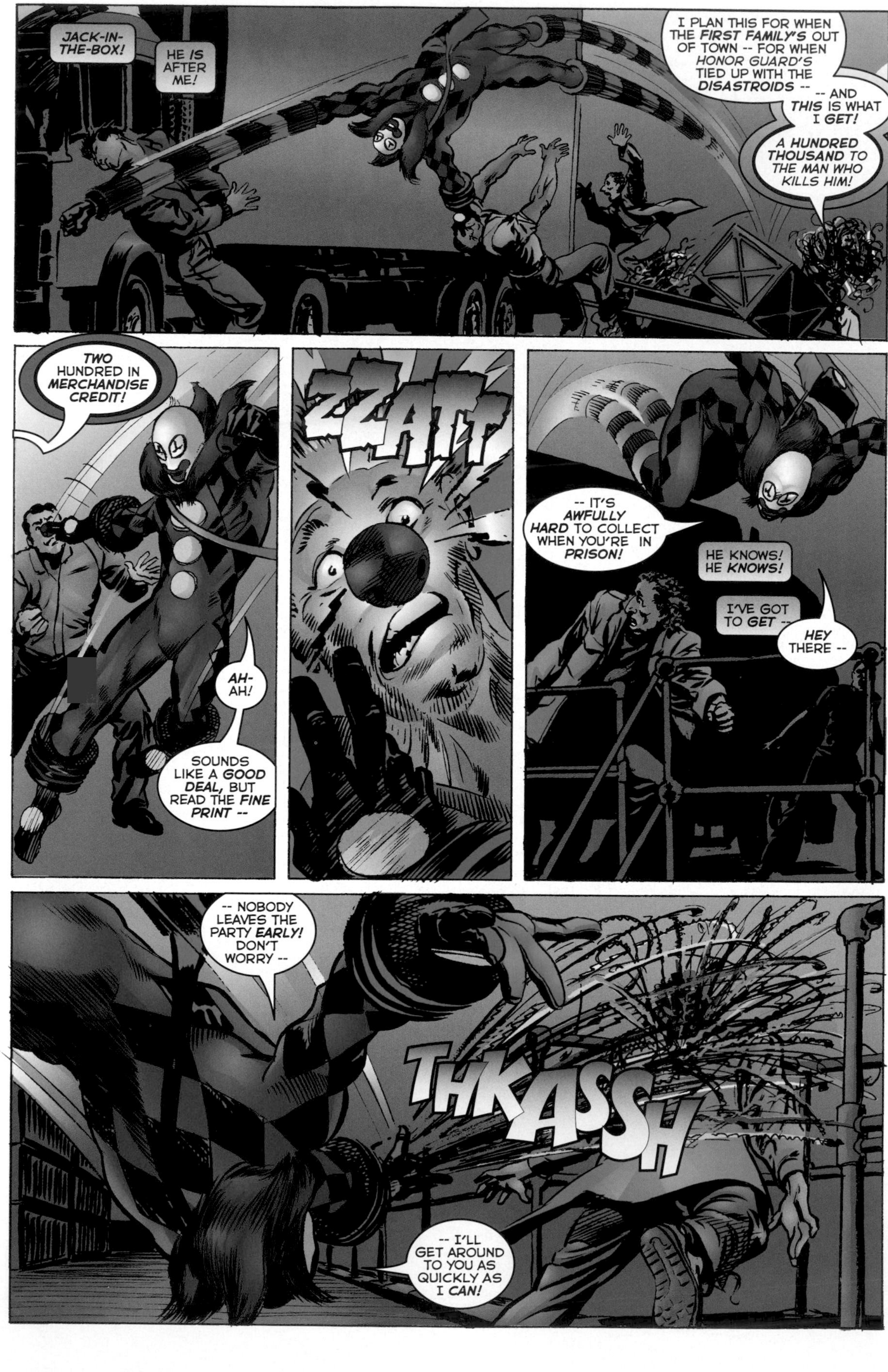
JACK-IN-THE-BOX!
HE IS AFTER ME!
I PLAN THIS FOR WHEN THE FIRST FAMILY'S OUT OF TOWN -- FOR WHEN HONOR GUARD'S TIED UP WITH THE DISASTROIDS --
-- AND THIS IS WHAT I GET!
A HUNDRED THOUSAND TO THE MAN WHO KILLS HIM!
TWO HUNDRED IN MERCHANDISE CREDIT!
AH-AH!
SOUNDS LIKE A GOOD DEAL, BUT READ THE FINE PRINT --
ZZATT
-- IT'S AWFULLY HARD TO COLLECT WHEN YOU'RE IN PRISON!
HE KNOWS! HE KNOWS!
I'VE GOT TO GET --
HEY THERE --
-- NOBODY LEAVES THE PARTY EARLY! DON'T WORRY --
THKASSH
-- I'LL GET AROUND TO YOU AS QUICKLY AS I CAN!

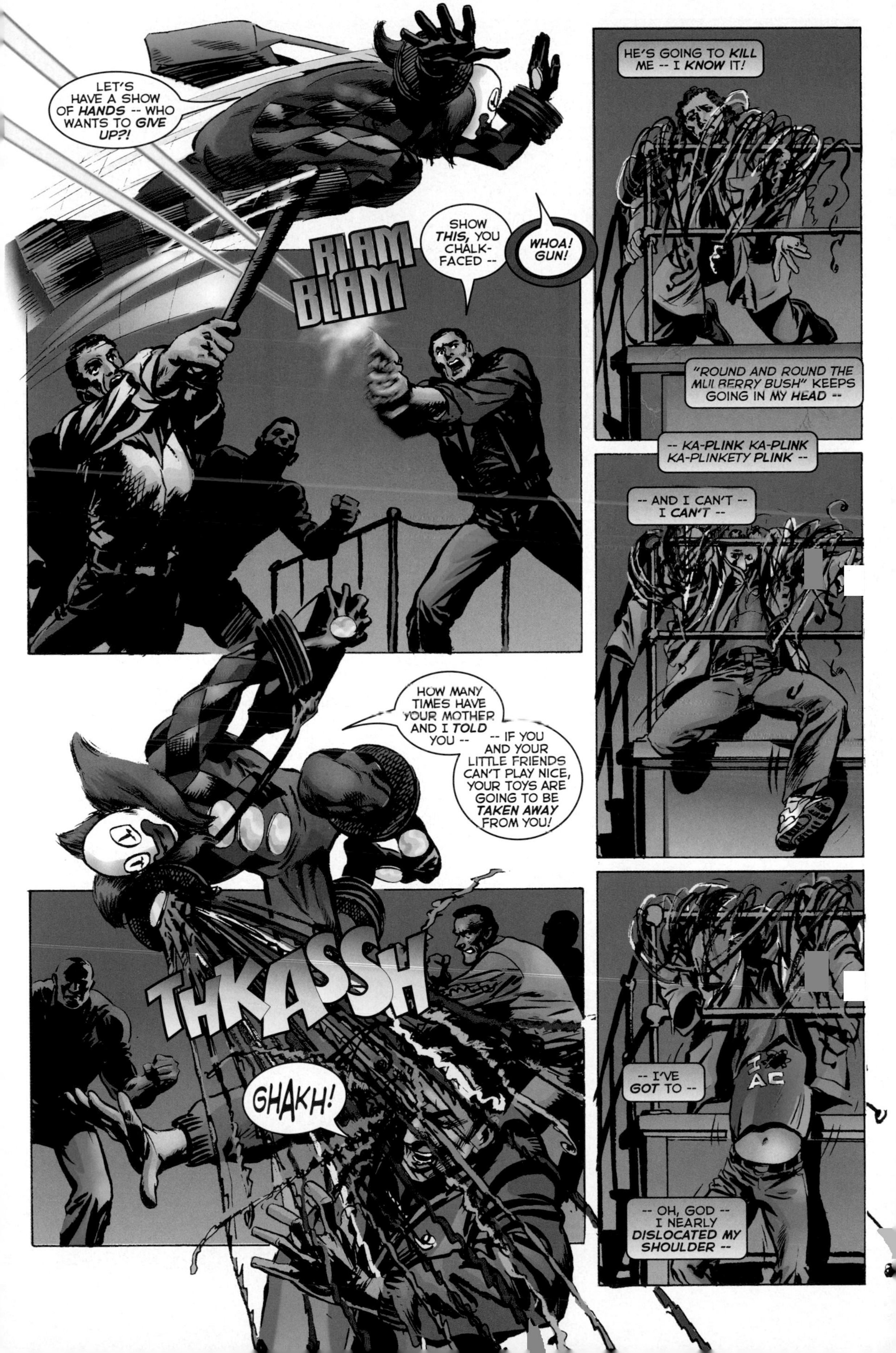

LET'S HAVE A SHOW OF HANDS -- WHO WANTS TO GIVE UP?!
BLAM BLAM
SHOW THIS, YOU CHALK-FACED --
WHOA! GUN!
HE'S GOING TO KILL ME -- I KNOW IT!
"ROUND AND ROUND THE MULBERRY BUSH" KEEPS GOING IN MY HEAD --
-- KA-PLINK KA-PLINK KA-PLINKETY PLINK --
-- AND I CAN'T -- I CAN'T --
HOW MANY TIMES HAVE YOUR MOTHER AND I TOLD YOU --
-- IF YOU AND YOUR LITTLE FRIENDS CAN'T PLAY NICE, YOUR TOYS ARE GOING TO BE TAKEN AWAY FROM YOU!
THKASSH
GHAKH!
-- I'VE GOT TO --
-- OH, GOD -- I NEARLY DISLOCATED MY SHOULDER --

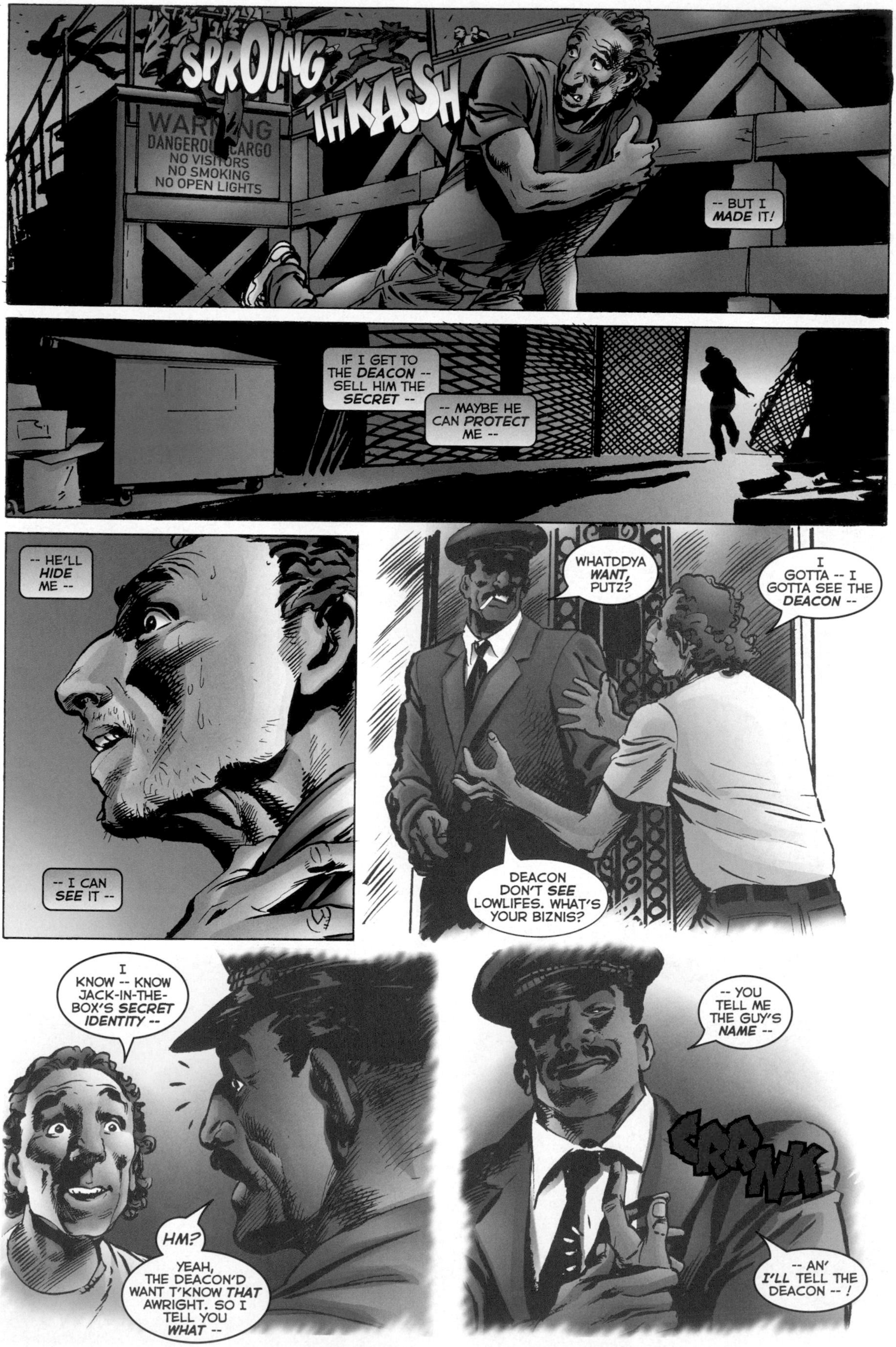
SPROING
THKASSH
WARNING DANGEROUS CARGO NO VISITORS NO SMOKING NO OPEN LIGHTS
-- BUT I MADE IT!
IF I GET TO THE DEACON -- SELL HIM THE SECRET --
-- MAYBE HE CAN PROTECT ME --
-- HE'LL HIDE ME --
-- I CAN SEE IT --
WHATDDYA WANT, PUTZ?
I GOTTA -- I GOTTA SEE THE DEACON --
DEACON DON'T SEE LOWLIFES. WHAT'S YOUR BIZNIS?
I KNOW -- KNOW JACK-IN-THE-BOX'S SECRET IDENTITY --
HM?
YEAH, THE DEACON'D WANT T'KNOW THAT AWRIGHT. SO I TELL YOU WHAT --
-- YOU TELL ME THE GUY'S NAME --
CRRNK
-- AN' I'LL TELL THE DEACON -- !

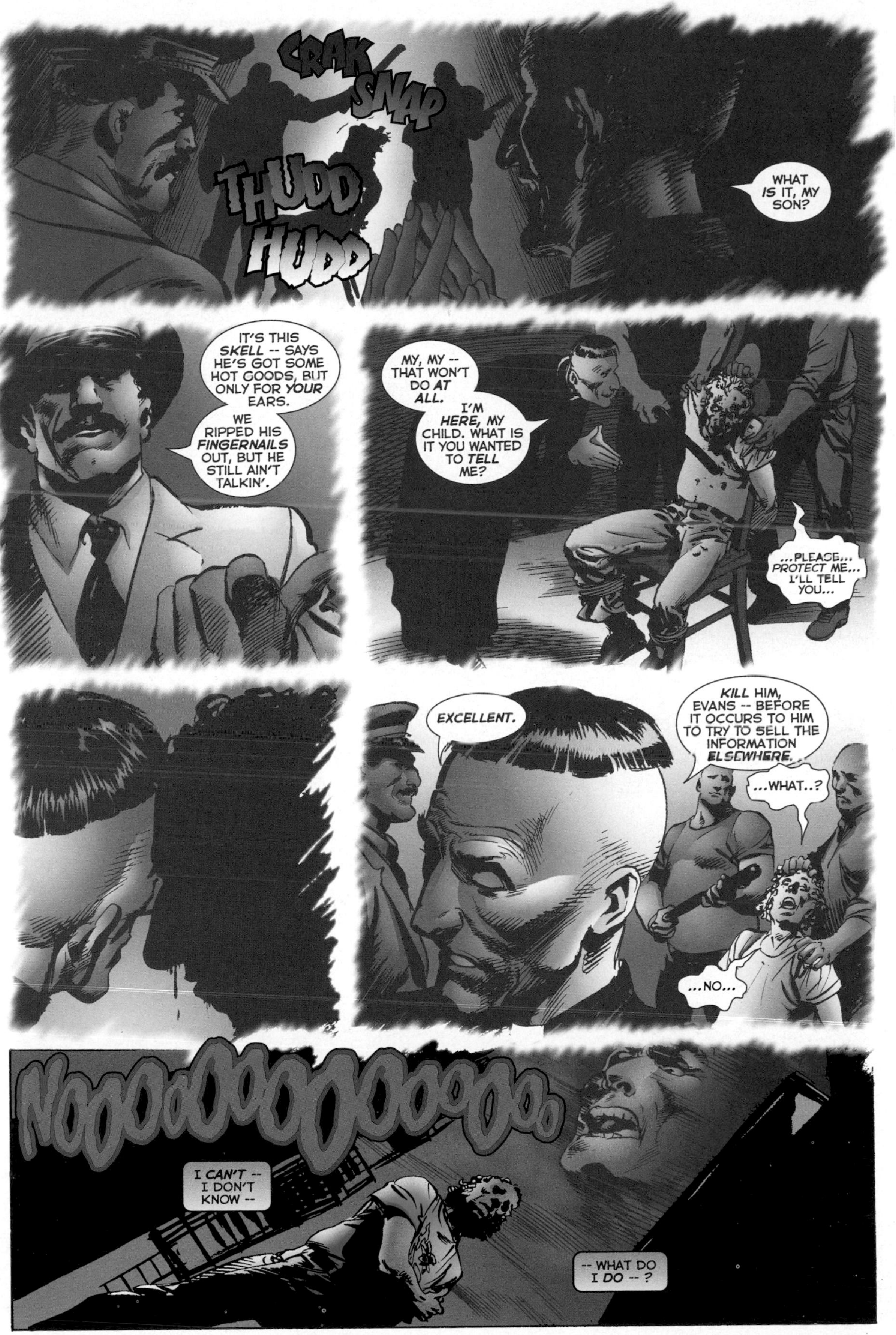
CRAK
SNAP
THUDD
HUDD
WHAT IS IT, MY SON?
IT'S THIS SKELL -- SAYS HE'S GOT SOME HOT GOODS, BUT ONLY FOR YOUR EARS.
WE RIPPED HIS FINGERNAILS OUT, BUT HE STILL AIN'T TALKIN'.
MY, MY -- THAT WON'T DO AT ALL.
I'M HERE, MY CHILD. WHAT IS IT YOU WANTED TO TELL ME?
...PLEASE... PROTECT ME... I'LL TELL YOU...
EXCELLENT.
KILL HIM, EVANS -- BEFORE IT OCCURS TO HIM TO TRY TO SELL THE INFORMATION ELSEWHERE.
...WHAT..?
...NO...
NOOOOOOOOOOOOooo
I CAN'T -- I DON'T KNOW --
-- WHAT DO I DO -- ?

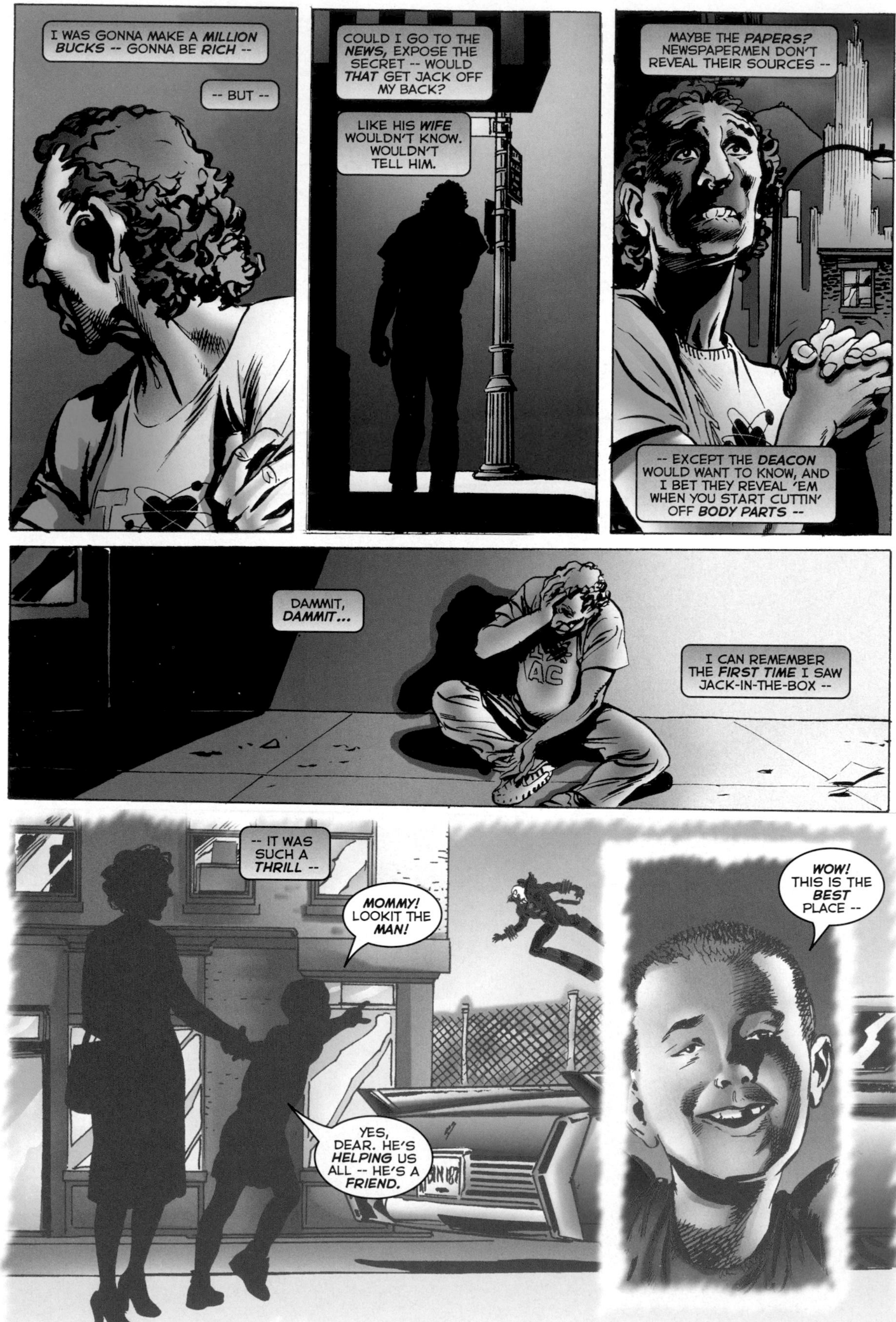
I WAS GONNA MAKE A *MILLION BUCKS* -- GONNA BE *RICH* --
-- BUT --
COULD I GO TO THE *NEWS,* EXPOSE THE SECRET -- WOULD *THAT* GET JACK OFF MY BACK?
LIKE HIS *WIFE* WOULDN'T KNOW. WOULDN'T TELL HIM.
MAYBE THE *PAPERS?* NEWSPAPERMEN DON'T REVEAL THEIR SOURCES --
-- EXCEPT THE *DEACON* WOULD WANT TO KNOW, AND I BET THEY REVEAL 'EM WHEN YOU START CUTTIN' OFF *BODY PARTS* --
DAMMIT, *DAMMIT...*
I CAN REMEMBER THE *FIRST TIME* I SAW JACK-IN-THE-BOX --
-- IT WAS SUCH A *THRILL* --
MOMMY! LOOKIT THE *MAN!*
YES, DEAR. HE'S *HELPING* US ALL -- HE'S A *FRIEND.*
WOW! THIS IS THE *BEST* PLACE --

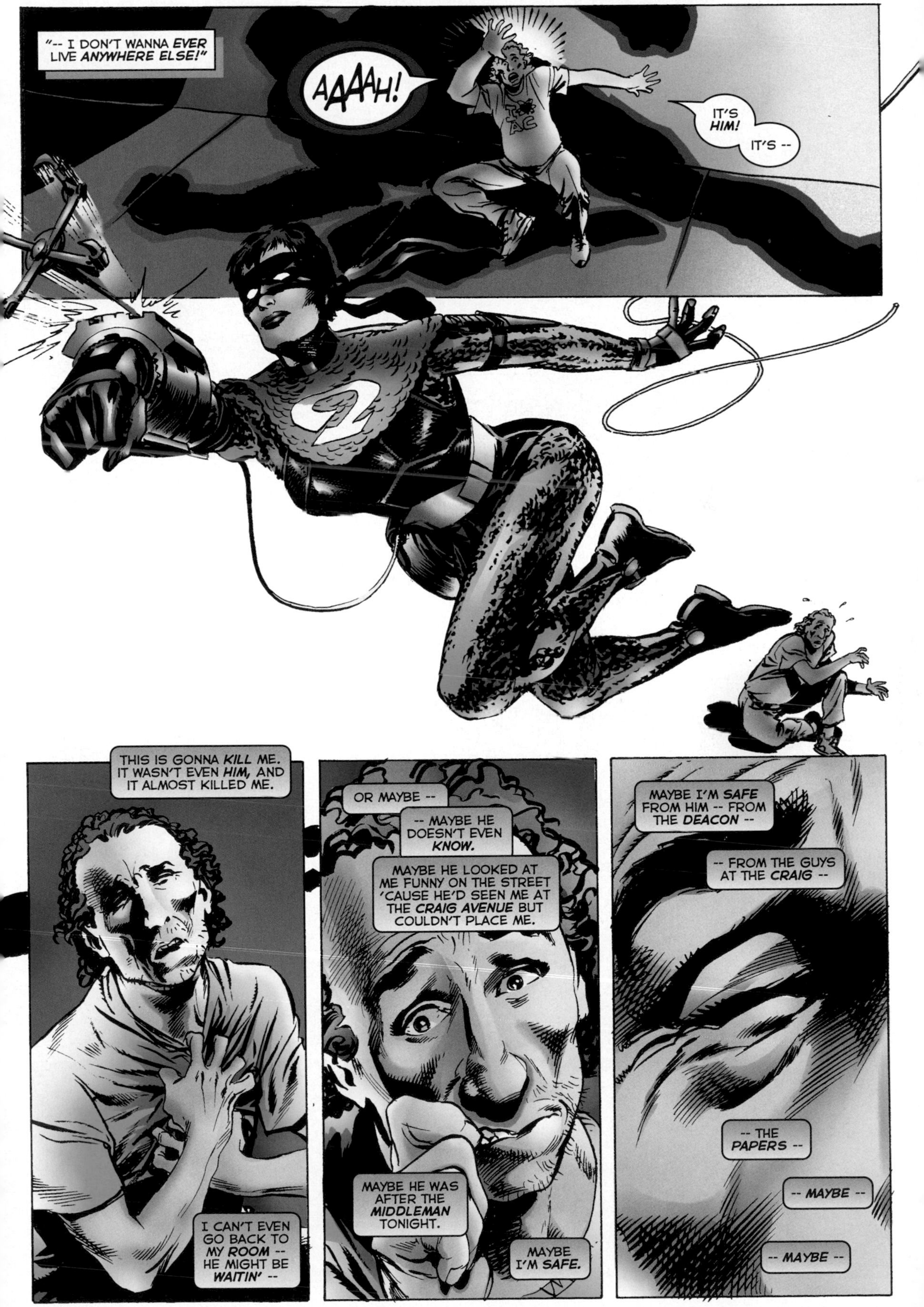
"-- I DON'T WANNA EVER LIVE ANYWHERE ELSE!"
AAAAH!
IT'S HIM!
IT'S --
THIS IS GONNA KILL ME. IT WASN'T EVEN HIM, AND IT ALMOST KILLED ME.
I CAN'T EVEN GO BACK TO MY ROOM -- HE MIGHT BE WAITIN' --
OR MAYBE --
-- MAYBE HE DOESN'T EVEN KNOW.
MAYBE HE LOOKED AT ME FUNNY ON THE STREET 'CAUSE HE'D SEEN ME AT THE CRAIG AVENUE BUT COULDN'T PLACE ME.
MAYBE HE WAS AFTER THE MIDDLEMAN TONIGHT.
MAYBE I'M SAFE.
MAYBE I'M SAFE FROM HIM -- FROM THE DEACON --
-- FROM THE GUYS AT THE CRAIG --
-- THE PAPERS --
-- MAYBE --
-- MAYBE --

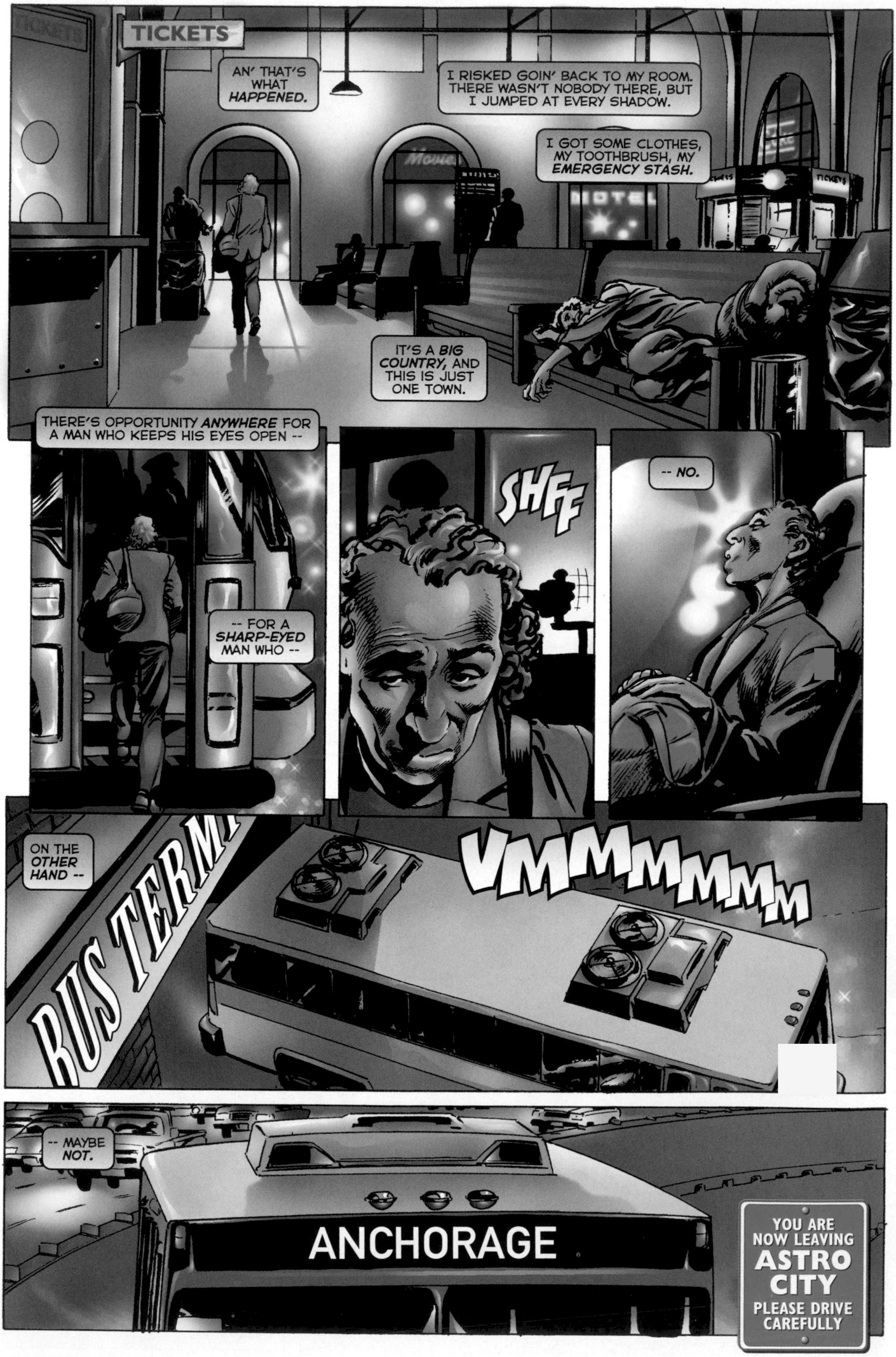
TICKETS
AN' THAT'S WHAT *HAPPENED.*
I RISKED GOIN' BACK TO MY ROOM. THERE WASN'T NOBODY THERE, BUT I JUMPED AT EVERY SHADOW.
I GOT SOME CLOTHES, MY TOOTHBRUSH, MY *EMERGENCY STASH.*
MOTEL
TICKETS
IT'S A *BIG COUNTRY,* AND THIS IS JUST ONE TOWN.
THERE'S OPPORTUNITY *ANYWHERE* FOR A MAN WHO KEEPS HIS EYES OPEN --
-- FOR A *SHARP-EYED* MAN WHO --
SHFF
-- *NO.*
ON THE *OTHER HAND* --
BUS TERM
VMMMMMMM
-- MAYBE *NOT.*
ANCHORAGE
YOU ARE NOW LEAVING ASTRO CITY PLEASE DRIVE CAREFULLY

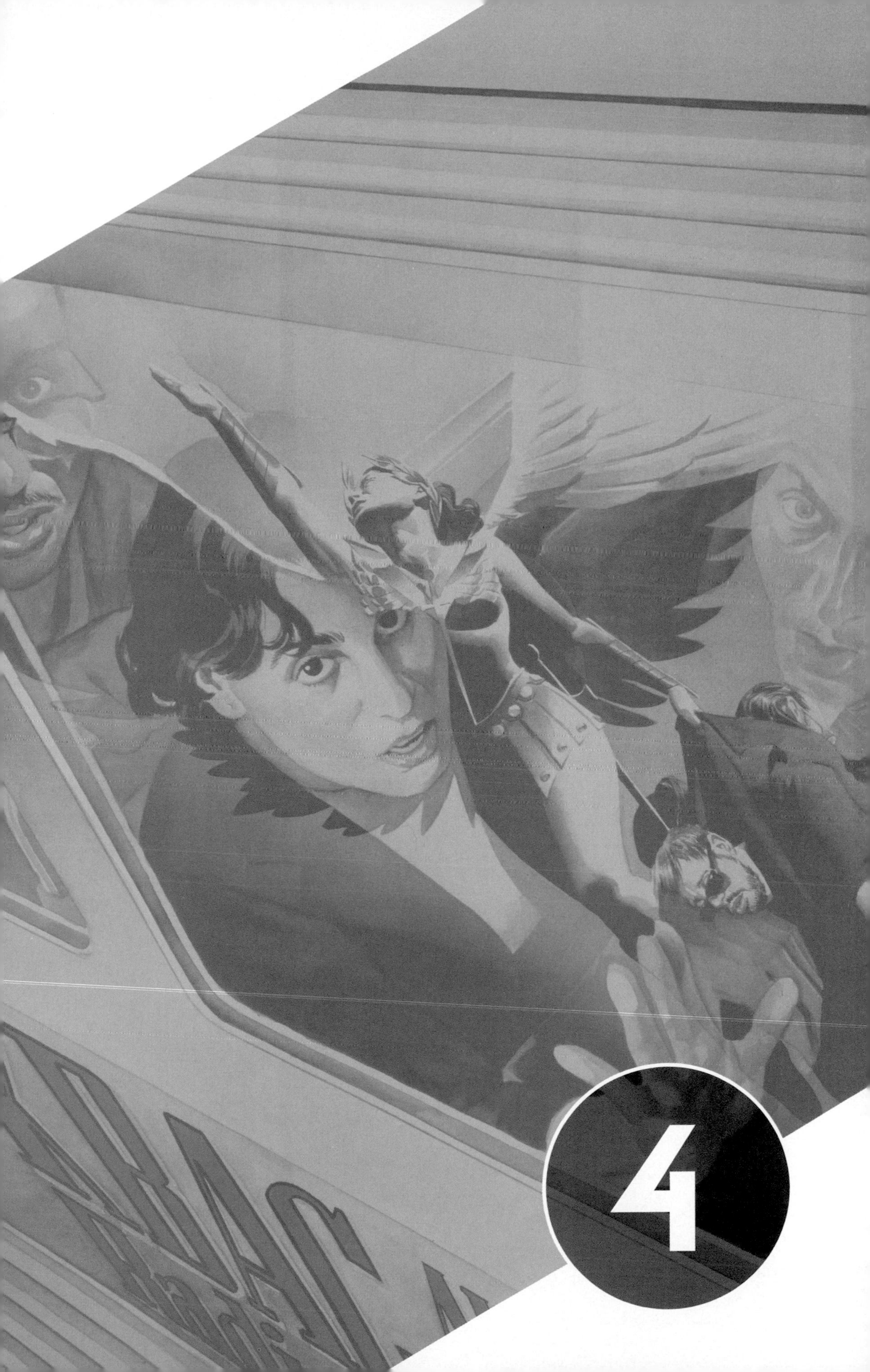

4

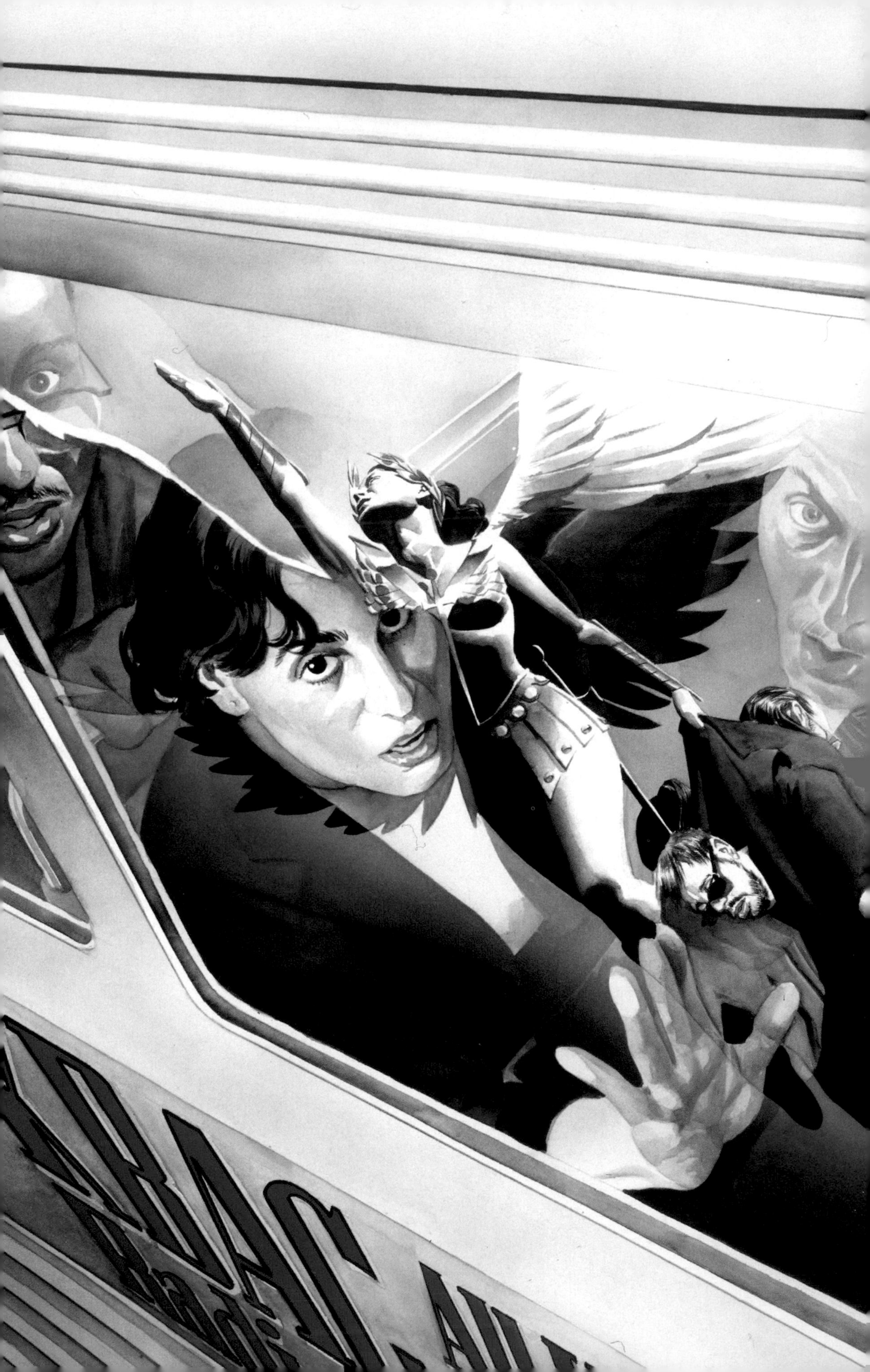

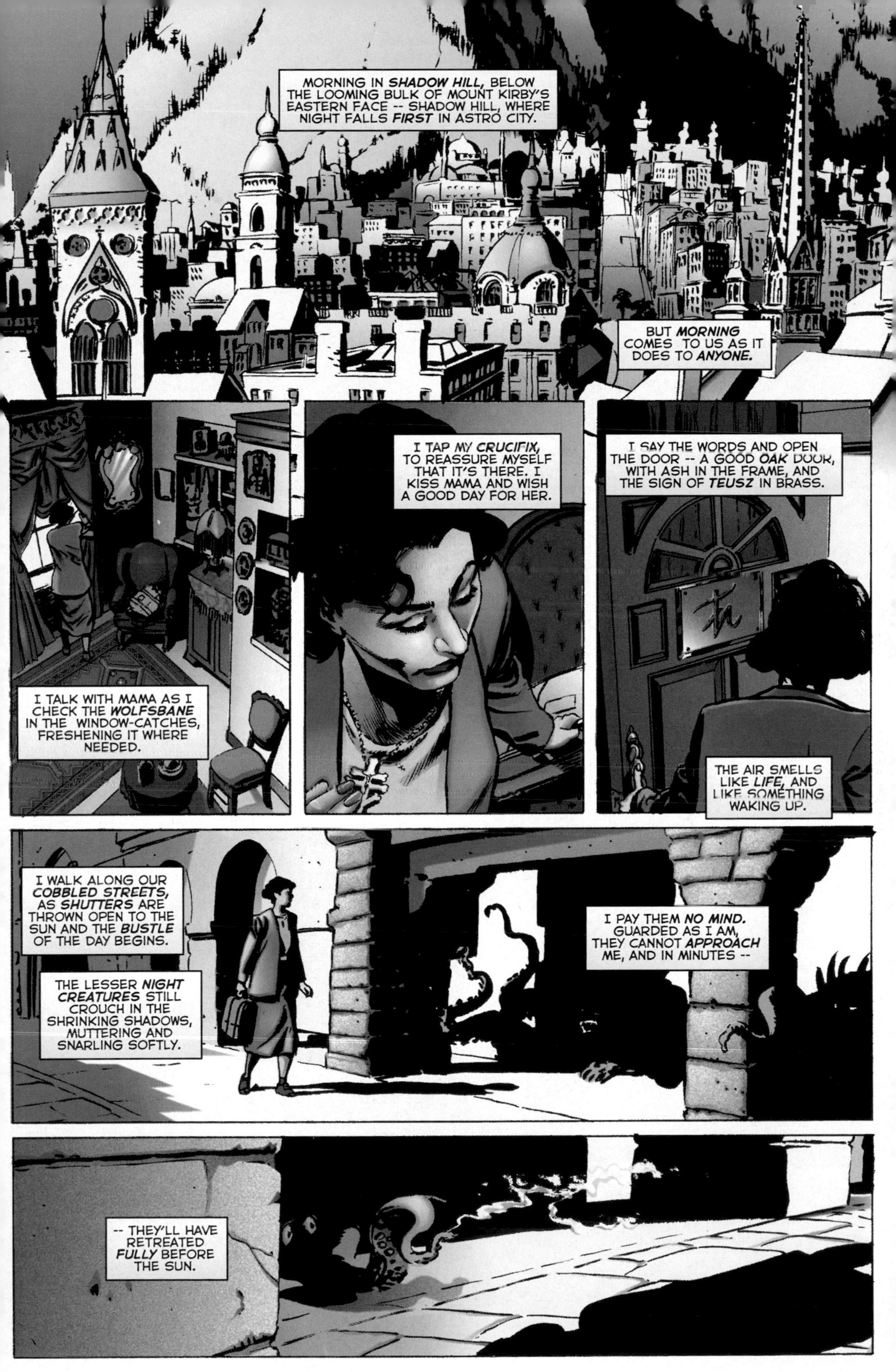
MORNING IN SHADOW HILL, BELOW THE LOOMING BULK OF MOUNT KIRBY'S EASTERN FACE -- SHADOW HILL, WHERE NIGHT FALLS FIRST IN ASTRO CITY.
BUT MORNING COMES TO US AS IT DOES TO ANYONE.
I TALK WITH MAMA AS I CHECK THE WOLFSBANE IN THE WINDOW-CATCHES, FRESHENING IT WHERE NEEDED.
I TAP MY CRUCIFIX, TO REASSURE MYSELF THAT IT'S THERE. I KISS MAMA AND WISH A GOOD DAY FOR HER.
I SAY THE WORDS AND OPEN THE DOOR -- A GOOD OAK DOOR, WITH ASH IN THE FRAME, AND THE SIGN OF TEUSZ IN BRASS.
THE AIR SMELLS LIKE LIFE, AND LIKE SOMETHING WAKING UP.
I WALK ALONG OUR COBBLED STREETS, AS SHUTTERS ARE THROWN OPEN TO THE SUN AND THE BUSTLE OF THE DAY BEGINS.
THE LESSER NIGHT CREATURES STILL CROUCH IN THE SHRINKING SHADOWS, MUTTERING AND SNARLING SOFTLY.
I PAY THEM NO MIND. GUARDED AS I AM, THEY CANNOT APPROACH ME, AND IN MINUTES --
-- THEY'LL HAVE RETREATED FULLY BEFORE THE SUN.

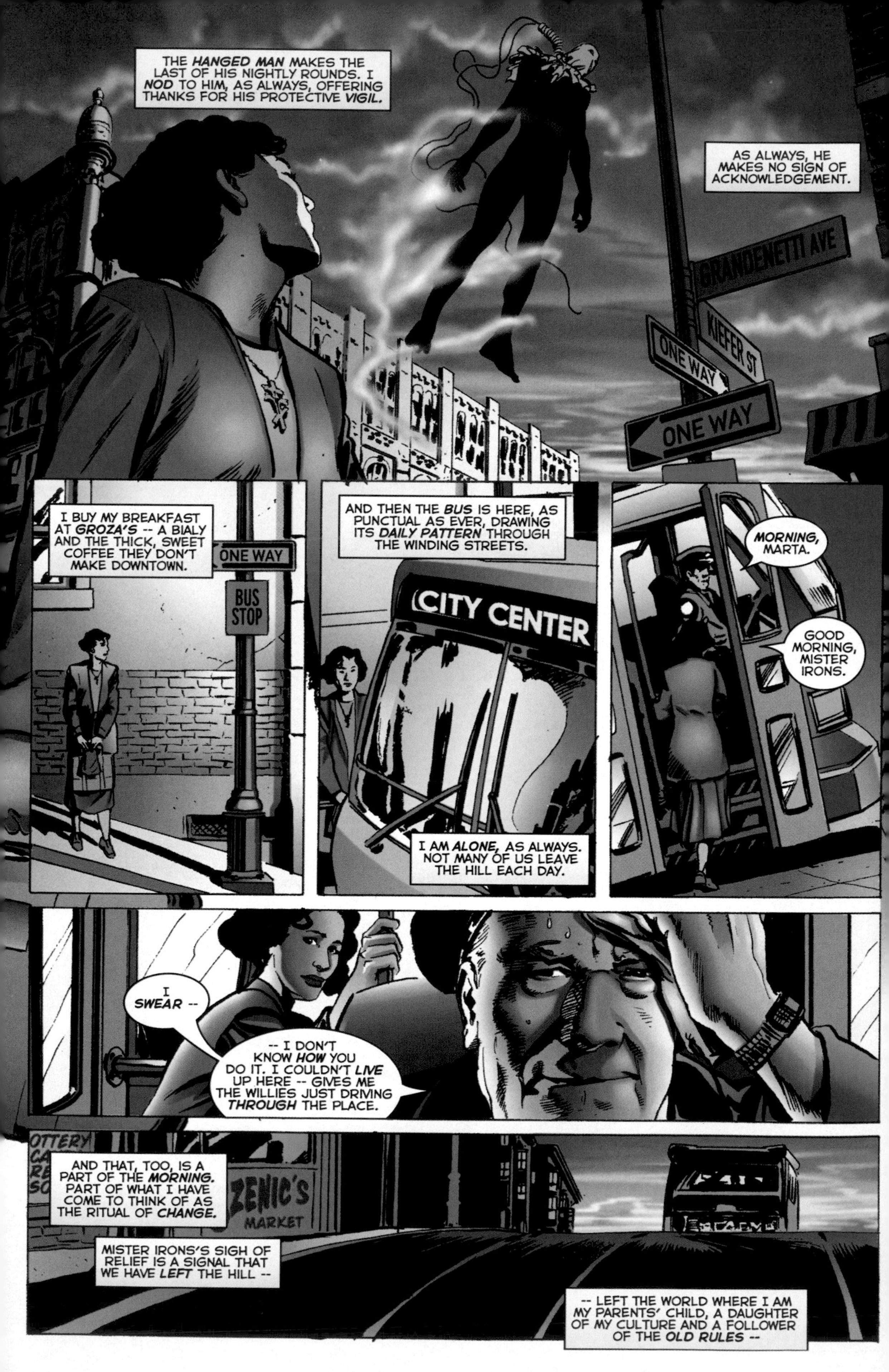
THE HANGED MAN MAKES THE LAST OF HIS NIGHTLY ROUNDS. I NOD TO HIM, AS ALWAYS, OFFERING THANKS FOR HIS PROTECTIVE VIGIL.
AS ALWAYS, HE MAKES NO SIGN OF ACKNOWLEDGEMENT.
GRANDENETTI AVE
KIEFER ST
ONE WAY
ONE WAY
I BUY MY BREAKFAST AT GROZA'S -- A BIALY AND THE THICK, SWEET COFFEE THEY DON'T MAKE DOWNTOWN.
ONE WAY
BUS STOP
AND THEN THE BUS IS HERE, AS PUNCTUAL AS EVER, DRAWING ITS DAILY PATTERN THROUGH THE WINDING STREETS.
CITY CENTER
I AM ALONE, AS ALWAYS. NOT MANY OF US LEAVE THE HILL EACH DAY.
MORNING, MARTA.
GOOD MORNING, MISTER IRONS.
I SWEAR --
-- I DON'T KNOW HOW YOU DO IT. I COULDN'T LIVE UP HERE -- GIVES ME THE WILLIES JUST DRIVING THROUGH THE PLACE.
AND THAT, TOO, IS A PART OF THE MORNING. PART OF WHAT I HAVE COME TO THINK OF AS THE RITUAL OF CHANGE.
ZENIC'S
MARKET
MISTER IRONS'S SIGH OF RELIEF IS A SIGNAL THAT WE HAVE LEFT THE HILL --
-- LEFT THE WORLD WHERE I AM MY PARENTS' CHILD, A DAUGHTER OF MY CULTURE AND A FOLLOWER OF THE OLD RULES --

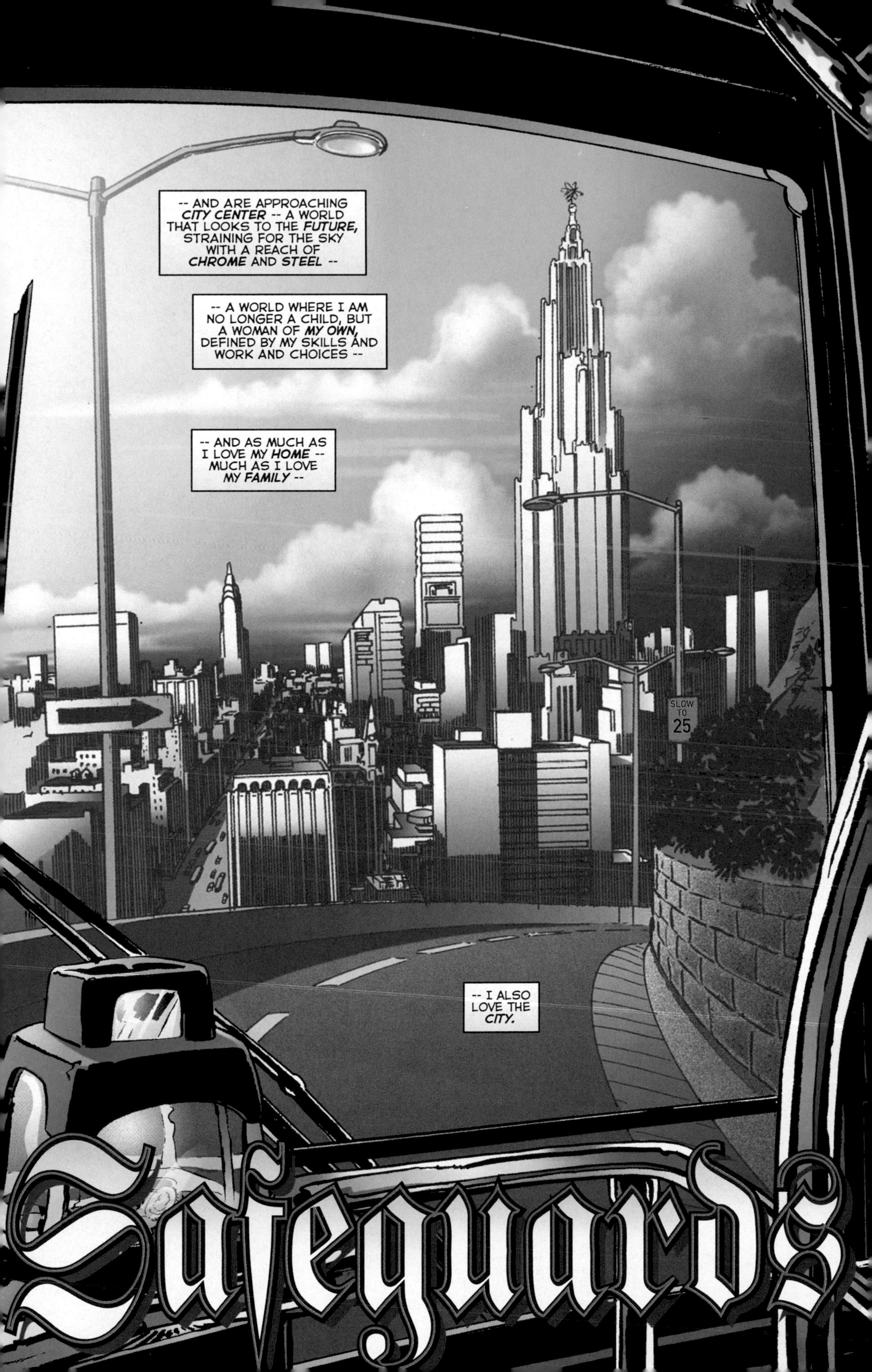
-- AND ARE APPROACHING CITY CENTER -- A WORLD THAT LOOKS TO THE FUTURE, STRAINING FOR THE SKY WITH A REACH OF CHROME AND STEEL --
-- A WORLD WHERE I AM NO LONGER A CHILD, BUT A WOMAN OF MY OWN, DEFINED BY MY SKILLS AND WORK AND CHOICES --
-- AND AS MUCH AS I LOVE MY HOME -- MUCH AS I LOVE MY FAMILY --
SLOW TO 25
-- I ALSO LOVE THE CITY.
Safeguards

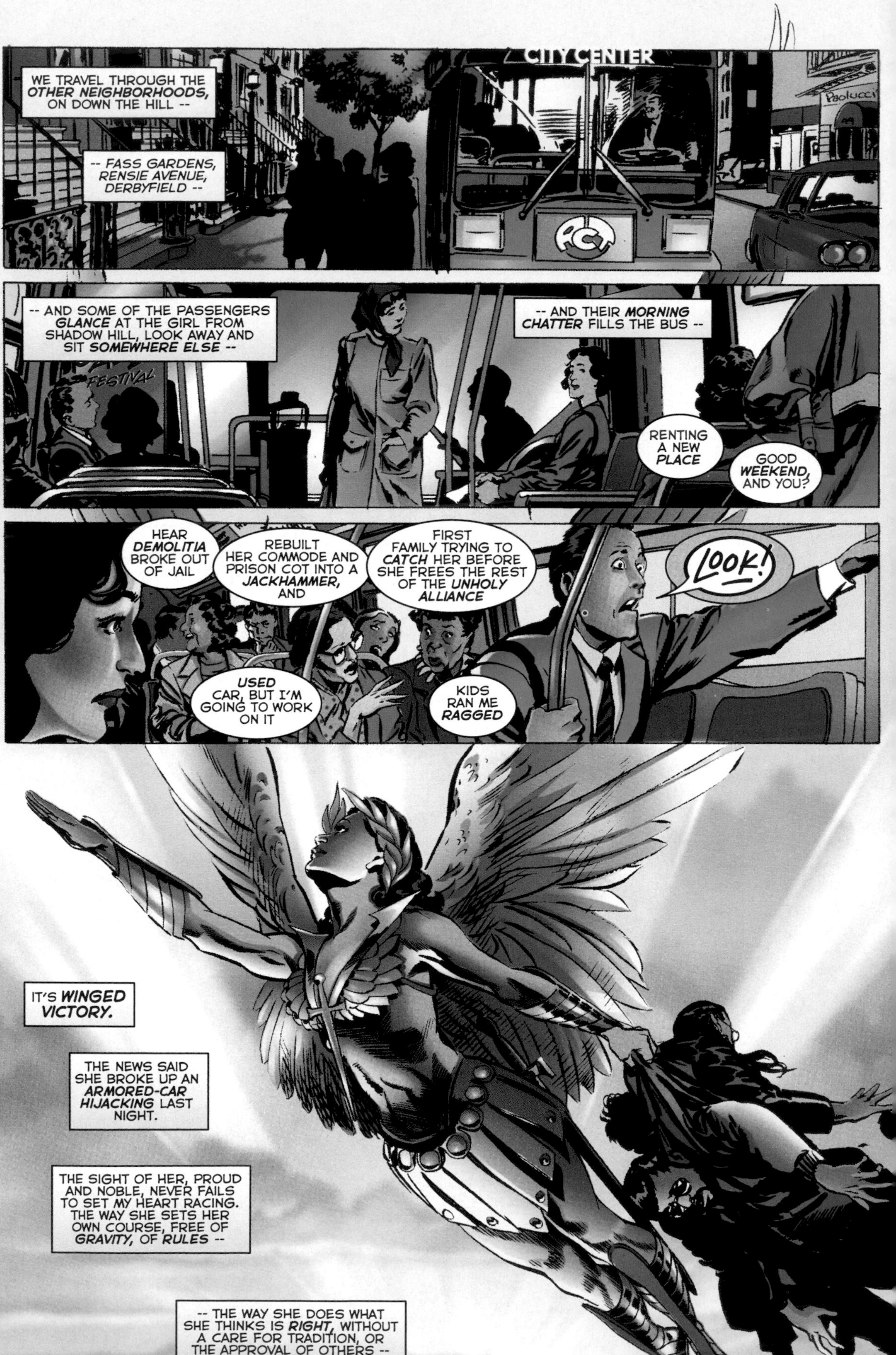
CITY CENTER
Paolucci
WE TRAVEL THROUGH THE OTHER NEIGHBORHOODS, ON DOWN THE HILL --
-- FASS GARDENS, RENSIE AVENUE, DERBYFIELD --
-- AND SOME OF THE PASSENGERS GLANCE AT THE GIRL FROM SHADOW HILL, LOOK AWAY AND SIT SOMEWHERE ELSE --
-- AND THEIR MORNING CHATTER FILLS THE BUS --
FESTIVAL
RENTING A NEW PLACE
GOOD WEEKEND, AND YOU?
HEAR DEMOLITIA BROKE OUT OF JAIL
REBUILT HER COMMODE AND PRISON COT INTO A JACKHAMMER, AND
FIRST FAMILY TRYING TO CATCH HER BEFORE SHE FREES THE REST OF THE UNHOLY ALLIANCE
LOOK!
USED CAR, BUT I'M GOING TO WORK ON IT
KIDS RAN ME RAGGED
IT'S WINGED VICTORY.
THE NEWS SAID SHE BROKE UP AN ARMORED-CAR HIJACKING LAST NIGHT.
THE SIGHT OF HER, PROUD AND NOBLE, NEVER FAILS TO SET MY HEART RACING. THE WAY SHE SETS HER OWN COURSE, FREE OF GRAVITY, OF RULES --
-- THE WAY SHE DOES WHAT SHE THINKS IS RIGHT, WITHOUT A CARE FOR TRADITION, OR THE APPROVAL OF OTHERS --

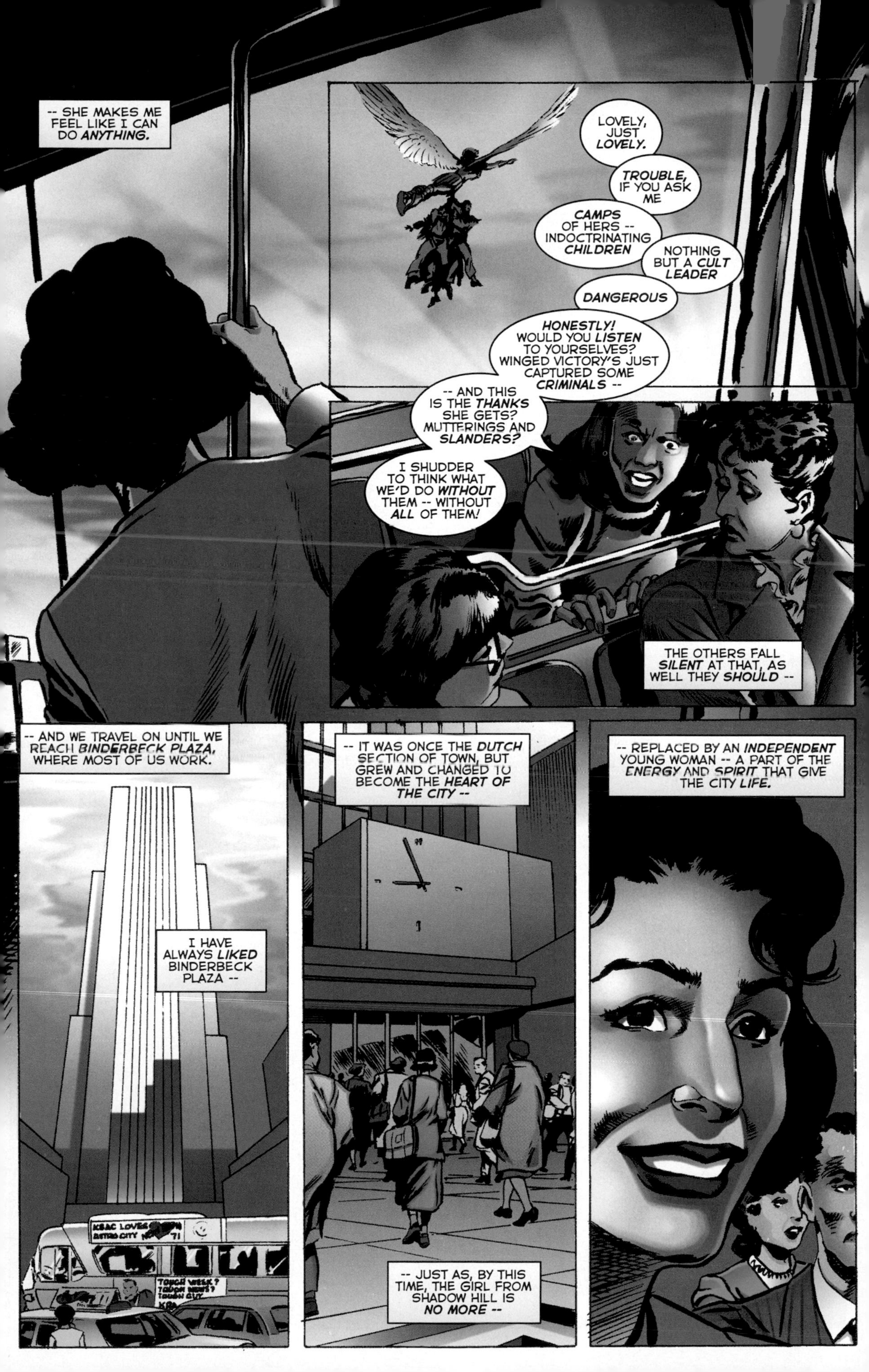
-- SHE MAKES ME FEEL LIKE I CAN DO ANYTHING.
LOVELY, JUST LOVELY.
TROUBLE, IF YOU ASK ME
CAMPS OF HERS -- INDOCTRINATING CHILDREN
NOTHING BUT A CULT LEADER
DANGEROUS
HONESTLY! WOULD YOU LISTEN TO YOURSELVES? WINGED VICTORY'S JUST CAPTURED SOME CRIMINALS --
-- AND THIS IS THE THANKS SHE GETS? MUTTERINGS AND SLANDERS?
I SHUDDER TO THINK WHAT WE'D DO WITHOUT THEM -- WITHOUT ALL OF THEM!
THE OTHERS FALL SILENT AT THAT, AS WELL THEY SHOULD --
-- AND WE TRAVEL ON UNTIL WE REACH BINDERBECK PLAZA, WHERE MOST OF US WORK.
I HAVE ALWAYS LIKED BINDERBECK PLAZA --
-- IT WAS ONCE THE DUTCH SECTION OF TOWN, BUT GREW AND CHANGED TO BECOME THE HEART OF THE CITY --
-- JUST AS, BY THIS TIME, THE GIRL FROM SHADOW HILL IS NO MORE --
-- REPLACED BY AN INDEPENDENT YOUNG WOMAN -- A PART OF THE ENERGY AND SPIRIT THAT GIVE THE CITY LIFE.

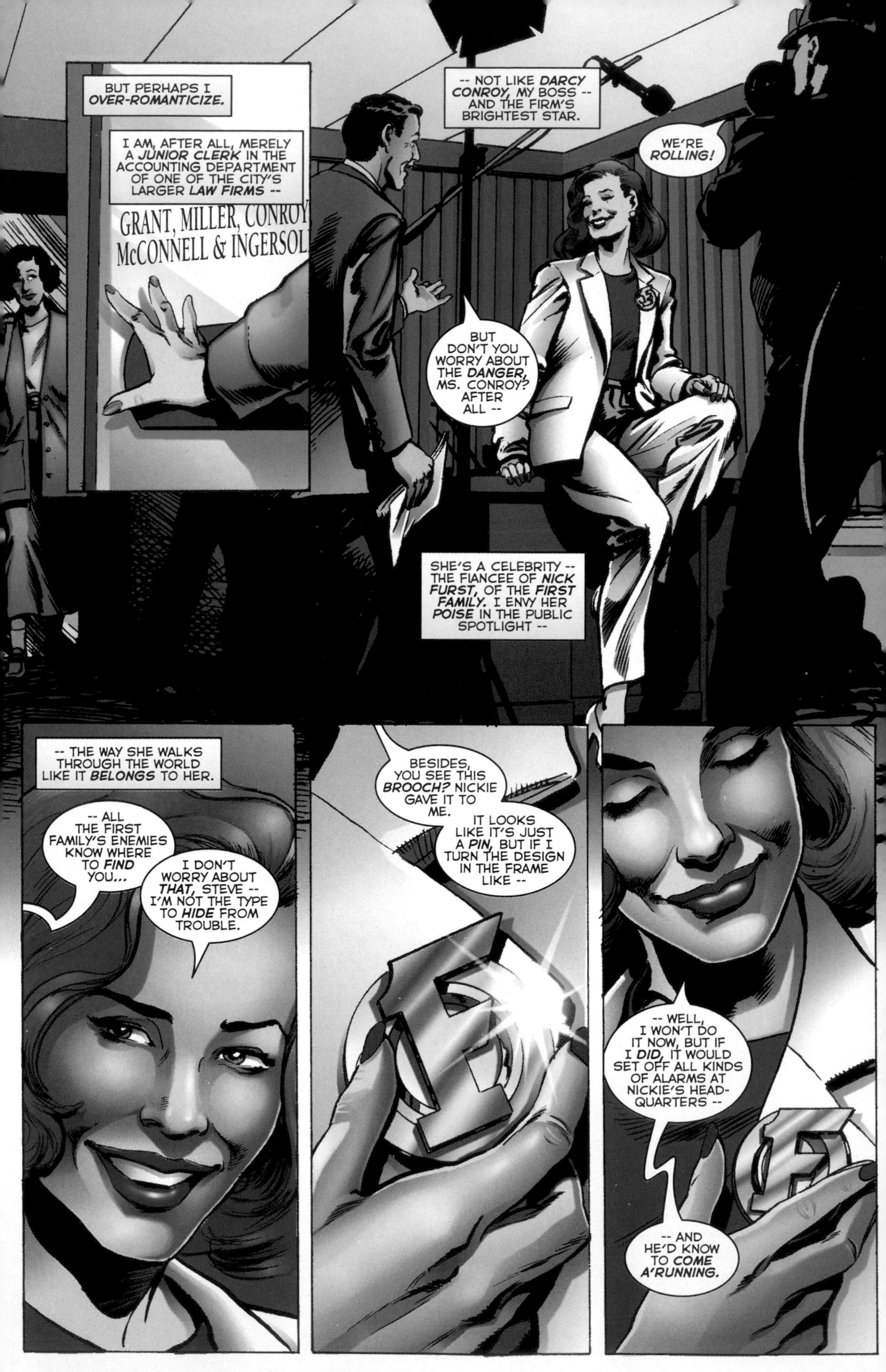

BUT PERHAPS I OVER-ROMANTICIZE.
I AM, AFTER ALL, MERELY A JUNIOR CLERK IN THE ACCOUNTING DEPARTMENT OF ONE OF THE CITY'S LARGER LAW FIRMS --
GRANT, MILLER, CONROY McCONNELL & INGERSOL
-- NOT LIKE DARCY CONROY, MY BOSS -- AND THE FIRM'S BRIGHTEST STAR.
WE'RE ROLLING!
BUT DON'T YOU WORRY ABOUT THE DANGER, MS. CONROY? AFTER ALL --
SHE'S A CELEBRITY -- THE FIANCEE OF NICK FURST, OF THE FIRST FAMILY. I ENVY HER POISE IN THE PUBLIC SPOTLIGHT --
-- THE WAY SHE WALKS THROUGH THE WORLD LIKE IT BELONGS TO HER.
-- ALL THE FIRST FAMILY'S ENEMIES KNOW WHERE TO FIND YOU...
I DON'T WORRY ABOUT THAT, STEVE -- I'M NOT THE TYPE TO HIDE FROM TROUBLE.
BESIDES, YOU SEE THIS BROOCH? NICKIE GAVE IT TO ME.
IT LOOKS LIKE IT'S JUST A PIN, BUT IF I TURN THE DESIGN IN THE FRAME LIKE --
-- WELL, I WON'T DO IT NOW, BUT IF I DID, IT WOULD SET OFF ALL KINDS OF ALARMS AT NICKIE'S HEAD-QUARTERS --
-- AND HE'D KNOW TO COME A'RUNNING.

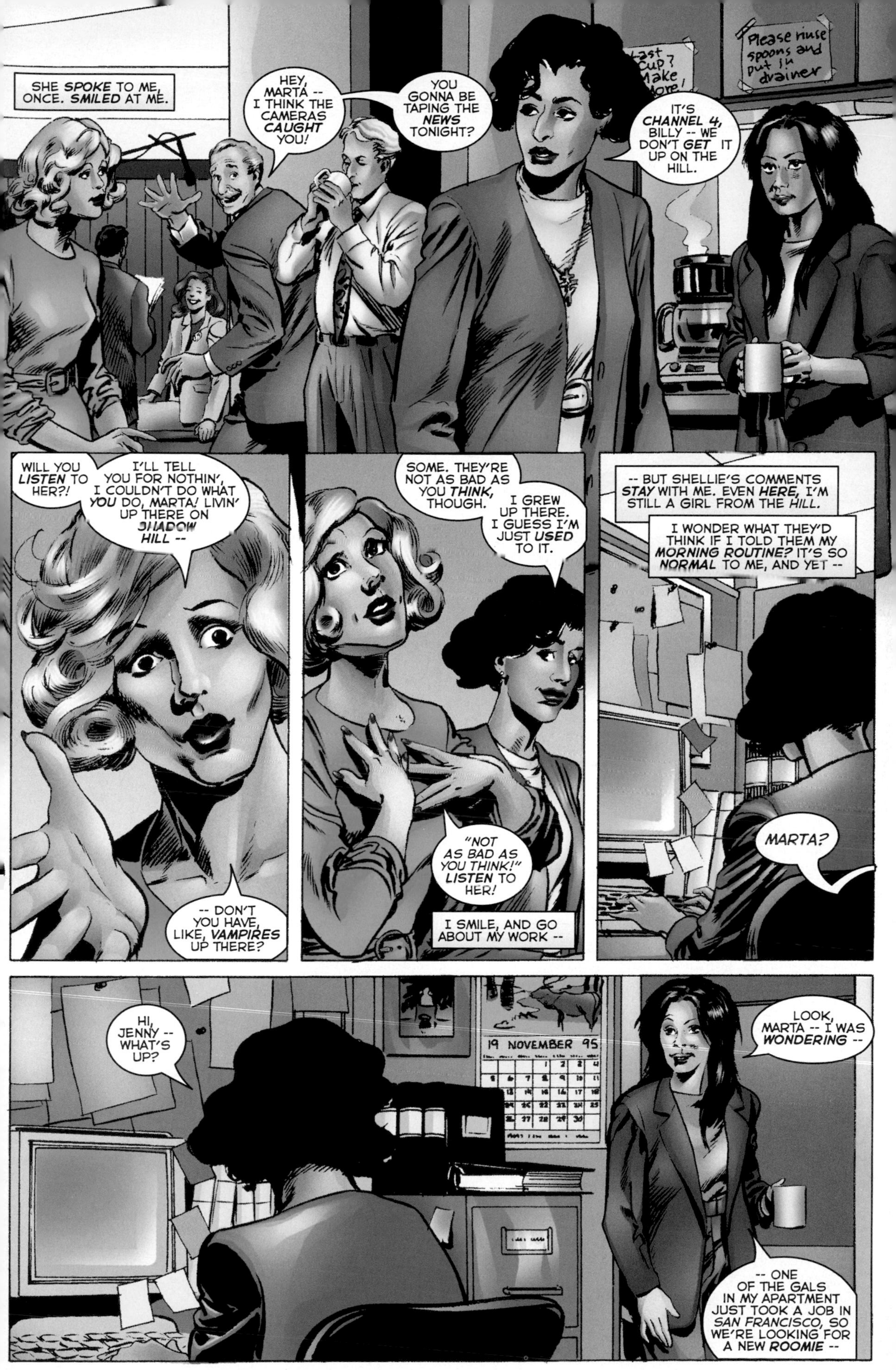
SHE SPOKE TO ME, ONCE. SMILED AT ME.
HEY, MARTA -- I THINK THE CAMERAS CAUGHT YOU!
YOU GONNA BE TAPING THE NEWS TONIGHT?
Please rinse spoons and put in drainer
CHANNEL 4, BILLY -- WE DON'T GET IT UP ON THE HILL.
WILL YOU LISTEN TO HER?!
I'LL TELL YOU FOR NOTHIN', I COULDN'T DO WHAT YOU DO, MARTA! LIVIN' UP THERE ON SHADOW HILL --
-- DON'T YOU HAVE, LIKE, VAMPIRES UP THERE?
SOME. THEY'RE NOT AS BAD AS YOU THINK, THOUGH.
I GREW UP THERE. I GUESS I'M JUST USED TO IT.
"NOT AS BAD AS YOU THINK!" LISTEN TO HER!
I SMILE, AND GO ABOUT MY WORK --
-- BUT SHELLIE'S COMMENTS STAY WITH ME. EVEN HERE, I'M STILL A GIRL FROM THE HILL.
I WONDER WHAT THEY'D THINK IF I TOLD THEM MY MORNING ROUTINE? IT'S SO NORMAL TO ME, AND YET --
MARTA?
HI, JENNY -- WHAT'S UP?
19 NOVEMBER 95
LOOK, MARTA -- I WAS WONDERING --
-- ONE OF THE GALS IN MY APARTMENT JUST TOOK A JOB IN SAN FRANCISCO, SO WE'RE LOOKING FOR A NEW ROOMIE --

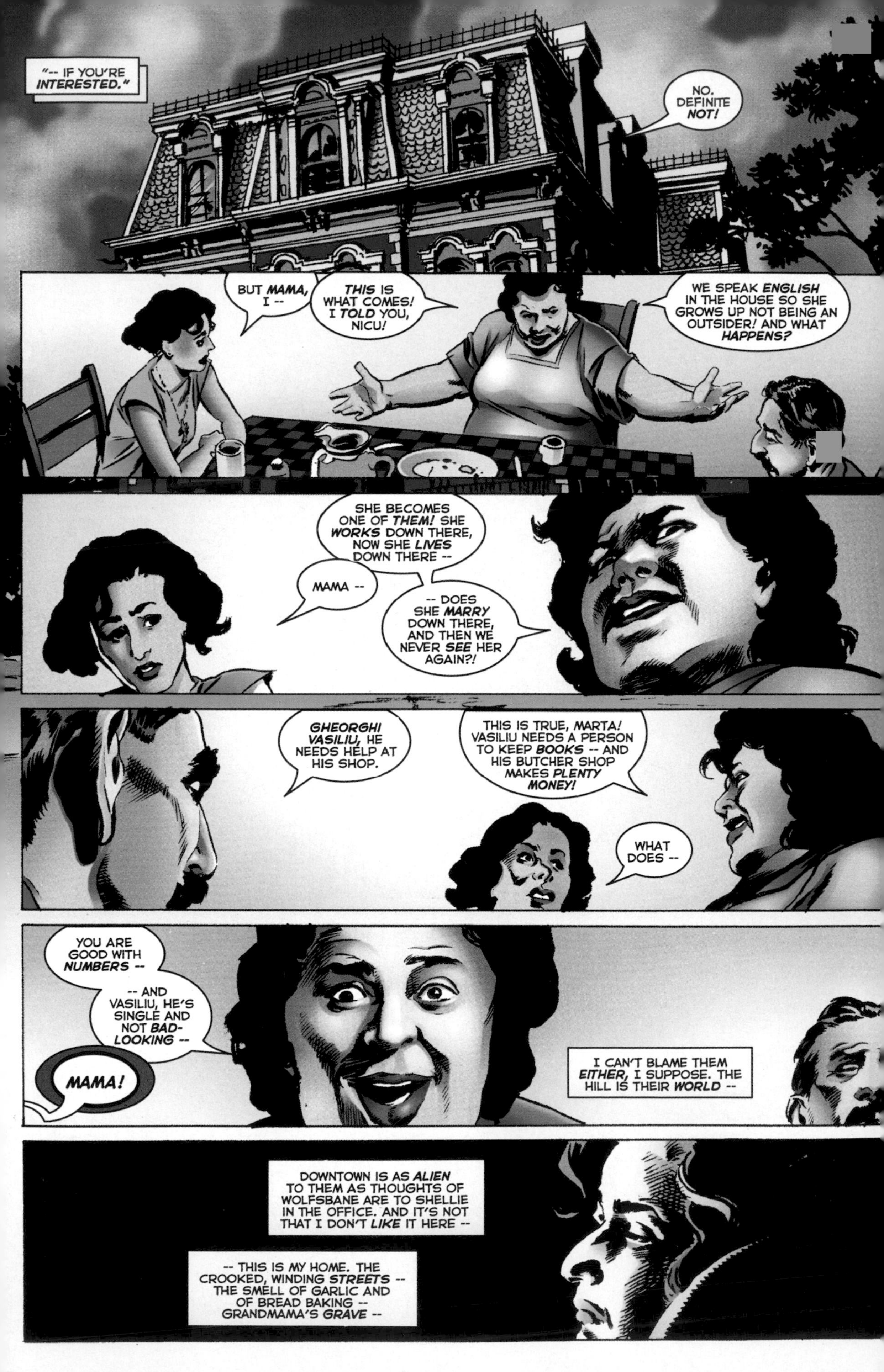
"-- IF YOU'RE INTERESTED."
NO. DEFINITE NOT!
BUT MAMA, I --
THIS IS WHAT COMES! I TOLD YOU, NICU!
WE SPEAK ENGLISH IN THE HOUSE SO SHE GROWS UP NOT BEING AN OUTSIDER! AND WHAT HAPPENS?
SHE BECOMES ONE OF THEM! SHE WORKS DOWN THERE, NOW SHE LIVES DOWN THERE --
MAMA --
-- DOES SHE MARRY DOWN THERE, AND THEN WE NEVER SEE HER AGAIN?!
GHEORGHI VASILIU, HE NEEDS HELP AT HIS SHOP.
THIS IS TRUE, MARTA! VASILIU NEEDS A PERSON TO KEEP BOOKS -- AND HIS BUTCHER SHOP MAKES PLENTY MONEY!
WHAT DOES --
YOU ARE GOOD WITH NUMBERS --
-- AND VASILIU, HE'S SINGLE AND NOT BAD-LOOKING --
MAMA!
I CAN'T BLAME THEM EITHER, I SUPPOSE. THE HILL IS THEIR WORLD --
DOWNTOWN IS AS ALIEN TO THEM AS THOUGHTS OF WOLFSBANE ARE TO SHELLIE IN THE OFFICE. AND IT'S NOT THAT I DON'T LIKE IT HERE --
-- THIS IS MY HOME. THE CROOKED, WINDING STREETS -- THE SMELL OF GARLIC AND OF BREAD BAKING -- GRANDMAMA'S GRAVE --

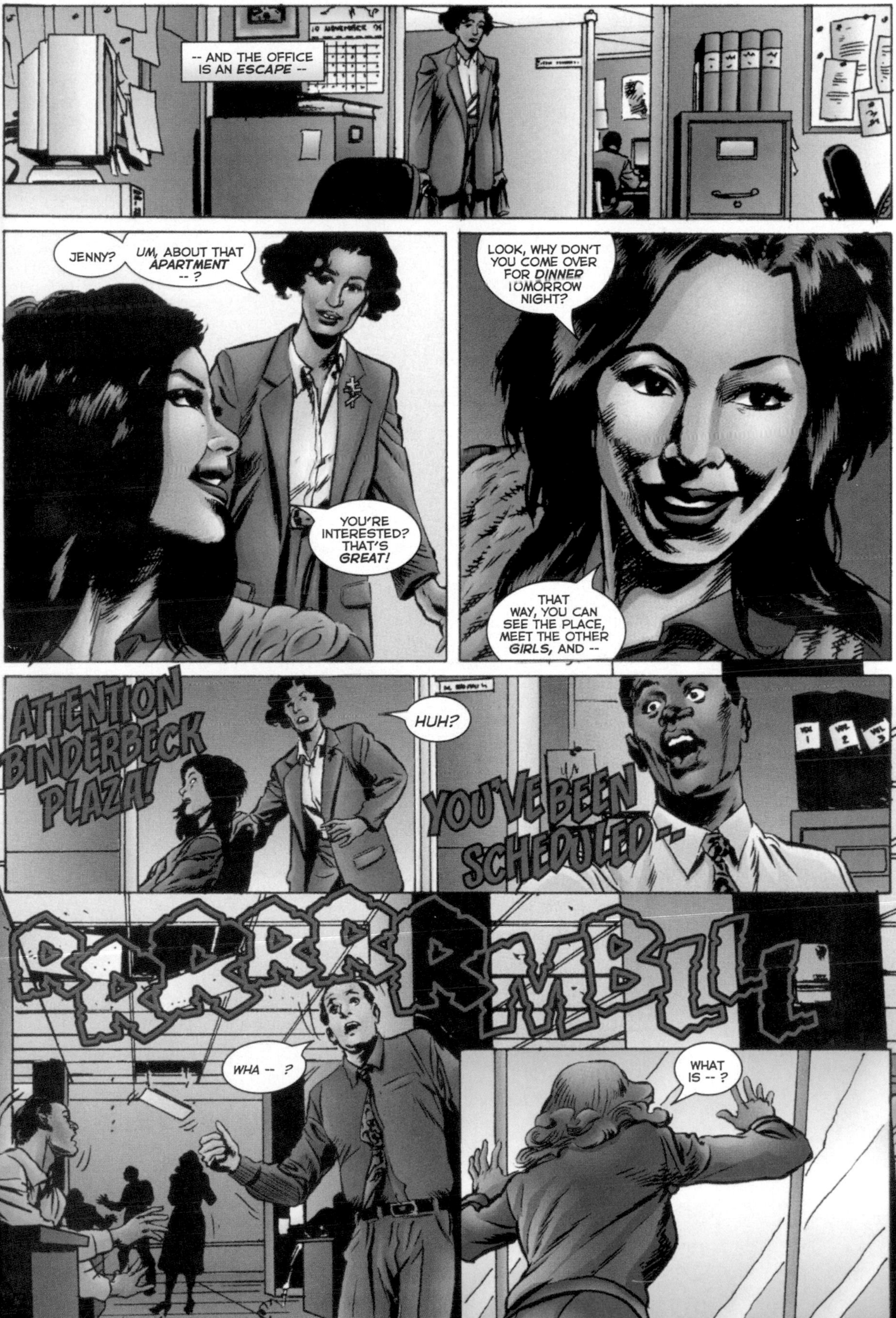

-- AND THE OFFICE IS AN ESCAPE --
JENNY?
UM, ABOUT THAT APARTMENT -- ?
YOU'RE INTERESTED? THAT'S GREAT!
LOOK, WHY DON'T YOU COME OVER FOR DINNER TOMORROW NIGHT?
THAT WAY, YOU CAN SEE THE PLACE, MEET THE OTHER GIRLS, AND --
ATTENTION BINDERBECK PLAZA!
HUH?
YOU'VE BEEN SCHEDULED --
WHA -- ?
WHAT IS -- ?

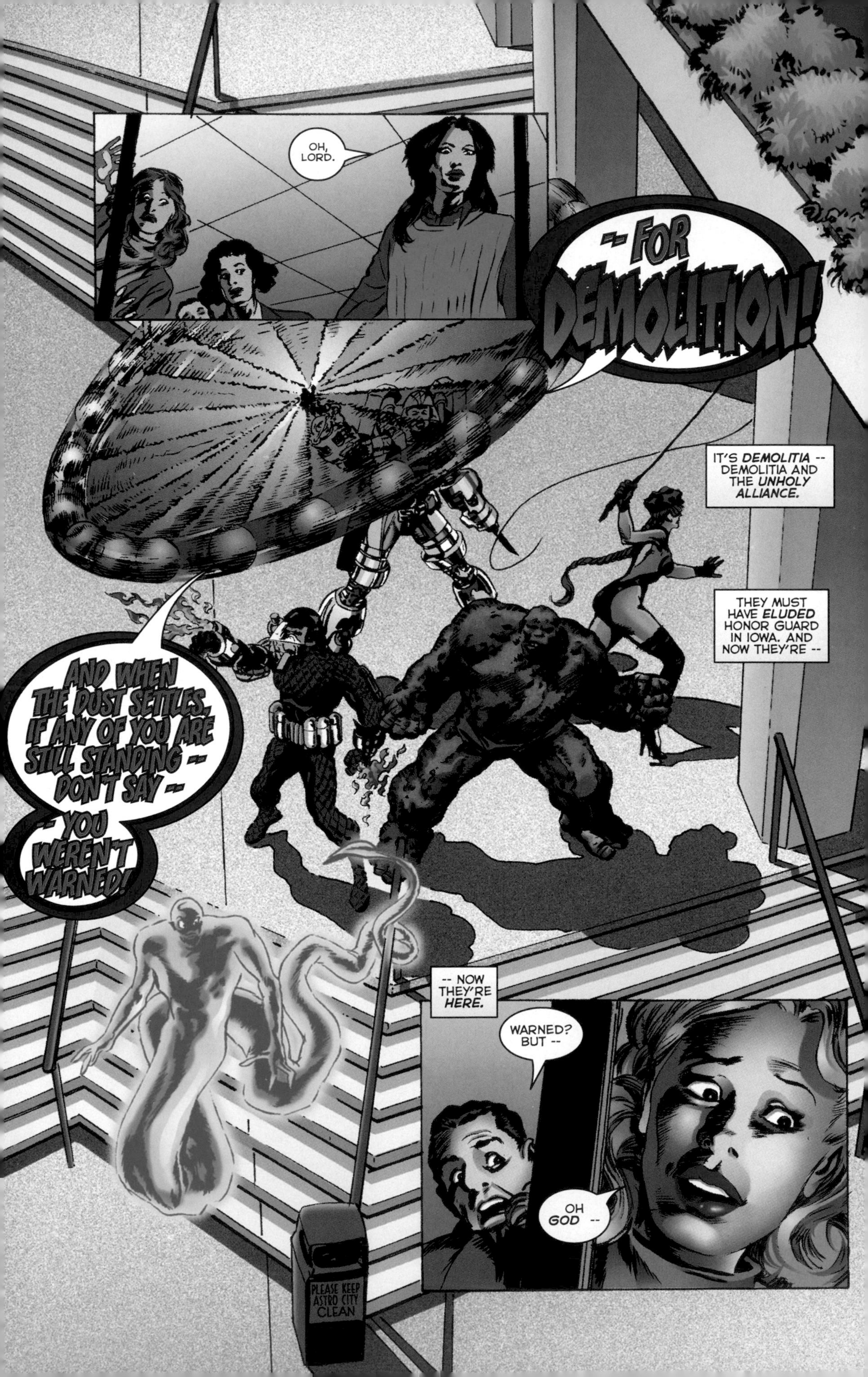
OH, LORD.
-- FOR DEMOLITION!
IT'S DEMOLITIA -- DEMOLITIA AND THE UNHOLY ALLIANCE.
THEY MUST HAVE ELUDED HONOR GUARD IN IOWA. AND NOW THEY'RE --
AND WHEN THE DUST SETTLES, IF ANY OF YOU ARE STILL STANDING -- DON'T SAY --
-- YOU WEREN'T WARNED!
-- NOW THEY'RE HERE.
WARNED? BUT --
OH GOD --
PLEASE KEEP ASTRO CITY CLEAN

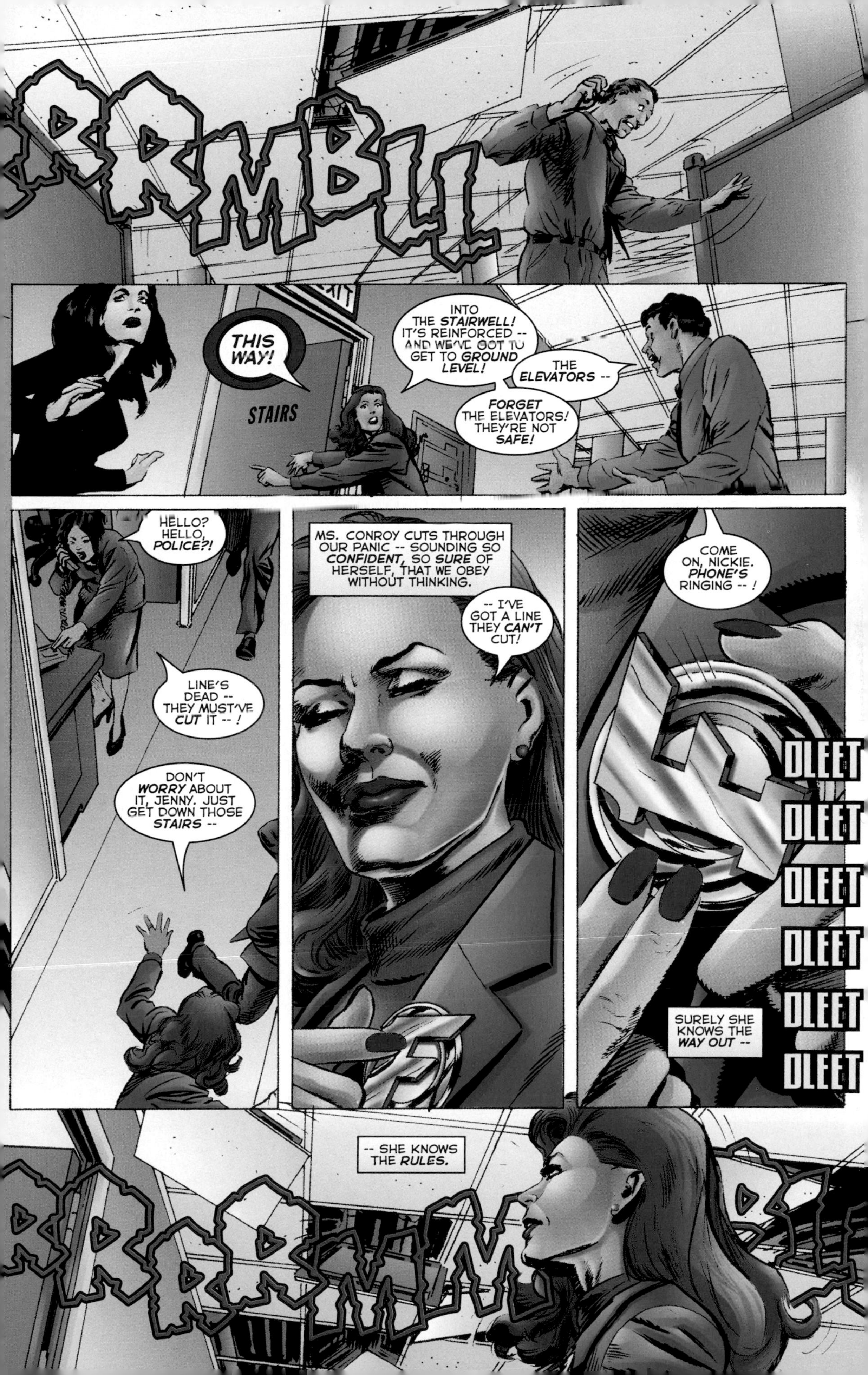
RRMBLL
THIS WAY!
STAIRS
INTO THE STAIRWELL! IT'S REINFORCED -- AND WE'VE GOT TO GET TO GROUND LEVEL!
THE ELEVATORS --
FORGET THE ELEVATORS! THEY'RE NOT SAFE!
HELLO? HELLO, POLICE?!
LINE'S DEAD -- THEY MUST'VE CUT IT -- !
DON'T WORRY ABOUT IT, JENNY. JUST GET DOWN THOSE STAIRS --
MS. CONROY CUTS THROUGH OUR PANIC -- SOUNDING SO CONFIDENT, SO SURE OF HERSELF, THAT WE OBEY WITHOUT THINKING.
-- I'VE GOT A LINE THEY CAN'T CUT!
COME ON, NICKIE. PHONE'S RINGING -- !
DLEET
DLEET
DLEET
DLEET
DLEET
DLEET
SURELY SHE KNOWS THE WAY OUT --
-- SHE KNOWS THE RULES.

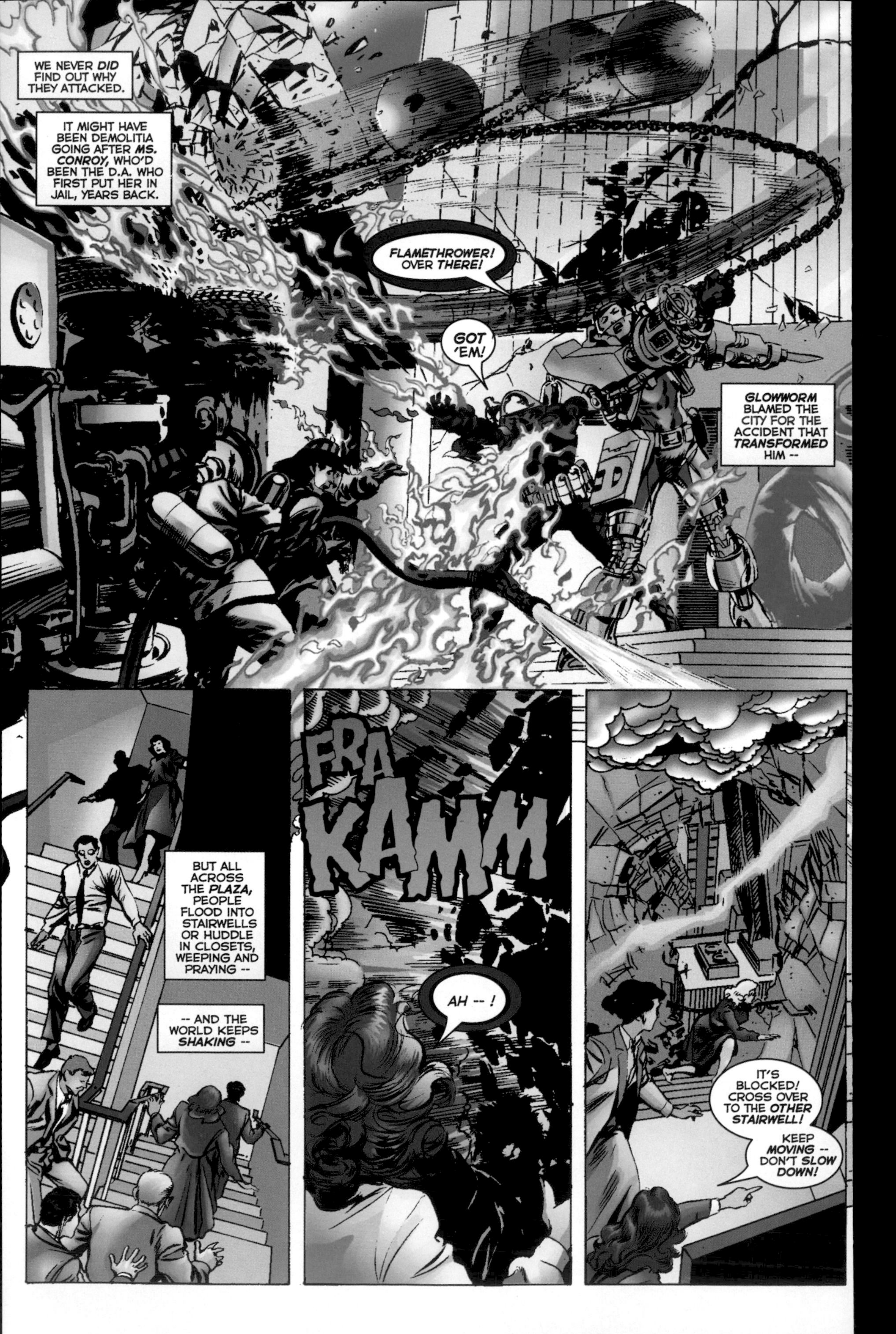
WE NEVER DID FIND OUT WHY THEY ATTACKED.
IT MIGHT HAVE BEEN DEMOLITIA GOING AFTER MS. CONROY, WHO'D BEEN THE D.A. WHO FIRST PUT HER IN JAIL, YEARS BACK.
FLAMETHROWER! OVER THERE!
GOT 'EM!
GLOWWORM BLAMED THE CITY FOR THE ACCIDENT THAT TRANSFORMED HIM --
BUT ALL ACROSS THE PLAZA, PEOPLE FLOOD INTO STAIRWELLS OR HUDDLE IN CLOSETS, WEEPING AND PRAYING --
-- AND THE WORLD KEEPS SHAKING --
FRA KAMM
AH -- !
IT'S BLOCKED! CROSS OVER TO THE OTHER STAIRWELL!
KEEP MOVING -- DON'T SLOW DOWN!

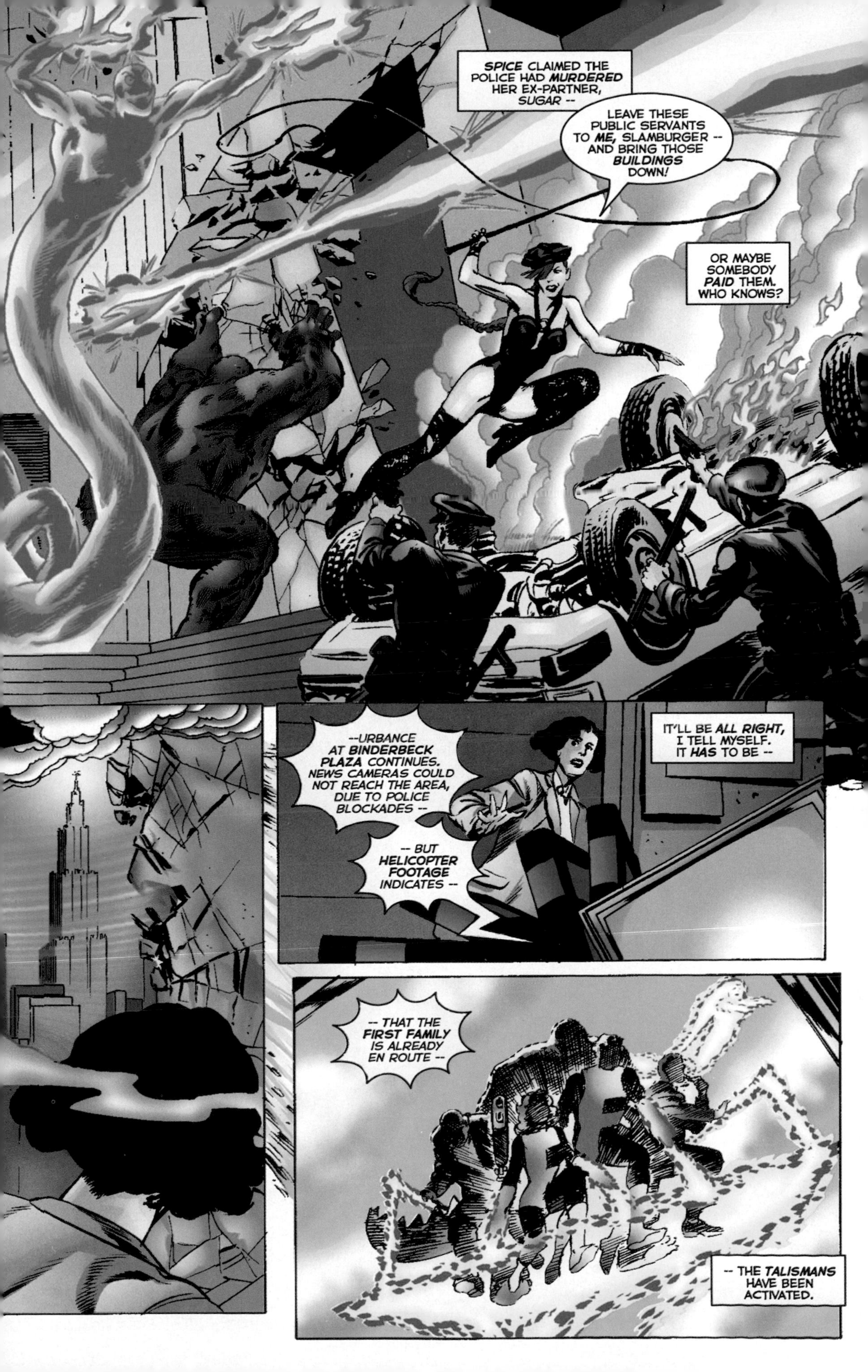

SPICE CLAIMED THE POLICE HAD MURDERED HER EX-PARTNER, SUGAR --
LEAVE THESE PUBLIC SERVANTS TO ME, SLAMBURGER -- AND BRING THOSE BUILDINGS DOWN!
OR MAYBE SOMEBODY PAID THEM. WHO KNOWS?
--URBANCE AT BINDERBECK PLAZA CONTINUES. NEWS CAMERAS COULD NOT REACH THE AREA, DUE TO POLICE BLOCKADES --
IT'LL BE ALL RIGHT, I TELL MYSELF. IT HAS TO BE --
-- BUT HELICOPTER FOOTAGE INDICATES --
-- THAT THE FIRST FAMILY IS ALREADY EN ROUTE --
-- THE TALISMANS HAVE BEEN ACTIVATED.

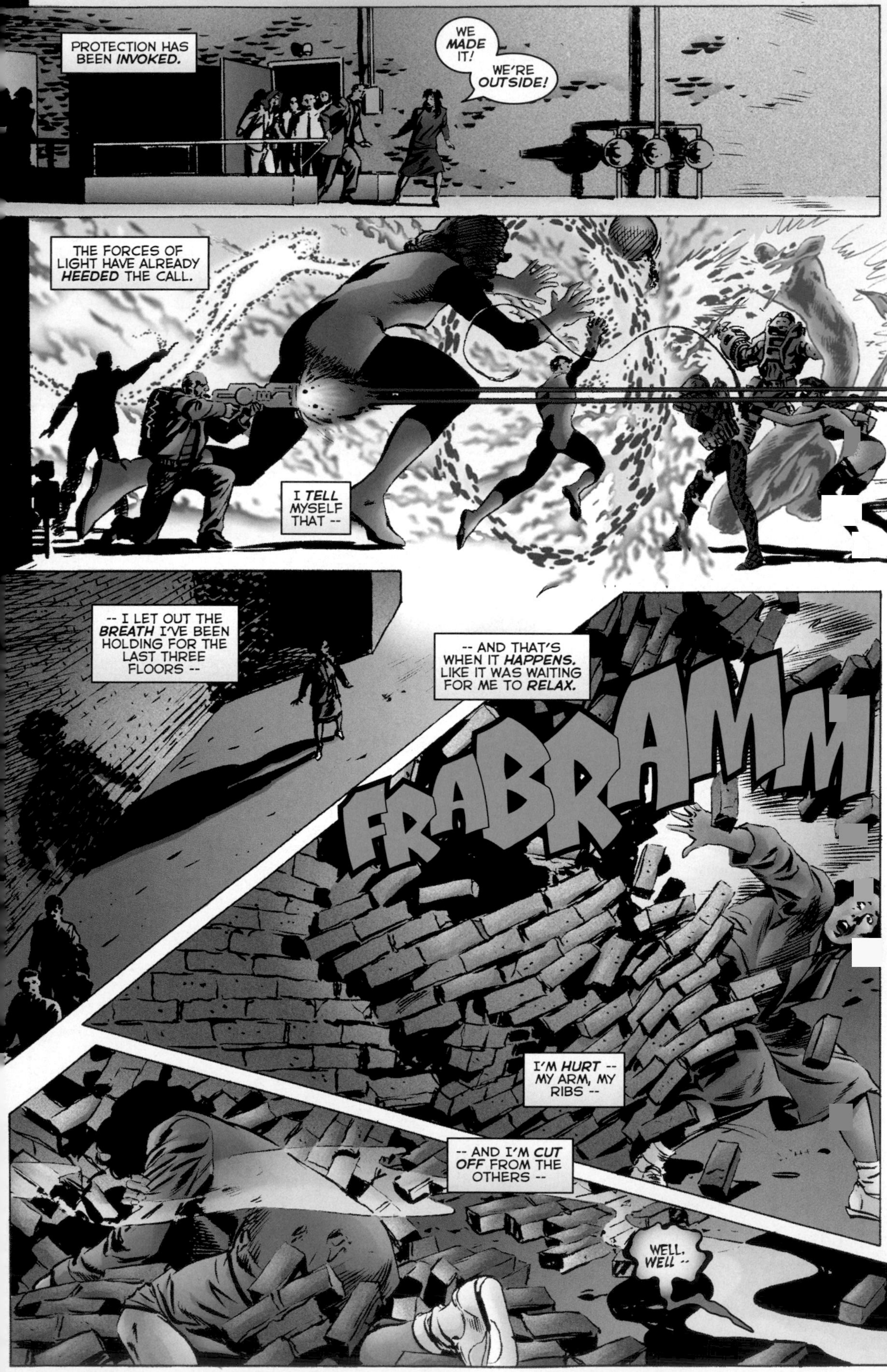
PROTECTION HAS BEEN INVOKED.
WE MADE IT!
WE'RE OUTSIDE!
THE FORCES OF LIGHT HAVE ALREADY HEEDED THE CALL.
I TELL MYSELF THAT --
-- I LET OUT THE BREATH I'VE BEEN HOLDING FOR THE LAST THREE FLOORS --
-- AND THAT'S WHEN IT HAPPENS. LIKE IT WAS WAITING FOR ME TO RELAX.
FRABRAMM
I'M HURT -- MY ARM, MY RIBS --
-- AND I'M CUT OFF FROM THE OTHERS --
WELL, WELL --

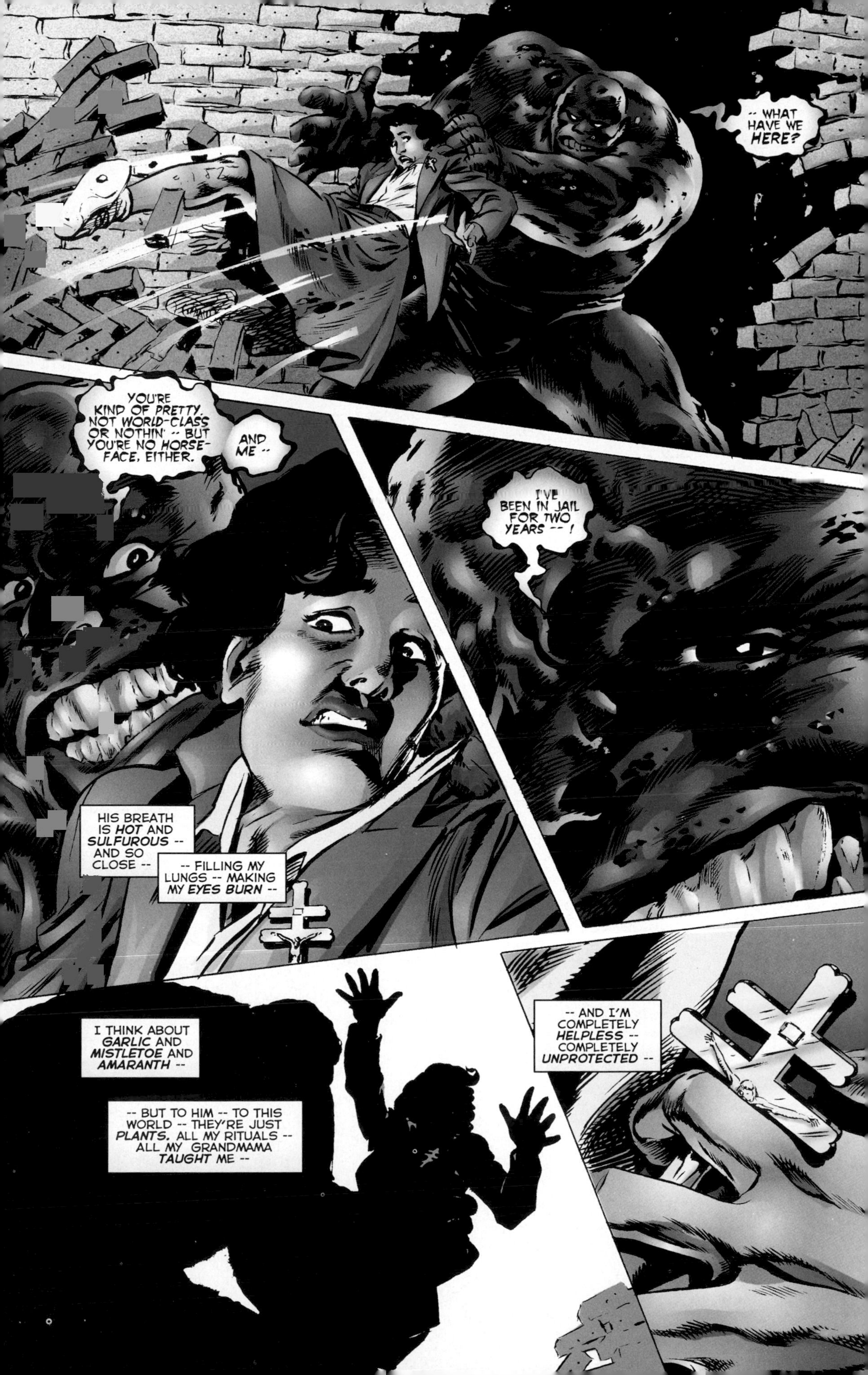
-- WHAT HAVE WE HERE?
YOU'RE KIND OF PRETTY. NOT WORLD-CLASS OR NOTHIN' -- BUT YOU'RE NO HORSE-FACE, EITHER.
AND ME --
I'VE BEEN IN JAIL FOR TWO YEARS -- !
HIS BREATH IS HOT AND SULFUROUS -- AND SO CLOSE --
-- FILLING MY LUNGS -- MAKING MY EYES BURN --
I THINK ABOUT GARLIC AND MISTLETOE AND AMARANTH --
-- BUT TO HIM -- TO THIS WORLD -- THEY'RE JUST PLANTS. ALL MY RITUALS -- ALL MY GRANDMAMA TAUGHT ME --
-- AND I'M COMPLETELY HELPLESS -- COMPLETELY UNPROTECTED --

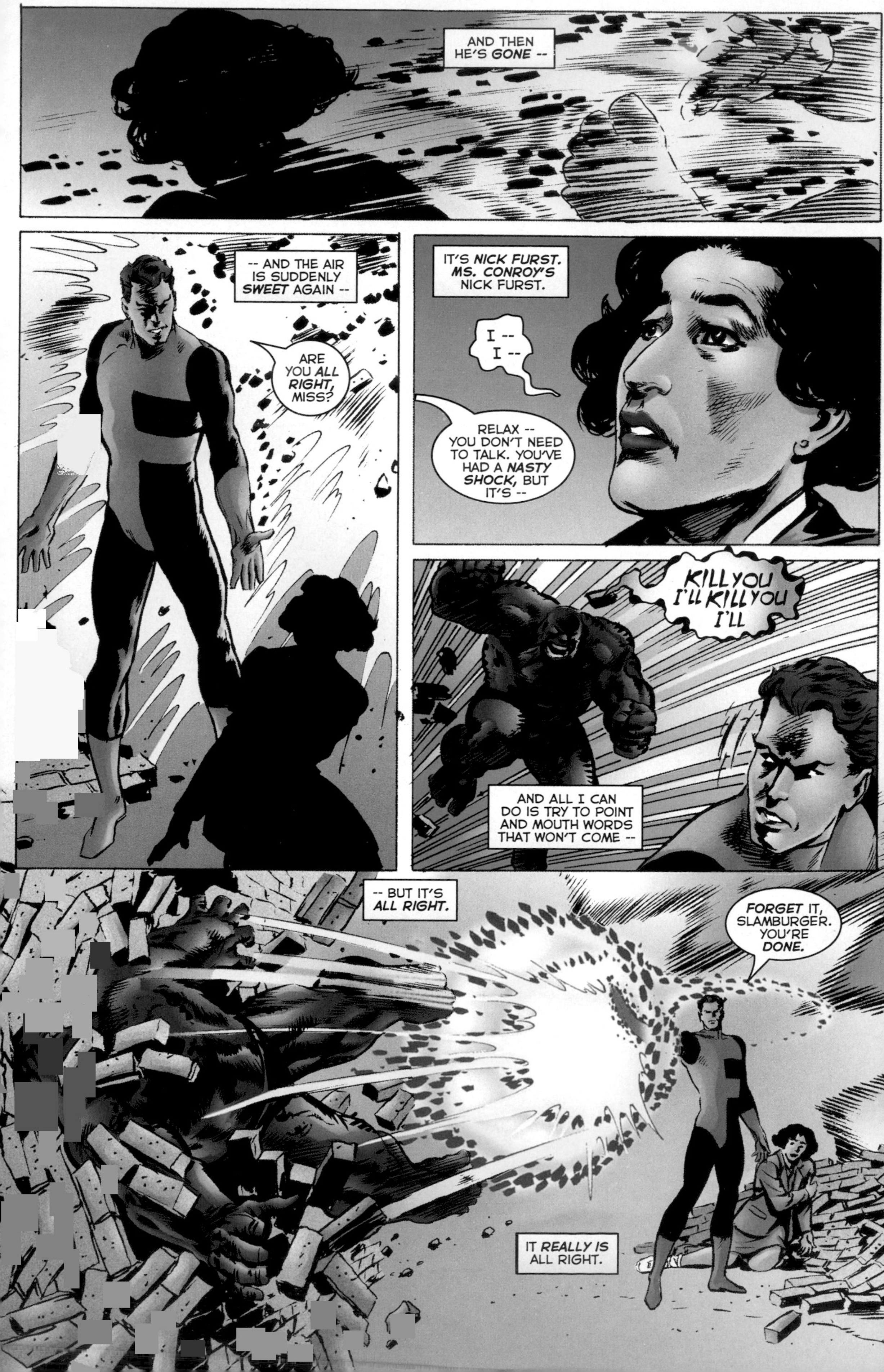
AND THEN HE'S GONE --
-- AND THE AIR IS SUDDENLY SWEET AGAIN --
ARE YOU ALL RIGHT, MISS?
IT'S NICK FURST. MS. CONROY'S NICK FURST.
I -- I --
RELAX -- YOU DON'T NEED TO TALK. YOU'VE HAD A NASTY SHOCK, BUT IT'S --
KILL YOU I'LL KILL YOU I'LL
AND ALL I CAN DO IS TRY TO POINT AND MOUTH WORDS THAT WON'T COME --
-- BUT IT'S ALL RIGHT.
FORGET IT, SLAMBURGER. YOU'RE DONE.
IT REALLY IS ALL RIGHT.

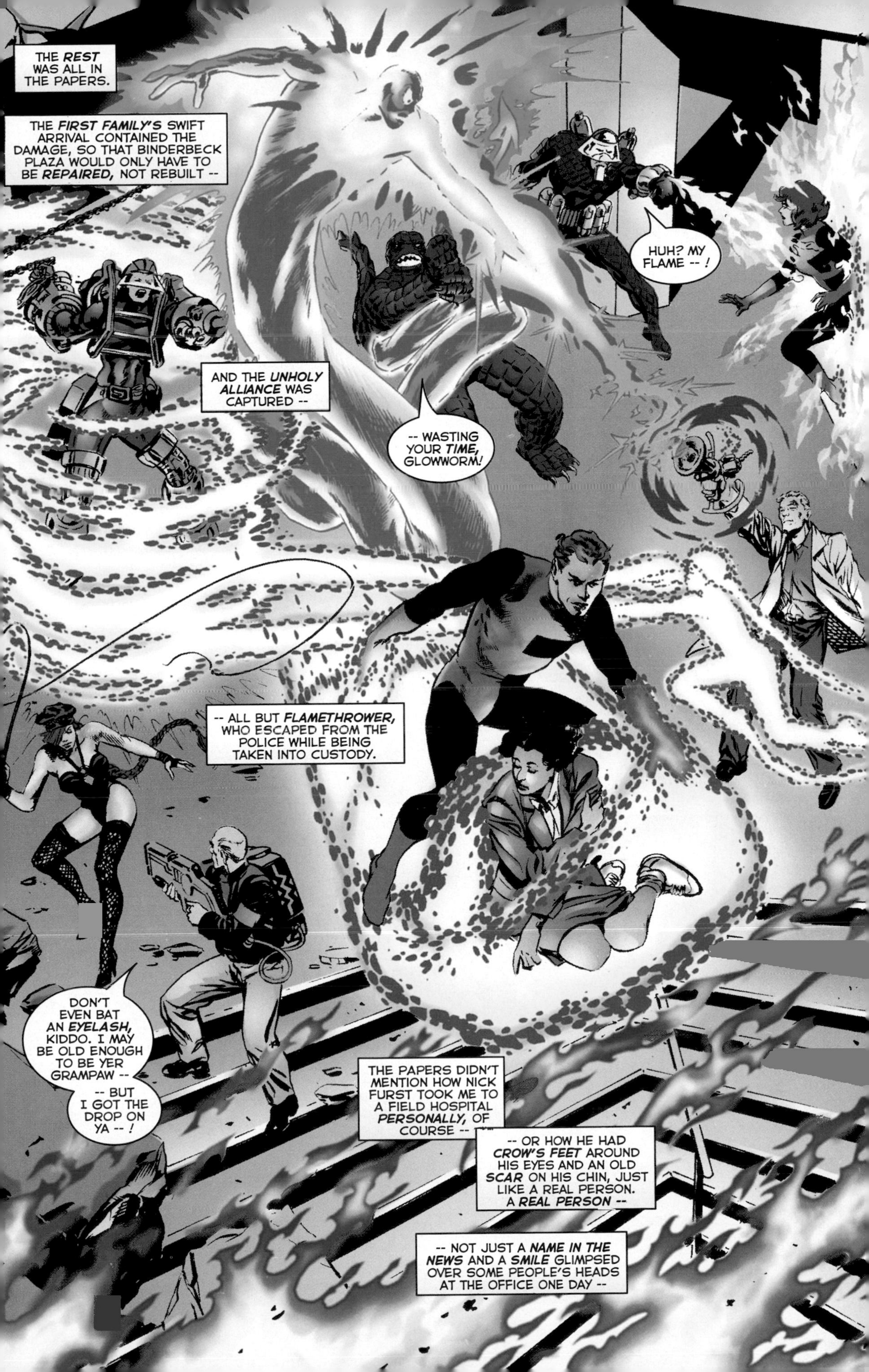
THE REST WAS ALL IN THE PAPERS.
THE FIRST FAMILY'S SWIFT ARRIVAL CONTAINED THE DAMAGE, SO THAT BINDERBECK PLAZA WOULD ONLY HAVE TO BE REPAIRED, NOT REBUILT --
HUH? MY FLAME -- !
AND THE UNHOLY ALLIANCE WAS CAPTURED --
-- WASTING YOUR TIME, GLOWWORM!
-- ALL BUT FLAMETHROWER, WHO ESCAPED FROM THE POLICE WHILE BEING TAKEN INTO CUSTODY.
DON'T EVEN BAT AN EYELASH, KIDDO. I MAY BE OLD ENOUGH TO BE YER GRAMPAW --
-- BUT I GOT THE DROP ON YA -- !
THE PAPERS DIDN'T MENTION HOW NICK FURST TOOK ME TO A FIELD HOSPITAL PERSONALLY, OF COURSE --
-- OR HOW HE HAD CROW'S FEET AROUND HIS EYES AND AN OLD SCAR ON HIS CHIN, JUST LIKE A REAL PERSON. A REAL PERSON --
-- NOT JUST A NAME IN THE NEWS AND A SMILE GLIMPSED OVER SOME PEOPLE'S HEADS AT THE OFFICE ONE DAY --

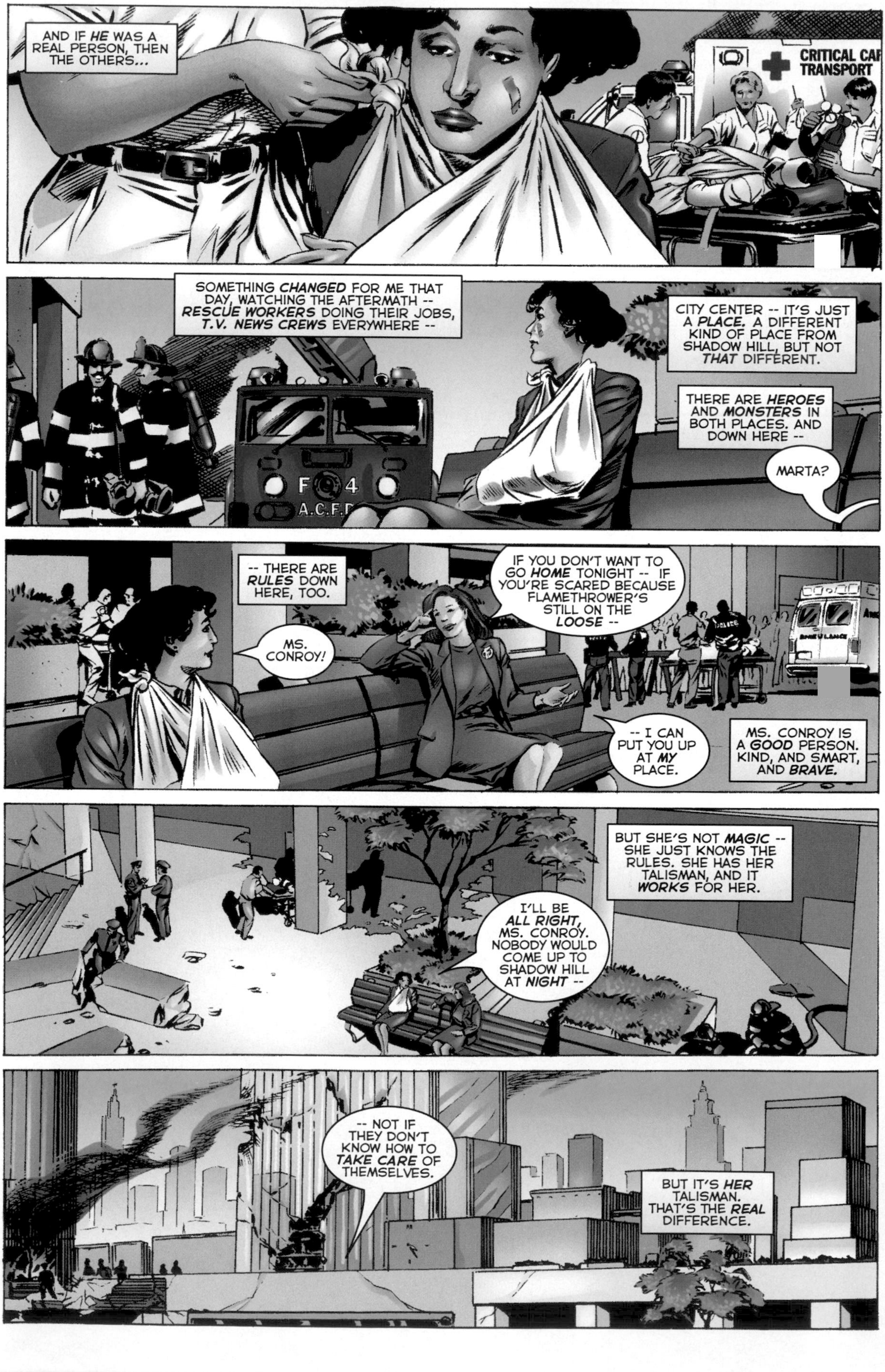

AND IF HE WAS A REAL PERSON, THEN THE OTHERS...
CRITICAL CAR
TRANSPORT
SOMETHING CHANGED FOR ME THAT DAY, WATCHING THE AFTERMATH -- RESCUE WORKERS DOING THEIR JOBS, T.V. NEWS CREWS EVERYWHERE --
F 4
A.C.F.D.
CITY CENTER -- IT'S JUST A PLACE. A DIFFERENT KIND OF PLACE FROM SHADOW HILL, BUT NOT THAT DIFFERENT.
THERE ARE HEROES AND MONSTERS IN BOTH PLACES. AND DOWN HERE --
MARTA?
-- THERE ARE RULES DOWN HERE, TOO.
MS. CONROY!
IF YOU DON'T WANT TO GO HOME TONIGHT -- IF YOU'RE SCARED BECAUSE FLAMETHROWER'S STILL ON THE LOOSE --
-- I CAN PUT YOU UP AT MY PLACE.
MS. CONROY IS A GOOD PERSON. KIND, AND SMART, AND BRAVE.
BUT SHE'S NOT MAGIC -- SHE JUST KNOWS THE RULES. SHE HAS HER TALISMAN, AND IT WORKS FOR HER.
I'LL BE ALL RIGHT, MS. CONROY. NOBODY WOULD COME UP TO SHADOW HILL AT NIGHT --
-- NOT IF THEY DON'T KNOW HOW TO TAKE CARE OF THEMSELVES.
BUT IT'S HER TALISMAN. THAT'S THE REAL DIFFERENCE.

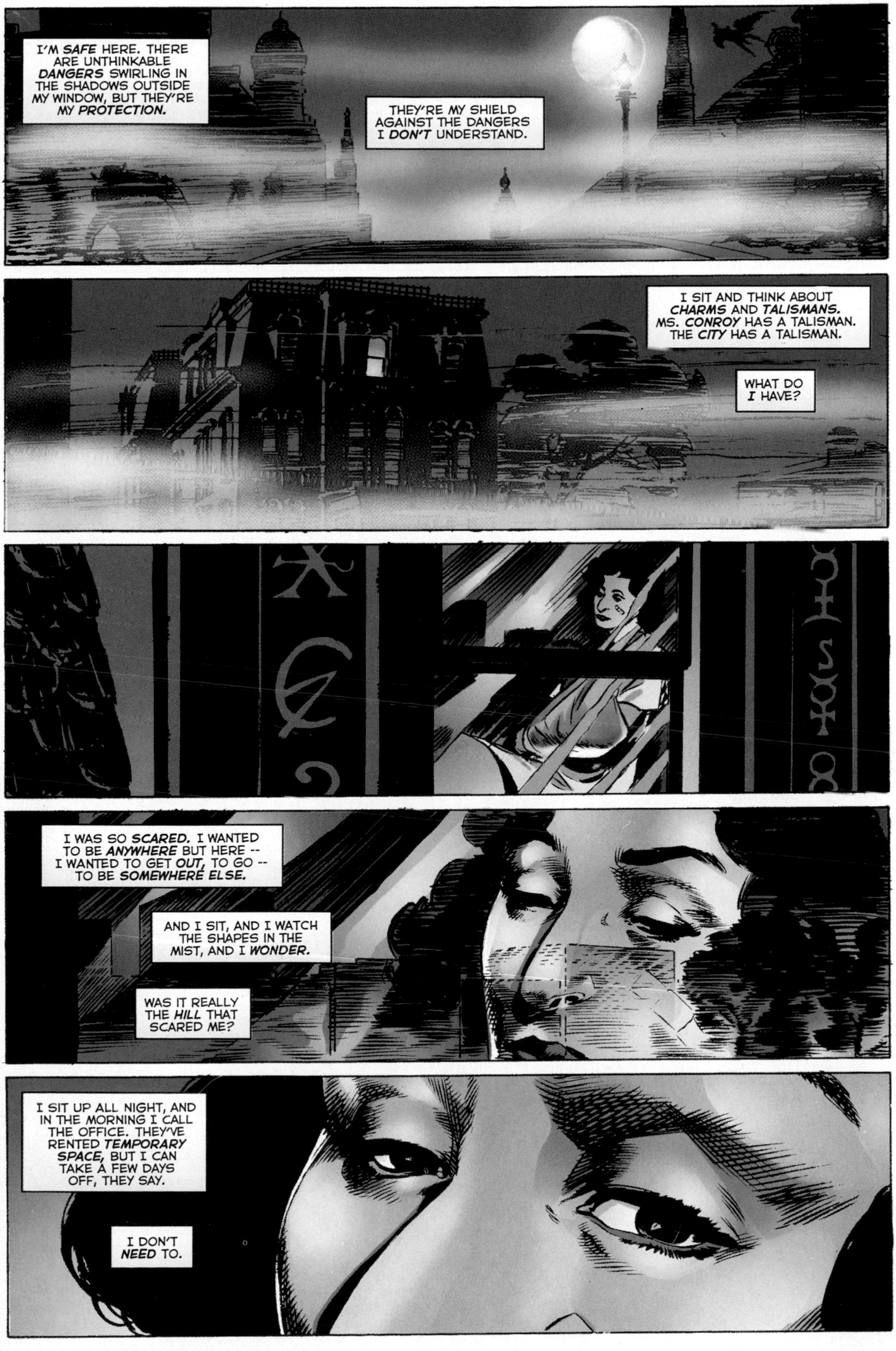

I'M SAFE HERE. THERE ARE UNTHINKABLE DANGERS SWIRLING IN THE SHADOWS OUTSIDE MY WINDOW, BUT THEY'RE MY PROTECTION.
THEY'RE MY SHIELD AGAINST THE DANGERS I DON'T UNDERSTAND.
I SIT AND THINK ABOUT CHARMS AND TALISMANS. MS. CONROY HAS A TALISMAN. THE CITY HAS A TALISMAN.
WHAT DO I HAVE?
I WAS SO SCARED. I WANTED TO BE ANYWHERE BUT HERE -- I WANTED TO GET OUT, TO GO -- TO BE SOMEWHERE ELSE.
AND I SIT, AND I WATCH THE SHAPES IN THE MIST, AND I WONDER.
WAS IT REALLY THE HILL THAT SCARED ME?
I SIT UP ALL NIGHT, AND IN THE MORNING I CALL THE OFFICE. THEY'VE RENTED TEMPORARY SPACE, BUT I CAN TAKE A FEW DAYS OFF, THEY SAY.
I DON'T NEED TO.

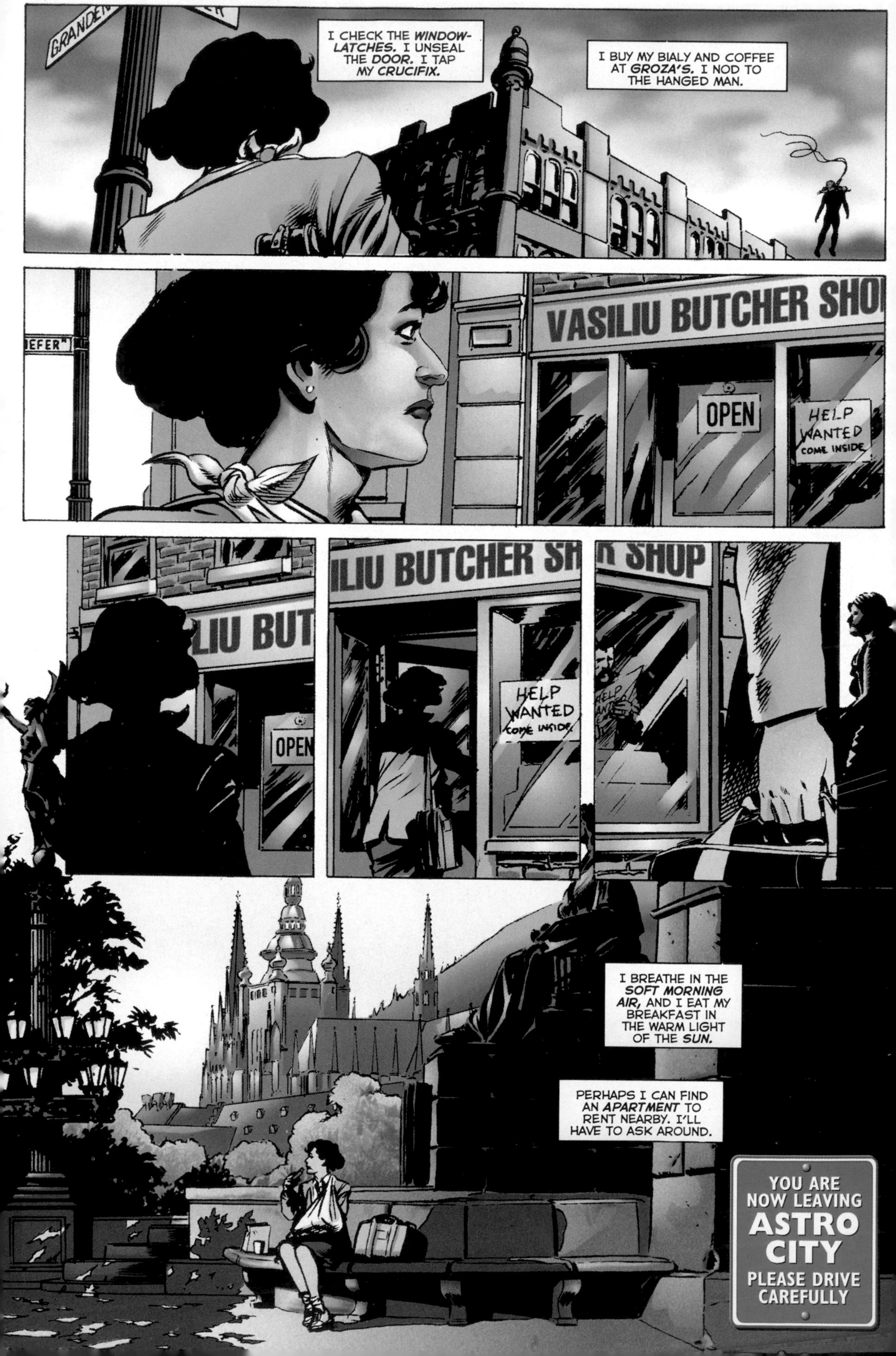
GRANDEN
I CHECK THE WINDOW-LATCHES. I UNSEAL THE DOOR. I TAP MY CRUCIFIX.
I BUY MY BIALY AND COFFEE AT GROZA'S. I NOD TO THE HANGED MAN.
EFER
VASILIU BUTCHER SHO
OPEN
HELP WANTED COME INSIDE
ILIU BUT
OPEN
ILIU BUTCHER SH R SHOP
HELP WANTED COME INSIDE
I BREATHE IN THE SOFT MORNING AIR, AND I EAT MY BREAKFAST IN THE WARM LIGHT OF THE SUN.
PERHAPS I CAN FIND AN APARTMENT TO RENT NEARBY. I'LL HAVE TO ASK AROUND.
YOU ARE NOW LEAVING ASTRO CITY PLEASE DRIVE CAREFULLY

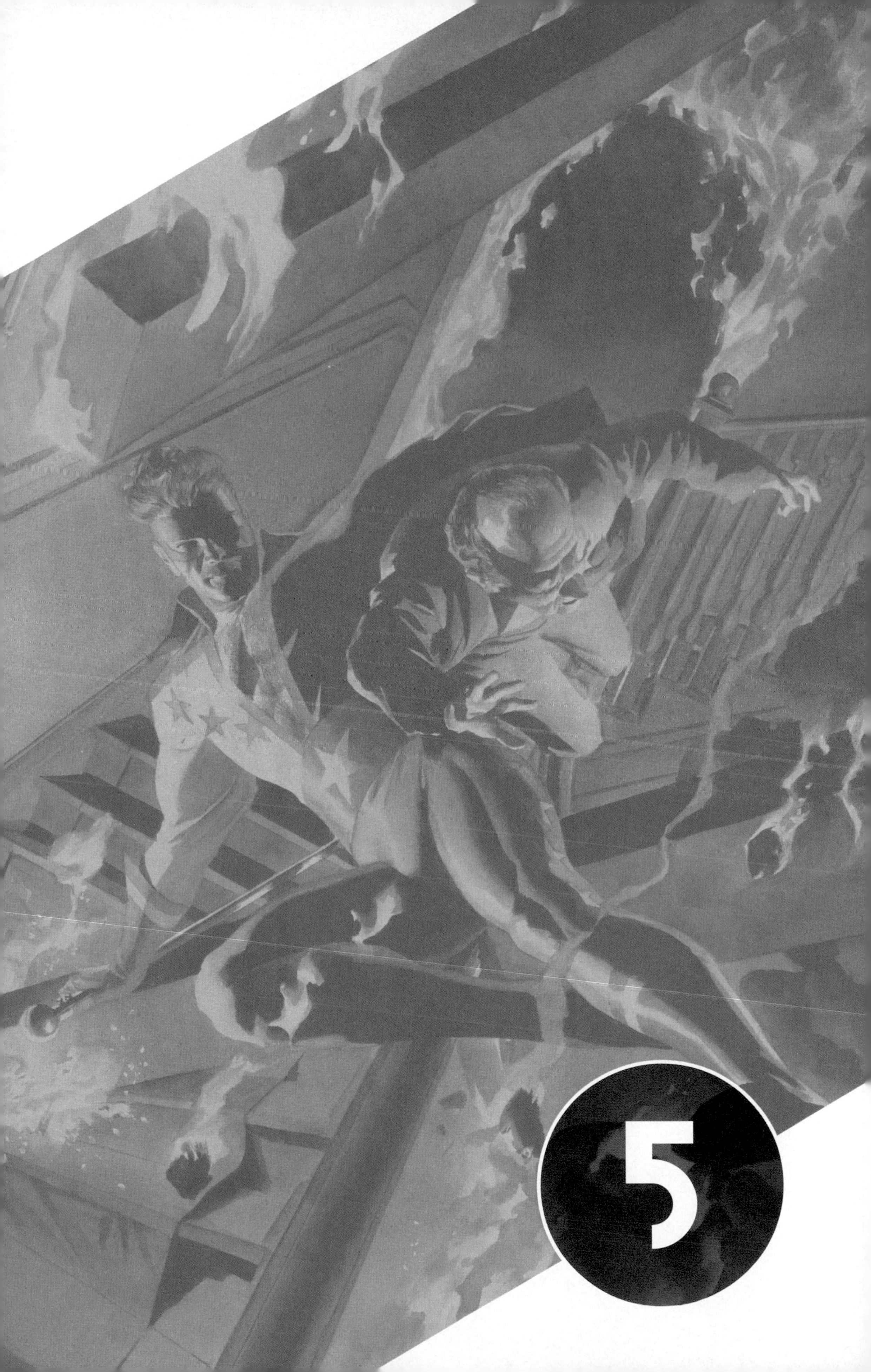
5

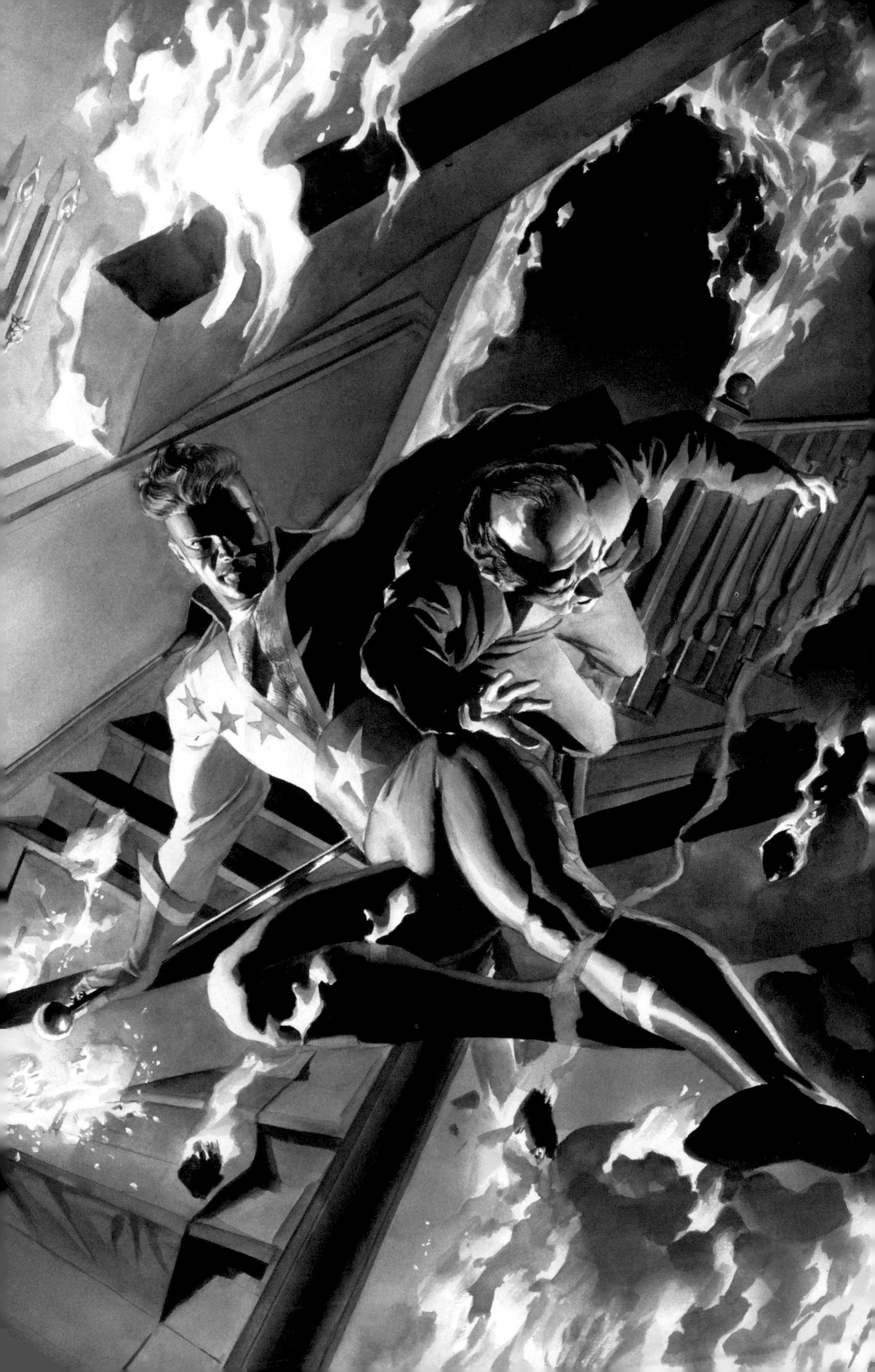

Once upon a time...

...there was a **little old man** who lived in an undistinguished rooming house on the **north side** of Astro City.

If you asked him, the little old man would say that he worked **forty-five** years as a draftsman in a basement room without windows, and he intended to spend his retirement out-of-doors as much as **possible,** breathing the air, looking at the **sun** and **sky** until he finally managed to flush the **fluorescent light** from his system.

Nordling's
Department Store
Affordable Quality Since 1921

But the little old man was a **liar.**

There was no **basement room.** There was no **fluorescent light.**

And he did not walk outside to look at the sun.

RECONNAISSANCE

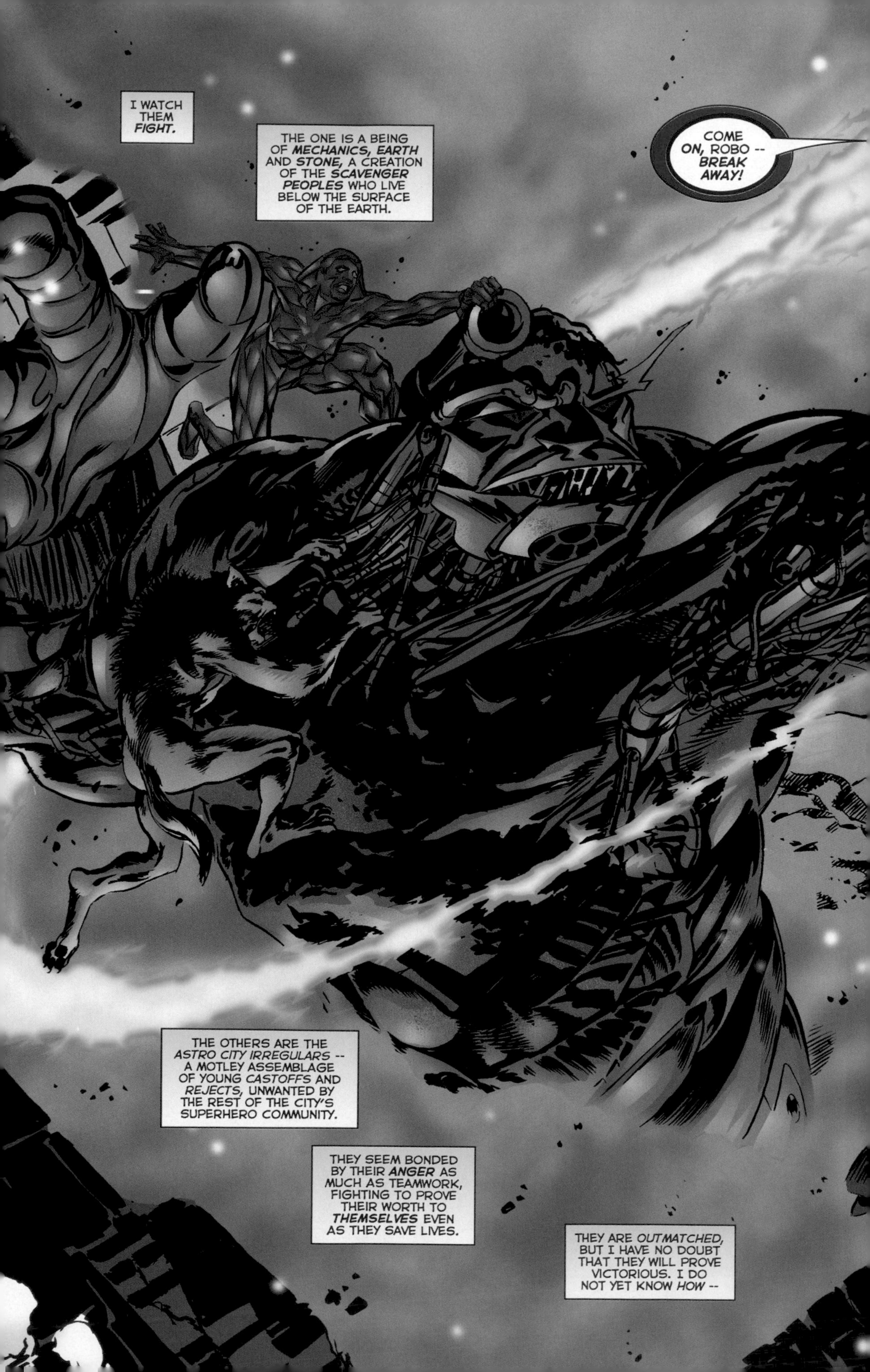
I WATCH THEM *FIGHT.*
THE ONE IS A BEING OF ***MECHANICS, EARTH*** AND ***STONE,*** A CREATION OF THE ***SCAVENGER PEOPLES*** WHO LIVE BELOW THE SURFACE OF THE EARTH.
COME ***ON,*** ROBO -- ***BREAK AWAY!***
THE OTHERS ARE THE *ASTRO CITY IRREGULARS* -- A MOTLEY ASSEMBLAGE OF YOUNG *CASTOFFS* AND *REJECTS,* UNWANTED BY THE REST OF THE CITY'S SUPERHERO COMMUNITY.
THEY SEEM BONDED BY THEIR ***ANGER*** AS MUCH AS TEAMWORK, FIGHTING TO PROVE THEIR WORTH TO ***THEMSELVES*** EVEN AS THEY SAVE LIVES.
THEY ARE *OUTMATCHED,* BUT I HAVE NO DOUBT THAT THEY WILL PROVE VICTORIOUS. I DO NOT YET KNOW *HOW* --

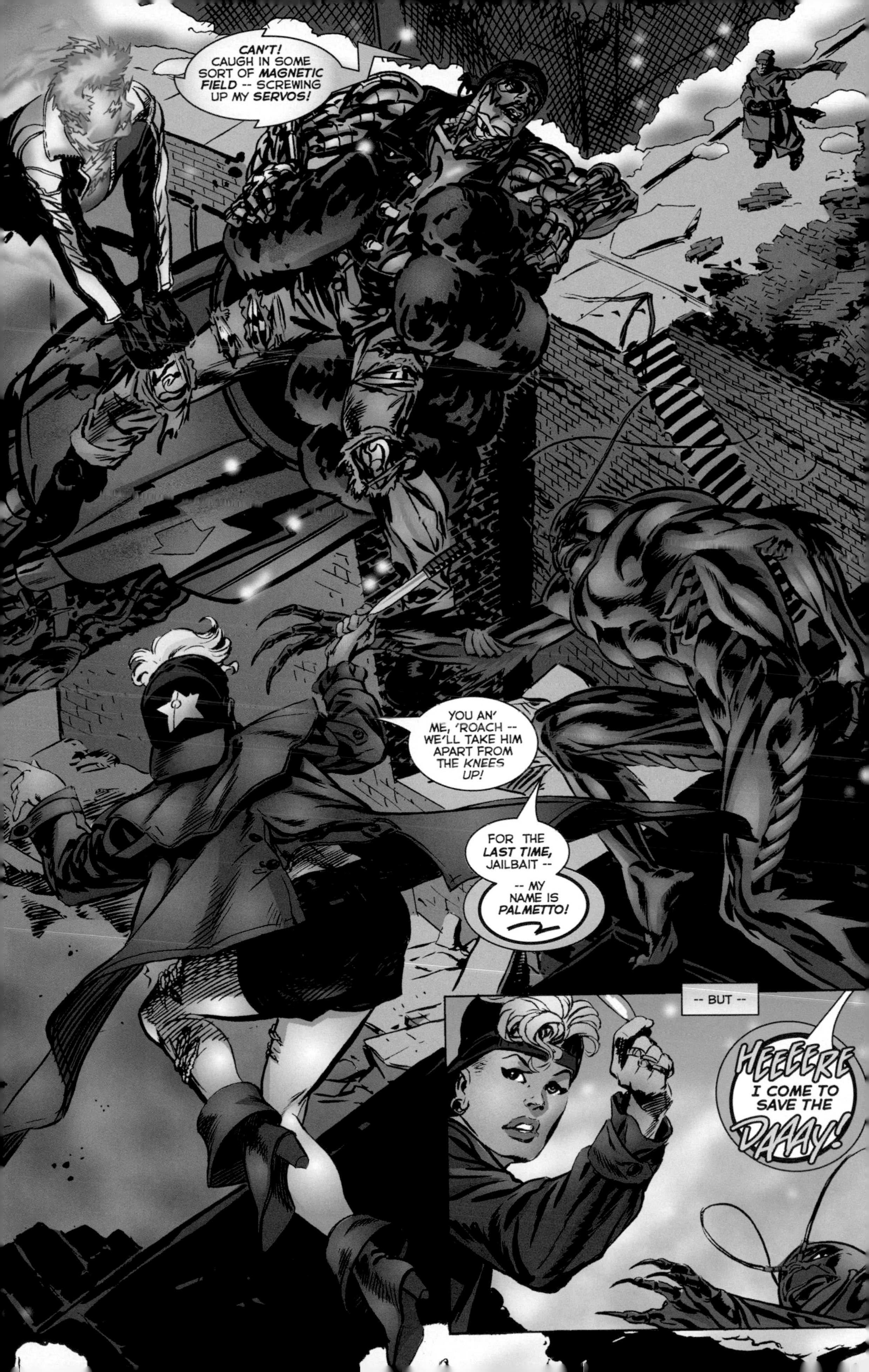
CAN'T! CAUGH IN SOME SORT OF MAGNETIC FIELD -- SCREWING UP MY SERVOS!
YOU AN' ME, 'ROACH -- WE'LL TAKE HIM APART FROM THE KNEES UP!
FOR THE LAST TIME, JAILBAIT --
-- MY NAME IS PALMETTO!
-- BUT --
HEEEERE I COME TO SAVE THE DAAAY!

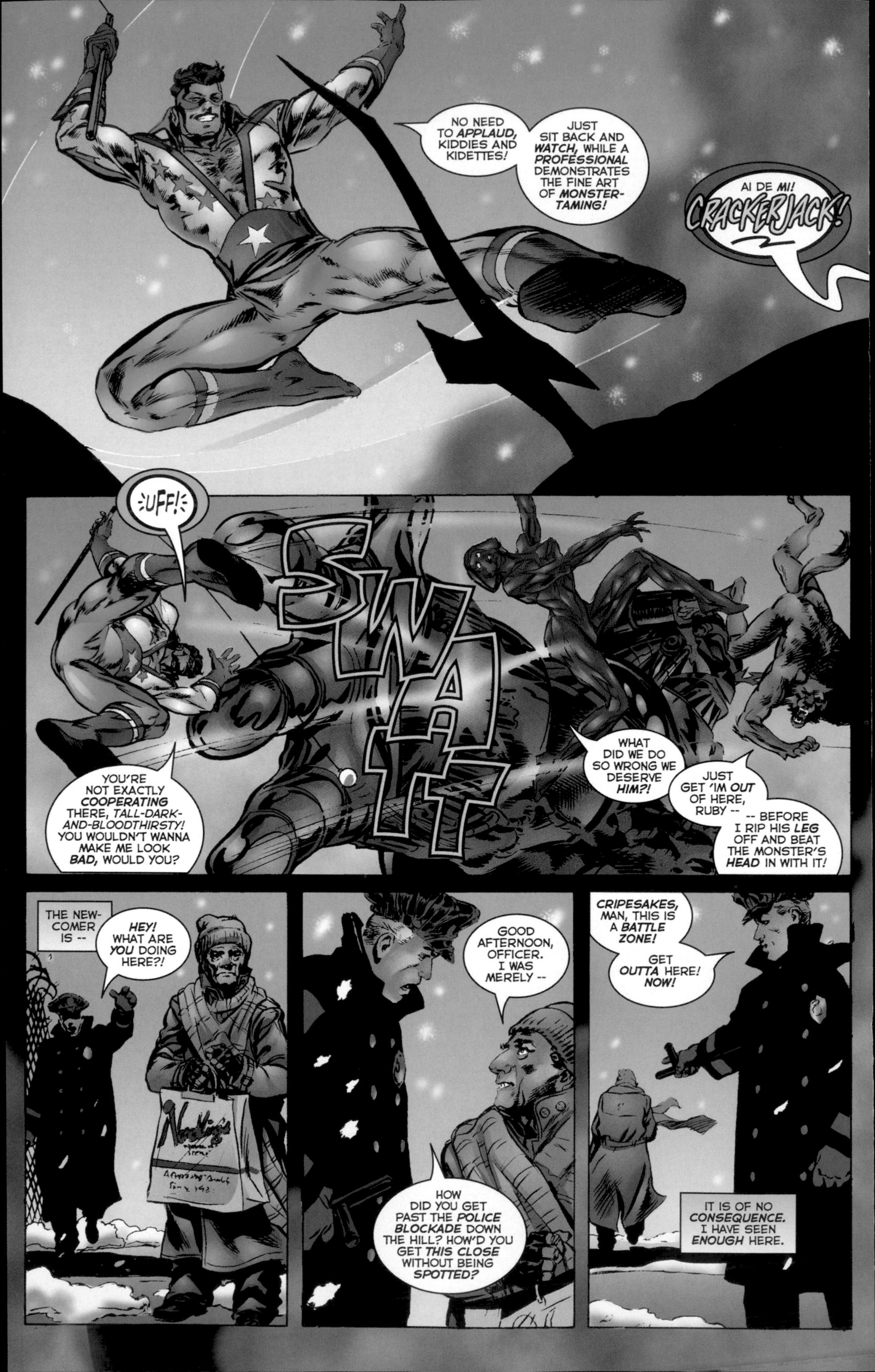
NO NEED TO APPLAUD, KIDDIES AND KIDETTES!
JUST SIT BACK AND WATCH, WHILE A PROFESSIONAL DEMONSTRATES THE FINE ART OF MONSTER-TAMING!
AI DE MI! CRACKERJACK!
UFF!
SWAT
YOU'RE NOT EXACTLY COOPERATING THERE, TALL-DARK-AND-BLOODTHIRSTY! YOU WOULDN'T WANNA MAKE ME LOOK BAD, WOULD YOU?
WHAT DID WE DO SO WRONG WE DESERVE HIM?!
JUST GET 'IM OUT OF HERE, RUBY --
-- BEFORE I RIP HIS LEG OFF AND BEAT THE MONSTER'S HEAD IN WITH IT!
THE NEW-COMER IS --
HEY! WHAT ARE YOU DOING HERE?!
GOOD AFTERNOON, OFFICER. I WAS MERELY --
HOW DID YOU GET PAST THE POLICE BLOCKADE DOWN THE HILL? HOW'D YOU GET THIS CLOSE WITHOUT BEING SPOTTED?
CRIPESAKES, MAN, THIS IS A BATTLE ZONE!
GET OUTTA HERE! NOW!
IT IS OF NO CONSEQUENCE. I HAVE SEEN ENOUGH HERE.

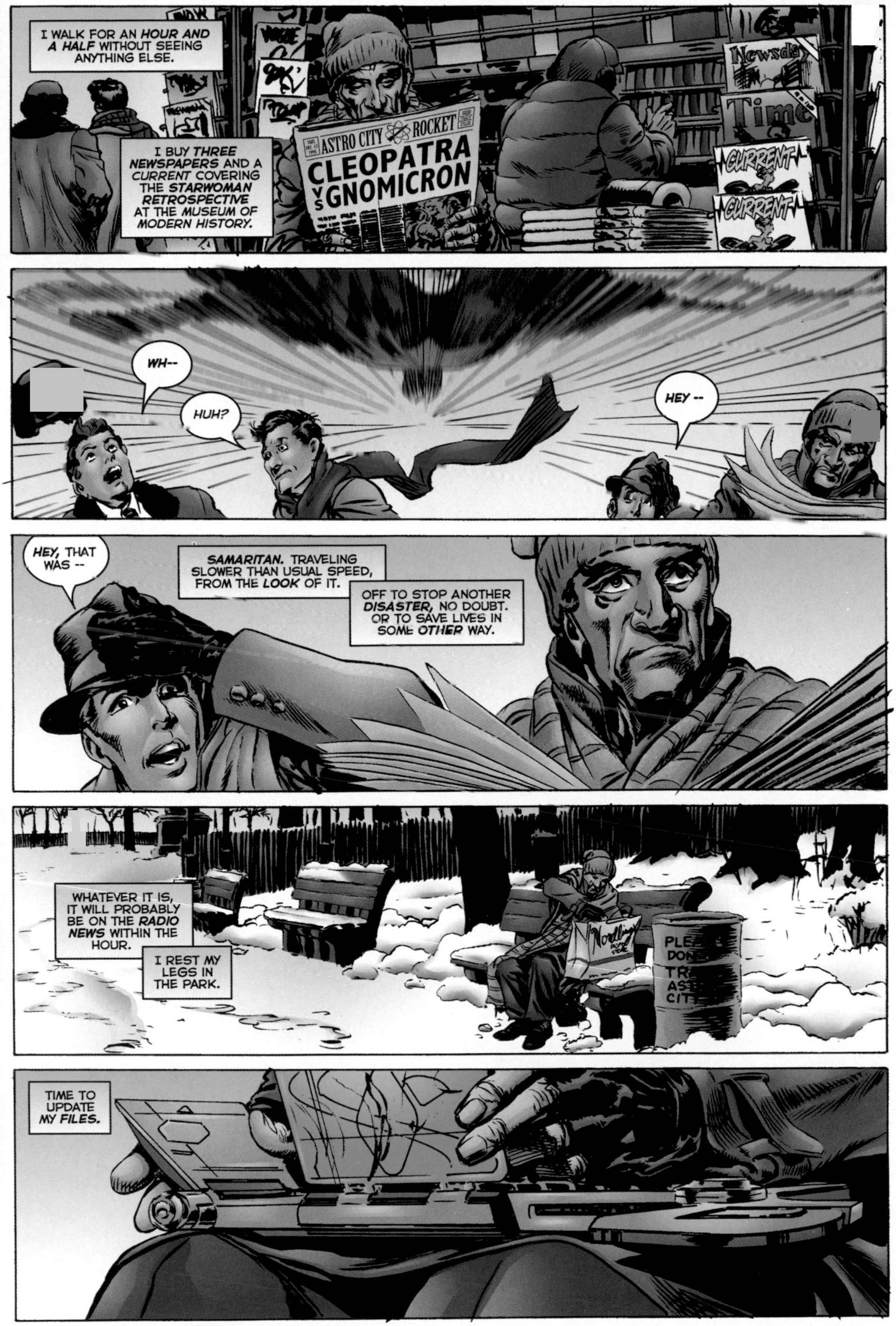
I WALK FOR AN HOUR AND A HALF WITHOUT SEEING ANYTHING ELSE.
I BUY THREE NEWSPAPERS AND A CURRENT COVERING THE STARWOMAN RETROSPECTIVE AT THE MUSEUM OF MODERN HISTORY.
ASTRO CITY ROCKET
CLEOPATRA VS GNOMICRON
Newsday
Time
CURRENT
CURRENT
WH--
HUH?
HEY --
HEY, THAT WAS --
SAMARITAN. TRAVELING SLOWER THAN USUAL SPEED, FROM THE LOOK OF IT.
OFF TO STOP ANOTHER DISASTER, NO DOUBT. OR TO SAVE LIVES IN SOME OTHER WAY.
WHATEVER IT IS, IT WILL PROBABLY BE ON THE RADIO NEWS WITHIN THE HOUR.
I REST MY LEGS IN THE PARK.
TIME TO UPDATE MY FILES.

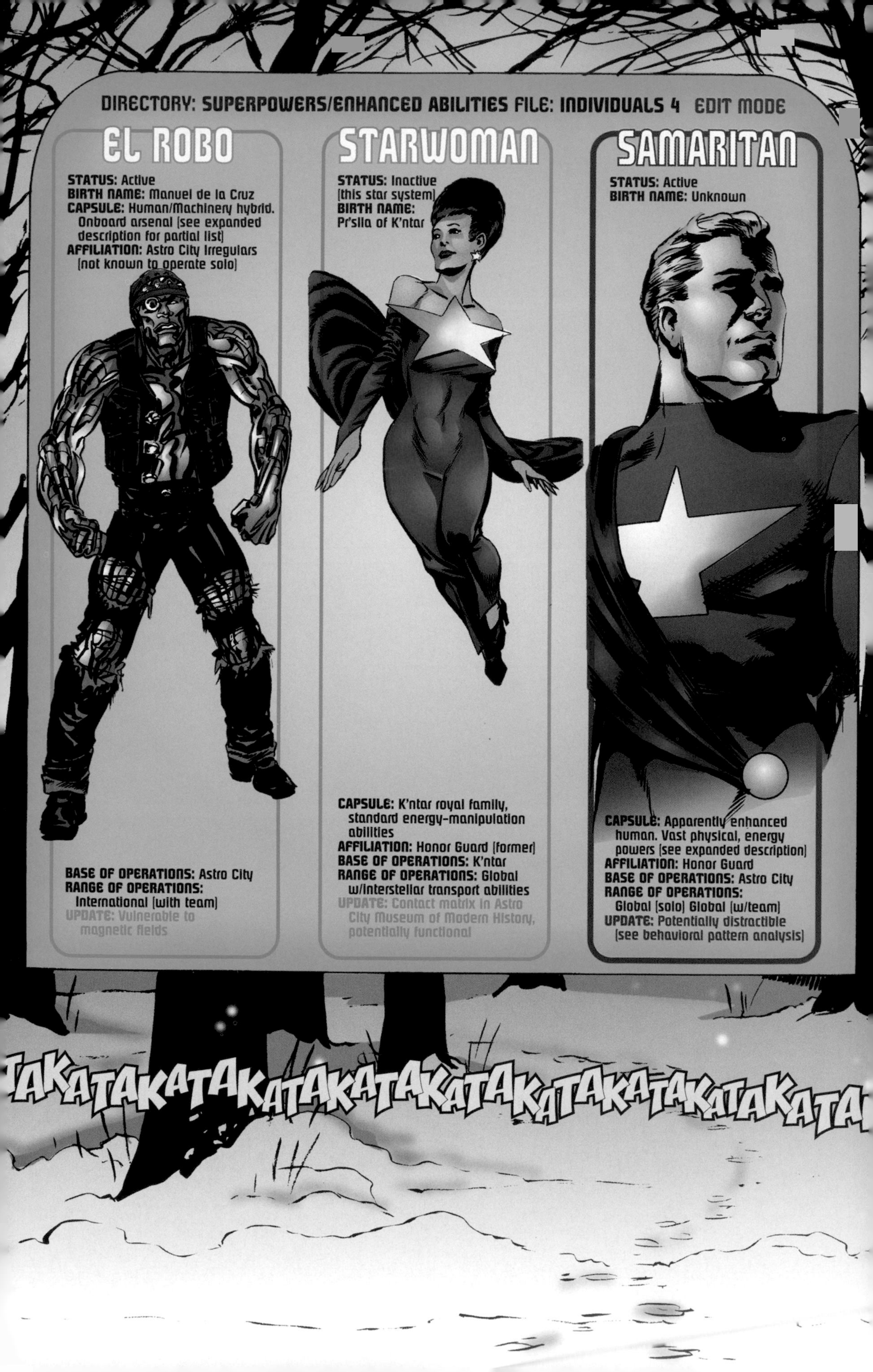
DIRECTORY: SUPERPOWERS/ENHANCED ABILITIES FILE: INDIVIDUALS 4 EDIT MODE
EL ROBO
STATUS: Active
BIRTH NAME: Manuel de la Cruz
CAPSULE: Human/Machinery hybrid. Onboard arsenal (see expanded description for partial list)
AFFILIATION: Astro City Irregulars (not known to operate solo)
BASE OF OPERATIONS: Astro City
RANGE OF OPERATIONS: International (with team)
UPDATE: Vulnerable to magnetic fields
STARWOMAN
STATUS: Inactive (this star system)
BIRTH NAME: Pr'slla of K'ntar
CAPSULE: K'ntar royal family, standard energy-manipulation abilities
AFFILIATION: Honor Guard (former)
BASE OF OPERATIONS: K'ntar
RANGE OF OPERATIONS: Global w/interstellar transport abilities
UPDATE: Contact matrix in Astro City Museum of Modern History, potentially functional
SAMARITAN
STATUS: Active
BIRTH NAME: Unknown
CAPSULE: Apparently enhanced human. Vast physical, energy powers (see expanded description)
AFFILIATION: Honor Guard
BASE OF OPERATIONS: Astro City
RANGE OF OPERATIONS: Global (solo) Global (w/team)
UPDATE: Potentially distractible (see behavioral pattern analysis)
TAKATAKATAKATAKATAKATAKATAKATAKATAKATAKATA

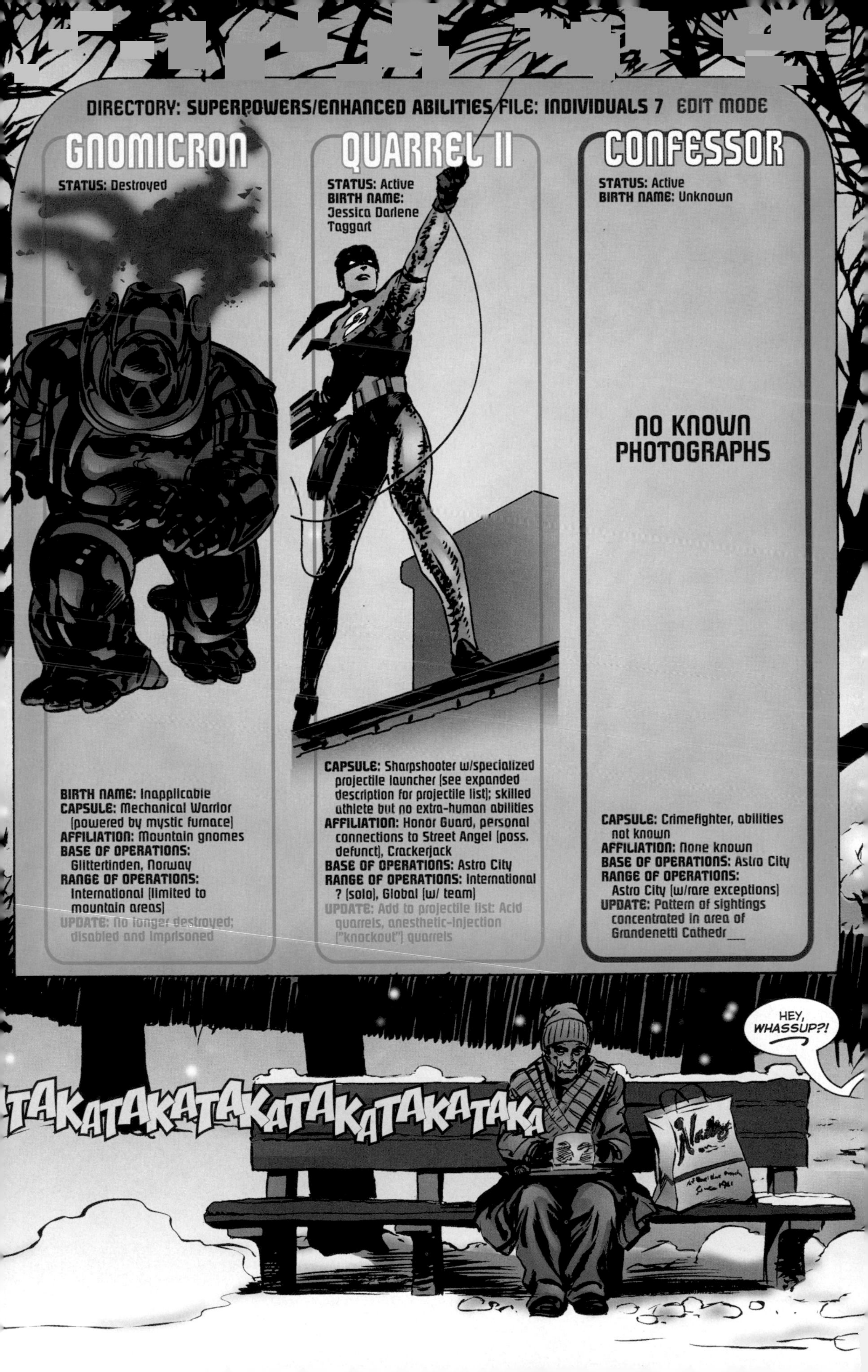
DIRECTORY: SUPERPOWERS/ENHANCED ABILITIES FILE: INDIVIDUALS 7 EDIT MODE
GNOMICRON
STATUS: Destroyed
BIRTH NAME: Inapplicable
CAPSULE: Mechanical Warrior (powered by mystic furnace)
AFFILIATION: Mountain gnomes
BASE OF OPERATIONS: Glittertinden, Norway
RANGE OF OPERATIONS: International (limited to mountain areas)
UPDATE: No longer destroyed; disabled and imprisoned
QUARREL II
STATUS: Active
BIRTH NAME: Jessica Darlene Taggart
CAPSULE: Sharpshooter w/specialized projectile launcher (see expanded description for projectile list); skilled athlete but no extra-human abilities
AFFILIATION: Honor Guard, personal connections to Street Angel (poss. defunct), Crackerjack
BASE OF OPERATIONS: Astro City
RANGE OF OPERATIONS: International ? (solo), Global (w/ team)
UPDATE: Add to projectile list: Acid quarrels, anesthetic-injection ("knockout") quarrels
CONFESSOR
STATUS: Active
BIRTH NAME: Unknown
NO KNOWN PHOTOGRAPHS
CAPSULE: Crimefighter, abilities not known
AFFILIATION: None known
BASE OF OPERATIONS: Astro City
RANGE OF OPERATIONS: Astro City (w/rare exceptions)
UPDATE: Pattern of sightings concentrated in area of Grandenetti Cathedr___
HEY, WHASSUP?!
TAKATAKATAKATAKATAKATAKA

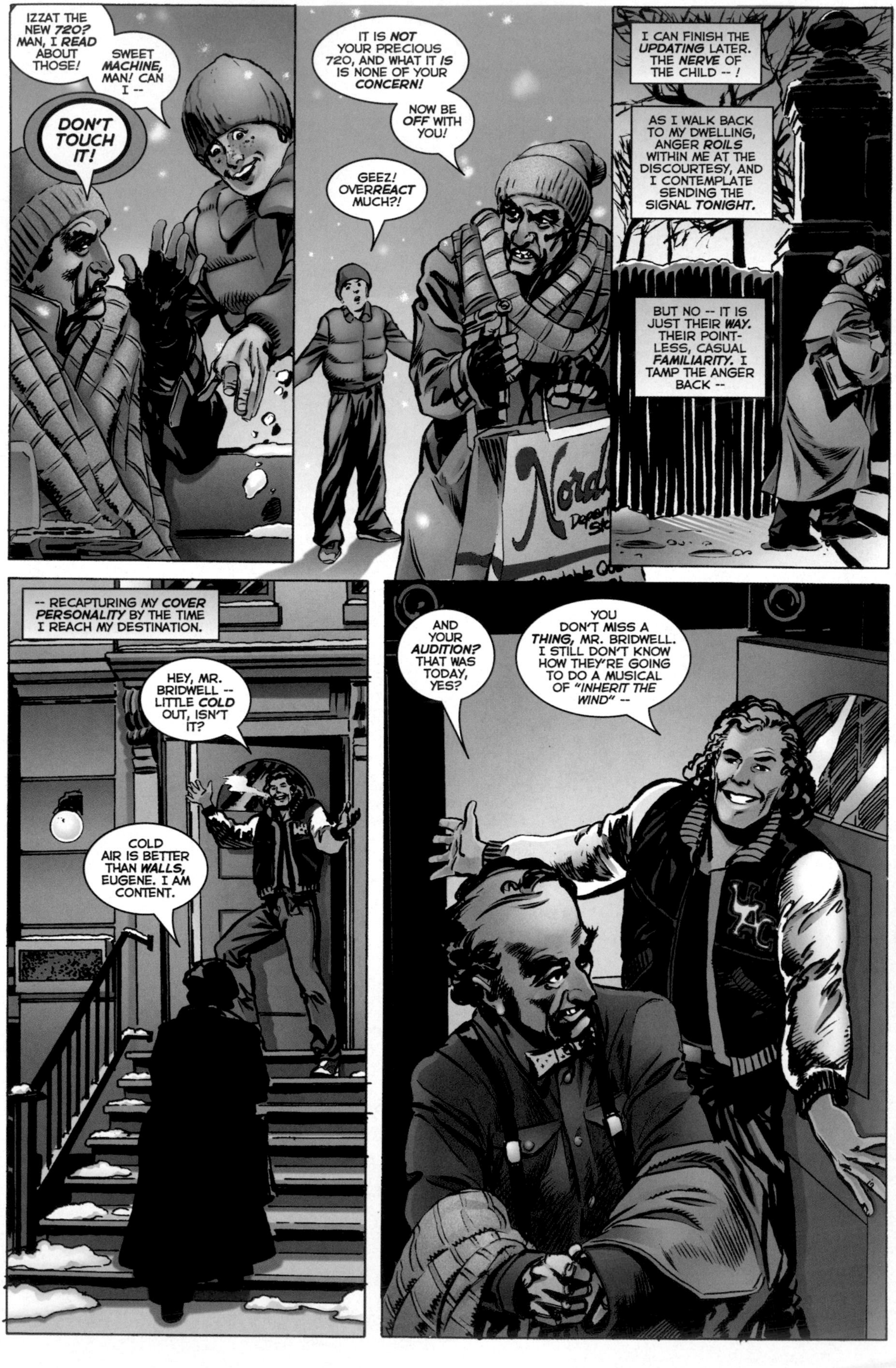
IZZAT THE NEW 720? MAN, I READ ABOUT THOSE!
SWEET MACHINE, MAN! CAN I --
DON'T TOUCH IT!
IT IS NOT YOUR PRECIOUS 720, AND WHAT IT IS IS NONE OF YOUR CONCERN!
NOW BE OFF WITH YOU!
GEEZ! OVERREACT MUCH?!
I CAN FINISH THE UPDATING LATER. THE NERVE OF THE CHILD -- !
AS I WALK BACK TO MY DWELLING, ANGER ROILS WITHIN ME AT THE DISCOURTESY, AND I CONTEMPLATE SENDING THE SIGNAL TONIGHT.
BUT NO -- IT IS JUST THEIR WAY. THEIR POINT-LESS, CASUAL FAMILIARITY. I TAMP THE ANGER BACK --
-- RECAPTURING MY COVER PERSONALITY BY THE TIME I REACH MY DESTINATION.
HEY, MR. BRIDWELL -- LITTLE COLD OUT, ISN'T IT?
COLD AIR IS BETTER THAN WALLS, EUGENE. I AM CONTENT.
AND YOUR AUDITION? THAT WAS TODAY, YES?
YOU DON'T MISS A THING, MR. BRIDWELL. I STILL DON'T KNOW HOW THEY'RE GOING TO DO A MUSICAL OF "INHERIT THE WIND" --

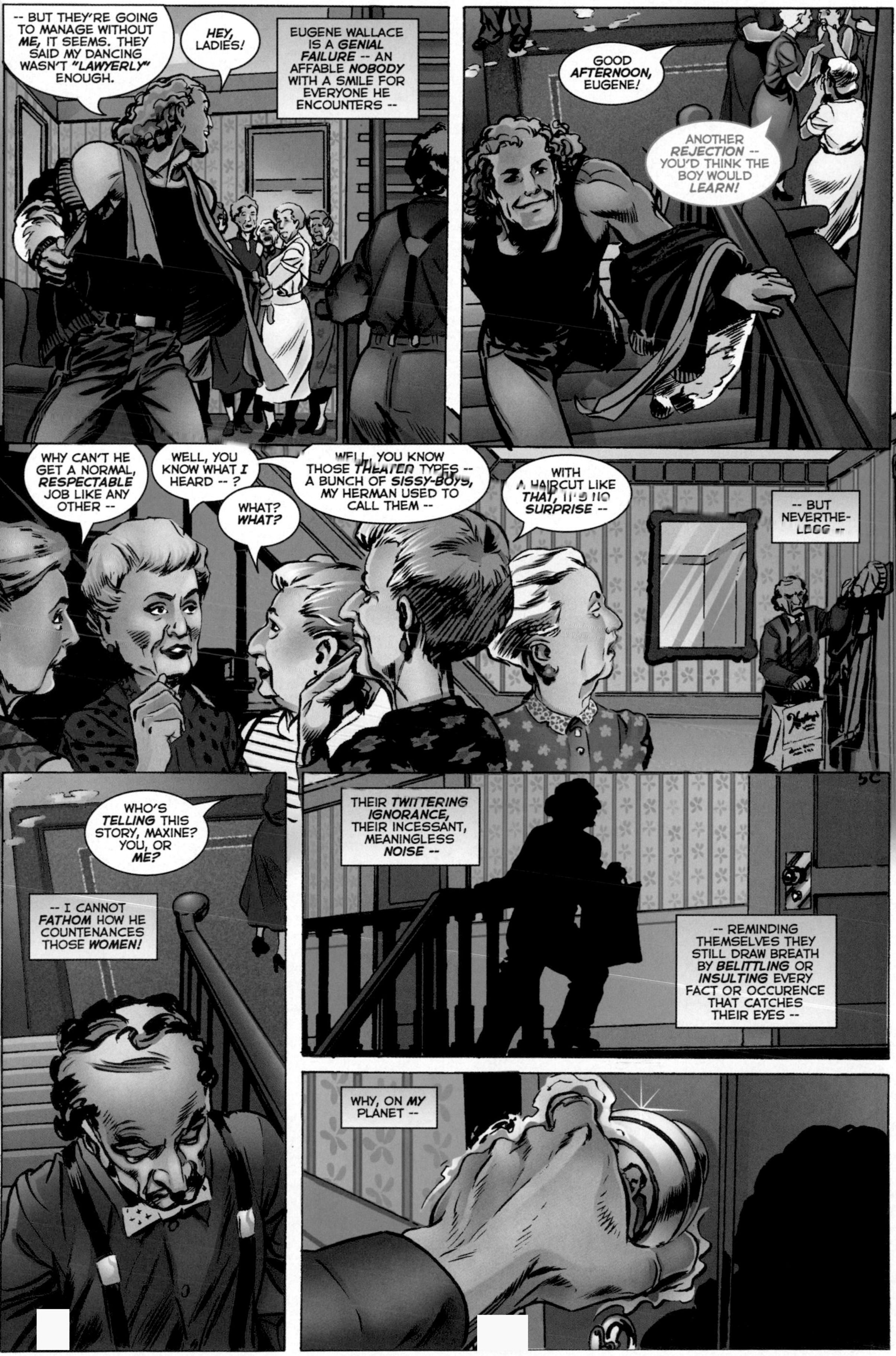
-- BUT THEY'RE GOING TO MANAGE WITHOUT ME, IT SEEMS. THEY SAID MY DANCING WASN'T "LAWYERLY" ENOUGH.
HEY, LADIES!
EUGENE WALLACE IS A GENIAL FAILURE -- AN AFFABLE NOBODY WITH A SMILE FOR EVERYONE HE ENCOUNTERS --
GOOD AFTERNOON, EUGENE!
ANOTHER REJECTION -- YOU'D THINK THE BOY WOULD LEARN!
WHY CAN'T HE GET A NORMAL, RESPECTABLE JOB LIKE ANY OTHER --
WELL, YOU KNOW WHAT I HEARD -- ?
WHAT? WHAT?
WELL, YOU KNOW THOSE THEATER TYPES -- A BUNCH OF SISSY-BOYS, MY HERMAN USED TO CALL THEM --
WITH A HAIRCUT LIKE THAT, IT'S NO SURPRISE --
-- BUT NEVERTHELESS --
WHO'S TELLING THIS STORY, MAXINE? YOU, OR ME?
-- I CANNOT FATHOM HOW HE COUNTENANCES THOSE WOMEN!
THEIR TWITTERING IGNORANCE, THEIR INCESSANT, MEANINGLESS NOISE --
-- REMINDING THEMSELVES THEY STILL DRAW BREATH BY BELITTLING OR INSULTING EVERY FACT OR OCCURENCE THAT CATCHES THEIR EYES --
WHY, ON MY PLANET --

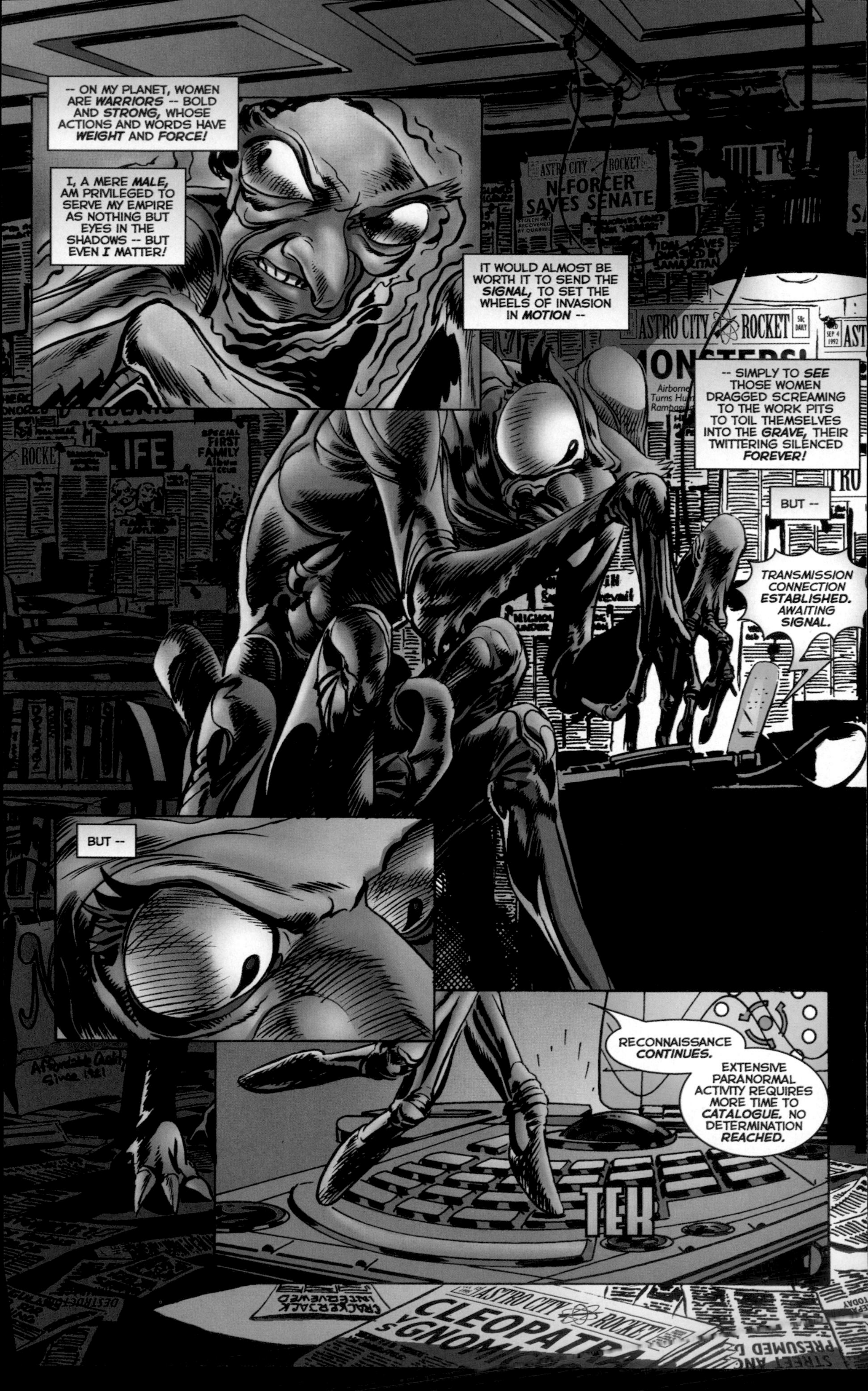
-- ON MY PLANET, WOMEN ARE WARRIORS -- BOLD AND STRONG, WHOSE ACTIONS AND WORDS HAVE WEIGHT AND FORCE!
I, A MERE MALE, AM PRIVILEGED TO SERVE MY EMPIRE AS NOTHING BUT EYES IN THE SHADOWS -- BUT EVEN I MATTER!
IT WOULD ALMOST BE WORTH IT TO SEND THE SIGNAL, TO SET THE WHEELS OF INVASION IN MOTION --
-- SIMPLY TO SEE THOSE WOMEN DRAGGED SCREAMING TO THE WORK PITS TO TOIL THEMSELVES INTO THE GRAVE, THEIR TWITTERING SILENCED FOREVER!
BUT --
TRANSMISSION CONNECTION ESTABLISHED. AWAITING SIGNAL.
BUT --
RECONNAISSANCE CONTINUES.
EXTENSIVE PARANORMAL ACTIVITY REQUIRES MORE TIME TO CATALOGUE. NO DETERMINATION REACHED.
TEK
ASTRO CITY ROCKET
N-FORCER SAVES SENATE
ASTRO CITY ROCKET
MONSTERS!
CLEOPATRA

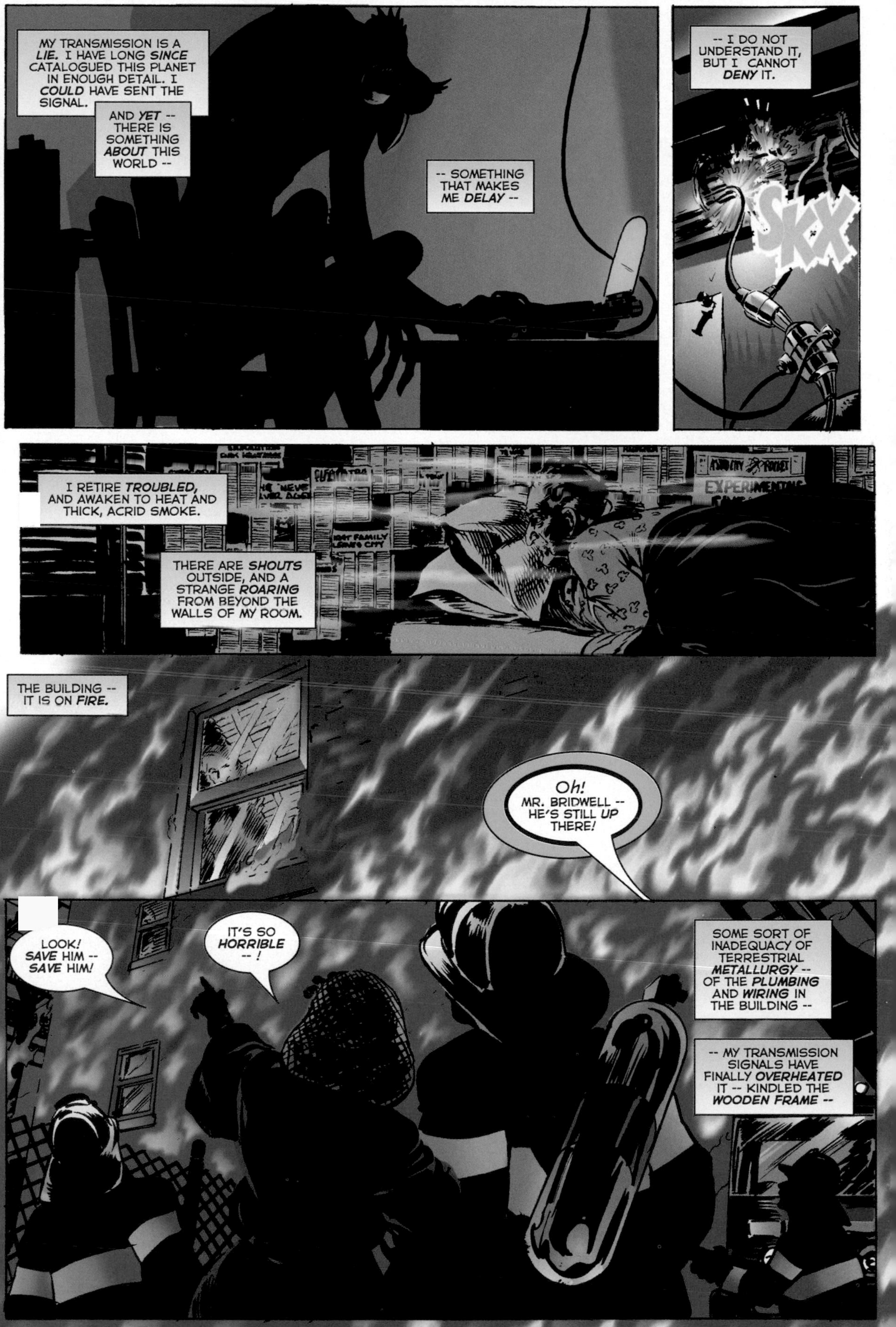
MY TRANSMISSION IS A LIE. I HAVE LONG SINCE CATALOGUED THIS PLANET IN ENOUGH DETAIL. I COULD HAVE SENT THE SIGNAL.
AND YET -- THERE IS SOMETHING ABOUT THIS WORLD --
-- SOMETHING THAT MAKES ME DELAY --
-- I DO NOT UNDERSTAND IT, BUT I CANNOT DENY IT.
SKX
I RETIRE TROUBLED, AND AWAKEN TO HEAT AND THICK, ACRID SMOKE.
THERE ARE SHOUTS OUTSIDE, AND A STRANGE ROARING FROM BEYOND THE WALLS OF MY ROOM.
THE BUILDING -- IT IS ON FIRE.
Oh! MR. BRIDWELL -- HE'S STILL UP THERE!
LOOK! SAVE HIM -- SAVE HIM!
IT'S SO HORRIBLE -- !
SOME SORT OF INADEQUACY OF TERRESTRIAL METALLURGY -- OF THE PLUMBING AND WIRING IN THE BUILDING --
-- MY TRANSMISSION SIGNALS HAVE FINALLY OVERHEATED IT -- KINDLED THE WOODEN FRAME --

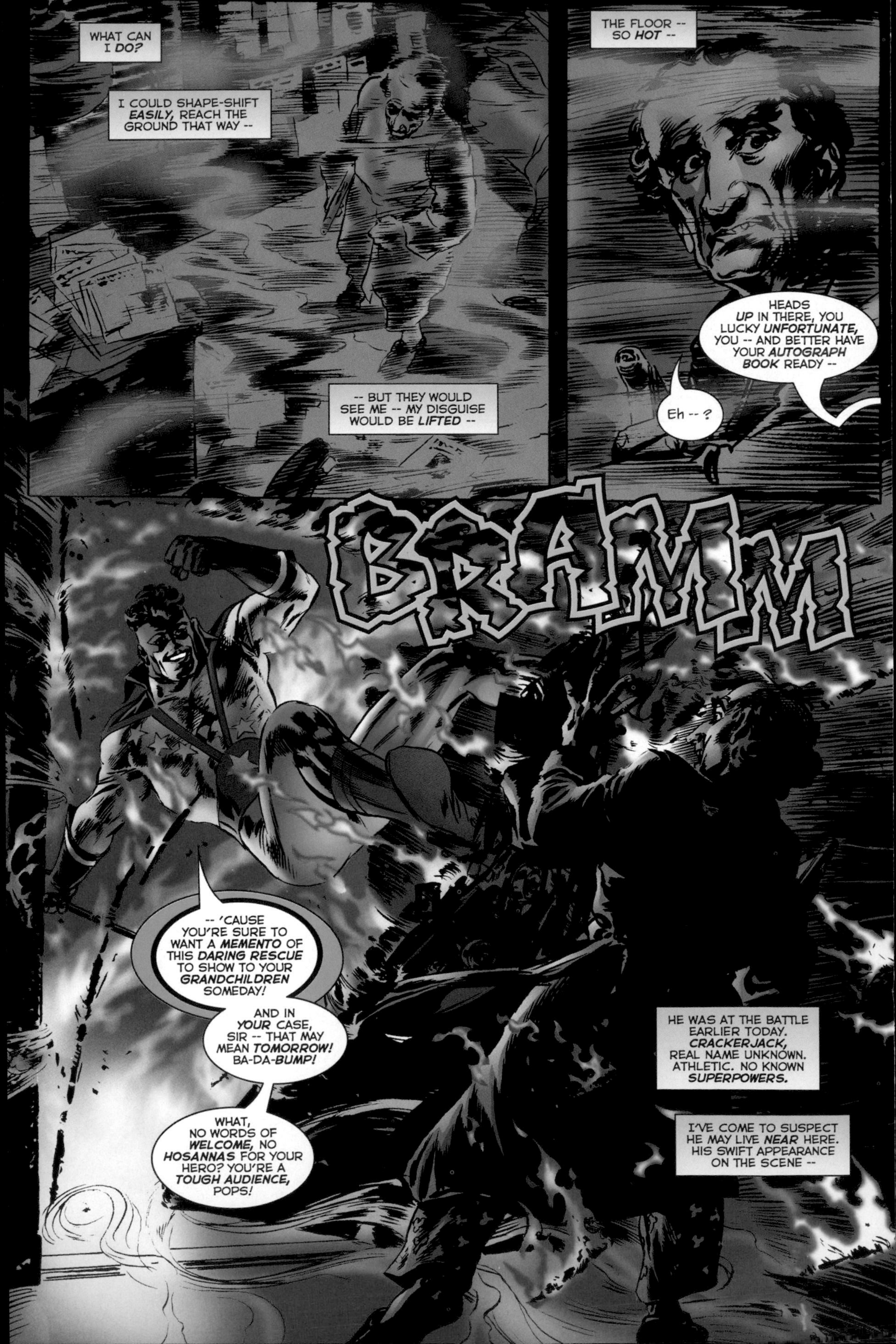

WHAT CAN I DO?
I COULD SHAPE-SHIFT EASILY, REACH THE GROUND THAT WAY --
-- BUT THEY WOULD SEE ME -- MY DISGUISE WOULD BE LIFTED --
THE FLOOR -- SO HOT --
HEADS UP IN THERE, YOU LUCKY UNFORTUNATE, YOU -- AND BETTER HAVE YOUR AUTOGRAPH BOOK READY --
Eh -- ?
BRAMM
-- 'CAUSE YOU'RE SURE TO WANT A MEMENTO OF THIS DARING RESCUE TO SHOW TO YOUR GRANDCHILDREN SOMEDAY!
AND IN YOUR CASE, SIR -- THAT MAY MEAN TOMORROW! BA-DA-BUMP!
WHAT, NO WORDS OF WELCOME, NO HOSANNAS FOR YOUR HERO? YOU'RE A TOUGH AUDIENCE, POPS!
HE WAS AT THE BATTLE EARLIER TODAY. CRACKERJACK, REAL NAME UNKNOWN. ATHLETIC. NO KNOWN SUPERPOWERS.
I'VE COME TO SUSPECT HE MAY LIVE NEAR HERE. HIS SWIFT APPEARANCE ON THE SCENE --

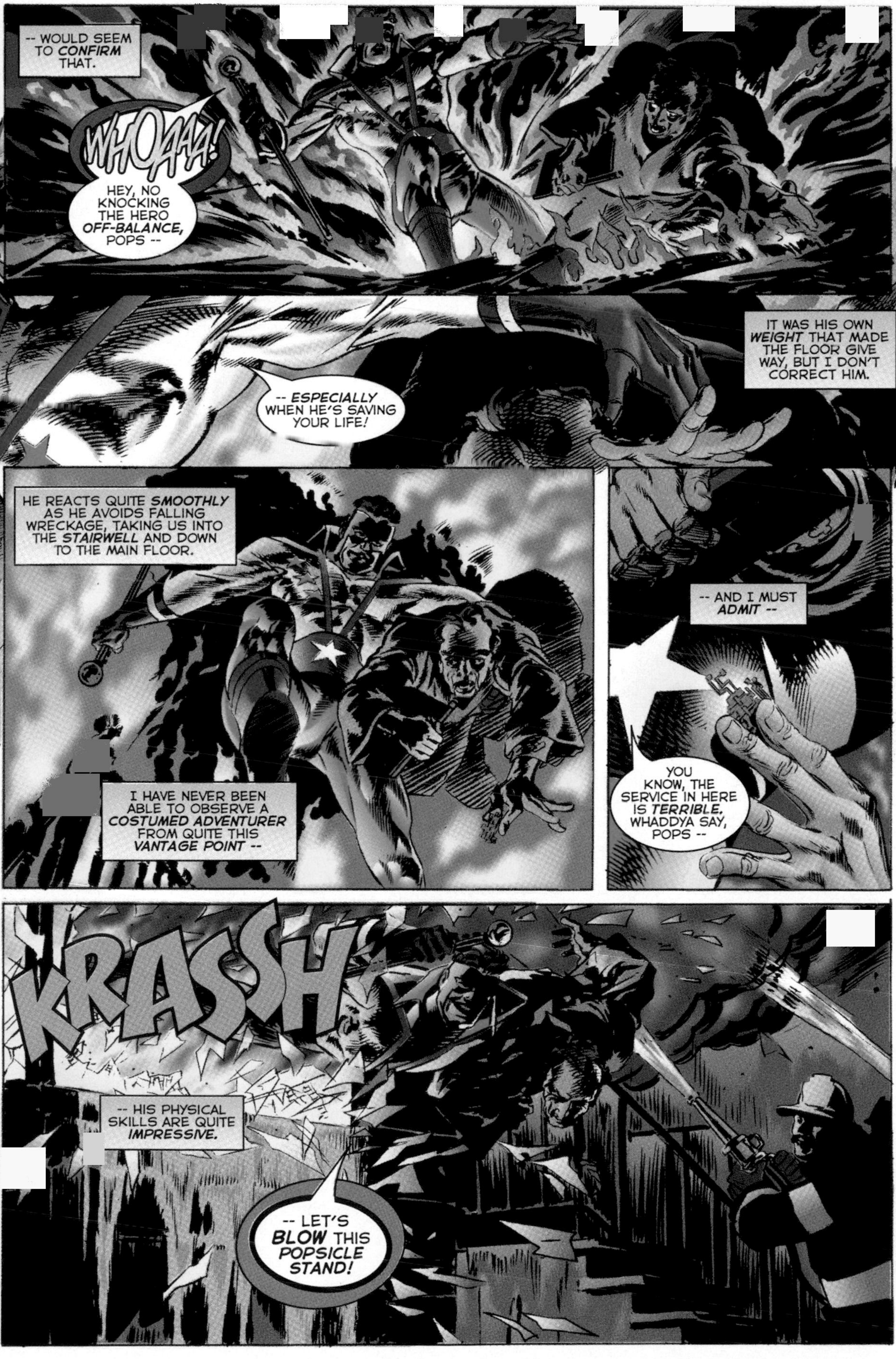
-- WOULD SEEM TO CONFIRM THAT.
WHOAAA!
HEY, NO KNOCKING THE HERO OFF-BALANCE, POPS --
-- ESPECIALLY WHEN HE'S SAVING YOUR LIFE!
IT WAS HIS OWN WEIGHT THAT MADE THE FLOOR GIVE WAY, BUT I DON'T CORRECT HIM.
HE REACTS QUITE SMOOTHLY AS HE AVOIDS FALLING WRECKAGE, TAKING US INTO THE STAIRWELL AND DOWN TO THE MAIN FLOOR.
I HAVE NEVER BEEN ABLE TO OBSERVE A COSTUMED ADVENTURER FROM QUITE THIS VANTAGE POINT --
-- AND I MUST ADMIT --
YOU KNOW, THE SERVICE IN HERE IS TERRIBLE. WHADDYA SAY, POPS --
KRASSH
-- HIS PHYSICAL SKILLS ARE QUITE IMPRESSIVE.
-- LET'S BLOW THIS POPSICLE STAND!

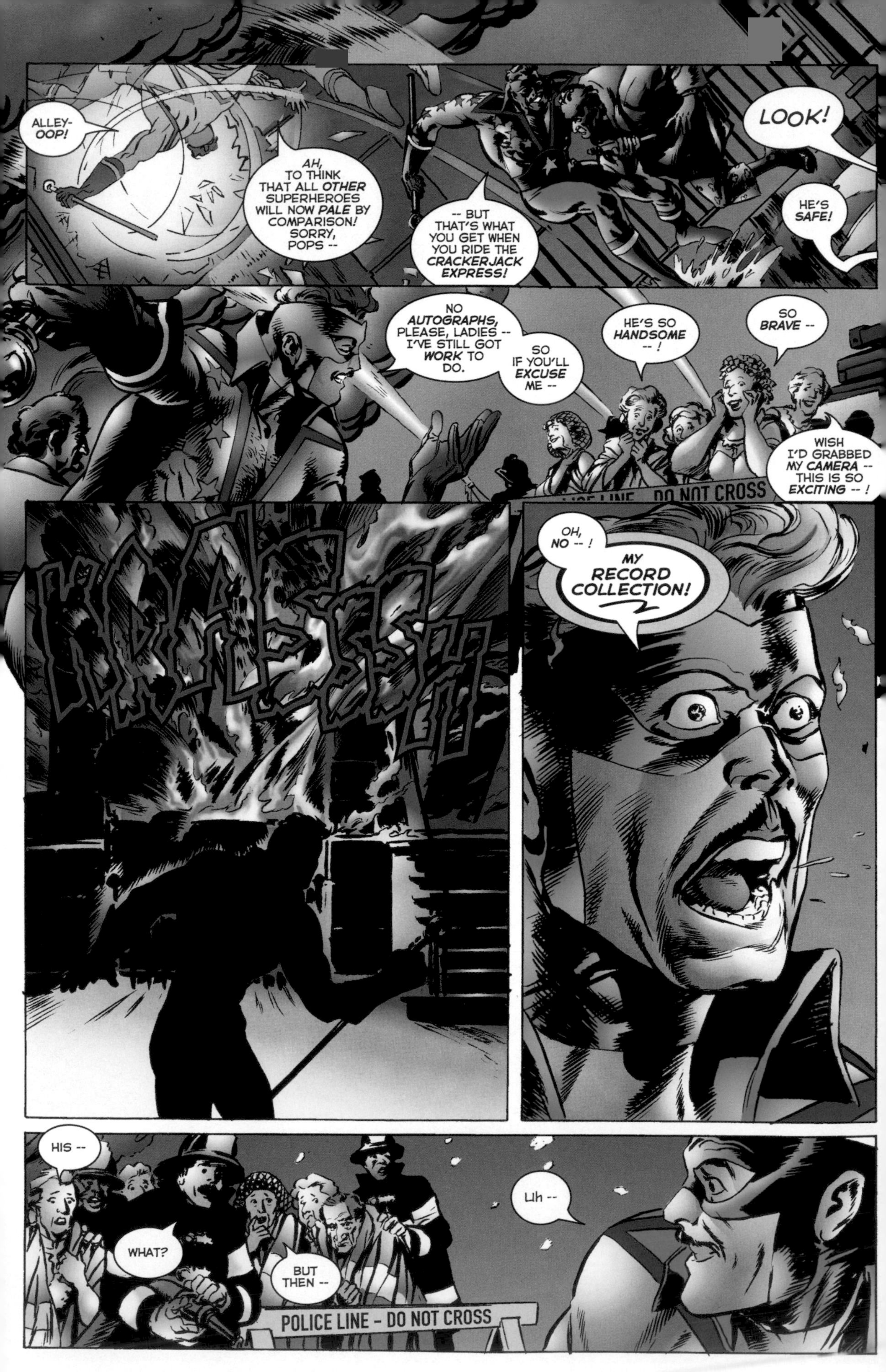
ALLEY-OOP!
AH, TO THINK THAT ALL OTHER SUPERHEROES WILL NOW PALE BY COMPARISON! SORRY, POPS --
-- BUT THAT'S WHAT YOU GET WHEN YOU RIDE THE CRACKERJACK EXPRESS!
LOOK!
HE'S SAFE!
NO AUTOGRAPHS, PLEASE, LADIES -- I'VE STILL GOT WORK TO DO.
SO IF YOU'LL EXCUSE ME --
HE'S SO HANDSOME -- !
SO BRAVE --
WISH I'D GRABBED MY CAMERA -- THIS IS SO EXCITING -- !
DO NOT CROSS
OH, NO -- !
MY RECORD COLLECTION!
HIS --
WHAT?
BUT THEN --
UH --
POLICE LINE - DO NOT CROSS

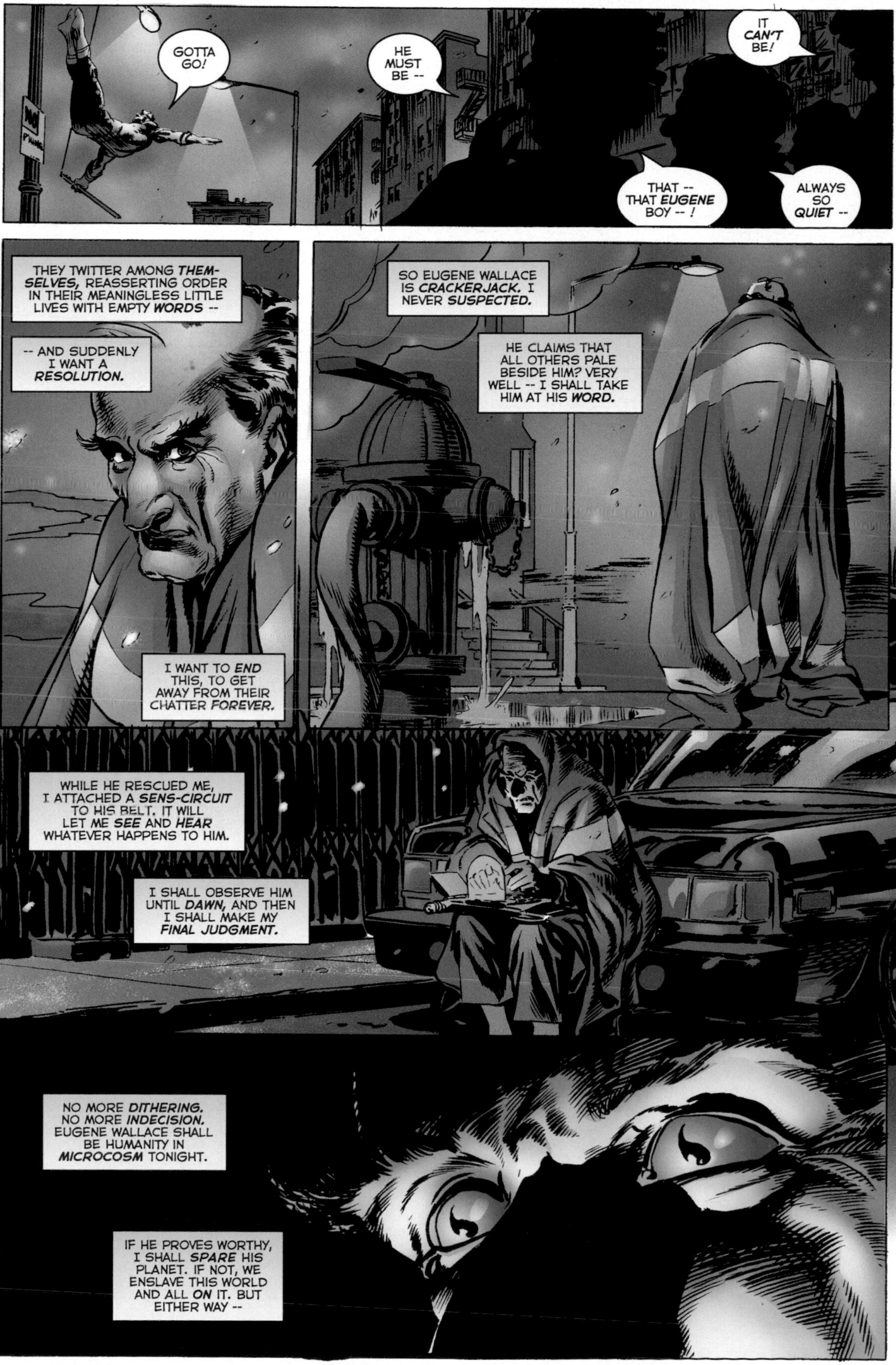
GOTTA GO!
HE MUST BE --
IT CAN'T BE!
THAT -- THAT EUGENE BOY -- !
ALWAYS SO QUIET --
THEY TWITTER AMONG THEMSELVES, REASSERTING ORDER IN THEIR MEANINGLESS LITTLE LIVES WITH EMPTY WORDS --
-- AND SUDDENLY I WANT A RESOLUTION.
I WANT TO END THIS, TO GET AWAY FROM THEIR CHATTER FOREVER.
SO EUGENE WALLACE IS CRACKERJACK. I NEVER SUSPECTED.
HE CLAIMS THAT ALL OTHERS PALE BESIDE HIM? VERY WELL -- I SHALL TAKE HIM AT HIS WORD.
WHILE HE RESCUED ME, I ATTACHED A SENS-CIRCUIT TO HIS BELT. IT WILL LET ME SEE AND HEAR WHATEVER HAPPENS TO HIM.
I SHALL OBSERVE HIM UNTIL DAWN, AND THEN I SHALL MAKE MY FINAL JUDGMENT.
NO MORE DITHERING. NO MORE INDECISION. EUGENE WALLACE SHALL BE HUMANITY IN MICROCOSM TONIGHT.
IF HE PROVES WORTHY, I SHALL SPARE HIS PLANET. IF NOT, WE ENSLAVE THIS WORLD AND ALL ON IT. BUT EITHER WAY --

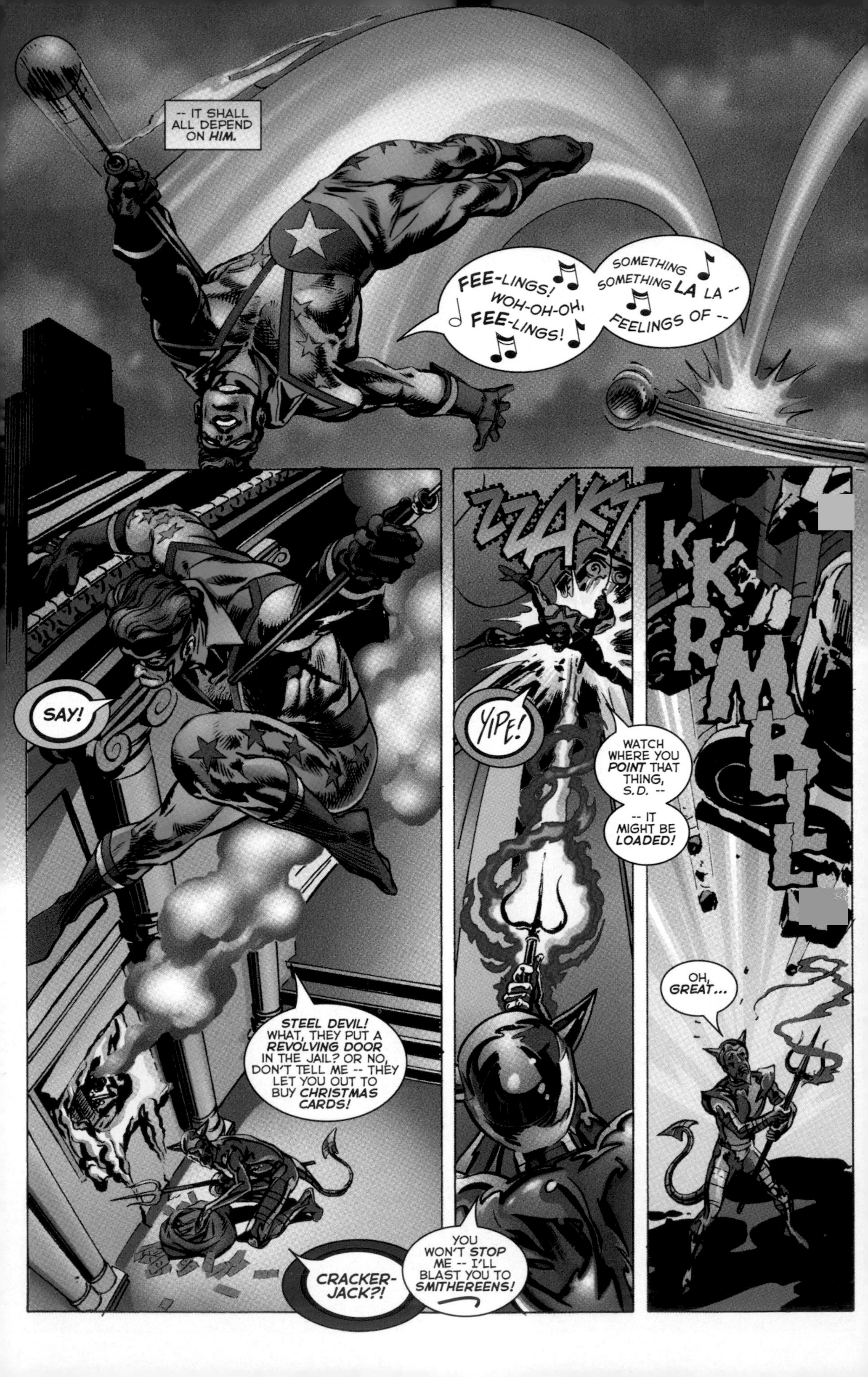

-- IT SHALL ALL DEPEND ON HIM.
FEE-LINGS! WOH-OH-OH, FEE-LINGS!
SOMETHING SOMETHING LA LA -- FEELINGS OF --
SAY!
STEEL DEVIL! WHAT, THEY PUT A REVOLVING DOOR IN THE JAIL? OR NO, DON'T TELL ME -- THEY LET YOU OUT TO BUY CHRISTMAS CARDS!
CRACKER-JACK?!
YOU WON'T STOP ME -- I'LL BLAST YOU TO SMITHEREENS!
ZZZAKT
YIPE!
WATCH WHERE YOU POINT THAT THING, S.D. --
-- IT MIGHT BE LOADED!
KKRMBL
OH, GREAT...

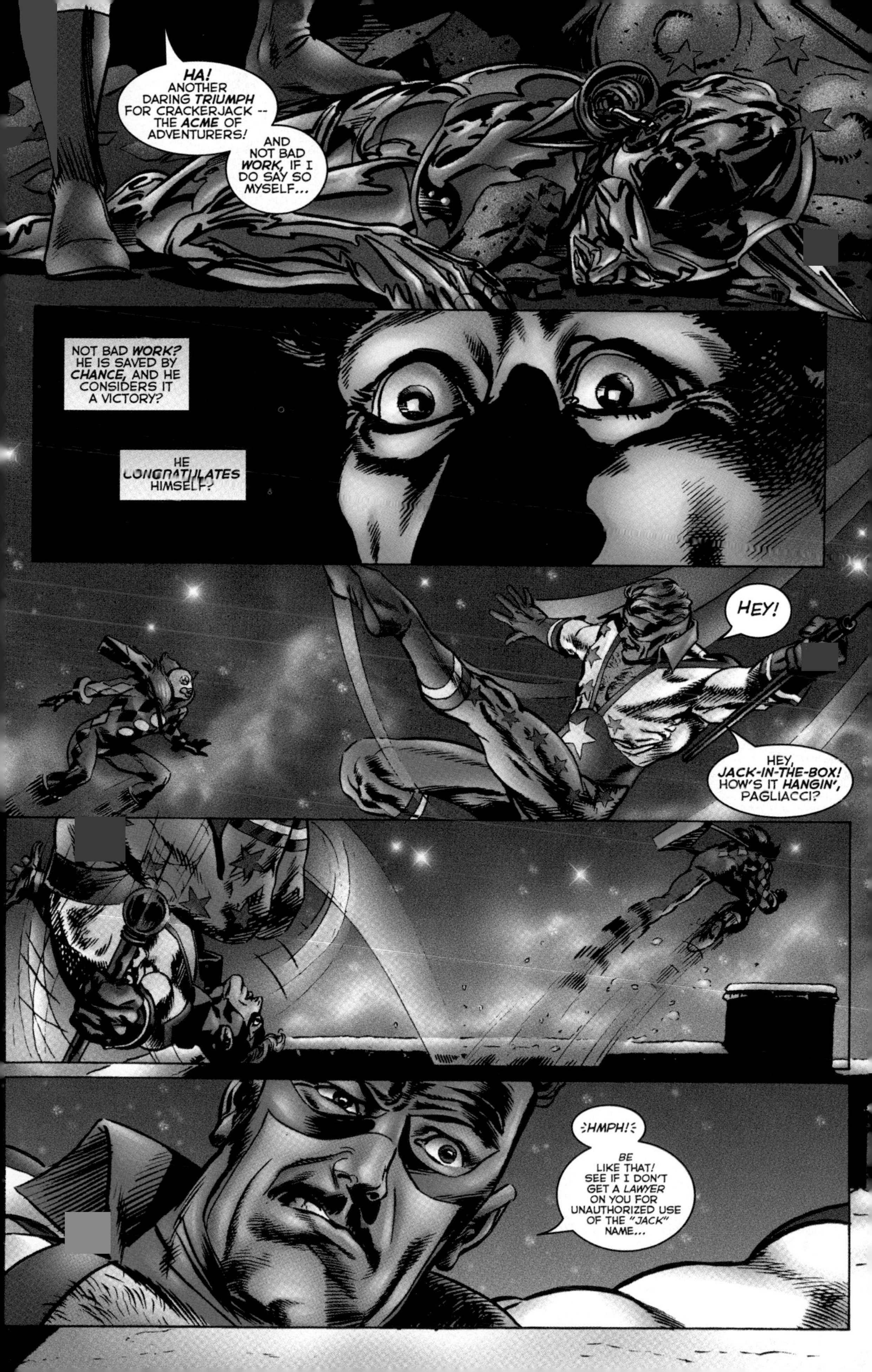

HA! ANOTHER DARING TRIUMPH FOR CRACKERJACK -- THE ACME OF ADVENTURERS!
AND NOT BAD WORK, IF I DO SAY SO MYSELF...
NOT BAD WORK? HE IS SAVED BY CHANCE, AND HE CONSIDERS IT A VICTORY?
HE CONGRATULATES HIMSELF?
HEY!
HEY, JACK-IN-THE-BOX! HOW'S IT HANGIN', PAGLIACCI?
HMPH!
BE LIKE THAT! SEE IF I DON'T GET A LAWYER ON YOU FOR UNAUTHORIZED USE OF THE "JACK" NAME...

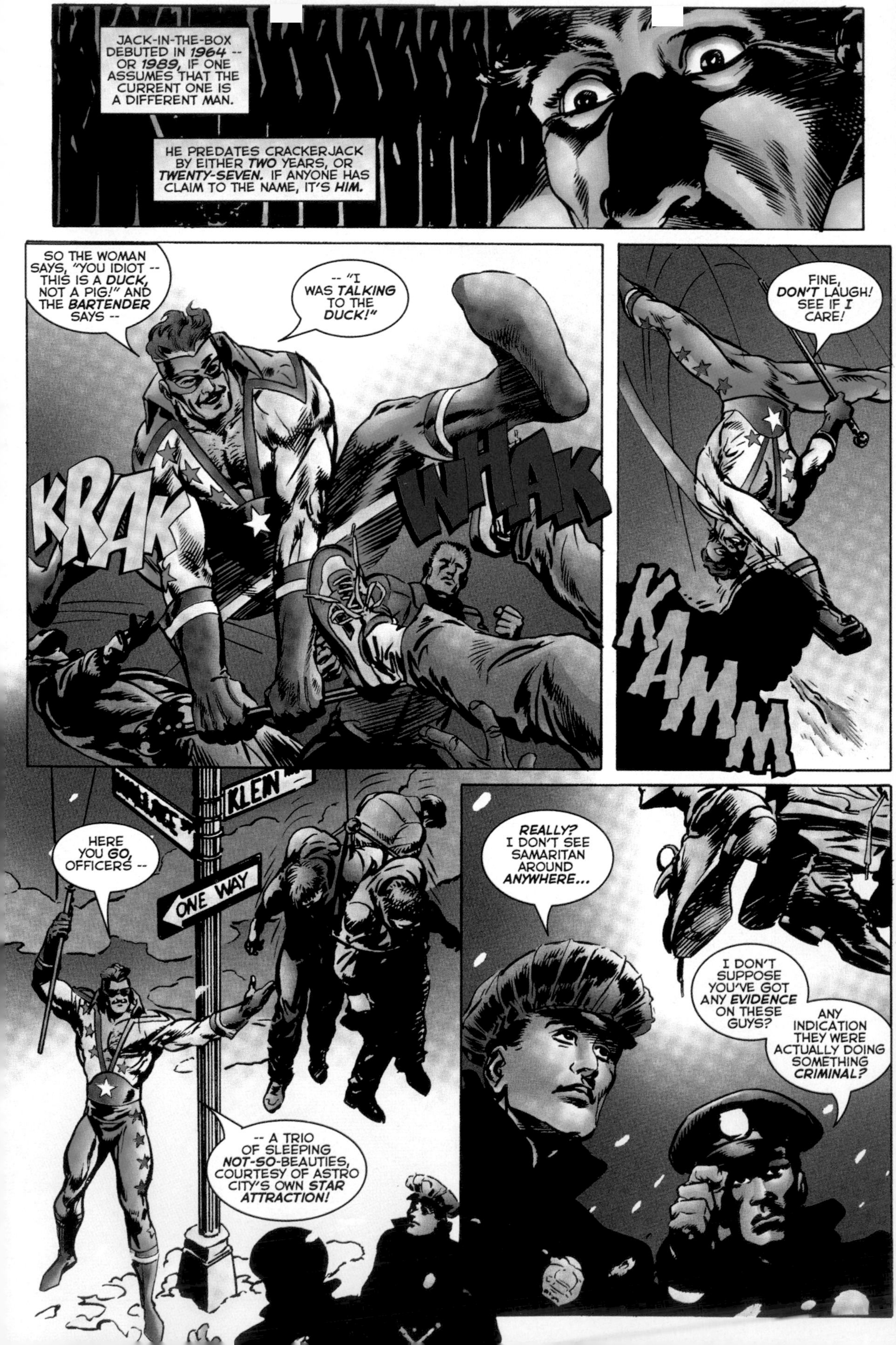
JACK-IN-THE-BOX DEBUTED IN 1964 -- OR 1989, IF ONE ASSUMES THAT THE CURRENT ONE IS A DIFFERENT MAN.
HE PREDATES CRACKERJACK BY EITHER TWO YEARS, OR TWENTY-SEVEN. IF ANYONE HAS CLAIM TO THE NAME, IT'S HIM.
SO THE WOMAN SAYS, "YOU IDIOT -- THIS IS A DUCK, NOT A PIG!" AND THE BARTENDER SAYS --
-- "I WAS TALKING TO THE DUCK!"
KRAK
WHAK
FINE, DON'T LAUGH! SEE IF I CARE!
KAMMM
KLEIN
ONE WAY
HERE YOU GO, OFFICERS --
-- A TRIO OF SLEEPING NOT-SO-BEAUTIES, COURTESY OF ASTRO CITY'S OWN STAR ATTRACTION!
REALLY? I DON'T SEE SAMARITAN AROUND ANYWHERE...
I DON'T SUPPOSE YOU'VE GOT ANY EVIDENCE ON THESE GUYS?
ANY INDICATION THEY WERE ACTUALLY DOING SOMETHING CRIMINAL?

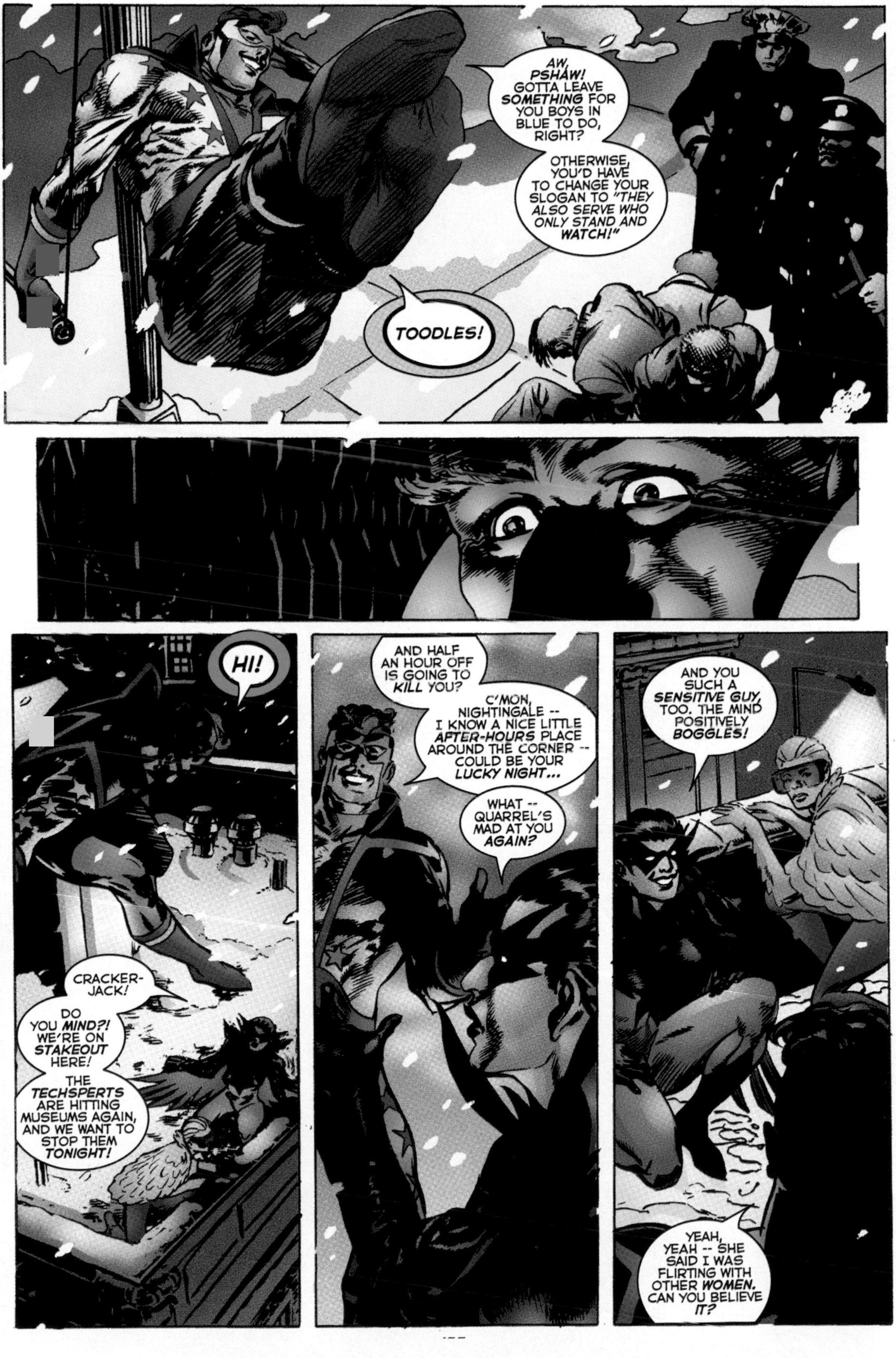
AW, PSHAW! GOTTA LEAVE SOMETHING FOR YOU BOYS IN BLUE TO DO, RIGHT?
OTHERWISE, YOU'D HAVE TO CHANGE YOUR SLOGAN TO "THEY ALSO SERVE WHO ONLY STAND AND WATCH!"
TOODLES!
HI!
CRACKER-JACK!
DO YOU MIND?! WE'RE ON STAKEOUT HERE!
THE TECHSPERTS ARE HITTING MUSEUMS AGAIN, AND WE WANT TO STOP THEM TONIGHT!
AND HALF AN HOUR OFF IS GOING TO KILL YOU?
C'MON, NIGHTINGALE -- I KNOW A NICE LITTLE AFTER-HOURS PLACE AROUND THE CORNER -- COULD BE YOUR LUCKY NIGHT...
WHAT -- QUARREL'S MAD AT YOU AGAIN?
YEAH, YEAH -- SHE SAID I WAS FLIRTING WITH OTHER WOMEN. CAN YOU BELIEVE IT?
AND YOU SUCH A SENSITIVE GUY, TOO. THE MIND POSITIVELY BOGGLES!

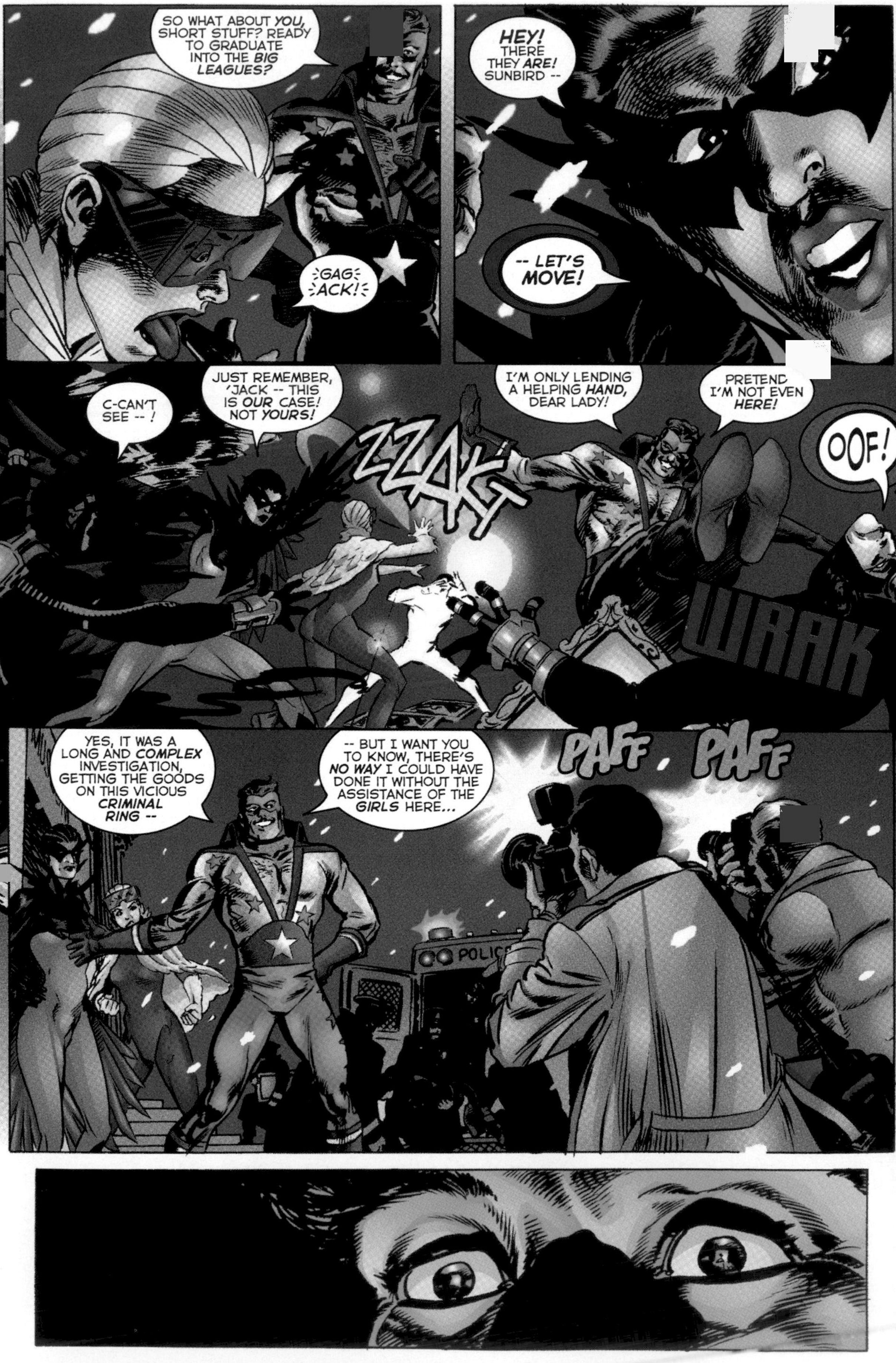
SO WHAT ABOUT *YOU*, SHORT STUFF? READY TO GRADUATE INTO THE *BIG LEAGUES?*
GAG ACK!
HEY! THERE THEY *ARE!* SUNBIRD --
-- *LET'S MOVE!*
C-CAN'T SEE -- !
JUST REMEMBER, 'JACK -- THIS IS *OUR* CASE! NOT *YOURS!*
ZZAKT
I'M ONLY LENDING A HELPING *HAND,* DEAR LADY!
PRETEND I'M NOT EVEN *HERE!*
OOF!
WRAK
YES, IT WAS A LONG AND *COMPLEX* INVESTIGATION, GETTING THE GOODS ON THIS VICIOUS *CRIMINAL RING* --
-- BUT I WANT YOU TO KNOW, THERE'S *NO WAY* I COULD HAVE DONE IT WITHOUT THE ASSISTANCE OF THE *GIRLS* HERE...
PAFF PAFF
POLICE

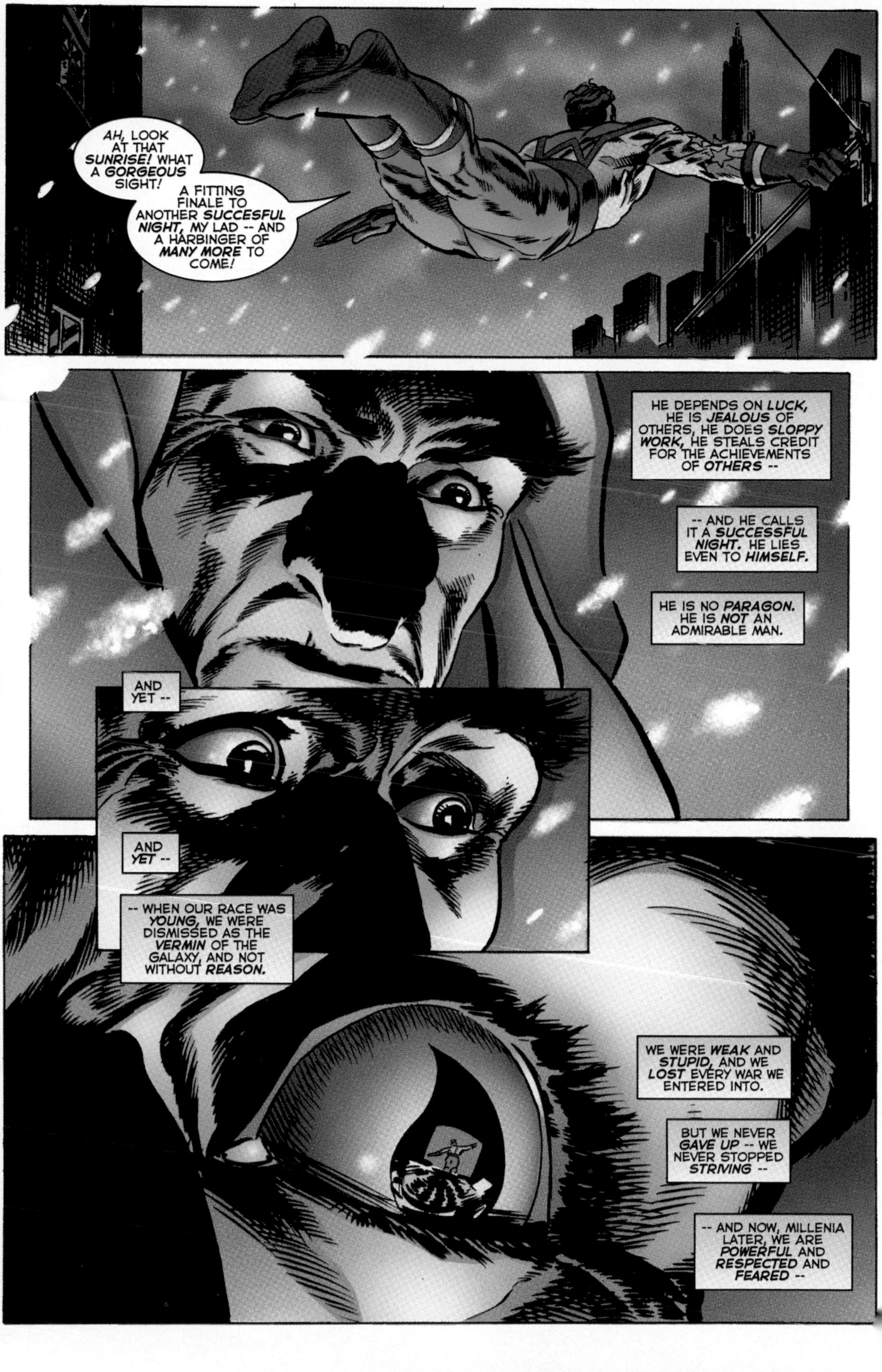
AH, LOOK AT THAT SUNRISE! WHAT A GORGEOUS SIGHT!
A FITTING FINALE TO ANOTHER SUCCESFUL NIGHT, MY LAD -- AND A HARBINGER OF MANY MORE TO COME!
HE DEPENDS ON LUCK, HE IS JEALOUS OF OTHERS, HE DOES SLOPPY WORK, HE STEALS CREDIT FOR THE ACHIEVEMENTS OF OTHERS --
-- AND HE CALLS IT A SUCCESSFUL NIGHT. HE LIES EVEN TO HIMSELF.
HE IS NO PARAGON. HE IS NOT AN ADMIRABLE MAN.
AND YET --
AND YET --
-- WHEN OUR RACE WAS YOUNG, WE WERE DISMISSED AS THE VERMIN OF THE GALAXY, AND NOT WITHOUT REASON.
WE WERE WEAK AND STUPID, AND WE LOST EVERY WAR WE ENTERED INTO.
BUT WE NEVER GAVE UP -- WE NEVER STOPPED STRIVING --
-- AND NOW, MILLENIA LATER, WE ARE POWERFUL AND RESPECTED AND FEARED --

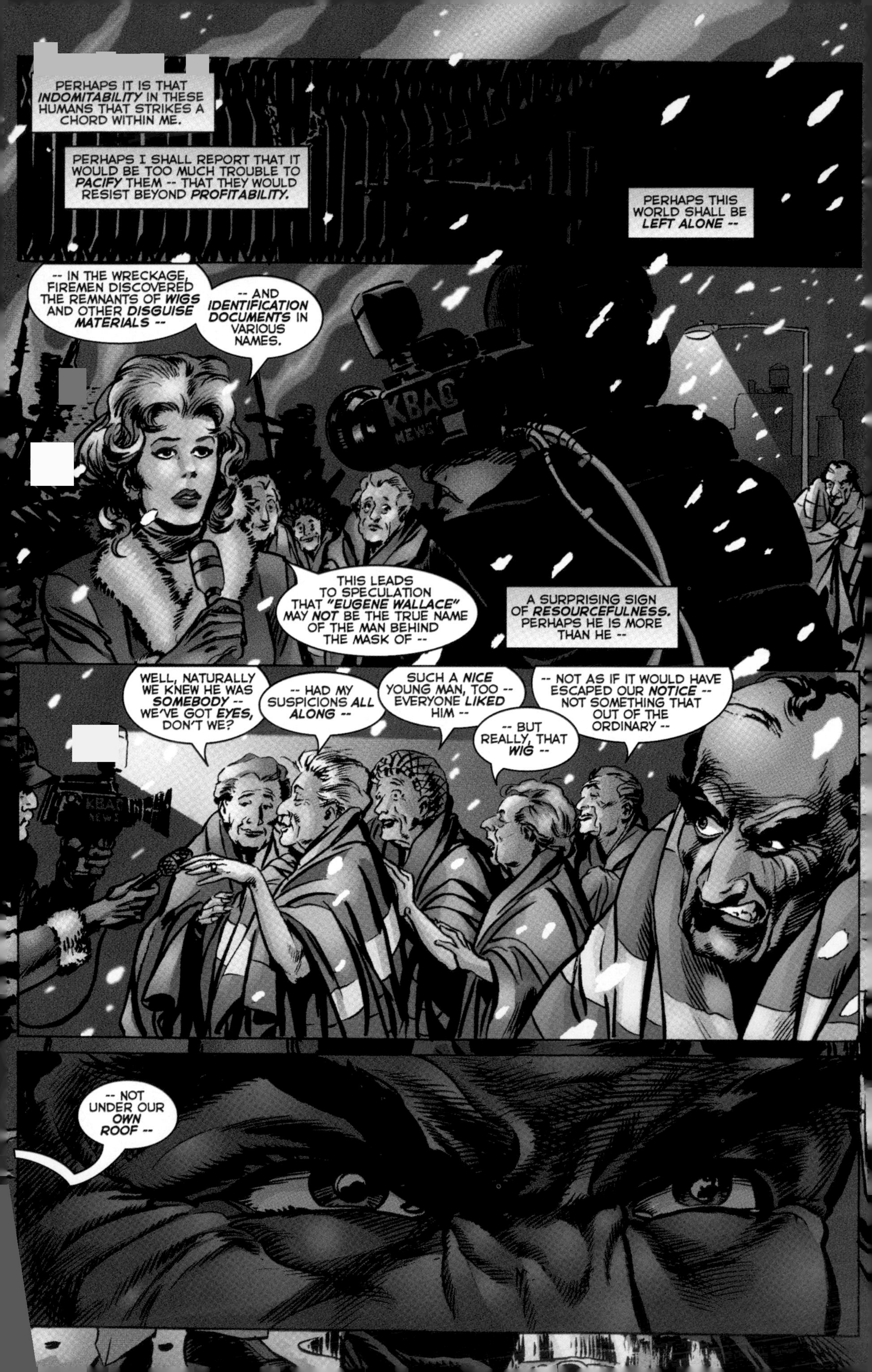
PERHAPS IT IS THAT INDOMITABILITY IN THESE HUMANS THAT STRIKES A CHORD WITHIN ME.
PERHAPS I SHALL REPORT THAT IT WOULD BE TOO MUCH TROUBLE TO PACIFY THEM -- THAT THEY WOULD RESIST BEYOND PROFITABILITY.
PERHAPS THIS WORLD SHALL BE LEFT ALONE --
-- IN THE WRECKAGE, FIREMEN DISCOVERED THE REMNANTS OF WIGS AND OTHER DISGUISE MATERIALS --
-- AND IDENTIFICATION DOCUMENTS IN VARIOUS NAMES.
KBAQ NEWS
THIS LEADS TO SPECULATION THAT "EUGENE WALLACE" MAY NOT BE THE TRUE NAME OF THE MAN BEHIND THE MASK OF --
A SURPRISING SIGN OF RESOURCEFULNESS. PERHAPS HE IS MORE THAN HE --
WELL, NATURALLY WE KNEW HE WAS SOMEBODY -- WE'VE GOT EYES, DON'T WE?
-- HAD MY SUSPICIONS ALL ALONG --
SUCH A NICE YOUNG MAN, TOO -- EVERYONE LIKED HIM --
-- BUT REALLY, THAT WIG --
-- NOT AS IF IT WOULD HAVE ESCAPED OUR NOTICE -- NOT SOMETHING THAT OUT OF THE ORDINARY --
-- NOT UNDER OUR OWN ROOF --

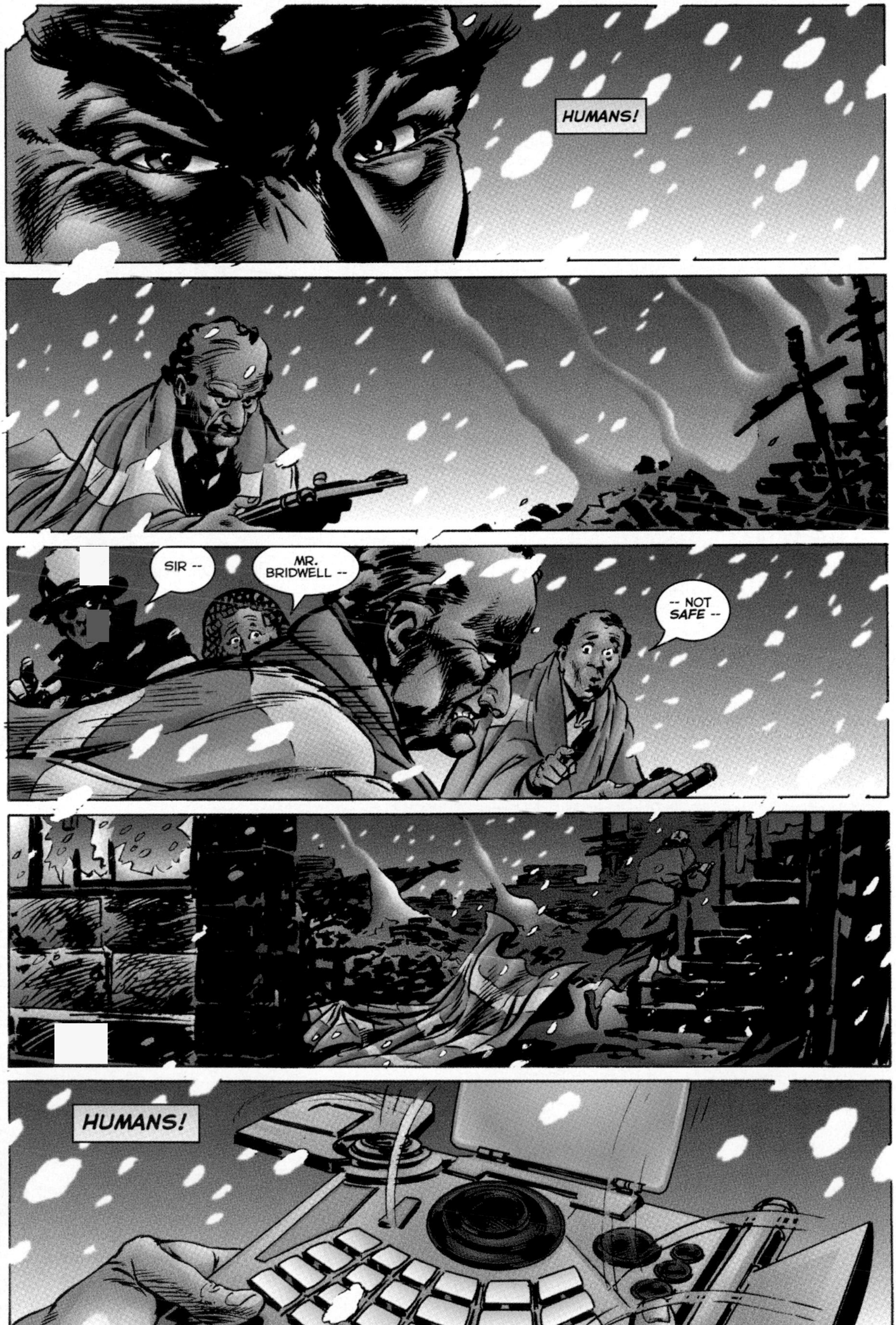
HUMANS!
SIR --
MR. BRIDWELL --
-- NOT SAFE --
HUMANS!

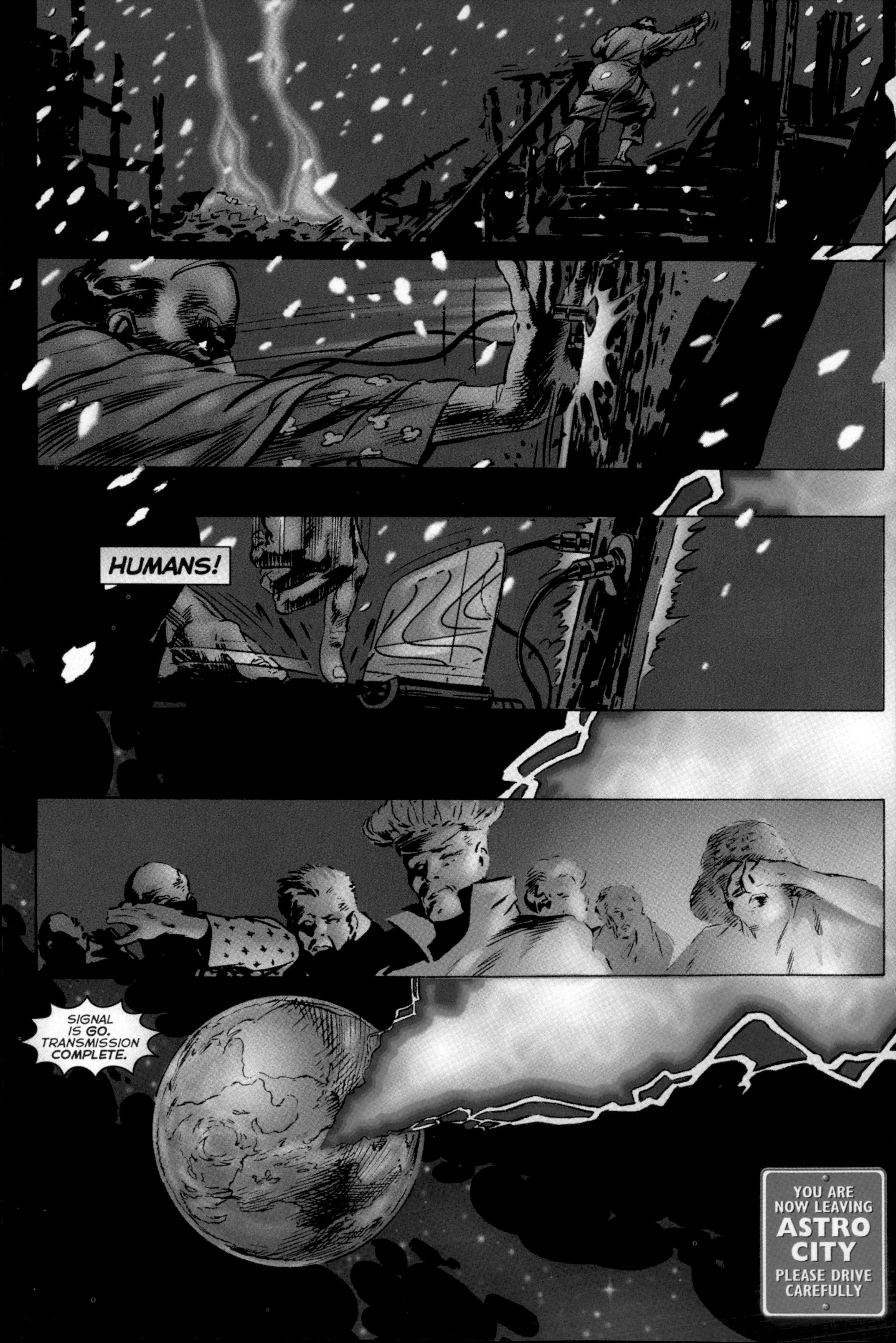
HUMANS!
SIGNAL IS GO. TRANSMISSION COMPLETE.
YOU ARE NOW LEAVING ASTRO CITY PLEASE DRIVE CAREFULLY

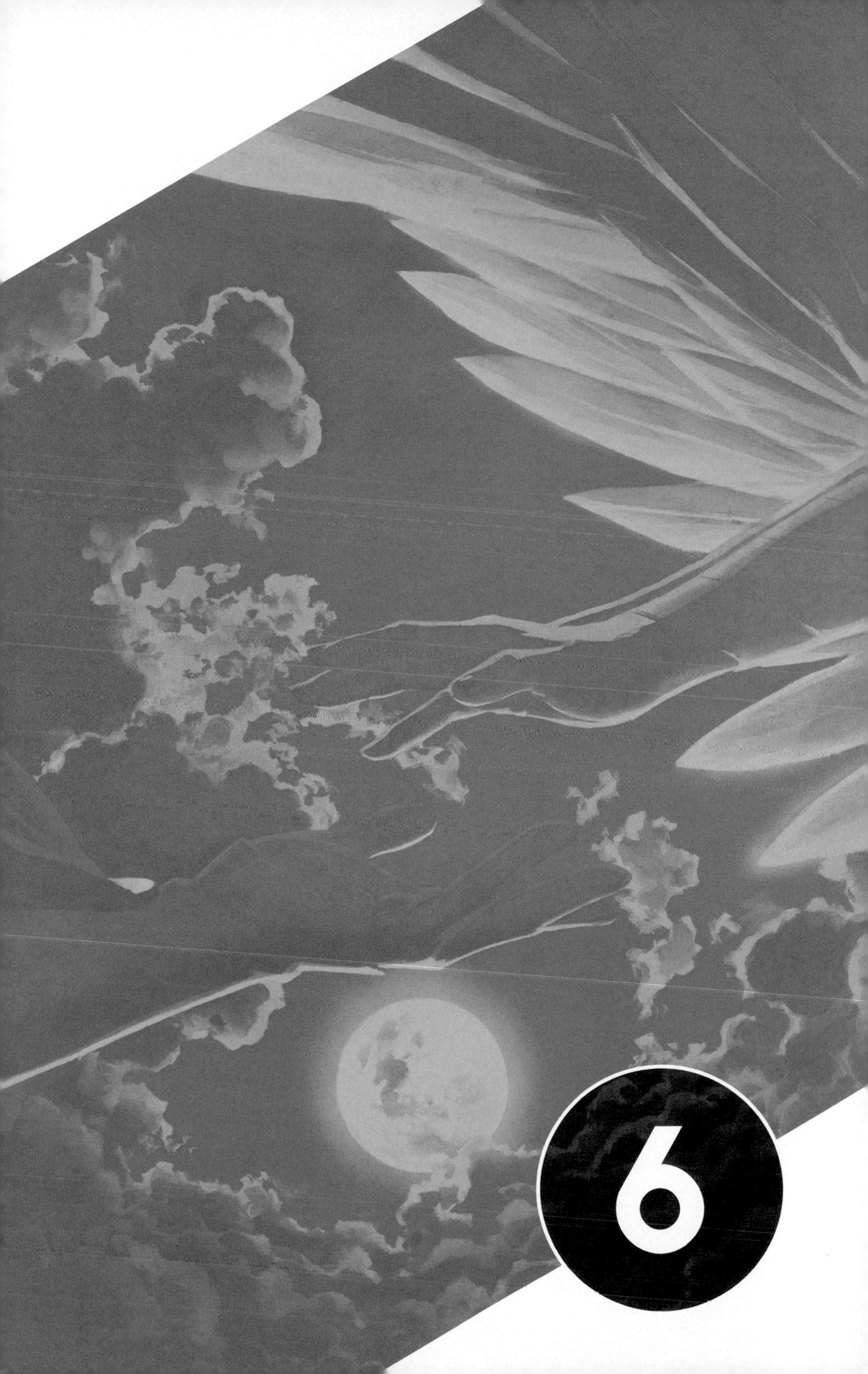
6

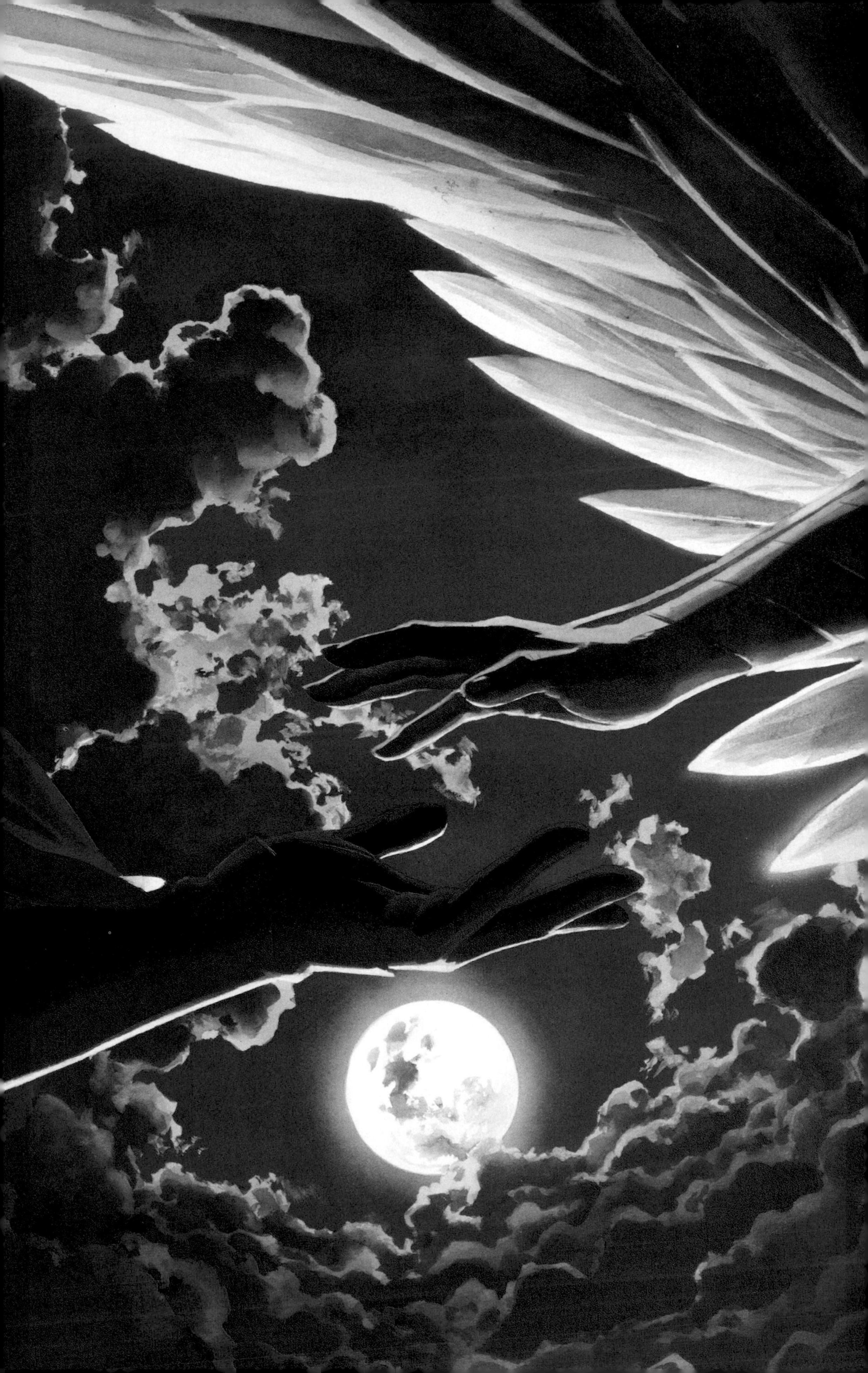

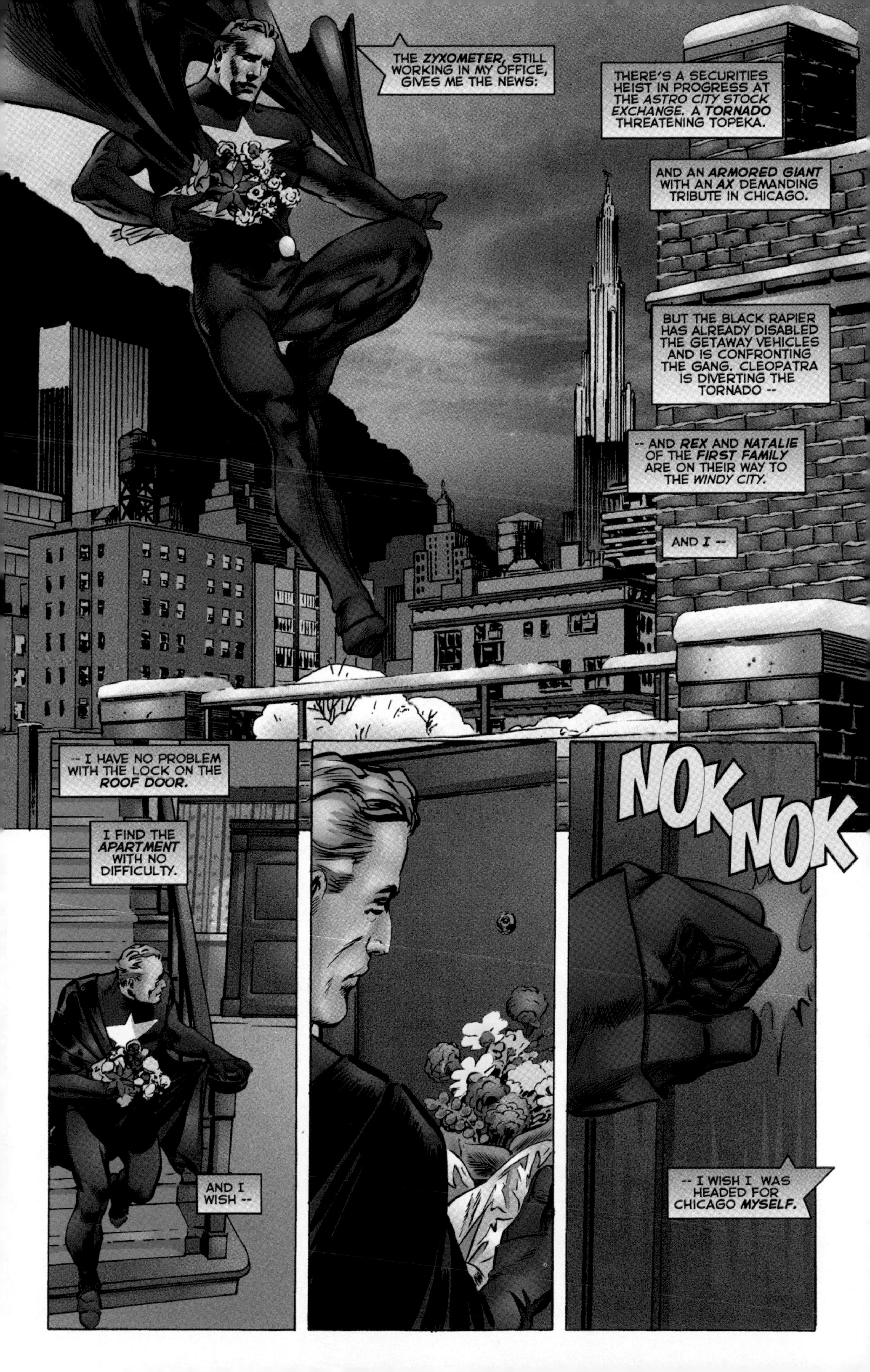

THE ZYXOMETER, STILL WORKING IN MY OFFICE, GIVES ME THE NEWS:
THERE'S A SECURITIES HEIST IN PROGRESS AT THE ASTRO CITY STOCK EXCHANGE. A TORNADO THREATENING TOPEKA.
AND AN ARMORED GIANT WITH AN AX DEMANDING TRIBUTE IN CHICAGO.
BUT THE BLACK RAPIER HAS ALREADY DISABLED THE GETAWAY VEHICLES AND IS CONFRONTING THE GANG. CLEOPATRA IS DIVERTING THE TORNADO --
-- AND REX AND NATALIE OF THE FIRST FAMILY ARE ON THEIR WAY TO THE WINDY CITY.
AND I --
-- I HAVE NO PROBLEM WITH THE LOCK ON THE ROOF DOOR.
I FIND THE APARTMENT WITH NO DIFFICULTY.
AND I WISH --
NOK NOK
-- I WISH I WAS HEADED FOR CHICAGO MYSELF.

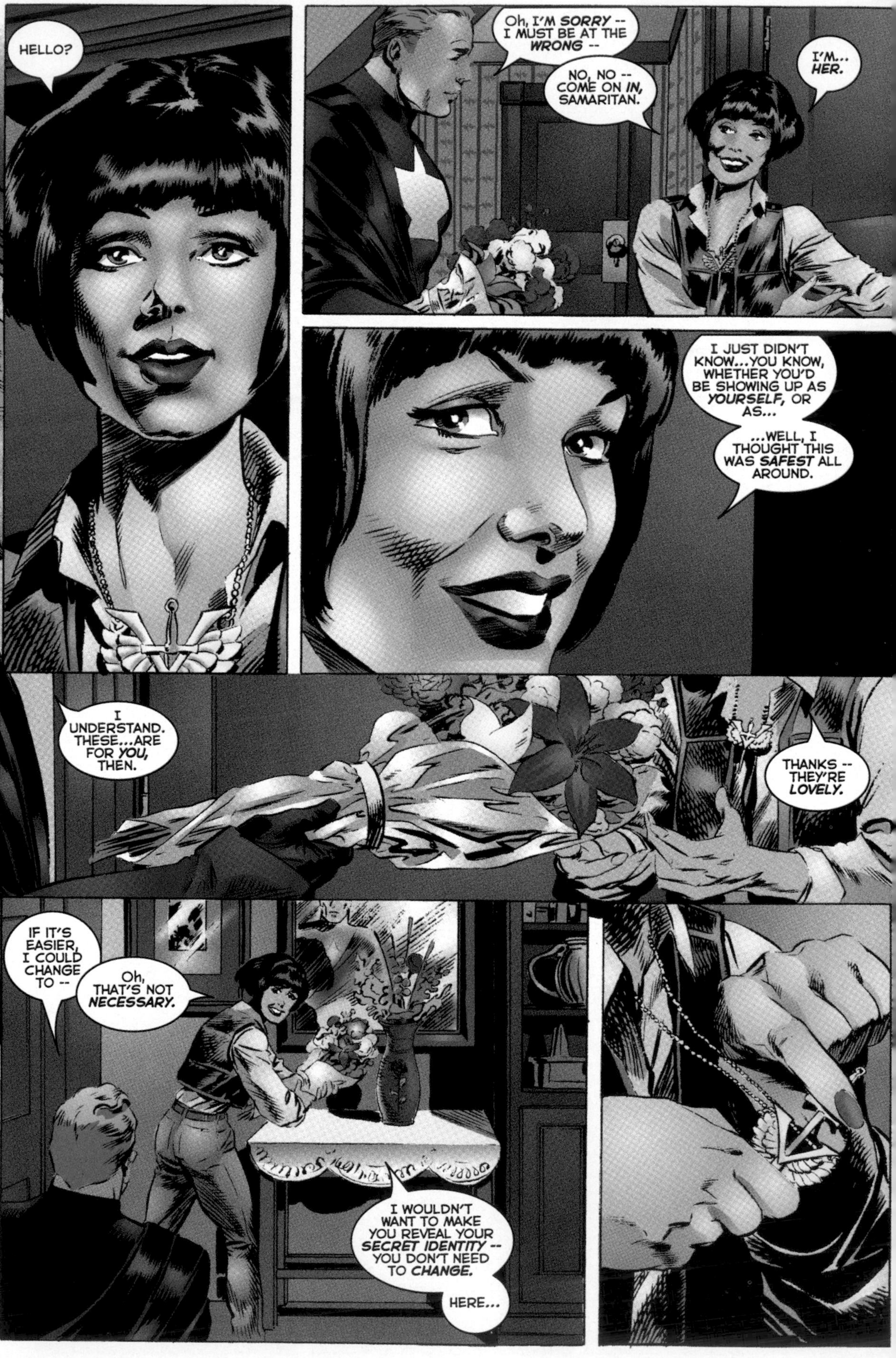
HELLO?
Oh, I'M SORRY -- I MUST BE AT THE WRONG --
NO, NO -- COME ON IN, SAMARITAN.
I'M... HER.
I JUST DIDN'T KNOW... YOU KNOW, WHETHER YOU'D BE SHOWING UP AS YOURSELF, OR AS...
...WELL, I THOUGHT THIS WAS SAFEST ALL AROUND.
I UNDERSTAND. THESE... ARE FOR YOU, THEN.
THANKS -- THEY'RE LOVELY.
IF IT'S EASIER, I COULD CHANGE TO --
Oh, THAT'S NOT NECESSARY.
I WOULDN'T WANT TO MAKE YOU REVEAL YOUR SECRET IDENTITY -- YOU DON'T NEED TO CHANGE.
HERE...

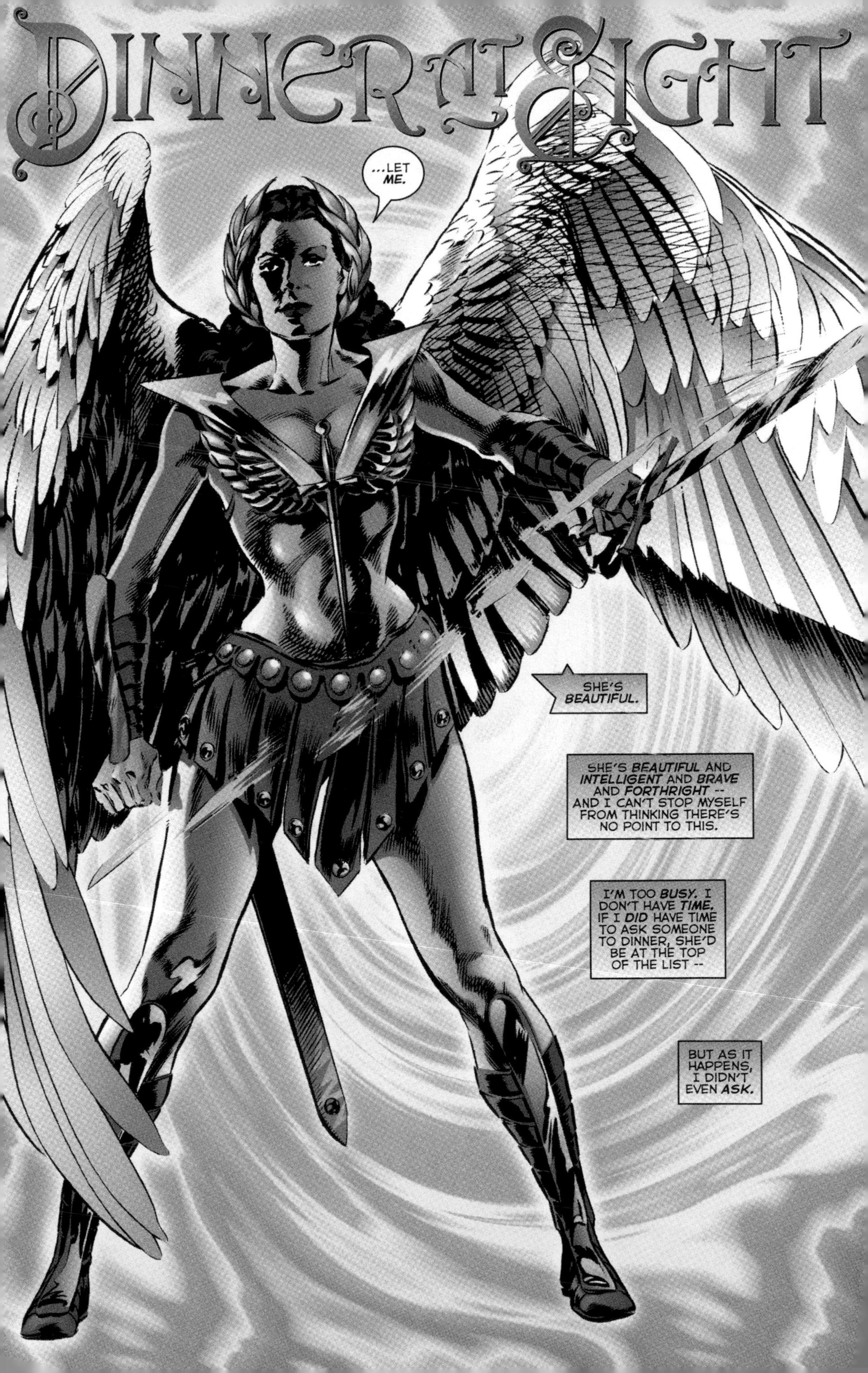
DINNER AT EIGHT
...LET ME.
SHE'S BEAUTIFUL.
SHE'S BEAUTIFUL AND INTELLIGENT AND BRAVE AND FORTHRIGHT -- AND I CAN'T STOP MYSELF FROM THINKING THERE'S NO POINT TO THIS.
I'M TOO BUSY. I DON'T HAVE TIME. IF I DID HAVE TIME TO ASK SOMEONE TO DINNER, SHE'D BE AT THE TOP OF THE LIST --
BUT AS IT HAPPENS, I DIDN'T EVEN ASK.

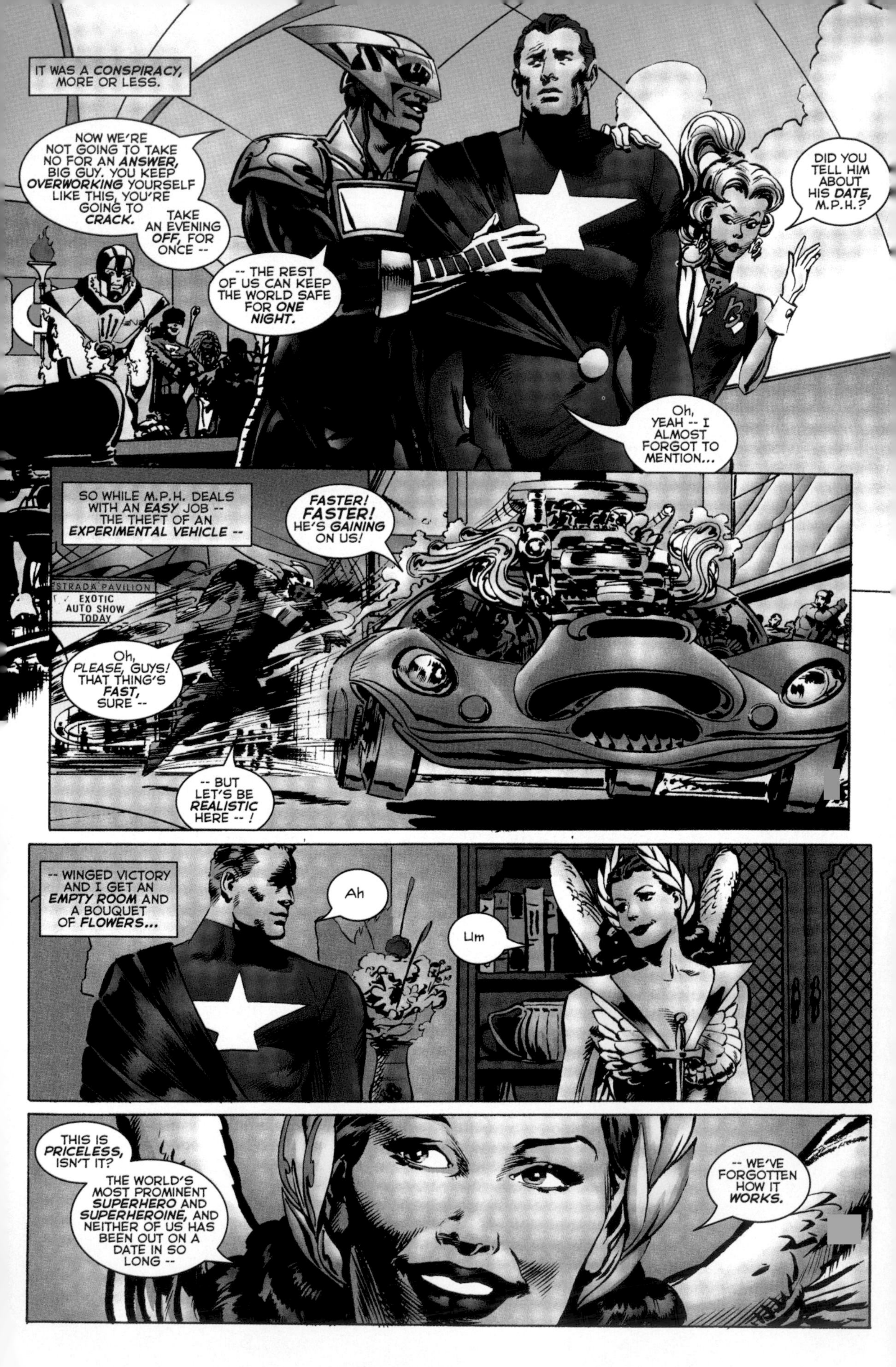
IT WAS A CONSPIRACY, MORE OR LESS.
NOW WE'RE NOT GOING TO TAKE NO FOR AN ANSWER, BIG GUY. YOU KEEP OVERWORKING YOURSELF LIKE THIS, YOU'RE GOING TO CRACK.
TAKE AN EVENING OFF, FOR ONCE --
-- THE REST OF US CAN KEEP THE WORLD SAFE FOR ONE NIGHT.
DID YOU TELL HIM ABOUT HIS DATE, M.P.H.?
Oh, YEAH -- I ALMOST FORGOT TO MENTION...
SO WHILE M.P.H. DEALS WITH AN EASY JOB -- THE THEFT OF AN EXPERIMENTAL VEHICLE --
FASTER! FASTER! HE'S GAINING ON US!
ESTRADA PAVILION
EXOTIC AUTO SHOW TODAY
Oh, PLEASE, GUYS! THAT THING'S FAST, SURE --
-- BUT LET'S BE REALISTIC HERE -- !
-- WINGED VICTORY AND I GET AN EMPTY ROOM AND A BOUQUET OF FLOWERS...
Ah
Um
THIS IS PRICELESS, ISN'T IT?
THE WORLD'S MOST PROMINENT SUPERHERO AND SUPERHEROINE, AND NEITHER OF US HAS BEEN OUT ON A DATE IN SO LONG --
-- WE'VE FORGOTTEN HOW IT WORKS.

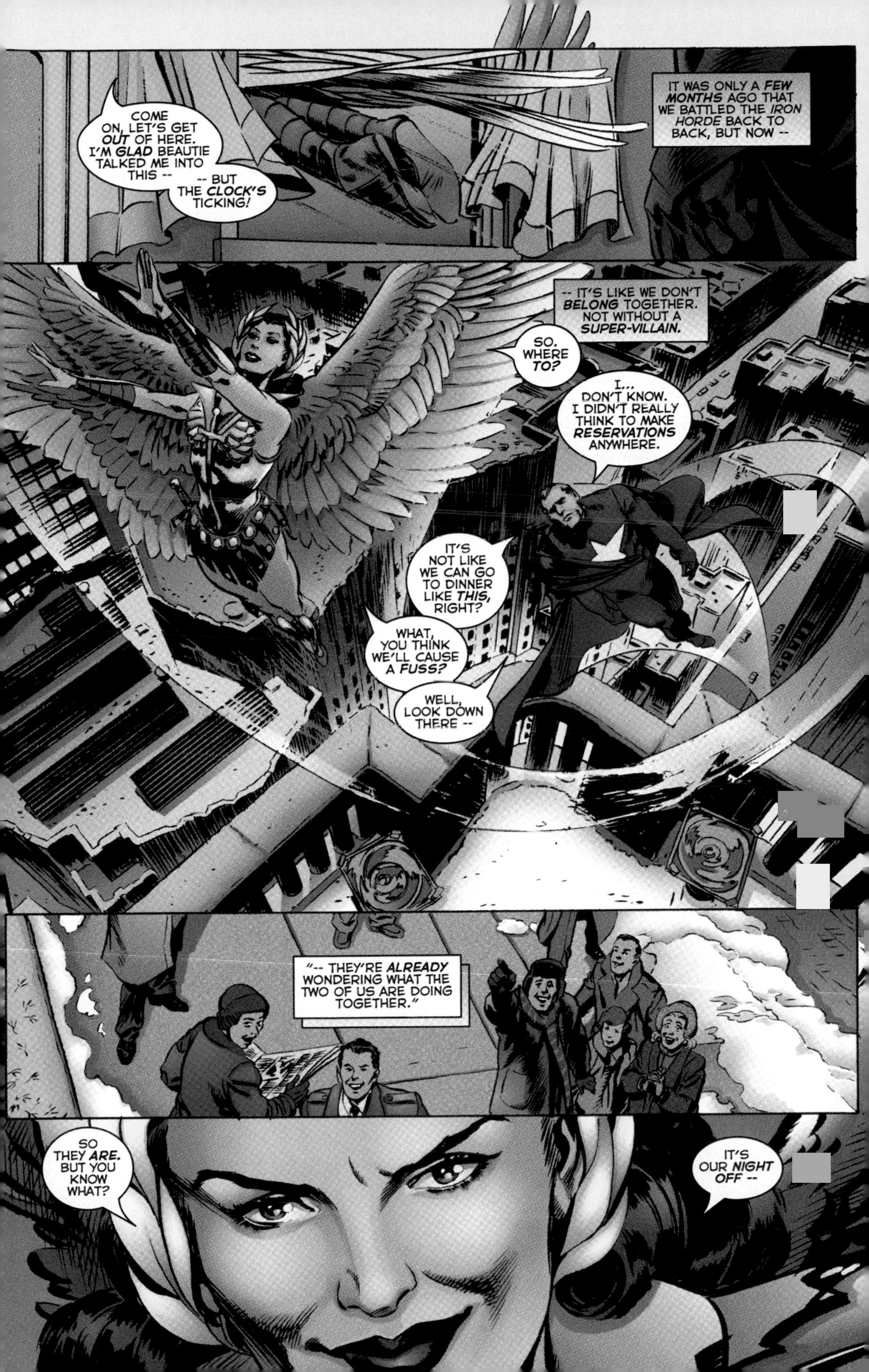
COME ON, LET'S GET OUT OF HERE. I'M GLAD BEAUTIE TALKED ME INTO THIS --
-- BUT THE CLOCK'S TICKING!
IT WAS ONLY A FEW MONTHS AGO THAT WE BATTLED THE IRON HORDE BACK TO BACK, BUT NOW --
-- IT'S LIKE WE DON'T BELONG TOGETHER. NOT WITHOUT A SUPER-VILLAIN.
SO. WHERE TO?
I... DON'T KNOW. I DIDN'T REALLY THINK TO MAKE RESERVATIONS ANYWHERE.
IT'S NOT LIKE WE CAN GO TO DINNER LIKE THIS, RIGHT?
WHAT, YOU THINK WE'LL CAUSE A FUSS?
WELL, LOOK DOWN THERE --
"-- THEY'RE ALREADY WONDERING WHAT THE TWO OF US ARE DOING TOGETHER."
SO THEY ARE. BUT YOU KNOW WHAT?
IT'S OUR NIGHT OFF --

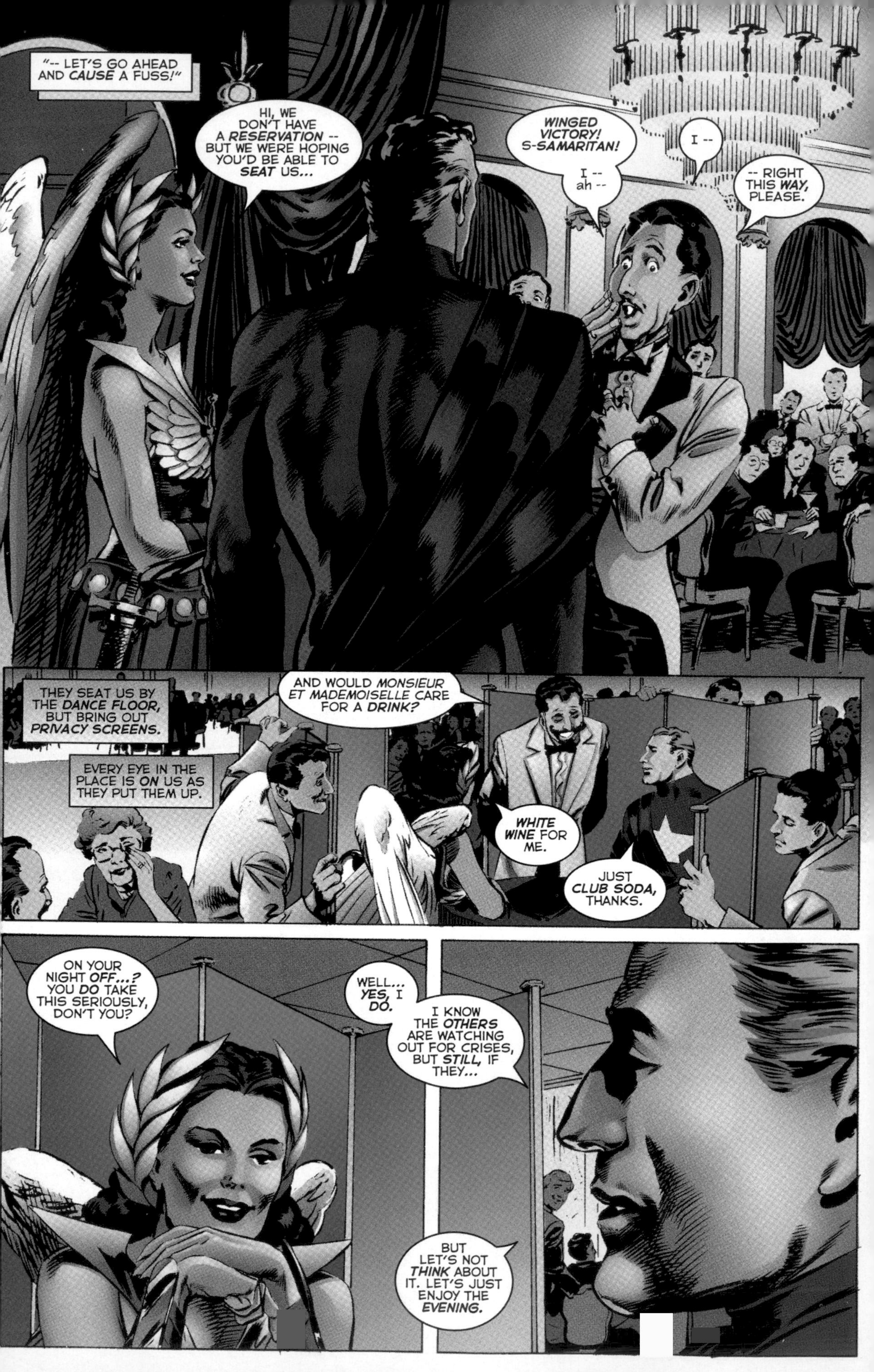
"-- LET'S GO AHEAD AND CAUSE A FUSS!"
HI, WE DON'T HAVE A RESERVATION -- BUT WE WERE HOPING YOU'D BE ABLE TO SEAT US...
WINGED VICTORY! S-SAMARITAN!
I -- ah --
I --
-- RIGHT THIS WAY, PLEASE.
THEY SEAT US BY THE DANCE FLOOR, BUT BRING OUT PRIVACY SCREENS.
EVERY EYE IN THE PLACE IS ON US AS THEY PUT THEM UP.
AND WOULD MONSIEUR ET MADEMOISELLE CARE FOR A DRINK?
WHITE WINE FOR ME.
JUST CLUB SODA, THANKS.
ON YOUR NIGHT OFF...? YOU DO TAKE THIS SERIOUSLY, DON'T YOU?
WELL... YES, I DO.
I KNOW THE OTHERS ARE WATCHING OUT FOR CRISES, BUT STILL, IF THEY...
BUT LET'S NOT THINK ABOUT IT. LET'S JUST ENJOY THE EVENING.

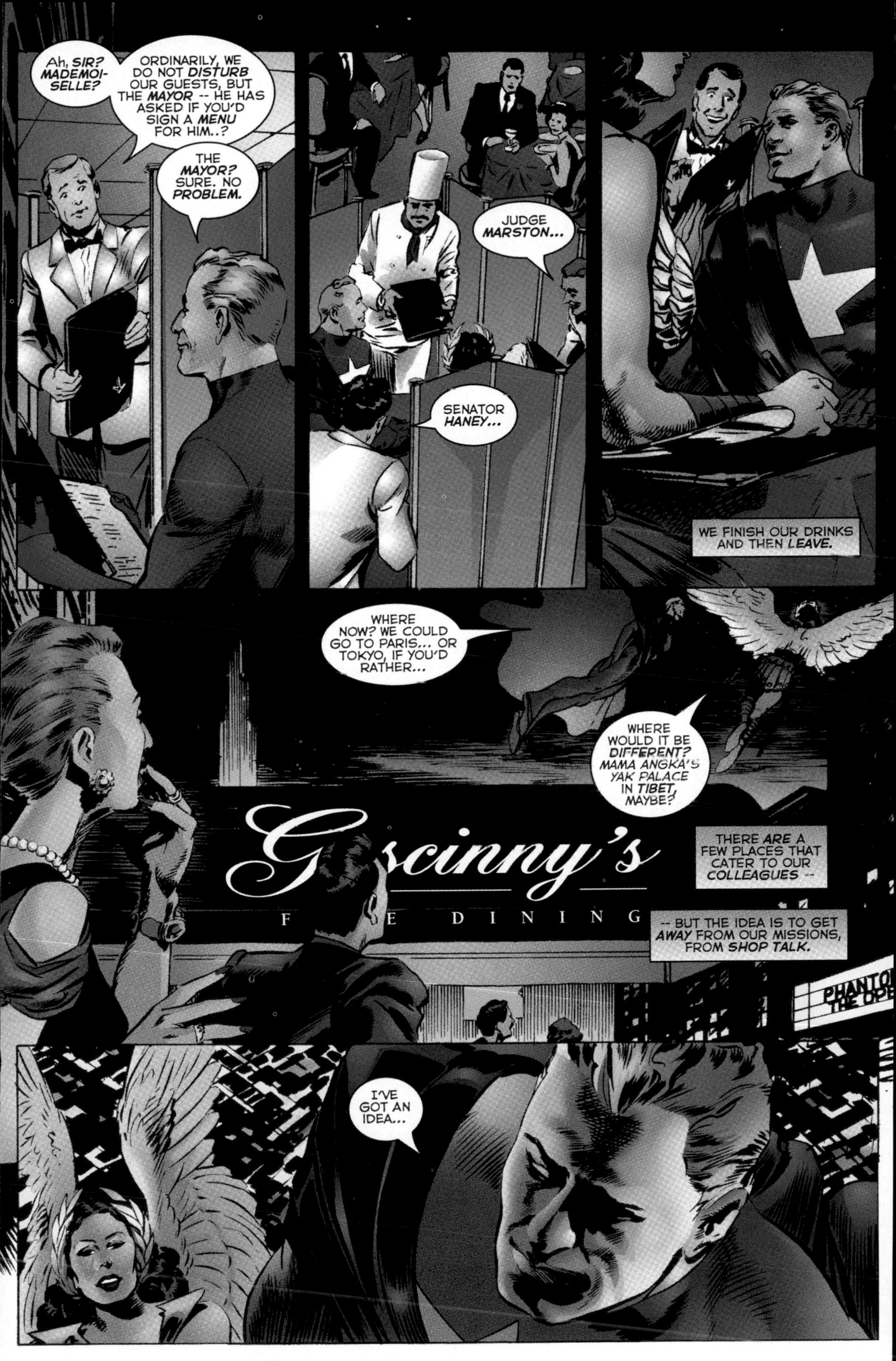

Ah, SIR? MADEMOISELLE?
ORDINARILY, WE DO NOT DISTURB OUR GUESTS, BUT THE MAYOR -- HE HAS ASKED IF YOU'D SIGN A MENU FOR HIM..?
THE MAYOR? SURE. NO PROBLEM.
JUDGE MARSTON...
SENATOR HANEY...
WE FINISH OUR DRINKS AND THEN LEAVE.
WHERE NOW? WE COULD GO TO PARIS... OR TOKYO, IF YOU'D RATHER...
WHERE WOULD IT BE DIFFERENT? MAMA ANGKA'S YAK PALACE IN TIBET, MAYBE?
THERE ARE A FEW PLACES THAT CATER TO OUR COLLEAGUES --
-- BUT THE IDEA IS TO GET AWAY FROM OUR MISSIONS, FROM SHOP TALK.
I'VE GOT AN IDEA...

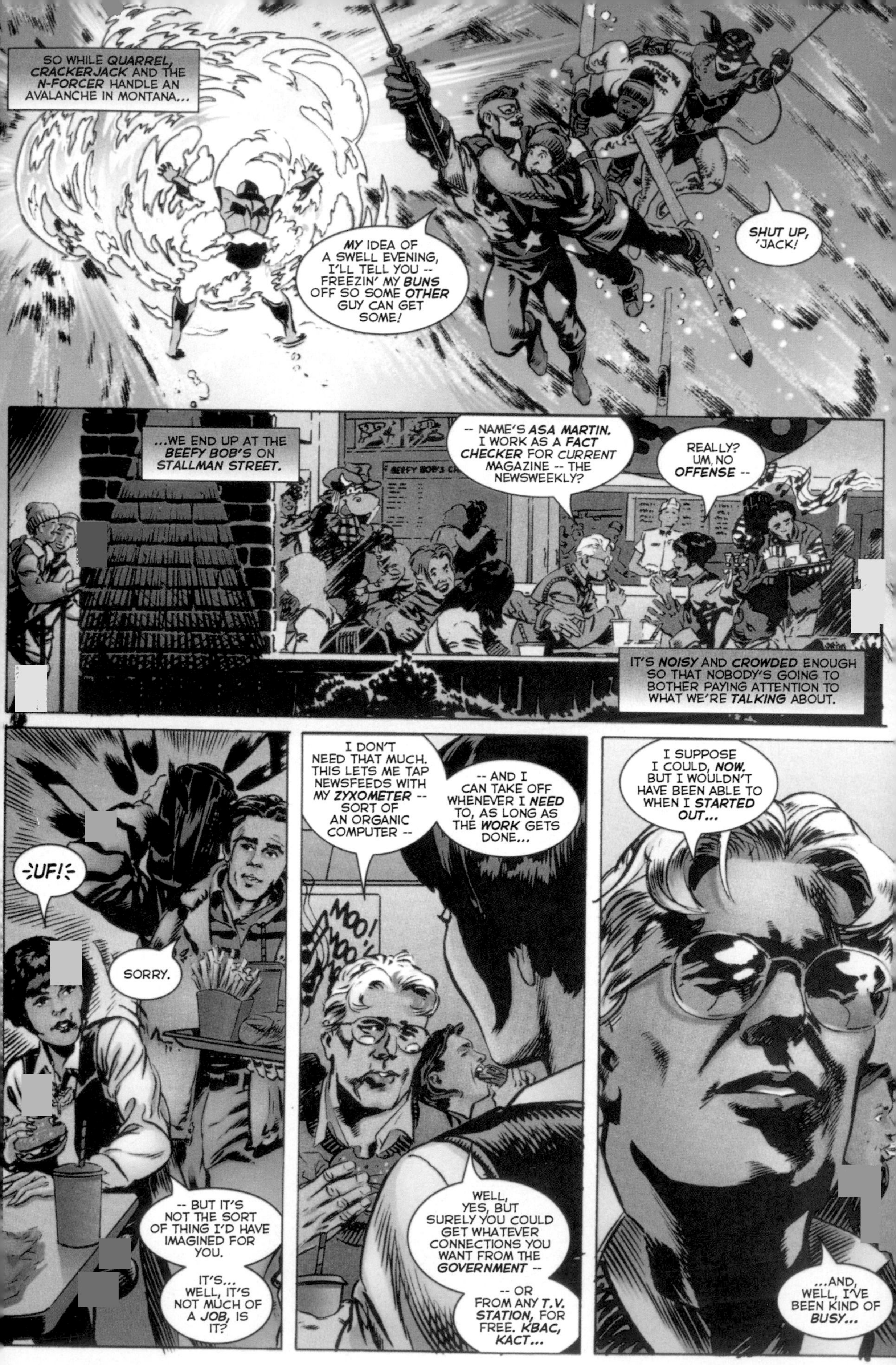

SO WHILE QUARREL, CRACKERJACK AND THE N-FORCER HANDLE AN AVALANCHE IN MONTANA...
MY IDEA OF A SWELL EVENING, I'LL TELL YOU -- FREEZIN' MY BUNS OFF SO SOME OTHER GUY CAN GET SOME!
SHUT UP, 'JACK!
...WE END UP AT THE BEEFY BOB'S ON STALLMAN STREET.
-- NAME'S ASA MARTIN. I WORK AS A FACT CHECKER FOR CURRENT MAGAZINE -- THE NEWSWEEKLY?
REALLY? UM, NO OFFENSE --
IT'S NOISY AND CROWDED ENOUGH SO THAT NOBODY'S GOING TO BOTHER PAYING ATTENTION TO WHAT WE'RE TALKING ABOUT.
-UF!-
SORRY.
-- BUT IT'S NOT THE SORT OF THING I'D HAVE IMAGINED FOR YOU.
IT'S... WELL, IT'S NOT MUCH OF A JOB, IS IT?
I DON'T NEED THAT MUCH. THIS LETS ME TAP NEWSFEEDS WITH MY ZYXOMETER -- SORT OF AN ORGANIC COMPUTER --
-- AND I CAN TAKE OFF WHENEVER I NEED TO, AS LONG AS THE WORK GETS DONE...
MOO!
WELL, YES, BUT SURELY YOU COULD GET WHATEVER CONNECTIONS YOU WANT FROM THE GOVERNMENT --
-- OR FROM ANY T.V. STATION, FOR FREE. KBAC, KACT...
I SUPPOSE I COULD, NOW. BUT I WOULDN'T HAVE BEEN ABLE TO WHEN I STARTED OUT...
...AND, WELL, I'VE BEEN KIND OF BUSY...

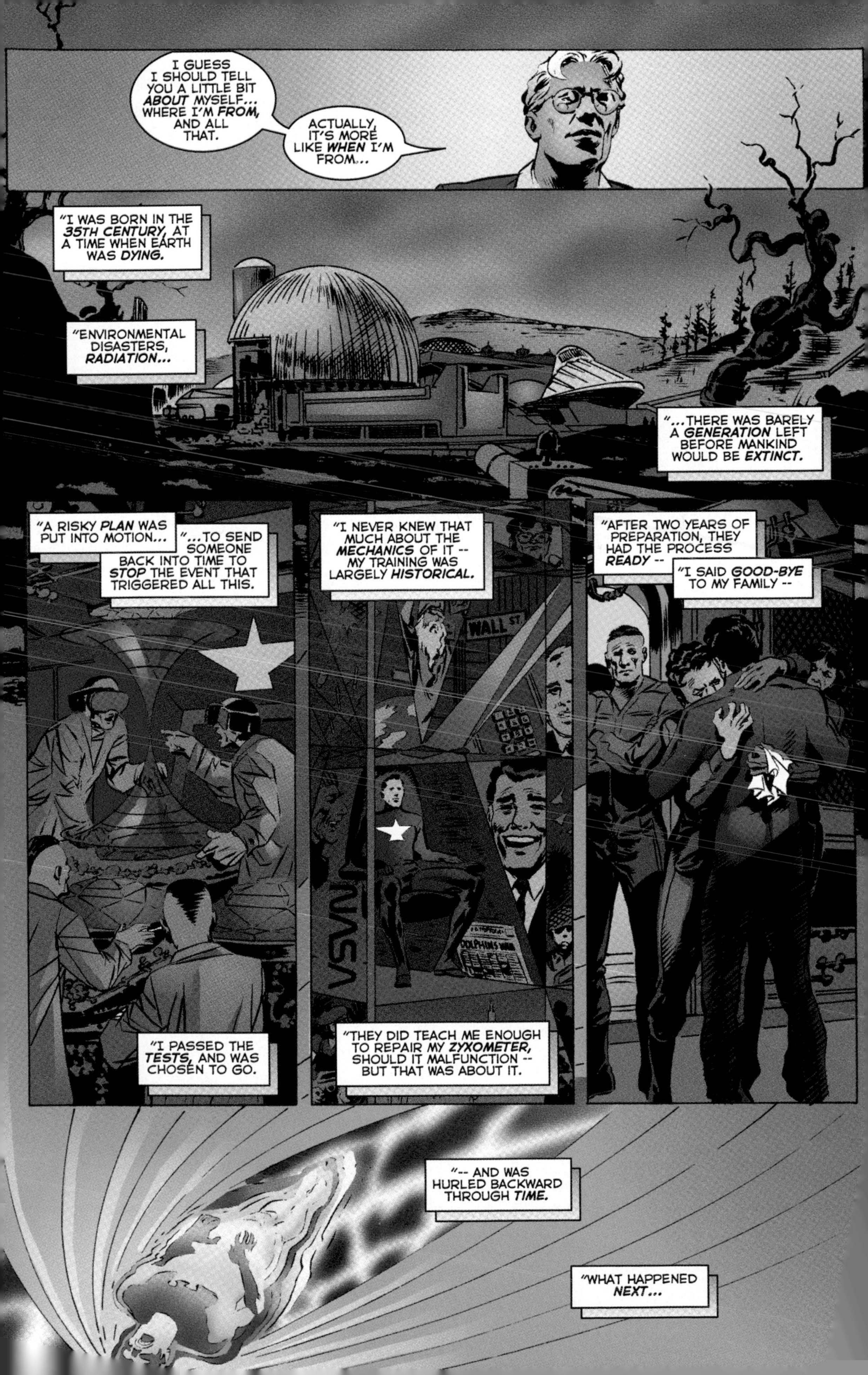
I GUESS I SHOULD TELL YOU A LITTLE BIT ABOUT MYSELF... WHERE I'M FROM, AND ALL THAT.
ACTUALLY, IT'S MORE LIKE WHEN I'M FROM...
"I WAS BORN IN THE 35TH CENTURY, AT A TIME WHEN EARTH WAS DYING.
"ENVIRONMENTAL DISASTERS, RADIATION...
"...THERE WAS BARELY A GENERATION LEFT BEFORE MANKIND WOULD BE EXTINCT.
"A RISKY PLAN WAS PUT INTO MOTION...
"...TO SEND SOMEONE BACK INTO TIME TO STOP THE EVENT THAT TRIGGERED ALL THIS.
"I PASSED THE TESTS, AND WAS CHOSEN TO GO.
"I NEVER KNEW THAT MUCH ABOUT THE MECHANICS OF IT -- MY TRAINING WAS LARGELY HISTORICAL.
WALL ST.
NASA
"THEY DID TEACH ME ENOUGH TO REPAIR MY ZYXOMETER, SHOULD IT MALFUNCTION -- BUT THAT WAS ABOUT IT.
"AFTER TWO YEARS OF PREPARATION, THEY HAD THE PROCESS READY --
"I SAID GOOD-BYE TO MY FAMILY --
"-- AND WAS HURLED BACKWARD THROUGH TIME.
"WHAT HAPPENED NEXT...

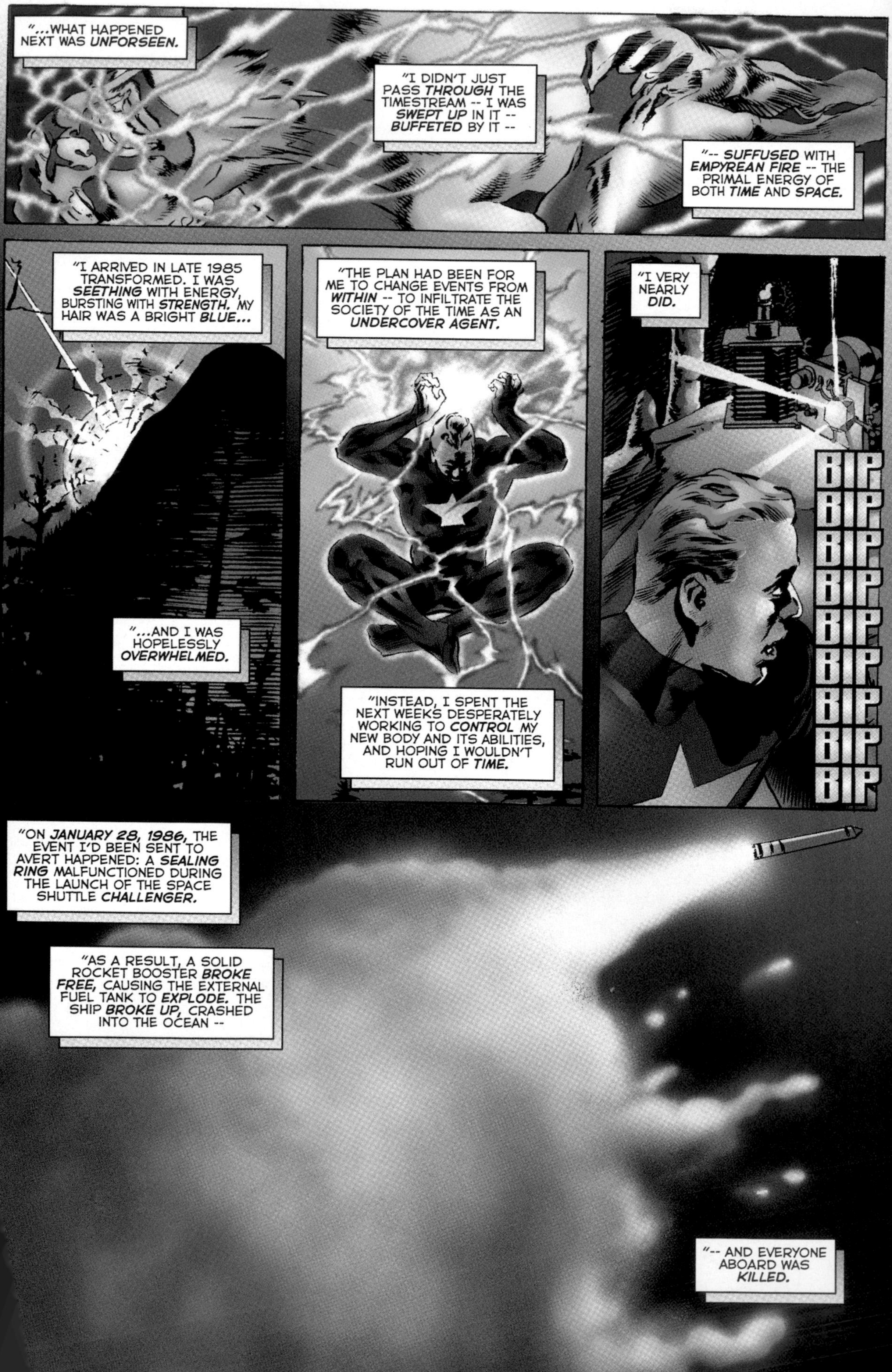
"...WHAT HAPPENED NEXT WAS UNFORSEEN.
"I DIDN'T JUST PASS THROUGH THE TIMESTREAM -- I WAS SWEPT UP IN IT -- BUFFETED BY IT --
"-- SUFFUSED WITH EMPYREAN FIRE -- THE PRIMAL ENERGY OF BOTH TIME AND SPACE.
"I ARRIVED IN LATE 1985 TRANSFORMED. I WAS SEETHING WITH ENERGY, BURSTING WITH STRENGTH. MY HAIR WAS A BRIGHT BLUE...
"...AND I WAS HOPELESSLY OVERWHELMED.
"THE PLAN HAD BEEN FOR ME TO CHANGE EVENTS FROM WITHIN -- TO INFILTRATE THE SOCIETY OF THE TIME AS AN UNDERCOVER AGENT.
"INSTEAD, I SPENT THE NEXT WEEKS DESPERATELY WORKING TO CONTROL MY NEW BODY AND ITS ABILITIES, AND HOPING I WOULDN'T RUN OUT OF TIME.
"I VERY NEARLY DID.
BIP BIP BIP BIP BIP BIP BIP BIP BIP
"ON JANUARY 28, 1986, THE EVENT I'D BEEN SENT TO AVERT HAPPENED: A SEALING RING MALFUNCTIONED DURING THE LAUNCH OF THE SPACE SHUTTLE CHALLENGER.
"AS A RESULT, A SOLID ROCKET BOOSTER BROKE FREE, CAUSING THE EXTERNAL FUEL TANK TO EXPLODE. THE SHIP BROKE UP, CRASHED INTO THE OCEAN --
"-- AND EVERYONE ABOARD WAS KILLED.

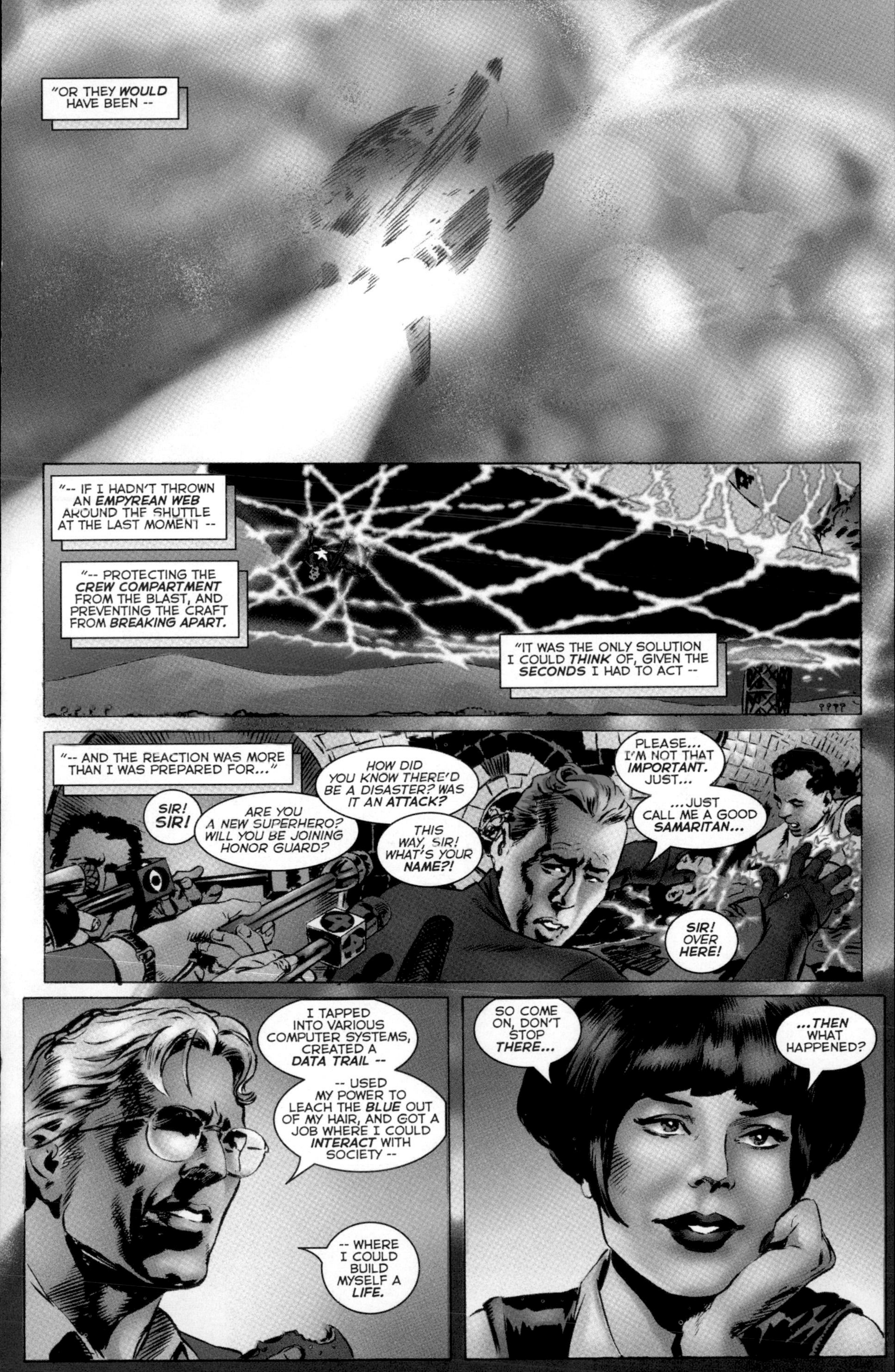
"OR THEY *WOULD* HAVE BEEN --
"-- IF I HADN'T THROWN AN *EMPYREAN WEB* AROUND THE SHUTTLE AT THE LAST MOMENT --
"-- PROTECTING THE *CREW COMPARTMENT* FROM THE BLAST, AND PREVENTING THE CRAFT FROM *BREAKING APART.*
"IT WAS THE ONLY SOLUTION I COULD *THINK* OF, GIVEN THE *SECONDS* I HAD TO ACT --
"-- AND THE REACTION WAS MORE THAN I WAS PREPARED FOR..."
SIR! SIR!
ARE YOU A NEW SUPERHERO? WILL YOU BE JOINING HONOR GUARD?
HOW DID YOU KNOW THERE'D BE A DISASTER? WAS IT AN ATTACK?
THIS WAY, SIR! WHAT'S YOUR NAME?!
PLEASE... I'M NOT THAT *IMPORTANT.* JUST...
...JUST CALL ME A GOOD *SAMARITAN...*
SIR! OVER HERE!
I TAPPED INTO VARIOUS COMPUTER SYSTEMS, CREATED A *DATA TRAIL* --
-- USED MY POWER TO LEACH THE *BLUE* OUT OF MY HAIR, AND GOT A JOB WHERE I COULD *INTERACT* WITH SOCIETY --
-- WHERE I COULD BUILD MYSELF A *LIFE.*
SO COME ON, DON'T STOP *THERE...*
...THEN WHAT HAPPENED?

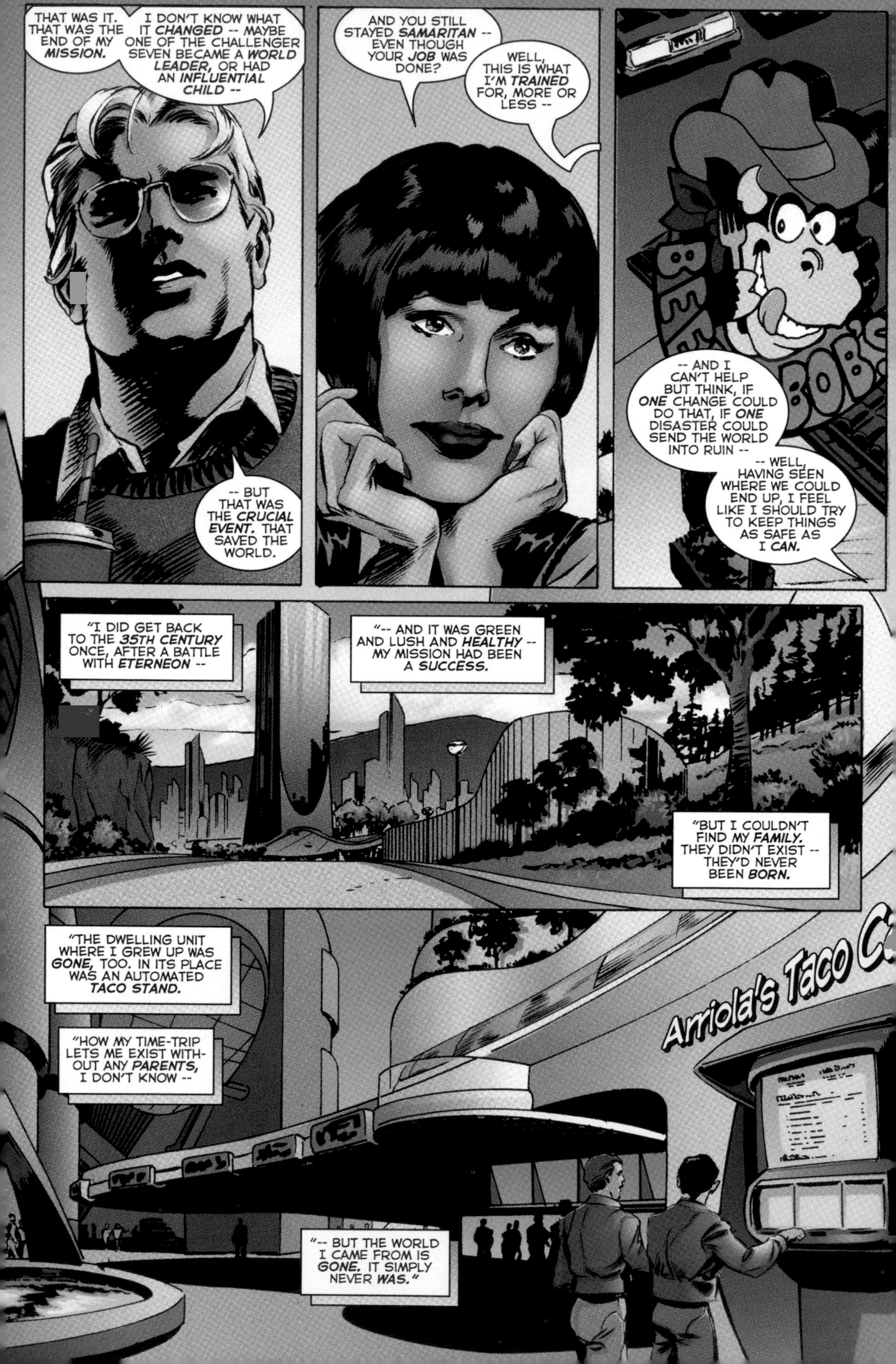
THAT WAS IT. THAT WAS THE END OF MY MISSION.
I DON'T KNOW WHAT IT CHANGED -- MAYBE ONE OF THE CHALLENGER SEVEN BECAME A WORLD LEADER, OR HAD AN INFLUENTIAL CHILD --
-- BUT THAT WAS THE CRUCIAL EVENT. THAT SAVED THE WORLD.
AND YOU STILL STAYED SAMARITAN -- EVEN THOUGH YOUR JOB WAS DONE?
WELL, THIS IS WHAT I'M TRAINED FOR, MORE OR LESS --
BOB'S
-- AND I CAN'T HELP BUT THINK, IF ONE CHANGE COULD DO THAT, IF ONE DISASTER COULD SEND THE WORLD INTO RUIN --
-- WELL, HAVING SEEN WHERE WE COULD END UP, I FEEL LIKE I SHOULD TRY TO KEEP THINGS AS SAFE AS I CAN.
"I DID GET BACK TO THE 35TH CENTURY ONCE, AFTER A BATTLE WITH ETERNEON --
"-- AND IT WAS GREEN AND LUSH AND HEALTHY -- MY MISSION HAD BEEN A SUCCESS.
"BUT I COULDN'T FIND MY FAMILY. THEY DIDN'T EXIST -- THEY'D NEVER BEEN BORN.
"THE DWELLING UNIT WHERE I GREW UP WAS GONE, TOO. IN ITS PLACE WAS AN AUTOMATED TACO STAND.
Arriola's Taco C
"HOW MY TIME-TRIP LETS ME EXIST WITHOUT ANY PARENTS, I DON'T KNOW --
"-- BUT THE WORLD I CAME FROM IS GONE. IT SIMPLY NEVER WAS."

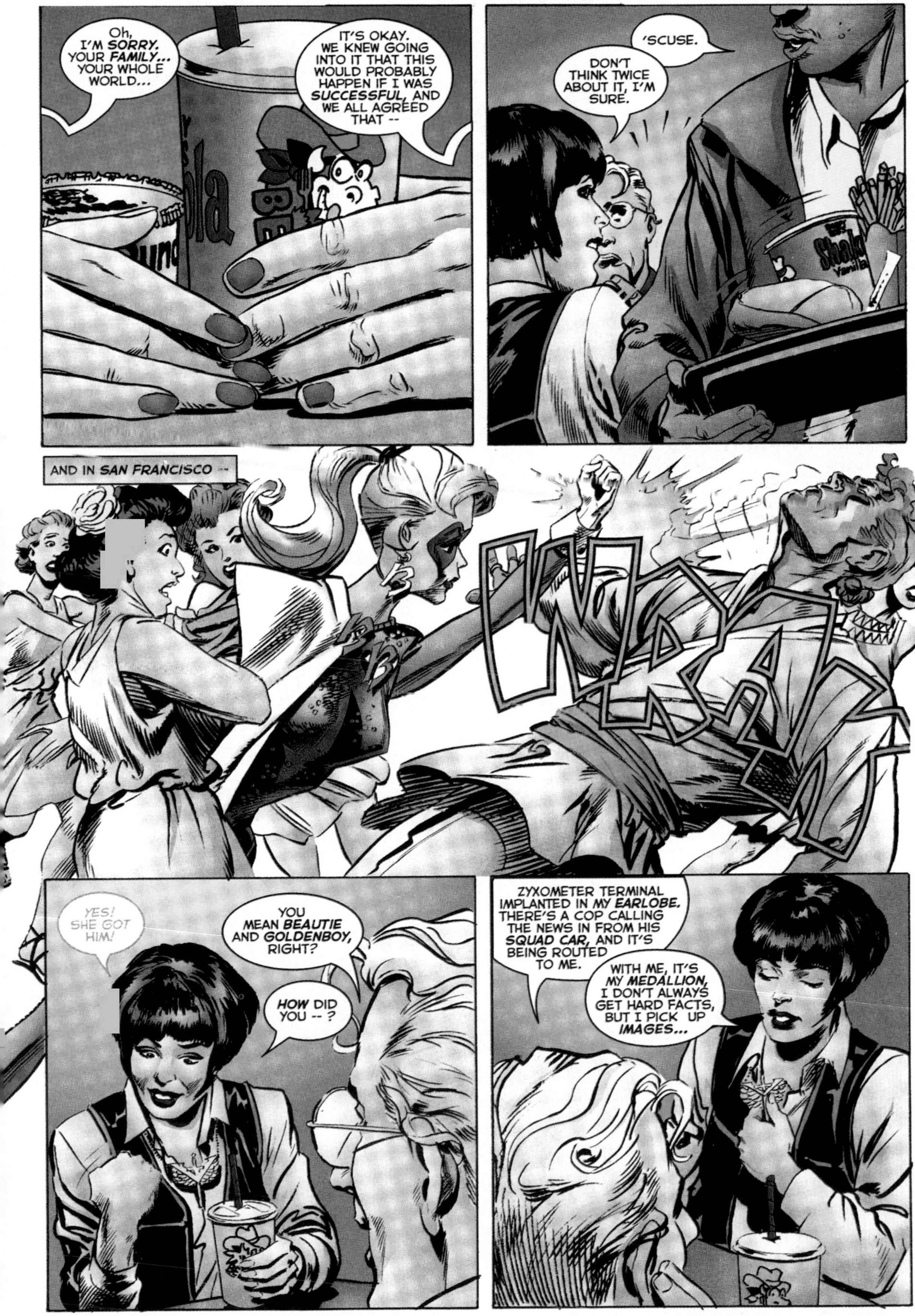
Oh, I'M SORRY. YOUR FAMILY... YOUR WHOLE WORLD...
IT'S OKAY. WE KNEW GOING INTO IT THAT THIS WOULD PROBABLY HAPPEN IF I WAS SUCCESSFUL, AND WE ALL AGREED THAT --
'SCUSE.
DON'T THINK TWICE ABOUT IT, I'M SURE.
AND IN SAN FRANCISCO --
YES! SHE GOT HIM!
YOU MEAN BEAUTIE AND GOLDENBOY, RIGHT?
HOW DID YOU -- ?
ZYXOMETER TERMINAL IMPLANTED IN MY EARLOBE. THERE'S A COP CALLING THE NEWS IN FROM HIS SQUAD CAR, AND IT'S BEING ROUTED TO ME.
WITH ME, IT'S MY MEDALLION. I DON'T ALWAYS GET HARD FACTS, BUT I PICK UP IMAGES...

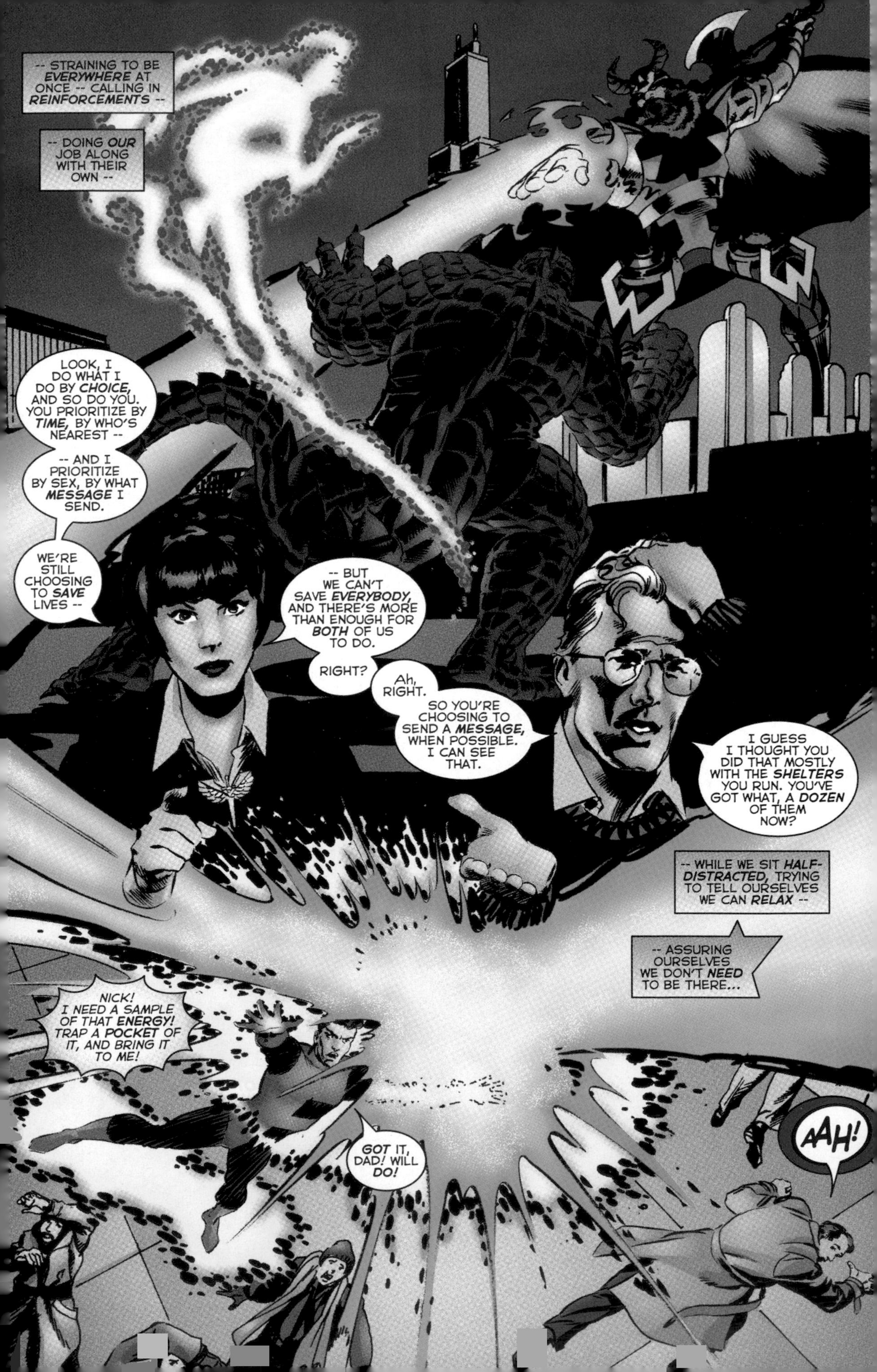
-- STRAINING TO BE EVERYWHERE AT ONCE -- CALLING IN REINFORCEMENTS --
-- DOING OUR JOB ALONG WITH THEIR OWN --
LOOK, I DO WHAT I DO BY CHOICE, AND SO DO YOU. YOU PRIORITIZE BY TIME, BY WHO'S NEAREST --
-- AND I PRIORITIZE BY SEX, BY WHAT MESSAGE I SEND.
WE'RE STILL CHOOSING TO SAVE LIVES --
-- BUT WE CAN'T SAVE EVERYBODY, AND THERE'S MORE THAN ENOUGH FOR BOTH OF US TO DO.
RIGHT?
Ah, RIGHT.
SO YOU'RE CHOOSING TO SEND A MESSAGE, WHEN POSSIBLE. I CAN SEE THAT.
I GUESS I THOUGHT YOU DID THAT MOSTLY WITH THE SHELTERS YOU RUN. YOU'VE GOT WHAT, A DOZEN OF THEM NOW?
-- WHILE WE SIT HALF-DISTRACTED, TRYING TO TELL OURSELVES WE CAN RELAX --
-- ASSURING OURSELVES WE DON'T NEED TO BE THERE...
NICK! I NEED A SAMPLE OF THAT ENERGY! TRAP A POCKET OF IT, AND BRING IT TO ME!
GOT IT, DAD! WILL DO!
AAH!

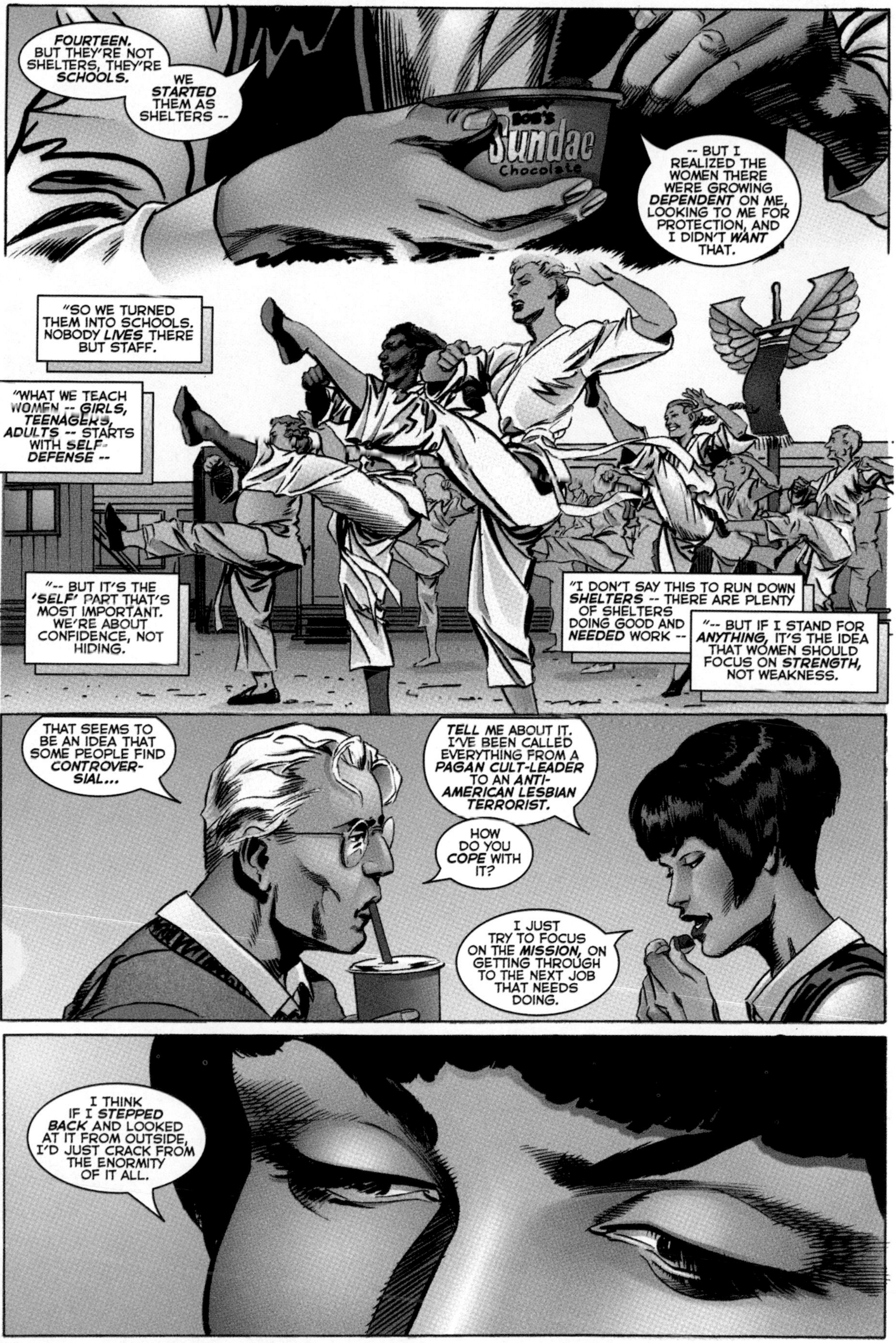
FOURTEEN. BUT THEY'RE NOT SHELTERS, THEY'RE SCHOOLS.
WE STARTED THEM AS SHELTERS --
BOB'S Sundae Chocolate
-- BUT I REALIZED THE WOMEN THERE WERE GROWING DEPENDENT ON ME, LOOKING TO ME FOR PROTECTION, AND I DIDN'T WANT THAT.
"SO WE TURNED THEM INTO SCHOOLS. NOBODY LIVES THERE BUT STAFF.
"WHAT WE TEACH WOMEN -- GIRLS, TEENAGERS, ADULTS -- STARTS WITH SELF-DEFENSE --
"-- BUT IT'S THE 'SELF' PART THAT'S MOST IMPORTANT. WE'RE ABOUT CONFIDENCE, NOT HIDING.
"I DON'T SAY THIS TO RUN DOWN SHELTERS -- THERE ARE PLENTY OF SHELTERS DOING GOOD AND NEEDED WORK --
"-- BUT IF I STAND FOR ANYTHING, IT'S THE IDEA THAT WOMEN SHOULD FOCUS ON STRENGTH, NOT WEAKNESS.
THAT SEEMS TO BE AN IDEA THAT SOME PEOPLE FIND CONTROVERSIAL...
TELL ME ABOUT IT. I'VE BEEN CALLED EVERYTHING FROM A PAGAN CULT-LEADER TO AN ANTI-AMERICAN LESBIAN TERRORIST.
HOW DO YOU COPE WITH IT?
I JUST TRY TO FOCUS ON THE MISSION, ON GETTING THROUGH TO THE NEXT JOB THAT NEEDS DOING.
I THINK IF I STEPPED BACK AND LOOKED AT IT FROM OUTSIDE, I'D JUST CRACK FROM THE ENORMITY OF IT ALL.

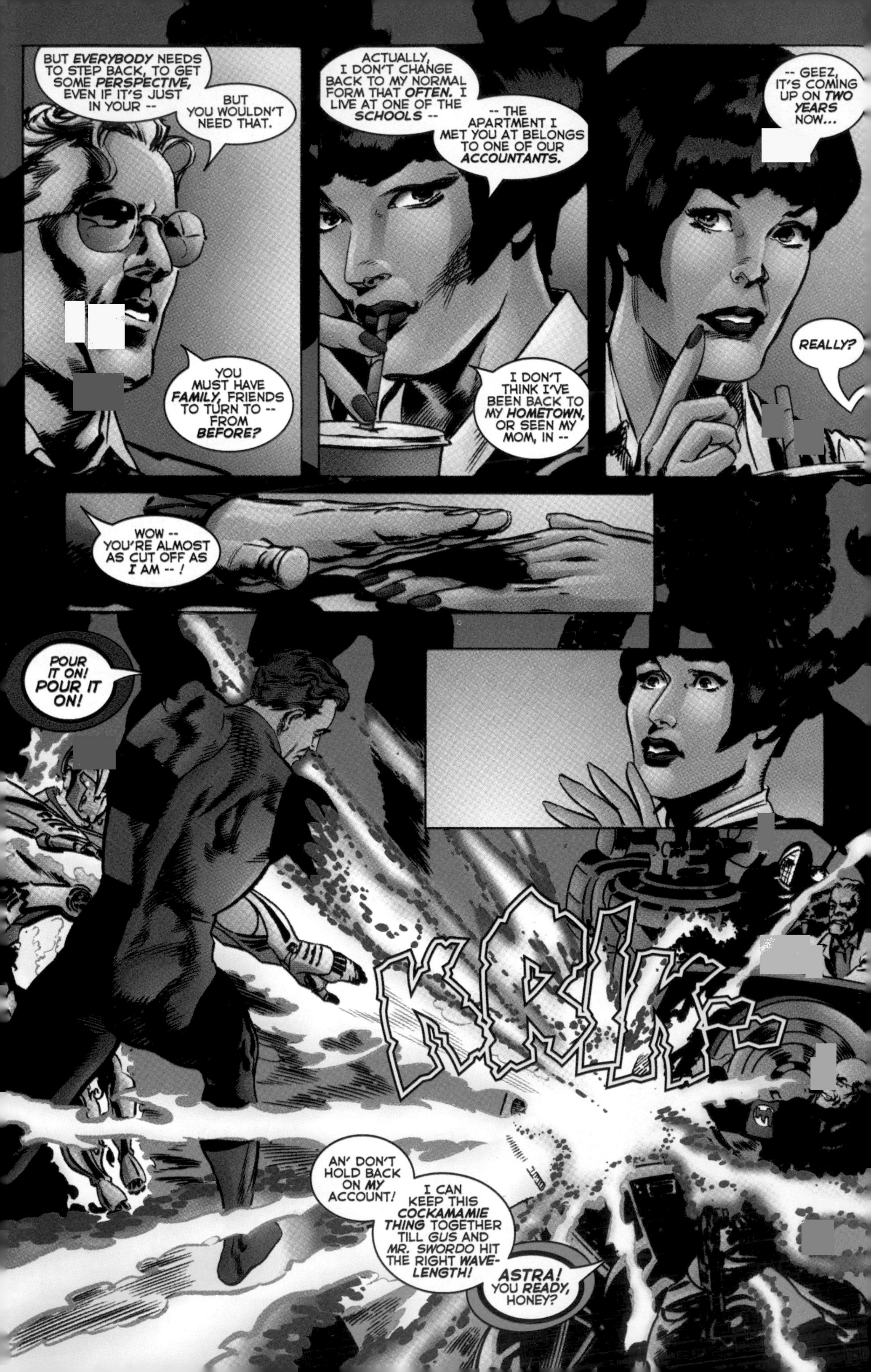
BUT EVERYBODY NEEDS TO STEP BACK, TO GET SOME PERSPECTIVE, EVEN IF IT'S JUST IN YOUR --
BUT YOU WOULDN'T NEED THAT.
YOU MUST HAVE FAMILY, FRIENDS TO TURN TO -- FROM BEFORE?
ACTUALLY, I DON'T CHANGE BACK TO MY NORMAL FORM THAT OFTEN. I LIVE AT ONE OF THE SCHOOLS --
-- THE APARTMENT I MET YOU AT BELONGS TO ONE OF OUR ACCOUNTANTS.
I DON'T THINK I'VE BEEN BACK TO MY HOMETOWN, OR SEEN MY MOM, IN --
-- GEEZ, IT'S COMING UP ON TWO YEARS NOW...
REALLY?
WOW -- YOU'RE ALMOST AS CUT OFF AS I AM -- !
POUR IT ON! POUR IT ON!
AN' DON'T HOLD BACK ON MY ACCOUNT!
I CAN KEEP THIS COCKAMAMIE THING TOGETHER TILL GUS AND MR. SWORDO HIT THE RIGHT WAVE-LENGTH!
ASTRA! YOU READY, HONEY?

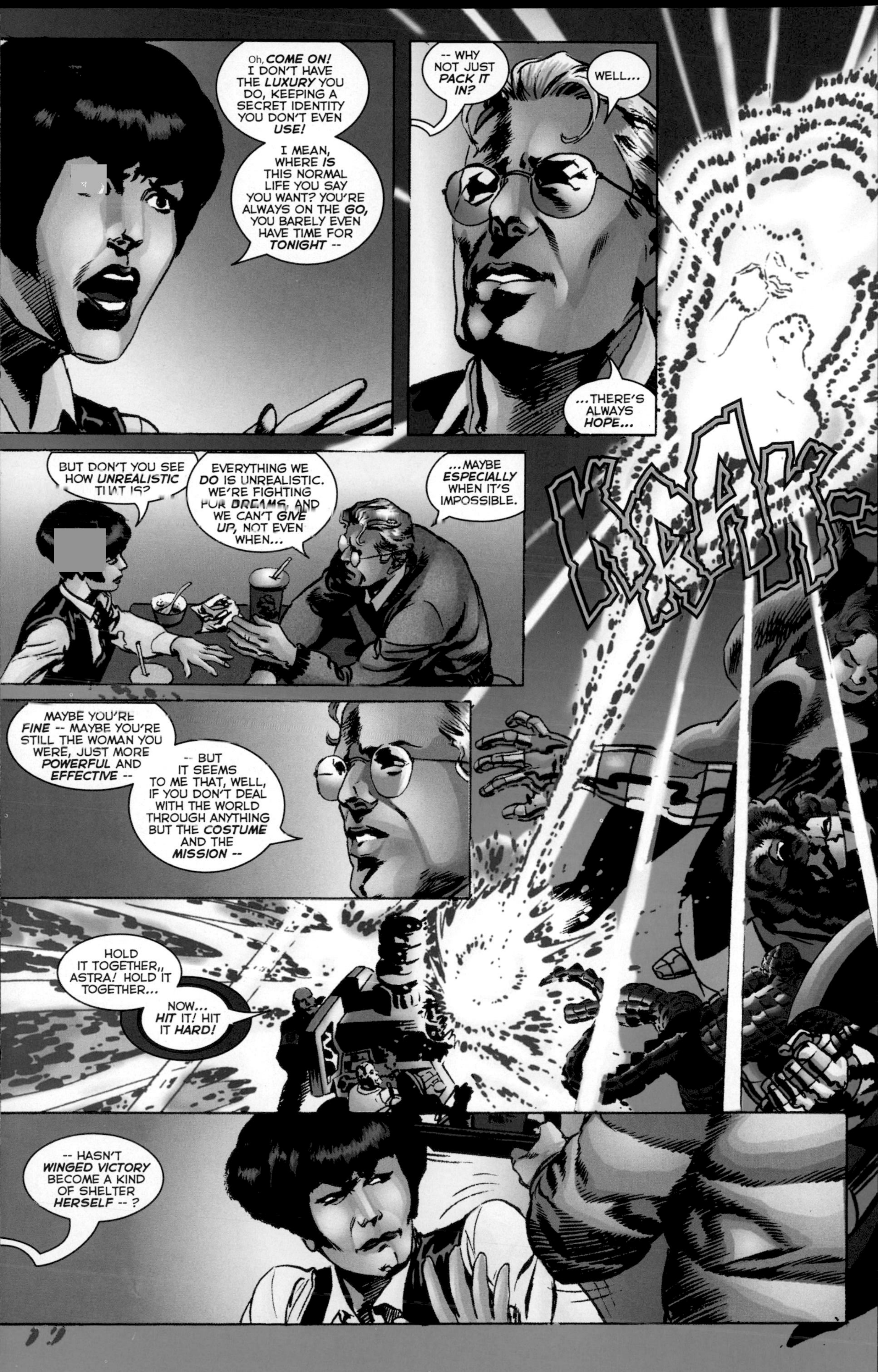
Oh, COME ON! I DON'T HAVE THE LUXURY YOU DO, KEEPING A SECRET IDENTITY YOU DON'T EVEN USE!
I MEAN, WHERE IS THIS NORMAL LIFE YOU SAY YOU WANT? YOU'RE ALWAYS ON THE GO, YOU BARELY EVEN HAVE TIME FOR TONIGHT --
-- WHY NOT JUST PACK IT IN?
WELL...
...THERE'S ALWAYS HOPE...
BUT DON'T YOU SEE HOW UNREALISTIC THAT IS?
EVERYTHING WE DO IS UNREALISTIC. WE'RE FIGHTING FOR DREAMS, AND WE CAN'T GIVE UP, NOT EVEN WHEN...
...MAYBE ESPECIALLY WHEN IT'S IMPOSSIBLE.
MAYBE YOU'RE FINE -- MAYBE YOU'RE STILL THE WOMAN YOU WERE, JUST MORE POWERFUL AND EFFECTIVE --
-- BUT IT SEEMS TO ME THAT, WELL, IF YOU DON'T DEAL WITH THE WORLD THROUGH ANYTHING BUT THE COSTUME AND THE MISSION --
HOLD IT TOGETHER,, ASTRA! HOLD IT TOGETHER...
NOW... HIT IT! HIT IT HARD!
-- HASN'T WINGED VICTORY BECOME A KIND OF SHELTER HERSELF -- ?

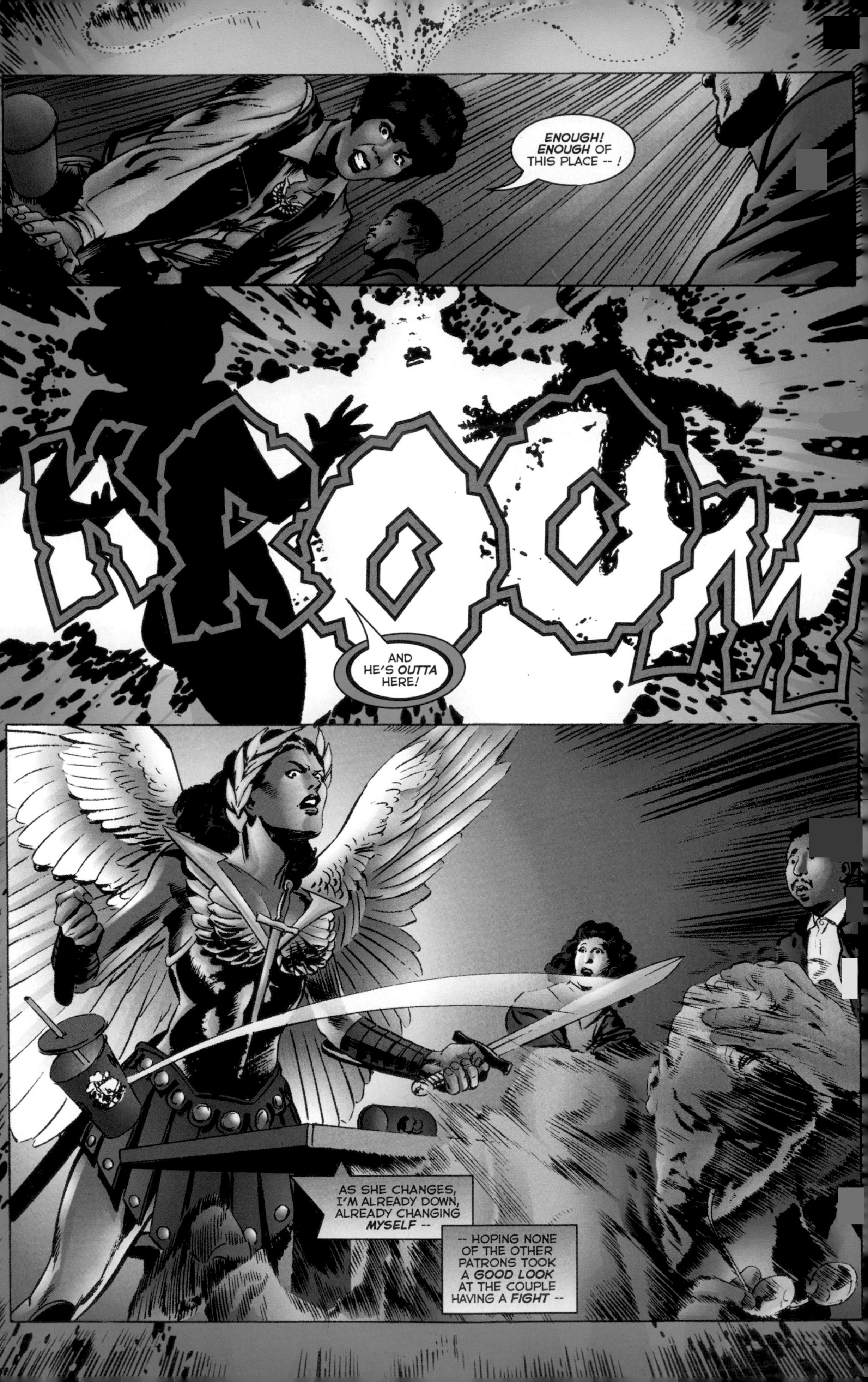
ENOUGH! ENOUGH OF THIS PLACE -- !
KROOM
AND HE'S OUTTA HERE!
AS SHE CHANGES, I'M ALREADY DOWN, ALREADY CHANGING MYSELF --
-- HOPING NONE OF THE OTHER PATRONS TOOK A GOOD LOOK AT THE COUPLE HAVING A FIGHT --

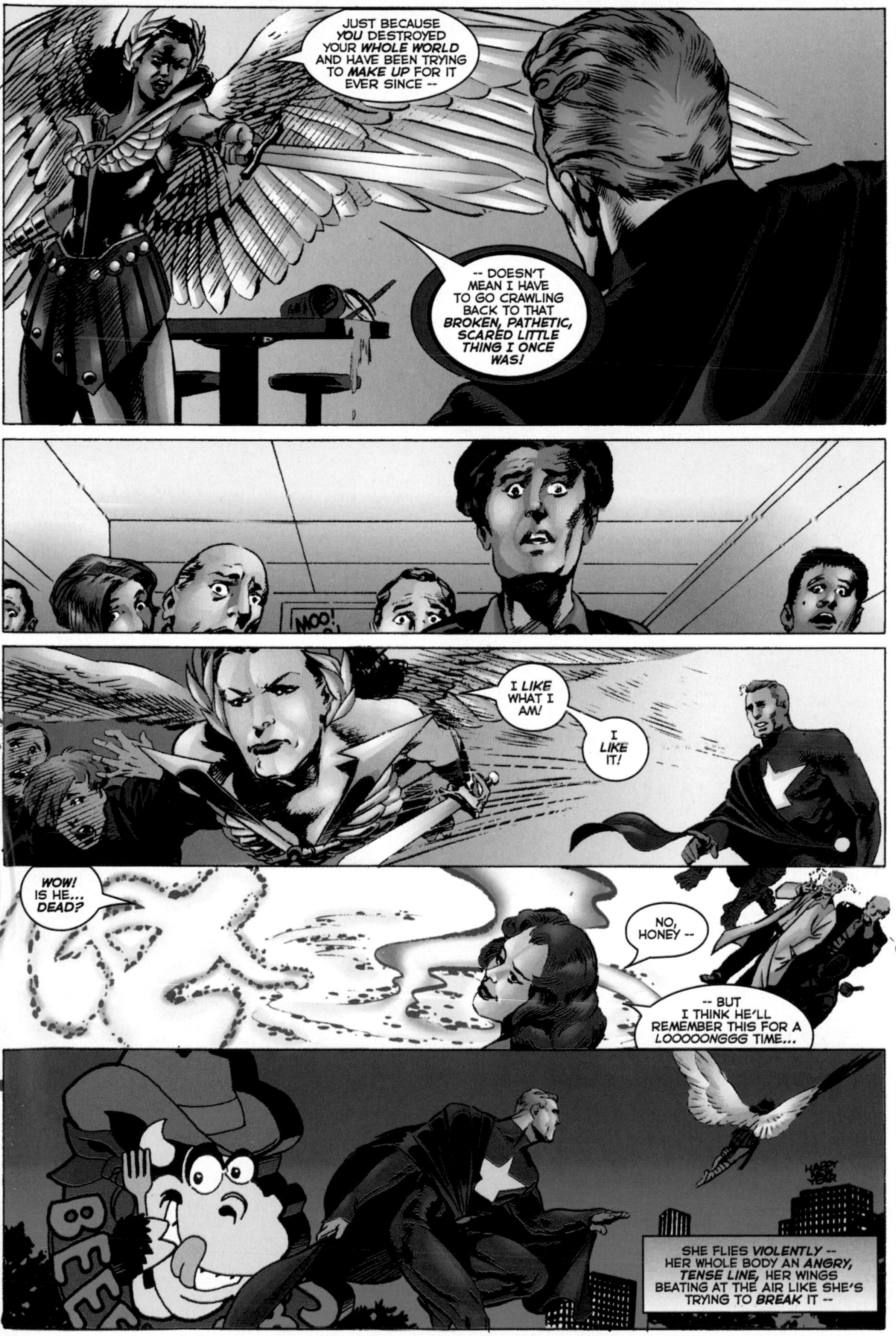
JUST BECAUSE YOU DESTROYED YOUR WHOLE WORLD AND HAVE BEEN TRYING TO MAKE UP FOR IT EVER SINCE --
-- DOESN'T MEAN I HAVE TO GO CRAWLING BACK TO THAT BROKEN, PATHETIC, SCARED LITTLE THING I ONCE WAS!
MOO!
I LIKE WHAT I AM!
I LIKE IT!
WOW! IS HE... DEAD?
NO, HONEY --
-- BUT I THINK HE'LL REMEMBER THIS FOR A LOOOOONGGG TIME...
HAPPY NEW YEAR
SHE FLIES VIOLENTLY -- HER WHOLE BODY AN ANGRY, TENSE LINE, HER WINGS BEATING AT THE AIR LIKE SHE'S TRYING TO BREAK IT --

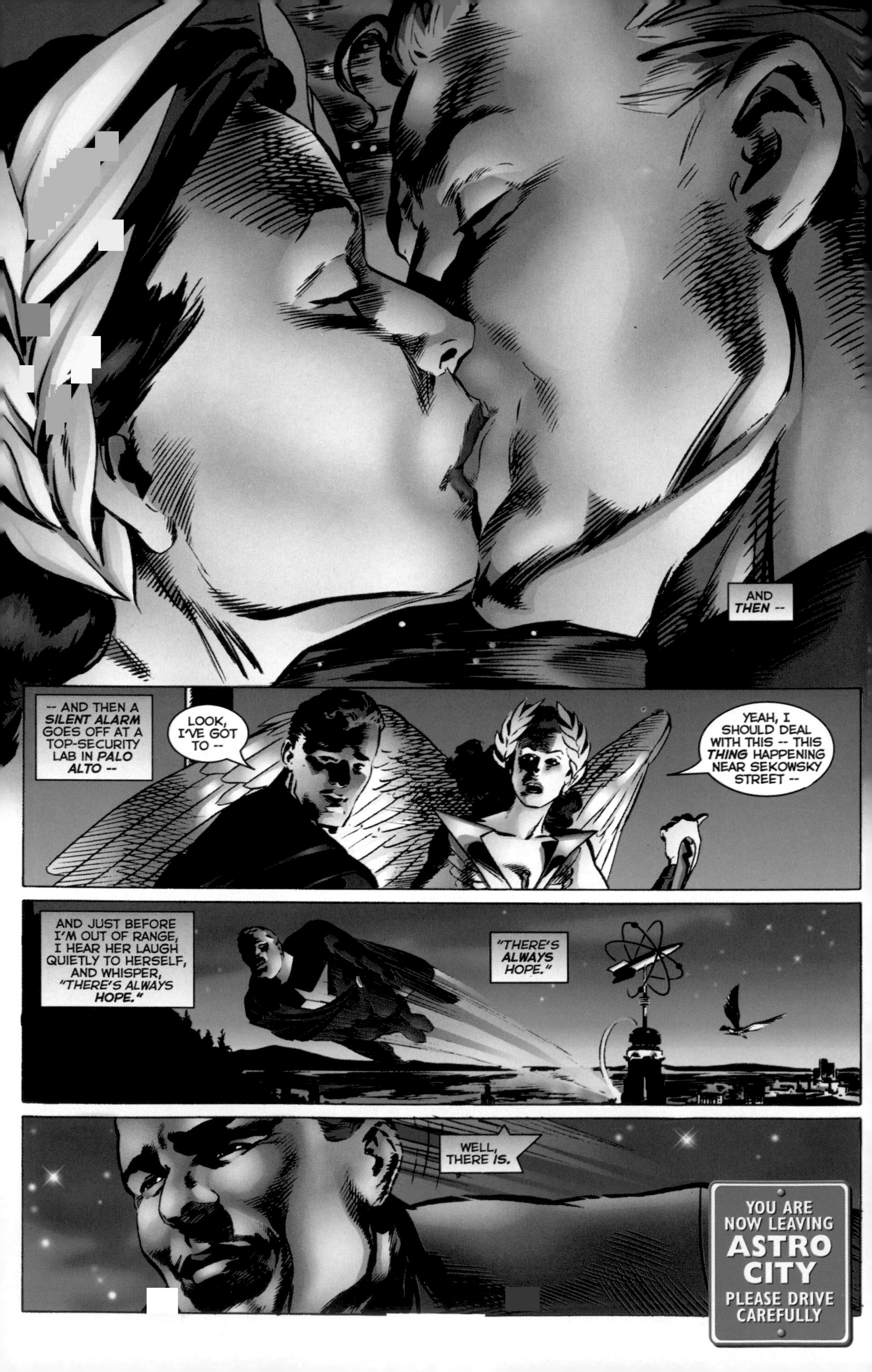
AND THEN --
-- AND THEN A SILENT ALARM GOES OFF AT A TOP-SECURITY LAB IN PALO ALTO --
LOOK, I'VE GOT TO --
YEAH, I SHOULD DEAL WITH THIS -- THIS THING HAPPENING NEAR SEKOWSKY STREET --
AND JUST BEFORE I'M OUT OF RANGE, I HEAR HER LAUGH QUIETLY TO HERSELF, AND WHISPER, "THERE'S ALWAYS HOPE."
"THERE'S ALWAYS HOPE."
WELL, THERE IS.
YOU ARE NOW LEAVING ASTRO CITY PLEASE DRIVE CAREFULLY

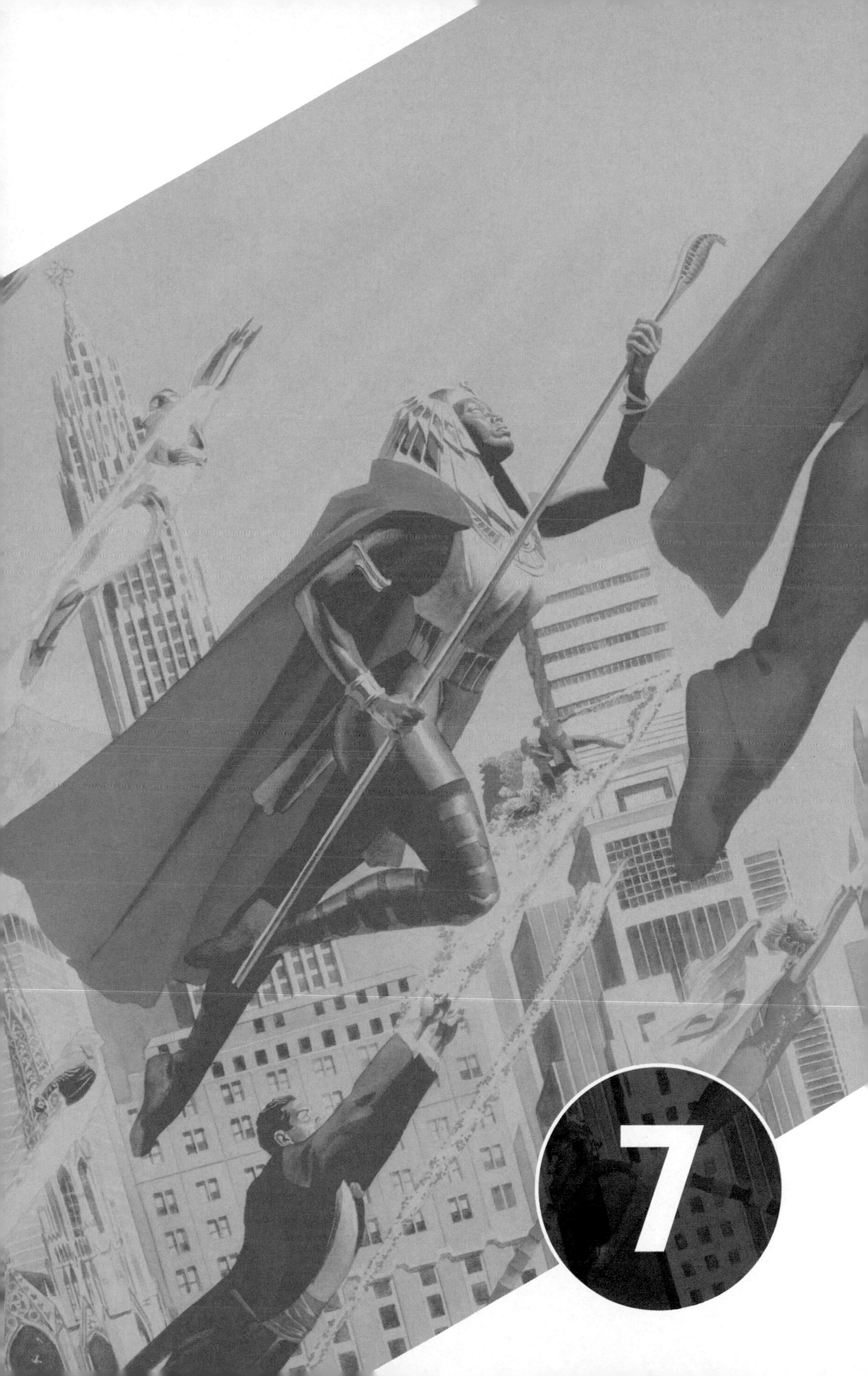
7

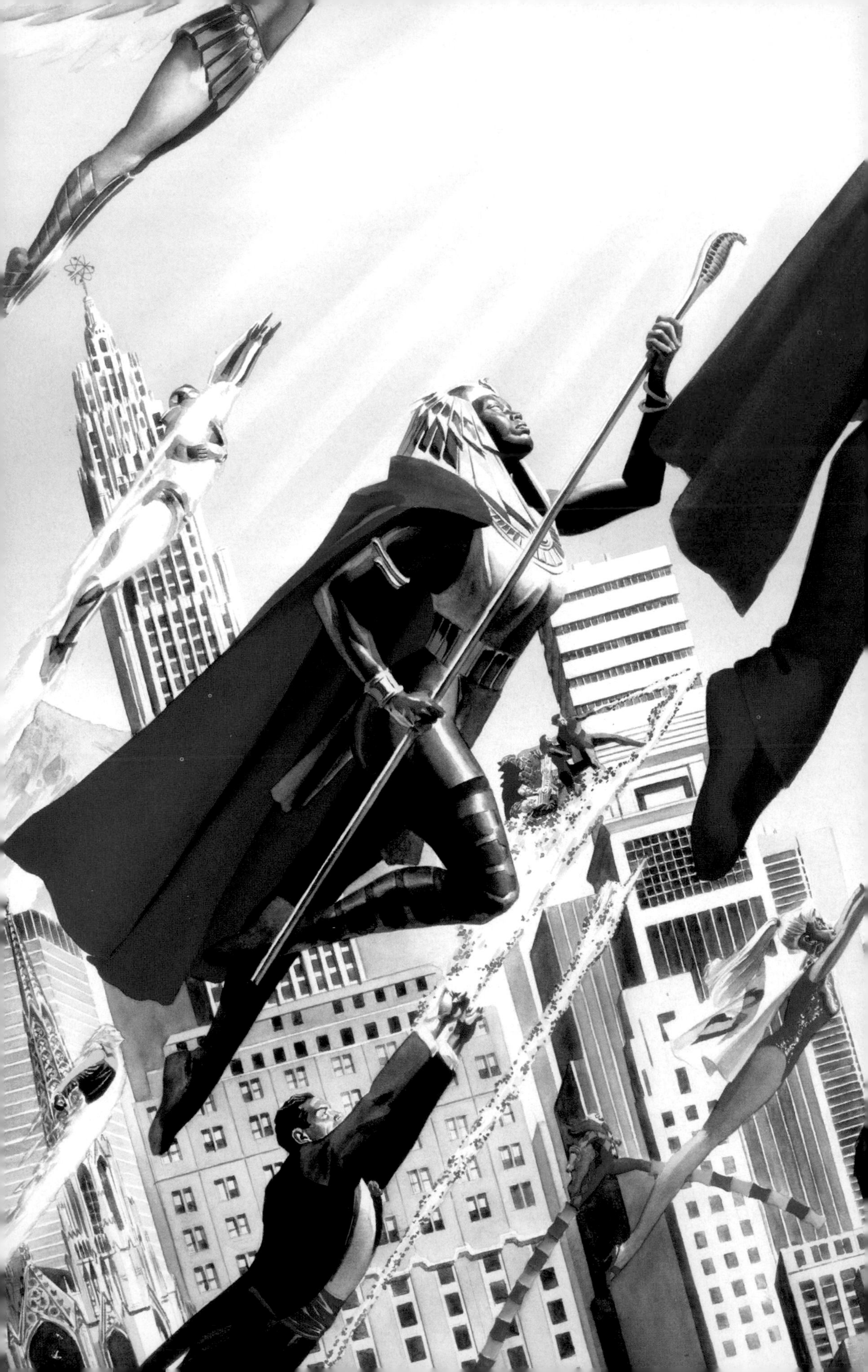

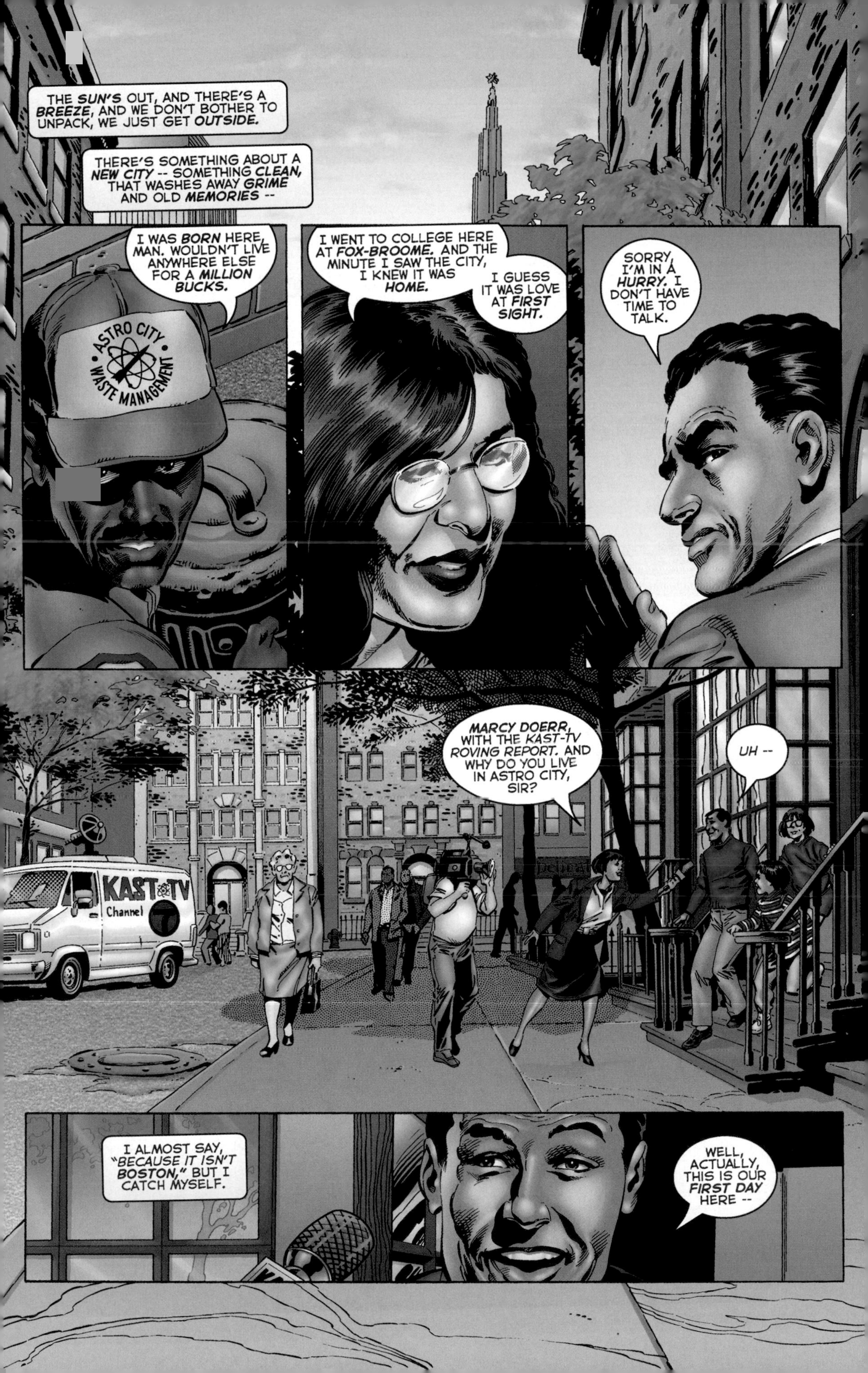
THE SUN'S OUT, AND THERE'S A BREEZE, AND WE DON'T BOTHER TO UNPACK, WE JUST GET OUTSIDE.
THERE'S SOMETHING ABOUT A NEW CITY -- SOMETHING CLEAN, THAT WASHES AWAY GRIME AND OLD MEMORIES --
I WAS BORN HERE, MAN. WOULDN'T LIVE ANYWHERE ELSE FOR A MILLION BUCKS.
ASTRO CITY WASTE MANAGEMENT
I WENT TO COLLEGE HERE AT FOX-BROOME. AND THE MINUTE I SAW THE CITY, I KNEW IT WAS HOME.
I GUESS IT WAS LOVE AT FIRST SIGHT.
SORRY, I'M IN A HURRY. I DON'T HAVE TIME TO TALK.
KAST TV
Channel
MARCY DOERR, WITH THE KAST-TV ROVING REPORT. AND WHY DO YOU LIVE IN ASTRO CITY, SIR?
UH --
I ALMOST SAY, "BECAUSE IT ISN'T BOSTON," BUT I CATCH MYSELF.
WELL, ACTUALLY, THIS IS OUR FIRST DAY HERE --

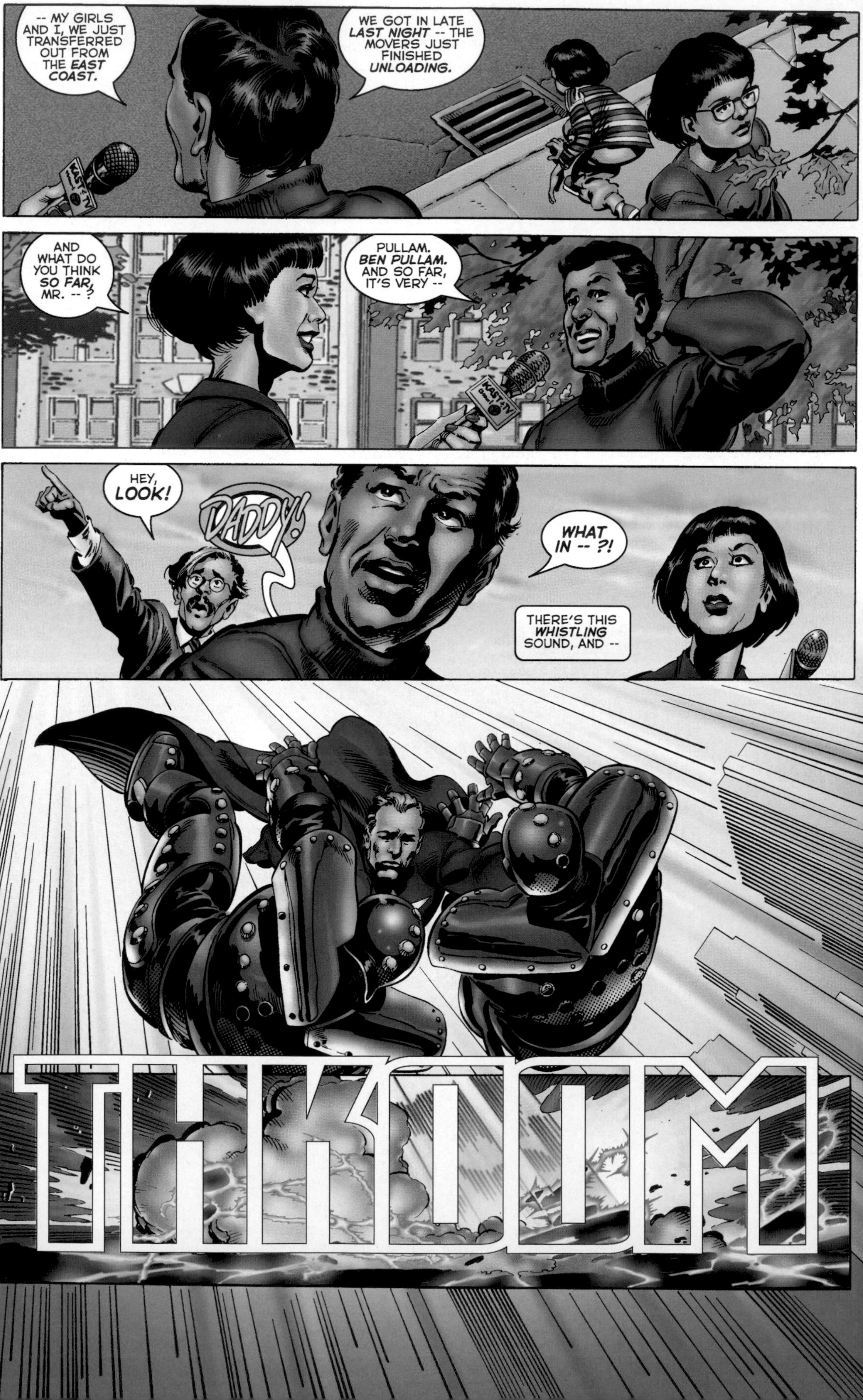
-- MY GIRLS AND I, WE JUST TRANSFERRED OUT FROM THE *EAST COAST.*
WE GOT IN LATE *LAST NIGHT* -- THE MOVERS JUST FINISHED *UNLOADING.*
AND WHAT DO YOU THINK *SO FAR,* MR. -- ?
PULLAM. *BEN PULLAM.* AND SO FAR, IT'S VERY --
HEY, *LOOK!*
DADDY!
WHAT IN -- ?!
THERE'S THIS *WHISTLING* SOUND, AND --
THKOOM

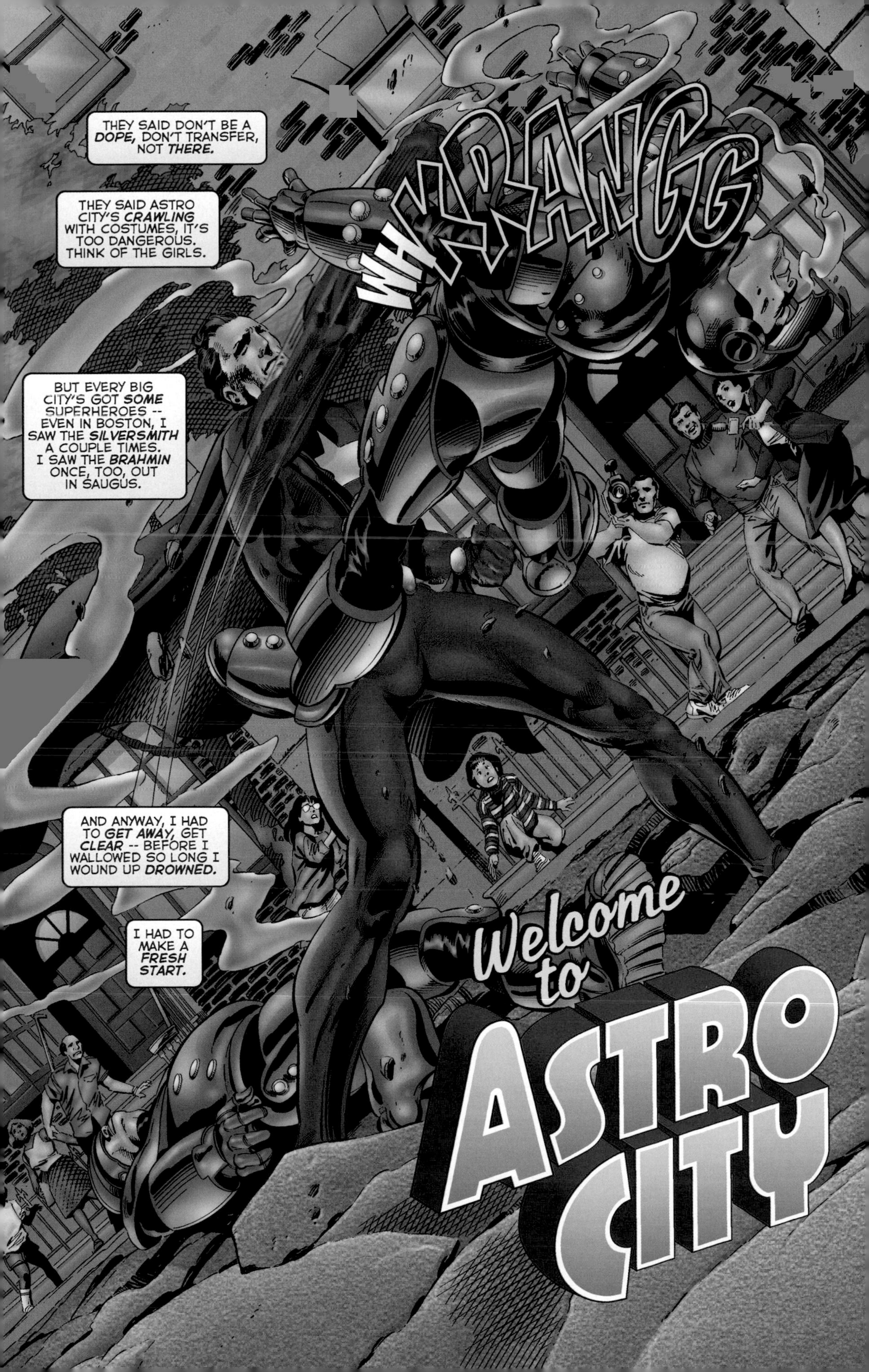
THEY SAID DON'T BE A DOPE, DON'T TRANSFER, NOT THERE.
THEY SAID ASTRO CITY'S CRAWLING WITH COSTUMES, IT'S TOO DANGEROUS. THINK OF THE GIRLS.
WHKRANGG
BUT EVERY BIG CITY'S GOT SOME SUPERHEROES -- EVEN IN BOSTON, I SAW THE SILVERSMITH A COUPLE TIMES. I SAW THE BRAHMIN ONCE, TOO, OUT IN SAUGUS.
AND ANYWAY, I HAD TO GET AWAY, GET CLEAR -- BEFORE I WALLOWED SO LONG I WOUND UP DROWNED.
I HAD TO MAKE A FRESH START.
Welcome to
ASTRO CITY

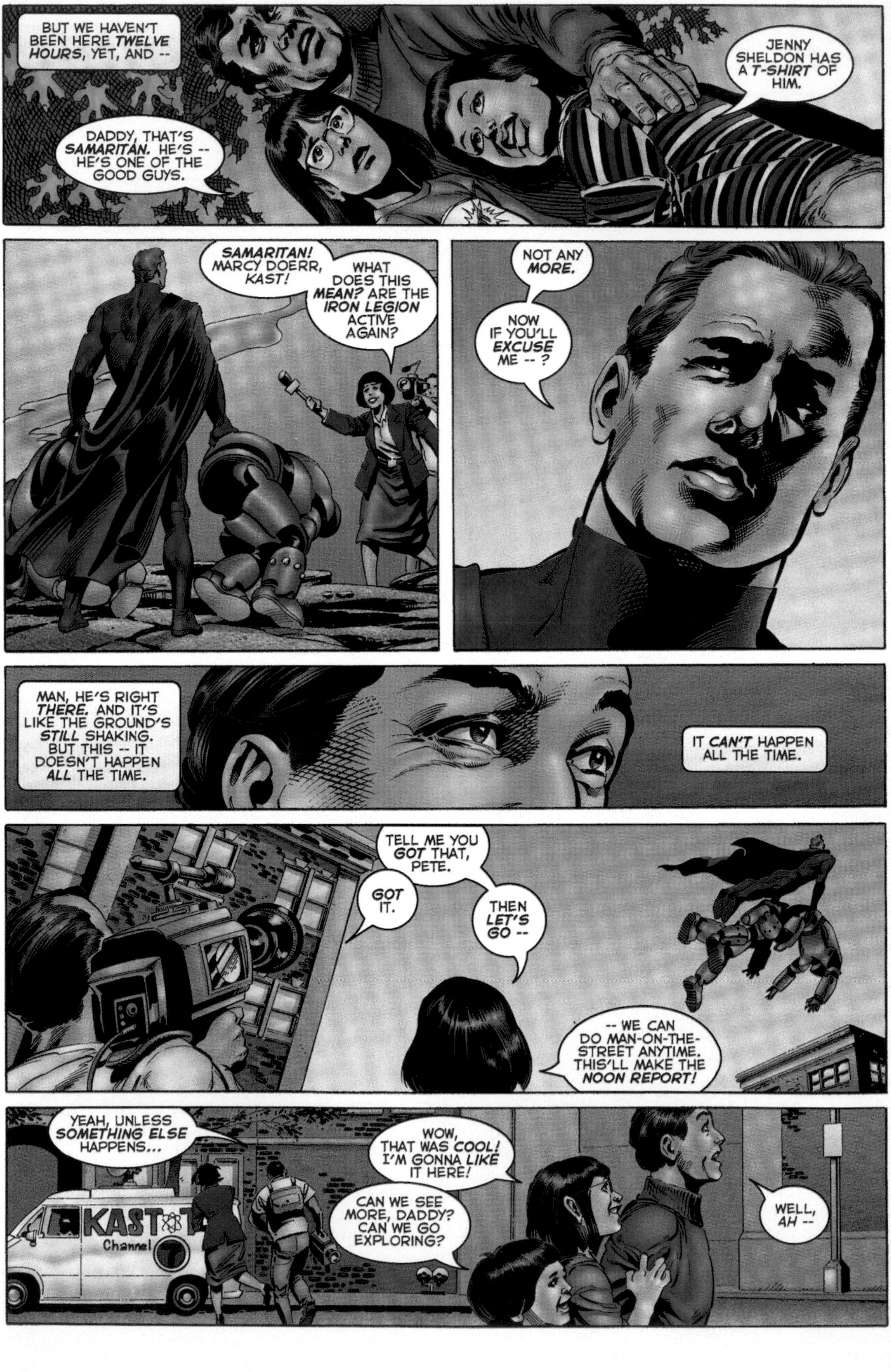
BUT WE HAVEN'T BEEN HERE TWELVE HOURS, YET, AND --
JENNY SHELDON HAS A T-SHIRT OF HIM.
DADDY, THAT'S SAMARITAN. HE'S -- HE'S ONE OF THE GOOD GUYS.
SAMARITAN! MARCY DOERR, KAST!
WHAT DOES THIS MEAN? ARE THE IRON LEGION ACTIVE AGAIN?
NOT ANY MORE.
NOW IF YOU'LL EXCUSE ME -- ?
MAN, HE'S RIGHT THERE. AND IT'S LIKE THE GROUND'S STILL SHAKING. BUT THIS -- IT DOESN'T HAPPEN ALL THE TIME.
IT CAN'T HAPPEN ALL THE TIME.
TELL ME YOU GOT THAT, PETE.
GOT IT.
THEN LET'S GO --
-- WE CAN DO MAN-ON-THE-STREET ANYTIME. THIS'LL MAKE THE NOON REPORT!
YEAH, UNLESS SOMETHING ELSE HAPPENS...
KAST
Channel
WOW, THAT WAS COOL! I'M GONNA LIKE IT HERE!
CAN WE SEE MORE, DADDY? CAN WE GO EXPLORING?
WELL, AH --

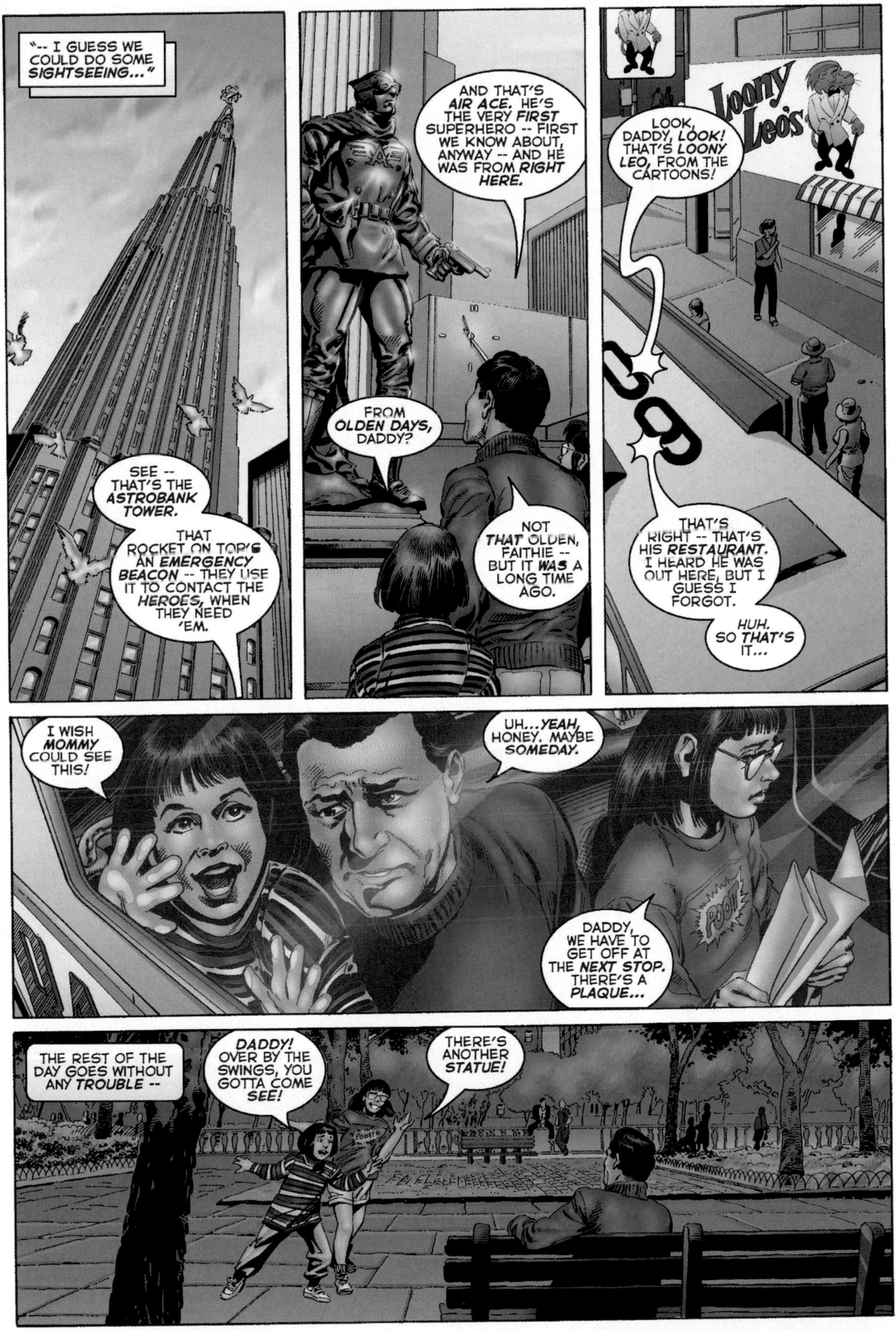
"-- I GUESS WE COULD DO SOME SIGHTSEEING..."
SEE -- THAT'S THE ASTROBANK TOWER.
THAT ROCKET ON TOP'S AN EMERGENCY BEACON -- THEY USE IT TO CONTACT THE HEROES, WHEN THEY NEED 'EM.
AND THAT'S AIR ACE. HE'S THE VERY FIRST SUPERHERO -- FIRST WE KNOW ABOUT, ANYWAY -- AND HE WAS FROM RIGHT HERE.
FROM OLDEN DAYS, DADDY?
NOT THAT OLDEN, FAITHIE -- BUT IT WAS A LONG TIME AGO.
Loony Leo's
LOOK, DADDY, LOOK! THAT'S LOONY LEO, FROM THE CARTOONS!
THAT'S RIGHT -- THAT'S HIS RESTAURANT. I HEARD HE WAS OUT HERE, BUT I GUESS I FORGOT.
HUH. SO THAT'S IT...
I WISH MOMMY COULD SEE THIS!
UH...YEAH, HONEY. MAYBE SOMEDAY.
DADDY, WE HAVE TO GET OFF AT THE NEXT STOP. THERE'S A PLAQUE...
THE REST OF THE DAY GOES WITHOUT ANY TROUBLE --
DADDY! OVER BY THE SWINGS, YOU GOTTA COME SEE!
THERE'S ANOTHER STATUE!

-- WELL, WITHOUT *MUCH* TROUBLE --

THAT'S THE *SILVER AGENT*, GIRLS. HE WAS AROUND WHEN I WAS A *BOY* -- I USED TO SEE HIM ON TV ALL THE TIME.

MAN, I USED TO HAVE A SILVER AGENT *JUNIOR PEACE OFFICER* BADGE AND *DETECTIVE KIT...*

WHAT'S THE *INSCRIPTION* MEAN?

ALAN CRAIG
THE SILVER AGENT
1932-1973
"TO OUR ETERNAL SHAME"

ETERNAL SHAME. HOW COME IT SAYS *"ETERNAL SHAME?"*

UH...I'LL EXPLAIN IT TO YOU WHEN YOU'RE *OLDER.*

WHEN *I'M* OLDER, OR WHEN *MEG'S* OLDER?

ALAN CRAIG
THE SILVER AGENT
1932-1973

WHEN YOU'RE *BOTH* OLDER, FAITHIE. NOW COME ON, LET'S GO HOME...

WHEN THEY'RE *OLDER.* WHO AM I KIDDING? THEY SOAK UP EVERYTHING WE *SAY* OR *DO,* LIKE LITTLE SPONGES.

AND WE'RE *ALWAYS* TEACHING THEM. LIKE IT OR NOT, WE'RE TEACHING THEM *SOMETHING.*

...IT'S GETTING A LITTLE *COLD...*

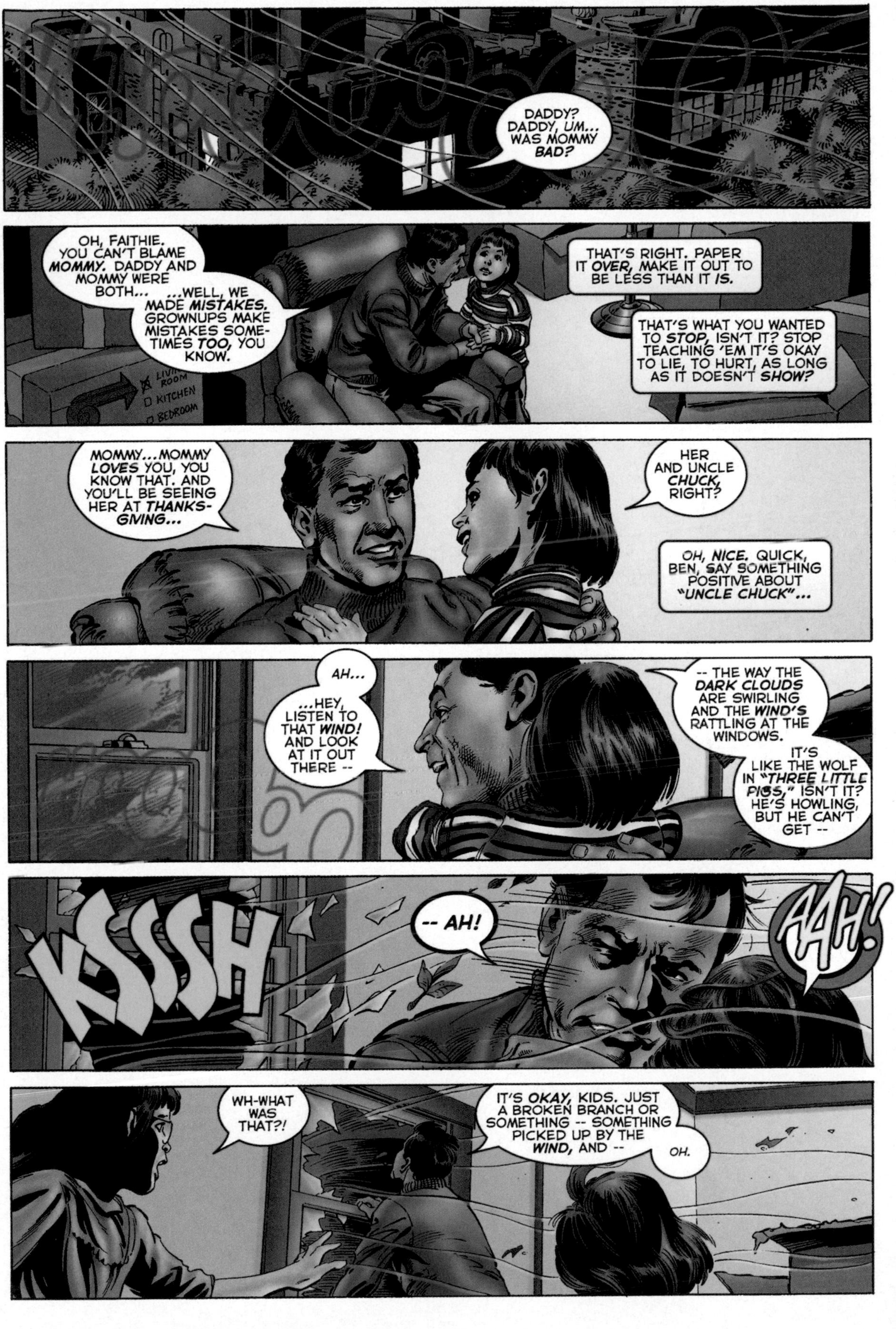
DADDY? DADDY, UM... WAS MOMMY BAD?
OH, FAITHIE. YOU CAN'T BLAME MOMMY. DADDY AND MOMMY WERE BOTH...
...WELL, WE MADE MISTAKES. GROWNUPS MAKE MISTAKES SOMETIMES TOO, YOU KNOW.
THAT'S RIGHT. PAPER IT OVER, MAKE IT OUT TO BE LESS THAN IT IS.
THAT'S WHAT YOU WANTED TO STOP, ISN'T IT? STOP TEACHING 'EM IT'S OKAY TO LIE, TO HURT, AS LONG AS IT DOESN'T SHOW?
KITCHEN
BEDROOM
MOMMY... MOMMY LOVES YOU, YOU KNOW THAT. AND YOU'LL BE SEEING HER AT THANKSGIVING...
HER AND UNCLE CHUCK, RIGHT?
OH, NICE. QUICK, BEN, SAY SOMETHING POSITIVE ABOUT "UNCLE CHUCK"...
AH...
...HEY, LISTEN TO THAT WIND! AND LOOK AT IT OUT THERE --
-- THE WAY THE DARK CLOUDS ARE SWIRLING AND THE WIND'S RATTLING AT THE WINDOWS.
IT'S LIKE THE WOLF IN "THREE LITTLE PIGS," ISN'T IT? HE'S HOWLING, BUT HE CAN'T GET --
KSSSH
-- AH!
AAH!
WH-WHAT WAS THAT?!
IT'S OKAY, KIDS. JUST A BROKEN BRANCH OR SOMETHING -- SOMETHING PICKED UP BY THE WIND, AND --
OH.

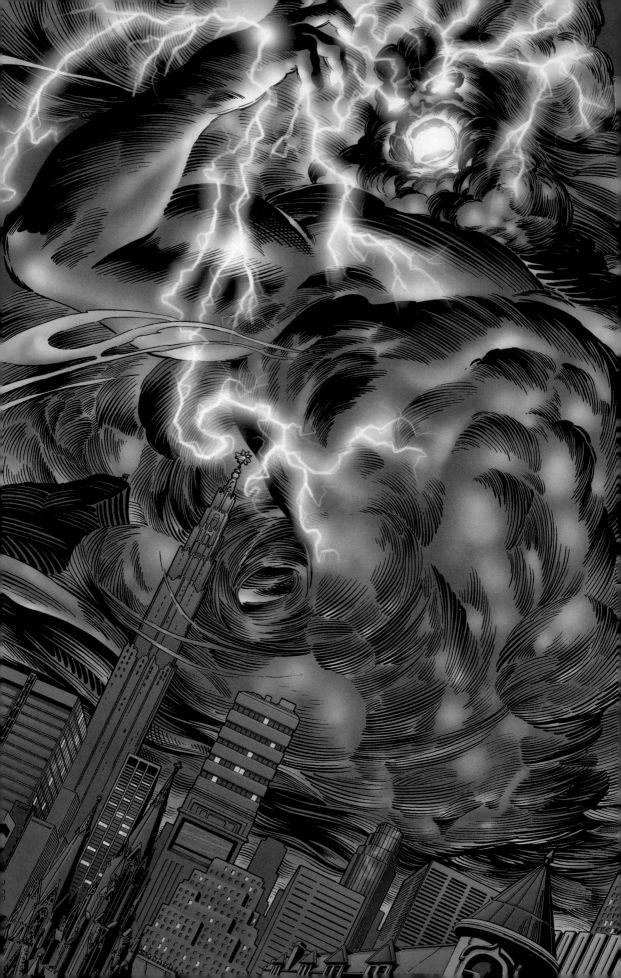

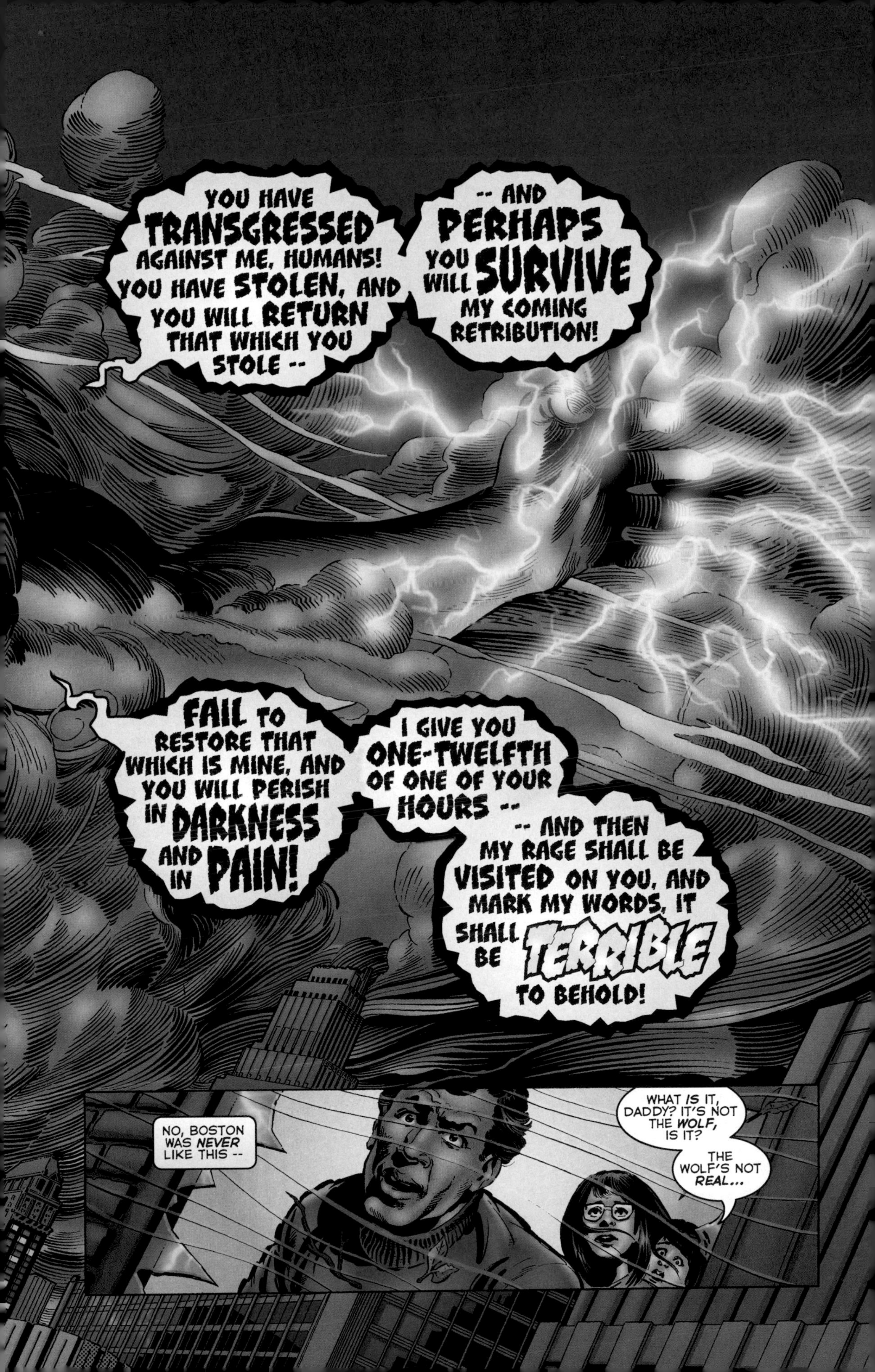
YOU HAVE TRANSGRESSED AGAINST ME, HUMANS! YOU HAVE STOLEN, AND YOU WILL RETURN THAT WHICH YOU STOLE --
-- AND PERHAPS YOU WILL SURVIVE MY COMING RETRIBUTION!
FAIL TO RESTORE THAT WHICH IS MINE, AND YOU WILL PERISH IN DARKNESS AND IN PAIN!
I GIVE YOU ONE-TWELFTH OF ONE OF YOUR HOURS --
-- AND THEN MY RAGE SHALL BE VISITED ON YOU, AND MARK MY WORDS, IT SHALL BE TERRIBLE TO BEHOLD!
NO, BOSTON WAS *NEVER* LIKE THIS --
WHAT *IS* IT, DADDY? IT'S NOT THE *WOLF,* IS IT?
THE WOLF'S NOT *REAL...*

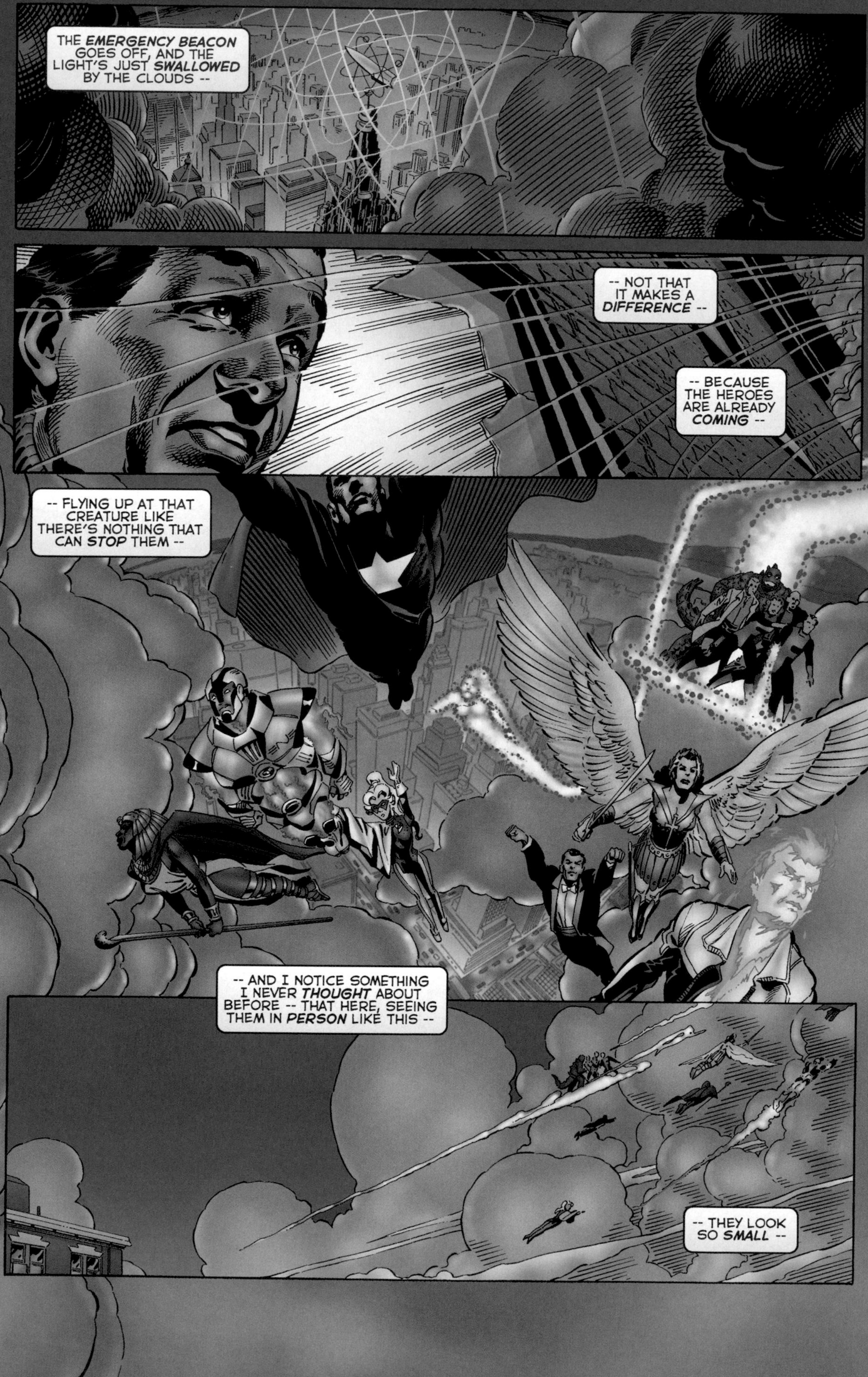
THE EMERGENCY BEACON GOES OFF, AND THE LIGHT'S JUST SWALLOWED BY THE CLOUDS --
-- NOT THAT IT MAKES A DIFFERENCE --
-- BECAUSE THE HEROES ARE ALREADY COMING --
-- FLYING UP AT THAT CREATURE LIKE THERE'S NOTHING THAT CAN STOP THEM --
-- AND I NOTICE SOMETHING I NEVER THOUGHT ABOUT BEFORE -- THAT HERE, SEEING THEM IN PERSON LIKE THIS --
-- THEY LOOK SO SMALL --

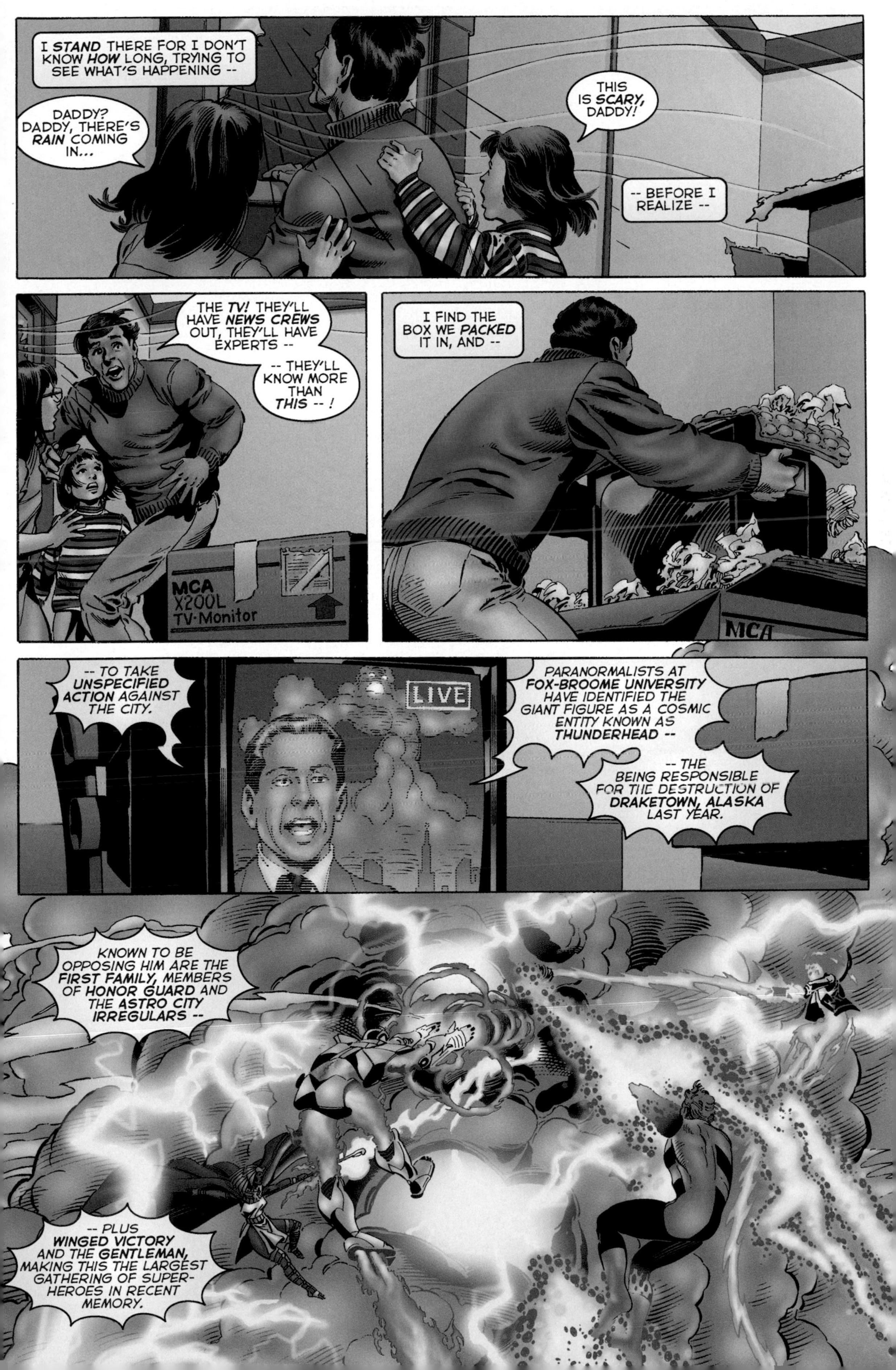

I STAND THERE FOR I DON'T KNOW HOW LONG, TRYING TO SEE WHAT'S HAPPENING --
DADDY? DADDY, THERE'S RAIN COMING IN...
THIS IS SCARY, DADDY!
-- BEFORE I REALIZE --
THE TV! THEY'LL HAVE NEWS CREWS OUT, THEY'LL HAVE EXPERTS --
-- THEY'LL KNOW MORE THAN THIS -- !
MCA X200L TV-Monitor
I FIND THE BOX WE PACKED IT IN, AND --
MCA
-- TO TAKE UNSPECIFIED ACTION AGAINST THE CITY.
LIVE
PARANORMALISTS AT FOX-BROOME UNIVERSITY HAVE IDENTIFIED THE GIANT FIGURE AS A COSMIC ENTITY KNOWN AS THUNDERHEAD --
-- THE BEING RESPONSIBLE FOR THE DESTRUCTION OF DRAKETOWN, ALASKA LAST YEAR.
KNOWN TO BE OPPOSING HIM ARE THE FIRST FAMILY, MEMBERS OF HONOR GUARD AND THE ASTRO CITY IRREGULARS --
-- PLUS WINGED VICTORY AND THE GENTLEMAN, MAKING THIS THE LARGEST GATHERING OF SUPER-HEROES IN RECENT MEMORY.

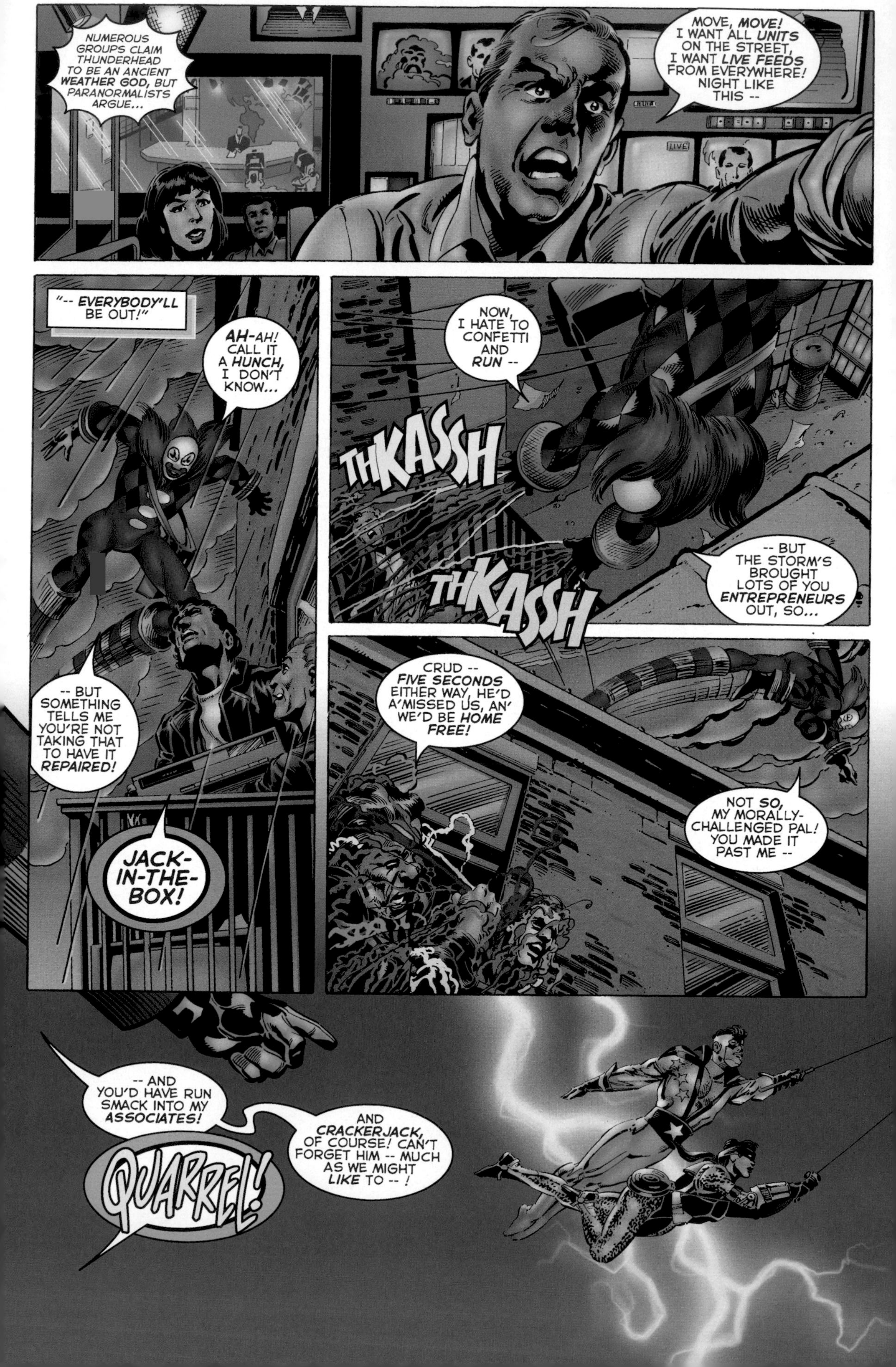
NUMEROUS GROUPS CLAIM THUNDERHEAD TO BE AN ANCIENT WEATHER GOD, BUT PARANORMALISTS ARGUE...
MOVE, MOVE! I WANT ALL UNITS ON THE STREET, I WANT LIVE FEEDS FROM EVERYWHERE! NIGHT LIKE THIS --
"-- EVERYBODY'LL BE OUT!"
AH-AH! CALL IT A HUNCH, I DON'T KNOW...
-- BUT SOMETHING TELLS ME YOU'RE NOT TAKING THAT TO HAVE IT REPAIRED!
JACK-IN-THE-BOX!
NOW, I HATE TO CONFETTI AND RUN --
THKASSH
THKASSH
-- BUT THE STORM'S BROUGHT LOTS OF YOU ENTREPRENEURS OUT, SO...
CRUD -- FIVE SECONDS EITHER WAY, HE'D A'MISSED US, AN' WE'D BE HOME FREE!
NOT SO, MY MORALLY-CHALLENGED PAL! YOU MADE IT PAST ME --
-- AND YOU'D HAVE RUN SMACK INTO MY ASSOCIATES!
QUARREL!
AND CRACKERJACK, OF COURSE! CAN'T FORGET HIM -- MUCH AS WE MIGHT LIKE TO -- !

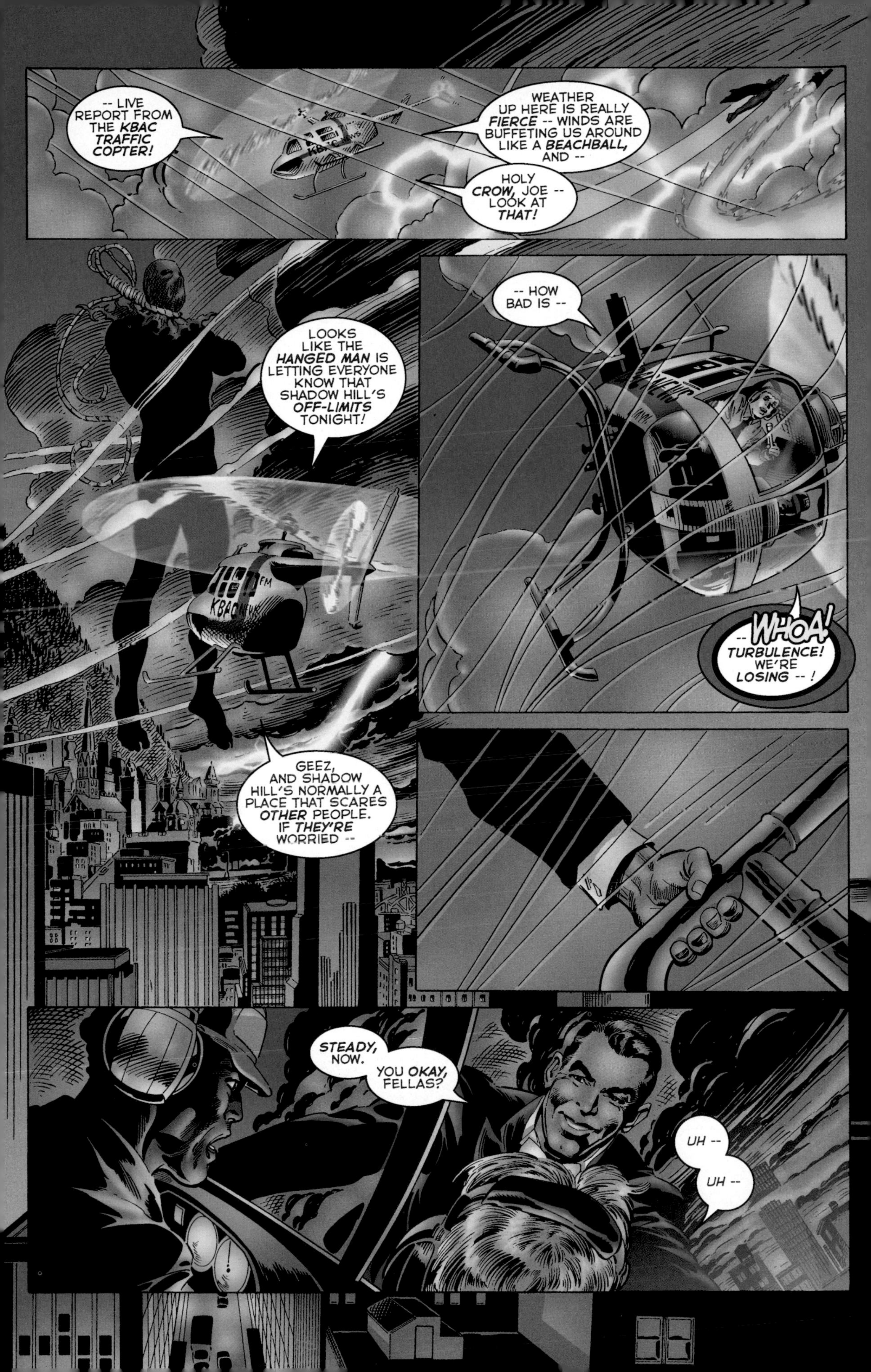
-- LIVE REPORT FROM THE KBAC TRAFFIC COPTER!
WEATHER UP HERE IS REALLY FIERCE -- WINDS ARE BUFFETING US AROUND LIKE A BEACHBALL, AND --
HOLY CROW, JOE -- LOOK AT THAT!
LOOKS LIKE THE HANGED MAN IS LETTING EVERYONE KNOW THAT SHADOW HILL'S OFF-LIMITS TONIGHT!
GEEZ, AND SHADOW HILL'S NORMALLY A PLACE THAT SCARES OTHER PEOPLE. IF THEY'RE WORRIED --
-- HOW BAD IS --
-- WHOA! TURBULENCE! WE'RE LOSING -- !
STEADY, NOW.
YOU OKAY, FELLAS?
UH --
UH --

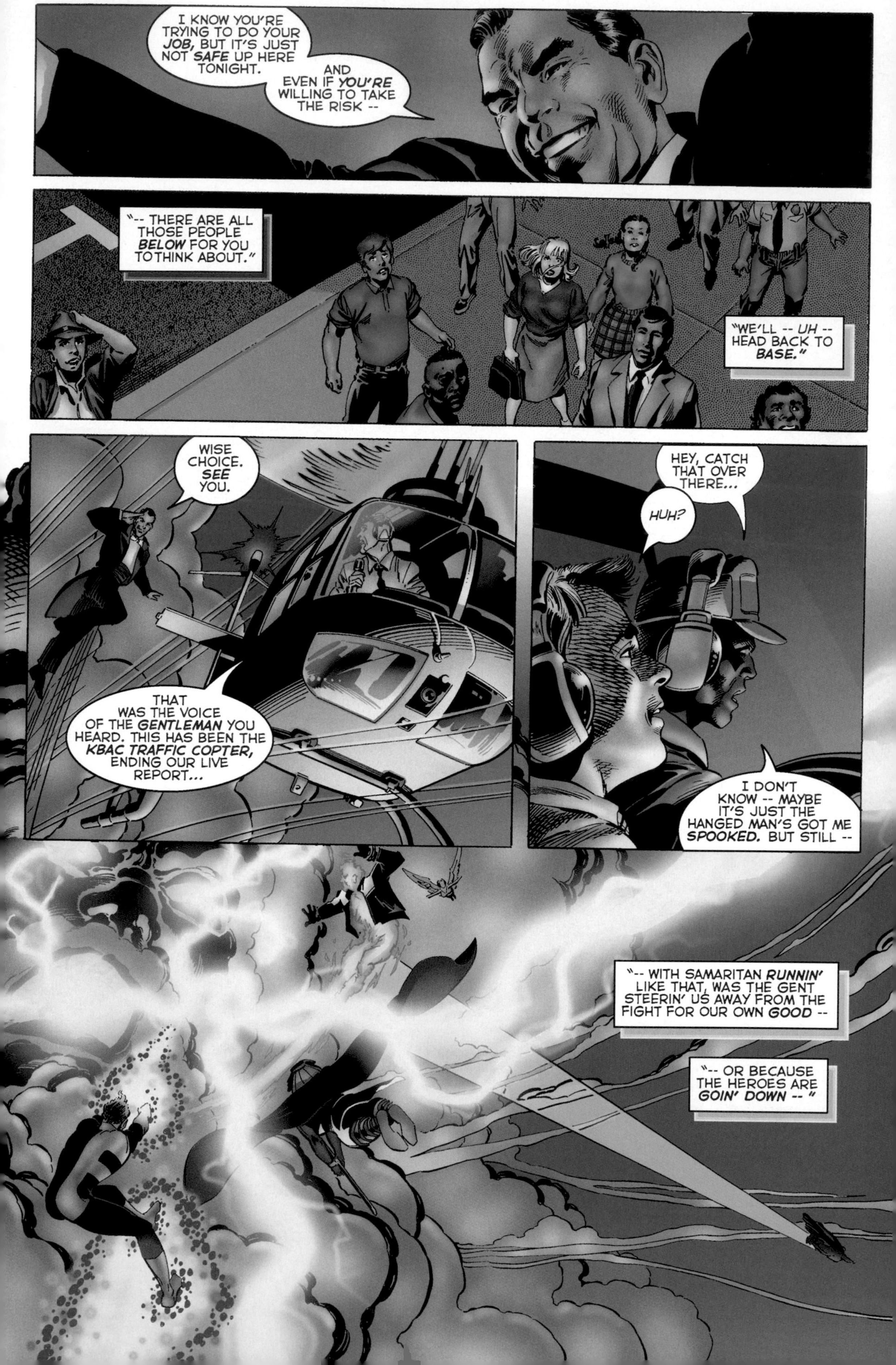

I KNOW YOU'RE TRYING TO DO YOUR JOB, BUT IT'S JUST NOT SAFE UP HERE TONIGHT.
AND EVEN IF YOU'RE WILLING TO TAKE THE RISK --
"-- THERE ARE ALL THOSE PEOPLE BELOW FOR YOU TO THINK ABOUT."
"WE'LL -- UH -- HEAD BACK TO BASE."
WISE CHOICE. SEE YOU.
THAT WAS THE VOICE OF THE GENTLEMAN YOU HEARD. THIS HAS BEEN THE KBAC TRAFFIC COPTER, ENDING OUR LIVE REPORT...
HEY, CATCH THAT OVER THERE...
HUH?
I DON'T KNOW -- MAYBE IT'S JUST THE HANGED MAN'S GOT ME SPOOKED. BUT STILL --
"-- WITH SAMARITAN RUNNIN' LIKE THAT, WAS THE GENT STEERIN' US AWAY FROM THE FIGHT FOR OUR OWN GOOD --
"-- OR BECAUSE THE HEROES ARE GOIN' DOWN -- "

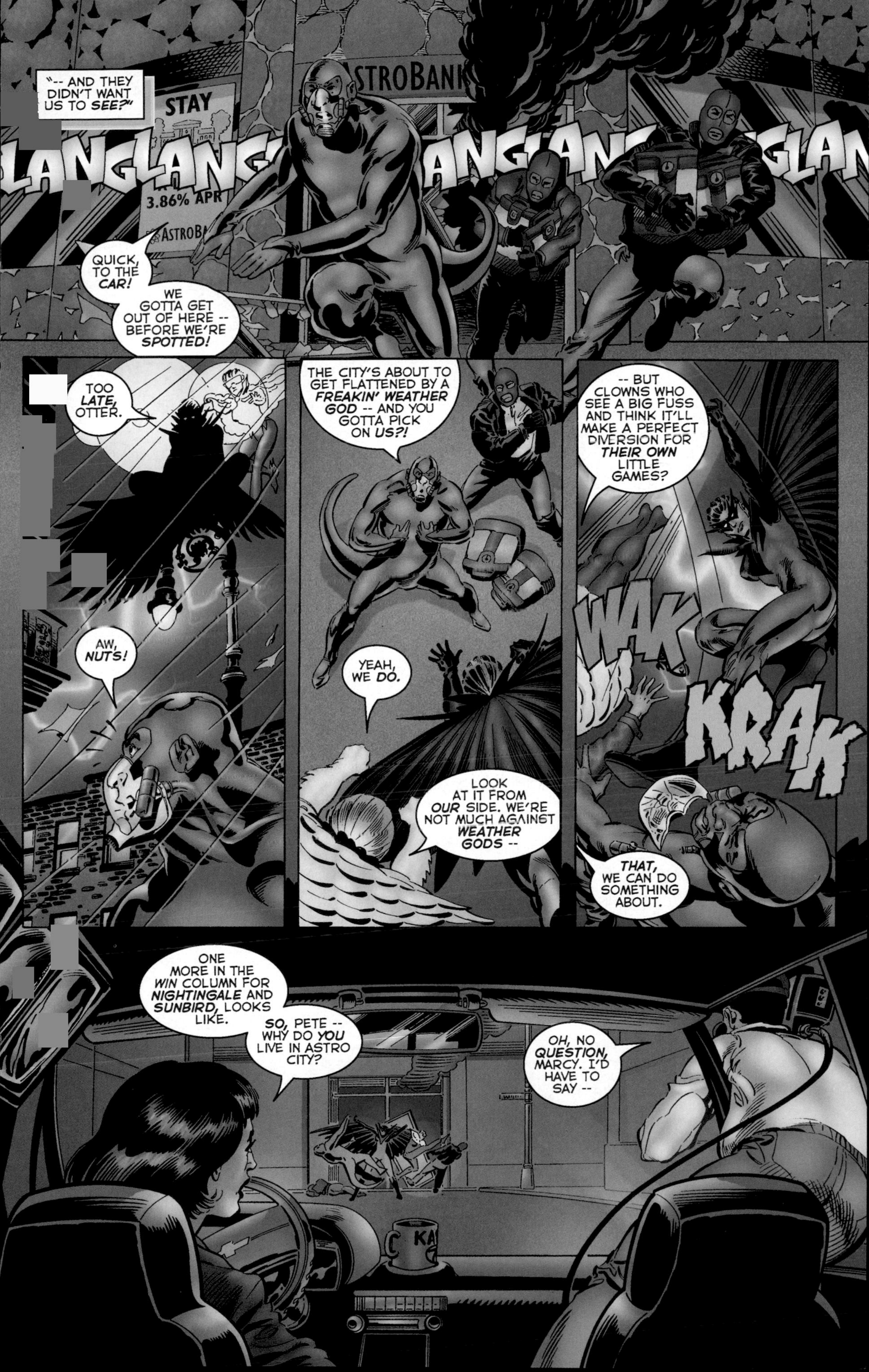
"-- AND THEY DIDN'T WANT US TO SEE?"
ASTROBANK
STAY
3.86% APR
LANGLANGLANGLANGLANGLANGLAN
QUICK, TO THE CAR!
WE GOTTA GET OUT OF HERE -- BEFORE WE'RE SPOTTED!
TOO LATE, OTTER.
AW, NUTS!
THE CITY'S ABOUT TO GET FLATTENED BY A FREAKIN' WEATHER GOD -- AND YOU GOTTA PICK ON US?!
YEAH, WE DO.
LOOK AT IT FROM OUR SIDE. WE'RE NOT MUCH AGAINST WEATHER GODS --
-- BUT CLOWNS WHO SEE A BIG FUSS AND THINK IT'LL MAKE A PERFECT DIVERSION FOR THEIR OWN LITTLE GAMES?
WAK
KRAK
THAT, WE CAN DO SOMETHING ABOUT.
ONE MORE IN THE WIN COLUMN FOR NIGHTINGALE AND SUNBIRD, LOOKS LIKE.
SO, PETE -- WHY DO YOU LIVE IN ASTRO CITY?
OH, NO QUESTION, MARCY. I'D HAVE TO SAY --

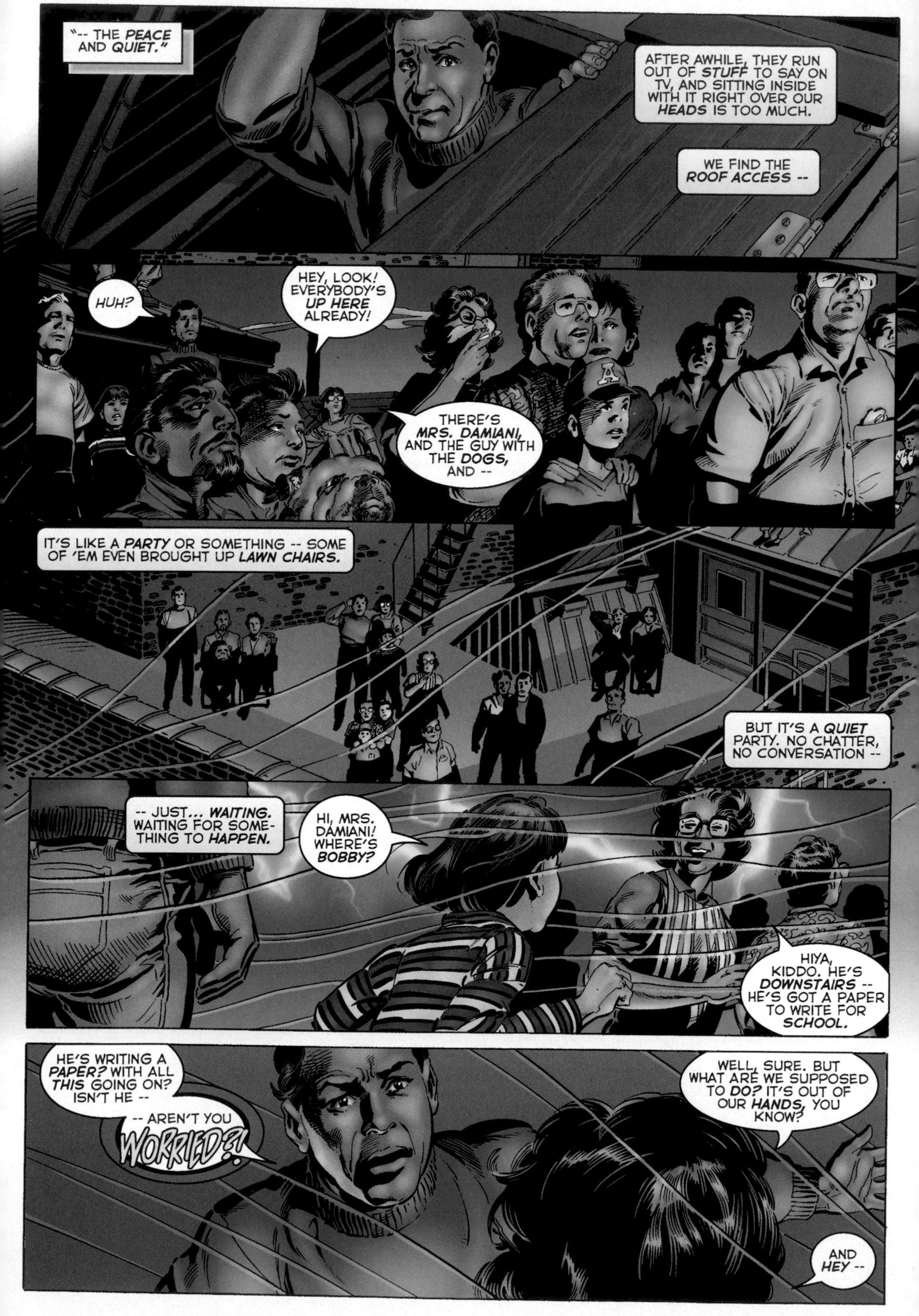
"-- THE PEACE AND QUIET."
AFTER AWHILE, THEY RUN OUT OF STUFF TO SAY ON TV, AND SITTING INSIDE WITH IT RIGHT OVER OUR HEADS IS TOO MUCH.
WE FIND THE ROOF ACCESS --
HUH?
HEY, LOOK! EVERYBODY'S UP HERE ALREADY!
THERE'S MRS. DAMIANI, AND THE GUY WITH THE DOGS, AND --
IT'S LIKE A PARTY OR SOMETHING -- SOME OF 'EM EVEN BROUGHT UP LAWN CHAIRS.
BUT IT'S A QUIET PARTY. NO CHATTER, NO CONVERSATION --
-- JUST... WAITING. WAITING FOR SOMETHING TO HAPPEN.
HI, MRS. DAMIANI! WHERE'S BOBBY?
HIYA, KIDDO. HE'S DOWNSTAIRS -- HE'S GOT A PAPER TO WRITE FOR SCHOOL.
HE'S WRITING A PAPER? WITH ALL THIS GOING ON? ISN'T HE --
-- AREN'T YOU WORRIED?!
WELL, SURE. BUT WHAT ARE WE SUPPOSED TO DO? IT'S OUT OF OUR HANDS, YOU KNOW?
AND HEY --

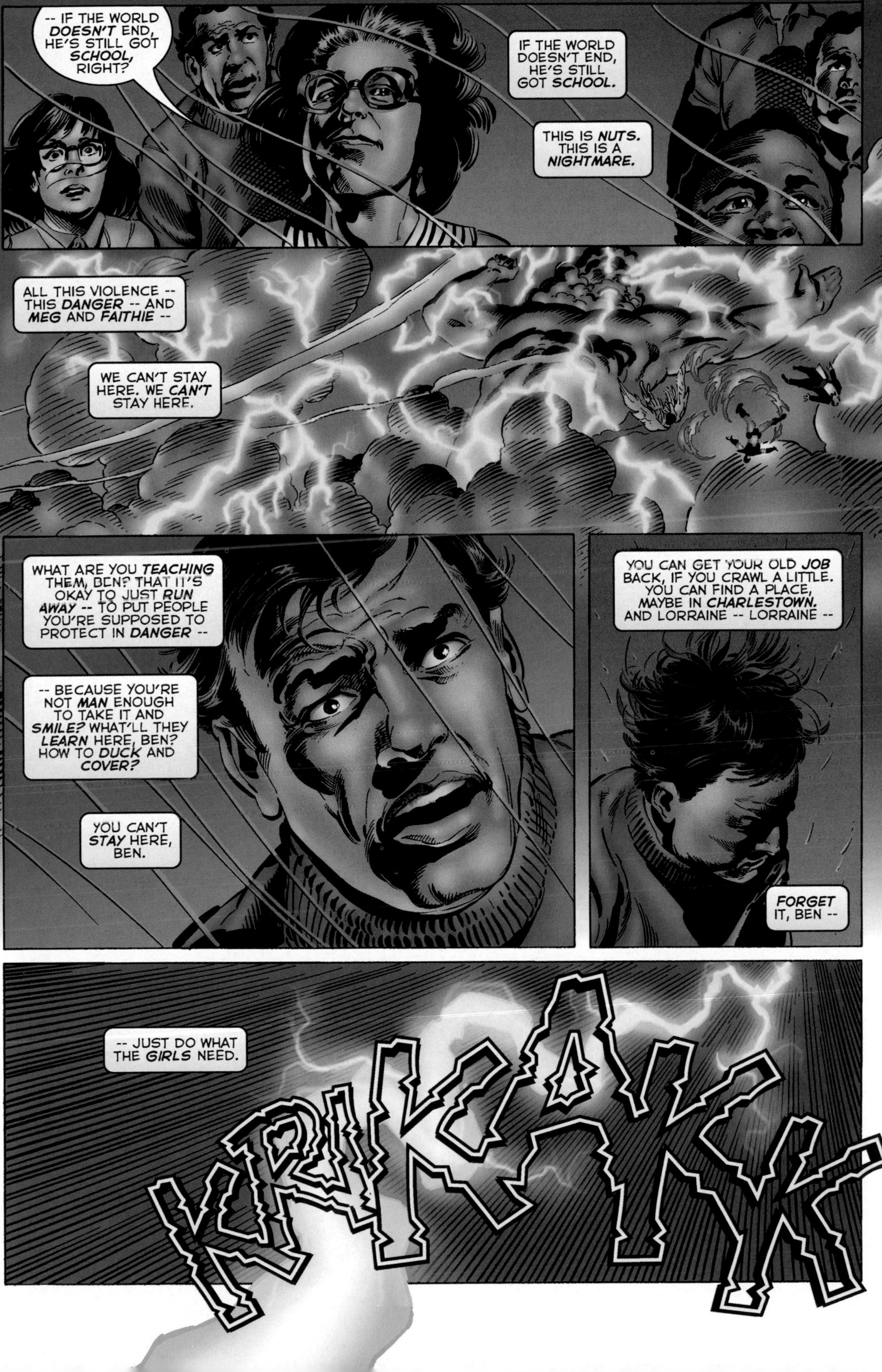
-- IF THE WORLD DOESN'T END, HE'S STILL GOT SCHOOL, RIGHT?
IF THE WORLD DOESN'T END, HE'S STILL GOT SCHOOL.
THIS IS NUTS. THIS IS A NIGHTMARE.
ALL THIS VIOLENCE -- THIS DANGER -- AND MEG AND FAITHIE --
WE CAN'T STAY HERE. WE CAN'T STAY HERE.
WHAT ARE YOU TEACHING THEM, BEN? THAT IT'S OKAY TO JUST RUN AWAY -- TO PUT PEOPLE YOU'RE SUPPOSED TO PROTECT IN DANGER --
-- BECAUSE YOU'RE NOT MAN ENOUGH TO TAKE IT AND SMILE? WHAT'LL THEY LEARN HERE, BEN? HOW TO DUCK AND COVER?
YOU CAN'T STAY HERE, BEN.
YOU CAN GET YOUR OLD JOB BACK, IF YOU CRAWL A LITTLE. YOU CAN FIND A PLACE, MAYBE IN CHARLESTOWN. AND LORRAINE -- LORRAINE --
FORGET IT, BEN --
-- JUST DO WHAT THE GIRLS NEED.
KRAKAKK

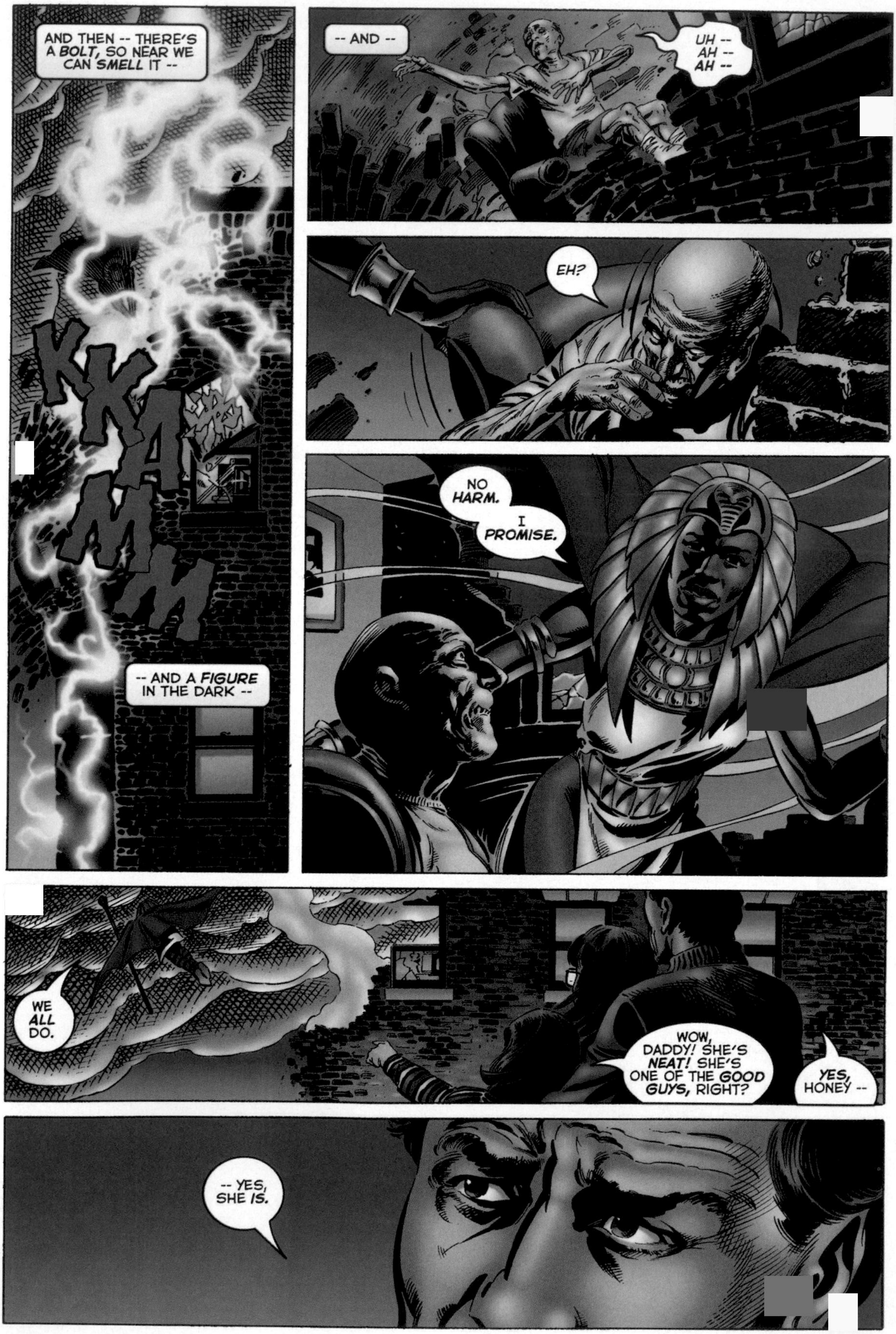
AND THEN -- THERE'S A BOLT, SO NEAR WE CAN SMELL IT --
KKAMMM
-- AND A FIGURE IN THE DARK --
-- AND --
UH -- AH -- AH --
EH?
NO HARM. I PROMISE.
WE ALL DO.
WOW, DADDY! SHE'S NEAT! SHE'S ONE OF THE GOOD GUYS, RIGHT?
YES, HONEY --
-- YES, SHE IS.

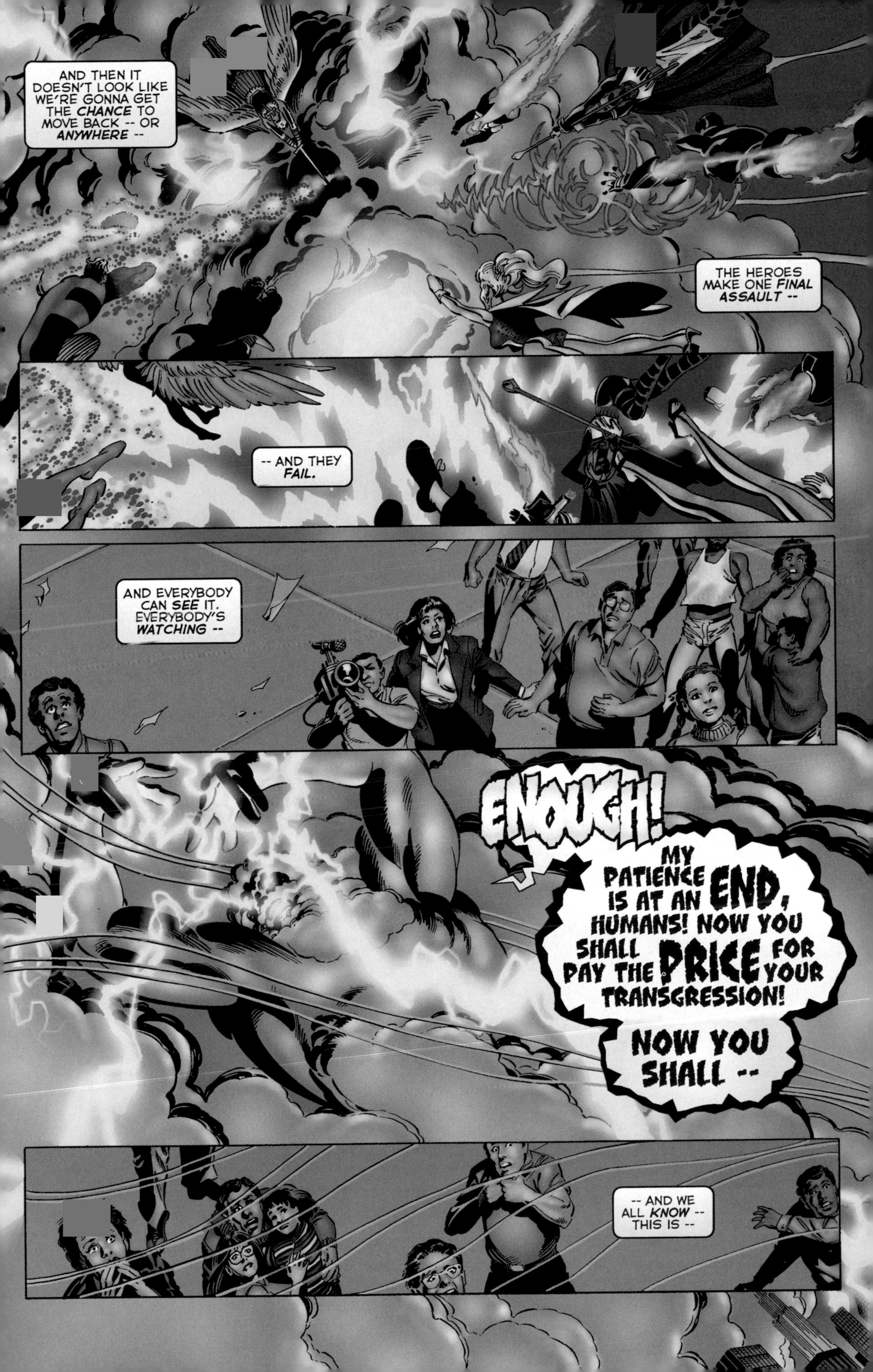
AND THEN IT DOESN'T LOOK LIKE WE'RE GONNA GET THE CHANCE TO MOVE BACK -- OR ANYWHERE --
THE HEROES MAKE ONE FINAL ASSAULT --
-- AND THEY FAIL.
AND EVERYBODY CAN SEE IT. EVERYBODY'S WATCHING --
ENOUGH!
MY PATIENCE IS AT AN END, HUMANS! NOW YOU SHALL PAY THE PRICE FOR YOUR TRANSGRESSION!
NOW YOU SHALL --
-- AND WE ALL KNOW -- THIS IS --

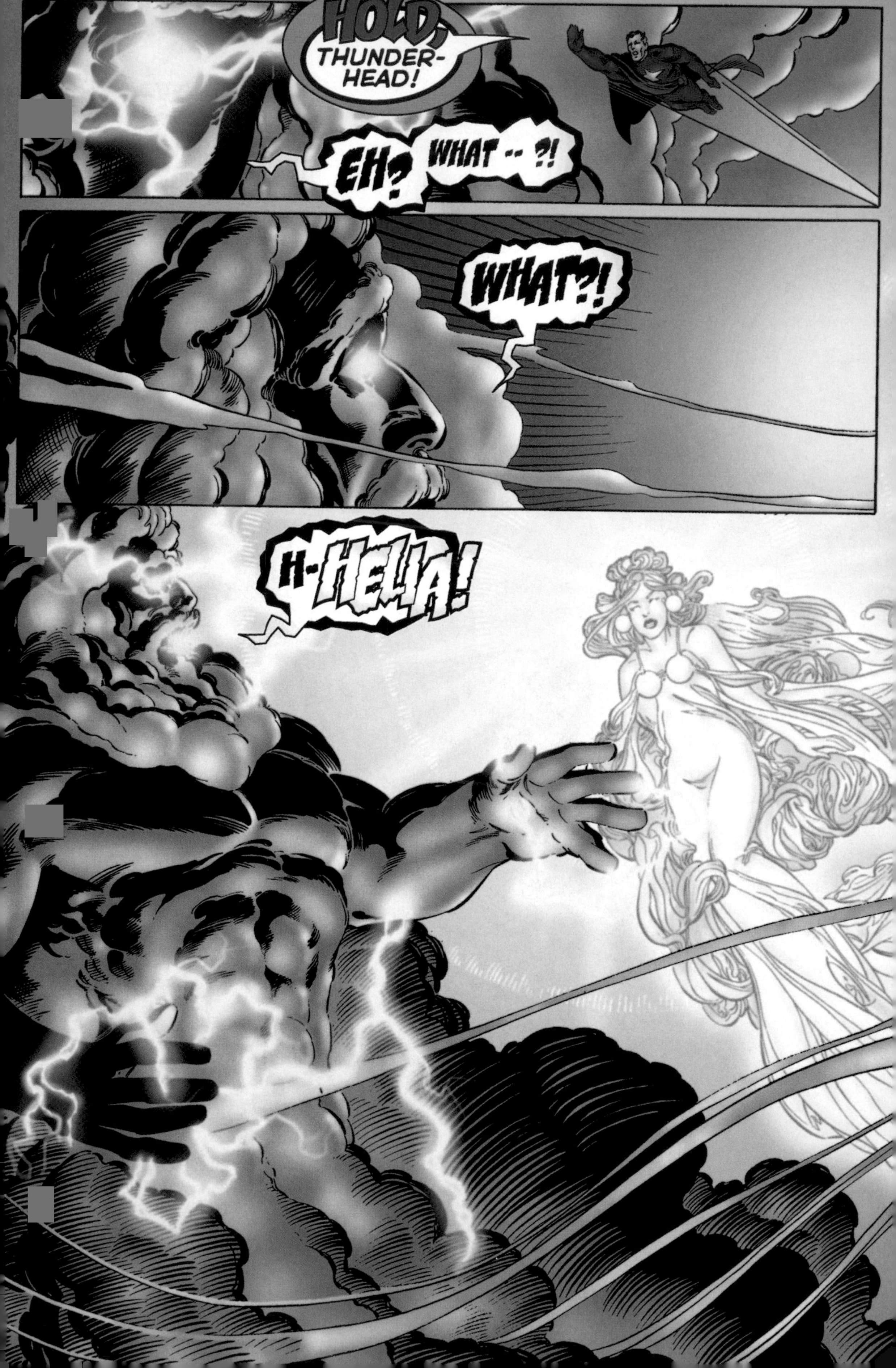
HOLD, THUNDER-HEAD!
EH?
WHAT -- ?!
WHAT?!
H-HELIA!

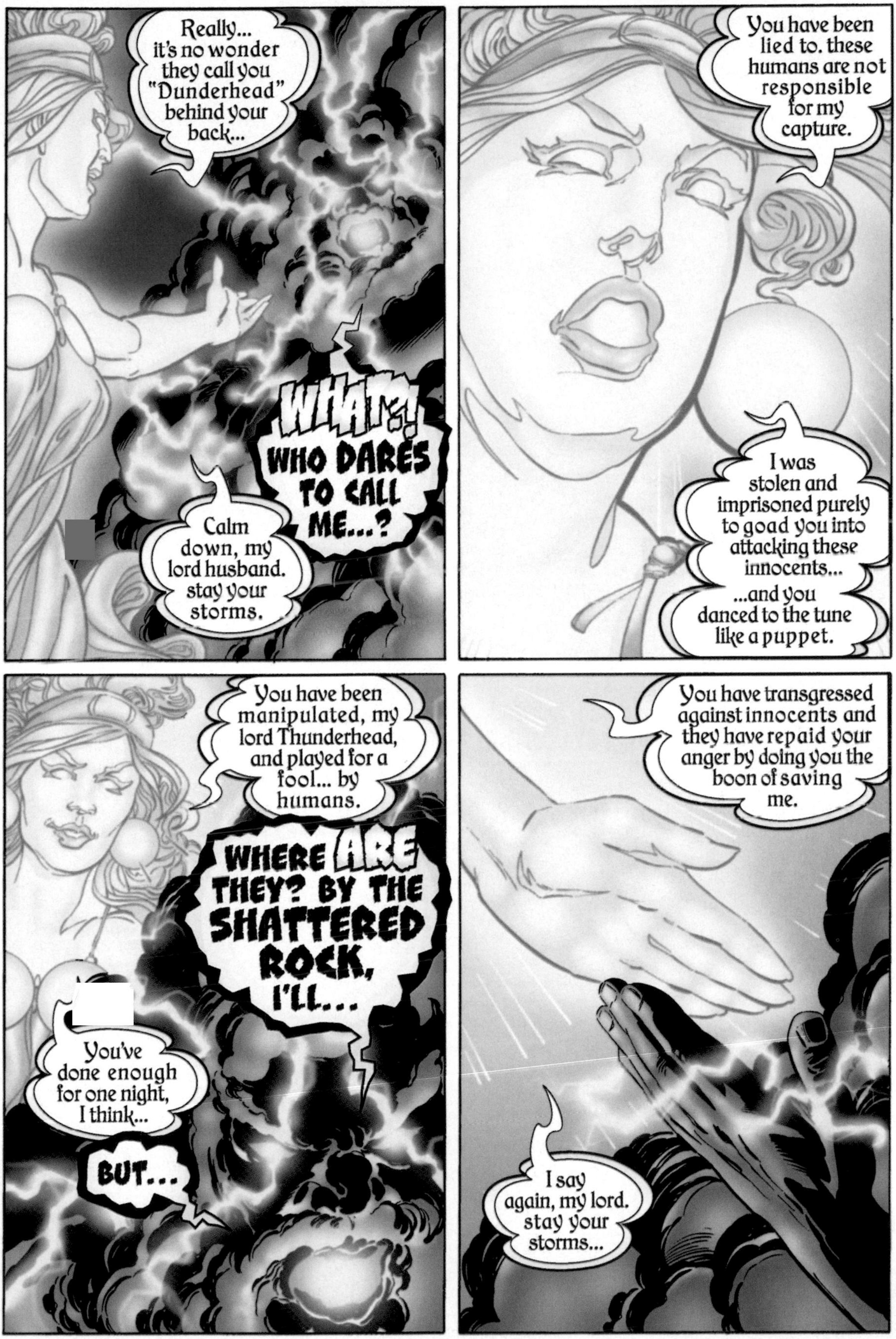
Really... it's no wonder they call you "Dunderhead" behind your back...
WHAT?! WHO DARES TO CALL ME...?
Calm down, my lord husband. stay your storms.
You have been lied to. these humans are not responsible for my capture.
I was stolen and imprisoned purely to goad you into attacking these innocents...
...and you danced to the tune like a puppet.
You have been manipulated, my lord Thunderhead, and played for a fool... by humans.
WHERE ARE THEY? BY THE SHATTERED ROCK, I'LL...
You've done enough for one night, I think...
BUT...
You have transgressed against innocents and they have repaid your anger by doing you the boon of saving me.
I say again, my lord. stay your storms...

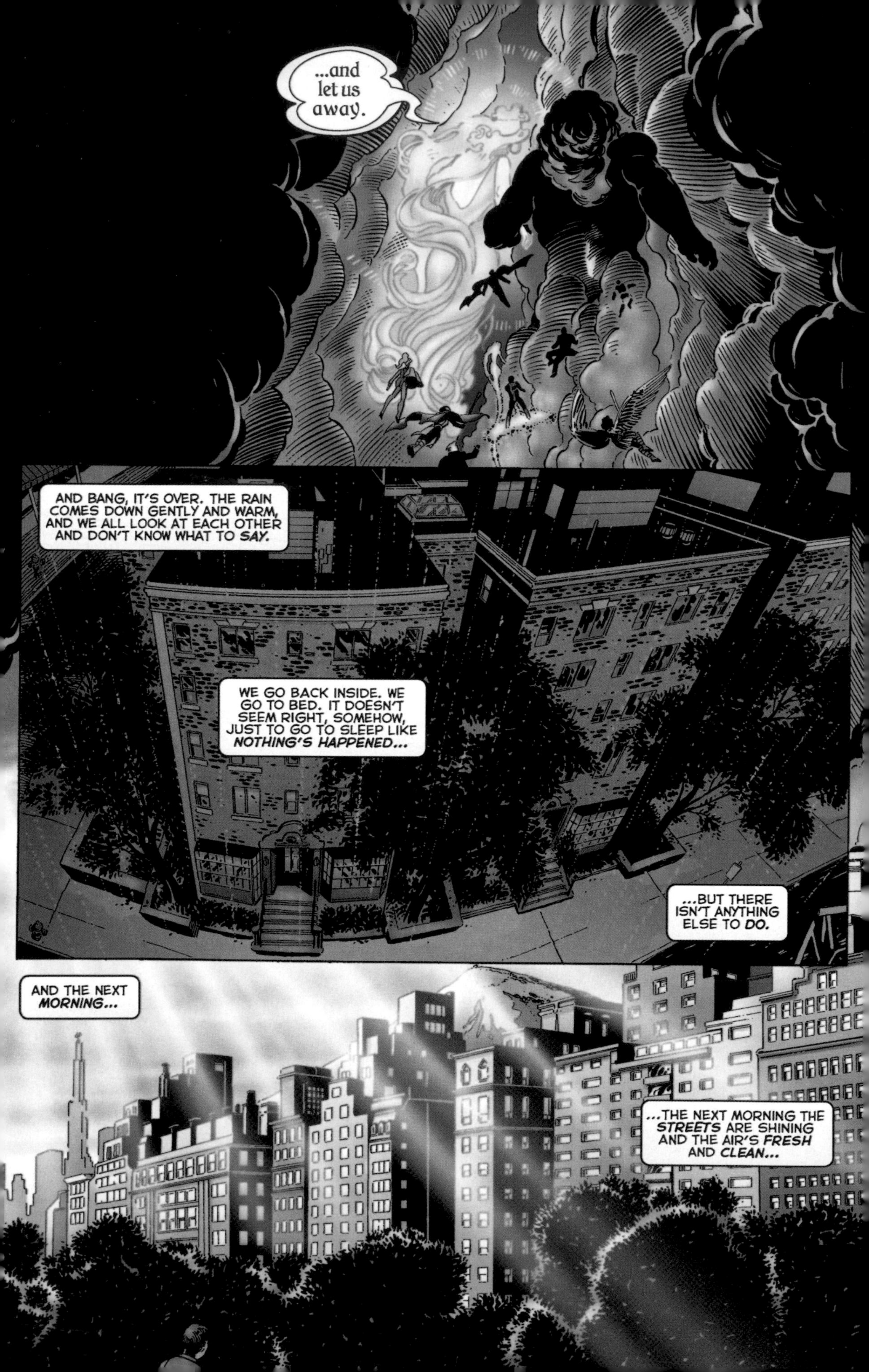
...and let us away.
AND BANG, IT'S OVER. THE RAIN COMES DOWN GENTLY AND WARM, AND WE ALL LOOK AT EACH OTHER AND DON'T KNOW WHAT TO SAY.
WE GO BACK INSIDE. WE GO TO BED. IT DOESN'T SEEM RIGHT, SOMEHOW, JUST TO GO TO SLEEP LIKE NOTHING'S HAPPENED...
...BUT THERE ISN'T ANYTHING ELSE TO DO.
AND THE NEXT MORNING...
...THE NEXT MORNING THE STREETS ARE SHINING AND THE AIR'S FRESH AND CLEAN...

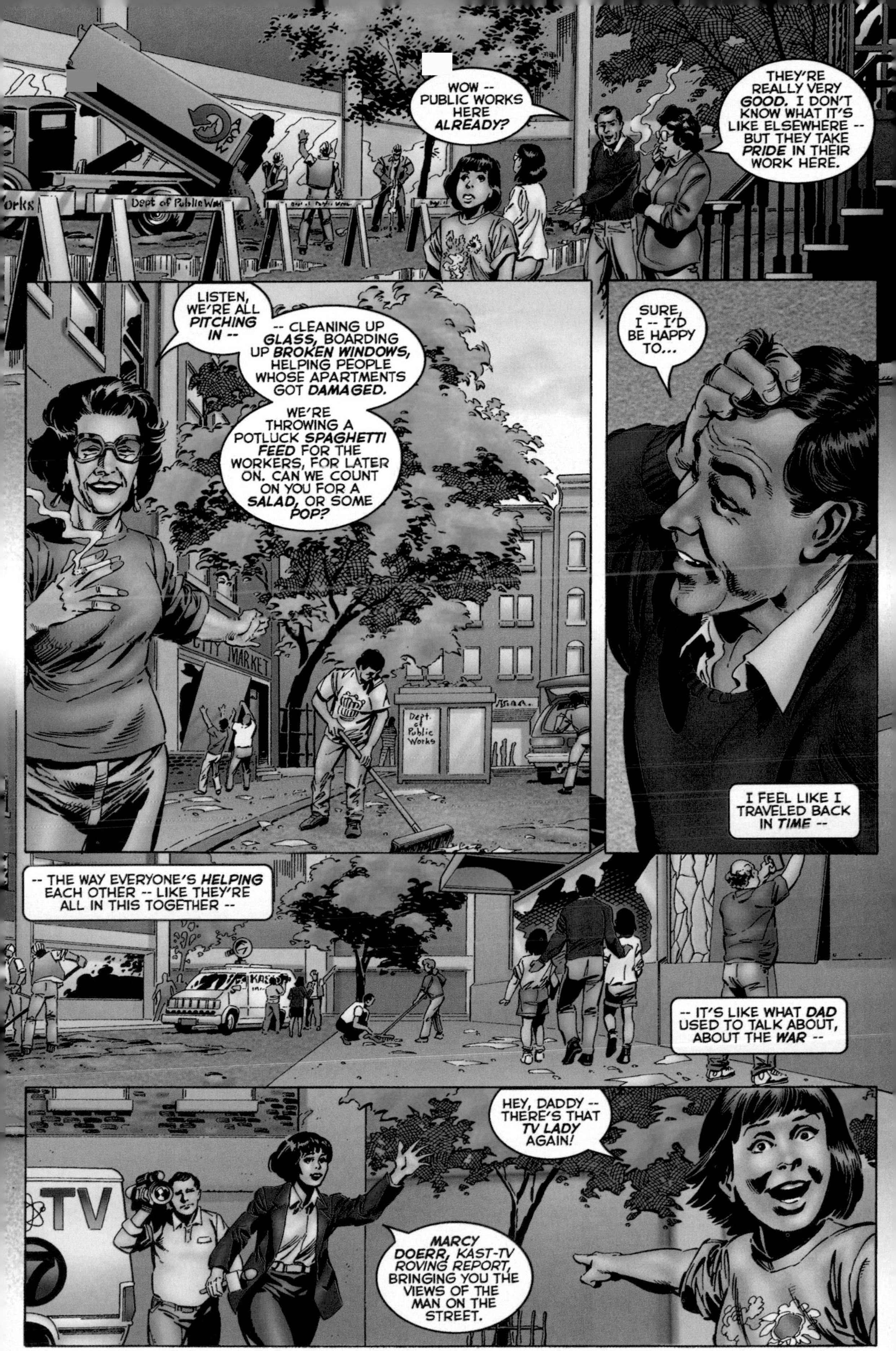
WOW -- PUBLIC WORKS HERE ALREADY?
THEY'RE REALLY VERY GOOD. I DON'T KNOW WHAT IT'S LIKE ELSEWHERE -- BUT THEY TAKE PRIDE IN THEIR WORK HERE.
Dept of Public Works
LISTEN, WE'RE ALL PITCHING IN --
-- CLEANING UP GLASS, BOARDING UP BROKEN WINDOWS, HELPING PEOPLE WHOSE APARTMENTS GOT DAMAGED.
WE'RE THROWING A POTLUCK SPAGHETTI FEED FOR THE WORKERS, FOR LATER ON. CAN WE COUNT ON YOU FOR A SALAD, OR SOME POP?
CITY MARKET
Dept. of Public Works
SURE, I -- I'D BE HAPPY TO...
I FEEL LIKE I TRAVELED BACK IN TIME --
-- THE WAY EVERYONE'S HELPING EACH OTHER -- LIKE THEY'RE ALL IN THIS TOGETHER --
-- IT'S LIKE WHAT DAD USED TO TALK ABOUT, ABOUT THE WAR --
HEY, DADDY -- THERE'S THAT TV LADY AGAIN!
TV
7
MARCY DOERR, KAST-TV ROVING REPORT, BRINGING YOU THE VIEWS OF THE MAN ON THE STREET.

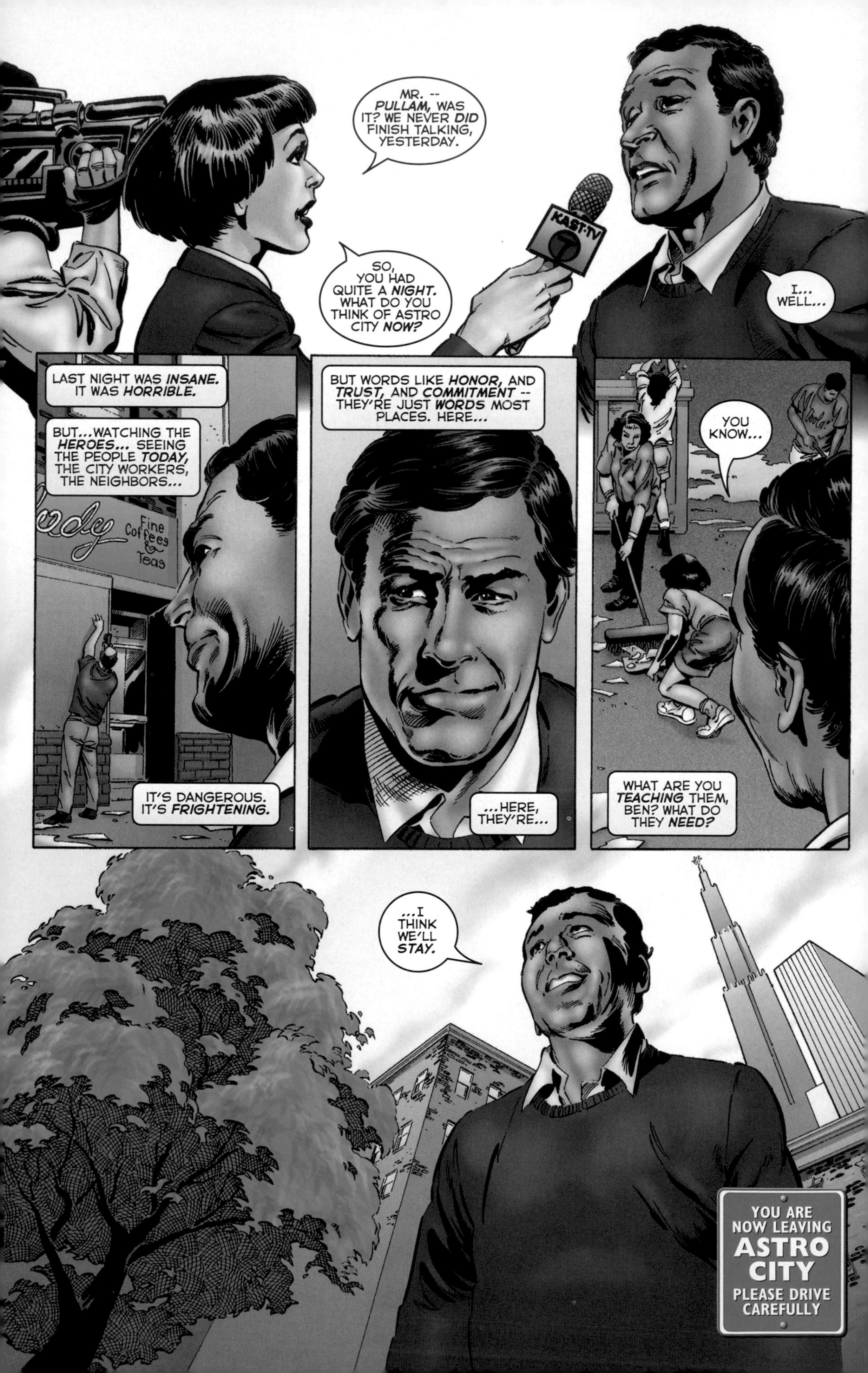
MR. -- PULLAM, WAS IT? WE NEVER DID FINISH TALKING, YESTERDAY.
SO, YOU HAD QUITE A NIGHT. WHAT DO YOU THINK OF ASTRO CITY NOW?
KAST-TV
I... WELL...
LAST NIGHT WAS INSANE. IT WAS HORRIBLE.
BUT...WATCHING THE HEROES... SEEING THE PEOPLE TODAY, THE CITY WORKERS, THE NEIGHBORS...
Fine Coffees & Teas
IT'S DANGEROUS. IT'S FRIGHTENING.
BUT WORDS LIKE HONOR, AND TRUST, AND COMMITMENT -- THEY'RE JUST WORDS MOST PLACES. HERE...
...HERE, THEY'RE...
YOU KNOW...
WHAT ARE YOU TEACHING THEM, BEN? WHAT DO THEY NEED?
...I THINK WE'LL STAY.
YOU ARE NOW LEAVING ASTRO CITY PLEASE DRIVE CAREFULLY

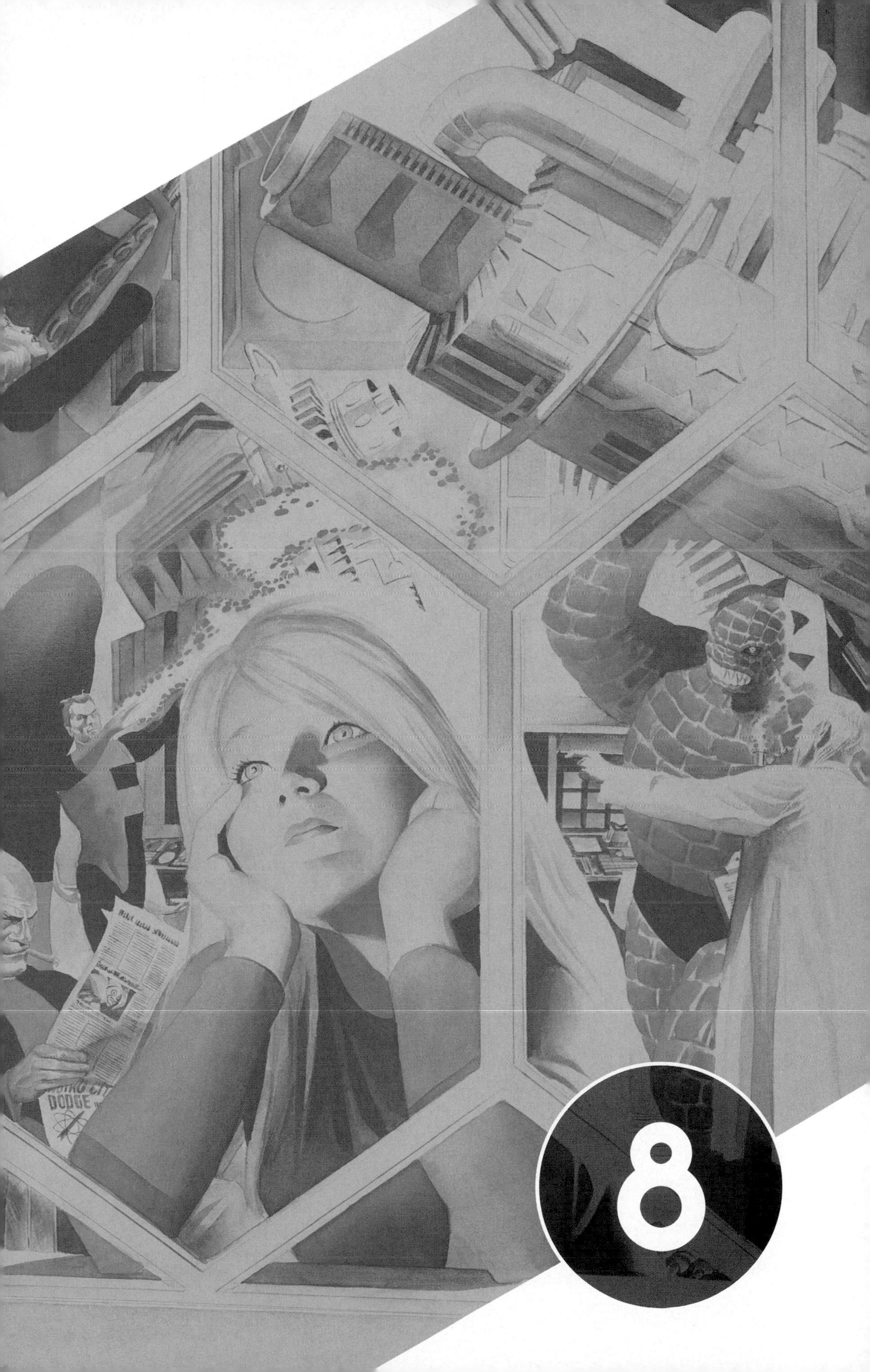
DODGE
8

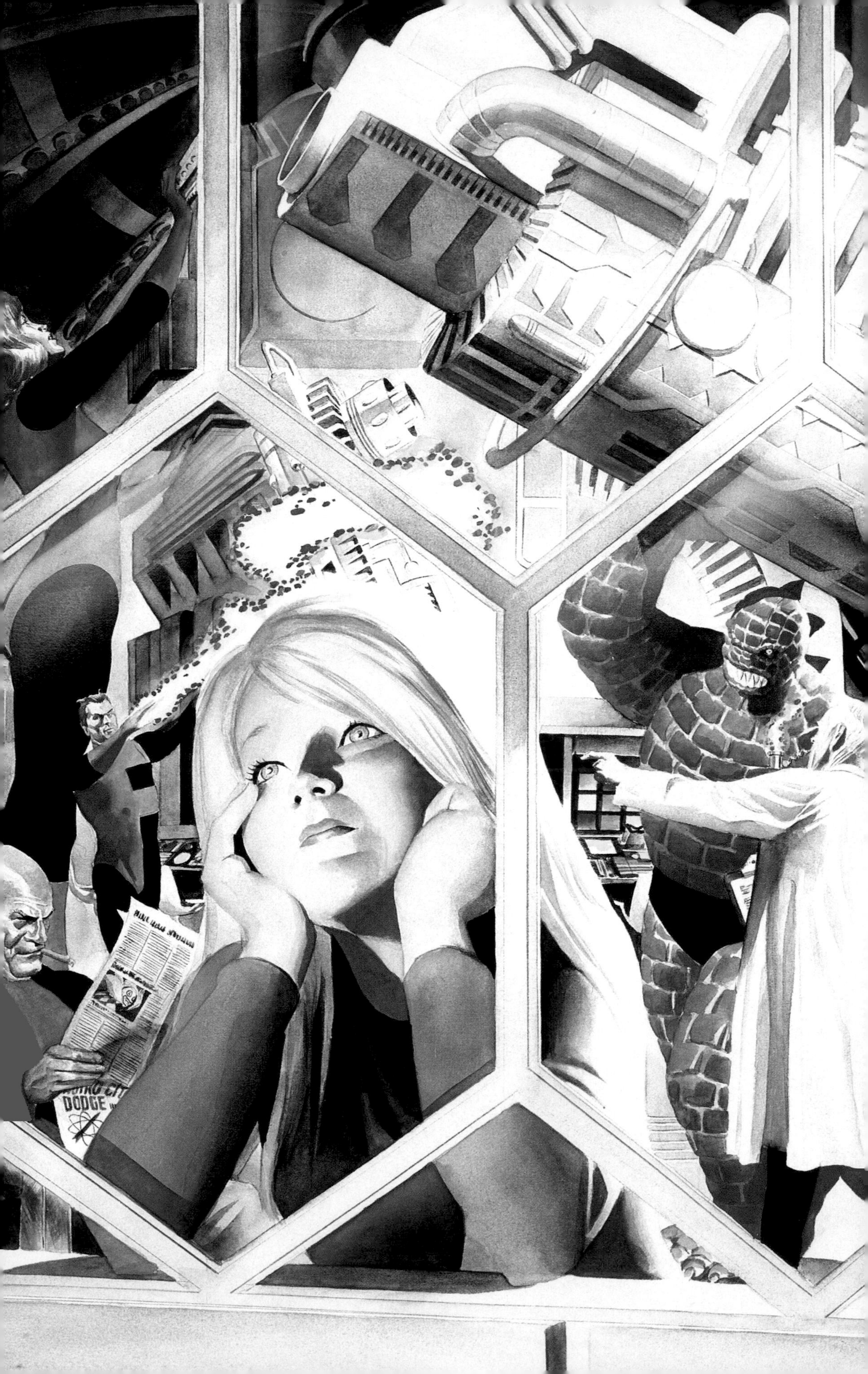
DODGE

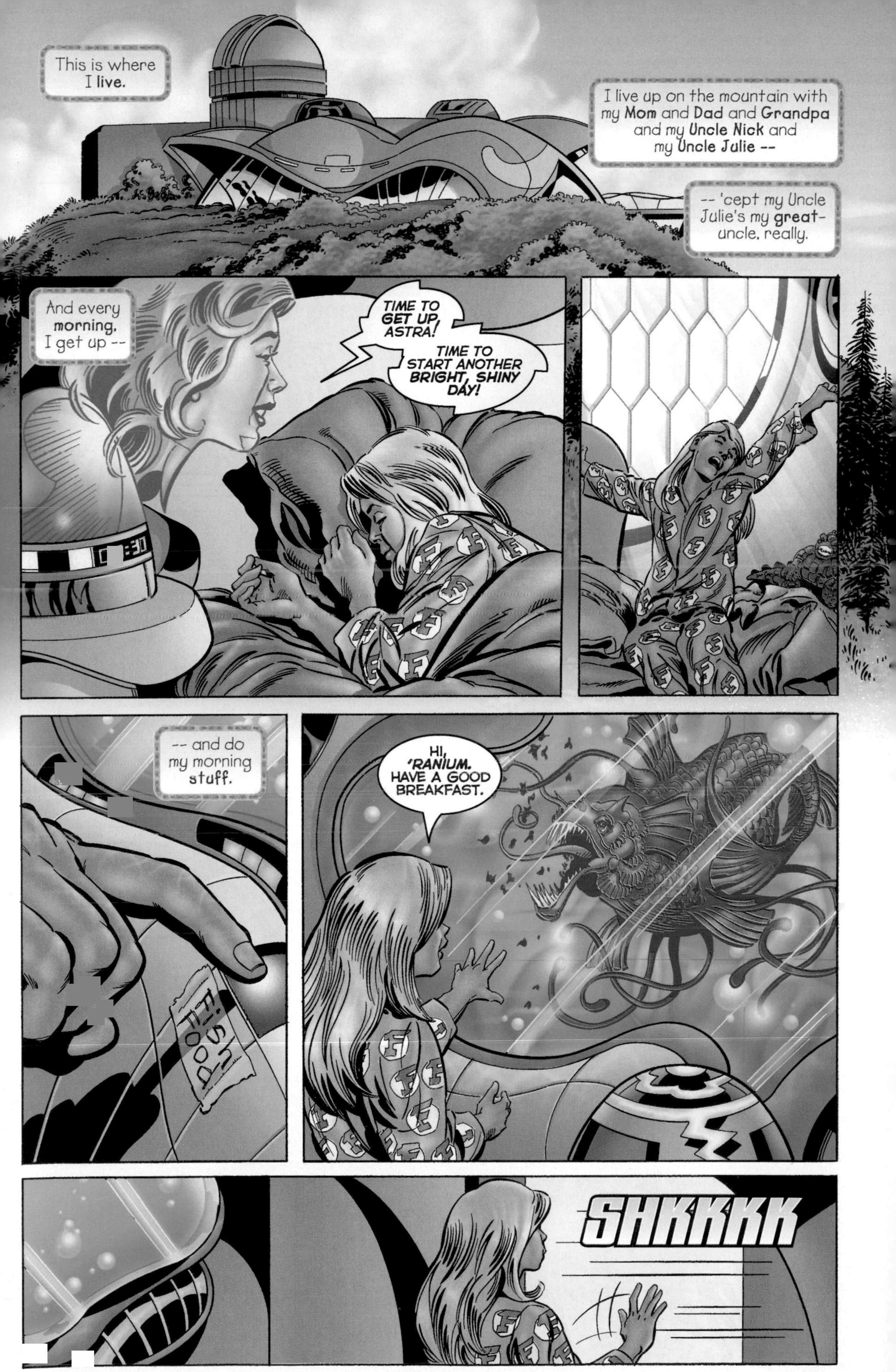

This is where I live.
I live up on the mountain with my Mom and Dad and Grandpa and my Uncle Nick and my Uncle Julie --
-- 'cept my Uncle Julie's my great-uncle, really.
And every morning, I get up --
TIME TO GET UP, ASTRA!
TIME TO START ANOTHER BRIGHT, SHINY DAY!
-- and do my morning stuff.
FISH FOOD
HI, 'RANIUM. HAVE A GOOD BREAKFAST.
SHKKKK

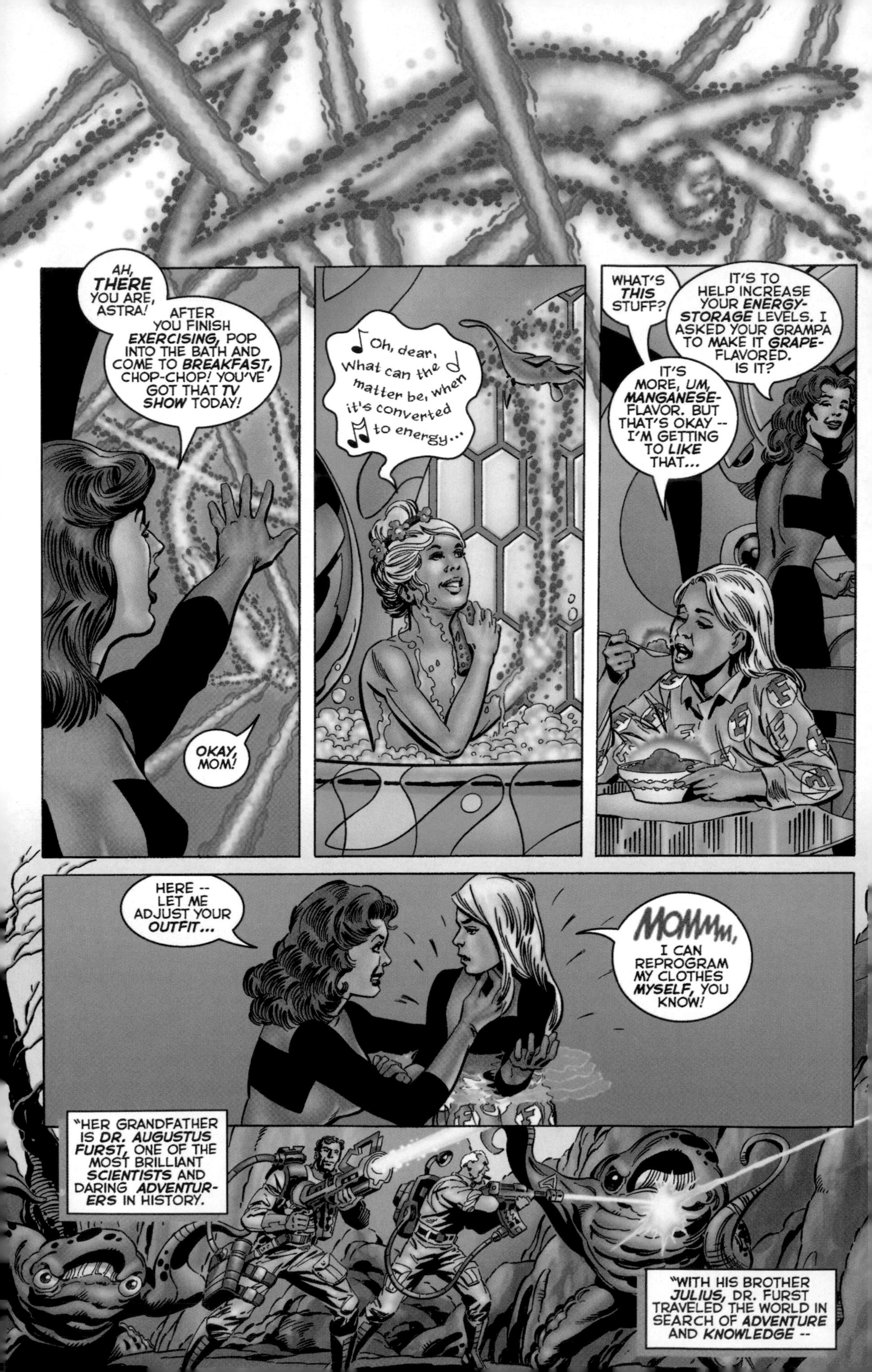
AH, THERE YOU ARE, ASTRA! AFTER YOU FINISH EXERCISING, POP INTO THE BATH AND COME TO BREAKFAST, CHOP-CHOP! YOU'VE GOT THAT TV SHOW TODAY!
OKAY, MOM!
Oh, dear, What can the matter be, when it's converted to energy...
WHAT'S THIS STUFF?
IT'S TO HELP INCREASE YOUR ENERGY-STORAGE LEVELS. I ASKED YOUR GRAMPA TO MAKE IT GRAPE-FLAVORED. IS IT?
IT'S MORE, UM, MANGANESE-FLAVOR. BUT THAT'S OKAY -- I'M GETTING TO LIKE THAT...
HERE -- LET ME ADJUST YOUR OUTFIT...
MOMMM, I CAN REPROGRAM MY CLOTHES MYSELF, YOU KNOW!
"HER GRANDFATHER IS DR. AUGUSTUS FURST, ONE OF THE MOST BRILLIANT SCIENTISTS AND DARING ADVENTURERS IN HISTORY.
"WITH HIS BROTHER JULIUS, DR. FURST TRAVELED THE WORLD IN SEARCH OF ADVENTURE AND KNOWLEDGE --

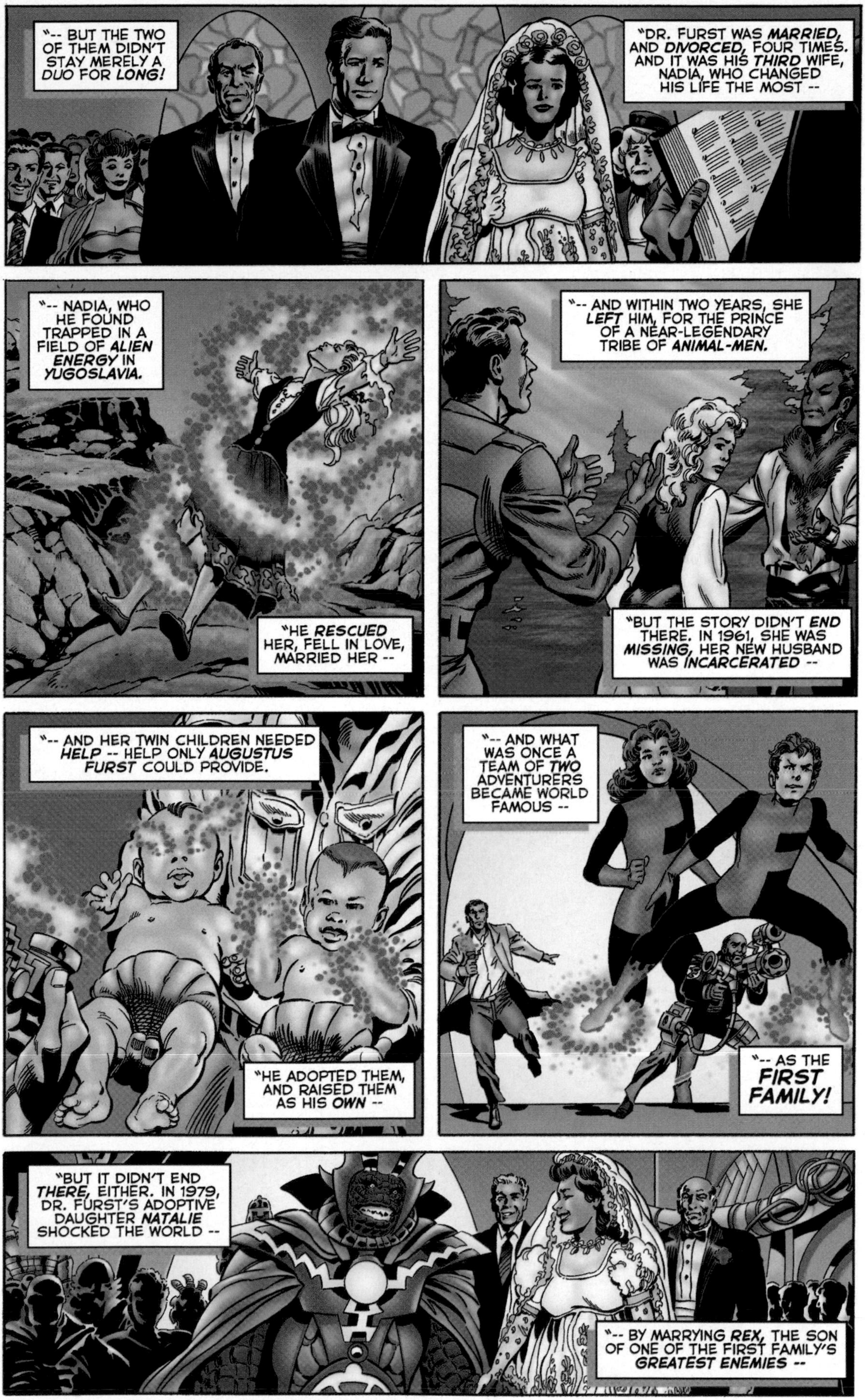
"-- BUT THE TWO OF THEM DIDN'T STAY MERELY A DUO FOR LONG!
"DR. FURST WAS MARRIED, AND DIVORCED, FOUR TIMES. AND IT WAS HIS THIRD WIFE, NADIA, WHO CHANGED HIS LIFE THE MOST --
"-- NADIA, WHO HE FOUND TRAPPED IN A FIELD OF ALIEN ENERGY IN YUGOSLAVIA.
"HE RESCUED HER, FELL IN LOVE, MARRIED HER --
"-- AND WITHIN TWO YEARS, SHE LEFT HIM, FOR THE PRINCE OF A NEAR-LEGENDARY TRIBE OF ANIMAL-MEN.
"BUT THE STORY DIDN'T END THERE. IN 1961, SHE WAS MISSING, HER NEW HUSBAND WAS INCARCERATED --
"-- AND HER TWIN CHILDREN NEEDED HELP -- HELP ONLY AUGUSTUS FURST COULD PROVIDE.
"HE ADOPTED THEM, AND RAISED THEM AS HIS OWN --
"-- AND WHAT WAS ONCE A TEAM OF TWO ADVENTURERS BECAME WORLD FAMOUS --
"-- AS THE FIRST FAMILY!
"BUT IT DIDN'T END THERE, EITHER. IN 1979, DR. FURST'S ADOPTIVE DAUGHTER NATALIE SHOCKED THE WORLD --
"-- BY MARRYING REX, THE SON OF ONE OF THE FIRST FAMILY'S GREATEST ENEMIES --

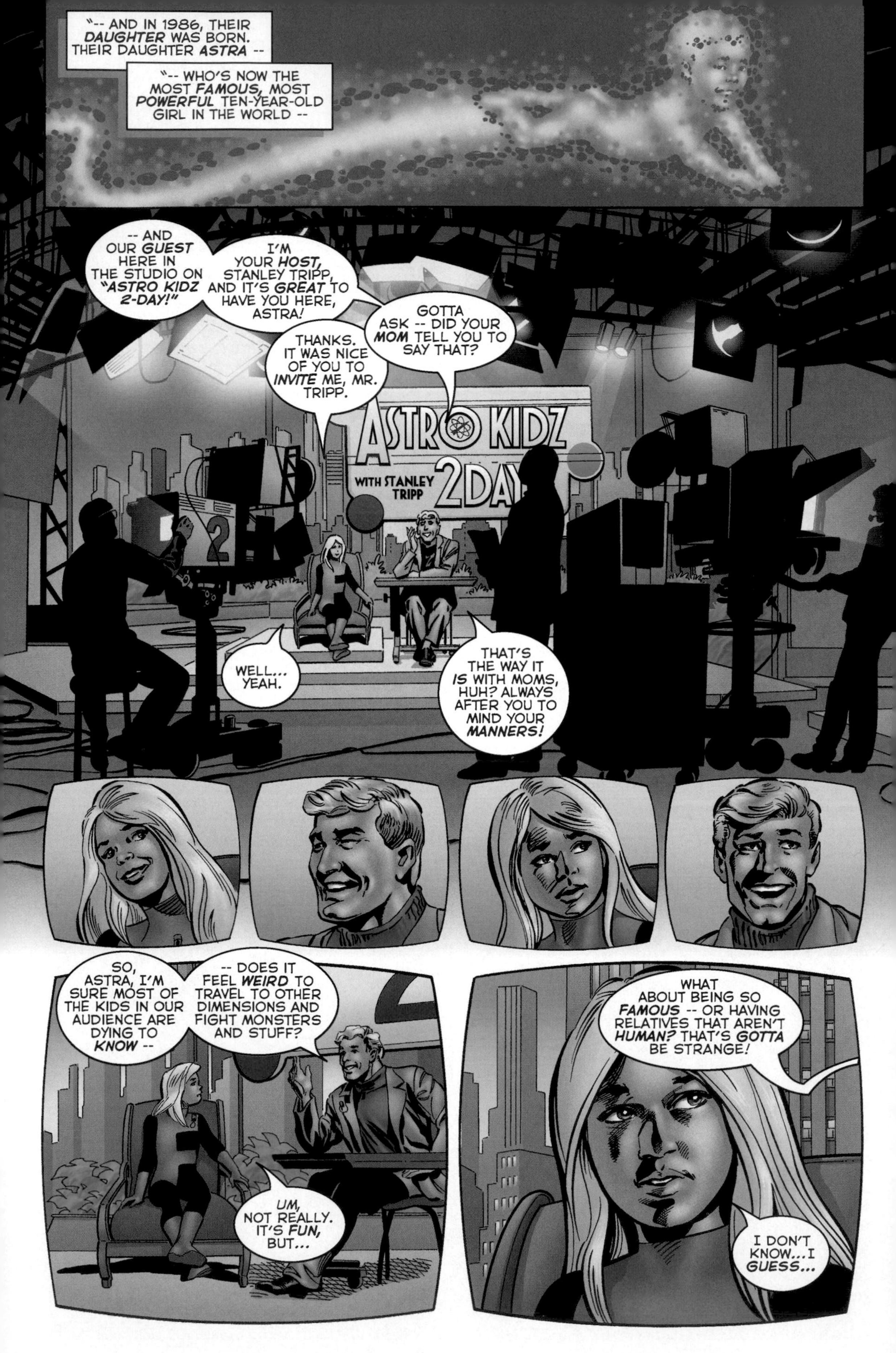
"-- AND IN 1986, THEIR DAUGHTER WAS BORN. THEIR DAUGHTER ASTRA --
"-- WHO'S NOW THE MOST FAMOUS, MOST POWERFUL TEN-YEAR-OLD GIRL IN THE WORLD --
-- AND OUR GUEST HERE IN THE STUDIO ON "ASTRO KIDZ 2-DAY!"
I'M YOUR HOST, STANLEY TRIPP, AND IT'S GREAT TO HAVE YOU HERE, ASTRA!
THANKS. IT WAS NICE OF YOU TO INVITE ME, MR. TRIPP.
GOTTA ASK -- DID YOUR MOM TELL YOU TO SAY THAT?
ASTRO KIDZ 2DAY
WITH STANLEY TRIPP
2
WELL... YEAH.
THAT'S THE WAY IT IS WITH MOMS, HUH? ALWAYS AFTER YOU TO MIND YOUR MANNERS!
SO, ASTRA, I'M SURE MOST OF THE KIDS IN OUR AUDIENCE ARE DYING TO KNOW --
-- DOES IT FEEL WEIRD TO TRAVEL TO OTHER DIMENSIONS AND FIGHT MONSTERS AND STUFF?
UM, NOT REALLY. IT'S FUN, BUT...
WHAT ABOUT BEING SO FAMOUS -- OR HAVING RELATIVES THAT AREN'T HUMAN? THAT'S GOTTA BE STRANGE!
I DON'T KNOW... I GUESS...

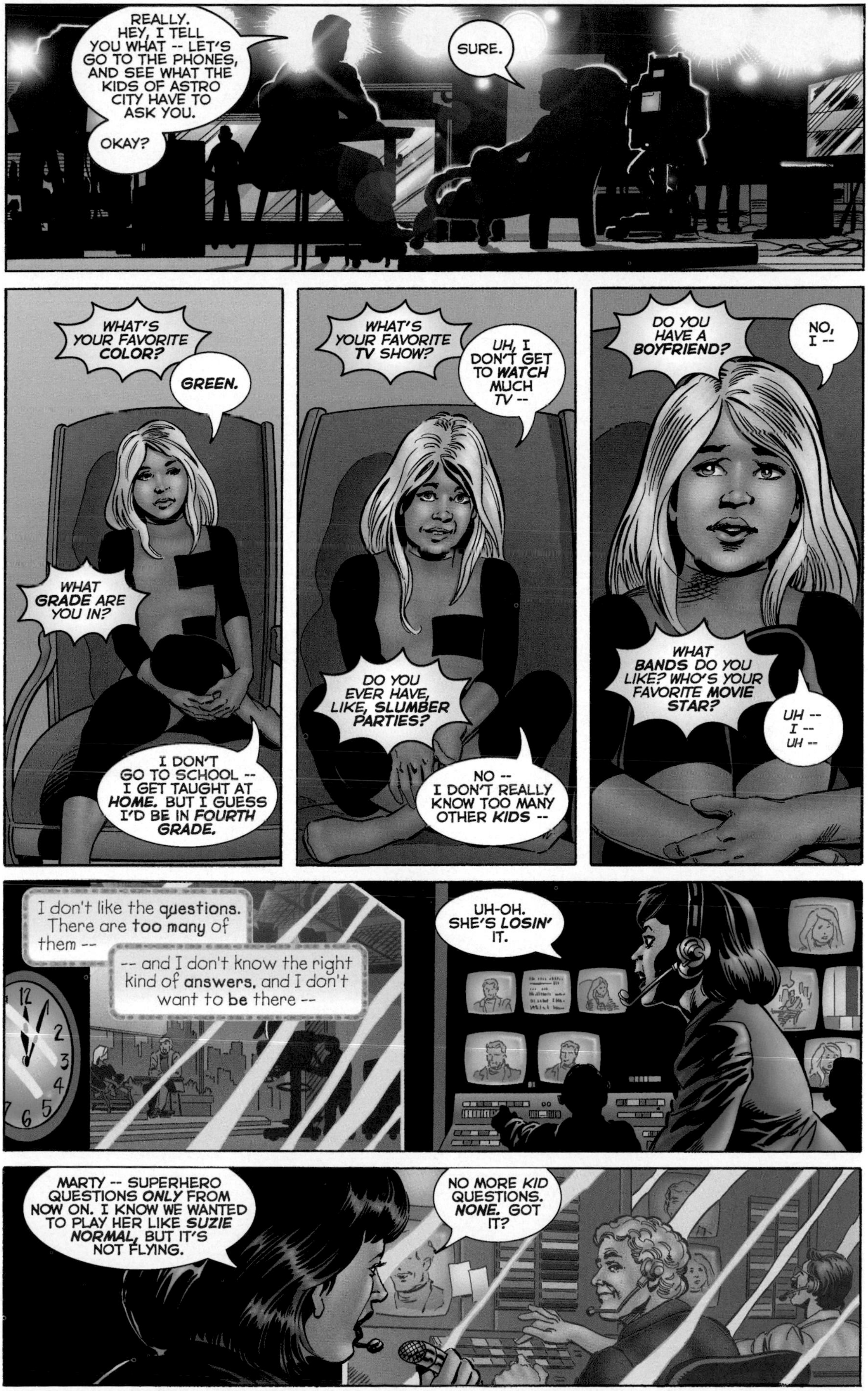
REALLY. HEY, I TELL YOU WHAT -- LET'S GO TO THE PHONES, AND SEE WHAT THE KIDS OF ASTRO CITY HAVE TO ASK YOU.
OKAY?
SURE.
WHAT'S YOUR FAVORITE COLOR?
GREEN.
WHAT GRADE ARE YOU IN?
I DON'T GO TO SCHOOL -- I GET TAUGHT AT HOME. BUT I GUESS I'D BE IN FOURTH GRADE.
WHAT'S YOUR FAVORITE TV SHOW?
UH, I DON'T GET TO WATCH MUCH TV --
DO YOU EVER HAVE, LIKE, SLUMBER PARTIES?
NO -- I DON'T REALLY KNOW TOO MANY OTHER KIDS --
DO YOU HAVE A BOYFRIEND?
NO, I --
WHAT BANDS DO YOU LIKE? WHO'S YOUR FAVORITE MOVIE STAR?
UH -- I -- UH --
I don't like the questions. There are too many of them --
-- and I don't know the right kind of answers, and I don't want to be there --
UH-OH. SHE'S LOSIN' IT.
MARTY -- SUPERHERO QUESTIONS ONLY FROM NOW ON. I KNOW WE WANTED TO PLAY HER LIKE SUZIE NORMAL, BUT IT'S NOT FLYING.
NO MORE KID QUESTIONS. NONE. GOT IT?

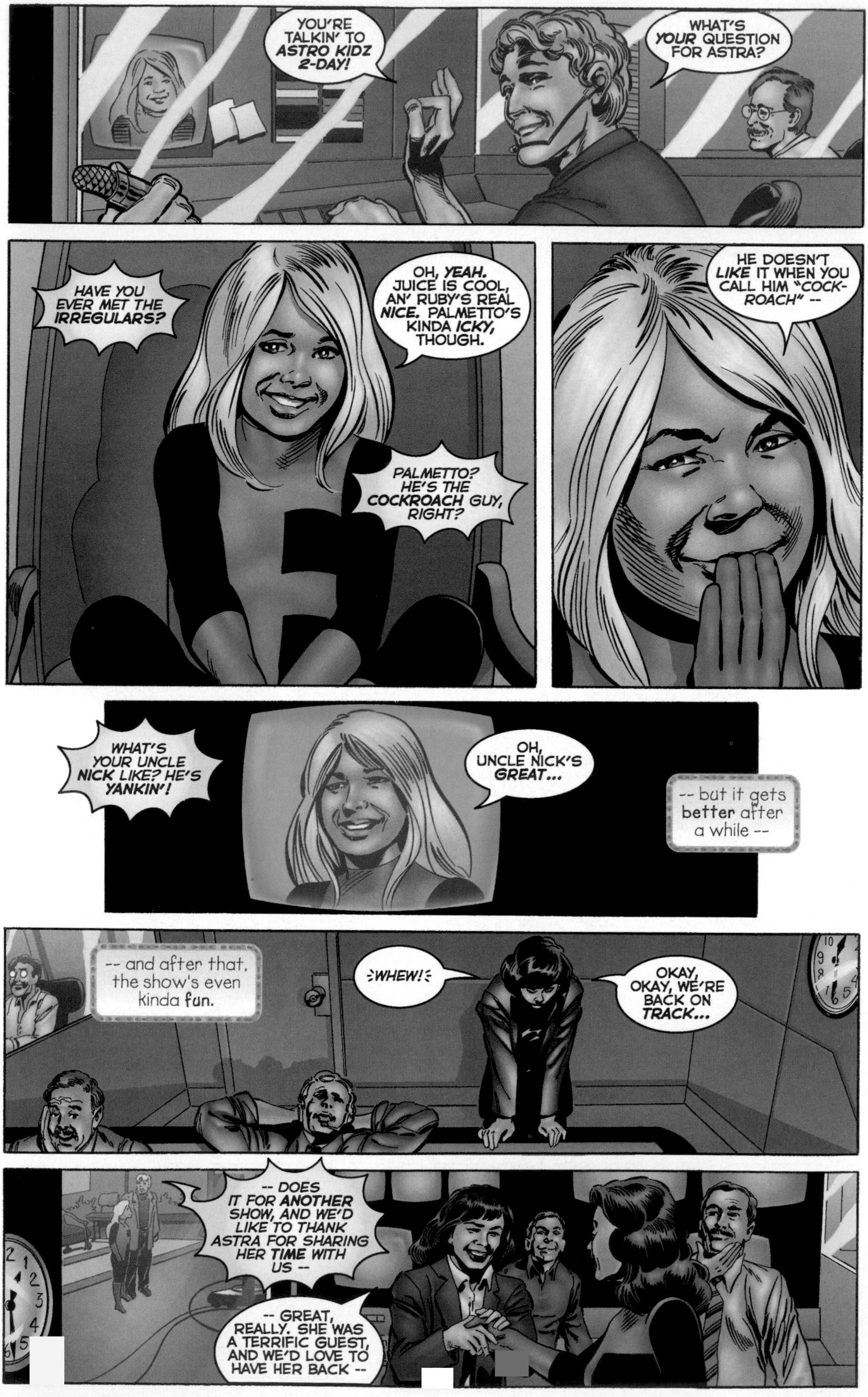
YOU'RE TALKIN' TO ASTRO KIDZ 2-DAY!
WHAT'S YOUR QUESTION FOR ASTRA?
HAVE YOU EVER MET THE IRREGULARS?
OH, YEAH. JUICE IS COOL, AN' RUBY'S REAL NICE. PALMETTO'S KINDA ICKY, THOUGH.
PALMETTO? HE'S THE COCKROACH GUY, RIGHT?
HE DOESN'T LIKE IT WHEN YOU CALL HIM "COCK-ROACH" --
WHAT'S YOUR UNCLE NICK LIKE? HE'S YANKIN'!
OH, UNCLE NICK'S GREAT...
-- but it gets better after a while --
-- and after that, the show's even kinda fun.
WHEW!
OKAY, OKAY, WE'RE BACK ON TRACK...
-- DOES IT FOR ANOTHER SHOW, AND WE'D LIKE TO THANK ASTRA FOR SHARING HER TIME WITH US --
-- GREAT, REALLY. SHE WAS A TERRIFIC GUEST, AND WE'D LOVE TO HAVE HER BACK --

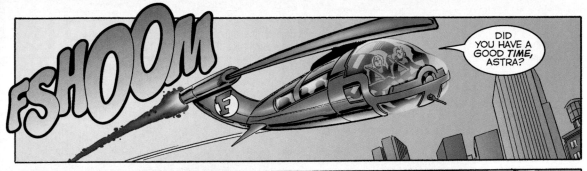

FSHOOM

DID YOU HAVE A GOOD *TIME*, ASTRA?

I *GUESS*.

Those *kids* down there -- they know all about T.V. and *boyfriends* and *slumber parties* and *bands*.

And me -- I know how a T.V. *works* --

-- but I don't even know what *game* they're playing.

MOM?

HOLD ON A SECOND, DEAR. I'M DOCKING *FAMILY-1...*

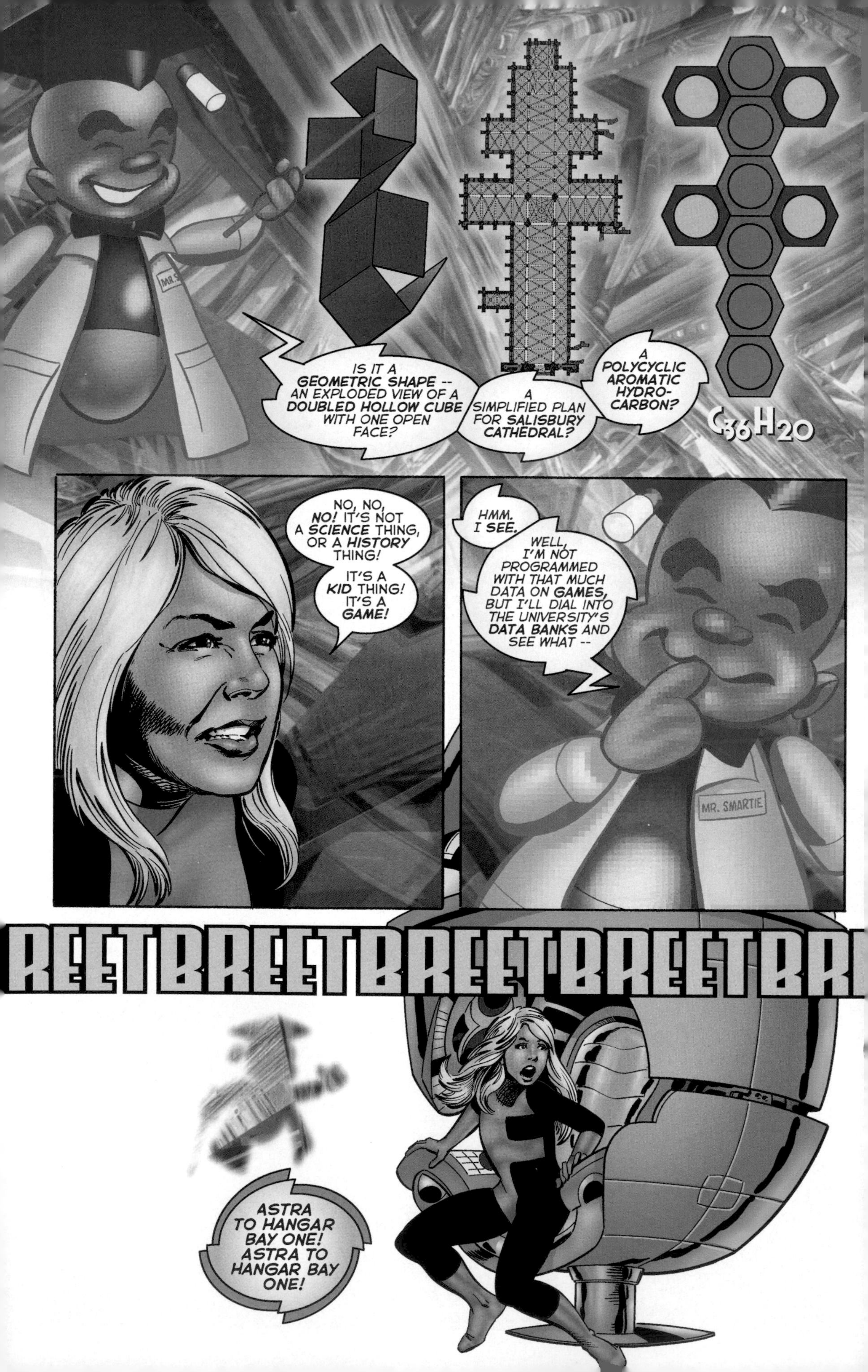
IS IT A GEOMETRIC SHAPE -- AN EXPLODED VIEW OF A DOUBLED HOLLOW CUBE WITH ONE OPEN FACE?
A SIMPLIFIED PLAN FOR SALISBURY CATHEDRAL?
A POLYCYCLIC AROMATIC HYDRO-CARBON?
C36H20
MR. S
NO, NO, NO! IT'S NOT A SCIENCE THING, OR A HISTORY THING!
IT'S A KID THING! IT'S A GAME!
HMM. I SEE.
WELL, I'M NOT PROGRAMMED WITH THAT MUCH DATA ON GAMES, BUT I'LL DIAL INTO THE UNIVERSITY'S DATA BANKS AND SEE WHAT --
MR. SMARTIE
REETBREETBREETBREETBR
ASTRA TO HANGAR BAY ONE! ASTRA TO HANGAR BAY ONE!

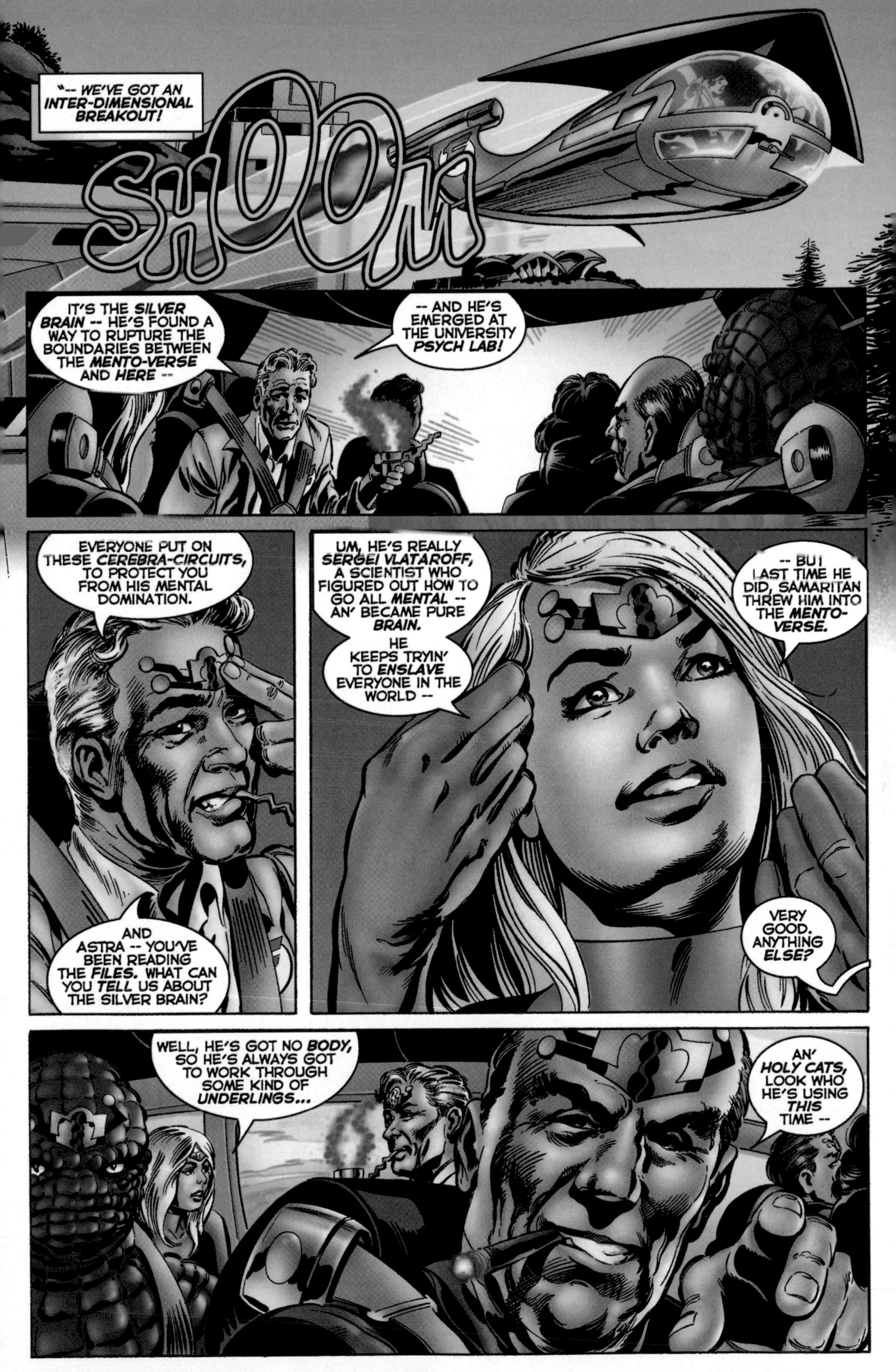
"-- WE'VE GOT AN INTER-DIMENSIONAL BREAKOUT!
SHOOM
IT'S THE SILVER BRAIN -- HE'S FOUND A WAY TO RUPTURE THE BOUNDARIES BETWEEN THE MENTO-VERSE AND HERE --
-- AND HE'S EMERGED AT THE UNIVERSITY PSYCH LAB!
EVERYONE PUT ON THESE CEREBRA-CIRCUITS, TO PROTECT YOU FROM HIS MENTAL DOMINATION.
AND ASTRA -- YOU'VE BEEN READING THE FILES. WHAT CAN YOU TELL US ABOUT THE SILVER BRAIN?
UM, HE'S REALLY SERGEI VLATAROFF, A SCIENTIST WHO FIGURED OUT HOW TO GO ALL MENTAL -- AN' BECAME PURE BRAIN.
HE KEEPS TRYIN' TO ENSLAVE EVERYONE IN THE WORLD --
-- BUT LAST TIME HE DID, SAMARITAN THREW HIM INTO THE MENTO-VERSE.
VERY GOOD. ANYTHING ELSE?
WELL, HE'S GOT NO BODY, SO HE'S ALWAYS GOT TO WORK THROUGH SOME KIND OF UNDERLINGS...
AN' HOLY CATS, LOOK WHO HE'S USING THIS TIME --

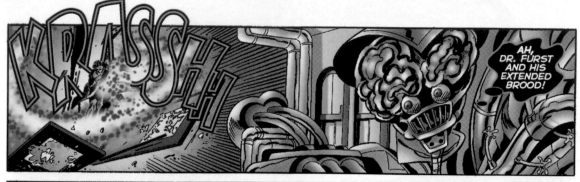

AH, DR. FURST AND HIS EXTENDED BROOD!

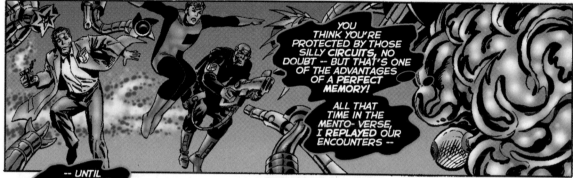

YOU THINK YOU'RE PROTECTED BY THOSE SILLY CIRCUITS, NO DOUBT -- BUT THAT'S ONE OF THE ADVANTAGES OF A PERFECT MEMORY!

ALL THAT TIME IN THE MENTO-VERSE, I REPLAYED OUR ENCOUNTERS --

-- UNTIL I DEDUCED YOUR CIRCUITS' FREQUENCY!

GUS?!

GRAMPA!

YOU SHOT MY GRAMPA!

ASTRA, WAIT! YOU'VE FORGOTTEN THE BRAIN'S LAST LINE OF DEFENSE --

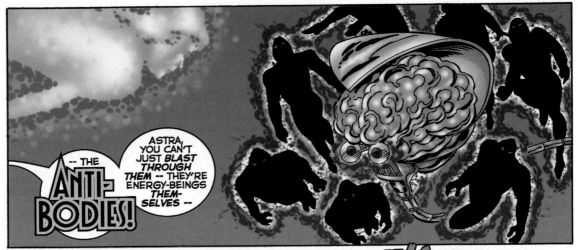

-- THE **ANTI-BODIES!**

ASTRA, YOU CAN'T JUST *BLAST* THROUGH *THEM* -- THEY'RE ENERGY-BEINGS *THEM-SELVES* --

-- AND THEY CAN GRAB *HOLD* OF YOU!

Yeah, duh!

ZKAK ZKAK

SHOOM

ASTRA!

WE'LL GETCHA BACK, KID!

Uncle Nick an' Uncle Julie are the ones who've forgotten what the Anti-Bodies do.

They grab onto the energy-blasts, just like they do any loose energy -- take *us* all to the power core --

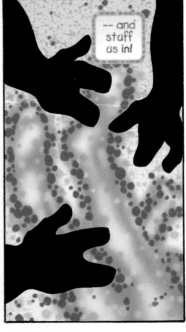

-- and stuff us *in!*

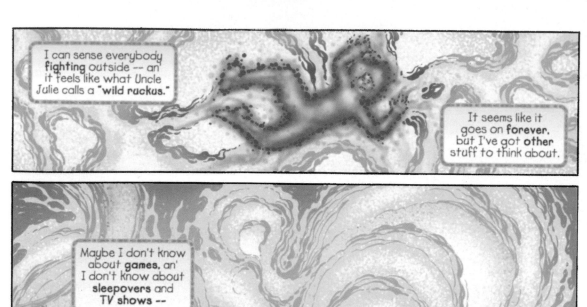

I can sense everybody **fighting** outside -- an' it feels like what Uncle Julie calls a "**wild ruckus.**"

It seems like it goes on **forever**, but I've got **other** stuff to think about.

Maybe I don't know about **games**, an' I don't know about **sleepovers** and **TV shows** --

-- but I **do** know about energy.

I reach out, an' let myself **dissolve** a little into the energy core --

-- an' I find where the core's powering all of the Silver Brain's **stuff** --

-- an' I shut it all **off.**

HUH?

WHAT?!

CLAK

THE DIMENSIONAL APERSTOMUM -- IT'S BEEN DE-ACTIVATED!

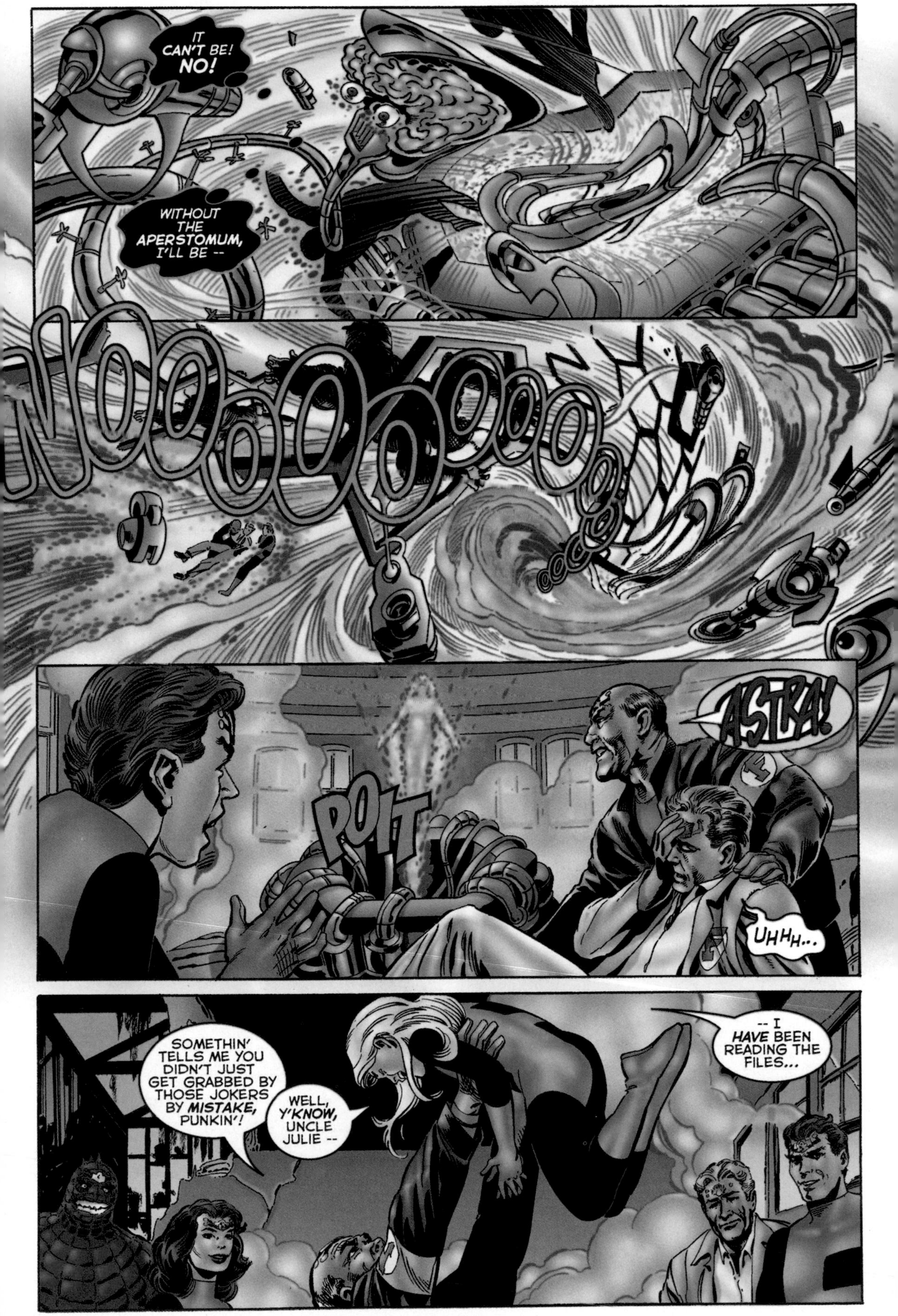
IT CAN'T BE! NO!
WITHOUT THE APERSTOMUM, I'LL BE --
NOOOOOOOOOOOOOOOOOOO
ASTRA!
POIT
UHHH...
SOMETHIN' TELLS ME YOU DIDN'T JUST GET GRABBED BY THOSE JOKERS BY MISTAKE, PUNKIN'!
WELL, Y'KNOW, UNCLE JULIE --
-- I HAVE BEEN READING THE FILES...

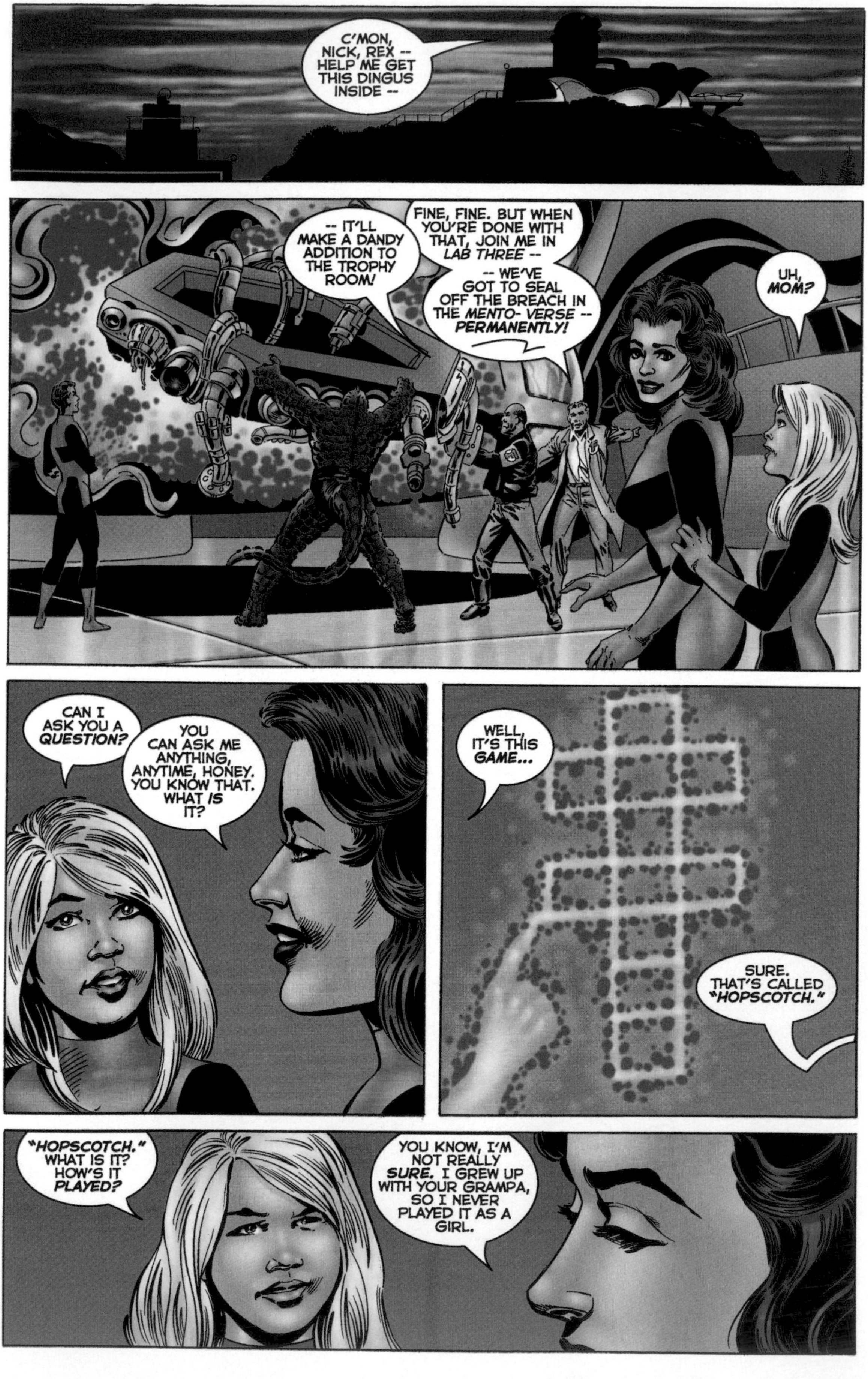
C'MON, NICK, REX -- HELP ME GET THIS DINGUS INSIDE --
-- IT'LL MAKE A DANDY ADDITION TO THE TROPHY ROOM!
FINE, FINE. BUT WHEN YOU'RE DONE WITH THAT, JOIN ME IN LAB THREE --
-- WE'VE GOT TO SEAL OFF THE BREACH IN THE MENTO-VERSE -- PERMANENTLY!
UH, MOM?
CAN I ASK YOU A QUESTION?
YOU CAN ASK ME ANYTHING, ANYTIME, HONEY. YOU KNOW THAT. WHAT IS IT?
WELL, IT'S THIS GAME...
SURE. THAT'S CALLED "HOPSCOTCH."
"HOPSCOTCH." WHAT IS IT? HOW'S IT PLAYED?
YOU KNOW, I'M NOT REALLY SURE. I GREW UP WITH YOUR GRAMPA, SO I NEVER PLAYED IT AS A GIRL.

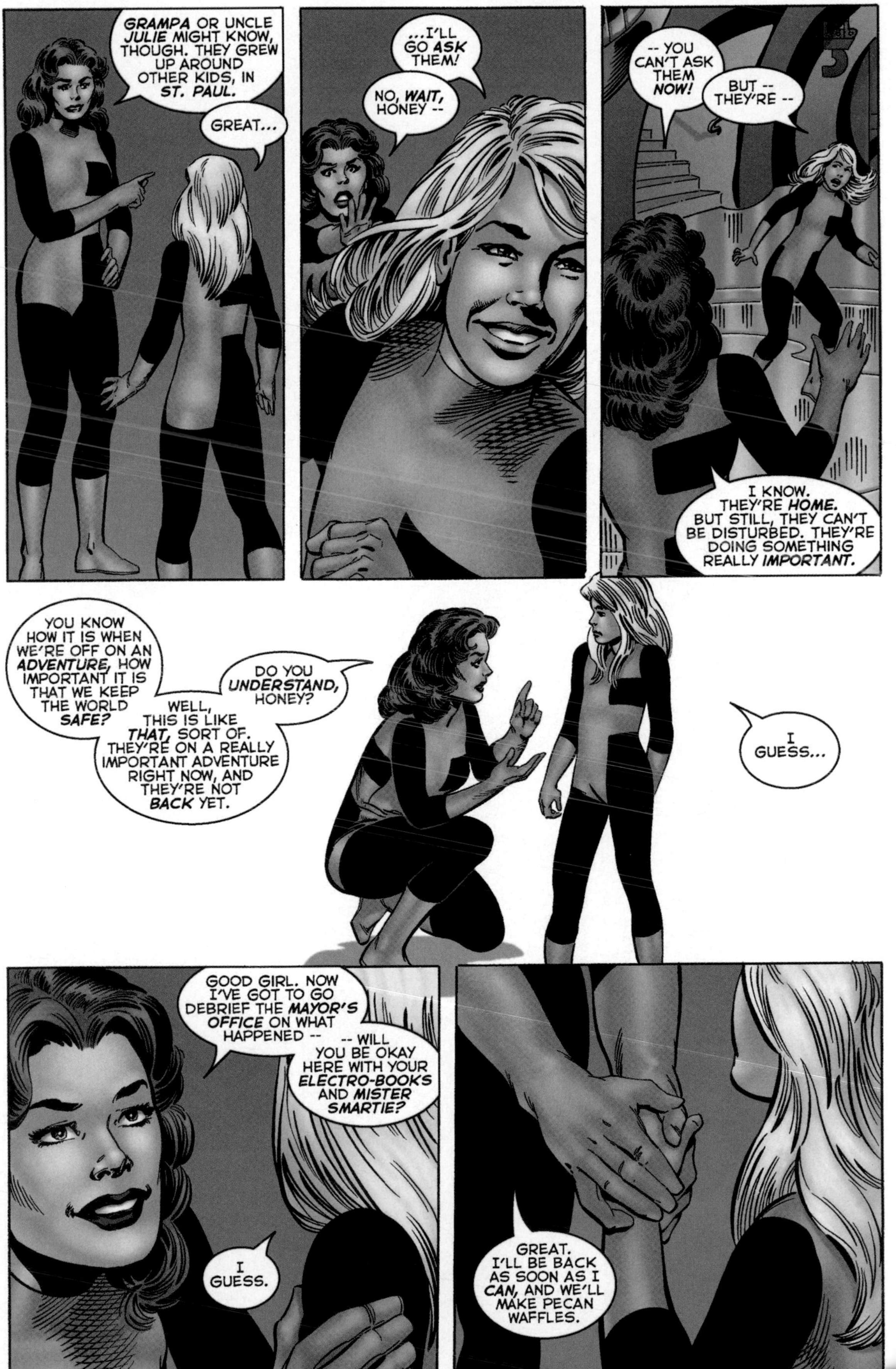
GRAMPA OR UNCLE JULIE MIGHT KNOW, THOUGH. THEY GREW UP AROUND OTHER KIDS, IN ST. PAUL.
GREAT...
...I'LL GO ASK THEM!
NO, WAIT, HONEY --
-- YOU CAN'T ASK THEM NOW!
BUT -- THEY'RE --
I KNOW. THEY'RE HOME. BUT STILL, THEY CAN'T BE DISTURBED. THEY'RE DOING SOMETHING REALLY IMPORTANT.
YOU KNOW HOW IT IS WHEN WE'RE OFF ON AN ADVENTURE, HOW IMPORTANT IT IS THAT WE KEEP THE WORLD SAFE?
WELL, THIS IS LIKE THAT, SORT OF. THEY'RE ON A REALLY IMPORTANT ADVENTURE RIGHT NOW, AND THEY'RE NOT BACK YET.
DO YOU UNDERSTAND, HONEY?
I GUESS...
GOOD GIRL. NOW I'VE GOT TO GO DEBRIEF THE MAYOR'S OFFICE ON WHAT HAPPENED --
-- WILL YOU BE OKAY HERE WITH YOUR ELECTRO-BOOKS AND MISTER SMARTIE?
I GUESS.
GREAT. I'LL BE BACK AS SOON AS I CAN, AND WE'LL MAKE PECAN WAFFLES.

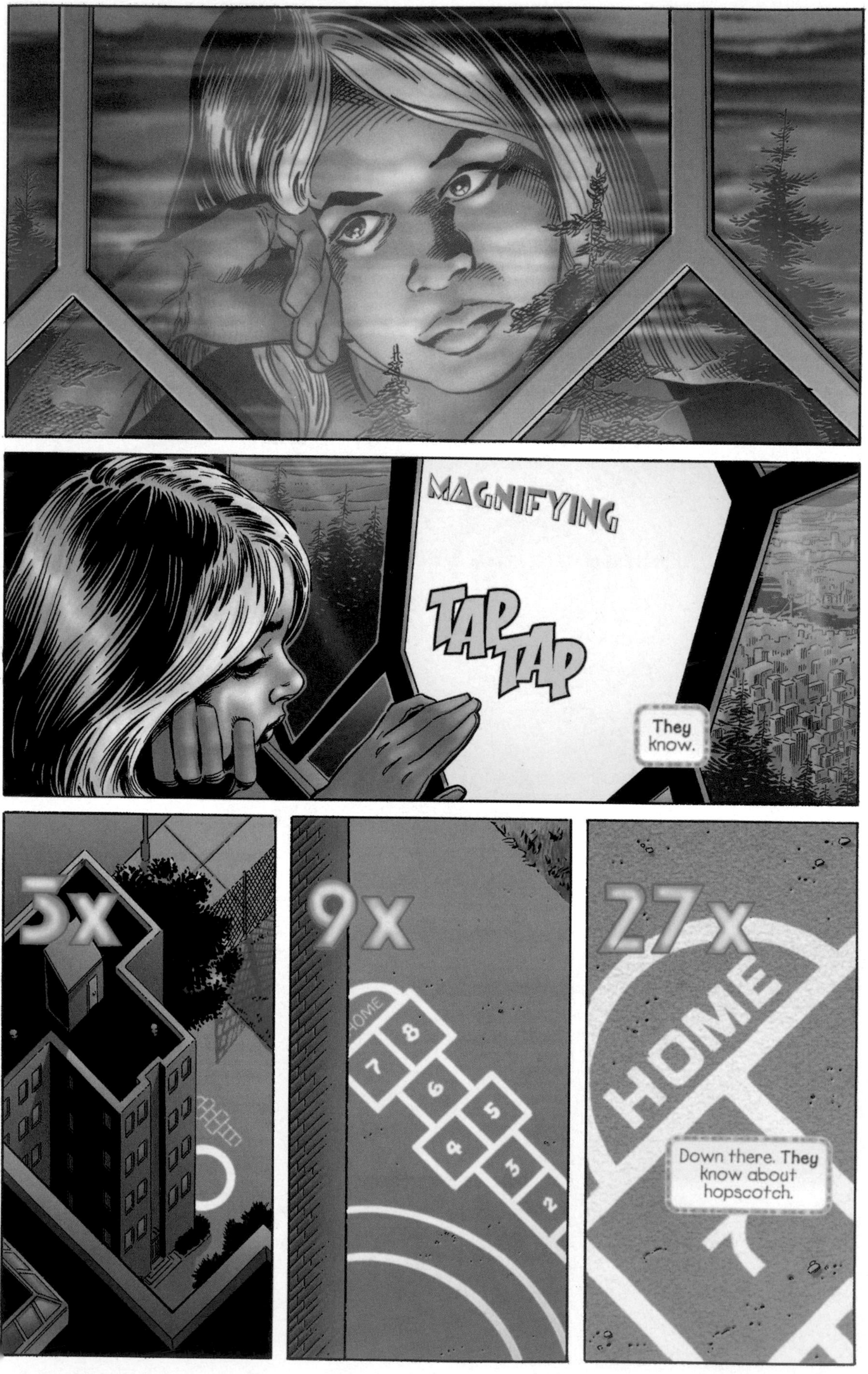
MAGNIFYING
TAP TAP
They know.
3x
9x
HOME
8
7
6
5
4
3
2
27x
HOME
Down there. They know about hopscotch.
7

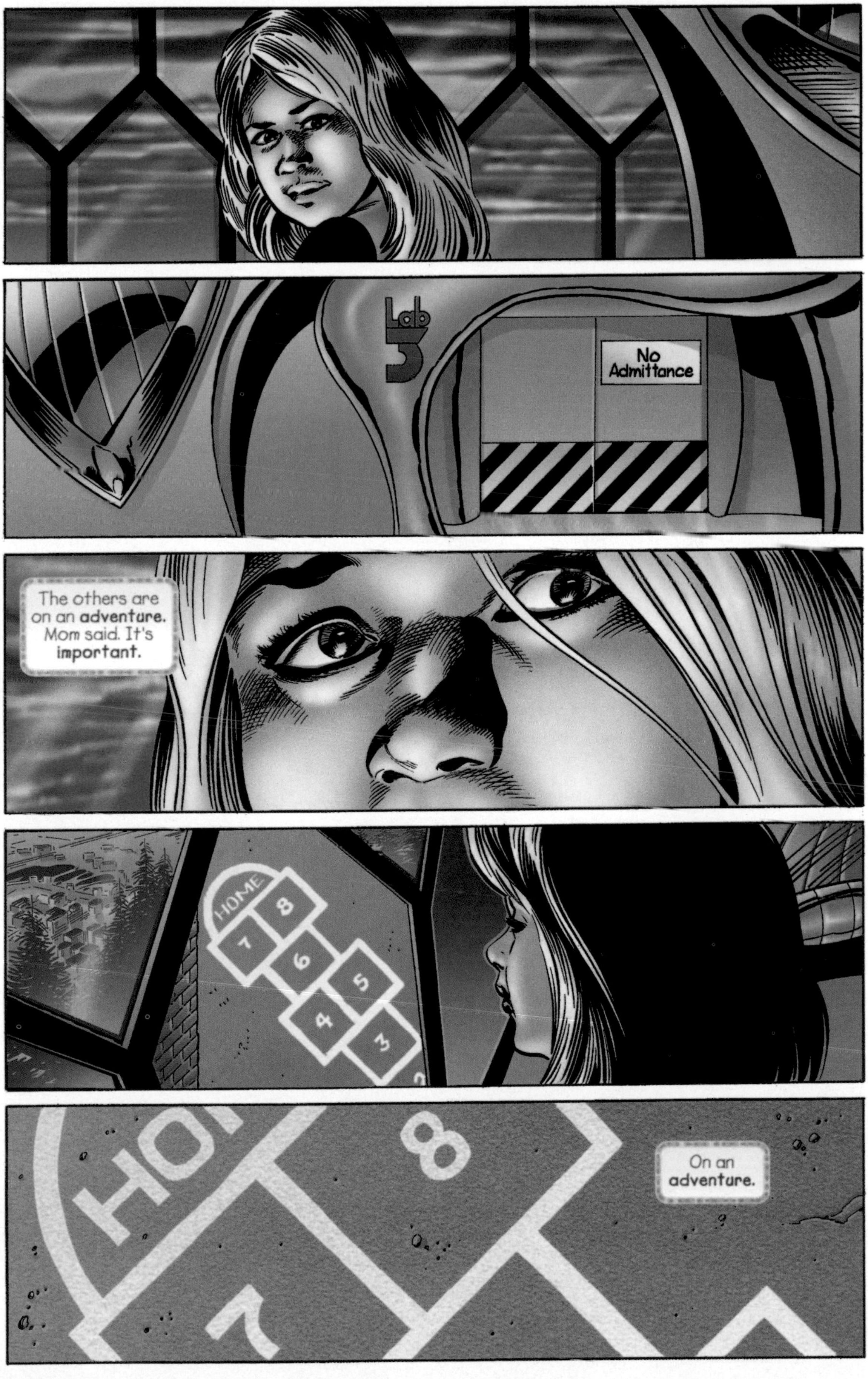
Lab 3
No Admittance
The others are on an adventure. Mom said. It's important.
HOME
8
7
6
5
4
3
On an adventure.

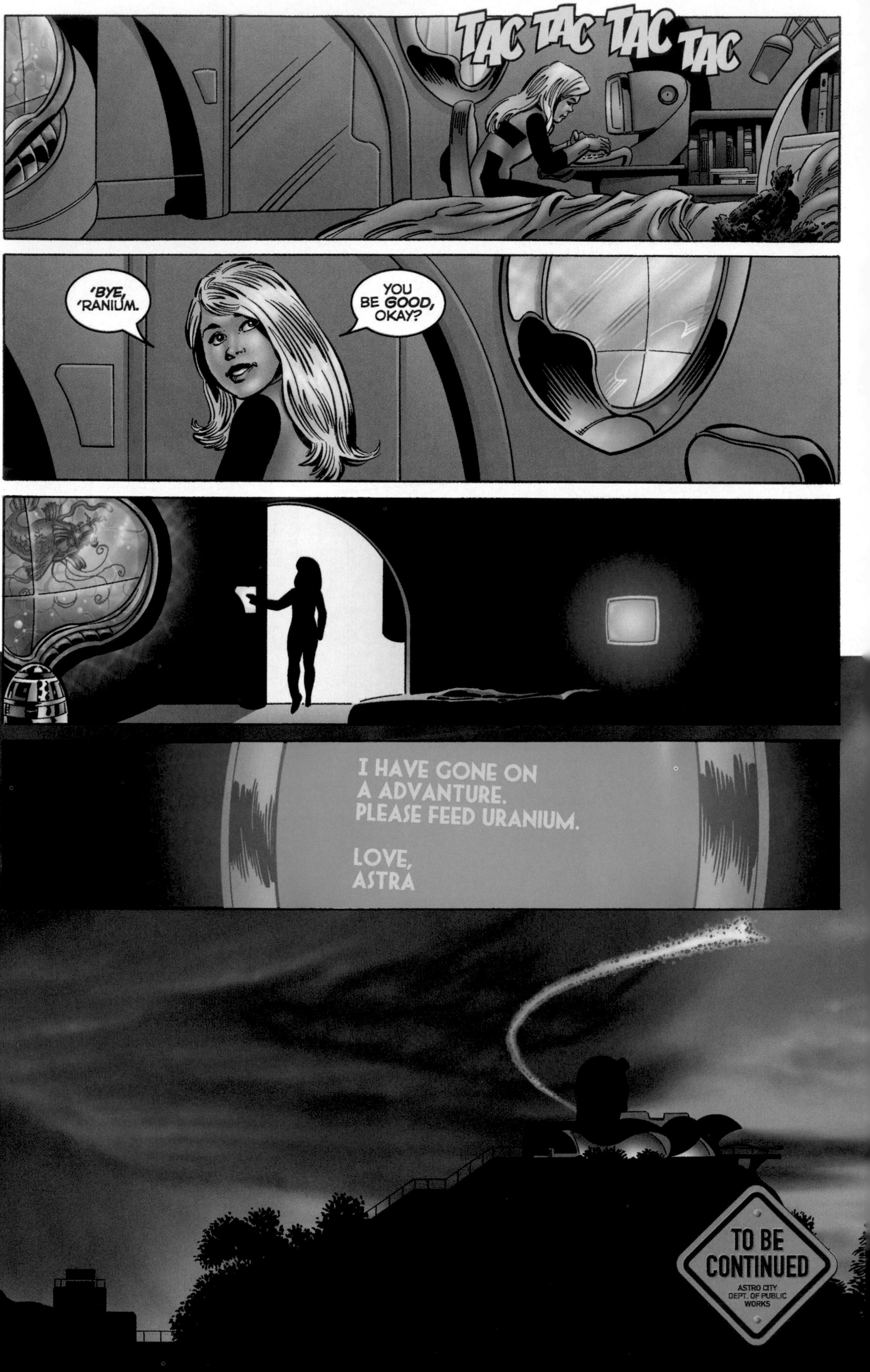
TAC TAC TAC TAC
'BYE, 'RANIUM.
YOU BE GOOD, OKAY?
I HAVE GONE ON
A ADVANTURE.
PLEASE FEED URANIUM.
LOVE,
ASTRA
TO BE CONTINUED
ASTRO CITY DEPT. OF PUBLIC WORKS

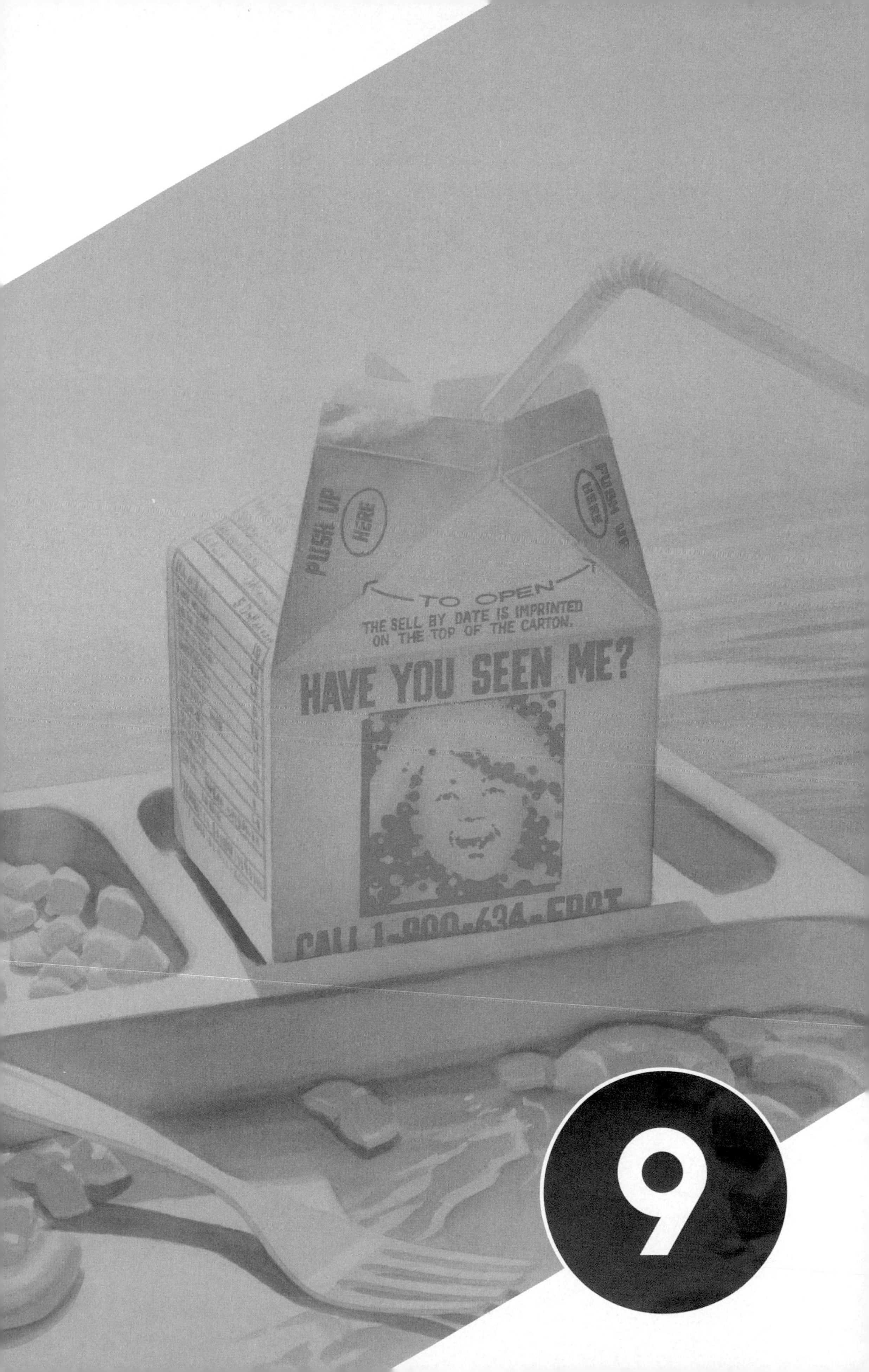
PUSH UP
HERE
PUSH UP
HERE
TO OPEN
THE SELL BY DATE IS IMPRINTED
ON THE TOP OF THE CARTON.
HAVE YOU SEEN ME?

9

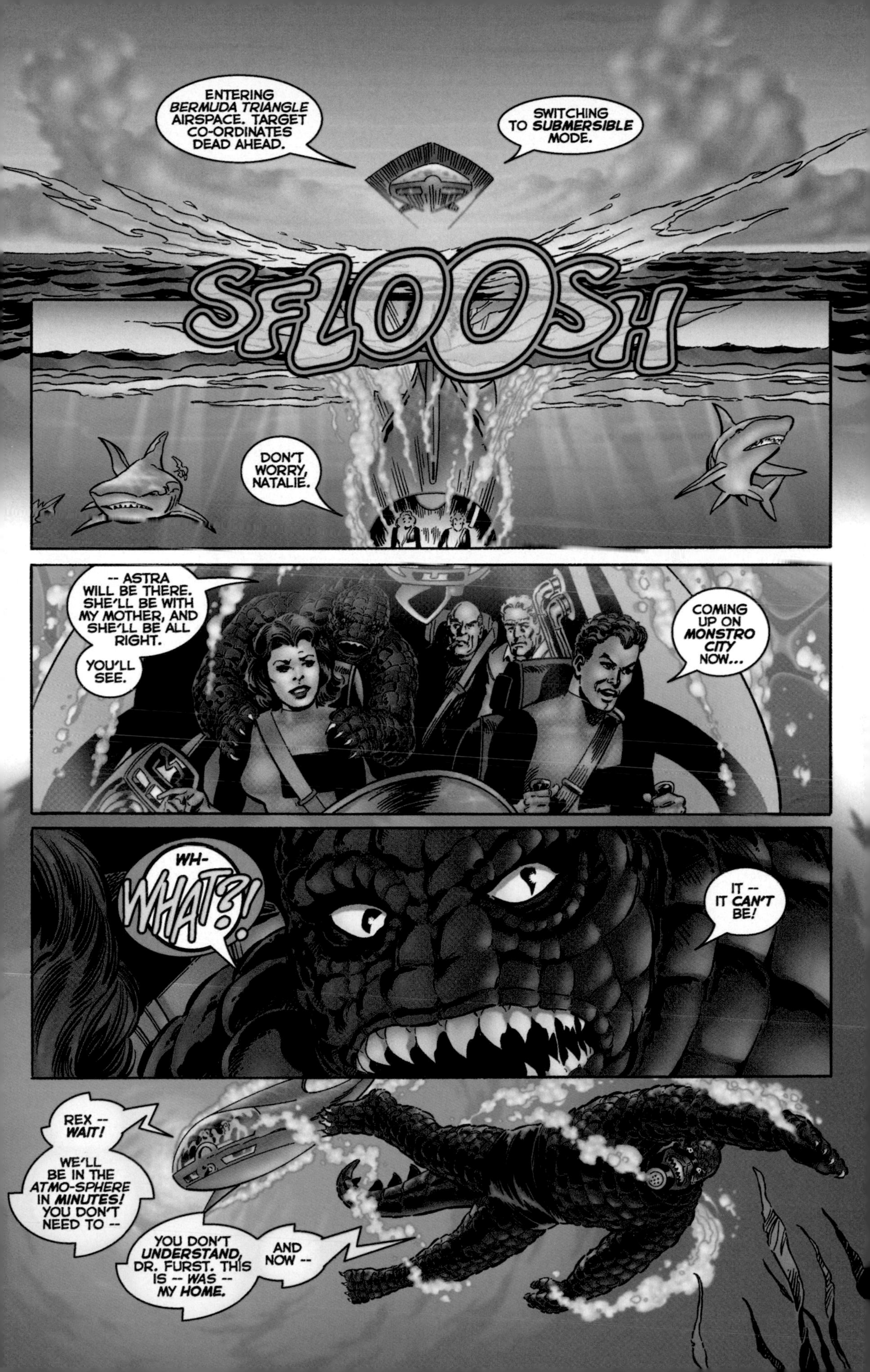
ENTERING BERMUDA TRIANGLE AIRSPACE. TARGET CO-ORDINATES DEAD AHEAD.
SWITCHING TO SUBMERSIBLE MODE.
SFLOOSH
DON'T WORRY, NATALIE.
-- ASTRA WILL BE THERE. SHE'LL BE WITH MY MOTHER, AND SHE'LL BE ALL RIGHT.
YOU'LL SEE.
COMING UP ON MONSTRO CITY NOW...
WH- WHAT?!
IT -- IT CAN'T BE!
REX -- WAIT!
WE'LL BE IN THE ATMO-SPHERE IN MINUTES! YOU DON'T NEED TO --
YOU DON'T UNDERSTAND, DR. FURST. THIS IS -- WAS -- MY HOME.
AND NOW --

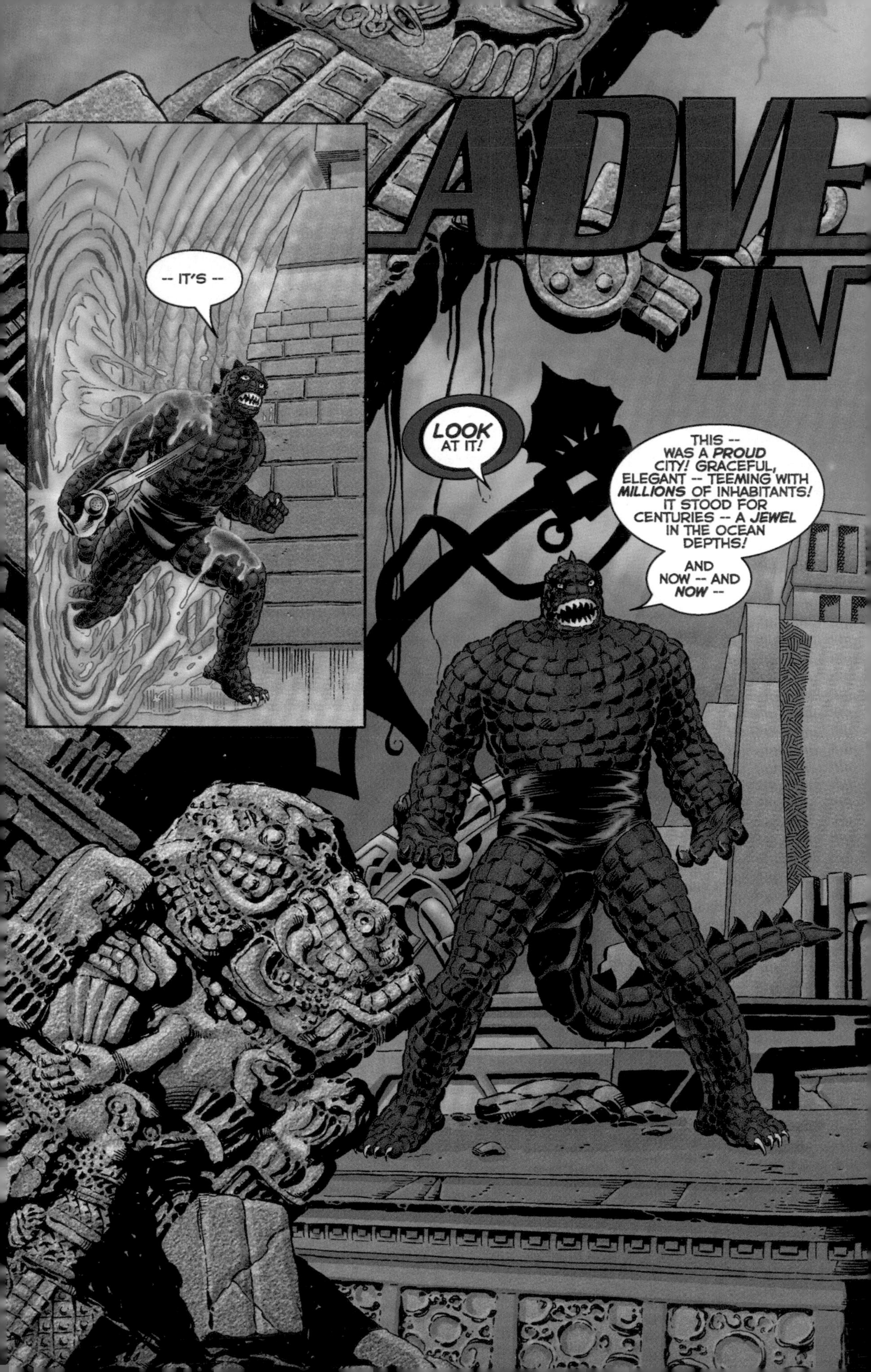
ADVE
IN
-- IT'S --
LOOK AT IT!
THIS -- WAS A PROUD CITY! GRACEFUL, ELEGANT -- TEEMING WITH MILLIONS OF INHABITANTS! IT STOOD FOR CENTURIES -- A JEWEL IN THE OCEAN DEPTHS!
AND NOW -- AND NOW --

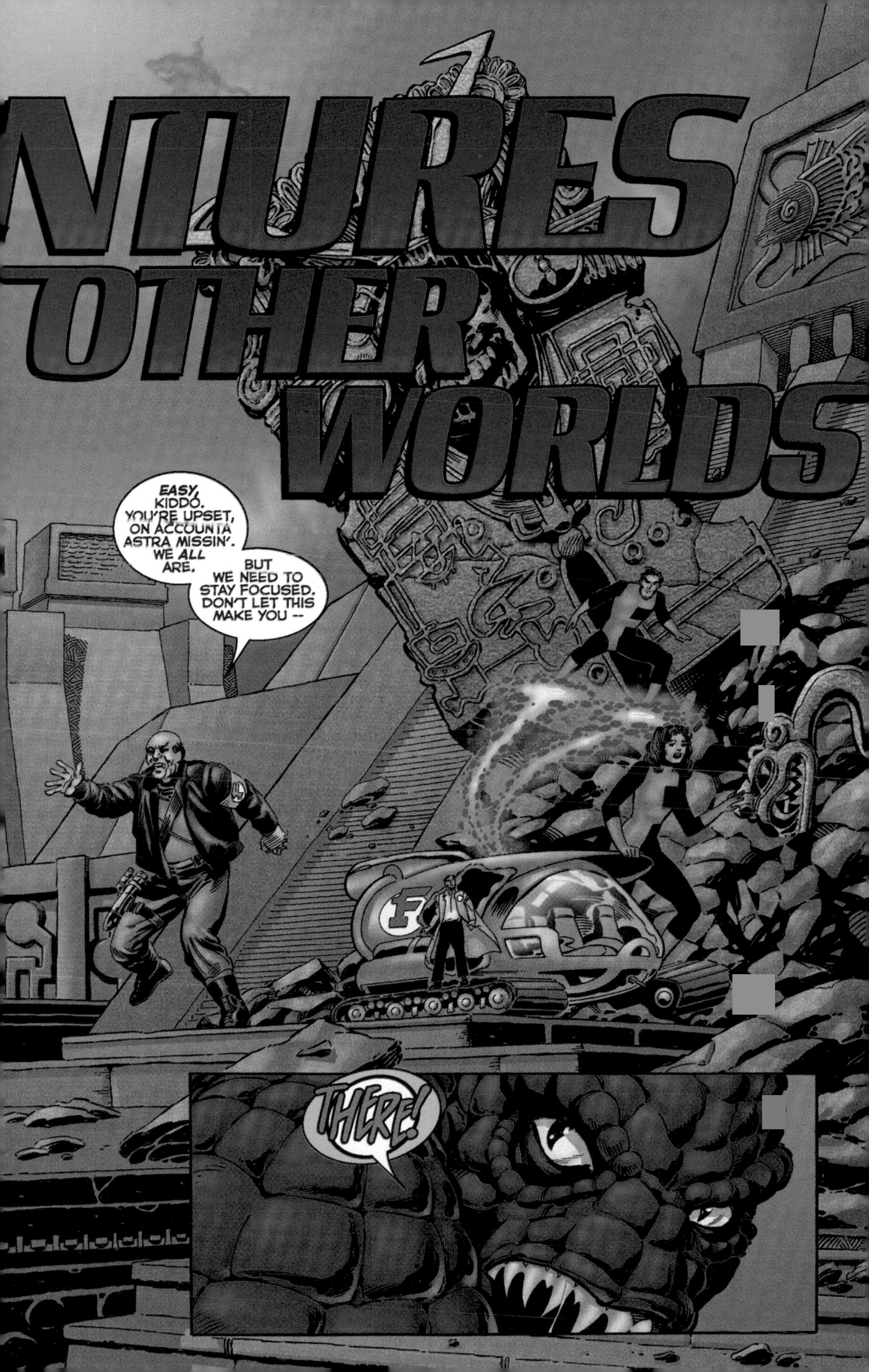
NTURES OTHER WORLDS
EASY, KIDDO. YOU'RE UPSET, ON ACCOUNTA ASTRA MISSIN'. WE ALL ARE.
BUT WE NEED TO STAY FOCUSED. DON'T LET THIS MAKE YOU --
THERE!

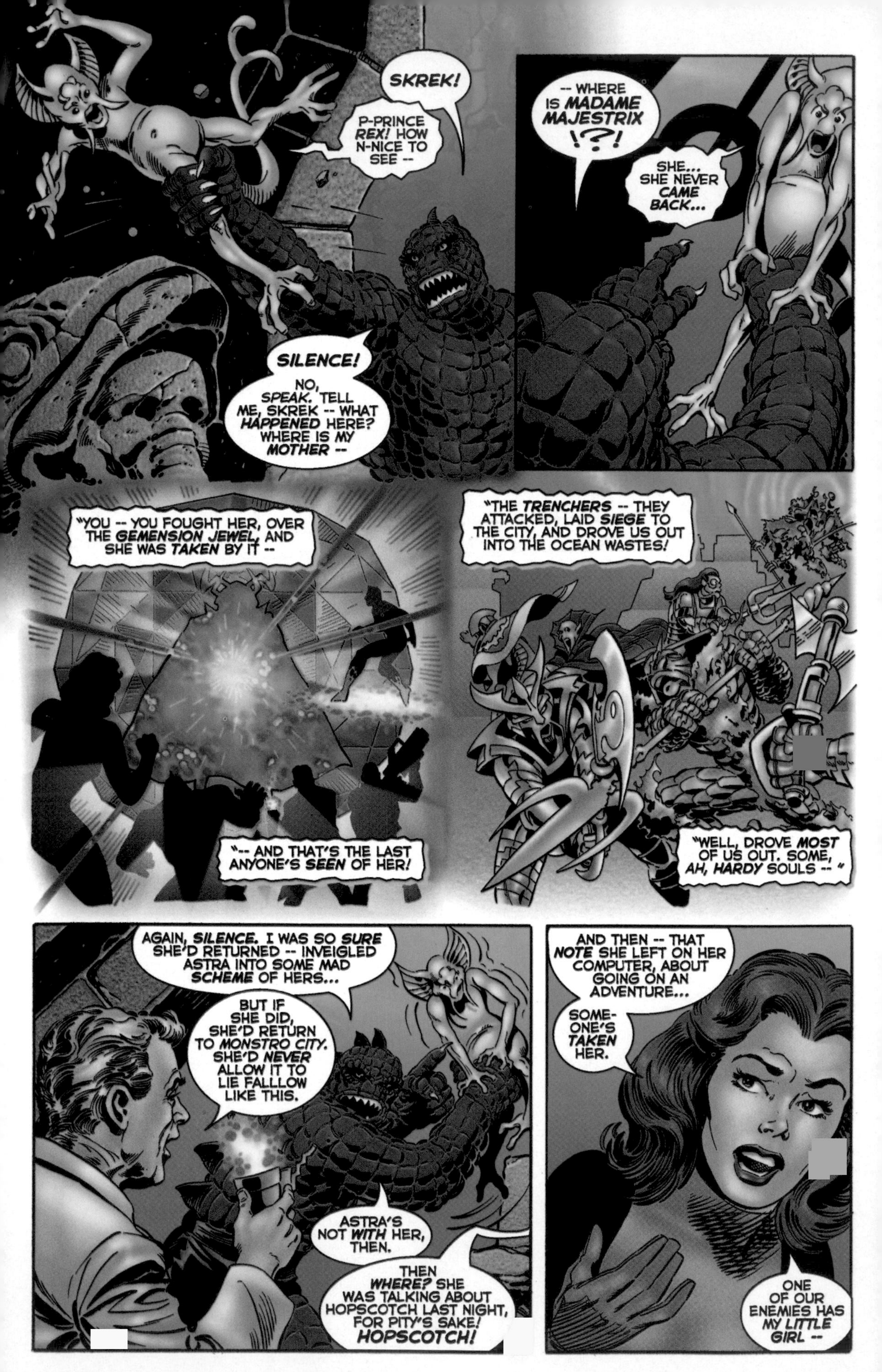
SKREK!
P-PRINCE REX! HOW N-NICE TO SEE --
SILENCE!
NO, SPEAK. TELL ME, SKREK -- WHAT HAPPENED HERE? WHERE IS MY MOTHER --
-- WHERE IS MADAME MAJESTRIX !?!
SHE... SHE NEVER CAME BACK...
"YOU -- YOU FOUGHT HER, OVER THE GEMENSION JEWEL, AND SHE WAS TAKEN BY IT --
"-- AND THAT'S THE LAST ANYONE'S SEEN OF HER!
"THE TRENCHERS -- THEY ATTACKED, LAID SIEGE TO THE CITY, AND DROVE US OUT INTO THE OCEAN WASTES!
"WELL, DROVE MOST OF US OUT. SOME, AH, HARDY SOULS -- "
AGAIN, SILENCE. I WAS SO SURE SHE'D RETURNED -- INVEIGLED ASTRA INTO SOME MAD SCHEME OF HERS...
BUT IF SHE DID, SHE'D RETURN TO MONSTRO CITY. SHE'D NEVER ALLOW IT TO LIE FALLLOW LIKE THIS.
ASTRA'S NOT WITH HER, THEN.
THEN WHERE? SHE WAS TALKING ABOUT HOPSCOTCH LAST NIGHT, FOR PITY'S SAKE! HOPSCOTCH!
AND THEN -- THAT NOTE SHE LEFT ON HER COMPUTER, ABOUT GOING ON AN ADVENTURE...
SOME-ONE'S TAKEN HER.
ONE OF OUR ENEMIES HAS MY LITTLE GIRL --

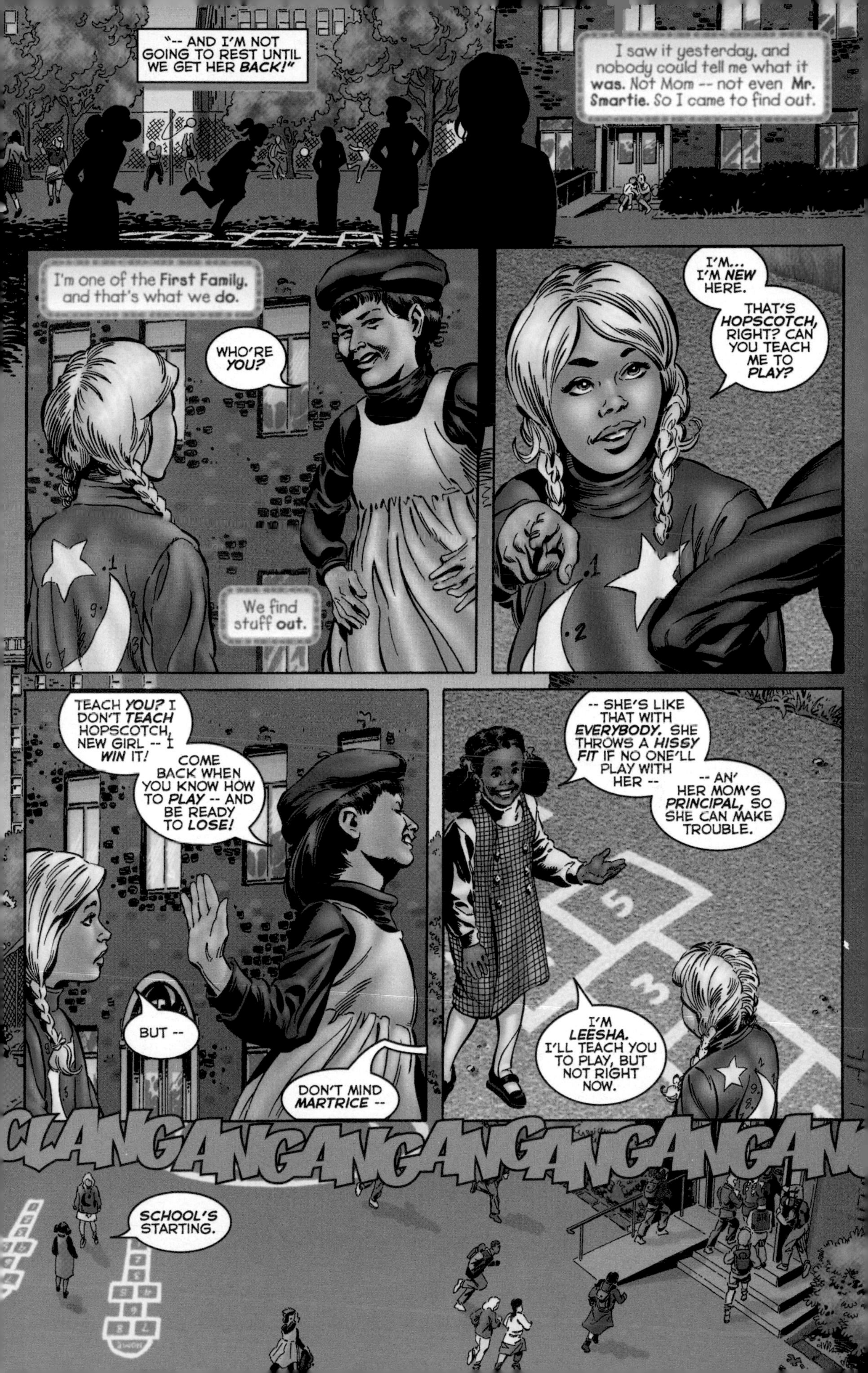
"-- AND I'M NOT GOING TO REST UNTIL WE GET HER BACK!"
I saw it yesterday, and nobody could tell me what it was. Not Mom -- not even Mr. Smartie. So I came to find out.
I'm one of the First Family, and that's what we do.
WHO'RE YOU?
We find stuff out.
I'M... I'M NEW HERE.
THAT'S HOPSCOTCH, RIGHT? CAN YOU TEACH ME TO PLAY?
TEACH YOU? I DON'T TEACH HOPSCOTCH, NEW GIRL -- I WIN IT!
COME BACK WHEN YOU KNOW HOW TO PLAY -- AND BE READY TO LOSE!
BUT --
DON'T MIND MARTRICE --
-- SHE'S LIKE THAT WITH EVERYBODY. SHE THROWS A HISSY FIT IF NO ONE'LL PLAY WITH HER --
-- AN' HER MOM'S PRINCIPAL, SO SHE CAN MAKE TROUBLE.
I'M LEESHA. I'LL TEACH YOU TO PLAY, BUT NOT RIGHT NOW.
CLANGANGANGANGANGANGANGAN
SCHOOL'S STARTING.

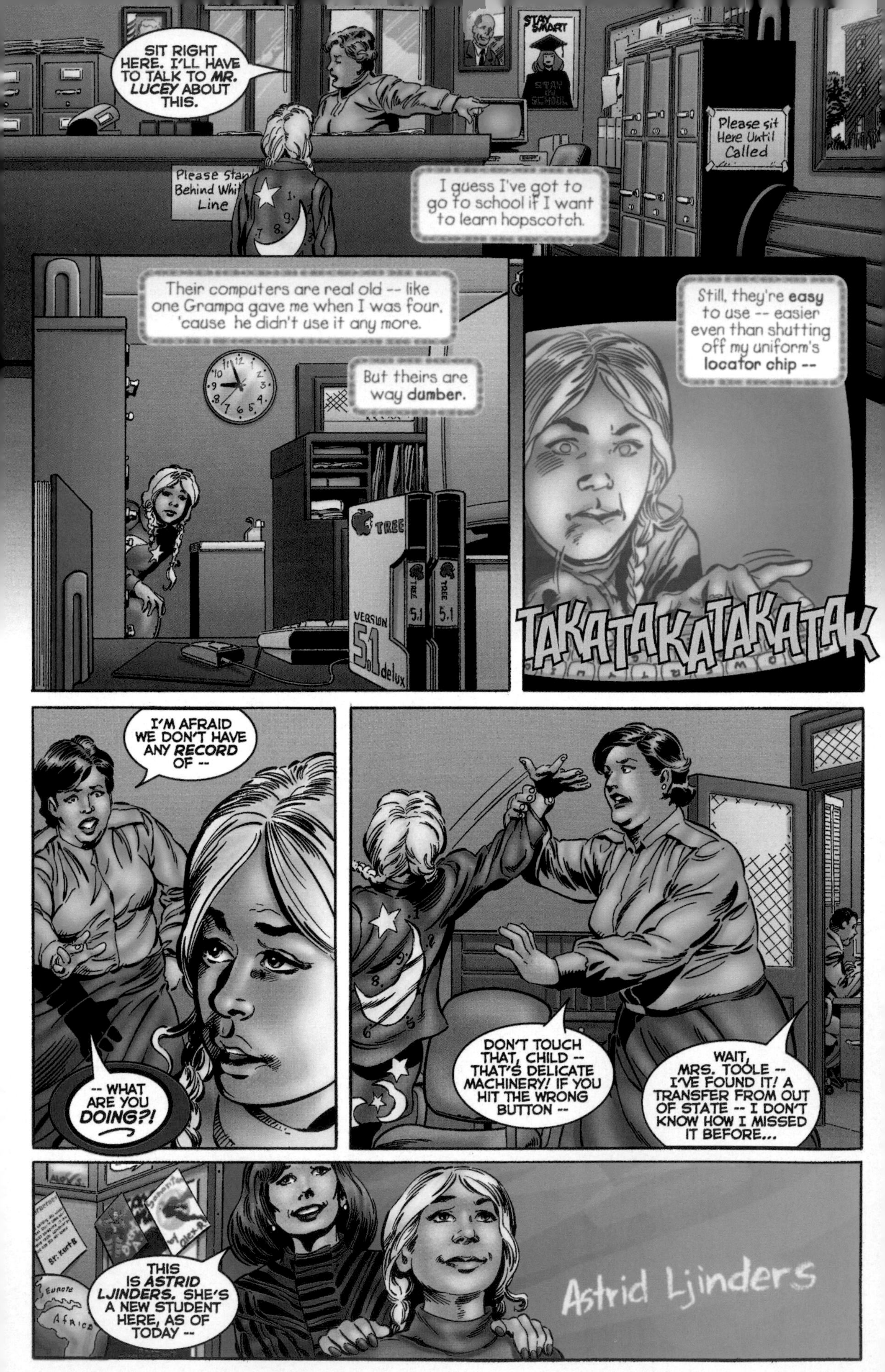

SIT RIGHT HERE. I'LL HAVE TO TALK TO MR. LUCEY ABOUT THIS.
STAY SMART
STAY IN SCHOOL
Please sit Here Until Called
Please Stan Behind Whi Line
I guess I've got to go to school if I want to learn hopscotch.
Their computers are real old -- like one Grampa gave me when I was four, 'cause he didn't use it any more.
But theirs are way dumber.
TREE
VERSION 5.1 delux
Still, they're easy to use -- easier even than shutting off my uniform's locator chip --
TAKATAKATAKATAK
I'M AFRAID WE DON'T HAVE ANY RECORD OF --
-- WHAT ARE YOU DOING?!
DON'T TOUCH THAT, CHILD -- THAT'S DELICATE MACHINERY! IF YOU HIT THE WRONG BUTTON --
WAIT, MRS. TOOLE -- I'VE FOUND IT! A TRANSFER FROM OUT OF STATE -- I DON'T KNOW HOW I MISSED IT BEFORE...
THIS IS ASTRID LJINDERS. SHE'S A NEW STUDENT HERE, AS OF TODAY --
Astrid Ljinders

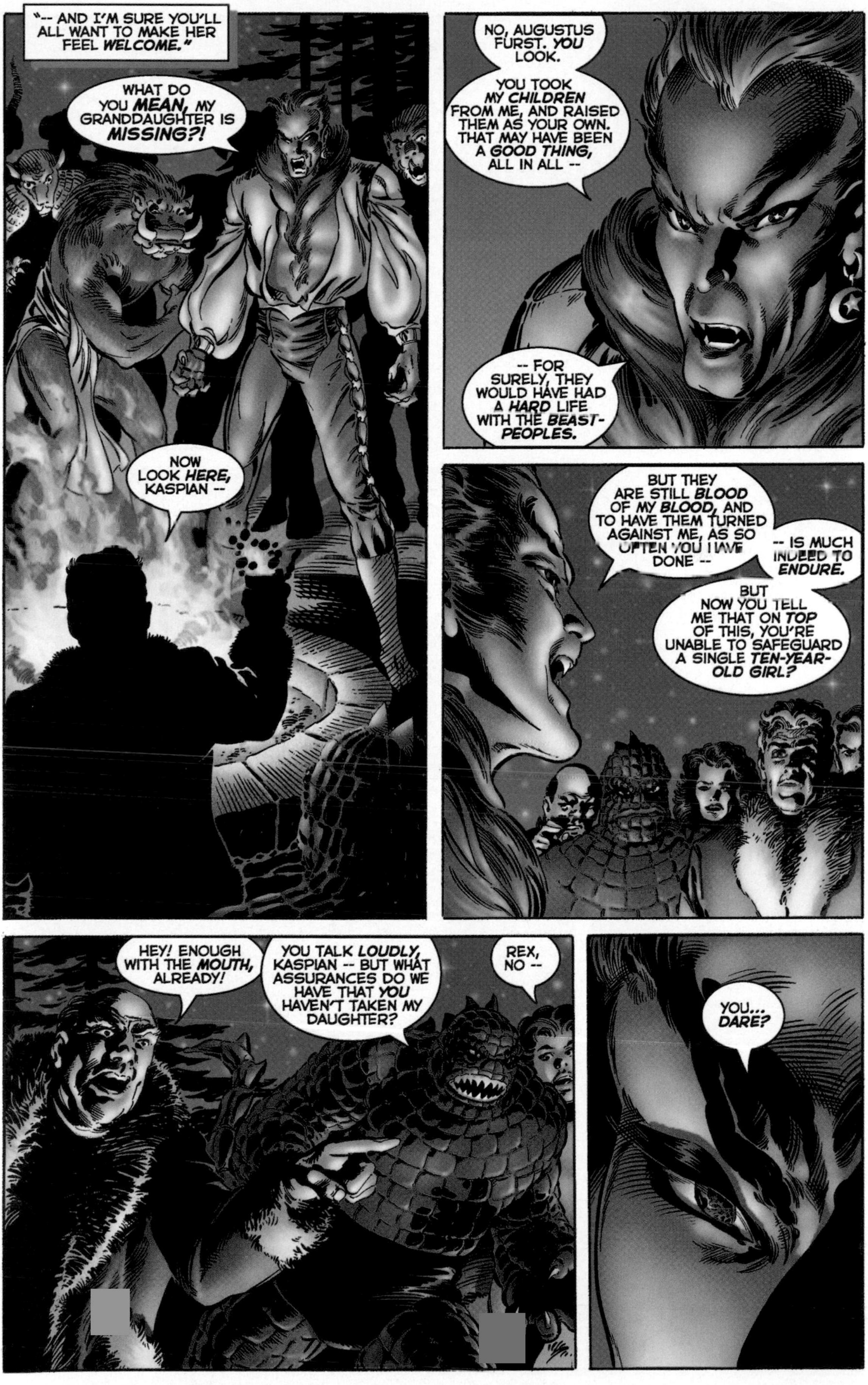
"-- AND I'M SURE YOU'LL ALL WANT TO MAKE HER FEEL WELCOME."
WHAT DO YOU MEAN, MY GRANDDAUGHTER IS MISSING?!
NOW LOOK HERE, KASPIAN --
NO, AUGUSTUS FURST. YOU LOOK.
YOU TOOK MY CHILDREN FROM ME, AND RAISED THEM AS YOUR OWN. THAT MAY HAVE BEEN A GOOD THING, ALL IN ALL --
-- FOR SURELY, THEY WOULD HAVE HAD A HARD LIFE WITH THE BEAST-PEOPLES.
BUT THEY ARE STILL BLOOD OF MY BLOOD, AND TO HAVE THEM TURNED AGAINST ME, AS SO OFTEN YOU HAVE DONE --
-- IS MUCH INDEED TO ENDURE.
BUT NOW YOU TELL ME THAT ON TOP OF THIS, YOU'RE UNABLE TO SAFEGUARD A SINGLE TEN-YEAR-OLD GIRL?
HEY! ENOUGH WITH THE MOUTH, ALREADY!
YOU TALK LOUDLY, KASPIAN -- BUT WHAT ASSURANCES DO WE HAVE THAT YOU HAVEN'T TAKEN MY DAUGHTER?
REX, NO --
YOU... DARE?

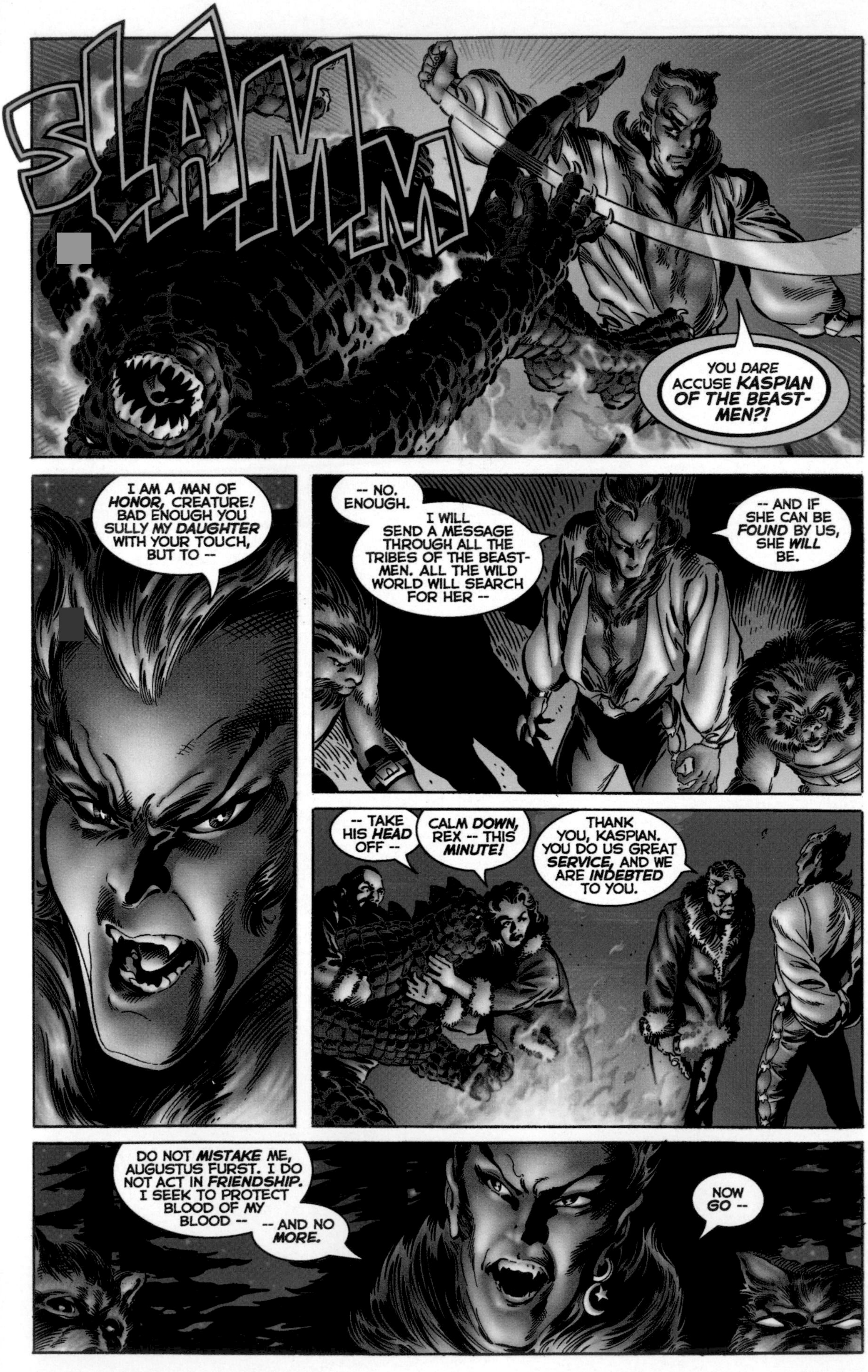
SLAMM
YOU DARE ACCUSE KASPIAN OF THE BEAST-MEN?!
I AM A MAN OF HONOR, CREATURE! BAD ENOUGH YOU SULLY MY DAUGHTER WITH YOUR TOUCH, BUT TO --
-- NO. ENOUGH.
I WILL SEND A MESSAGE THROUGH ALL THE TRIBES OF THE BEAST-MEN. ALL THE WILD WORLD WILL SEARCH FOR HER --
-- AND IF SHE CAN BE FOUND BY US, SHE WILL BE.
-- TAKE HIS HEAD OFF --
CALM DOWN, REX -- THIS MINUTE!
THANK YOU, KASPIAN. YOU DO US GREAT SERVICE, AND WE ARE INDEBTED TO YOU.
DO NOT MISTAKE ME, AUGUSTUS FURST. I DO NOT ACT IN FRIENDSHIP. I SEEK TO PROTECT BLOOD OF MY BLOOD --
-- AND NO MORE.
NOW GO --

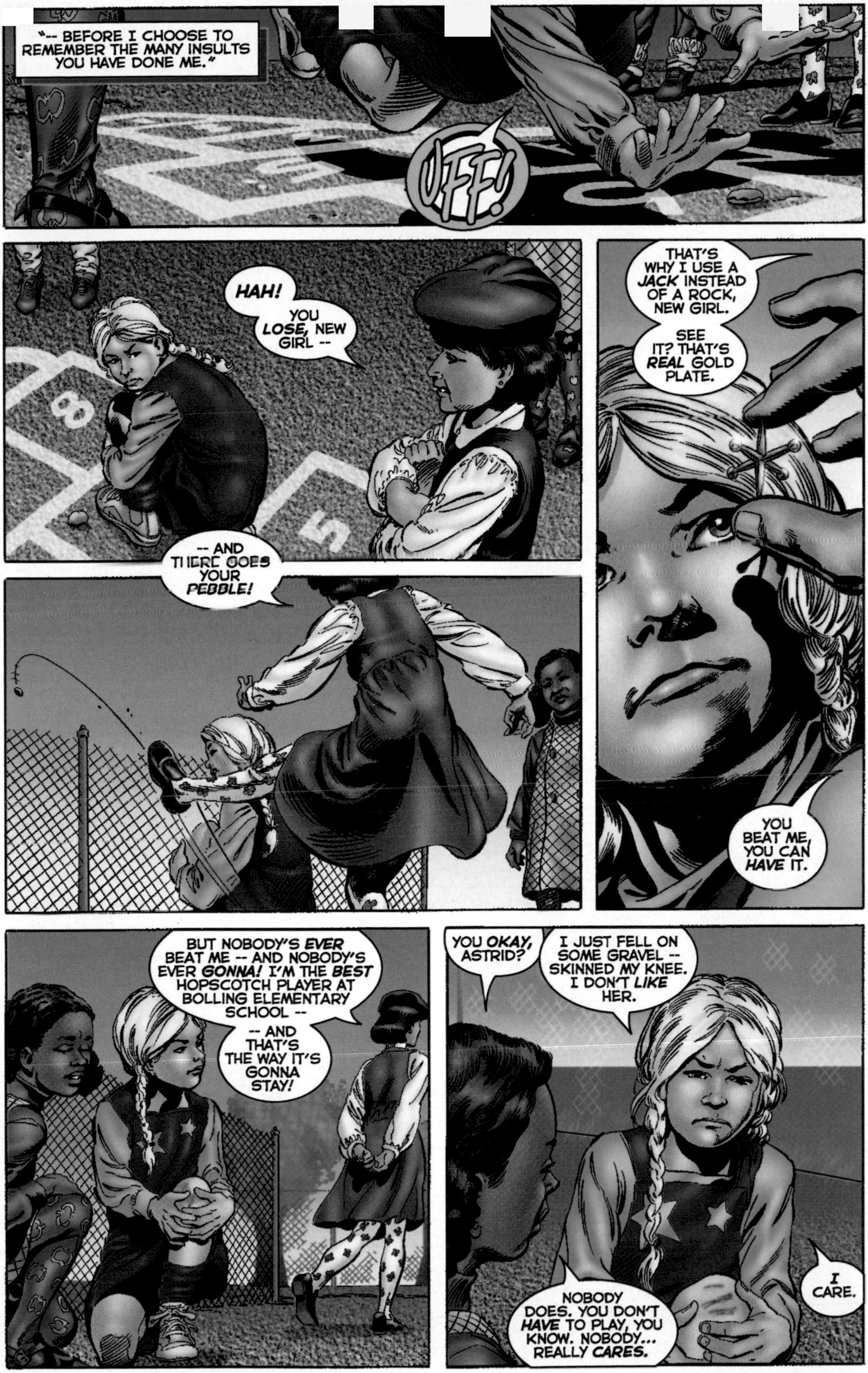
"-- BEFORE I CHOOSE TO REMEMBER THE MANY INSULTS YOU HAVE DONE ME."
OFF!
HAH!
YOU LOSE, NEW GIRL --
THAT'S WHY I USE A JACK INSTEAD OF A ROCK, NEW GIRL.
SEE IT? THAT'S REAL GOLD PLATE.
-- AND THERE GOES YOUR PEBBLE!
YOU BEAT ME, YOU CAN HAVE IT.
BUT NOBODY'S EVER BEAT ME -- AND NOBODY'S EVER GONNA! I'M THE BEST HOPSCOTCH PLAYER AT BOLLING ELEMENTARY SCHOOL --
-- AND THAT'S THE WAY IT'S GONNA STAY!
YOU OKAY, ASTRID?
I JUST FELL ON SOME GRAVEL -- SKINNED MY KNEE. I DON'T LIKE HER.
NOBODY DOES. YOU DON'T HAVE TO PLAY, YOU KNOW. NOBODY... REALLY CARES.
I CARE.

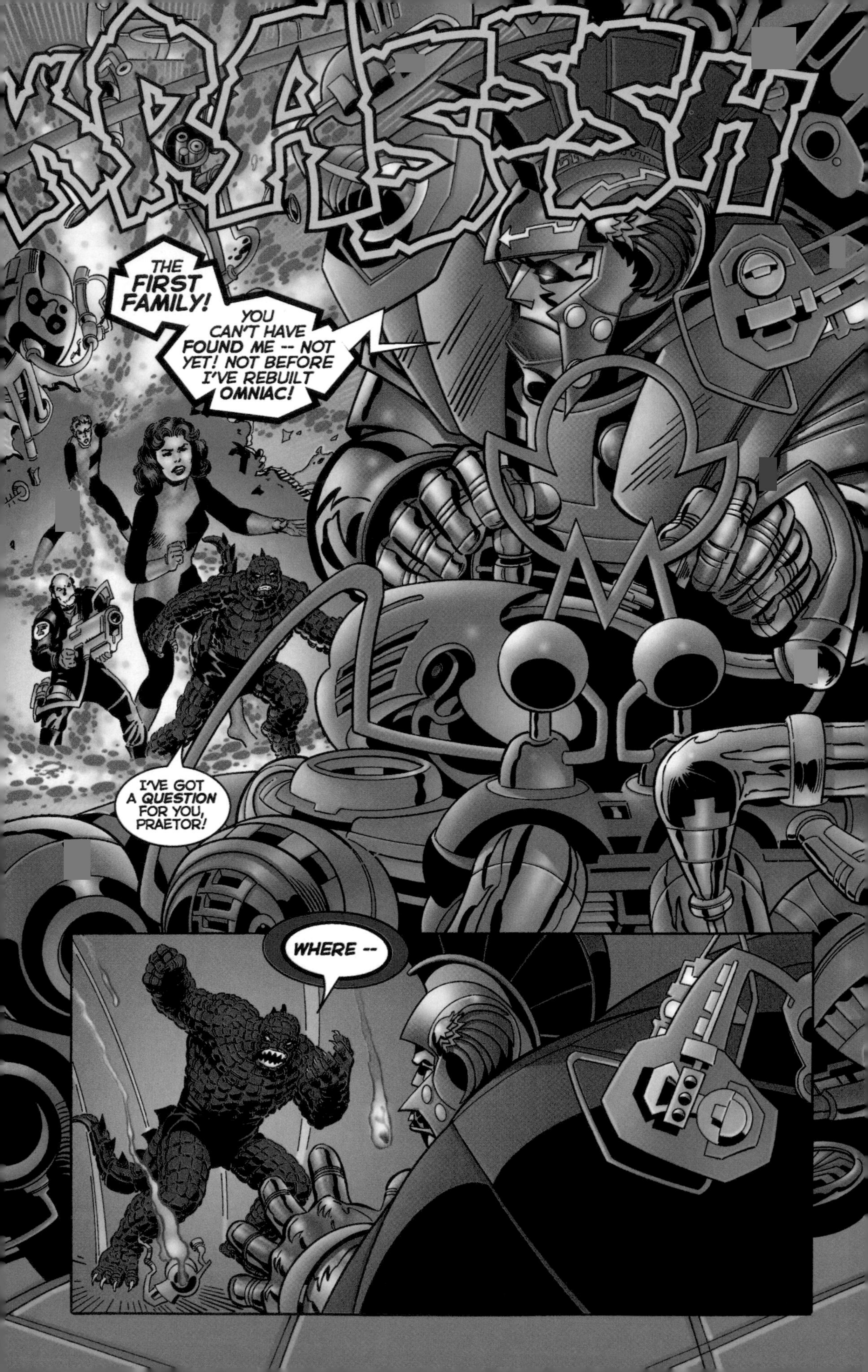
THE FIRST FAMILY!
YOU CAN'T HAVE FOUND ME -- NOT YET! NOT BEFORE I'VE REBUILT OMNIAC!
I'VE GOT A QUESTION FOR YOU, PRAETOR!
WHERE --

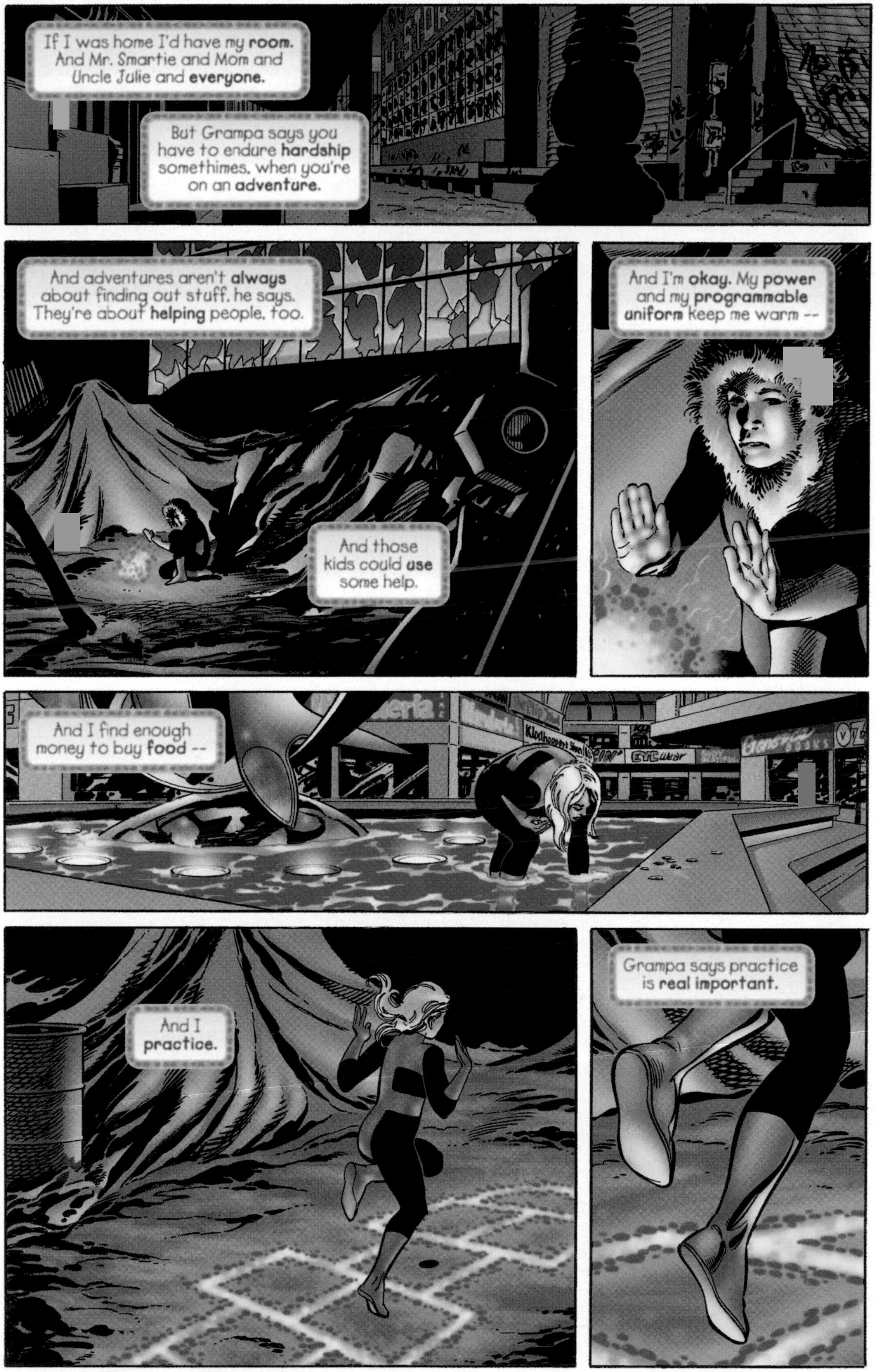

If I was home I'd have my room. And Mr. Smartie and Mom and Uncle Julie and everyone.
But Grampa says you have to endure hardship somethimes, when you're on an adventure.
And adventures aren't always about finding out stuff, he says. They're about helping people, too.
And those kids could use some help.
And I'm okay. My power and my programmable uniform keep me warm --
And I find enough money to buy food --
And I practice.
Grampa says practice is real important.

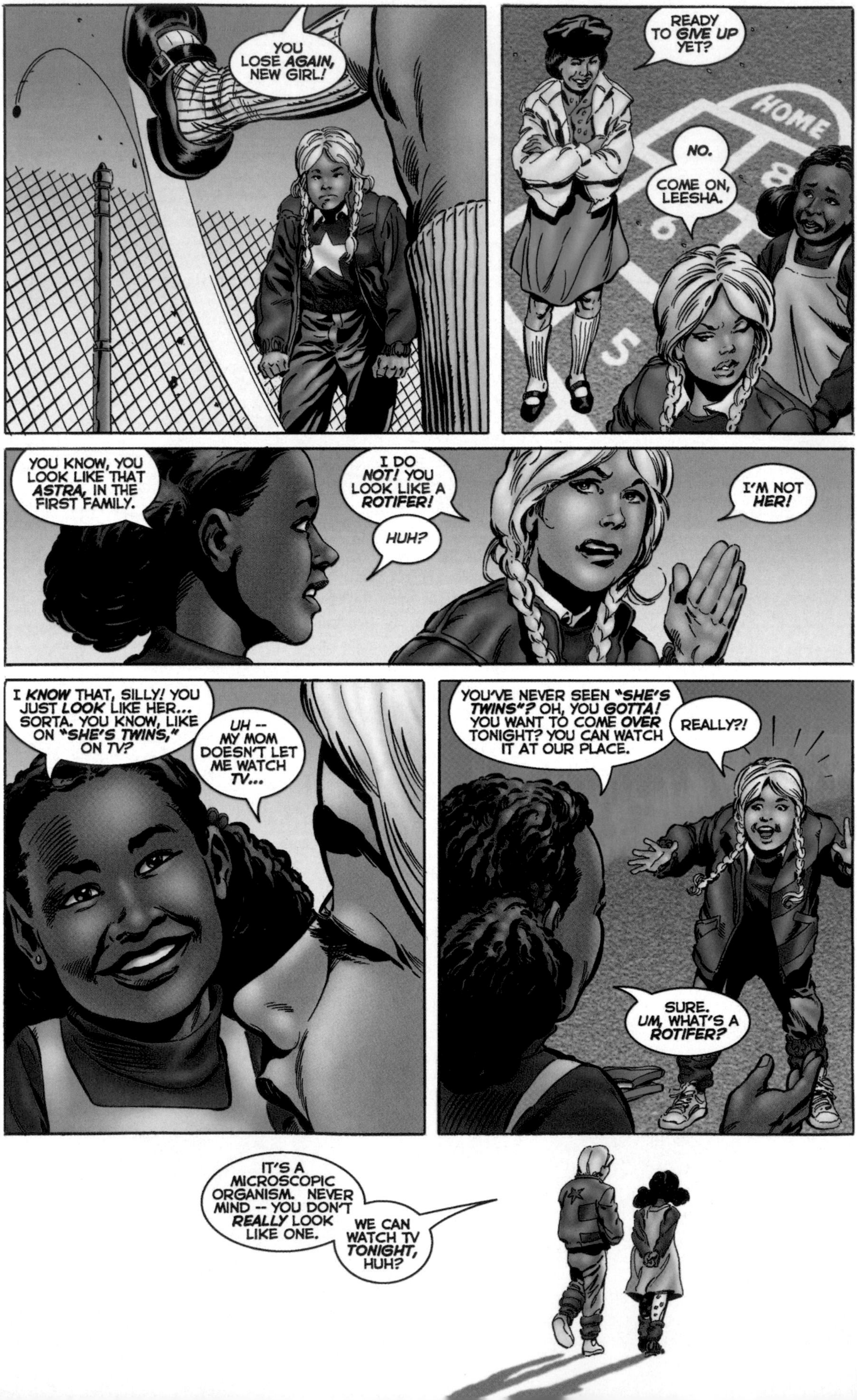
YOU LOSE AGAIN, NEW GIRL!
READY TO GIVE UP YET?
HOME
NO.
COME ON, LEESHA.
YOU KNOW, YOU LOOK LIKE THAT ASTRA, IN THE FIRST FAMILY.
I DO NOT! YOU LOOK LIKE A ROTIFER!
HUH?
I'M NOT HER!
I KNOW THAT, SILLY! YOU JUST LOOK LIKE HER... SORTA. YOU KNOW, LIKE ON "SHE'S TWINS," ON TV?
UH -- MY MOM DOESN'T LET ME WATCH TV...
YOU'VE NEVER SEEN "SHE'S TWINS"? OH, YOU GOTTA! YOU WANT TO COME OVER TONIGHT? YOU CAN WATCH IT AT OUR PLACE.
REALLY?!
SURE. UM, WHAT'S A ROTIFER?
IT'S A MICROSCOPIC ORGANISM. NEVER MIND -- YOU DON'T REALLY LOOK LIKE ONE.
WE CAN WATCH TV TONIGHT, HUH?

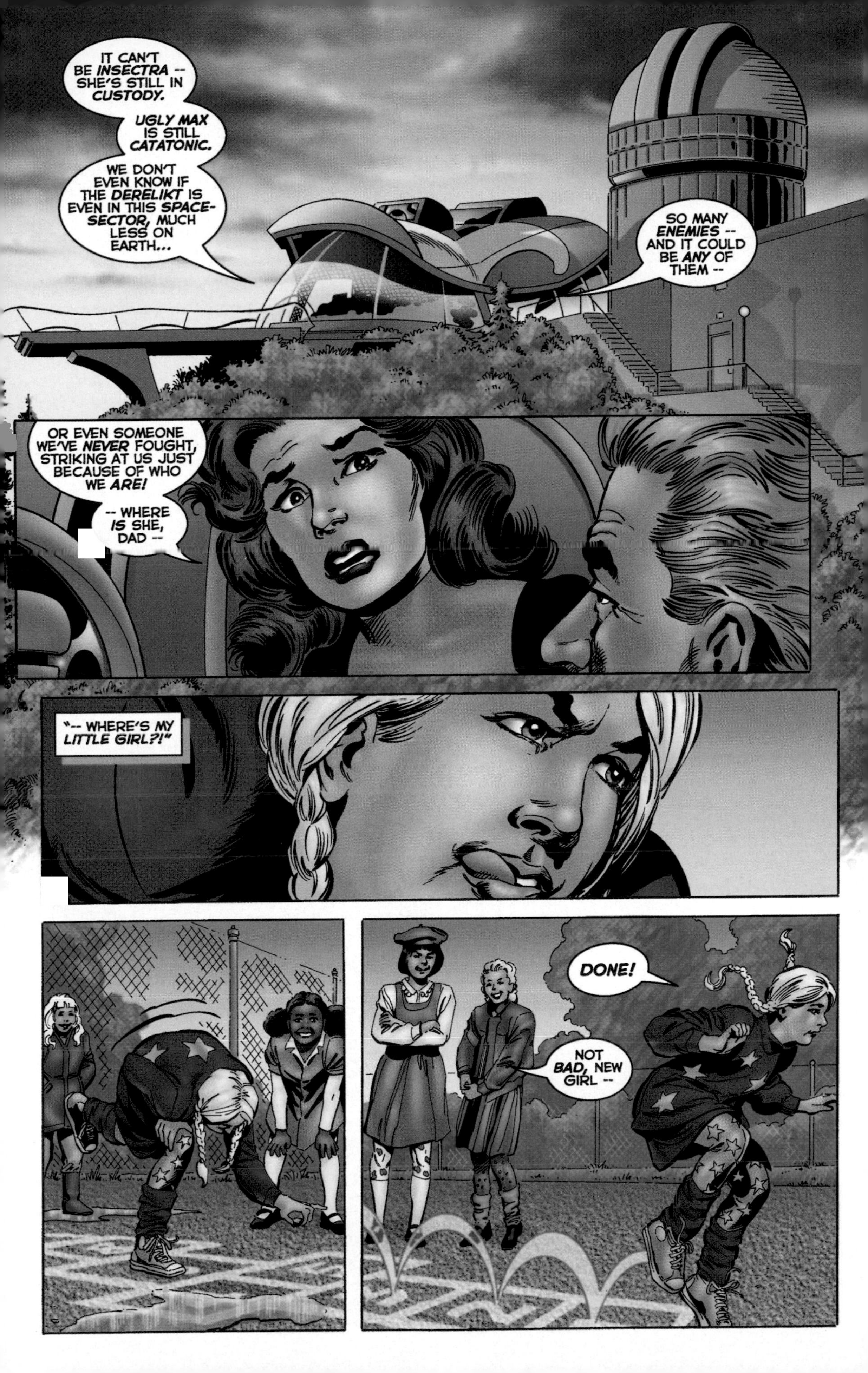
IT CAN'T BE INSECTRA -- SHE'S STILL IN CUSTODY.
UGLY MAX IS STILL CATATONIC.
WE DON'T EVEN KNOW IF THE DERELIKT IS EVEN IN THIS SPACE-SECTOR, MUCH LESS ON EARTH...
SO MANY ENEMIES -- AND IT COULD BE ANY OF THEM --
OR EVEN SOMEONE WE'VE NEVER FOUGHT, STRIKING AT US JUST BECAUSE OF WHO WE ARE!
-- WHERE IS SHE, DAD --
"-- WHERE'S MY LITTLE GIRL?!"
DONE!
NOT BAD, NEW GIRL --

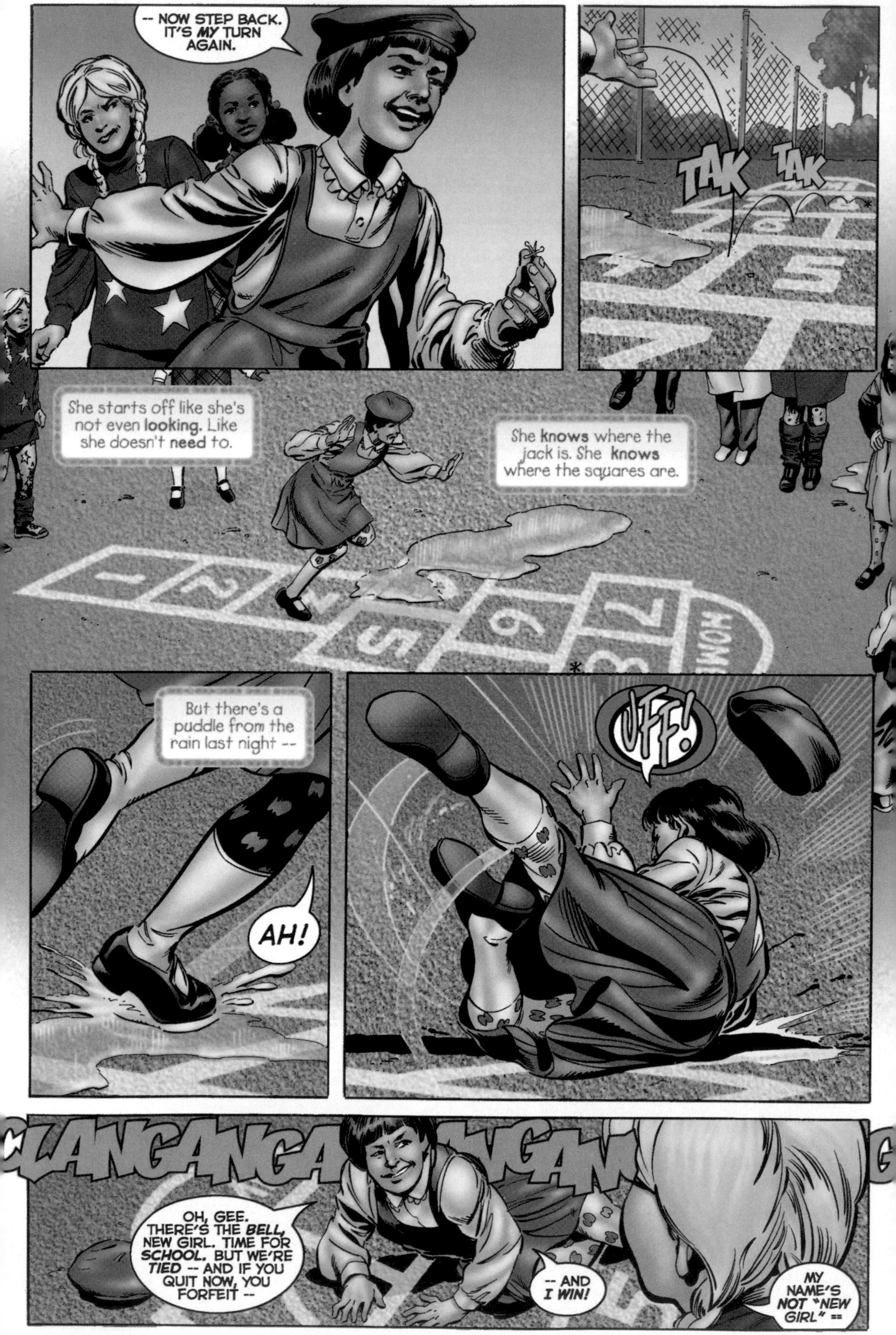

-- NOW STEP BACK. IT'S MY TURN AGAIN.
TAK
TAK
She starts off like she's not even looking. Like she doesn't need to.
She knows where the jack is. She knows where the squares are.
But there's a puddle from the rain last night --
AH!
UFF!
CLANGANGANGANGANG
OH, GEE. THERE'S THE BELL, NEW GIRL. TIME FOR SCHOOL. BUT WE'RE TIED -- AND IF YOU QUIT NOW, YOU FORFEIT --
-- AND I WIN!
MY NAME'S NOT "NEW GIRL" --

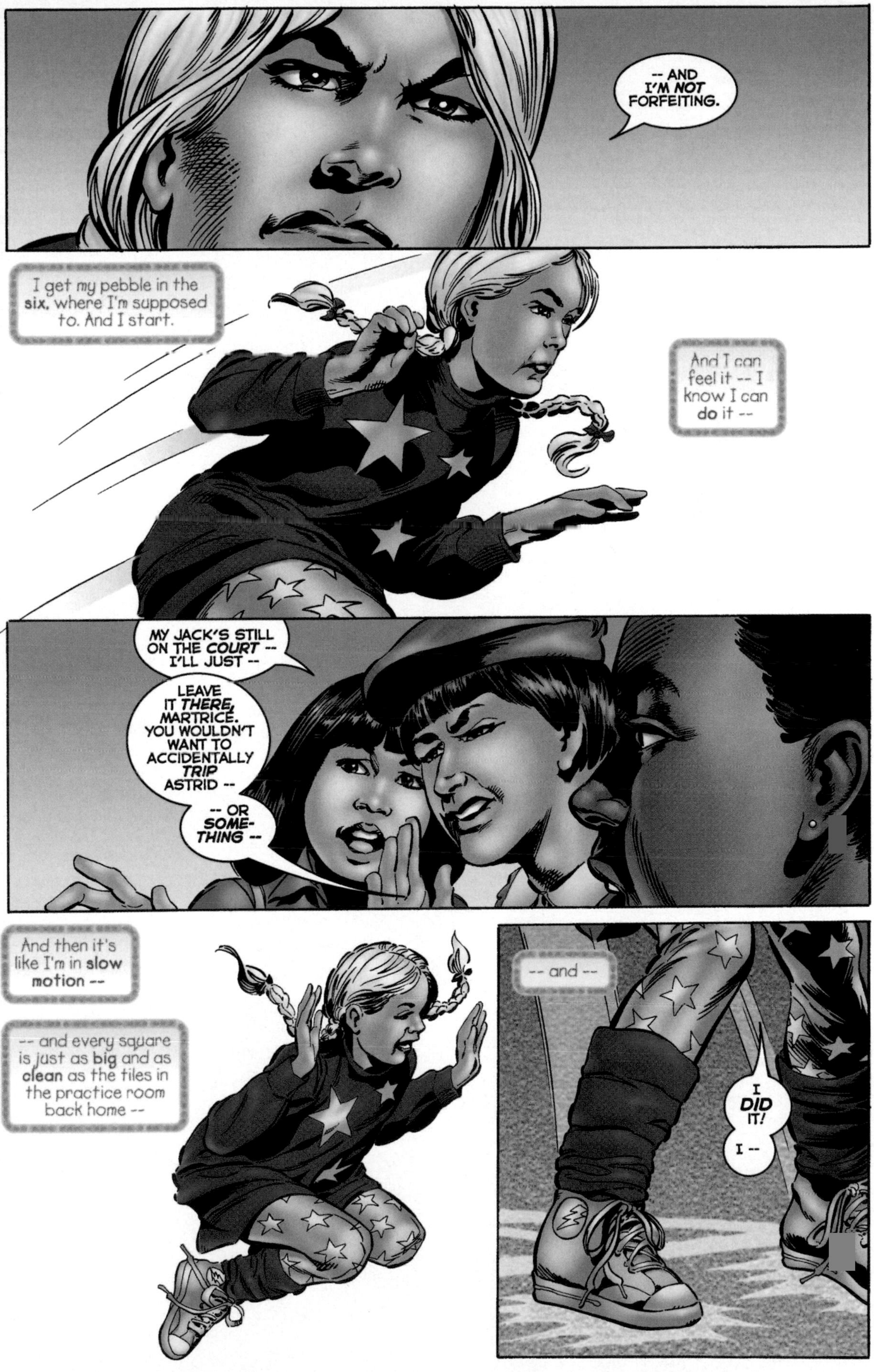
-- AND I'M NOT FORFEITING.
I get my pebble in the six, where I'm supposed to. And I start.
And I can feel it -- I know I can do it --
MY JACK'S STILL ON THE COURT -- I'LL JUST --
LEAVE IT THERE, MARTRICE. YOU WOULDN'T WANT TO ACCIDENTALLY TRIP ASTRID --
-- OR SOME-THING --
And then it's like I'm in slow motion --
-- and every square is just as big and as clean as the tiles in the practice room back home --
-- and --
I DID IT!
I --

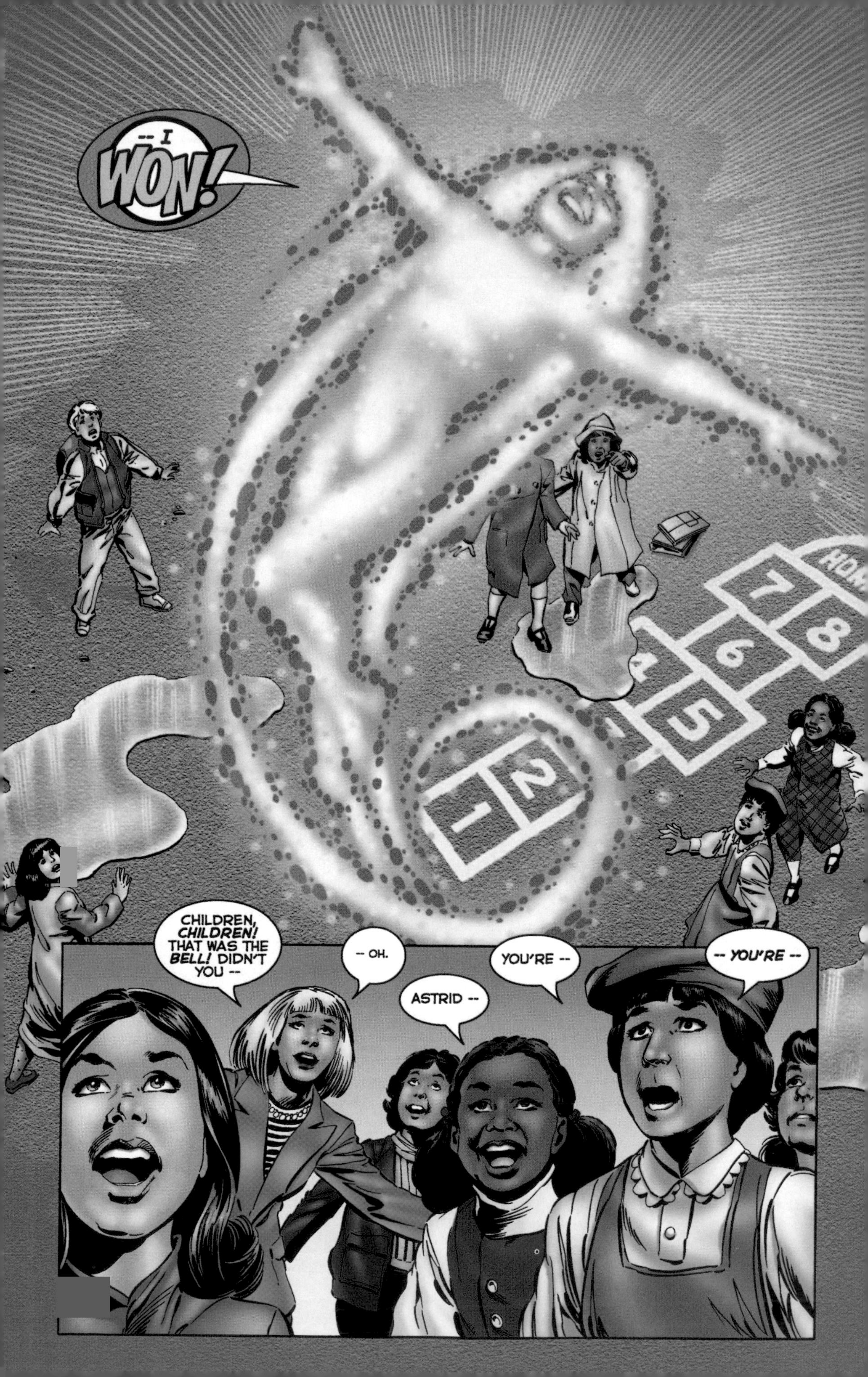
-- I WON!
CHILDREN, CHILDREN! THAT WAS THE BELL! DIDN'T YOU --
-- OH.
ASTRID --
YOU'RE --
-- YOU'RE --

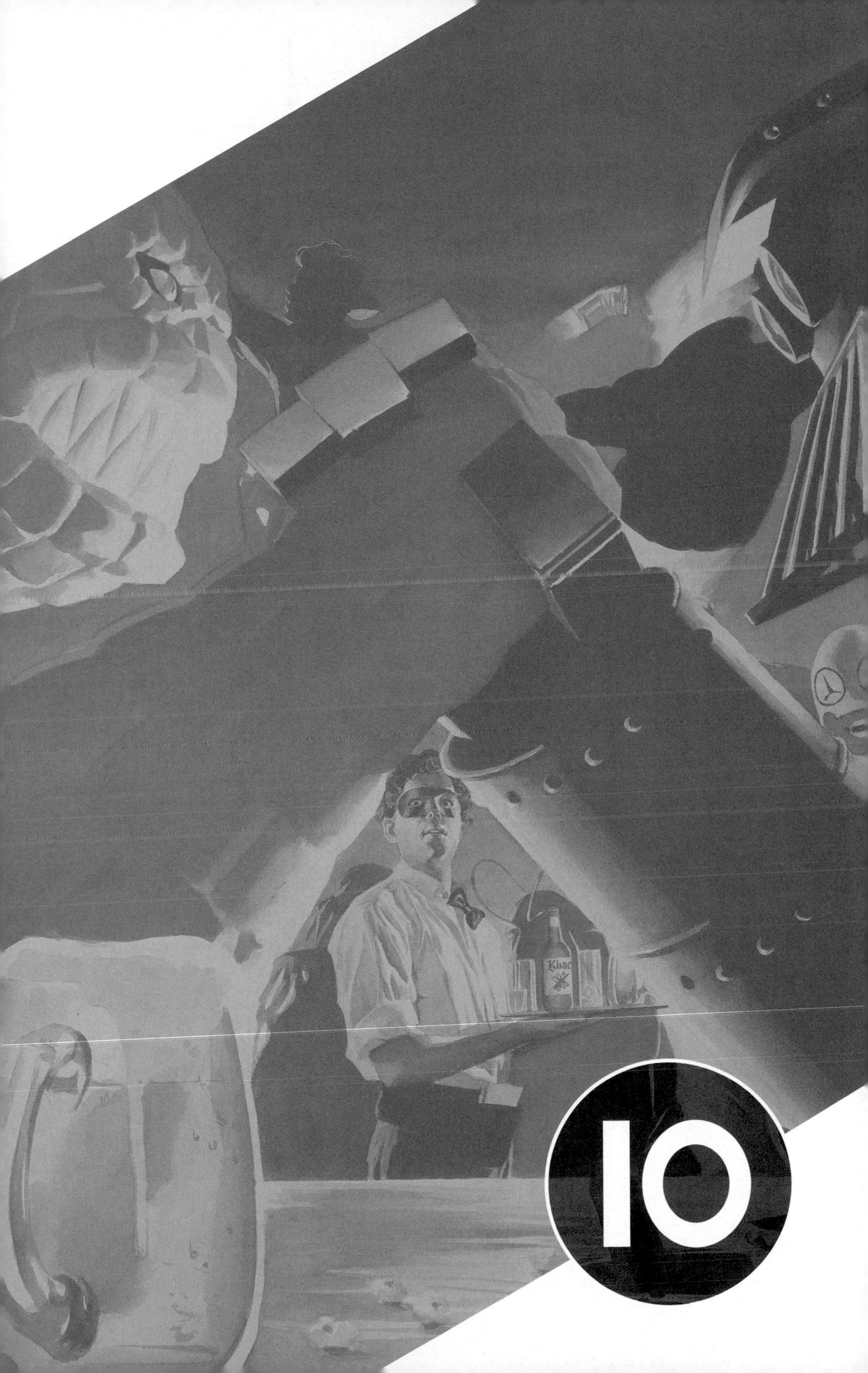

10

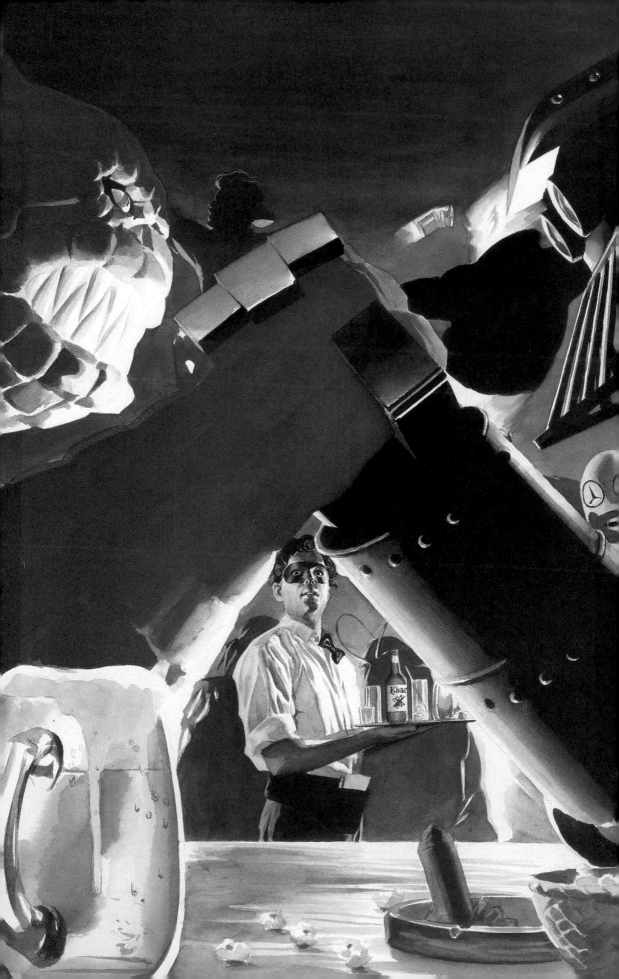

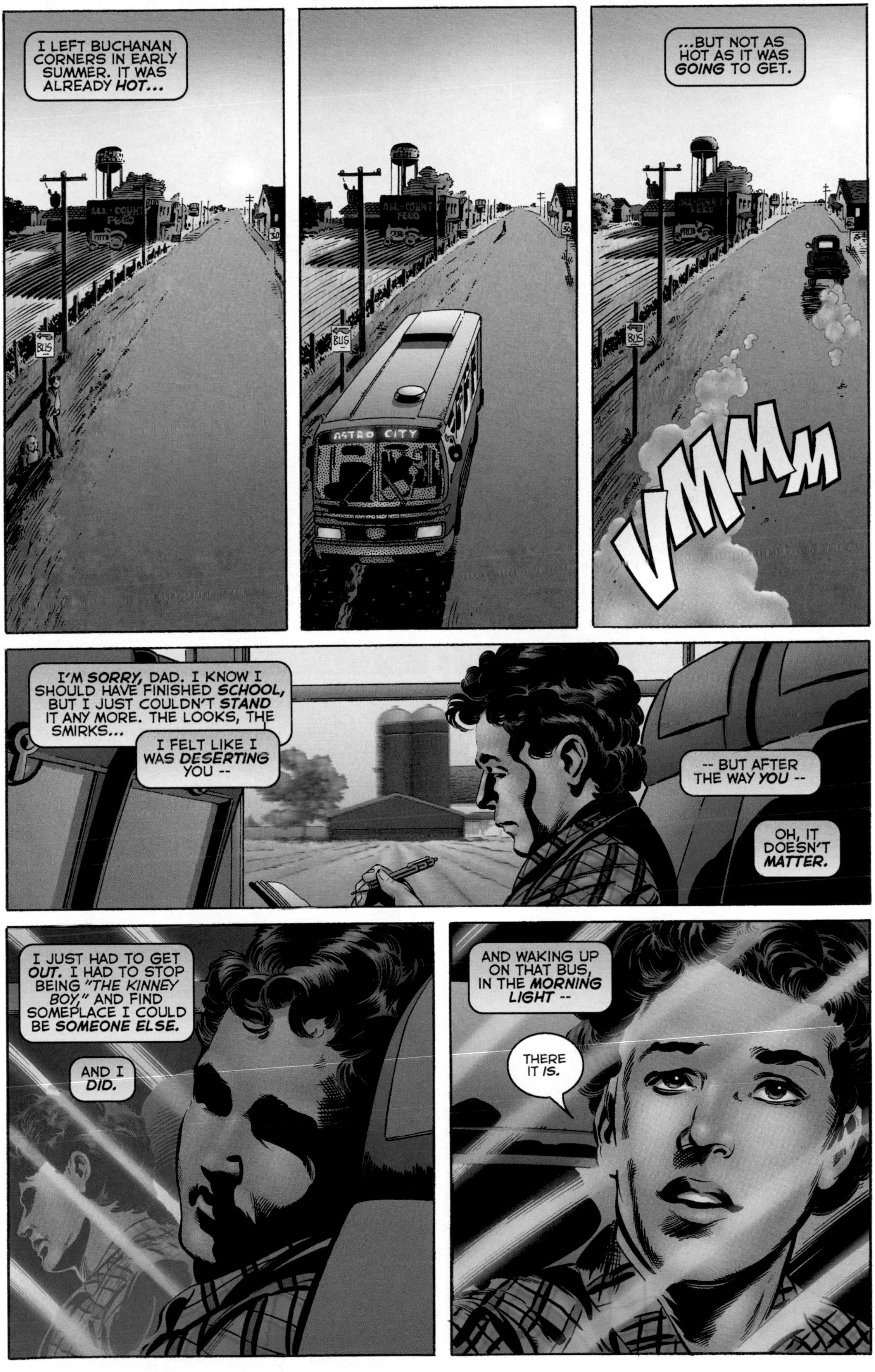

I LEFT BUCHANAN CORNERS IN EARLY SUMMER. IT WAS ALREADY HOT...
ASTRO CITY
...BUT NOT AS HOT AS IT WAS GOING TO GET.
VMMMM
I'M SORRY, DAD. I KNOW I SHOULD HAVE FINISHED SCHOOL, BUT I JUST COULDN'T STAND IT ANY MORE. THE LOOKS, THE SMIRKS...
I FELT LIKE I WAS DESERTING YOU --
-- BUT AFTER THE WAY YOU --
OH, IT DOESN'T MATTER.
I JUST HAD TO GET OUT. I HAD TO STOP BEING "THE KINNEY BOY," AND FIND SOMEPLACE I COULD BE SOMEONE ELSE.
AND I DID.
AND WAKING UP ON THAT BUS, IN THE MORNING LIGHT --
THERE IT IS.

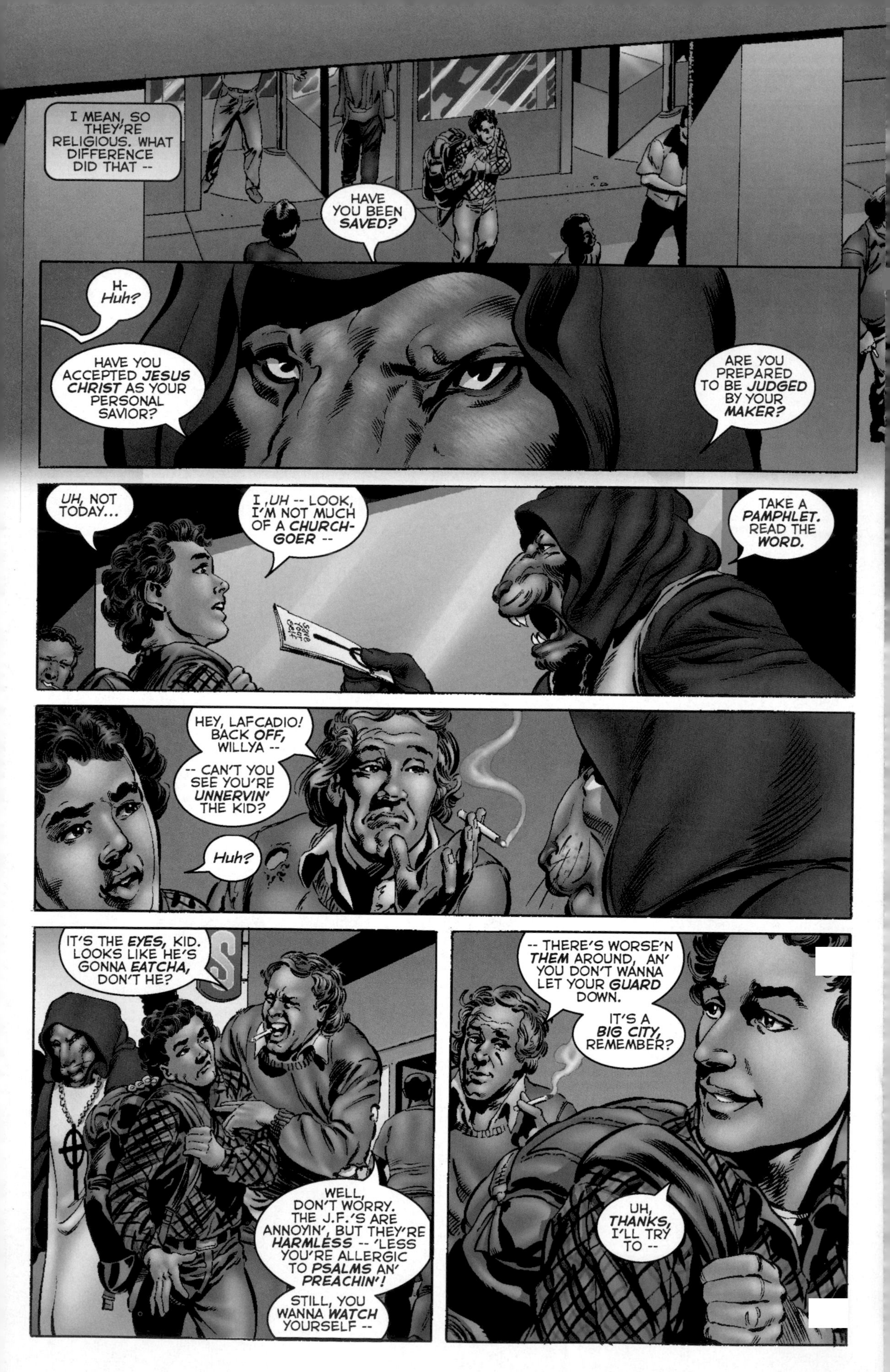
I MEAN, SO THEY'RE RELIGIOUS. WHAT DIFFERENCE DID THAT --
HAVE YOU BEEN SAVED?
H- Huh?
HAVE YOU ACCEPTED JESUS CHRIST AS YOUR PERSONAL SAVIOR?
ARE YOU PREPARED TO BE JUDGED BY YOUR MAKER?
UH, NOT TODAY...
I, UH -- LOOK, I'M NOT MUCH OF A CHURCH-GOER --
TAKE A PAMPHLET. READ THE WORD.
Save Your Self
HEY, LAFCADIO! BACK OFF, WILLYA --
-- CAN'T YOU SEE YOU'RE UNNERVIN' THE KID?
Huh?
IT'S THE EYES, KID. LOOKS LIKE HE'S GONNA EATCHA, DON'T HE?
WELL, DON'T WORRY. THE J.F.'S ARE ANNOYIN', BUT THEY'RE HARMLESS -- 'LESS YOU'RE ALLERGIC TO PSALMS AN' PREACHIN'!
STILL, YOU WANNA WATCH YOURSELF --
-- THERE'S WORSE'N THEM AROUND, AN' YOU DON'T WANNA LET YOUR GUARD DOWN.
IT'S A BIG CITY, REMEMBER?
UH, THANKS, I'LL TRY TO --

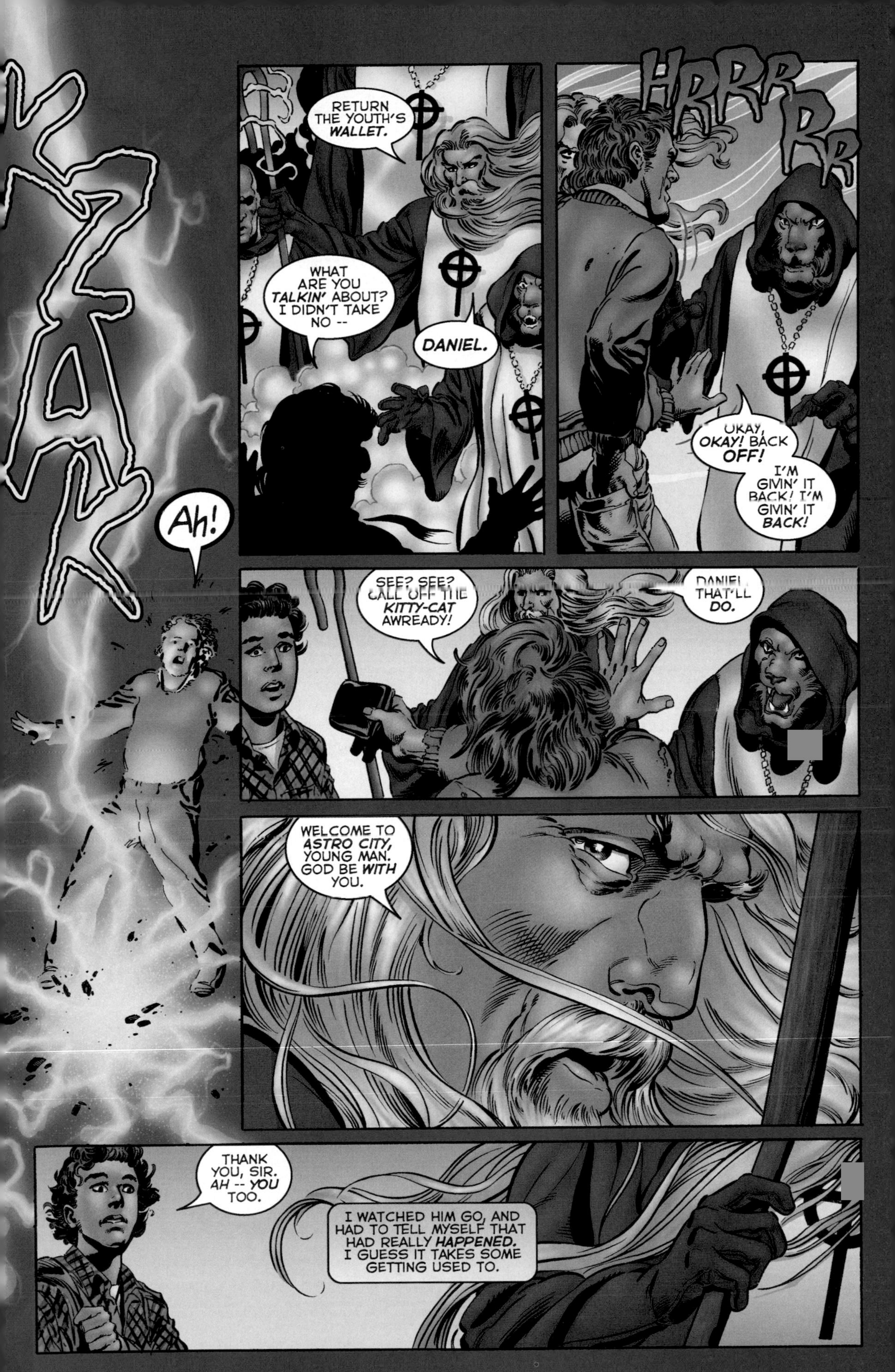
KZZAK
Ah!
RETURN THE YOUTH'S WALLET.
WHAT ARE YOU TALKIN' ABOUT? I DIDN'T TAKE NO --
DANIEL.
HRRRRRR
OKAY, OKAY! BACK OFF!
I'M GIVIN' IT BACK! I'M GIVIN' IT BACK!
SEE? SEE? CALL OFF THE KITTY-CAT AWREADY!
DANIEL. THAT'LL DO.
WELCOME TO ASTRO CITY, YOUNG MAN. GOD BE WITH YOU.
THANK YOU, SIR. AH -- YOU TOO.
I WATCHED HIM GO, AND HAD TO TELL MYSELF THAT HAD REALLY HAPPENED. I GUESS IT TAKES SOME GETTING USED TO.

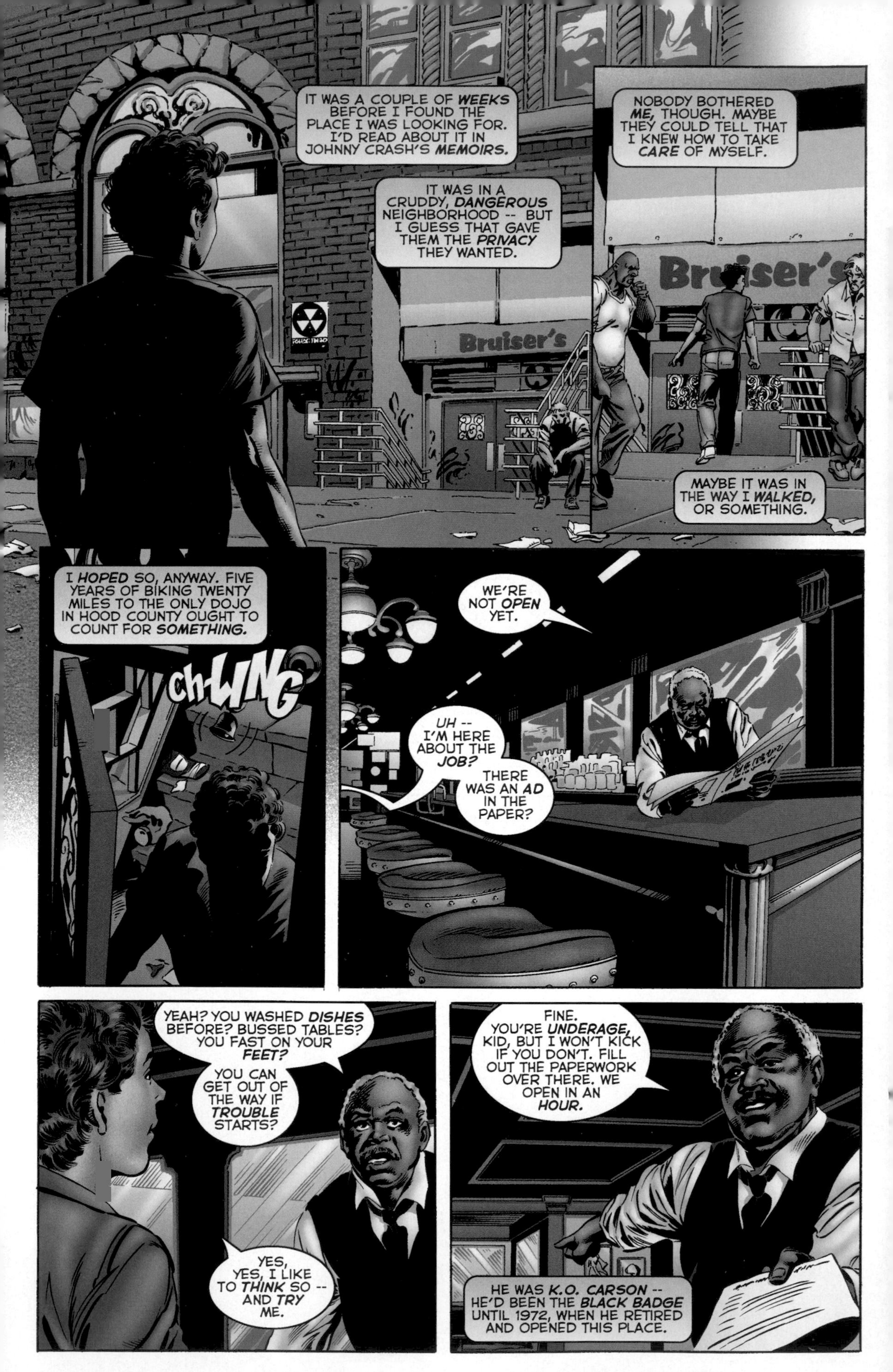
IT WAS A COUPLE OF WEEKS BEFORE I FOUND THE PLACE I WAS LOOKING FOR. I'D READ ABOUT IT IN JOHNNY CRASH'S MEMOIRS.
IT WAS IN A CRUDDY, DANGEROUS NEIGHBORHOOD -- BUT I GUESS THAT GAVE THEM THE PRIVACY THEY WANTED.
Bruiser's
NOBODY BOTHERED ME, THOUGH. MAYBE THEY COULD TELL THAT I KNEW HOW TO TAKE CARE OF MYSELF.
Bruiser's
MAYBE IT WAS IN THE WAY I WALKED, OR SOMETHING.
I HOPED SO, ANYWAY. FIVE YEARS OF BIKING TWENTY MILES TO THE ONLY DOJO IN HOOD COUNTY OUGHT TO COUNT FOR SOMETHING.
ch-LING
WE'RE NOT OPEN YET.
UH -- I'M HERE ABOUT THE JOB?
THERE WAS AN AD IN THE PAPER?
YEAH? YOU WASHED DISHES BEFORE? BUSSED TABLES? YOU FAST ON YOUR FEET?
YOU CAN GET OUT OF THE WAY IF TROUBLE STARTS?
YES, YES, I LIKE TO THINK SO -- AND TRY ME.
FINE. YOU'RE UNDERAGE, KID, BUT I WON'T KICK IF YOU DON'T. FILL OUT THE PAPERWORK OVER THERE. WE OPEN IN AN HOUR.
HE WAS K.O. CARSON -- HE'D BEEN THE BLACK BADGE UNTIL 1972, WHEN HE RETIRED AND OPENED THIS PLACE.

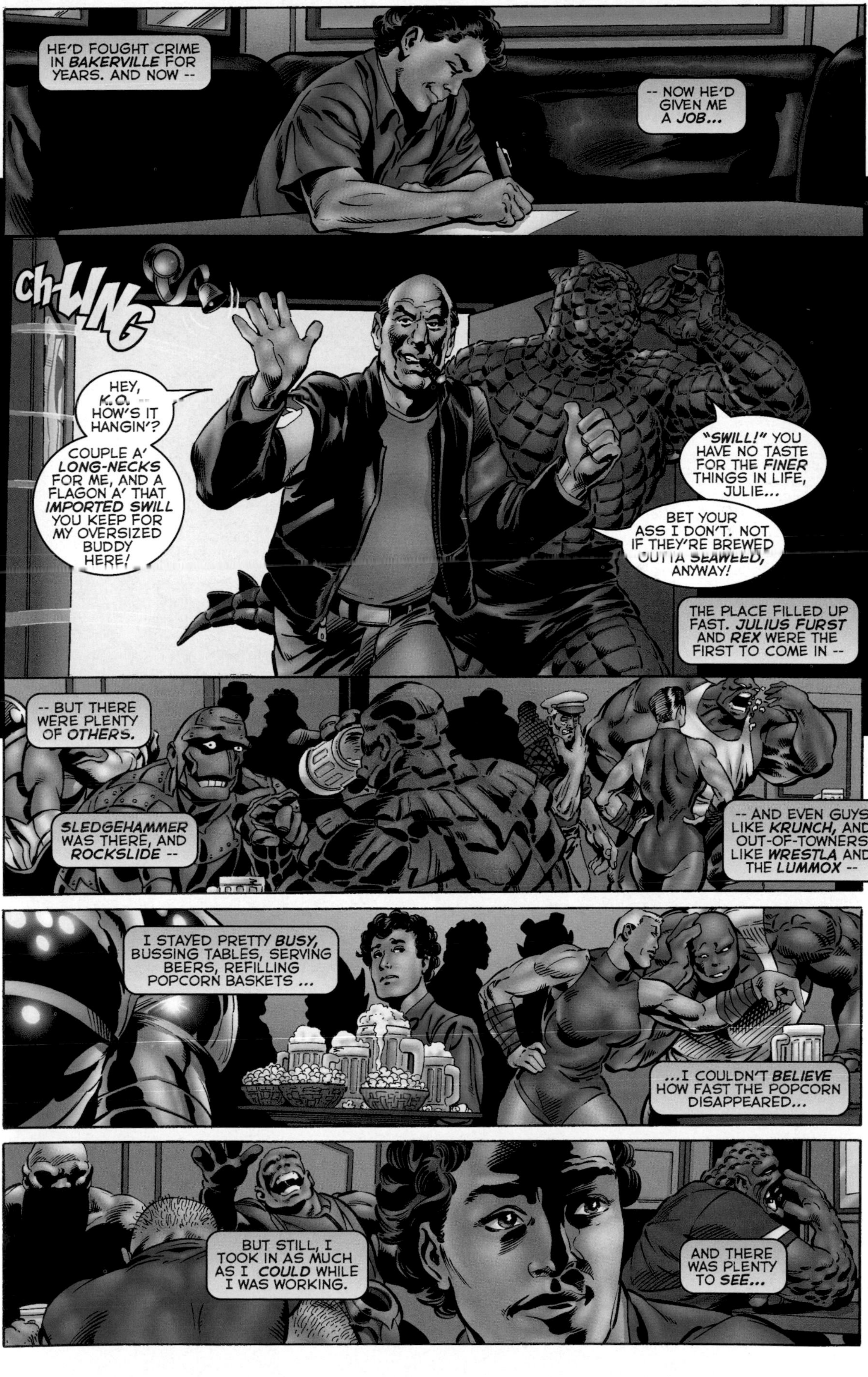
HE'D FOUGHT CRIME IN BAKERVILLE FOR YEARS. AND NOW --
-- NOW HE'D GIVEN ME A JOB...
CH-LING
HEY, K.O. -- HOW'S IT HANGIN'?
COUPLE A' LONG-NECKS FOR ME, AND A FLAGON A' THAT IMPORTED SWILL YOU KEEP FOR MY OVERSIZED BUDDY HERE!
"SWILL!" YOU HAVE NO TASTE FOR THE FINER THINGS IN LIFE, JULIE...
BET YOUR ASS I DON'T. NOT IF THEY'RE BREWED OUTTA SEAWEED, ANYWAY!
THE PLACE FILLED UP FAST. JULIUS FURST AND REX WERE THE FIRST TO COME IN --
-- BUT THERE WERE PLENTY OF OTHERS.
SLEDGEHAMMER WAS THERE, AND ROCKSLIDE --
-- AND EVEN GUYS LIKE KRUNCH, AND OUT-OF-TOWNERS LIKE WRESTLA AND THE LUMMOX --
I STAYED PRETTY BUSY, BUSSING TABLES, SERVING BEERS, REFILLING POPCORN BASKETS ...
...I COULDN'T BELIEVE HOW FAST THE POPCORN DISAPPEARED...
BUT STILL, I TOOK IN AS MUCH AS I COULD WHILE I WAS WORKING.
AND THERE WAS PLENTY TO SEE...

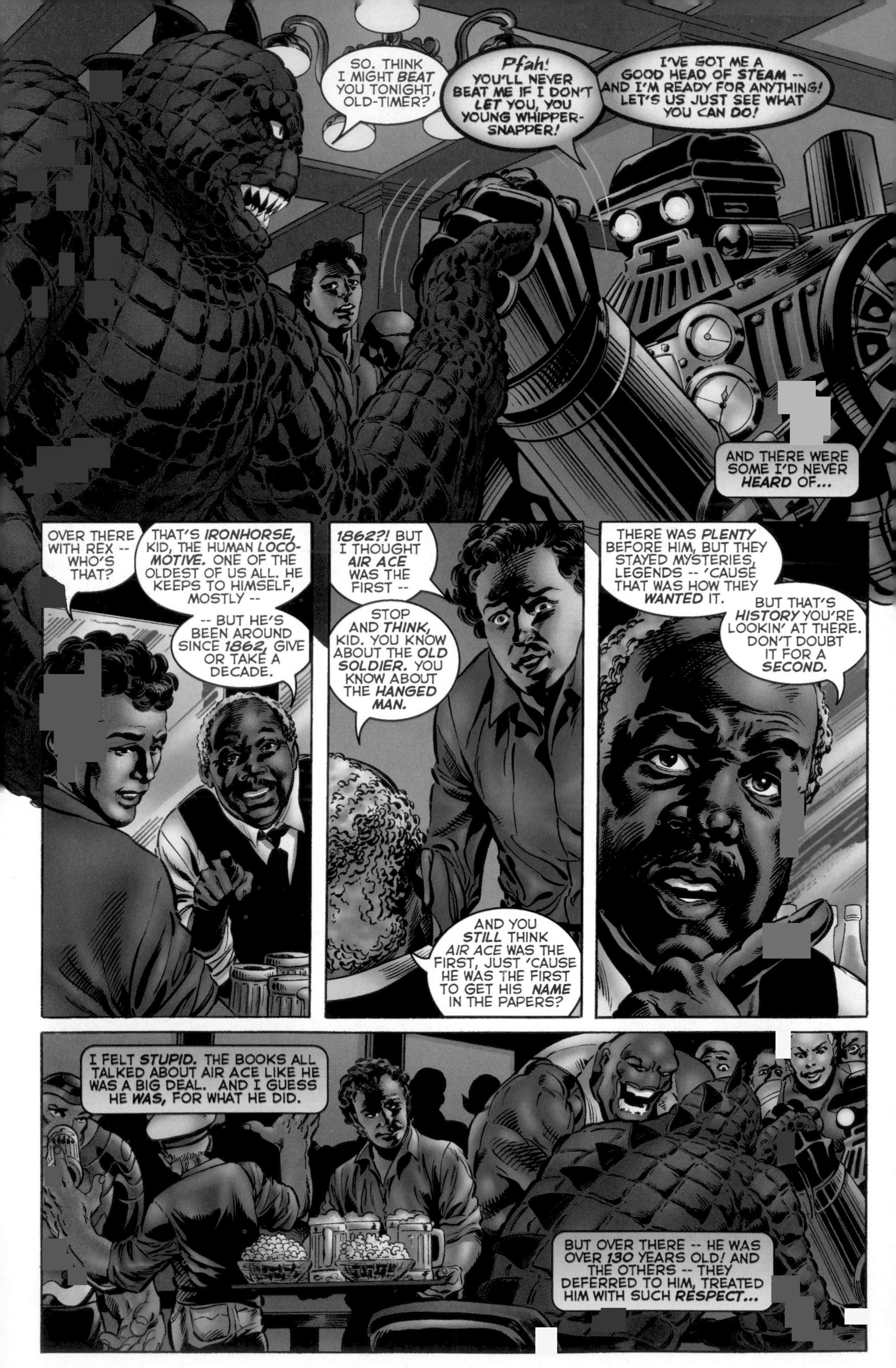
SO. THINK I MIGHT BEAT YOU TONIGHT, OLD-TIMER?
Pfah! YOU'LL NEVER BEAT ME IF I DON'T LET YOU, YOU YOUNG WHIPPER-SNAPPER!
I'VE GOT ME A GOOD HEAD OF STEAM -- AND I'M READY FOR ANYTHING! LET'S US JUST SEE WHAT YOU CAN DO!
AND THERE WERE SOME I'D NEVER HEARD OF...
OVER THERE WITH REX -- WHO'S THAT?
THAT'S IRONHORSE, KID, THE HUMAN LOCO-MOTIVE. ONE OF THE OLDEST OF US ALL. HE KEEPS TO HIMSELF, MOSTLY --
-- BUT HE'S BEEN AROUND SINCE 1862, GIVE OR TAKE A DECADE.
1862?! BUT I THOUGHT AIR ACE WAS THE FIRST --
STOP AND THINK, KID. YOU KNOW ABOUT THE OLD SOLDIER. YOU KNOW ABOUT THE HANGED MAN.
AND YOU STILL THINK AIR ACE WAS THE FIRST, JUST 'CAUSE HE WAS THE FIRST TO GET HIS NAME IN THE PAPERS?
THERE WAS PLENTY BEFORE HIM, BUT THEY STAYED MYSTERIES, LEGENDS -- 'CAUSE THAT WAS HOW THEY WANTED IT.
BUT THAT'S HISTORY YOU'RE LOOKIN' AT THERE. DON'T DOUBT IT FOR A SECOND.
I FELT STUPID. THE BOOKS ALL TALKED ABOUT AIR ACE LIKE HE WAS A BIG DEAL. AND I GUESS HE WAS, FOR WHAT HE DID.
BUT OVER THERE -- HE WAS OVER 130 YEARS OLD! AND THE OTHERS -- THEY DEFERRED TO HIM, TREATED HIM WITH SUCH RESPECT...

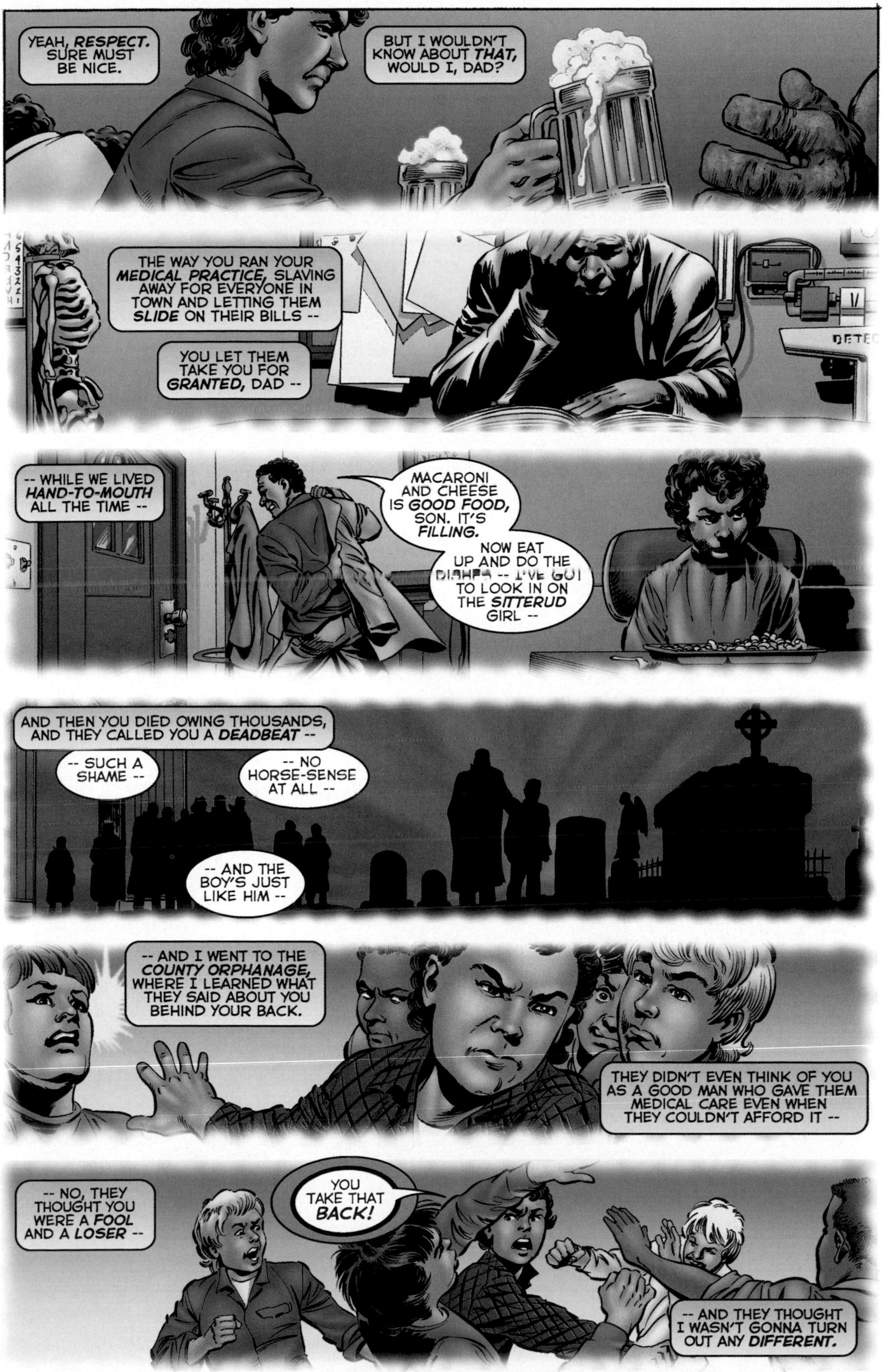
YEAH, RESPECT. SURE MUST BE NICE.
BUT I WOULDN'T KNOW ABOUT THAT, WOULD I, DAD?
THE WAY YOU RAN YOUR MEDICAL PRACTICE, SLAVING AWAY FOR EVERYONE IN TOWN AND LETTING THEM SLIDE ON THEIR BILLS --
YOU LET THEM TAKE YOU FOR GRANTED, DAD --
DETEC
-- WHILE WE LIVED HAND-TO-MOUTH ALL THE TIME --
MACARONI AND CHEESE IS GOOD FOOD, SON. IT'S FILLING.
NOW EAT UP AND DO THE DISHES -- I'VE GOT TO LOOK IN ON THE SITTERUD GIRL --
AND THEN YOU DIED OWING THOUSANDS, AND THEY CALLED YOU A DEADBEAT --
-- SUCH A SHAME --
-- NO HORSE-SENSE AT ALL --
-- AND THE BOY'S JUST LIKE HIM --
-- AND I WENT TO THE COUNTY ORPHANAGE, WHERE I LEARNED WHAT THEY SAID ABOUT YOU BEHIND YOUR BACK.
THEY DIDN'T EVEN THINK OF YOU AS A GOOD MAN WHO GAVE THEM MEDICAL CARE EVEN WHEN THEY COULDN'T AFFORD IT --
-- NO, THEY THOUGHT YOU WERE A FOOL AND A LOSER --
YOU TAKE THAT BACK!
-- AND THEY THOUGHT I WASN'T GONNA TURN OUT ANY DIFFERENT.

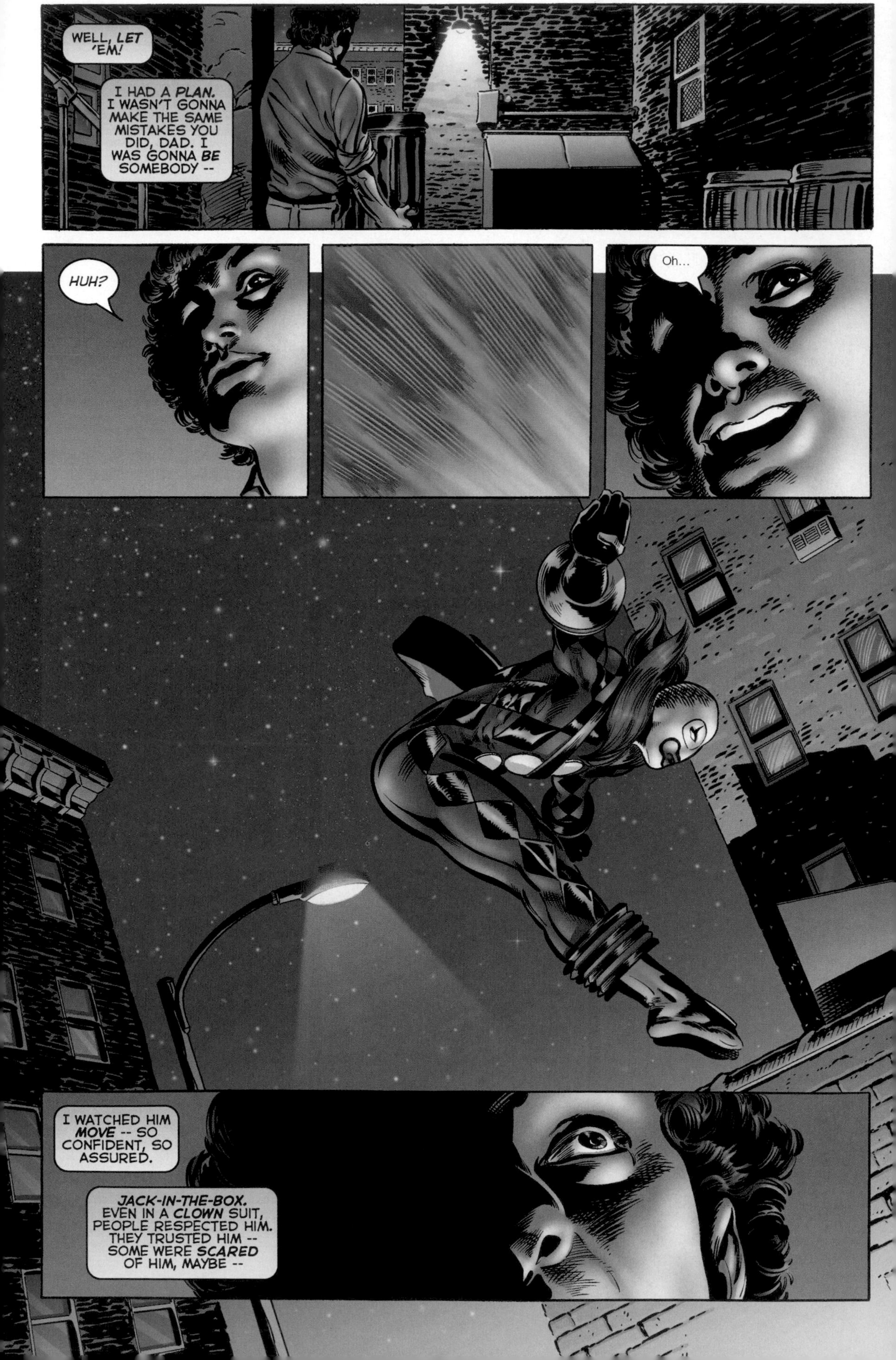
WELL, LET 'EM!
I HAD A PLAN. I WASN'T GONNA MAKE THE SAME MISTAKES YOU DID, DAD. I WAS GONNA BE SOMEBODY --
HUH?
Oh...
I WATCHED HIM MOVE -- SO CONFIDENT, SO ASSURED.
JACK-IN-THE-BOX. EVEN IN A CLOWN SUIT, PEOPLE RESPECTED HIM. THEY TRUSTED HIM -- SOME WERE SCARED OF HIM, MAYBE --

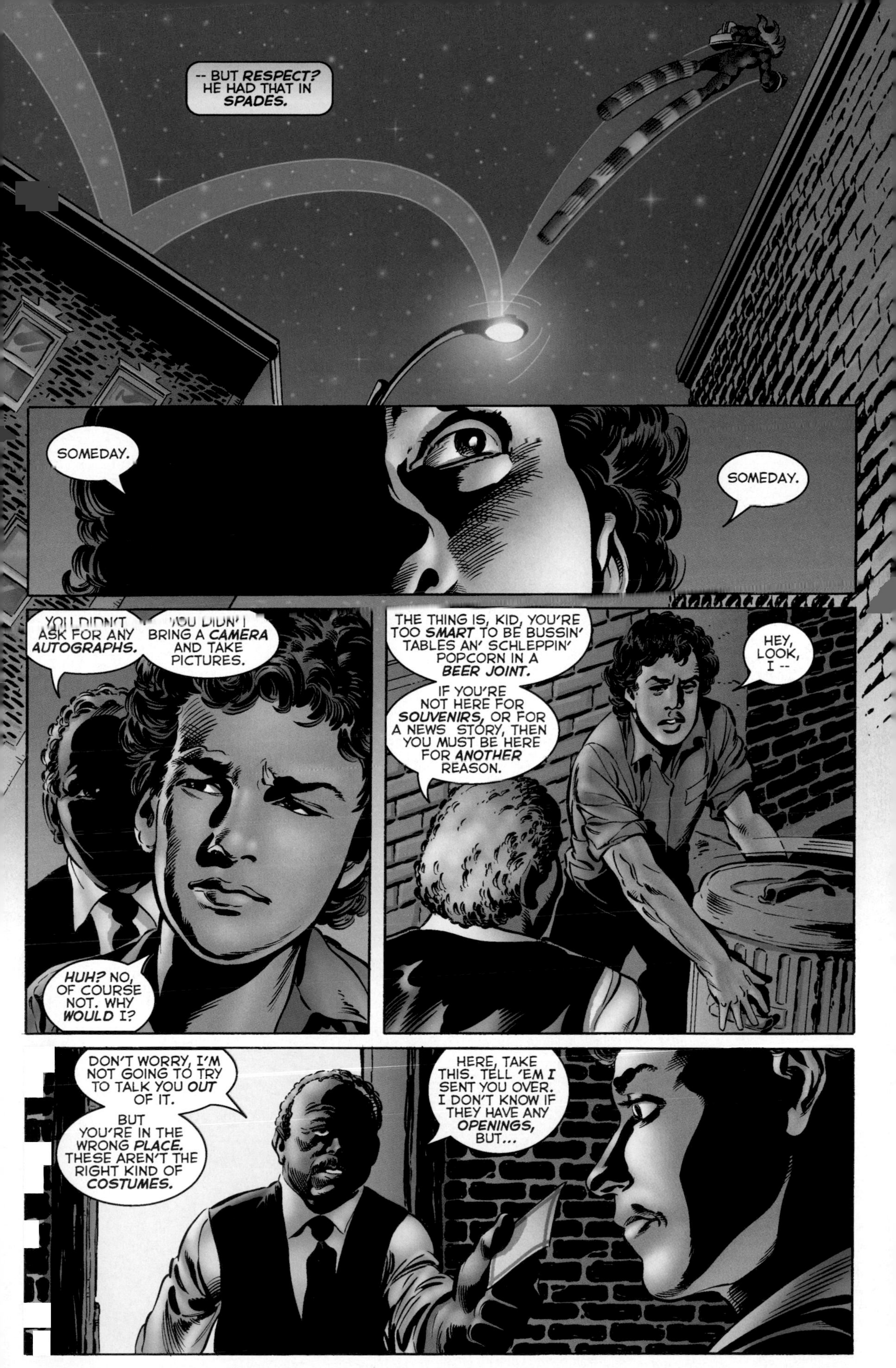
-- BUT RESPECT? HE HAD THAT IN SPADES.
SOMEDAY.
SOMEDAY.
YOU DIDN'T ASK FOR ANY AUTOGRAPHS.
YOU DIDN'T BRING A CAMERA AND TAKE PICTURES.
HUH? NO, OF COURSE NOT. WHY WOULD I?
THE THING IS, KID, YOU'RE TOO SMART TO BE BUSSIN' TABLES AN' SCHLEPPIN' POPCORN IN A BEER JOINT.
IF YOU'RE NOT HERE FOR SOUVENIRS, OR FOR A NEWS STORY, THEN YOU MUST BE HERE FOR ANOTHER REASON.
HEY, LOOK, I --
DON'T WORRY, I'M NOT GOING TO TRY TO TALK YOU OUT OF IT.
BUT YOU'RE IN THE WRONG PLACE. THESE AREN'T THE RIGHT KIND OF COSTUMES.
HERE, TAKE THIS. TELL 'EM I SENT YOU OVER. I DON'T KNOW IF THEY HAVE ANY OPENINGS, BUT...

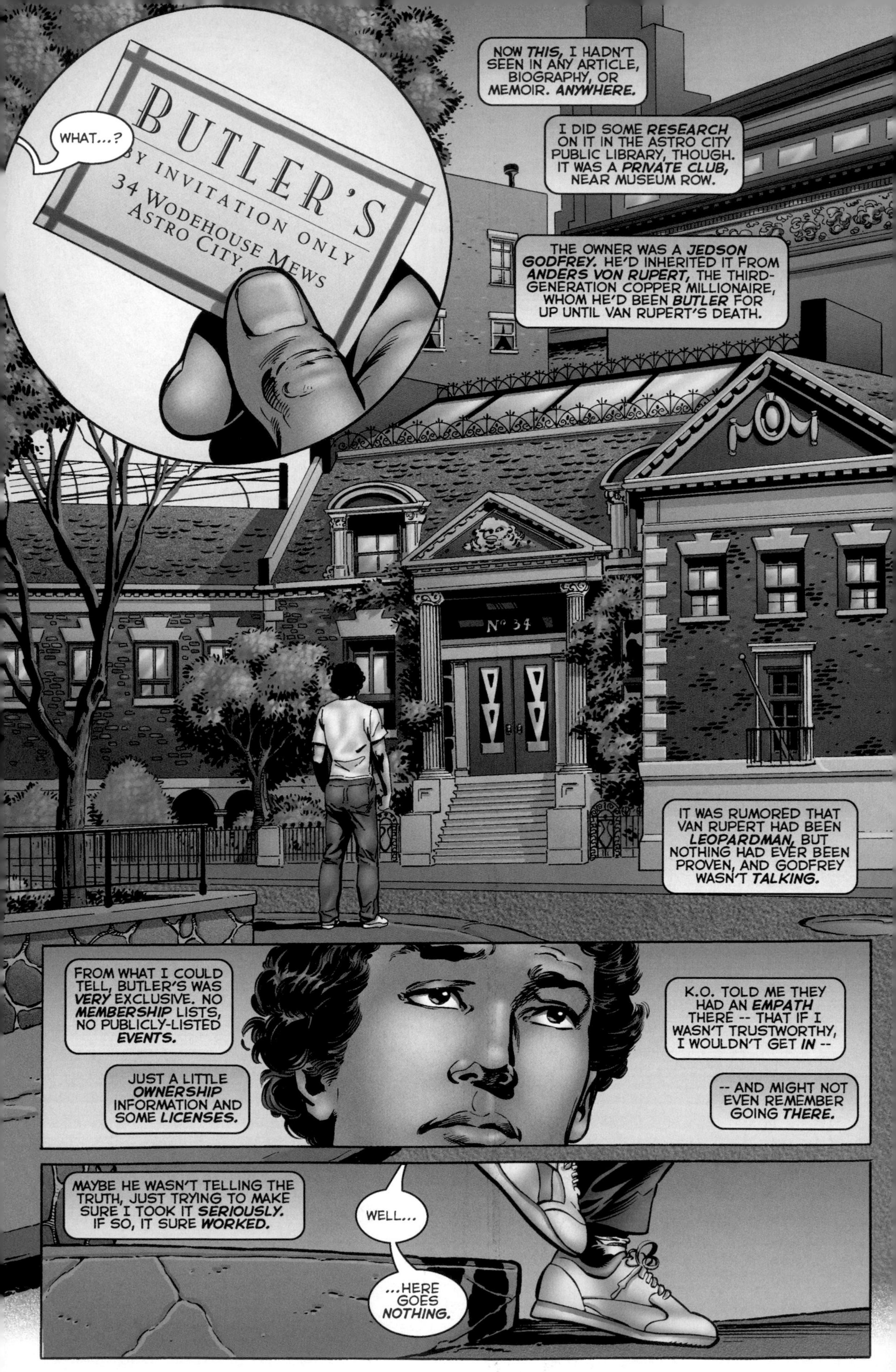
BUTLER'S
BY INVITATION ONLY
34 WODEHOUSE MEWS
ASTRO CITY,
WHAT...?
NOW THIS, I HADN'T SEEN IN ANY ARTICLE, BIOGRAPHY, OR MEMOIR. ANYWHERE.
I DID SOME RESEARCH ON IT IN THE ASTRO CITY PUBLIC LIBRARY, THOUGH. IT WAS A PRIVATE CLUB, NEAR MUSEUM ROW.
THE OWNER WAS A JEDSON GODFREY. HE'D INHERITED IT FROM ANDERS VON RUPERT, THE THIRD-GENERATION COPPER MILLIONAIRE, WHOM HE'D BEEN BUTLER FOR UP UNTIL VAN RUPERT'S DEATH.
Nº 34
IT WAS RUMORED THAT VAN RUPERT HAD BEEN LEOPARDMAN, BUT NOTHING HAD EVER BEEN PROVEN, AND GODFREY WASN'T TALKING.
FROM WHAT I COULD TELL, BUTLER'S WAS VERY EXCLUSIVE. NO MEMBERSHIP LISTS, NO PUBLICLY-LISTED EVENTS.
JUST A LITTLE OWNERSHIP INFORMATION AND SOME LICENSES.
K.O. TOLD ME THEY HAD AN EMPATH THERE -- THAT IF I WASN'T TRUSTWORTHY, I WOULDN'T GET IN --
-- AND MIGHT NOT EVEN REMEMBER GOING THERE.
MAYBE HE WASN'T TELLING THE TRUTH, JUST TRYING TO MAKE SURE I TOOK IT SERIOUSLY. IF SO, IT SURE WORKED.
WELL...
...HERE GOES NOTHING.

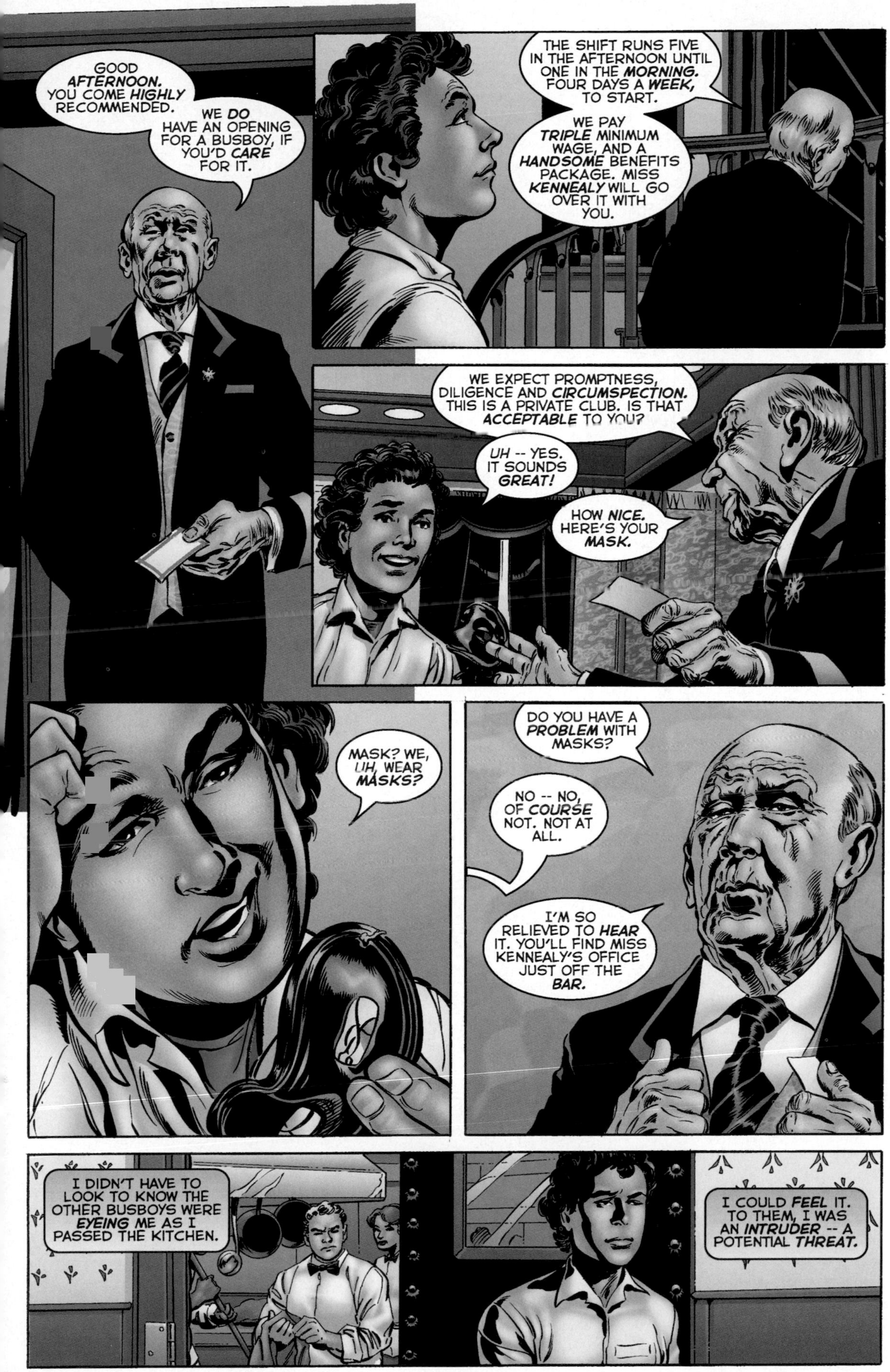
GOOD AFTERNOON. YOU COME HIGHLY RECOMMENDED.
WE DO HAVE AN OPENING FOR A BUSBOY, IF YOU'D CARE FOR IT.
THE SHIFT RUNS FIVE IN THE AFTERNOON UNTIL ONE IN THE MORNING. FOUR DAYS A WEEK, TO START.
WE PAY TRIPLE MINIMUM WAGE, AND A HANDSOME BENEFITS PACKAGE. MISS KENNEALY WILL GO OVER IT WITH YOU.
WE EXPECT PROMPTNESS, DILIGENCE AND CIRCUMSPECTION. THIS IS A PRIVATE CLUB. IS THAT ACCEPTABLE TO YOU?
UH -- YES. IT SOUNDS GREAT!
HOW NICE. HERE'S YOUR MASK.
MASK? WE, UH, WEAR MASKS?
DO YOU HAVE A PROBLEM WITH MASKS?
NO -- NO, OF COURSE NOT. NOT AT ALL.
I'M SO RELIEVED TO HEAR IT. YOU'LL FIND MISS KENNEALY'S OFFICE JUST OFF THE BAR.
I DIDN'T HAVE TO LOOK TO KNOW THE OTHER BUSBOYS WERE EYEING ME AS I PASSED THE KITCHEN.
I COULD FEEL IT. TO THEM, I WAS AN INTRUDER -- A POTENTIAL THREAT.

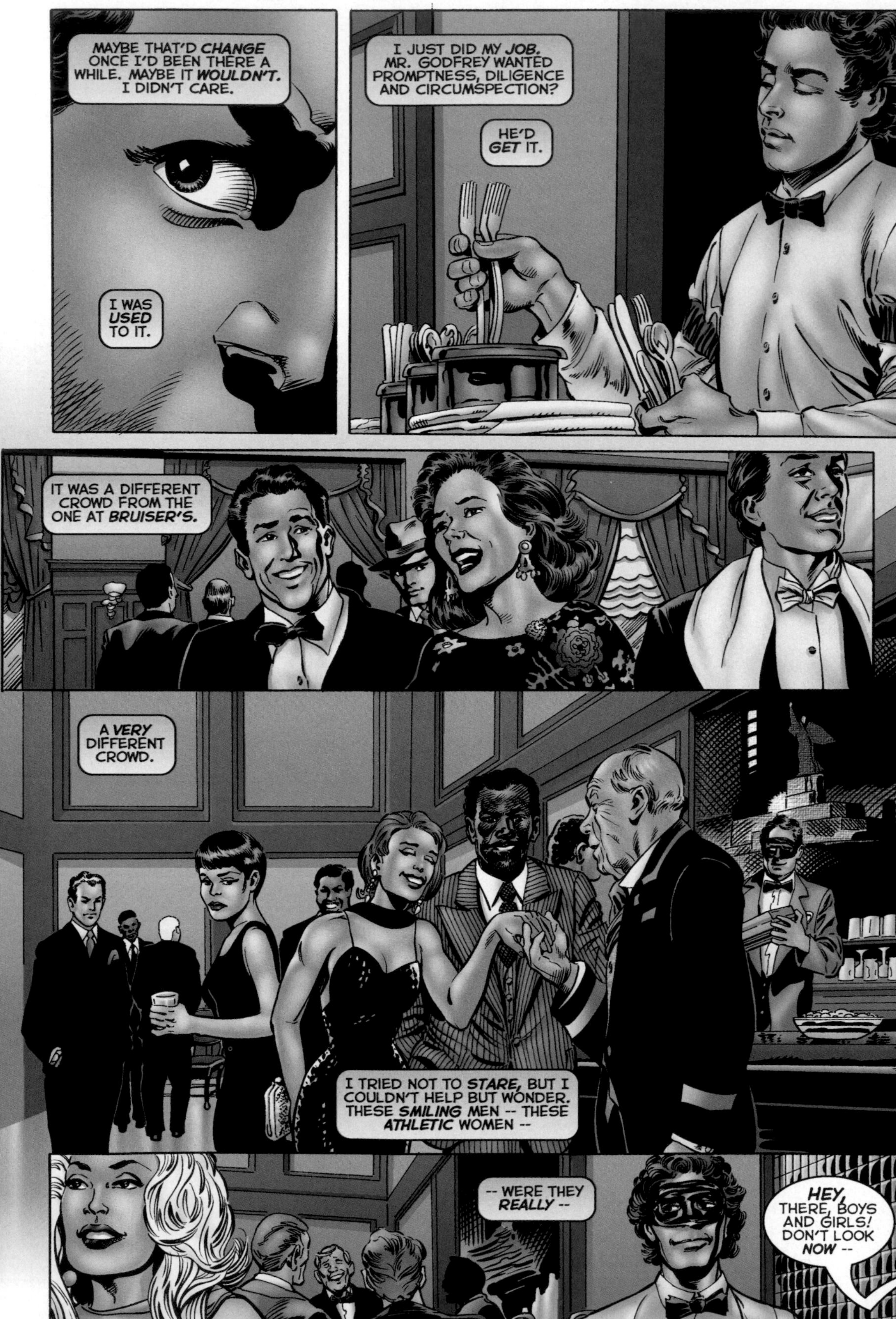
MAYBE THAT'D CHANGE ONCE I'D BEEN THERE A WHILE. MAYBE IT WOULDN'T. I DIDN'T CARE.
I WAS USED TO IT.
I JUST DID MY JOB. MR. GODFREY WANTED PROMPTNESS, DILIGENCE AND CIRCUMSPECTION?
HE'D GET IT.
IT WAS A DIFFERENT CROWD FROM THE ONE AT BRUISER'S.
A VERY DIFFERENT CROWD.
I TRIED NOT TO STARE, BUT I COULDN'T HELP BUT WONDER. THESE SMILING MEN -- THESE ATHLETIC WOMEN --
-- WERE THEY REALLY --
HEY, THERE, BOYS AND GIRLS! DON'T LOOK NOW --

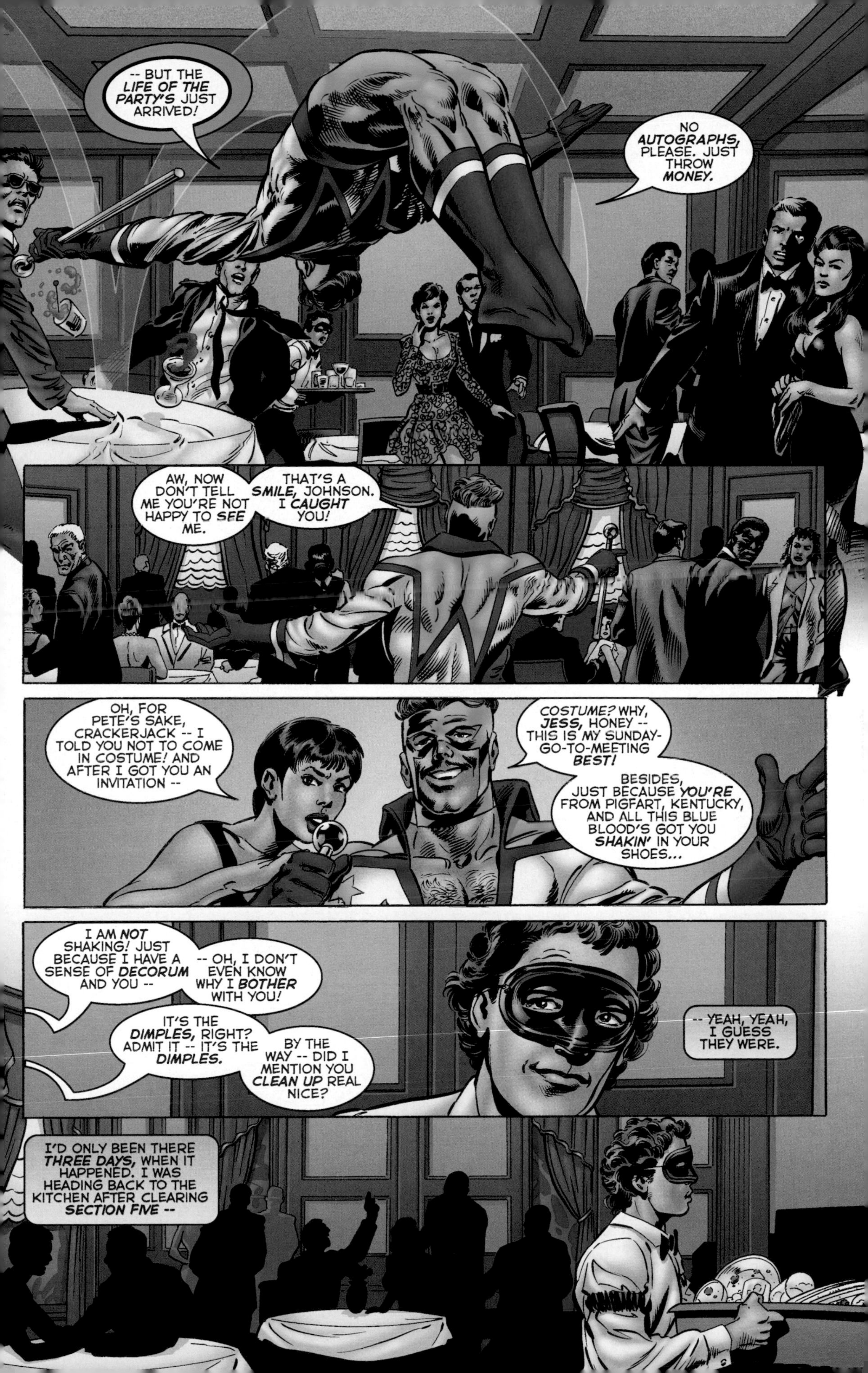

-- BUT THE LIFE OF THE PARTY'S JUST ARRIVED!
NO AUTOGRAPHS, PLEASE. JUST THROW MONEY.
AW, NOW DON'T TELL ME YOU'RE NOT HAPPY TO SEE ME.
THAT'S A SMILE, JOHNSON. I CAUGHT YOU!
OH, FOR PETE'S SAKE, CRACKERJACK -- I TOLD YOU NOT TO COME IN COSTUME! AND AFTER I GOT YOU AN INVITATION --
COSTUME? WHY, JESS, HONEY -- THIS IS MY SUNDAY-GO-TO-MEETING BEST!
BESIDES, JUST BECAUSE YOU'RE FROM PIGFART, KENTUCKY, AND ALL THIS BLUE BLOOD'S GOT YOU SHAKIN' IN YOUR SHOES...
I AM NOT SHAKING! JUST BECAUSE I HAVE A SENSE OF DECORUM AND YOU --
-- OH, I DON'T EVEN KNOW WHY I BOTHER WITH YOU!
IT'S THE DIMPLES, RIGHT? ADMIT IT -- IT'S THE DIMPLES.
BY THE WAY -- DID I MENTION YOU CLEAN UP REAL NICE?
-- YEAH, YEAH, I GUESS THEY WERE.
I'D ONLY BEEN THERE THREE DAYS, WHEN IT HAPPENED. I WAS HEADING BACK TO THE KITCHEN AFTER CLEARING SECTION FIVE --

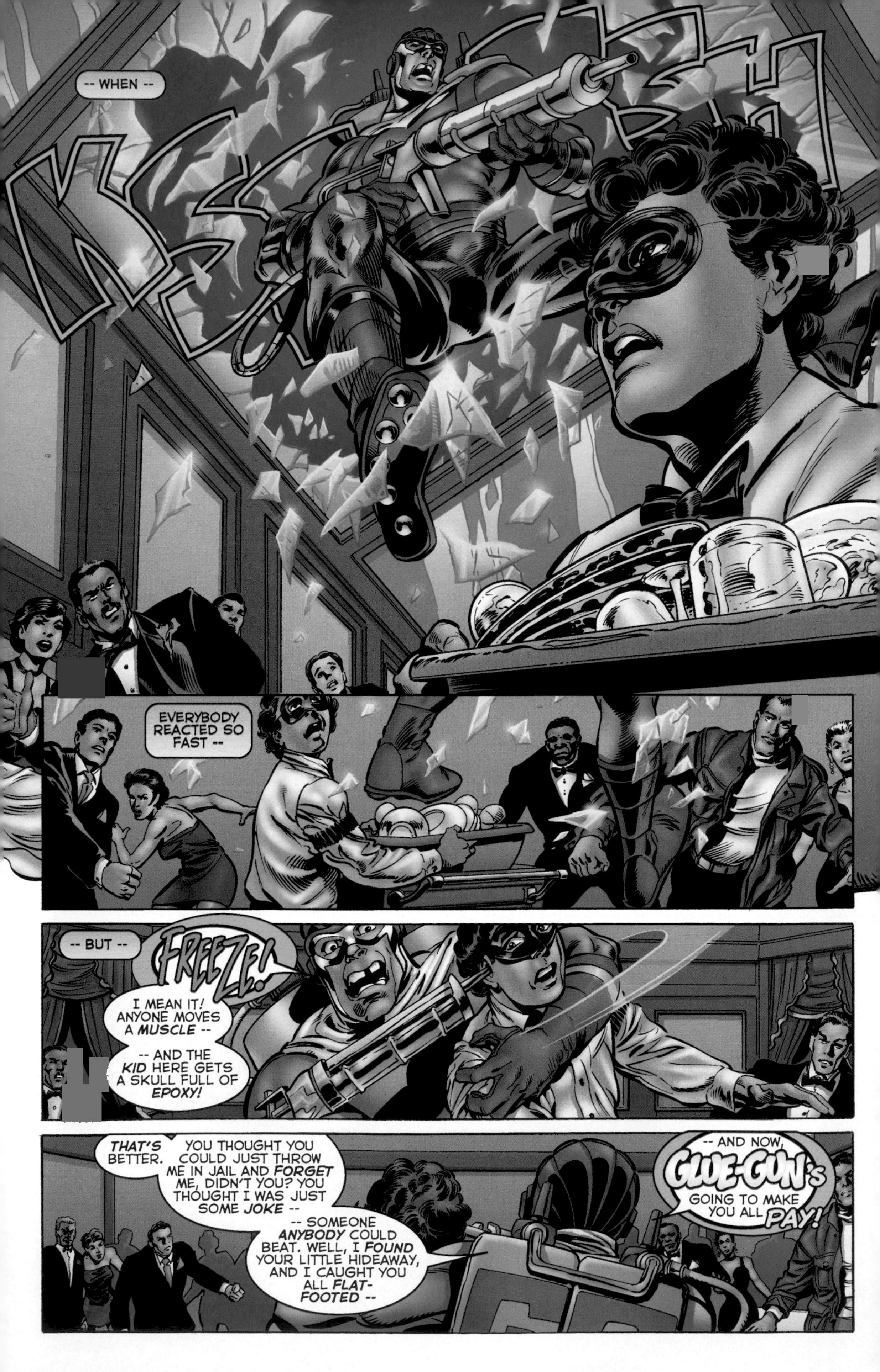
-- WHEN --
EVERYBODY REACTED SO FAST --
-- BUT --
FREEZE!
I MEAN IT! ANYONE MOVES A MUSCLE --
-- AND THE KID HERE GETS A SKULL FULL OF EPOXY!
THAT'S BETTER.
YOU THOUGHT YOU COULD JUST THROW ME IN JAIL AND FORGET ME, DIDN'T YOU? YOU THOUGHT I WAS JUST SOME JOKE --
-- SOMEONE ANYBODY COULD BEAT. WELL, I FOUND YOUR LITTLE HIDEAWAY, AND I CAUGHT YOU ALL FLAT-FOOTED --
-- AND NOW, GLUE-GUN'S GOING TO MAKE YOU ALL PAY!

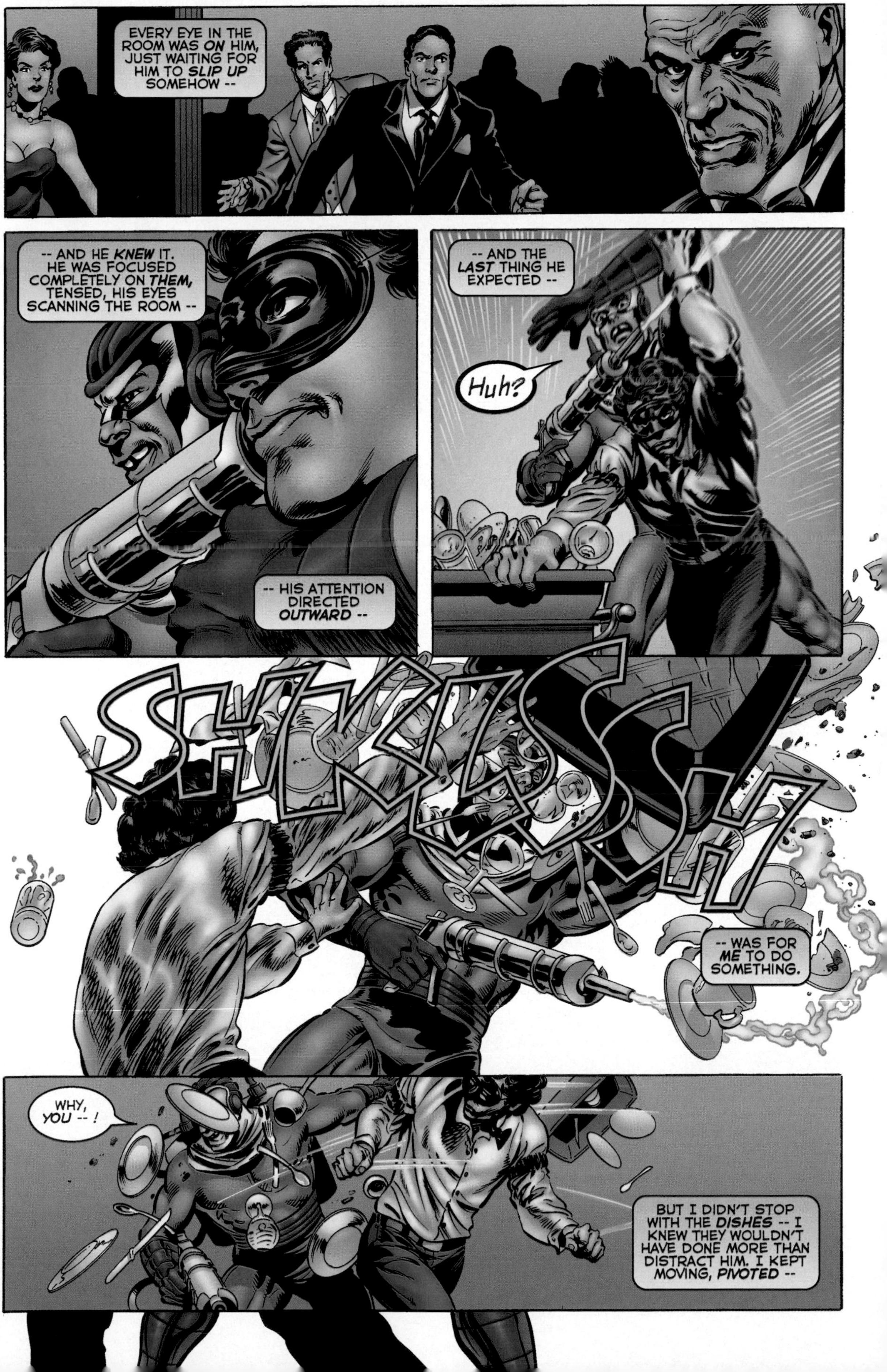

EVERY EYE IN THE ROOM WAS ON HIM, JUST WAITING FOR HIM TO SLIP UP SOMEHOW --
-- AND HE KNEW IT. HE WAS FOCUSED COMPLETELY ON THEM, TENSED, HIS EYES SCANNING THE ROOM --
-- HIS ATTENTION DIRECTED OUTWARD --
-- AND THE LAST THING HE EXPECTED --
Huh?
SHKRSSH
-- WAS FOR ME TO DO SOMETHING.
WHY, YOU -- !
BUT I DIDN'T STOP WITH THE DISHES -- I KNEW THEY WOULDN'T HAVE DONE MORE THAN DISTRACT HIM. I KEPT MOVING, PIVOTED --

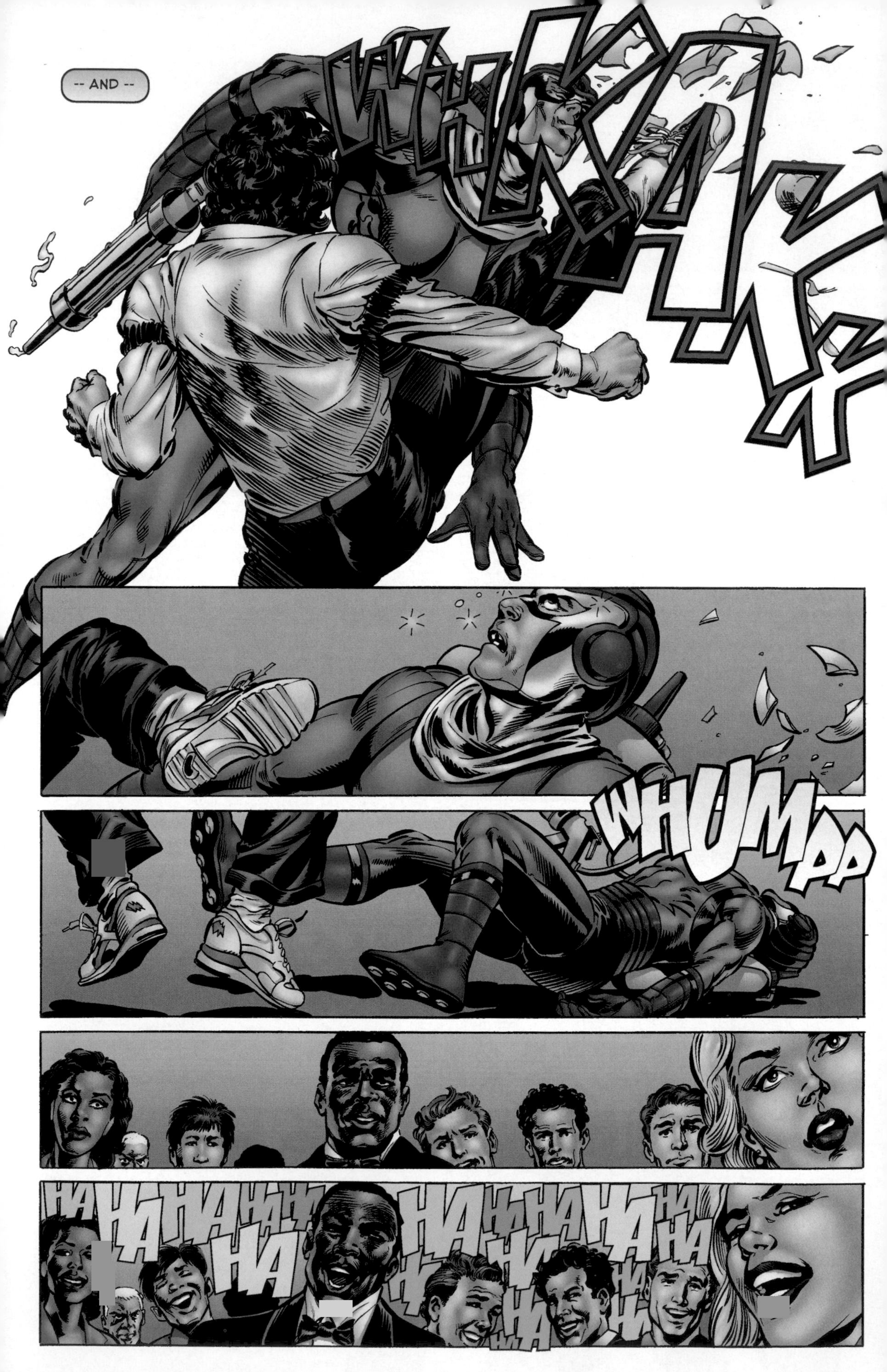

-- AND --
WHUMPP
HA HA HA HA HA HA HA HA HA HA

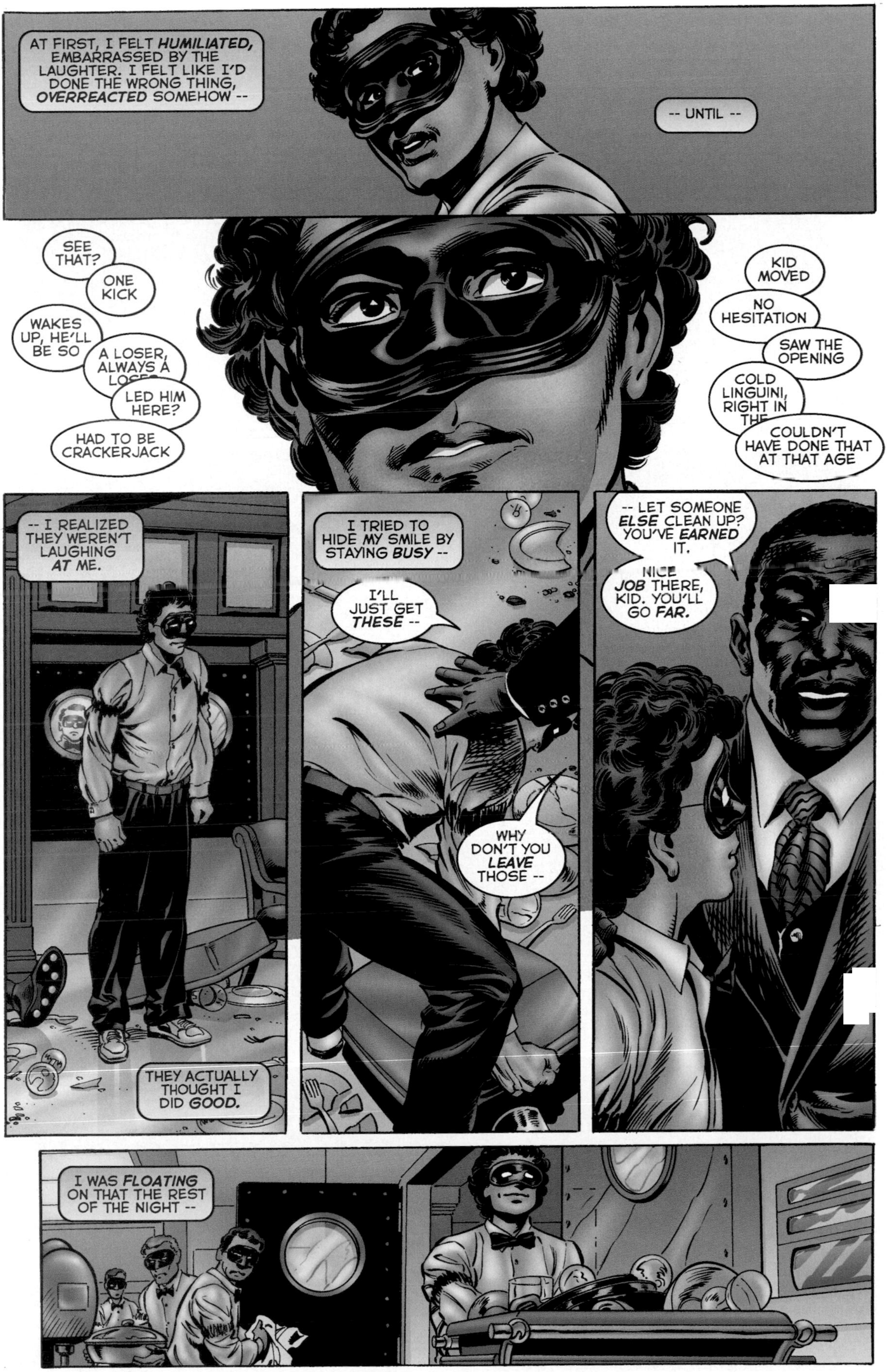
AT FIRST, I FELT HUMILIATED, EMBARRASSED BY THE LAUGHTER. I FELT LIKE I'D DONE THE WRONG THING, OVERREACTED SOMEHOW --
-- UNTIL --
SEE THAT?
ONE KICK
WAKES UP, HE'LL BE SO
A LOSER, ALWAYS A
LED HIM HERE?
HAD TO BE CRACKERJACK
KID MOVED
NO HESITATION
SAW THE OPENING
COLD LINGUINI, RIGHT IN THE
COULDN'T HAVE DONE THAT AT THAT AGE
-- I REALIZED THEY WEREN'T LAUGHING AT ME.
THEY ACTUALLY THOUGHT I DID GOOD.
I TRIED TO HIDE MY SMILE BY STAYING BUSY --
I'LL JUST GET THESE --
WHY DON'T YOU LEAVE THOSE --
-- LET SOMEONE ELSE CLEAN UP? YOU'VE EARNED IT.
NICE JOB THERE, KID. YOU'LL GO FAR.
I WAS FLOATING ON THAT THE REST OF THE NIGHT --

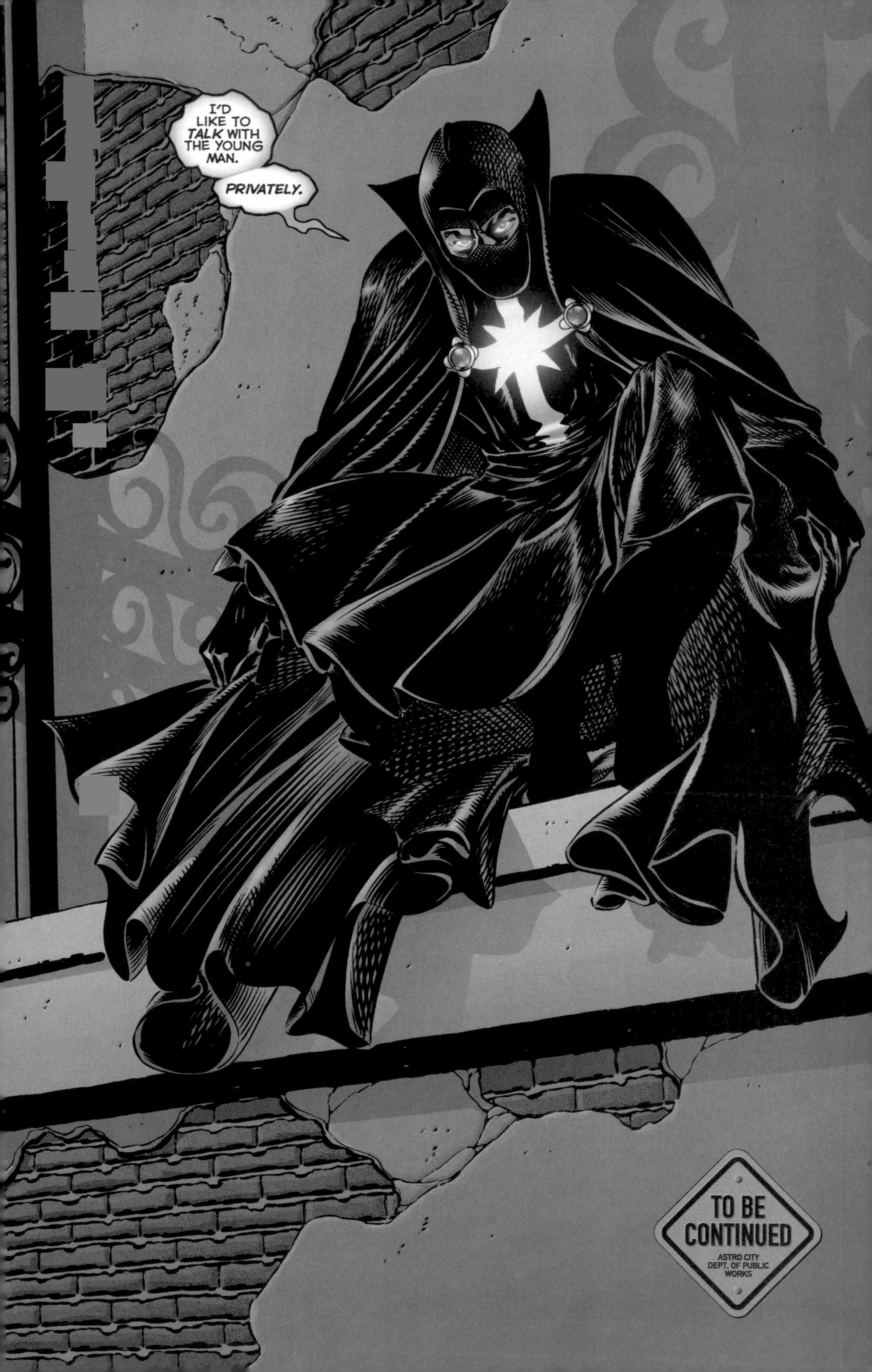
I'D LIKE TO TALK WITH THE YOUNG MAN.
PRIVATELY.
TO BE CONTINUED
ASTRO CITY DEPT. OF PUBLIC WORKS

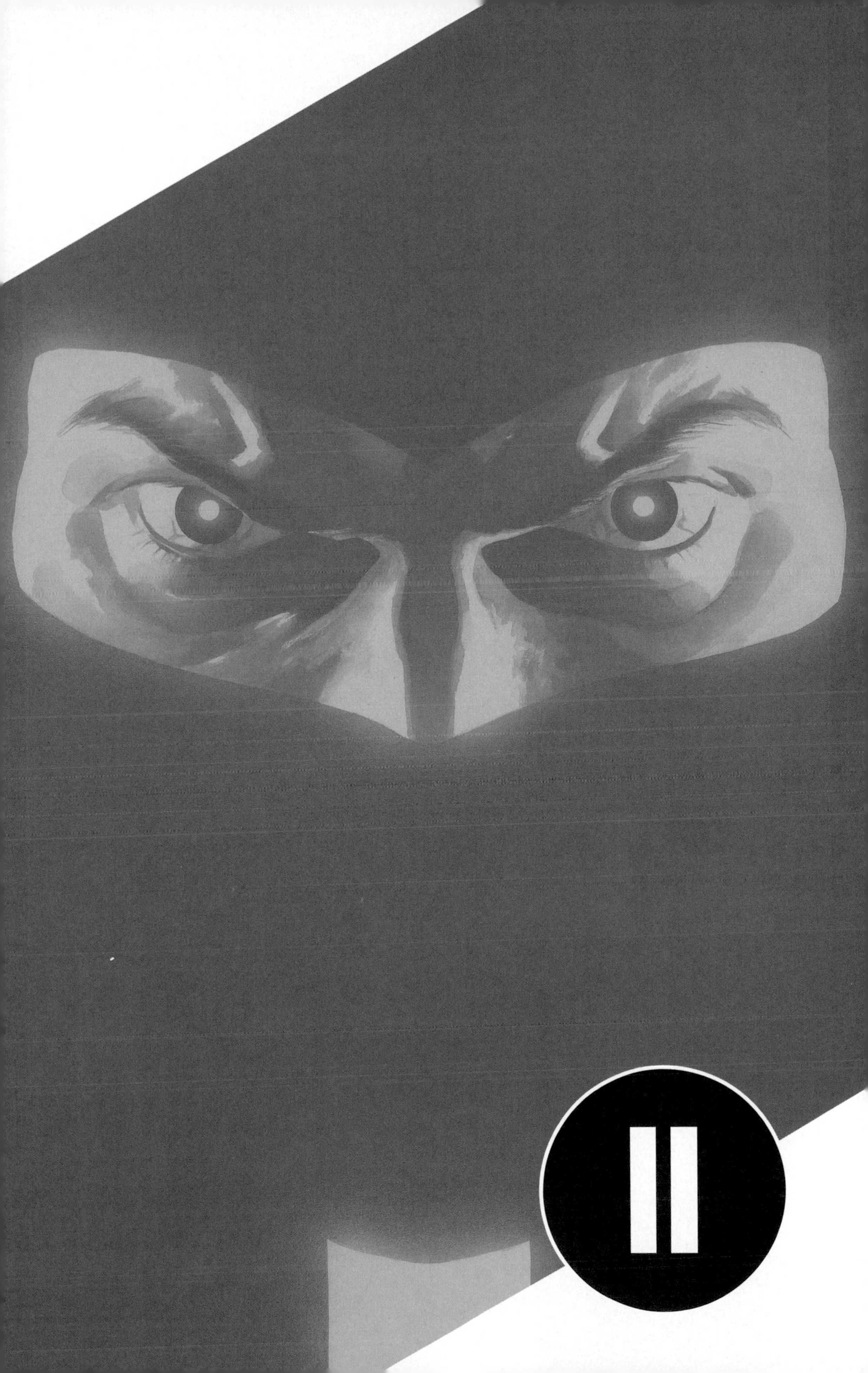
II

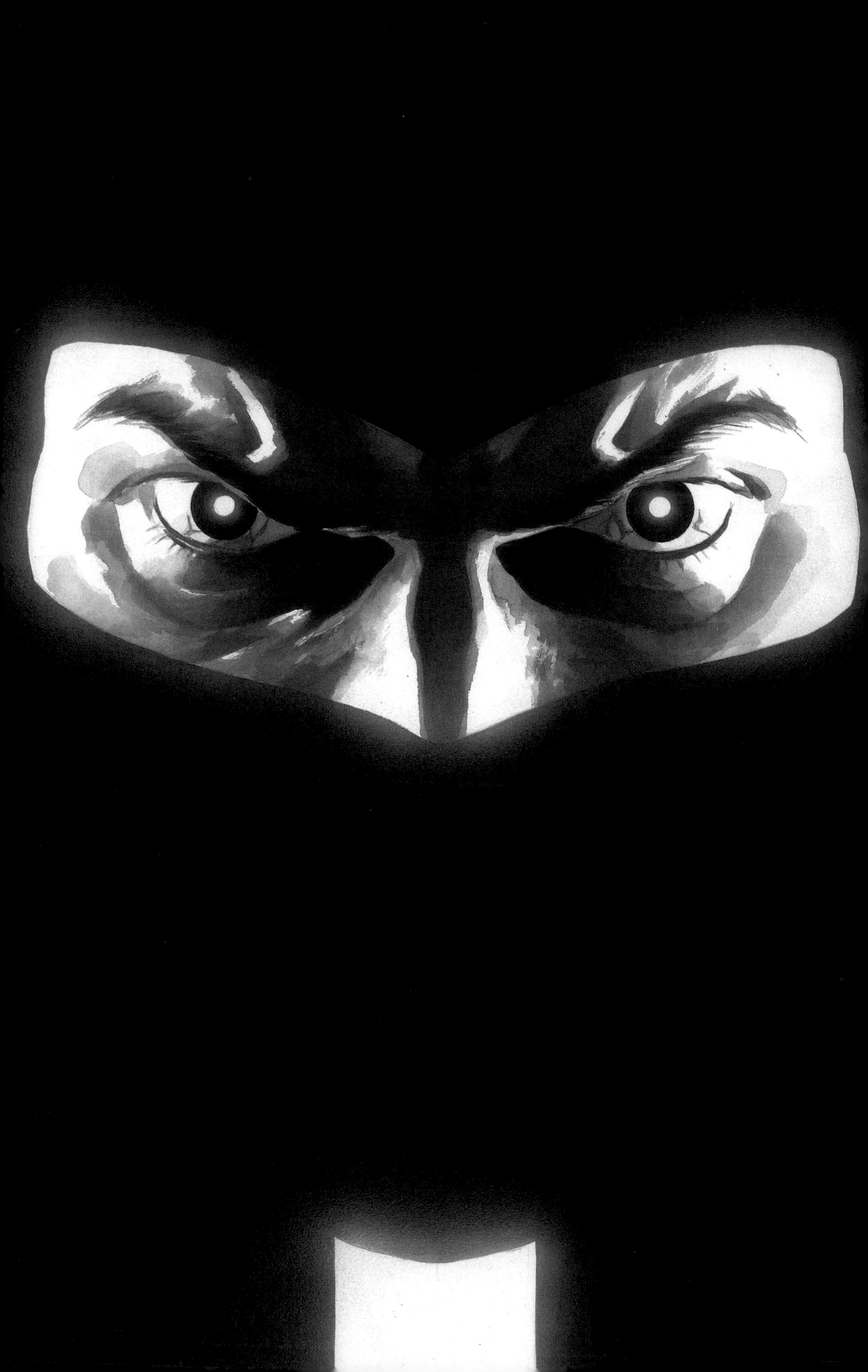

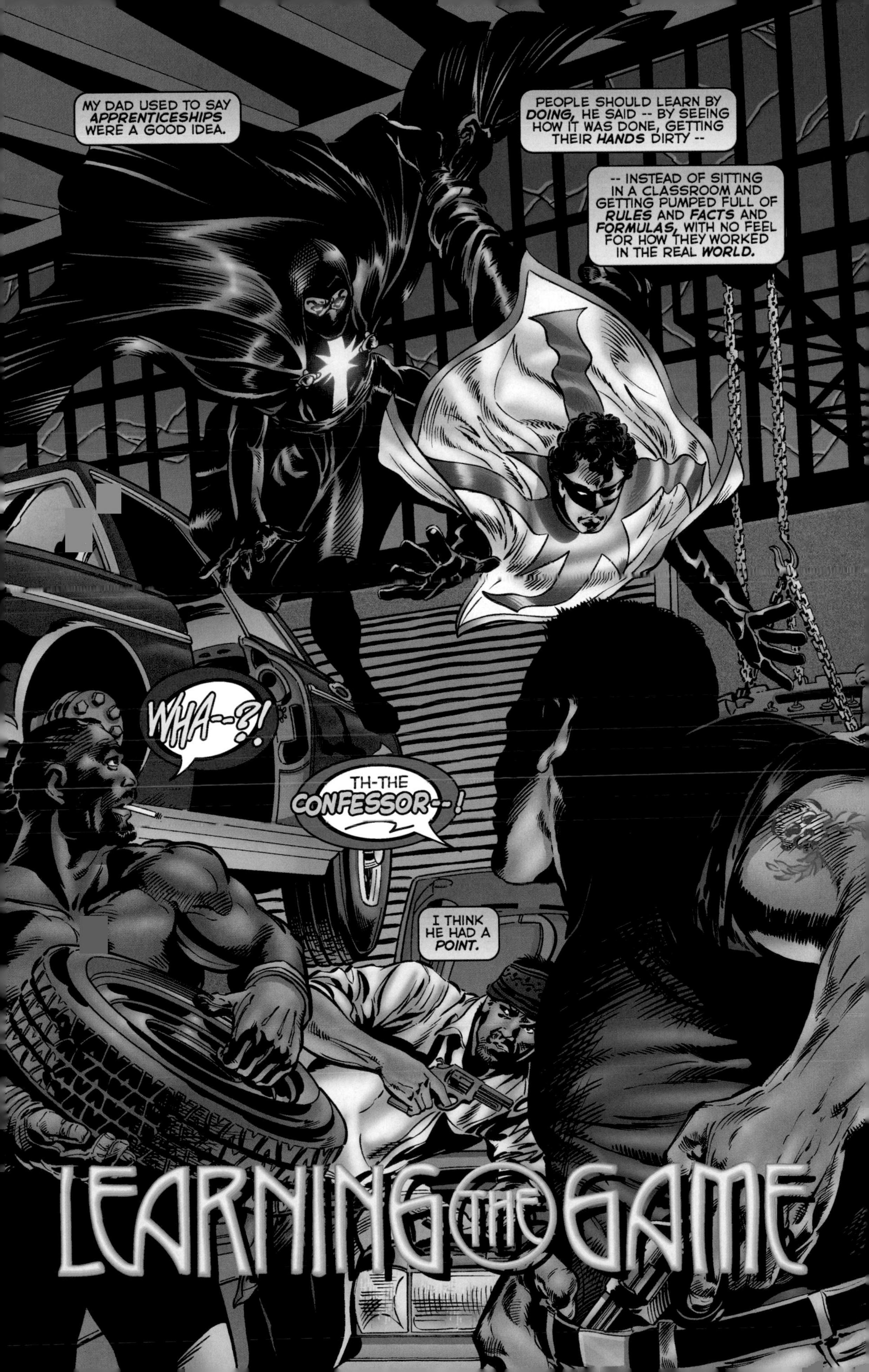

MY DAD USED TO SAY APPRENTICESHIPS WERE A GOOD IDEA.
PEOPLE SHOULD LEARN BY DOING, HE SAID -- BY SEEING HOW IT WAS DONE, GETTING THEIR HANDS DIRTY --
-- INSTEAD OF SITTING IN A CLASSROOM AND GETTING PUMPED FULL OF RULES AND FACTS AND FORMULAS, WITH NO FEEL FOR HOW THEY WORKED IN THE REAL WORLD.
WHA--?!
TH-THE CONFESSOR--!
I THINK HE HAD A POINT.
LEARNING THE GAME

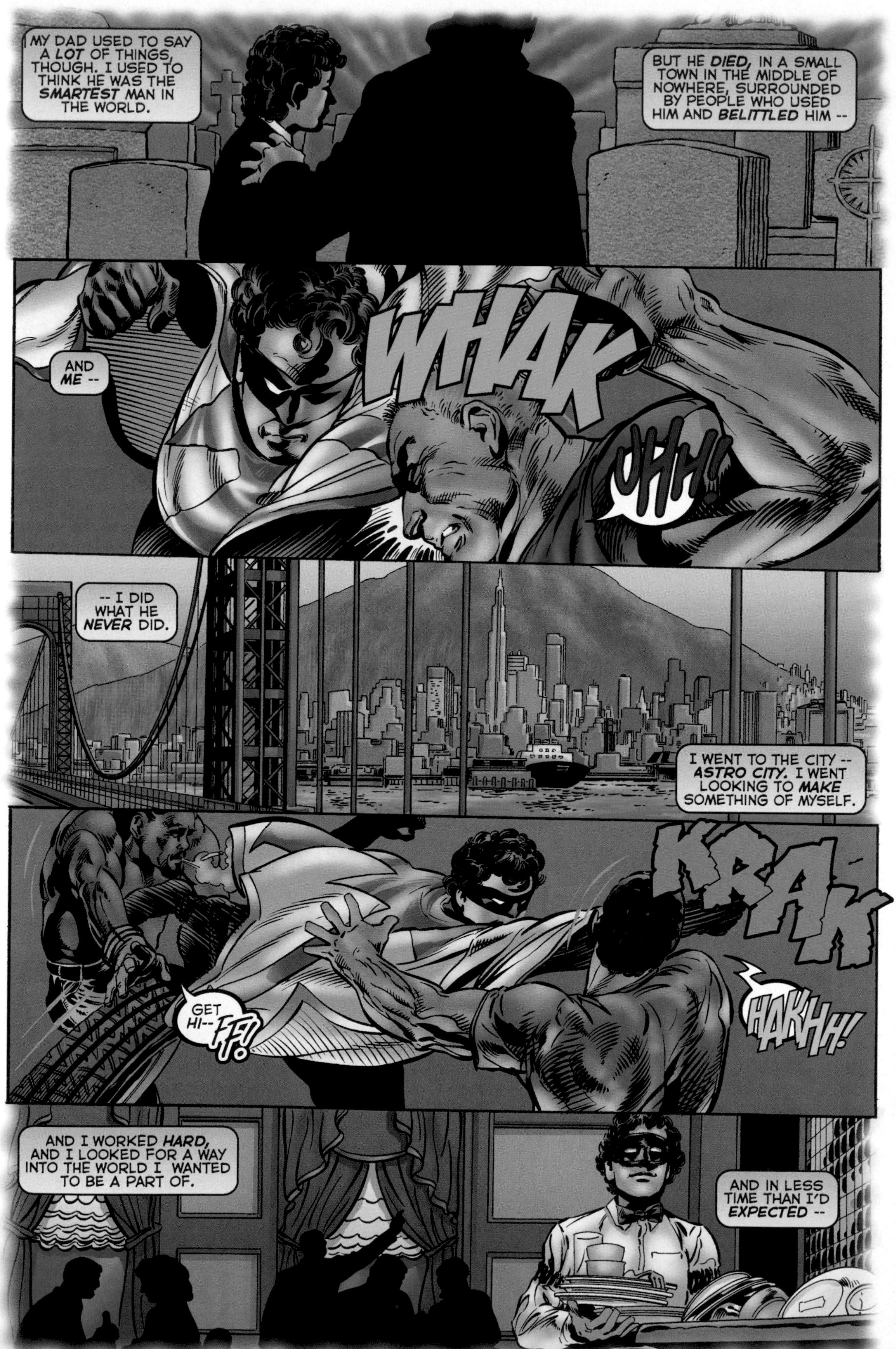

MY DAD USED TO SAY A LOT OF THINGS, THOUGH. I USED TO THINK HE WAS THE SMARTEST MAN IN THE WORLD.
BUT HE DIED, IN A SMALL TOWN IN THE MIDDLE OF NOWHERE, SURROUNDED BY PEOPLE WHO USED HIM AND BELITTLED HIM --
AND ME --
WHAK
UHH!
-- I DID WHAT HE NEVER DID.
I WENT TO THE CITY -- ASTRO CITY. I WENT LOOKING TO MAKE SOMETHING OF MYSELF.
KRAK
GET HI--FF!
HAKHH!
AND I WORKED HARD, AND I LOOKED FOR A WAY INTO THE WORLD I WANTED TO BE A PART OF.
AND IN LESS TIME THAN I'D EXPECTED --

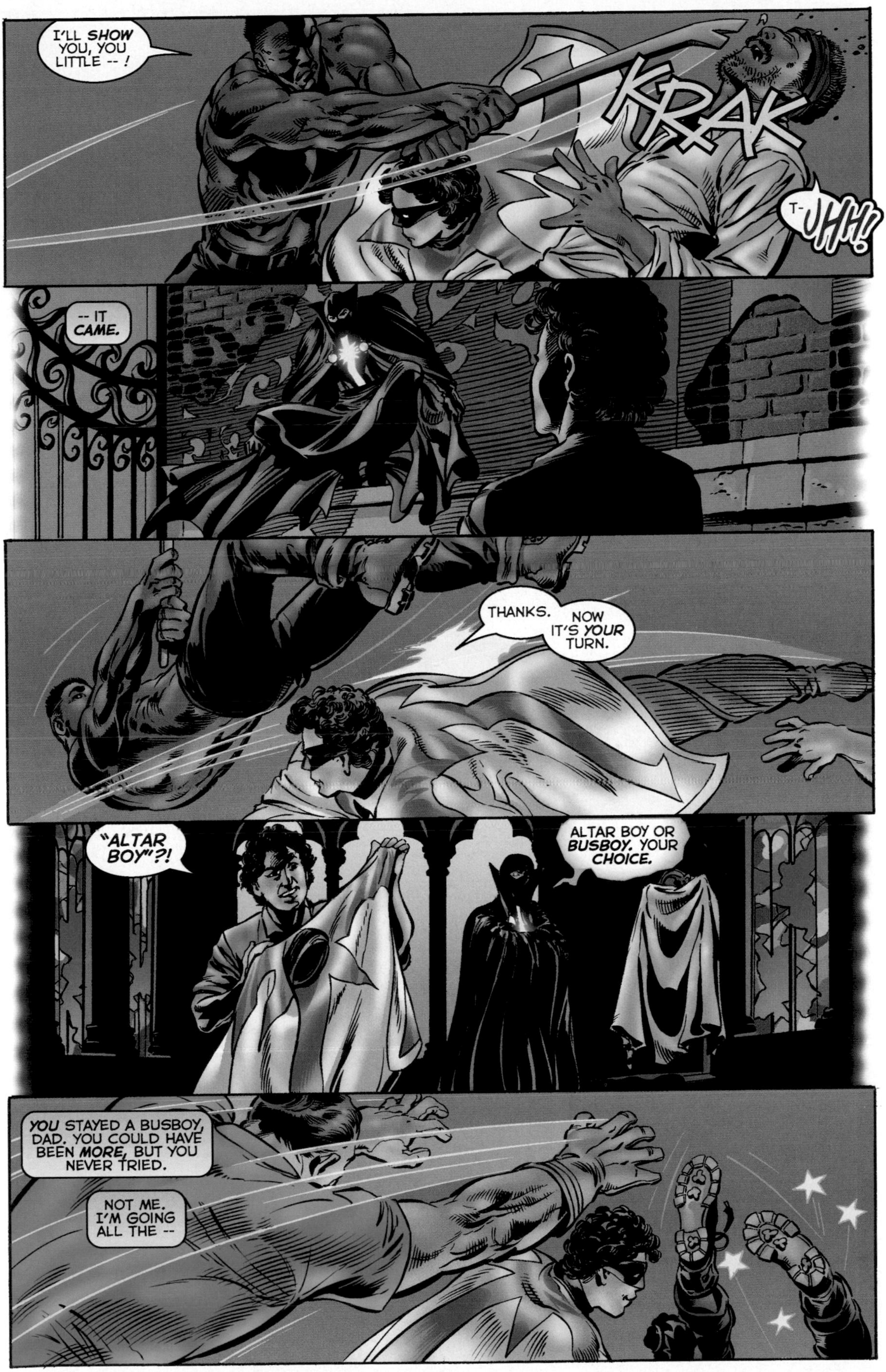

I'LL SHOW YOU, YOU LITTLE -- !
KRAK
T-UHH!
-- IT CAME.
THANKS.
NOW IT'S YOUR TURN.
"ALTAR BOY"?!
ALTAR BOY OR BUSBOY. YOUR CHOICE.
YOU STAYED A BUSBOY, DAD. YOU COULD HAVE BEEN MORE, BUT YOU NEVER TRIED.
NOT ME. I'M GOING ALL THE --

KRAK

BEHIND YOU. ALWAYS KEEP A SENSE OF WHERE *EVERYONE* IS. FOCUS IN ONE DIRECTION, AND YOU'LL *LOSE.*

UH, *THANKS!* I'LL REMEMBER THAT NEXT --

--TIIII--!

BRADADADATATT

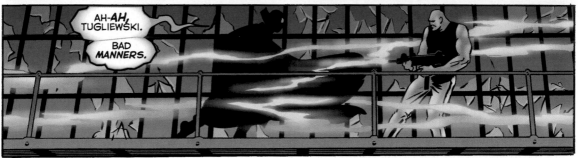

AH-*AH,* TUGLIEWSKI.

BAD *MANNERS.*

WHAK

HUH? HOW DID YOU -- ?!

THE COSTUME WORKED OUT *WELL?* THE WEIGHTED HEM OF THE SURPLICE KEPT IT OUT OF YOUR *WAY?*

AND THE LOW-FRICTION COATING KEPT THEM FROM *GRABBING* YOU BY IT?

UH, YEAH, I *GUESS.* BUT HOW --

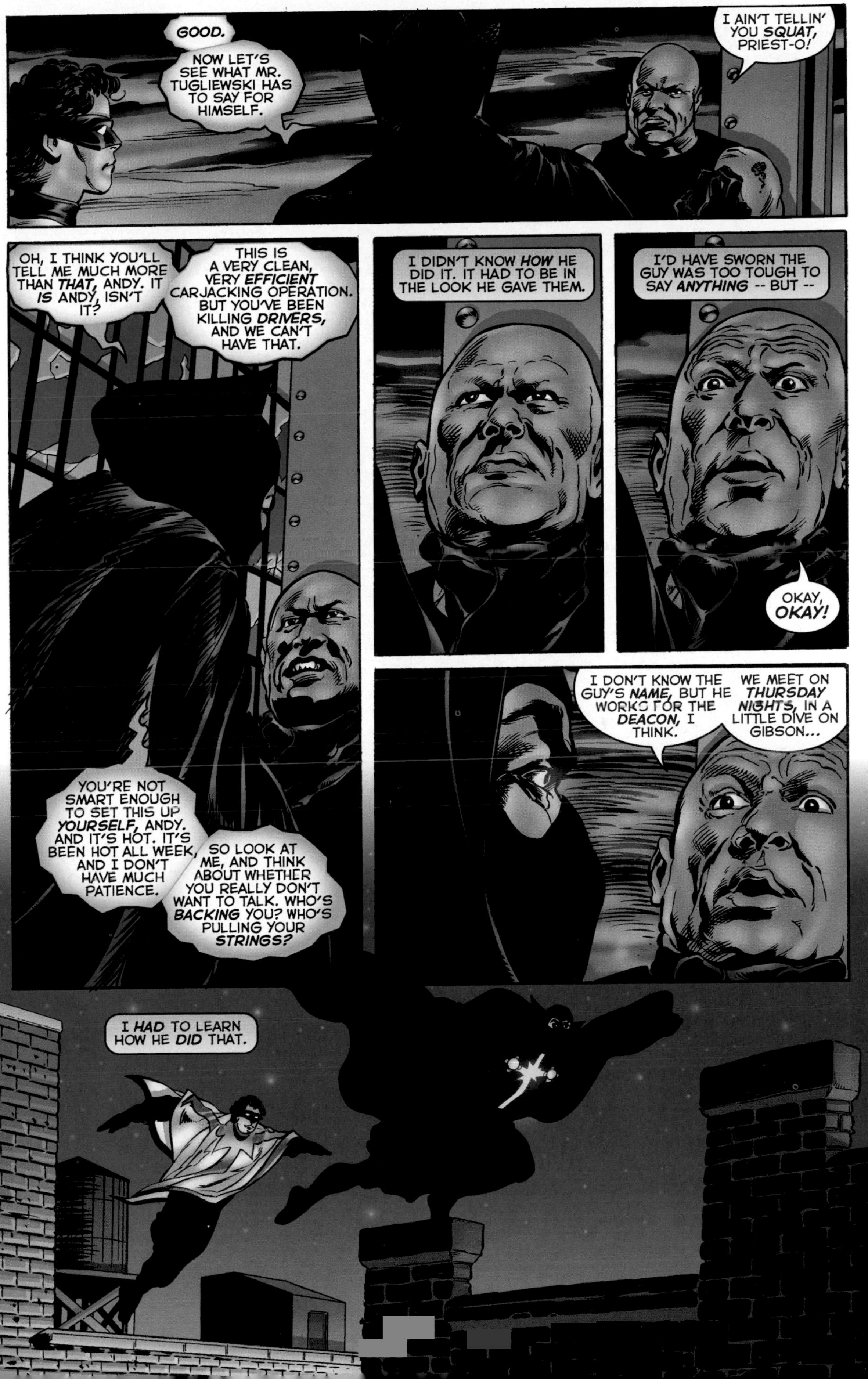
GOOD.
NOW LET'S SEE WHAT MR. TUGLIEWSKI HAS TO SAY FOR HIMSELF.
I AIN'T TELLIN' YOU SQUAT, PRIEST-O!
OH, I THINK YOU'LL TELL ME MUCH MORE THAN THAT, ANDY. IT IS ANDY, ISN'T IT?
THIS IS A VERY CLEAN, VERY EFFICIENT CARJACKING OPERATION. BUT YOU'VE BEEN KILLING DRIVERS, AND WE CAN'T HAVE THAT.
YOU'RE NOT SMART ENOUGH TO SET THIS UP YOURSELF, ANDY. AND IT'S HOT. IT'S BEEN HOT ALL WEEK, AND I DON'T HAVE MUCH PATIENCE.
SO LOOK AT ME, AND THINK ABOUT WHETHER YOU REALLY DON'T WANT TO TALK. WHO'S BACKING YOU? WHO'S PULLING YOUR STRINGS?
I DIDN'T KNOW HOW HE DID IT. IT HAD TO BE IN THE LOOK HE GAVE THEM.
I'D HAVE SWORN THE GUY WAS TOO TOUGH TO SAY ANYTHING -- BUT --
OKAY, OKAY!
I DON'T KNOW THE GUY'S NAME, BUT HE WORKS FOR THE DEACON, I THINK.
WE MEET ON THURSDAY NIGHTS, IN A LITTLE DIVE ON GIBSON...
I HAD TO LEARN HOW HE DID THAT.

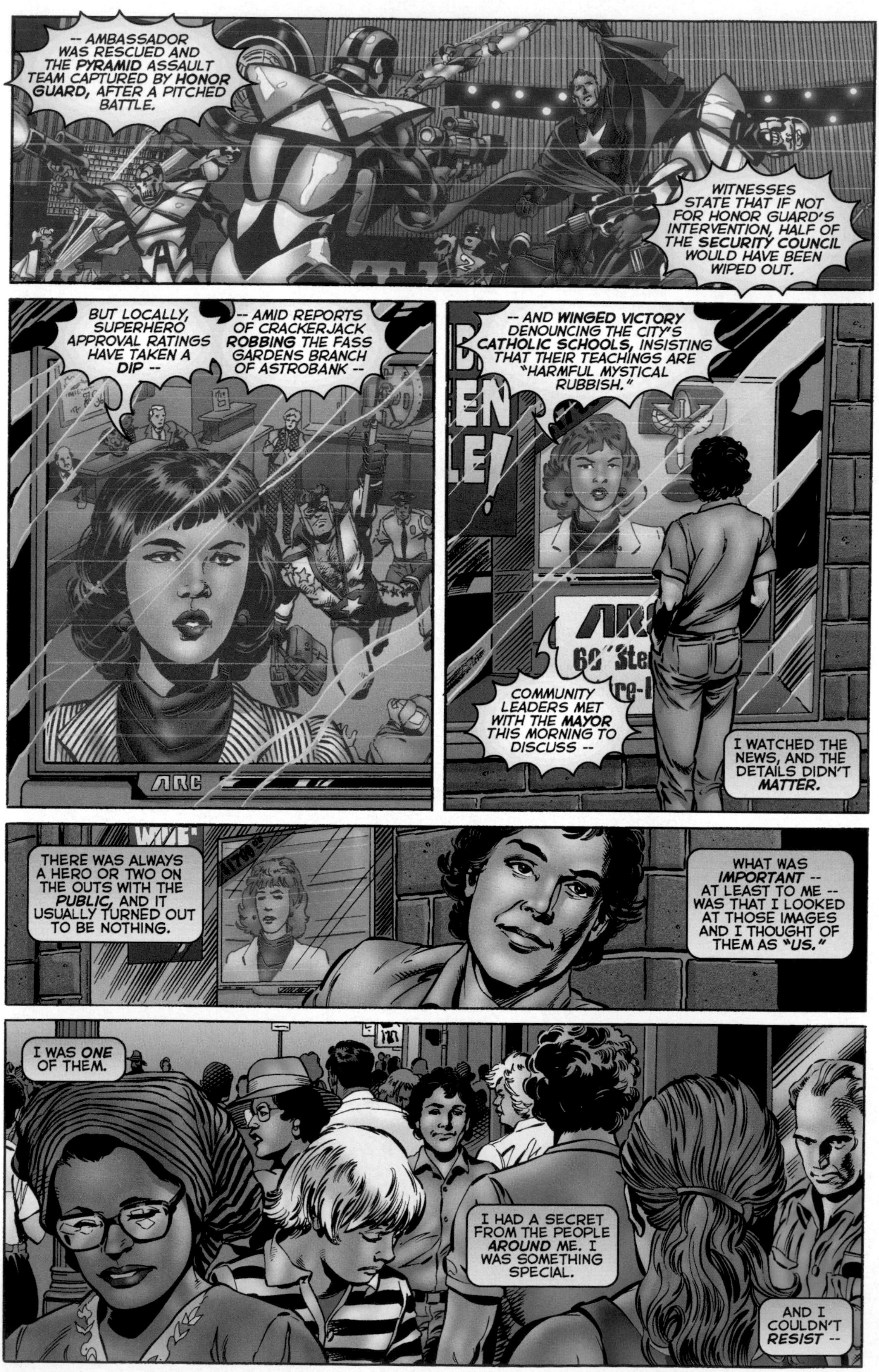
-- AMBASSADOR WAS RESCUED AND THE PYRAMID ASSAULT TEAM CAPTURED BY HONOR GUARD, AFTER A PITCHED BATTLE.
WITNESSES STATE THAT IF NOT FOR HONOR GUARD'S INTERVENTION, HALF OF THE SECURITY COUNCIL WOULD HAVE BEEN WIPED OUT.
BUT LOCALLY, SUPERHERO APPROVAL RATINGS HAVE TAKEN A DIP --
-- AMID REPORTS OF CRACKERJACK ROBBING THE FASS GARDENS BRANCH OF ASTROBANK --
ARC
-- AND WINGED VICTORY DENOUNCING THE CITY'S CATHOLIC SCHOOLS, INSISTING THAT THEIR TEACHINGS ARE "HARMFUL MYSTICAL RUBBISH."
COMMUNITY LEADERS MET WITH THE MAYOR THIS MORNING TO DISCUSS --
I WATCHED THE NEWS, AND THE DETAILS DIDN'T MATTER.
THERE WAS ALWAYS A HERO OR TWO ON THE OUTS WITH THE PUBLIC, AND IT USUALLY TURNED OUT TO BE NOTHING.
WHAT WAS IMPORTANT -- AT LEAST TO ME -- WAS THAT I LOOKED AT THOSE IMAGES AND I THOUGHT OF THEM AS "US."
I WAS ONE OF THEM.
I HAD A SECRET FROM THE PEOPLE AROUND ME. I WAS SOMETHING SPECIAL.
AND I COULDN'T RESIST --

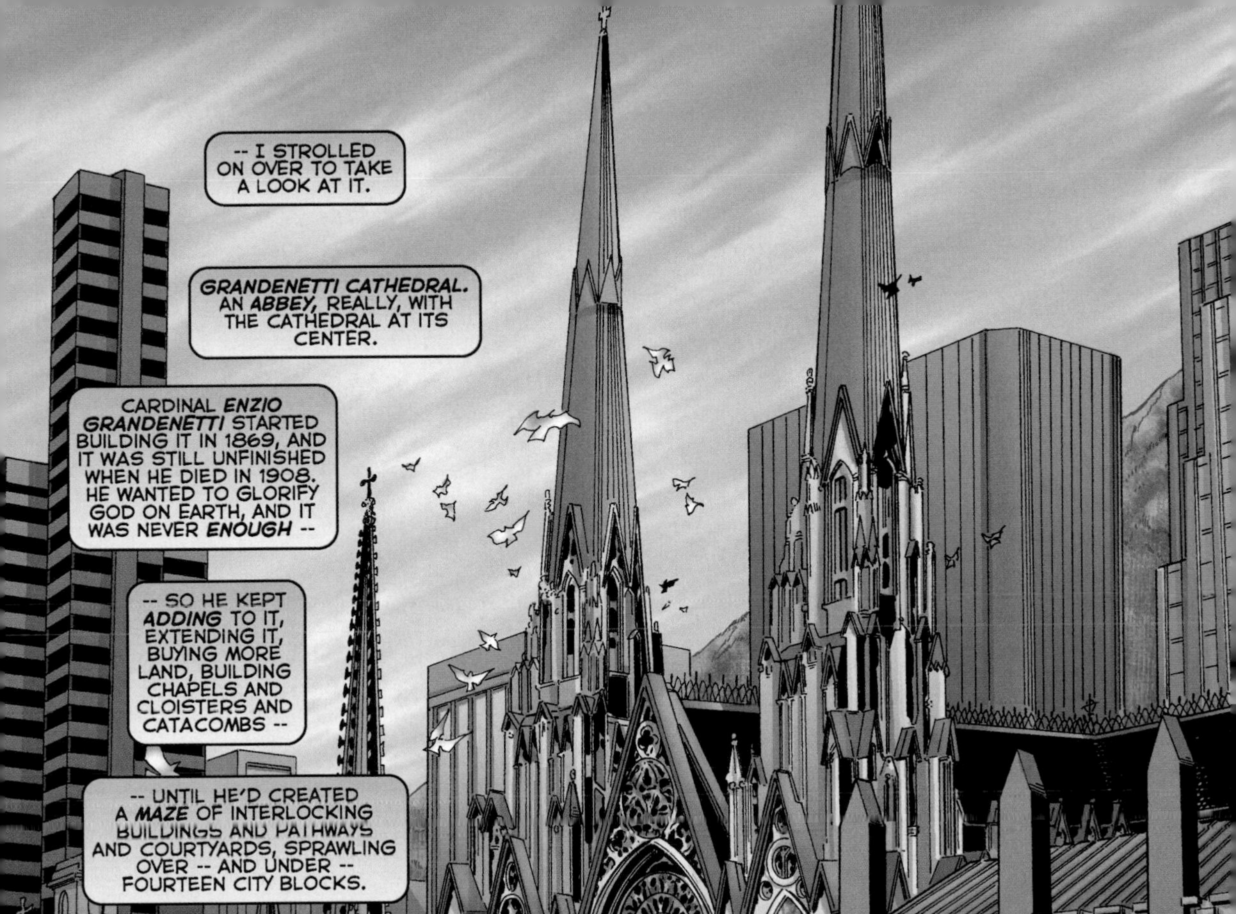
-- I STROLLED ON OVER TO TAKE A LOOK AT IT.
GRANDENETTI CATHEDRAL. AN ABBEY, REALLY, WITH THE CATHEDRAL AT ITS CENTER.
CARDINAL ENZIO GRANDENETTI STARTED BUILDING IT IN 1869, AND IT WAS STILL UNFINISHED WHEN HE DIED IN 1908. HE WANTED TO GLORIFY GOD ON EARTH, AND IT WAS NEVER ENOUGH --
-- SO HE KEPT ADDING TO IT, EXTENDING IT, BUYING MORE LAND, BUILDING CHAPELS AND CLOISTERS AND CATACOMBS --
-- UNTIL HE'D CREATED A MAZE OF INTERLOCKING BUILDINGS AND PATHWAYS AND COURTYARDS, SPRAWLING OVER -- AND UNDER -- FOURTEEN CITY BLOCKS.
"A CHARMING AND EDUCATIONAL SITE FOR A SUNNY AFTERNOON'S EXPLORING," THE GUIDEBOOKS CALLED IT.
BUT THAT WAS BY DAY. BY NIGHT --
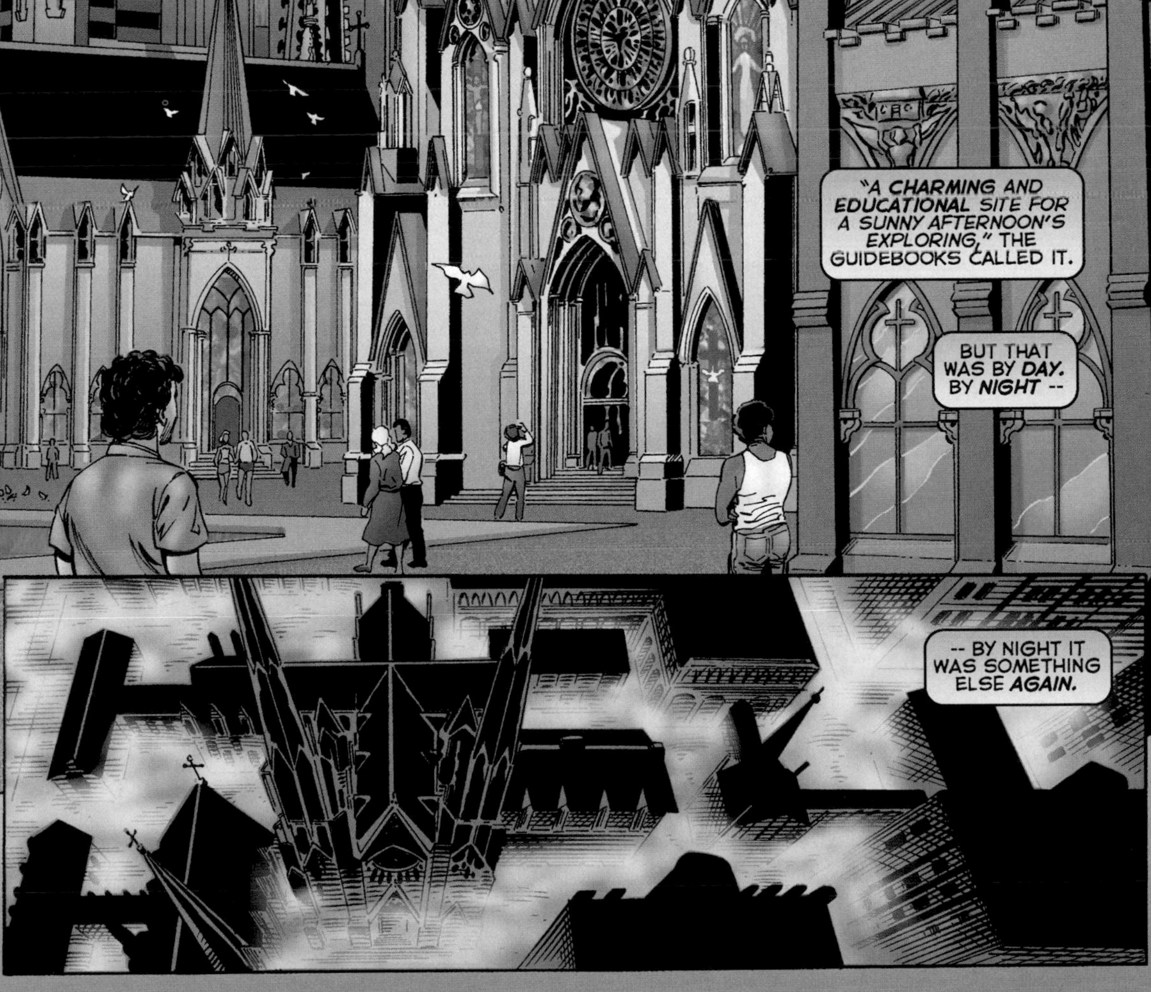
-- BY NIGHT IT WAS SOMETHING ELSE AGAIN.

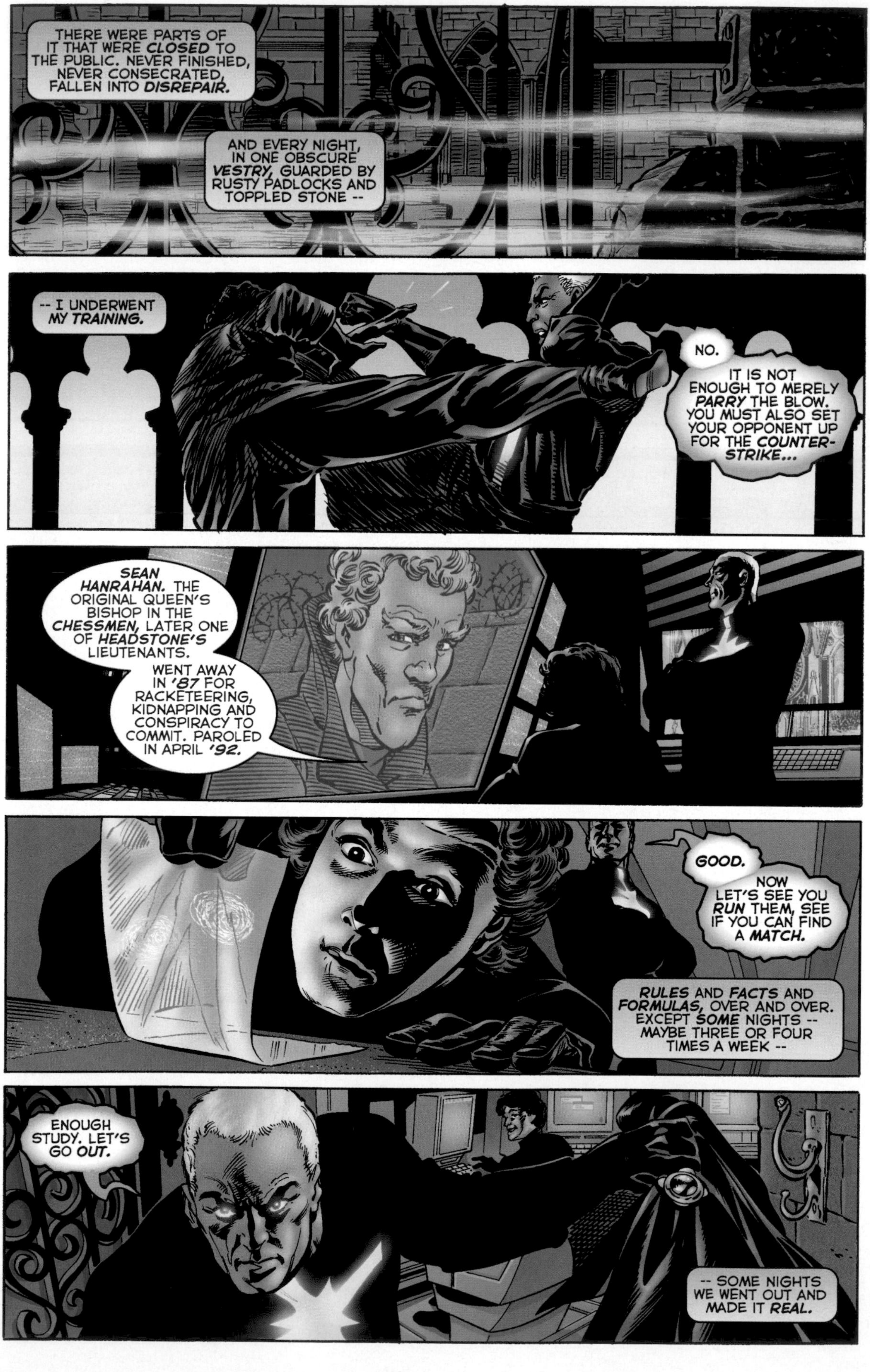

THERE WERE PARTS OF IT THAT WERE CLOSED TO THE PUBLIC. NEVER FINISHED, NEVER CONSECRATED, FALLEN INTO DISREPAIR.
AND EVERY NIGHT, IN ONE OBSCURE VESTRY, GUARDED BY RUSTY PADLOCKS AND TOPPLED STONE --
-- I UNDERWENT MY TRAINING.
NO.
IT IS NOT ENOUGH TO MERELY PARRY THE BLOW. YOU MUST ALSO SET YOUR OPPONENT UP FOR THE COUNTER-STRIKE...
SEAN HANRAHAN. THE ORIGINAL QUEEN'S BISHOP IN THE CHESSMEN, LATER ONE OF HEADSTONE'S LIEUTENANTS.
WENT AWAY IN '87 FOR RACKETEERING, KIDNAPPING AND CONSPIRACY TO COMMIT. PAROLED IN APRIL '92.
GOOD.
NOW LET'S SEE YOU RUN THEM, SEE IF YOU CAN FIND A MATCH.
RULES AND FACTS AND FORMULAS, OVER AND OVER. EXCEPT SOME NIGHTS -- MAYBE THREE OR FOUR TIMES A WEEK --
ENOUGH STUDY. LET'S GO OUT.
-- SOME NIGHTS WE WENT OUT AND MADE IT REAL.

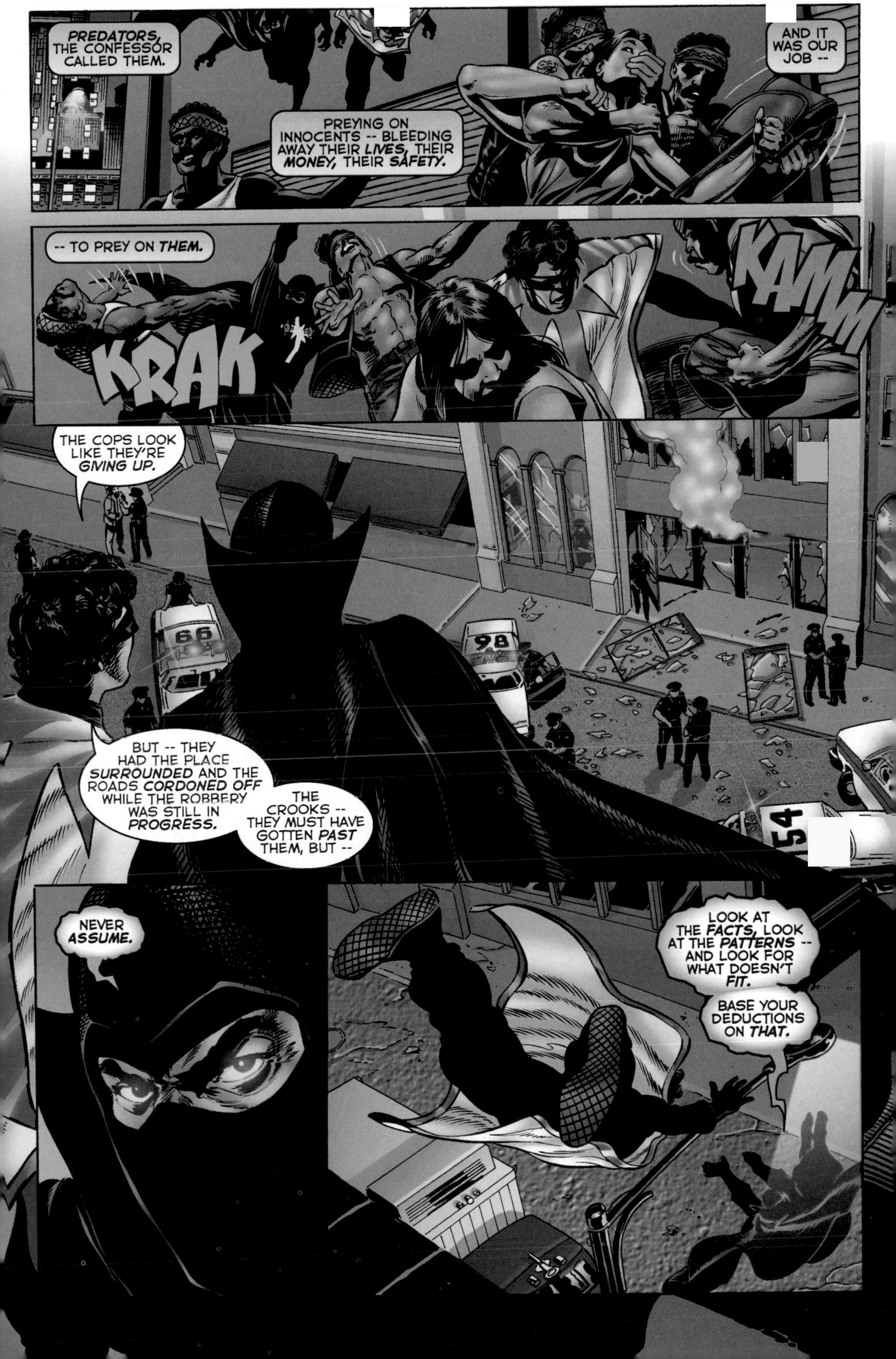
PREDATORS, THE CONFESSOR CALLED THEM.
PREYING ON INNOCENTS -- BLEEDING AWAY THEIR LIVES, THEIR MONEY, THEIR SAFETY.
AND IT WAS OUR JOB --
-- TO PREY ON THEM.
KRAK
KAWWM
THE COPS LOOK LIKE THEY'RE GIVING UP.
BUT -- THEY HAD THE PLACE SURROUNDED AND THE ROADS CORDONED OFF WHILE THE ROBBERY WAS STILL IN PROGRESS.
THE CROOKS -- THEY MUST HAVE GOTTEN PAST THEM, BUT --
NEVER ASSUME.
LOOK AT THE FACTS, LOOK AT THE PATTERNS -- AND LOOK FOR WHAT DOESN'T FIT.
BASE YOUR DEDUCTIONS ON THAT.

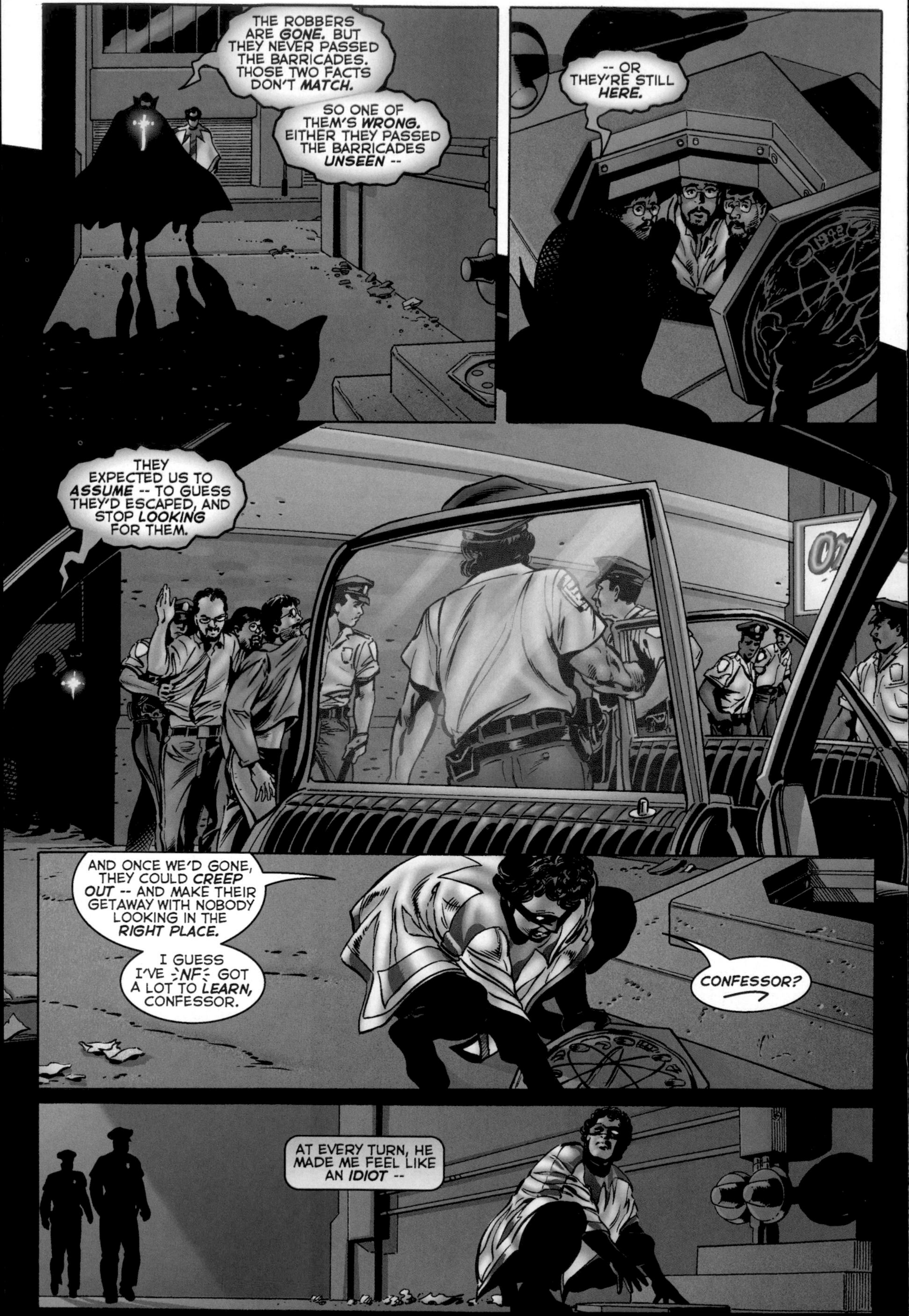
THE ROBBERS ARE GONE. BUT THEY NEVER PASSED THE BARRICADES. THOSE TWO FACTS DON'T MATCH.
SO ONE OF THEM'S WRONG. EITHER THEY PASSED THE BARRICADES UNSEEN --
-- OR THEY'RE STILL HERE.
THEY EXPECTED US TO ASSUME -- TO GUESS THEY'D ESCAPED, AND STOP LOOKING FOR THEM.
AND ONCE WE'D GONE, THEY COULD CREEP OUT -- AND MAKE THEIR GETAWAY WITH NOBODY LOOKING IN THE RIGHT PLACE.
I GUESS I'VE NF GOT A LOT TO LEARN, CONFESSOR.
CONFESSOR?
AT EVERY TURN, HE MADE ME FEEL LIKE AN IDIOT --

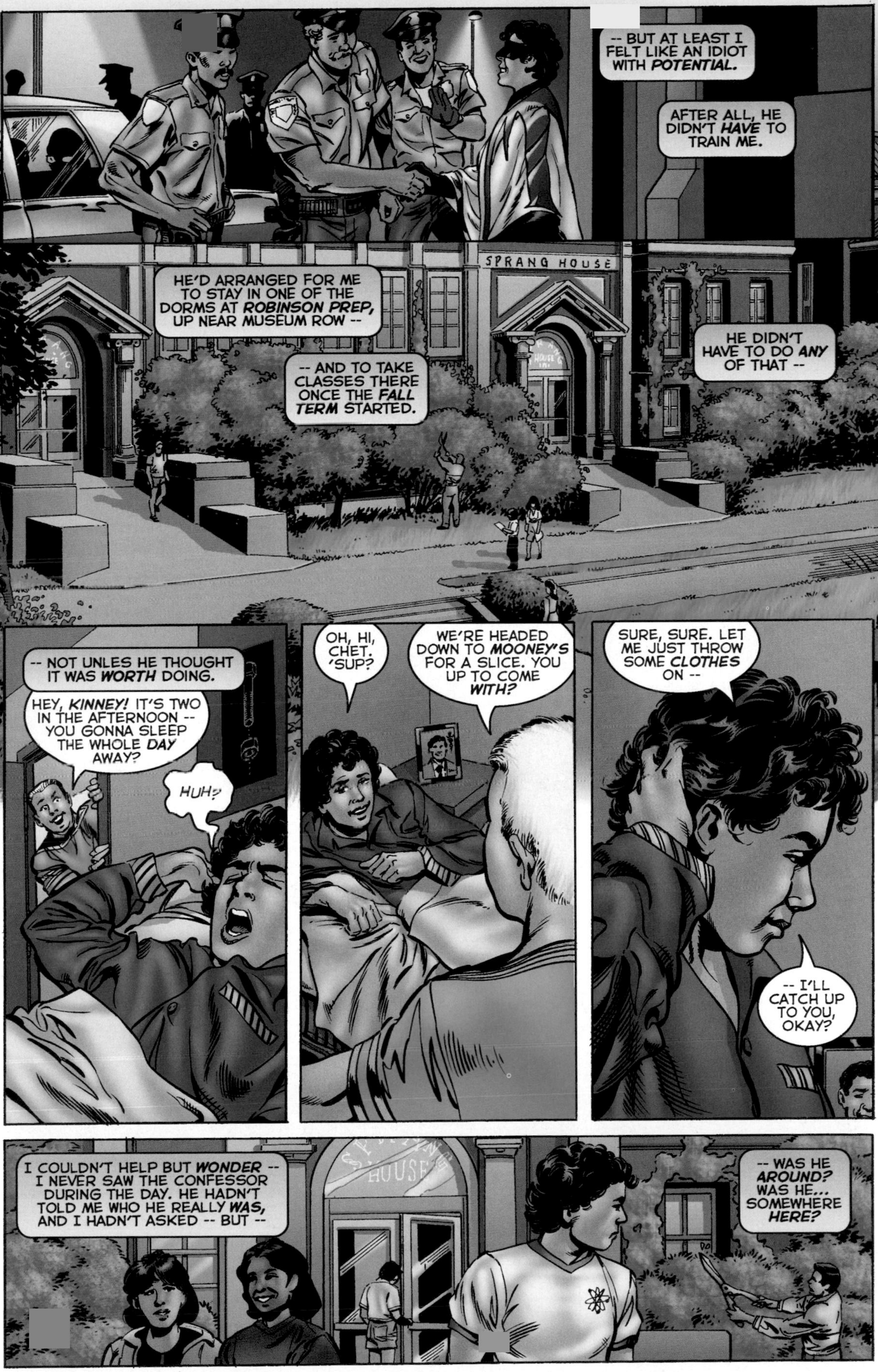
-- BUT AT LEAST I FELT LIKE AN IDIOT WITH POTENTIAL.
AFTER ALL, HE DIDN'T HAVE TO TRAIN ME.
SPRANG HOUSE
HE'D ARRANGED FOR ME TO STAY IN ONE OF THE DORMS AT ROBINSON PREP, UP NEAR MUSEUM ROW --
-- AND TO TAKE CLASSES THERE ONCE THE FALL TERM STARTED.
HE DIDN'T HAVE TO DO ANY OF THAT --
-- NOT UNLES HE THOUGHT IT WAS WORTH DOING.
HEY, KINNEY! IT'S TWO IN THE AFTERNOON -- YOU GONNA SLEEP THE WHOLE DAY AWAY?
HUH?
OH, HI, CHET. 'SUP?
WE'RE HEADED DOWN TO MOONEY'S FOR A SLICE. YOU UP TO COME WITH?
SURE, SURE. LET ME JUST THROW SOME CLOTHES ON --
-- I'LL CATCH UP TO YOU, OKAY?
I COULDN'T HELP BUT WONDER -- I NEVER SAW THE CONFESSOR DURING THE DAY. HE HADN'T TOLD ME WHO HE REALLY WAS, AND I HADN'T ASKED -- BUT --
-- WAS HE AROUND? WAS HE... SOMEWHERE HERE?

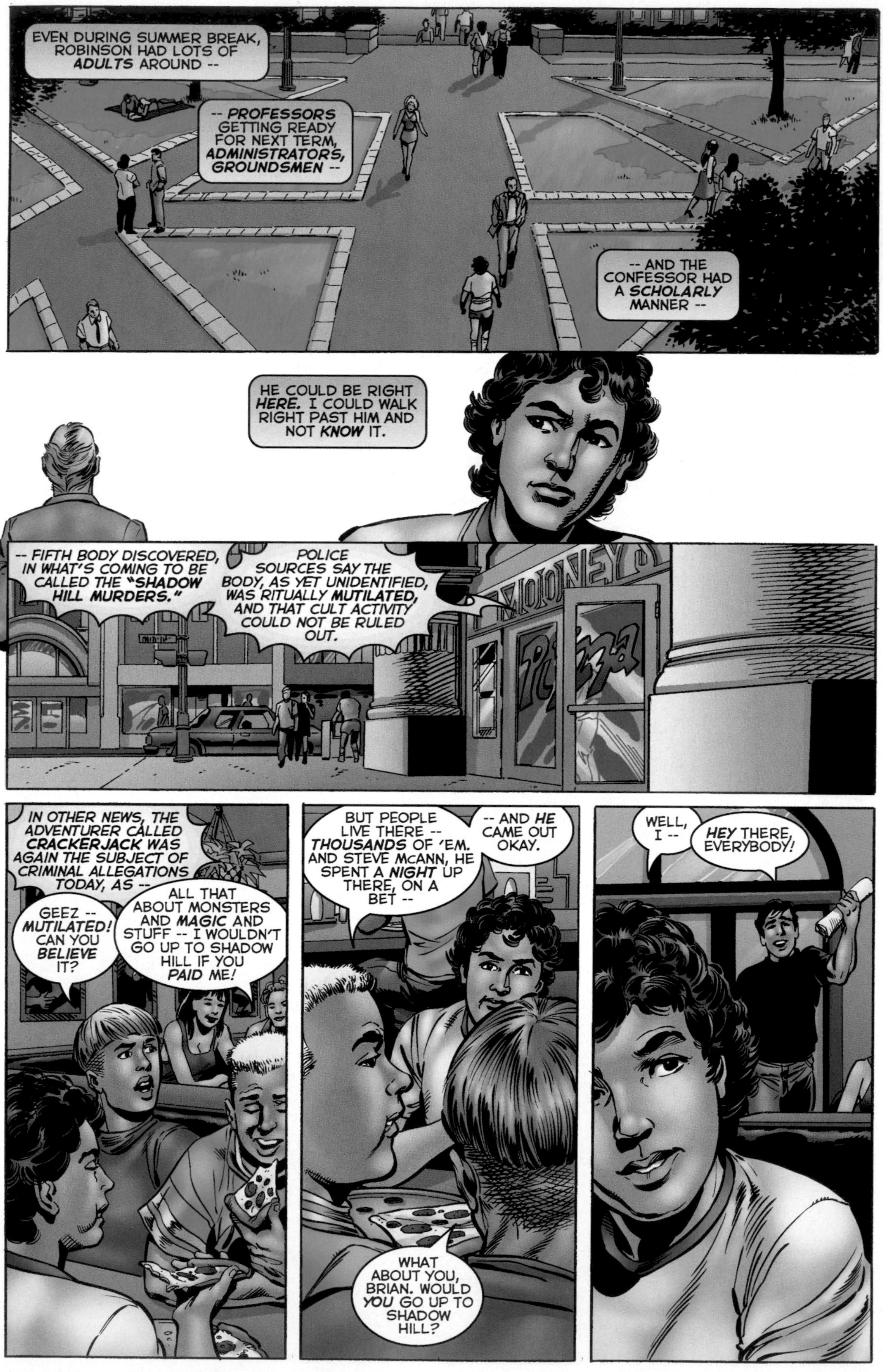
EVEN DURING SUMMER BREAK, ROBINSON HAD LOTS OF ADULTS AROUND --
-- PROFESSORS GETTING READY FOR NEXT TERM, ADMINISTRATORS, GROUNDSMEN --
-- AND THE CONFESSOR HAD A SCHOLARLY MANNER --
HE COULD BE RIGHT HERE. I COULD WALK RIGHT PAST HIM AND NOT KNOW IT.
-- FIFTH BODY DISCOVERED, IN WHAT'S COMING TO BE CALLED THE "SHADOW HILL MURDERS."
POLICE SOURCES SAY THE BODY, AS YET UNIDENTIFIED, WAS RITUALLY MUTILATED, AND THAT CULT ACTIVITY COULD NOT BE RULED OUT.
MOONEY'S
Pizza
IN OTHER NEWS, THE ADVENTURER CALLED CRACKERJACK WAS AGAIN THE SUBJECT OF CRIMINAL ALLEGATIONS TODAY, AS --
GEEZ -- MUTILATED! CAN YOU BELIEVE IT?
ALL THAT ABOUT MONSTERS AND MAGIC AND STUFF -- I WOULDN'T GO UP TO SHADOW HILL IF YOU PAID ME!
BUT PEOPLE LIVE THERE -- THOUSANDS OF 'EM. AND STEVE McCANN, HE SPENT A NIGHT UP THERE, ON A BET --
-- AND HE CAME OUT OKAY.
WHAT ABOUT YOU, BRIAN. WOULD YOU GO UP TO SHADOW HILL?
WELL, I --
HEY THERE, EVERYBODY!

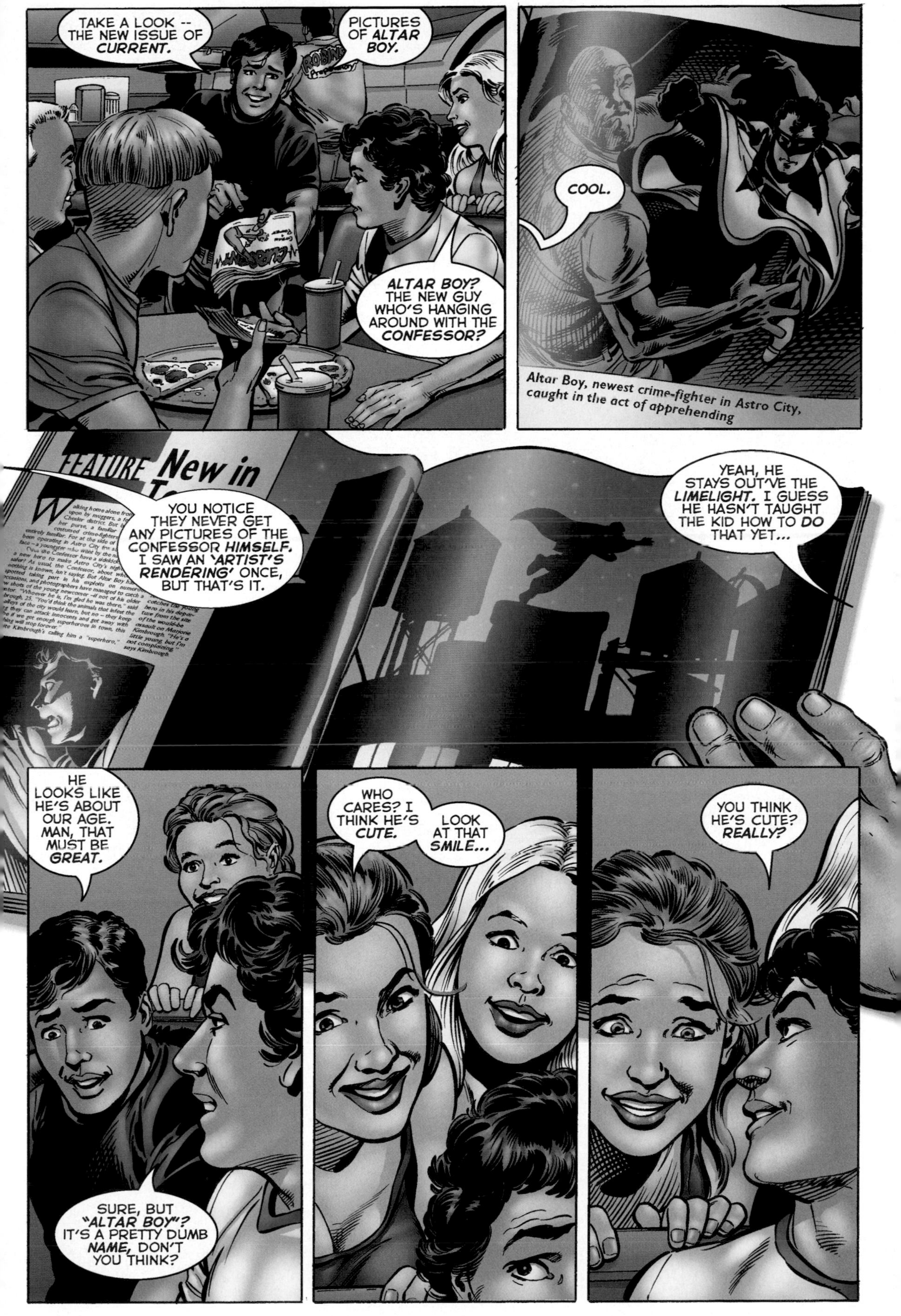
TAKE A LOOK -- THE NEW ISSUE OF CURRENT.
PICTURES OF ALTAR BOY.
ALTAR BOY? THE NEW GUY WHO'S HANGING AROUND WITH THE CONFESSOR?
COOL.
Altar Boy, newest crime-fighter in Astro City, caught in the act of apprehending
FEATURE New in
YOU NOTICE THEY NEVER GET ANY PICTURES OF THE CONFESSOR HIMSELF. I SAW AN 'ARTIST'S RENDERING' ONCE, BUT THAT'S IT.
YEAH, HE STAYS OUT'VE THE LIMELIGHT. I GUESS HE HASN'T TAUGHT THE KID HOW TO DO THAT YET...
HE LOOKS LIKE HE'S ABOUT OUR AGE. MAN, THAT MUST BE GREAT.
SURE, BUT "ALTAR BOY"? IT'S A PRETTY DUMB NAME, DON'T YOU THINK?
WHO CARES? I THINK HE'S CUTE.
LOOK AT THAT SMILE...
YOU THINK HE'S CUTE? REALLY?

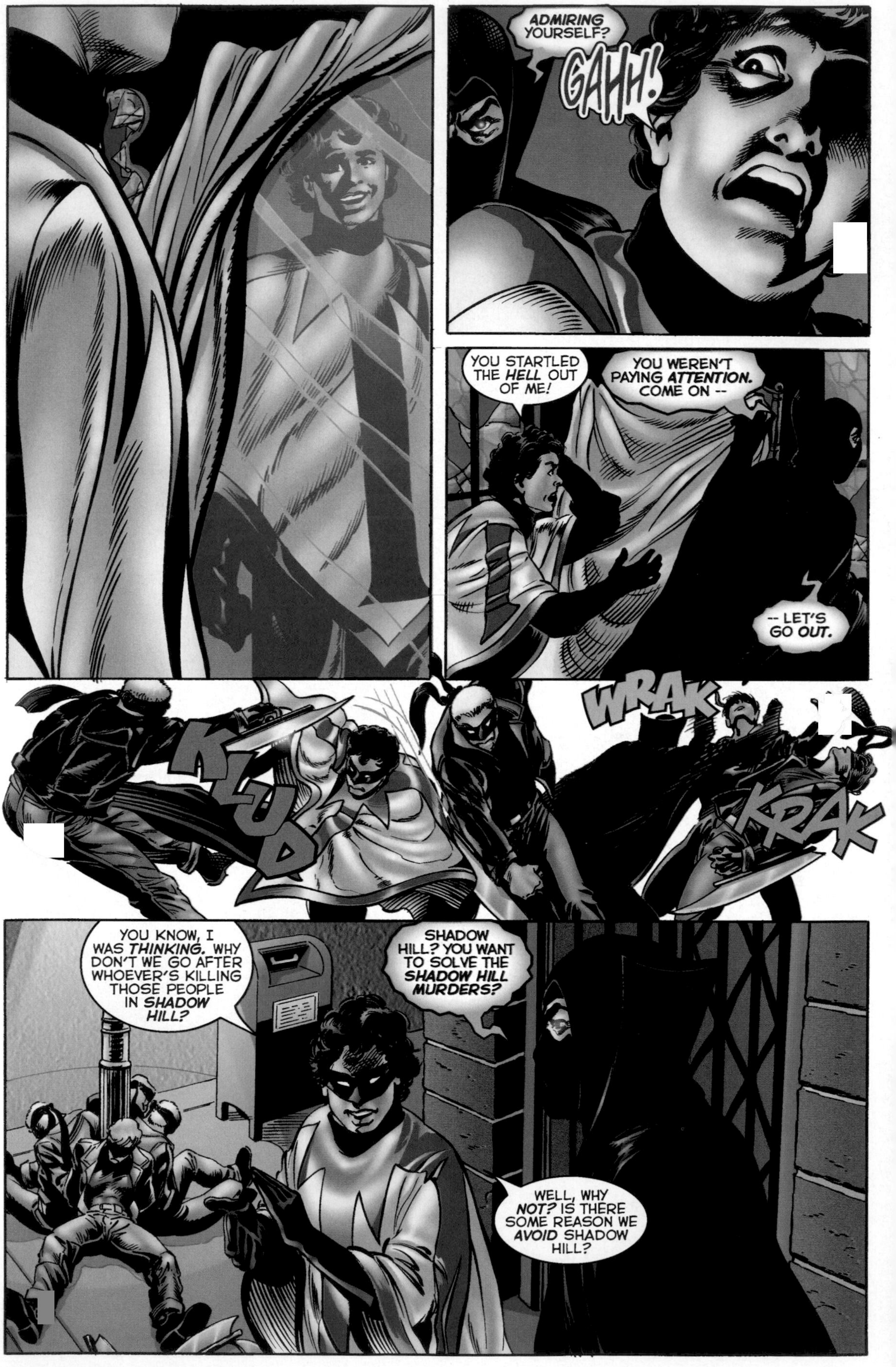
ADMIRING YOURSELF?
GAHH!
YOU STARTLED THE HELL OUT OF ME!
YOU WEREN'T PAYING ATTENTION. COME ON --
-- LET'S GO OUT.
KLUD
WRAK
KRAK
YOU KNOW, I WAS THINKING. WHY DON'T WE GO AFTER WHOEVER'S KILLING THOSE PEOPLE IN SHADOW HILL?
SHADOW HILL? YOU WANT TO SOLVE THE SHADOW HILL MURDERS?
WELL, WHY NOT? IS THERE SOME REASON WE AVOID SHADOW HILL?

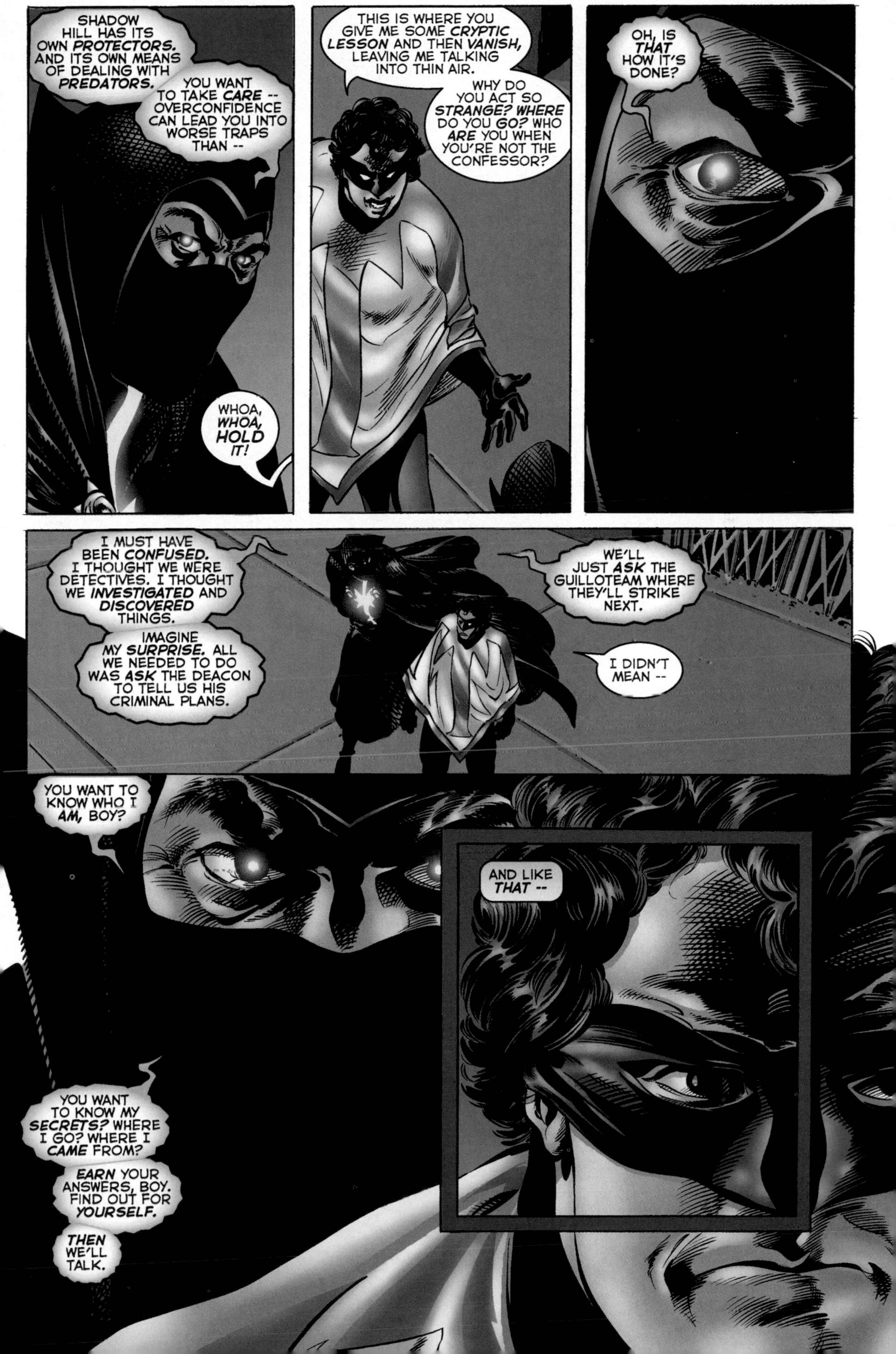
SHADOW HILL HAS ITS OWN PROTECTORS. AND ITS OWN MEANS OF DEALING WITH PREDATORS.
YOU WANT TO TAKE CARE -- OVERCONFIDENCE CAN LEAD YOU INTO WORSE TRAPS THAN --
WHOA, WHOA, HOLD IT!
THIS IS WHERE YOU GIVE ME SOME CRYPTIC LESSON AND THEN VANISH, LEAVING ME TALKING INTO THIN AIR.
WHY DO YOU ACT SO STRANGE? WHERE DO YOU GO? WHO ARE YOU WHEN YOU'RE NOT THE CONFESSOR?
OH, IS THAT HOW IT'S DONE?
I MUST HAVE BEEN CONFUSED. I THOUGHT WE WERE DETECTIVES. I THOUGHT WE INVESTIGATED AND DISCOVERED THINGS.
IMAGINE MY SURPRISE. ALL WE NEEDED TO DO WAS ASK THE DEACON TO TELL US HIS CRIMINAL PLANS.
WE'LL JUST ASK THE GUILLOTEAM WHERE THEY'LL STRIKE NEXT.
I DIDN'T MEAN --
YOU WANT TO KNOW WHO I AM, BOY?
AND LIKE THAT --
YOU WANT TO KNOW MY SECRETS? WHERE I GO? WHERE I CAME FROM?
EARN YOUR ANSWERS, BOY. FIND OUT FOR YOURSELF.
THEN WE'LL TALK.

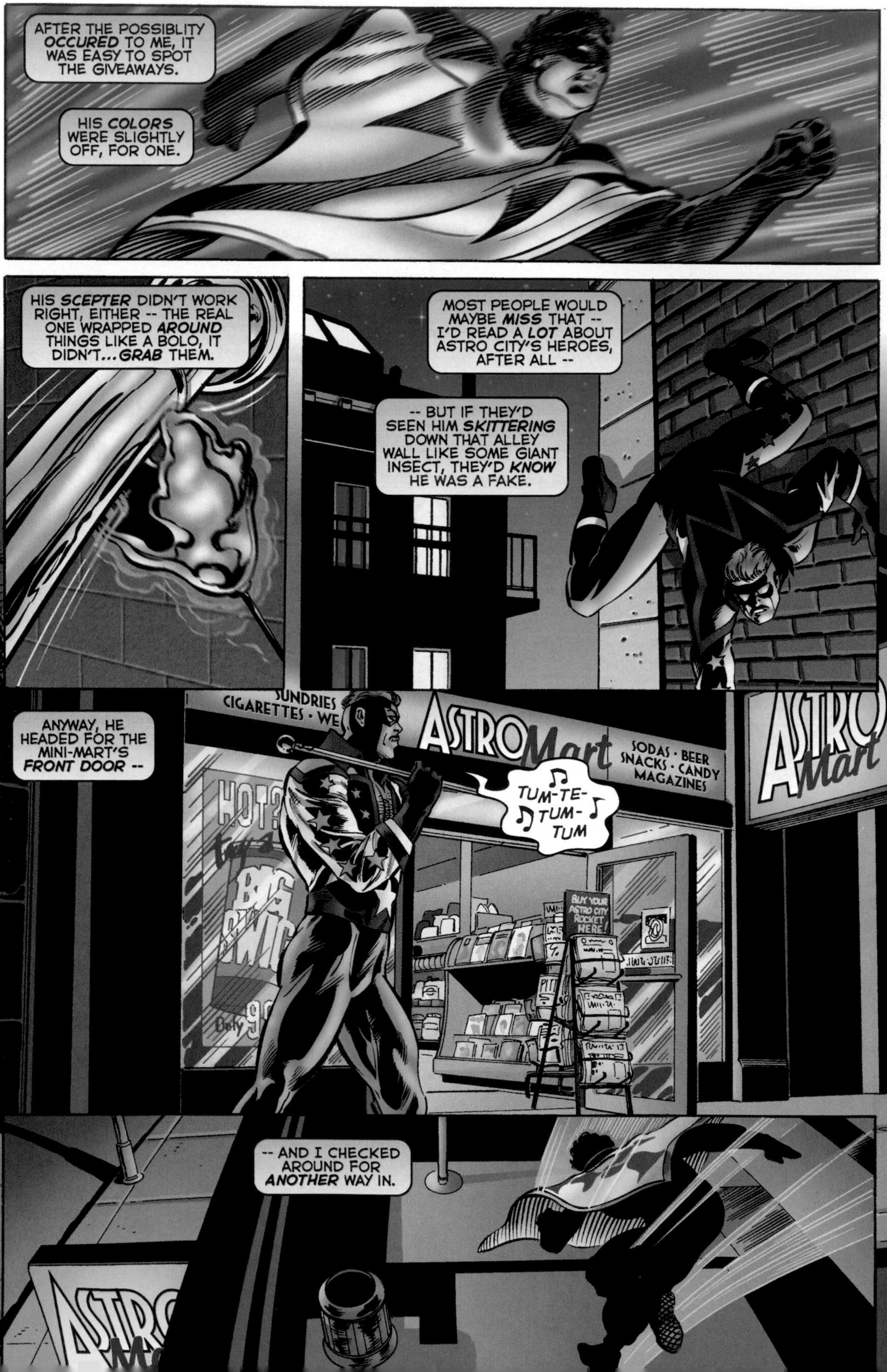
AFTER THE POSSIBLITY OCCURED TO ME, IT WAS EASY TO SPOT THE GIVEAWAYS.
HIS COLORS WERE SLIGHTLY OFF, FOR ONE.
HIS SCEPTER DIDN'T WORK RIGHT, EITHER -- THE REAL ONE WRAPPED AROUND THINGS LIKE A BOLO, IT DIDN'T...GRAB THEM.
MOST PEOPLE WOULD MAYBE MISS THAT -- I'D READ A LOT ABOUT ASTRO CITY'S HEROES, AFTER ALL --
-- BUT IF THEY'D SEEN HIM SKITTERING DOWN THAT ALLEY WALL LIKE SOME GIANT INSECT, THEY'D KNOW HE WAS A FAKE.
ANYWAY, HE HEADED FOR THE MINI-MART'S FRONT DOOR --
SUNDRIES
CIGARETTES · WE
ASTRO Mart
SODAS · BEER
SNACKS · CANDY
MAGAZINES
TUM-TE-TUM-TUM
ASTRO Mart
BUY YOUR ASTRO CITY ROCKET HERE!
-- AND I CHECKED AROUND FOR ANOTHER WAY IN.

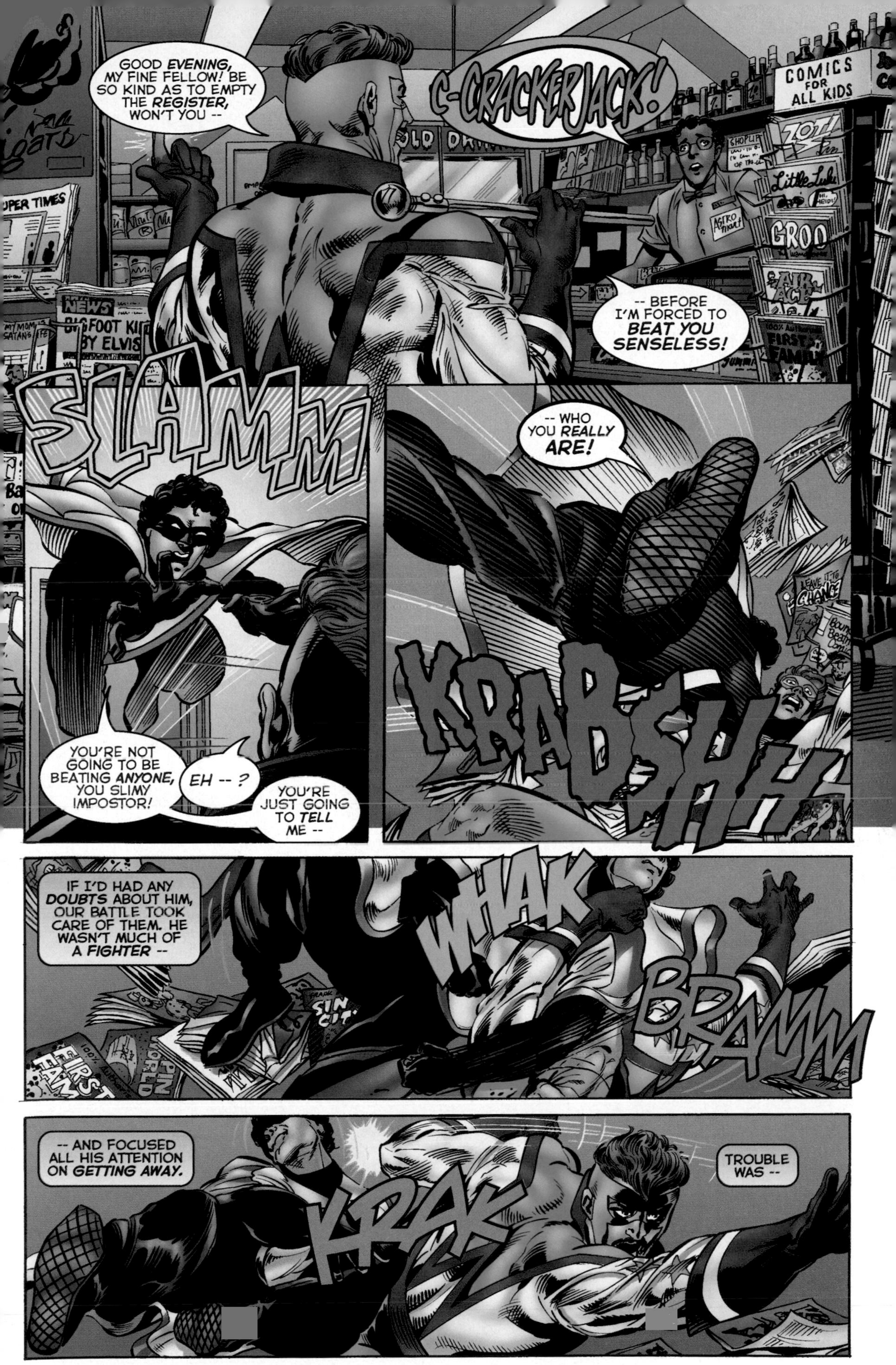
GOOD EVENING, MY FINE FELLOW! BE SO KIND AS TO EMPTY THE REGISTER, WON'T YOU --
C-CRACKERJACK!
COMICS FOR ALL KIDS
-- BEFORE I'M FORCED TO BEAT YOU SENSELESS!
SLAMMM
-- WHO YOU REALLY ARE!
YOU'RE NOT GOING TO BE BEATING ANYONE, YOU SLIMY IMPOSTOR!
EH -- ?
YOU'RE JUST GOING TO TELL ME --
KRABSHH
IF I'D HAD ANY DOUBTS ABOUT HIM, OUR BATTLE TOOK CARE OF THEM. HE WASN'T MUCH OF A FIGHTER --
WHAK
BRAMM
-- AND FOCUSED ALL HIS ATTENTION ON GETTING AWAY.
TROUBLE WAS --
KRAK

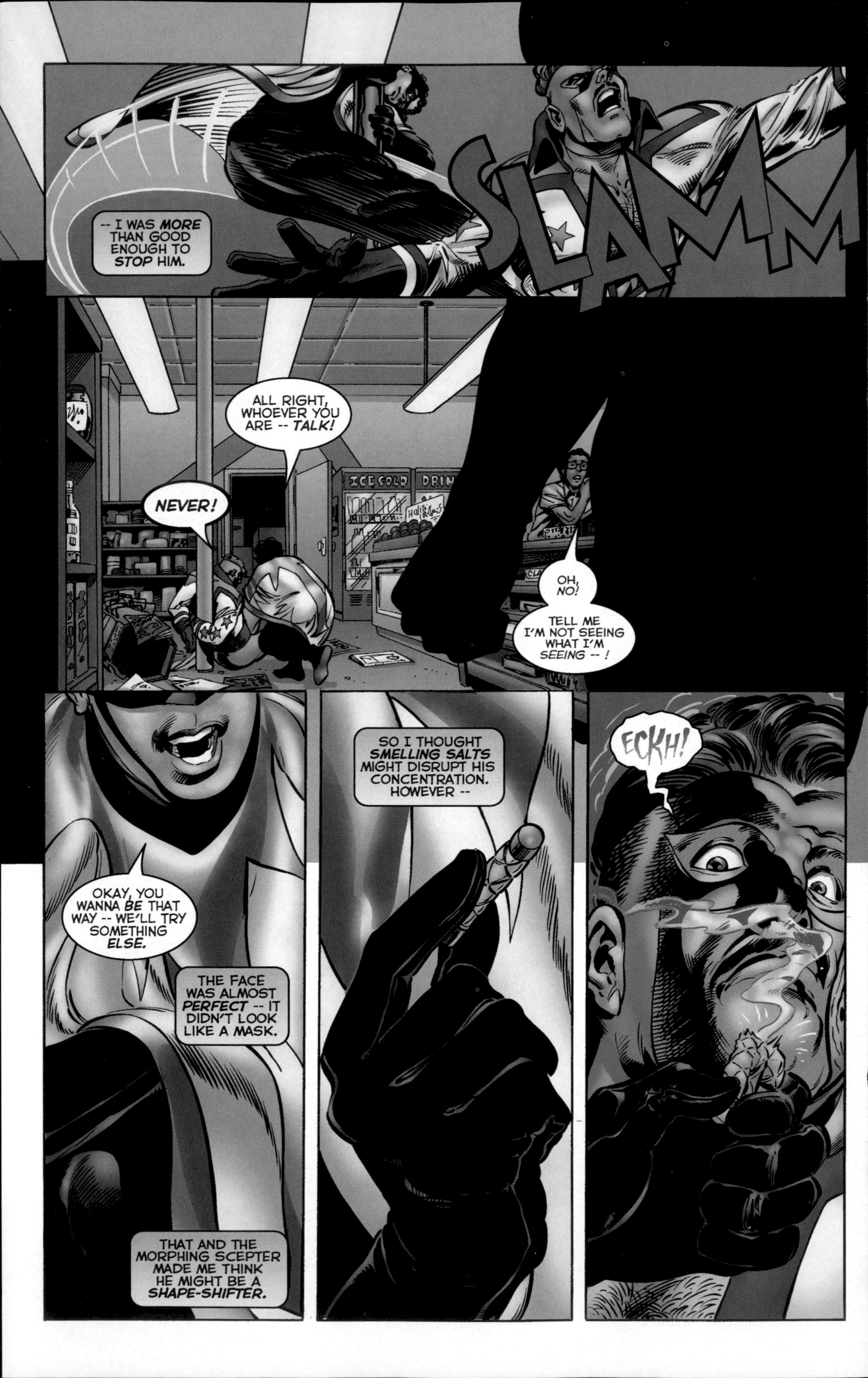
-- I WAS MORE THAN GOOD ENOUGH TO STOP HIM.
SLAMM
ALL RIGHT, WHOEVER YOU ARE -- TALK!
NEVER!
ICE COLD
OH, NO!
TELL ME I'M NOT SEEING WHAT I'M SEEING -- !
OKAY, YOU WANNA BE THAT WAY -- WE'LL TRY SOMETHING ELSE.
THE FACE WAS ALMOST PERFECT -- IT DIDN'T LOOK LIKE A MASK.
THAT AND THE MORPHING SCEPTER MADE ME THINK HE MIGHT BE A SHAPE-SHIFTER.
SO I THOUGHT SMELLING SALTS MIGHT DISRUPT HIS CONCENTRATION. HOWEVER --
ECKH!

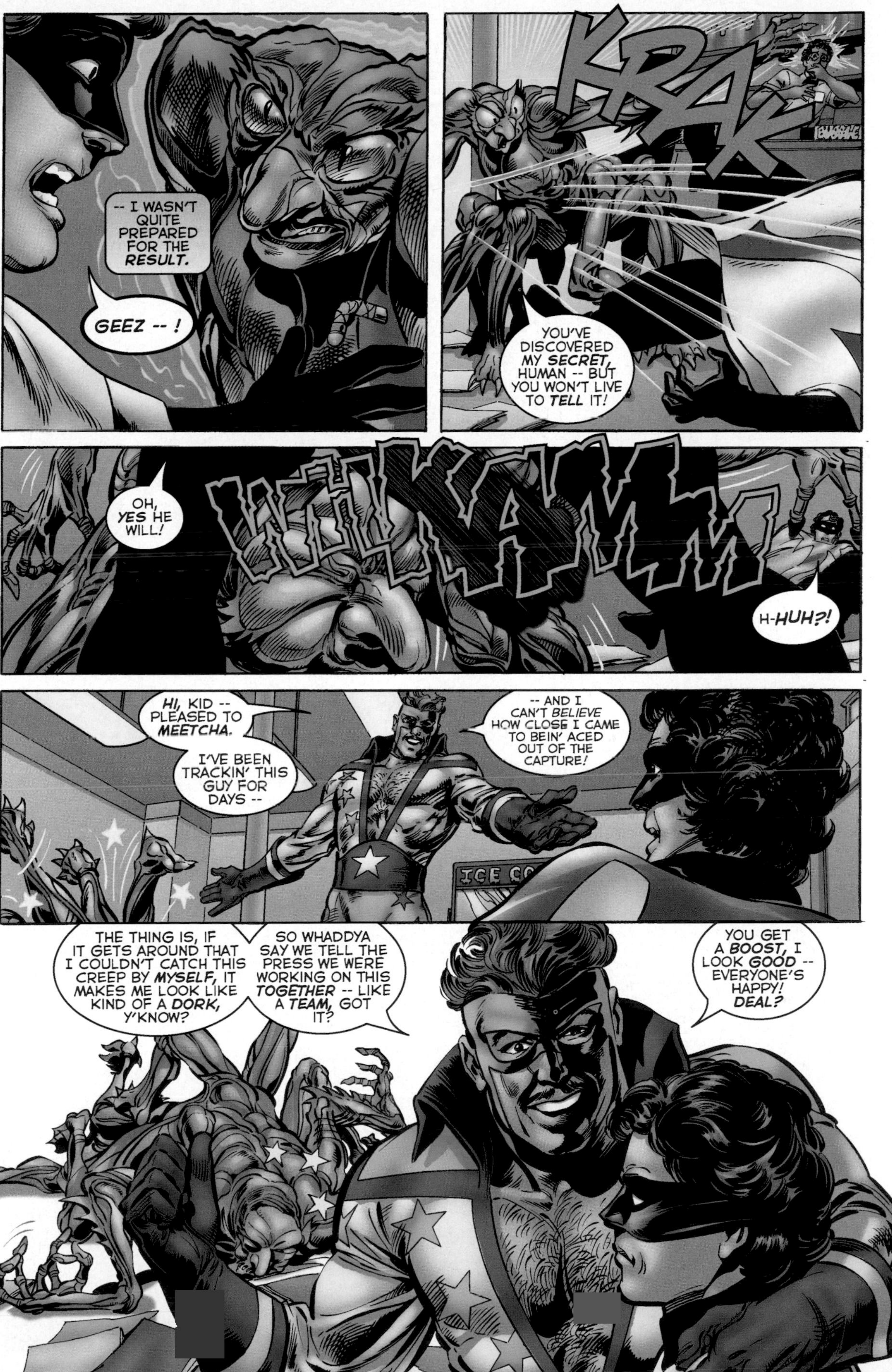
-- I WASN'T QUITE PREPARED FOR THE RESULT.
GEEZ -- !
KRAK
YOU'VE DISCOVERED MY SECRET, HUMAN -- BUT YOU WON'T LIVE TO TELL IT!
OH, YES HE WILL!
H-HUH?!
HI, KID -- PLEASED TO MEETCHA.
I'VE BEEN TRACKIN' THIS GUY FOR DAYS --
-- AND I CAN'T BELIEVE HOW CLOSE I CAME TO BEIN' ACED OUT OF THE CAPTURE!
THE THING IS, IF IT GETS AROUND THAT I COULDN'T CATCH THIS CREEP BY MYSELF, IT MAKES ME LOOK LIKE KIND OF A DORK, Y'KNOW?
SO WHADDYA SAY WE TELL THE PRESS WE WERE WORKING ON THIS TOGETHER -- LIKE A TEAM, GOT IT?
YOU GET A BOOST, I LOOK GOOD -- EVERYONE'S HAPPY! DEAL?

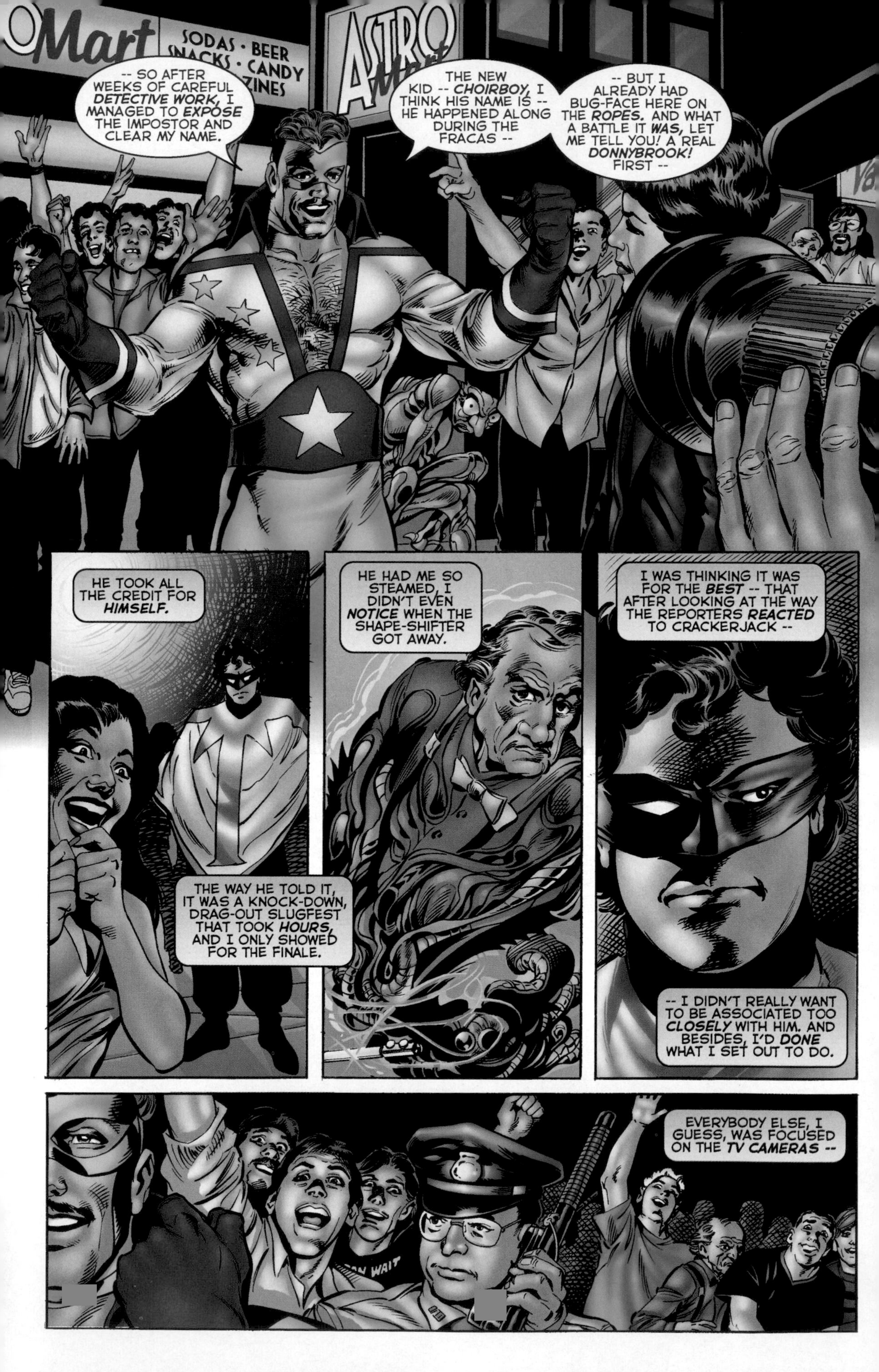

MART
SODAS · BEER
SNACKS · CANDY
ZINES
ASTRO
-- SO AFTER WEEKS OF CAREFUL DETECTIVE WORK, I MANAGED TO EXPOSE THE IMPOSTOR AND CLEAR MY NAME.
THE NEW KID -- CHOIRBOY, I THINK HIS NAME IS -- HE HAPPENED ALONG DURING THE FRACAS --
-- BUT I ALREADY HAD BUG-FACE HERE ON THE ROPES. AND WHAT A BATTLE IT WAS, LET ME TELL YOU! A REAL DONNYBROOK! FIRST --
HE TOOK ALL THE CREDIT FOR HIMSELF.
THE WAY HE TOLD IT, IT WAS A KNOCK-DOWN, DRAG-OUT SLUGFEST THAT TOOK HOURS, AND I ONLY SHOWED FOR THE FINALE.
HE HAD ME SO STEAMED, I DIDN'T EVEN NOTICE WHEN THE SHAPE-SHIFTER GOT AWAY.
I WAS THINKING IT WAS FOR THE BEST -- THAT AFTER LOOKING AT THE WAY THE REPORTERS REACTED TO CRACKERJACK --
-- I DIDN'T REALLY WANT TO BE ASSOCIATED TOO CLOSELY WITH HIM. AND BESIDES, I'D DONE WHAT I SET OUT TO DO.
EVERYBODY ELSE, I GUESS, WAS FOCUSED ON THE TV CAMERAS --

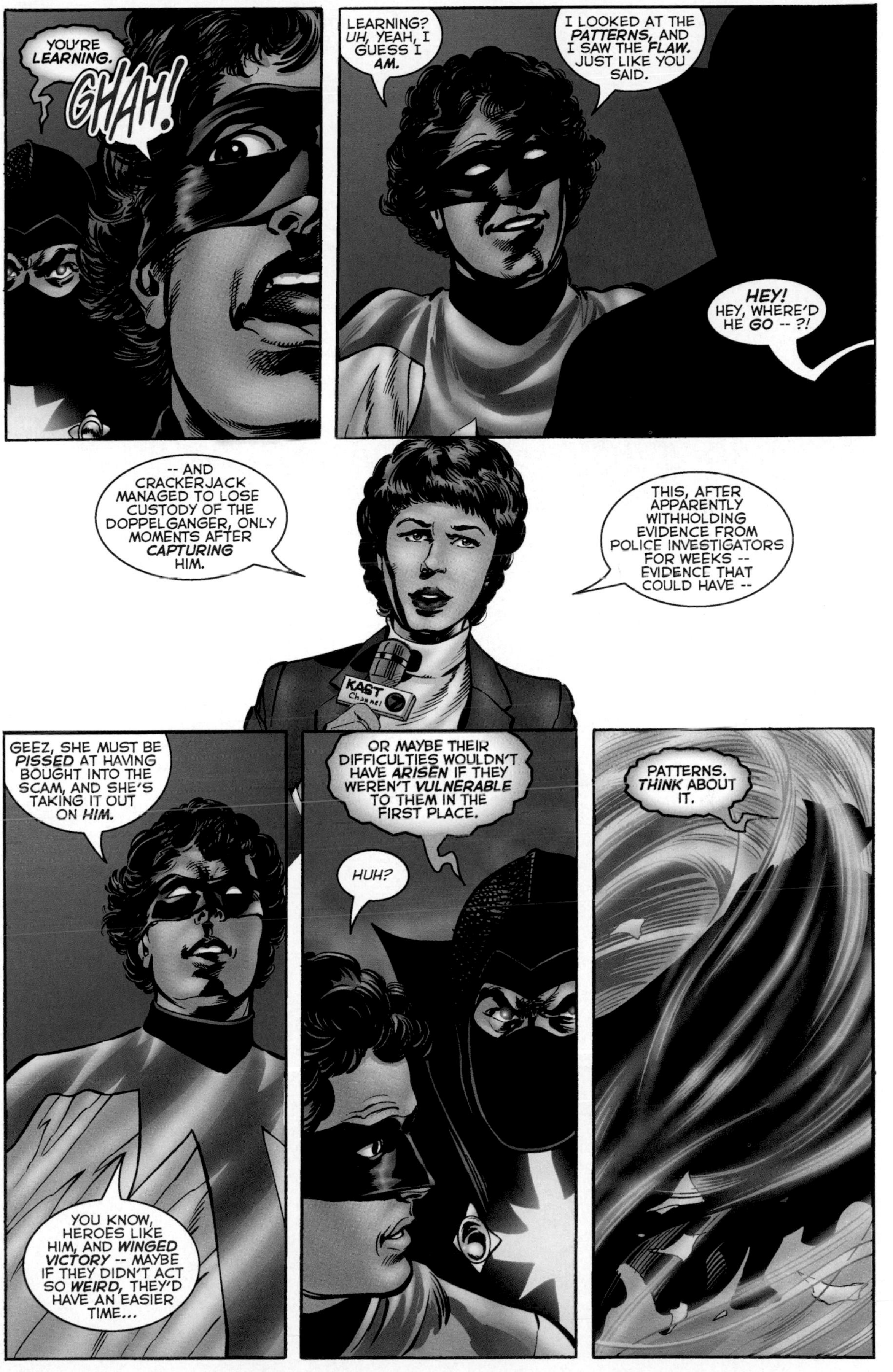
YOU'RE LEARNING.
GHAH!
LEARNING? UH, YEAH, I GUESS I AM.
I LOOKED AT THE PATTERNS, AND I SAW THE FLAW. JUST LIKE YOU SAID.
HEY! HEY, WHERE'D HE GO -- ?!
-- AND CRACKERJACK MANAGED TO LOSE CUSTODY OF THE DOPPELGANGER, ONLY MOMENTS AFTER CAPTURING HIM.
THIS, AFTER APPARENTLY WITHHOLDING EVIDENCE FROM POLICE INVESTIGATORS FOR WEEKS -- EVIDENCE THAT COULD HAVE --
KAST Channel 7
GEEZ, SHE MUST BE PISSED AT HAVING BOUGHT INTO THE SCAM, AND SHE'S TAKING IT OUT ON HIM.
YOU KNOW, HEROES LIKE HIM, AND WINGED VICTORY -- MAYBE IF THEY DIDN'T ACT SO WEIRD, THEY'D HAVE AN EASIER TIME...
OR MAYBE THEIR DIFFICULTIES WOULDN'T HAVE ARISEN IF THEY WEREN'T VULNERABLE TO THEM IN THE FIRST PLACE.
HUH?
PATTERNS. THINK ABOUT IT.

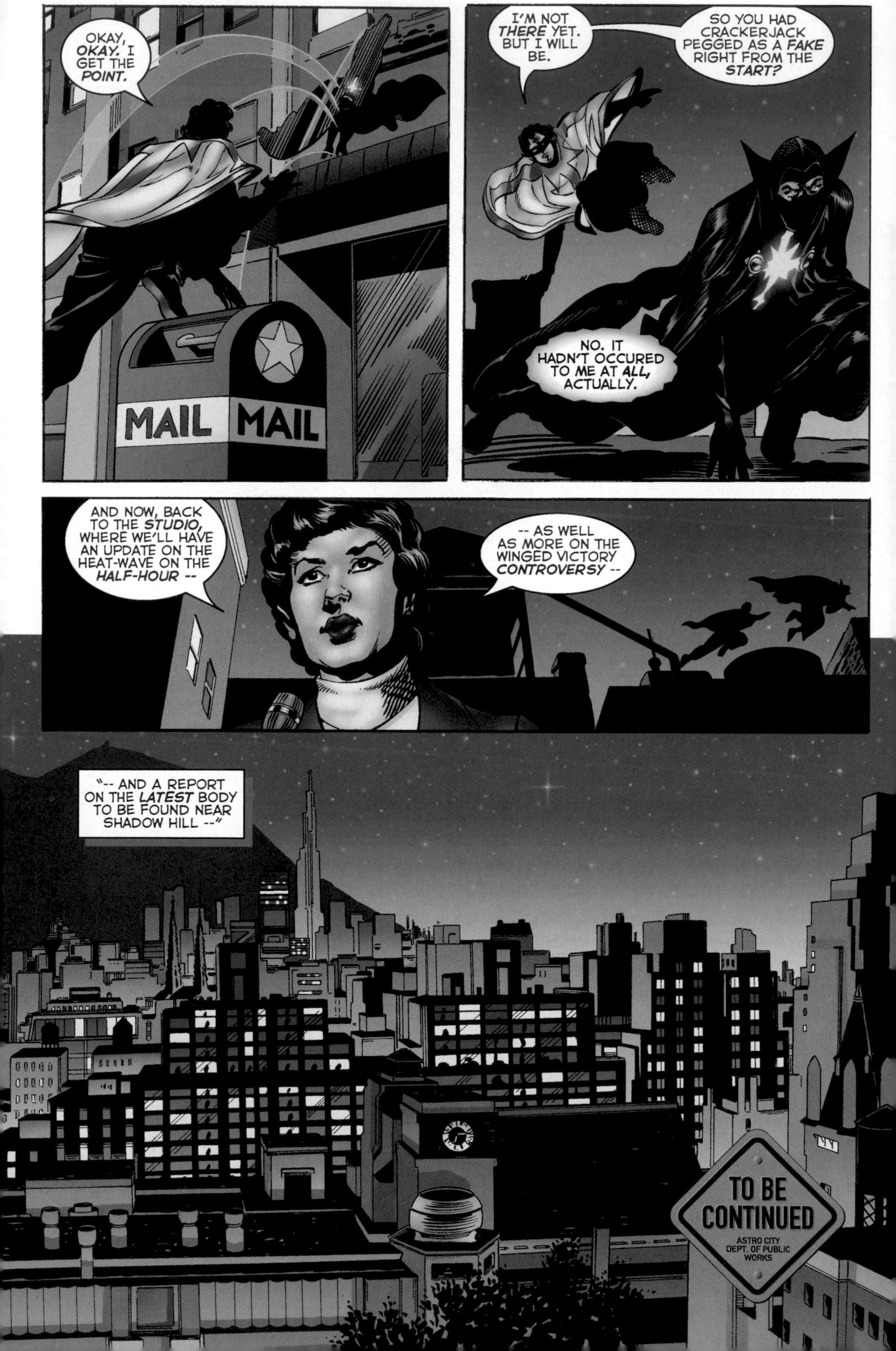
OKAY, OKAY. I GET THE POINT.
SO YOU HAD CRACKERJACK PEGGED AS A FAKE RIGHT FROM THE START?
I'M NOT THERE YET. BUT I WILL BE.
NO. IT HADN'T OCCURED TO ME AT ALL, ACTUALLY.
MAIL
MAIL
AND NOW, BACK TO THE STUDIO, WHERE WE'LL HAVE AN UPDATE ON THE HEAT-WAVE ON THE HALF-HOUR --
-- AS WELL AS MORE ON THE WINGED VICTORY CONTROVERSY --
"-- AND A REPORT ON THE LATEST BODY TO BE FOUND NEAR SHADOW HILL --"
TO BE CONTINUED
ASTRO CITY DEPT. OF PUBLIC WORKS

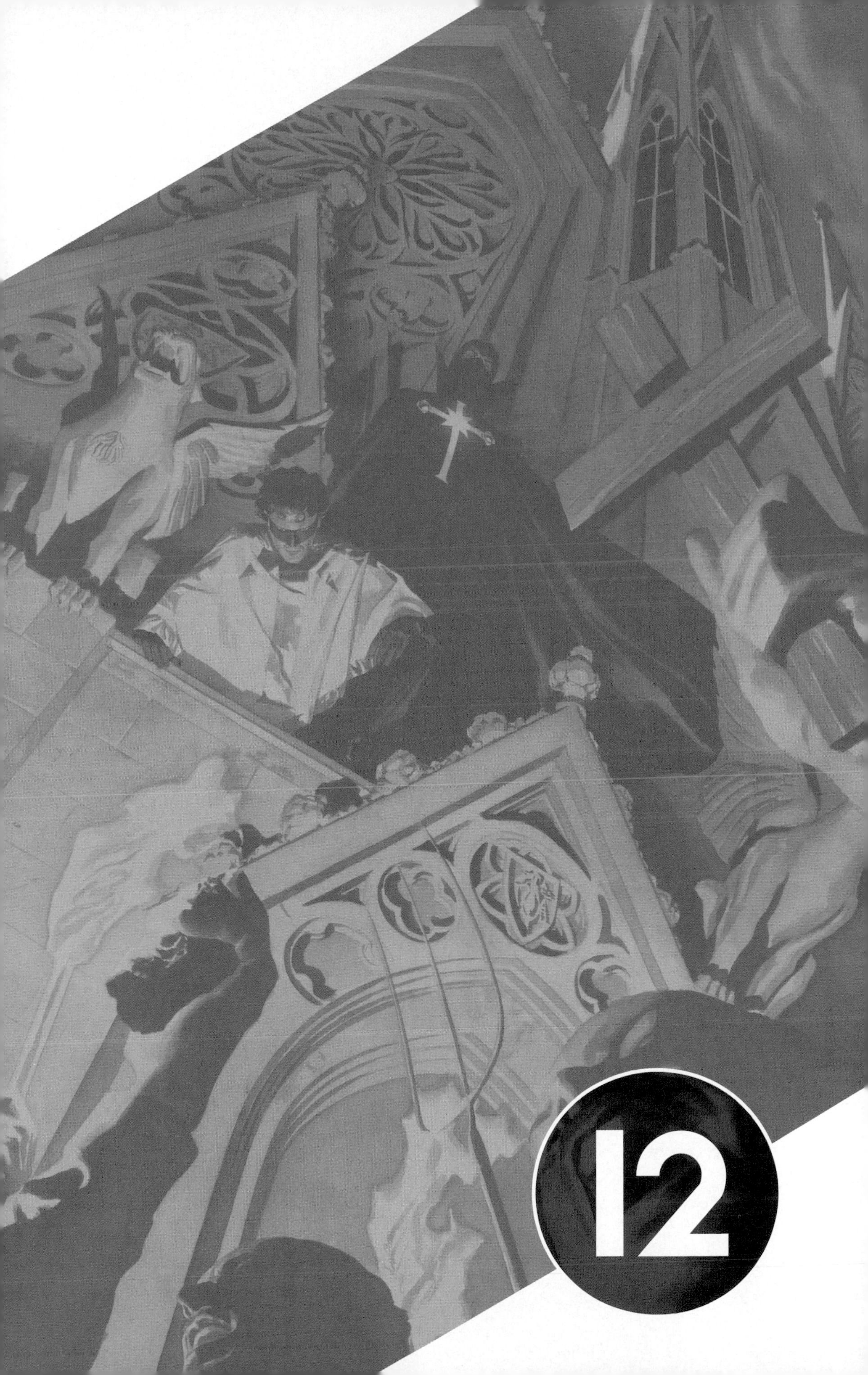

12

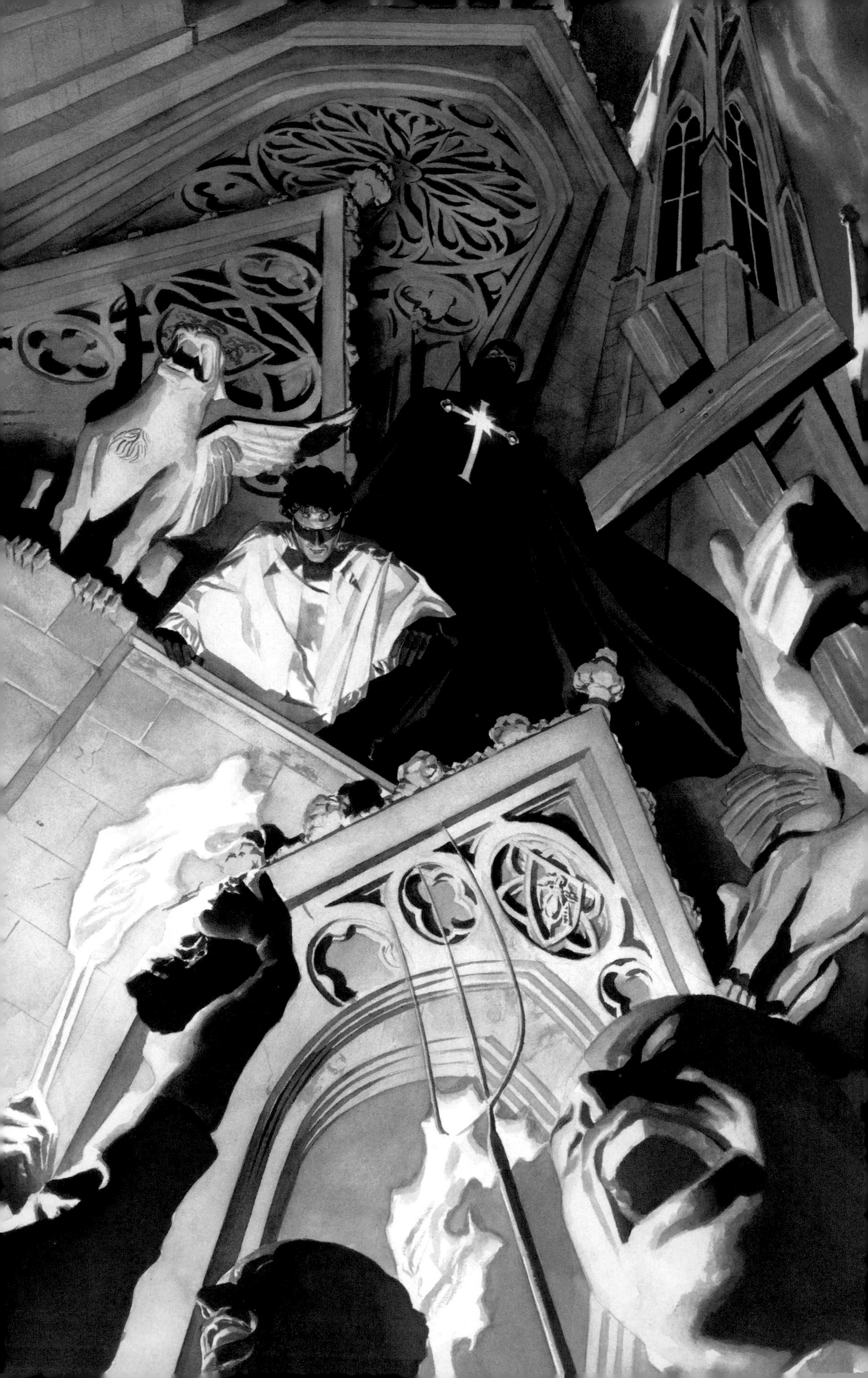

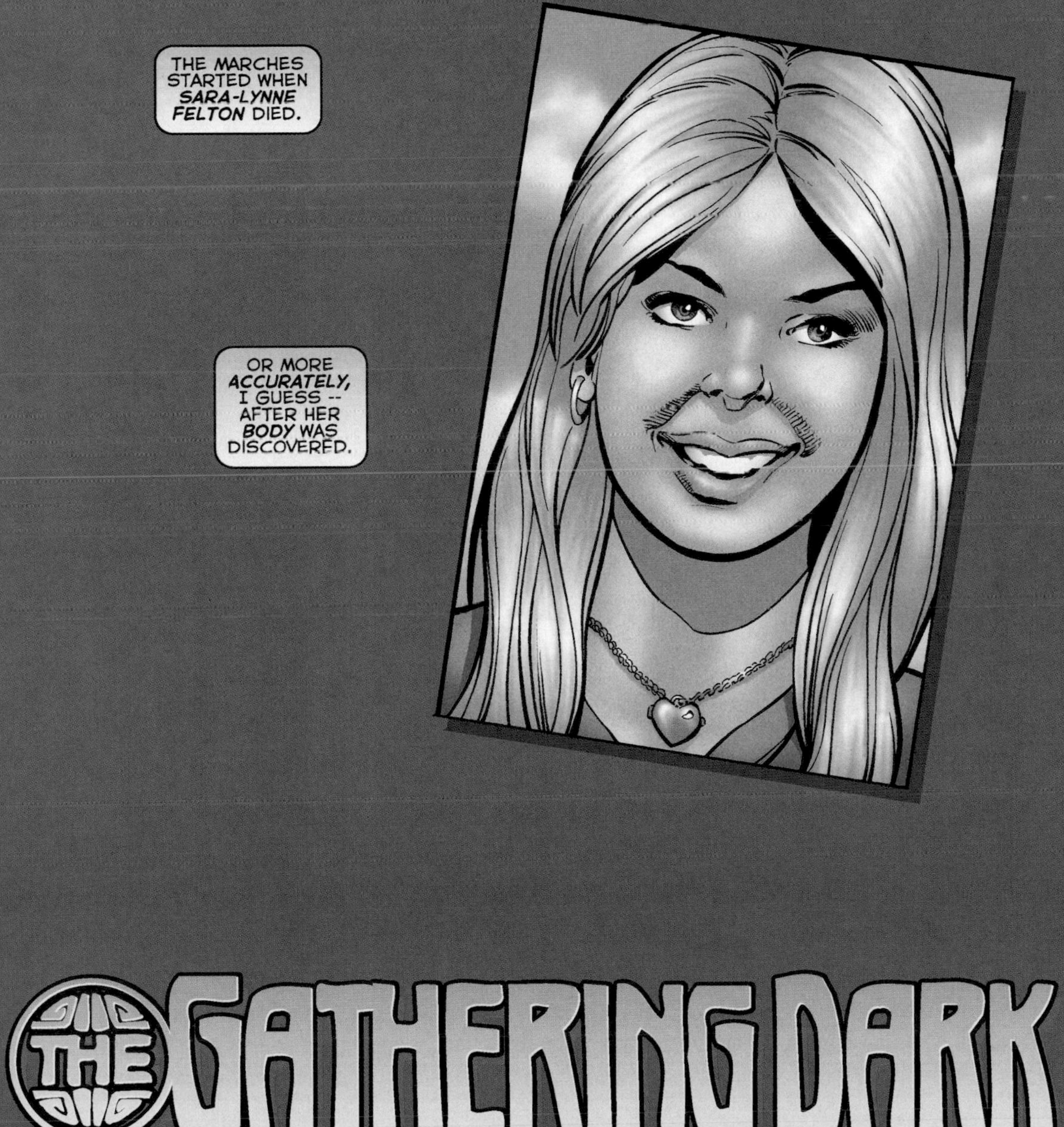
THE MARCHES STARTED WHEN SARA-LYNNE FELTON DIED.
OR MORE ACCURATELY, I GUESS -- AFTER HER BODY WAS DISCOVERED.
THE GATHERING DARK

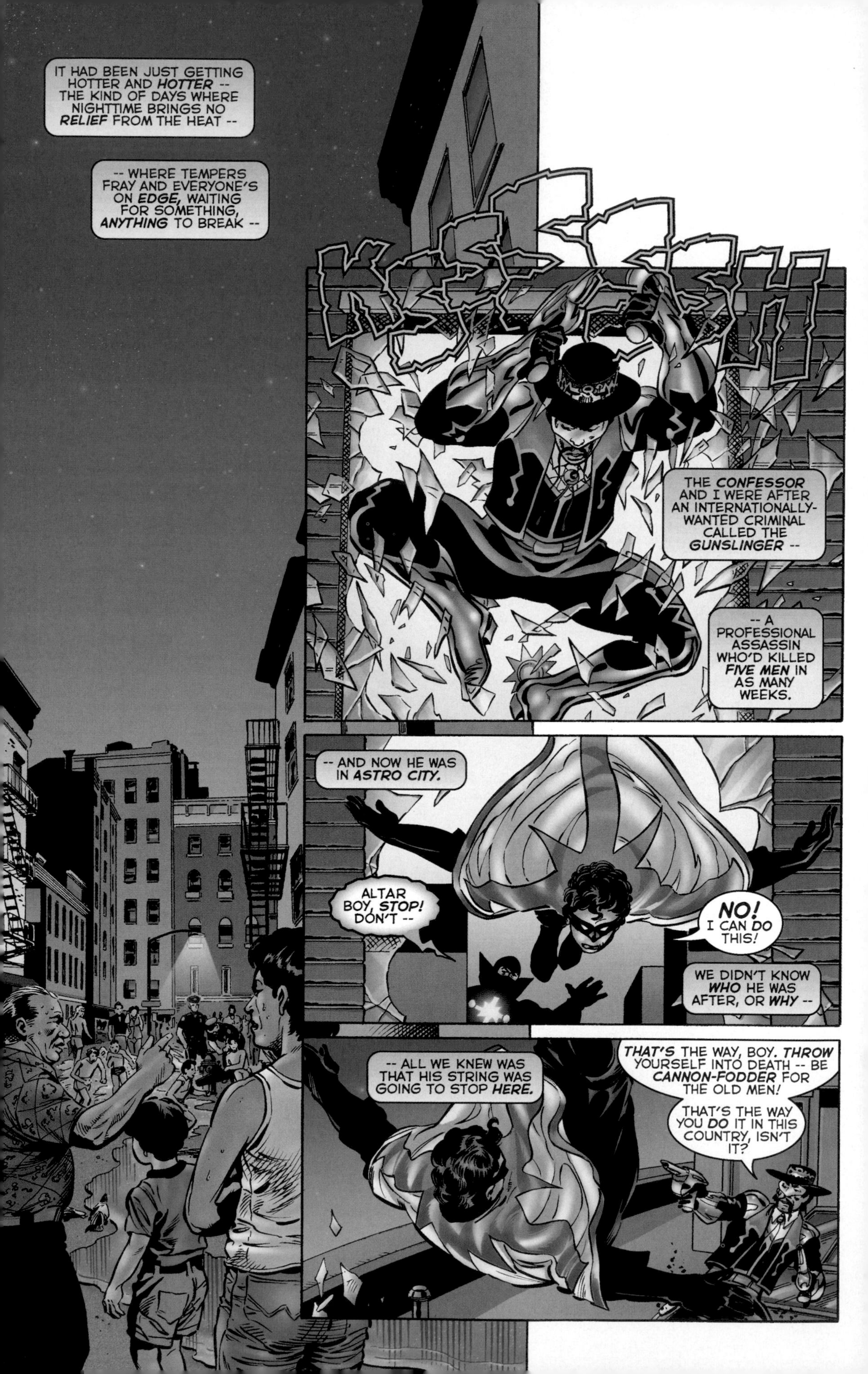
IT HAD BEEN JUST GETTING HOTTER AND HOTTER -- THE KIND OF DAYS WHERE NIGHTTIME BRINGS NO RELIEF FROM THE HEAT --
-- WHERE TEMPERS FRAY AND EVERYONE'S ON EDGE, WAITING FOR SOMETHING, ANYTHING TO BREAK --
THE CONFESSOR AND I WERE AFTER AN INTERNATIONALLY-WANTED CRIMINAL CALLED THE GUNSLINGER --
-- A PROFESSIONAL ASSASSIN WHO'D KILLED FIVE MEN IN AS MANY WEEKS.
-- AND NOW HE WAS IN ASTRO CITY.
ALTAR BOY, STOP! DON'T --
NO! I CAN DO THIS!
WE DIDN'T KNOW WHO HE WAS AFTER, OR WHY --
-- ALL WE KNEW WAS THAT HIS STRING WAS GOING TO STOP HERE.
THAT'S THE WAY, BOY. THROW YOURSELF INTO DEATH -- BE CANNON-FODDER FOR THE OLD MEN!
THAT'S THE WAY YOU DO IT IN THIS COUNTRY, ISN'T IT?

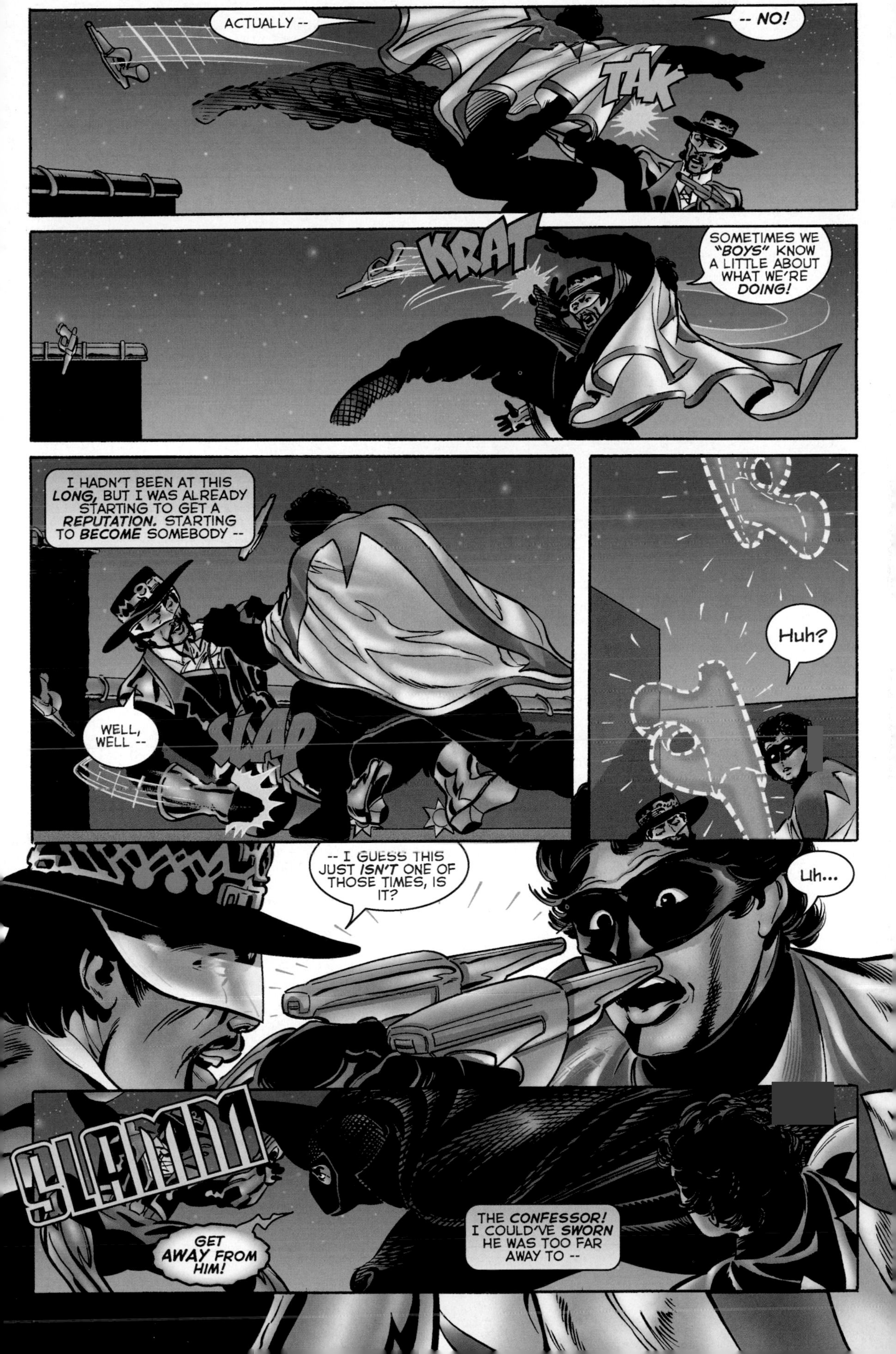
ACTUALLY --
-- NO!
TAK
KRAT
SOMETIMES WE "BOYS" KNOW A LITTLE ABOUT WHAT WE'RE DOING!
I HADN'T BEEN AT THIS LONG, BUT I WAS ALREADY STARTING TO GET A REPUTATION. STARTING TO BECOME SOMEBODY --
WELL, WELL --
SLAP
Huh?
-- I GUESS THIS JUST ISN'T ONE OF THOSE TIMES, IS IT?
Uh...
SLAMM
GET AWAY FROM HIM!
THE CONFESSOR! I COULD'VE SWORN HE WAS TOO FAR AWAY TO --

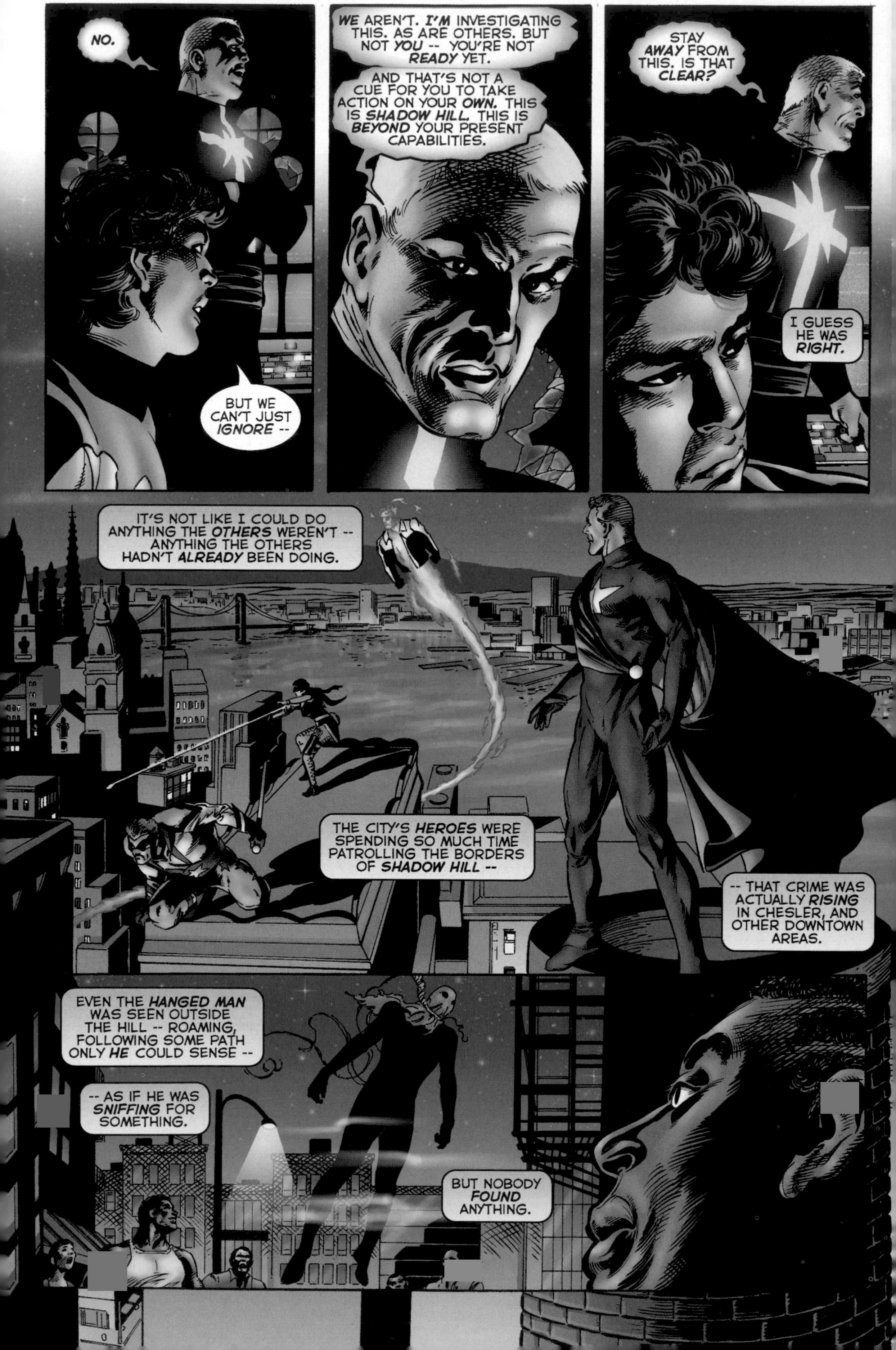
NO.
BUT WE CAN'T JUST IGNORE --
WE AREN'T. I'M INVESTIGATING THIS. AS ARE OTHERS. BUT NOT YOU -- YOU'RE NOT READY YET.
AND THAT'S NOT A CUE FOR YOU TO TAKE ACTION ON YOUR OWN. THIS IS SHADOW HILL. THIS IS BEYOND YOUR PRESENT CAPABILITIES.
STAY AWAY FROM THIS. IS THAT CLEAR?
I GUESS HE WAS RIGHT.
IT'S NOT LIKE I COULD DO ANYTHING THE OTHERS WEREN'T -- ANYTHING THE OTHERS HADN'T ALREADY BEEN DOING.
THE CITY'S HEROES WERE SPENDING SO MUCH TIME PATROLLING THE BORDERS OF SHADOW HILL --
-- THAT CRIME WAS ACTUALLY RISING IN CHESLER, AND OTHER DOWNTOWN AREAS.
EVEN THE HANGED MAN WAS SEEN OUTSIDE THE HILL -- ROAMING, FOLLOWING SOME PATH ONLY HE COULD SENSE --
-- AS IF HE WAS SNIFFING FOR SOMETHING.
BUT NOBODY FOUND ANYTHING.

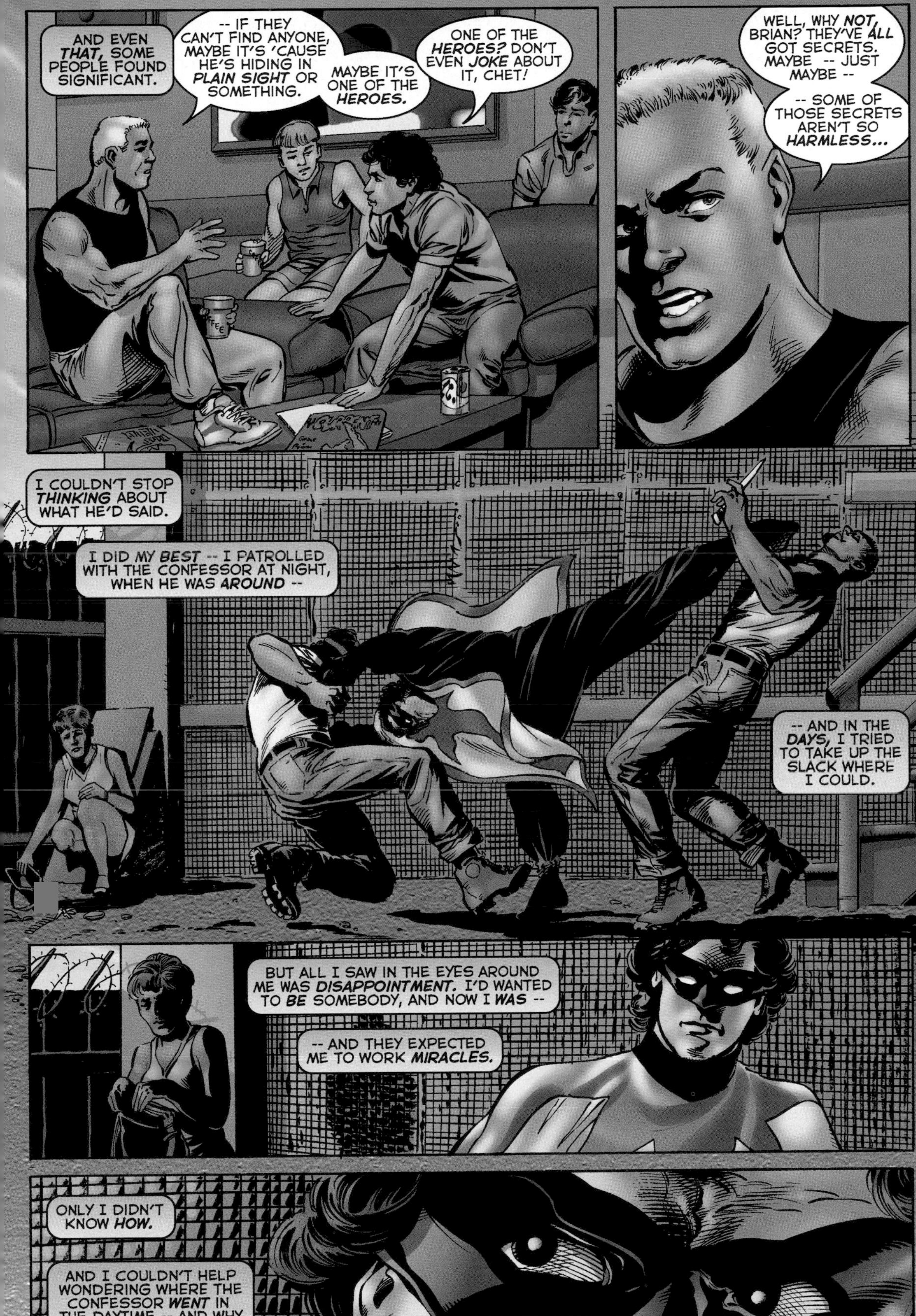
AND EVEN THAT, SOME PEOPLE FOUND SIGNIFICANT.
-- IF THEY CAN'T FIND ANYONE, MAYBE IT'S 'CAUSE HE'S HIDING IN PLAIN SIGHT OR SOMETHING.
MAYBE IT'S ONE OF THE HEROES.
ONE OF THE HEROES? DON'T EVEN JOKE ABOUT IT, CHET!
WELL, WHY NOT, BRIAN? THEY'VE ALL GOT SECRETS. MAYBE -- JUST MAYBE --
-- SOME OF THOSE SECRETS AREN'T SO HARMLESS...
I COULDN'T STOP THINKING ABOUT WHAT HE'D SAID.
I DID MY BEST -- I PATROLLED WITH THE CONFESSOR AT NIGHT, WHEN HE WAS AROUND --
-- AND IN THE DAYS, I TRIED TO TAKE UP THE SLACK WHERE I COULD.
BUT ALL I SAW IN THE EYES AROUND ME WAS DISAPPOINTMENT. I'D WANTED TO BE SOMEBODY, AND NOW I WAS --
-- AND THEY EXPECTED ME TO WORK MIRACLES.
ONLY I DIDN'T KNOW HOW.
AND I COULDN'T HELP WONDERING WHERE THE CONFESSOR WENT IN THE DAYTIME -- AND WHY HE ACTED SO STRANGE SOMETIMES --

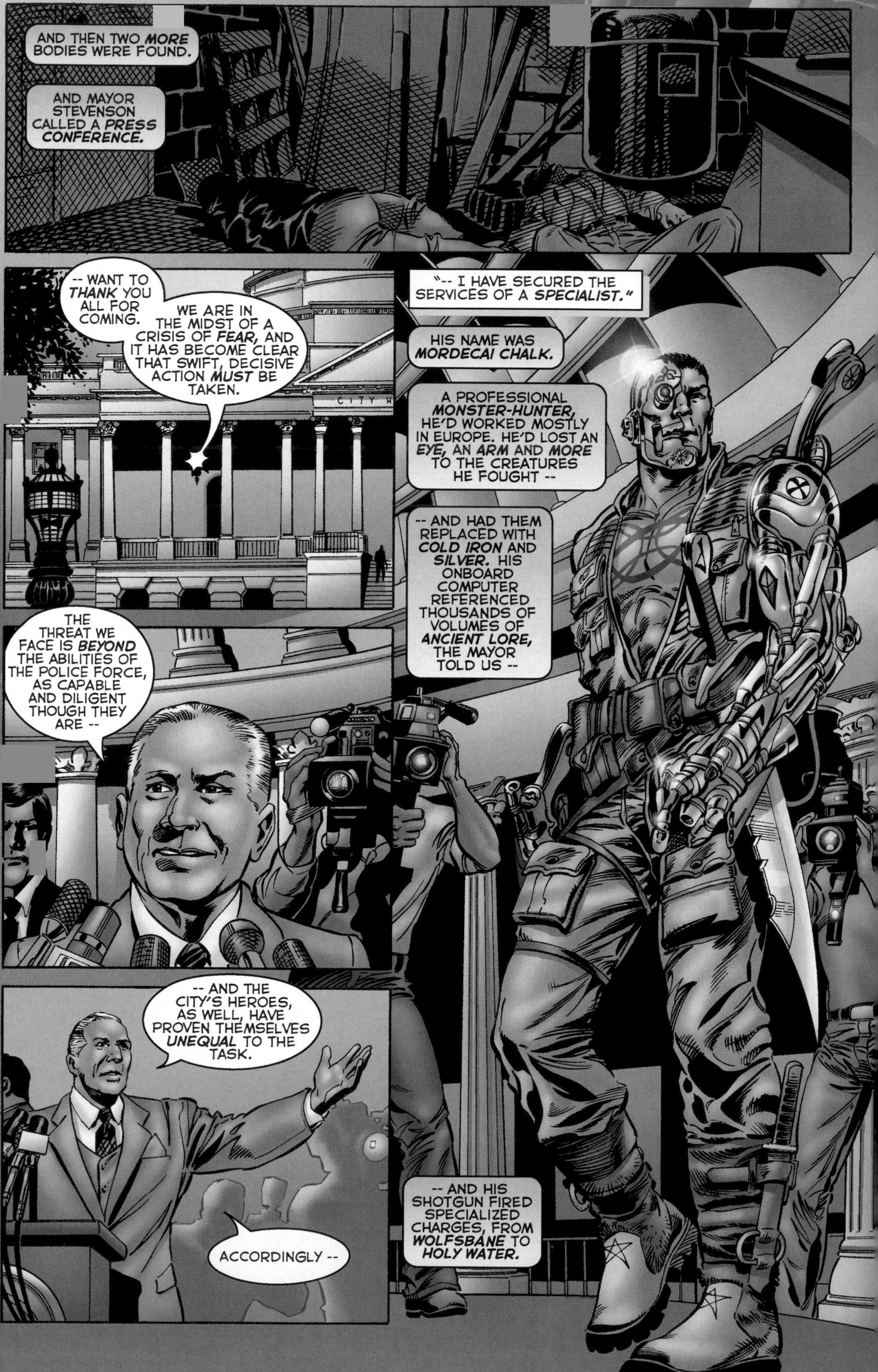
AND THEN TWO MORE BODIES WERE FOUND.
AND MAYOR STEVENSON CALLED A PRESS CONFERENCE.
-- WANT TO THANK YOU ALL FOR COMING.
WE ARE IN THE MIDST OF A CRISIS OF FEAR, AND IT HAS BECOME CLEAR THAT SWIFT, DECISIVE ACTION MUST BE TAKEN.
CITY H
THE THREAT WE FACE IS BEYOND THE ABILITIES OF THE POLICE FORCE, AS CAPABLE AND DILIGENT THOUGH THEY ARE --
-- AND THE CITY'S HEROES, AS WELL, HAVE PROVEN THEMSELVES UNEQUAL TO THE TASK.
ACCORDINGLY --
"-- I HAVE SECURED THE SERVICES OF A SPECIALIST."
HIS NAME WAS MORDECAI CHALK.
A PROFESSIONAL MONSTER-HUNTER, HE'D WORKED MOSTLY IN EUROPE. HE'D LOST AN EYE, AN ARM AND MORE TO THE CREATURES HE FOUGHT --
-- AND HAD THEM REPLACED WITH COLD IRON AND SILVER. HIS ONBOARD COMPUTER REFERENCED THOUSANDS OF VOLUMES OF ANCIENT LORE, THE MAYOR TOLD US --
-- AND HIS SHOTGUN FIRED SPECIALIZED CHARGES, FROM WOLFSBANE TO HOLY WATER.

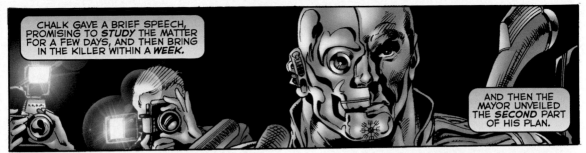

CHALK GAVE A BRIEF SPEECH, PROMISING TO *STUDY* THE MATTER FOR A FEW DAYS, AND THEN BRING IN THE KILLER WITHIN A *WEEK*.

AND THEN THE MAYOR UNVEILED THE *SECOND* PART OF HIS PLAN.

IT IS WITH DEEP DELIBERATION AND *CONCERN* THAT I TAKE THIS STEP --

-- FOR I'D HATE TO JEOPARDIZE RELATIONS WITH THE *SUPERHUMAN* COMMUNITY.

BUT IT SEEMS OBVIOUS WE FACE AN *UNKNOWN* SUPERHUMAN HERE --

-- AND WE MUST INVESTIGATE ALL AVENUES. ACCORDINGLY, THE CITY WILL BEGIN TO *REGISTER* SUPERHUMANS --

-- IN ORDER TO GATHER INFORMATION TO HELP US *TRACK DOWN* THE KILLER. ALL INFORMATION WILL BE KEPT *CONFIDENTIAL*, AND --

MR. *MAYOR!* DO YOU PLAN TO REGISTER *ALL* THE HEROES?

FOR NOW, WE'LL ONLY BE REGISTERING THOSE WITH *MYSTIC POWERS*. IT'S *INFORMATION* WE'RE INTERESTED IN, NOT CONTROL.

AND WHAT IF THE HEROES WON'T *COOPERATE?*

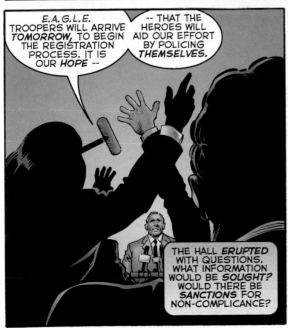

E.A.G.L.E. TROOPERS WILL ARRIVE *TOMORROW*, TO BEGIN THE REGISTRATION PROCESS. IT IS OUR *HOPE* --

-- THAT THE HEROES WILL AID OUR EFFORT BY POLICING *THEMSELVES*.

THE HALL *ERUPTED* WITH QUESTIONS. WHAT INFORMATION WOULD BE *SOUGHT?* WOULD THERE BE *SANCTIONS* FOR NON-COMPLIANCE?

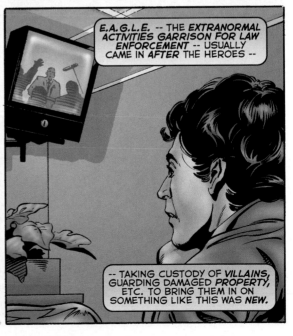

E.A.G.L.E. -- THE *EXTRANORMAL ACTIVITIES GARRISON FOR LAW ENFORCEMENT* -- USUALLY CAME IN *AFTER* THE HEROES --

-- TAKING CUSTODY OF *VILLAINS*, GUARDING DAMAGED *PROPERTY*, ETC. TO BRING THEM IN ON SOMETHING LIKE THIS WAS *NEW*.

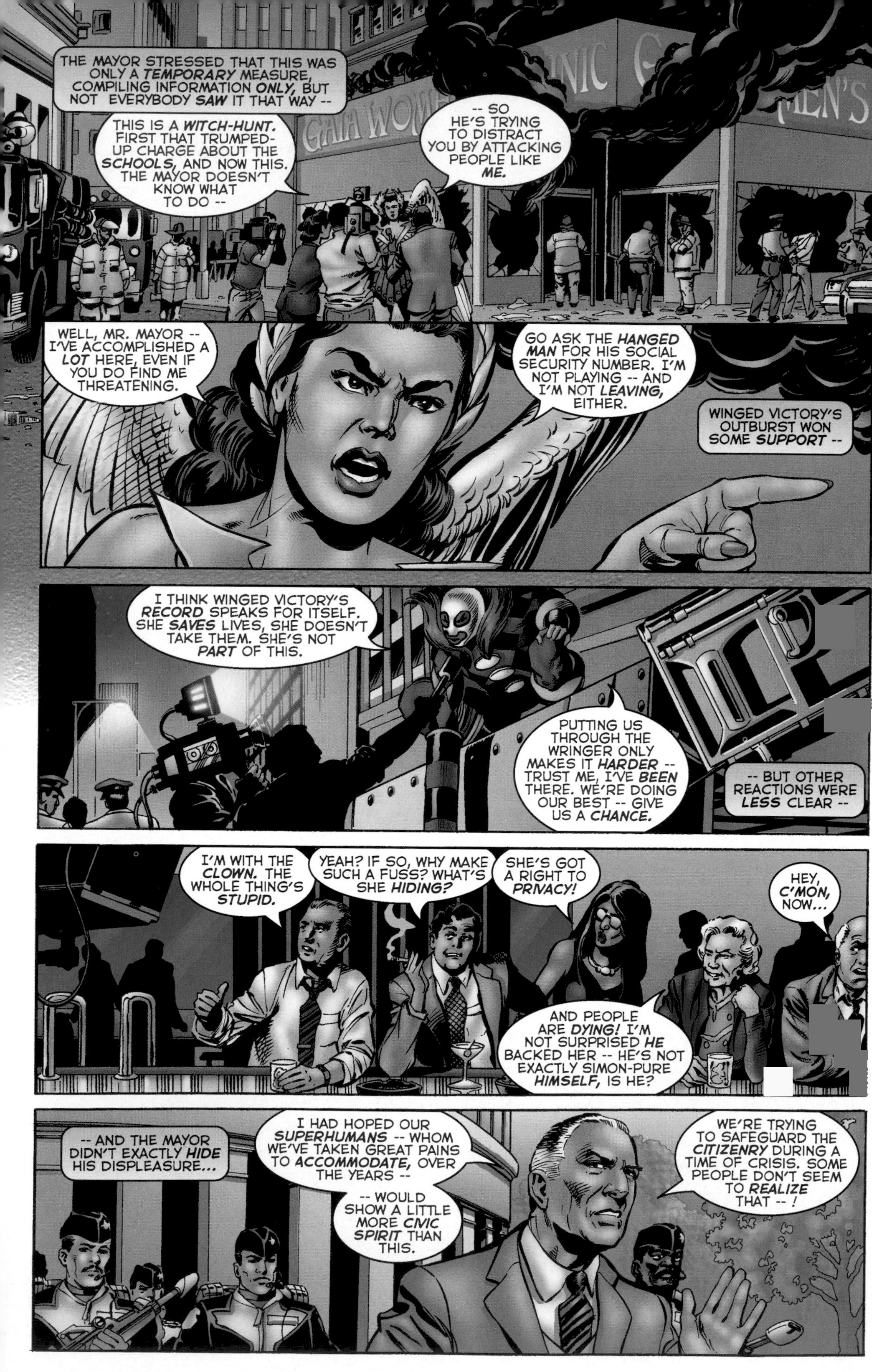

THE MAYOR STRESSED THAT THIS WAS ONLY A TEMPORARY MEASURE, COMPILING INFORMATION ONLY, BUT NOT EVERYBODY SAW IT THAT WAY --
THIS IS A WITCH-HUNT. FIRST THAT TRUMPED-UP CHARGE ABOUT THE SCHOOLS, AND NOW THIS. THE MAYOR DOESN'T KNOW WHAT TO DO --
-- SO HE'S TRYING TO DISTRACT YOU BY ATTACKING PEOPLE LIKE ME.
GAIA WOMEN'S CLINIC
WELL, MR. MAYOR -- I'VE ACCOMPLISHED A LOT HERE, EVEN IF YOU DO FIND ME THREATENING.
GO ASK THE HANGED MAN FOR HIS SOCIAL SECURITY NUMBER. I'M NOT PLAYING -- AND I'M NOT LEAVING, EITHER.
WINGED VICTORY'S OUTBURST WON SOME SUPPORT --
I THINK WINGED VICTORY'S RECORD SPEAKS FOR ITSELF. SHE SAVES LIVES, SHE DOESN'T TAKE THEM. SHE'S NOT PART OF THIS.
PUTTING US THROUGH THE WRINGER ONLY MAKES IT HARDER -- TRUST ME, I'VE BEEN THERE. WE'RE DOING OUR BEST -- GIVE US A CHANCE.
-- BUT OTHER REACTIONS WERE LESS CLEAR --
I'M WITH THE CLOWN. THE WHOLE THING'S STUPID.
YEAH? IF SO, WHY MAKE SUCH A FUSS? WHAT'S SHE HIDING?
SHE'S GOT A RIGHT TO PRIVACY!
AND PEOPLE ARE DYING! I'M NOT SURPRISED HE BACKED HER -- HE'S NOT EXACTLY SIMON-PURE HIMSELF, IS HE?
HEY, C'MON, NOW...
-- AND THE MAYOR DIDN'T EXACTLY HIDE HIS DISPLEASURE...
I HAD HOPED OUR SUPERHUMANS -- WHOM WE'VE TAKEN GREAT PAINS TO ACCOMMODATE, OVER THE YEARS --
-- WOULD SHOW A LITTLE MORE CIVIC SPIRIT THAN THIS.
WE'RE TRYING TO SAFEGUARD THE CITIZENRY DURING A TIME OF CRISIS. SOME PEOPLE DON'T SEEM TO REALIZE THAT -- !

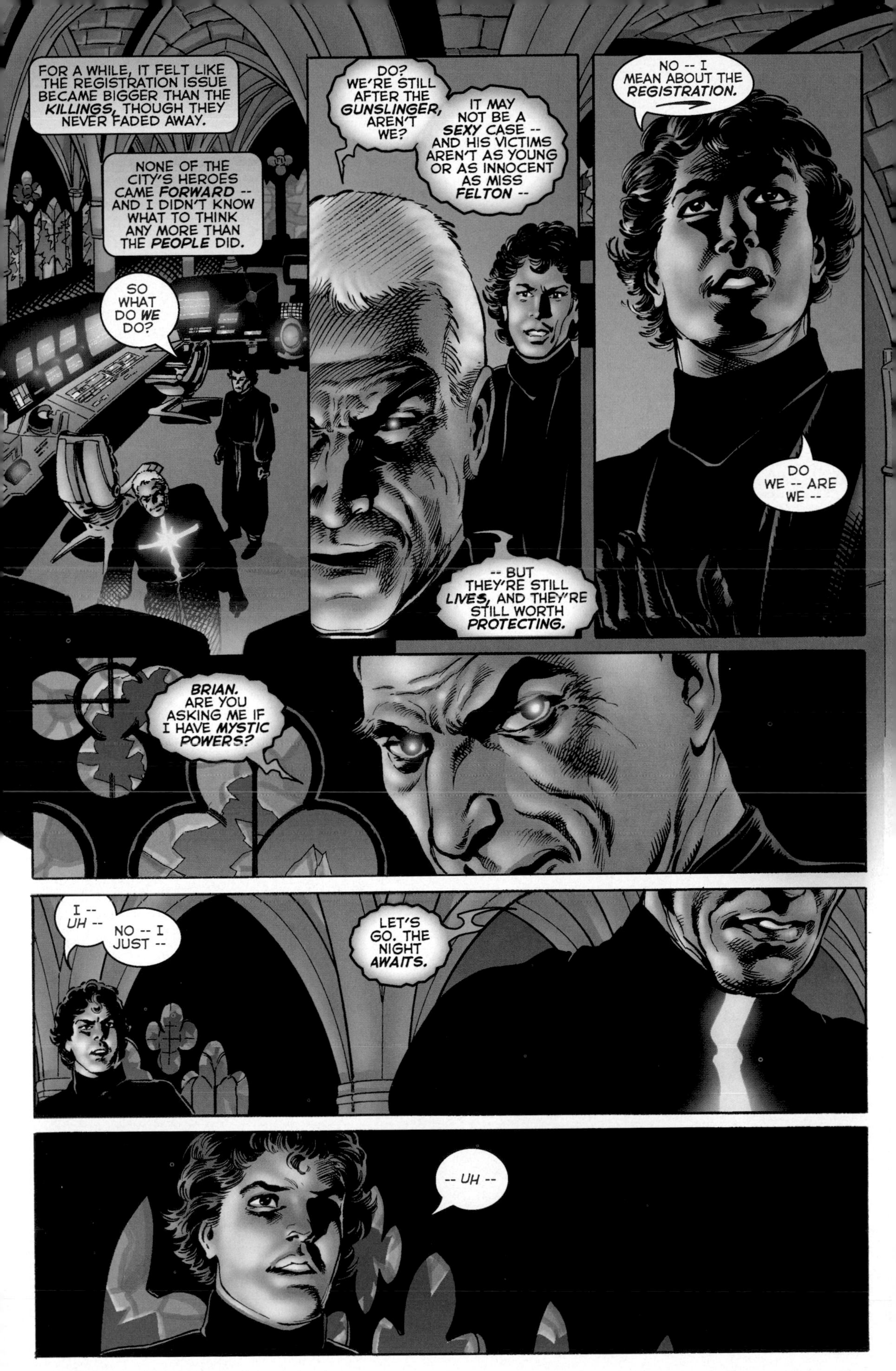
FOR A WHILE, IT FELT LIKE THE REGISTRATION ISSUE BECAME BIGGER THAN THE KILLINGS, THOUGH THEY NEVER FADED AWAY.
NONE OF THE CITY'S HEROES CAME FORWARD -- AND I DIDN'T KNOW WHAT TO THINK ANY MORE THAN THE PEOPLE DID.
SO WHAT DO WE DO?
DO? WE'RE STILL AFTER THE GUNSLINGER, AREN'T WE?
IT MAY NOT BE A SEXY CASE -- AND HIS VICTIMS AREN'T AS YOUNG OR AS INNOCENT AS MISS FELTON --
-- BUT THEY'RE STILL LIVES, AND THEY'RE STILL WORTH PROTECTING.
NO -- I MEAN ABOUT THE REGISTRATION.
DO WE -- ARE WE --
BRIAN. ARE YOU ASKING ME IF I HAVE MYSTIC POWERS?
I -- UH --
NO -- I JUST --
LET'S GO. THE NIGHT AWAITS.
-- UH --

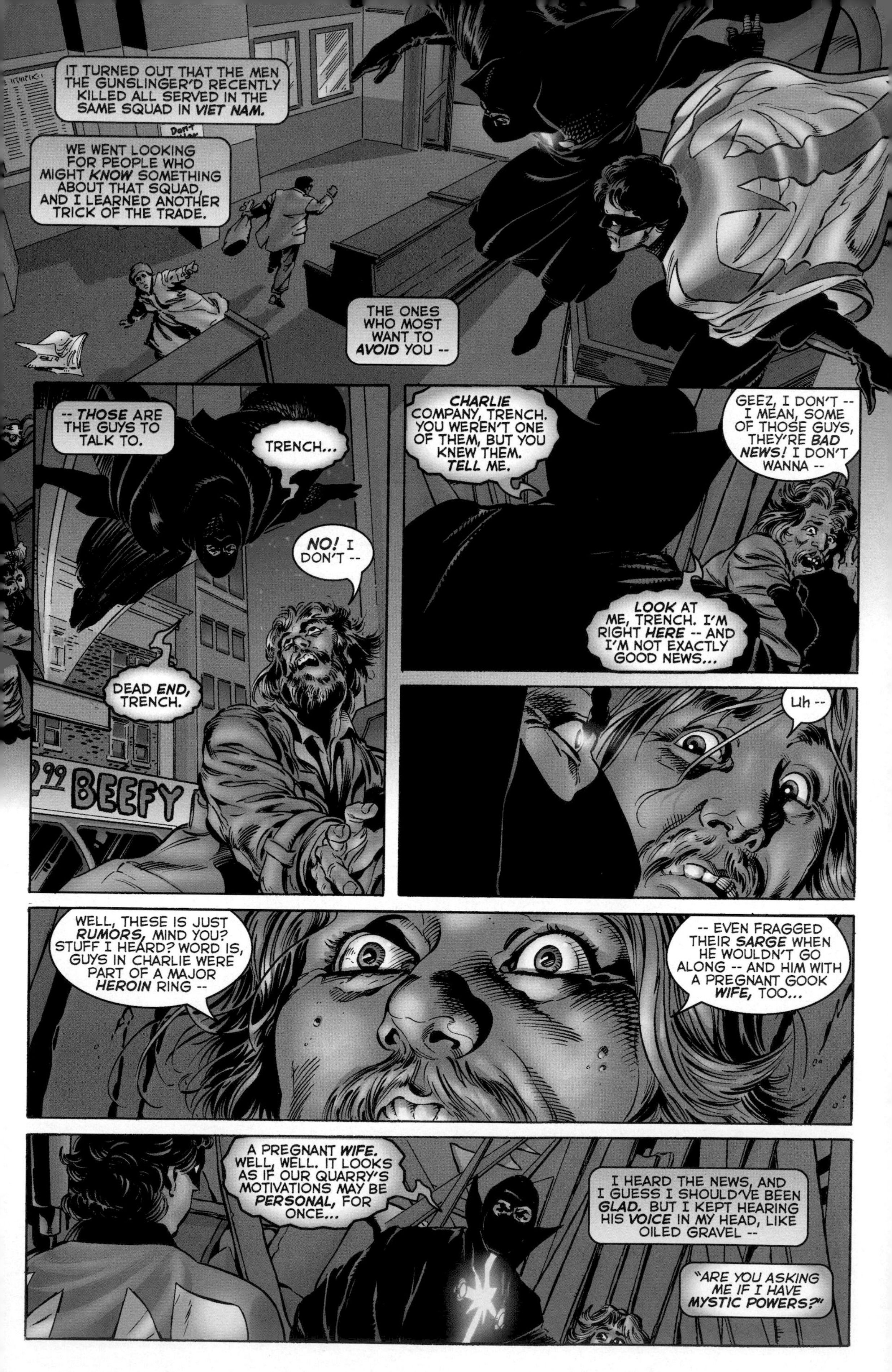
IT TURNED OUT THAT THE MEN THE GUNSLINGER'D RECENTLY KILLED ALL SERVED IN THE SAME SQUAD IN VIET NAM.
WE WENT LOOKING FOR PEOPLE WHO MIGHT KNOW SOMETHING ABOUT THAT SQUAD, AND I LEARNED ANOTHER TRICK OF THE TRADE.
THE ONES WHO MOST WANT TO AVOID YOU --
-- THOSE ARE THE GUYS TO TALK TO.
TRENCH...
NO! I DON'T --
DEAD END, TRENCH.
BEEFY
CHARLIE COMPANY, TRENCH. YOU WEREN'T ONE OF THEM, BUT YOU KNEW THEM. TELL ME.
GEEZ, I DON'T -- I MEAN, SOME OF THOSE GUYS, THEY'RE BAD NEWS! I DON'T WANNA --
LOOK AT ME, TRENCH. I'M RIGHT HERE -- AND I'M NOT EXACTLY GOOD NEWS...
UH --
WELL, THESE IS JUST RUMORS, MIND YOU? STUFF I HEARD? WORD IS, GUYS IN CHARLIE WERE PART OF A MAJOR HEROIN RING --
-- EVEN FRAGGED THEIR SARGE WHEN HE WOULDN'T GO ALONG -- AND HIM WITH A PREGNANT GOOK WIFE, TOO...
A PREGNANT WIFE. WELL, WELL. IT LOOKS AS IF OUR QUARRY'S MOTIVATIONS MAY BE PERSONAL, FOR ONCE...
I HEARD THE NEWS, AND I GUESS I SHOULD'VE BEEN GLAD. BUT I KEPT HEARING HIS VOICE IN MY HEAD, LIKE OILED GRAVEL --
"ARE YOU ASKING ME IF I HAVE MYSTIC POWERS?"

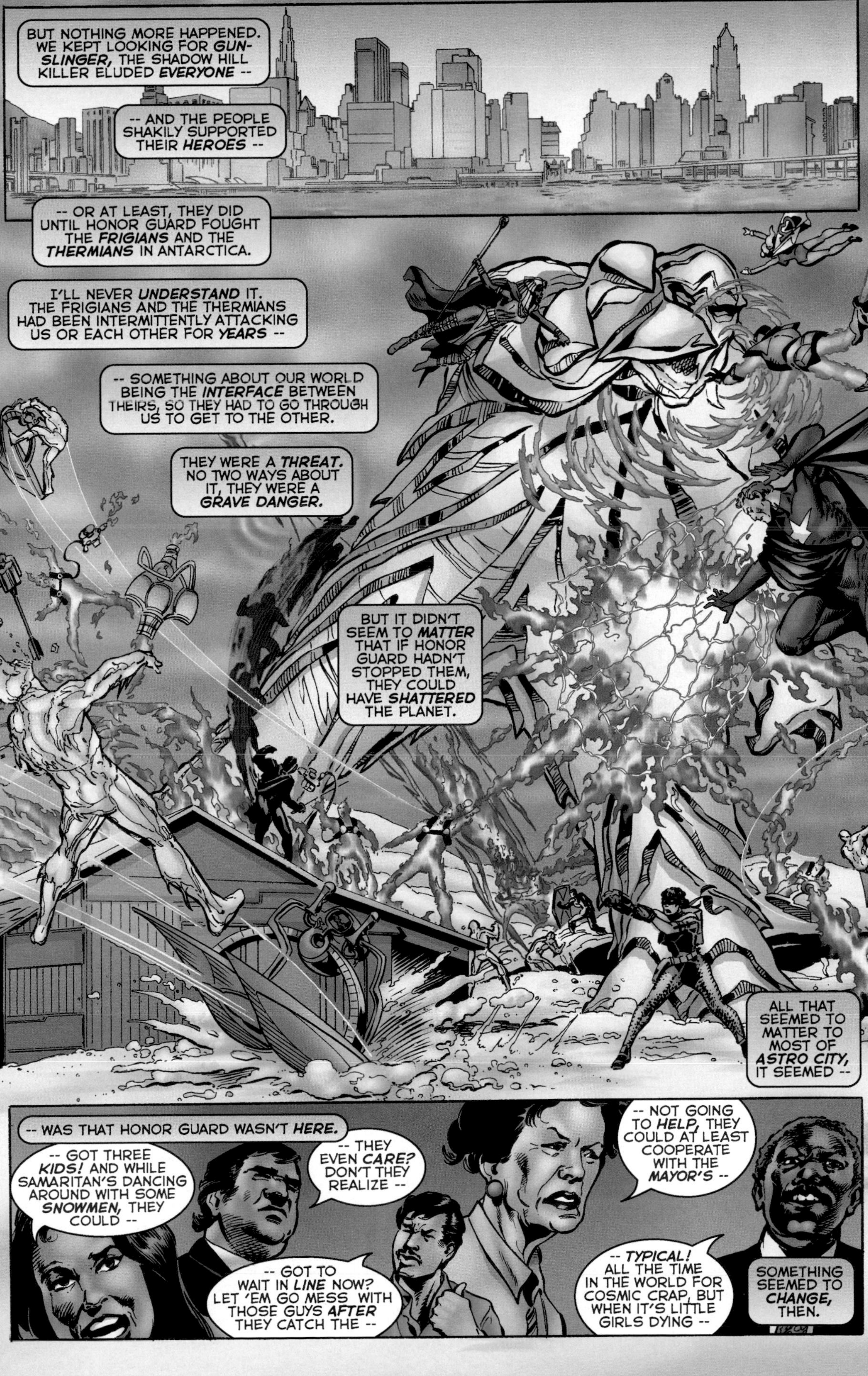
BUT NOTHING MORE HAPPENED. WE KEPT LOOKING FOR GUNSLINGER, THE SHADOW HILL KILLER ELUDED EVERYONE --
-- AND THE PEOPLE SHAKILY SUPPORTED THEIR HEROES --
-- OR AT LEAST, THEY DID UNTIL HONOR GUARD FOUGHT THE FRIGIANS AND THE THERMIANS IN ANTARCTICA.
I'LL NEVER UNDERSTAND IT. THE FRIGIANS AND THE THERMIANS HAD BEEN INTERMITTENTLY ATTACKING US OR EACH OTHER FOR YEARS --
-- SOMETHING ABOUT OUR WORLD BEING THE INTERFACE BETWEEN THEIRS, SO THEY HAD TO GO THROUGH US TO GET TO THE OTHER.
THEY WERE A THREAT. NO TWO WAYS ABOUT IT, THEY WERE A GRAVE DANGER.
BUT IT DIDN'T SEEM TO MATTER THAT IF HONOR GUARD HADN'T STOPPED THEM, THEY COULD HAVE SHATTERED THE PLANET.
ALL THAT SEEMED TO MATTER TO MOST OF ASTRO CITY, IT SEEMED --
-- WAS THAT HONOR GUARD WASN'T HERE.
-- GOT THREE KIDS! AND WHILE SAMARITAN'S DANCING AROUND WITH SOME SNOWMEN, THEY COULD --
-- THEY EVEN CARE? DON'T THEY REALIZE --
-- NOT GOING TO HELP, THEY COULD AT LEAST COOPERATE WITH THE MAYOR'S --
-- GOT TO WAIT IN LINE NOW? LET 'EM GO MESS WITH THOSE GUYS AFTER THEY CATCH THE --
-- TYPICAL! ALL THE TIME IN THE WORLD FOR COSMIC CRAP, BUT WHEN IT'S LITTLE GIRLS DYING --
SOMETHING SEEMED TO CHANGE, THEN.

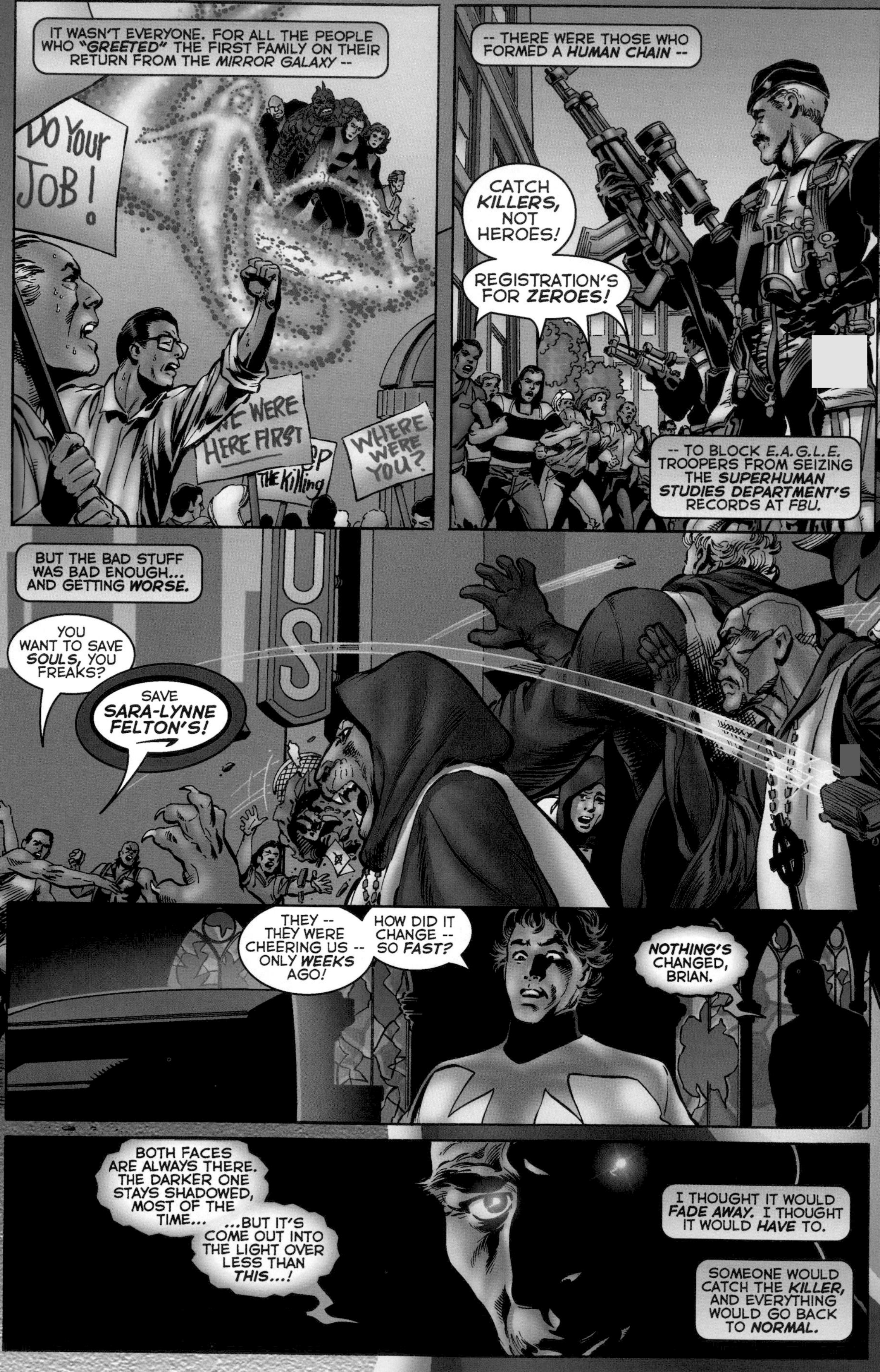
IT WASN'T EVERYONE. FOR ALL THE PEOPLE WHO "GREETED" THE FIRST FAMILY ON THEIR RETURN FROM THE MIRROR GALAXY --
DO YOUR JOB!
WE WERE HERE FIRST
STOP THE KILLING
WHERE WERE YOU?
-- THERE WERE THOSE WHO FORMED A HUMAN CHAIN --
CATCH KILLERS, NOT HEROES!
REGISTRATION'S FOR ZEROES!
-- TO BLOCK E.A.G.L.E. TROOPERS FROM SEIZING THE SUPERHUMAN STUDIES DEPARTMENT'S RECORDS AT FBU.
BUT THE BAD STUFF WAS BAD ENOUGH... AND GETTING WORSE.
YOU WANT TO SAVE SOULS, YOU FREAKS?
SAVE SARA-LYNNE FELTON'S!
THEY -- THEY WERE CHEERING US -- ONLY WEEKS AGO!
HOW DID IT CHANGE -- SO FAST?
NOTHING'S CHANGED, BRIAN.
BOTH FACES ARE ALWAYS THERE. THE DARKER ONE STAYS SHADOWED, MOST OF THE TIME...
...BUT IT'S COME OUT INTO THE LIGHT OVER LESS THAN THIS...!
I THOUGHT IT WOULD FADE AWAY. I THOUGHT IT WOULD HAVE TO.
SOMEONE WOULD CATCH THE KILLER, AND EVERYTHING WOULD GO BACK TO NORMAL.

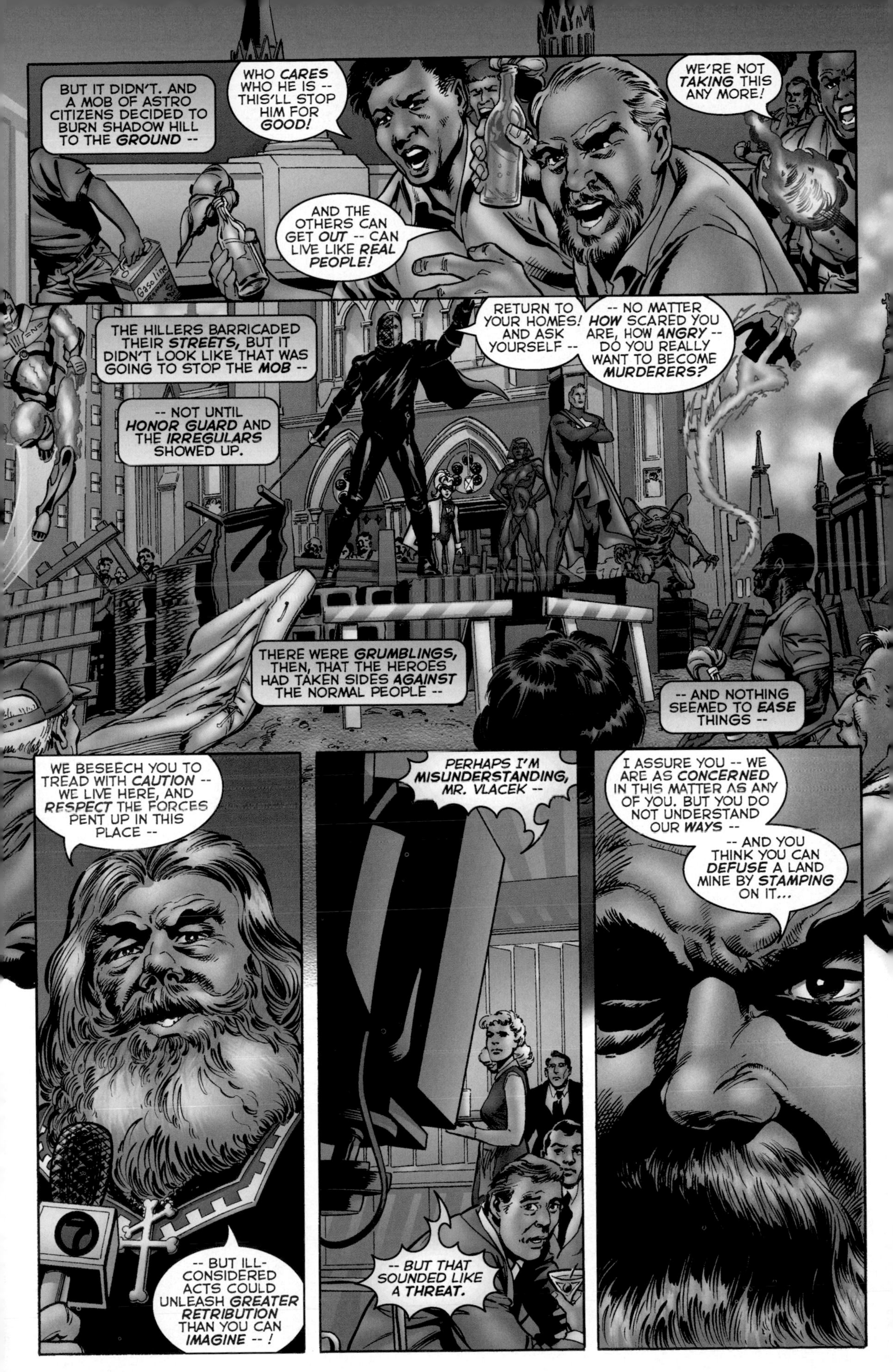
BUT IT DIDN'T. AND A MOB OF ASTRO CITIZENS DECIDED TO BURN SHADOW HILL TO THE GROUND --
WHO CARES WHO HE IS -- THIS'LL STOP HIM FOR GOOD!
WE'RE NOT TAKING THIS ANY MORE!
AND THE OTHERS CAN GET OUT -- CAN LIVE LIKE REAL PEOPLE!
Gasoline
THE HILLERS BARRICADED THEIR STREETS, BUT IT DIDN'T LOOK LIKE THAT WAS GOING TO STOP THE MOB --
-- NOT UNTIL HONOR GUARD AND THE IRREGULARS SHOWED UP.
RETURN TO YOUR HOMES! AND ASK YOURSELF --
-- NO MATTER HOW SCARED YOU ARE, HOW ANGRY -- DO YOU REALLY WANT TO BECOME MURDERERS?
THERE WERE GRUMBLINGS, THEN, THAT THE HEROES HAD TAKEN SIDES AGAINST THE NORMAL PEOPLE --
-- AND NOTHING SEEMED TO EASE THINGS --
WE BESEECH YOU TO TREAD WITH CAUTION -- WE LIVE HERE, AND RESPECT THE FORCES PENT UP IN THIS PLACE --
7
-- BUT ILL-CONSIDERED ACTS COULD UNLEASH GREATER RETRIBUTION THAN YOU CAN IMAGINE -- !
PERHAPS I'M MISUNDERSTANDING, MR. VLACEK --
-- BUT THAT SOUNDED LIKE A THREAT.
I ASSURE YOU -- WE ARE AS CONCERNED IN THIS MATTER AS ANY OF YOU. BUT YOU DO NOT UNDERSTAND OUR WAYS --
-- AND YOU THINK YOU CAN DEFUSE A LAND MINE BY STAMPING ON IT...

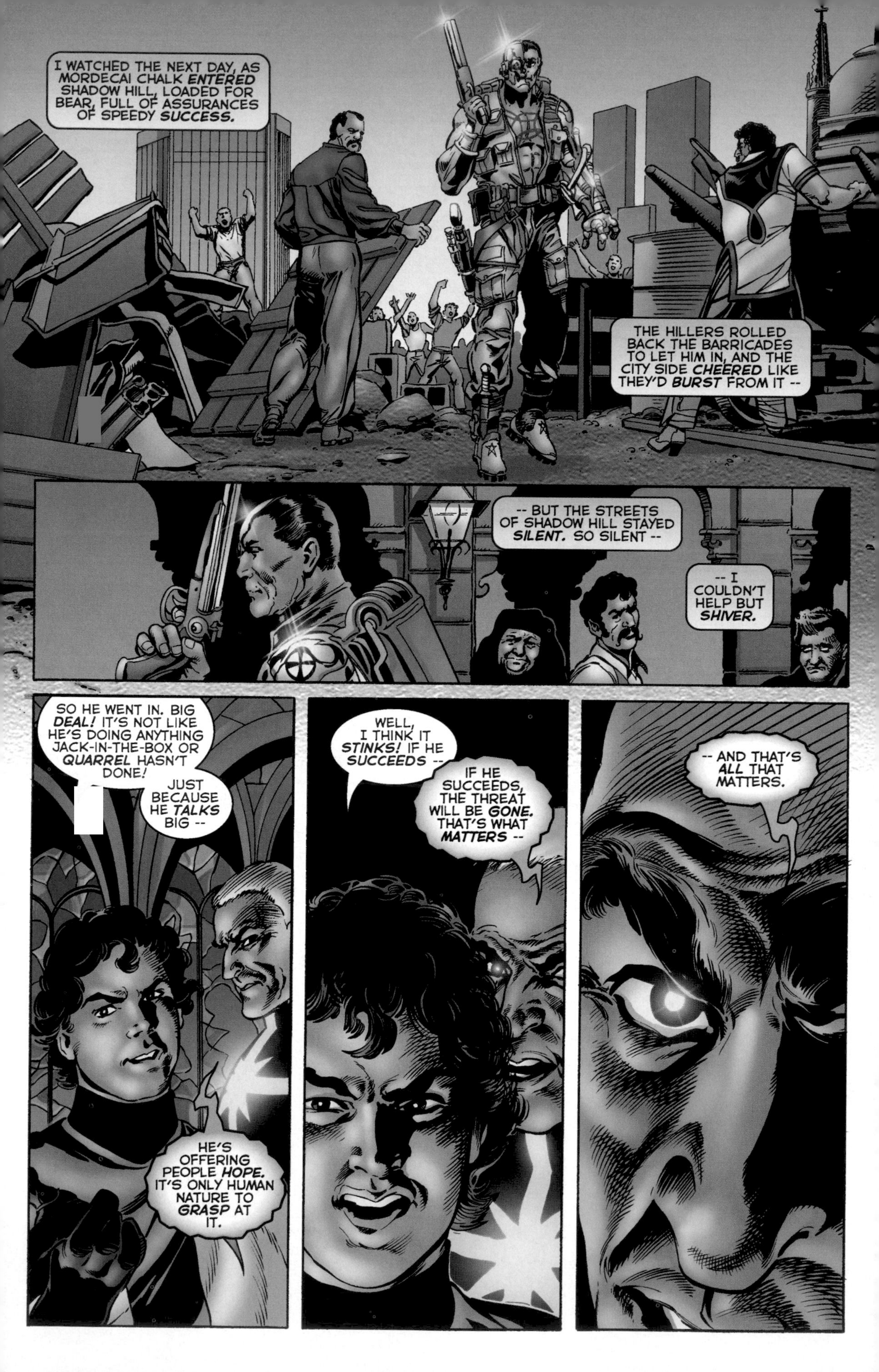
I WATCHED THE NEXT DAY, AS MORDECAI CHALK ENTERED SHADOW HILL, LOADED FOR BEAR, FULL OF ASSURANCES OF SPEEDY SUCCESS.
THE HILLERS ROLLED BACK THE BARRICADES TO LET HIM IN, AND THE CITY SIDE CHEERED LIKE THEY'D BURST FROM IT --
-- BUT THE STREETS OF SHADOW HILL STAYED SILENT. SO SILENT --
-- I COULDN'T HELP BUT SHIVER.
SO HE WENT IN. BIG DEAL! IT'S NOT LIKE HE'S DOING ANYTHING JACK-IN-THE-BOX OR QUARREL HASN'T DONE!
JUST BECAUSE HE TALKS BIG --
HE'S OFFERING PEOPLE HOPE. IT'S ONLY HUMAN NATURE TO GRASP AT IT.
WELL, I THINK IT STINKS! IF HE SUCCEEDS --
IF HE SUCCEEDS, THE THREAT WILL BE GONE. THAT'S WHAT MATTERS --
-- AND THAT'S ALL THAT MATTERS.

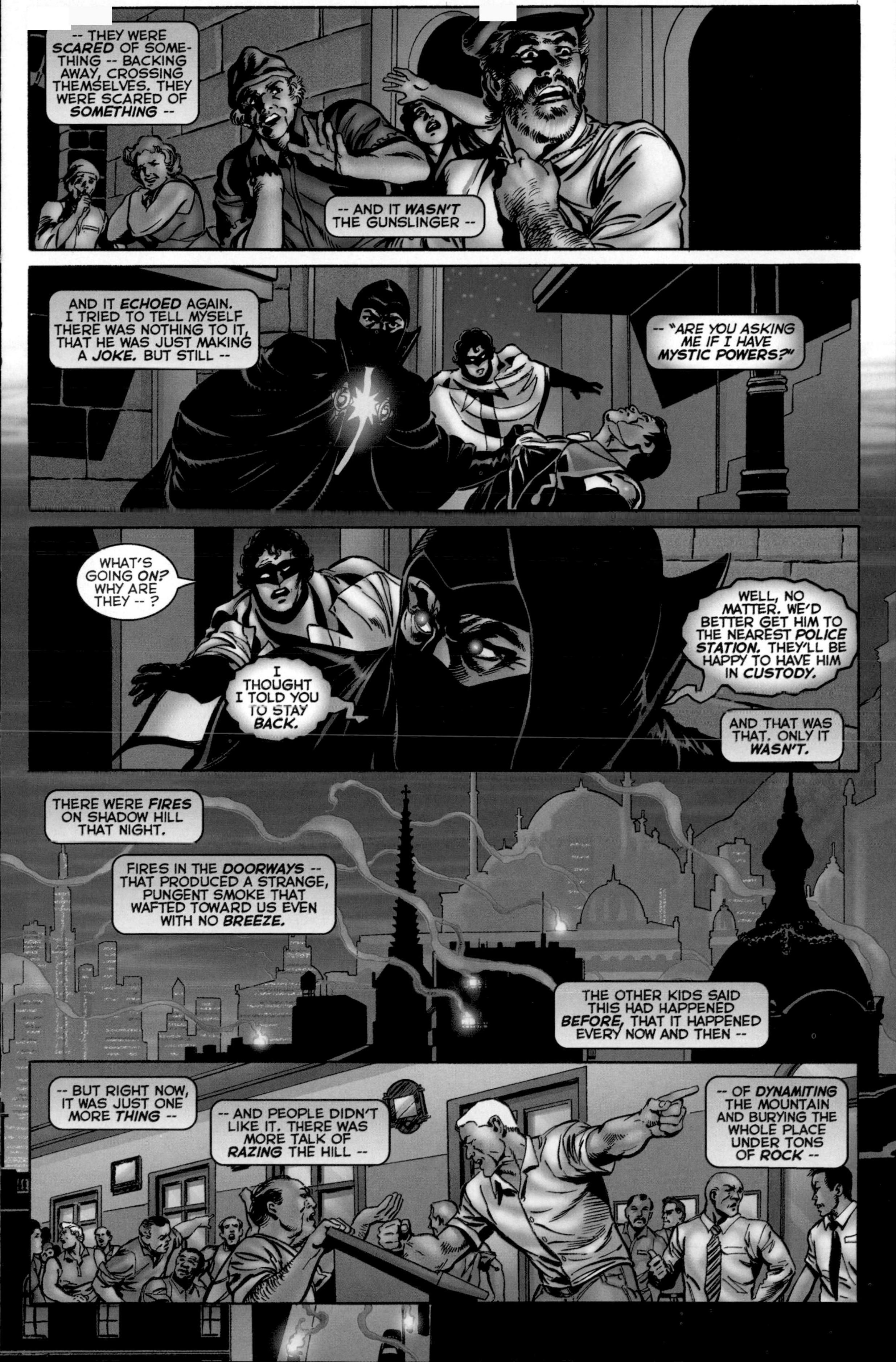
-- THEY WERE SCARED OF SOMETHING -- BACKING AWAY, CROSSING THEMSELVES. THEY WERE SCARED OF SOMETHING --
-- AND IT WASN'T THE GUNSLINGER --
AND IT ECHOED AGAIN. I TRIED TO TELL MYSELF THERE WAS NOTHING TO IT, THAT HE WAS JUST MAKING A JOKE. BUT STILL --
-- "ARE YOU ASKING ME IF I HAVE MYSTIC POWERS?"
WHAT'S GOING ON? WHY ARE THEY -- ?
I THOUGHT I TOLD YOU TO STAY BACK.
WELL, NO MATTER. WE'D BETTER GET HIM TO THE NEAREST POLICE STATION. THEY'LL BE HAPPY TO HAVE HIM IN CUSTODY.
AND THAT WAS THAT. ONLY IT WASN'T.
THERE WERE FIRES ON SHADOW HILL THAT NIGHT.
FIRES IN THE DOORWAYS -- THAT PRODUCED A STRANGE, PUNGENT SMOKE THAT WAFTED TOWARD US EVEN WITH NO BREEZE.
THE OTHER KIDS SAID THIS HAD HAPPENED BEFORE, THAT IT HAPPENED EVERY NOW AND THEN --
-- BUT RIGHT NOW, IT WAS JUST ONE MORE THING --
-- AND PEOPLE DIDN'T LIKE IT. THERE WAS MORE TALK OF RAZING THE HILL --
-- OF DYNAMITING THE MOUNTAIN AND BURYING THE WHOLE PLACE UNDER TONS OF ROCK --

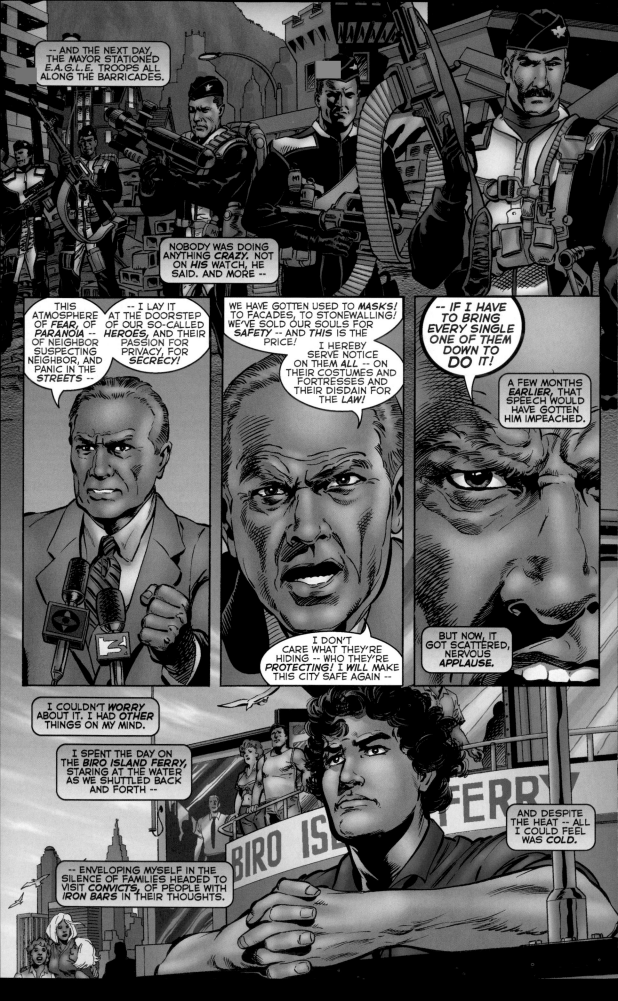

-- AND THE NEXT DAY, THE MAYOR STATIONED *E.A.G.L.E.* TROOPS ALL ALONG THE BARRICADES.

NOBODY WAS DOING ANYTHING *CRAZY*. NOT ON *HIS* WATCH, HE SAID. AND MORE --

THIS ATMOSPHERE OF *FEAR*, OF *PARANOIA* -- OF NEIGHBOR SUSPECTING NEIGHBOR, AND PANIC IN THE *STREETS* --

-- I LAY IT AT THE DOORSTEP OF OUR SO-CALLED *HEROES*, AND THEIR PASSION FOR PRIVACY, FOR *SECRECY*!

WE HAVE GOTTEN USED TO *MASKS*! TO FACADES, TO STONEWALLING! WE'VE SOLD OUR SOULS FOR *SAFETY* -- AND *THIS* IS THE PRICE!

I HEREBY SERVE NOTICE ON THEM *ALL* -- ON THEIR COSTUMES AND FORTRESSES AND THEIR DISDAIN FOR THE *LAW*!

I DON'T CARE WHAT THEY'RE *HIDING* -- WHO THEY'RE *PROTECTING*! I *WILL* MAKE THIS CITY SAFE AGAIN --

-- IF I HAVE TO BRING EVERY SINGLE ONE OF THEM DOWN TO *DO* IT!

A FEW MONTHS *EARLIER*, THAT SPEECH WOULD HAVE GOTTEN HIM IMPEACHED.

BUT NOW, IT GOT SCATTERED, NERVOUS *APPLAUSE*.

I COULDN'T *WORRY* ABOUT IT. I HAD *OTHER* THINGS ON MY MIND.

I SPENT THE DAY ON THE *BIRO ISLAND FERRY*, STARING AT THE WATER AS WE SHUTTLED BACK AND FORTH --

-- ENVELOPING MYSELF IN THE SILENCE OF FAMILIES HEADED TO VISIT *CONVICTS*, OF PEOPLE WITH *IRON BARS* IN THEIR THOUGHTS.

AND DESPITE THE HEAT -- ALL I COULD FEEL WAS *COLD*.

BIRO ISLAND FERRY

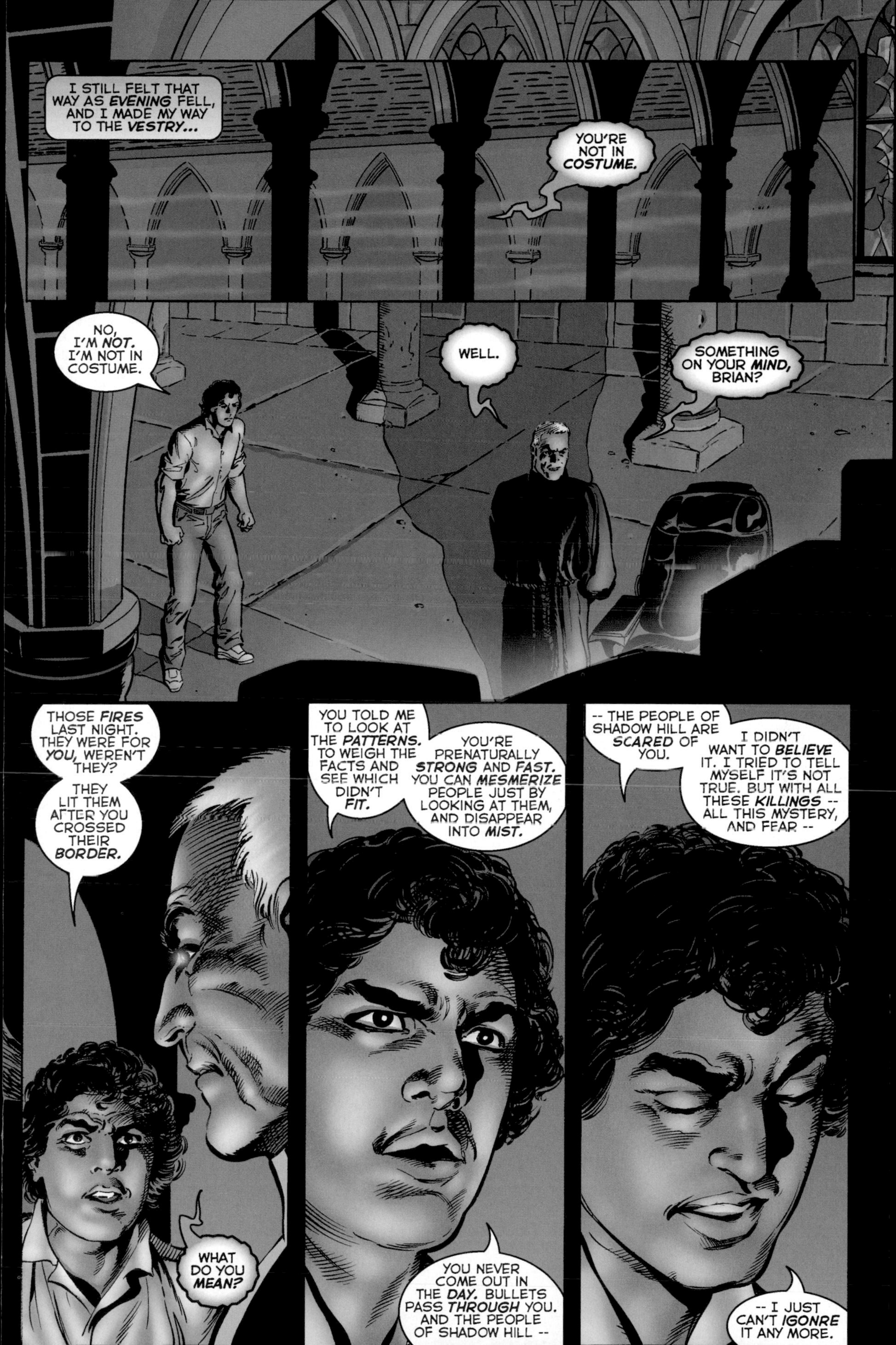

I STILL FELT THAT WAY AS EVENING FELL, AND I MADE MY WAY TO THE VESTRY...
YOU'RE NOT IN COSTUME.
NO, I'M NOT. I'M NOT IN COSTUME.
WELL.
SOMETHING ON YOUR MIND, BRIAN?
THOSE FIRES LAST NIGHT. THEY WERE FOR YOU, WEREN'T THEY?
THEY LIT THEM AFTER YOU CROSSED THEIR BORDER.
WHAT DO YOU MEAN?
YOU TOLD ME TO LOOK AT THE PATTERNS. TO WEIGH THE FACTS AND SEE WHICH DIDN'T FIT.
YOU'RE PRENATURALLY STRONG AND FAST. YOU CAN MESMERIZE PEOPLE JUST BY LOOKING AT THEM, AND DISAPPEAR INTO MIST.
YOU NEVER COME OUT IN THE DAY. BULLETS PASS THROUGH YOU. AND THE PEOPLE OF SHADOW HILL --
-- THE PEOPLE OF SHADOW HILL ARE SCARED OF YOU.
I DIDN'T WANT TO BELIEVE IT. I TRIED TO TELL MYSELF IT'S NOT TRUE. BUT WITH ALL THESE KILLINGS -- ALL THIS MYSTERY, AND FEAR --
-- I JUST CAN'T IGONRE IT ANY MORE.

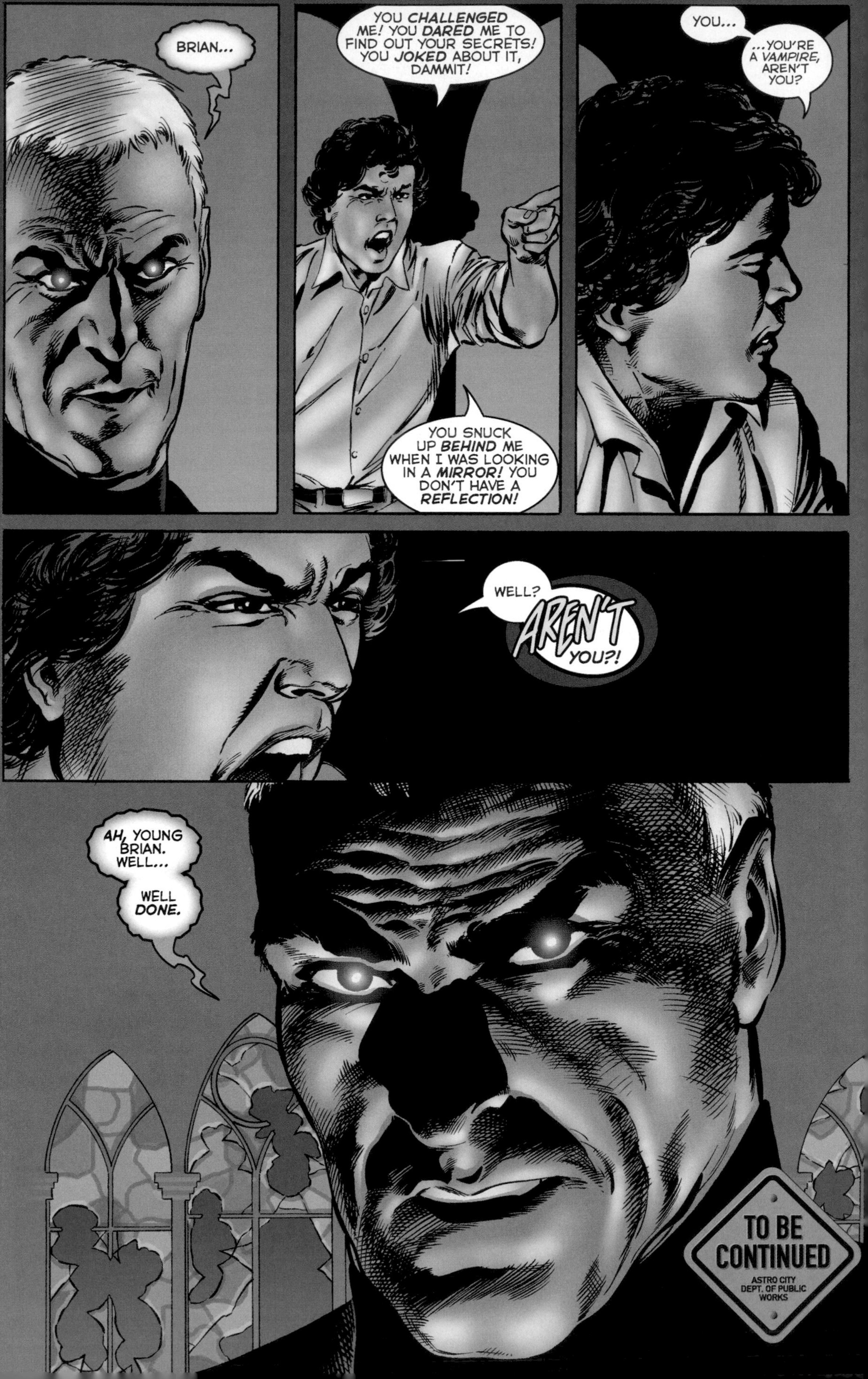
BRIAN...
YOU CHALLENGED ME! YOU DARED ME TO FIND OUT YOUR SECRETS! YOU JOKED ABOUT IT, DAMMIT!
YOU SNUCK UP BEHIND ME WHEN I WAS LOOKING IN A MIRROR! YOU DON'T HAVE A REFLECTION!
YOU...
...YOU'RE A VAMPIRE, AREN'T YOU?
WELL?
AREN'T YOU?!
AH, YOUNG BRIAN. WELL...
WELL DONE.
TO BE CONTINUED
ASTRO CITY DEPT. OF PUBLIC WORKS

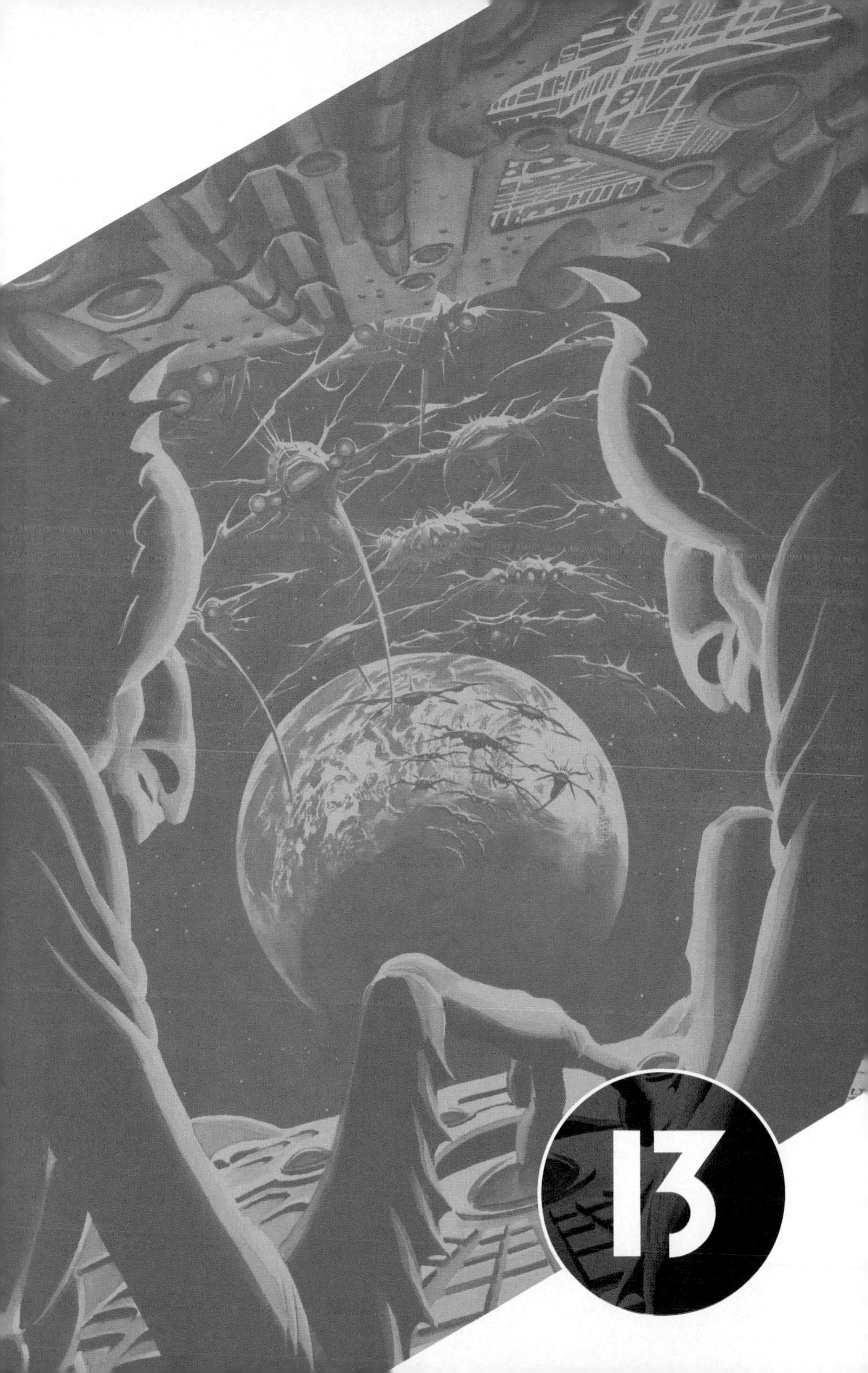

13

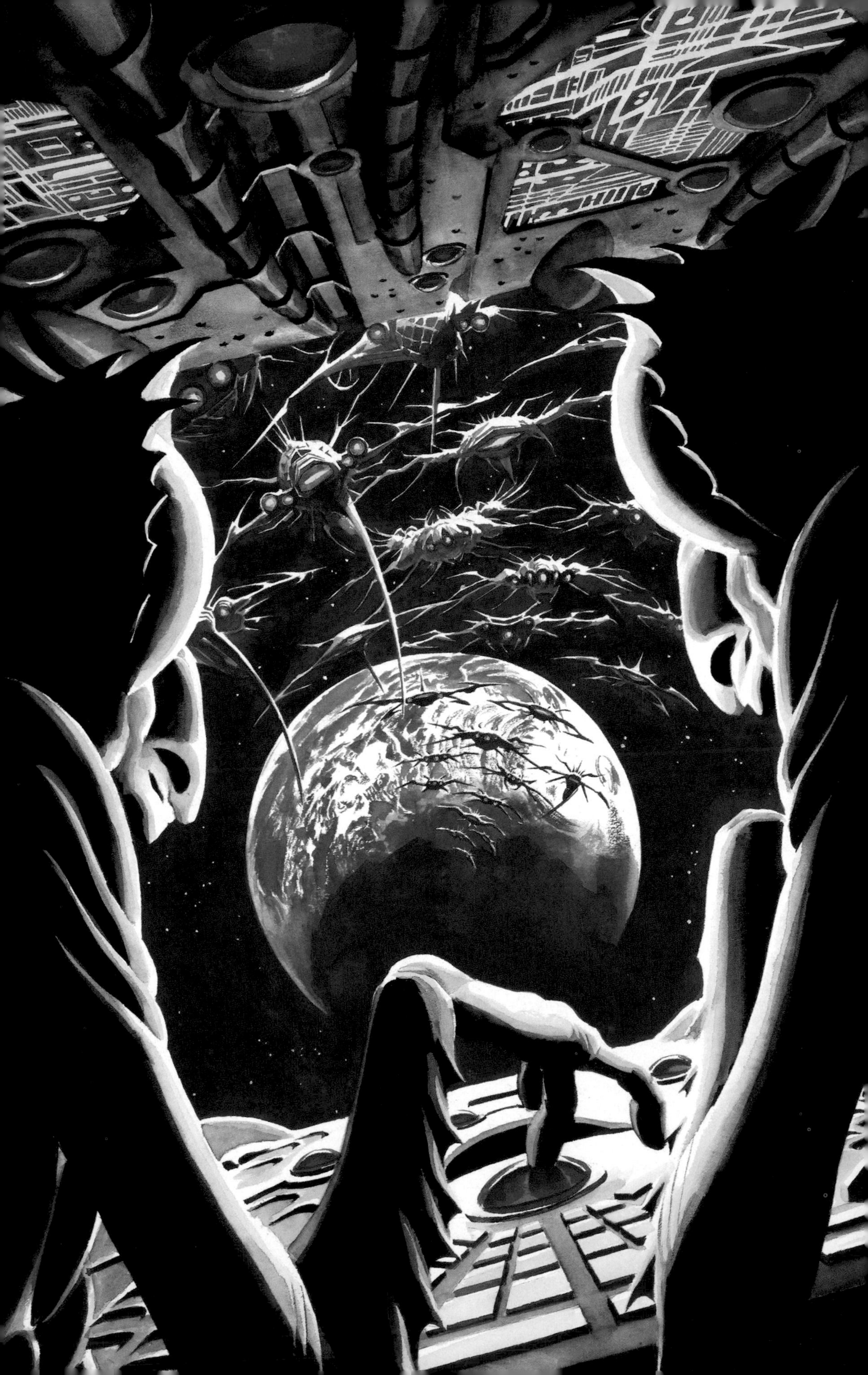

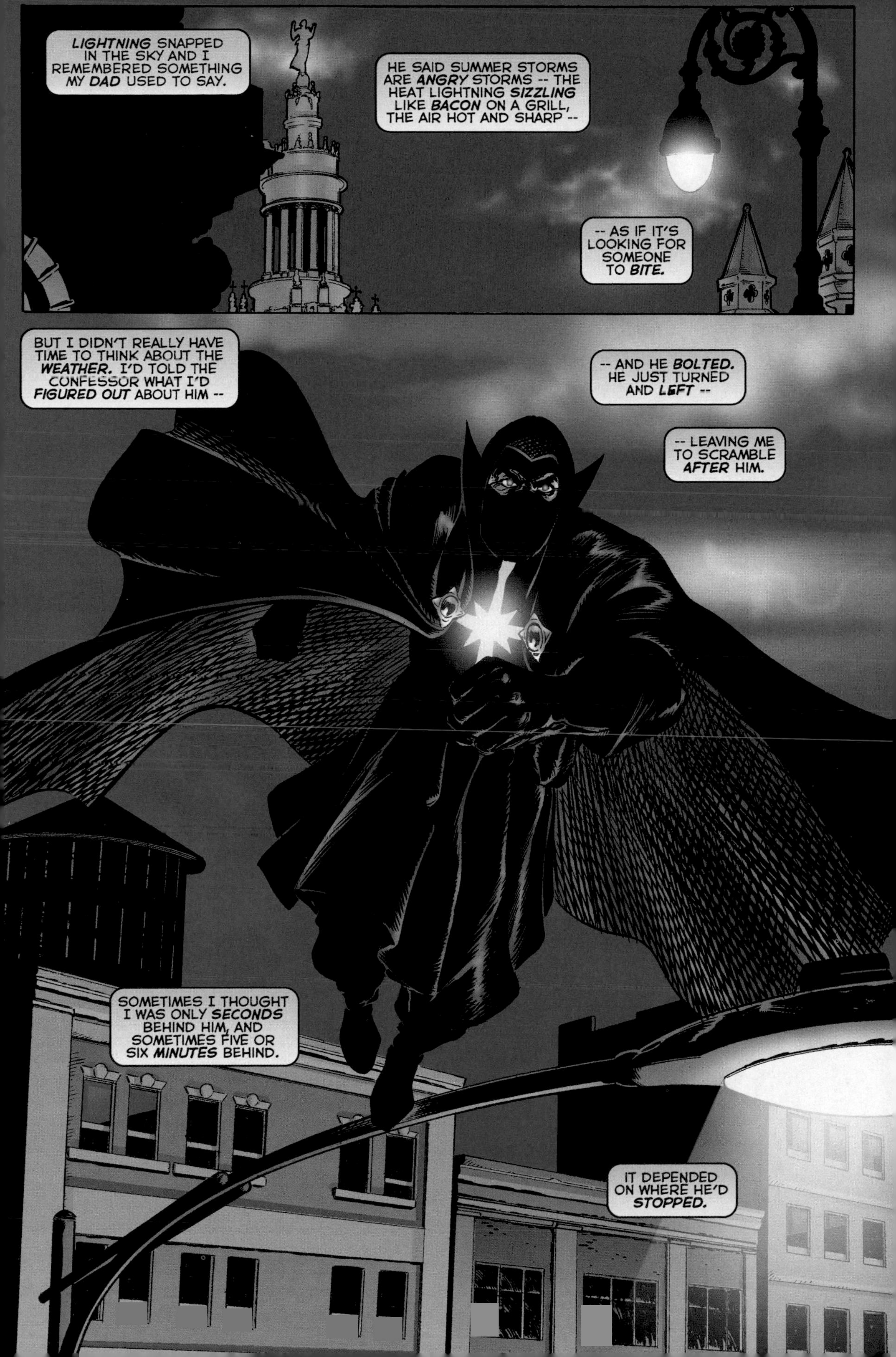
LIGHTNING SNAPPED IN THE SKY AND I REMEMBERED SOMETHING MY DAD USED TO SAY.
HE SAID SUMMER STORMS ARE ANGRY STORMS -- THE HEAT LIGHTNING SIZZLING LIKE BACON ON A GRILL, THE AIR HOT AND SHARP --
-- AS IF IT'S LOOKING FOR SOMEONE TO BITE.
BUT I DIDN'T REALLY HAVE TIME TO THINK ABOUT THE WEATHER. I'D TOLD THE CONFESSOR WHAT I'D FIGURED OUT ABOUT HIM --
-- AND HE BOLTED. HE JUST TURNED AND LEFT --
-- LEAVING ME TO SCRAMBLE AFTER HIM.
SOMETIMES I THOUGHT I WAS ONLY SECONDS BEHIND HIM, AND SOMETIMES FIVE OR SIX MINUTES BEHIND.
IT DEPENDED ON WHERE HE'D STOPPED.

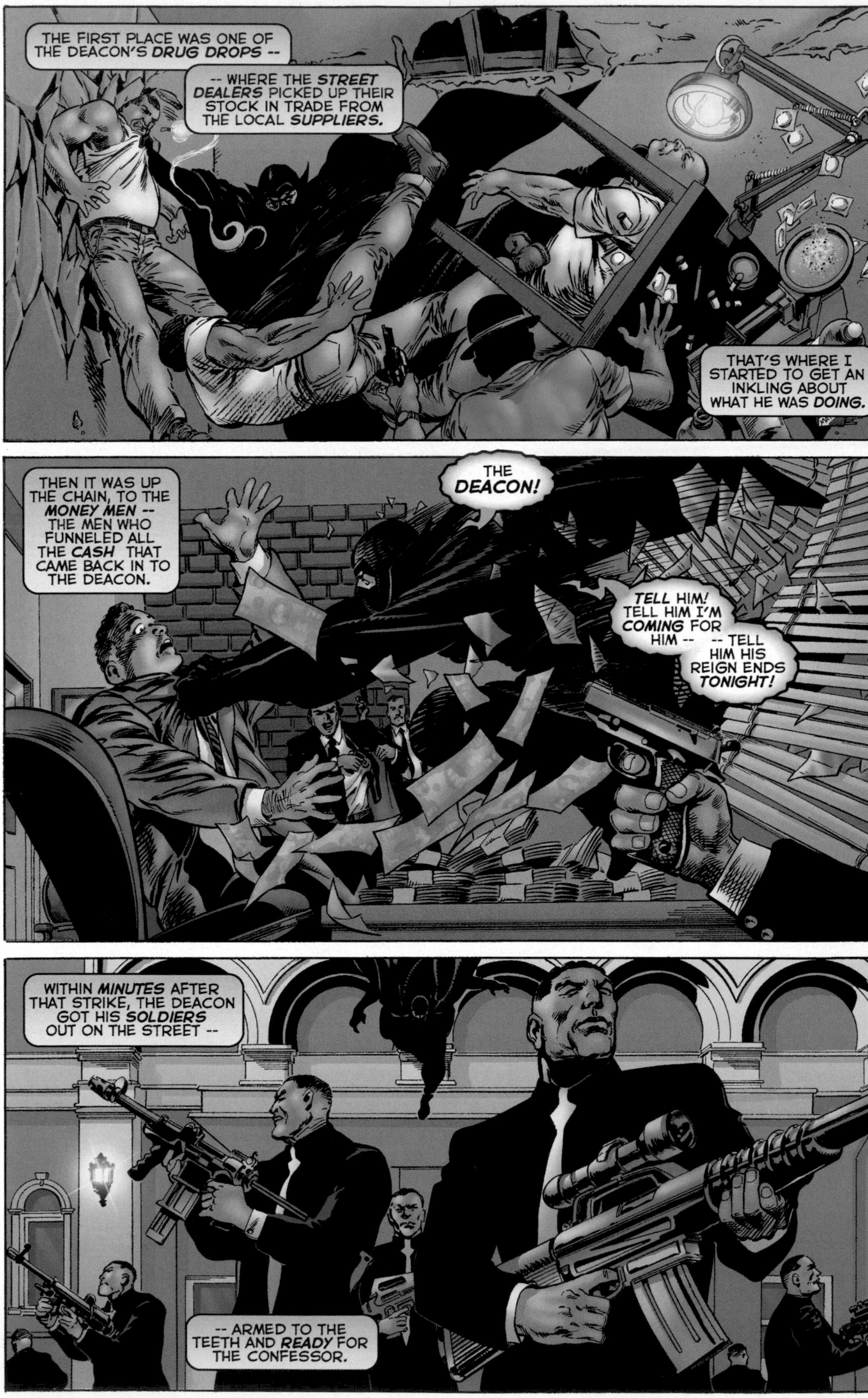
THE FIRST PLACE WAS ONE OF THE DEACON'S DRUG DROPS --
-- WHERE THE STREET DEALERS PICKED UP THEIR STOCK IN TRADE FROM THE LOCAL SUPPLIERS.
THAT'S WHERE I STARTED TO GET AN INKLING ABOUT WHAT HE WAS DOING.
THEN IT WAS UP THE CHAIN, TO THE MONEY MEN -- THE MEN WHO FUNNELED ALL THE CASH THAT CAME BACK IN TO THE DEACON.
THE DEACON!
TELL HIM! TELL HIM I'M COMING FOR HIM --
-- TELL HIM HIS REIGN ENDS TONIGHT!
WITHIN MINUTES AFTER THAT STRIKE, THE DEACON GOT HIS SOLDIERS OUT ON THE STREET --
-- ARMED TO THE TEETH AND READY FOR THE CONFESSOR.

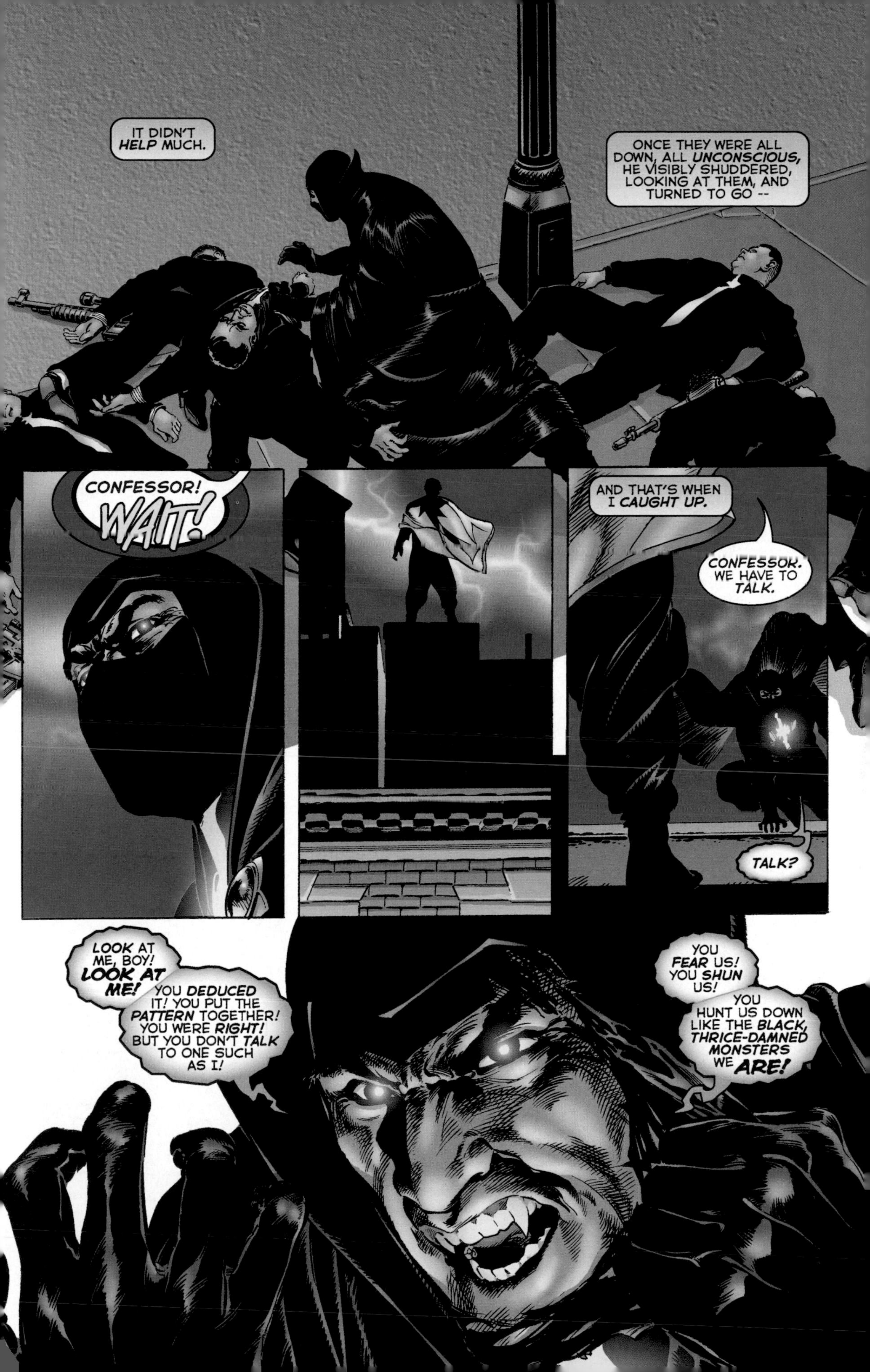
IT DIDN'T HELP MUCH.
ONCE THEY WERE ALL DOWN, ALL UNCONSCIOUS, HE VISIBLY SHUDDERED, LOOKING AT THEM, AND TURNED TO GO --
CONFESSOR! WAIT!
AND THAT'S WHEN I CAUGHT UP.
CONFESSOR. WE HAVE TO TALK.
TALK?
LOOK AT ME, BOY! LOOK AT ME!
YOU DEDUCED IT! YOU PUT THE PATTERN TOGETHER! YOU WERE RIGHT! BUT YOU DON'T TALK TO ONE SUCH AS I!
YOU FEAR US! YOU SHUN US!
YOU HUNT US DOWN LIKE THE BLACK, THRICE-DAMNED MONSTERS WE ARE!

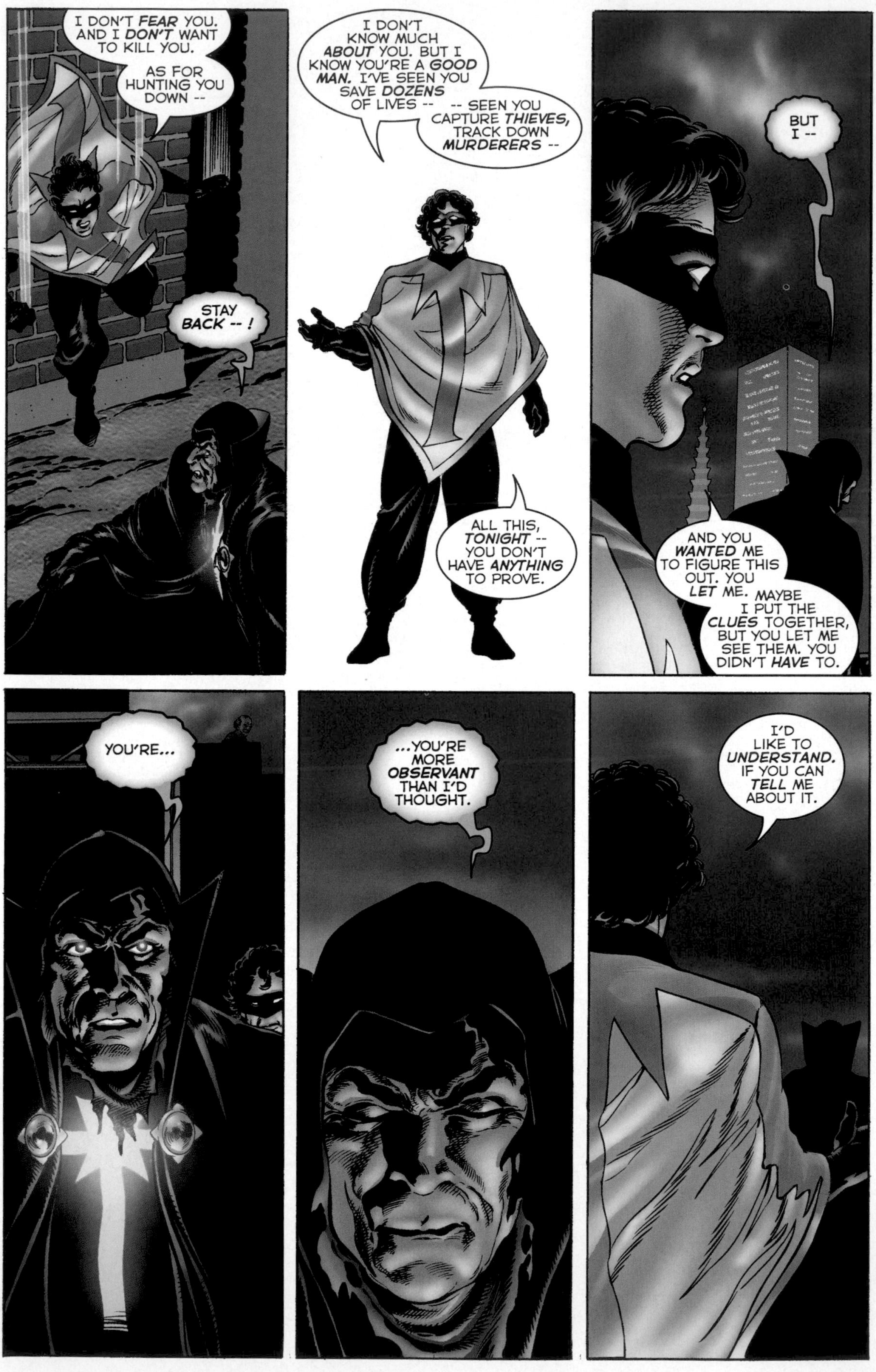
I DON'T FEAR YOU. AND I DON'T WANT TO KILL YOU.
AS FOR HUNTING YOU DOWN --
STAY BACK -- !
I DON'T KNOW MUCH ABOUT YOU. BUT I KNOW YOU'RE A GOOD MAN. I'VE SEEN YOU SAVE DOZENS OF LIVES --
-- SEEN YOU CAPTURE THIEVES, TRACK DOWN MURDERERS --
ALL THIS, TONIGHT -- YOU DON'T HAVE ANYTHING TO PROVE.
BUT I --
AND YOU WANTED ME TO FIGURE THIS OUT. YOU LET ME.
MAYBE I PUT THE CLUES TOGETHER, BUT YOU LET ME SEE THEM. YOU DIDN'T HAVE TO.
YOU'RE...
...YOU'RE MORE OBSERVANT THAN I'D THOUGHT.
I'D LIKE TO UNDERSTAND. IF YOU CAN TELL ME ABOUT IT.

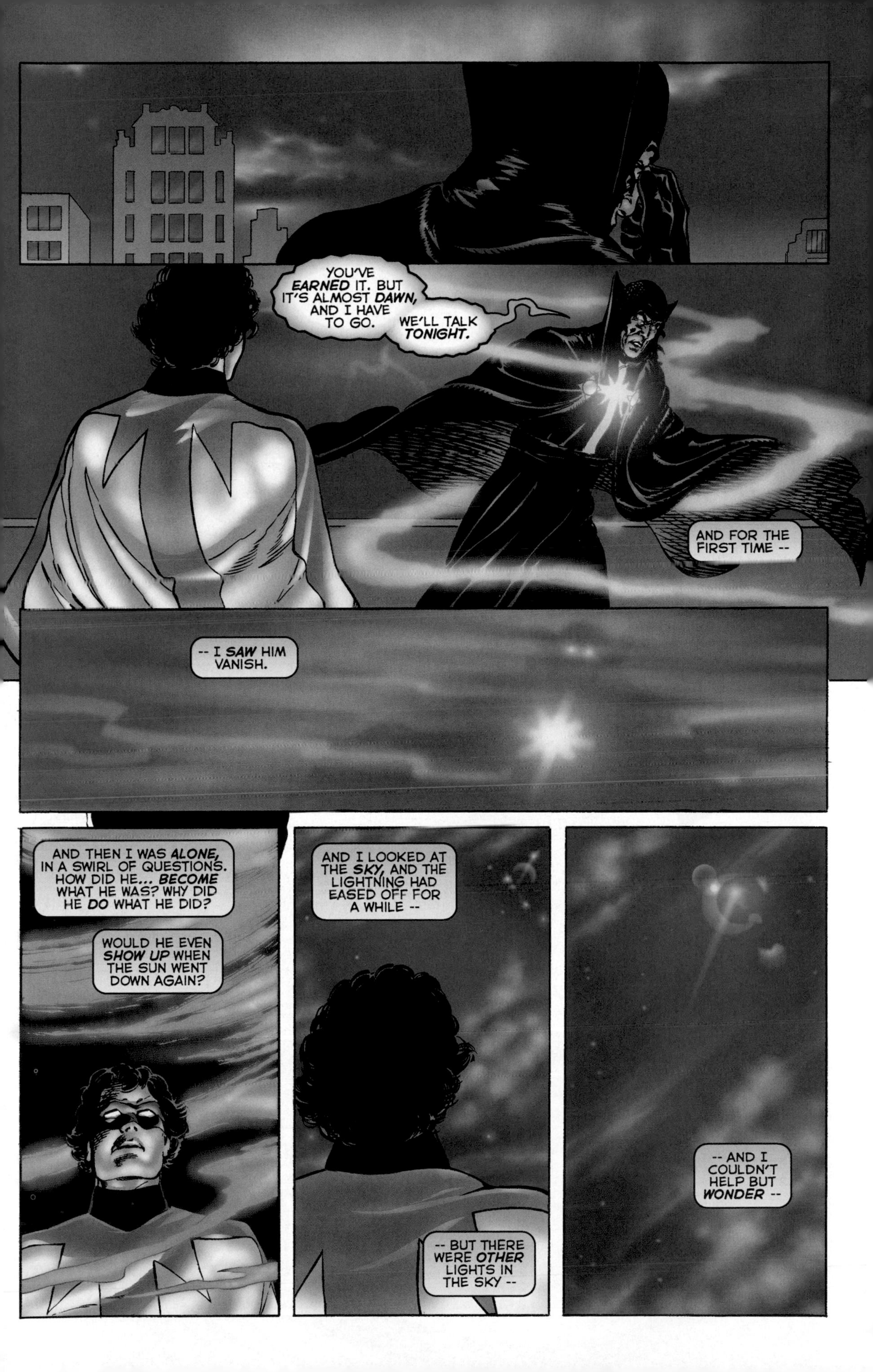
YOU'VE EARNED IT. BUT IT'S ALMOST DAWN, AND I HAVE TO GO.
WE'LL TALK TONIGHT.
AND FOR THE FIRST TIME --
-- I SAW HIM VANISH.
AND THEN I WAS ALONE, IN A SWIRL OF QUESTIONS. HOW DID HE... BECOME WHAT HE WAS? WHY DID HE DO WHAT HE DID?
WOULD HE EVEN SHOW UP WHEN THE SUN WENT DOWN AGAIN?
AND I LOOKED AT THE SKY, AND THE LIGHTNING HAD EASED OFF FOR A WHILE --
-- BUT THERE WERE OTHER LIGHTS IN THE SKY --
-- AND I COULDN'T HELP BUT WONDER --

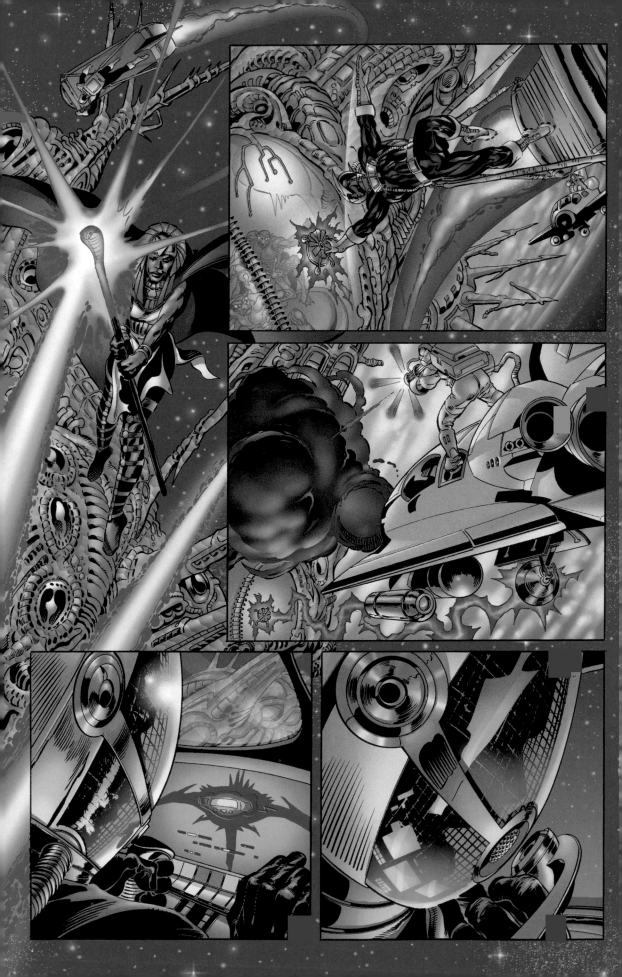

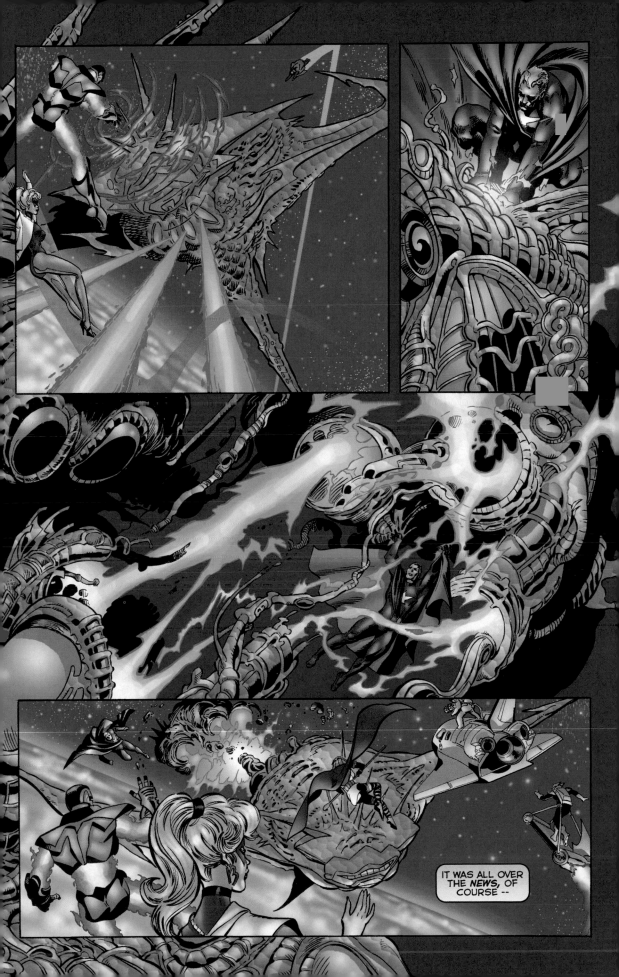

IT WAS ALL OVER THE *NEWS*, OF COURSE --

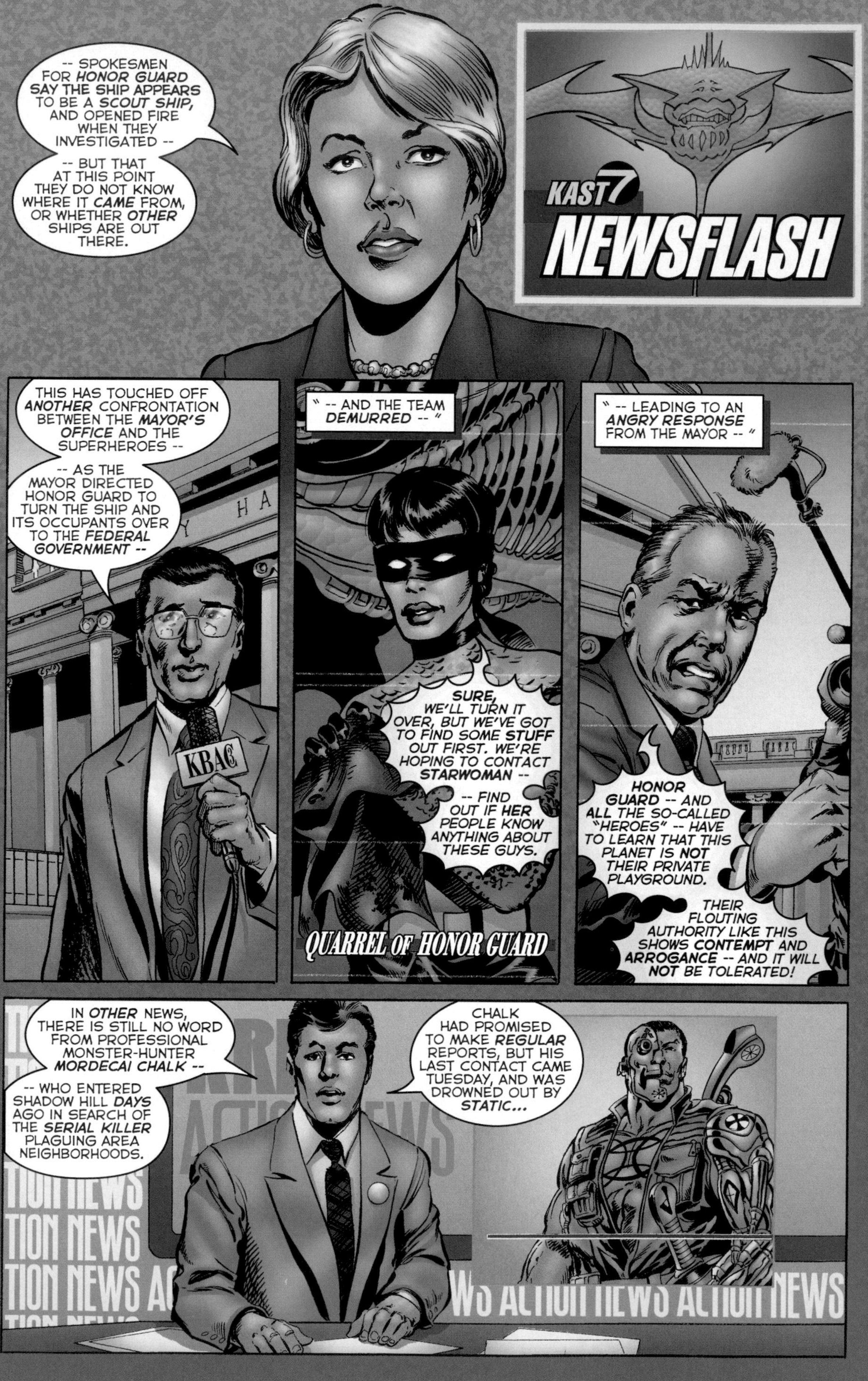
-- SPOKESMEN FOR HONOR GUARD SAY THE SHIP APPEARS TO BE A SCOUT SHIP, AND OPENED FIRE WHEN THEY INVESTIGATED --
-- BUT THAT AT THIS POINT THEY DO NOT KNOW WHERE IT CAME FROM, OR WHETHER OTHER SHIPS ARE OUT THERE.
KAST 7
NEWSFLASH
THIS HAS TOUCHED OFF ANOTHER CONFRONTATION BETWEEN THE MAYOR'S OFFICE AND THE SUPERHEROES --
-- AS THE MAYOR DIRECTED HONOR GUARD TO TURN THE SHIP AND ITS OCCUPANTS OVER TO THE FEDERAL GOVERNMENT --
KBAC
" -- AND THE TEAM DEMURRED -- "
SURE, WE'LL TURN IT OVER, BUT WE'VE GOT TO FIND SOME STUFF OUT FIRST. WE'RE HOPING TO CONTACT STARWOMAN --
-- FIND OUT IF HER PEOPLE KNOW ANYTHING ABOUT THESE GUYS.
QUARREL OF HONOR GUARD
" -- LEADING TO AN ANGRY RESPONSE FROM THE MAYOR -- "
HONOR GUARD -- AND ALL THE SO-CALLED "HEROES" -- HAVE TO LEARN THAT THIS PLANET IS NOT THEIR PRIVATE PLAYGROUND.
THEIR FLOUTING AUTHORITY LIKE THIS SHOWS CONTEMPT AND ARROGANCE -- AND IT WILL NOT BE TOLERATED!
IN OTHER NEWS, THERE IS STILL NO WORD FROM PROFESSIONAL MONSTER-HUNTER MORDECAI CHALK --
-- WHO ENTERED SHADOW HILL DAYS AGO IN SEARCH OF THE SERIAL KILLER PLAGUING AREA NEIGHBORHOODS.
CHALK HAD PROMISED TO MAKE REGULAR REPORTS, BUT HIS LAST CONTACT CAME TUESDAY, AND WAS DROWNED OUT BY STATIC...

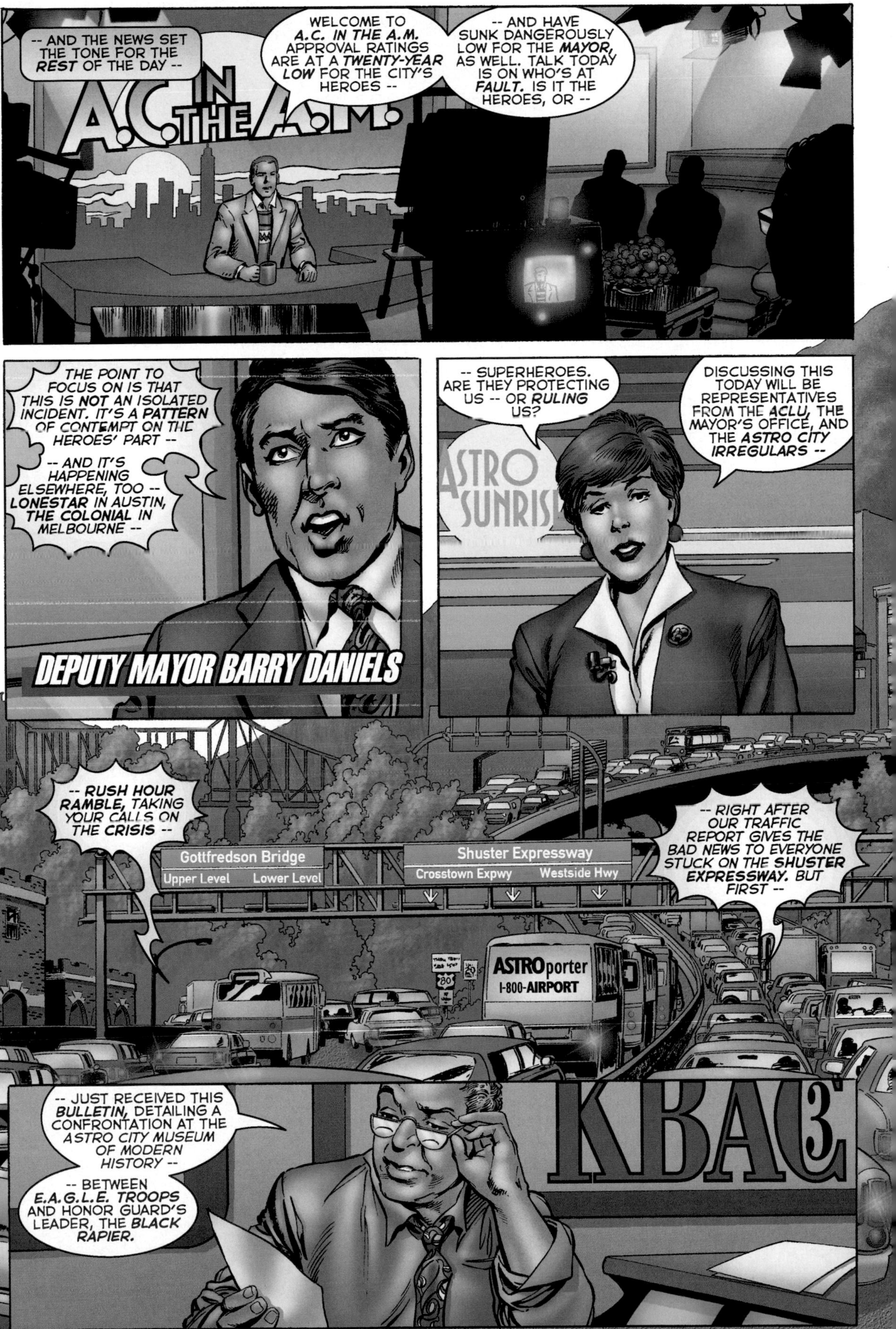
-- AND THE NEWS SET THE TONE FOR THE REST OF THE DAY --
A.C. IN THE A.M.
WELCOME TO A.C. IN THE A.M. APPROVAL RATINGS ARE AT A TWENTY-YEAR LOW FOR THE CITY'S HEROES --
-- AND HAVE SUNK DANGEROUSLY LOW FOR THE MAYOR, AS WELL. TALK TODAY IS ON WHO'S AT FAULT. IS IT THE HEROES, OR --
THE POINT TO FOCUS ON IS THAT THIS IS NOT AN ISOLATED INCIDENT. IT'S A PATTERN OF CONTEMPT ON THE HEROES' PART --
-- AND IT'S HAPPENING ELSEWHERE, TOO -- LONESTAR IN AUSTIN, THE COLONIAL IN MELBOURNE --
DEPUTY MAYOR BARRY DANIELS
-- SUPERHEROES. ARE THEY PROTECTING US -- OR RULING US?
DISCUSSING THIS TODAY WILL BE REPRESENTATIVES FROM THE ACLU, THE MAYOR'S OFFICE, AND THE ASTRO CITY IRREGULARS --
ASTRO SUNRIS
-- RUSH HOUR RAMBLE, TAKING YOUR CALLS ON THE CRISIS --
-- RIGHT AFTER OUR TRAFFIC REPORT GIVES THE BAD NEWS TO EVERYONE STUCK ON THE SHUSTER EXPRESSWAY. BUT FIRST --
Gottfredson Bridge
Upper Level Lower Level
Shuster Expressway
Crosstown Expwy Westside Hwy
ASTROporter
1-800-AIRPORT
80
-- JUST RECEIVED THIS BULLETIN, DETAILING A CONFRONTATION AT THE ASTRO CITY MUSEUM OF MODERN HISTORY --
-- BETWEEN E.A.G.L.E. TROOPS AND HONOR GUARD'S LEADER, THE BLACK RAPIER.
KBAC3

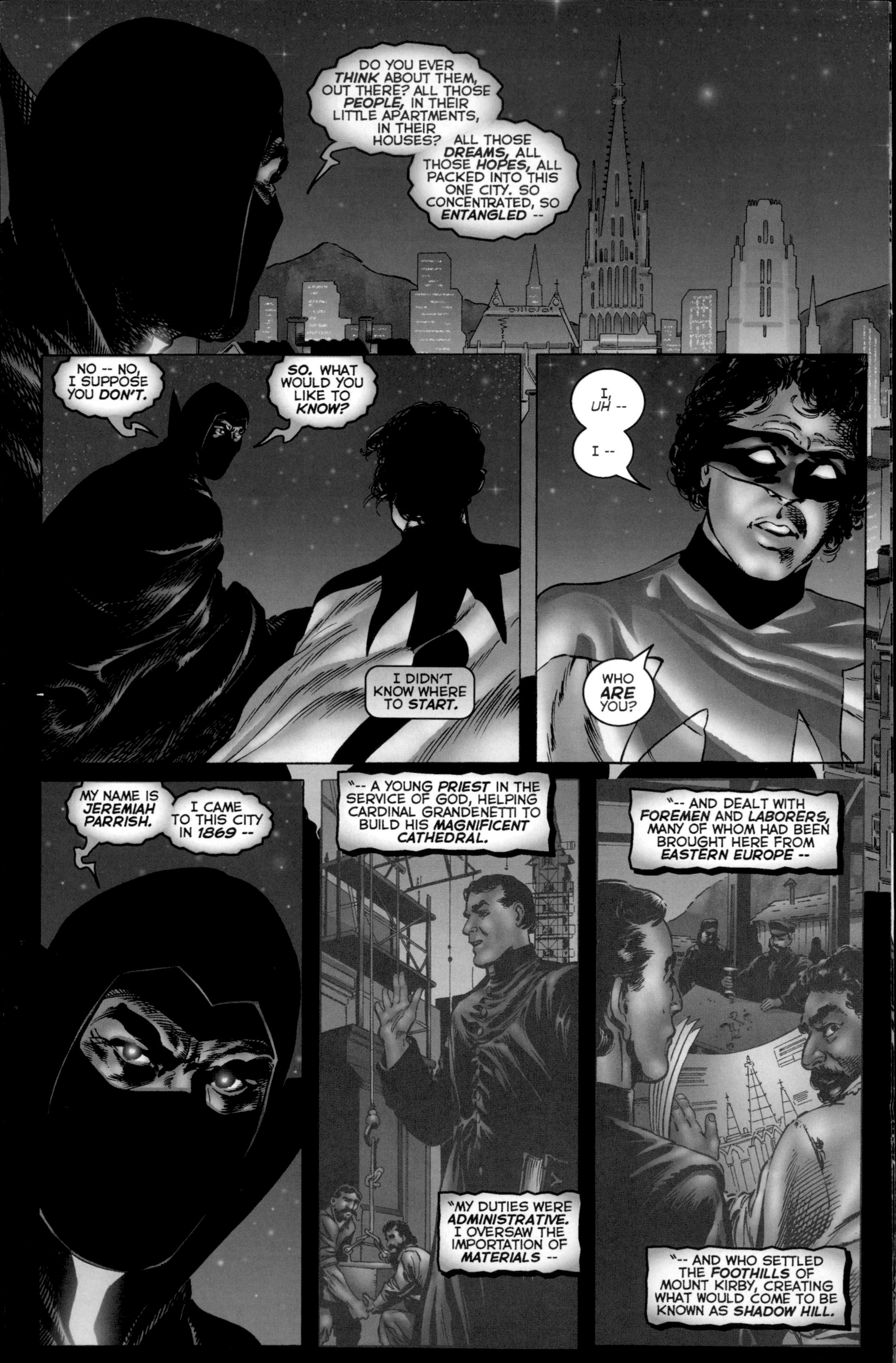
DO YOU EVER THINK ABOUT THEM, OUT THERE? ALL THOSE PEOPLE, IN THEIR LITTLE APARTMENTS, IN THEIR HOUSES?
ALL THOSE DREAMS, ALL THOSE HOPES, ALL PACKED INTO THIS ONE CITY. SO CONCENTRATED, SO ENTANGLED --
NO -- NO, I SUPPOSE YOU DON'T.
SO. WHAT WOULD YOU LIKE TO KNOW?
I DIDN'T KNOW WHERE TO START.
I, UH --
I --
WHO ARE YOU?
MY NAME IS JEREMIAH PARRISH.
I CAME TO THIS CITY IN 1869 --
"-- A YOUNG PRIEST IN THE SERVICE OF GOD, HELPING CARDINAL GRANDENETTI TO BUILD HIS MAGNIFICENT CATHEDRAL.
"MY DUTIES WERE ADMINISTRATIVE. I OVERSAW THE IMPORTATION OF MATERIALS --
"-- AND DEALT WITH FOREMEN AND LABORERS, MANY OF WHOM HAD BEEN BROUGHT HERE FROM EASTERN EUROPE --
"-- AND WHO SETTLED THE FOOTHILLS OF MOUNT KIRBY, CREATING WHAT WOULD COME TO BE KNOWN AS SHADOW HILL.

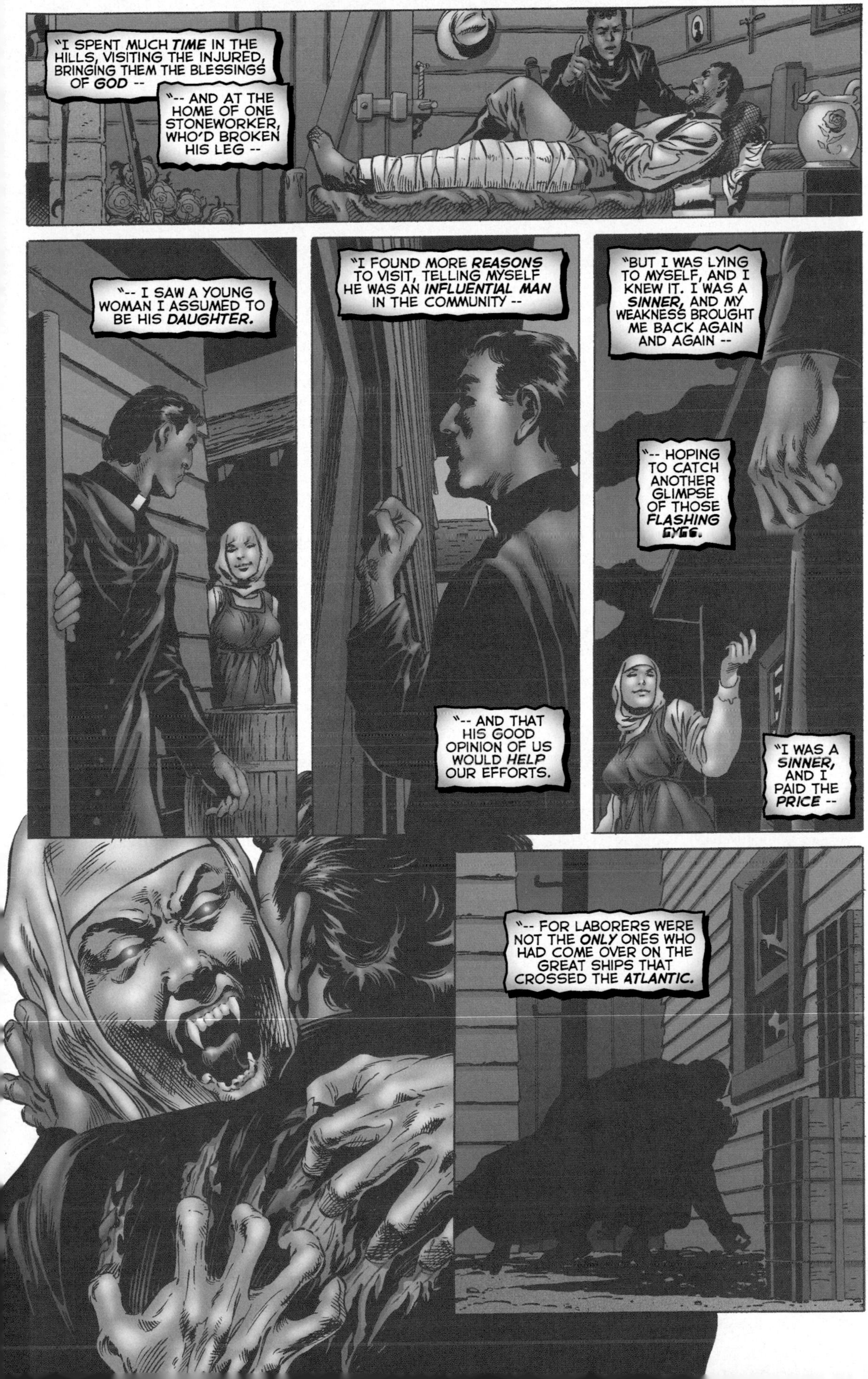
"I SPENT MUCH TIME IN THE HILLS, VISITING THE INJURED, BRINGING THEM THE BLESSINGS OF GOD --
"-- AND AT THE HOME OF ONE STONEWORKER, WHO'D BROKEN HIS LEG --
"-- I SAW A YOUNG WOMAN I ASSUMED TO BE HIS DAUGHTER.
"I FOUND MORE REASONS TO VISIT, TELLING MYSELF HE WAS AN INFLUENTIAL MAN IN THE COMMUNITY --
"-- AND THAT HIS GOOD OPINION OF US WOULD HELP OUR EFFORTS.
"BUT I WAS LYING TO MYSELF, AND I KNEW IT. I WAS A SINNER, AND MY WEAKNESS BROUGHT ME BACK AGAIN AND AGAIN --
"-- HOPING TO CATCH ANOTHER GLIMPSE OF THOSE FLASHING EYES.
"I WAS A SINNER, AND I PAID THE PRICE --
"-- FOR LABORERS WERE NOT THE ONLY ONES WHO HAD COME OVER ON THE GREAT SHIPS THAT CROSSED THE ATLANTIC.

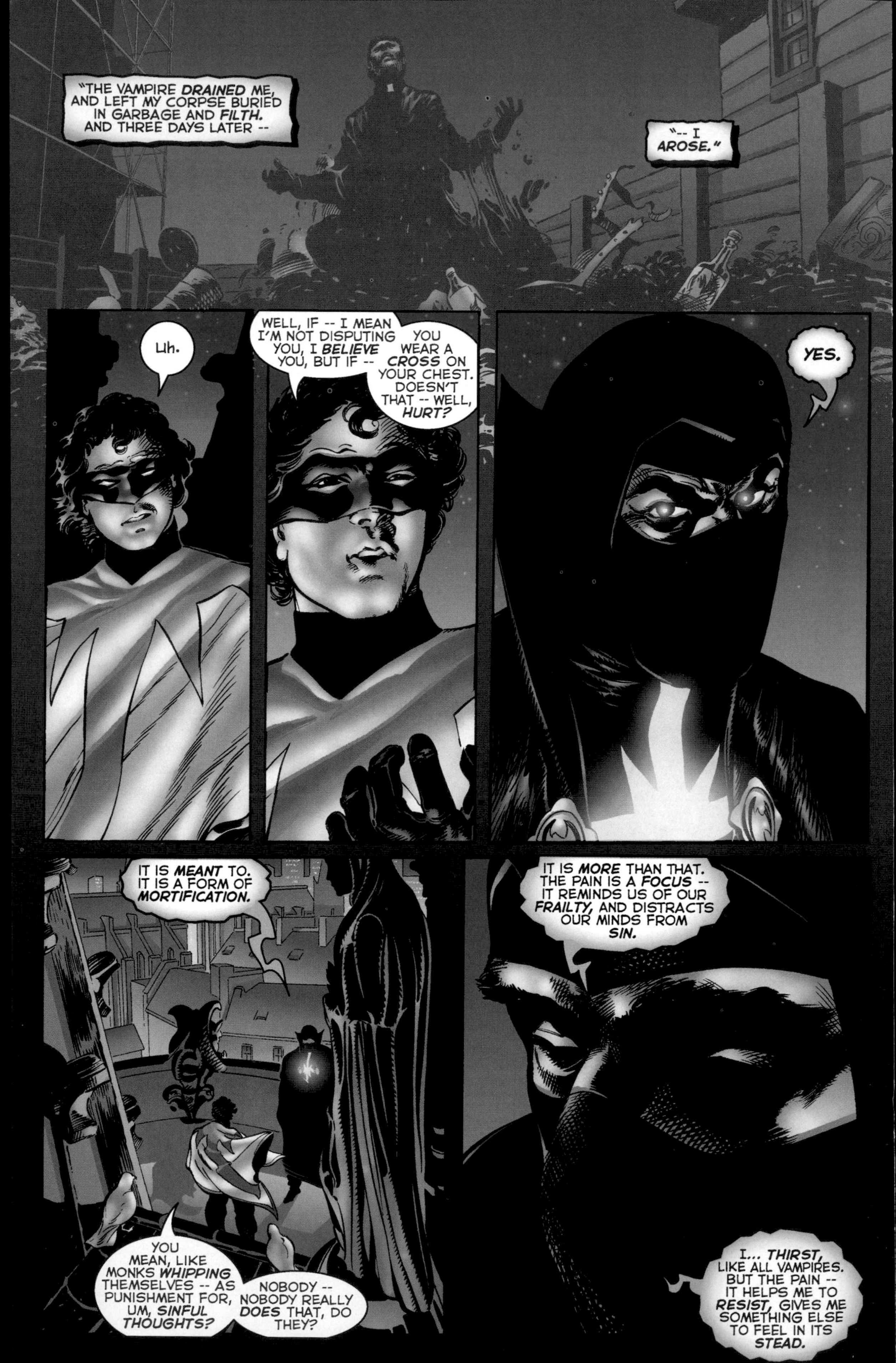
"THE VAMPIRE DRAINED ME, AND LEFT MY CORPSE BURIED IN GARBAGE AND FILTH. AND THREE DAYS LATER --
"-- I AROSE."
Uh.
WELL, IF -- I MEAN I'M NOT DISPUTING YOU, I BELIEVE YOU, BUT IF --
YOU WEAR A CROSS ON YOUR CHEST. DOESN'T THAT -- WELL, HURT?
YES.
IT IS MEANT TO. IT IS A FORM OF MORTIFICATION.
YOU MEAN, LIKE MONKS WHIPPING THEMSELVES -- AS PUNISHMENT FOR, UM, SINFUL THOUGHTS?
NOBODY -- NOBODY REALLY DOES THAT, DO THEY?
IT IS MORE THAN THAT. THE PAIN IS A FOCUS -- IT REMINDS US OF OUR FRAILTY, AND DISTRACTS OUR MINDS FROM SIN.
I... THIRST, LIKE ALL VAMPIRES. BUT THE PAIN -- IT HELPS ME TO RESIST, GIVES ME SOMETHING ELSE TO FEEL IN ITS STEAD.

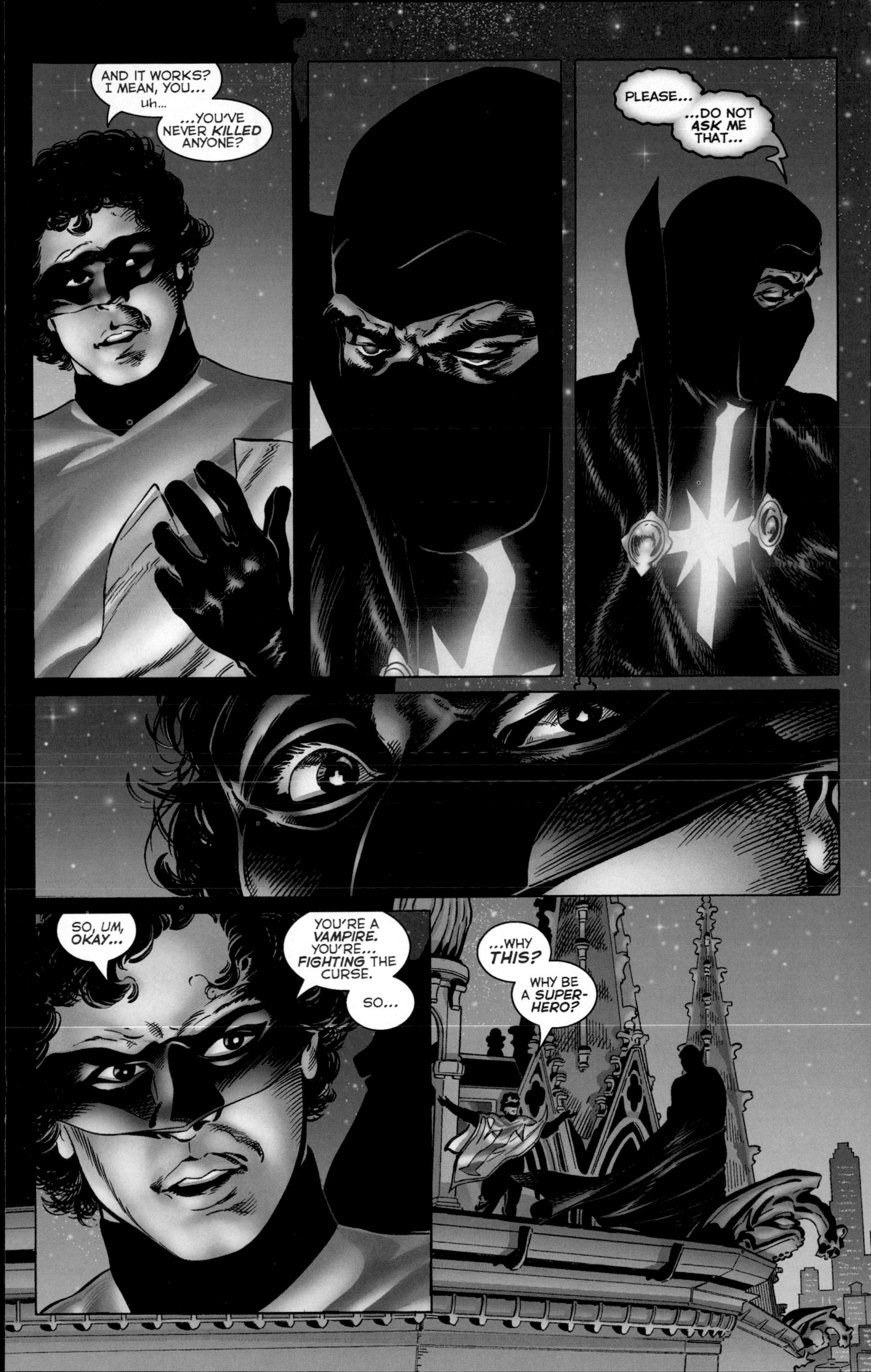
AND IT WORKS? I MEAN, YOU...
uh...
...YOU'VE NEVER KILLED ANYONE?
PLEASE...
...DO NOT ASK ME THAT...
SO, UM, OKAY...
YOU'RE A VAMPIRE. YOU'RE... FIGHTING THE CURSE.
SO...
...WHY THIS?
WHY BE A SUPER-HERO?

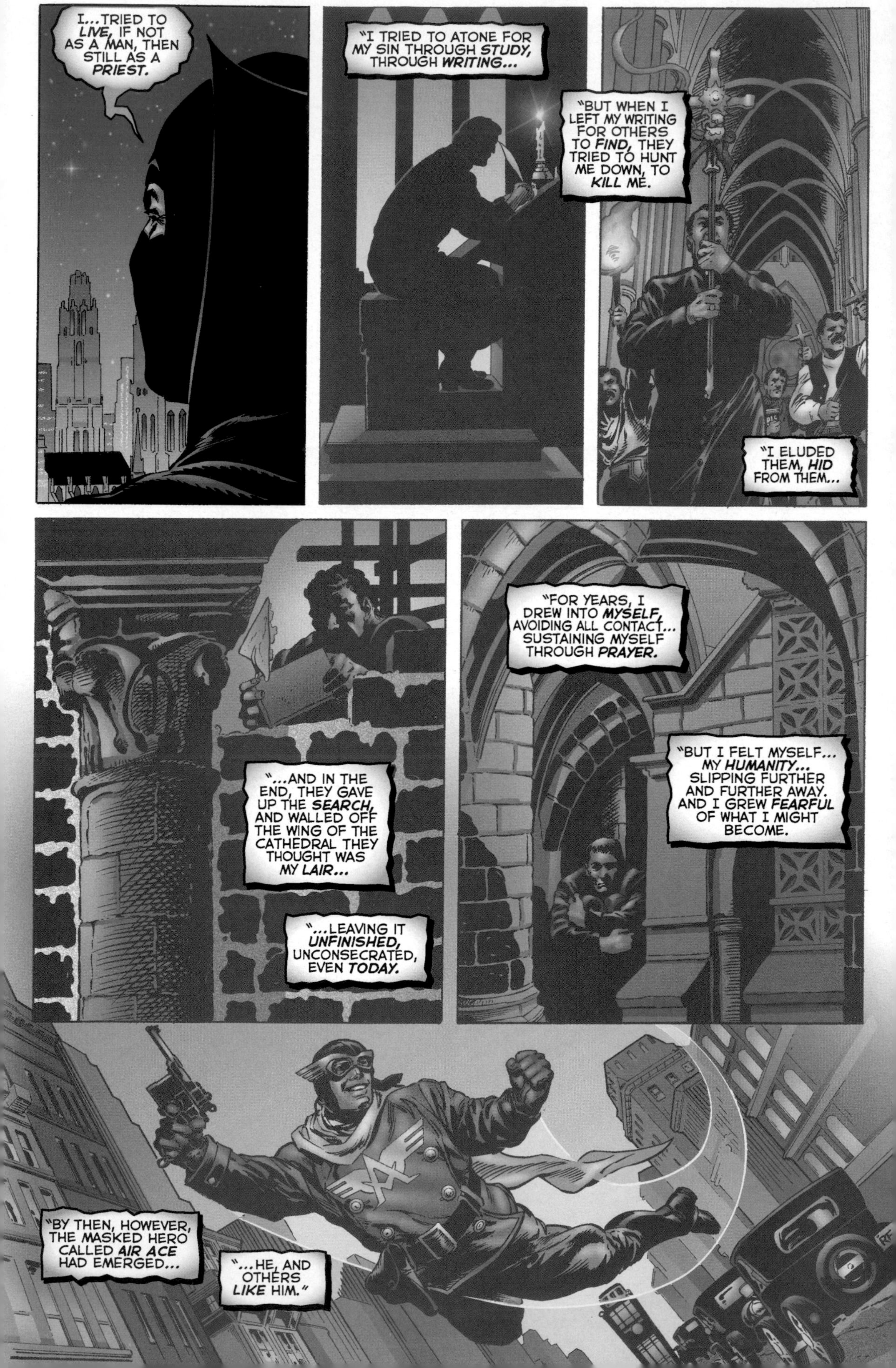
I...TRIED TO LIVE, IF NOT AS A MAN, THEN STILL AS A PRIEST.
"I TRIED TO ATONE FOR MY SIN THROUGH STUDY, THROUGH WRITING...
"BUT WHEN I LEFT MY WRITING FOR OTHERS TO FIND, THEY TRIED TO HUNT ME DOWN, TO KILL ME.
"I ELUDED THEM, HID FROM THEM...
"...AND IN THE END, THEY GAVE UP THE SEARCH, AND WALLED OFF THE WING OF THE CATHEDRAL THEY THOUGHT WAS MY LAIR...
"...LEAVING IT UNFINISHED, UNCONSECRATED, EVEN TODAY.
"FOR YEARS, I DREW INTO MYSELF, AVOIDING ALL CONTACT... SUSTAINING MYSELF THROUGH PRAYER.
"BUT I FELT MYSELF... MY HUMANITY... SLIPPING FURTHER AND FURTHER AWAY. AND I GREW FEARFUL OF WHAT I MIGHT BECOME.
"BY THEN, HOWEVER, THE MASKED HERO CALLED AIR ACE HAD EMERGED...
"...HE, AND OTHERS LIKE HIM."

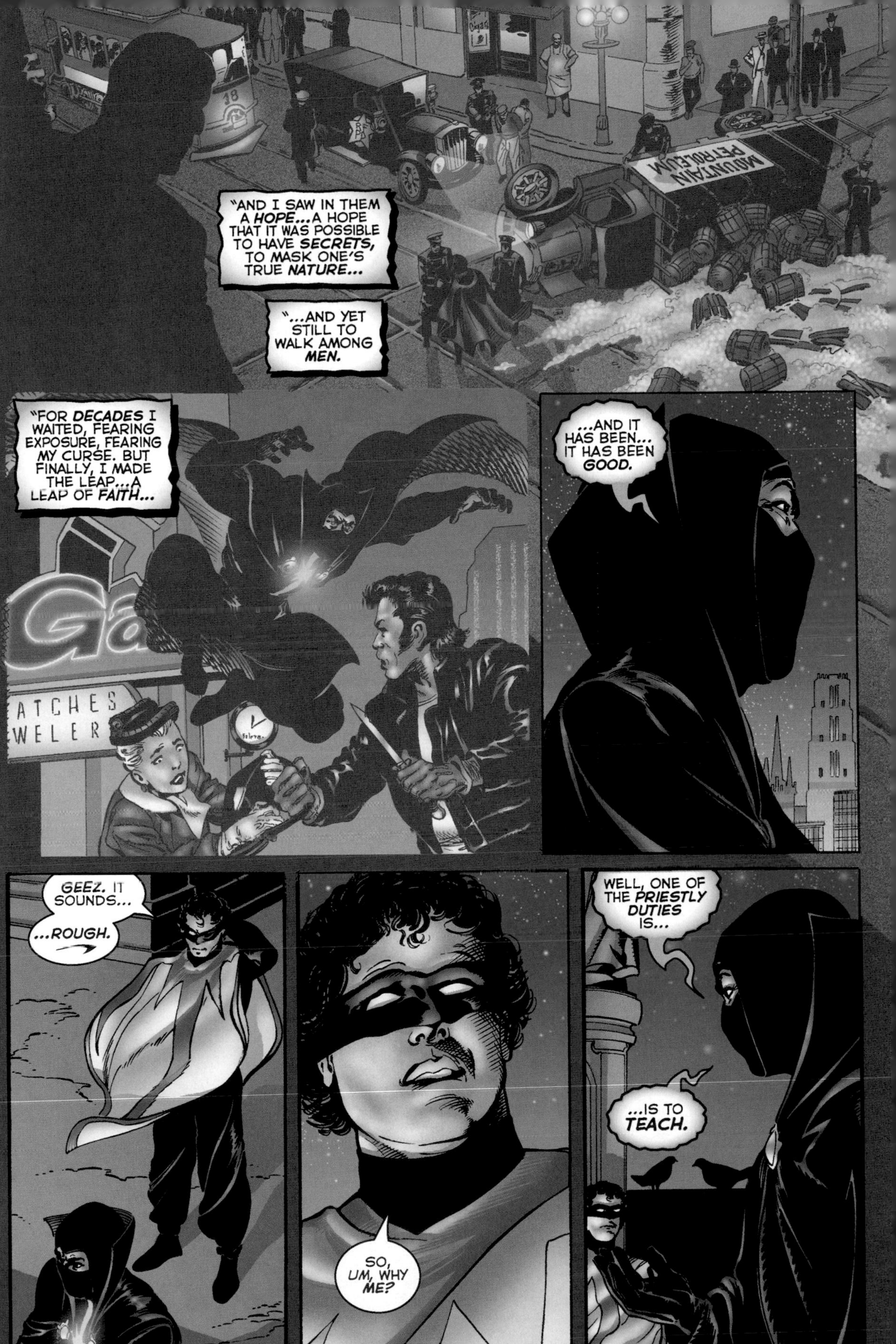
"AND I SAW IN THEM A HOPE... A HOPE THAT IT WAS POSSIBLE TO HAVE SECRETS, TO MASK ONE'S TRUE NATURE...
"...AND YET STILL TO WALK AMONG MEN.
MOUNTAIN PETROLEUM
"FOR DECADES I WAITED, FEARING EXPOSURE, FEARING MY CURSE. BUT FINALLY, I MADE THE LEAP... A LEAP OF FAITH...
...AND IT HAS BEEN... IT HAS BEEN GOOD.
ATCHES
WELER
GEEZ. IT SOUNDS...
...ROUGH.
SO, UM, WHY ME?
WELL, ONE OF THE PRIESTLY DUTIES IS...
...IS TO TEACH.

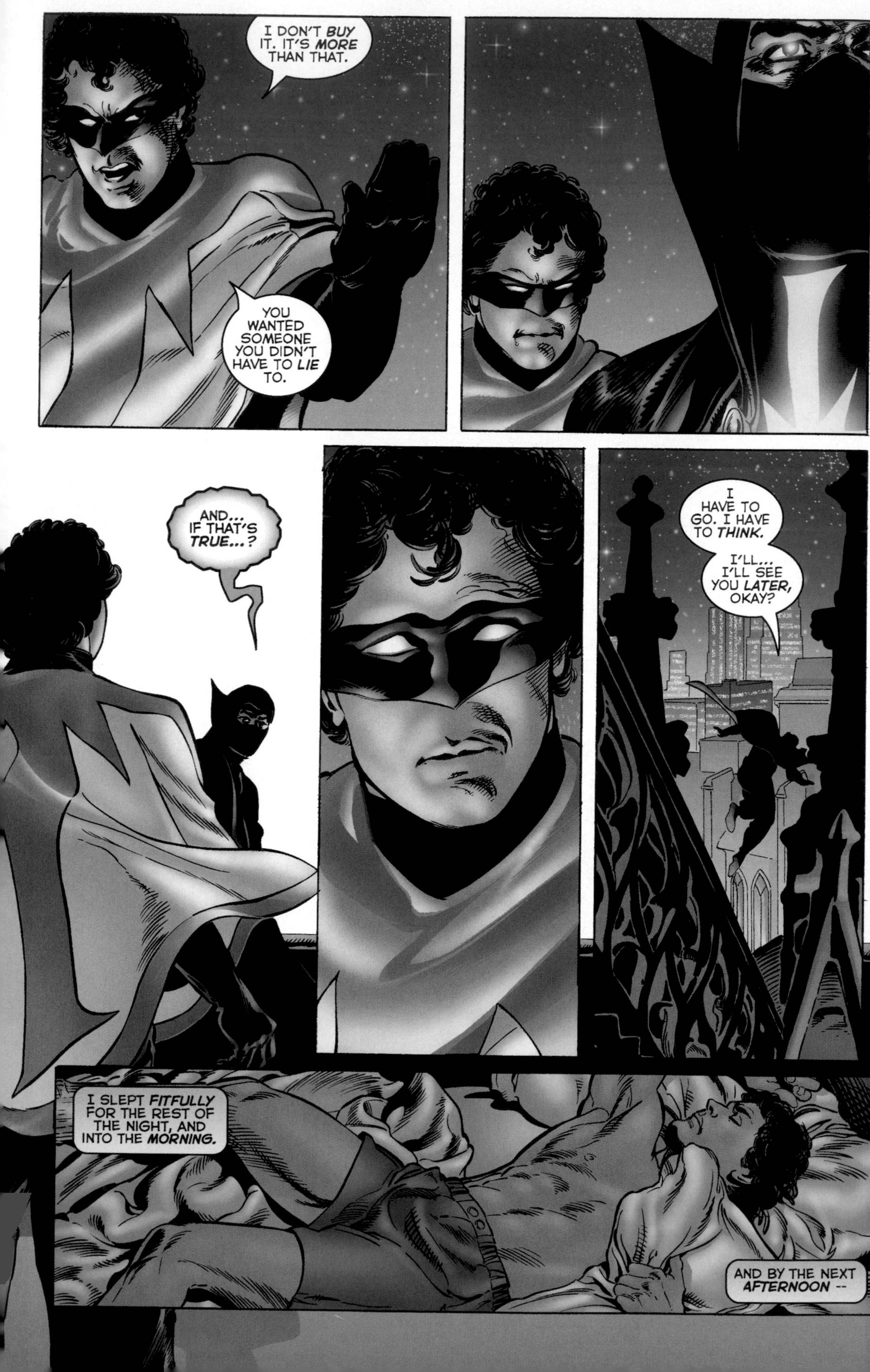
I DON'T *BUY* IT. IT'S *MORE* THAN THAT.
YOU WANTED SOMEONE YOU DIDN'T HAVE TO *LIE* TO.
AND... IF THAT'S *TRUE*...?
I HAVE TO GO. I HAVE TO *THINK.*
I'LL... I'LL SEE YOU *LATER,* OKAY?
I SLEPT *FITFULLY* FOR THE REST OF THE NIGHT, AND INTO THE *MORNING.*
AND BY THE NEXT *AFTERNOON* --

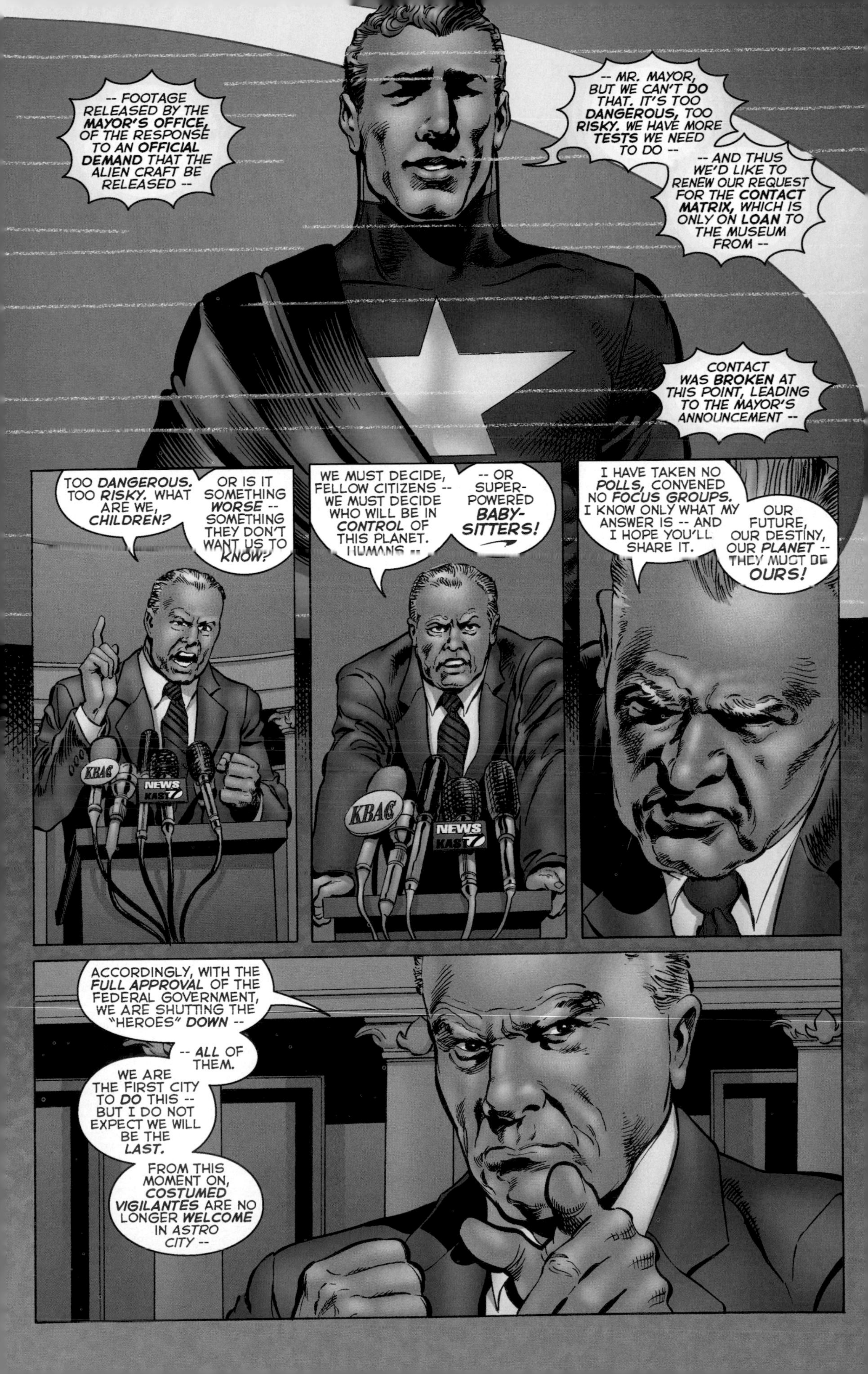

-- FOOTAGE RELEASED BY THE MAYOR'S OFFICE, OF THE RESPONSE TO AN OFFICIAL DEMAND THAT THE ALIEN CRAFT BE RELEASED --
-- MR. MAYOR, BUT WE CAN'T DO THAT. IT'S TOO DANGEROUS, TOO RISKY. WE HAVE MORE TESTS WE NEED TO DO --
-- AND THUS WE'D LIKE TO RENEW OUR REQUEST FOR THE CONTACT MATRIX, WHICH IS ONLY ON LOAN TO THE MUSEUM FROM --
CONTACT WAS BROKEN AT THIS POINT, LEADING TO THE MAYOR'S ANNOUNCEMENT --
TOO DANGEROUS. TOO RISKY. WHAT ARE WE, CHILDREN?
OR IS IT SOMETHING WORSE -- SOMETHING THEY DON'T WANT US TO KNOW?
KBAC
NEWS KAST 7
WE MUST DECIDE, FELLOW CITIZENS -- WE MUST DECIDE WHO WILL BE IN CONTROL OF THIS PLANET. HUMANS --
-- OR SUPER-POWERED BABY-SITTERS!
I HAVE TAKEN NO POLLS, CONVENED NO FOCUS GROUPS. I KNOW ONLY WHAT MY ANSWER IS -- AND I HOPE YOU'LL SHARE IT.
OUR FUTURE, OUR DESTINY, OUR PLANET -- THEY MUST BE OURS!
ACCORDINGLY, WITH THE FULL APPROVAL OF THE FEDERAL GOVERNMENT, WE ARE SHUTTING THE "HEROES" DOWN --
-- ALL OF THEM.
WE ARE THE FIRST CITY TO DO THIS -- BUT I DO NOT EXPECT WE WILL BE THE LAST.
FROM THIS MOMENT ON, COSTUMED VIGILANTES ARE NO LONGER WELCOME IN ASTRO CITY --

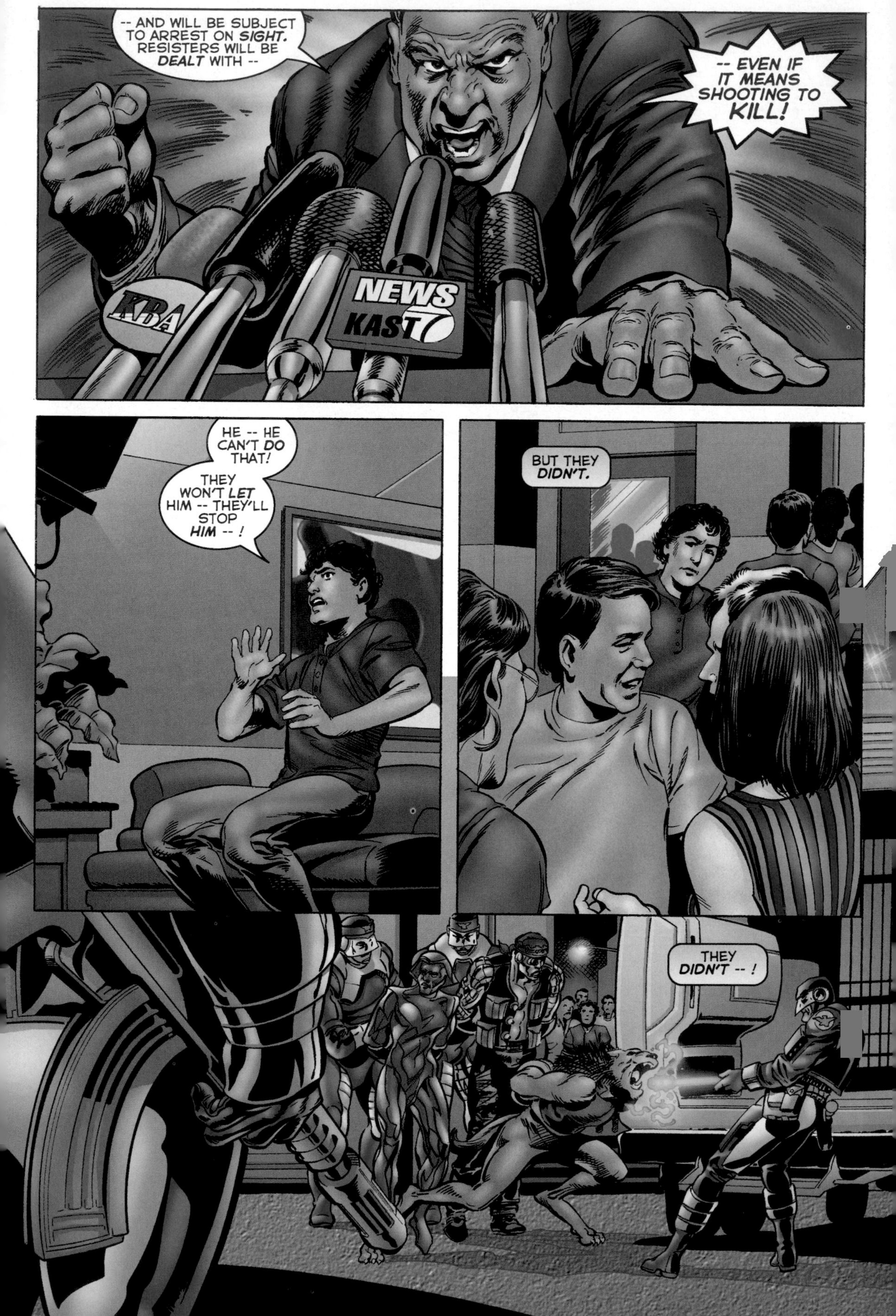
-- AND WILL BE SUBJECT TO ARREST ON SIGHT. RESISTERS WILL BE DEALT WITH --
-- EVEN IF IT MEANS SHOOTING TO KILL!
KBA
NEWS
KAST 7
HE -- HE CAN'T DO THAT!
THEY WON'T LET HIM -- THEY'LL STOP HIM -- !
BUT THEY DIDN'T.
THEY DIDN'T -- !

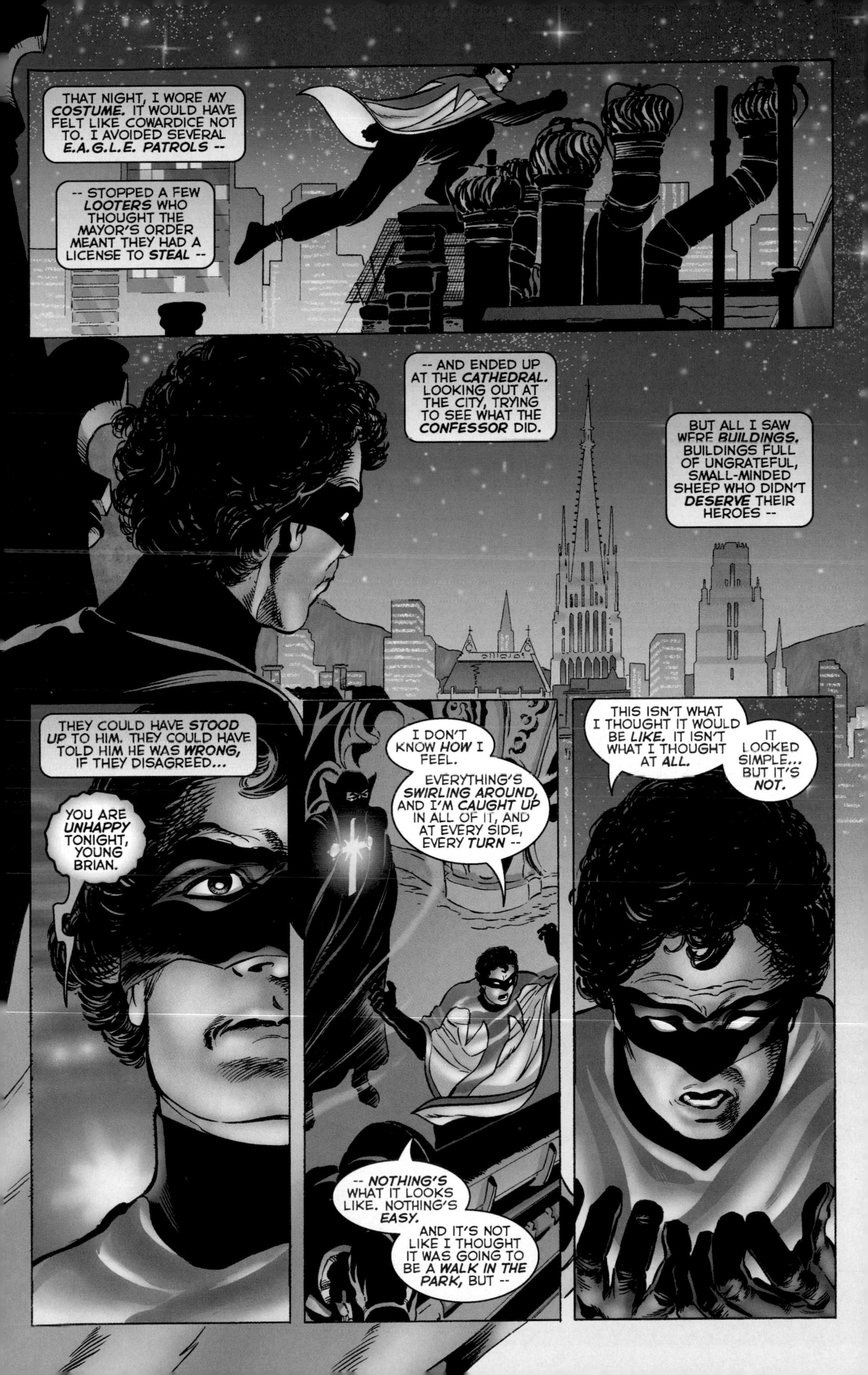
THAT NIGHT, I WORE MY COSTUME. IT WOULD HAVE FELT LIKE COWARDICE NOT TO. I AVOIDED SEVERAL E.A.G.L.E. PATROLS --
-- STOPPED A FEW LOOTERS WHO THOUGHT THE MAYOR'S ORDER MEANT THEY HAD A LICENSE TO STEAL --
-- AND ENDED UP AT THE CATHEDRAL. LOOKING OUT AT THE CITY, TRYING TO SEE WHAT THE CONFESSOR DID.
BUT ALL I SAW WERE BUILDINGS. BUILDINGS FULL OF UNGRATEFUL, SMALL-MINDED SHEEP WHO DIDN'T DESERVE THEIR HEROES --
THEY COULD HAVE STOOD UP TO HIM. THEY COULD HAVE TOLD HIM HE WAS WRONG, IF THEY DISAGREED...
YOU ARE UNHAPPY TONIGHT, YOUNG BRIAN.
I DON'T KNOW HOW I FEEL.
EVERYTHING'S SWIRLING AROUND, AND I'M CAUGHT UP IN ALL OF IT, AND AT EVERY SIDE, EVERY TURN --
-- NOTHING'S WHAT IT LOOKS LIKE. NOTHING'S EASY.
AND IT'S NOT LIKE I THOUGHT IT WAS GOING TO BE A WALK IN THE PARK, BUT --
THIS ISN'T WHAT I THOUGHT IT WOULD BE LIKE. IT ISN'T WHAT I THOUGHT AT ALL.
IT LOOKED SIMPLE... BUT IT'S NOT.

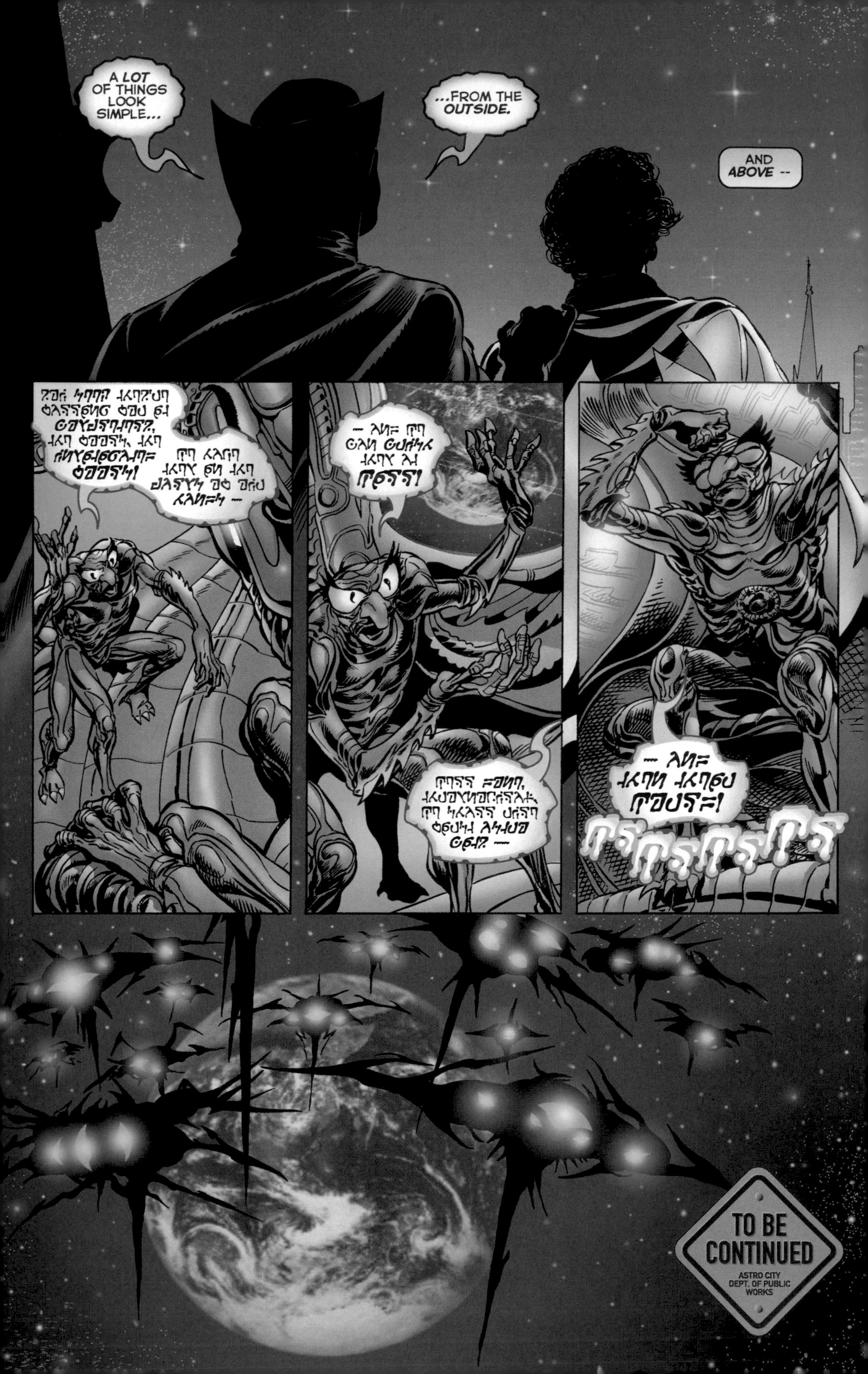
A LOT OF THINGS LOOK SIMPLE...
...FROM THE OUTSIDE.
AND ABOVE --
TO BE CONTINUED
ASTRO CITY DEPT. OF PUBLIC WORKS

14

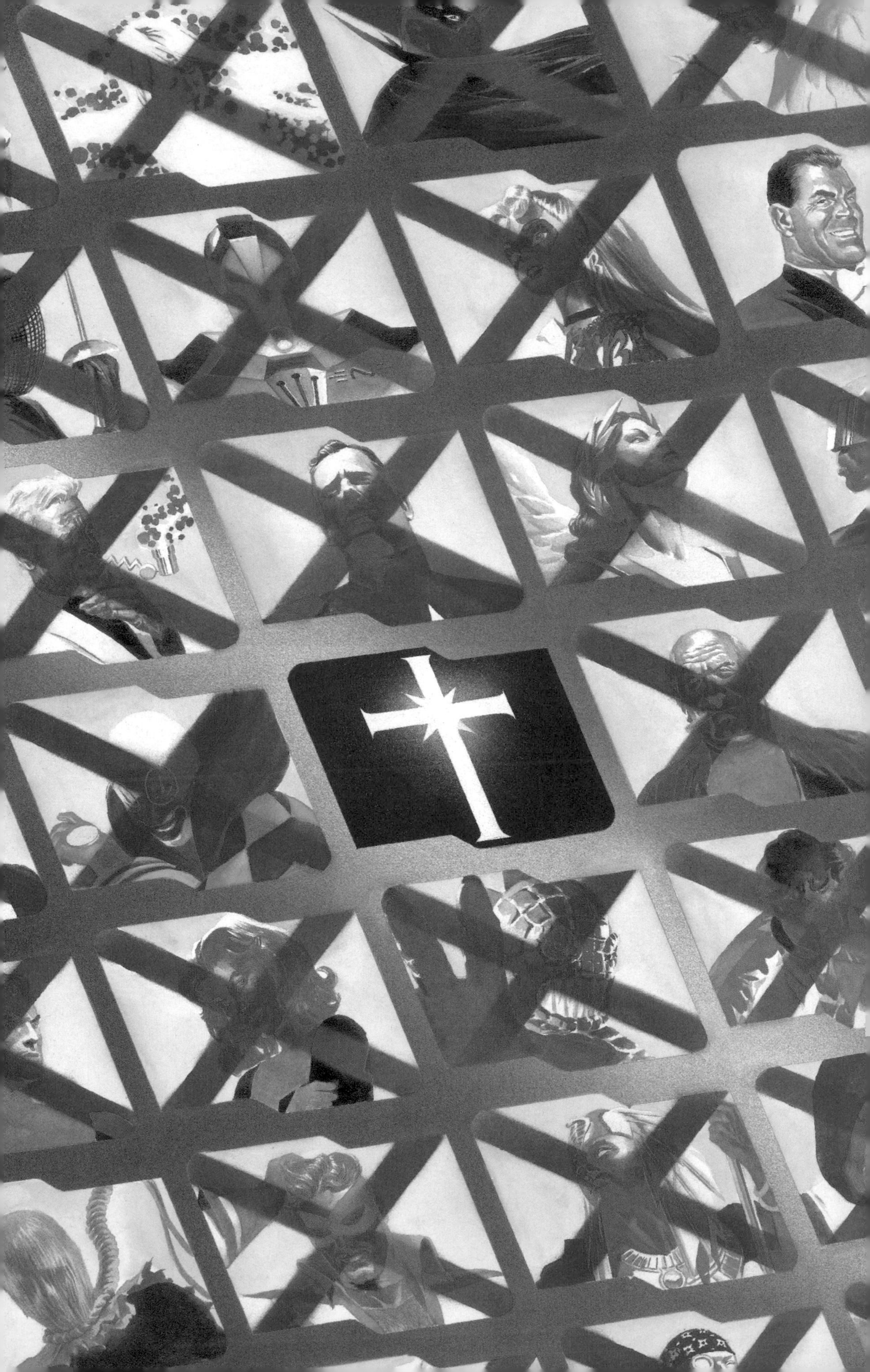

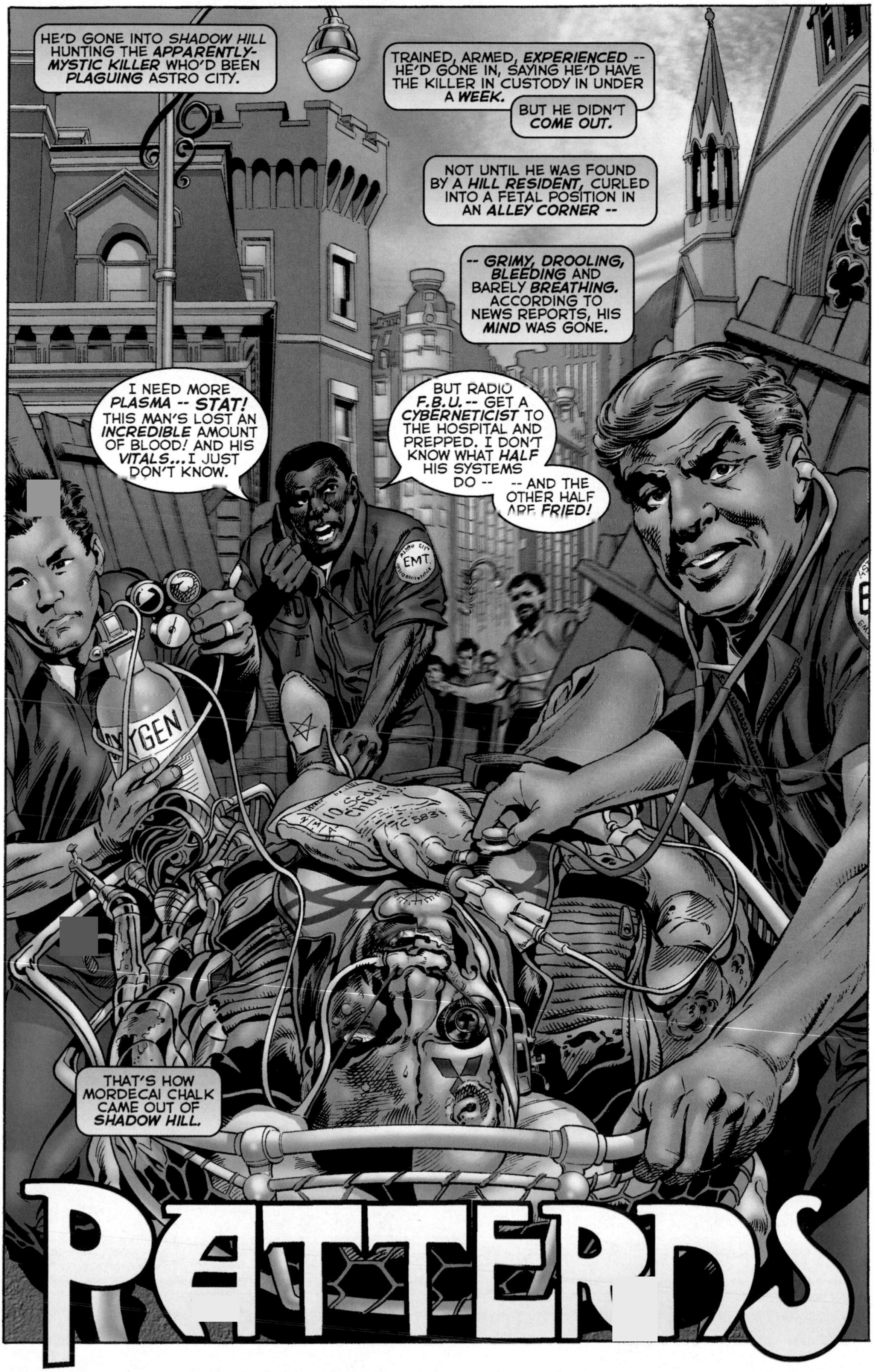
HE'D GONE INTO SHADOW HILL HUNTING THE APPARENTLY-MYSTIC KILLER WHO'D BEEN PLAGUING ASTRO CITY.
TRAINED, ARMED, EXPERIENCED -- HE'D GONE IN, SAYING HE'D HAVE THE KILLER IN CUSTODY IN UNDER A WEEK.
BUT HE DIDN'T COME OUT.
NOT UNTIL HE WAS FOUND BY A HILL RESIDENT, CURLED INTO A FETAL POSITION IN AN ALLEY CORNER --
-- GRIMY, DROOLING, BLEEDING AND BARELY BREATHING. ACCORDING TO NEWS REPORTS, HIS MIND WAS GONE.
I NEED MORE PLASMA -- STAT! THIS MAN'S LOST AN INCREDIBLE AMOUNT OF BLOOD! AND HIS VITALS... I JUST DON'T KNOW.
BUT RADIO F.B.U. -- GET A CYBERNETICIST TO THE HOSPITAL AND PREPPED. I DON'T KNOW WHAT HALF HIS SYSTEMS DO --
-- AND THE OTHER HALF ARE FRIED!
EMT
OXYGEN
THAT'S HOW MORDECAI CHALK CAME OUT OF SHADOW HILL.
PATTERNS

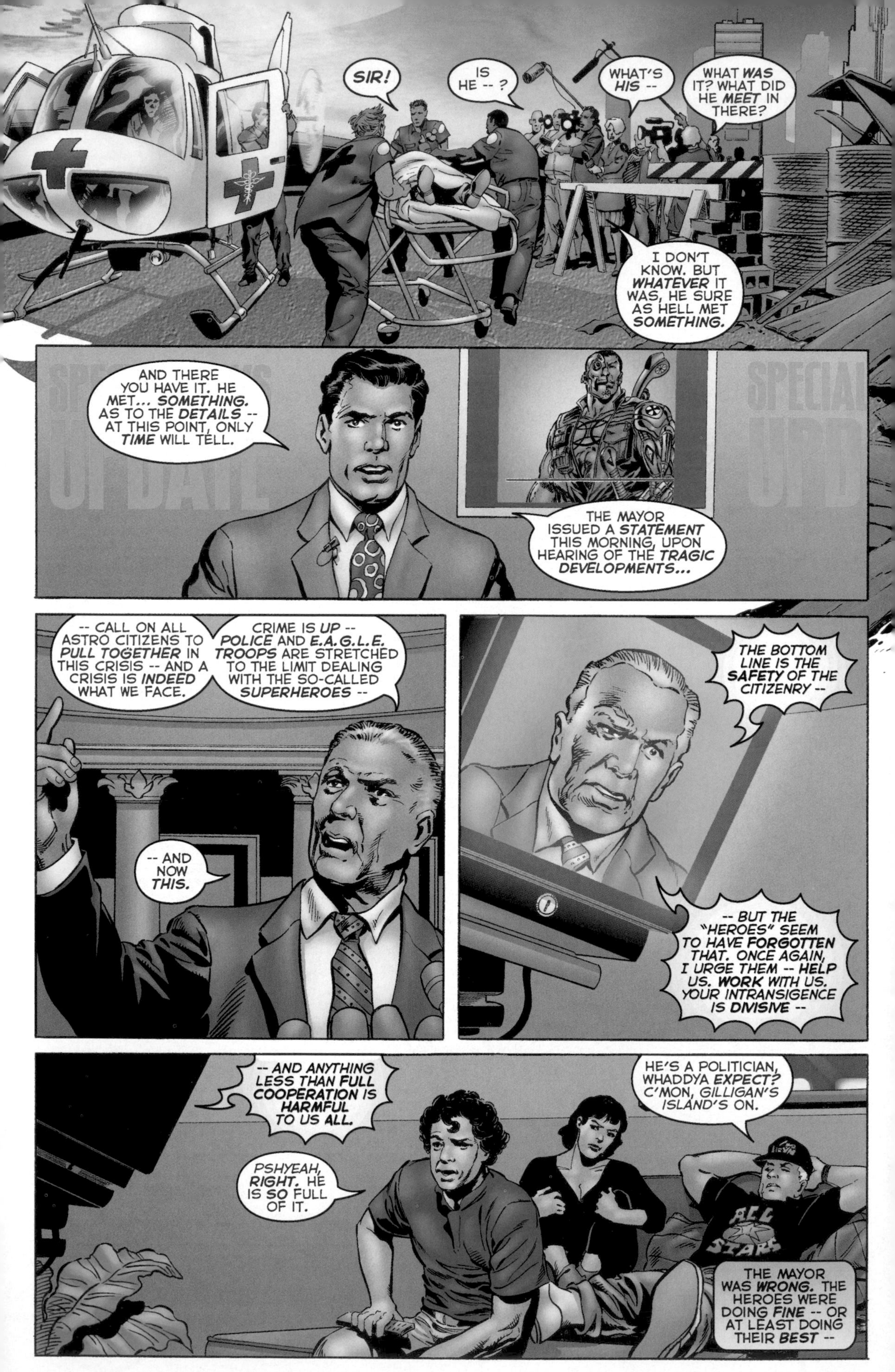
SIR!
IS HE -- ?
WHAT'S HIS --
WHAT WAS IT? WHAT DID HE MEET IN THERE?
I DON'T KNOW. BUT WHATEVER IT WAS, HE SURE AS HELL MET SOMETHING.
AND THERE YOU HAVE IT. HE MET... SOMETHING. AS TO THE DETAILS -- AT THIS POINT, ONLY TIME WILL TELL.
THE MAYOR ISSUED A STATEMENT THIS MORNING, UPON HEARING OF THE TRAGIC DEVELOPMENTS...
-- CALL ON ALL ASTRO CITIZENS TO PULL TOGETHER IN THIS CRISIS -- AND A CRISIS IS INDEED WHAT WE FACE.
CRIME IS UP -- POLICE AND E.A.G.L.E. TROOPS ARE STRETCHED TO THE LIMIT DEALING WITH THE SO-CALLED SUPERHEROES --
-- AND NOW THIS.
THE BOTTOM LINE IS THE SAFETY OF THE CITIZENRY --
-- BUT THE "HEROES" SEEM TO HAVE FORGOTTEN THAT. ONCE AGAIN, I URGE THEM -- HELP US. WORK WITH US. YOUR INTRANSIGENCE IS DIVISIVE --
-- AND ANYTHING LESS THAN FULL COOPERATION IS HARMFUL TO US ALL.
PSHYEAH, RIGHT. HE IS SO FULL OF IT.
HE'S A POLITICIAN, WHADDYA EXPECT? C'MON, GILLIGAN'S ISLAND'S ON.
THE MAYOR WAS WRONG. THE HEROES WERE DOING FINE -- OR AT LEAST DOING THEIR BEST --

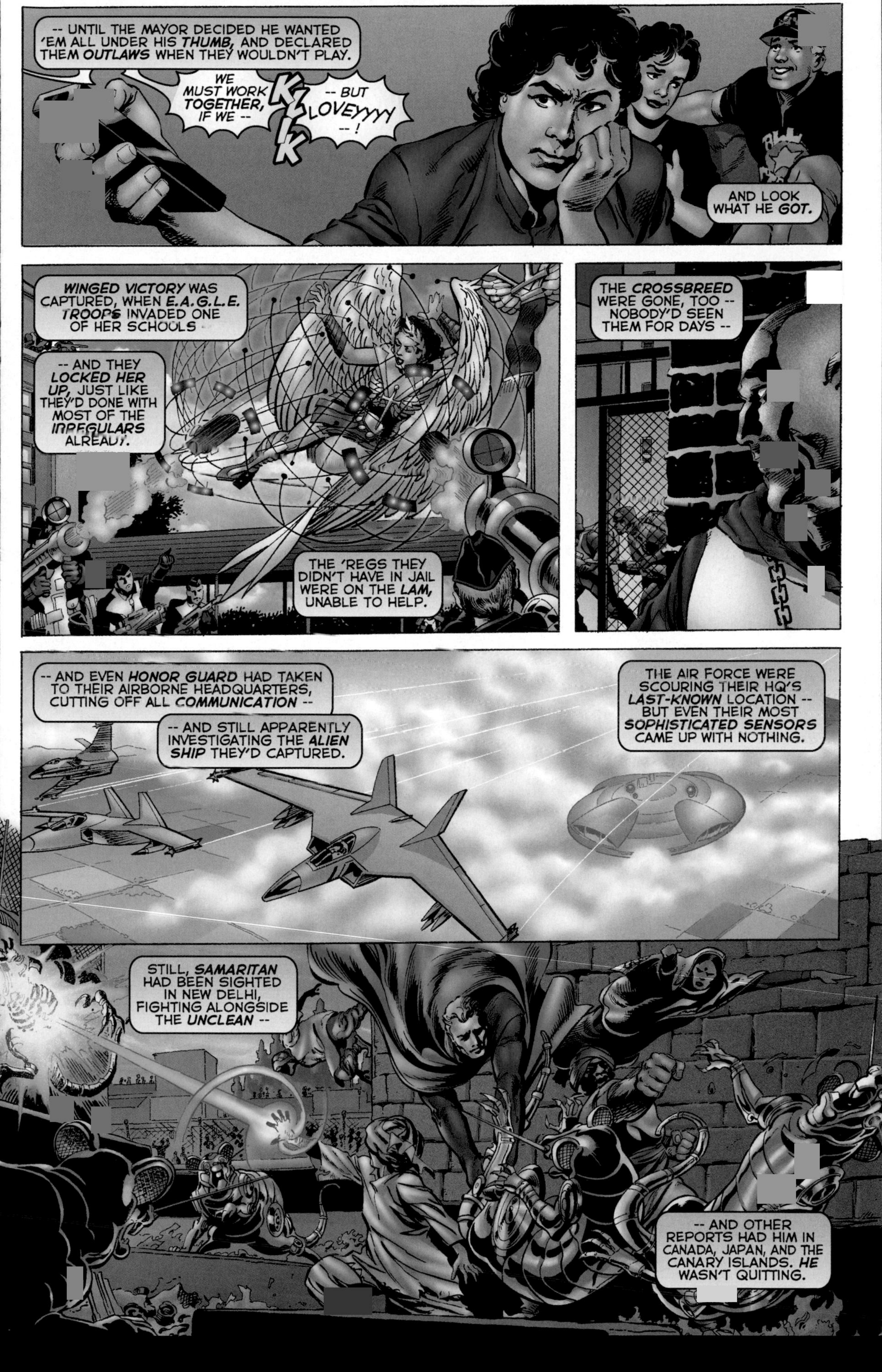
-- UNTIL THE MAYOR DECIDED HE WANTED 'EM ALL UNDER HIS THUMB, AND DECLARED THEM OUTLAWS WHEN THEY WOULDN'T PLAY.
WE MUST WORK TOGETHER, IF WE --
KLIK
-- BUT LOVEYYYY --!
AND LOOK WHAT HE GOT.
WINGED VICTORY WAS CAPTURED, WHEN E.A.G.L.E. TROOPS INVADED ONE OF HER SCHOOLS --
-- AND THEY LOCKED HER UP, JUST LIKE THEY'D DONE WITH MOST OF THE IRREGULARS ALREADY.
THE 'REGS THEY DIDN'T HAVE IN JAIL WERE ON THE LAM, UNABLE TO HELP.
THE CROSSBREED WERE GONE, TOO -- NOBODY'D SEEN THEM FOR DAYS --
-- AND EVEN HONOR GUARD HAD TAKEN TO THEIR AIRBORNE HEADQUARTERS, CUTTING OFF ALL COMMUNICATION --
-- AND STILL APPARENTLY INVESTIGATING THE ALIEN SHIP THEY'D CAPTURED.
THE AIR FORCE WERE SCOURING THEIR HQ'S LAST-KNOWN LOCATION -- BUT EVEN THEIR MOST SOPHISTICATED SENSORS CAME UP WITH NOTHING.
STILL, SAMARITAN HAD BEEN SIGHTED IN NEW DELHI, FIGHTING ALONGSIDE THE UNCLEAN --
-- AND OTHER REPORTS HAD HIM IN CANADA, JAPAN, AND THE CANARY ISLANDS. HE WASN'T QUITTING.

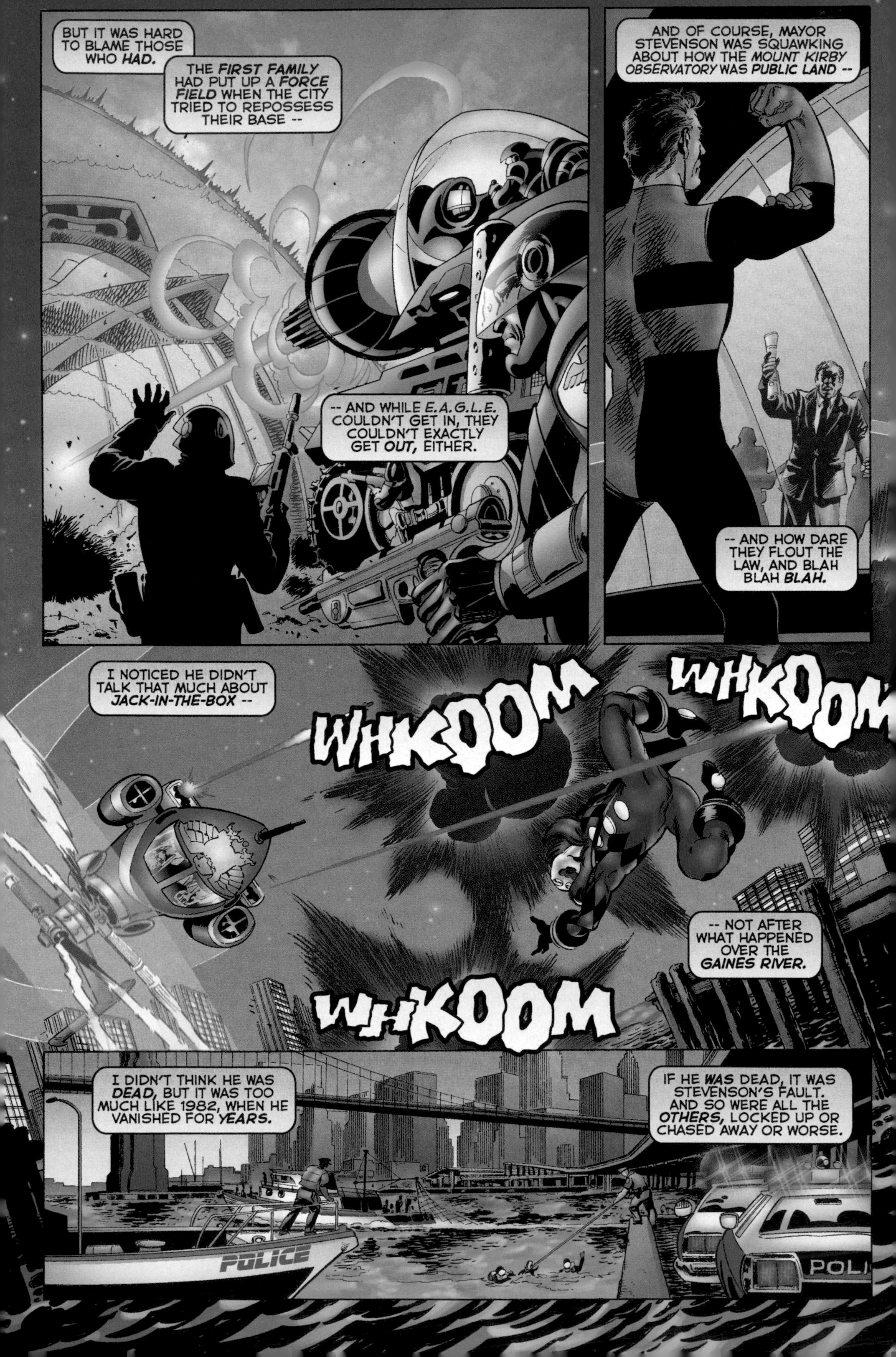

BUT IT WAS HARD TO BLAME THOSE WHO *HAD.*
THE *FIRST FAMILY* HAD PUT UP A *FORCE FIELD* WHEN THE CITY TRIED TO REPOSSESS THEIR BASE --
-- AND WHILE *E.A.G.L.E.* COULDN'T GET IN, THEY COULDN'T EXACTLY GET *OUT,* EITHER.
AND OF COURSE, MAYOR STEVENSON WAS SQUAWKING ABOUT HOW THE *MOUNT KIRBY OBSERVATORY* WAS *PUBLIC LAND* --
-- AND HOW DARE THEY FLOUT THE LAW, AND BLAH BLAH *BLAH.*
I NOTICED HE DIDN'T TALK THAT MUCH ABOUT *JACK-IN-THE-BOX* --
WHKOOM
WHKOOM
-- NOT AFTER WHAT HAPPENED OVER THE *GAINES RIVER.*
WHKOOM
I DIDN'T THINK HE WAS *DEAD,* BUT IT WAS TOO MUCH LIKE 1982, WHEN HE VANISHED FOR *YEARS.*
IF HE *WAS* DEAD, IT WAS STEVENSON'S FAULT. AND SO WERE ALL THE *OTHERS,* LOCKED UP OR CHASED AWAY OR WORSE.
POLICE

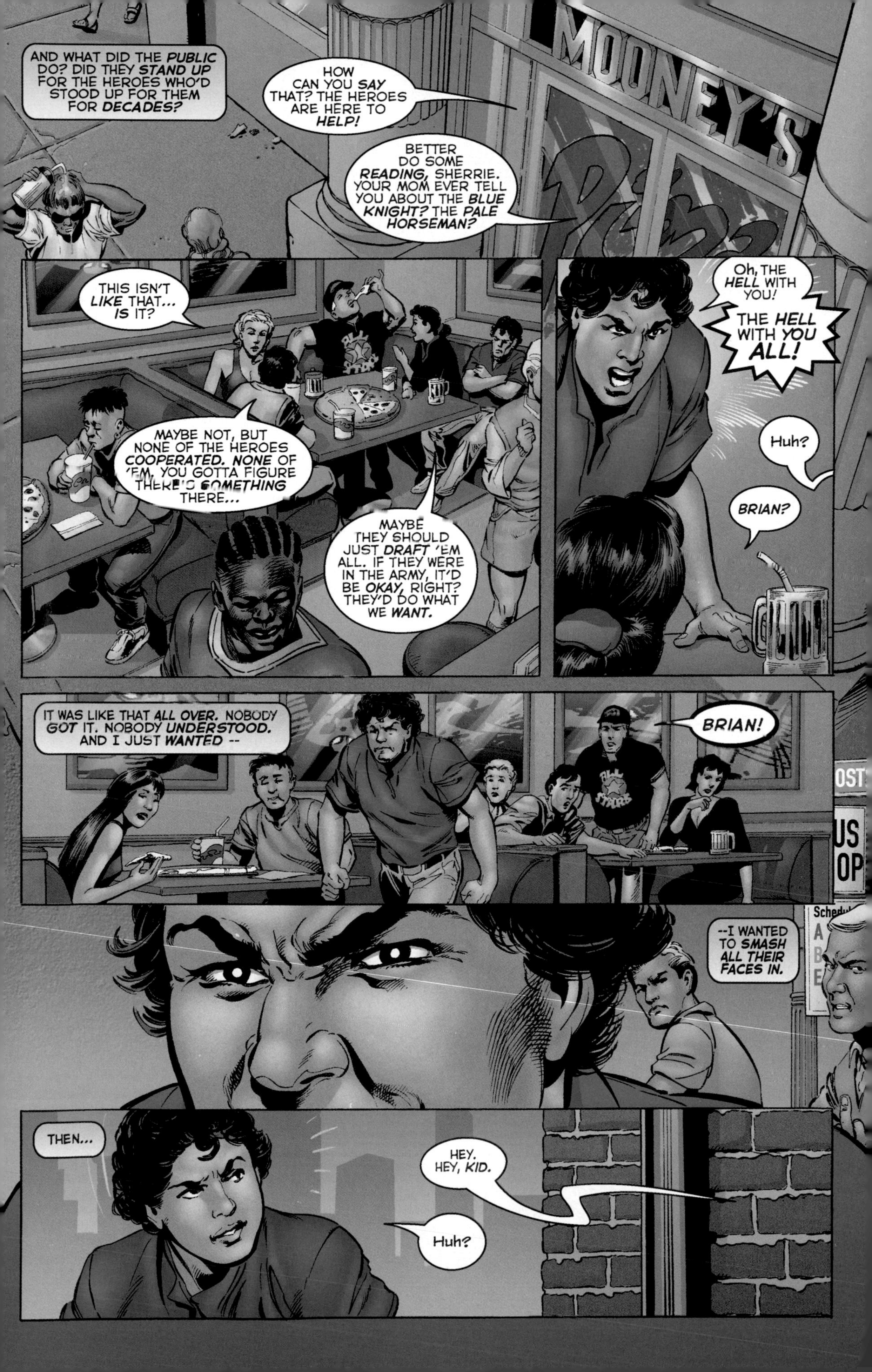

MOONEY'S
AND WHAT DID THE PUBLIC DO? DID THEY STAND UP FOR THE HEROES WHO'D STOOD UP FOR THEM FOR DECADES?
HOW CAN YOU SAY THAT? THE HEROES ARE HERE TO HELP!
BETTER DO SOME READING, SHERRIE. YOUR MOM EVER TELL YOU ABOUT THE BLUE KNIGHT? THE PALE HORSEMAN?
THIS ISN'T LIKE THAT... IS IT?
MAYBE NOT, BUT NONE OF THE HEROES COOPERATED. NONE OF 'EM. YOU GOTTA FIGURE THERE'S SOMETHING THERE...
MAYBE THEY SHOULD JUST DRAFT 'EM ALL. IF THEY WERE IN THE ARMY, IT'D BE OKAY, RIGHT? THEY'D DO WHAT WE WANT.
Oh, THE HELL WITH YOU!
THE HELL WITH YOU ALL!
Huh?
BRIAN?
IT WAS LIKE THAT ALL OVER. NOBODY GOT IT. NOBODY UNDERSTOOD. AND I JUST WANTED --
BRIAN!
--I WANTED TO SMASH ALL THEIR FACES IN.
THEN...
HEY. HEY, KID.
Huh?

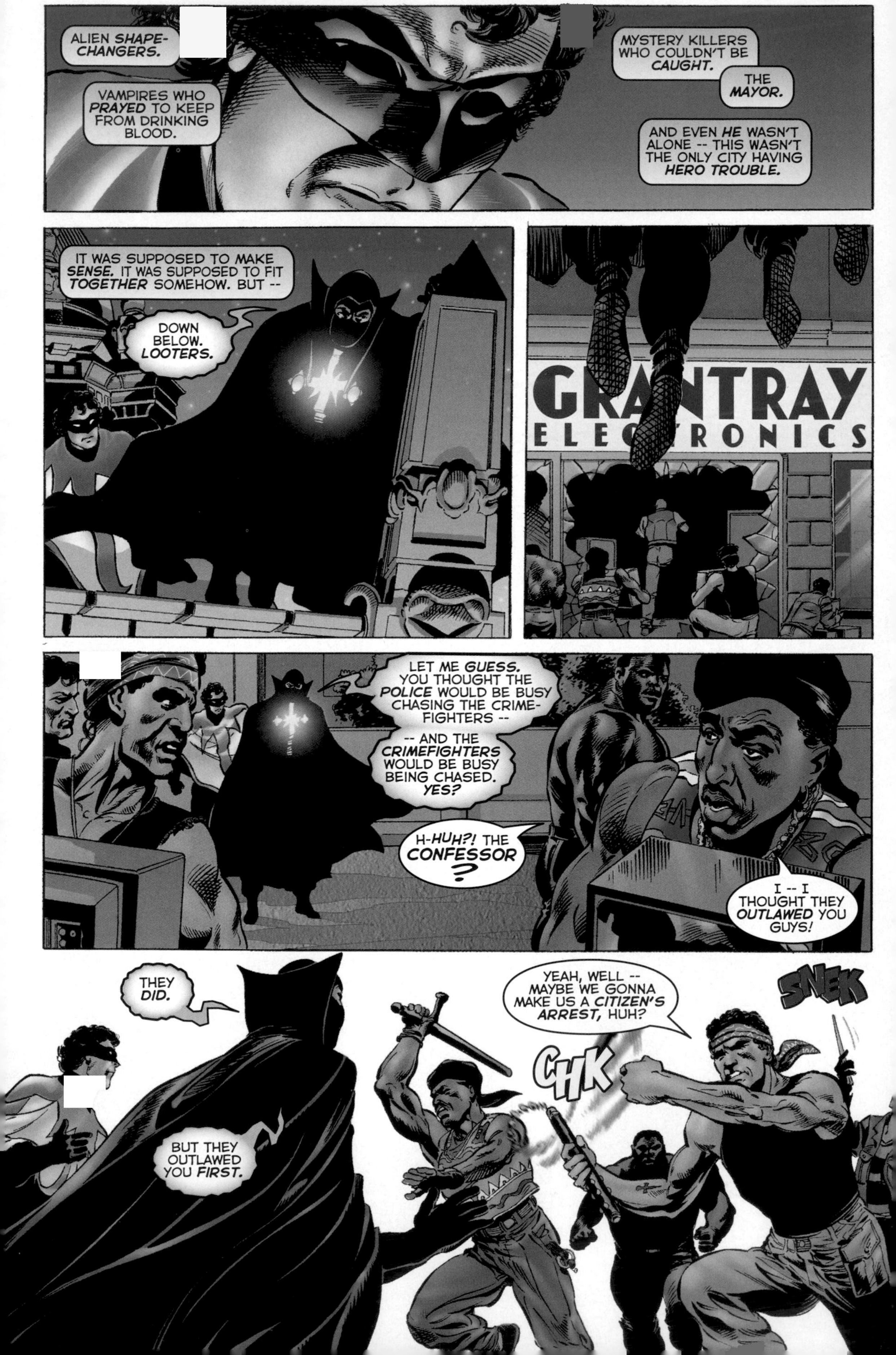
ALIEN SHAPE-CHANGERS.
VAMPIRES WHO PRAYED TO KEEP FROM DRINKING BLOOD.
MYSTERY KILLERS WHO COULDN'T BE CAUGHT.
THE MAYOR.
AND EVEN HE WASN'T ALONE -- THIS WASN'T THE ONLY CITY HAVING HERO TROUBLE.
IT WAS SUPPOSED TO MAKE SENSE. IT WAS SUPPOSED TO FIT TOGETHER SOMEHOW. BUT --
DOWN BELOW. LOOTERS.
GRANTRAY ELECTRONICS
LET ME GUESS. YOU THOUGHT THE POLICE WOULD BE BUSY CHASING THE CRIME-FIGHTERS --
-- AND THE CRIMEFIGHTERS WOULD BE BUSY BEING CHASED. YES?
H-HUH?! THE CONFESSOR?
I -- I THOUGHT THEY OUTLAWED YOU GUYS!
THEY DID.
BUT THEY OUTLAWED YOU FIRST.
YEAH, WELL -- MAYBE WE GONNA MAKE US A CITIZEN'S ARREST, HUH?
SNEK
CHK

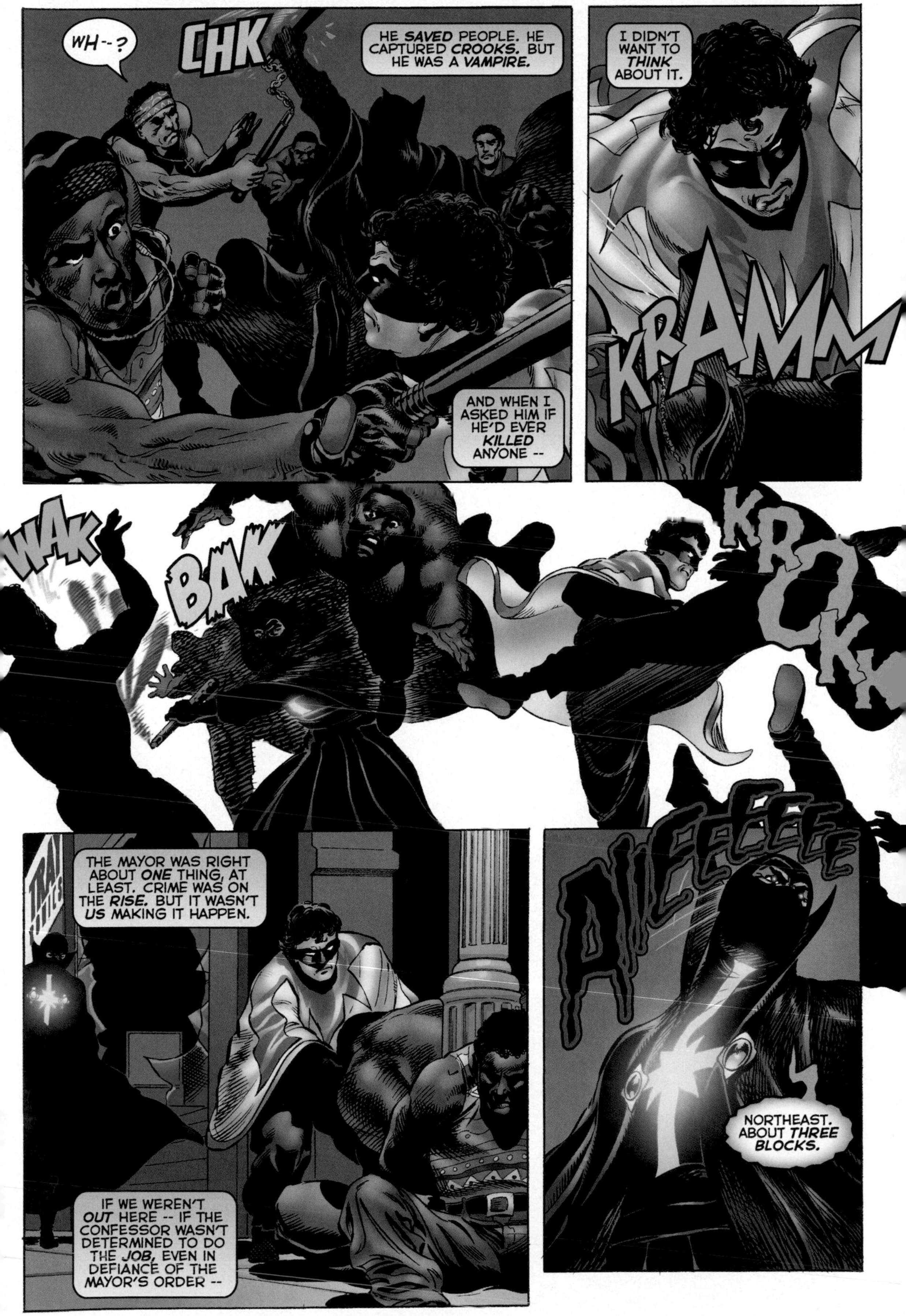
WH--?
CHK
HE SAVED PEOPLE. HE CAPTURED CROOKS. BUT HE WAS A VAMPIRE.
AND WHEN I ASKED HIM IF HE'D EVER KILLED ANYONE --
I DIDN'T WANT TO THINK ABOUT IT.
KRAMM
WAK
BAK
KROCKK
THE MAYOR WAS RIGHT ABOUT ONE THING, AT LEAST. CRIME WAS ON THE RISE. BUT IT WASN'T US MAKING IT HAPPEN.
IF WE WEREN'T OUT HERE -- IF THE CONFESSOR WASN'T DETERMINED TO DO THE JOB, EVEN IN DEFIANCE OF THE MAYOR'S ORDER --
AIEEEEEE
NORTHEAST. ABOUT THREE BLOCKS.

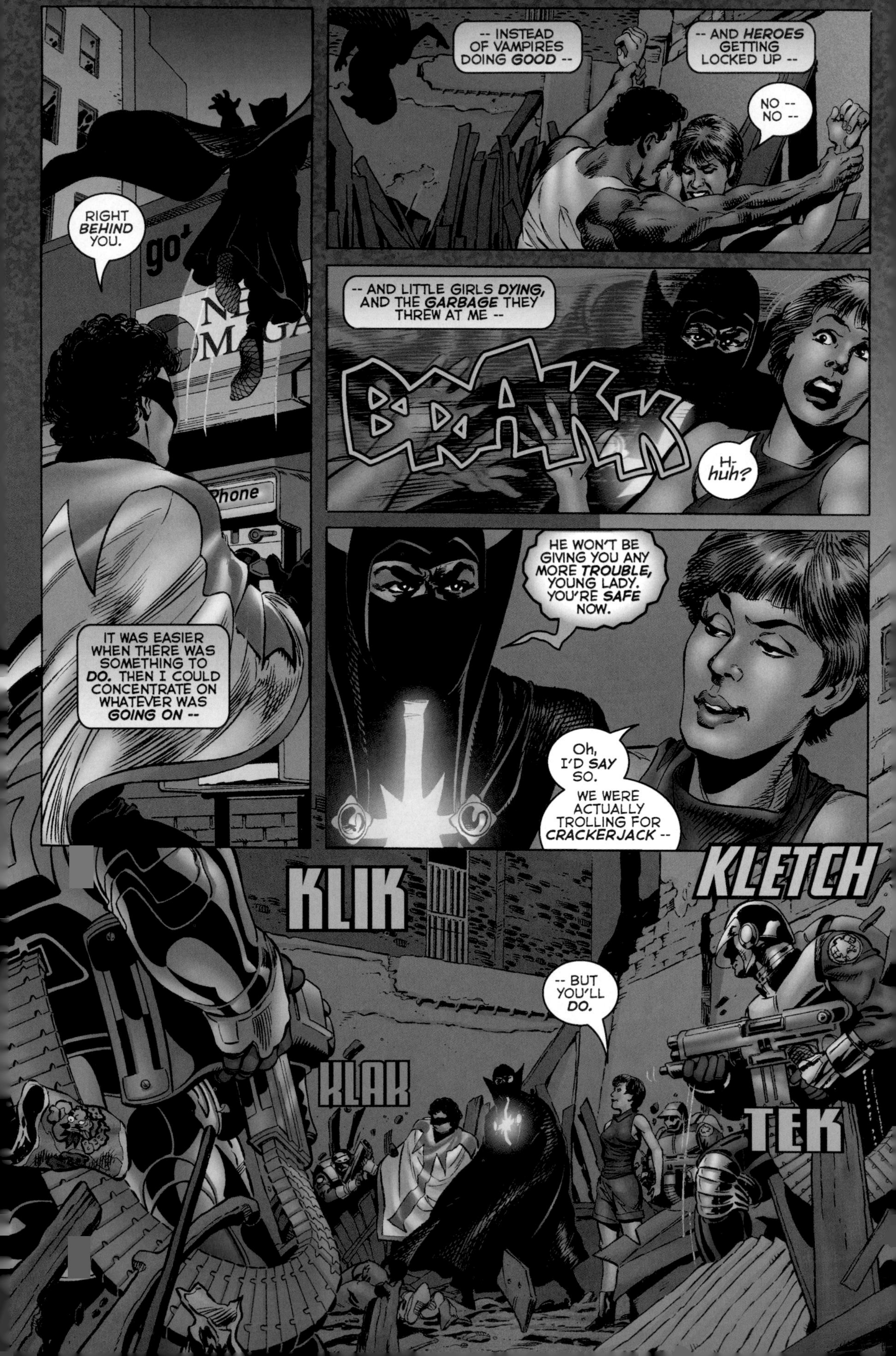
RIGHT BEHIND YOU.
IT WAS EASIER WHEN THERE WAS SOMETHING TO DO. THEN I COULD CONCENTRATE ON WHATEVER WAS GOING ON --
-- INSTEAD OF VAMPIRES DOING GOOD --
-- AND HEROES GETTING LOCKED UP --
NO -- NO --
-- AND LITTLE GIRLS DYING, AND THE GARBAGE THEY THREW AT ME --
BRAKK
H-huh?
HE WON'T BE GIVING YOU ANY MORE TROUBLE, YOUNG LADY. YOU'RE SAFE NOW.
Oh, I'D SAY SO.
WE WERE ACTUALLY TROLLING FOR CRACKERJACK --
KLIK
KLETCH
-- BUT YOU'LL DO.
KLAK
TEK

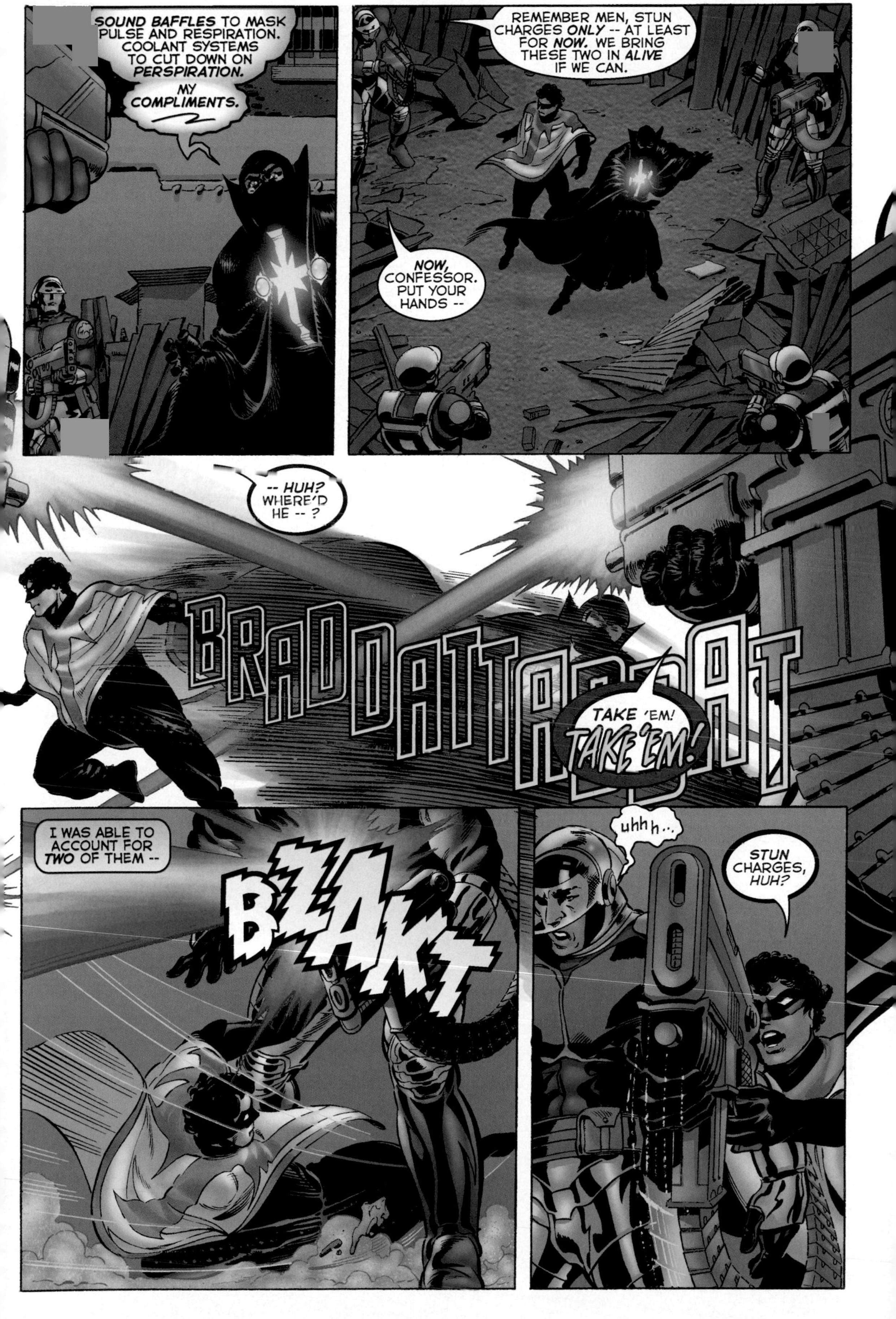
SOUND BAFFLES TO MASK PULSE AND RESPIRATION. COOLANT SYSTEMS TO CUT DOWN ON PERSPIRATION.
MY COMPLIMENTS.
REMEMBER MEN, STUN CHARGES ONLY -- AT LEAST FOR NOW. WE BRING THESE TWO IN ALIVE IF WE CAN.
NOW, CONFESSOR. PUT YOUR HANDS --
-- HUH? WHERE'D HE -- ?
BRADDATTADDAT
TAKE 'EM! TAKE 'EM!
I WAS ABLE TO ACCOUNT FOR TWO OF THEM --
BZAKT
uhhh...
STUN CHARGES, HUH?

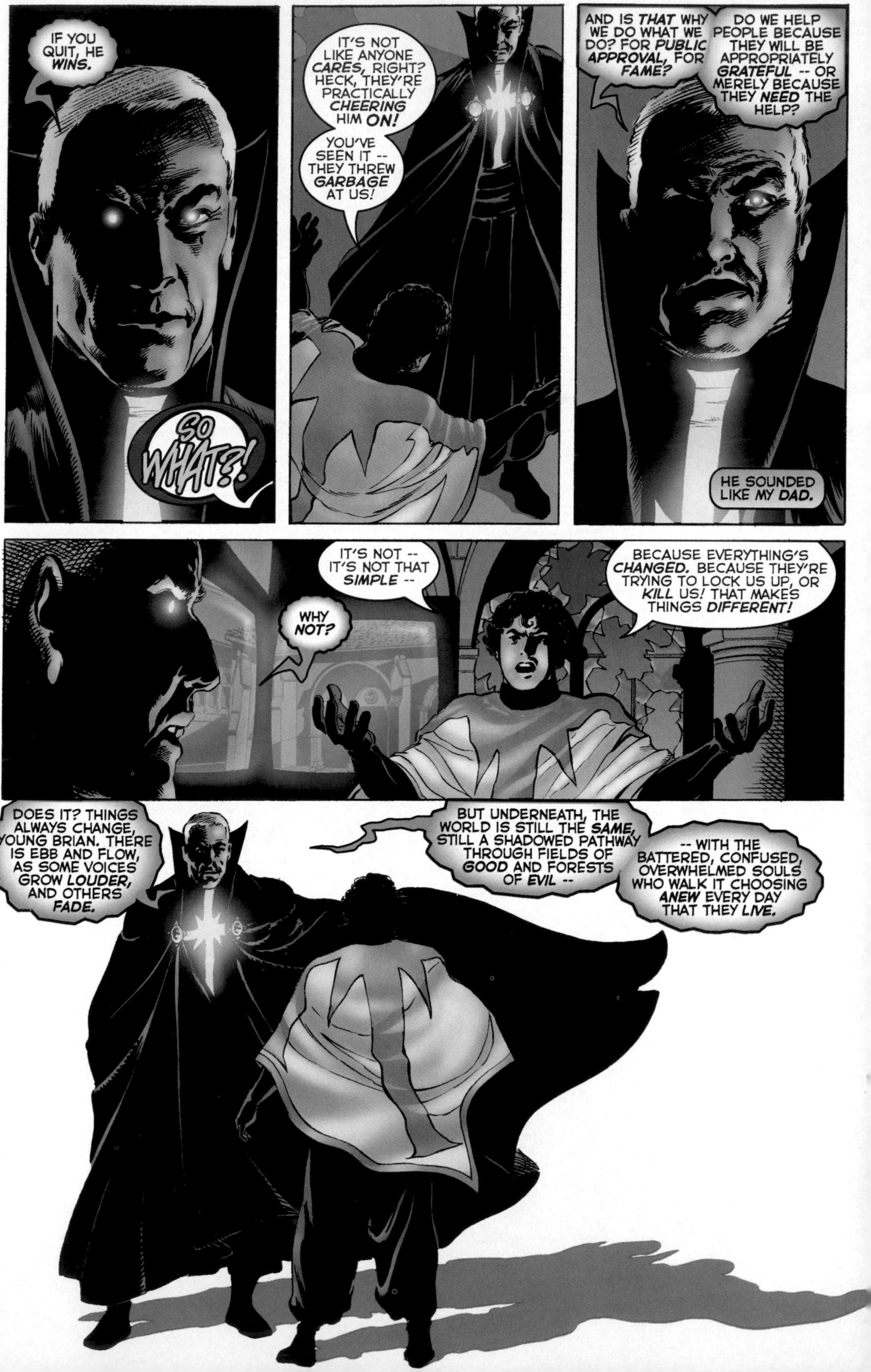
IF YOU QUIT, HE WINS.
SO WHAT?!
IT'S NOT LIKE ANYONE CARES, RIGHT? HECK, THEY'RE PRACTICALLY CHEERING HIM ON!
YOU'VE SEEN IT -- THEY THREW GARBAGE AT US!
AND IS THAT WHY WE DO WHAT WE DO? FOR PUBLIC APPROVAL, FOR FAME?
DO WE HELP PEOPLE BECAUSE THEY WILL BE APPROPRIATELY GRATEFUL -- OR MERELY BECAUSE THEY NEED THE HELP?
HE SOUNDED LIKE MY DAD.
IT'S NOT -- IT'S NOT THAT SIMPLE --
WHY NOT?
BECAUSE EVERYTHING'S CHANGED. BECAUSE THEY'RE TRYING TO LOCK US UP, OR KILL US! THAT MAKES THINGS DIFFERENT!
DOES IT? THINGS ALWAYS CHANGE, YOUNG BRIAN. THERE IS EBB AND FLOW, AS SOME VOICES GROW LOUDER, AND OTHERS FADE.
BUT UNDERNEATH, THE WORLD IS STILL THE SAME, STILL A SHADOWED PATHWAY THROUGH FIELDS OF GOOD AND FORESTS OF EVIL --
-- WITH THE BATTERED, CONFUSED, OVERWHELMED SOULS WHO WALK IT CHOOSING ANEW EVERY DAY THAT THEY LIVE.

AND IF THE FORCES OF ANGER AND UNREASON ARE *GROWING*, IF HUMANITY IS LOSING SIGHT OF THEIR *PATH* -- -- THEN IS IT NOT ALL THE *MORE* CRUCIAL THAT THEY BE SHOWN THEIR *CHOICE*? THAT THEY BE SHOWN THE *WAY*?

I TAKE IT *BACK*. YOU'RE *WORSE* THAN MY DAD.

YOUR FATHER SOUNDS LIKE A VERY *ADMIRABLE* MAN. I'D LIKE TO HAVE *MET* HIM.

MY FATHER WAS AN *IDIOT* -- WHO DIED BROKE AND *LAUGHED* AT! AND YOU, A *VAMPIRE*, TALKING ABOUT THIS KIND OF --

-- DO YOU THINK FOR A *MINUTE* THAT ANYONE WOULD LISTEN TO YOU IF -- IF --

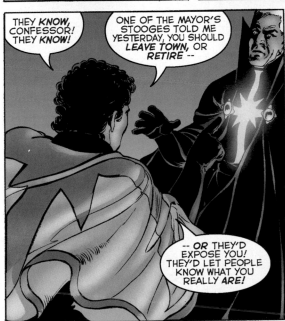

THEY *KNOW*, CONFESSOR! THEY *KNOW*!

ONE OF THE MAYOR'S STOOGES TOLD ME YESTERDAY, YOU SHOULD *LEAVE TOWN*, OR *RETIRE* --

-- OR THEY'D *EXPOSE* YOU! THEY'D LET PEOPLE KNOW WHAT YOU REALLY *ARE*!

THINK ABOUT HOW THEY'D *REACT* -- AND THEN ASK YOURSELF IF YOU STILL *WANT* TO SAVE 'EM ALL!

THEY...

...THEY *KNOW*?

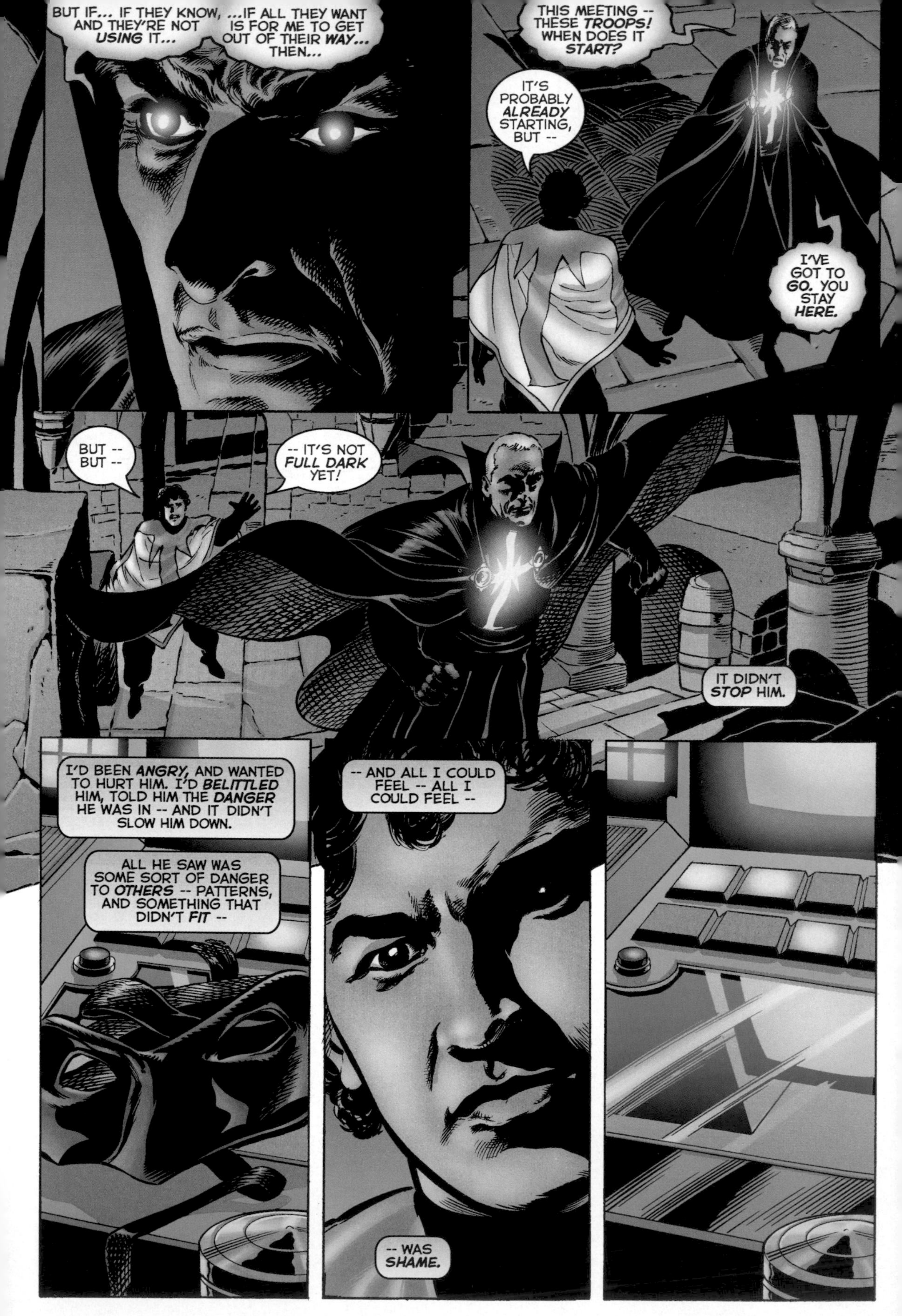
BUT IF... IF THEY KNOW, AND THEY'RE NOT USING IT...
...IF ALL THEY WANT IS FOR ME TO GET OUT OF THEIR WAY... THEN...
THIS MEETING -- THESE TROOPS! WHEN DOES IT START?
IT'S PROBABLY ALREADY STARTING, BUT --
I'VE GOT TO GO. YOU STAY HERE.
BUT -- BUT --
-- IT'S NOT FULL DARK YET!
IT DIDN'T STOP HIM.
I'D BEEN ANGRY, AND WANTED TO HURT HIM. I'D BELITTLED HIM, TOLD HIM THE DANGER HE WAS IN -- AND IT DIDN'T SLOW HIM DOWN.
ALL HE SAW WAS SOME SORT OF DANGER TO OTHERS -- PATTERNS, AND SOMETHING THAT DIDN'T FIT --
-- AND ALL I COULD FEEL -- ALL I COULD FEEL --
-- WAS SHAME.

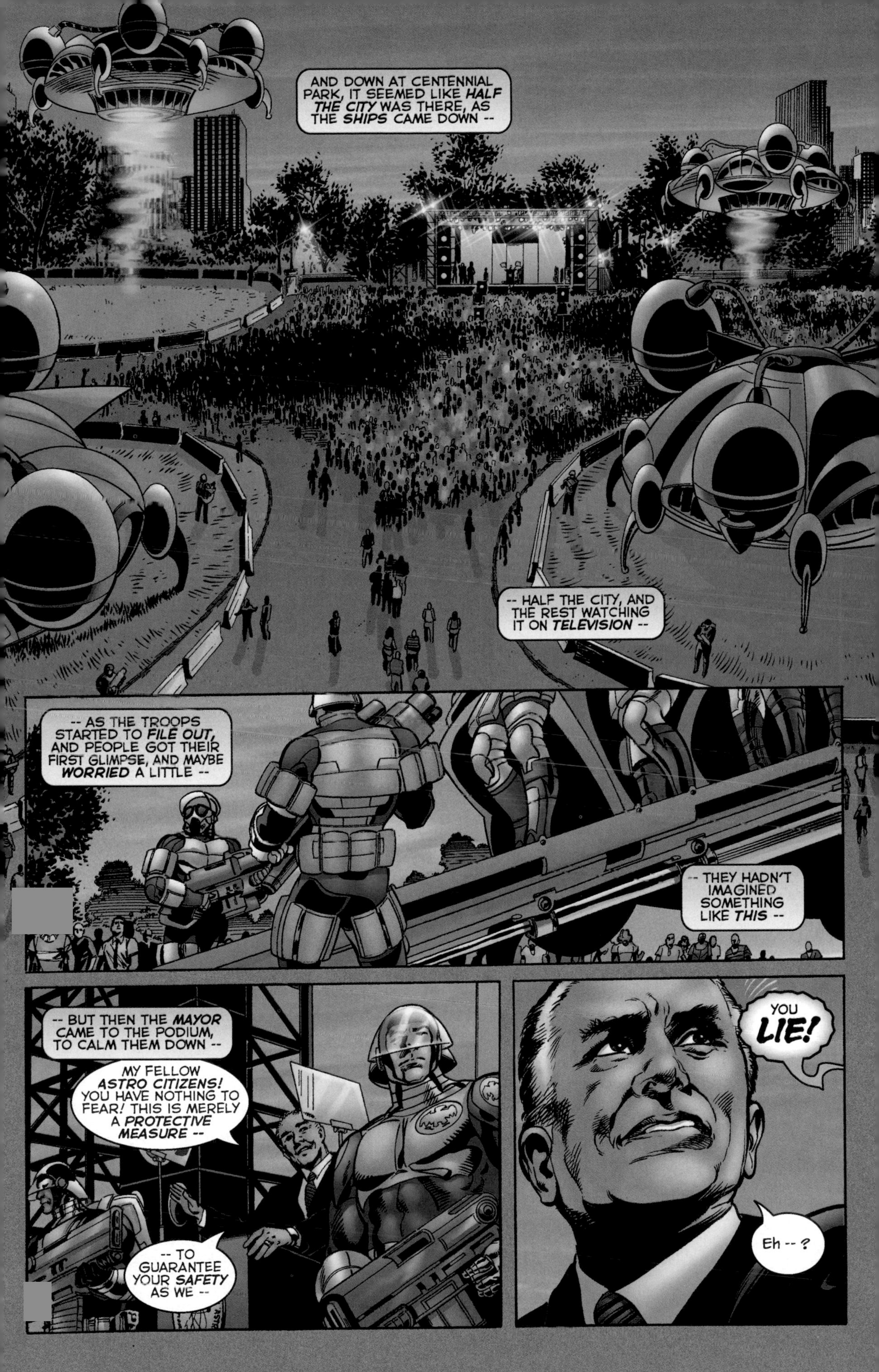
AND DOWN AT CENTENNIAL PARK, IT SEEMED LIKE HALF THE CITY WAS THERE, AS THE SHIPS CAME DOWN --
-- HALF THE CITY, AND THE REST WATCHING IT ON TELEVISION --
-- AS THE TROOPS STARTED TO FILE OUT, AND PEOPLE GOT THEIR FIRST GLIMPSE, AND MAYBE WORRIED A LITTLE --
-- THEY HADN'T IMAGINED SOMETHING LIKE THIS --
-- BUT THEN THE MAYOR CAME TO THE PODIUM, TO CALM THEM DOWN --
MY FELLOW ASTRO CITIZENS! YOU HAVE NOTHING TO FEAR! THIS IS MERELY A PROTECTIVE MEASURE --
-- TO GUARANTEE YOUR SAFETY AS WE --
YOU LIE!
Eh -- ?

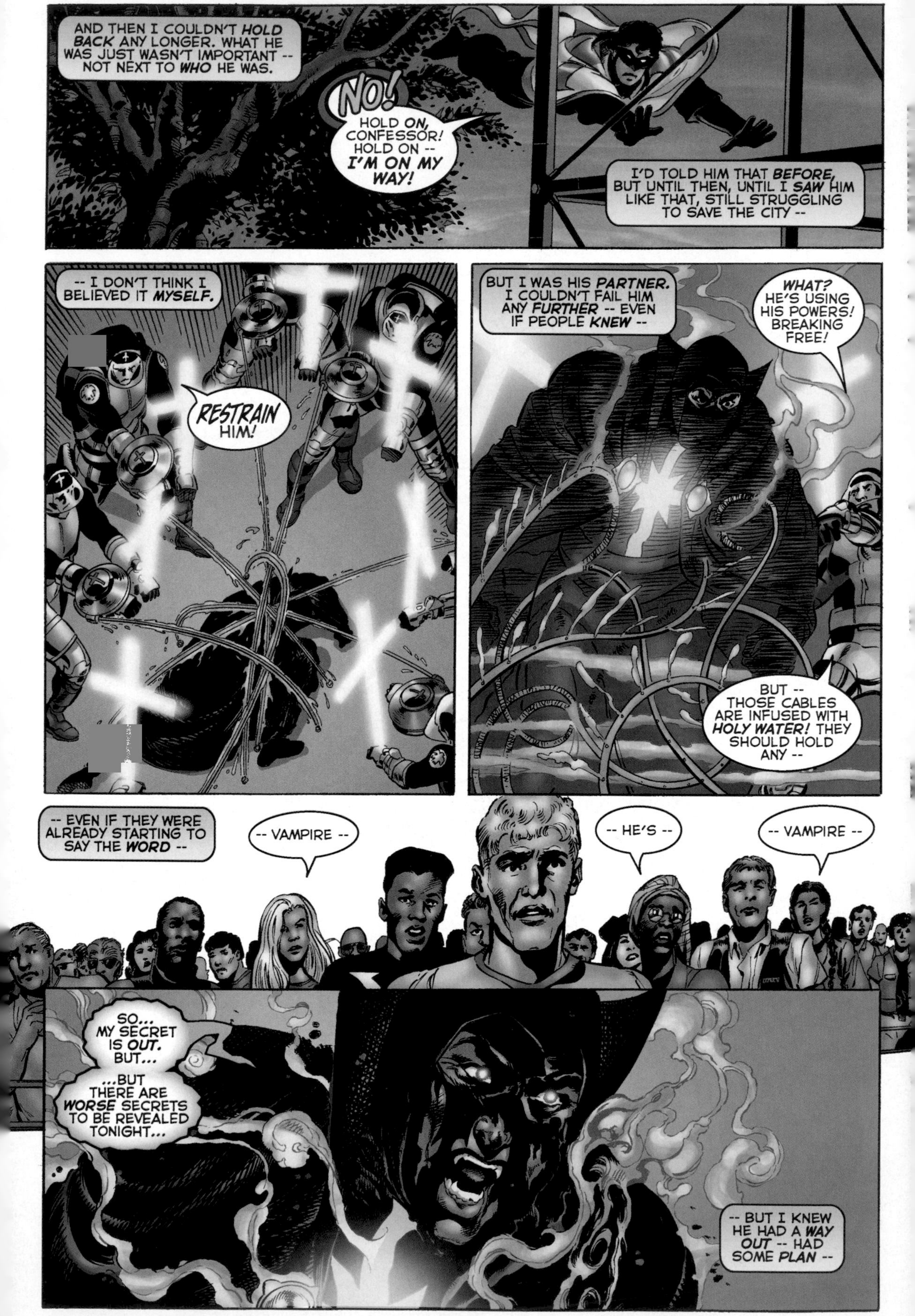
AND THEN I COULDN'T HOLD BACK ANY LONGER. WHAT HE WAS JUST WASN'T IMPORTANT -- NOT NEXT TO WHO HE WAS.
NO!
HOLD ON, CONFESSOR! HOLD ON -- I'M ON MY WAY!
I'D TOLD HIM THAT BEFORE, BUT UNTIL THEN, UNTIL I SAW HIM LIKE THAT, STILL STRUGGLING TO SAVE THE CITY --
-- I DON'T THINK I BELIEVED IT MYSELF.
RESTRAIN HIM!
BUT I WAS HIS PARTNER. I COULDN'T FAIL HIM ANY FURTHER -- EVEN IF PEOPLE KNEW --
WHAT? HE'S USING HIS POWERS! BREAKING FREE!
BUT -- THOSE CABLES ARE INFUSED WITH HOLY WATER! THEY SHOULD HOLD ANY --
-- EVEN IF THEY WERE ALREADY STARTING TO SAY THE WORD --
-- VAMPIRE --
-- HE'S --
-- VAMPIRE --
SO... MY SECRET IS OUT. BUT...
...BUT THERE ARE WORSE SECRETS TO BE REVEALED TONIGHT...
-- BUT I KNEW HE HAD A WAY OUT -- HAD SOME PLAN --

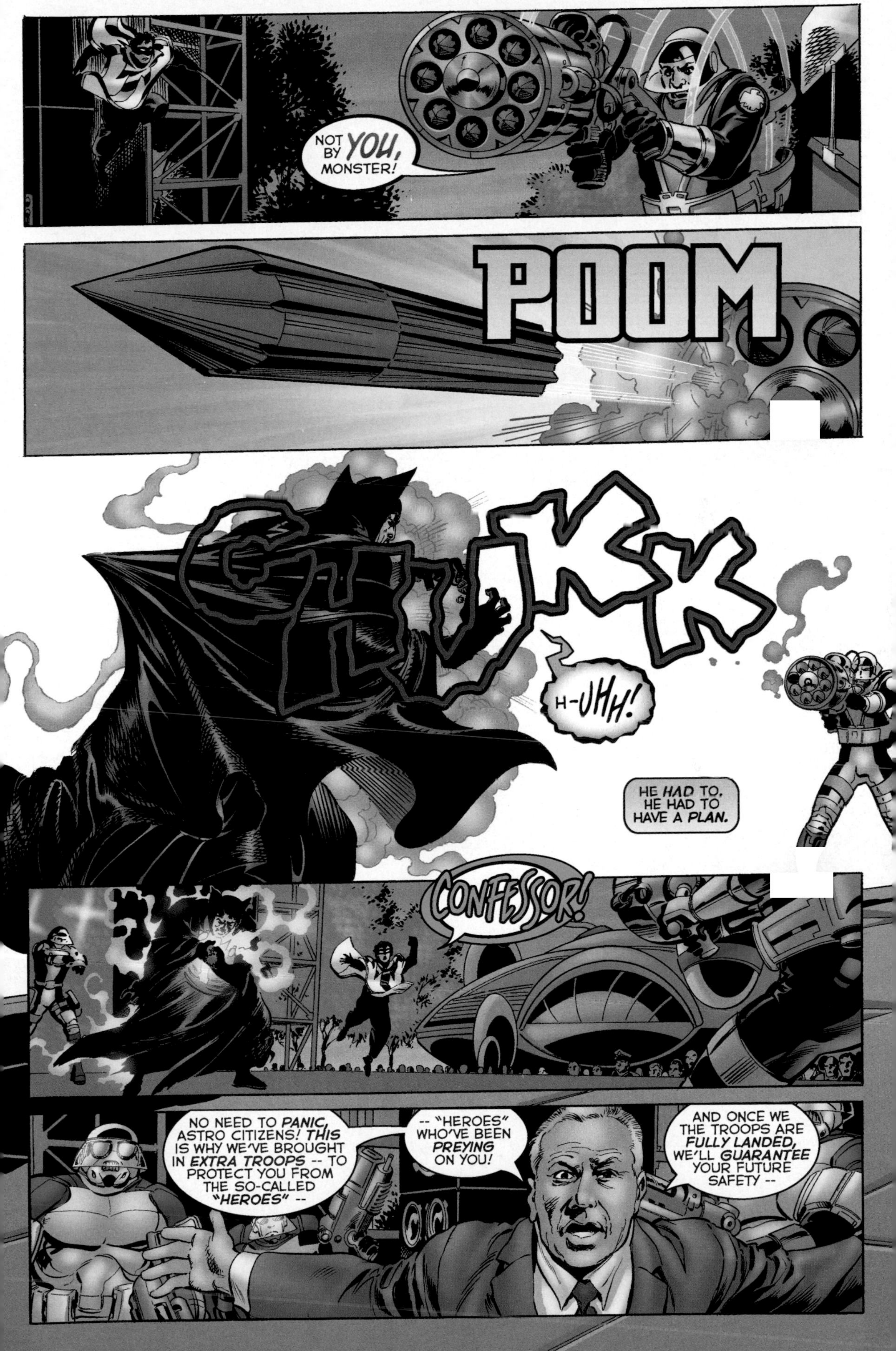
NOT BY YOU, MONSTER!
POOM
CHUKK
H-UHH!
HE HAD TO. HE HAD TO HAVE A PLAN.
CONFESSOR!
NO NEED TO PANIC, ASTRO CITIZENS! THIS IS WHY WE'VE BROUGHT IN EXTRA TROOPS -- TO PROTECT YOU FROM THE SO-CALLED "HEROES" --
-- "HEROES" WHO'VE BEEN PREYING ON YOU!
AND ONCE WE THE TROOPS ARE FULLY LANDED, WE'LL GUARANTEE YOUR FUTURE SAFETY --

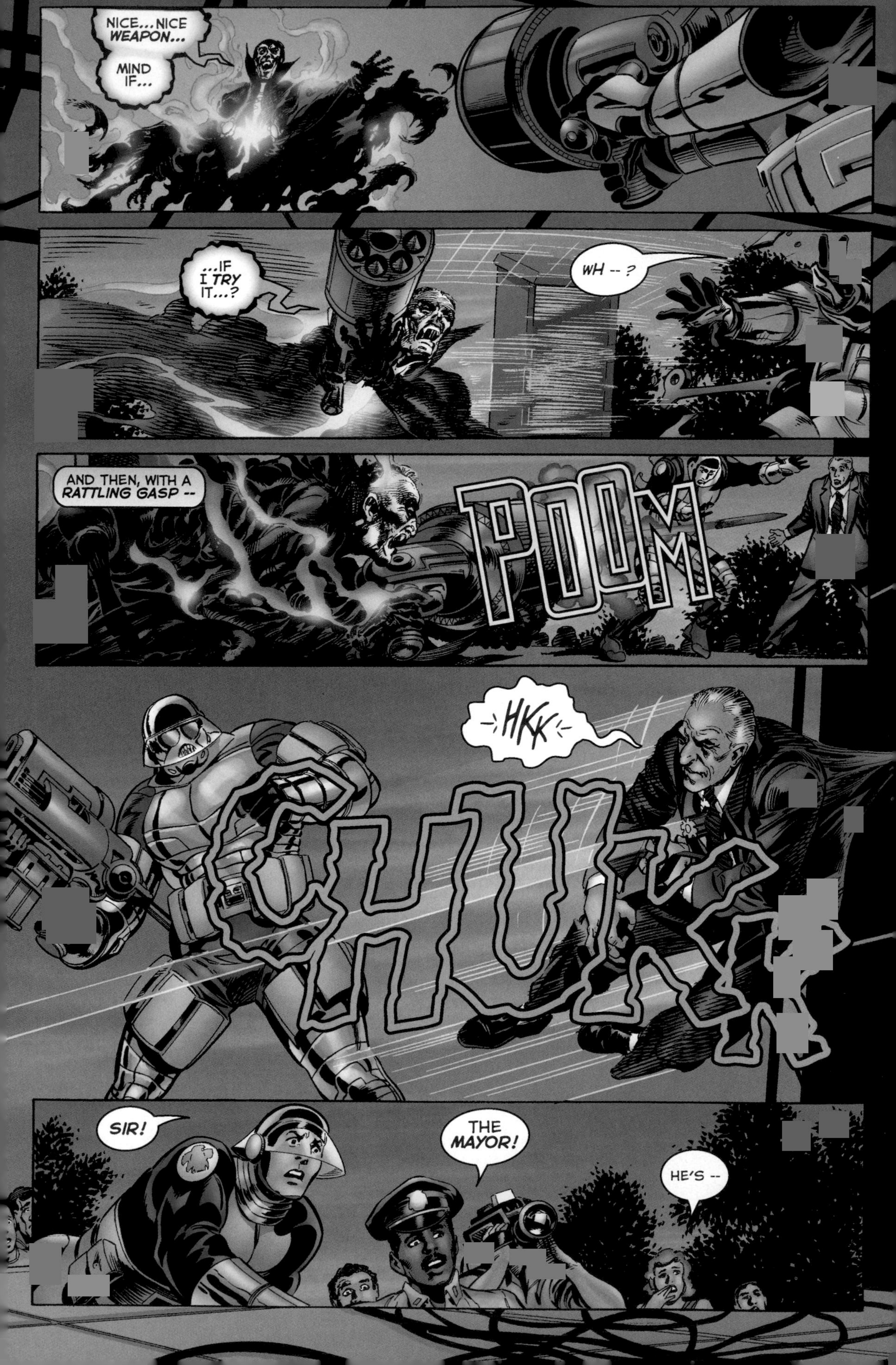
NICE...NICE WEAPON...
MIND IF...
...IF I TRY IT...?
WH -- ?
AND THEN, WITH A RATTLING GASP --
POOM
-HKK-
CHUK
SIR!
THE MAYOR!
HE'S --

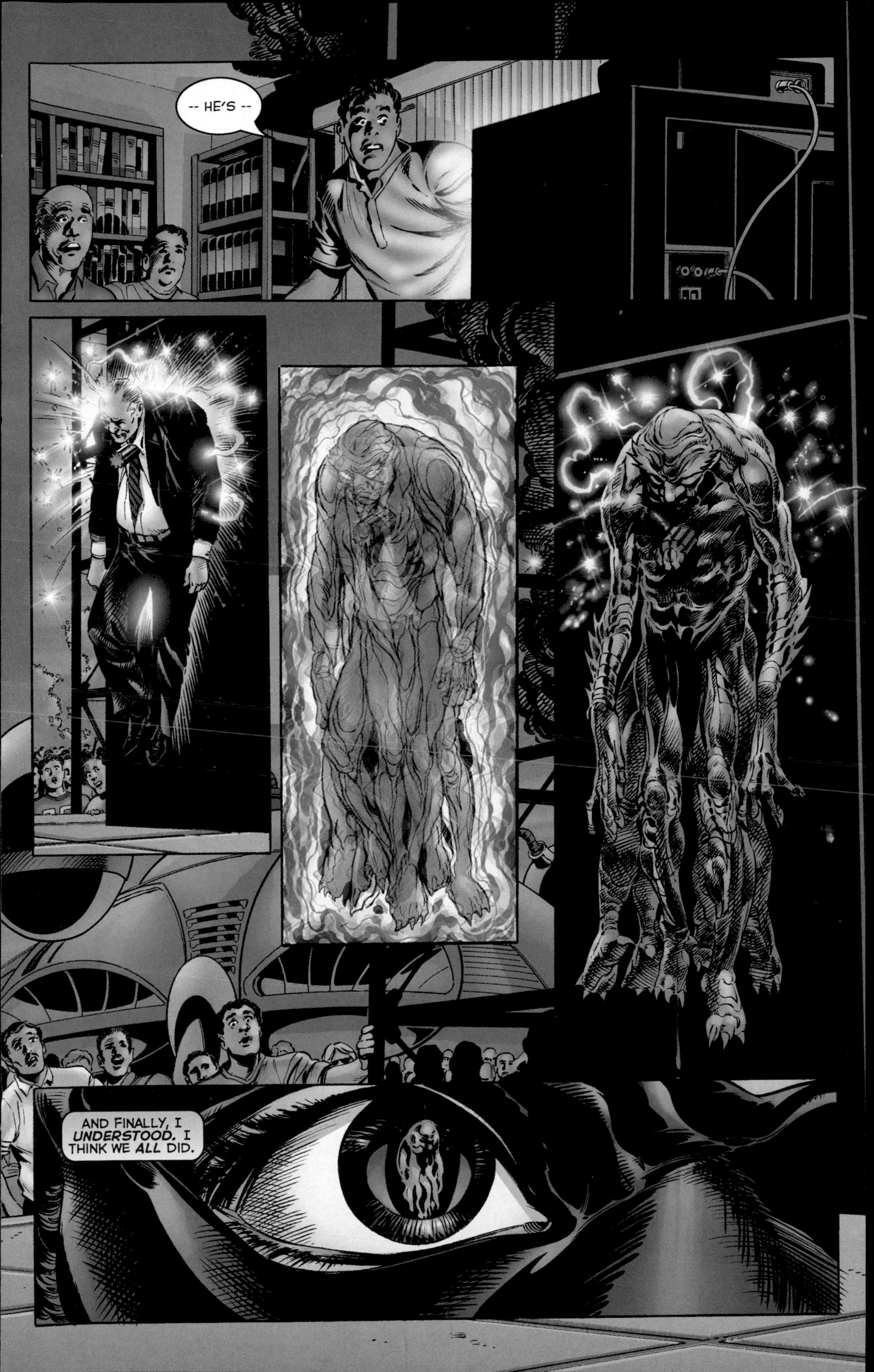
-- HE'S --
AND FINALLY, I UNDERSTOOD. I THINK WE ALL DID.

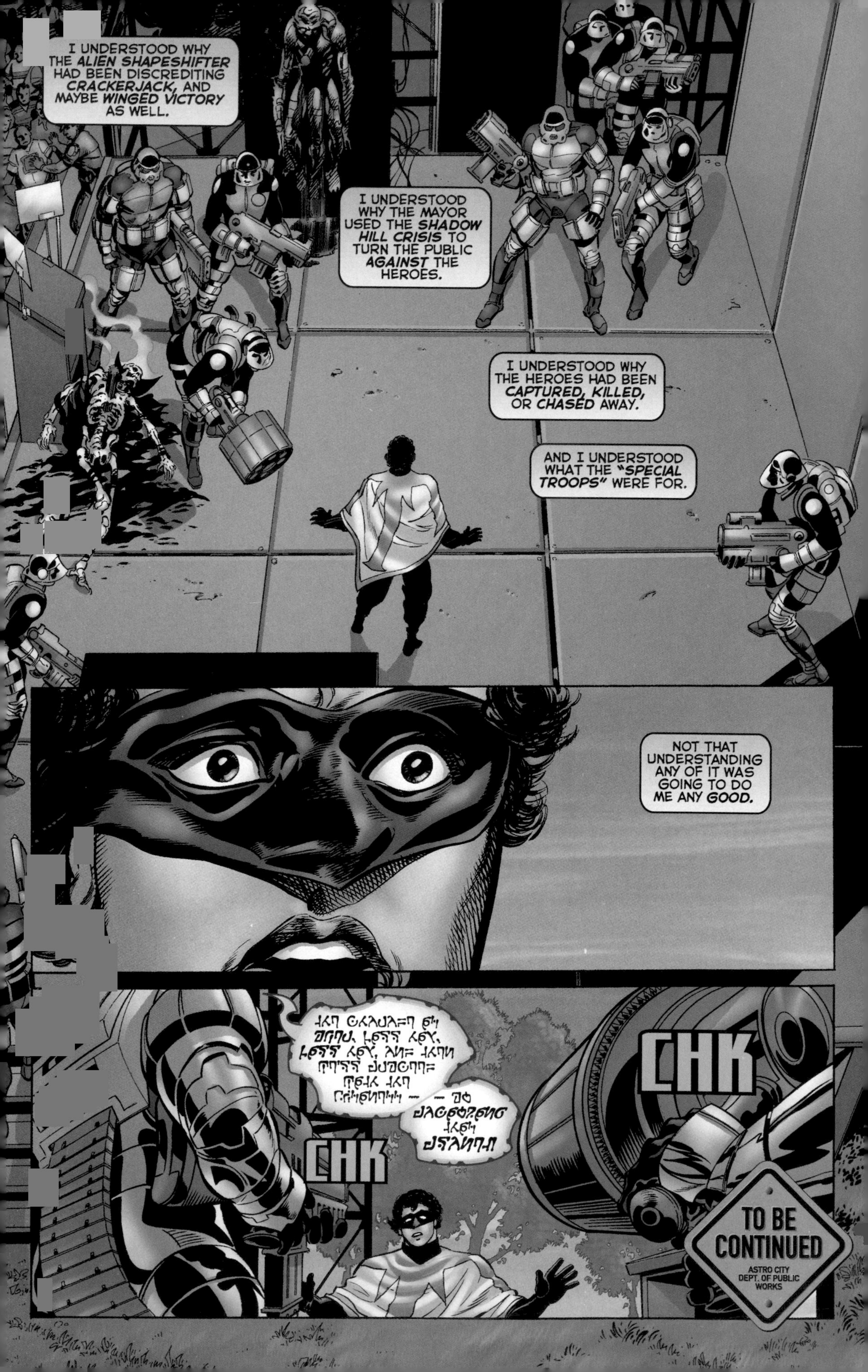
I UNDERSTOOD WHY THE ALIEN SHAPESHIFTER HAD BEEN DISCREDITING CRACKERJACK, AND MAYBE WINGED VICTORY AS WELL.
I UNDERSTOOD WHY THE MAYOR USED THE SHADOW HILL CRISIS TO TURN THE PUBLIC AGAINST THE HEROES.
I UNDERSTOOD WHY THE HEROES HAD BEEN CAPTURED, KILLED, OR CHASED AWAY.
AND I UNDERSTOOD WHAT THE "SPECIAL TROOPS" WERE FOR.
NOT THAT UNDERSTANDING ANY OF IT WAS GOING TO DO ME ANY GOOD.
CHK
CHK
TO BE CONTINUED
ASTRO CITY DEPT. OF PUBLIC WORKS

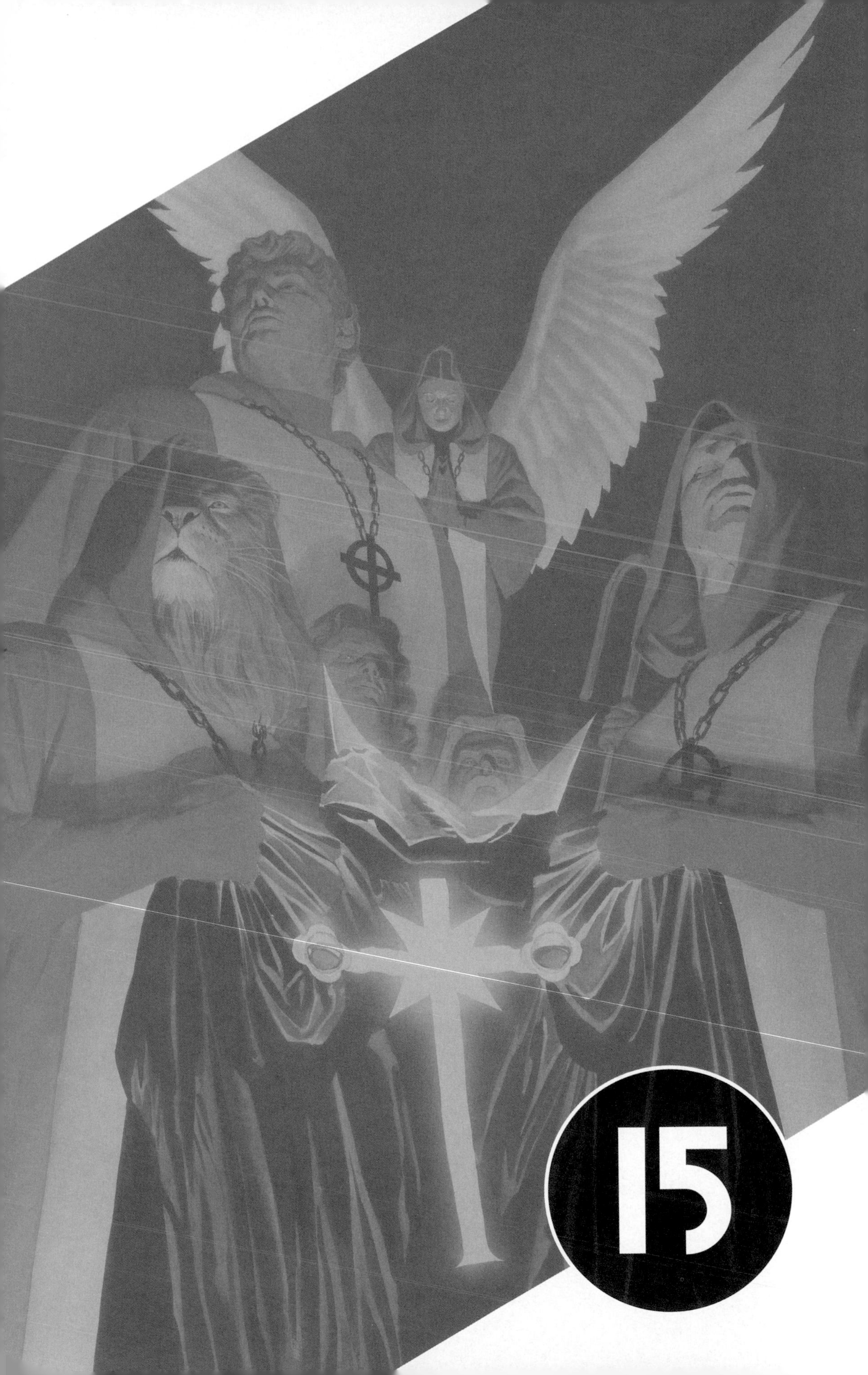
15

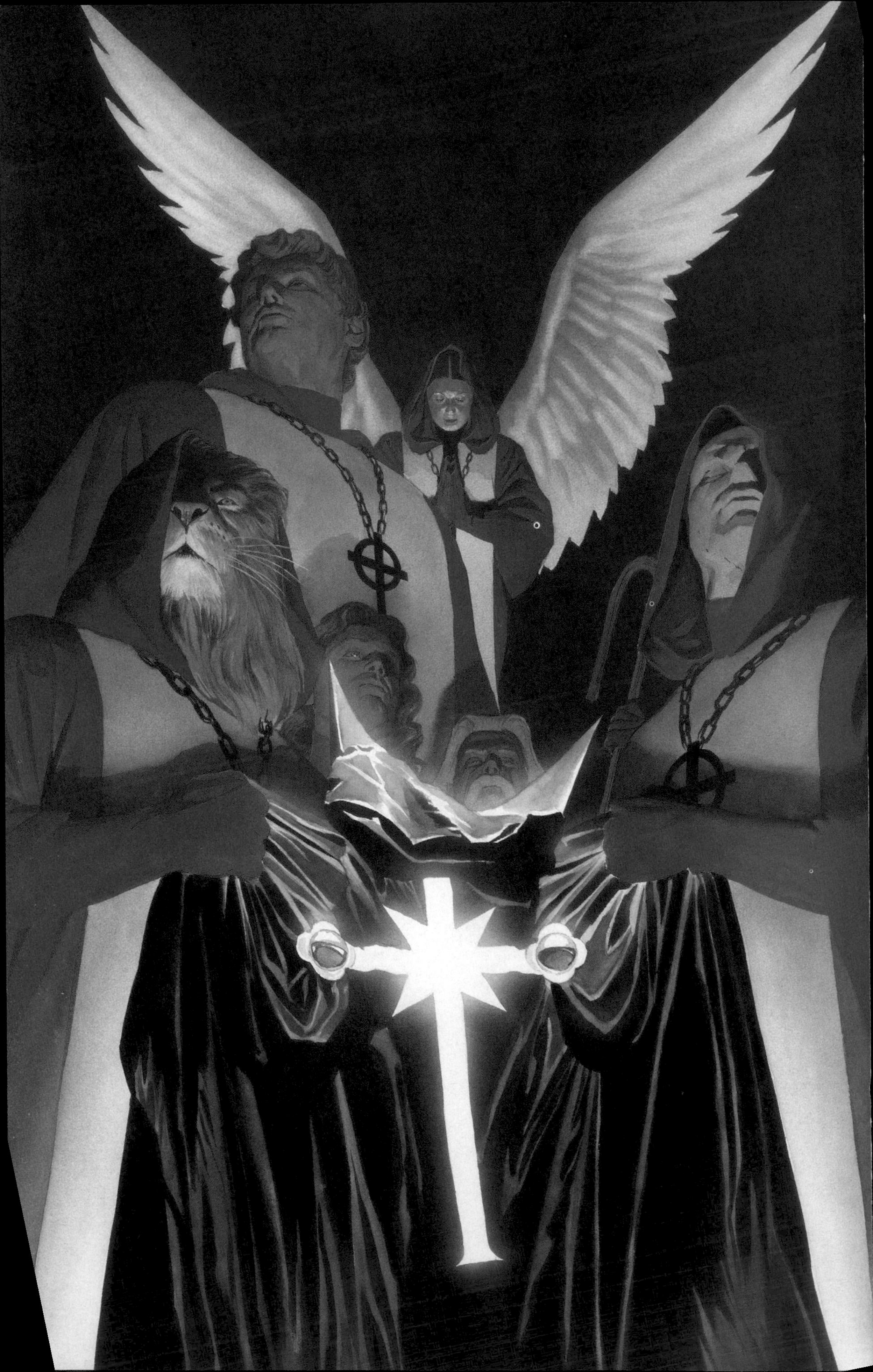

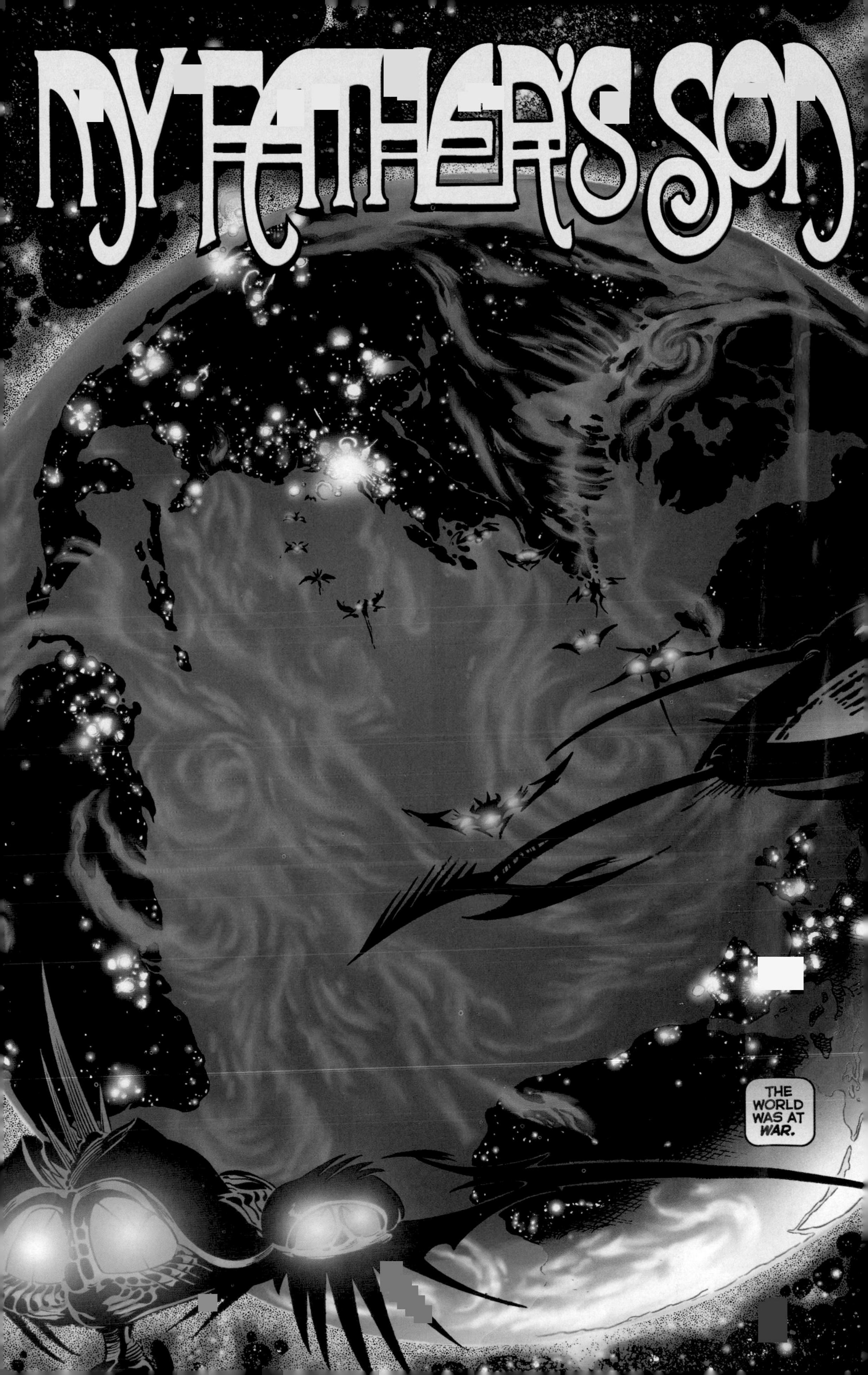
MY FATHER'S SON
THE WORLD WAS AT WAR.

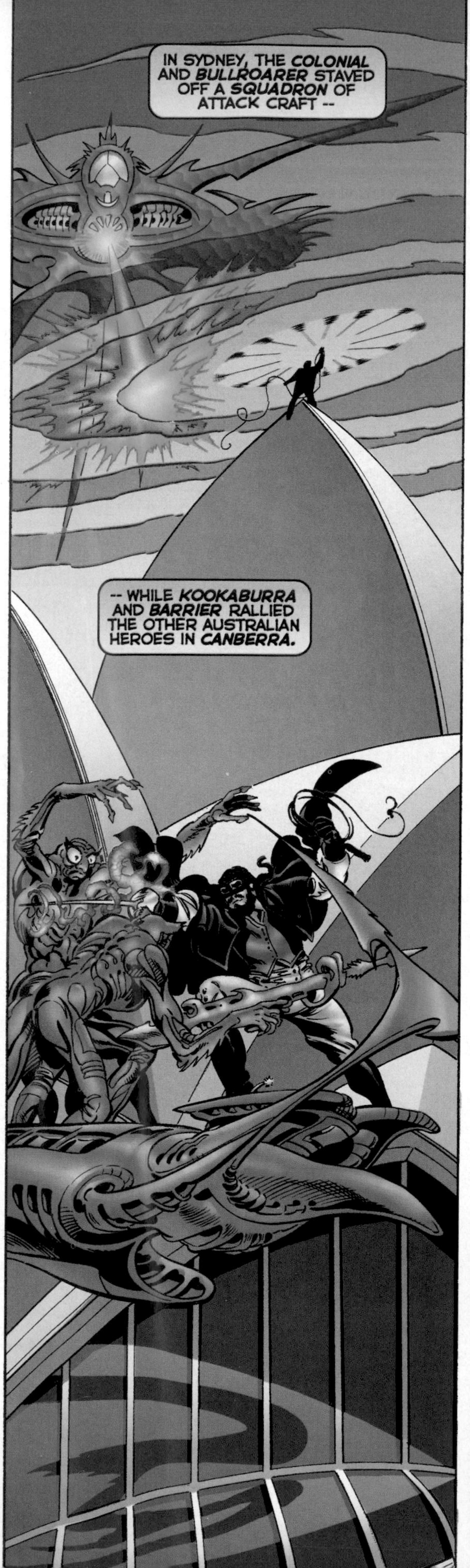
IN SYDNEY, THE COLONIAL AND BULLROARER STAVED OFF A SQUADRON OF ATTACK CRAFT --
-- WHILE KOOKABURRA AND BARRIER RALLIED THE OTHER AUSTRALIAN HEROES IN CANBERRA.
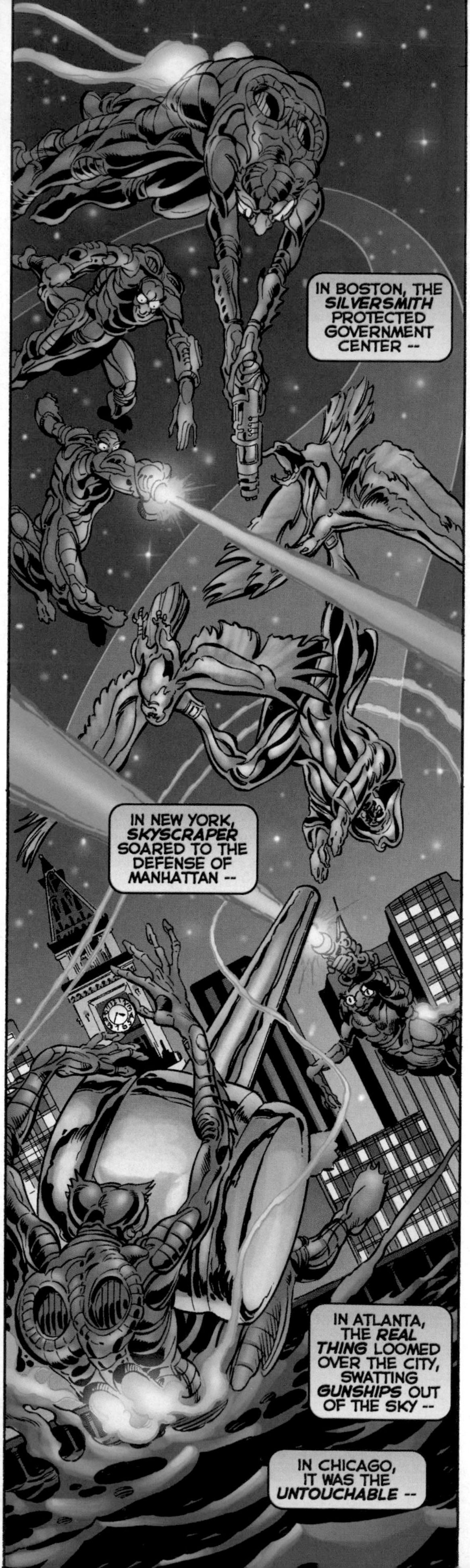
IN BOSTON, THE SILVERSMITH PROTECTED GOVERNMENT CENTER --
IN NEW YORK, SKYSCRAPER SOARED TO THE DEFENSE OF MANHATTAN --
IN ATLANTA, THE REAL THING LOOMED OVER THE CITY, SWATTING GUNSHIPS OUT OF THE SKY --
IN CHICAGO, IT WAS THE UNTOUCHABLE --

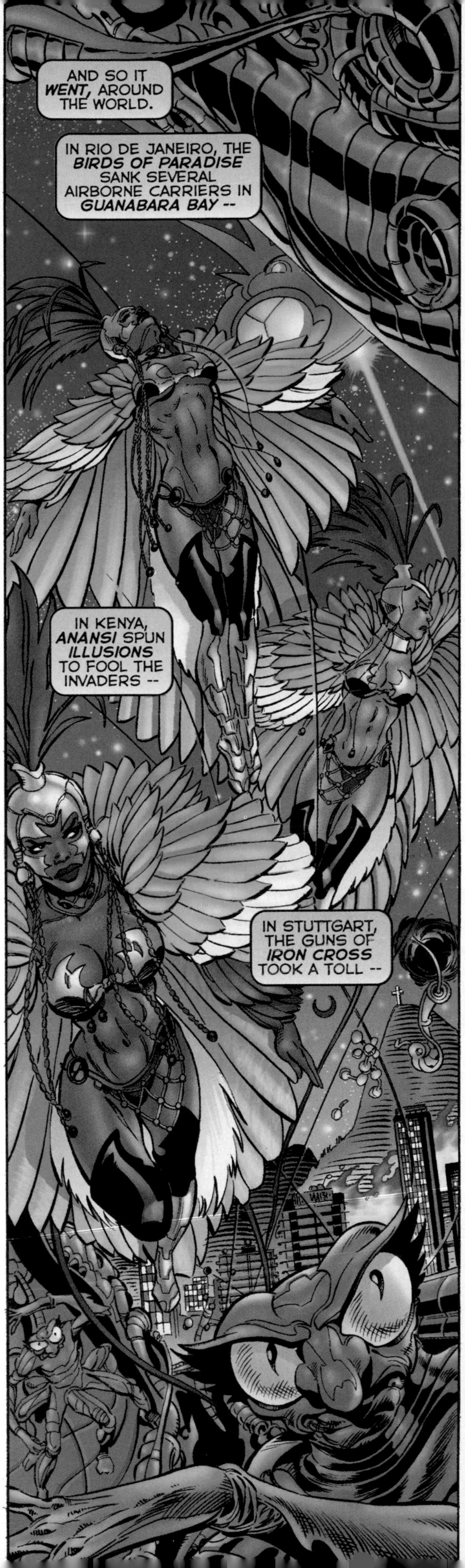
AND SO IT WENT, AROUND THE WORLD.
IN RIO DE JANEIRO, THE BIRDS OF PARADISE SANK SEVERAL AIRBORNE CARRIERS IN GUANABARA BAY --
IN KENYA, ANANSI SPUN ILLUSIONS TO FOOL THE INVADERS --
IN STUTTGART, THE GUNS OF IRON CROSS TOOK A TOLL --

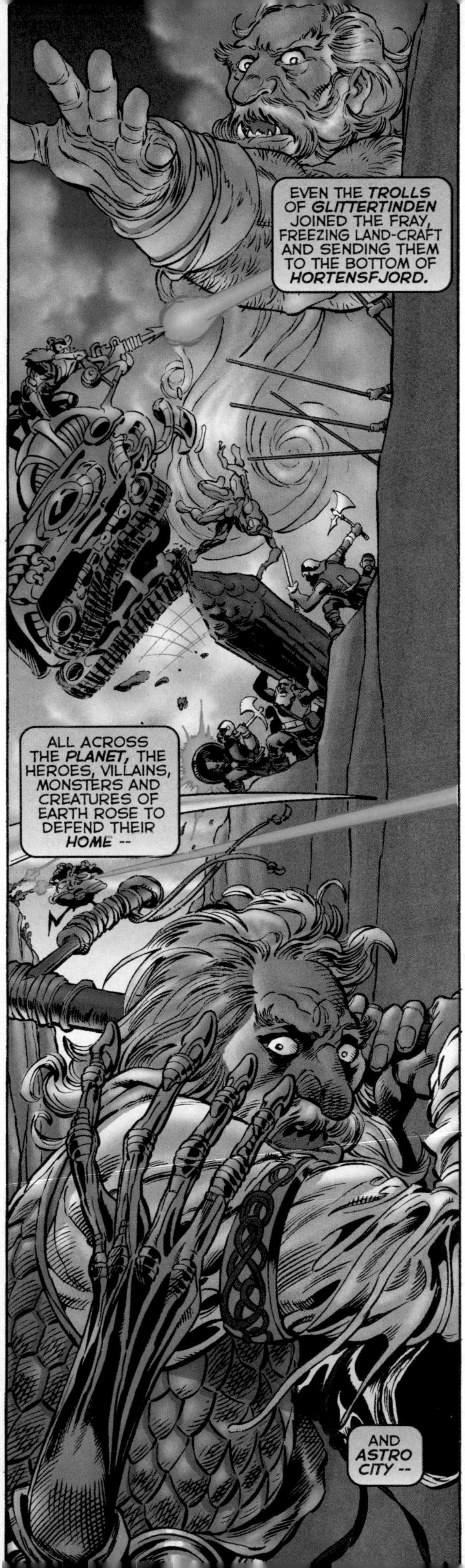
EVEN THE TROLLS OF GLITTERTINDEN JOINED THE FRAY, FREEZING LAND-CRAFT AND SENDING THEM TO THE BOTTOM OF HORTENSFJORD.
ALL ACROSS THE PLANET, THE HEROES, VILLAINS, MONSTERS AND CREATURES OF EARTH ROSE TO DEFEND THEIR HOME --
AND ASTRO CITY --

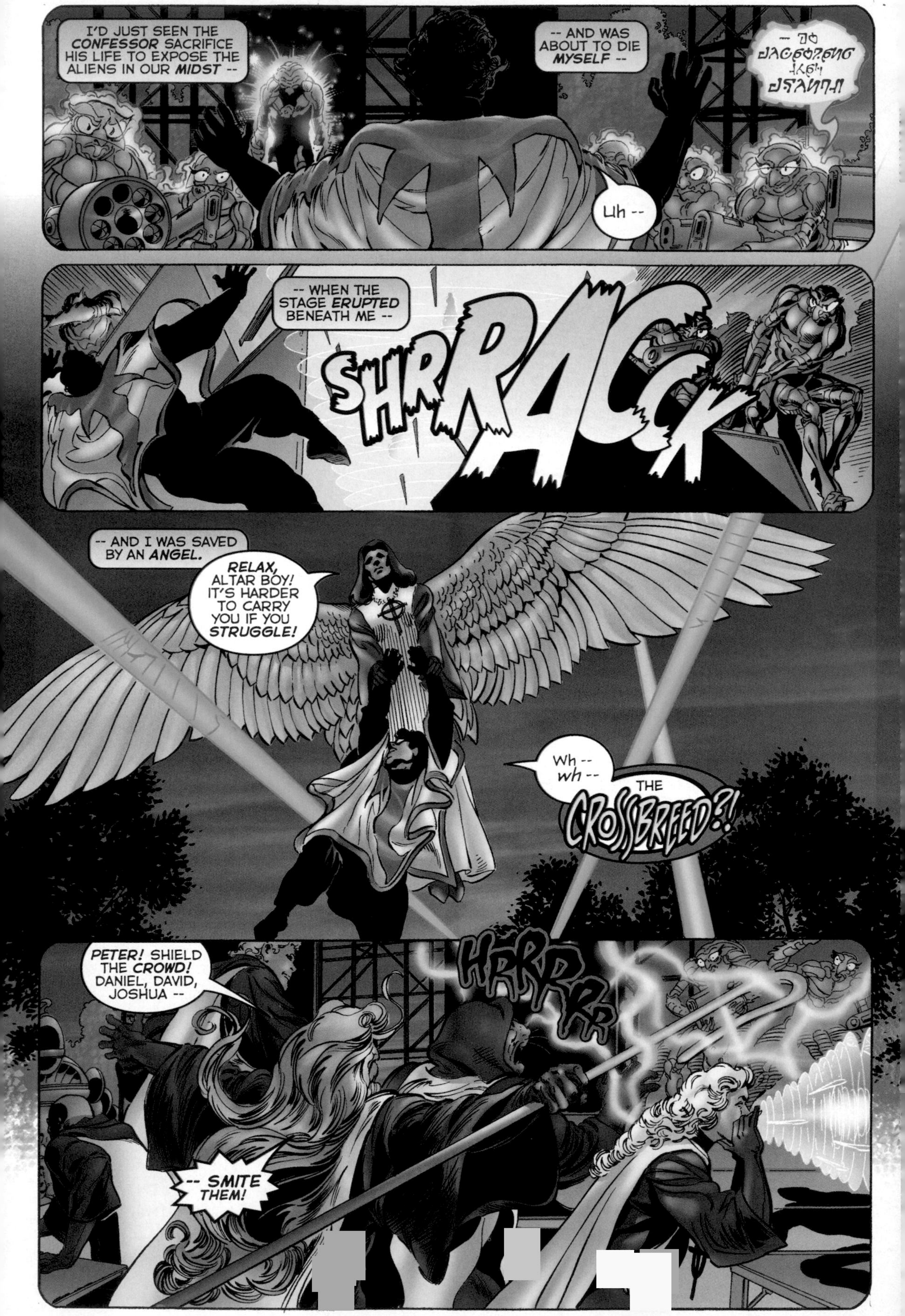
I'D JUST SEEN THE CONFESSOR SACRIFICE HIS LIFE TO EXPOSE THE ALIENS IN OUR MIDST --
-- AND WAS ABOUT TO DIE MYSELF --
Uh --
-- WHEN THE STAGE ERUPTED BENEATH ME --
SHRRACK
-- AND I WAS SAVED BY AN ANGEL.
RELAX, ALTAR BOY! IT'S HARDER TO CARRY YOU IF YOU STRUGGLE!
Wh -- wh -- THE CROSSBREED?!
PETER! SHIELD THE CROWD! DANIEL, DAVID, JOSHUA --
HRRRRRR
-- SMITE THEM!

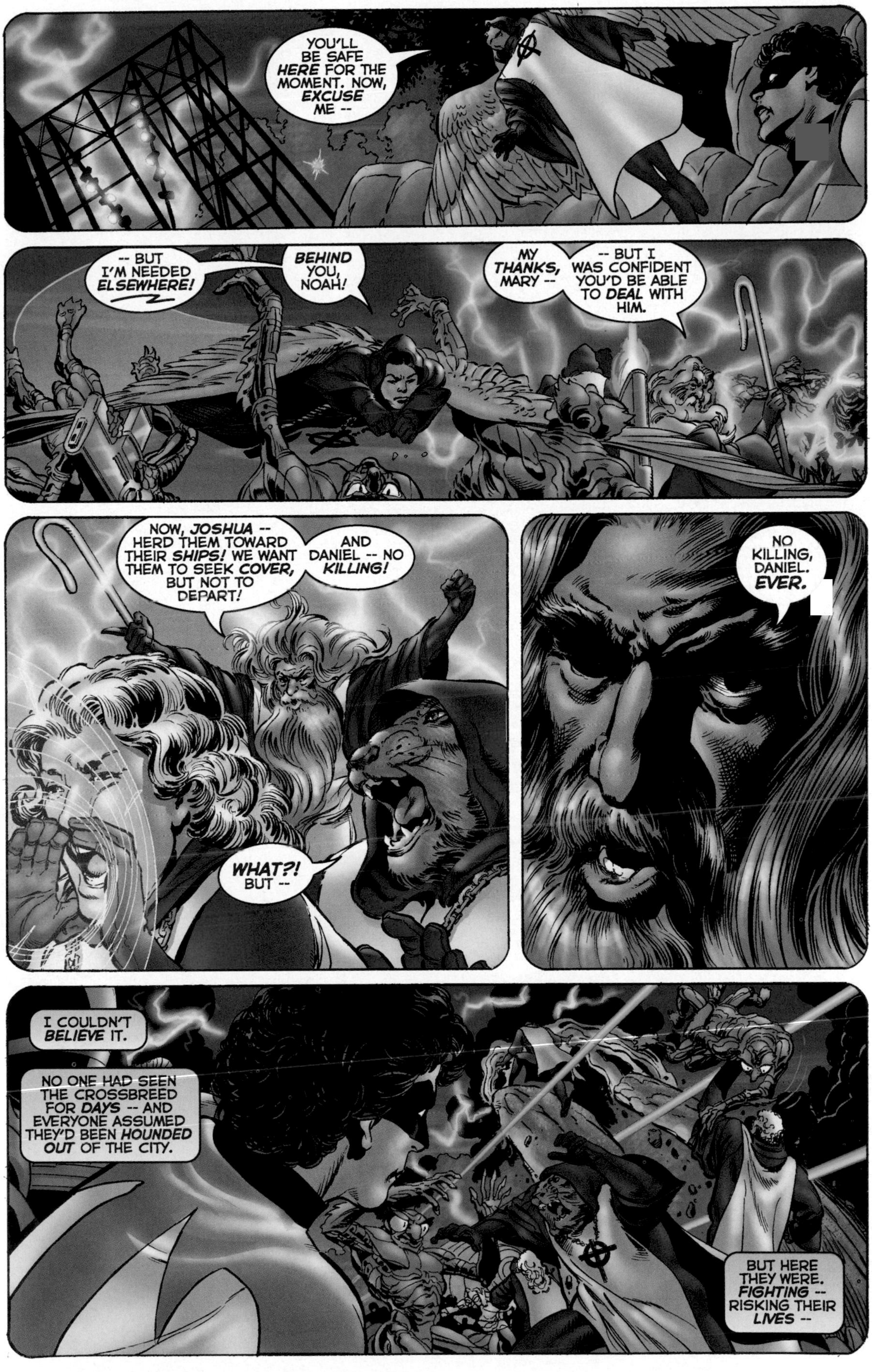
YOU'LL BE SAFE HERE FOR THE MOMENT. NOW, EXCUSE ME --
-- BUT I'M NEEDED ELSEWHERE!
BEHIND YOU, NOAH!
MY THANKS, MARY --
-- BUT I WAS CONFIDENT YOU'D BE ABLE TO DEAL WITH HIM.
NOW, JOSHUA -- HERD THEM TOWARD THEIR SHIPS! WE WANT THEM TO SEEK COVER, BUT NOT TO DEPART!
AND DANIEL -- NO KILLING!
WHAT?! BUT --
NO KILLING, DANIEL. EVER.
I COULDN'T BELIEVE IT.
NO ONE HAD SEEN THE CROSSBREED FOR DAYS -- AND EVERYONE ASSUMED THEY'D BEEN HOUNDED OUT OF THE CITY.
BUT HERE THEY WERE. FIGHTING -- RISKING THEIR LIVES --

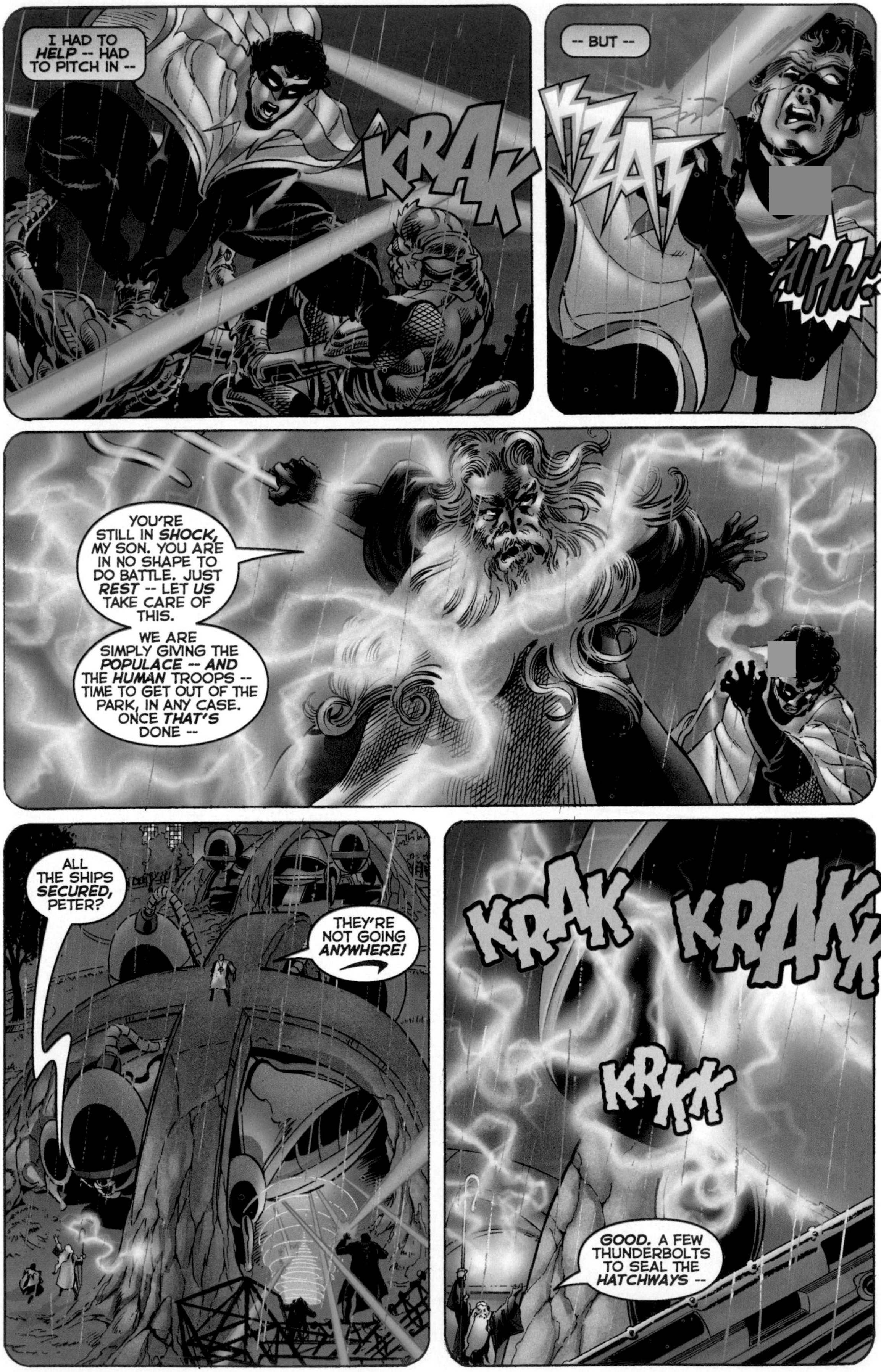

I HAD TO HELP -- HAD TO PITCH IN --
KRAK
-- BUT --
KZZAT
AIHH!
YOU'RE STILL IN SHOCK, MY SON. YOU ARE IN NO SHAPE TO DO BATTLE. JUST REST -- LET US TAKE CARE OF THIS.
WE ARE SIMPLY GIVING THE POPULACE -- AND THE HUMAN TROOPS -- TIME TO GET OUT OF THE PARK, IN ANY CASE. ONCE THAT'S DONE --
ALL THE SHIPS SECURED, PETER?
THEY'RE NOT GOING ANYWHERE!
KRAK
KRAKK
KRKK
GOOD. A FEW THUNDERBOLTS TO SEAL THE HATCHWAYS --

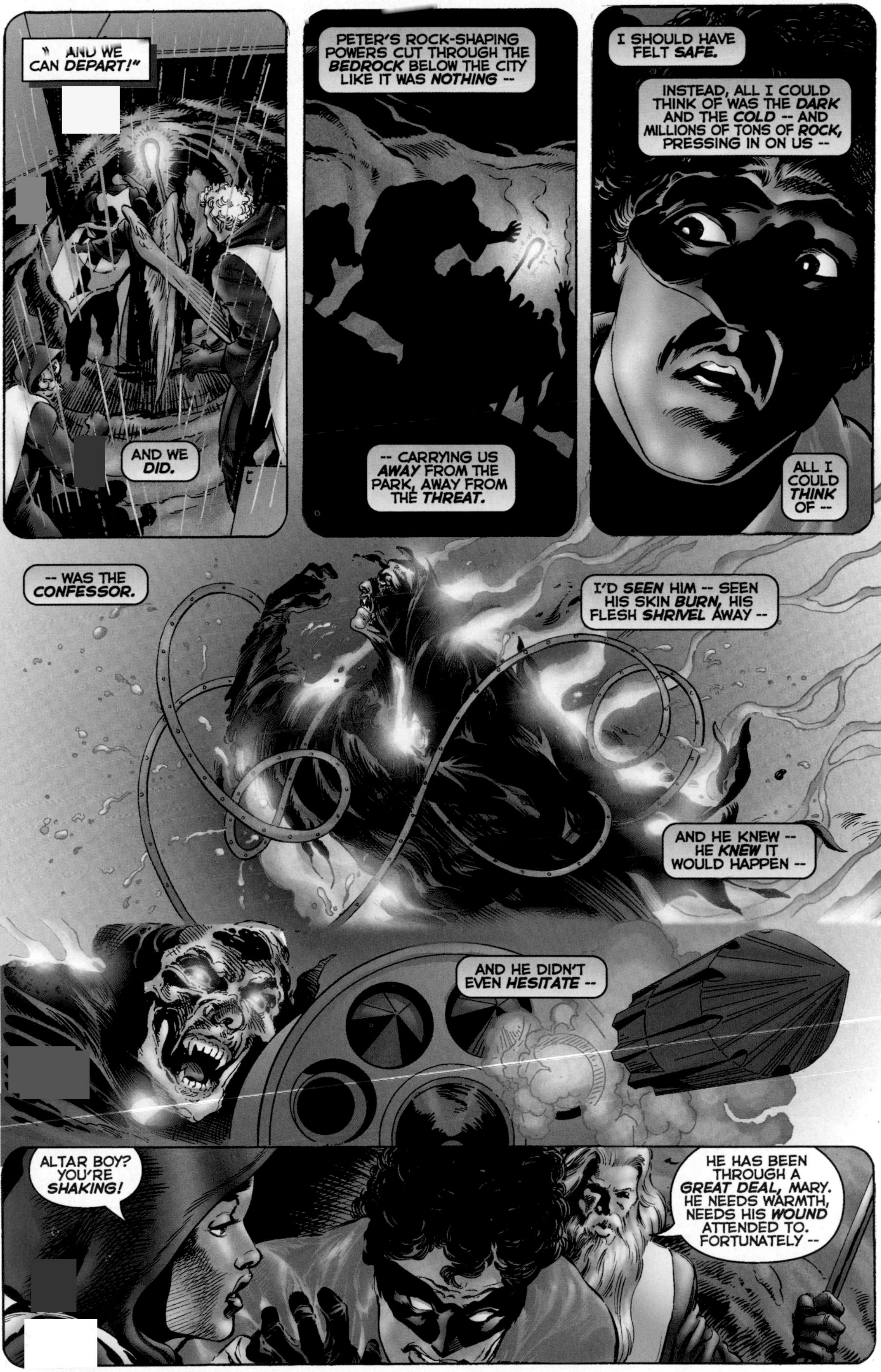
"... AND WE CAN DEPART!"
AND WE DID.
PETER'S ROCK-SHAPING POWERS CUT THROUGH THE BEDROCK BELOW THE CITY LIKE IT WAS NOTHING --
-- CARRYING US AWAY FROM THE PARK, AWAY FROM THE THREAT.
I SHOULD HAVE FELT SAFE.
INSTEAD, ALL I COULD THINK OF WAS THE DARK AND THE COLD -- AND MILLIONS OF TONS OF ROCK, PRESSING IN ON US --
ALL I COULD THINK OF --
-- WAS THE CONFESSOR.
I'D SEEN HIM -- SEEN HIS SKIN BURN, HIS FLESH SHRIVEL AWAY --
AND HE KNEW -- HE KNEW IT WOULD HAPPEN --
AND HE DIDN'T EVEN HESITATE --
ALTAR BOY? YOU'RE SHAKING!
HE HAS BEEN THROUGH A GREAT DEAL, MARY. HE NEEDS WARMTH, NEEDS HIS WOUND ATTENDED TO. FORTUNATELY --

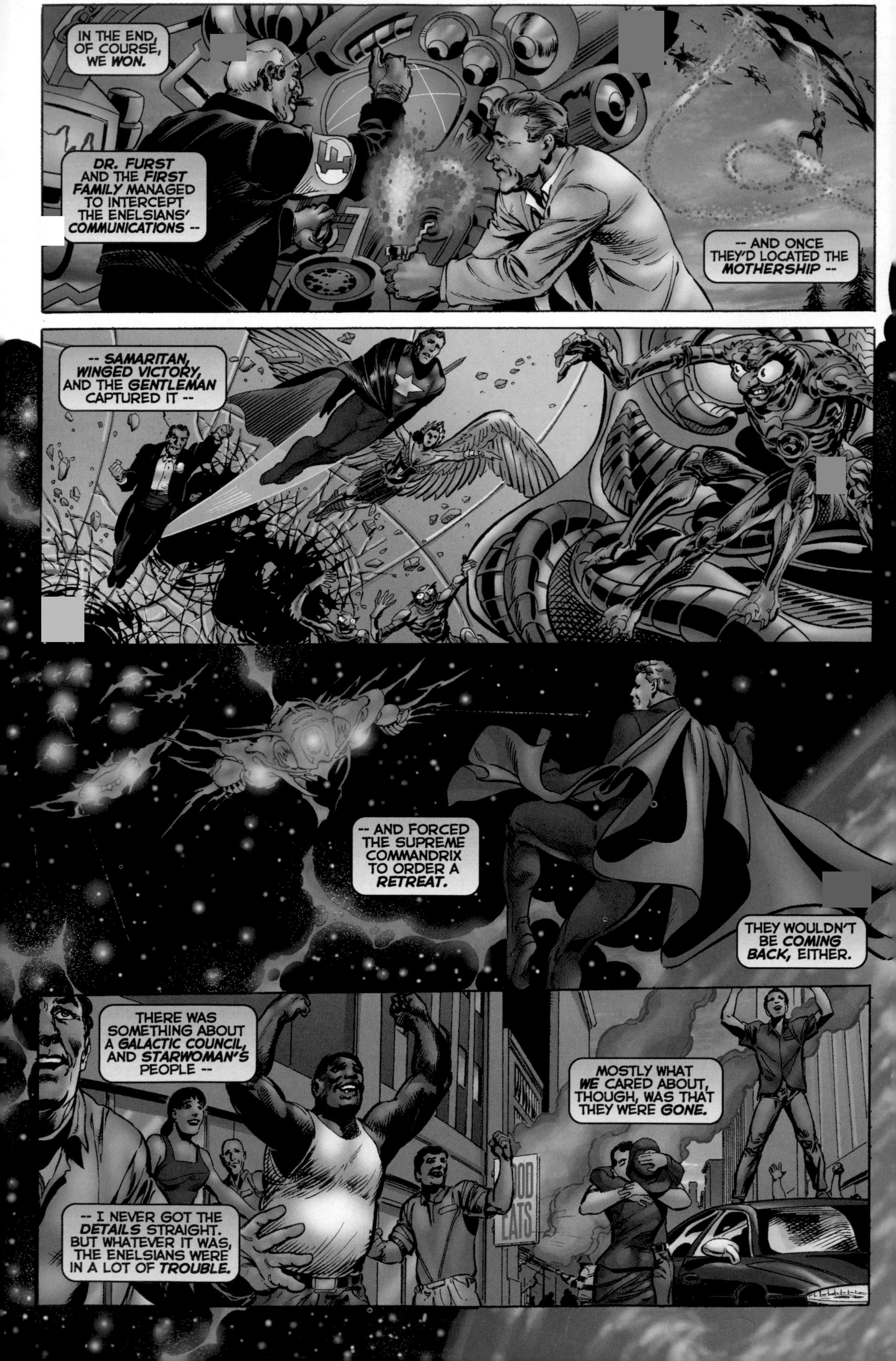
IN THE END, OF COURSE, WE WON.
DR. FURST AND THE FIRST FAMILY MANAGED TO INTERCEPT THE ENELSIANS' COMMUNICATIONS --
-- AND ONCE THEY'D LOCATED THE MOTHERSHIP --
-- SAMARITAN, WINGED VICTORY, AND THE GENTLEMAN CAPTURED IT --
-- AND FORCED THE SUPREME COMMANDRIX TO ORDER A RETREAT.
THEY WOULDN'T BE COMING BACK, EITHER.
THERE WAS SOMETHING ABOUT A GALACTIC COUNCIL, AND STARWOMAN'S PEOPLE --
-- I NEVER GOT THE DETAILS STRAIGHT. BUT WHATEVER IT WAS, THE ENELSIANS WERE IN A LOT OF TROUBLE.
MOSTLY WHAT WE CARED ABOUT, THOUGH, WAS THAT THEY WERE GONE.
GOOD EATS

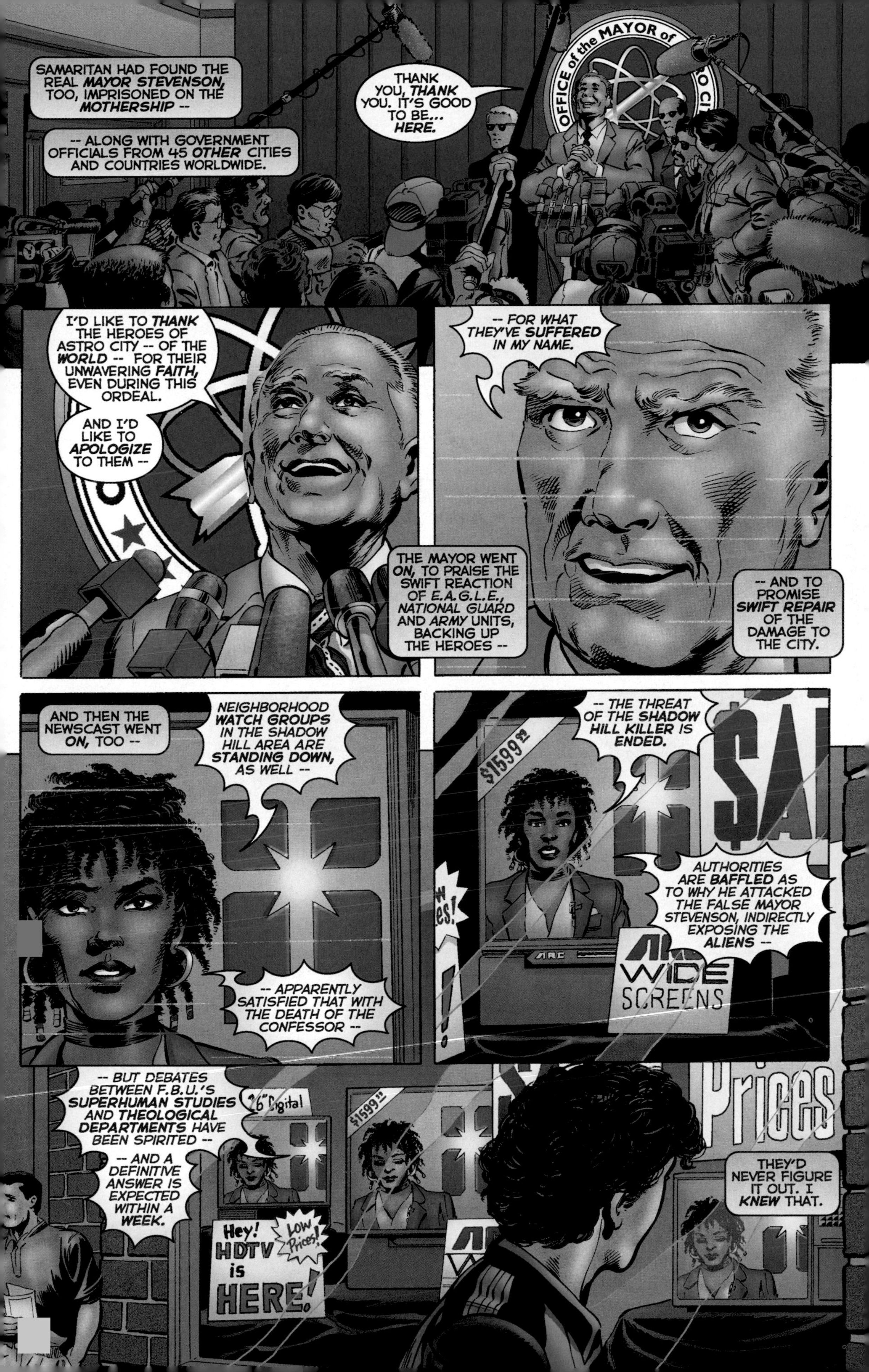
SAMARITAN HAD FOUND THE REAL MAYOR STEVENSON, TOO, IMPRISONED ON THE MOTHERSHIP --
-- ALONG WITH GOVERNMENT OFFICIALS FROM 45 OTHER CITIES AND COUNTRIES WORLDWIDE.
THANK YOU, THANK YOU. IT'S GOOD TO BE... HERE.
OFFICE of the MAYOR of
I'D LIKE TO THANK THE HEROES OF ASTRO CITY -- OF THE WORLD -- FOR THEIR UNWAVERING FAITH, EVEN DURING THIS ORDEAL.
AND I'D LIKE TO APOLOGIZE TO THEM --
-- FOR WHAT THEY'VE SUFFERED IN MY NAME.
THE MAYOR WENT ON, TO PRAISE THE SWIFT REACTION OF E.A.G.L.E., NATIONAL GUARD AND ARMY UNITS, BACKING UP THE HEROES --
-- AND TO PROMISE SWIFT REPAIR OF THE DAMAGE TO THE CITY.
AND THEN THE NEWSCAST WENT ON, TOO --
NEIGHBORHOOD WATCH GROUPS IN THE SHADOW HILL AREA ARE STANDING DOWN, AS WELL --
-- APPARENTLY SATISFIED THAT WITH THE DEATH OF THE CONFESSOR --
-- THE THREAT OF THE SHADOW HILL KILLER IS ENDED.
$1599.99
AUTHORITIES ARE BAFFLED AS TO WHY HE ATTACKED THE FALSE MAYOR STEVENSON, INDIRECTLY EXPOSING THE ALIENS --
ARC
WIDE SCREENS
-- BUT DEBATES BETWEEN F.B.U.'S SUPERHUMAN STUDIES AND THEOLOGICAL DEPARTMENTS HAVE BEEN SPIRITED --
-- AND A DEFINITIVE ANSWER IS EXPECTED WITHIN A WEEK.
26" Digital
$1599.99
Prices
Hey! HDTV is HERE!
Low Prices!
THEY'D NEVER FIGURE IT OUT. I KNEW THAT.

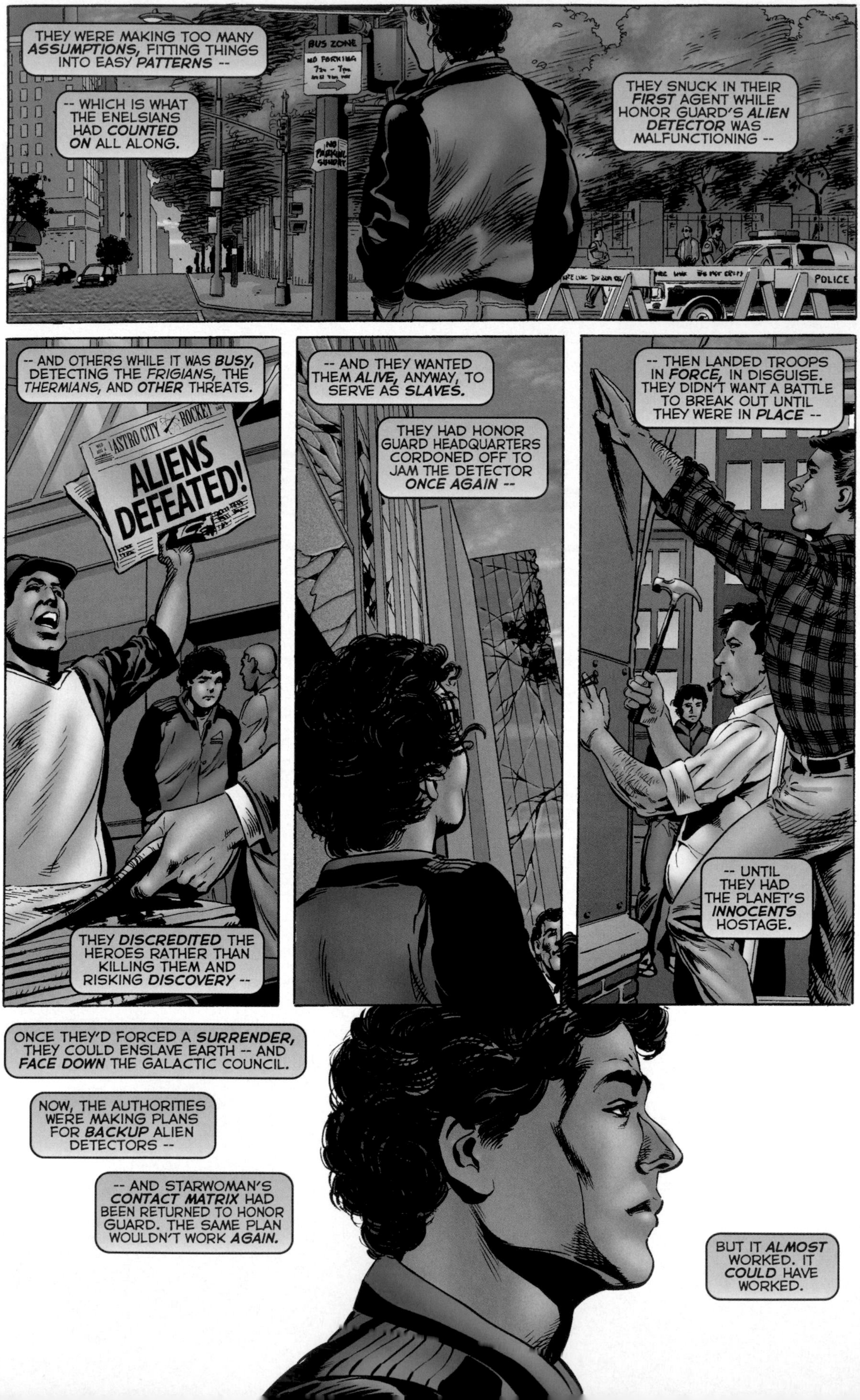
THEY WERE MAKING TOO MANY ASSUMPTIONS, FITTING THINGS INTO EASY PATTERNS --
-- WHICH IS WHAT THE ENELSIANS HAD COUNTED ON ALL ALONG.
BUS ZONE
THEY SNUCK IN THEIR FIRST AGENT WHILE HONOR GUARD'S ALIEN DETECTOR WAS MALFUNCTIONING --
POLICE
-- AND OTHERS WHILE IT WAS BUSY, DETECTING THE FRIGIANS, THE THERMIANS, AND OTHER THREATS.
ASTRO CITY ROCKET
ALIENS DEFEATED!
THEY DISCREDITED THE HEROES RATHER THAN KILLING THEM AND RISKING DISCOVERY --
-- AND THEY WANTED THEM ALIVE, ANYWAY, TO SERVE AS SLAVES.
THEY HAD HONOR GUARD HEADQUARTERS CORDONED OFF TO JAM THE DETECTOR ONCE AGAIN --
-- THEN LANDED TROOPS IN FORCE, IN DISGUISE. THEY DIDN'T WANT A BATTLE TO BREAK OUT UNTIL THEY WERE IN PLACE --
-- UNTIL THEY HAD THE PLANET'S INNOCENTS HOSTAGE.
ONCE THEY'D FORCED A SURRENDER, THEY COULD ENSLAVE EARTH -- AND FACE DOWN THE GALACTIC COUNCIL.
NOW, THE AUTHORITIES WERE MAKING PLANS FOR BACKUP ALIEN DETECTORS --
-- AND STARWOMAN'S CONTACT MATRIX HAD BEEN RETURNED TO HONOR GUARD. THE SAME PLAN WOULDN'T WORK AGAIN.
BUT IT ALMOST WORKED. IT COULD HAVE WORKED.

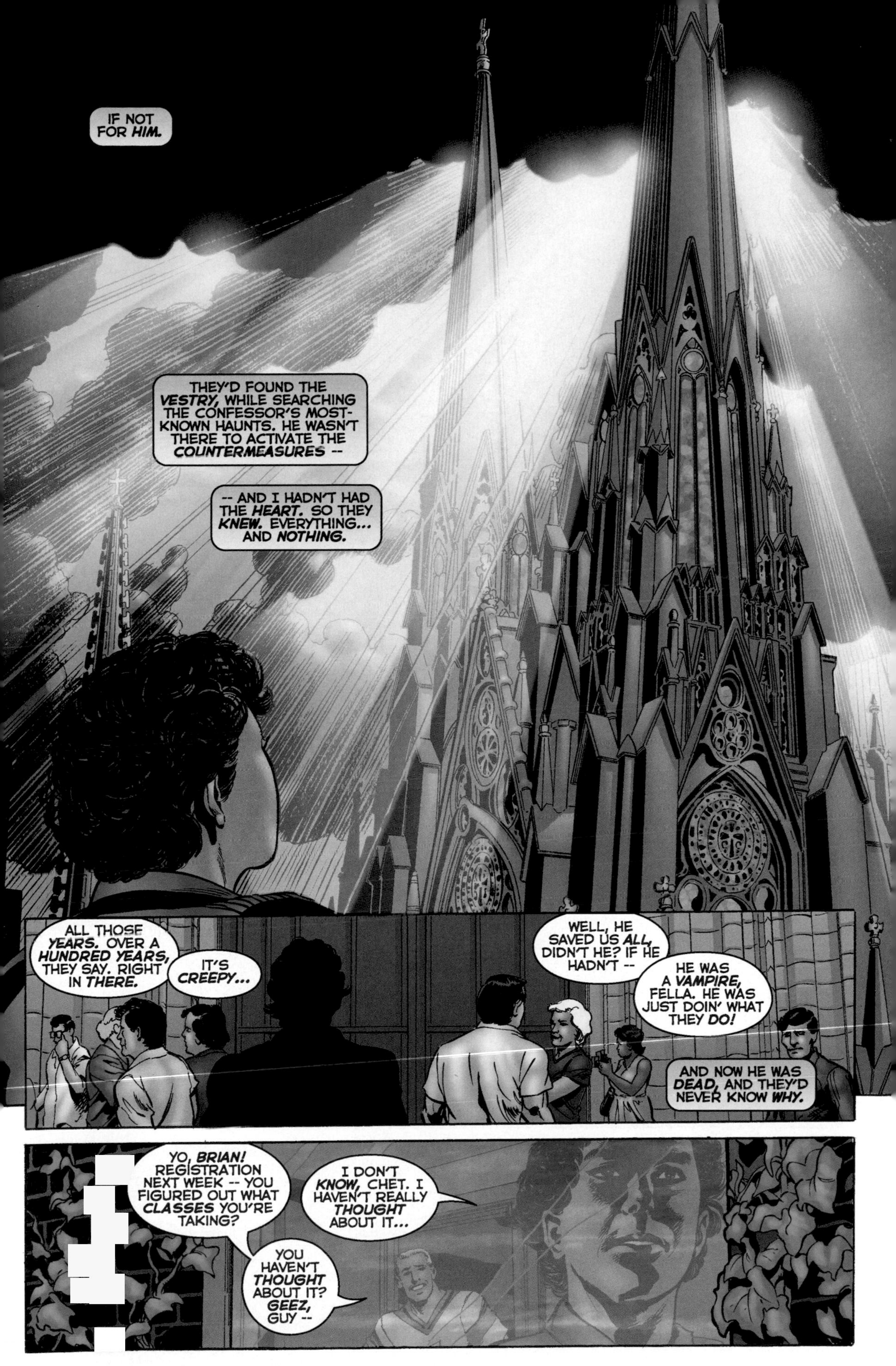
IF NOT FOR HIM.
THEY'D FOUND THE VESTRY, WHILE SEARCHING THE CONFESSOR'S MOST-KNOWN HAUNTS. HE WASN'T THERE TO ACTIVATE THE COUNTERMEASURES --
-- AND I HADN'T HAD THE HEART. SO THEY KNEW. EVERYTHING... AND NOTHING.
ALL THOSE YEARS. OVER A HUNDRED YEARS, THEY SAY. RIGHT IN THERE.
IT'S CREEPY...
WELL, HE SAVED US ALL, DIDN'T HE? IF HE HADN'T --
HE WAS A VAMPIRE, FELLA. HE WAS JUST DOIN' WHAT THEY DO!
AND NOW HE WAS DEAD, AND THEY'D NEVER KNOW WHY.
YO, BRIAN! REGISTRATION NEXT WEEK -- YOU FIGURED OUT WHAT CLASSES YOU'RE TAKING?
I DON'T KNOW, CHET. I HAVEN'T REALLY THOUGHT ABOUT IT...
YOU HAVEN'T THOUGHT ABOUT IT? GEEZ, GUY --

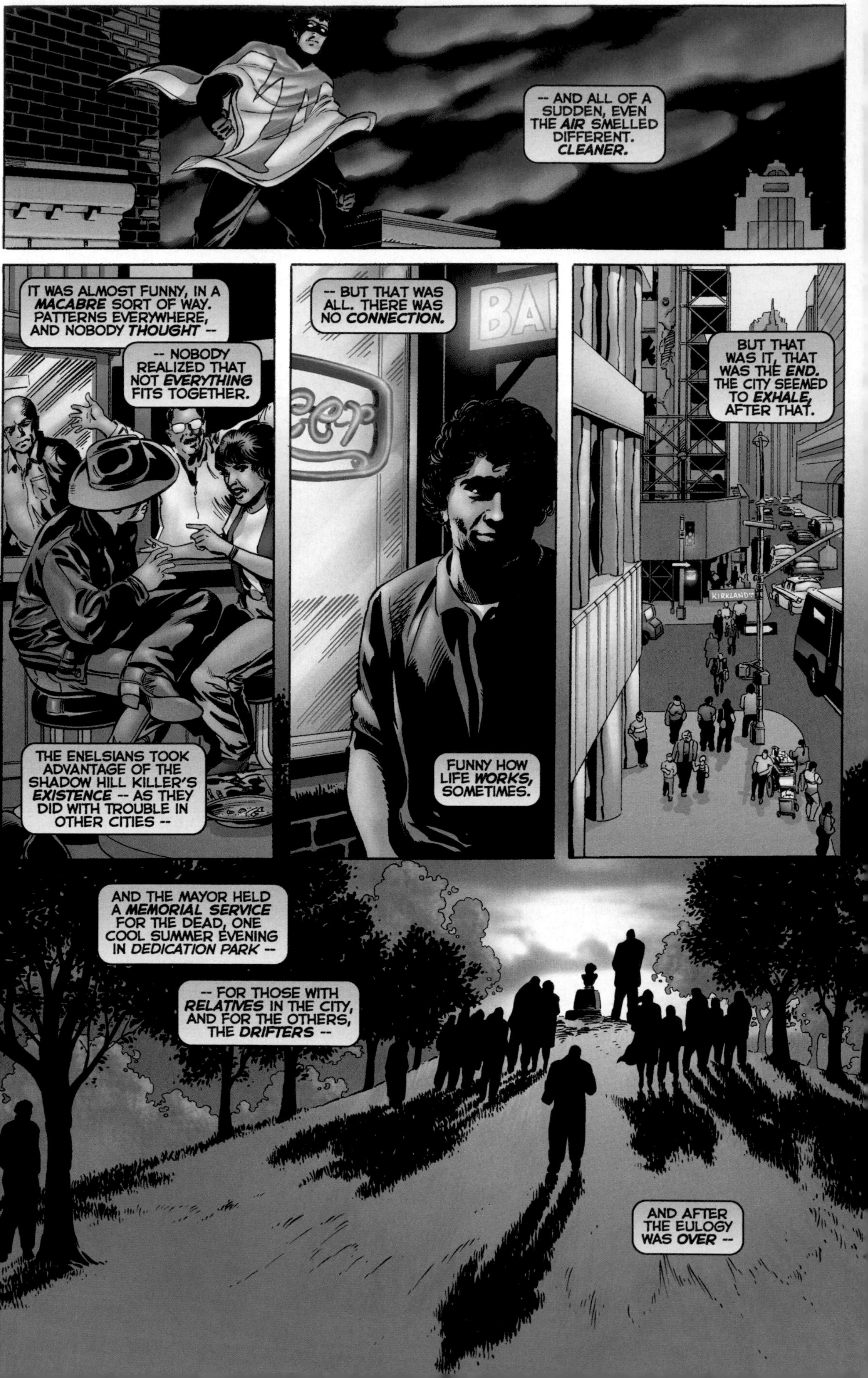
-- AND ALL OF A SUDDEN, EVEN THE AIR SMELLED DIFFERENT. CLEANER.
IT WAS ALMOST FUNNY, IN A MACABRE SORT OF WAY. PATTERNS EVERYWHERE, AND NOBODY THOUGHT --
-- NOBODY REALIZED THAT NOT EVERYTHING FITS TOGETHER.
THE ENELSIANS TOOK ADVANTAGE OF THE SHADOW HILL KILLER'S EXISTENCE -- AS THEY DID WITH TROUBLE IN OTHER CITIES --
-- BUT THAT WAS ALL. THERE WAS NO CONNECTION.
FUNNY HOW LIFE WORKS, SOMETIMES.
BUT THAT WAS IT, THAT WAS THE END. THE CITY SEEMED TO EXHALE, AFTER THAT.
KIRKLAND
AND THE MAYOR HELD A MEMORIAL SERVICE FOR THE DEAD, ONE COOL SUMMER EVENING IN DEDICATION PARK --
-- FOR THOSE WITH RELATIVES IN THE CITY, AND FOR THE OTHERS, THE DRIFTERS --
AND AFTER THE EULOGY WAS OVER --

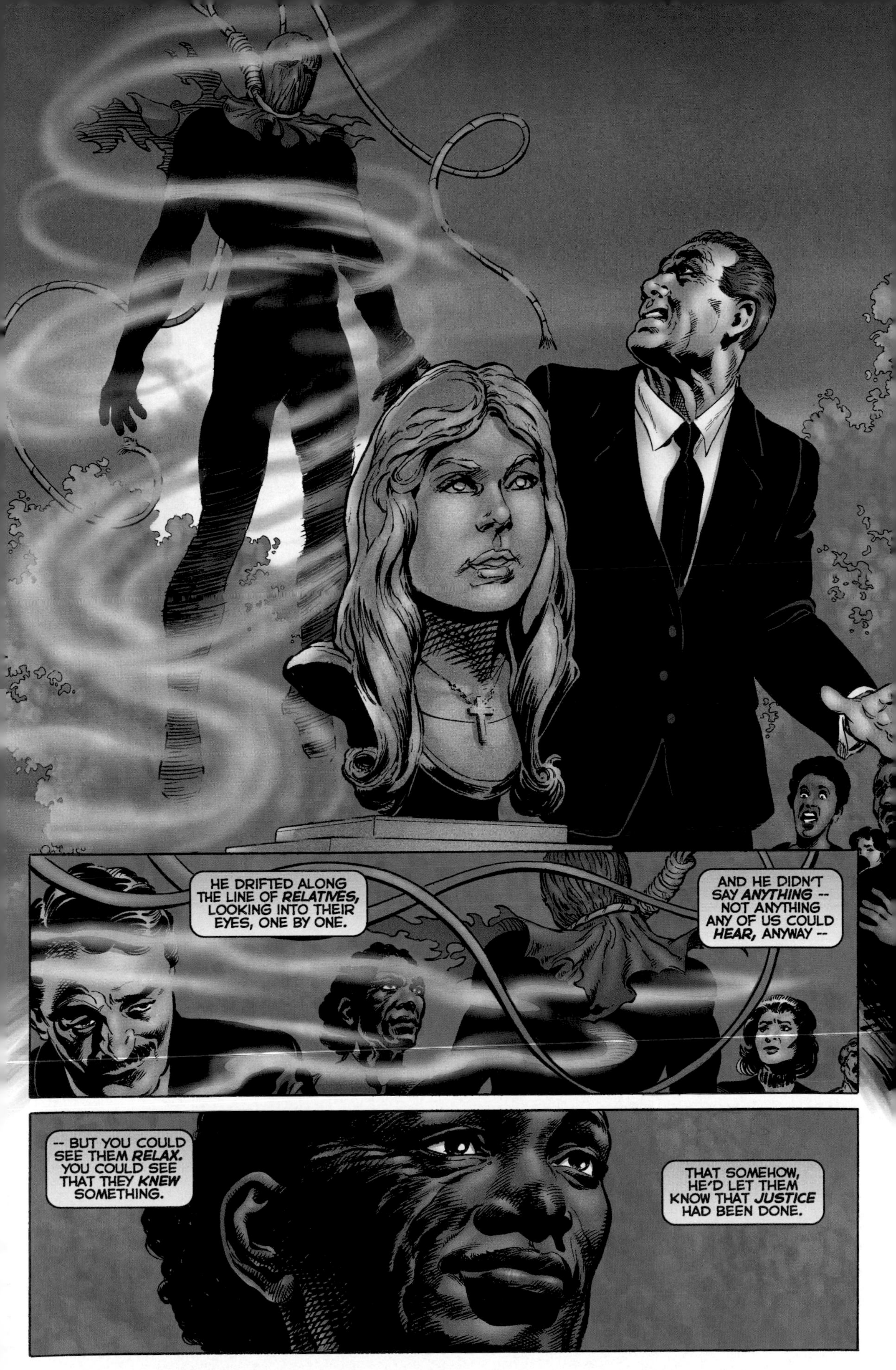
HE DRIFTED ALONG THE LINE OF RELATIVES, LOOKING INTO THEIR EYES, ONE BY ONE.
AND HE DIDN'T SAY ANYTHING -- NOT ANYTHING ANY OF US COULD HEAR, ANYWAY --
-- BUT YOU COULD SEE THEM RELAX. YOU COULD SEE THAT THEY KNEW SOMETHING.
THAT SOMEHOW, HE'D LET THEM KNOW THAT JUSTICE HAD BEEN DONE.

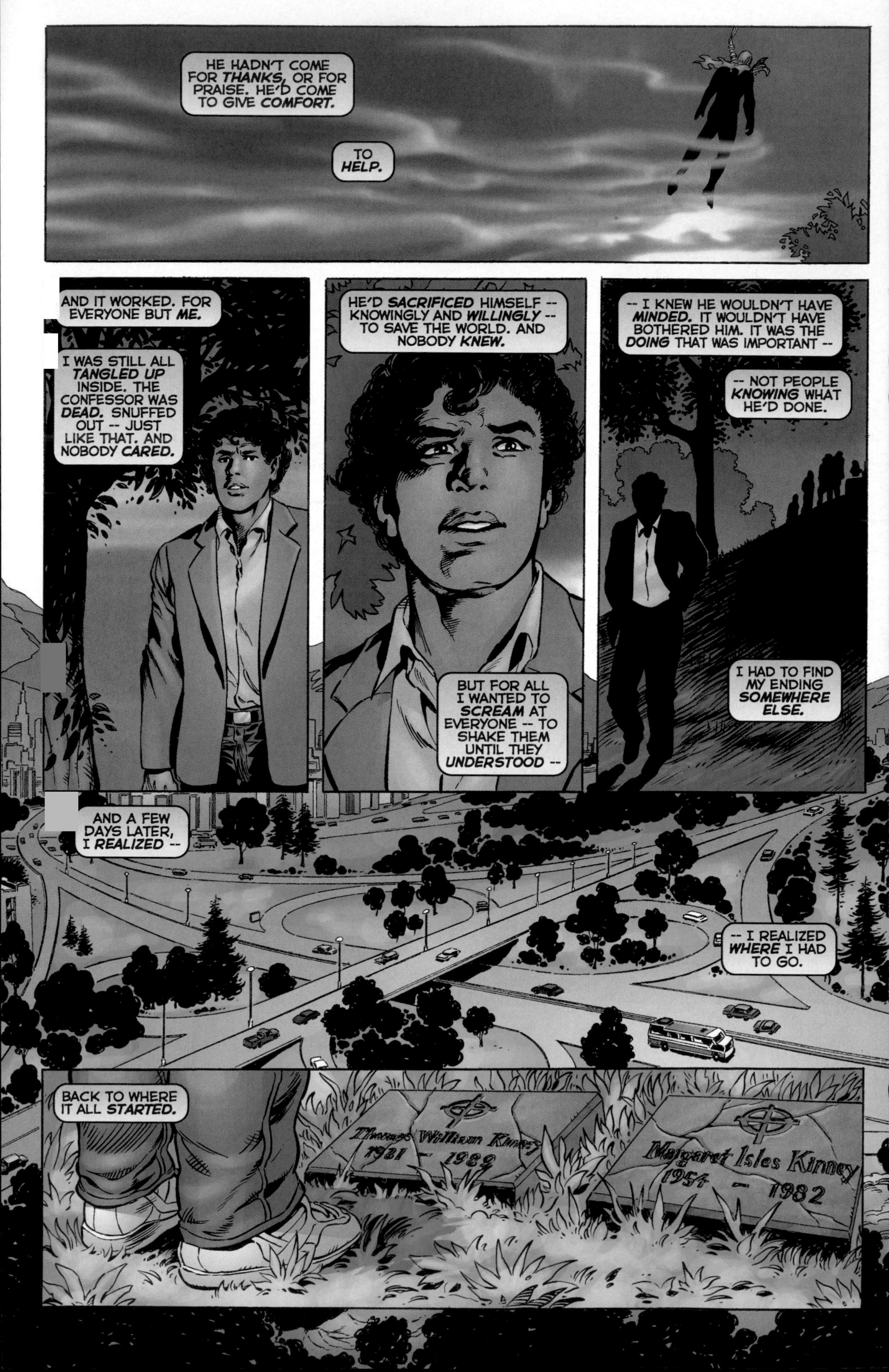
HE HADN'T COME FOR THANKS, OR FOR PRAISE. HE'D COME TO GIVE COMFORT.
TO HELP.
AND IT WORKED. FOR EVERYONE BUT ME.
I WAS STILL ALL TANGLED UP INSIDE. THE CONFESSOR WAS DEAD. SNUFFED OUT -- JUST LIKE THAT. AND NOBODY CARED.
HE'D SACRIFICED HIMSELF -- KNOWINGLY AND WILLINGLY -- TO SAVE THE WORLD. AND NOBODY KNEW.
BUT FOR ALL I WANTED TO SCREAM AT EVERYONE -- TO SHAKE THEM UNTIL THEY UNDERSTOOD --
-- I KNEW HE WOULDN'T HAVE MINDED. IT WOULDN'T HAVE BOTHERED HIM. IT WAS THE DOING THAT WAS IMPORTANT --
-- NOT PEOPLE KNOWING WHAT HE'D DONE.
I HAD TO FIND MY ENDING SOMEWHERE ELSE.
AND A FEW DAYS LATER, I REALIZED --
-- I REALIZED WHERE I HAD TO GO.
BACK TO WHERE IT ALL STARTED.
Margaret Isles Kinney
1954 - 1982

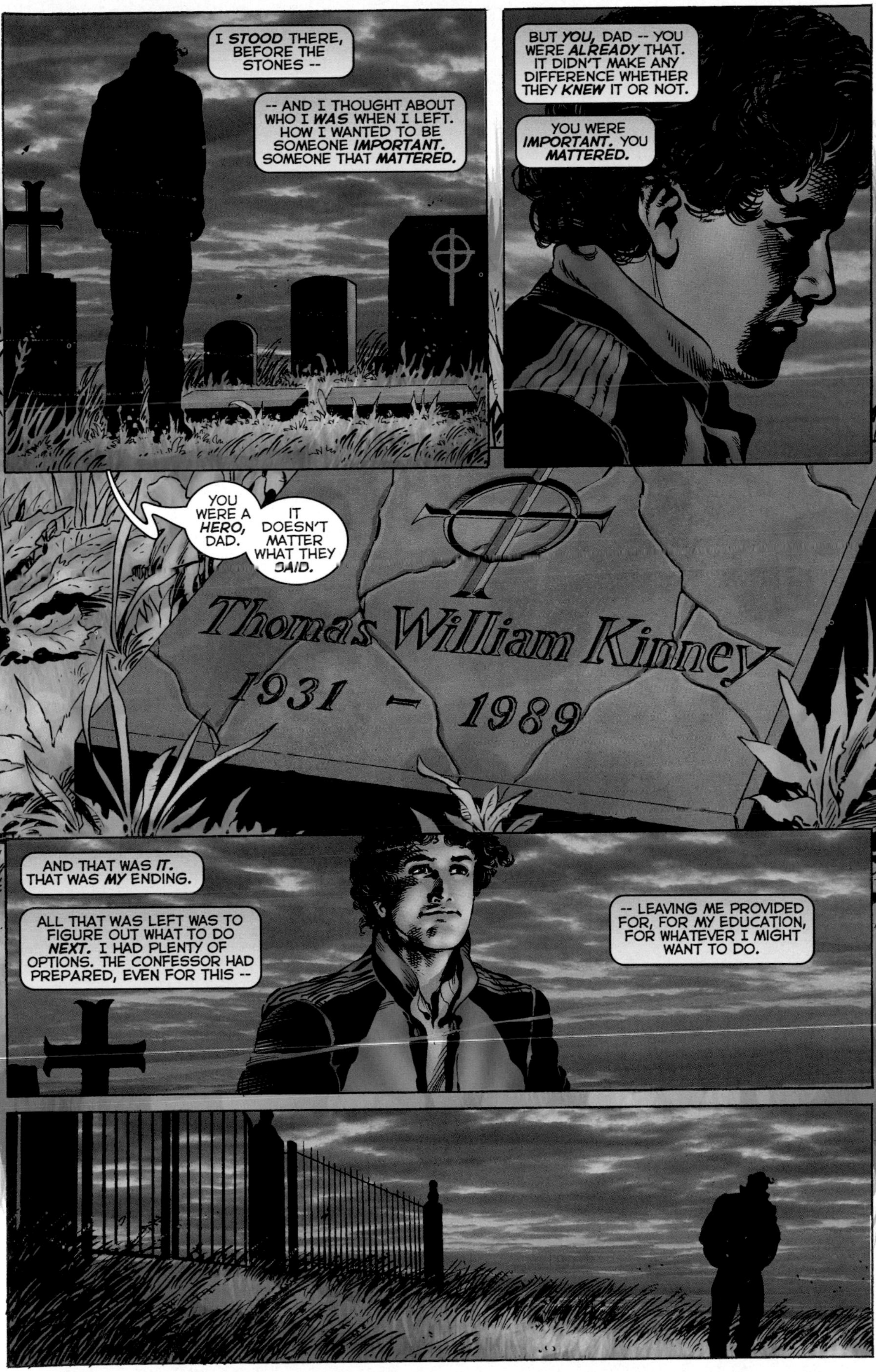

I STOOD THERE, BEFORE THE STONES --
-- AND I THOUGHT ABOUT WHO I WAS WHEN I LEFT. HOW I WANTED TO BE SOMEONE IMPORTANT. SOMEONE THAT MATTERED.
BUT YOU, DAD -- YOU WERE ALREADY THAT. IT DIDN'T MAKE ANY DIFFERENCE WHETHER THEY KNEW IT OR NOT.
YOU WERE IMPORTANT. YOU MATTERED.
YOU WERE A HERO, DAD.
IT DOESN'T MATTER WHAT THEY SAID.
Thomas William Kinney
1931 – 1989
AND THAT WAS IT. THAT WAS MY ENDING.
ALL THAT WAS LEFT WAS TO FIGURE OUT WHAT TO DO NEXT. I HAD PLENTY OF OPTIONS. THE CONFESSOR HAD PREPARED, EVEN FOR THIS --
-- LEAVING ME PROVIDED FOR, FOR MY EDUCATION, FOR WHATEVER I MIGHT WANT TO DO.

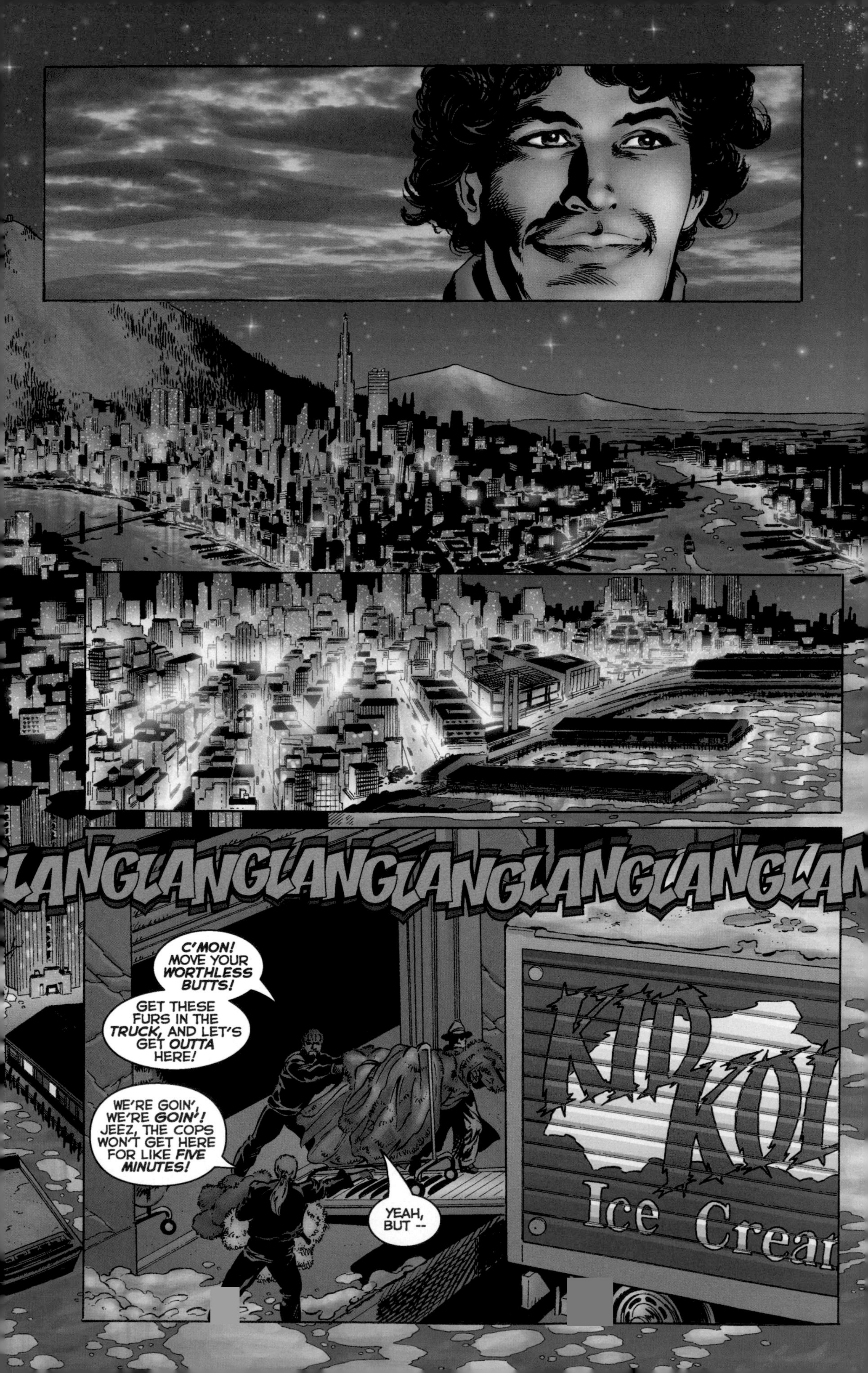

LANGLANGLANGLANGLANGLANGLANGLAN
C'MON! MOVE YOUR WORTHLESS BUTTS!
GET THESE FURS IN THE TRUCK, AND LET'S GET OUTTA HERE!
WE'RE GOIN', WE'RE GOIN'! JEEZ, THE COPS WON'T GET HERE FOR LIKE FIVE MINUTES!
YEAH, BUT --
Ice Crea

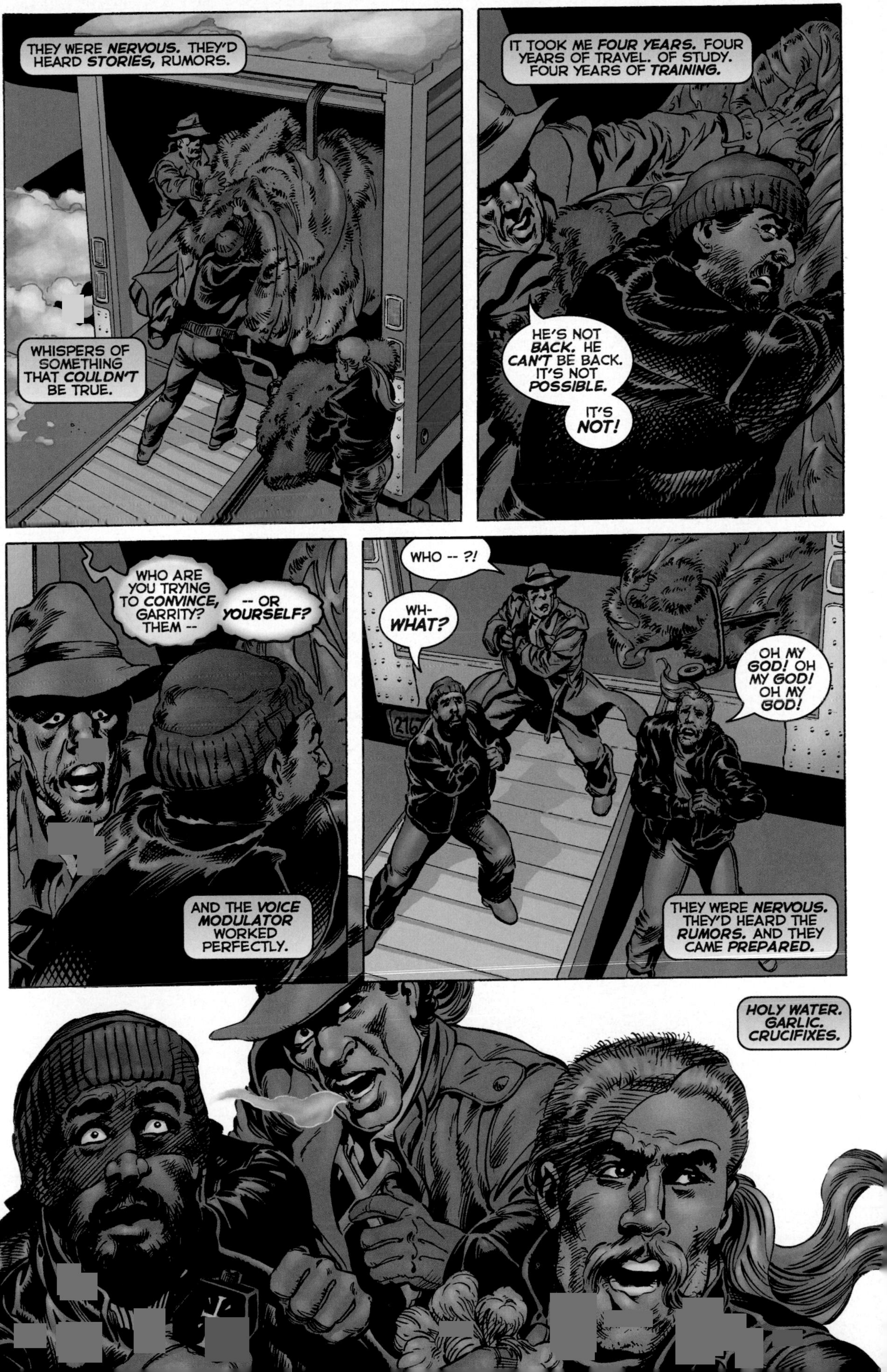
THEY WERE NERVOUS. THEY'D HEARD STORIES, RUMORS.
WHISPERS OF SOMETHING THAT COULDN'T BE TRUE.
IT TOOK ME FOUR YEARS. FOUR YEARS OF TRAVEL. OF STUDY. FOUR YEARS OF TRAINING.
HE'S NOT BACK. HE CAN'T BE BACK. IT'S NOT POSSIBLE.
IT'S NOT!
WHO ARE YOU TRYING TO CONVINCE, GARRITY? THEM --
-- OR YOURSELF?
AND THE VOICE MODULATOR WORKED PERFECTLY.
WHO -- ?!
WH- WHAT?
OH MY GOD! OH MY GOD! OH MY GOD!
THEY WERE NERVOUS. THEY'D HEARD THE RUMORS. AND THEY CAME PREPARED.
HOLY WATER. GARLIC. CRUCIFIXES.

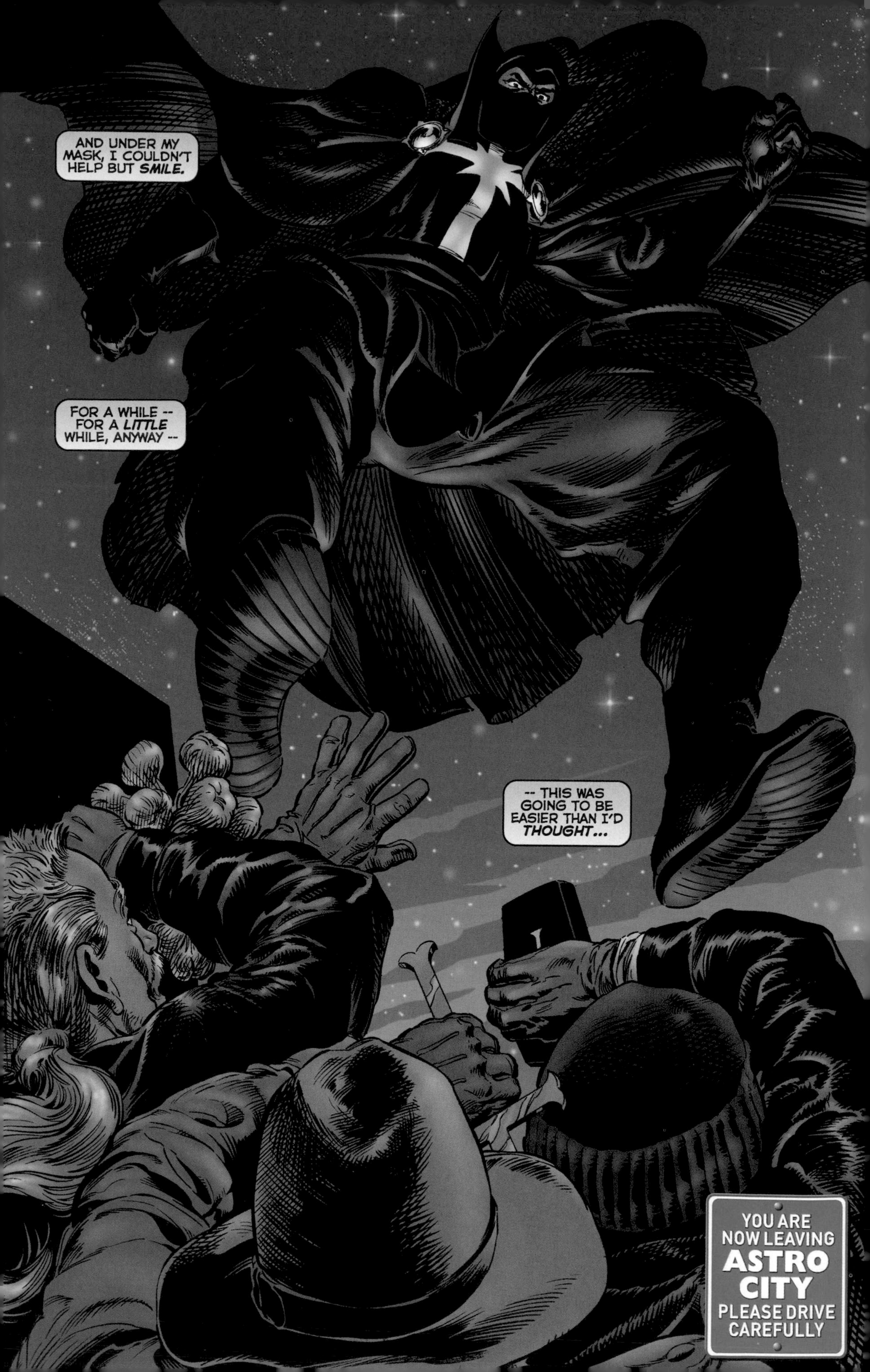
AND UNDER MY MASK, I COULDN'T HELP BUT SMILE.
FOR A WHILE -- FOR A LITTLE WHILE, ANYWAY --
-- THIS WAS GOING TO BE EASIER THAN I'D THOUGHT...
YOU ARE NOW LEAVING ASTRO CITY PLEASE DRIVE CAREFULLY

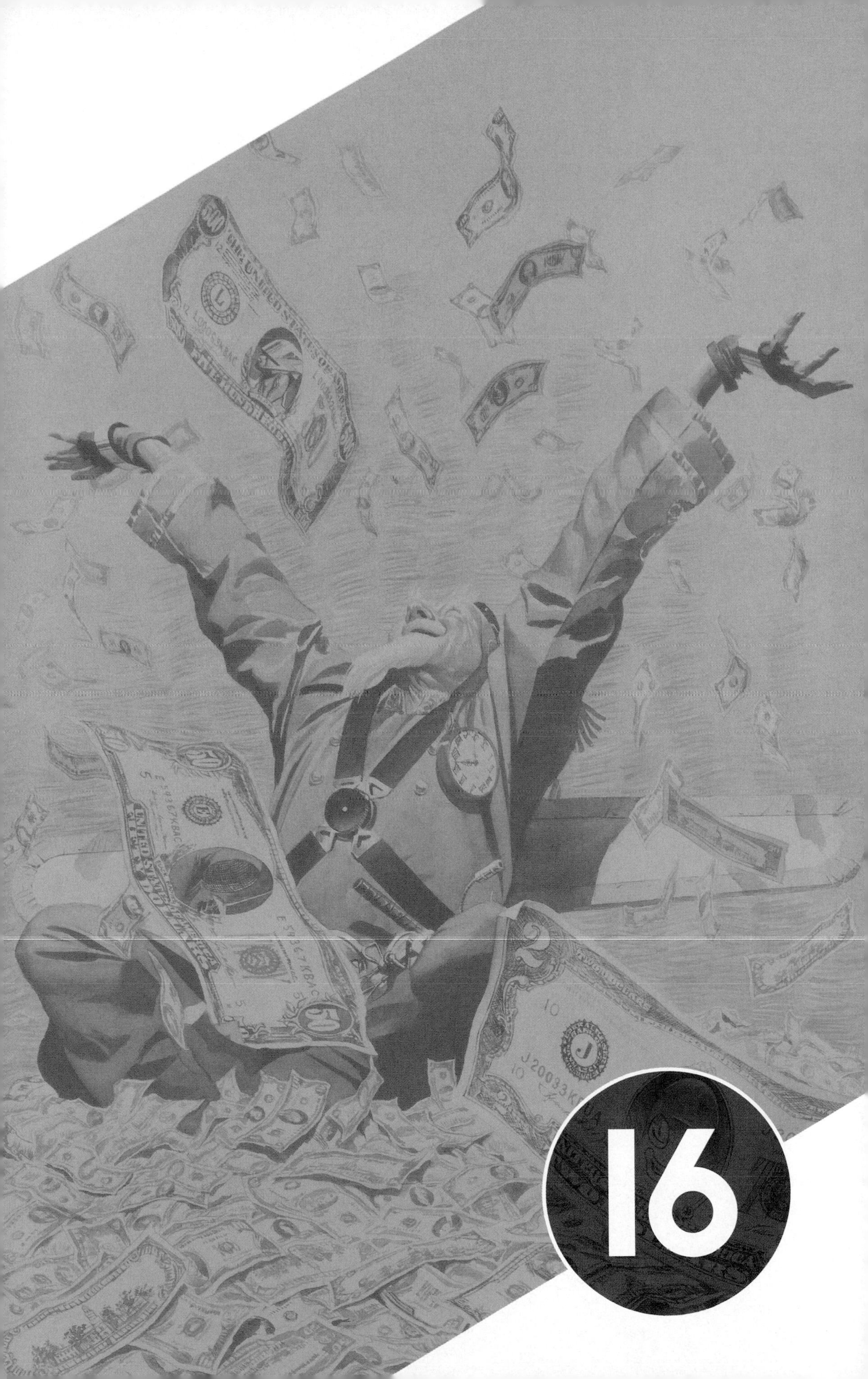

16

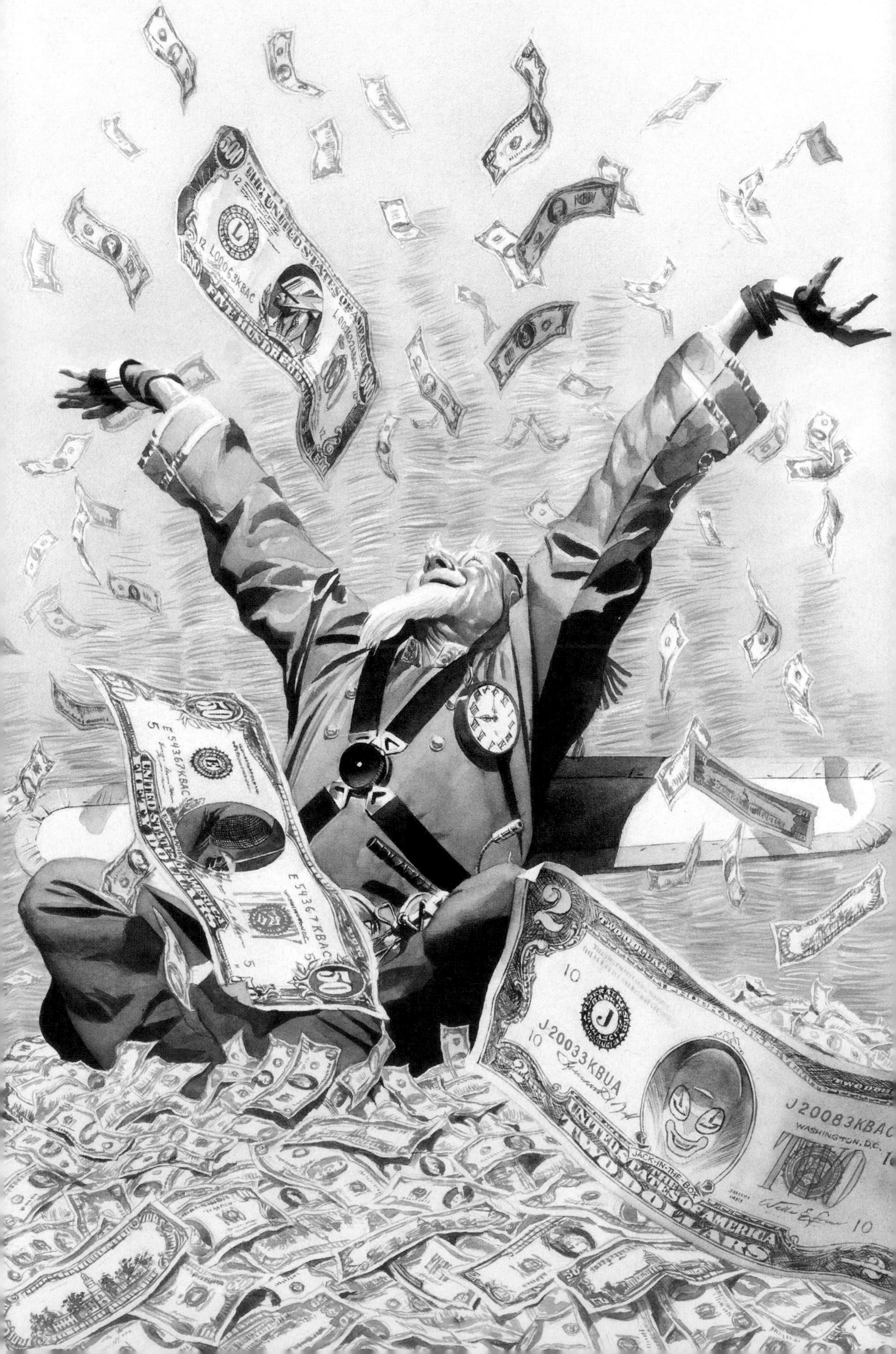

E 54367KBAC
J-20033KBUA
J20083KBAC
WASHINGTON, D.C.
JACK-IN-THE-BOX

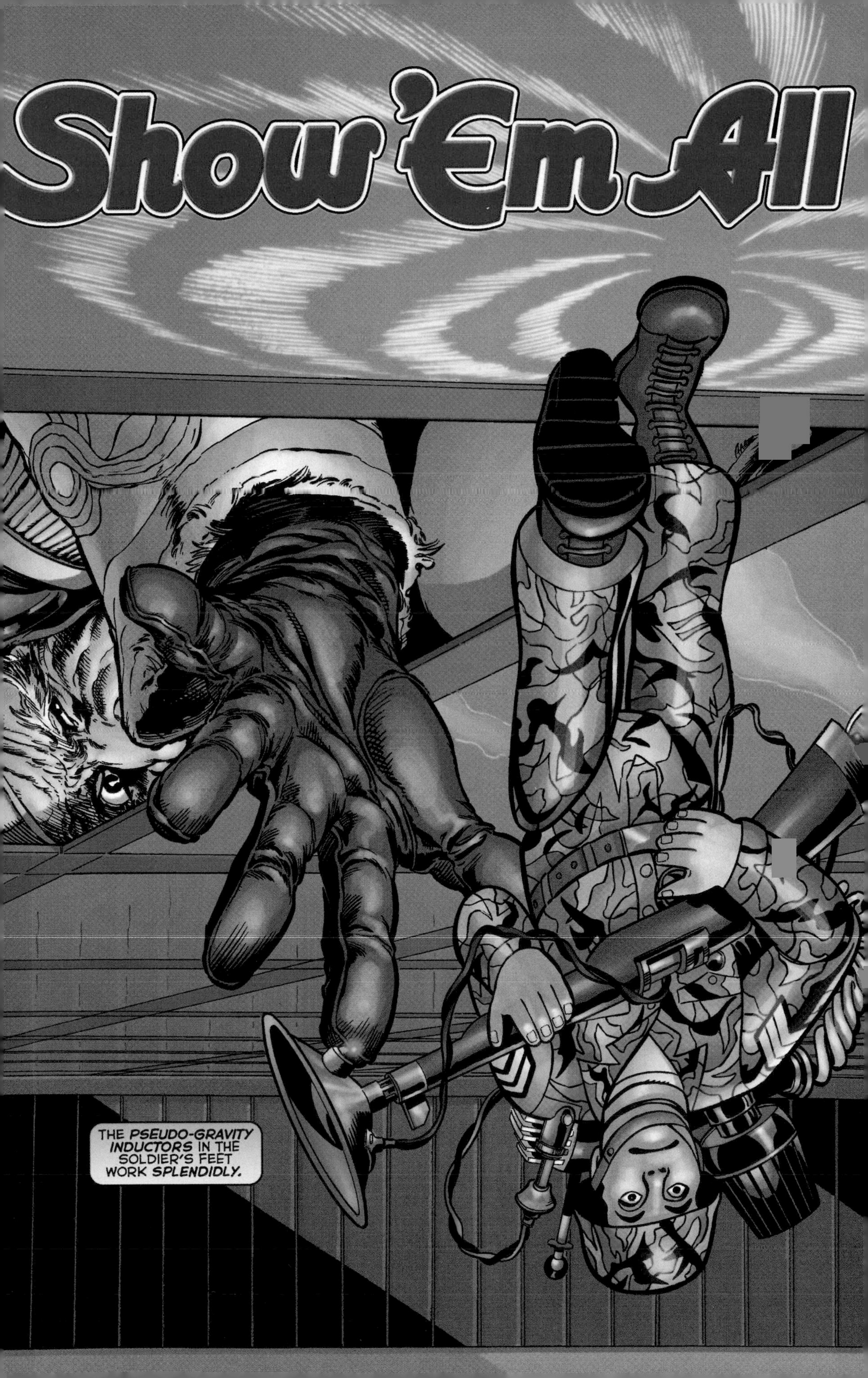
Show 'Em All
THE PSEUDO-GRAVITY INDUCTORS IN THE SOLDIER'S FEET WORK SPLENDIDLY.

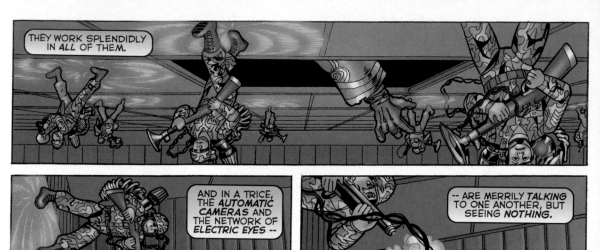

THEY WORK SPLENDIDLY IN *ALL* OF THEM.

AND IN A TRICE, THE *AUTOMATIC CAMERAS* AND THE NETWORK OF *ELECTRIC EYES* --

-- ARE MERRILY *TALKING* TO ONE ANOTHER, BUT SEEING *NOTHING.*

THEY ADDED THE ELECTRIC EYES AFTER THE *TECHSPERTS* BROKE IN, TWO YEARS AGO, AND WERE CAUGHT BY *QUARREL.*

THEY PUT *PRESSURE SENSORS* INTO THE FLOOR, TOO. BUT THEY'RE NO *GREAT DIFFICULTY.*

THE JUNKMAN COMES *PREPARED.*

HMM   HMM

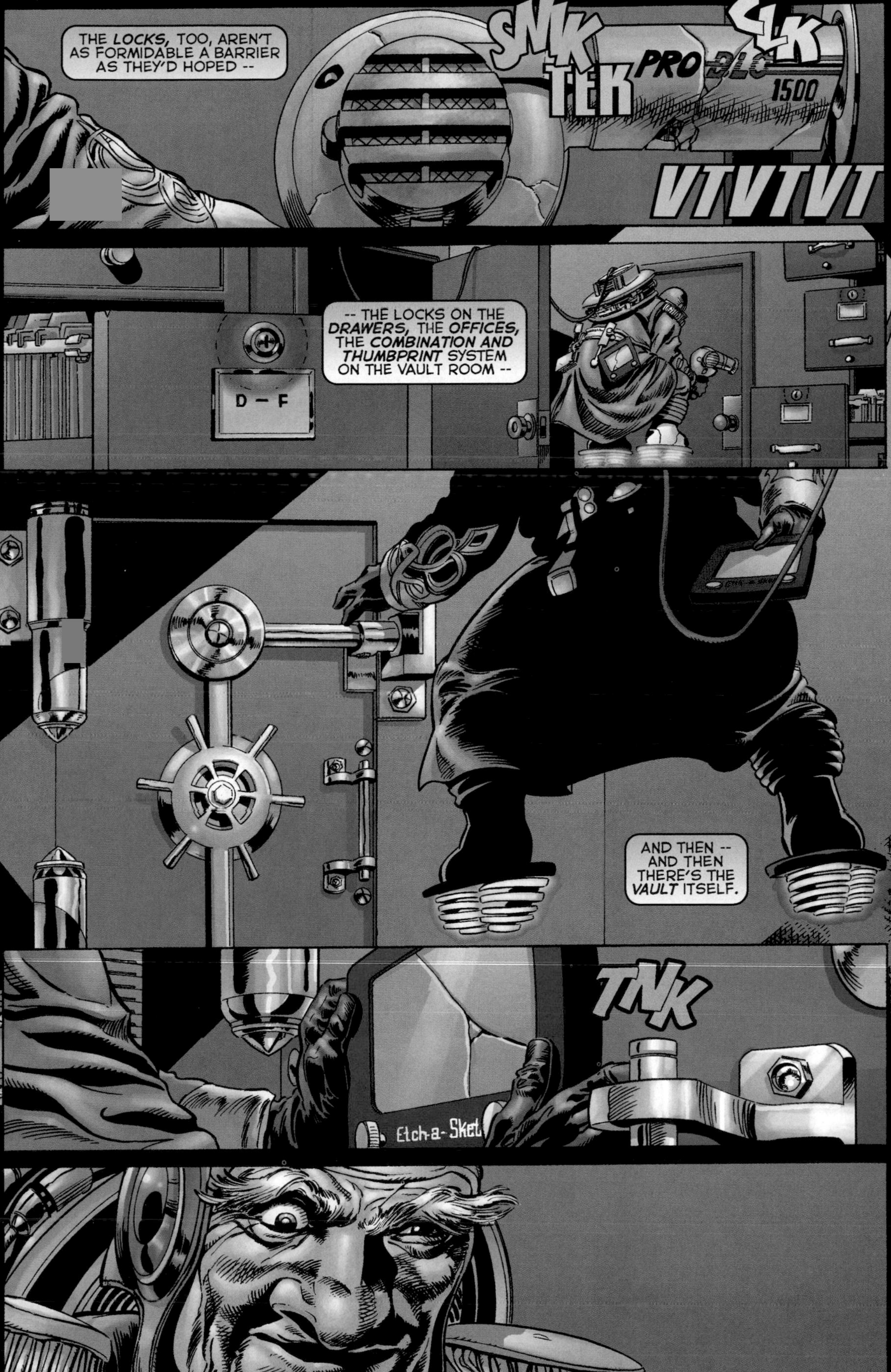
THE LOCKS, TOO, AREN'T AS FORMIDABLE A BARRIER AS THEY'D HOPED --
SNIK
TEK
PRO
CLK
1500
VTVTVT
-- THE LOCKS ON THE DRAWERS, THE OFFICES, THE COMBINATION AND THUMBPRINT SYSTEM ON THE VAULT ROOM --
D — F
AND THEN -- AND THEN THERE'S THE VAULT ITSELF.
TNK
Etch-a-Sket

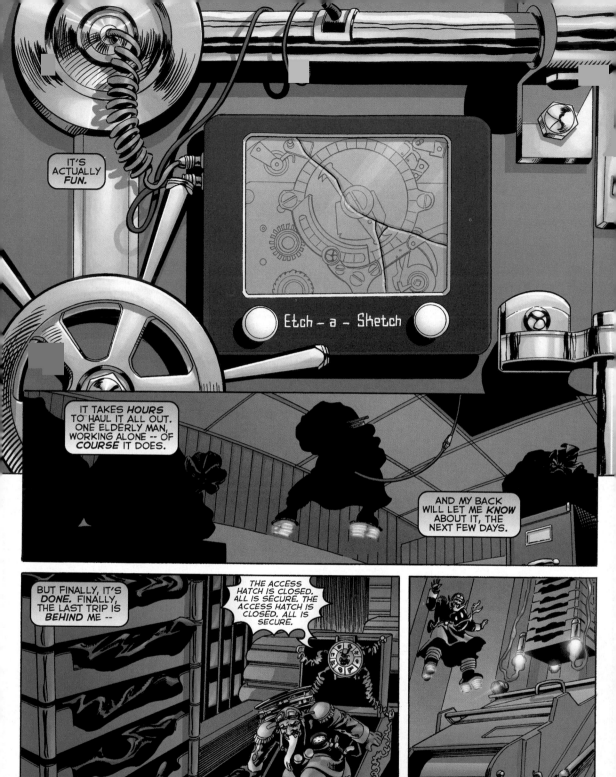

IT'S ACTUALLY *FUN.*

Etch - a - Sketch

IT TAKES *HOURS* TO HAUL IT ALL OUT. ONE ELDERLY MAN, WORKING ALONE -- OF *COURSE* IT DOES.

AND MY BACK WILL LET ME *KNOW* ABOUT IT, THE NEXT FEW DAYS.

BUT FINALLY, IT'S *DONE.* FINALLY, THE LAST TRIP IS *BEHIND* ME --

THE *ACCESS HATCH* IS *CLOSED.* ALL IS *SECURE.* THE *ACCESS HATCH* IS *CLOSED.* ALL IS *SECURE.*

-- AND ALL THAT REMAINS IS TO *FLOAT* IT *DOWN* TO THE *TRUCK.*

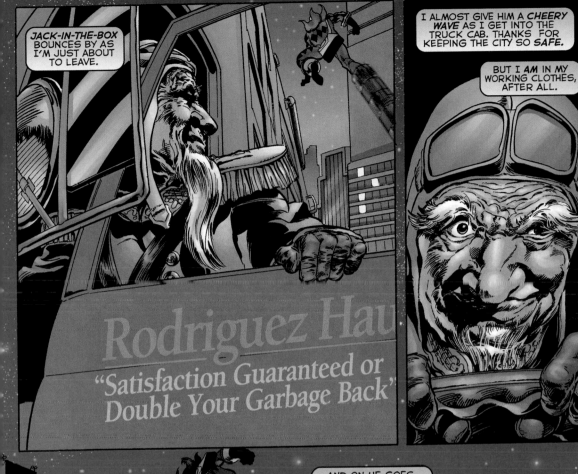

JACK-IN-THE-BOX BOUNCES BY AS I'M JUST ABOUT TO LEAVE.

I ALMOST GIVE HIM A *CHEERY WAVE* AS I GET INTO THE TRUCK CAB. THANKS FOR KEEPING THE CITY SO *SAFE.*

BUT I *AM* IN MY WORKING CLOTHES, AFTER ALL.

Rodriguez Hau

"Satisfaction Guaranteed or Double Your Garbage Back"

AND ON HE GOES, WITH THE ENERGY OF *YOUTH.* INTENT ON HIS *NOBLE CRUSADE.*

AND HE DOESN'T KNOW A *THING.*

BRUM BRUM PKTOW

NONE OF THEM KNOW A *THING.*

AstroBank

BRMMMMMMMMMMM

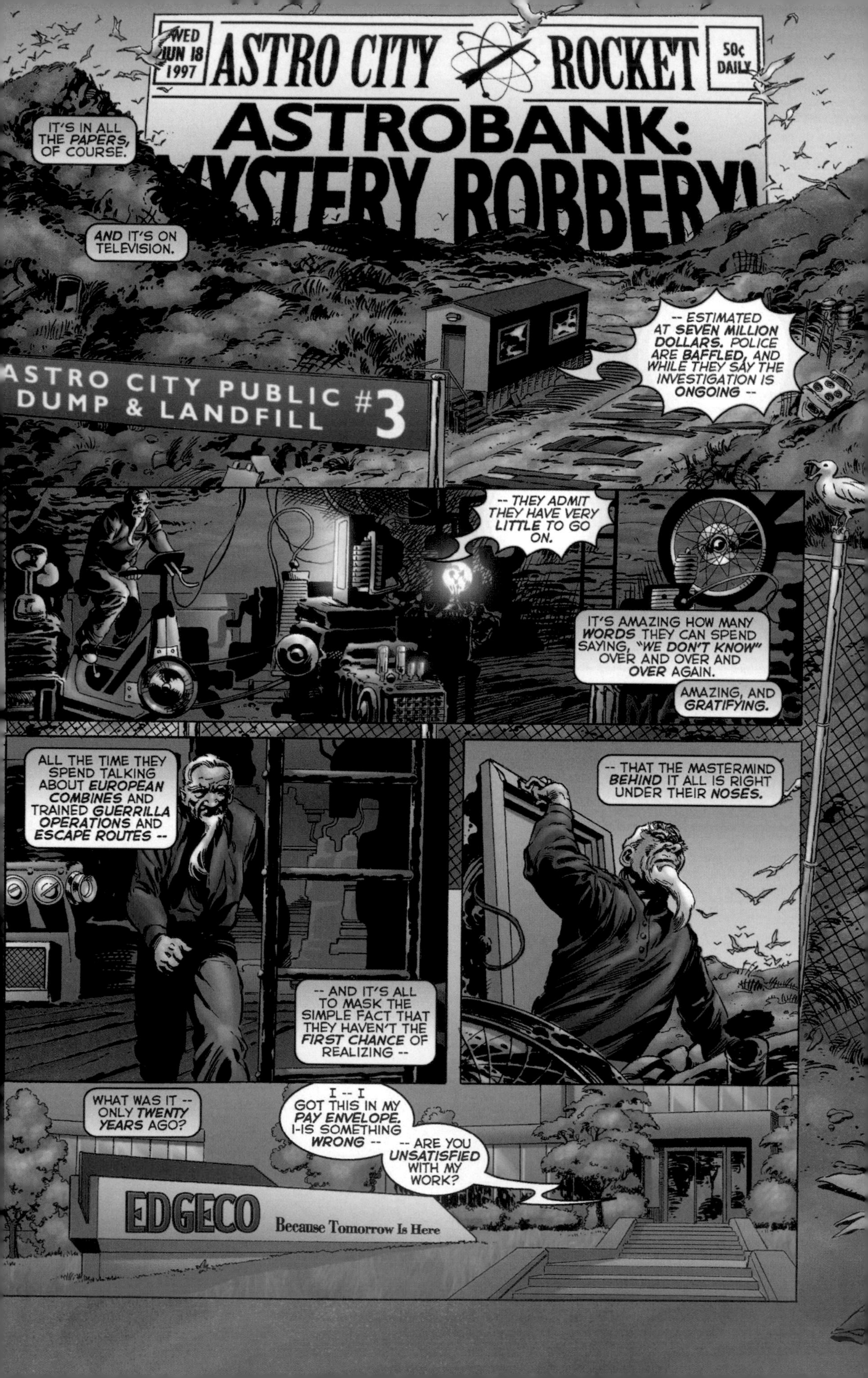
WED JUN 18 1997
ASTRO CITY ROCKET
50¢ DAILY
ASTROBANK: MYSTERY ROBBERY!
IT'S IN ALL THE PAPERS, OF COURSE.
AND IT'S ON TELEVISION.
ASTRO CITY PUBLIC DUMP & LANDFILL #3
-- ESTIMATED AT SEVEN MILLION DOLLARS. POLICE ARE BAFFLED, AND WHILE THEY SAY THE INVESTIGATION IS ONGOING --
-- THEY ADMIT THEY HAVE VERY LITTLE TO GO ON.
IT'S AMAZING HOW MANY WORDS THEY CAN SPEND SAYING, "WE DON'T KNOW" OVER AND OVER AND OVER AGAIN.
AMAZING, AND GRATIFYING.
ALL THE TIME THEY SPEND TALKING ABOUT EUROPEAN COMBINES AND TRAINED GUERRILLA OPERATIONS AND ESCAPE ROUTES --
-- AND IT'S ALL TO MASK THE SIMPLE FACT THAT THEY HAVEN'T THE FIRST CHANCE OF REALIZING --
-- THAT THE MASTERMIND BEHIND IT ALL IS RIGHT UNDER THEIR NOSES.
WHAT WAS IT -- ONLY TWENTY YEARS AGO?
I -- I GOT THIS IN MY PAY ENVELOPE. I-IS SOMETHING WRONG --
-- ARE YOU UNSATISFIED WITH MY WORK?
EDGECO
Because Tomorrow Is Here

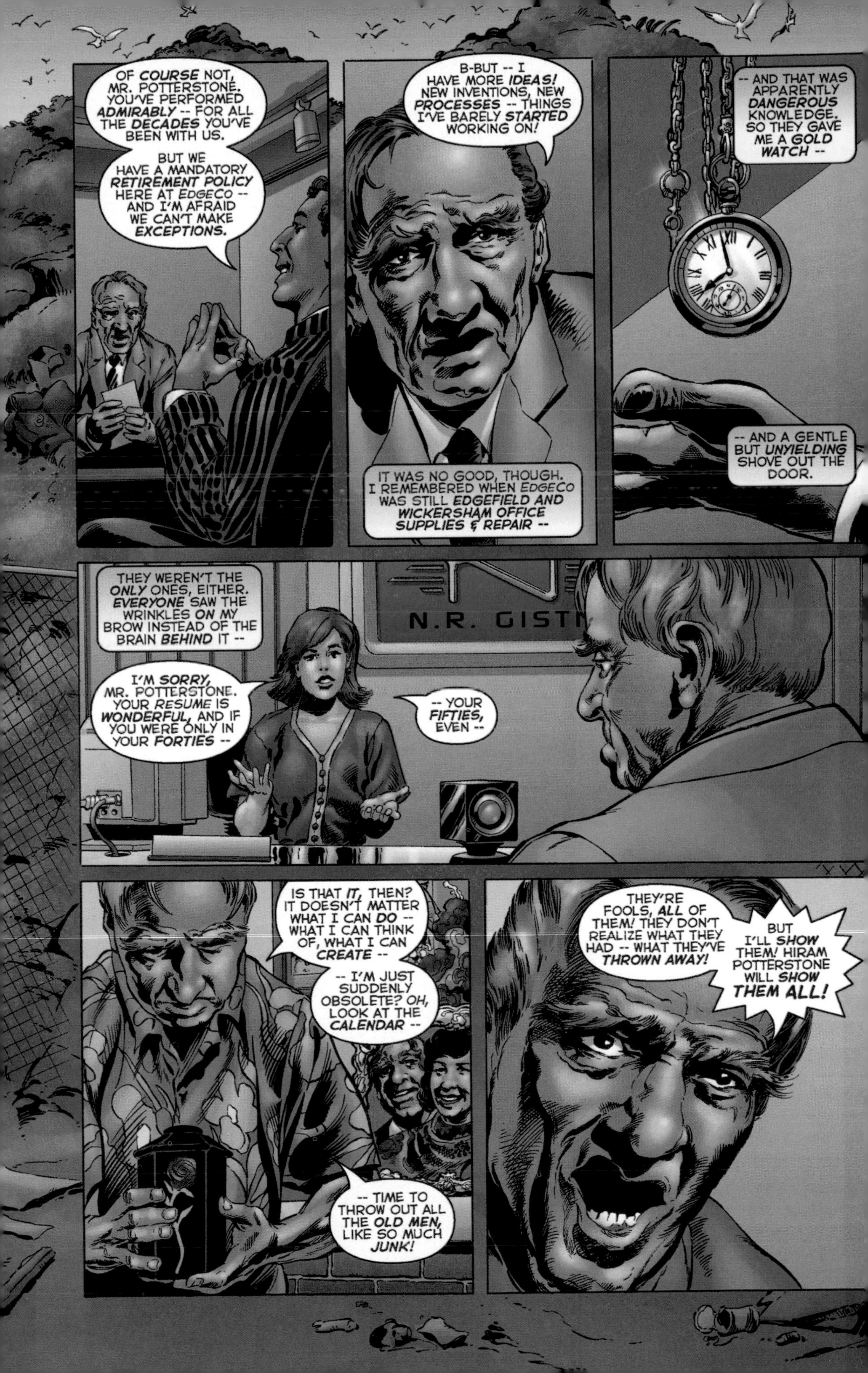
OF COURSE NOT, MR. POTTERSTONE. YOU'VE PERFORMED ADMIRABLY -- FOR ALL THE DECADES YOU'VE BEEN WITH US.
BUT WE HAVE A MANDATORY RETIREMENT POLICY HERE AT EDGECO -- AND I'M AFRAID WE CAN'T MAKE EXCEPTIONS.
B-BUT -- I HAVE MORE IDEAS! NEW INVENTIONS, NEW PROCESSES -- THINGS I'VE BARELY STARTED WORKING ON!
IT WAS NO GOOD, THOUGH. I REMEMBERED WHEN EDGECO WAS STILL EDGEFIELD AND WICKERSHAM OFFICE SUPPLIES & REPAIR --
-- AND THAT WAS APPARENTLY DANGEROUS KNOWLEDGE. SO THEY GAVE ME A GOLD WATCH --
-- AND A GENTLE BUT UNYIELDING SHOVE OUT THE DOOR.
THEY WEREN'T THE ONLY ONES, EITHER. EVERYONE SAW THE WRINKLES ON MY BROW INSTEAD OF THE BRAIN BEHIND IT --
N.R. GIST
I'M SORRY, MR. POTTERSTONE. YOUR RESUME IS WONDERFUL, AND IF YOU WERE ONLY IN YOUR FORTIES --
-- YOUR FIFTIES, EVEN --
IS THAT IT, THEN? IT DOESN'T MATTER WHAT I CAN DO -- WHAT I CAN THINK OF, WHAT I CAN CREATE --
-- I'M JUST SUDDENLY OBSOLETE? OH, LOOK AT THE CALENDAR --
-- TIME TO THROW OUT ALL THE OLD MEN, LIKE SO MUCH JUNK!
THEY'RE FOOLS, ALL OF THEM! THEY DON'T REALIZE WHAT THEY HAD -- WHAT THEY'VE THROWN AWAY!
BUT I'LL SHOW THEM! HIRAM POTTERSTONE WILL SHOW THEM ALL!

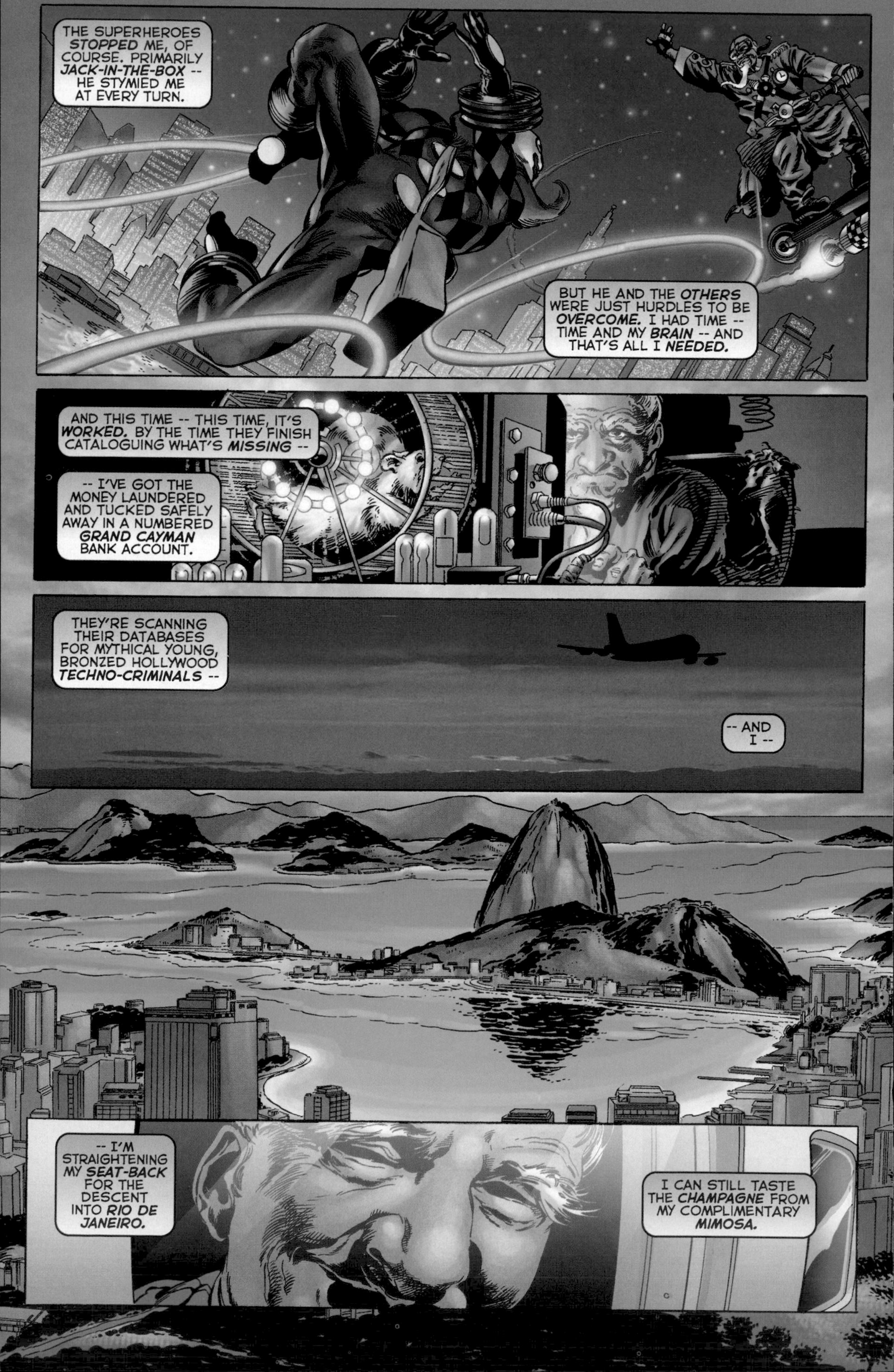
THE SUPERHEROES *STOPPED* ME, OF COURSE. PRIMARILY *JACK-IN-THE-BOX* -- HE STYMIED ME AT EVERY TURN.
BUT HE AND THE *OTHERS* WERE JUST HURDLES TO BE *OVERCOME.* I HAD TIME -- TIME AND MY *BRAIN* -- AND THAT'S ALL I *NEEDED.*
AND THIS TIME -- THIS TIME, IT'S *WORKED.* BY THE TIME THEY FINISH CATALOGUING WHAT'S *MISSING* --
-- I'VE GOT THE MONEY LAUNDERED AND TUCKED SAFELY AWAY IN A NUMBERED *GRAND CAYMAN* BANK ACCOUNT.
THEY'RE SCANNING THEIR DATABASES FOR MYTHICAL YOUNG, BRONZED HOLLYWOOD *TECHNO-CRIMINALS* --
-- AND I --
-- I'M STRAIGHTENING MY *SEAT-BACK* FOR THE DESCENT INTO *RIO DE JANEIRO.*
I CAN STILL TASTE THE *CHAMPAGNE* FROM MY COMPLIMENTARY *MIMOSA.*

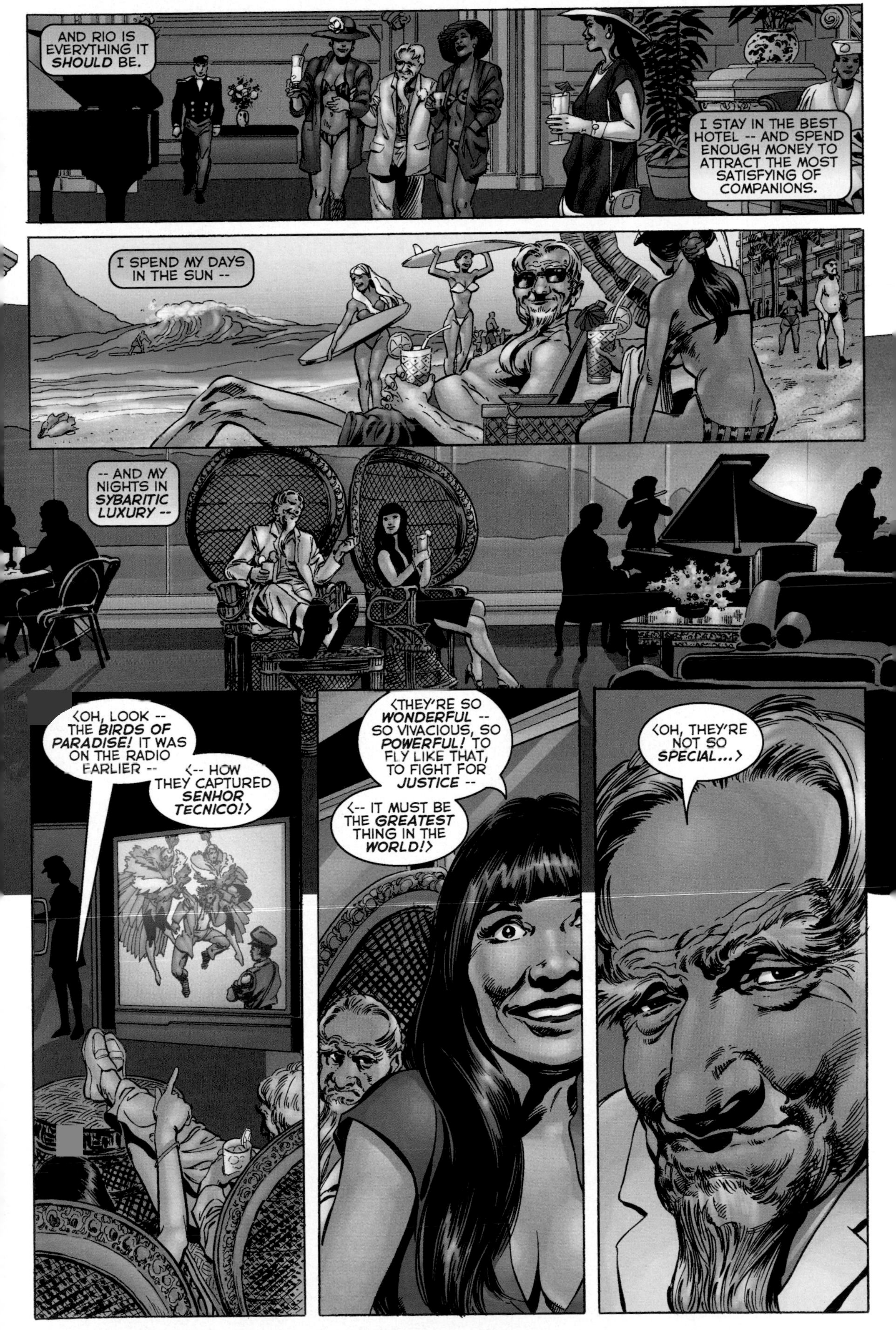

AND RIO IS EVERYTHING IT SHOULD BE.
I STAY IN THE BEST HOTEL -- AND SPEND ENOUGH MONEY TO ATTRACT THE MOST SATISFYING OF COMPANIONS.
I SPEND MY DAYS IN THE SUN --
-- AND MY NIGHTS IN SYBARITIC LUXURY --
<OH, LOOK -- THE BIRDS OF PARADISE! IT WAS ON THE RADIO EARLIER --
<-- HOW THEY CAPTURED SENHOR TECNICO!>
<THEY'RE SO WONDERFUL -- SO VIVACIOUS, SO POWERFUL! TO FLY LIKE THAT, TO FIGHT FOR JUSTICE --
<-- IT MUST BE THE GREATEST THING IN THE WORLD!>
<OH, THEY'RE NOT SO SPECIAL...>

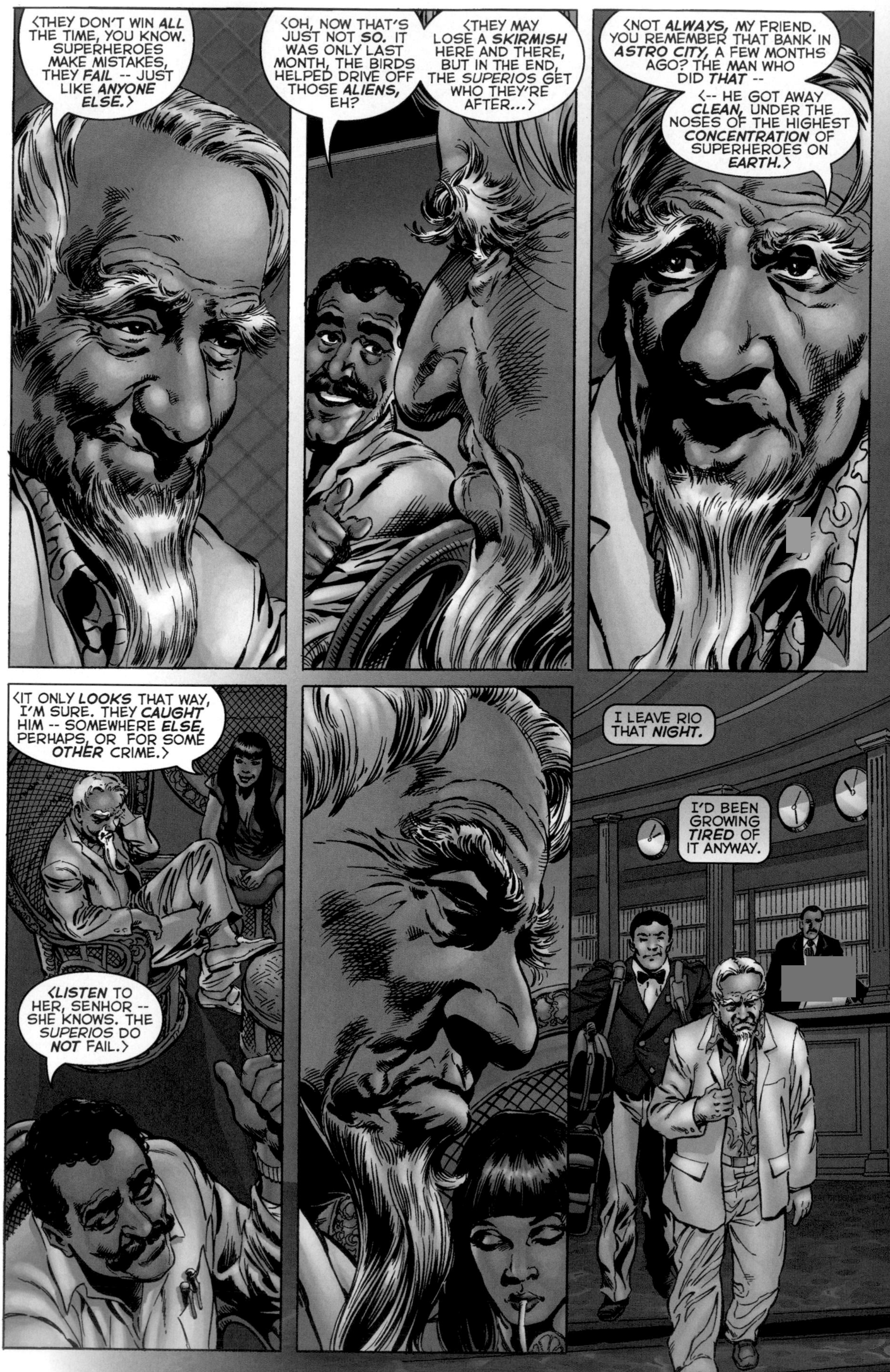

<THEY DON'T WIN ALL THE TIME, YOU KNOW. SUPERHEROES MAKE MISTAKES, THEY FAIL -- JUST LIKE ANYONE ELSE.>
<OH, NOW THAT'S JUST NOT SO. IT WAS ONLY LAST MONTH, THE BIRDS HELPED DRIVE OFF THOSE ALIENS, EH?
<THEY MAY LOSE A SKIRMISH HERE AND THERE, BUT IN THE END, THE SUPERIOS GET WHO THEY'RE AFTER...>
<NOT ALWAYS, MY FRIEND. YOU REMEMBER THAT BANK IN ASTRO CITY, A FEW MONTHS AGO? THE MAN WHO DID THAT --
<-- HE GOT AWAY CLEAN, UNDER THE NOSES OF THE HIGHEST CONCENTRATION OF SUPERHEROES ON EARTH.>
<IT ONLY LOOKS THAT WAY, I'M SURE. THEY CAUGHT HIM -- SOMEWHERE ELSE, PERHAPS, OR FOR SOME OTHER CRIME.>
<LISTEN TO HER, SENHOR -- SHE KNOWS. THE SUPERIOS DO NOT FAIL.>
I LEAVE RIO THAT NIGHT.
I'D BEEN GROWING TIRED OF IT ANYWAY.

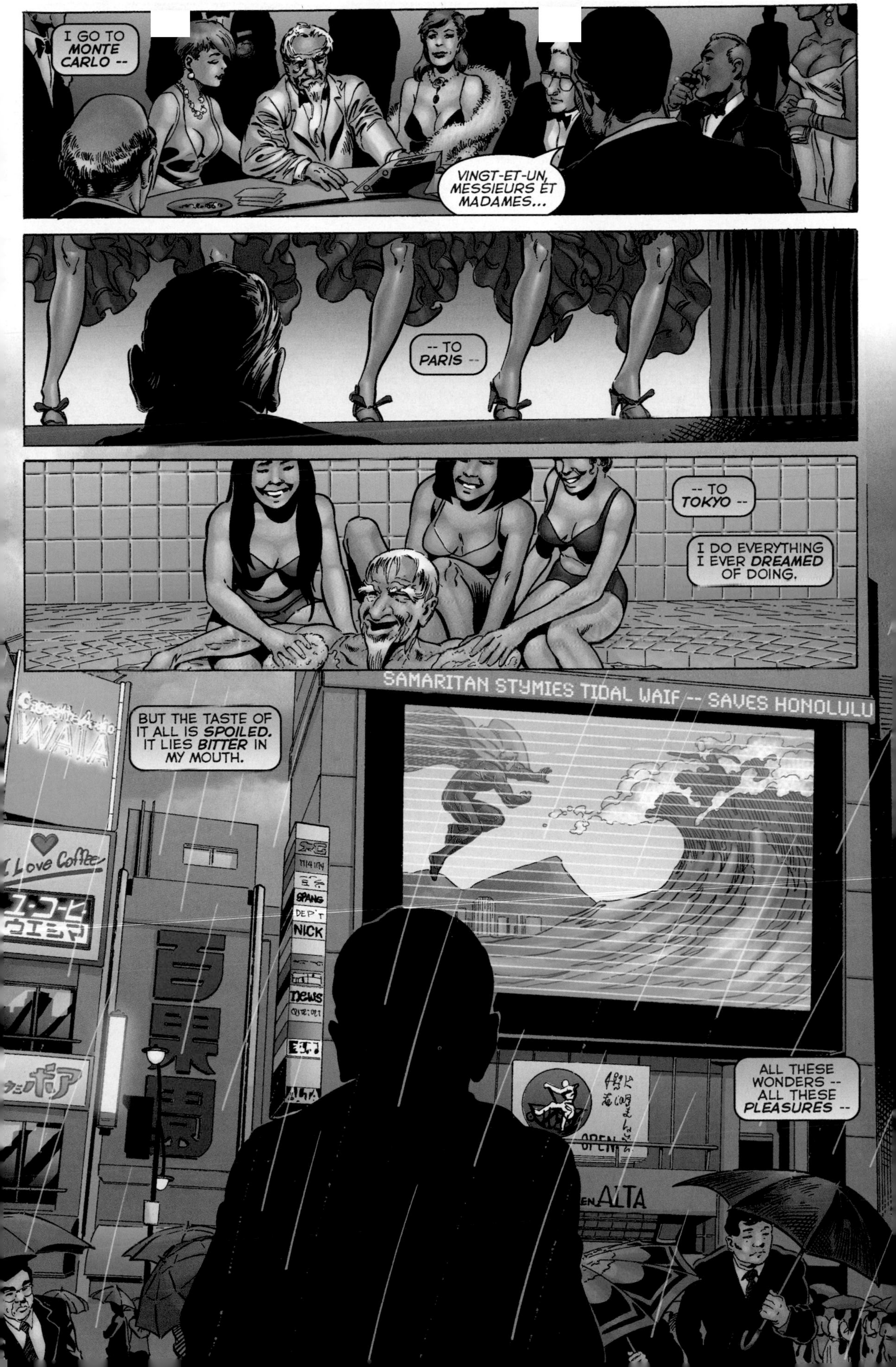
I GO TO MONTE CARLO --
VINGT-ET-UN, MESSIEURS ET MADAMES...
-- TO PARIS --
-- TO TOKYO --
I DO EVERYTHING I EVER DREAMED OF DOING.
SAMARITAN STYMIES TIDAL WAIF -- SAVES HONOLULU
BUT THE TASTE OF IT ALL IS SPOILED. IT LIES BITTER IN MY MOUTH.
I Love Coffee
SPANG
DEP'T
NICK
News
ALTA
OPEN
ALL THESE WONDERS -- ALL THESE PLEASURES --

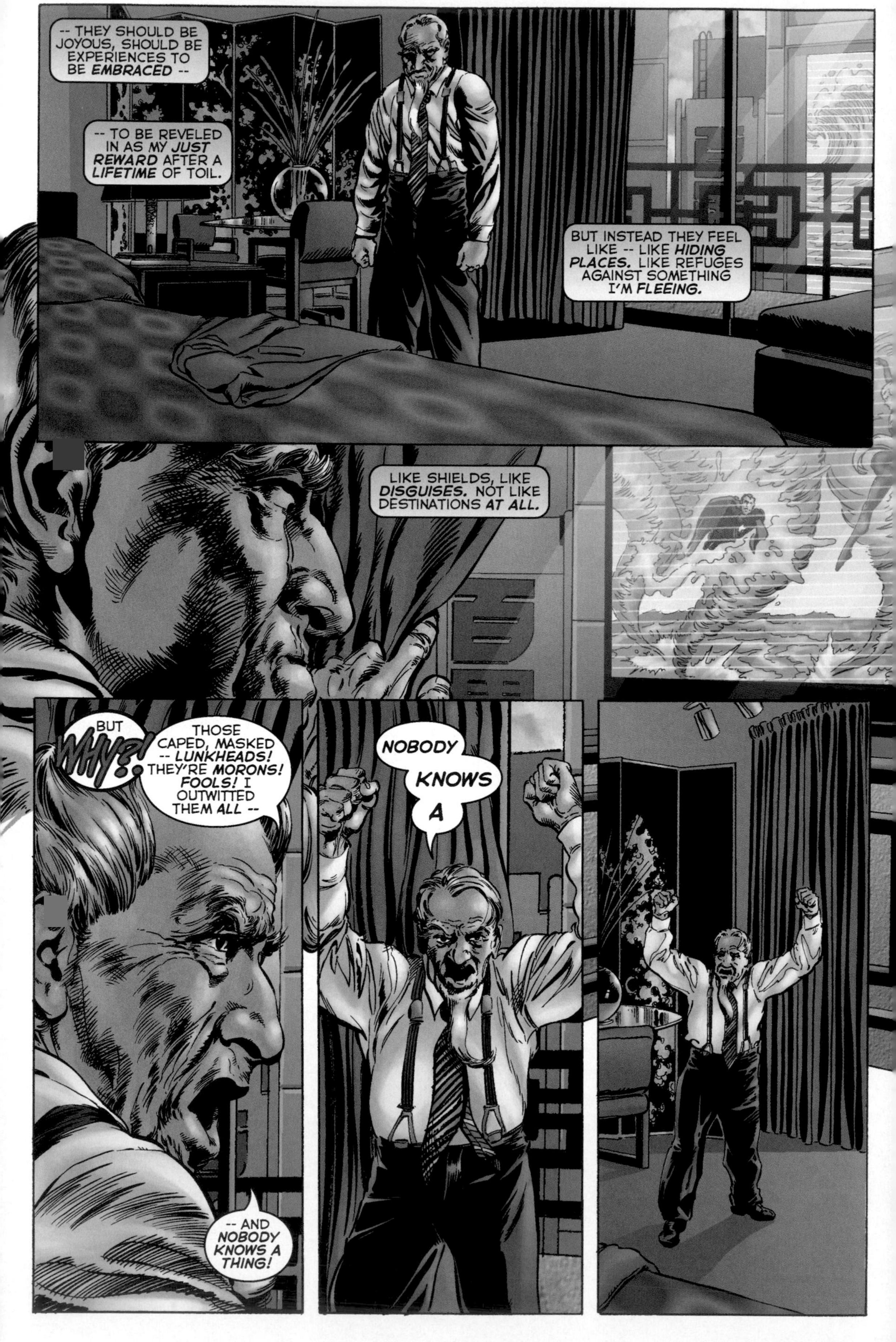
-- THEY SHOULD BE JOYOUS, SHOULD BE EXPERIENCES TO BE EMBRACED --
-- TO BE REVELED IN AS MY JUST REWARD AFTER A LIFETIME OF TOIL.
BUT INSTEAD THEY FEEL LIKE -- LIKE HIDING PLACES. LIKE REFUGES AGAINST SOMETHING I'M FLEEING.
LIKE SHIELDS, LIKE DISGUISES. NOT LIKE DESTINATIONS AT ALL.
BUT WHY?!
THOSE CAPED, MASKED -- LUNKHEADS! THEY'RE MORONS! FOOLS! I OUTWITTED THEM ALL --
-- AND NOBODY KNOWS A THING!
NOBODY KNOWS A

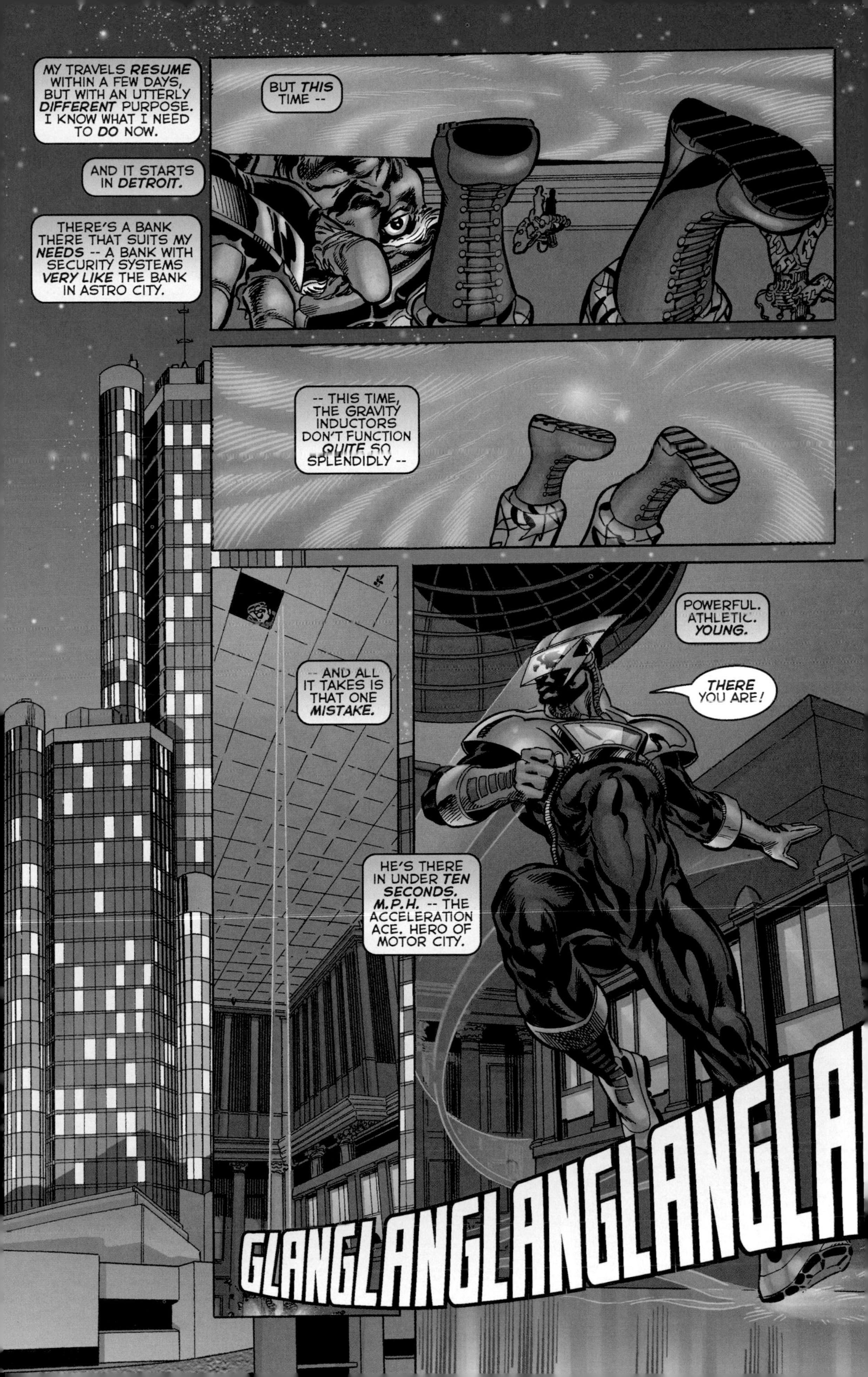

MY TRAVELS RESUME WITHIN A FEW DAYS, BUT WITH AN UTTERLY DIFFERENT PURPOSE. I KNOW WHAT I NEED TO DO NOW.
AND IT STARTS IN DETROIT.
THERE'S A BANK THERE THAT SUITS MY NEEDS -- A BANK WITH SECURITY SYSTEMS VERY LIKE THE BANK IN ASTRO CITY.
BUT THIS TIME --
-- THIS TIME, THE GRAVITY INDUCTORS DON'T FUNCTION QUITE SO SPLENDIDLY --
-- AND ALL IT TAKES IS THAT ONE MISTAKE.
POWERFUL. ATHLETIC. YOUNG.
THERE YOU ARE!
HE'S THERE IN UNDER TEN SECONDS. M.P.H. -- THE ACCELERATION ACE. HERO OF MOTOR CITY.
GLANGLANGLANGLANGLA

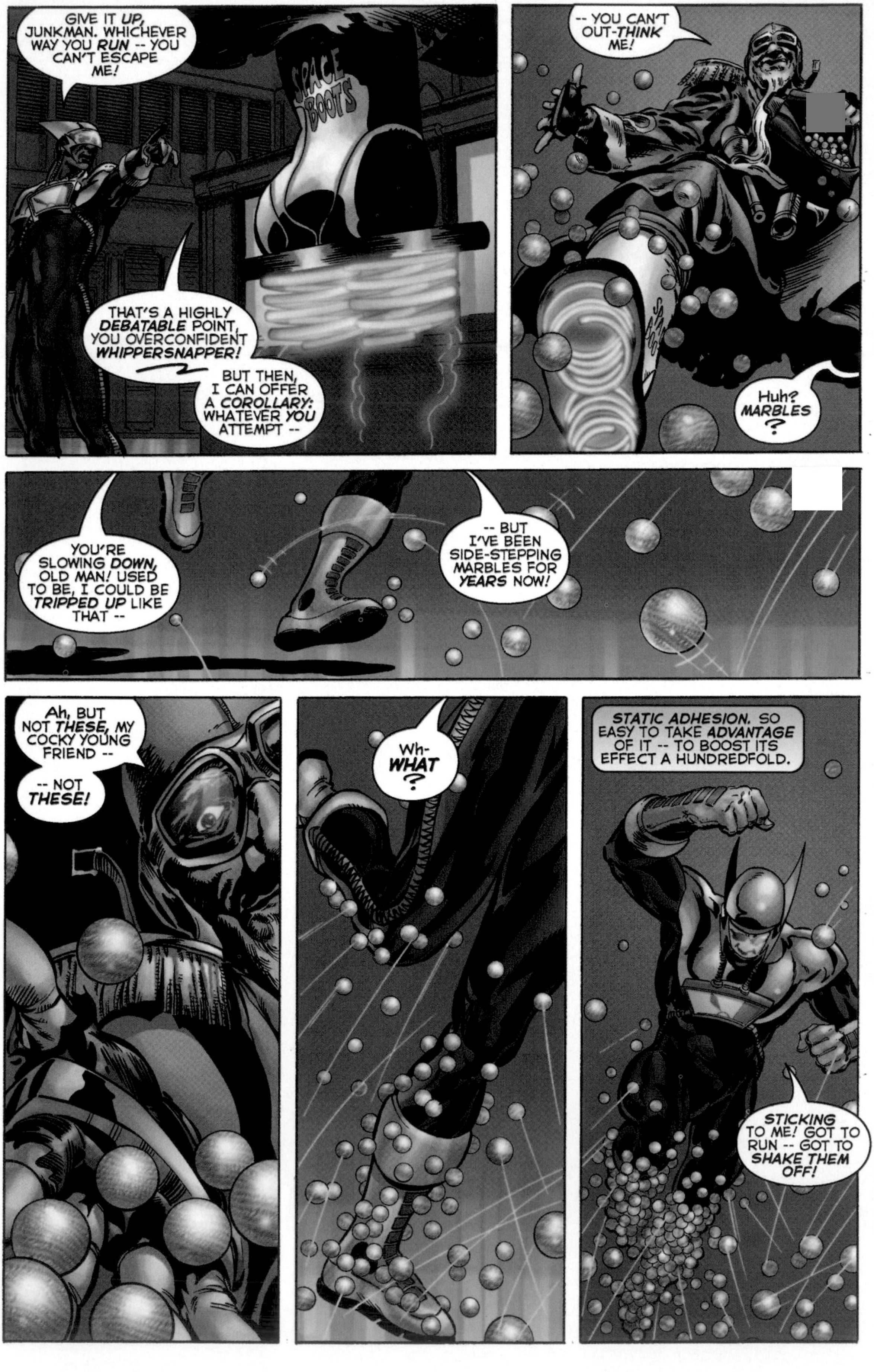
GIVE IT UP, JUNKMAN. WHICHEVER WAY YOU RUN -- YOU CAN'T ESCAPE ME!
THAT'S A HIGHLY DEBATABLE POINT, YOU OVERCONFIDENT WHIPPERSNAPPER!
BUT THEN, I CAN OFFER A COROLLARY: WHATEVER YOU ATTEMPT --
SPACE BOOTS
-- YOU CAN'T OUT-THINK ME!
Huh? MARBLES?
YOU'RE SLOWING DOWN, OLD MAN! USED TO BE, I COULD BE TRIPPED UP LIKE THAT --
-- BUT I'VE BEEN SIDE-STEPPING MARBLES FOR YEARS NOW!
Ah, BUT NOT THESE, MY COCKY YOUNG FRIEND --
-- NOT THESE!
Wh- WHAT?
STATIC ADHESION. SO EASY TO TAKE ADVANTAGE OF IT -- TO BOOST ITS EFFECT A HUNDREDFOLD.
STICKING TO ME! GOT TO RUN -- GOT TO SHAKE THEM OFF!

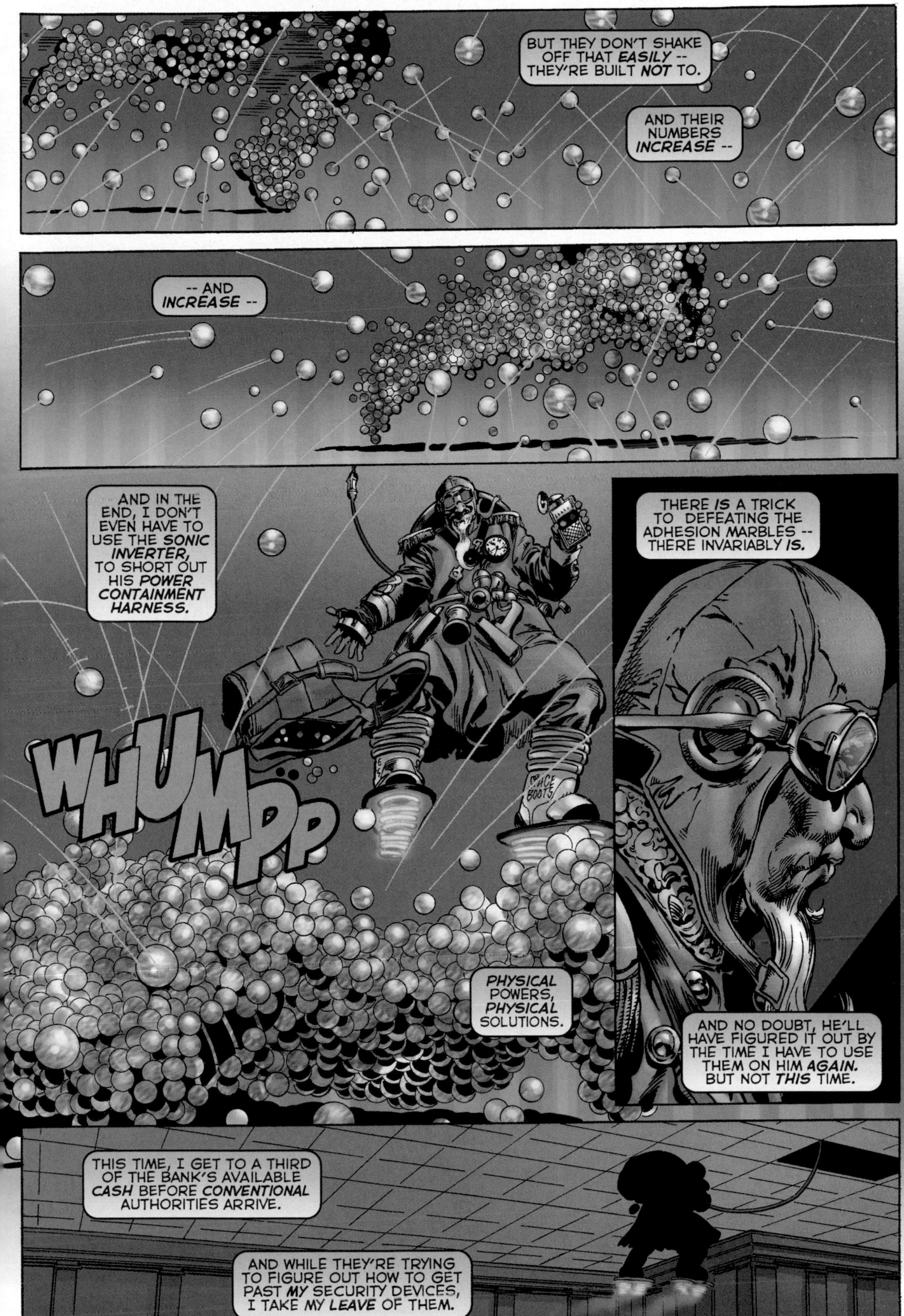
BUT THEY DON'T SHAKE OFF THAT EASILY -- THEY'RE BUILT NOT TO.
AND THEIR NUMBERS INCREASE --
-- AND INCREASE --
AND IN THE END, I DON'T EVEN HAVE TO USE THE SONIC INVERTER, TO SHORT OUT HIS POWER CONTAINMENT HARNESS.
WHUMPP
PHYSICAL POWERS, PHYSICAL SOLUTIONS.
THERE IS A TRICK TO DEFEATING THE ADHESION MARBLES -- THERE INVARIABLY IS.
AND NO DOUBT, HE'LL HAVE FIGURED IT OUT BY THE TIME I HAVE TO USE THEM ON HIM AGAIN. BUT NOT THIS TIME.
THIS TIME, I GET TO A THIRD OF THE BANK'S AVAILABLE CASH BEFORE CONVENTIONAL AUTHORITIES ARRIVE.
AND WHILE THEY'RE TRYING TO FIGURE OUT HOW TO GET PAST MY SECURITY DEVICES, I TAKE MY LEAVE OF THEM.

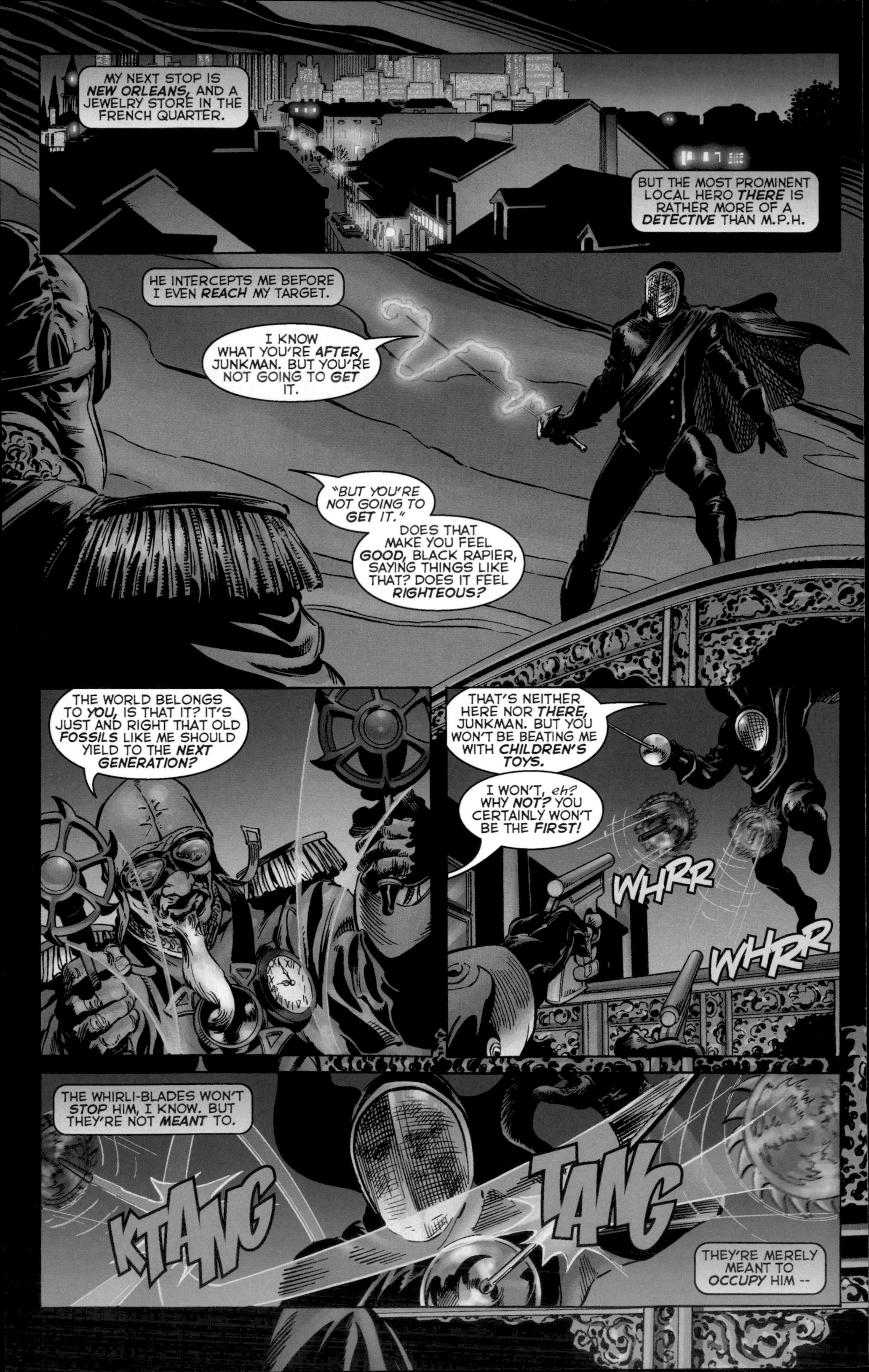
MY NEXT STOP IS NEW ORLEANS, AND A JEWELRY STORE IN THE FRENCH QUARTER.
BUT THE MOST PROMINENT LOCAL HERO THERE IS RATHER MORE OF A DETECTIVE THAN M.P.H.
HE INTERCEPTS ME BEFORE I EVEN REACH MY TARGET.
I KNOW WHAT YOU'RE AFTER, JUNKMAN. BUT YOU'RE NOT GOING TO GET IT.
"BUT YOU'RE NOT GOING TO GET IT." DOES THAT MAKE YOU FEEL GOOD, BLACK RAPIER, SAYING THINGS LIKE THAT? DOES IT FEEL RIGHTEOUS?
THE WORLD BELONGS TO YOU, IS THAT IT? IT'S JUST AND RIGHT THAT OLD FOSSILS LIKE ME SHOULD YIELD TO THE NEXT GENERATION?
THAT'S NEITHER HERE NOR THERE, JUNKMAN. BUT YOU WON'T BE BEATING ME WITH CHILDREN'S TOYS.
I WON'T, eh? WHY NOT? YOU CERTAINLY WON'T BE THE FIRST!
WHRR
WHRR
THE WHIRLI-BLADES WON'T STOP HIM, I KNOW. BUT THEY'RE NOT MEANT TO.
KTANG
TANG
THEY'RE MERELY MEANT TO OCCUPY HIM --

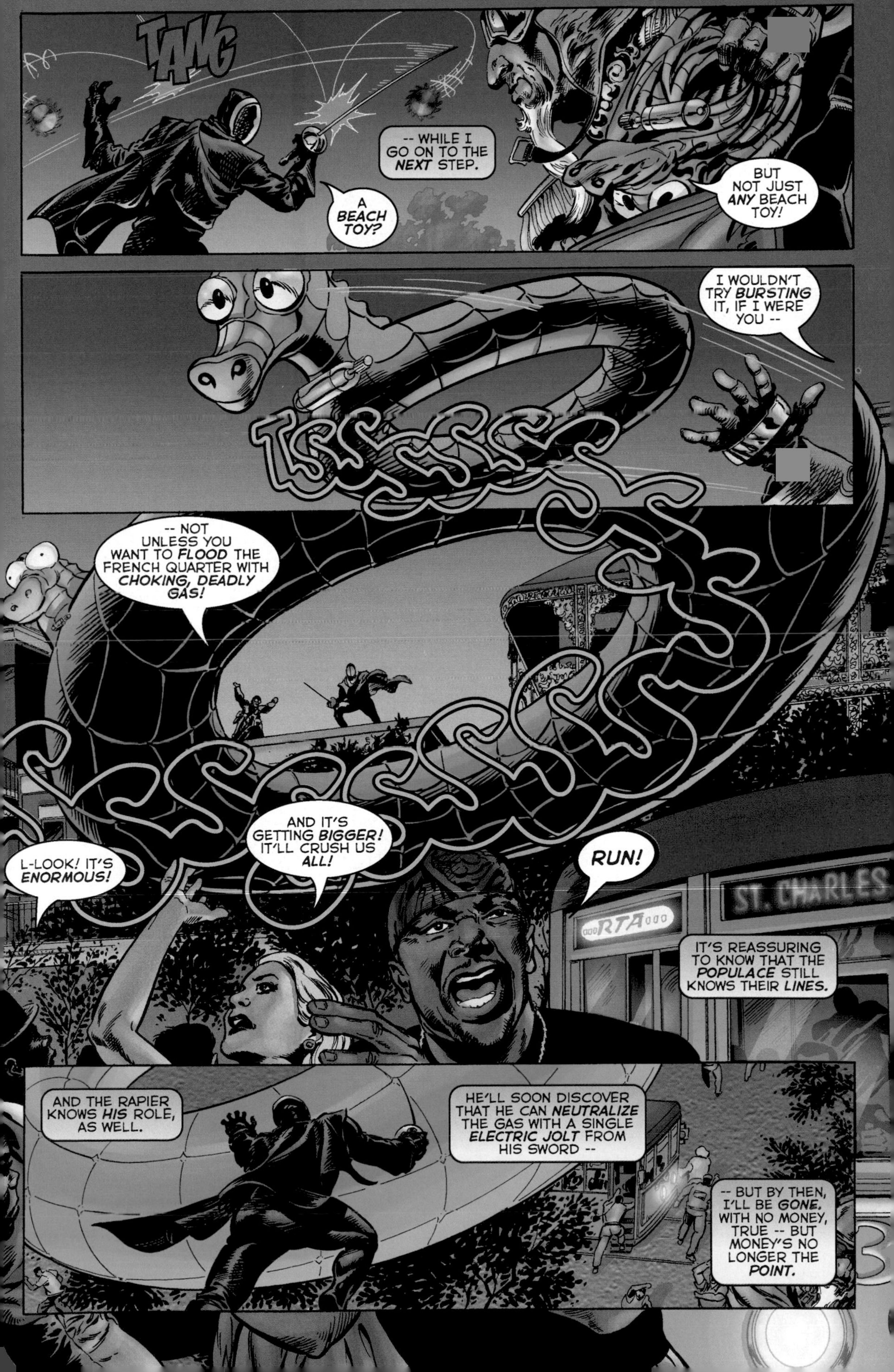
TANG
-- WHILE I GO ON TO THE NEXT STEP.
A BEACH TOY?
BUT NOT JUST ANY BEACH TOY!
I WOULDN'T TRY BURSTING IT, IF I WERE YOU --
-- NOT UNLESS YOU WANT TO FLOOD THE FRENCH QUARTER WITH CHOKING, DEADLY GAS!
L-LOOK! IT'S ENORMOUS!
AND IT'S GETTING BIGGER! IT'LL CRUSH US ALL!
RUN!
ST. CHARLES
RTA
IT'S REASSURING TO KNOW THAT THE POPULACE STILL KNOWS THEIR LINES.
AND THE RAPIER KNOWS HIS ROLE, AS WELL.
HE'LL SOON DISCOVER THAT HE CAN NEUTRALIZE THE GAS WITH A SINGLE ELECTRIC JOLT FROM HIS SWORD --
-- BUT BY THEN, I'LL BE GONE, WITH NO MONEY, TRUE -- BUT MONEY'S NO LONGER THE POINT.

THEY'RE STARTING TO PUT IT *TOGETHER.*

-- DARING TWILIGHT BATTLE BETWEEN THE BLACK RAPIER AND THE NOTORIOUS *JUNKMAN* --

THEY'VE REALIZED THE FIRST BANK WAS *MINE* -- AND THEY'RE EVEN STARTING TO FIGURE OUT HOW I *DID* IT.

Detroit Free Press EXTRA EDITION

EXTRA EDITION

JUNKMAN ON CRIME SPREE?

'M.O. in AstroBank Heist is His As Well' S Authori

Wary Banks Up Security

Oldster Eludes Speedster

Astro City **Current**

The **AstroBank Robbery:** First Clues Come to Ligh

• The Man Whe Counts the Crime
• America's Most Powerful Schoo Elementary Schoo A Report Card
• urant R

I CAN JUST PICTURE YOUNG *YUMIKO -- YOU SEE,* SENHOR, THEY WILL *CATCH HIM NOW...*

FOR THAT MATTER, THE MEDIA IS GIVING THE CREDIT TO THE *HEROES* --

-- EXCLUSIVE CAMCORDER FOOTAGE OF THE *NEW ORLEANS STANDOFF,* AND THE *BLACK RAPIER'S HEROIC* --

-- M.P.H. INTERRUPTS BANK ROBBERY, BLACK RAPIER THWARTS SUPERVILLAIN, YADDITA YADDITA *YADDITA.*

WHO'LL STOP THE JUNKMAN'S CRIME SPREE? *THAT'S* THEIR TACK. BUT THEY'LL *LEARN.* THEY'LL *ALL* LEARN.

THAT'S WHAT I'M *DOING* HERE, FIVE MONTHS TO THE DAY FROM WHEN I *LEFT.* THAT'S WHY I'M *BACK* IN *ASTRO CITY.*

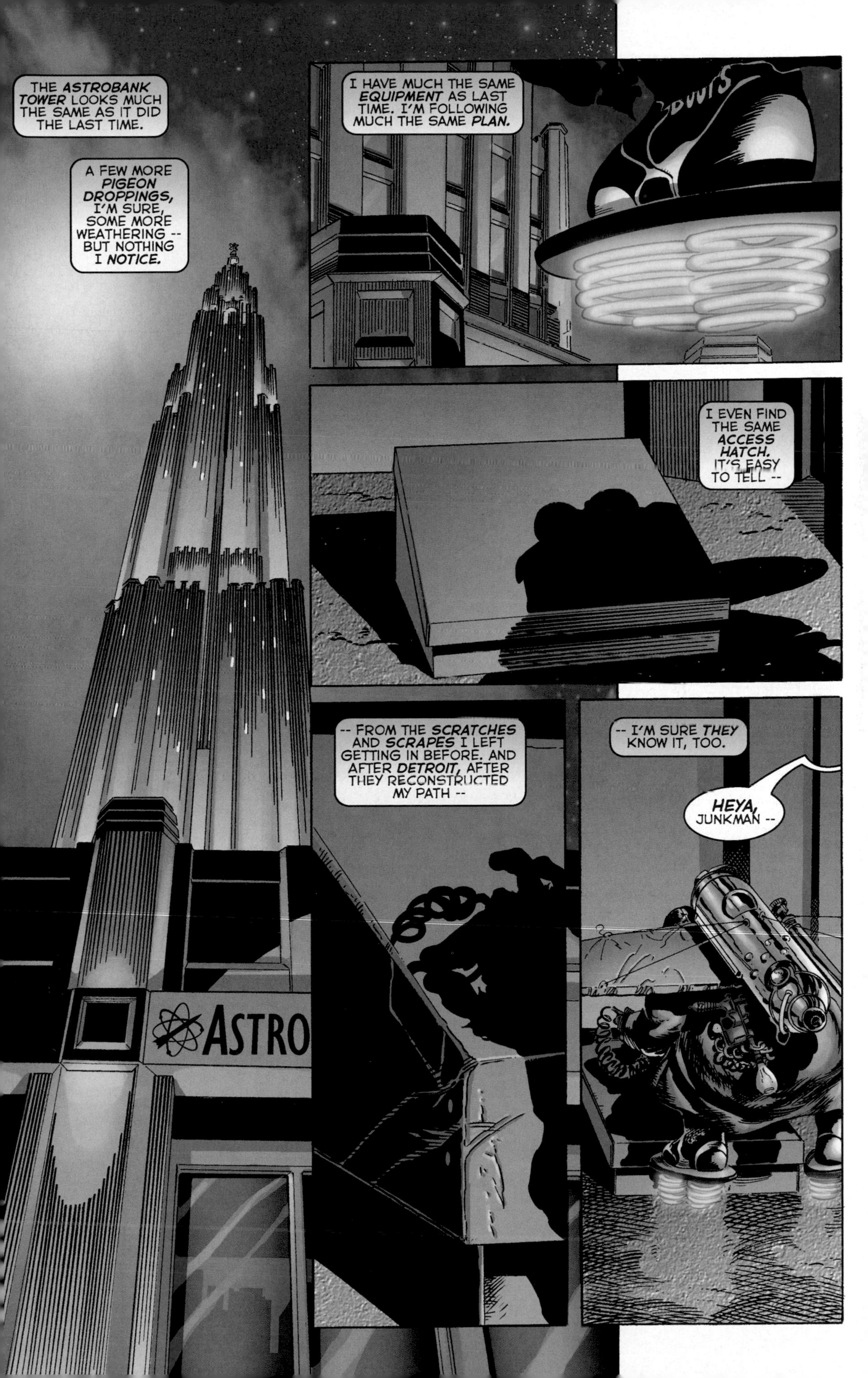
THE ASTROBANK TOWER LOOKS MUCH THE SAME AS IT DID THE LAST TIME.
A FEW MORE PIGEON DROPPINGS, I'M SURE, SOME MORE WEATHERING -- BUT NOTHING I NOTICE.
ASTRO
I HAVE MUCH THE SAME EQUIPMENT AS LAST TIME. I'M FOLLOWING MUCH THE SAME PLAN.
BOOTS
I EVEN FIND THE SAME ACCESS HATCH. IT'S EASY TO TELL --
-- FROM THE SCRATCHES AND SCRAPES I LEFT GETTING IN BEFORE. AND AFTER DETROIT, AFTER THEY RECONSTRUCTED MY PATH --
-- I'M SURE THEY KNOW IT, TOO.
HEYA, JUNKMAN --

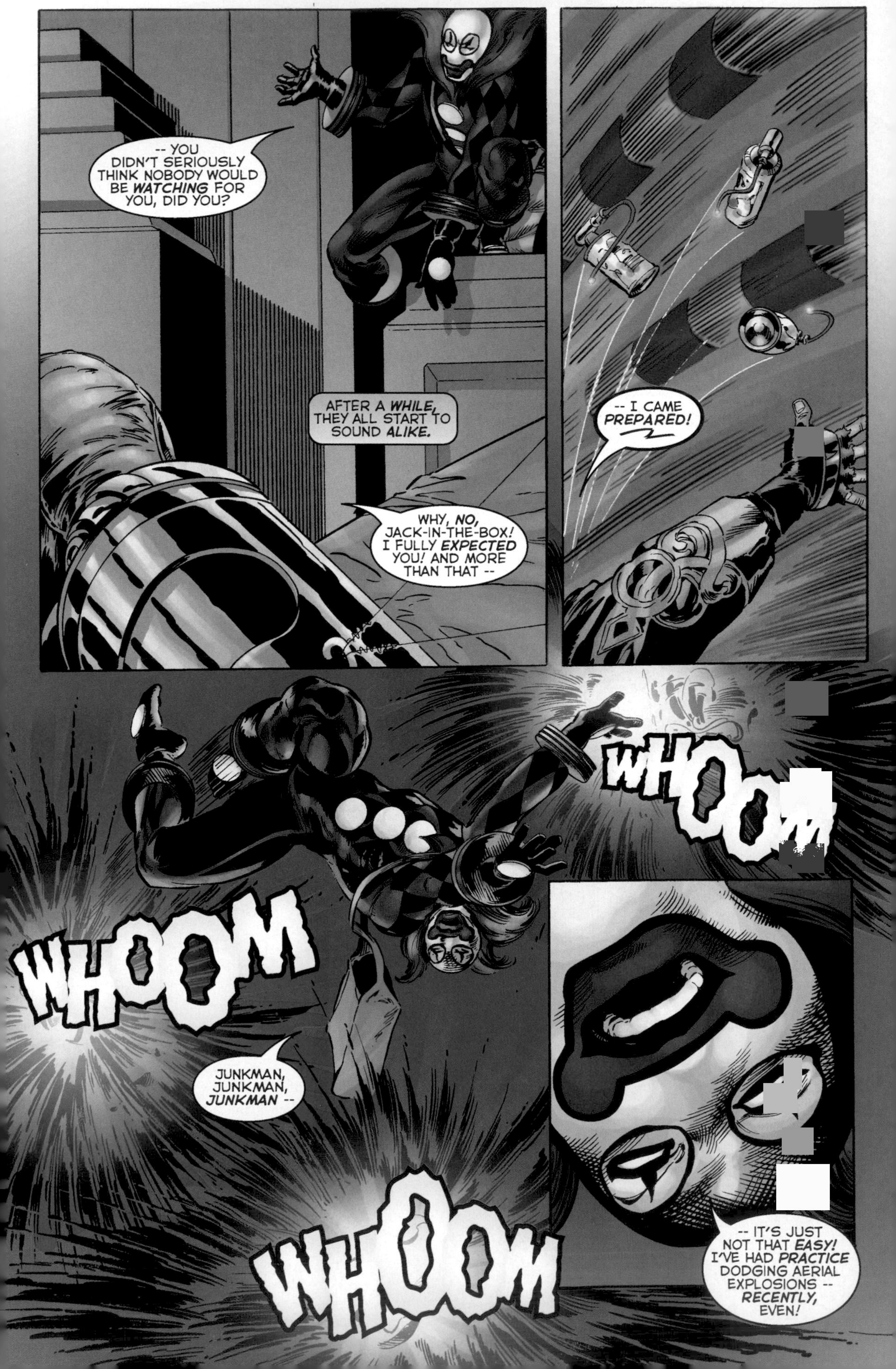
-- YOU DIDN'T SERIOUSLY THINK NOBODY WOULD BE WATCHING FOR YOU, DID YOU?
AFTER A WHILE, THEY ALL START TO SOUND ALIKE.
WHY, NO, JACK-IN-THE-BOX! I FULLY EXPECTED YOU! AND MORE THAN THAT --
-- I CAME PREPARED!
WHOOM
WHOOM
JUNKMAN, JUNKMAN, JUNKMAN --
WHOOM
-- IT'S JUST NOT THAT EASY! I'VE HAD PRACTICE DODGING AERIAL EXPLOSIONS -- RECENTLY, EVEN!

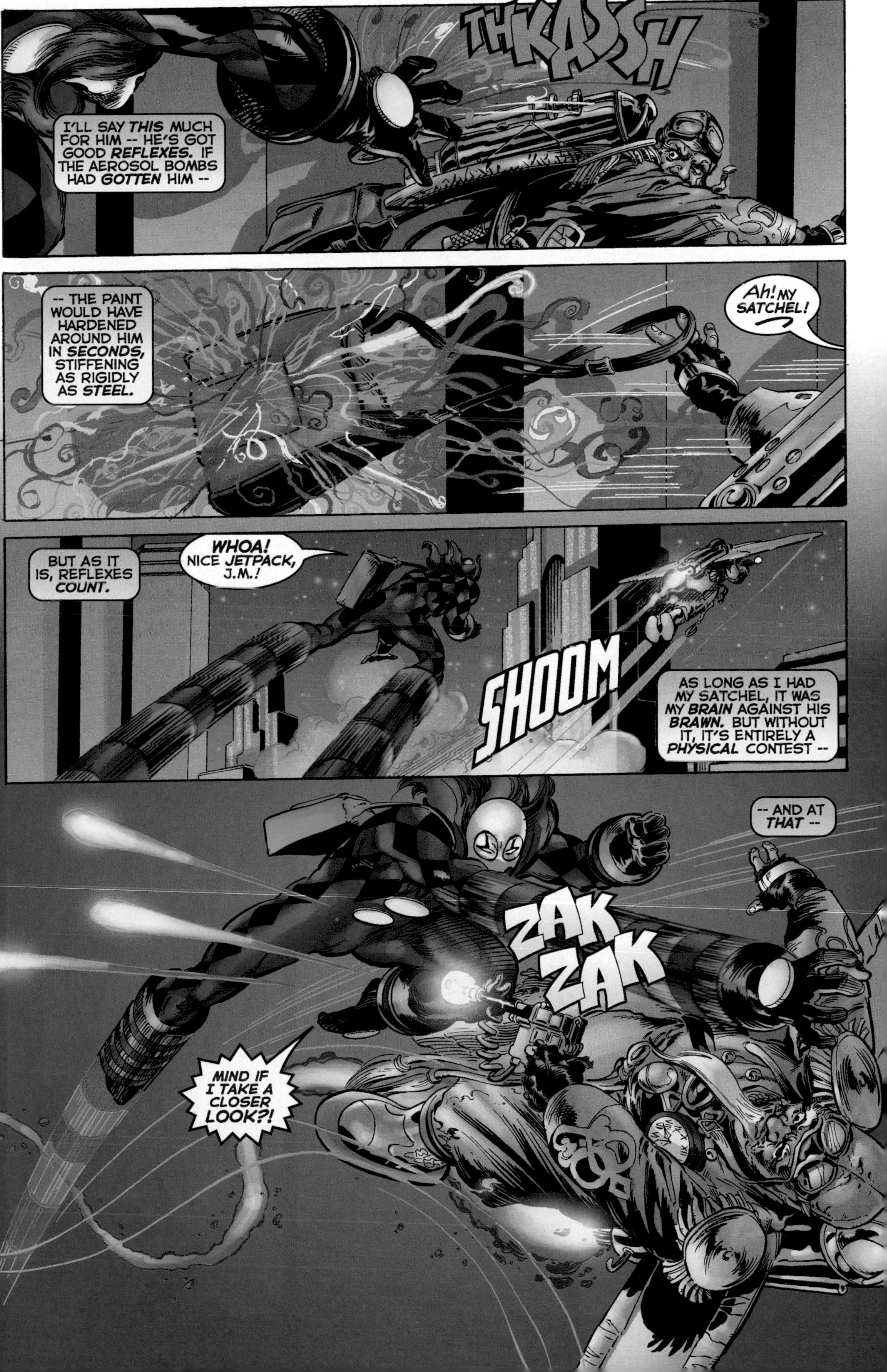
THKASSH
I'LL SAY THIS MUCH FOR HIM -- HE'S GOT GOOD REFLEXES. IF THE AEROSOL BOMBS HAD GOTTEN HIM --
-- THE PAINT WOULD HAVE HARDENED AROUND HIM IN SECONDS, STIFFENING AS RIGIDLY AS STEEL.
Ah! MY SATCHEL!
BUT AS IT IS, REFLEXES COUNT.
WHOA! NICE JETPACK, J.M.!
SHOOM
AS LONG AS I HAD MY SATCHEL, IT WAS MY BRAIN AGAINST HIS BRAWN. BUT WITHOUT IT, IT'S ENTIRELY A PHYSICAL CONTEST --
-- AND AT THAT --
ZAK ZAK
MIND IF I TAKE A CLOSER LOOK?!

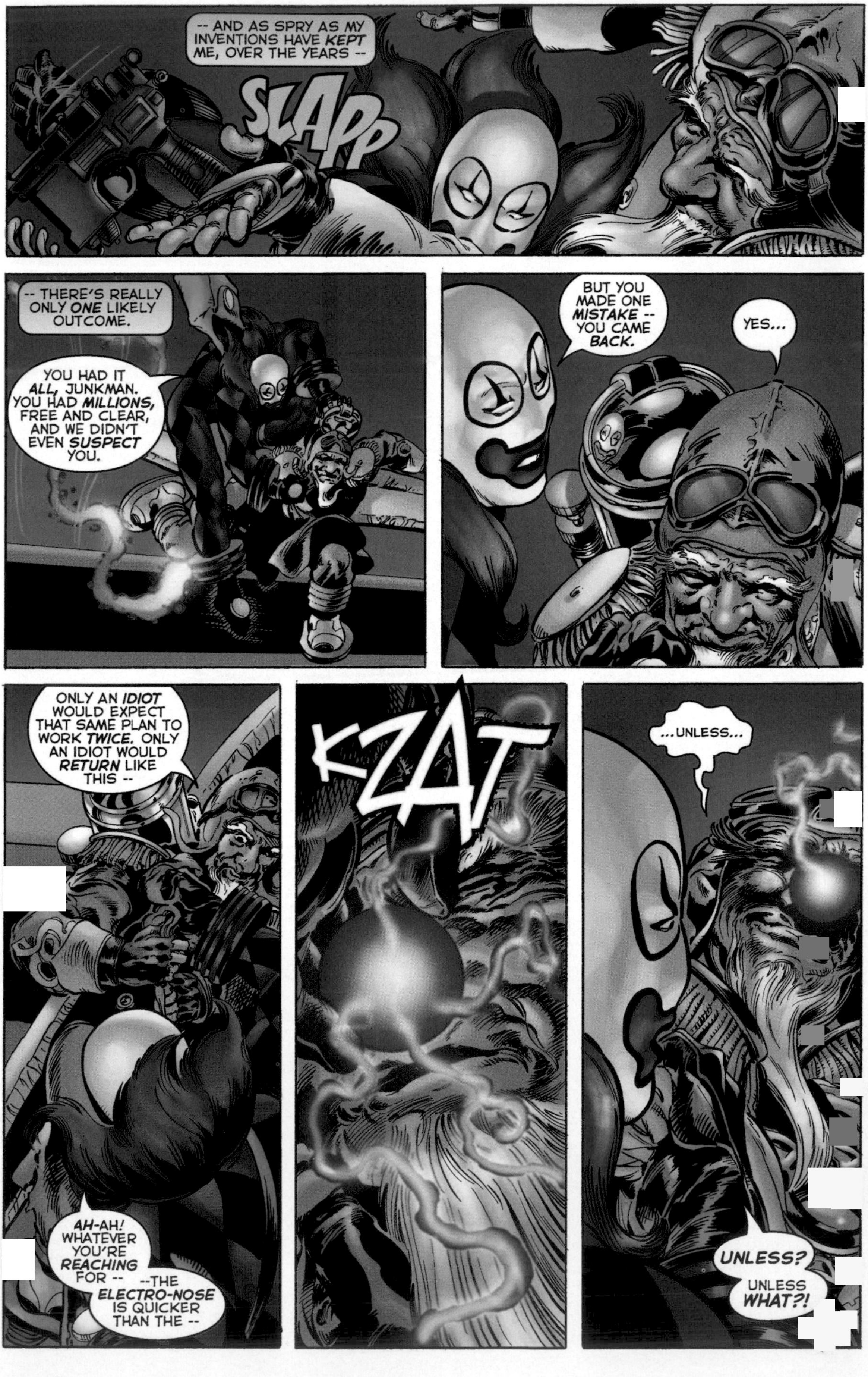
-- AND AS SPRY AS MY INVENTIONS HAVE KEPT ME, OVER THE YEARS --
SLAPP
-- THERE'S REALLY ONLY ONE LIKELY OUTCOME.
YOU HAD IT ALL, JUNKMAN. YOU HAD MILLIONS, FREE AND CLEAR, AND WE DIDN'T EVEN SUSPECT YOU.
BUT YOU MADE ONE MISTAKE -- YOU CAME BACK.
YES...
ONLY AN IDIOT WOULD EXPECT THAT SAME PLAN TO WORK TWICE. ONLY AN IDIOT WOULD RETURN LIKE THIS --
AH-AH! WHATEVER YOU'RE REACHING FOR --
--THE ELECTRO-NOSE IS QUICKER THAN THE --
KZAT
...UNLESS...
UNLESS? UNLESS WHAT?!

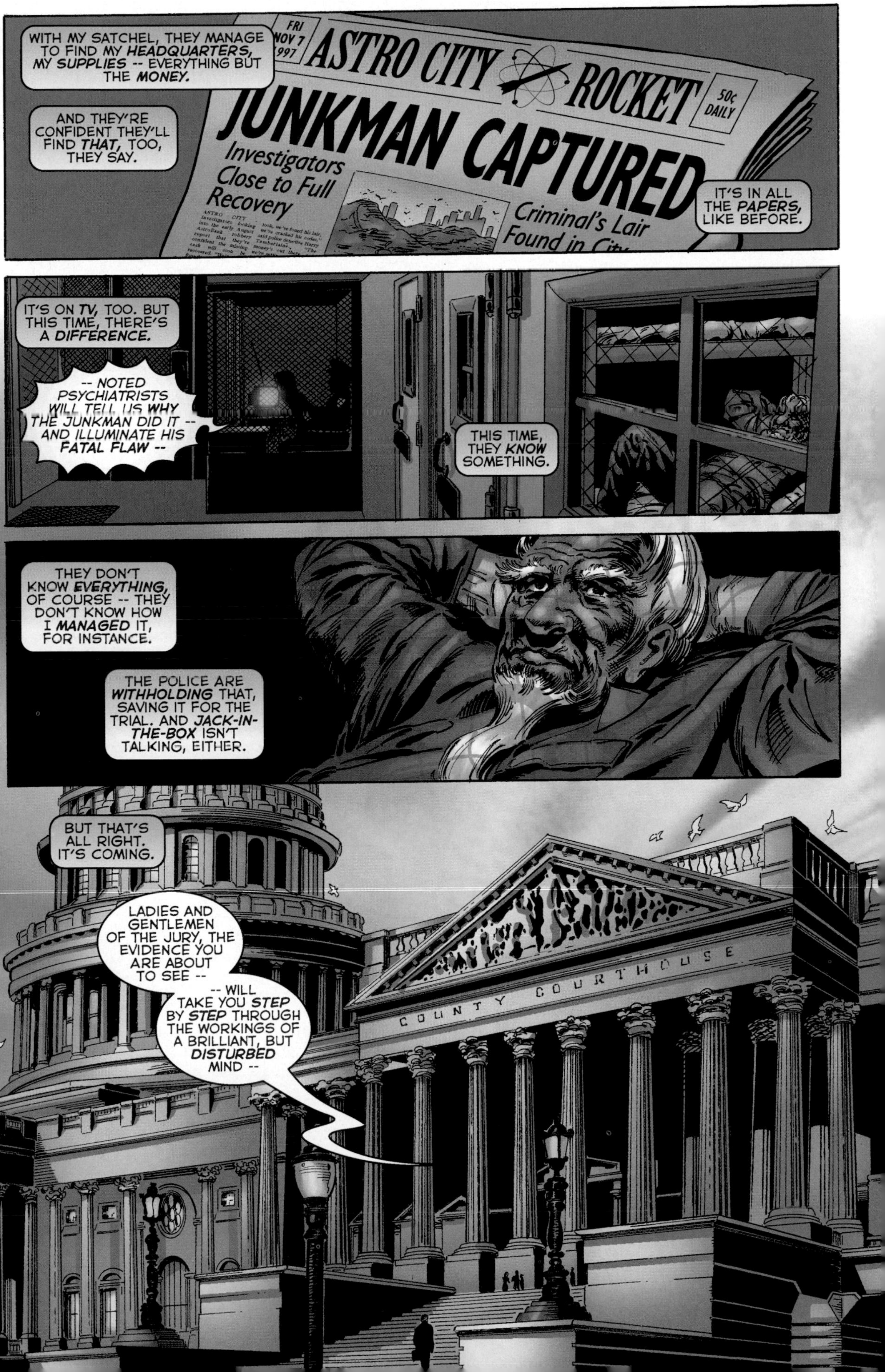
WITH MY SATCHEL, THEY MANAGE TO FIND MY HEADQUARTERS, MY SUPPLIES -- EVERYTHING BUT THE MONEY.
AND THEY'RE CONFIDENT THEY'LL FIND THAT, TOO, THEY SAY.
FRI NOV 7 1997
ASTRO CITY ROCKET
50¢ DAILY
JUNKMAN CAPTURED
Investigators Close to Full Recovery
Criminal's Lair Found in City
IT'S IN ALL THE PAPERS, LIKE BEFORE.
IT'S ON TV, TOO. BUT THIS TIME, THERE'S A DIFFERENCE.
-- NOTED PSYCHIATRISTS WILL TELL US WHY THE JUNKMAN DID IT -- AND ILLUMINATE HIS FATAL FLAW --
THIS TIME, THEY KNOW SOMETHING.
THEY DON'T KNOW EVERYTHING, OF COURSE -- THEY DON'T KNOW HOW I MANAGED IT, FOR INSTANCE.
THE POLICE ARE WITHHOLDING THAT, SAVING IT FOR THE TRIAL. AND JACK-IN-THE-BOX ISN'T TALKING, EITHER.
BUT THAT'S ALL RIGHT. IT'S COMING.
LADIES AND GENTLEMEN OF THE JURY, THE EVIDENCE YOU ARE ABOUT TO SEE --
-- WILL TAKE YOU STEP BY STEP THROUGH THE WORKINGS OF A BRILLIANT, BUT DISTURBED MIND --
COUNTY COURTHOUSE

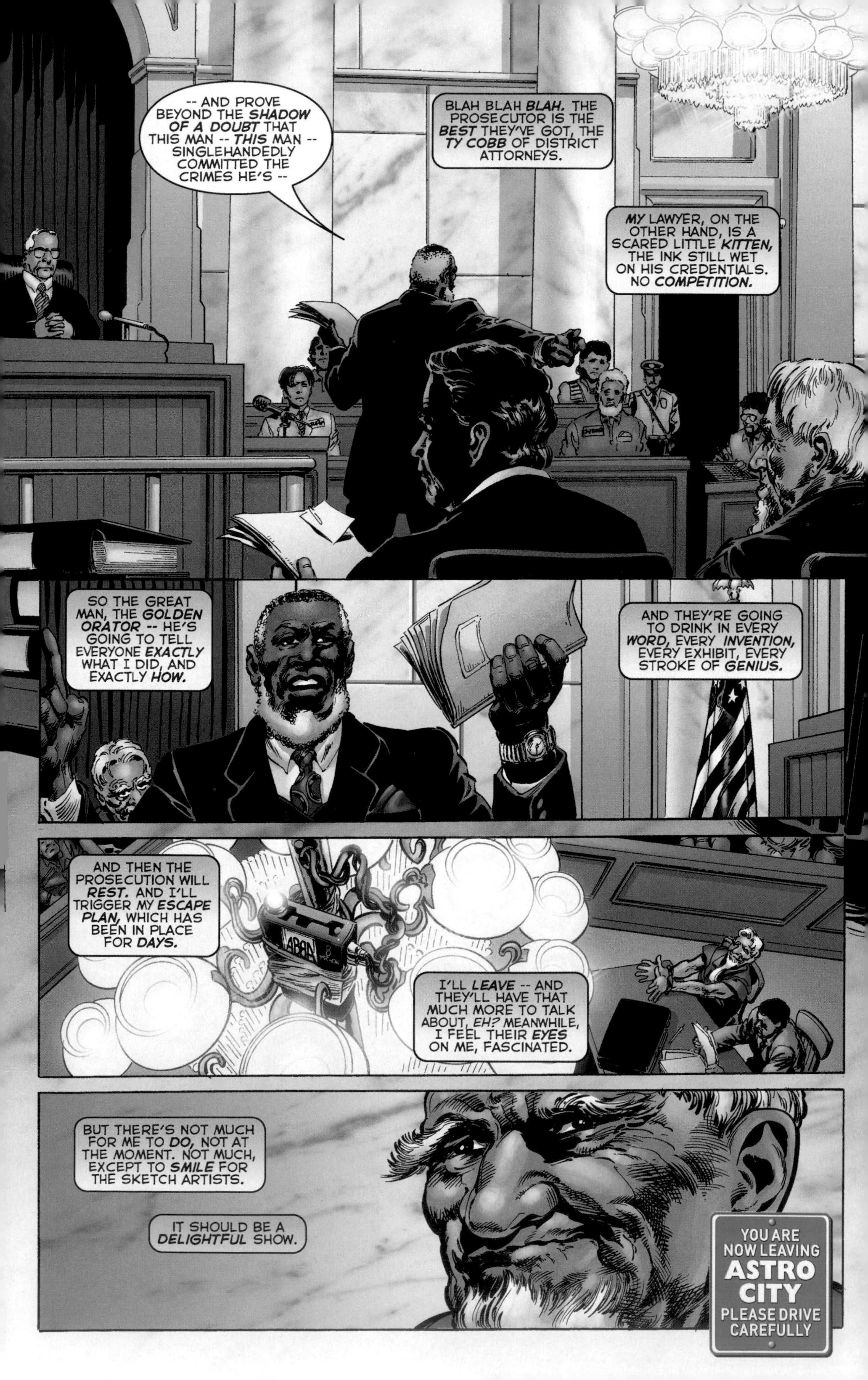
-- AND PROVE BEYOND THE SHADOW OF A DOUBT THAT THIS MAN -- THIS MAN -- SINGLEHANDEDLY COMMITTED THE CRIMES HE'S --
BLAH BLAH BLAH. THE PROSECUTOR IS THE BEST THEY'VE GOT, THE TY COBB OF DISTRICT ATTORNEYS.
MY LAWYER, ON THE OTHER HAND, IS A SCARED LITTLE KITTEN, THE INK STILL WET ON HIS CREDENTIALS. NO COMPETITION.
SO THE GREAT MAN, THE GOLDEN ORATOR -- HE'S GOING TO TELL EVERYONE EXACTLY WHAT I DID, AND EXACTLY HOW.
AND THEY'RE GOING TO DRINK IN EVERY WORD, EVERY INVENTION, EVERY EXHIBIT, EVERY STROKE OF GENIUS.
AND THEN THE PROSECUTION WILL REST. AND I'LL TRIGGER MY ESCAPE PLAN, WHICH HAS BEEN IN PLACE FOR DAYS.
I'LL LEAVE -- AND THEY'LL HAVE THAT MUCH MORE TO TALK ABOUT, EH? MEANWHILE, I FEEL THEIR EYES ON ME, FASCINATED.
BUT THERE'S NOT MUCH FOR ME TO DO, NOT AT THE MOMENT. NOT MUCH, EXCEPT TO SMILE FOR THE SKETCH ARTISTS.
IT SHOULD BE A DELIGHTFUL SHOW.
YOU ARE NOW LEAVING ASTRO CITY PLEASE DRIVE CAREFULLY

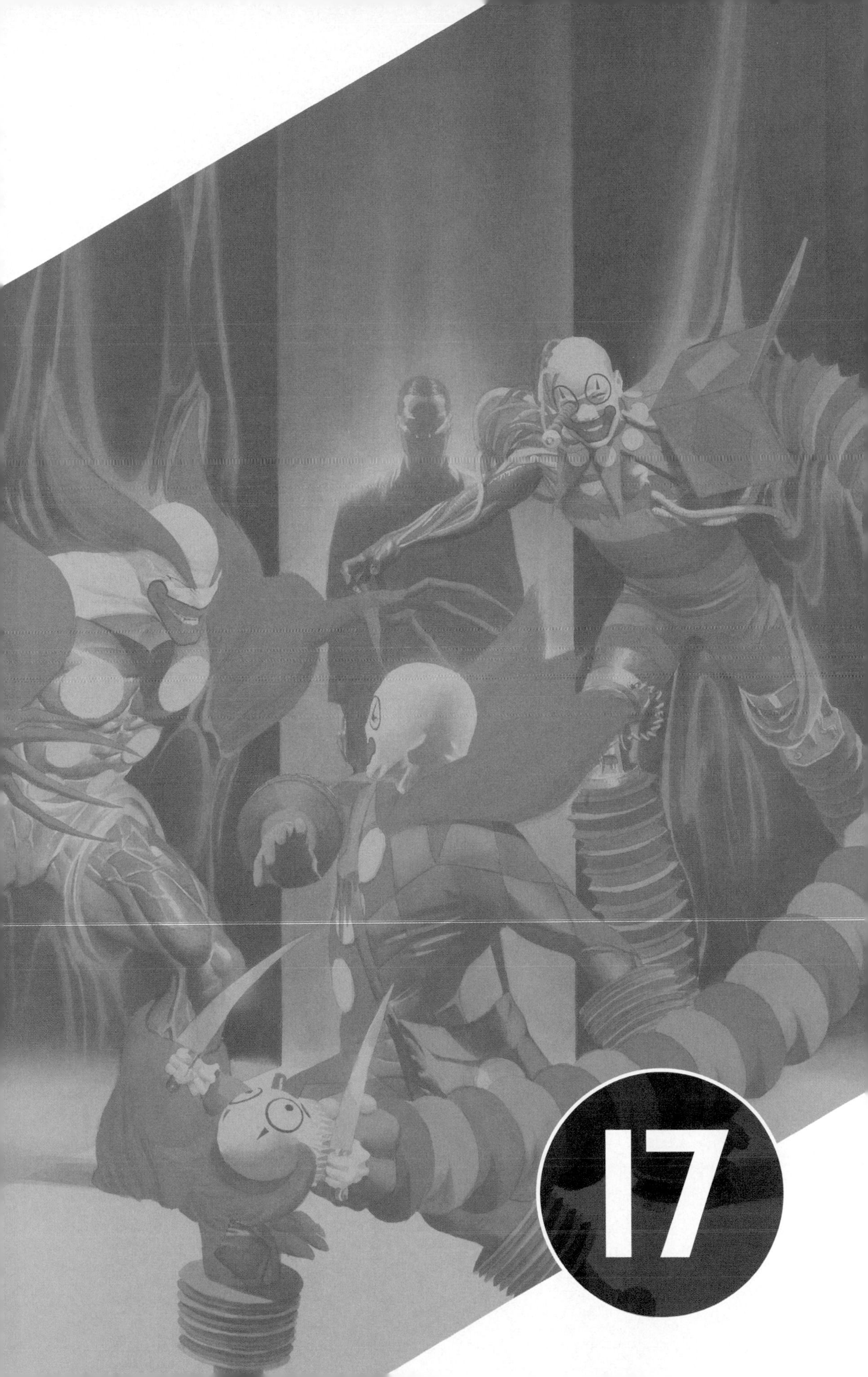

17

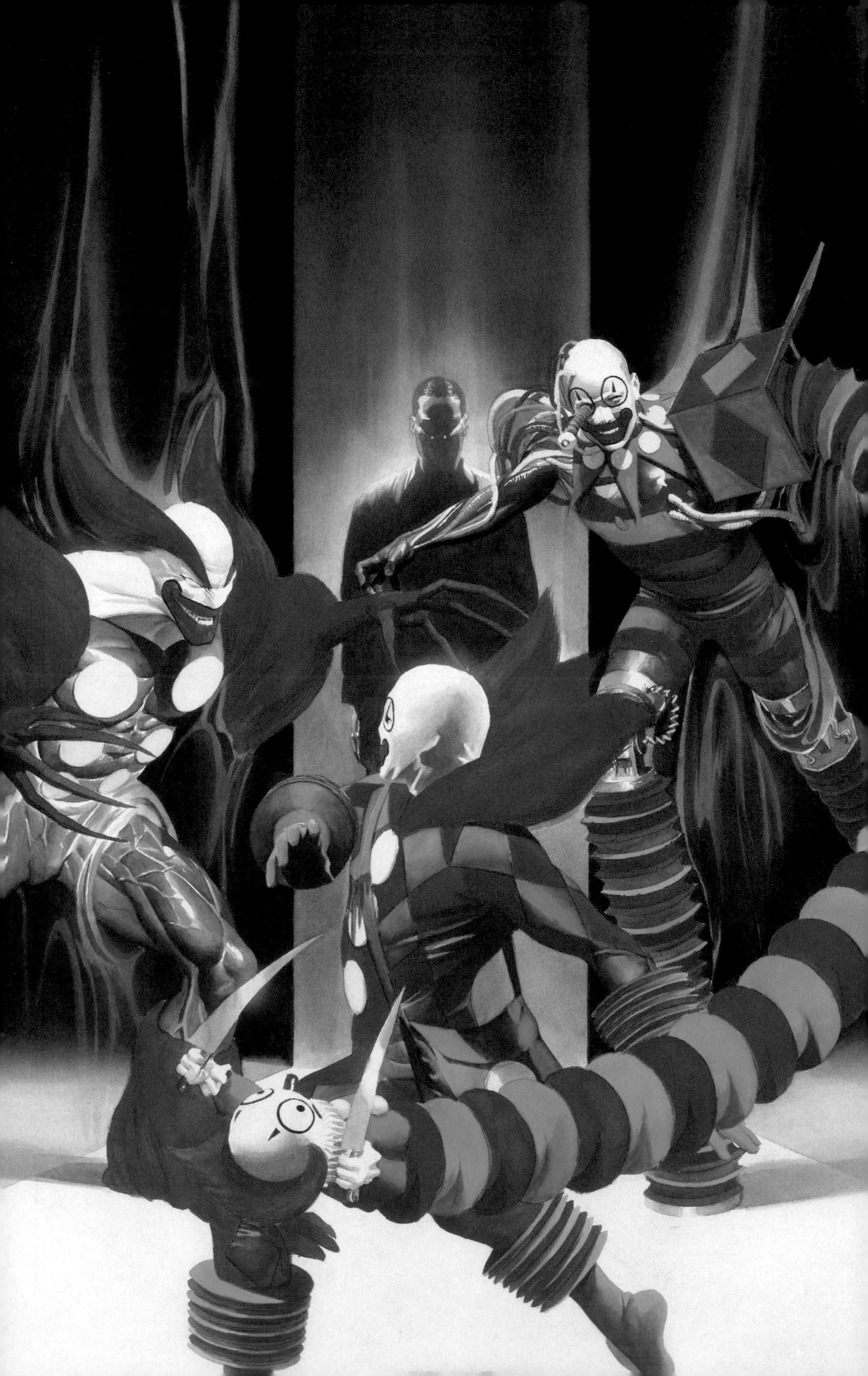

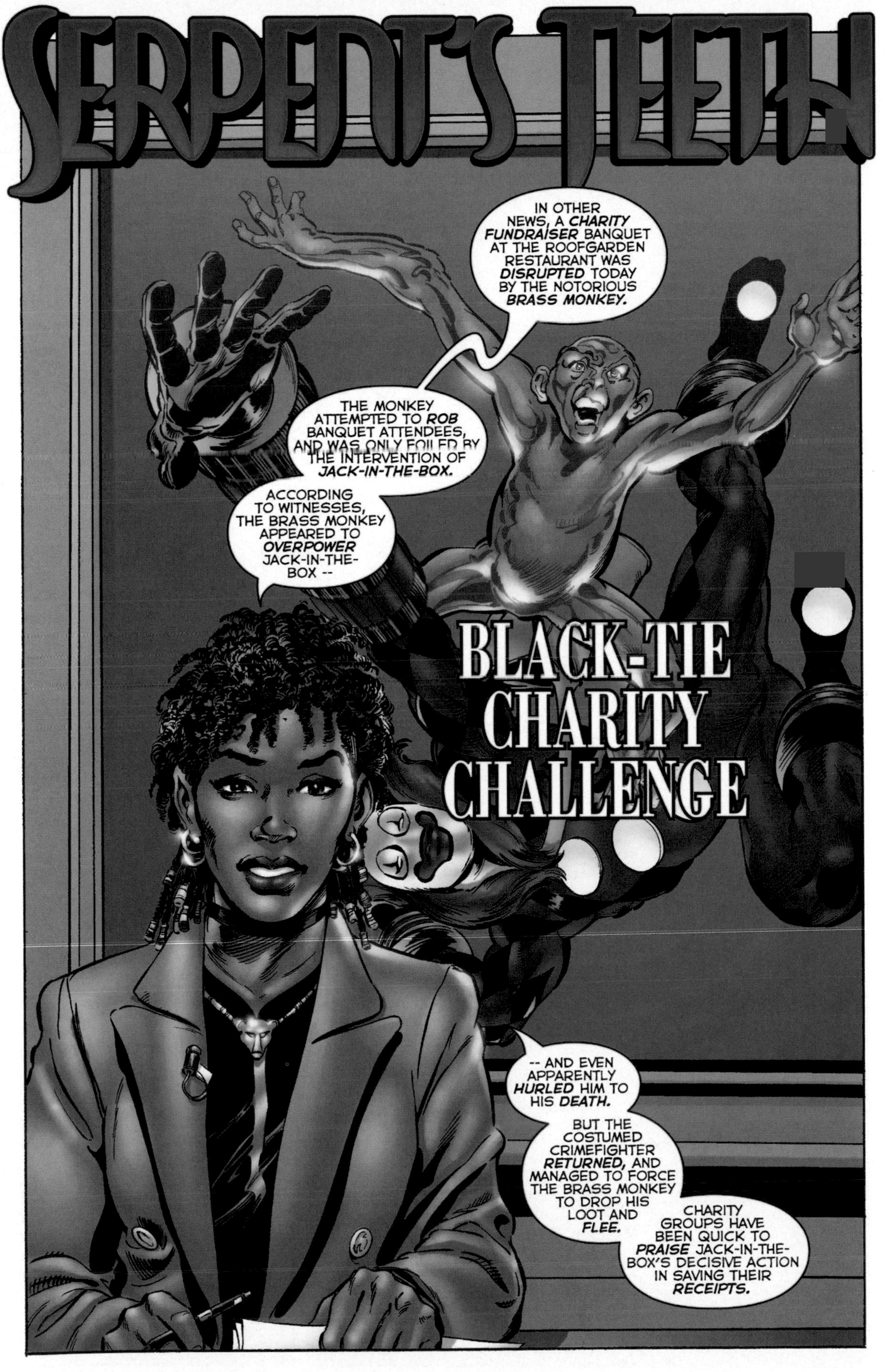
SERPENT'S TEETH
IN OTHER NEWS, A CHARITY FUNDRAISER BANQUET AT THE ROOFGARDEN RESTAURANT WAS DISRUPTED TODAY BY THE NOTORIOUS BRASS MONKEY.
THE MONKEY ATTEMPTED TO ROB BANQUET ATTENDEES, AND WAS ONLY FOILED BY THE INTERVENTION OF JACK-IN-THE-BOX.
ACCORDING TO WITNESSES, THE BRASS MONKEY APPEARED TO OVERPOWER JACK-IN-THE-BOX --
BLACK-TIE CHARITY CHALLENGE
-- AND EVEN APPARENTLY HURLED HIM TO HIS DEATH.
BUT THE COSTUMED CRIMEFIGHTER RETURNED, AND MANAGED TO FORCE THE BRASS MONKEY TO DROP HIS LOOT AND FLEE.
CHARITY GROUPS HAVE BEEN QUICK TO PRAISE JACK-IN-THE-BOX'S DECISIVE ACTION IN SAVING THEIR RECEIPTS.

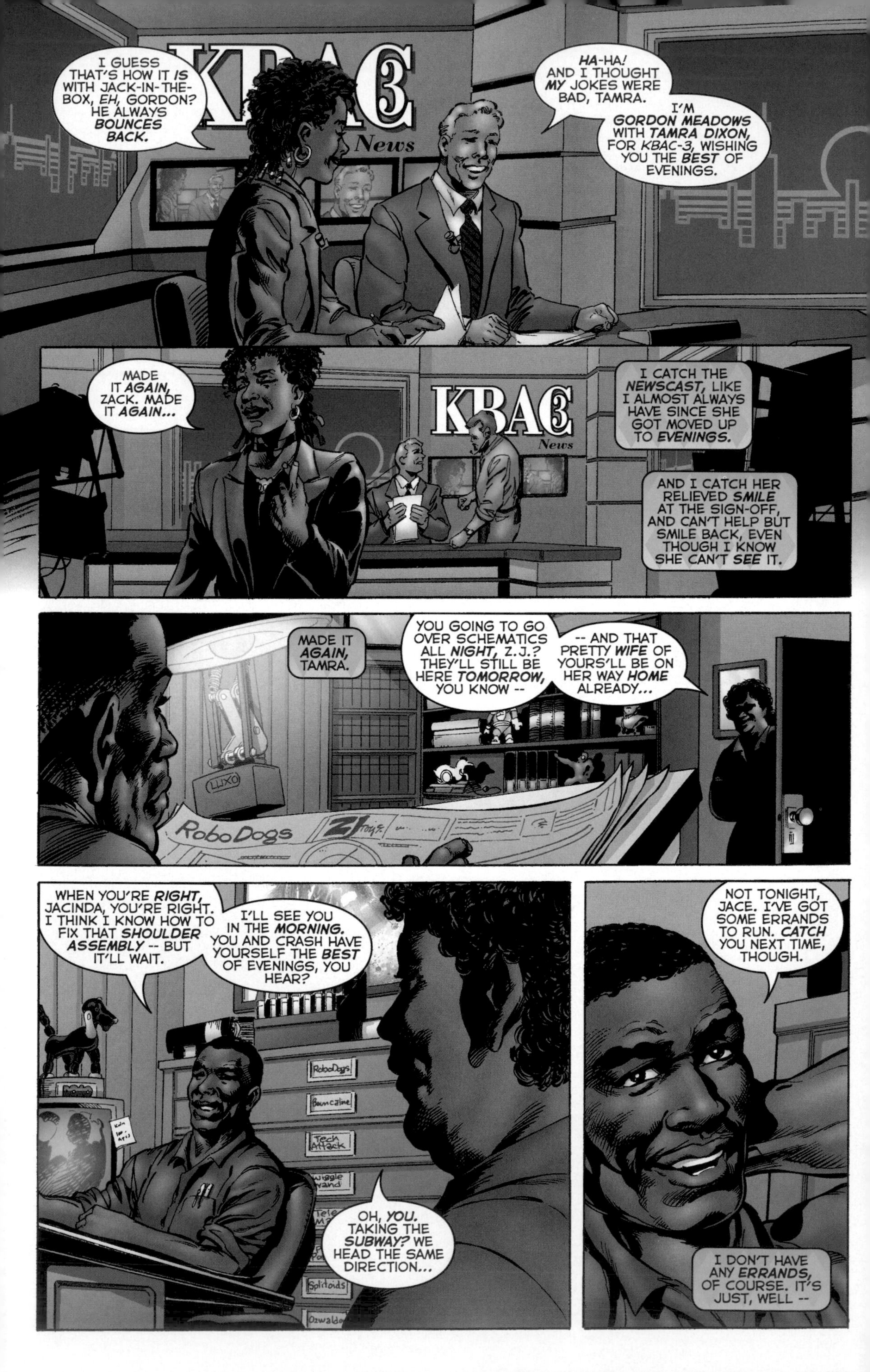
KBAC 3 News
I GUESS THAT'S HOW IT *IS* WITH JACK-IN-THE-BOX, *EH,* GORDON? HE ALWAYS *BOUNCES BACK.*
HA-HA! AND I THOUGHT *MY* JOKES WERE BAD, TAMRA.
I'M *GORDON MEADOWS* WITH *TAMRA DIXON,* FOR *KBAC-3,* WISHING YOU THE *BEST* OF EVENINGS.
MADE IT *AGAIN,* ZACK. MADE IT *AGAIN...*
KBAC 3 News
I CATCH THE *NEWSCAST,* LIKE I ALMOST ALWAYS HAVE SINCE SHE GOT MOVED UP TO *EVENINGS.*
AND I CATCH HER RELIEVED *SMILE* AT THE SIGN-OFF, AND CAN'T HELP BUT SMILE BACK, EVEN THOUGH I KNOW SHE *CAN'T SEE* IT.
MADE IT *AGAIN,* TAMRA.
YOU GOING TO GO OVER SCHEMATICS ALL *NIGHT,* Z.J.? THEY'LL STILL BE HERE *TOMORROW,* YOU KNOW --
-- AND THAT PRETTY *WIFE* OF YOURS'LL BE ON HER WAY *HOME* ALREADY...
LUXO
RoboDogs
WHEN YOU'RE *RIGHT,* JACINDA, YOU'RE RIGHT. I THINK I KNOW HOW TO FIX THAT *SHOULDER ASSEMBLY* -- BUT IT'LL WAIT.
I'LL SEE YOU IN THE *MORNING.* YOU AND CRASH HAVE YOURSELF THE *BEST* OF EVENINGS, YOU HEAR?
RoboDogs
Bouncaine
Tech Attack
OH, *YOU.* TAKING THE *SUBWAY?* WE HEAD THE SAME DIRECTION...
Splitoids
NOT TONIGHT, JACE. I'VE GOT SOME ERRANDS TO RUN. *CATCH* YOU NEXT TIME, THOUGH.
I DON'T HAVE ANY *ERRANDS,* OF COURSE. IT'S JUST, WELL --

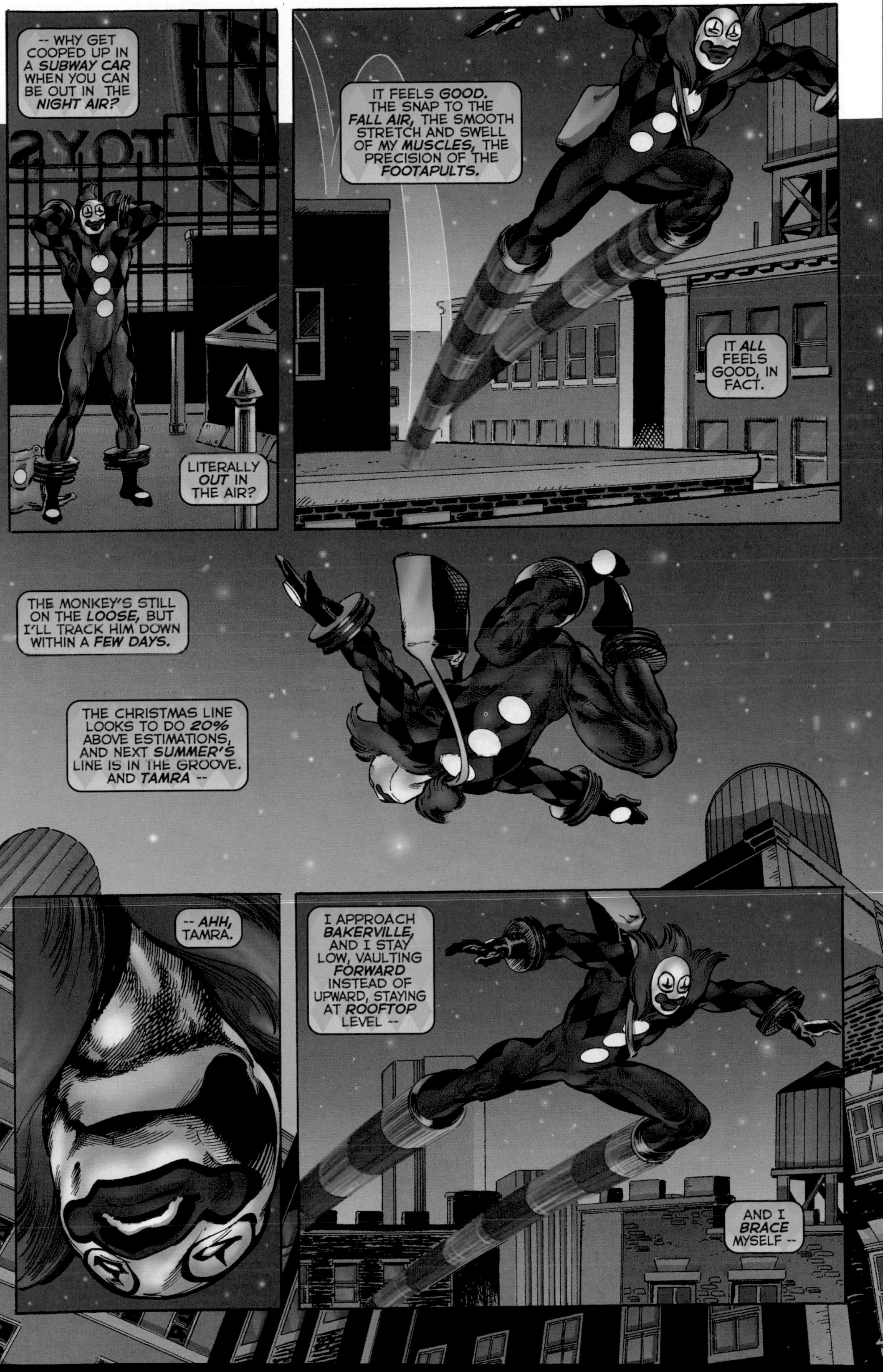
-- WHY GET COOPED UP IN A SUBWAY CAR WHEN YOU CAN BE OUT IN THE NIGHT AIR?
TOYS
LITERALLY OUT IN THE AIR?
IT FEELS GOOD. THE SNAP TO THE FALL AIR, THE SMOOTH STRETCH AND SWELL OF MY MUSCLES, THE PRECISION OF THE FOOTAPULTS.
IT ALL FEELS GOOD, IN FACT.
THE MONKEY'S STILL ON THE LOOSE, BUT I'LL TRACK HIM DOWN WITHIN A FEW DAYS.
THE CHRISTMAS LINE LOOKS TO DO 20% ABOVE ESTIMATIONS, AND NEXT SUMMER'S LINE IS IN THE GROOVE. AND TAMRA --
-- AHH, TAMRA.
I APPROACH BAKERVILLE, AND I STAY LOW, VAULTING FORWARD INSTEAD OF UPWARD, STAYING AT ROOFTOP LEVEL --
AND I BRACE MYSELF --

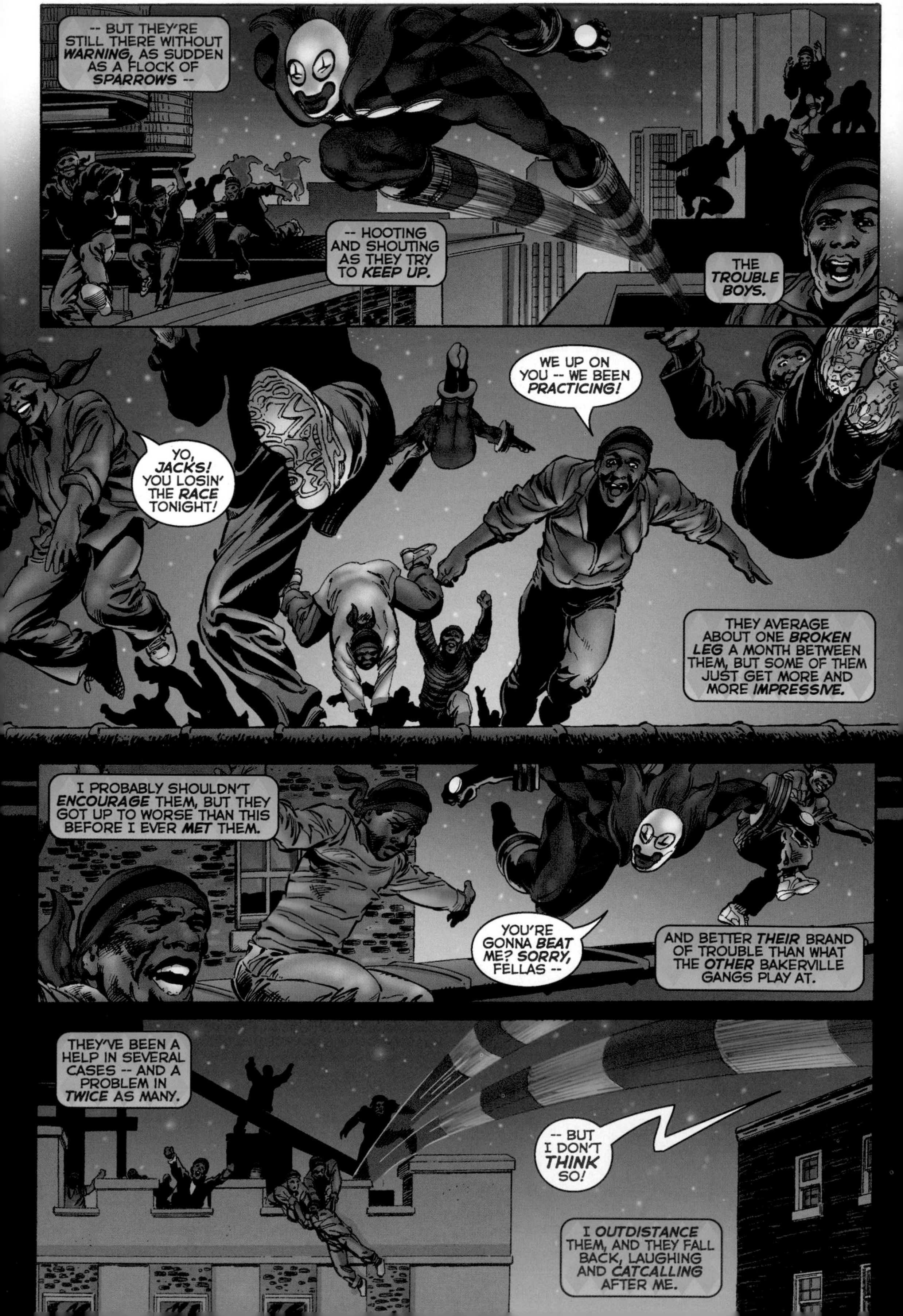
-- BUT THEY'RE STILL THERE WITHOUT WARNING, AS SUDDEN AS A FLOCK OF SPARROWS --
-- HOOTING AND SHOUTING AS THEY TRY TO KEEP UP.
THE TROUBLE BOYS.
YO, JACKS! YOU LOSIN' THE RACE TONIGHT!
WE UP ON YOU -- WE BEEN PRACTICING!
THEY AVERAGE ABOUT ONE BROKEN LEG A MONTH BETWEEN THEM, BUT SOME OF THEM JUST GET MORE AND MORE IMPRESSIVE.
I PROBABLY SHOULDN'T ENCOURAGE THEM, BUT THEY GOT UP TO WORSE THAN THIS BEFORE I EVER MET THEM.
YOU'RE GONNA BEAT ME? SORRY, FELLAS --
AND BETTER THEIR BRAND OF TROUBLE THAN WHAT THE OTHER BAKERVILLE GANGS PLAY AT.
THEY'VE BEEN A HELP IN SEVERAL CASES -- AND A PROBLEM IN TWICE AS MANY.
-- BUT I DON'T THINK SO!
I OUTDISTANCE THEM, AND THEY FALL BACK, LAUGHING AND CATCALLING AFTER ME.

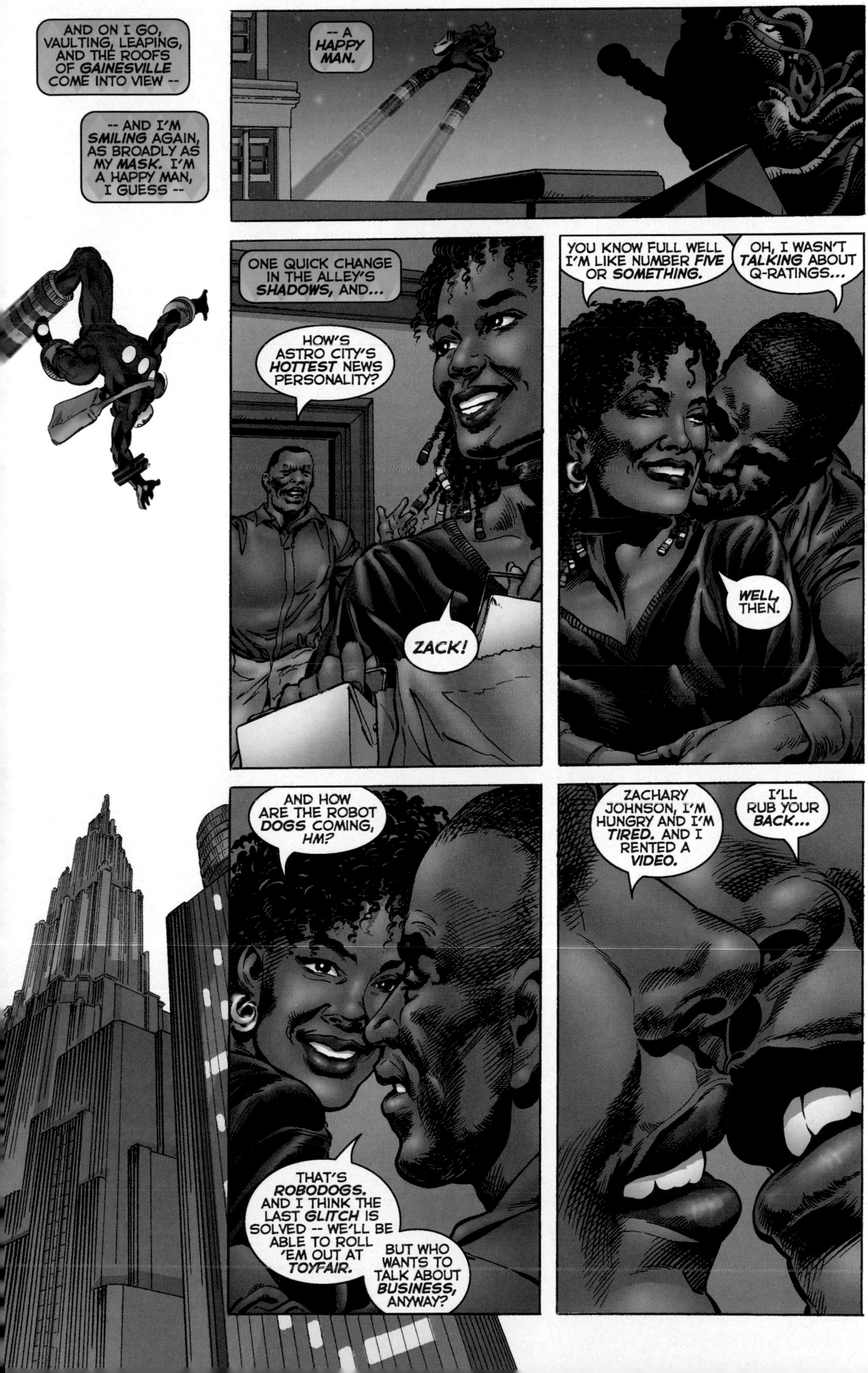
AND ON I GO, VAULTING, LEAPING, AND THE ROOFS OF GAINESVILLE COME INTO VIEW --
-- AND I'M SMILING AGAIN, AS BROADLY AS MY MASK. I'M A HAPPY MAN, I GUESS --
-- A HAPPY MAN.
ONE QUICK CHANGE IN THE ALLEY'S SHADOWS, AND...
HOW'S ASTRO CITY'S HOTTEST NEWS PERSONALITY?
ZACK!
YOU KNOW FULL WELL I'M LIKE NUMBER FIVE OR SOMETHING.
OH, I WASN'T TALKING ABOUT Q-RATINGS...
WELL, THEN.
AND HOW ARE THE ROBOT DOGS COMING, HM?
THAT'S ROBODOGS. AND I THINK THE LAST GLITCH IS SOLVED -- WE'LL BE ABLE TO ROLL 'EM OUT AT TOYFAIR.
BUT WHO WANTS TO TALK ABOUT BUSINESS, ANYWAY?
ZACHARY JOHNSON, I'M HUNGRY AND I'M TIRED. AND I RENTED A VIDEO.
I'LL RUB YOUR BACK...

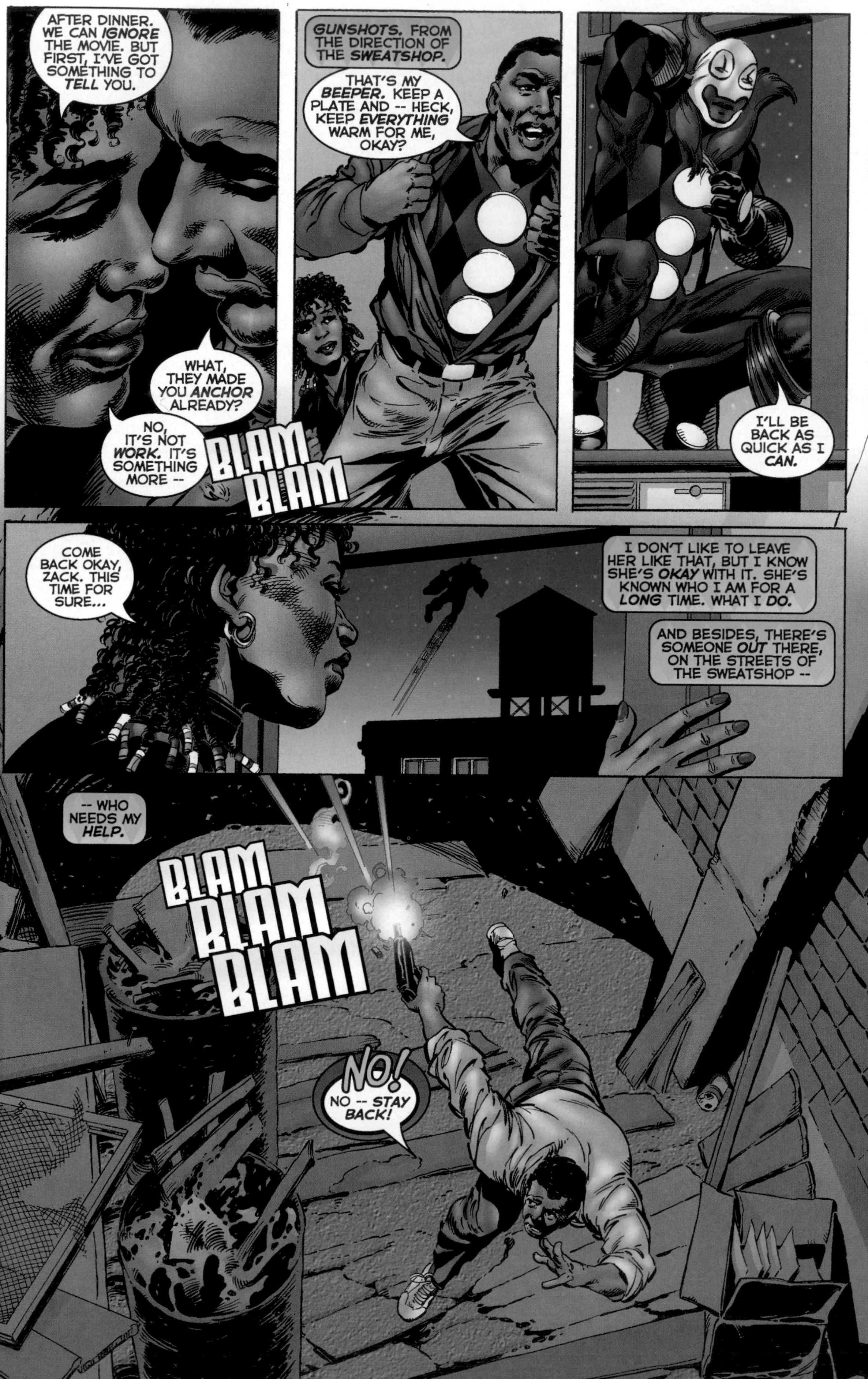

AFTER DINNER. WE CAN IGNORE THE MOVIE. BUT FIRST, I'VE GOT SOMETHING TO TELL YOU.
WHAT, THEY MADE YOU ANCHOR ALREADY?
NO, IT'S NOT WORK. IT'S SOMETHING MORE --
BLAM BLAM
GUNSHOTS. FROM THE DIRECTION OF THE SWEATSHOP.
THAT'S MY BEEPER. KEEP A PLATE AND -- HECK, KEEP EVERYTHING WARM FOR ME, OKAY?
I'LL BE BACK AS QUICK AS I CAN.
COME BACK OKAY, ZACK. THIS TIME FOR SURE...
I DON'T LIKE TO LEAVE HER LIKE THAT, BUT I KNOW SHE'S OKAY WITH IT. SHE'S KNOWN WHO I AM FOR A LONG TIME. WHAT I DO.
AND BESIDES, THERE'S SOMEONE OUT THERE, ON THE STREETS OF THE SWEATSHOP --
-- WHO NEEDS MY HELP.
BLAM BLAM BLAM
NO!
NO -- STAY BACK!

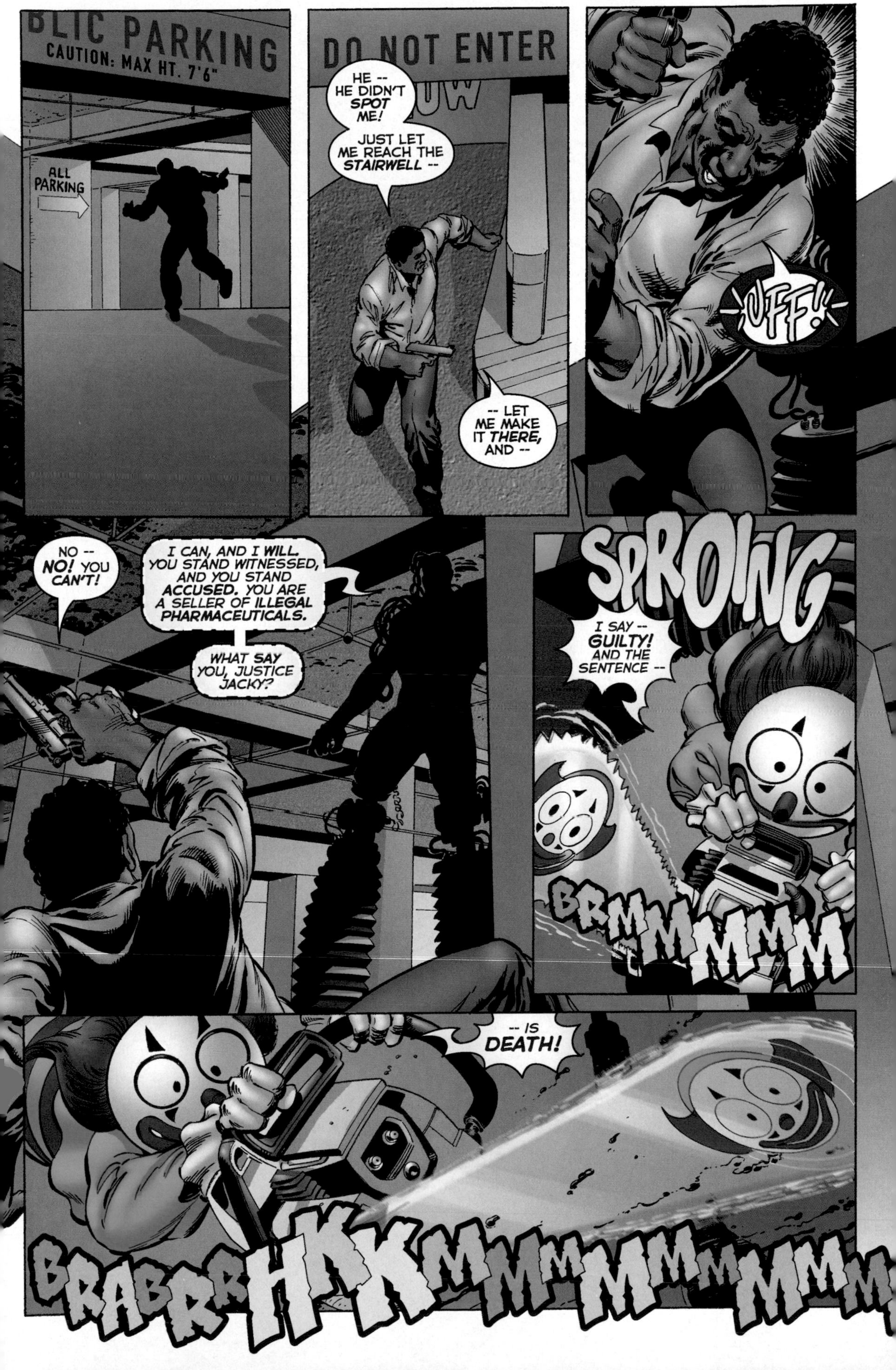
BLIC PARKING
CAUTION: MAX HT. 7'6"
ALL PARKING
DO NOT ENTER
HE -- HE DIDN'T SPOT ME!
JUST LET ME REACH THE STAIRWELL --
-- LET ME MAKE IT THERE, AND --
UFF!
NO -- NO! YOU CAN'T!
I CAN, AND I WILL. YOU STAND WITNESSED, AND YOU STAND ACCUSED. YOU ARE A SELLER OF ILLEGAL PHARMACEUTICALS.
WHAT SAY YOU, JUSTICE JACKY?
SPROING
I SAY -- GUILTY! AND THE SENTENCE --
BRMMMMMM
-- IS DEATH!
BRABRRHKMMMMMMMMMMM

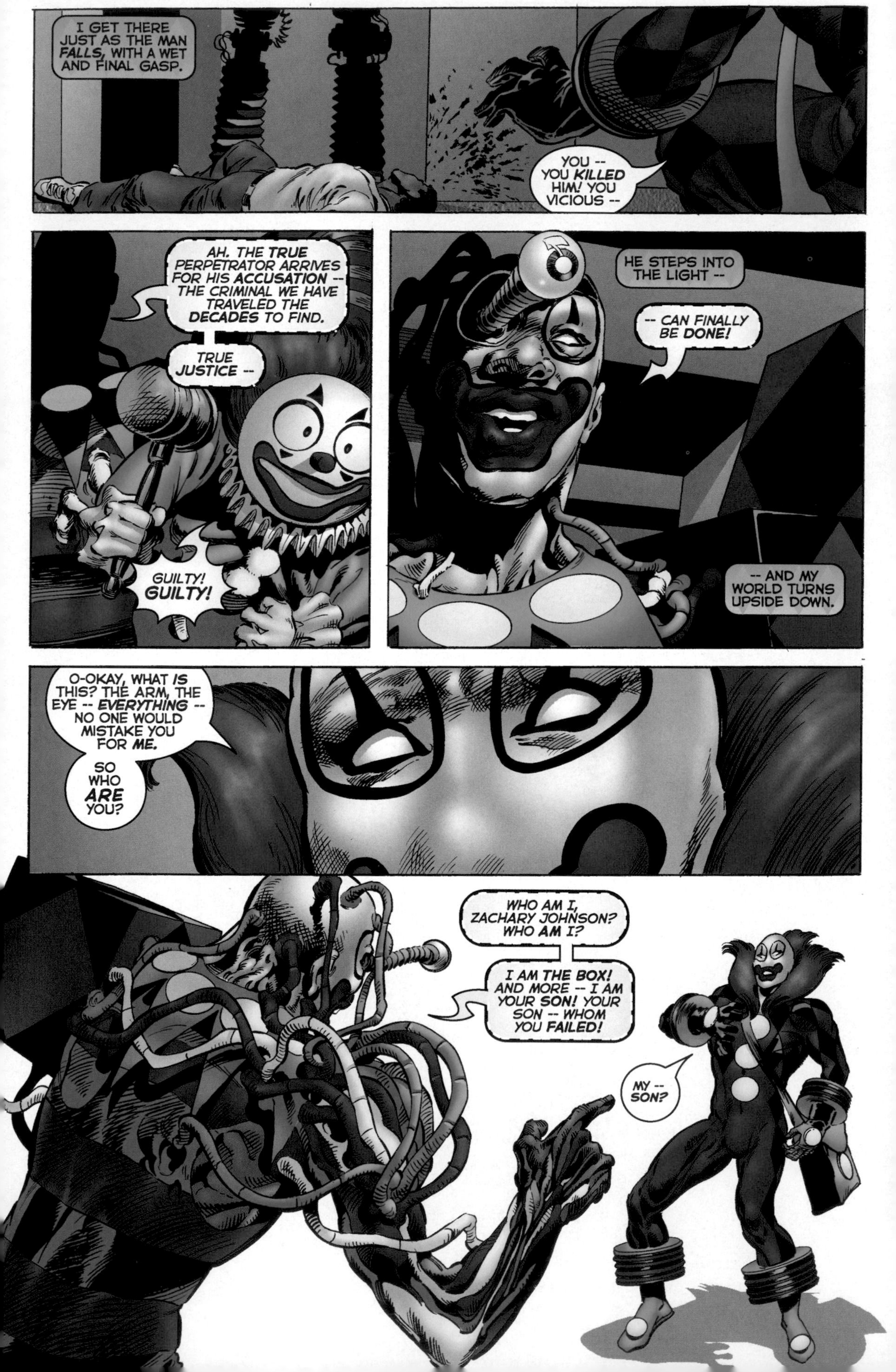

I GET THERE JUST AS THE MAN FALLS, WITH A WET AND FINAL GASP.
YOU -- YOU KILLED HIM! YOU VICIOUS --
AH. THE TRUE PERPETRATOR ARRIVES FOR HIS ACCUSATION -- THE CRIMINAL WE HAVE TRAVELED THE DECADES TO FIND.
TRUE JUSTICE --
GUILTY! GUILTY!
HE STEPS INTO THE LIGHT --
-- CAN FINALLY BE DONE!
-- AND MY WORLD TURNS UPSIDE DOWN.
O-OKAY, WHAT IS THIS? THE ARM, THE EYE -- EVERYTHING -- NO ONE WOULD MISTAKE YOU FOR ME.
SO WHO ARE YOU?
WHO AM I, ZACHARY JOHNSON? WHO AM I?
I AM THE BOX! AND MORE -- I AM YOUR SON! YOUR SON -- WHOM YOU FAILED!
MY -- SON?

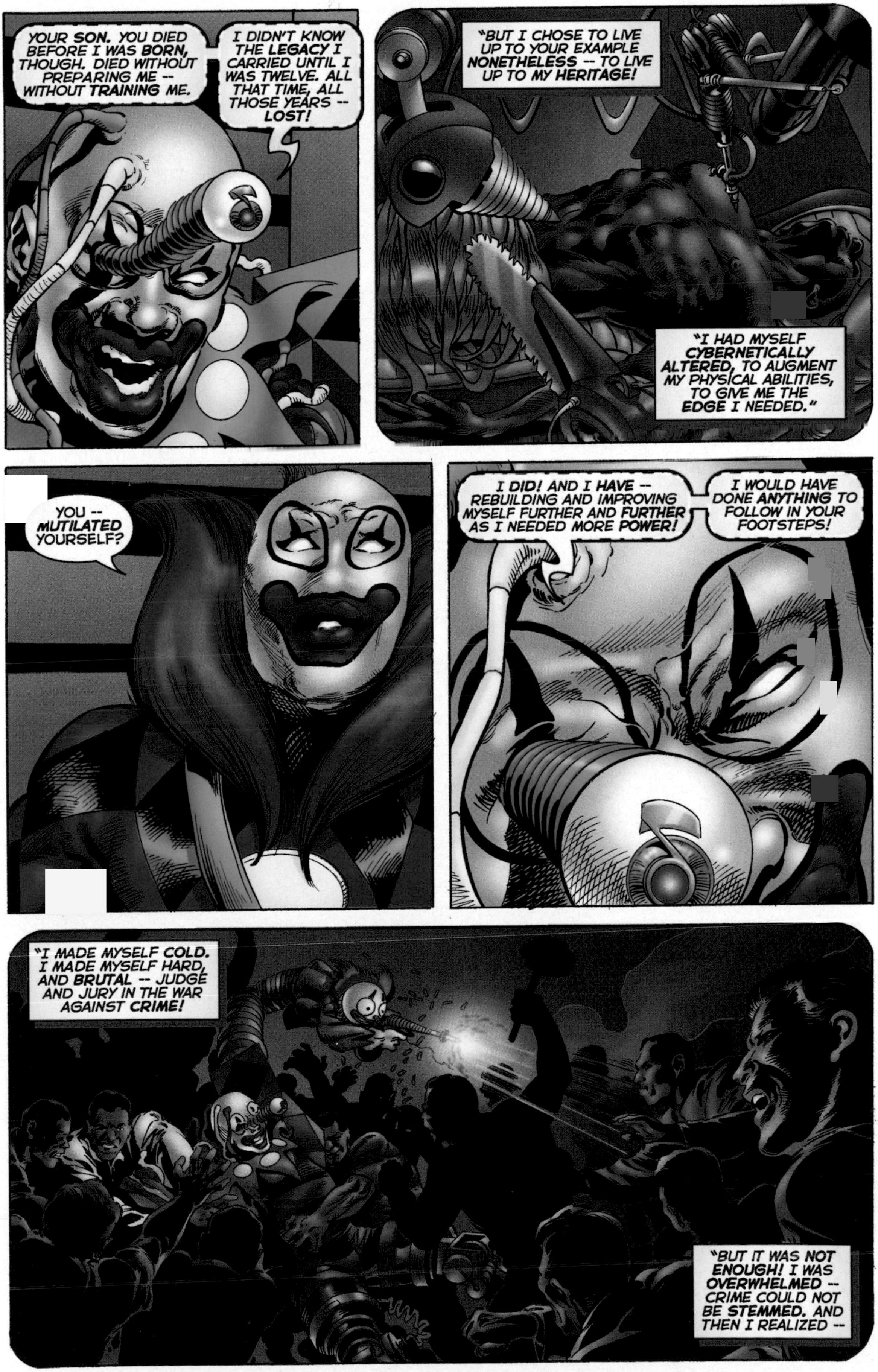
YOUR SON. YOU DIED BEFORE I WAS BORN, THOUGH. DIED WITHOUT PREPARING ME -- WITHOUT TRAINING ME.
I DIDN'T KNOW THE LEGACY I CARRIED UNTIL I WAS TWELVE. ALL THAT TIME, ALL THOSE YEARS -- LOST!
"BUT I CHOSE TO LIVE UP TO YOUR EXAMPLE NONETHELESS -- TO LIVE UP TO MY HERITAGE!
"I HAD MYSELF CYBERNETICALLY ALTERED, TO AUGMENT MY PHYSICAL ABILITIES, TO GIVE ME THE EDGE I NEEDED."
YOU -- MUTILATED YOURSELF?
I DID! AND I HAVE -- REBUILDING AND IMPROVING MYSELF FURTHER AND FURTHER AS I NEEDED MORE POWER!
I WOULD HAVE DONE ANYTHING TO FOLLOW IN YOUR FOOTSTEPS!
"I MADE MYSELF COLD. I MADE MYSELF HARD, AND BRUTAL -- JUDGE AND JURY IN THE WAR AGAINST CRIME!
"BUT IT WAS NOT ENOUGH! I WAS OVERWHELMED -- CRIME COULD NOT BE STEMMED. AND THEN I REALIZED --

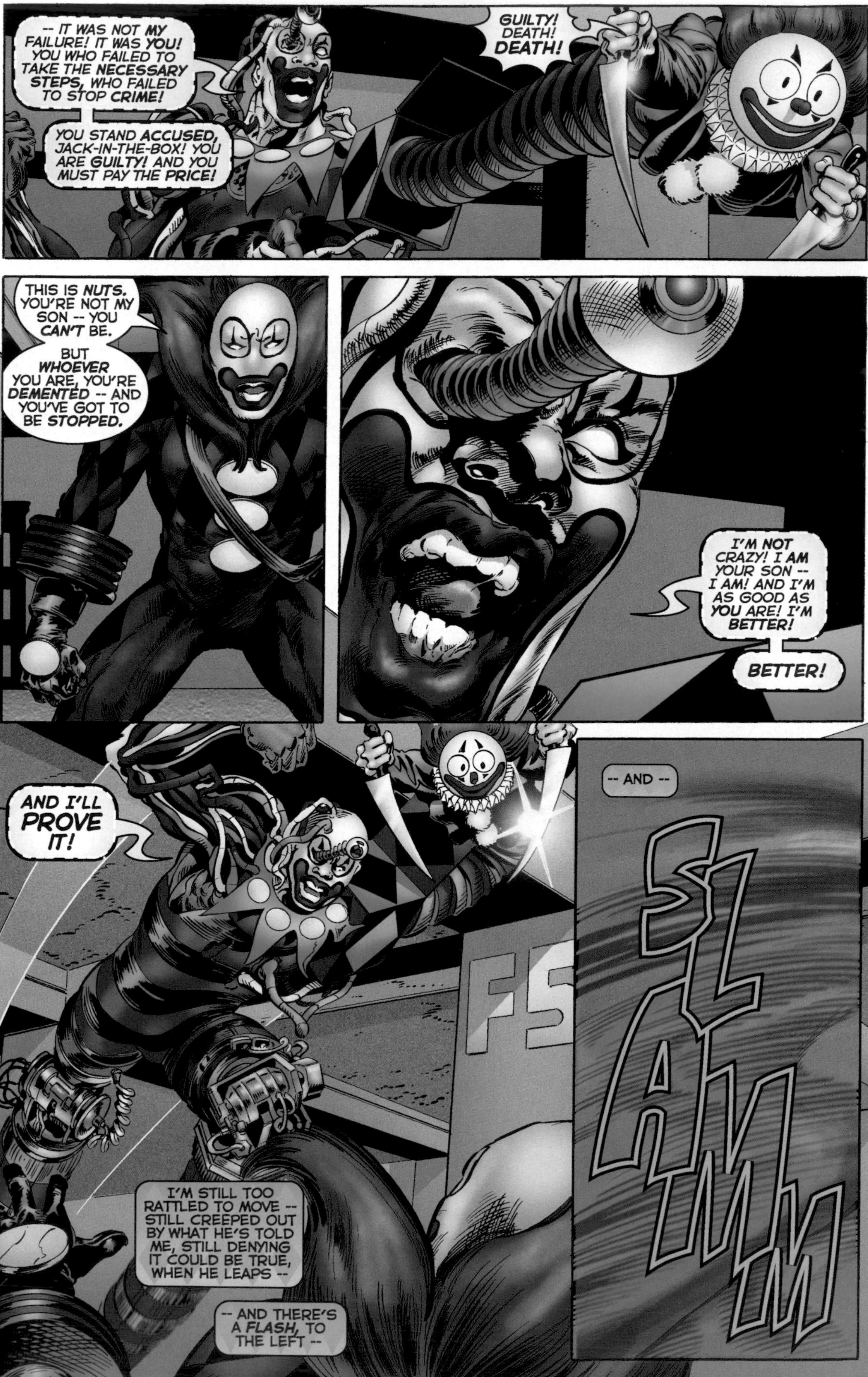
-- IT WAS NOT MY FAILURE! IT WAS YOU! YOU WHO FAILED TO TAKE THE NECESSARY STEPS, WHO FAILED TO STOP CRIME!
YOU STAND ACCUSED, JACK-IN-THE-BOX! YOU ARE GUILTY! AND YOU MUST PAY THE PRICE!
GUILTY! DEATH! DEATH!
THIS IS NUTS. YOU'RE NOT MY SON -- YOU CAN'T BE.
BUT WHOEVER YOU ARE, YOU'RE DEMENTED -- AND YOU'VE GOT TO BE STOPPED.
I'M NOT CRAZY! I AM YOUR SON -- I AM! AND I'M AS GOOD AS YOU ARE! I'M BETTER!
BETTER!
AND I'LL PROVE IT!
I'M STILL TOO RATTLED TO MOVE -- STILL CREEPED OUT BY WHAT HE'S TOLD ME, STILL DENYING IT COULD BE TRUE, WHEN HE LEAPS --
-- AND THERE'S A FLASH, TO THE LEFT --
-- AND --
SLAMM

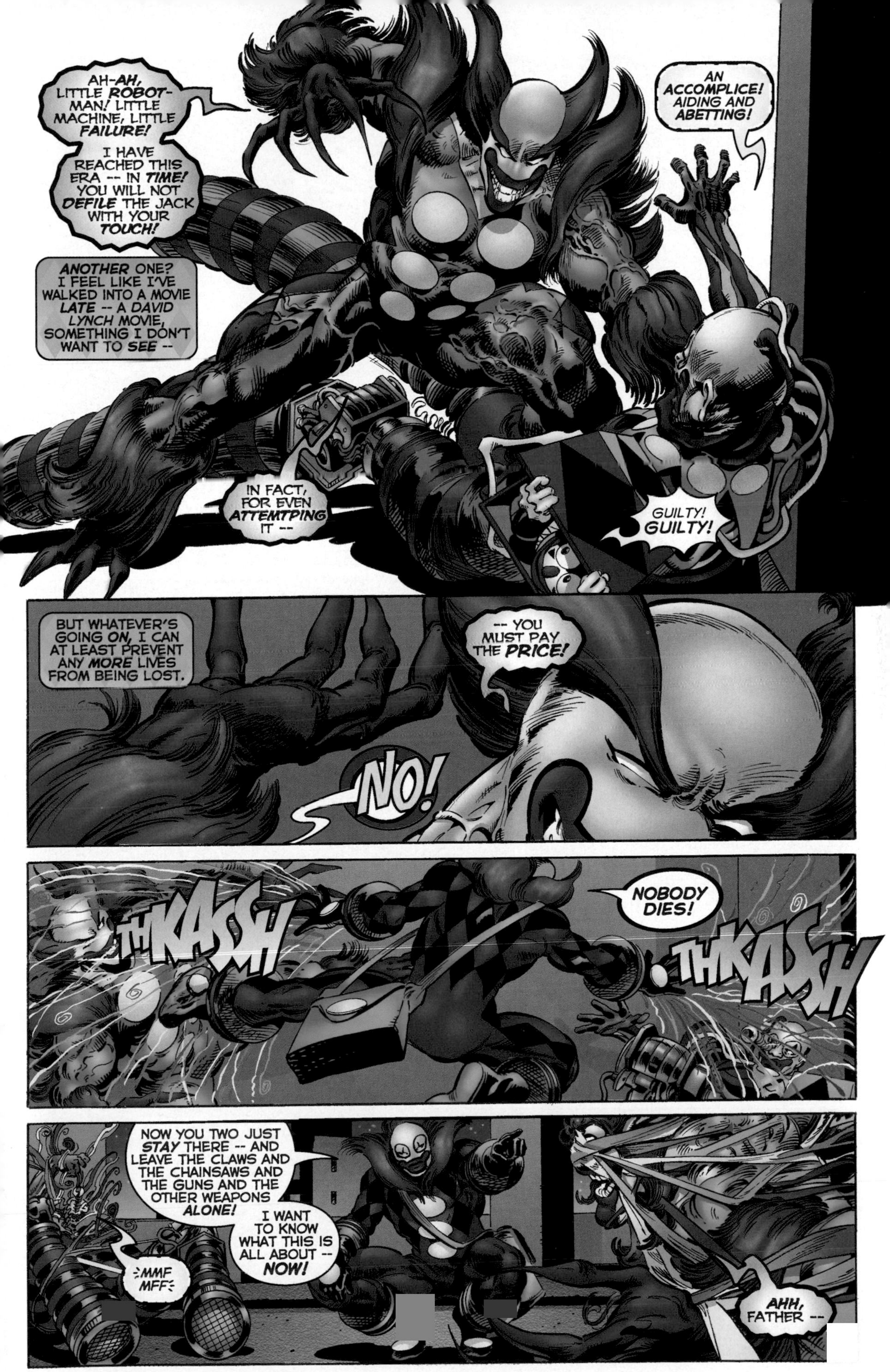
AH-AH, LITTLE ROBOT-MAN! LITTLE MACHINE, LITTLE FAILURE!
I HAVE REACHED THIS ERA -- IN TIME! YOU WILL NOT DEFILE THE JACK WITH YOUR TOUCH!
AN ACCOMPLICE! AIDING AND ABETTING!
ANOTHER ONE? I FEEL LIKE I'VE WALKED INTO A MOVIE LATE -- A DAVID LYNCH MOVIE, SOMETHING I DON'T WANT TO SEE --
IN FACT, FOR EVEN ATTEMTPING IT --
GUILTY! GUILTY!
BUT WHATEVER'S GOING ON, I CAN AT LEAST PREVENT ANY MORE LIVES FROM BEING LOST.
-- YOU MUST PAY THE PRICE!
NO!
THKASH
NOBODY DIES!
THKASH
NOW YOU TWO JUST STAY THERE -- AND LEAVE THE CLAWS AND THE CHAINSAWS AND THE GUNS AND THE OTHER WEAPONS ALONE!
I WANT TO KNOW WHAT THIS IS ALL ABOUT -- NOW!
MMF MFF
AHH, FATHER --

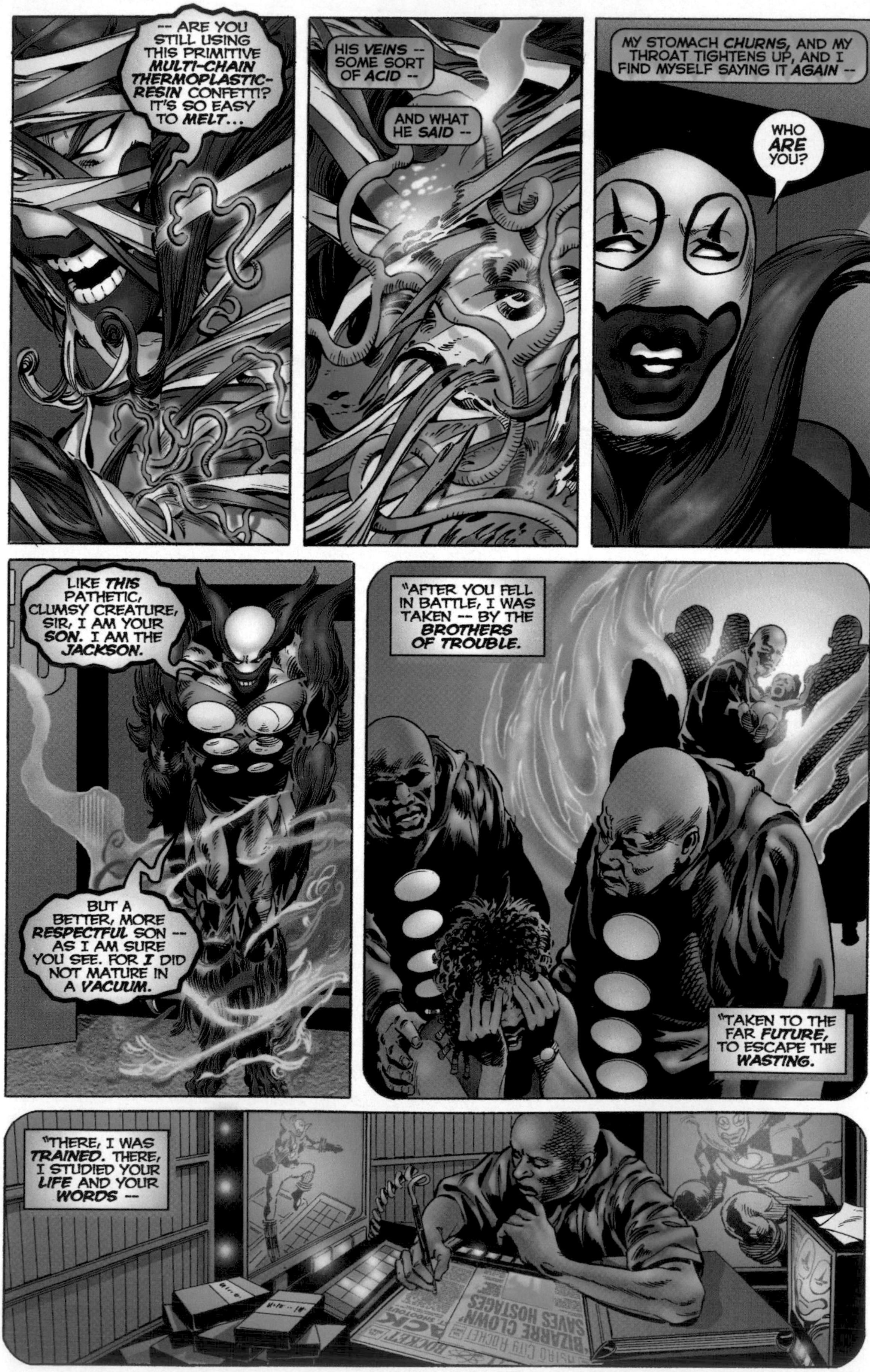
-- ARE YOU STILL USING THIS PRIMITIVE MULTI-CHAIN THERMOPLASTIC-RESIN CONFETTI? IT'S SO EASY TO MELT...
HIS VEINS -- SOME SORT OF ACID --
AND WHAT HE SAID --
MY STOMACH CHURNS, AND MY THROAT TIGHTENS UP, AND I FIND MYSELF SAYING IT AGAIN --
WHO ARE YOU?
LIKE THIS PATHETIC, CLUMSY CREATURE, SIR, I AM YOUR SON. I AM THE JACKSON.
BUT A BETTER, MORE RESPECTFUL SON -- AS I AM SURE YOU SEE. FOR I DID NOT MATURE IN A VACUUM.
"AFTER YOU FELL IN BATTLE, I WAS TAKEN -- BY THE BROTHERS OF TROUBLE.
"TAKEN TO THE FAR FUTURE, TO ESCAPE THE WASTING.
"THERE, I WAS TRAINED. THERE, I STUDIED YOUR LIFE AND YOUR WORDS --
BIZARRE CLOWN SAVES HOSTAGES

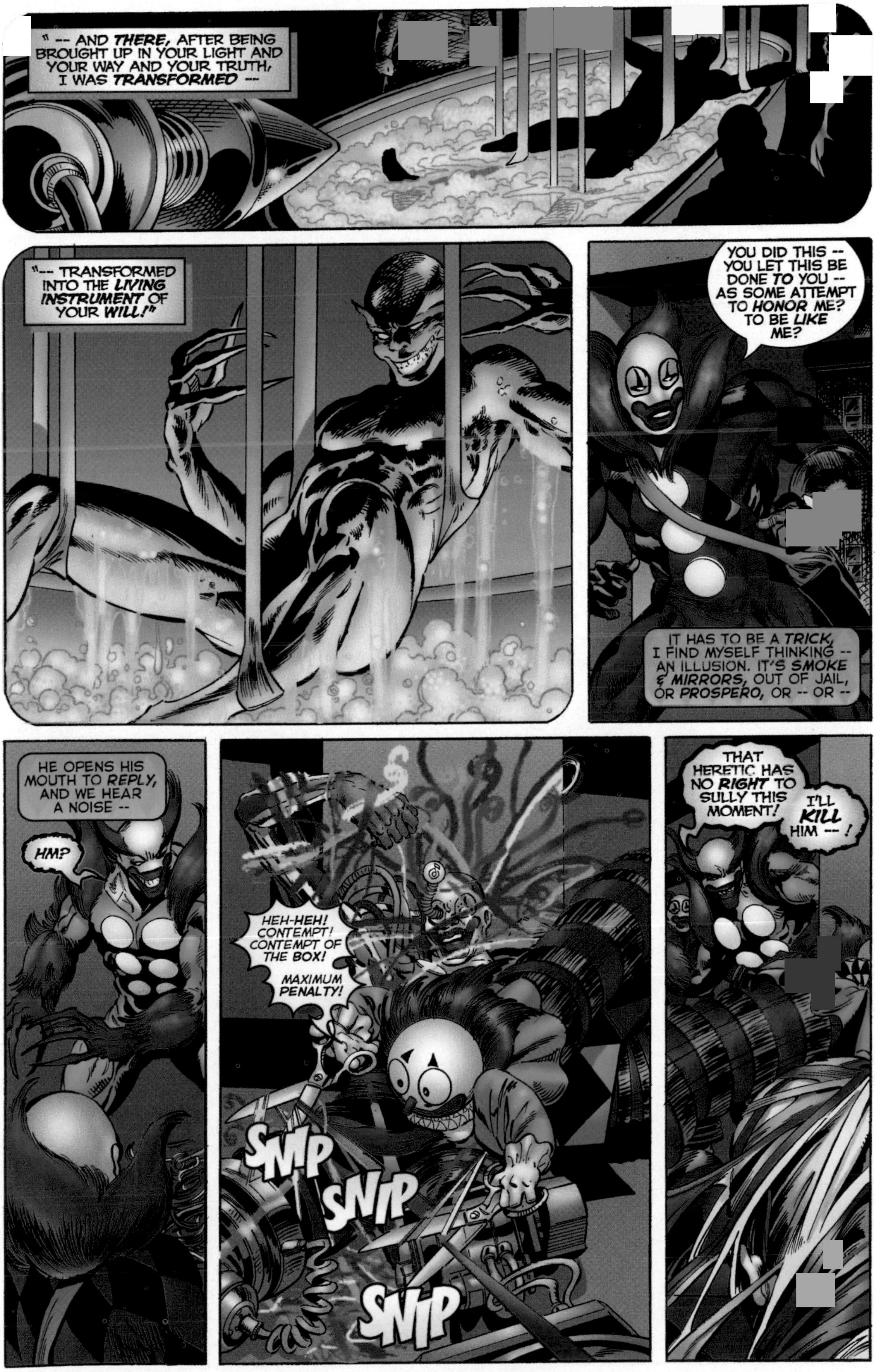
" -- AND THERE, AFTER BEING BROUGHT UP IN YOUR LIGHT AND YOUR WAY AND YOUR TRUTH, I WAS TRANSFORMED --
"-- TRANSFORMED INTO THE LIVING INSTRUMENT OF YOUR WILL!"
YOU DID THIS -- YOU LET THIS BE DONE TO YOU -- AS SOME ATTEMPT TO HONOR ME? TO BE LIKE ME?
IT HAS TO BE A TRICK, I FIND MYSELF THINKING -- AN ILLUSION. IT'S SMOKE & MIRRORS, OUT OF JAIL, OR PROSPERO, OR -- OR --
HE OPENS HIS MOUTH TO REPLY, AND WE HEAR A NOISE --
HM?
HEH-HEH! CONTEMPT! CONTEMPT OF THE BOX!
MAXIMUM PENALTY!
SNIP
SNIP
SNIP
THAT HERETIC HAS NO RIGHT TO SULLY THIS MOMENT!
I'LL KILL HIM -- !

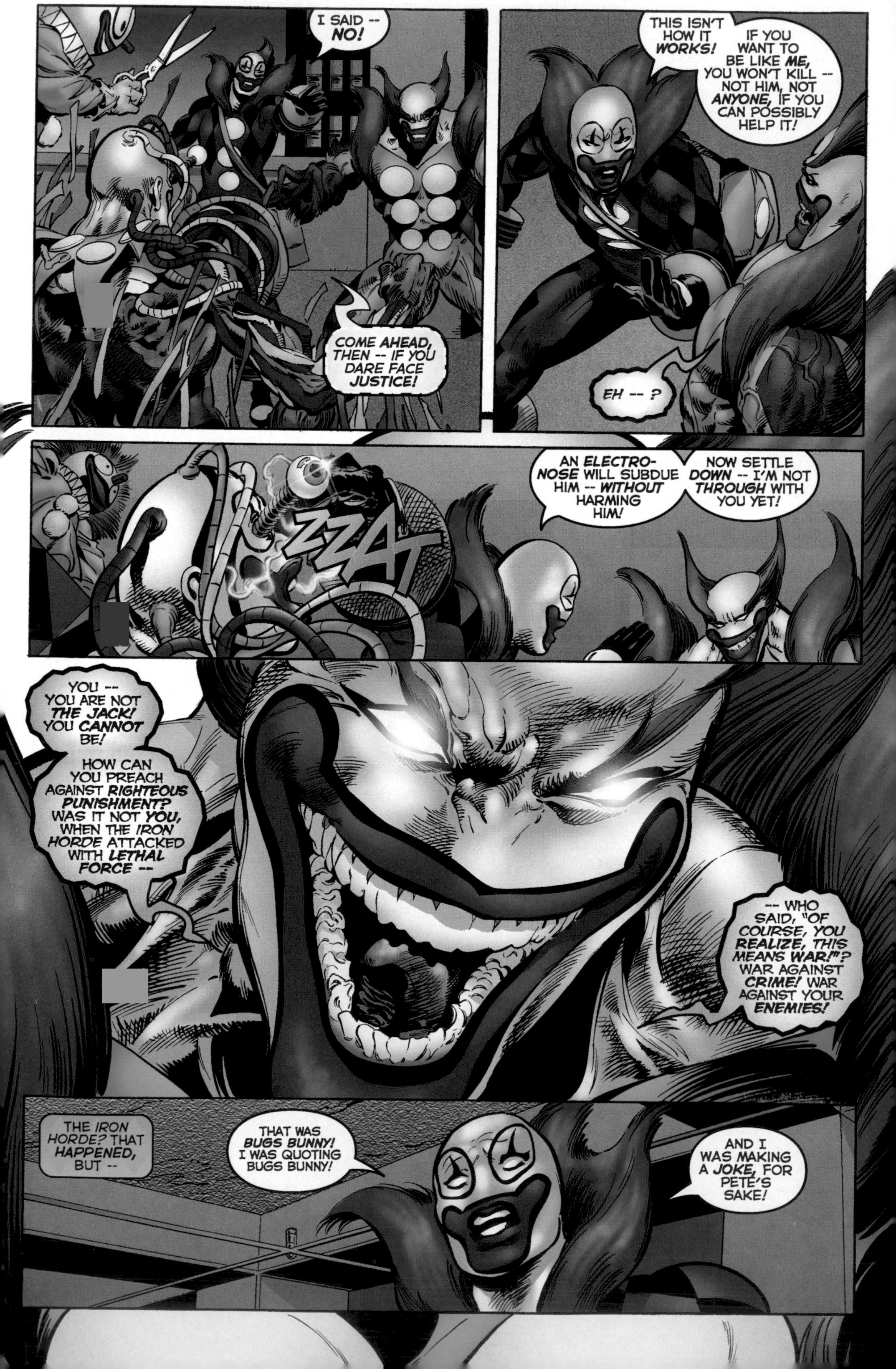
I SAID -- NO!
COME AHEAD, THEN -- IF YOU DARE FACE JUSTICE!
THIS ISN'T HOW IT WORKS!
IF YOU WANT TO BE LIKE ME, YOU WON'T KILL -- NOT HIM, NOT ANYONE, IF YOU CAN POSSIBLY HELP IT!
EH -- ?
ZZAT
AN ELECTRO-NOSE WILL SUBDUE HIM -- WITHOUT HARMING HIM!
NOW SETTLE DOWN -- I'M NOT THROUGH WITH YOU YET!
YOU -- YOU ARE NOT THE JACK! YOU CANNOT BE!
HOW CAN YOU PREACH AGAINST RIGHTEOUS PUNISHMENT? WAS IT NOT YOU, WHEN THE IRON HORDE ATTACKED WITH LETHAL FORCE --
-- WHO SAID, "OF COURSE, YOU REALIZE, THIS MEANS WAR!"? WAR AGAINST CRIME! WAR AGAINST YOUR ENEMIES!
THE IRON HORDE? THAT HAPPENED, BUT --
THAT WAS BUGS BUNNY! I WAS QUOTING BUGS BUNNY!
AND I WAS MAKING A JOKE, FOR PETE'S SAKE!

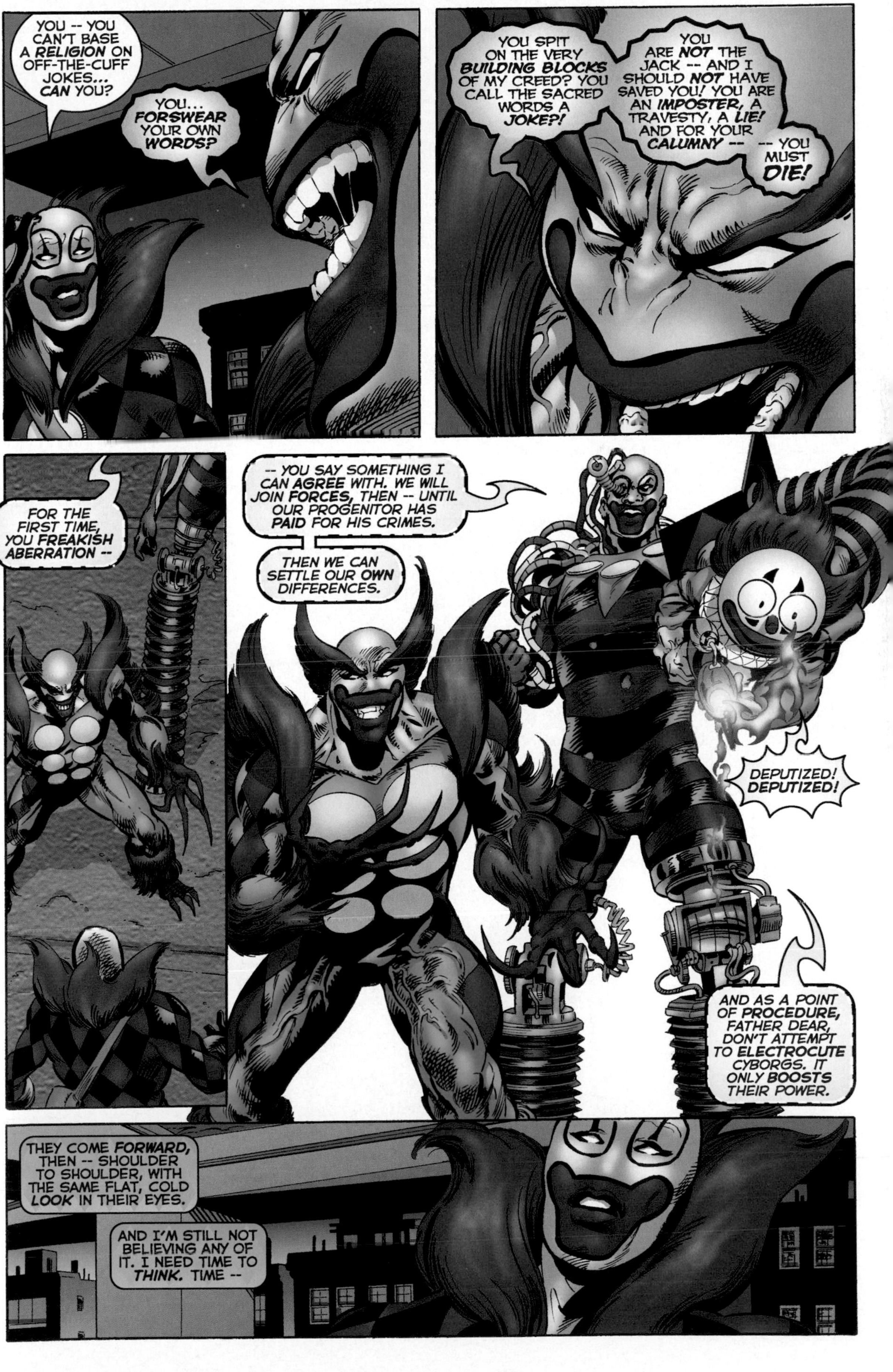
YOU -- YOU CAN'T BASE A RELIGION ON OFF-THE-CUFF JOKES... CAN YOU?
YOU... FORSWEAR YOUR OWN WORDS?
YOU SPIT ON THE VERY BUILDING BLOCKS OF MY CREED? YOU CALL THE SACRED WORDS A JOKE?!
YOU ARE NOT THE JACK -- AND I SHOULD NOT HAVE SAVED YOU! YOU ARE AN IMPOSTER, A TRAVESTY, A LIE! AND FOR YOUR CALUMNY --
-- YOU MUST DIE!
FOR THE FIRST TIME, YOU FREAKISH ABERRATION --
-- YOU SAY SOMETHING I CAN AGREE WITH. WE WILL JOIN FORCES, THEN -- UNTIL OUR PROGENITOR HAS PAID FOR HIS CRIMES.
THEN WE CAN SETTLE OUR OWN DIFFERENCES.
DEPUTIZED! DEPUTIZED!
AND AS A POINT OF PROCEDURE, FATHER DEAR, DON'T ATTEMPT TO ELECTROCUTE CYBORGS. IT ONLY BOOSTS THEIR POWER.
THEY COME FORWARD, THEN -- SHOULDER TO SHOULDER, WITH THE SAME FLAT, COLD LOOK IN THEIR EYES.
AND I'M STILL NOT BELIEVING ANY OF IT. I NEED TIME TO THINK. TIME --

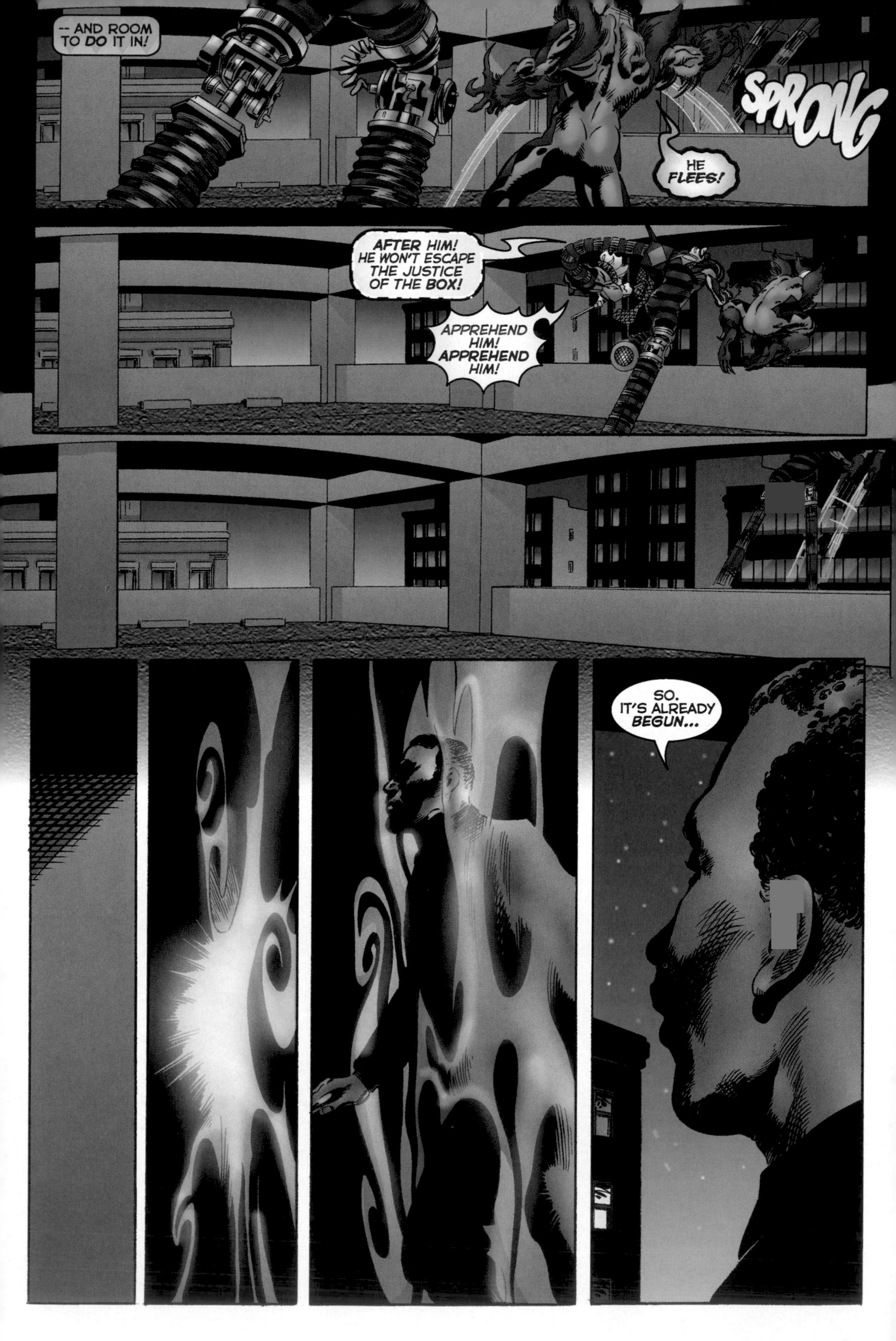
-- AND ROOM TO DO IT IN!
SPRONG
HE FLEES!
AFTER HIM! HE WON'T ESCAPE THE JUSTICE OF THE BOX!
APPREHEND HIM! APPREHEND HIM!
SO. IT'S ALREADY BEGUN...

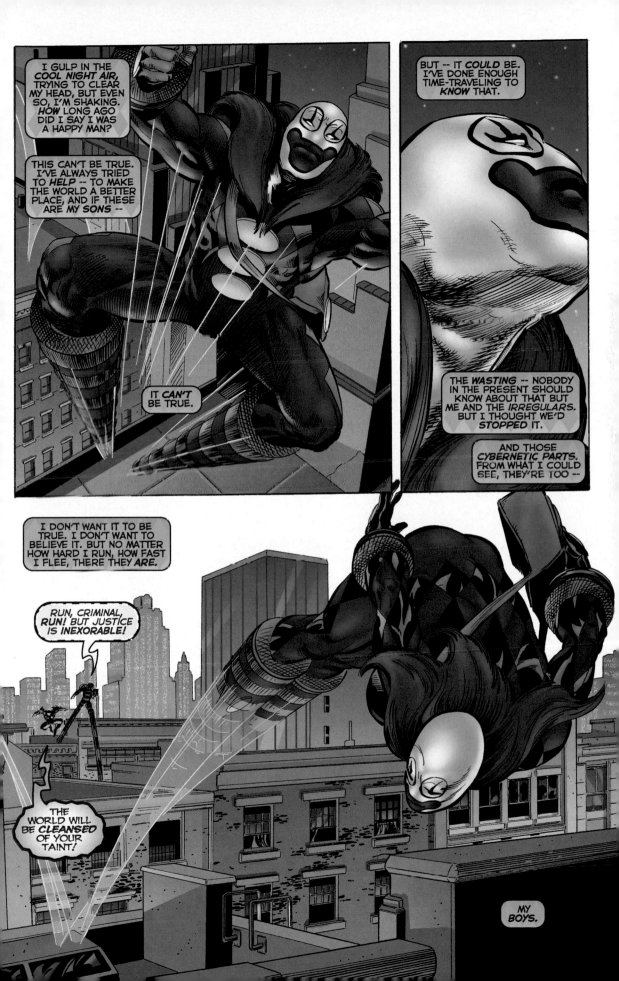

I GULP IN THE **COOL NIGHT AIR**, TRYING TO CLEAR MY HEAD, BUT EVEN SO, I'M SHAKING. **HOW** LONG AGO DID I SAY I WAS A **HAPPY MAN?**

THIS CAN'T BE TRUE. I'VE ALWAYS TRIED TO **HELP** -- TO MAKE THE WORLD A BETTER PLACE, AND IF THESE ARE MY **SONS** --

IT **CAN'T** BE TRUE.

BUT -- IT **COULD** BE. I'VE DONE ENOUGH TIME-TRAVELING TO **KNOW** THAT.

THE **WASTING** -- NOBODY IN THE PRESENT SHOULD KNOW ABOUT THAT BUT ME AND THE **IRREGULARS.** BUT I THOUGHT WE'D **STOPPED** IT.

AND THOSE **CYBERNETIC PARTS.** FROM WHAT I COULD SEE, THEY'RE TOO --

I DON'T WANT IT TO BE TRUE. I DON'T WANT TO BELIEVE IT. BUT NO MATTER HOW HARD I RUN, HOW FAST I FLEE, THERE THEY **ARE.**

RUN, CRIMINAL, **RUN!** BUT JUSTICE IS **INEXORABLE!**

THE WORLD WILL BE **CLEANSED** OF YOUR **TAINT!**

MY BOYS.

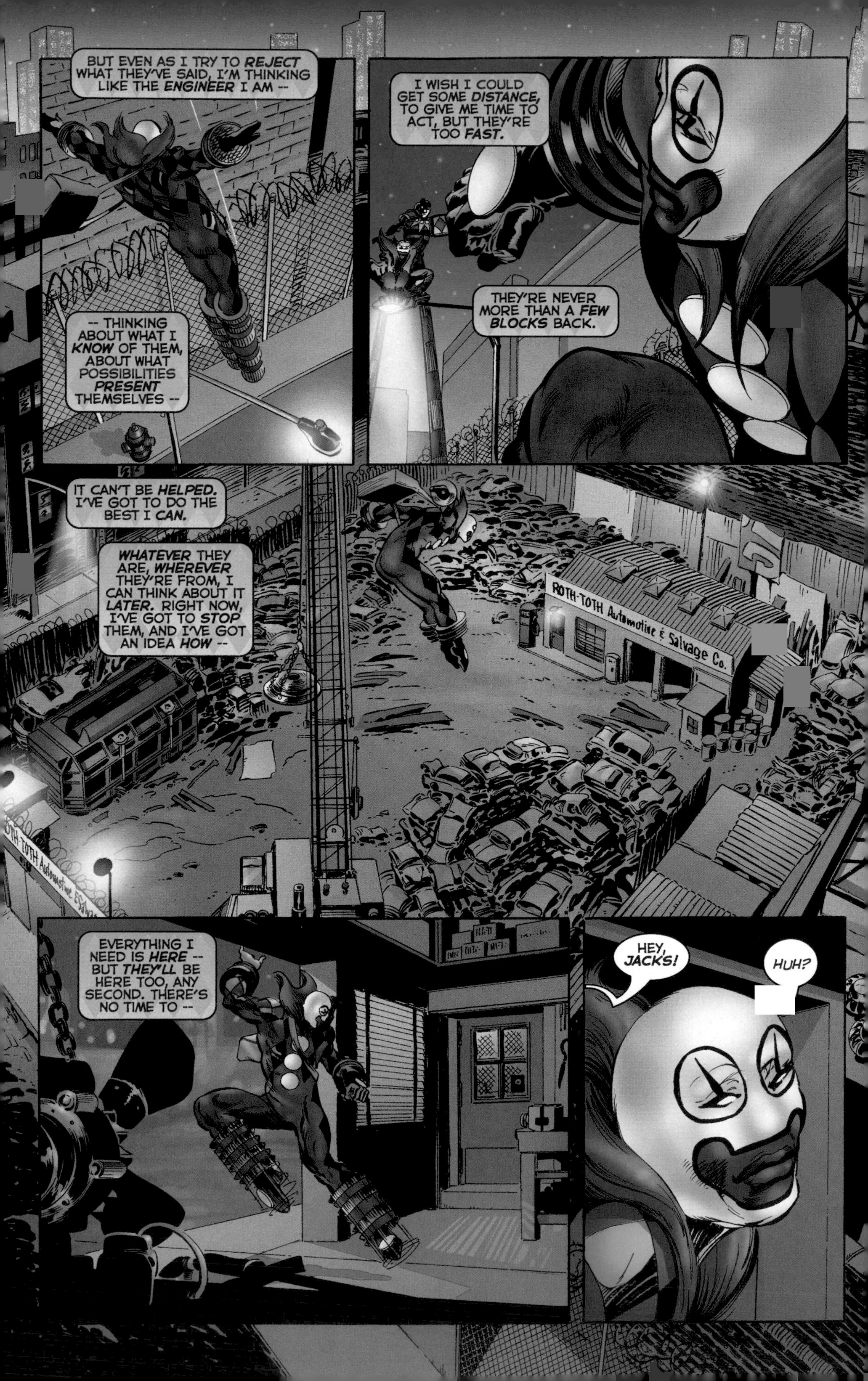

BUT EVEN AS I TRY TO REJECT WHAT THEY'VE SAID, I'M THINKING LIKE THE ENGINEER I AM --
-- THINKING ABOUT WHAT I KNOW OF THEM, ABOUT WHAT POSSIBILITIES PRESENT THEMSELVES --
I WISH I COULD GET SOME DISTANCE, TO GIVE ME TIME TO ACT, BUT THEY'RE TOO FAST.
THEY'RE NEVER MORE THAN A FEW BLOCKS BACK.
IT CAN'T BE HELPED. I'VE GOT TO DO THE BEST I CAN.
WHATEVER THEY ARE, WHEREVER THEY'RE FROM, I CAN THINK ABOUT IT LATER. RIGHT NOW, I'VE GOT TO STOP THEM, AND I'VE GOT AN IDEA HOW --
ROTH-TOTH Automotive & Salvage Co.
EVERYTHING I NEED IS HERE -- BUT THEY'LL BE HERE TOO, ANY SECOND. THERE'S NO TIME TO --
HEY, JACKS!
HUH?

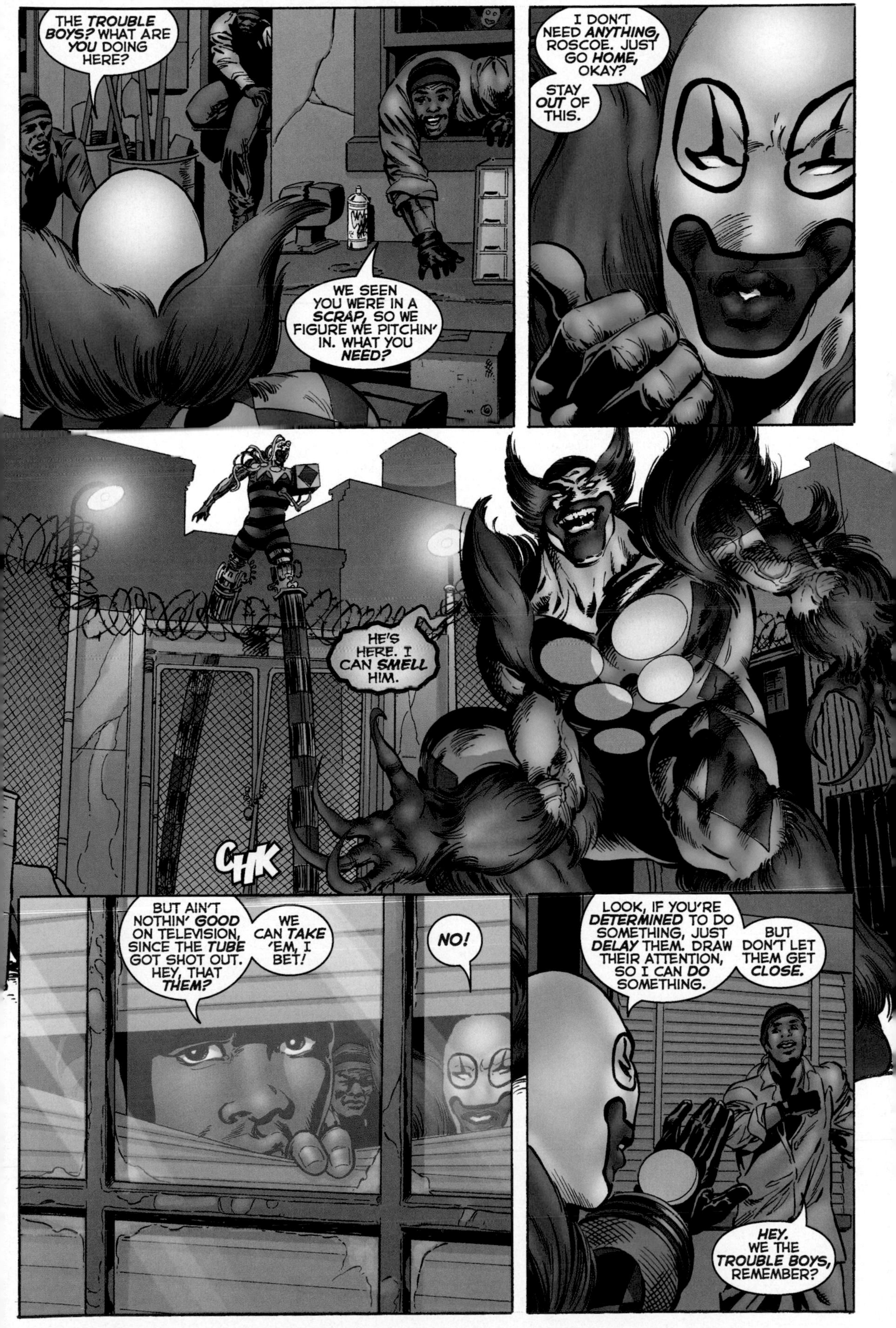
THE TROUBLE BOYS? WHAT ARE YOU DOING HERE?
WE SEEN YOU WERE IN A SCRAP, SO WE FIGURE WE PITCHIN' IN. WHAT YOU NEED?
I DON'T NEED ANYTHING, ROSCOE. JUST GO HOME, OKAY?
STAY OUT OF THIS.
HE'S HERE. I CAN SMELL HIM.
CHK
BUT AIN'T NOTHIN' GOOD ON TELEVISION, SINCE THE TUBE GOT SHOT OUT. HEY, THAT THEM?
WE CAN TAKE 'EM, I BET!
NO!
LOOK, IF YOU'RE DETERMINED TO DO SOMETHING, JUST DELAY THEM. DRAW THEIR ATTENTION, SO I CAN DO SOMETHING.
BUT DON'T LET THEM GET CLOSE.
HEY. WE THE TROUBLE BOYS, REMEMBER?

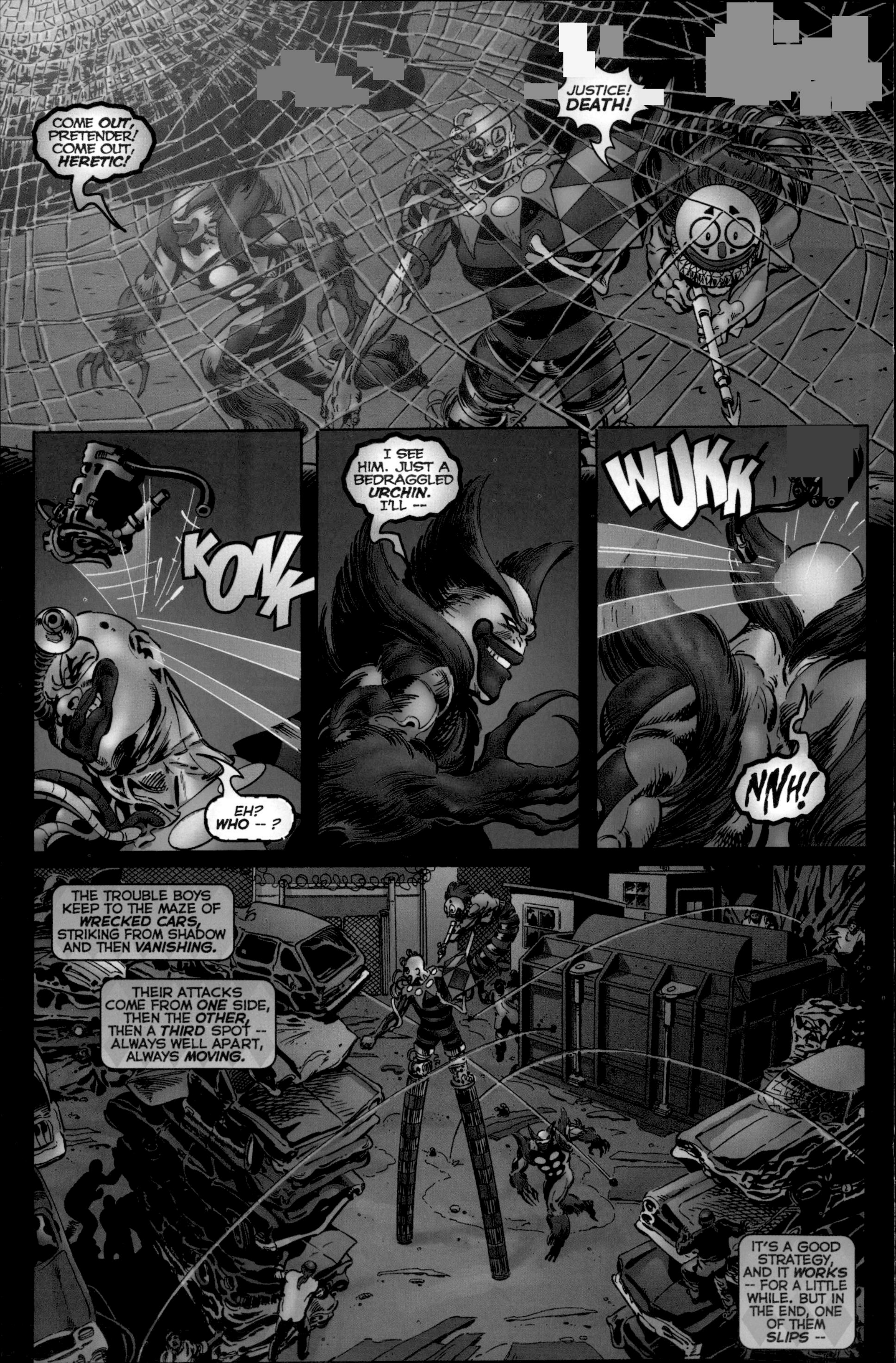

COME OUT, PRETENDER! COME OUT, HERETIC!
JUSTICE! DEATH!
KONK
EH? WHO -- ?
I SEE HIM. JUST A BEDRAGGLED URCHIN. I'LL --
WUKK
NNH!
THE TROUBLE BOYS KEEP TO THE MAZE OF WRECKED CARS, STRIKING FROM SHADOW AND THEN VANISHING.
THEIR ATTACKS COME FROM ONE SIDE, THEN THE OTHER, THEN A THIRD SPOT -- ALWAYS WELL APART, ALWAYS MOVING.
IT'S A GOOD STRATEGY, AND IT WORKS -- FOR A LITTLE WHILE. BUT IN THE END, ONE OF THEM SLIPS --

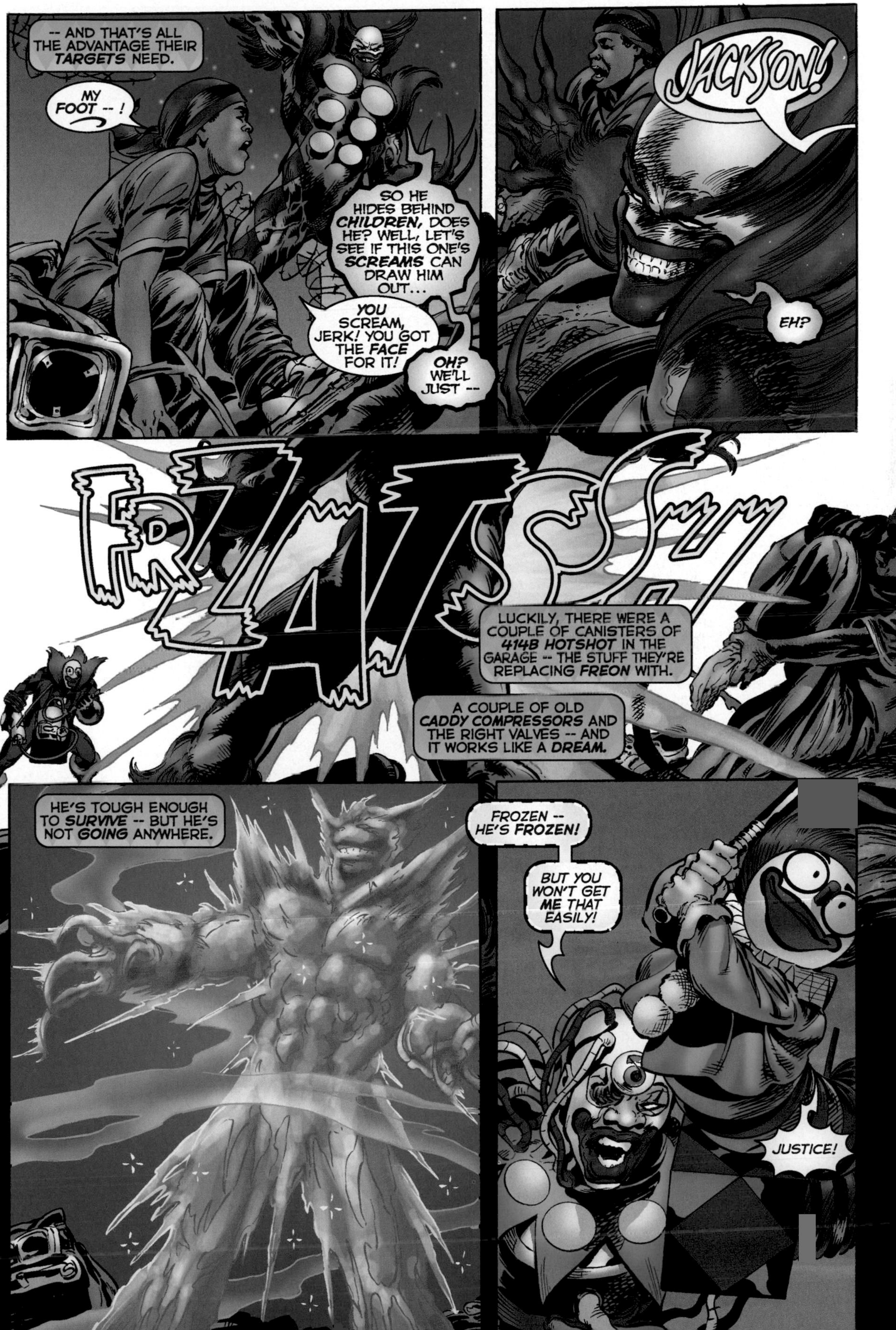

-- AND THAT'S ALL THE ADVANTAGE THEIR TARGETS NEED.
MY FOOT -- !
SO HE HIDES BEHIND CHILDREN, DOES HE? WELL, LET'S SEE IF THIS ONE'S SCREAMS CAN DRAW HIM OUT...
YOU SCREAM, JERK! YOU GOT THE FACE FOR IT!
OH? WE'LL JUST --
JACKSON!
EH?
FRZATSH!
LUCKILY, THERE WERE A COUPLE OF CANISTERS OF 414B HOTSHOT IN THE GARAGE -- THE STUFF THEY'RE REPLACING FREON WITH.
A COUPLE OF OLD CADDY COMPRESSORS AND THE RIGHT VALVES -- AND IT WORKS LIKE A DREAM.
HE'S TOUGH ENOUGH TO SURVIVE -- BUT HE'S NOT GOING ANYWHERE.
FROZEN -- HE'S FROZEN!
BUT YOU WON'T GET ME THAT EASILY!
JUSTICE!

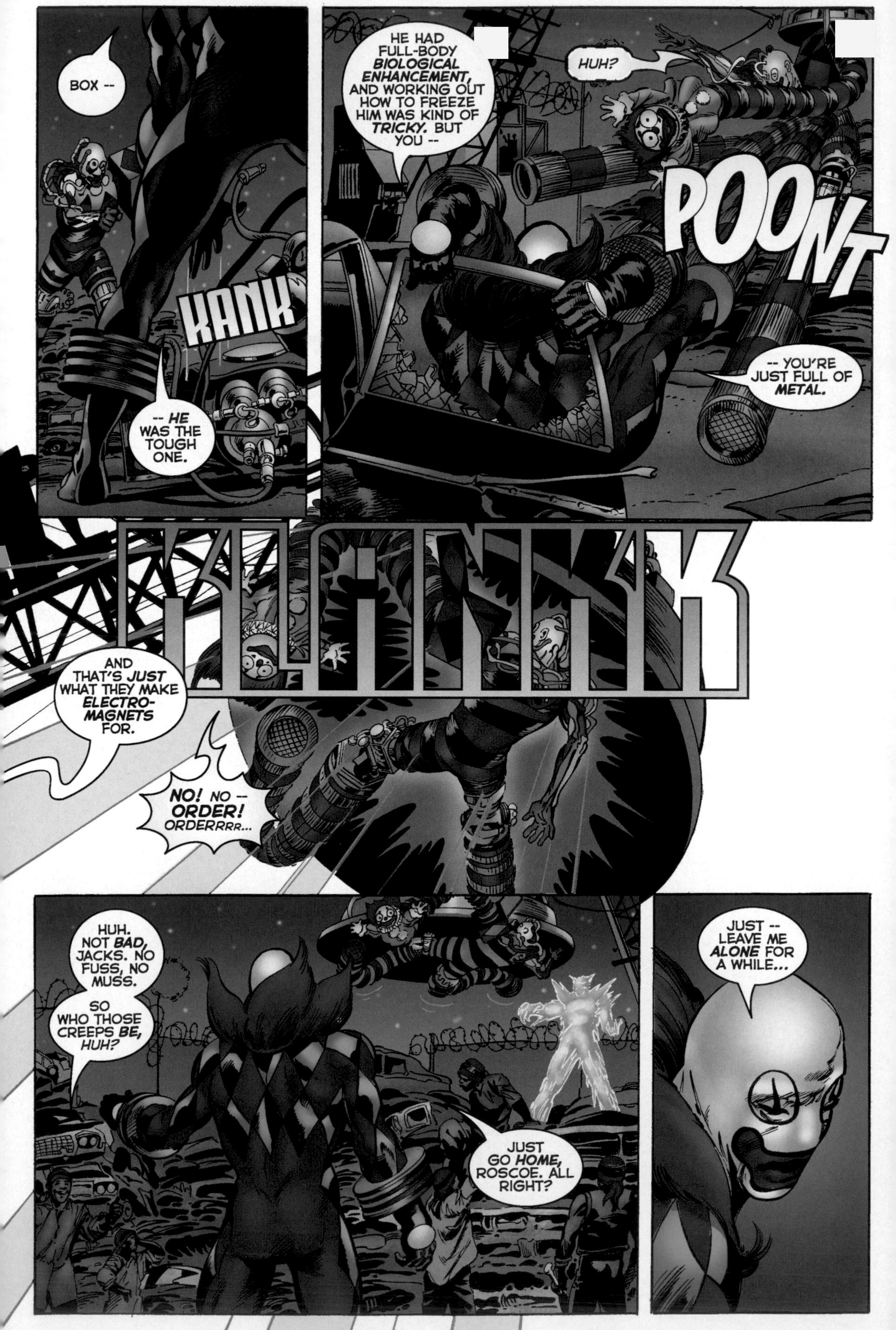
BOX --
KANK
-- HE WAS THE TOUGH ONE.
HE HAD FULL-BODY BIOLOGICAL ENHANCEMENT, AND WORKING OUT HOW TO FREEZE HIM WAS KIND OF TRICKY. BUT YOU --
HUH?
POOONT
-- YOU'RE JUST FULL OF METAL.
KLANKK
AND THAT'S JUST WHAT THEY MAKE ELECTRO-MAGNETS FOR.
NO! NO -- ORDER! ORDERRRR...
HUH. NOT BAD, JACKS. NO FUSS, NO MUSS.
SO WHO THOSE CREEPS BE, HUH?
JUST GO HOME, ROSCOE. ALL RIGHT?
JUST -- LEAVE ME ALONE FOR A WHILE...

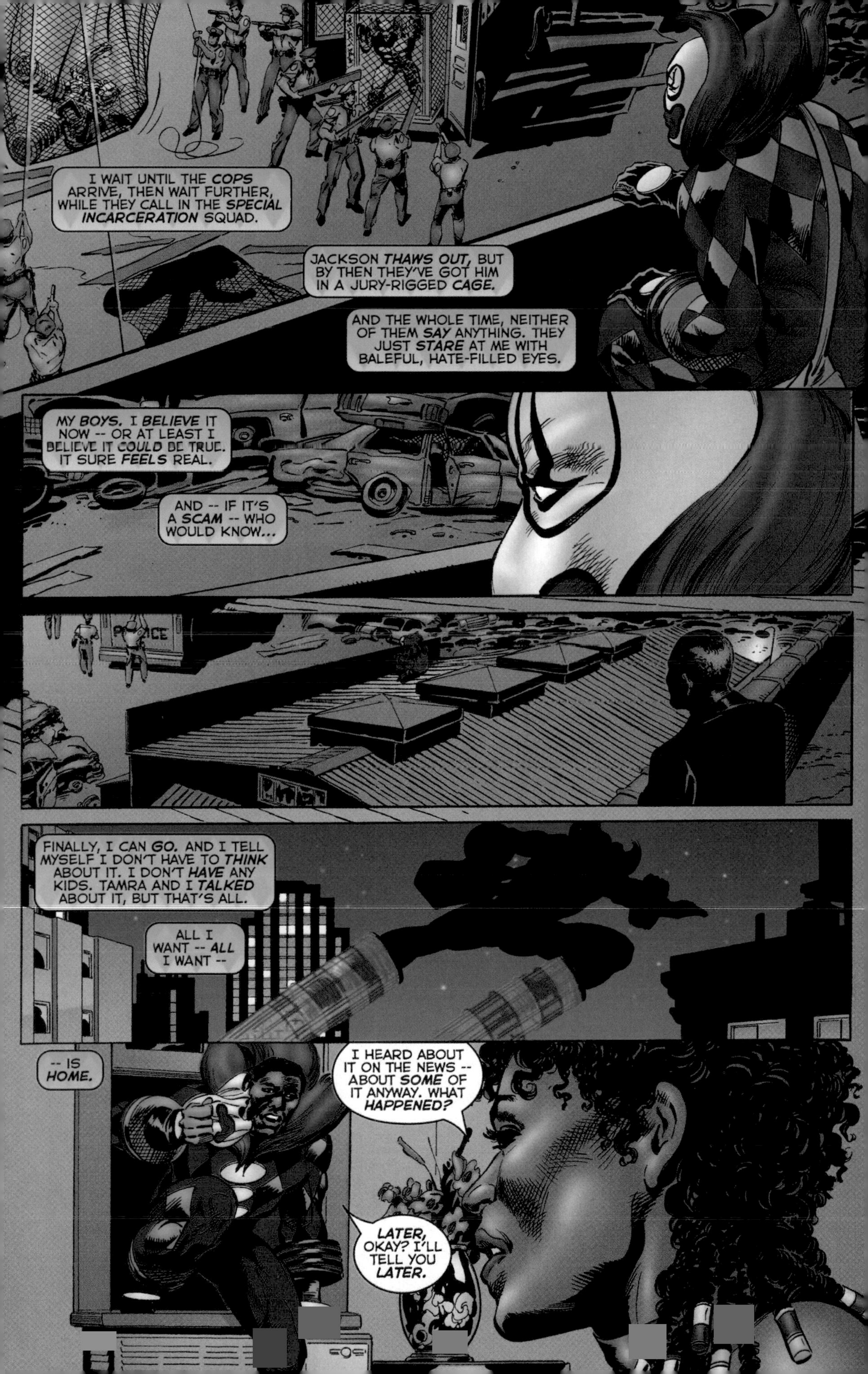
I WAIT UNTIL THE COPS ARRIVE, THEN WAIT FURTHER, WHILE THEY CALL IN THE SPECIAL INCARCERATION SQUAD.
JACKSON THAWS OUT, BUT BY THEN THEY'VE GOT HIM IN A JURY-RIGGED CAGE.
AND THE WHOLE TIME, NEITHER OF THEM SAY ANYTHING. THEY JUST STARE AT ME WITH BALEFUL, HATE-FILLED EYES.
MY BOYS. I BELIEVE IT NOW -- OR AT LEAST I BELIEVE IT COULD BE TRUE. IT SURE FEELS REAL.
AND -- IF IT'S A SCAM -- WHO WOULD KNOW...
FINALLY, I CAN GO. AND I TELL MYSELF I DON'T HAVE TO THINK ABOUT IT. I DON'T HAVE ANY KIDS. TAMRA AND I TALKED ABOUT IT, BUT THAT'S ALL.
ALL I WANT -- ALL I WANT --
-- IS HOME.
I HEARD ABOUT IT ON THE NEWS -- ABOUT SOME OF IT ANYWAY. WHAT HAPPENED?
LATER, OKAY? I'LL TELL YOU LATER.

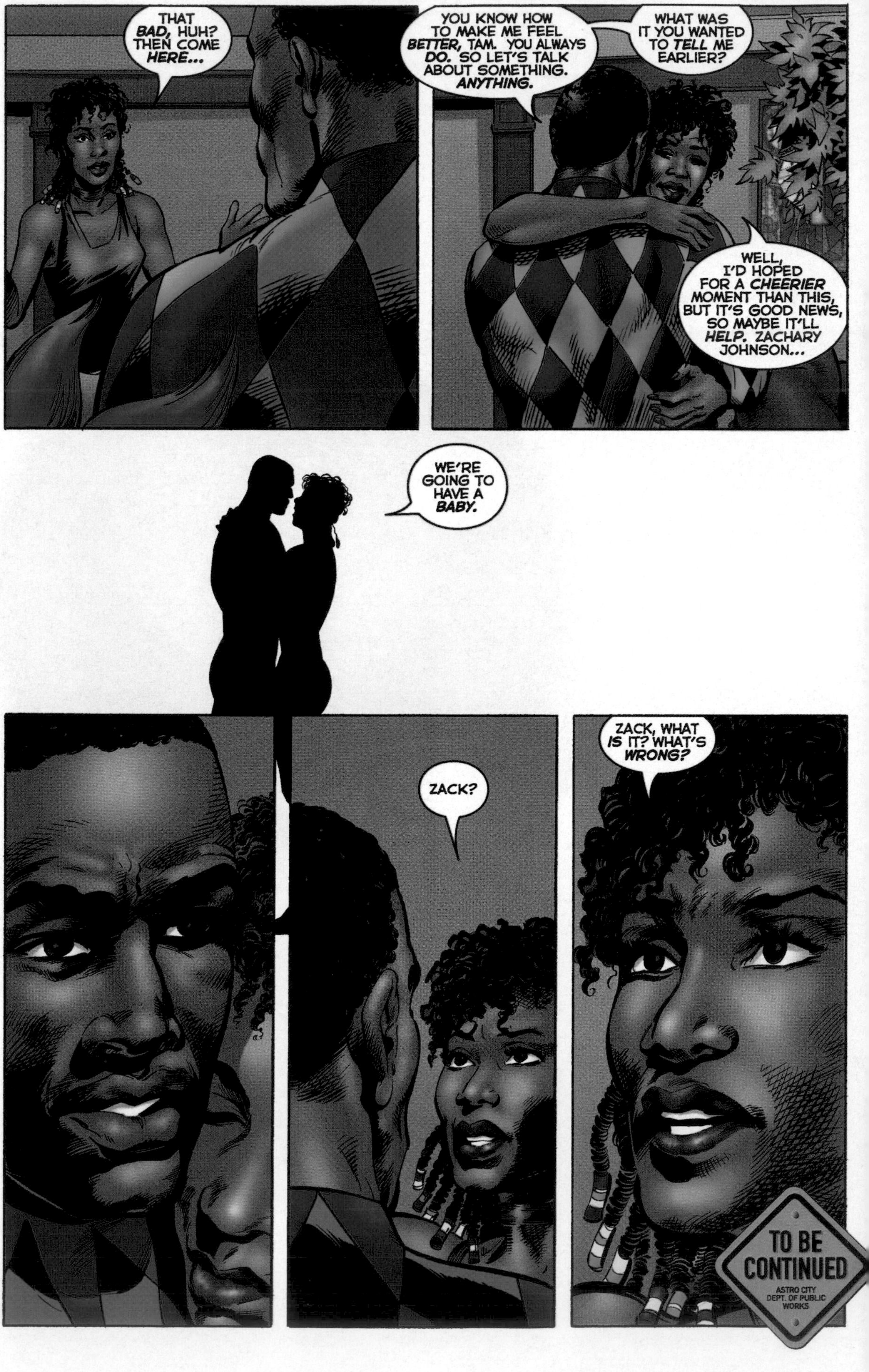
THAT BAD, HUH? THEN COME HERE...
YOU KNOW HOW TO MAKE ME FEEL BETTER, TAM. YOU ALWAYS DO. SO LET'S TALK ABOUT SOMETHING. ANYTHING.
WHAT WAS IT YOU WANTED TO TELL ME EARLIER?
WELL, I'D HOPED FOR A CHEERIER MOMENT THAN THIS, BUT IT'S GOOD NEWS, SO MAYBE IT'LL HELP. ZACHARY JOHNSON...
WE'RE GOING TO HAVE A BABY.
ZACK?
ZACK, WHAT IS IT? WHAT'S WRONG?
TO BE CONTINUED
ASTRO CITY DEPT. OF PUBLIC WORKS

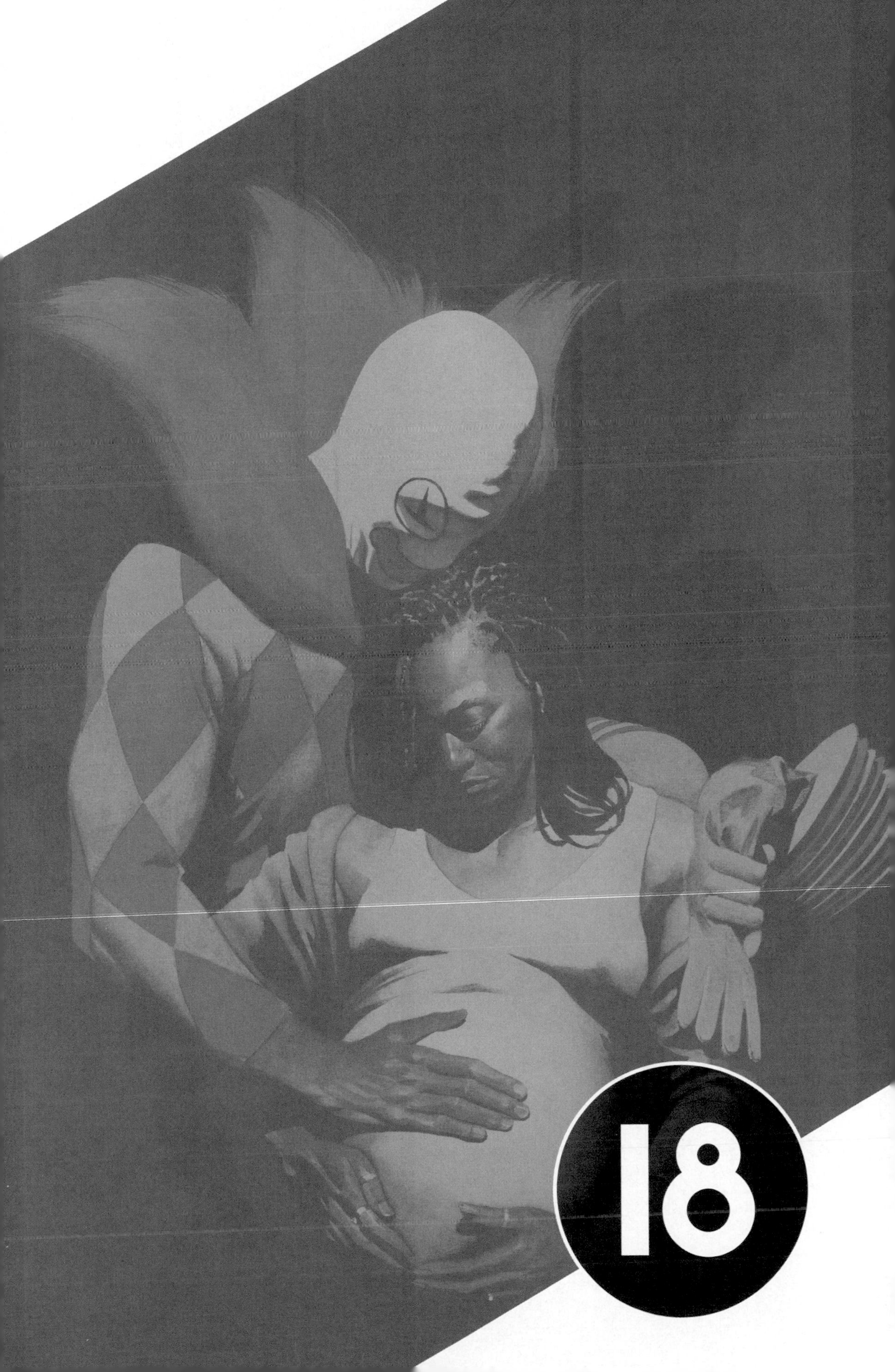
18

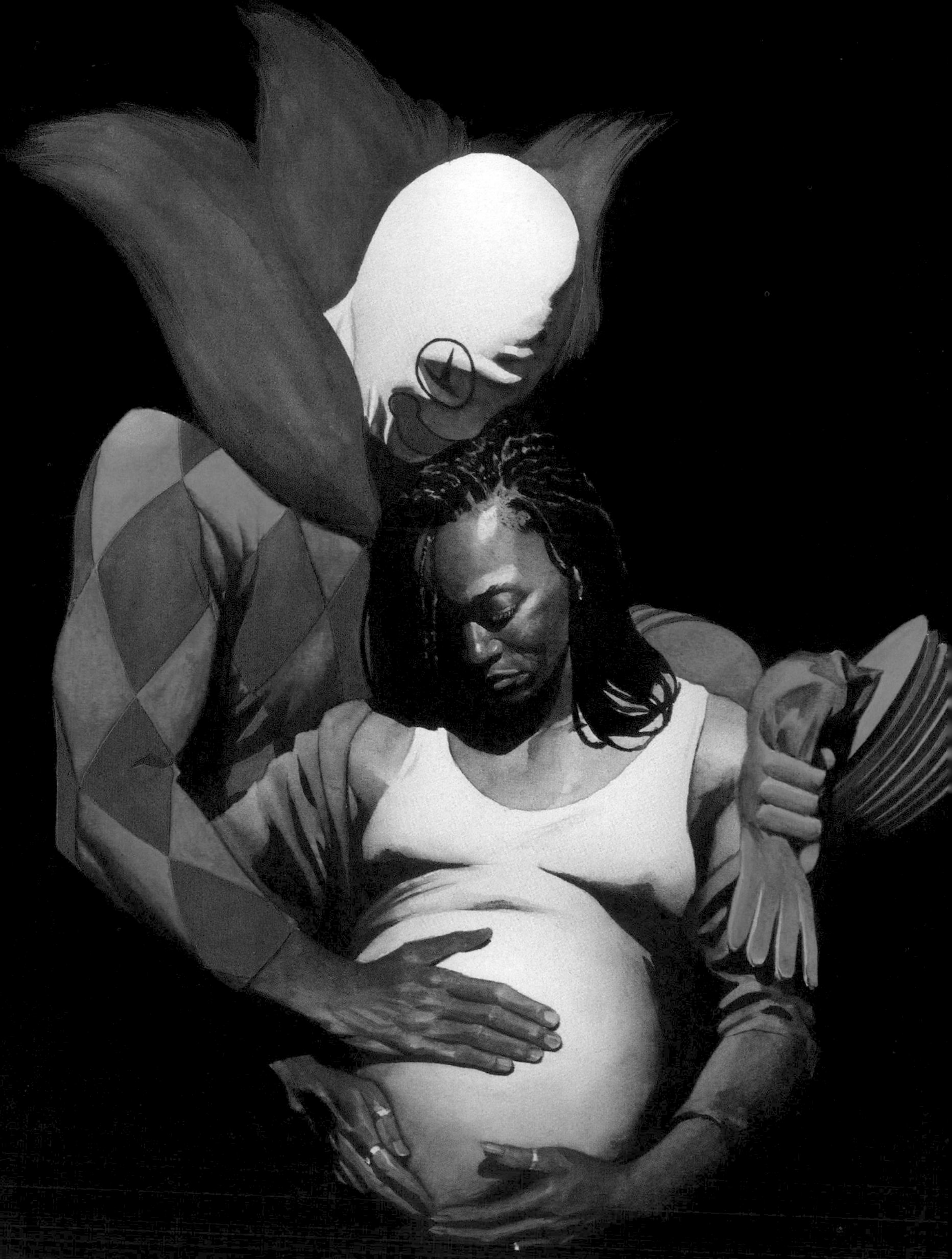

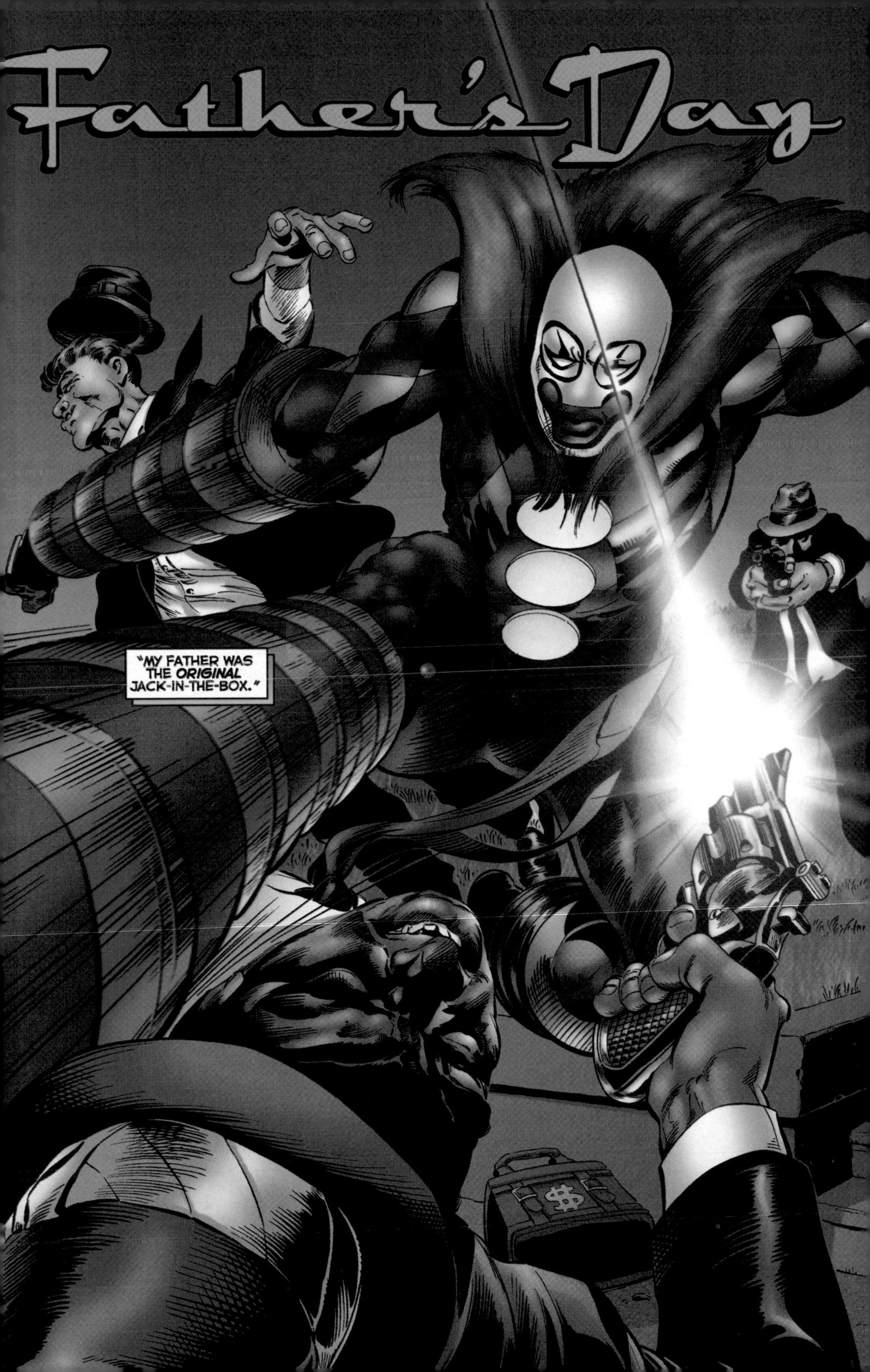
Father's Day
"MY FATHER WAS THE ORIGINAL JACK-IN-THE-BOX."

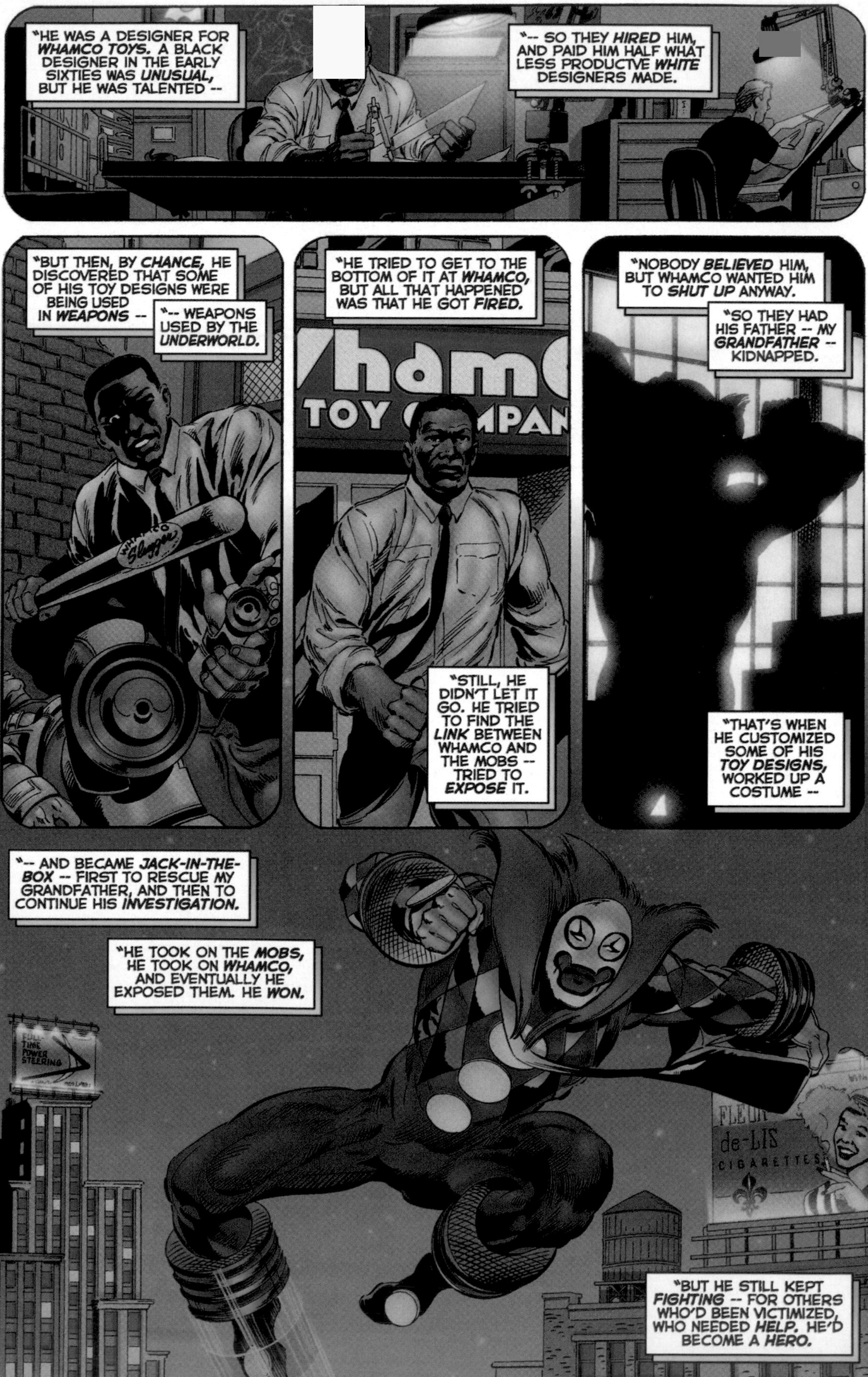
"HE WAS A DESIGNER FOR *WHAMCO TOYS.* A BLACK DESIGNER IN THE EARLY SIXTIES WAS *UNUSUAL,* BUT HE WAS TALENTED --
"-- SO THEY *HIRED* HIM, AND PAID HIM HALF WHAT LESS PRODUCTVE *WHITE* DESIGNERS MADE.
"BUT THEN, BY *CHANCE,* HE DISCOVERED THAT SOME OF HIS TOY DESIGNS WERE BEING USED IN *WEAPONS* --
"-- WEAPONS USED BY THE *UNDERWORLD.*
"HE TRIED TO GET TO THE BOTTOM OF IT AT *WHAMCO,* BUT ALL THAT HAPPENED WAS THAT HE GOT *FIRED.*
"STILL, HE DIDN'T LET IT GO. HE TRIED TO FIND THE *LINK* BETWEEN WHAMCO AND THE MOBS -- TRIED TO *EXPOSE* IT.
"NOBODY *BELIEVED* HIM, BUT WHAMCO WANTED HIM TO *SHUT UP* ANYWAY.
"SO THEY HAD HIS FATHER -- MY *GRANDFATHER* -- KIDNAPPED.
"THAT'S WHEN HE CUSTOMIZED SOME OF HIS *TOY DESIGNS,* WORKED UP A COSTUME --
"-- AND BECAME *JACK-IN-THE-BOX* -- FIRST TO RESCUE MY GRANDFATHER, AND THEN TO CONTINUE HIS *INVESTIGATION.*
"HE TOOK ON THE *MOBS,* HE TOOK ON *WHAMCO,* AND EVENTUALLY HE EXPOSED THEM. HE *WON.*
FULL-TIME POWER STEERING
FLEUR de-LIS CIGARETTES
"BUT HE STILL KEPT *FIGHTING* -- FOR OTHERS WHO'D BEEN VICTIMIZED, WHO NEEDED *HELP.* HE'D BECOME A *HERO.*

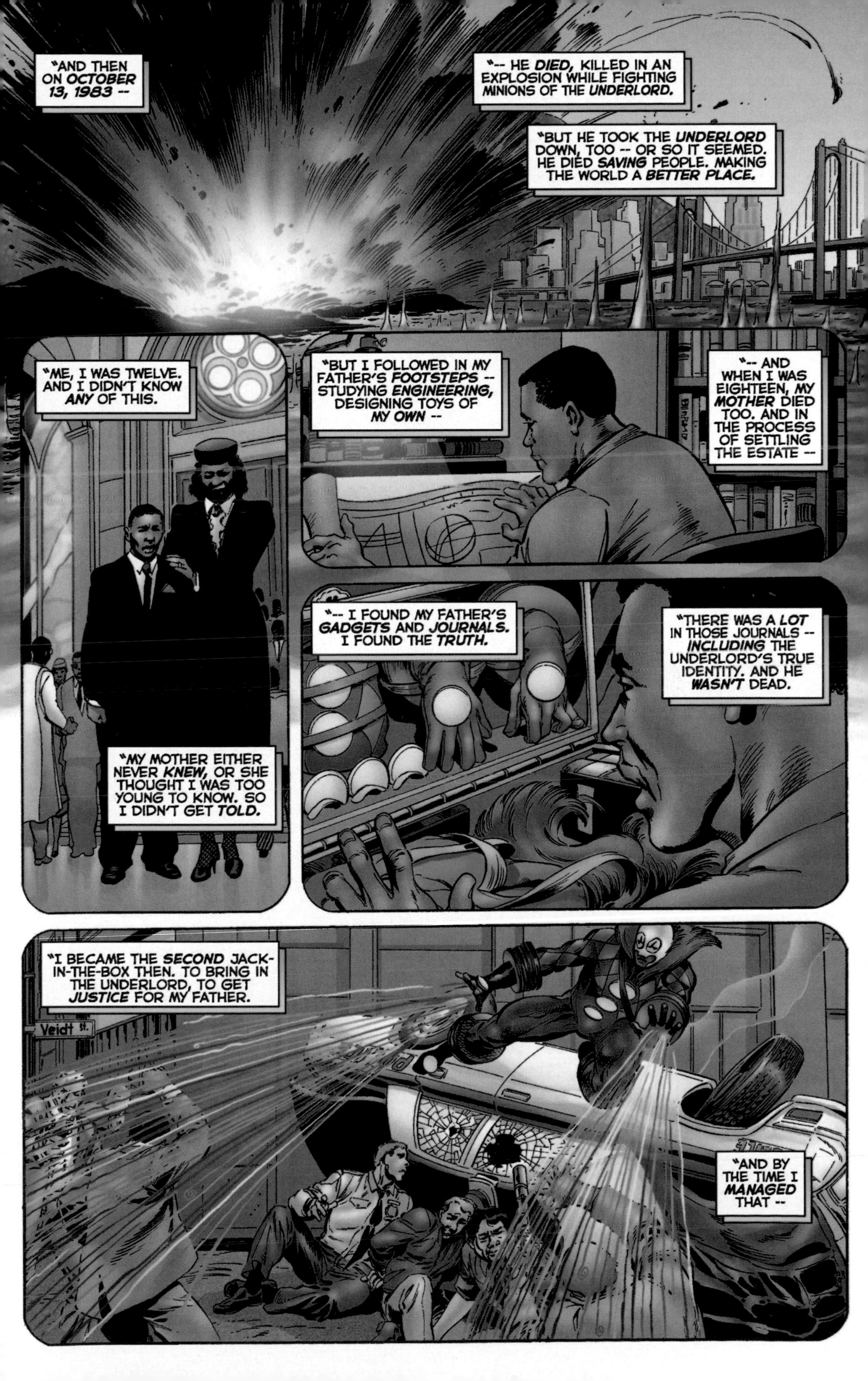
"AND THEN ON OCTOBER 13, 1983 --
"-- HE DIED, KILLED IN AN EXPLOSION WHILE FIGHTING MINIONS OF THE UNDERLORD.
"BUT HE TOOK THE UNDERLORD DOWN, TOO -- OR SO IT SEEMED. HE DIED SAVING PEOPLE. MAKING THE WORLD A BETTER PLACE.
"ME, I WAS TWELVE. AND I DIDN'T KNOW ANY OF THIS.
"MY MOTHER EITHER NEVER KNEW, OR SHE THOUGHT I WAS TOO YOUNG TO KNOW. SO I DIDN'T GET TOLD.
"BUT I FOLLOWED IN MY FATHER'S FOOTSTEPS -- STUDYING ENGINEERING, DESIGNING TOYS OF MY OWN --
"-- AND WHEN I WAS EIGHTEEN, MY MOTHER DIED TOO. AND IN THE PROCESS OF SETTLING THE ESTATE --
"-- I FOUND MY FATHER'S GADGETS AND JOURNALS. I FOUND THE TRUTH.
"THERE WAS A LOT IN THOSE JOURNALS -- INCLUDING THE UNDERLORD'S TRUE IDENTITY. AND HE WASN'T DEAD.
"I BECAME THE SECOND JACK-IN-THE-BOX THEN. TO BRING IN THE UNDERLORD, TO GET JUSTICE FOR MY FATHER.
Veidt St.
"AND BY THE TIME I MANAGED THAT --

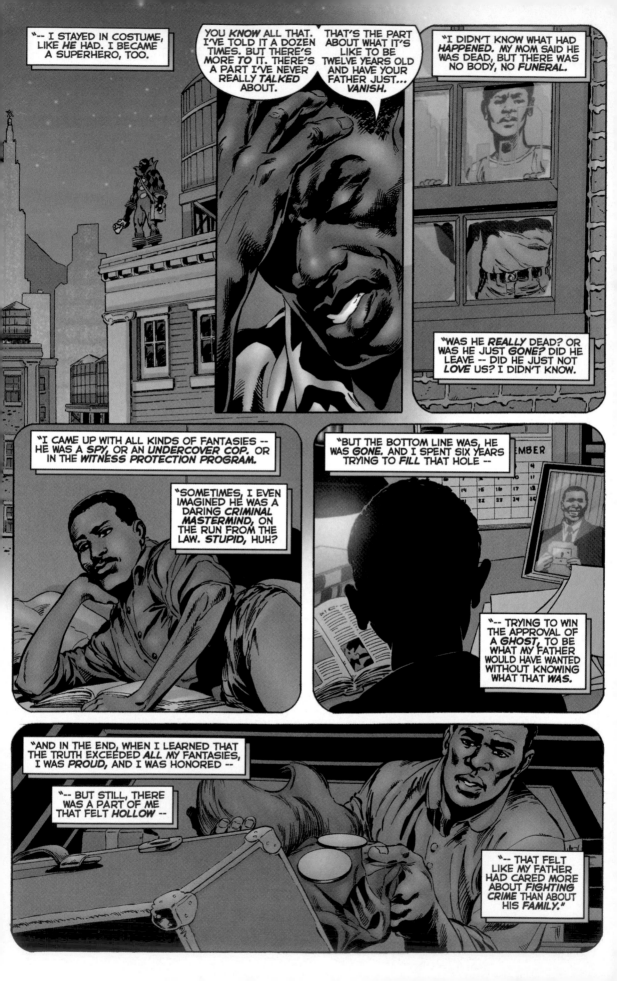

"-- I STAYED IN COSTUME, LIKE *HE* HAD. I BECAME A SUPERHERO, TOO."

YOU *KNOW* ALL THAT. I'VE TOLD IT A DOZEN TIMES. BUT THERE'S MORE *TO* IT. THERE'S A PART I'VE NEVER REALLY *TALKED* ABOUT.

THAT'S THE PART ABOUT WHAT IT'S LIKE TO BE TWELVE YEARS OLD AND HAVE YOUR FATHER JUST... *VANISH.*

"I DIDN'T KNOW WHAT HAD *HAPPENED.* MY MOM SAID HE WAS DEAD, BUT THERE WAS NO BODY, NO *FUNERAL.*"

"WAS HE *REALLY* DEAD? OR WAS HE JUST *GONE?* DID HE LEAVE -- DID HE JUST NOT *LOVE* US? I DIDN'T KNOW."

"I CAME UP WITH ALL KINDS OF FANTASIES -- HE WAS A *SPY,* OR AN *UNDERCOVER COP.* OR IN THE *WITNESS PROTECTION PROGRAM.*"

"SOMETIMES, I EVEN IMAGINED HE WAS A DARING *CRIMINAL MASTERMIND,* ON THE RUN FROM THE LAW. *STUPID,* HUH?"

"BUT THE BOTTOM LINE WAS, HE WAS *GONE.* AND I SPENT SIX YEARS TRYING TO *FILL* THAT HOLE --"

"-- TRYING TO WIN THE APPROVAL OF A *GHOST,* TO BE WHAT MY FATHER WOULD HAVE WANTED WITHOUT KNOWING WHAT THAT *WAS.*"

"AND IN THE END, WHEN I LEARNED THAT THE TRUTH EXCEEDED *ALL MY FANTASIES,* I WAS *PROUD,* AND I WAS HONORED --"

"-- BUT STILL, THERE WAS A PART OF ME THAT FELT *HOLLOW* --"

"-- THAT FELT LIKE MY FATHER HAD CARED MORE ABOUT *FIGHTING CRIME* THAN ABOUT HIS *FAMILY.*"

SO NOW, WHEN YOU TELL ME YOU'RE *PREGNANT* -- AND *I'M* THE ONE GOING OUT THERE EVERY NIGHT --

I -- I THOUGHT YOU *WANTED* KIDS. I THOUGHT YOU *WANTED* THIS!

I DO, TAMRA, I *DO*. IT'S JUST --

-- I DIDN'T THINK WE'D BE HAVING KIDS THIS *SOON*. I DIDN'T THINK ABOUT WHAT IT *MEANT* --

"AND AFTER WHAT HAPPENED *TONIGHT*, WITH THOSE -- THOSE TWISTED VERSIONS OF WHAT OUR CHILD COULD *BECOME* --

"-- IT'S MADE ME THINK ABOUT WHAT COULD *HAPPEN*, AND WHAT THAT COULD MEAN TO A *BABY*.

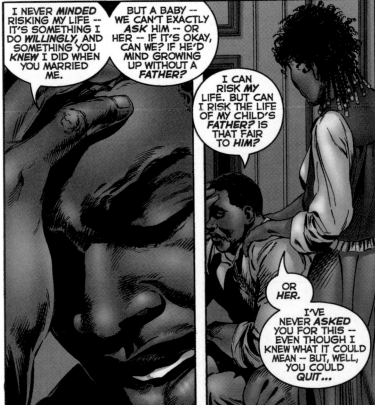

I NEVER *MINDED* RISKING MY LIFE -- IT'S SOMETHING I DO *WILLINGLY*, AND SOMETHING YOU *KNEW* I DID WHEN YOU MARRIED ME.

BUT A BABY -- WE CAN'T EXACTLY *ASK* HIM -- OR HER -- IF IT'S OKAY, CAN WE? IF HE'D MIND GROWING UP WITHOUT A *FATHER*?

I CAN RISK *MY* LIFE. BUT CAN I RISK THE LIFE OF MY CHILD'S *FATHER*? IS THAT FAIR TO *HIM*?

OR *HER*. I'VE NEVER *ASKED* YOU FOR THIS -- EVEN THOUGH I KNEW WHAT IT COULD MEAN -- BUT, WELL, YOU COULD *QUIT*...

HOW? CAN I READ IN THE PAPER ABOUT MURDER -- ABOUT *RAPE*, AND MORE -- AND KNOW I COULD HAVE *STOPPED* IT?

HOW COULD I *LIVE* WITH MYSELF?

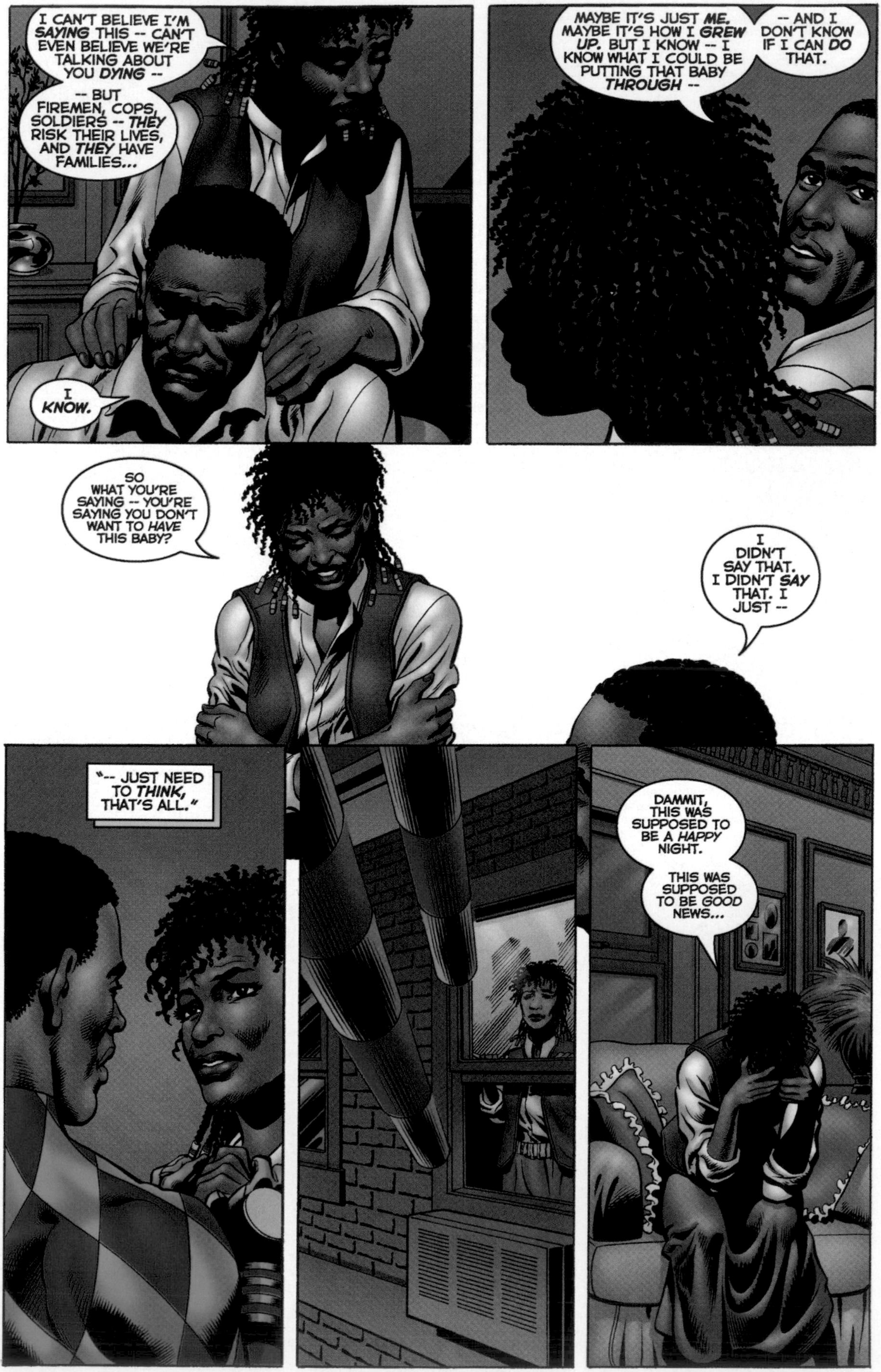
I CAN'T BELIEVE I'M SAYING THIS -- CAN'T EVEN BELIEVE WE'RE TALKING ABOUT YOU DYING --
-- BUT FIREMEN, COPS, SOLDIERS -- THEY RISK THEIR LIVES, AND THEY HAVE FAMILIES...
I KNOW.
MAYBE IT'S JUST ME. MAYBE IT'S HOW I GREW UP. BUT I KNOW -- I KNOW WHAT I COULD BE PUTTING THAT BABY THROUGH --
-- AND I DON'T KNOW IF I CAN DO THAT.
SO WHAT YOU'RE SAYING -- YOU'RE SAYING YOU DON'T WANT TO HAVE THIS BABY?
I DIDN'T SAY THAT. I DIDN'T SAY THAT. I JUST --
"-- JUST NEED TO THINK, THAT'S ALL."
DAMMIT, THIS WAS SUPPOSED TO BE A HAPPY NIGHT.
THIS WAS SUPPOSED TO BE GOOD NEWS...

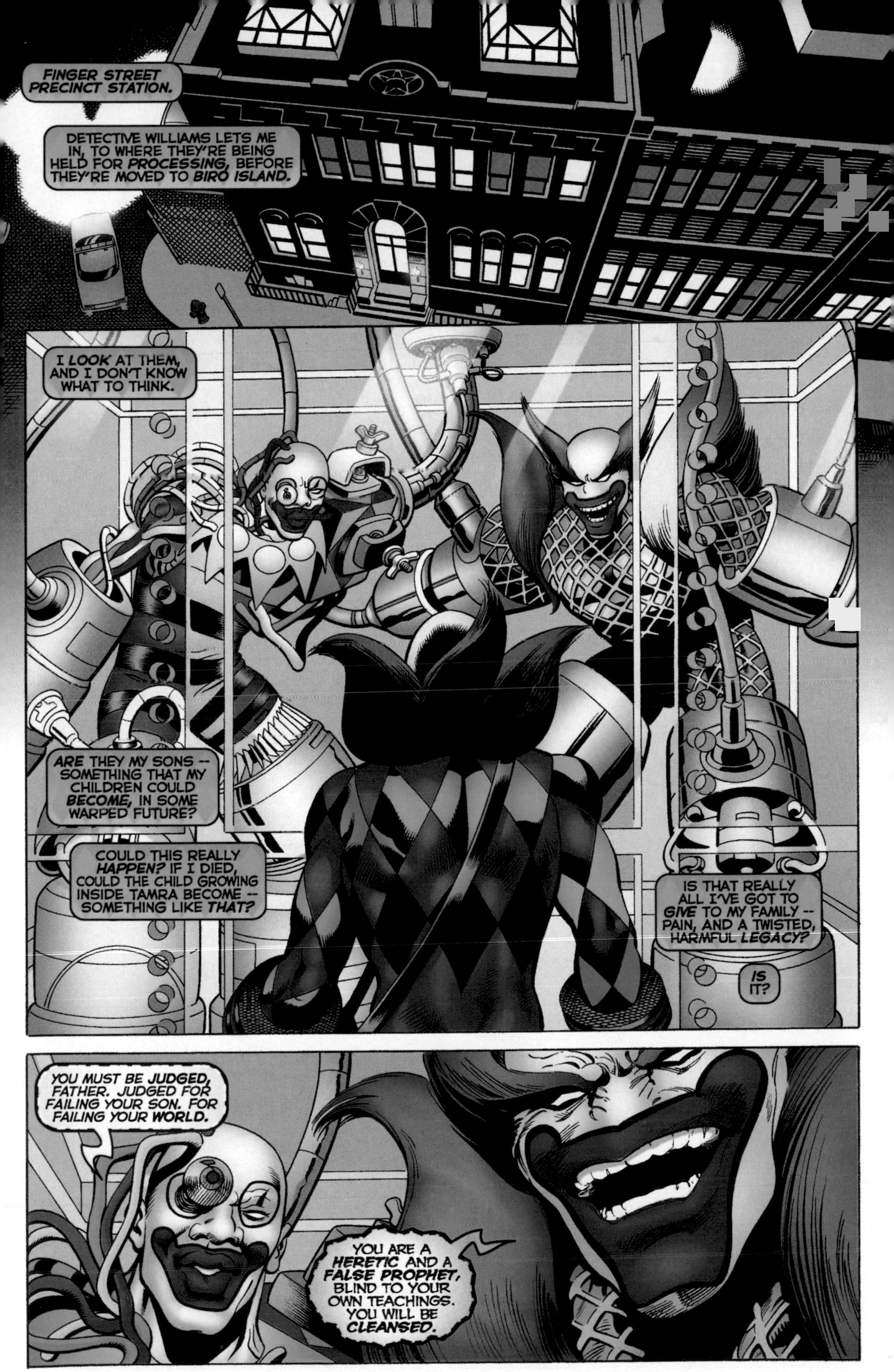

FINGER STREET PRECINCT STATION.
DETECTIVE WILLIAMS LETS ME IN, TO WHERE THEY'RE BEING HELD FOR PROCESSING, BEFORE THEY'RE MOVED TO BIRO ISLAND.
I LOOK AT THEM, AND I DON'T KNOW WHAT TO THINK.
ARE THEY MY SONS -- SOMETHING THAT MY CHILDREN COULD BECOME, IN SOME WARPED FUTURE?
COULD THIS REALLY HAPPEN? IF I DIED, COULD THE CHILD GROWING INSIDE TAMRA BECOME -- SOMETHING LIKE THAT?
IS THAT REALLY ALL I'VE GOT TO GIVE TO MY FAMILY -- PAIN, AND A TWISTED, HARMFUL LEGACY?
IS IT?
YOU MUST BE JUDGED, FATHER. JUDGED FOR FAILING YOUR SON. FOR FAILING YOUR WORLD.
YOU ARE A HERETIC AND A FALSE PROPHET, BLIND TO YOUR OWN TEACHINGS. YOU WILL BE CLEANSED.

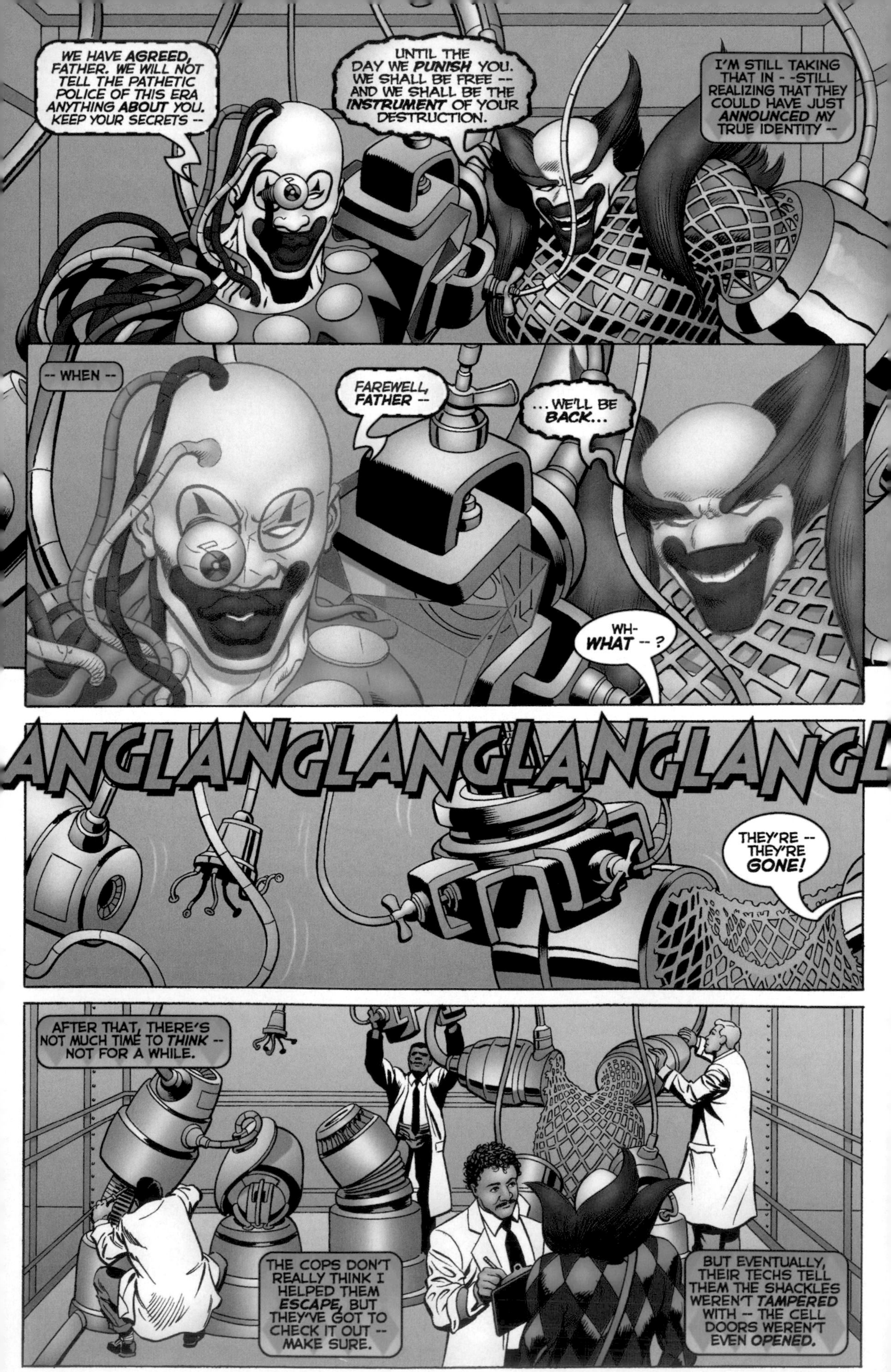

WE HAVE AGREED, FATHER. WE WILL NOT TELL THE PATHETIC POLICE OF THIS ERA ANYTHING ABOUT YOU. KEEP YOUR SECRETS --
UNTIL THE DAY WE PUNISH YOU. WE SHALL BE FREE -- AND WE SHALL BE THE INSTRUMENT OF YOUR DESTRUCTION.
I'M STILL TAKING THAT IN - -STILL REALIZING THAT THEY COULD HAVE JUST ANNOUNCED MY TRUE IDENTITY --
-- WHEN --
FAREWELL, FATHER --
...WE'LL BE BACK...
WH- WHAT -- ?
ANGLANGLANGLANGLANGLANGL
THEY'RE -- THEY'RE GONE!
AFTER THAT, THERE'S NOT MUCH TIME TO THINK -- NOT FOR A WHILE.
THE COPS DON'T REALLY THINK I HELPED THEM ESCAPE, BUT THEY'VE GOT TO CHECK IT OUT -- MAKE SURE.
BUT EVENTUALLY, THEIR TECHS TELL THEM THE SHACKLES WEREN'T TAMPERED WITH -- THE CELL DOORS WEREN'T EVEN OPENED.

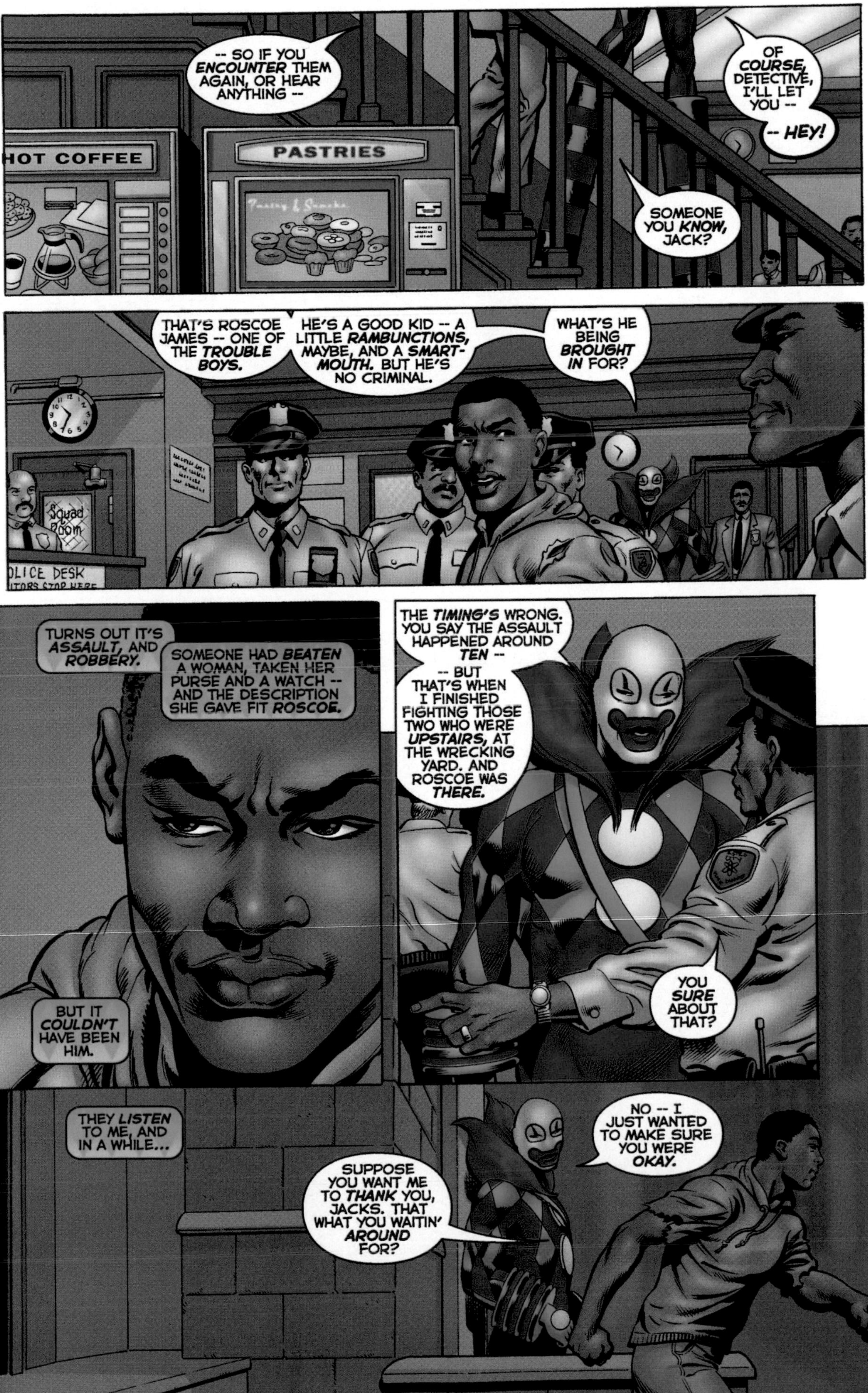
-- SO IF YOU ENCOUNTER THEM AGAIN, OR HEAR ANYTHING --
OF COURSE, DETECTIVE, I'LL LET YOU --
-- HEY!
HOT COFFEE
PASTRIES
SOMEONE YOU KNOW, JACK?
THAT'S ROSCOE JAMES -- ONE OF THE TROUBLE BOYS.
HE'S A GOOD KID -- A LITTLE RAMBUNCTIONS, MAYBE, AND A SMART-MOUTH. BUT HE'S NO CRIMINAL.
WHAT'S HE BEING BROUGHT IN FOR?
Squad Room
POLICE DESK
TURNS OUT IT'S ASSAULT, AND ROBBERY.
SOMEONE HAD BEATEN A WOMAN, TAKEN HER PURSE AND A WATCH -- AND THE DESCRIPTION SHE GAVE FIT ROSCOE.
BUT IT COULDN'T HAVE BEEN HIM.
THE TIMING'S WRONG. YOU SAY THE ASSAULT HAPPENED AROUND TEN --
-- BUT THAT'S WHEN I FINISHED FIGHTING THOSE TWO WHO WERE UPSTAIRS, AT THE WRECKING YARD. AND ROSCOE WAS THERE.
YOU SURE ABOUT THAT?
THEY LISTEN TO ME, AND IN A WHILE...
NO -- I JUST WANTED TO MAKE SURE YOU WERE OKAY.
SUPPOSE YOU WANT ME TO THANK YOU, JACKS. THAT WHAT YOU WAITIN' AROUND FOR?

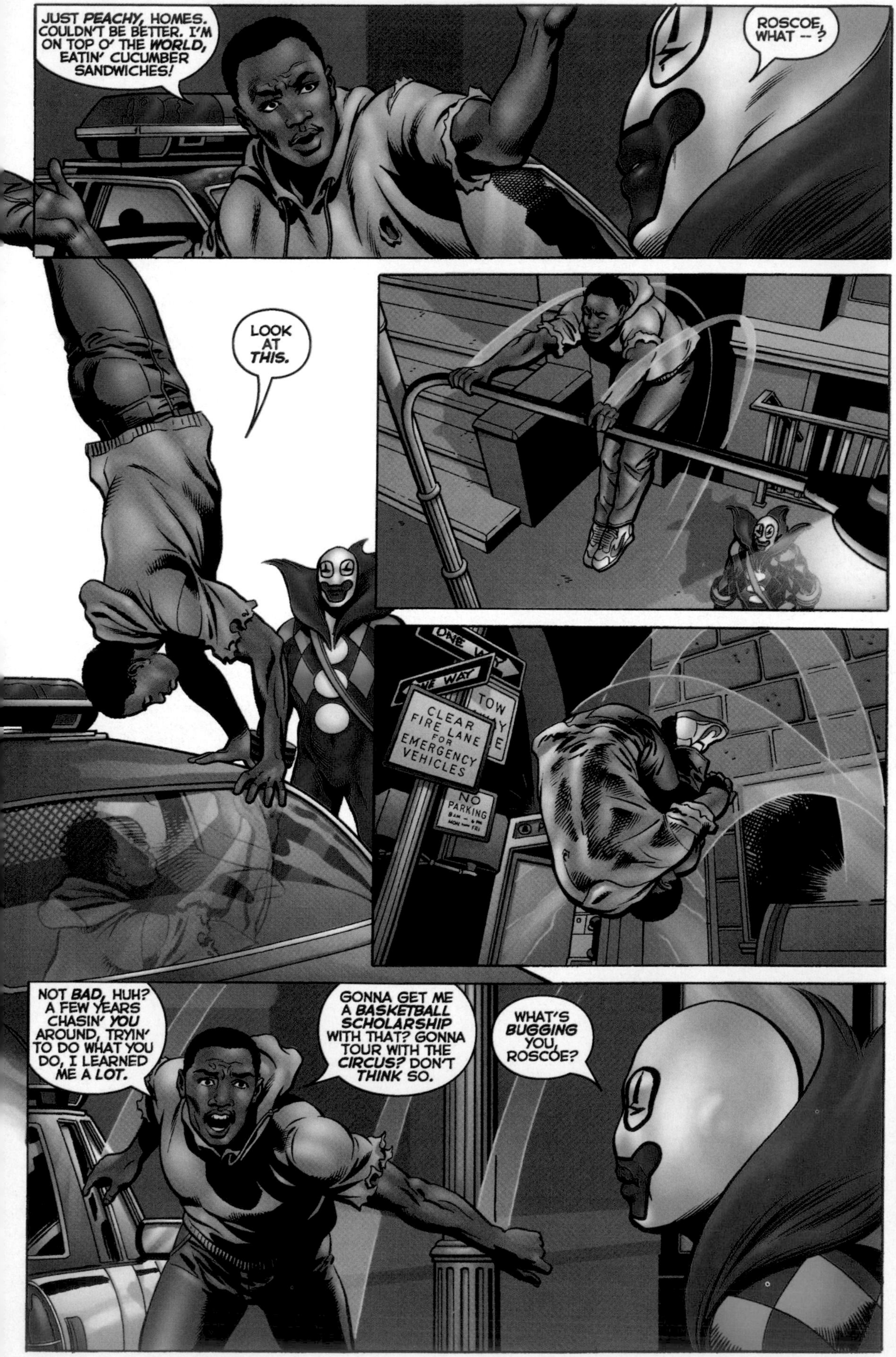
JUST PEACHY, HOMES. COULDN'T BE BETTER. I'M ON TOP O' THE WORLD, EATIN' CUCUMBER SANDWICHES!
ROSCOE, WHAT -- ?
LOOK AT THIS.
ONE WAY
ONE WAY
CLEAR FIRE LANE FOR EMERGENCY VEHICLES
TOW
NO PARKING
NOT BAD, HUH? A FEW YEARS CHASIN' YOU AROUND, TRYIN' TO DO WHAT YOU DO, I LEARNED ME A LOT.
GONNA GET ME A BASKETBALL SCHOLARSHIP WITH THAT? GONNA TOUR WITH THE CIRCUS? DON'T THINK SO.
WHAT'S BUGGING YOU, ROSCOE?

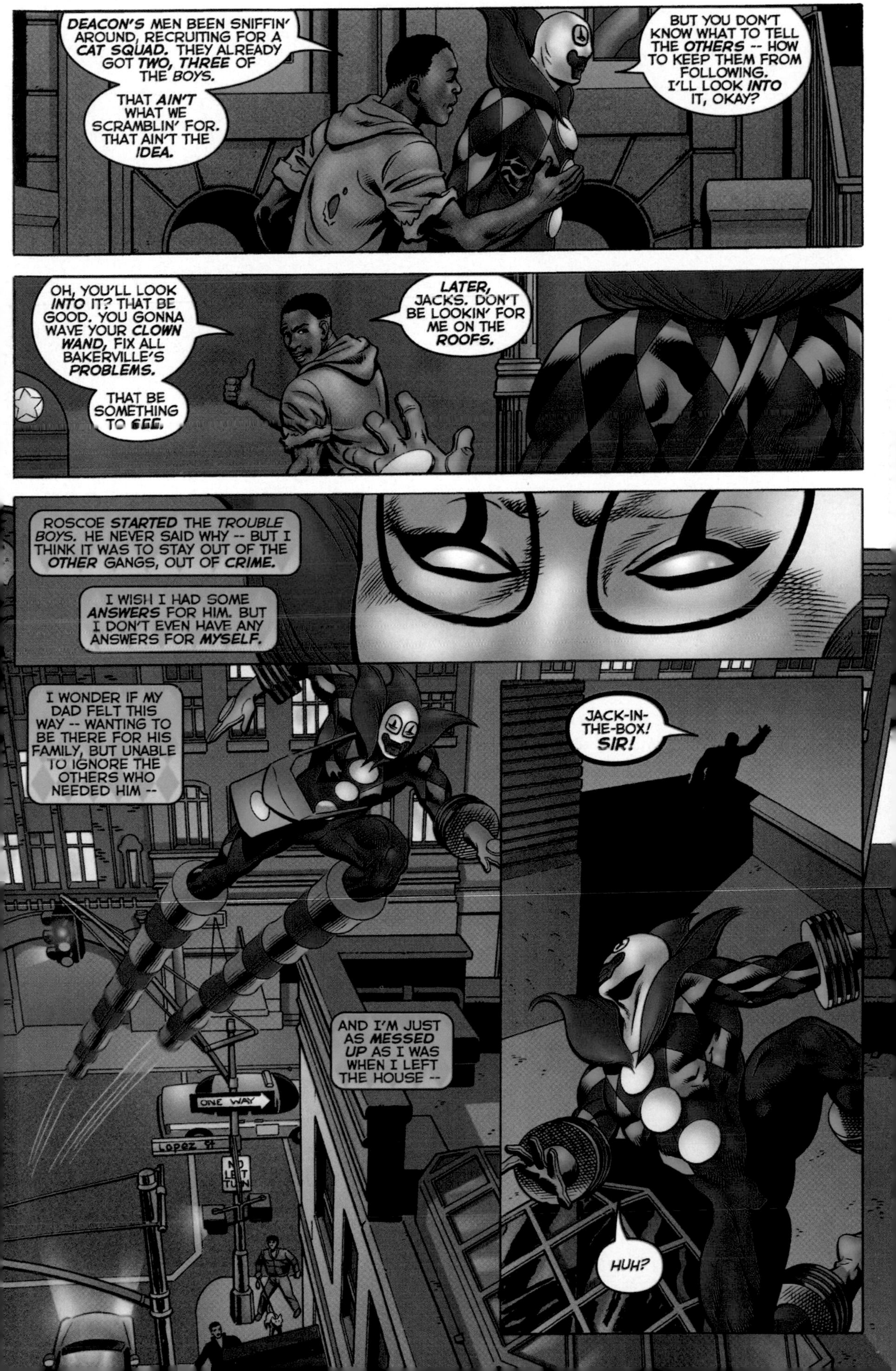
DEACON'S MEN BEEN SNIFFIN' AROUND, RECRUITING FOR A CAT SQUAD. THEY ALREADY GOT TWO, THREE OF THE BOYS.
THAT AIN'T WHAT WE SCRAMBLIN' FOR. THAT AIN'T THE IDEA.
BUT YOU DON'T KNOW WHAT TO TELL THE OTHERS -- HOW TO KEEP THEM FROM FOLLOWING. I'LL LOOK INTO IT, OKAY?
OH, YOU'LL LOOK INTO IT? THAT BE GOOD. YOU GONNA WAVE YOUR CLOWN WAND, FIX ALL BAKERVILLE'S PROBLEMS.
THAT BE SOMETHING TO SEE.
LATER, JACKS. DON'T BE LOOKIN' FOR ME ON THE ROOFS.
ROSCOE STARTED THE TROUBLE BOYS. HE NEVER SAID WHY -- BUT I THINK IT WAS TO STAY OUT OF THE OTHER GANGS, OUT OF CRIME.
I WISH I HAD SOME ANSWERS FOR HIM. BUT I DON'T EVEN HAVE ANY ANSWERS FOR MYSELF.
I WONDER IF MY DAD FELT THIS WAY -- WANTING TO BE THERE FOR HIS FAMILY, BUT UNABLE TO IGNORE THE OTHERS WHO NEEDED HIM --
ONE WAY
Lopez St
NO LEFT TURN
AND I'M JUST AS MESSED UP AS I WAS WHEN I LEFT THE HOUSE --
JACK-IN-THE-BOX! SIR!
HUH?

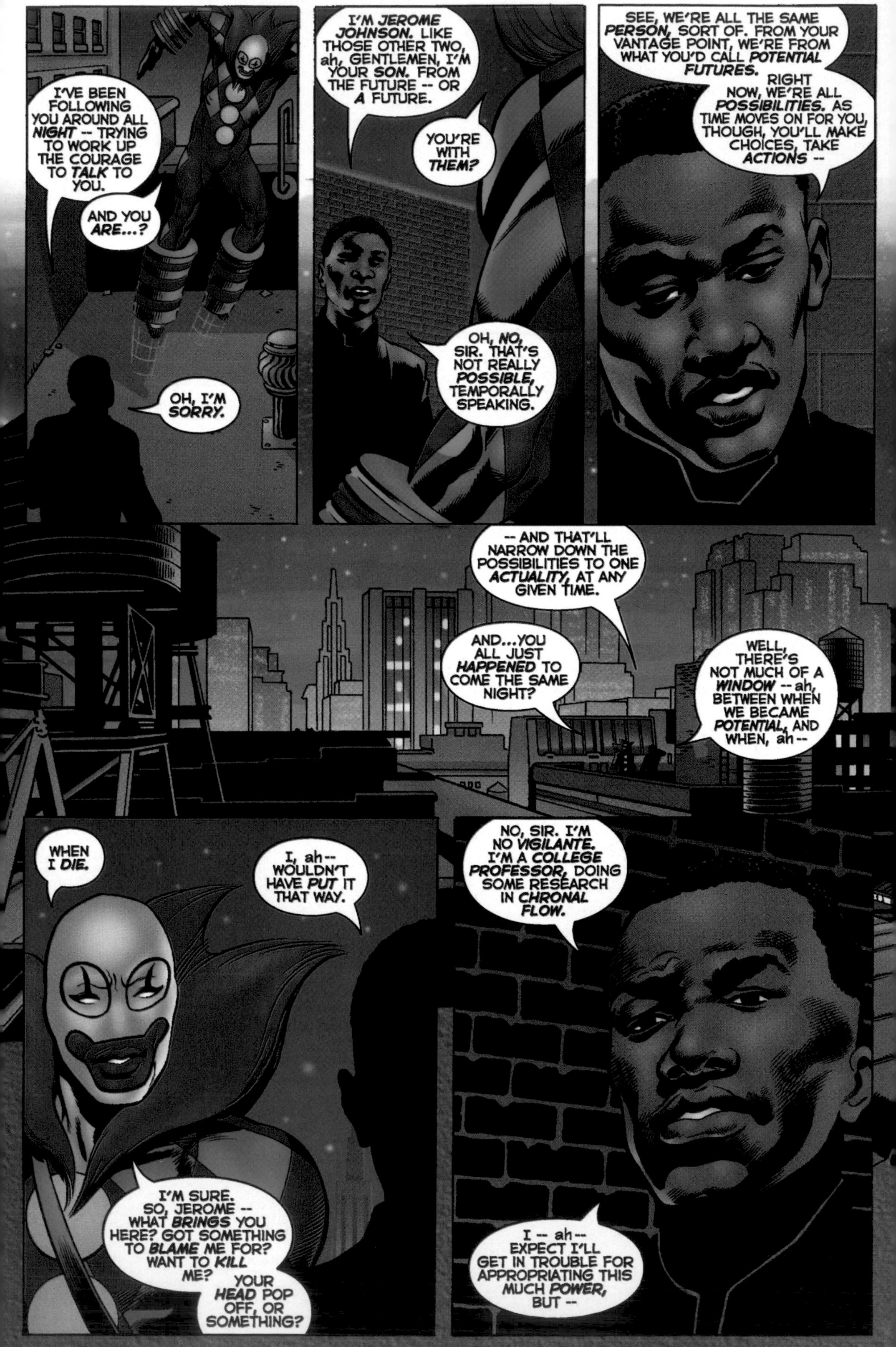
I'VE BEEN FOLLOWING YOU AROUND ALL NIGHT -- TRYING TO WORK UP THE COURAGE TO TALK TO YOU.
AND YOU ARE...?
OH, I'M SORRY.
I'M JEROME JOHNSON. LIKE THOSE OTHER TWO, ah, GENTLEMEN, I'M YOUR SON. FROM THE FUTURE -- OR A FUTURE.
YOU'RE WITH THEM?
OH, NO, SIR. THAT'S NOT REALLY POSSIBLE, TEMPORALLY SPEAKING.
SEE, WE'RE ALL THE SAME PERSON, SORT OF. FROM YOUR VANTAGE POINT, WE'RE FROM WHAT YOU'D CALL POTENTIAL FUTURES.
RIGHT NOW, WE'RE ALL POSSIBILITIES. AS TIME MOVES ON FOR YOU, THOUGH, YOU'LL MAKE CHOICES, TAKE ACTIONS --
-- AND THAT'LL NARROW DOWN THE POSSIBILITIES TO ONE ACTUALITY, AT ANY GIVEN TIME.
AND...YOU ALL JUST HAPPENED TO COME THE SAME NIGHT?
WELL, THERE'S NOT MUCH OF A WINDOW -- ah, BETWEEN WHEN WE BECAME POTENTIAL, AND WHEN, ah --
WHEN I DIE.
I, ah -- WOULDN'T HAVE PUT IT THAT WAY.
I'M SURE. SO, JEROME -- WHAT BRINGS YOU HERE? GOT SOMETHING TO BLAME ME FOR? WANT TO KILL ME?
YOUR HEAD POP OFF, OR SOMETHING?
NO, SIR. I'M NO VIGILANTE. I'M A COLLEGE PROFESSOR, DOING SOME RESEARCH IN CHRONAL FLOW.
I -- ah -- EXPECT I'LL GET IN TROUBLE FOR APPROPRIATING THIS MUCH POWER, BUT --

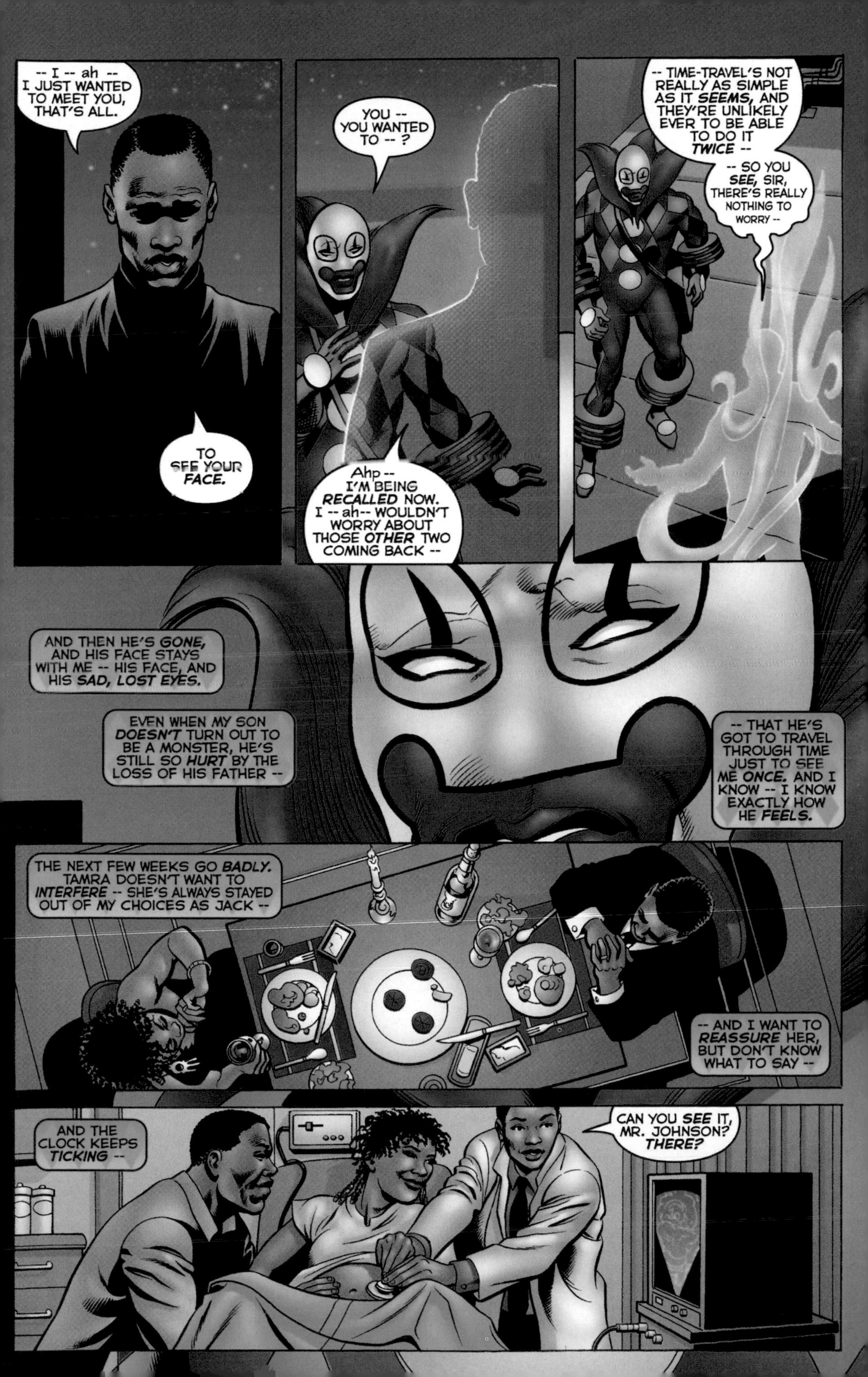
-- I -- ah -- I JUST WANTED TO MEET YOU, THAT'S ALL.
TO SEE YOUR FACE.
YOU -- YOU WANTED TO -- ?
Ahp -- I'M BEING RECALLED NOW. I -- ah-- WOULDN'T WORRY ABOUT THOSE OTHER TWO COMING BACK --
-- TIME-TRAVEL'S NOT REALLY AS SIMPLE AS IT SEEMS, AND THEY'RE UNLIKELY EVER TO BE ABLE TO DO IT TWICE --
-- SO YOU SEE, SIR, THERE'S REALLY NOTHING TO WORRY --
AND THEN HE'S GONE, AND HIS FACE STAYS WITH ME -- HIS FACE, AND HIS SAD, LOST EYES.
EVEN WHEN MY SON DOESN'T TURN OUT TO BE A MONSTER, HE'S STILL SO HURT BY THE LOSS OF HIS FATHER --
-- THAT HE'S GOT TO TRAVEL THROUGH TIME JUST TO SEE ME ONCE. AND I KNOW -- I KNOW EXACTLY HOW HE FEELS.
THE NEXT FEW WEEKS GO BADLY. TAMRA DOESN'T WANT TO INTERFERE -- SHE'S ALWAYS STAYED OUT OF MY CHOICES AS JACK --
-- AND I WANT TO REASSURE HER, BUT DON'T KNOW WHAT TO SAY --
AND THE CLOCK KEEPS TICKING --
CAN YOU SEE IT, MR. JOHNSON? THERE?

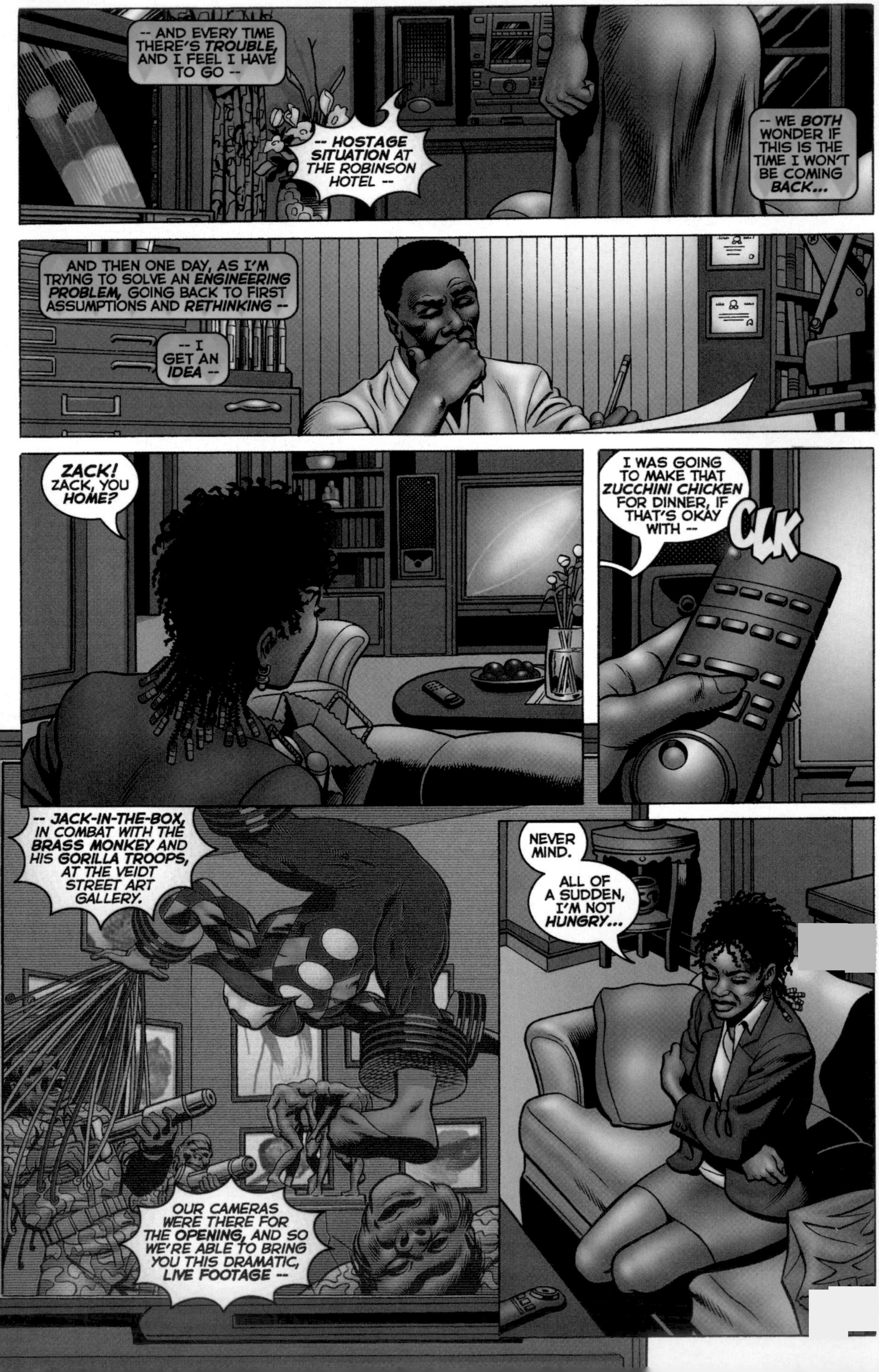
-- AND EVERY TIME THERE'S TROUBLE, AND I FEEL I HAVE TO GO --
-- HOSTAGE SITUATION AT THE ROBINSON HOTEL --
-- WE BOTH WONDER IF THIS IS THE TIME I WON'T BE COMING BACK...
AND THEN ONE DAY, AS I'M TRYING TO SOLVE AN ENGINEERING PROBLEM, GOING BACK TO FIRST ASSUMPTIONS AND RETHINKING --
-- I GET AN IDEA --
ZACK! ZACK, YOU HOME?
I WAS GOING TO MAKE THAT ZUCCHINI CHICKEN FOR DINNER, IF THAT'S OKAY WITH --
CLK
-- JACK-IN-THE-BOX, IN COMBAT WITH THE BRASS MONKEY AND HIS GORILLA TROOPS, AT THE VEIDT STREET ART GALLERY.
OUR CAMERAS WERE THERE FOR THE OPENING, AND SO WE'RE ABLE TO BRING YOU THIS DRAMATIC, LIVE FOOTAGE --
NEVER MIND.
ALL OF A SUDDEN, I'M NOT HUNGRY...

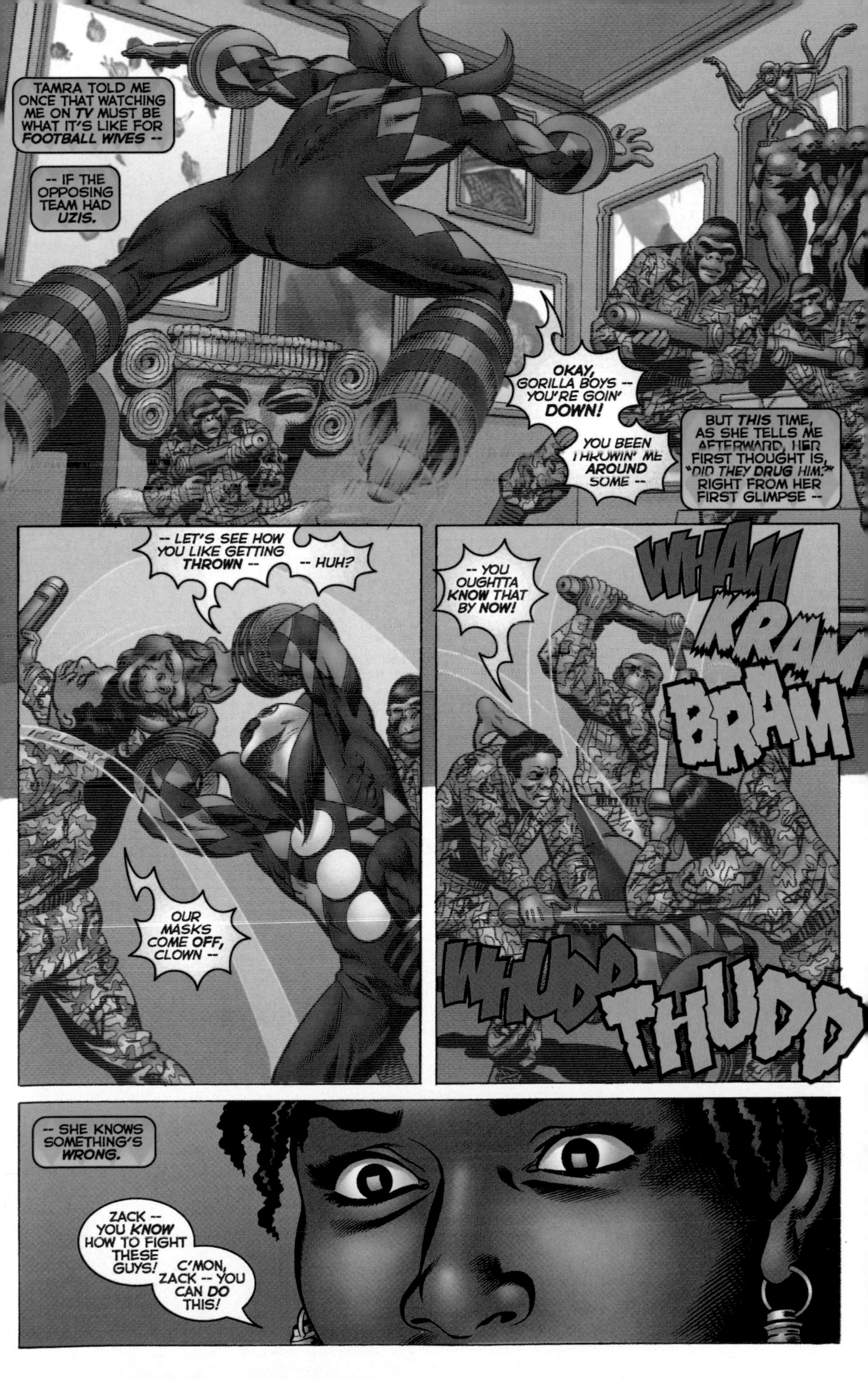
TAMRA TOLD ME ONCE THAT WATCHING ME ON TV MUST BE WHAT IT'S LIKE FOR FOOTBALL WIVES --
-- IF THE OPPOSING TEAM HAD UZIS.
OKAY, GORILLA BOYS -- YOU'RE GOIN' DOWN!
YOU BEEN THROWIN' ME AROUND SOME --
BUT THIS TIME, AS SHE TELLS ME AFTERWARD, HER FIRST THOUGHT IS, "DID THEY DRUG HIM?" RIGHT FROM HER FIRST GLIMPSE --
-- LET'S SEE HOW YOU LIKE GETTING THROWN --
-- HUH?
OUR MASKS COME OFF, CLOWN --
-- YOU OUGHTTA KNOW THAT BY NOW!
WHAM
KRAM
BRAM
WHUDD
THUDD
-- SHE KNOWS SOMETHING'S WRONG.
ZACK -- YOU KNOW HOW TO FIGHT THESE GUYS!
C'MON, ZACK -- YOU CAN DO THIS!

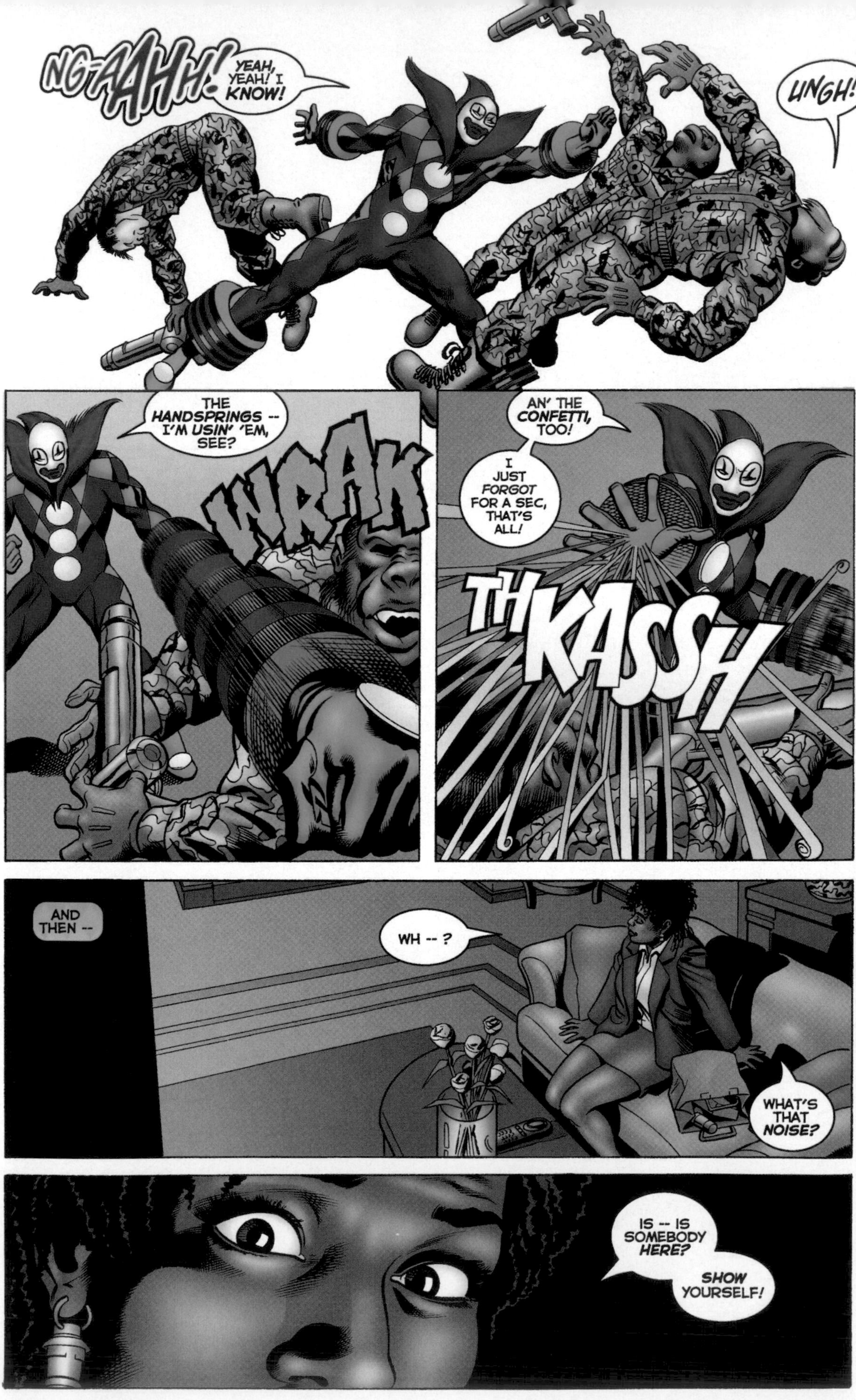
NG-AAHH!
YEAH, YEAH! I KNOW!
UNGH!
THE HANDSPRINGS -- I'M USIN' 'EM, SEE?
WRAK
AN' THE CONFETTI, TOO!
I JUST FORGOT FOR A SEC, THAT'S ALL!
THKASSH
AND THEN --
WH -- ?
WHAT'S THAT NOISE?
IS -- IS SOMEBODY HERE?
SHOW YOURSELF!

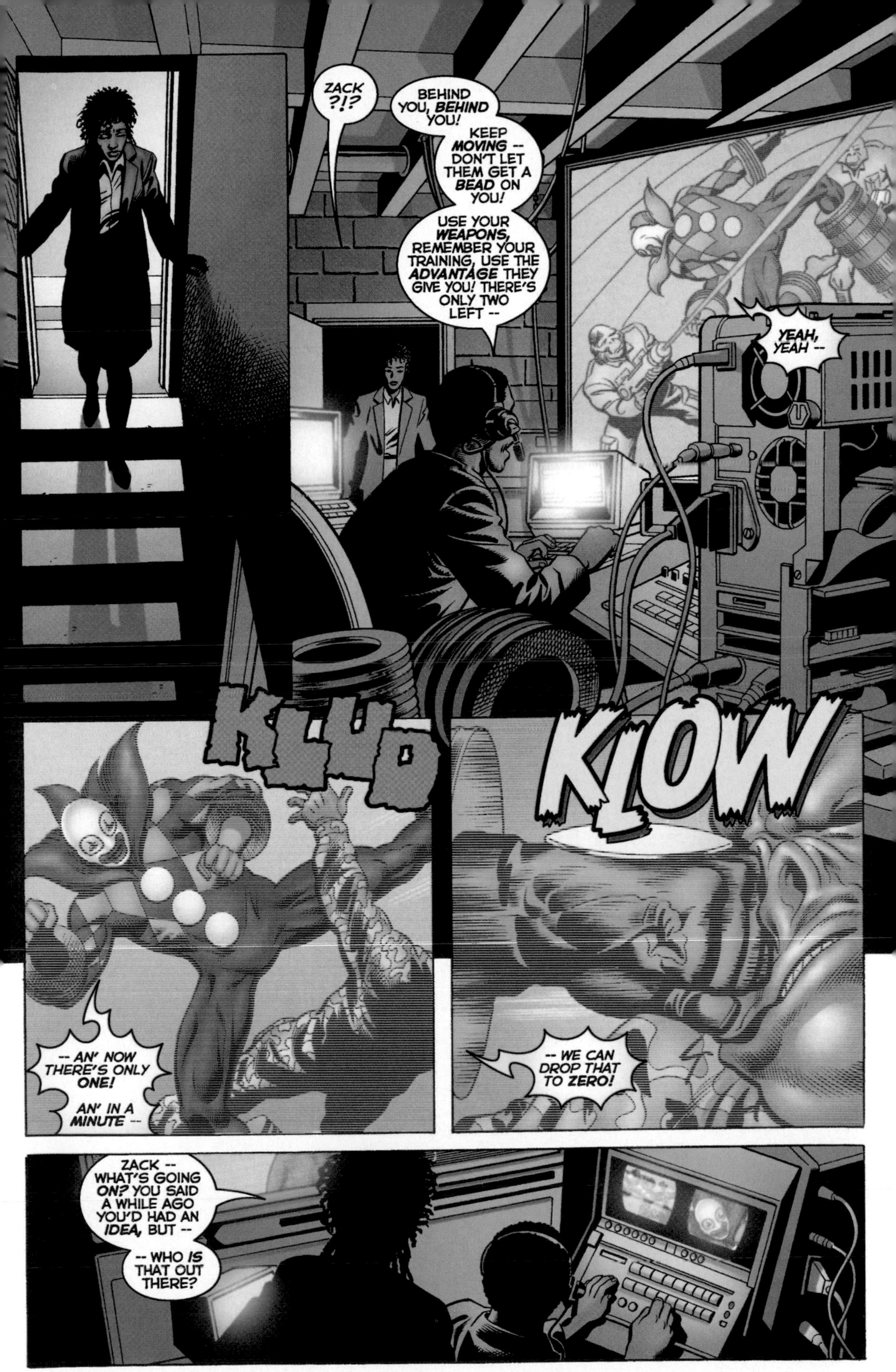
ZACK ?!?
BEHIND YOU, BEHIND YOU!
KEEP MOVING -- DON'T LET THEM GET A BEAD ON YOU!
USE YOUR WEAPONS, REMEMBER YOUR TRAINING, USE THE ADVANTAGE THEY GIVE YOU! THERE'S ONLY TWO LEFT --
YEAH, YEAH --
KLUD
KLOW
-- AN' NOW THERE'S ONLY ONE!
AN' IN A MINUTE --
-- WE CAN DROP THAT TO ZERO!
ZACK -- WHAT'S GOING ON? YOU SAID A WHILE AGO YOU'D HAD AN IDEA, BUT --
-- WHO IS THAT OUT THERE?

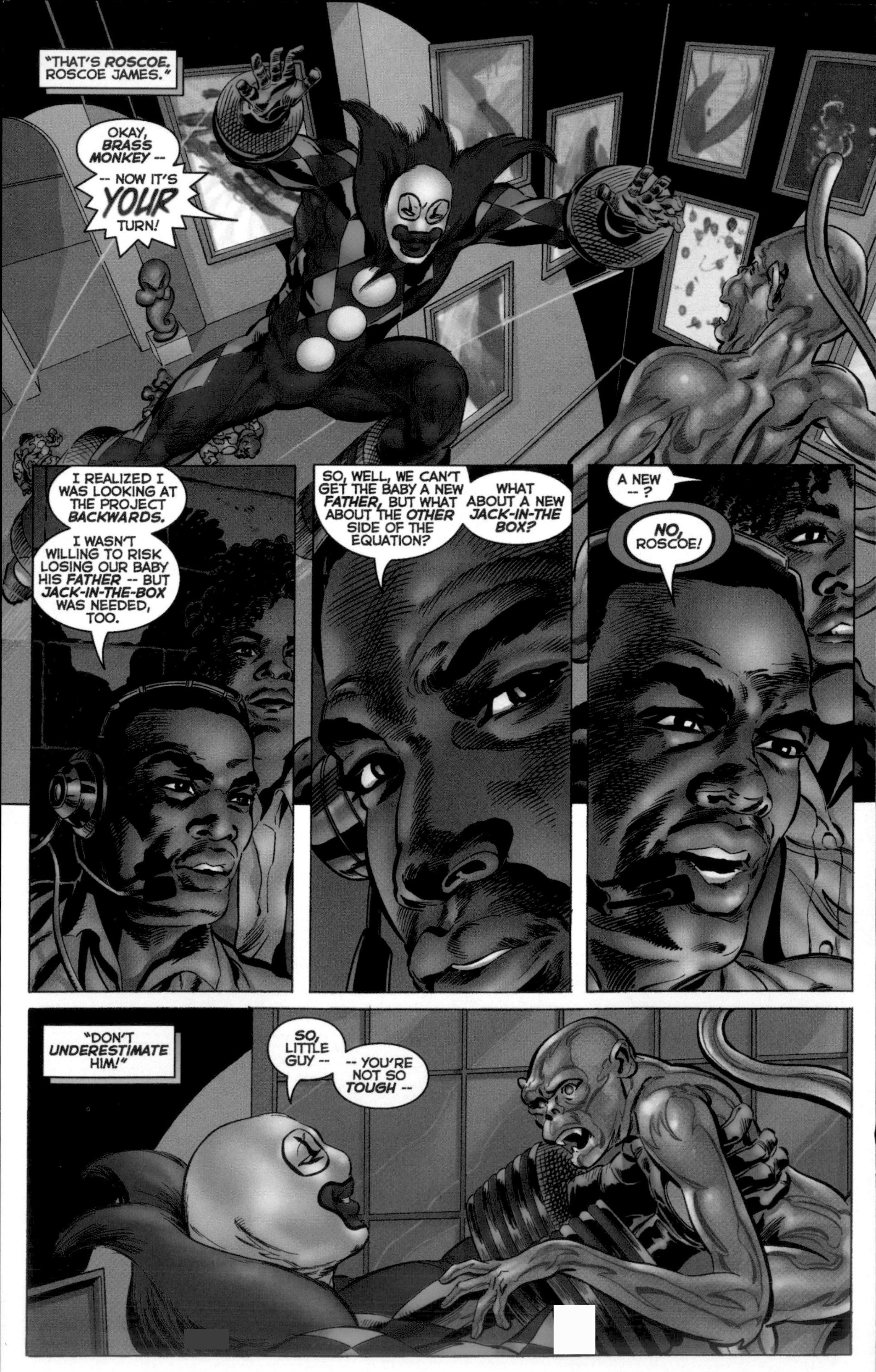
"THAT'S ROSCOE. ROSCOE JAMES."
OKAY, BRASS MONKEY --
-- NOW IT'S YOUR TURN!
I REALIZED I WAS LOOKING AT THE PROJECT BACKWARDS.
I WASN'T WILLING TO RISK LOSING OUR BABY HIS FATHER -- BUT JACK-IN-THE-BOX WAS NEEDED, TOO.
SO, WELL, WE CAN'T GET THE BABY A NEW FATHER, BUT WHAT ABOUT THE OTHER SIDE OF THE EQUATION?
WHAT ABOUT A NEW JACK-IN-THE BOX?
A NEW -- ?
NO, ROSCOE!
"DON'T UNDERESTIMATE HIM!"
SO, LITTLE GUY --
-- YOU'RE NOT SO TOUGH --

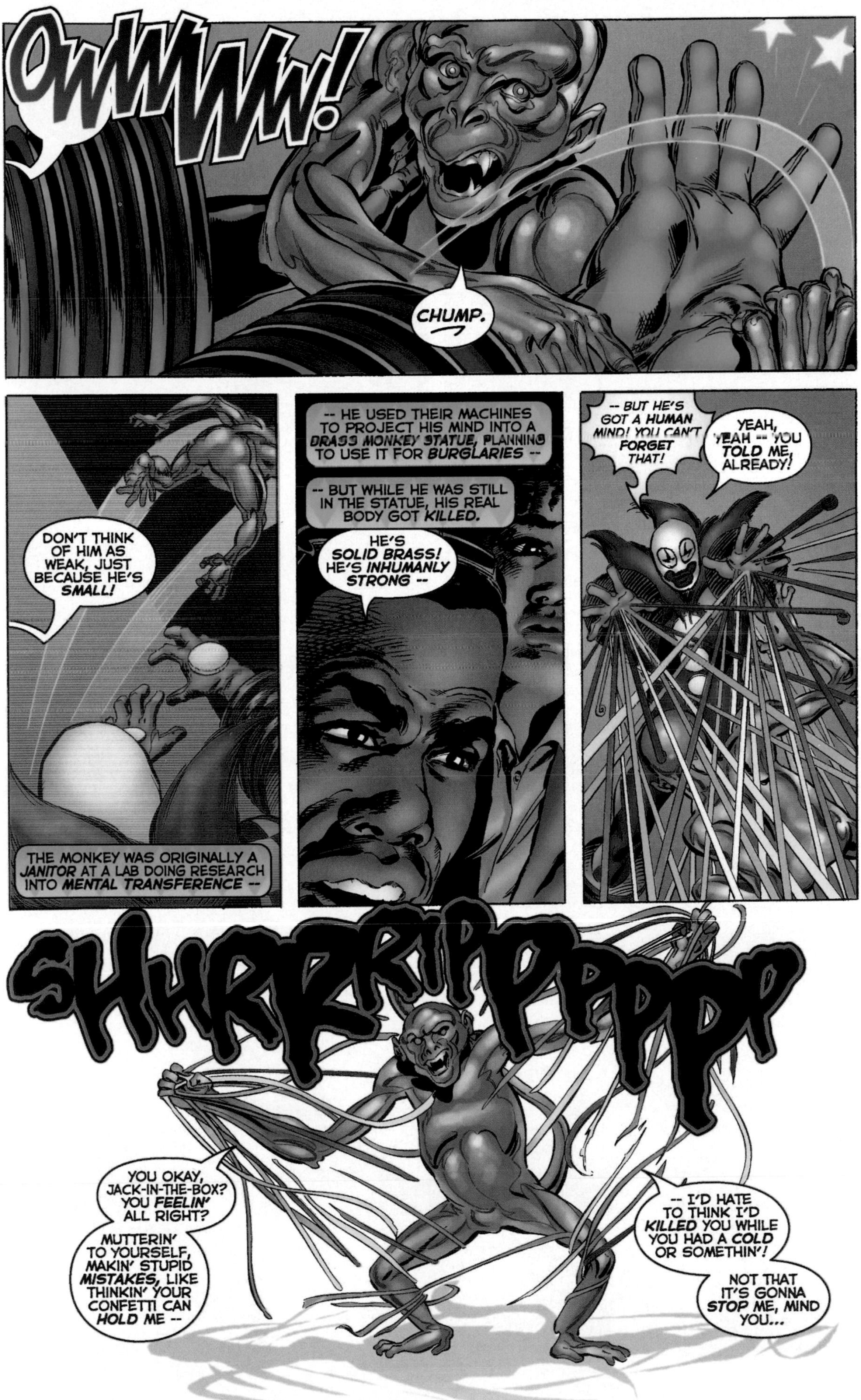
OWWWWW!
CHUMP.
THE MONKEY WAS ORIGINALLY A JANITOR AT A LAB DOING RESEARCH INTO MENTAL TRANSFERENCE --
DON'T THINK OF HIM AS WEAK, JUST BECAUSE HE'S SMALL!
-- HE USED THEIR MACHINES TO PROJECT HIS MIND INTO A BRASS MONKEY STATUE, PLANNING TO USE IT FOR BURGLARIES --
-- BUT WHILE HE WAS STILL IN THE STATUE, HIS REAL BODY GOT KILLED.
HE'S SOLID BRASS! HE'S INHUMANLY STRONG --
-- BUT HE'S GOT A HUMAN MIND! YOU CAN'T FORGET THAT!
YEAH, YEAH -- YOU TOLD ME, ALREADY!
SHHRRRIPPPPPP
YOU OKAY, JACK-IN-THE-BOX? YOU FEELIN' ALL RIGHT?
MUTTERIN' TO YOURSELF, MAKIN' STUPID MISTAKES, LIKE THINKIN' YOUR CONFETTI CAN HOLD ME --
-- I'D HATE TO THINK I'D KILLED YOU WHILE YOU HAD A COLD OR SOMETHIN'!
NOT THAT IT'S GONNA STOP ME, MIND YOU...

USE THE FOOTAPULTS, ROSCOE -- STAY AWAY FROM HIM!

DON'T LET HIM GRAPPLE WITH YOU -- HE'S TOO STRONG!

ARE YOU SURE IT'S OKAY TO *RECRUIT* HIM? THE RISK --

IT'S A *RISK*, YEAH. BUT AT LEAST *HE* CAN ACCEPT IT *CONSCIOUSLY* --

-- AND IT'S NOT LIKE THE STREETS OF BAKERVILLE ARE A WALK IN THE *PARK*. BELIEVE ME, HE *KNEW* WHAT HE WAS AGREEING TO.

HE NEEDS A WAY *OUT* -- AND THIS WAY, I CAN GIVE HIM SOME MONEY FOR SCHOOL, FOR *COLLEGE* --

-- AND HE'LL *TAKE* IT. HE WOULDN'T HAVE TAKEN *CHARITY*.

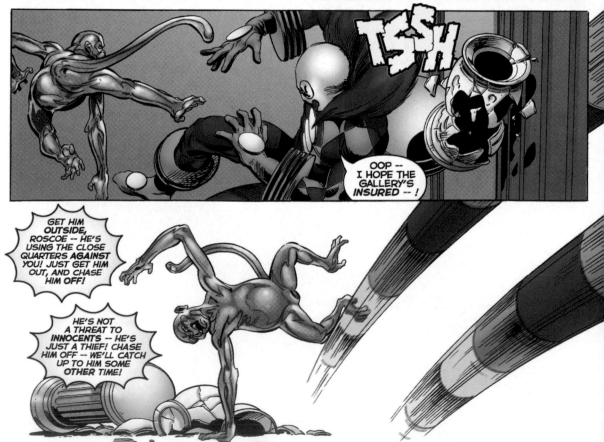

TSSH

OOP -- I HOPE THE GALLERY'S *INSURED* -- !

GET HIM OUTSIDE, ROSCOE -- HE'S USING THE CLOSE QUARTERS AGAINST YOU! JUST GET HIM OUT, AND CHASE HIM OFF!

HE'S NOT A THREAT TO *INNOCENTS* -- HE'S JUST A THIEF! CHASE HIM OFF -- WE'LL CATCH UP TO HIM SOME OTHER TIME!

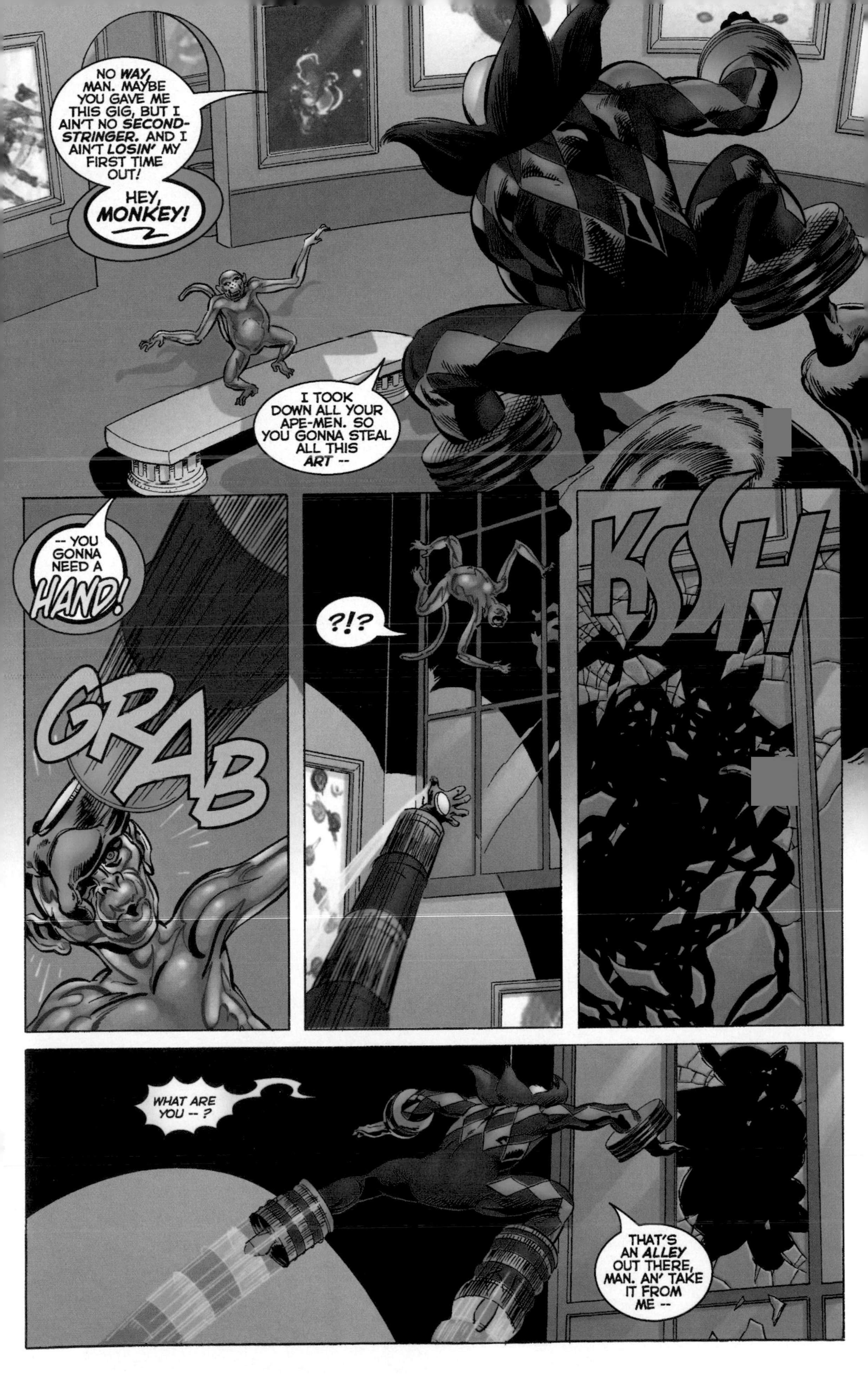
NO WAY, MAN. MAYBE YOU GAVE ME THIS GIG, BUT I AIN'T NO SECOND-STRINGER. AND I AIN'T LOSIN' MY FIRST TIME OUT!
HEY, MONKEY!
I TOOK DOWN ALL YOUR APE-MEN. SO YOU GONNA STEAL ALL THIS ART --
-- YOU GONNA NEED A HAND!
GRAB
?!?
KSSH
WHAT ARE YOU -- ?
THAT'S AN ALLEY OUT THERE, MAN. AN' TAKE IT FROM ME --

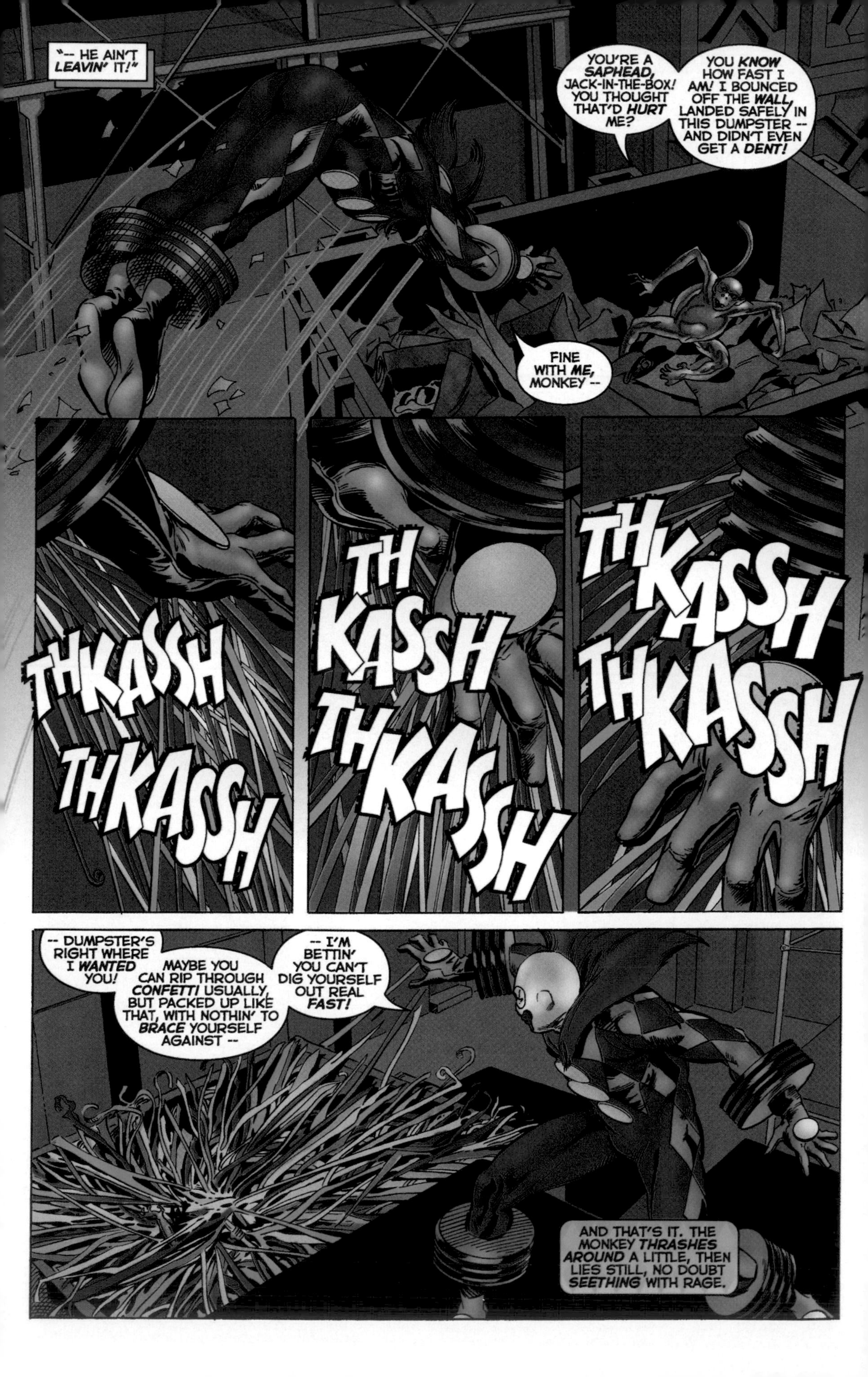
"-- HE AIN'T LEAVIN' IT!"
YOU'RE A SAPHEAD, JACK-IN-THE-BOX! YOU THOUGHT THAT'D HURT ME?
YOU KNOW HOW FAST I AM! I BOUNCED OFF THE WALL, LANDED SAFELY IN THIS DUMPSTER -- AND DIDN'T EVEN GET A DENT!
FINE WITH ME, MONKEY --
THKASSH THKASSH
THKASSH THKASSH
THKASSH THKASSH
-- DUMPSTER'S RIGHT WHERE I WANTED YOU!
MAYBE YOU CAN RIP THROUGH CONFETTI USUALLY, BUT PACKED UP LIKE THAT, WITH NOTHIN' TO BRACE YOURSELF AGAINST --
-- I'M BETTIN' YOU CAN'T DIG YOURSELF OUT REAL FAST!
AND THAT'S IT. THE MONKEY THRASHES AROUND A LITTLE, THEN LIES STILL, NO DOUBT SEETHING WITH RAGE.

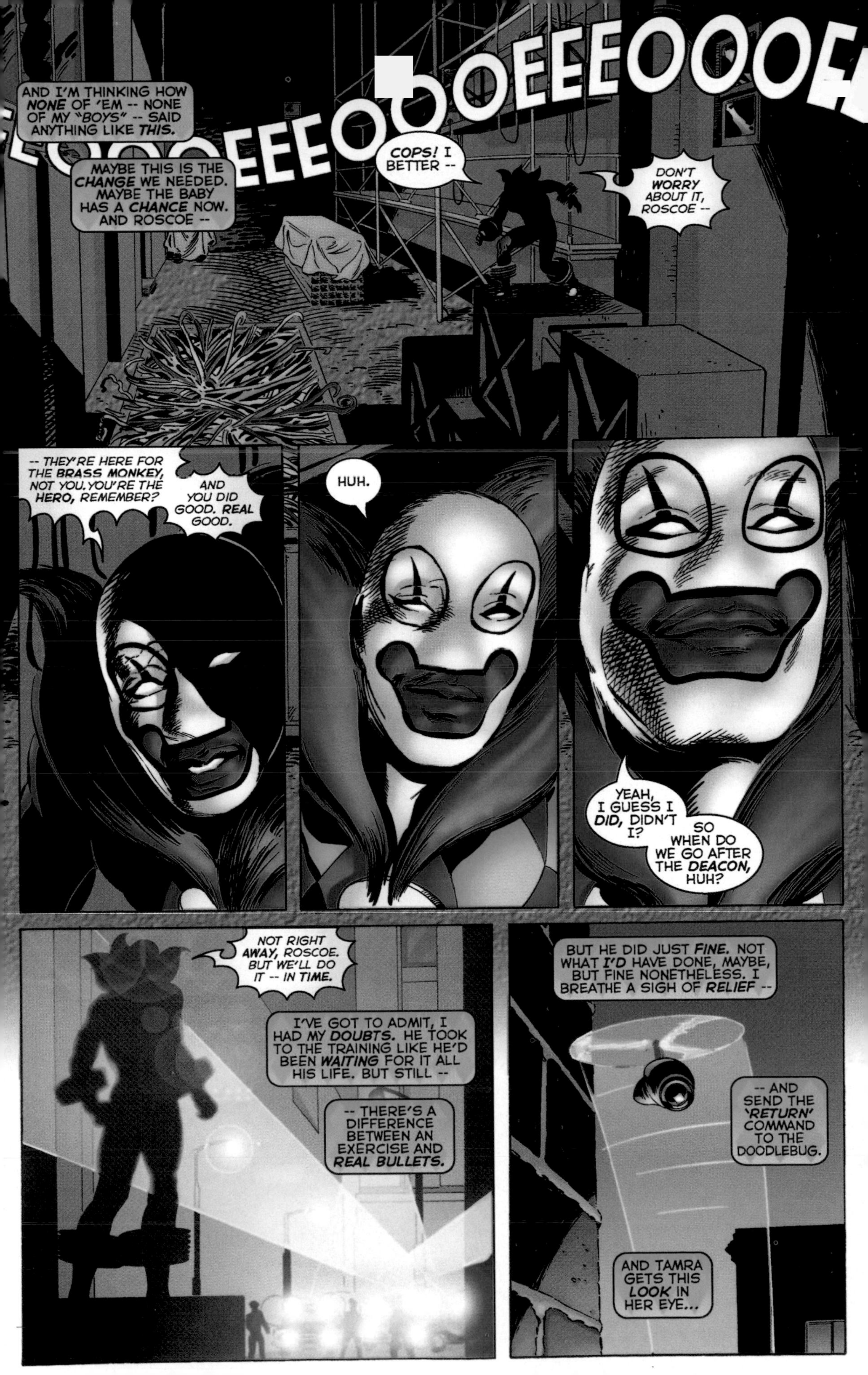

EEEOOOOEEEOOOOE
AND I'M THINKING HOW NONE OF 'EM -- NONE OF MY "BOYS" -- SAID ANYTHING LIKE THIS.
MAYBE THIS IS THE CHANGE WE NEEDED. MAYBE THE BABY HAS A CHANCE NOW. AND ROSCOE --
COPS! I BETTER --
DON'T WORRY ABOUT IT, ROSCOE --
-- THEY'RE HERE FOR THE BRASS MONKEY, NOT YOU. YOU'RE THE HERO, REMEMBER?
AND YOU DID GOOD. REAL GOOD.
HUH.
YEAH, I GUESS I DID, DIDN'T I?
SO WHEN DO WE GO AFTER THE DEACON, HUH?
NOT RIGHT AWAY, ROSCOE. BUT WE'LL DO IT -- IN TIME.
I'VE GOT TO ADMIT, I HAD MY DOUBTS. HE TOOK TO THE TRAINING LIKE HE'D BEEN WAITING FOR IT ALL HIS LIFE. BUT STILL --
-- THERE'S A DIFFERENCE BETWEEN AN EXERCISE AND REAL BULLETS.
BUT HE DID JUST FINE. NOT WHAT I'D HAVE DONE, MAYBE, BUT FINE NONETHELESS. I BREATHE A SIGH OF RELIEF --
-- AND SEND THE 'RETURN' COMMAND TO THE DOODLEBUG.
AND TAMRA GETS THIS LOOK IN HER EYE...

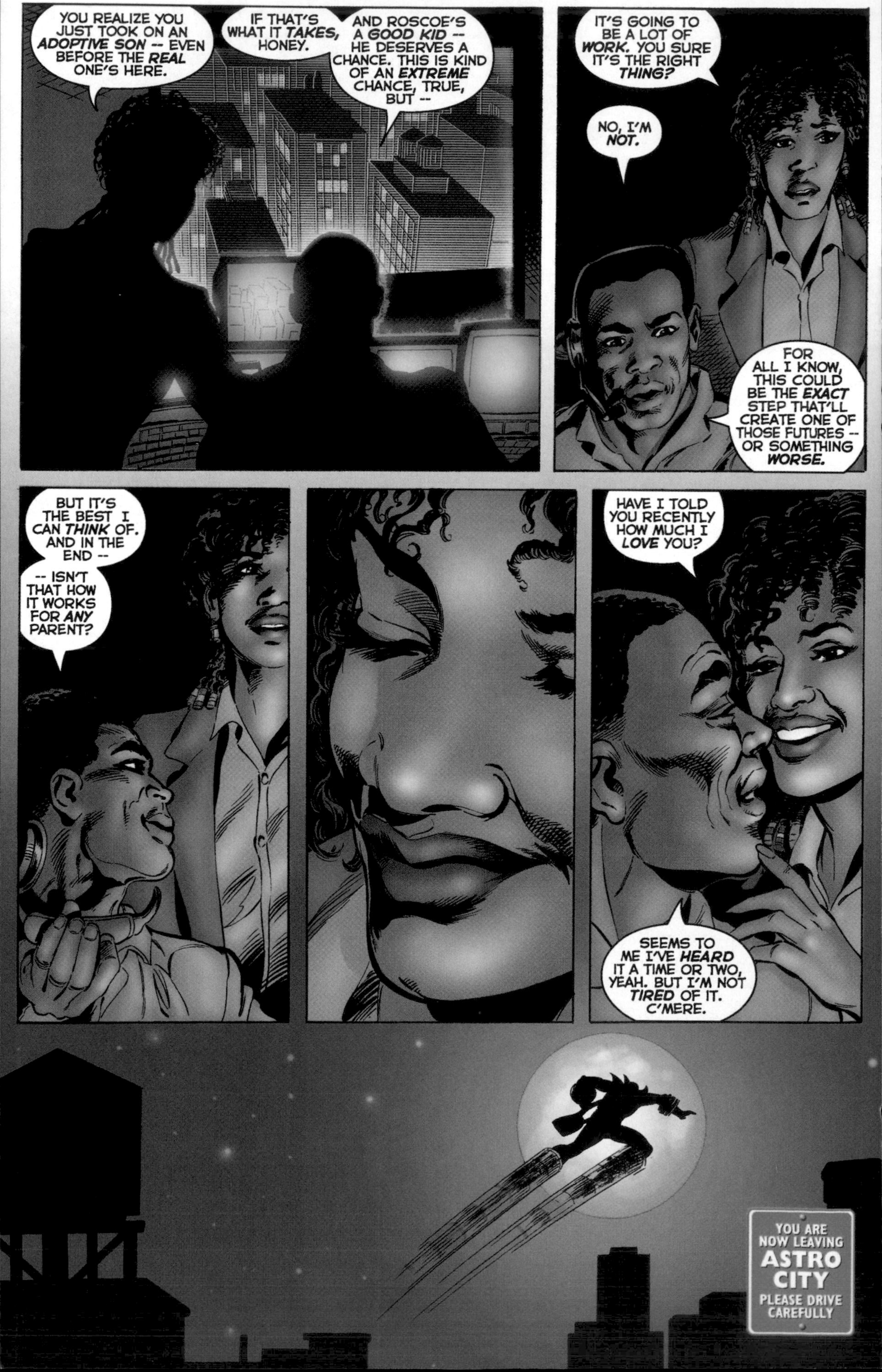
YOU REALIZE YOU JUST TOOK ON AN ADOPTIVE SON -- EVEN BEFORE THE REAL ONE'S HERE.
IF THAT'S WHAT IT TAKES, HONEY.
AND ROSCOE'S A GOOD KID -- HE DESERVES A CHANCE. THIS IS KIND OF AN EXTREME CHANCE, TRUE, BUT --
IT'S GOING TO BE A LOT OF WORK. YOU SURE IT'S THE RIGHT THING?
NO, I'M NOT.
FOR ALL I KNOW, THIS COULD BE THE EXACT STEP THAT'LL CREATE ONE OF THOSE FUTURES -- OR SOMETHING WORSE.
BUT IT'S THE BEST I CAN THINK OF. AND IN THE END --
-- ISN'T THAT HOW IT WORKS FOR ANY PARENT?
HAVE I TOLD YOU RECENTLY HOW MUCH I LOVE YOU?
SEEMS TO ME I'VE HEARD IT A TIME OR TWO, YEAH. BUT I'M NOT TIRED OF IT. C'MERE.
YOU ARE NOW LEAVING ASTRO CITY PLEASE DRIVE CAREFULLY

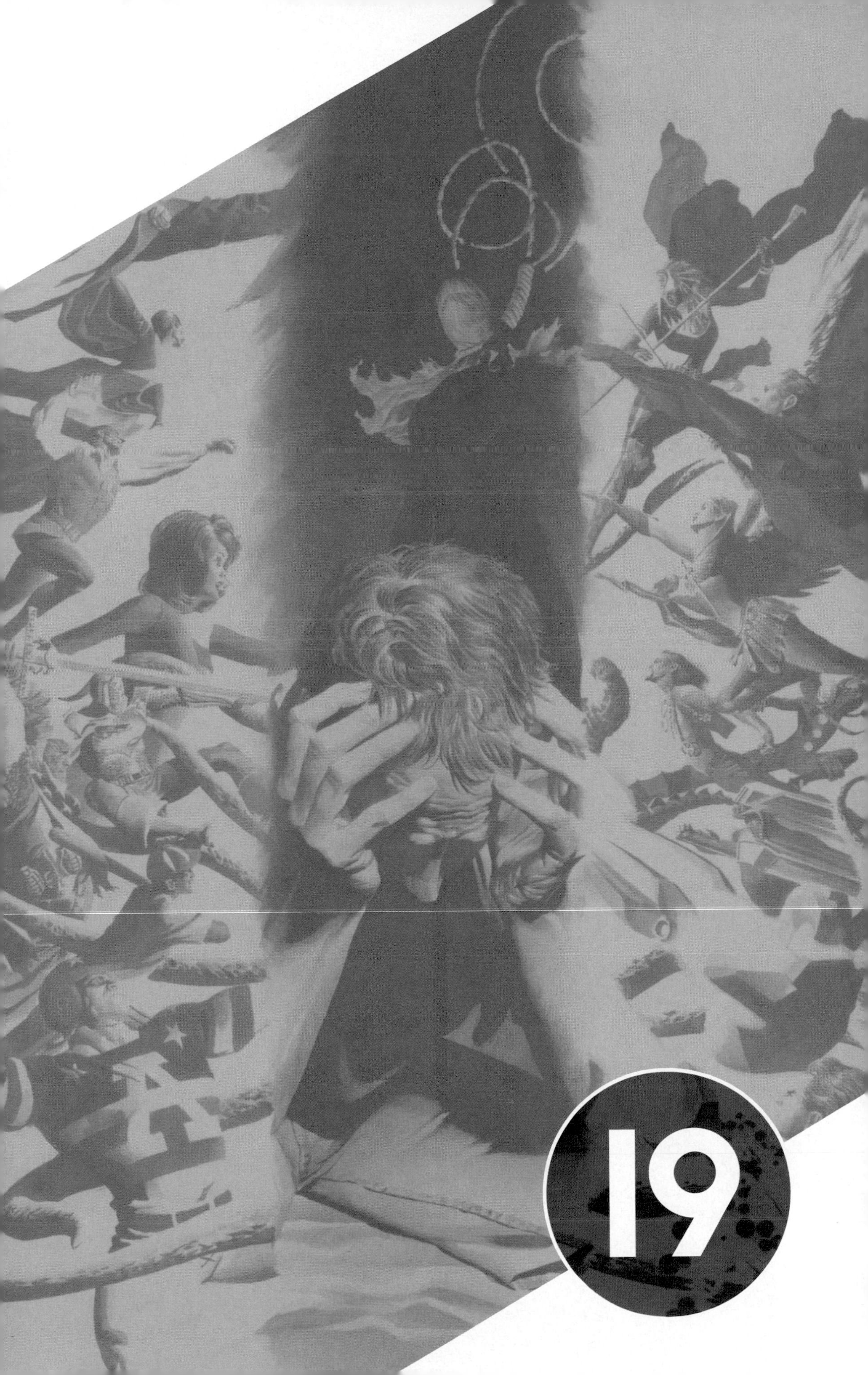
19

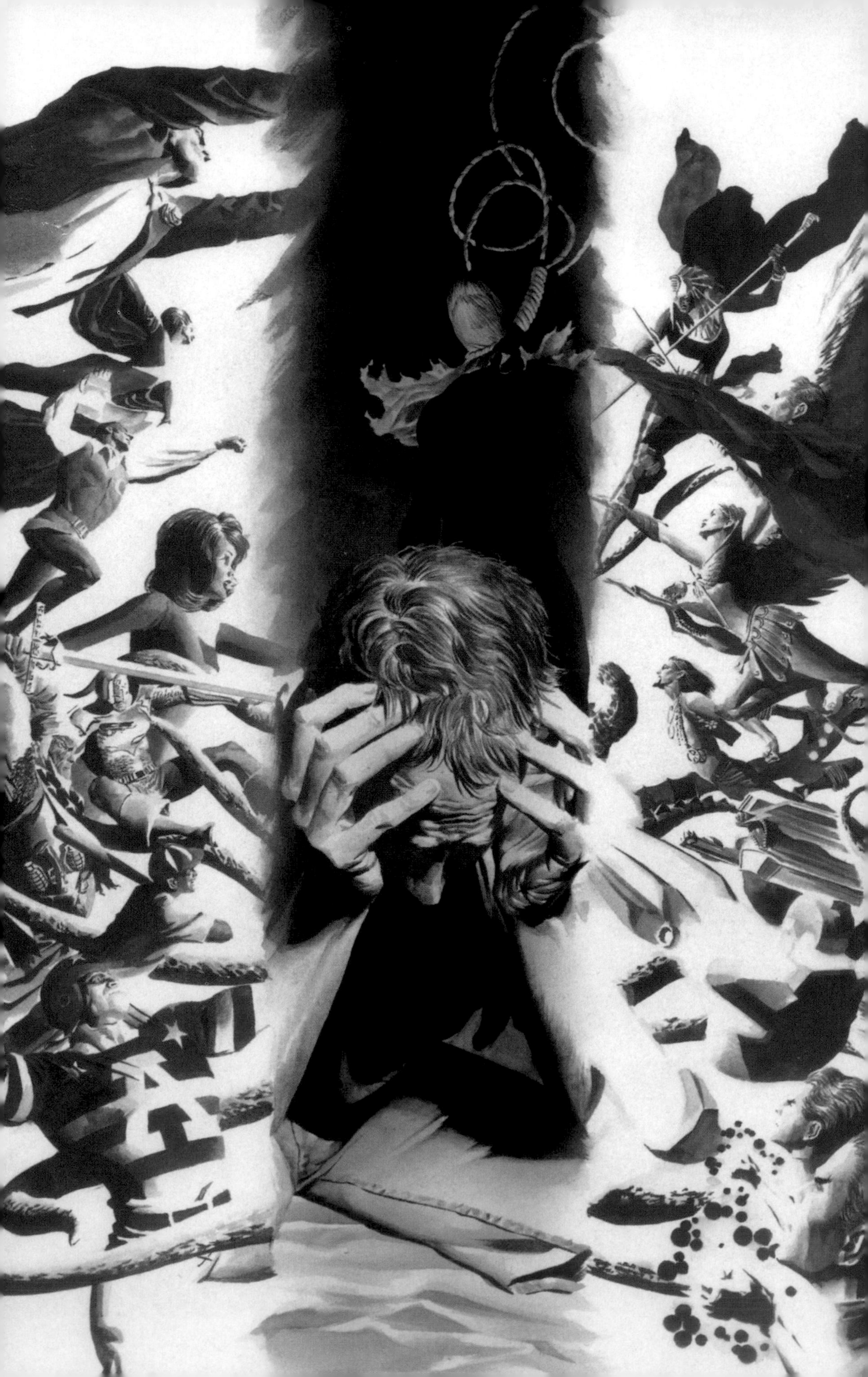

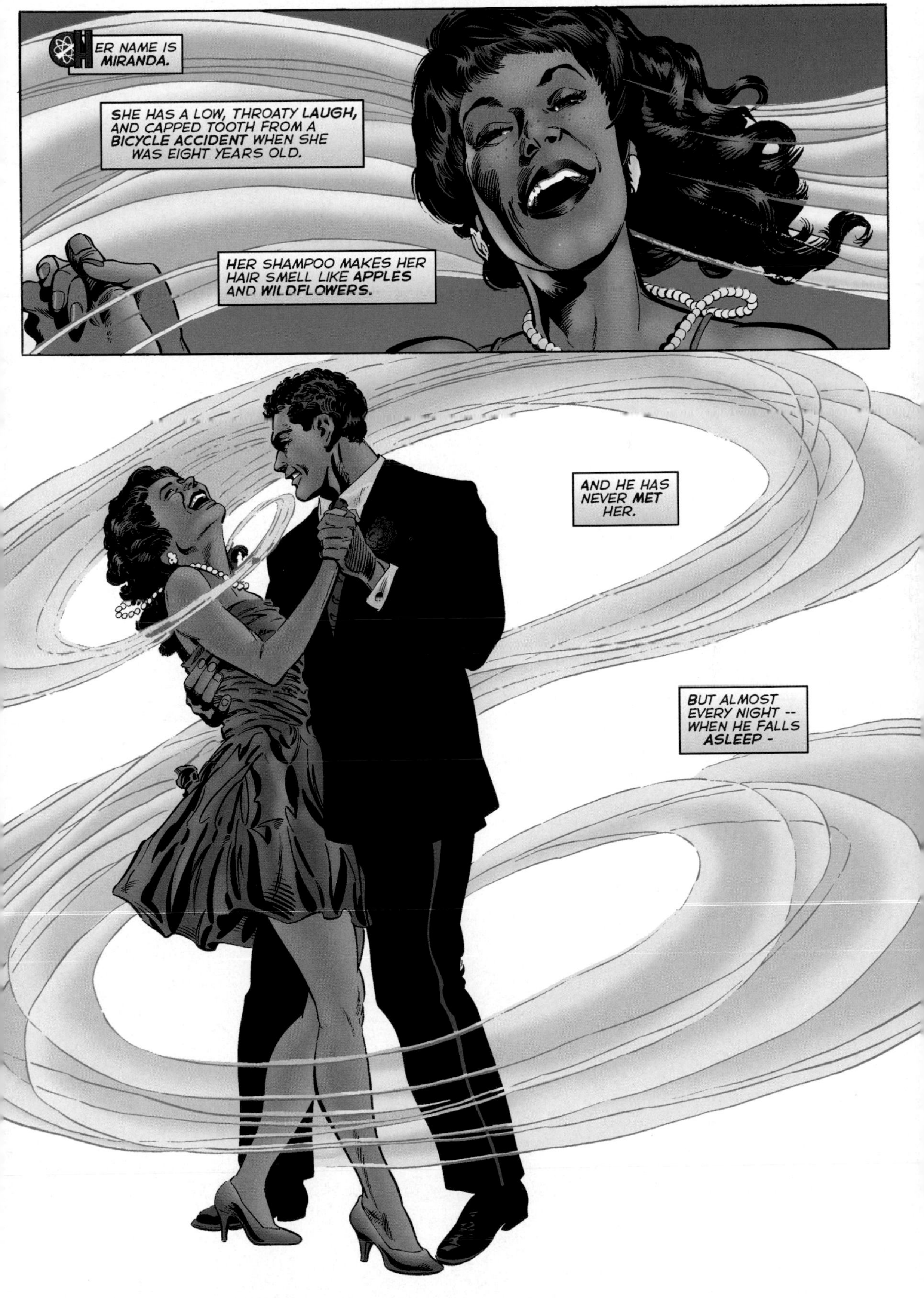
HER NAME IS MIRANDA.
SHE HAS A LOW, THROATY LAUGH, AND CAPPED TOOTH FROM A BICYCLE ACCIDENT WHEN SHE WAS EIGHT YEARS OLD.
HER SHAMPOO MAKES HER HAIR SMELL LIKE APPLES AND WILDFLOWERS.
AND HE HAS NEVER MET HER.
BUT ALMOST EVERY NIGHT -- WHEN HE FALLS ASLEEP -

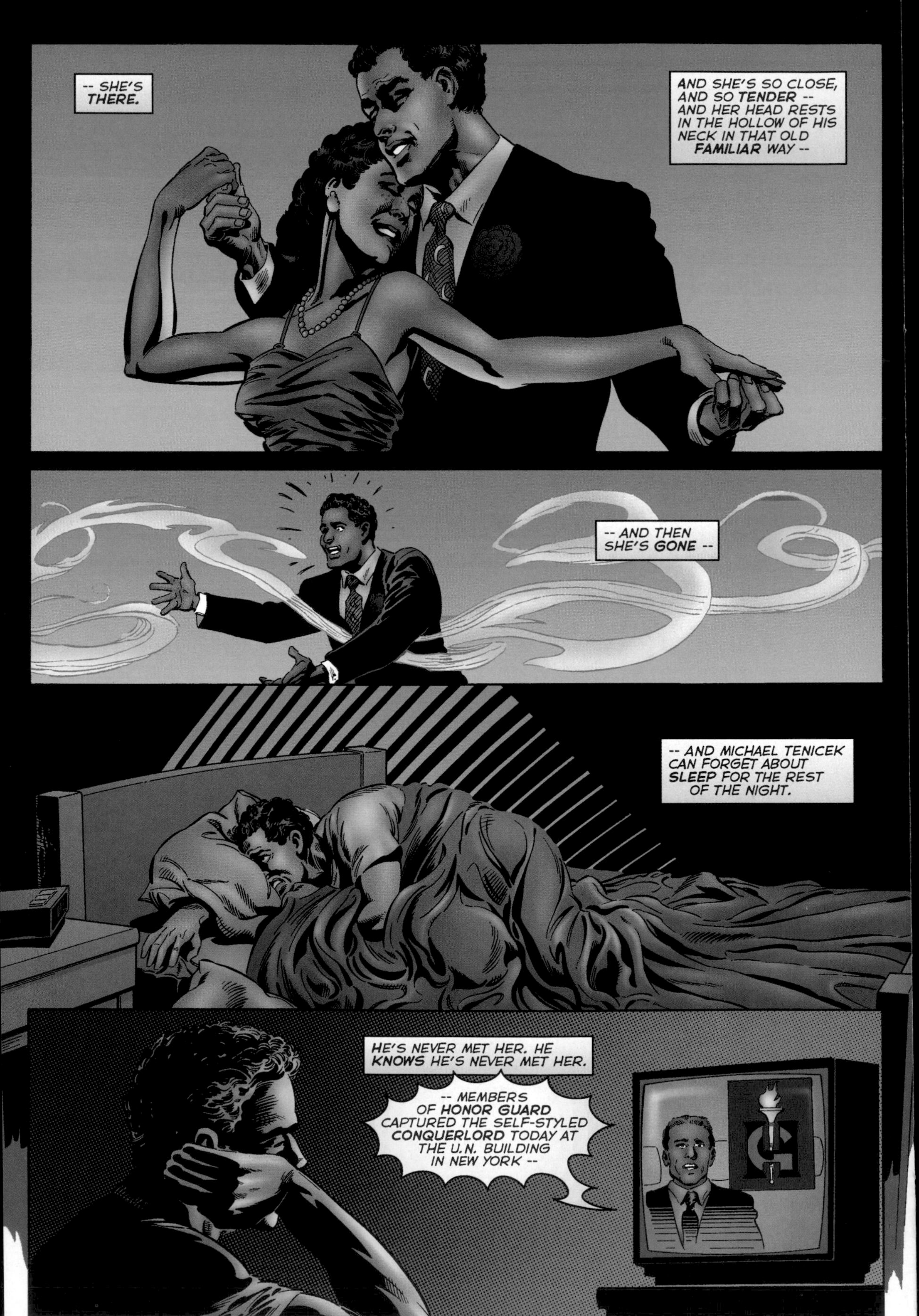
-- SHE'S THERE.
AND SHE'S SO CLOSE, AND SO TENDER -- AND HER HEAD RESTS IN THE HOLLOW OF HIS NECK IN THAT OLD FAMILIAR WAY --
-- AND THEN SHE'S GONE --
-- AND MICHAEL TENICEK CAN FORGET ABOUT SLEEP FOR THE REST OF THE NIGHT.
HE'S NEVER MET HER. HE KNOWS HE'S NEVER MET HER.
-- MEMBERS OF HONOR GUARD CAPTURED THE SELF-STYLED CONQUERLORD TODAY AT THE U.N. BUILDING IN NEW YORK --

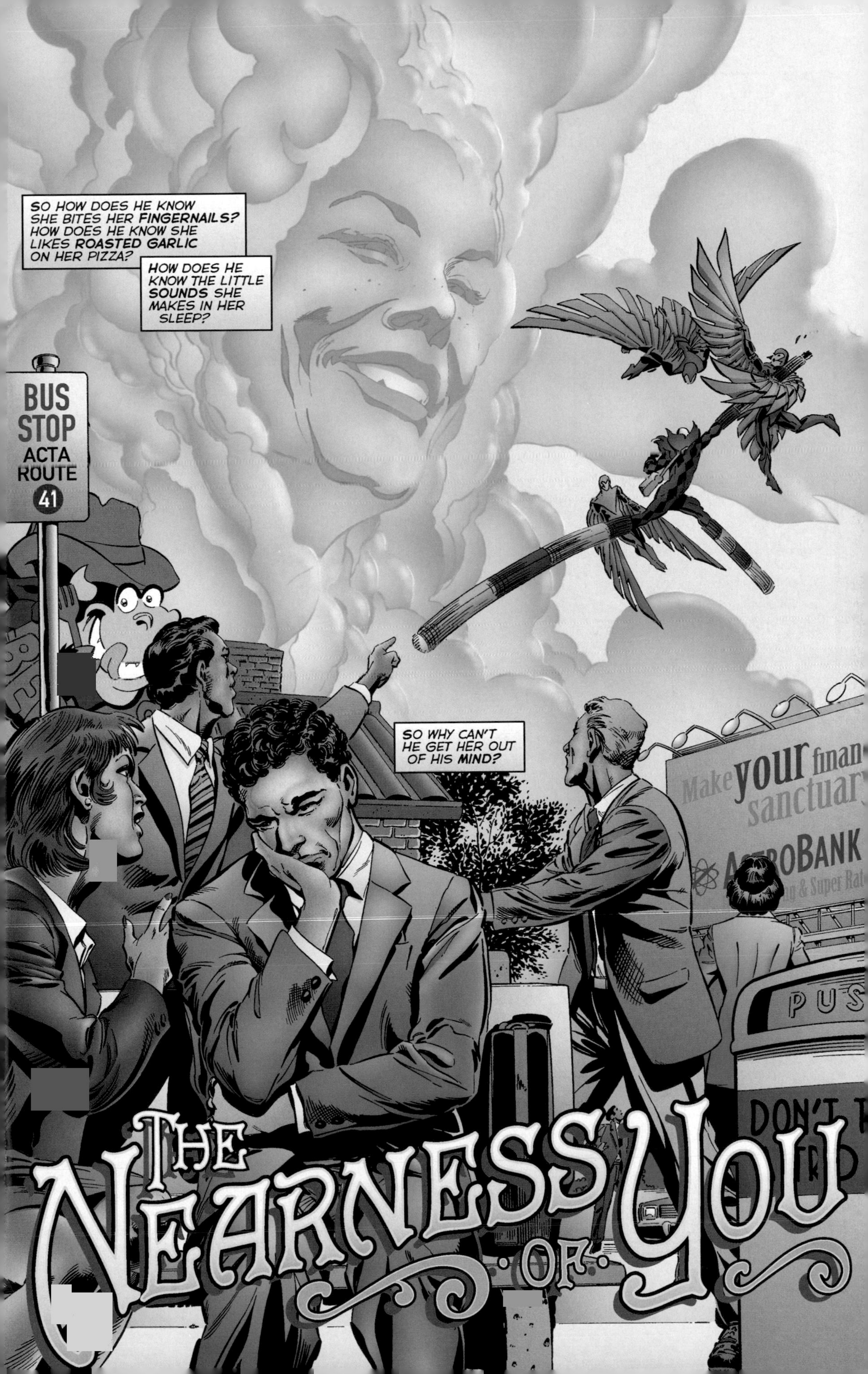
SO HOW DOES HE KNOW SHE BITES HER **FINGERNAILS?** HOW DOES HE KNOW SHE LIKES **ROASTED GARLIC** ON HER PIZZA?
HOW DOES HE KNOW THE LITTLE **SOUNDS** SHE MAKES IN HER SLEEP?
BUS STOP ACTA ROUTE 41
SO WHY CAN'T HE GET HER OUT OF HIS **MIND?**
DON'T
THE NEARNESS OF YOU

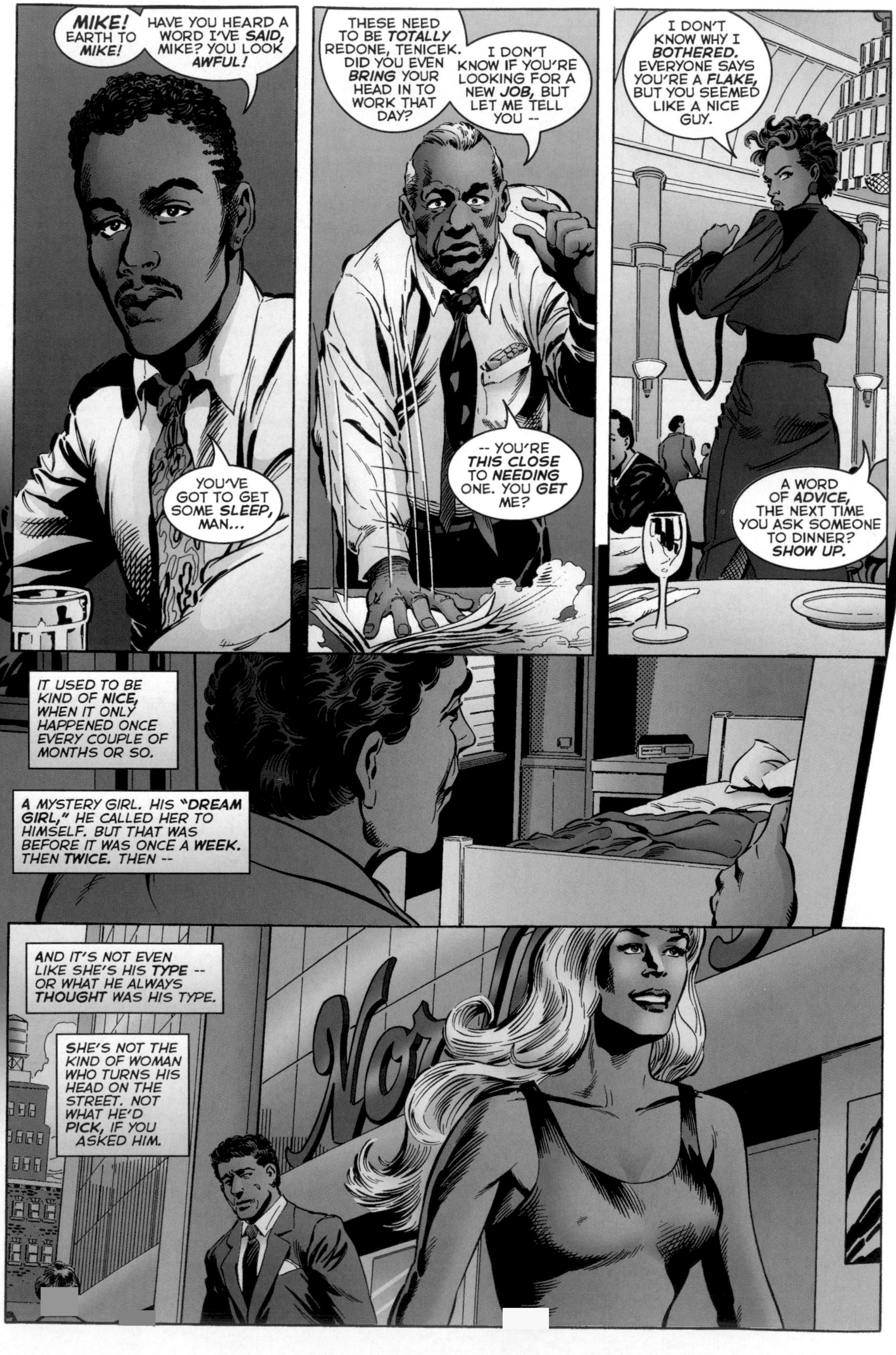

MIKE! EARTH TO MIKE!
HAVE YOU HEARD A WORD I'VE SAID, MIKE? YOU LOOK AWFUL!
YOU'VE GOT TO GET SOME SLEEP, MAN...
THESE NEED TO BE TOTALLY REDONE, TENICEK. DID YOU EVEN BRING YOUR HEAD IN TO WORK THAT DAY?
I DON'T KNOW IF YOU'RE LOOKING FOR A NEW JOB, BUT LET ME TELL YOU --
-- YOU'RE THIS CLOSE TO NEEDING ONE. YOU GET ME?
I DON'T KNOW WHY I BOTHERED. EVERYONE SAYS YOU'RE A FLAKE, BUT YOU SEEMED LIKE A NICE GUY.
A WORD OF ADVICE, THE NEXT TIME YOU ASK SOMEONE TO DINNER? SHOW UP.
IT USED TO BE KIND OF NICE, WHEN IT ONLY HAPPENED ONCE EVERY COUPLE OF MONTHS OR SO.
A MYSTERY GIRL. HIS "DREAM GIRL," HE CALLED HER TO HIMSELF. BUT THAT WAS BEFORE IT WAS ONCE A WEEK. THEN TWICE. THEN --
AND IT'S NOT EVEN LIKE SHE'S HIS TYPE -- OR WHAT HE ALWAYS THOUGHT WAS HIS TYPE.
SHE'S NOT THE KIND OF WOMAN WHO TURNS HIS HEAD ON THE STREET. NOT WHAT HE'D PICK, IF YOU ASKED HIM.

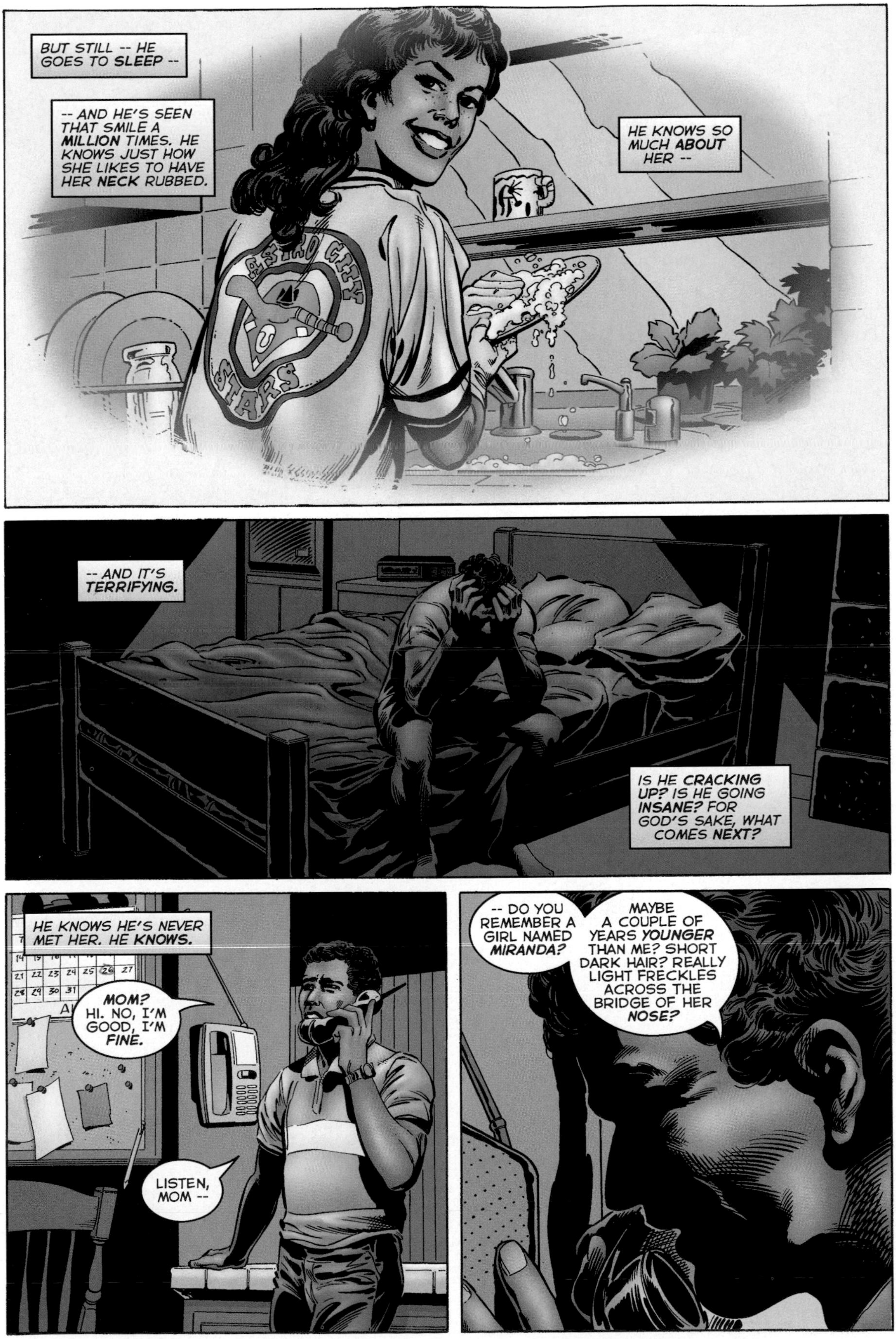
BUT STILL -- HE GOES TO SLEEP --
-- AND HE'S SEEN THAT SMILE A MILLION TIMES. HE KNOWS JUST HOW SHE LIKES TO HAVE HER NECK RUBBED.
HE KNOWS SO MUCH ABOUT HER --
-- AND IT'S TERRIFYING.
IS HE CRACKING UP? IS HE GOING INSANE? FOR GOD'S SAKE, WHAT COMES NEXT?
HE KNOWS HE'S NEVER MET HER. HE KNOWS.
MOM? HI. NO, I'M GOOD, I'M FINE.
LISTEN, MOM --
-- DO YOU REMEMBER A GIRL NAMED MIRANDA?
MAYBE A COUPLE OF YEARS YOUNGER THAN ME? SHORT DARK HAIR? REALLY LIGHT FRECKLES ACROSS THE BRIDGE OF HER NOSE?

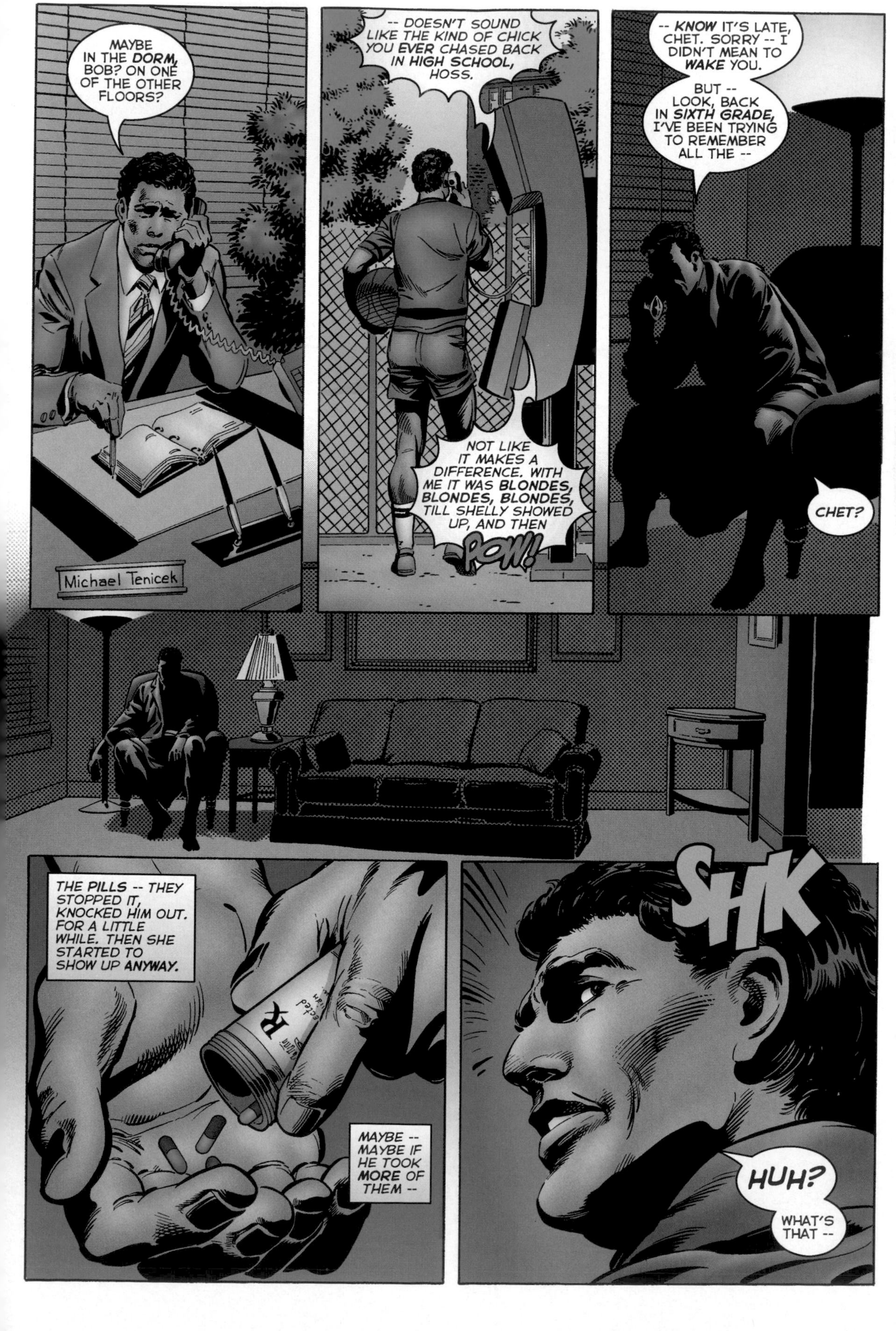
MAYBE IN THE DORM, BOB? ON ONE OF THE OTHER FLOORS?
Michael Tenicek
-- DOESN'T SOUND LIKE THE KIND OF CHICK YOU EVER CHASED BACK IN HIGH SCHOOL, HOSS.
NOT LIKE IT MAKES A DIFFERENCE. WITH ME IT WAS BLONDES, BLONDES, BLONDES, TILL SHELLY SHOWED UP, AND THEN
POW!
-- KNOW IT'S LATE, CHET. SORRY -- I DIDN'T MEAN TO WAKE YOU.
BUT -- LOOK, BACK IN SIXTH GRADE, I'VE BEEN TRYING TO REMEMBER ALL THE --
CHET?
THE PILLS -- THEY STOPPED IT, KNOCKED HIM OUT. FOR A LITTLE WHILE. THEN SHE STARTED TO SHOW UP ANYWAY.
MAYBE -- MAYBE IF HE TOOK MORE OF THEM --
SHK
HUH?
WHAT'S THAT --

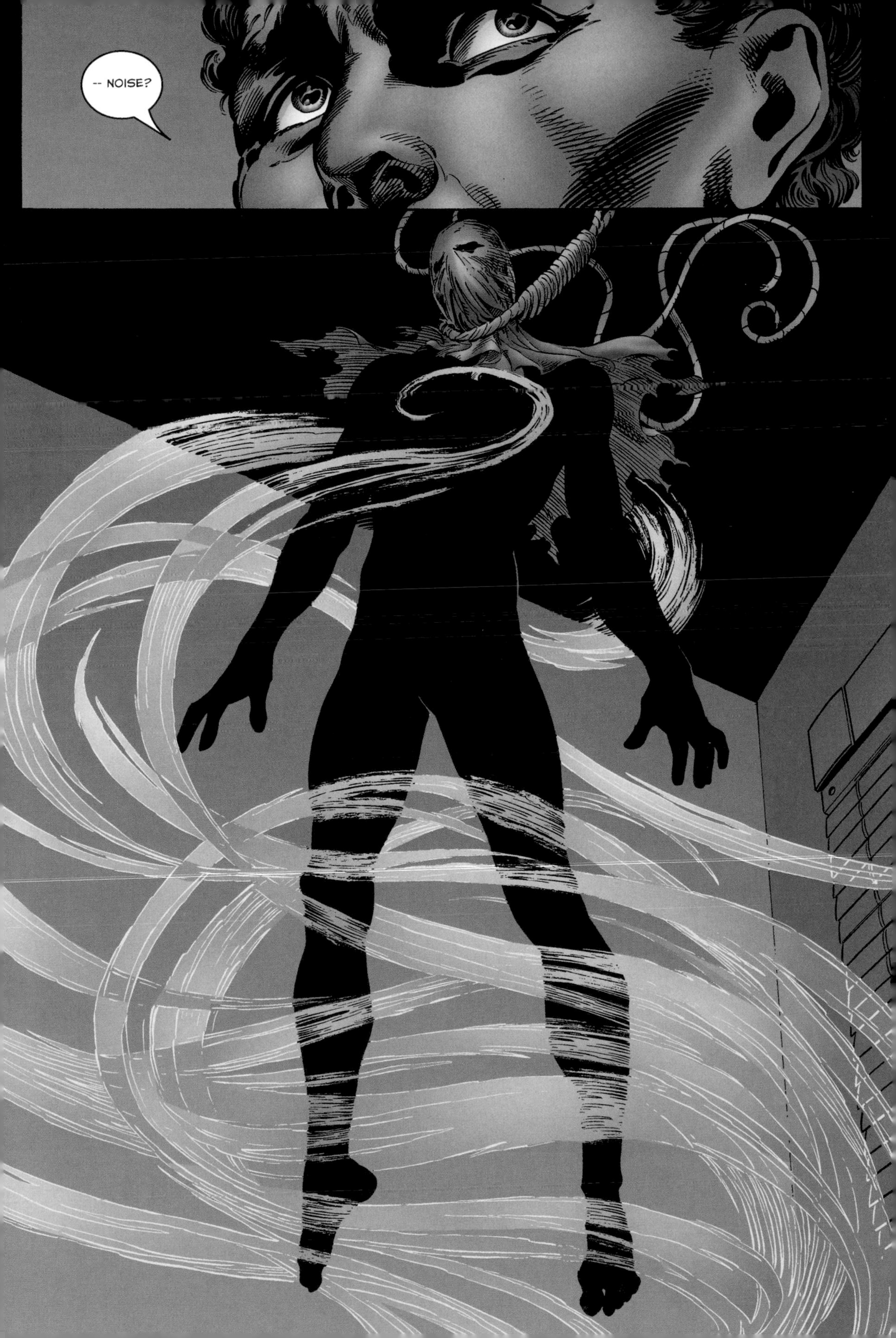
-- NOISE?

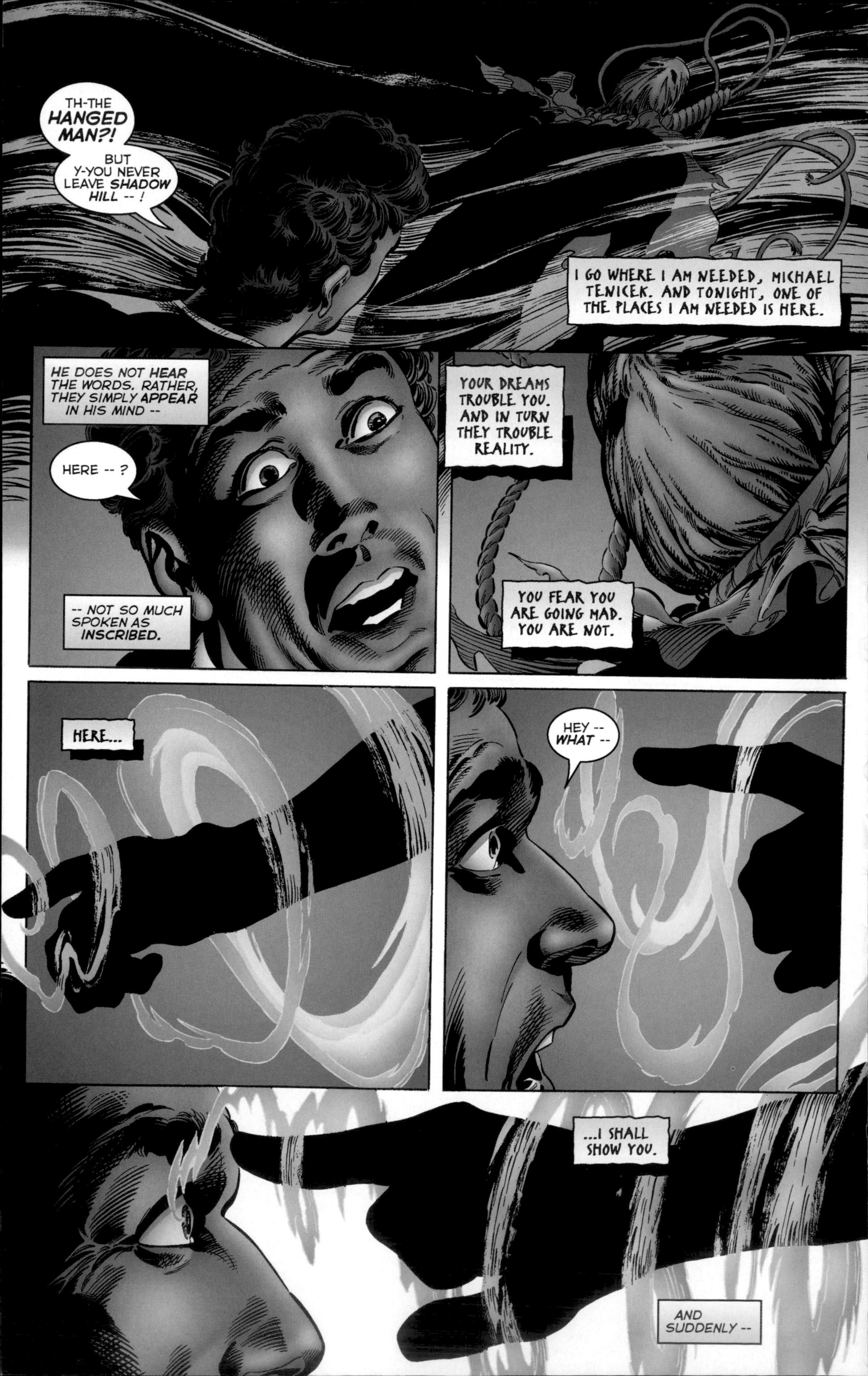
TH-THE HANGED MAN?!
BUT Y-YOU NEVER LEAVE SHADOW HILL -- !
I GO WHERE I AM NEEDED, MICHAEL TENICEK. AND TONIGHT, ONE OF THE PLACES I AM NEEDED IS HERE.
HE DOES NOT HEAR THE WORDS. RATHER, THEY SIMPLY APPEAR IN HIS MIND --
HERE -- ?
-- NOT SO MUCH SPOKEN AS INSCRIBED.
YOUR DREAMS TROUBLE YOU. AND IN TURN THEY TROUBLE REALITY.
YOU FEAR YOU ARE GOING MAD. YOU ARE NOT.
HERE...
HEY -- WHAT --
...I SHALL SHOW YOU.
AND SUDDENLY --

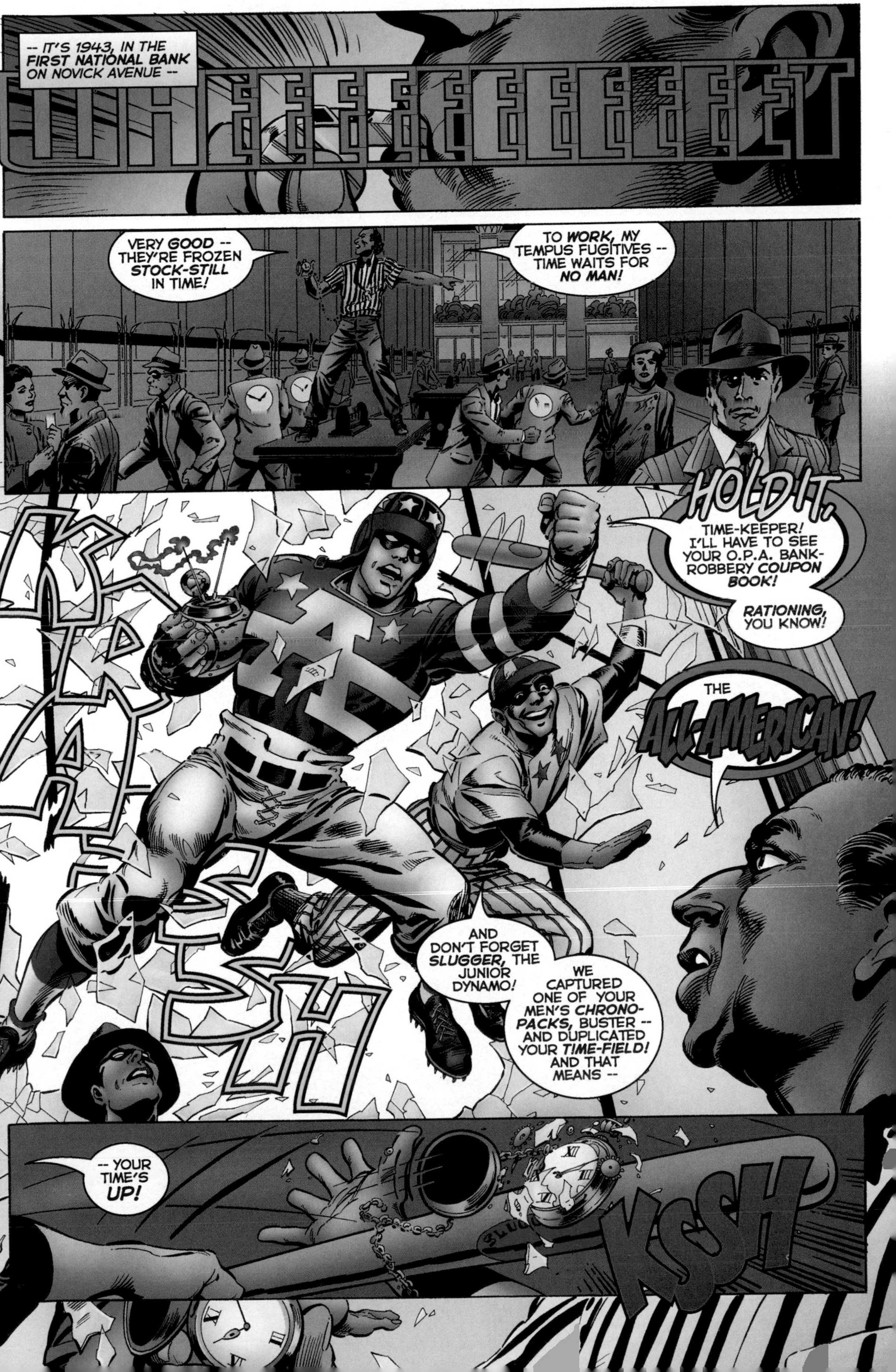
-- IT'S 1943, IN THE FIRST NATIONAL BANK ON NOVICK AVENUE --
THEEEEEEEEEET
VERY GOOD -- THEY'RE FROZEN STOCK-STILL IN TIME!
TO WORK, MY TEMPUS FUGITIVES -- TIME WAITS FOR NO MAN!
KRASH
HOLD IT, TIME-KEEPER! I'LL HAVE TO SEE YOUR O.P.A. BANK-ROBBERY COUPON BOOK!
RATIONING, YOU KNOW!
THE ALL-AMERICAN!
AND DON'T FORGET SLUGGER, THE JUNIOR DYNAMO!
WE CAPTURED ONE OF YOUR MEN'S CHRONO-PACKS, BUSTER -- AND DUPLICATED YOUR TIME-FIELD! AND THAT MEANS --
-- YOUR TIME'S UP!
KSSH

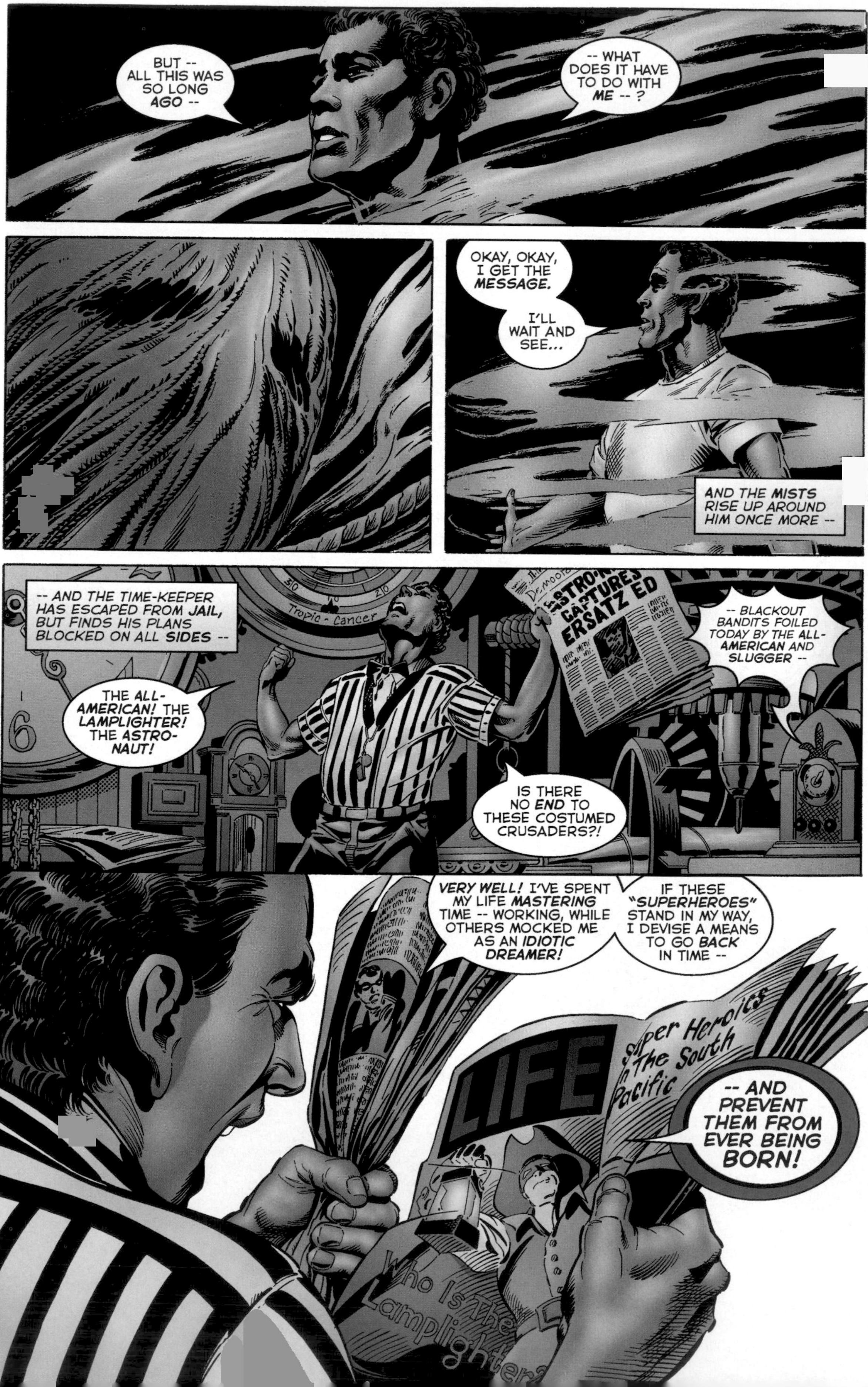
BUT -- ALL THIS WAS SO LONG AGO --
-- WHAT DOES IT HAVE TO DO WITH ME -- ?
OKAY, OKAY, I GET THE MESSAGE.
I'LL WAIT AND SEE...
AND THE MISTS RISE UP AROUND HIM ONCE MORE --
-- AND THE TIME-KEEPER HAS ESCAPED FROM JAIL, BUT FINDS HIS PLANS BLOCKED ON ALL SIDES --
Tropic - Cancer
ASTRONAUT CAPTURES ERSATZ ED
THE ALL-AMERICAN! THE LAMPLIGHTER! THE ASTRONAUT!
-- BLACKOUT BANDITS FOILED TODAY BY THE ALL-AMERICAN AND SLUGGER --
IS THERE NO END TO THESE COSTUMED CRUSADERS?!
VERY WELL! I'VE SPENT MY LIFE MASTERING TIME -- WORKING, WHILE OTHERS MOCKED ME AS AN IDIOTIC DREAMER!
IF THESE "SUPERHEROES" STAND IN MY WAY, I DEVISE A MEANS TO GO BACK IN TIME --
LIFE
Super Heroics in The South Pacific
-- AND PREVENT THEM FROM EVER BEING BORN!
Who Is The Lamplighter?

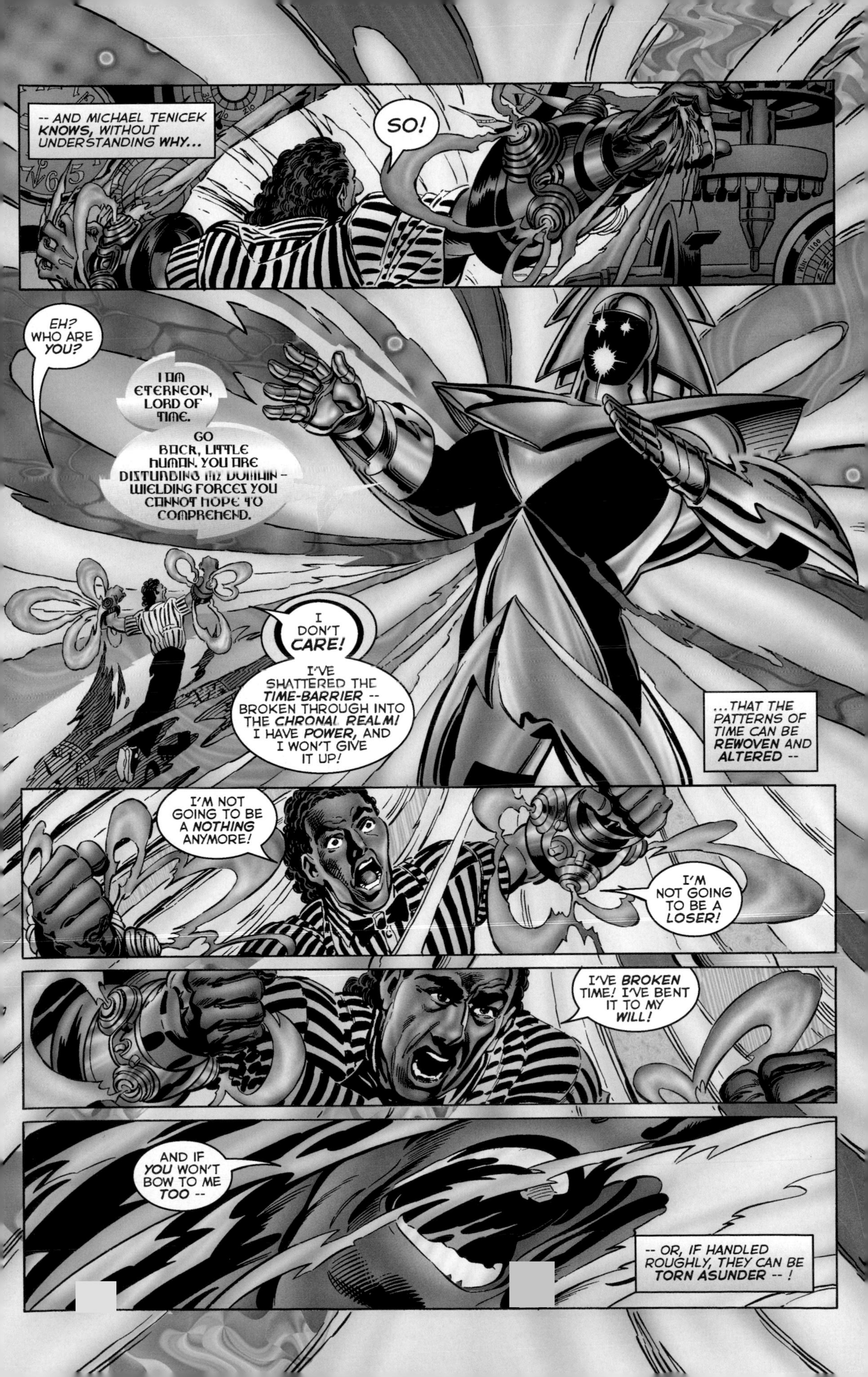
-- AND MICHAEL TENICEK KNOWS, WITHOUT UNDERSTANDING WHY...
SO!
EH? WHO ARE YOU?
I AM ETERNEON, LORD OF TIME.
GO BACK, LITTLE HUMAN. YOU ARE DISTURBING MY DOMAIN -- WIELDING FORCES YOU CANNOT HOPE TO COMPREHEND.
I DON'T CARE!
I'VE SHATTERED THE TIME-BARRIER -- BROKEN THROUGH INTO THE CHRONAL REALM! I HAVE POWER, AND I WON'T GIVE IT UP!
...THAT THE PATTERNS OF TIME CAN BE REWOVEN AND ALTERED --
I'M NOT GOING TO BE A NOTHING ANYMORE!
I'M NOT GOING TO BE A LOSER!
I'VE BROKEN TIME! I'VE BENT IT TO MY WILL!
AND IF YOU WON'T BOW TO ME TOO --
-- OR, IF HANDLED ROUGHLY, THEY CAN BE TORN ASUNDER -- !

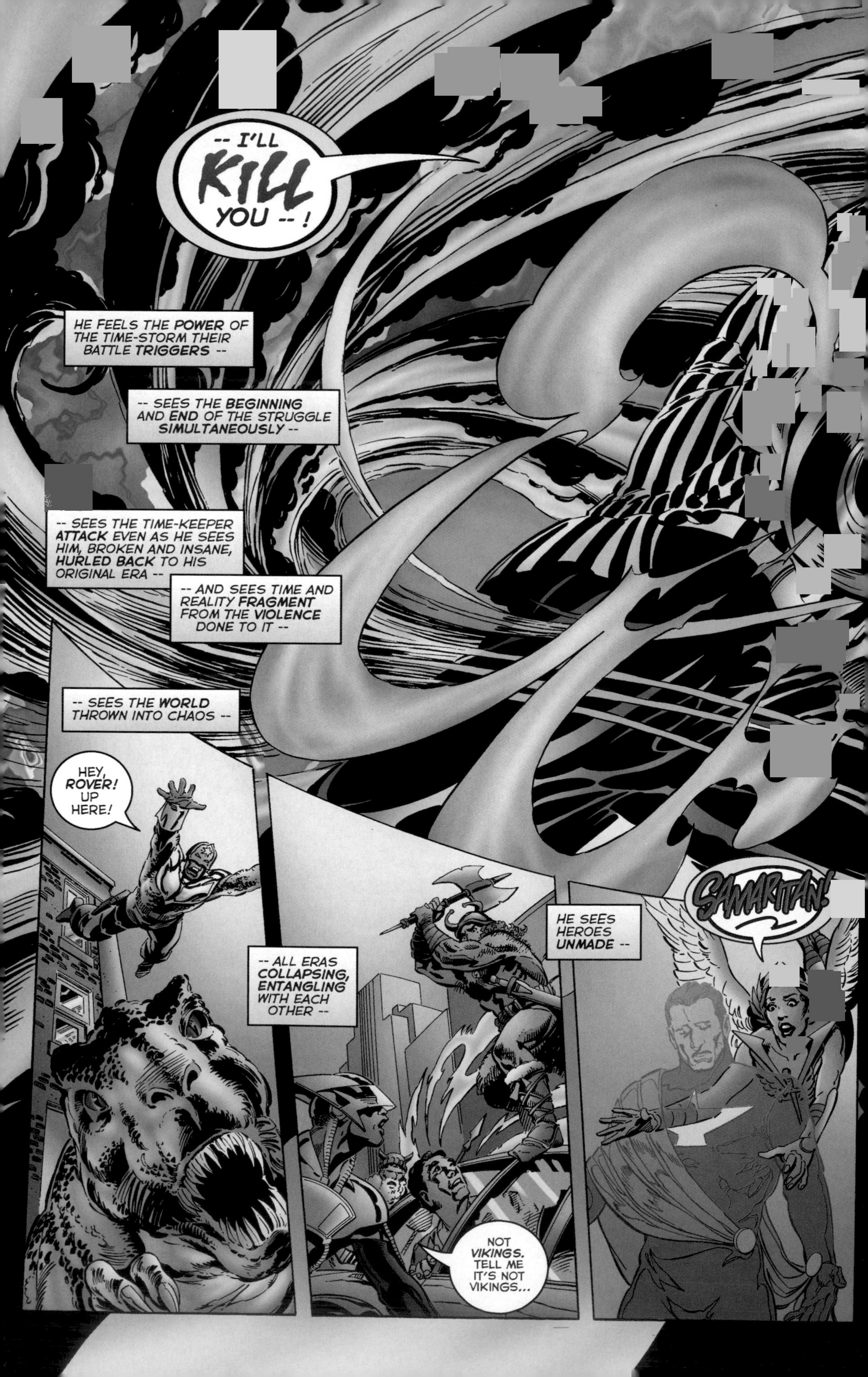

-- I'LL KILL YOU -- !
HE FEELS THE POWER OF THE TIME-STORM THEIR BATTLE TRIGGERS --
-- SEES THE BEGINNING AND END OF THE STRUGGLE SIMULTANEOUSLY --
-- SEES THE TIME-KEEPER ATTACK EVEN AS HE SEES HIM, BROKEN AND INSANE, HURLED BACK TO HIS ORIGINAL ERA --
-- AND SEES TIME AND REALITY FRAGMENT FROM THE VIOLENCE DONE TO IT --
-- SEES THE WORLD THROWN INTO CHAOS --
HEY, ROVER! UP HERE!
-- ALL ERAS COLLAPSING, ENTANGLING WITH EACH OTHER --
NOT VIKINGS. TELL ME IT'S NOT VIKINGS...
HE SEES HEROES UNMADE --
SAMARITAN!

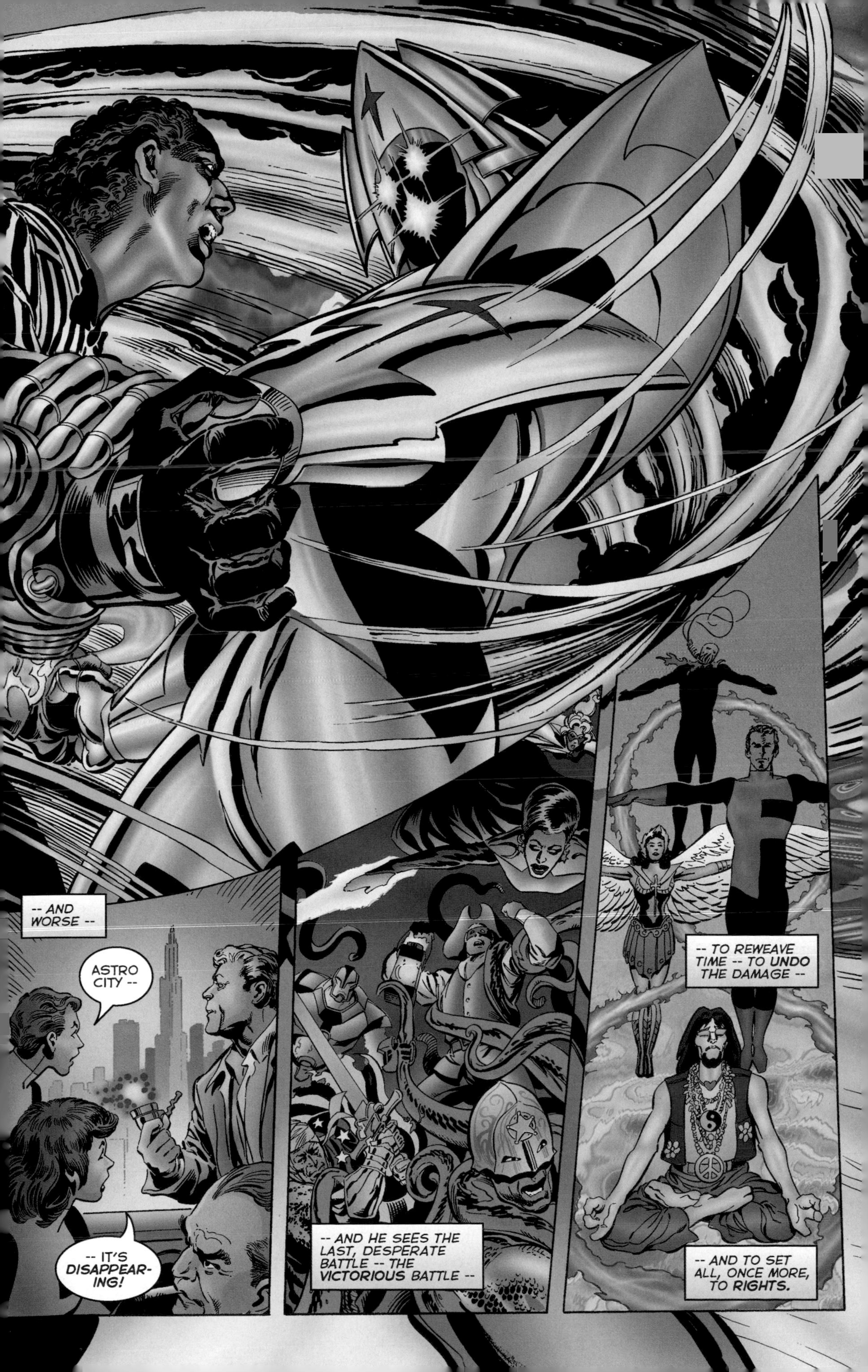
-- AND WORSE --
ASTRO CITY --
-- IT'S DISAPPEAR-ING!
-- AND HE SEES THE LAST, DESPERATE BATTLE -- THE VICTORIOUS BATTLE --
-- TO REWEAVE TIME -- TO UNDO THE DAMAGE --
-- AND TO SET ALL, ONCE MORE, TO RIGHTS.

WHEN... WHEN DID THIS ALL HAPPEN?

YESTERDAY. FIVE DECADES AGO. DOES IT MATTER?

I... UNDERSTAND, I THINK.

SHE DIED, DIDN'T SHE? I KNEW HER, AND SHE DIED IN THAT...THAT MAELSTROM...

SHE WAS YOUR WIFE. AND SHE NEVER EXISTED.

THE CHRONAL RECONSTRUCTION WAS NOT EXACT.

MY... WIFE?

AIR ACE FIRST BATTLED THE BARNSTORMERS ON A SUNDAY, NOT A MONDAY... AND AS A RESULT, HER GRANDPARENTS NEVER MET.

FOR THE MOST PART, THE NEW REALITY IS A WHOLE. BUT CLOSE BONDS SUCH AS YOURS... THEY CREATE A WEAKNESS IN THE FABRIC OF TIME...

...ONE THAT COULD LET THROUGH... DANGEROUS THINGS. BUT THE WEAKNESS IS HEALED BY YOUR UNDERSTANDING.

I CANNOT RETURN HER TO YOU... THAT IS BEYOND EVEN MY POWER. BUT IF THE PAIN IS TOO MUCH...

... I CAN ALLOW YOU TO FORGET...

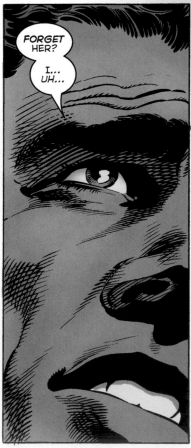

FORGET HER?

I... UH...

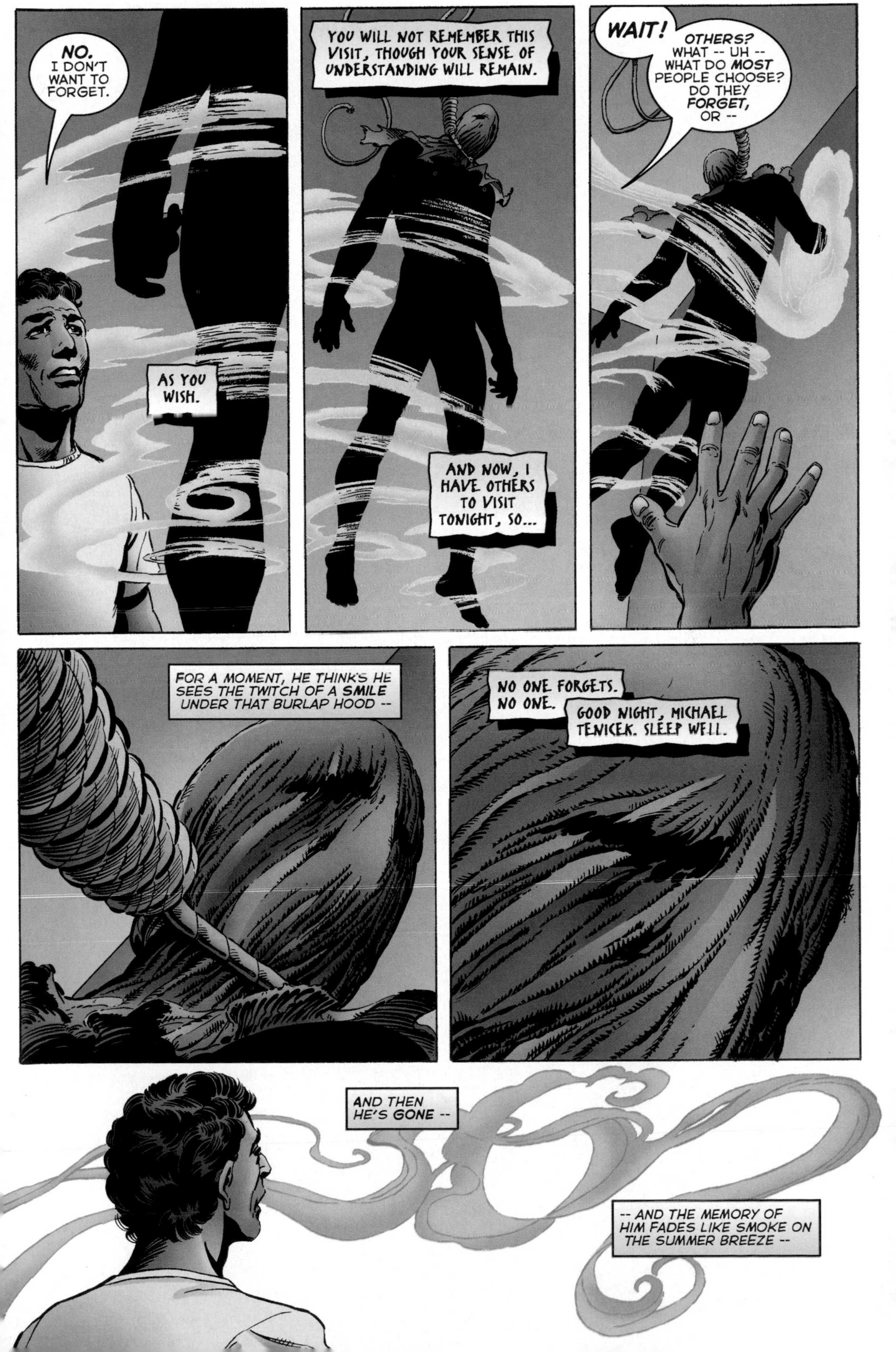
NO. I DON'T WANT TO FORGET.
AS YOU WISH.
YOU WILL NOT REMEMBER THIS VISIT, THOUGH YOUR SENSE OF UNDERSTANDING WILL REMAIN.
AND NOW, I HAVE OTHERS TO VISIT TONIGHT, SO...
WAIT!
OTHERS? WHAT -- UH -- WHAT DO MOST PEOPLE CHOOSE? DO THEY FORGET, OR --
FOR A MOMENT, HE THINKS HE SEES THE TWITCH OF A SMILE UNDER THAT BURLAP HOOD --
NO ONE FORGETS. NO ONE.
GOOD NIGHT, MICHAEL TENICEK. SLEEP WELL.
AND THEN HE'S GONE --
-- AND THE MEMORY OF HIM FADES LIKE SMOKE ON THE SUMMER BREEZE --

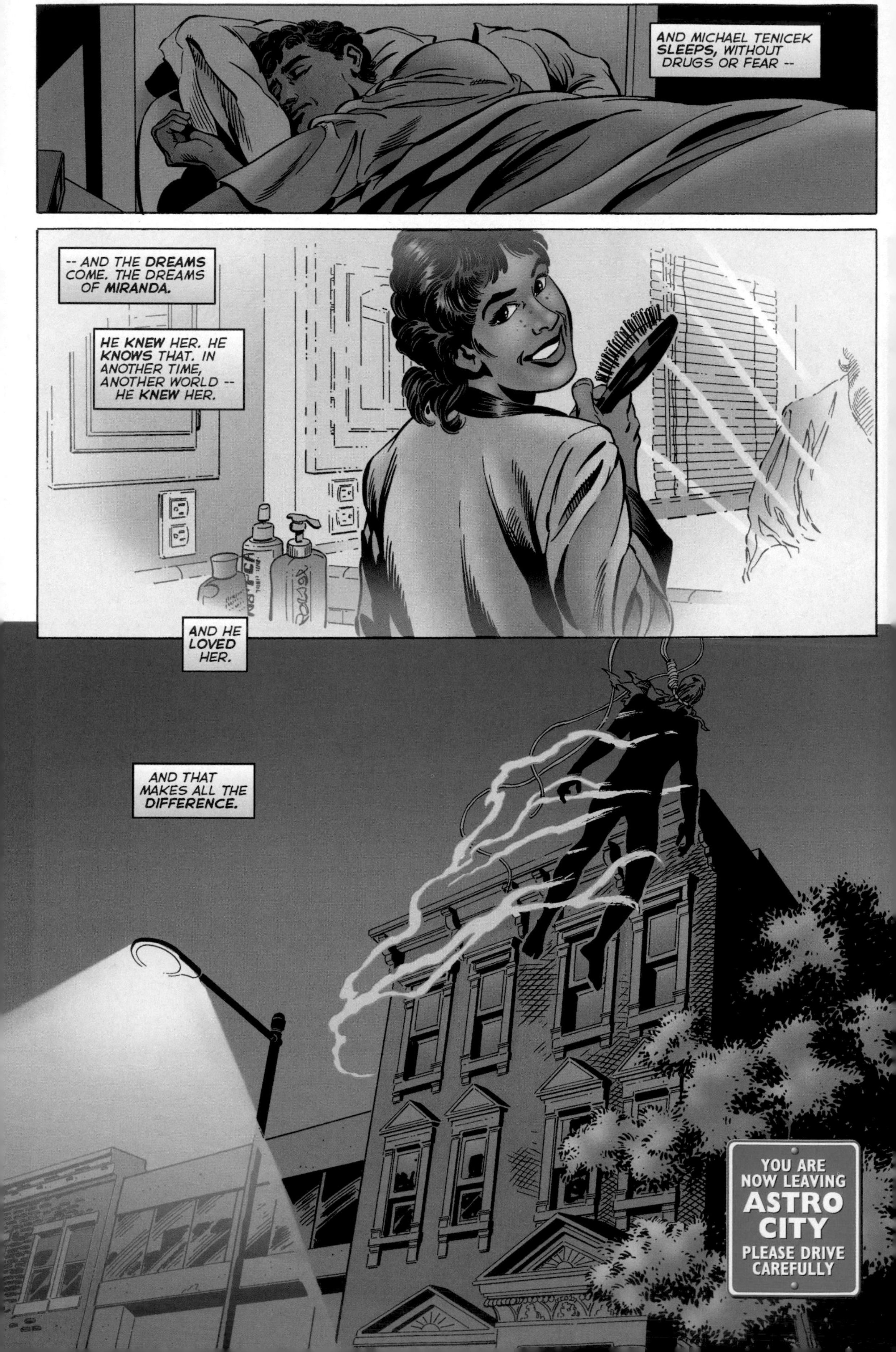
AND MICHAEL TENICEK SLEEPS, WITHOUT DRUGS OR FEAR --
-- AND THE DREAMS COME. THE DREAMS OF MIRANDA.
HE KNEW HER. HE KNOWS THAT. IN ANOTHER TIME, ANOTHER WORLD -- HE KNEW HER.
AND HE LOVED HER.
AND THAT MAKES ALL THE DIFFERENCE.
YOU ARE NOW LEAVING ASTRO CITY PLEASE DRIVE CAREFULLY

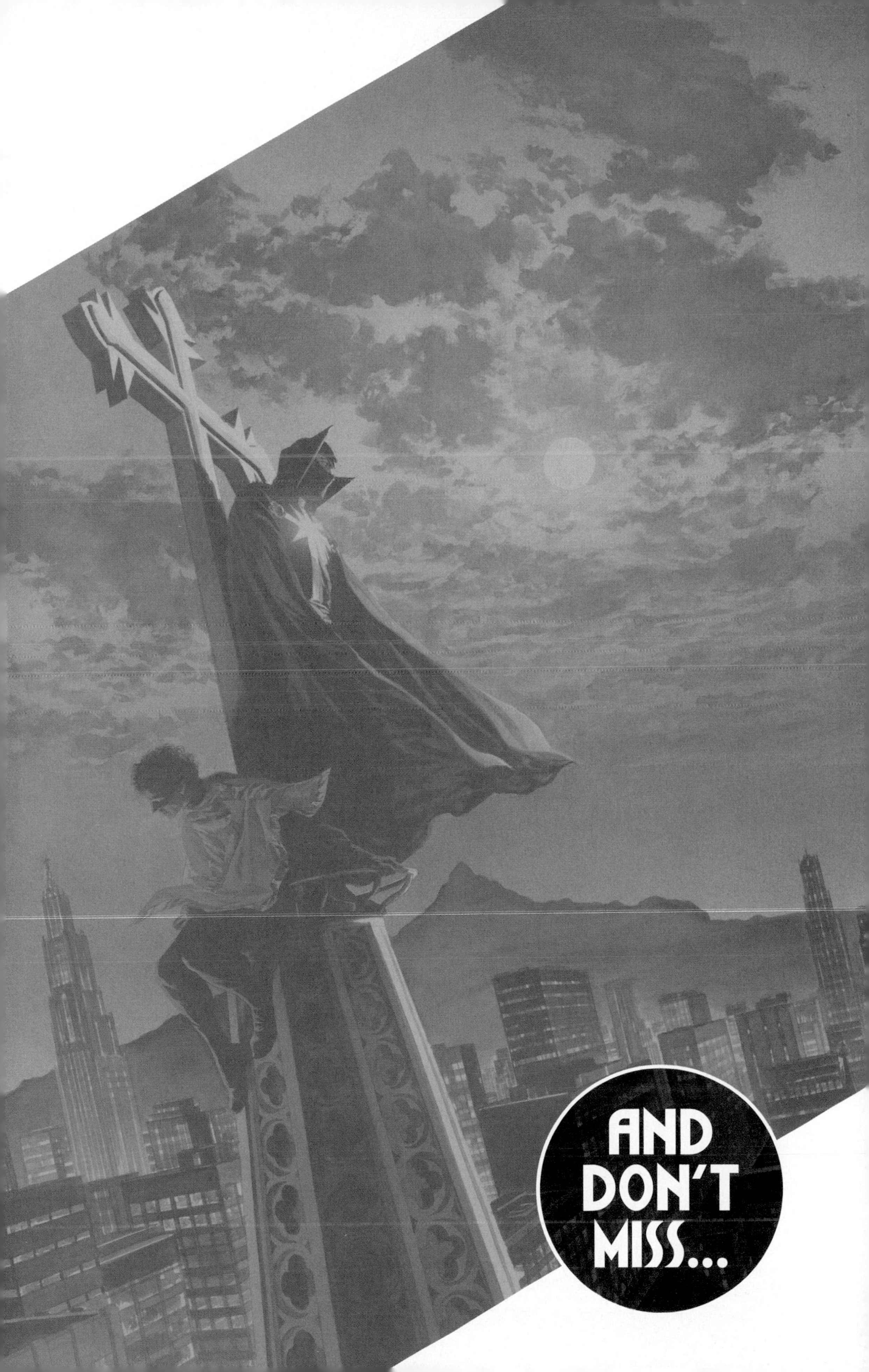

AND DON'T MISS...

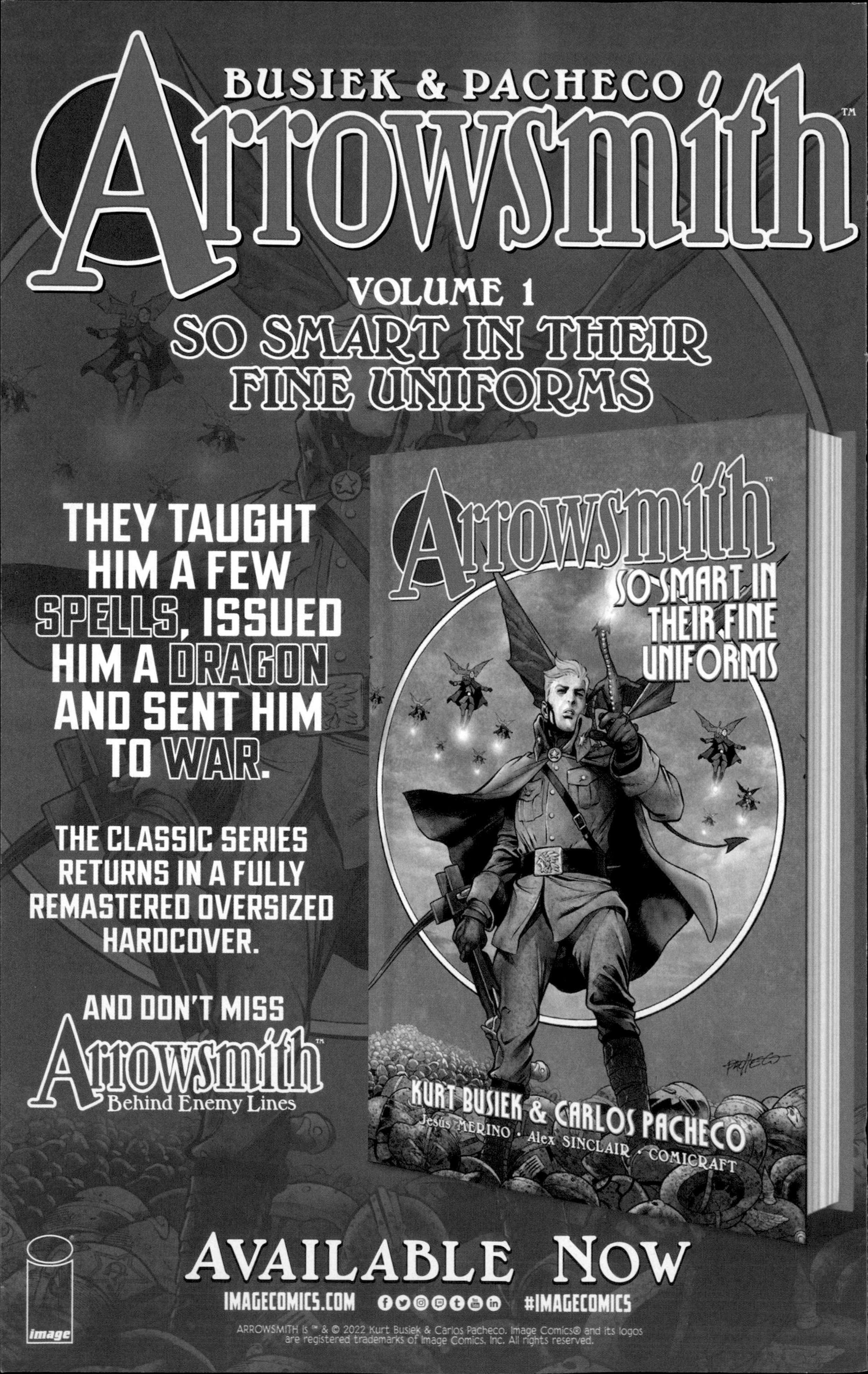
BUSIEK & PACHECO
Arrowsmith™
VOLUME 1
SO SMART IN THEIR FINE UNIFORMS
THEY TAUGHT HIM A FEW SPELLS, ISSUED HIM A DRAGON AND SENT HIM TO WAR.
THE CLASSIC SERIES RETURNS IN A FULLY REMASTERED OVERSIZED HARDCOVER.
AND DON'T MISS
Arrowsmith™ Behind Enemy Lines
Arrowsmith™
SO SMART IN THEIR FINE UNIFORMS
KURT BUSIEK & CARLOS PACHECO
Jesús MERINO · Alex SINCLAIR · COMICRAFT
AVAILABLE NOW
IMAGECOMICS.COM
#IMAGECOMICS
image

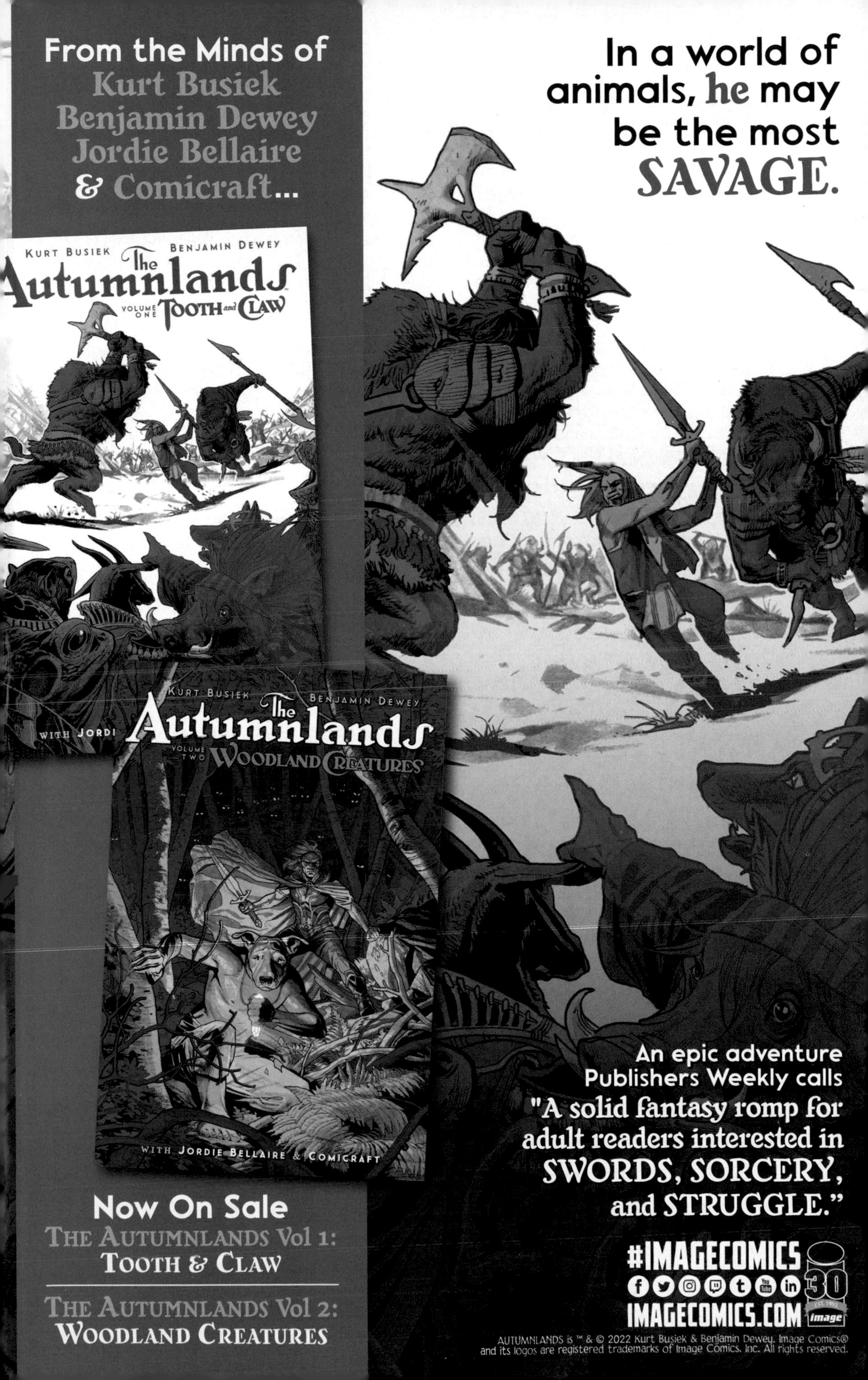

From the Minds of
Kurt Busiek
Benjamin Dewey
Jordie Bellaire
& Comicraft...
In a world of animals, he may be the most SAVAGE.
KURT BUSIEK BENJAMIN DEWEY
The Autumnlands
VOLUME ONE TOOTH and CLAW
KURT BUSIEK BENJAMIN DEWEY
The Autumnlands
VOLUME TWO WOODLAND CREATURES
WITH JORDIE BELLAIRE & COMICRAFT
Now On Sale
THE AUTUMNLANDS Vol 1: TOOTH & CLAW
THE AUTUMNLANDS Vol 2: WOODLAND CREATURES
An epic adventure Publishers Weekly calls "A solid fantasy romp for adult readers interested in SWORDS, SORCERY, and STRUGGLE."
#IMAGECOMICS
IMAGECOMICS.COM
AUTUMNLANDS is ™ & © 2022 Kurt Busiek & Benjamin Dewey. Image Comics® and its logos are registered trademarks of Image Comics, Inc. All rights reserved.

ABOUT THE CREATORS

KURT BUSIEK is a New York Times bestselling and Eisner Award-winning writer of celebrated runs on Avengers, Superman and more, including the breakout hit *Marvels* (with Ross), and has co-created ARROWSMITH, AUTUMNLANDS and *Thunderbolts*, among others. He lives in the Portland Oregon area with his wife Ann and their children Dan and Kat.

BRENT ERIC ANDERSON began making his own comics in junior high school, and graduated to professional work less than a decade later. He's drawn such projects as *Ka-Zar the Savage, X-Men: God Loves Man Kills, Strikeforce: Morituri, Somerset Holmes, Rising Stars* and, of course, ASTRO CITY, for which he's won multiple Eisner and Harvey Awards. He makes his home in Northern California.

ALEX ROSS is the artist and co-creator of multiple painted projects, including *Marvels, Kingdom Come, Superman: Peace on Earth*, and *Justice*. His work outside of comics includes magazine and album covers, as well as the poster for the 2002 Academy Awards. He has also been the subject of multiple books, including *Mythology: The DC Comics Art of Alex Ross* and *Marvelocity: The Marvel Comics Art of Alex Ross*.

WILL BLYBERG first inked Brent Anderson on *Anima* for DC Comics, which led to the ASTRO CITY assignment. He's also inked such series as *Deathstroke, Wonder Woman* and *DNAgents*, and collects vintage radio programs.

ALEX SINCLAIR has colored virtually every character in the DC stable and many others besides. Best known for his award-winning work with Jim Lee and Scott Williams, he's graced such books as ARROWSMITH, *Batman: Hush, Superman: For Tomorrow, Wonder Woman, Amazing Spider-Man, Star Wars* and *Venom*.

STEVE BUCCELLATO is an award-winning art director and illustrator who's worked in comics as a colorist, writer, penciler and editor on series from *Batman* to *X-Men* to *The Flintstones*, including his own *Weasel Guy* and *Joey Berserk and Claire*. His latest venture is Legendhaus, combining his experiences, interests and love of story.

COMICRAFT is the award-winning design and lettering studio founded by Richard Starkings with John Roshell in 1992, famous for pioneering the process of digitally lettering comic books. Their work has appeared in comics from *Avengers* to *X-Men*, as well as television, movies, phone apps and video games. Tyler Smith is the latest designer to join the Comicraft ranks, working on comics for Blizzard, Riot! and DC Comics. He lives and works alongside Richard in Chattanooga, Tennessee.